THE TRIALS OF

APOLLO

◄ 1 ►

THE HIDDEN ORACLE

RICK RIORDAN

THE TRIALS OF APOLLO

◄ 1 ►

THE HIDDEN ORACLE

Disney • HYPERION

Los Angeles   New York

First Hardcover Edition, May 2016
First Paperback Edition, October 2017

"Percy Jackson and the Singer of Apollo" was first published in a
short story anthology, *Guys Read: Other Worlds*, edited by Jon Scieszka,
published by HarperCollins in September 2013

Map illustration by Kayley LeFavier

SUSTAINABLE
FORESTRY
INITIATIVE

Certified Chain of Custody
Promoting Sustainable Forestry

www.sfiprogram.org
SFI-01054

The SFI label applies to the text stock

10 9 8 7
FAC-025438-19221
Printed in the United States of America

This book is set in Danton, Gauthier FY/Fontspring;
Goudy, Goudy Oldstyle, Sabon/Monotype

Library of Congress Control Number for Hardcover Edition: 2015045235
ISBN 978-1-4847-4641-7

Visit www.DisneyBooks.com

To the Muse Calliope
This is long overdue. Please don't hurt me.

CAMP HALF-BLOOD

Western Hills

The Northern Woods

Satyrs

Grove of Dodona

Zeus's Fist

Council of Cloven Elders Meeting Grove

Wolves

Bunker 9

Myrmekes' Lair

Zephyros Creek

Maenad Party Area

Geysers

Wreckage of Old Automatons

Longer Drakons

The Southern Woods

Pegasus Stables

To Peach Orchard

Archery Range

Combat Arena

Strawberry Fields

N
W E
S

K. LeFaiver

LONG ISLAND SOUND

The Beach
The Dunes
Eastern Hills

Euros Creek
Climbing Wall
Dining Pavilion
Canoe Lake
Athena Parthenos

Cabins
Green
Hestia's Hearth
Arts & Crafts
Thalia's Pine & Golden Fleece
Half-Blood Hill

Armory
Amphitheater
Cave of the Oracle

Forge
Campfire

Volleyball Court
Big House
Strawberry Fields

Farm Road 3.141
To Montauk, etc.

1

Hoodlums punch my face
I would smite them if I could
Mortality blows

MY NAME IS APOLLO. I used to be a god.

In my four thousand six hundred and twelve years, I have done many things. I inflicted a plague on the Greeks who besieged Troy. I blessed Babe Ruth with three home runs in game four of the 1926 World Series. I visited my wrath upon Britney Spears at the 2007 MTV Video Music Awards.

But in all my immortal life, I never before crash-landed in a Dumpster.

I'm not even sure how it happened.

I simply woke up falling. Skyscrapers spiraled in and out of view. Flames streamed off my body. I tried to fly. I tried to change into a cloud or teleport across the world or do a hundred other things that should have been easy for me, but I just kept falling. I plunged into a narrow canyon between two buildings and *BAM!*

Is anything sadder than the sound of a god hitting a pile of garbage bags?

I lay groaning and aching in the open Dumpster. My nostrils burned with the stench of rancid bologna and used diapers. My ribs felt broken, though that shouldn't have been possible.

My mind stewed in confusion, but one memory floated to the surface—the voice of my father, Zeus: *YOUR FAULT. YOUR PUNISHMENT.*

I realized what had happened to me. And I sobbed in despair.

Even for a god of poetry such as myself, it is difficult to describe how I felt. How could you—a mere mortal—possibly understand? Imagine being stripped of your clothes, then blasted with a fire hose in front of a laughing crowd. Imagine the ice-cold water filling your mouth and lungs, the pressure bruising your skin, turning your joints to putty. Imagine feeling helpless, ashamed, completely vulnerable—publicly and brutally stripped of everything that makes you *you*. My humiliation was worse than that.

YOUR FAULT, Zeus's voice rang in my head.

"No!" I cried miserably. "No, it wasn't! Please!"

Nobody answered. On either side of me, rusty fire escapes zigzagged up brick walls. Above, the winter sky was gray and unforgiving.

I tried to remember the details of my sentencing. Had my father told me how long this punishment would last? What was I supposed to do to regain his favor?

My memory was too fuzzy. I could barely recall what Zeus looked like, much less why he'd decided to toss me to earth. There'd been a war with the giants, I thought. The gods had been caught off guard, embarrassed, almost defeated.

The only thing I knew for certain: my punishment was

unfair. Zeus needed someone to blame, so of course he'd picked the handsomest, most talented, most popular god in the pantheon: me.

I lay in the garbage, staring at the label inside the Dumpster lid: FOR PICK-UP, CALL 1-555-STENCHY.

Zeus will reconsider, I told myself. *He's just trying to scare me. Any moment, he will yank me back to Olympus and let me off with a warning.*

"Yes . . ." My voice sounded hollow and desperate. "Yes, that's it."

I tried to move. I wanted to be on my feet when Zeus came to apologize. My ribs throbbed. My stomach clenched. I clawed the rim of the Dumpster and managed to drag myself over the side. I toppled out and landed on my shoulder, which made a cracking sound against the asphalt.

"*Araggeeddeee,*" I whimpered through the pain. "Stand up. Stand up."

Getting to my feet was not easy. My head spun. I almost passed out from the effort. I stood in a dead-end alley. About fifty feet away, the only exit opened onto a street with grimy storefronts for a bail bondsman's office and a pawnshop. I was somewhere on the west side of Manhattan, I guessed, or perhaps Crown Heights, in Brooklyn. Zeus must have been really angry with me.

I inspected my new body. I appeared to be a teenaged Caucasian male, clad in sneakers, blue jeans, and a green polo shirt. How utterly *drab.* I felt sick, weak, and so, so human.

I will never understand how you mortals tolerate it. You live your entire life trapped in a sack of meat, unable to enjoy simple pleasures like changing into a hummingbird or dissolving into pure light.

And now, heavens help me, I was one of you—just another meat sack.

I fumbled through my pants pockets, hoping I still had the keys to my sun chariot. No such luck. I found a cheap nylon wallet containing a hundred dollars in American currency—lunch money for my first day as a mortal, perhaps—along with a New York State junior driver's license featuring a photo of a dorky, curly-haired teen who could not possibly be me, with the name *Lester Papadopoulos*. The cruelty of Zeus knew no bounds!

I peered into the Dumpster, hoping my bow, quiver, and lyre might have fallen to earth with me. I would have settled for my harmonica. There was nothing.

I took a deep breath. *Cheer up*, I told myself. *I must have retained some of my godly abilities. Matters could be worse.*

A raspy voice called, "Hey, Cade, take a look at this loser."

Blocking the alley's exit were two young men: one squat and platinum blond, the other tall and redheaded. Both wore oversize hoodies and baggy pants. Serpentine tattoo designs covered their necks. All they were missing were the words I'M A THUG printed in large letters across their foreheads.

The redhead zeroed in on the wallet in my hand. "Now, be nice, Mikey. This guy looks friendly enough." He grinned and pulled a hunting knife from his belt. "In fact, I bet he wants to give us all his money."

———

I blame my disorientation for what happened next.

I knew my immortality had been stripped away, but I still considered myself the mighty Apollo! One cannot change one's way of thinking as easily as one might, say, turn into a snow leopard.

Also, on previous occasions when Zeus had punished me by making me mortal (yes, it had happened twice before), I had retained massive strength and at least some of my godly powers. I assumed the same would be true now.

I was *not* going to allow two young mortal ruffians to take Lester Papadopoulos's wallet.

I stood up straight, hoping Cade and Mikey would be intimidated by my regal bearing and divine beauty. (Surely those qualities could not be taken from me, no matter what my driver's license photo looked like.) I ignored the warm Dumpster juice trickling down my neck.

"I am Apollo," I announced. "You mortals have three choices: offer me tribute, flee, or be destroyed."

I wanted my words to echo through the alley, shake the towers of New York, and cause the skies to rain smoking ruin. None of that happened. On the word *destroyed*, my voice squeaked.

The redhead Cade grinned even wider. I thought how amusing it would be if I could make the snake tattoos around his neck come alive and strangle him to death.

"What do you think, Mikey?" he asked his friend. "Should we give this guy tribute?"

Mikey scowled. With his bristly blond hair, his cruel small eyes, and his thick frame, he reminded me of the monstrous sow that terrorized the village of Crommyon back in the good old days.

"Not feeling the tribute, Cade." His voice sounded like he'd been eating lit cigarettes. "What were the other options?"

"Fleeing?" said Cade.

"Nah," said Mikey.

"Being destroyed?"

Mikey snorted. "How about we destroy *him* instead?"

Cade flipped his knife and caught it by the handle. "I can live with that. After you."

I slipped the wallet into my back pocket. I raised my fists. I did not like the idea of flattening mortals into flesh waffles, but I was sure I could do it. Even in my weakened state, I would be far stronger than any human.

"I warned you," I said. "My powers are far beyond your comprehension."

Mikey cracked his knuckles. "Uh-huh."

He lumbered forward.

As soon as he was in range, I struck. I put all my wrath into that punch. It should have been enough to vaporize Mikey and leave a thug-shaped impression on the asphalt.

Instead he ducked, which I found quite annoying.

I stumbled forward. I have to say that when Prometheus fashioned you humans out of clay he did a shoddy job. Mortal legs are clumsy. I tried to compensate, drawing upon my boundless reserves of agility, but Mikey kicked me in the back. I fell on my divine face.

My nostrils inflated like air bags. My ears popped. The

taste of copper filled my mouth. I rolled over, groaning, and found the two blurry thugs staring down at me.

"Mikey," said Cade, "are you comprehending this guy's power?"

"Nah," said Mikey. "I'm not comprehending it."

"Fools!" I croaked. "I will destroy you!"

"Yeah, sure." Cade tossed away his knife. "But first I think we'll stomp you."

Cade raised his boot over my face, and the world went black.

2

A girl from nowhere
Completes my embarrassment
Stupid bananas

I HAD NOT BEEN STOMPED so badly since my guitar contest against Chuck Berry in 1957.

As Cade and Mikey kicked me, I curled into a ball, trying to protect my ribs and head. The pain was intolerable. I retched and shuddered. I blacked out and came to, my vision swimming with red splotches. When my attackers got tired of kicking me, they hit me over the head with a bag of garbage, which burst and covered me in coffee grounds and moldy fruit peels.

At last they stepped away, breathing heavily. Rough hands patted me down and took my wallet.

"Lookee here," said Cade. "Some cash and an ID for . . . Lester Papadopoulos."

Mikey laughed. "*Lester?* That's even worse than Apollo."

I touched my nose, which felt roughly the size and texture of a water-bed mattress. My fingers came away glistening red.

"Blood," I muttered. "That's not possible."

"It's very possible, Lester." Cade crouched next to me. "And there might be more blood in your near future. You want to explain why you don't have a credit card? Or a phone? I'd hate to think I did all that stomping for just a hundred bucks."

I stared at the blood on my fingertips. I was a god. I did not *have* blood. Even when I'd been turned mortal before, golden ichor still ran through my veins. I had never before been so . . . *converted*. It must be a mistake. A trick. Something.

I tried to sit up.

My hand hit a banana peel and I fell again. My attackers howled in delight.

"I love this guy!" Mikey said.

"Yeah, but the boss told us he'd be loaded," Cade complained.

"Boss . . ." I muttered. "Boss?"

"That's right, Lester." Cade flicked a finger against the side of my head. "'Go to that alley,' the boss told us. 'Easy score.' He said we should rough you up, take whatever you had. But this"—he waved the cash under my nose—"this isn't much of a payday."

Despite my predicament, I felt a surge of hopefulness. If these thugs had been sent here to find me, their "boss" must be a god. No mortal could have known I would fall to earth at this spot. Perhaps Cade and Mikey were not human either. Perhaps they were cleverly disguised monsters or spirits. At least that would explain why they had beaten me so easily.

"Who—who is your boss?" I struggled to my feet, coffee grounds dribbling from my shoulders. My dizziness made me feel as if I were flying too close to the fumes of primordial

Chaos, but I refused to be humbled. "Did Zeus send you? Or perhaps Ares? I demand an audience!"

Mikey and Cade looked at each other as if to say, *Can you believe this guy?*

Cade picked up his knife. "You don't take a hint, do you, Lester?"

Mikey pulled off his belt—a length of bike chain—and wrapped it around his fist.

I decided to sing them into submission. They may have resisted my fists, but no mortal could resist my golden voice. I was trying to decide between "You Send Me" and an original composition, "I'm Your Poetry God, Baby," when a voice yelled, "HEY!"

The hooligans turned. Above us, on the second-story fire escape landing, stood a girl of about twelve. "Leave him alone," she ordered.

My first thought was that Artemis had come to my aid. My sister often appeared as a twelve-year-old girl for reasons I'd never fully understood. But something told me this was not she.

The girl on the fire escape did not exactly inspire fear. She was small and pudgy, with dark hair chopped in a messy pageboy style and black cat-eye glasses with rhinestones glittering in the corners. Despite the cold, she wore no coat. Her outfit looked like it had been picked by a kindergartener—red sneakers, yellow tights, and a green tank dress. Perhaps she was on her way to a costume party dressed as a traffic light.

Still . . . there was something fierce in her expression.

She had the same obstinate scowl my old girlfriend Cyrene used to get whenever she wrestled lions.

Mikey and Cade did not seem impressed.

"Get lost, kid," Mikey told her.

The girl stamped her foot, causing the fire escape to shudder. "My alley. My rules!" Her bossy nasal voice made her sound like she was chiding a playmate in a game of make-believe. "Whatever that loser has is mine, including his money!"

"Why is everyone calling me a loser?" I asked weakly. The comment seemed unfair, even if I was beat-up and covered in garbage; but no one paid me any attention.

Cade glared at the girl. The red from his hair seemed to be seeping into his face. "You've got to be kidding me. Beat it, you brat!" He picked up a rotten apple and threw it.

The girl didn't flinch. The fruit landed at her feet and rolled harmlessly to a stop.

"You want to play with food?" The girl wiped her nose. "Okay."

I didn't see her kick the apple, but it came flying back with deadly accuracy and hit Cade in the nose. He collapsed on his rump.

Mikey snarled. He marched toward the fire escape ladder, but a banana peel seemed to slither directly into his path. He slipped and fell hard. "OWWW!"

I backed away from the fallen thugs. I wondered if I should make a run for it, but I could barely hobble. I also did not want to be assaulted with old fruit.

The girl climbed over the railing. She dropped to the

ground with surprising nimbleness and grabbed a sack of garbage from the Dumpster.

"Stop!" Cade did a sort of scuttling crab walk to get away from the girl. "Let's talk about this!"

Mikey groaned and rolled onto his back.

The girl pouted. Her lips were chapped. She had wispy black fuzz at the corners of her mouth.

"I don't like you guys," she said. "You should go."

"Yeah!" Cade said. "Sure! Just . . ."

He reached for the money scattered among the coffee grounds.

The girl swung her garbage bag. In mid arc the plastic exploded, disgorging an impossible number of rotten bananas. They knocked Cade flat. Mikey was plastered with so many peels he looked like he was being attacked by carnivorous starfish.

"Leave my alley," the girl said. "Now."

In the Dumpster, more trash bags burst like popcorn kernels, showering Cade and Mikey with radishes, potato peelings, and other compost material. Miraculously, none of it got on me. Despite their injuries, the two thugs scrambled to their feet and ran away, screaming.

I turned toward my pint-size savior. I was no stranger to dangerous women. My sister could rain down arrows of death. My stepmother, Hera, regularly drove mortals mad so that they would hack each other to pieces. But this garbage-wielding twelve-year-old made me nervous.

"Thank you," I ventured.

The girl crossed her arms. On her middle fingers she wore matching gold rings with crescent signets. Her eyes glinted darkly like a crow's. (I can make that comparison because I invented crows.)

"Don't thank me," she said. "You're still in my alley."

She walked a full circle around me, scrutinizing my appearance as if I were a prize cow. (I can also make that comparison, because I used to collect prize cows.)

"You're the god Apollo?" She sounded less than awestruck. She also didn't seem fazed by the idea of gods walking among mortals.

"You were listening, then?"

She nodded. "You don't look like a god."

"I'm not at my best," I admitted. "My father, Zeus, has exiled me from Olympus. And who are you?"

She smelled faintly of apple pie, which was surprising, since she looked so grubby. Part of me wanted to find a fresh towel, clean her face, and give her money for a hot meal. Part of me wanted to fend her off with a chair in case she decided to bite me. She reminded me of the strays my sister was always adopting: dogs, panthers, homeless maidens, small dragons.

"Name is Meg," she said.

"Short for Megara? Or Margaret?"

"Margaret. But don't ever call me Margaret."

"And are you a demigod, Meg?"

She pushed up her glasses. "Why would you think that?"

Again she didn't seem surprised by the question. I sensed she had heard the term *demigod* before.

"Well," I said, "you obviously have some power. You chased off those hooligans with rotten fruit. Perhaps you have banana-kinesis? Or you can control garbage? I once knew a Roman goddess, Cloacina, who presided over the city's sewer system. Perhaps you're related . . . ?"

Meg pouted. I got the impression I might have said something wrong, though I couldn't imagine what.

"I think I'll just take your money," Meg said. "Go on. Get out of here."

"No, wait!" Desperation crept into my voice. "Please, I—I may need a bit of assistance."

I felt ridiculous, of course. Me—the god of prophecy, plague, archery, healing, music, and several other things I couldn't remember at the moment—asking a colorfully dressed street urchin for help. But I had no one else. If this child chose to take my money and kick me into the cruel winter streets, I didn't think I could stop her.

"Say I believe you . . ." Meg's voice took on a singsong tone, as if she were about to announce the rules of the game: *I'll be the princess, and you'll be the scullery maid.* "Say I decide to help. What then?"

Good question, I thought. "We . . . we are in Manhattan?"

"Mm-hmm." She twirled and did a playful skip-kick. "Hell's Kitchen."

It seemed wrong for a child to say *Hell's Kitchen*. Then again, it seemed wrong for a child to live in an alley and have garbage fights with thugs.

I considered walking to the Empire State Building. That was the modern gateway to Mount Olympus, but I doubted the guards would let me up to the secret six hundredth floor. Zeus would not make it so easy.

Perhaps I could find my old friend Chiron the centaur. He had a training camp on Long Island. He could offer me shelter and guidance. But that would be a dangerous journey. A defenseless god makes for a juicy target. Any monster along the way would cheerfully disembowel me. Jealous spirits and minor gods might also welcome the opportunity. Then there was Cade and Mikey's mysterious "boss." I had no idea who he was, or whether he had other, worse minions to send against me.

Even if I made it to Long Island, my new mortal eyes might not be able to *find* Chiron's camp in its magically camouflaged valley. I needed a guide to get me there—someone experienced and close by. . . .

"I have an idea." I stood as straight as my injuries allowed. It wasn't easy to look confident with a bloody nose and coffee grounds dripping off my clothes. "I know someone who might help. He lives on the Upper East Side. Take me to him, and I shall reward you."

Meg made a sound between a sneeze and a laugh. "Reward me with what?" She danced around, plucking twenty-dollar bills from the trash. "I'm already taking all your money."

"Hey!"

She tossed me my wallet, now empty except for Lester Papadopoulos's junior driver's license.

Meg sang, "I've got your money, I've got your money."

I stifled a growl. "Listen, child, I won't be mortal forever. Someday I will become a god again. Then I will reward those who helped me—and punish those who didn't."

She put her hands on her hips. "How do *you* know what will happen? Have you ever been mortal before?"

"Yes, actually. Twice! Both times, my punishment only lasted a few years at most!"

"Oh, yeah? And how did you get back to being all goddy or whatever?"

"*Goddy* is not a word," I pointed out, though my poetic sensibilities were already thinking of ways I might use it. "Usually Zeus requires me to work as a slave for some important demigod. This fellow uptown I mentioned, for instance. He'd be perfect! I do whatever tasks my new master requires for a few years. As long as I behave, I am allowed back to Olympus. Right now I just have to recover my strength and figure out—"

"How do you know for sure which demigod?"

I blinked. "What?"

"Which demigod you're supposed to serve, dummy."

"I . . . uh. Well, it's usually obvious. I just sort of run into them. That's why I want to get to the Upper East Side. My new master will claim my service and—"

"I'm Meg McCaffrey!" Meg blew me a raspberry. "And I claim your service!"

Overhead, thunder rumbled in the gray sky. The sound echoed through the city canyons like divine laughter.

Whatever was left of my pride turned to ice water and trickled into my socks. "I walked right into that, didn't I?"

"Yep!" Meg bounced up and down in her red sneakers. "We're going to have fun!"

With great difficulty, I resisted the urge to weep. "Are you sure you're not Artemis in disguise?"

"I'm that other thing," Meg said, counting my money. "The thing you said before. A demigod."

"How do you know?"

"Just do." She gave me a smug smile. "And now I have a sidekick god named Lester!"

I raised my face to the heavens. "Please, Father, I get the point. Please, I can't do this!"

Zeus did not answer. He was probably too busy recording my humiliation to share on Snapchat.

"Cheer up," Meg told me. "Who's that guy you wanted to see—the guy on the Upper East Side?"

"Another demigod," I said. "He knows the way to a camp where I might find shelter, guidance, food—"

"Food?" Meg's ears perked up almost as much as the points on her glasses. "*Good* food?"

"Well, normally I just eat ambrosia, but, yes, I suppose."

"Then that's my first order! We're going to find this guy to take us to the camp place!"

I sighed miserably. It was going to be a very long servitude.

"As you wish," I said. "Let's find Percy Jackson."

3

Used to be goddy
Now uptown feeling shoddy
Bah, haiku don't rhyme

AS WE TRUDGED up Madison Avenue, my mind swirled with questions: Why hadn't Zeus given me a winter coat? Why did Percy Jackson live so far uptown? Why did pedestrians keep staring at me?

I wondered if my divine radiance was starting to return. Perhaps the New Yorkers were awed by my obvious power and unearthly good looks.

Meg McCaffrey set me straight.

"You smell," she said. "You look like you've just been mugged."

"I *have* just been mugged. Also enslaved by a small child."

"It's not slavery." She chewed off a piece of her thumb cuticle and spit it out. "It's more like mutual cooperation."

"Mutual in the sense that you give orders and I am forced to cooperate?"

"Yep." She stopped in front of a storefront window. "See? You look gross."

My reflection stared back at me, except it was *not* my

reflection. It couldn't be. The face was the same as on Lester Papadopoulos's ID.

I looked about sixteen. My medium-length hair was dark and curly—a style I had rocked in Athenian times, and again in the 1970s. My eyes were blue. My face was pleasing enough in a dorkish way, but it was marred by a swollen eggplant-colored nose, which had dripped a gruesome mustache of blood down my upper lip. Even worse, my cheeks were covered with some sort of rash that looked suspiciously like . . . My heart climbed into my throat.

"Horrors!" I cried. "Is that— Is that *acne?*"

Immortal gods do not *get* acne. It is one of our inalienable rights. Yet I leaned closer to the glass and saw that my skin was indeed a scarred landscape of whiteheads and pustules.

I balled my fists and wailed to the cruel sky, "Zeus, what have I done to deserve this?"

Meg tugged at my sleeve. "You're going to get yourself arrested."

"What does it matter? I have been made a teenager, and not even one with perfect skin! I bet I don't even have . . ." With a cold sense of dread, I lifted my shirt. My midriff was covered with a floral pattern of bruises from my fall into the Dumpster and my subsequent kicking. But even worse, I had *flab*.

"Oh, no, no, no." I staggered around the sidewalk, hoping the flab would not follow me. "Where are my eight-pack abs? I *always* have eight-pack abs. I *never* have love handles. Never in four thousand years!"

Meg made another snorting laugh. "Sheesh, crybaby, you're fine."

"I'm fat!"

"You're average. Average people don't have eight-pack abs. C'mon."

I wanted to protest that I was not average *nor* a person, but with growing despair, I realized the term now fit me perfectly.

On the other side of the storefront window, a security guard's face loomed, scowling at me. I allowed Meg to pull me farther down the street.

She skipped along, occasionally stopping to pick up a coin or swing herself around a streetlamp. The child seemed unfazed by the cold weather, the dangerous journey ahead, and the fact that I was suffering from acne.

"How are you so calm?" I demanded. "You are a demigod, walking with a god, on your way to a camp to meet others of your kind. Doesn't any of that surprise you?"

"Eh." She folded one of my twenty-dollar bills into a paper airplane. "I've seen a bunch of weird stuff."

I was tempted to ask what could be weirder than the morning we had just had. I decided I might not be able to stand the stress of knowing. "Where are you from?"

"I told you. The alley."

"No, but . . . your parents? Family? Friends?"

A ripple of discomfort passed over her face. She returned her attention to her twenty-dollar airplane. "Not important."

My highly advanced people-reading skills told me she was hiding something, but that was not unusual for demigods. For children blessed with an immortal parent, they were strangely sensitive about their backgrounds. "And you've never heard of Camp Half-Blood? Or Camp Jupiter?"

"Nuh-uh." She tested the airplane's point on her fingertip. "How much farther to Perry's house?"

"Percy's. I'm not sure. A few more blocks . . . I think."

That seemed to satisfy Meg. She hopscotched ahead, throwing the cash airplane and retrieving it. She cartwheeled through the intersection at East Seventy-Second Street—her clothes a flurry of traffic-light colors so bright I worried the drivers might get confused and run her down. Fortunately, New York drivers were used to swerving around oblivious pedestrians.

I decided Meg must be a feral demigod. They were rare but not unheard of. Without any support network, without being discovered by other demigods or taken in for proper training, she had still managed to survive. But her luck would not last. Monsters usually began hunting down and killing young heroes around the time they turned thirteen, when their true powers began to manifest. Meg did not have long. She needed to be brought to Camp Half-Blood as much as I did. She was fortunate to have met me.

(I know that last statement seems obvious. *Everyone* who meets me is fortunate, but you take my meaning.)

Had I been my usual omniscient self, I could have gleaned Meg's destiny. I could have looked into her soul and seen all I needed to know about her godly parentage, her powers, her motives and secrets.

Now I was blind to such things. I could only be sure she was a demigod because she had successfully claimed my service. Zeus had affirmed her right with a clap of thunder. I felt the binding upon me like a shroud of tightly wrapped banana peels. Whoever Meg McCaffrey was, however she had happened to find me, our fates were now intertwined.

It was almost as embarrassing as the acne.

We turned east on Eighty-Second Street.

By the time we reached Second Avenue, the neighborhood started to look familiar—rows of apartment buildings, hardware shops, convenience stores, and Indian restaurants. I knew that Percy Jackson lived around here somewhere, but my trips across the sky in the sun chariot had given me something of a Google Earth orientation. I wasn't used to traveling at street level.

Also, in this mortal form, my flawless memory had become . . . flawed. Mortal fears and needs clouded my thoughts. I wanted to eat. I wanted to use the restroom. My body hurt. My clothes stank. I felt as if my brain had been stuffed with wet cotton. Honestly, how do you humans stand it?

After a few more blocks, a mixture of sleet and rain began to fall. Meg tried to catch the precipitation on her tongue, which I thought a very ineffective way to get a drink—and of dirty water, no less. I shivered and concentrated on happy thoughts: the Bahamas, the Nine Muses in perfect harmony, the many horrible punishments I would visit on Cade and Mikey when I became a god again.

I still wondered about their boss, and how he had known where I would fall to earth. No mortal could've had that knowledge. In fact, the more I thought about it, I didn't see how even a god (other than myself) could have foreseen the future so accurately. After all, I had been the god of prophecy, master of the Oracle of Delphi, distributor of the highest quality sneak previews of destiny for millennia.

Of course, I had no shortage of enemies. One of the natural consequences of being so awesome is that I attracted envy from all quarters. But I could only think of one adversary who might be able to tell the future. And if *he* came looking for me in my weakened state . . .

I tamped down that thought. I had enough to worry about. No point scaring myself to death with what-ifs.

We began searching side streets, checking names on apartment mailboxes and intercom panels. The Upper East Side had a surprising number of Jacksons. I found that annoying.

After several failed attempts, we turned a corner and there—parked under a crape myrtle—sat an older model blue Prius. Its hood bore the unmistakable dents of pegasus hooves. (How was I sure? I know my hoof marks. Also, normal horses do not gallop over Toyotas. Pegasi often do.)

"Aha," I told Meg. "We're getting close."

Half a block down, I recognized the building: a five-story brick row house with rusty air conditioner units sagging from the windows. *"Voilà!"* I cried.

At the front steps, Meg stopped as if she'd run into an invisible barrier. She stared back toward Second Avenue, her dark eyes turbulent.

"What's wrong?" I asked.

"Thought I saw them again."

"Them?" I followed her gaze but saw nothing unusual. "The thugs from the alley?"

"No. Couple of . . ." She waggled her fingers. "Shiny blobs. Saw them back on Park Avenue."

My pulse increased from an andante tempo to a lively allegretto. "Shiny blobs? Why didn't you say anything?"

She tapped the temples of her glasses. "I've seen a lot of weird stuff. Told you that. Mostly, things don't bother me, but . . ."

"But if they are following us," I said, "that would be bad."

I scanned the street again. I saw nothing amiss, but I didn't doubt Meg had seen shiny blobs. Many spirits could appear that way. My own father, Zeus, once took the form of a shiny blob to woo a mortal woman. (Why the mortal woman found that attractive, I have no idea.)

"We should get inside," I said. "Percy Jackson will help us."

Still, Meg held back. She had shown no fear while pelting muggers with garbage in a blind alley, but now she seemed to be having second thoughts about ringing a doorbell. It occurred to me she might have met demigods before. Perhaps those meetings had not gone well.

"Meg," I said, "I realize some demigods are not good. I could tell you stories of all the ones I've had to kill or transform into herbs—"

"Herbs?"

"But Percy Jackson has always been reliable. You have nothing to fear. Besides, he likes me. I taught him everything he knows."

She frowned. "You did?"

I found her innocence somewhat charming. So many obvious things she did not know. "Of course. Now let's go up."

I rang the buzzer. A few moments later, the garbled voice of a woman answered, "Yes?"

"Hello," I said. "This is Apollo."

Static.

"The *god* Apollo," I said, thinking perhaps I should be more specific. "Is Percy home?"

More static, followed by two voices in muted conversation. The front door buzzed. I pushed it open. Just before I stepped inside, I caught a flash of movement in the corner of my eye. I peered down the sidewalk but again saw nothing.

Perhaps it had been a reflection. Or a whirl of sleet. Or perhaps it had been a shiny blob. My scalp tingled with apprehension.

"What?" Meg asked.

"Probably nothing." I forced a cheerful tone. I did not want Meg bolting off when we were so close to reaching safety. We were bound together now. I would have to follow her if she ordered me to, and I did not fancy living in the alley with her forever. "Let's go up. We can't keep our hosts waiting."

After all I had done for Percy Jackson, I expected delight upon my arrival. A tearful welcome, a few burnt offerings, and a small festival in my honor would not have been inappropriate.

Instead, the young man swung open the apartment door and said, "Why?"

As usual, I was struck by his resemblance to his father, Poseidon. He had the same sea-green eyes, the same dark tousled hair, the same handsome features that could shift from humor to anger so easily. However, Percy Jackson did not favor his father's chosen garb of beach shorts and Hawaiian shirts. He was dressed in ragged jeans and a blue hoodie with the words AHS SWIM TEAM stitched across the front.

Meg inched back into the hallway, hiding behind me.

I tried for a smile. "Percy Jackson, my blessings upon you! I am in need of assistance."

Percy's eyes darted from me to Meg. "Who's your friend?"

"This is Meg McCaffrey," I said, "a demigod who must be taken to Camp Half-Blood. She rescued me from street thugs."

"Rescued . . ." Percy scanned my battered face. "You mean the 'beat-up teenager' look isn't just a disguise? Dude, what happened to you?"

"I may have mentioned the street thugs."

"But you're a god."

"About that . . . I *was* a god."

Percy blinked. "*Was?*"

"Also," I said, "I'm fairly certain we're being followed by malicious spirits."

If I didn't know how much Percy Jackson adored me, I would have sworn he was about to punch me in my already-broken nose.

He sighed. "Maybe you two should come inside."

4

Casa de Jackson
No gold-plated throne for guests
Seriously, dude?

ANOTHER THING I have never understood: How can you mortals live in such tiny places? Where is your pride? Your sense of style?

The Jackson apartment had no grand throne room, no colonnades, no terraces or banquet halls or even a thermal bath. It had a tiny living room with an attached kitchen and a single hallway leading to what I assumed were the bedrooms. The place was on the fifth floor, and while I wasn't so picky as to expect an elevator, I did find it odd there was no landing deck for flying chariots. What did they do when guests from the sky wanted to visit?

Standing behind the kitchen counter, making a smoothie, was a strikingly attractive mortal woman of about forty. Her long brown hair had a few gray streaks, but her bright eyes, quick smile, and festive tie-dyed sundress made her look younger.

As we entered, she turned off the blender and stepped out from behind the counter.

"Sacred Sibyl!" I cried. "Madam, there is something wrong with your midsection!"

The woman stopped, mystified, and looked down at her hugely swollen belly. "Well, I'm seven months pregnant."

I wanted to cry for her. Carrying such a weight didn't seem natural. My sister, Artemis, had experience with midwifery, but I had always found it one area of the healing arts best left to others. "How can you bear it?" I asked. "My mother, Leto, suffered through a long pregnancy, but only because Hera cursed her. Are you cursed?"

Percy stepped to my side. "Um, Apollo? She's not cursed. And can you not mention Hera?"

"You poor woman." I shook my head. "A goddess would never allow herself to be so encumbered. She would give birth as soon as she felt like it."

"That must be nice," the woman agreed.

Percy Jackson coughed. "So anyway. Mom, this is Apollo and his friend Meg. Guys, this is my mom."

The Mother of Jackson smiled and shook our hands. "Call me Sally."

Her eyes narrowed as she studied my busted nose. "Dear, that looks painful. What happened?"

I attempted to explain, but I choked on my words. I, the silver-tongued god of poetry, could not bring myself to describe my fall from grace to this kind woman.

I understood why Poseidon had been so smitten with her. Sally Jackson possessed just the right combination of compassion, strength, and beauty. She was one of those rare mortal women who could connect spiritually with a god as an equal—to be neither terrified of us nor greedy for what we can offer, but to provide us with true companionship.

If I had still been an immortal, I might have flirted

with her myself. But I was now a sixteen-year-old boy. My mortal form was working its way upon my state of mind. I saw Sally Jackson as a mom—a fact that both consternated and embarrassed me. I thought about how long it had been since I had called my own mother. I should probably take her to lunch when I got back to Olympus.

"I tell you what." Sally patted my shoulder. "Percy can help you get bandaged and cleaned up."

"I can?" asked Percy.

Sally gave him the slightest motherly eyebrow raise. "There's a first-aid kit in your bathroom, sweetheart. Apollo can take a shower, then wear your extra clothes. You two are about the same size."

"That," Percy said, "is truly depressing."

Sally cupped her hand under Meg's chin. Thankfully, Meg did not bite her. Sally's expression remained gentle and reassuring, but I could see the worry in her eyes. No doubt she was thinking, *Who dressed this poor girl like a traffic light?*

"I have some clothes that might fit you, dear," Sally said. "Pre-pregnancy clothes, of course. Let's get you cleaned up. Then we'll get you something to eat."

"I like food," Meg muttered.

Sally laughed. "Well, we have that in common. Percy, you take Apollo. We'll meet you back here in a while."

In short order, I was showered, bandaged, and dressed in Jacksonesque hand-me-downs. Percy left me alone in the bathroom to take care of all this myself, for which I was grateful. He offered me some ambrosia and nectar—food and drink of the gods—to heal my wounds, but I was not sure it would be safe to consume in my mortal state. I didn't want to self-combust, so I stuck with mortal first-aid supplies.

When I was done, I stared at my battered face in the bathroom mirror. Perhaps teenage angst had permeated the clothes, because I felt more like a sulky high schooler than ever. I thought how unfair it was that I was being punished, how lame my father was, how no one else in the history of time had ever experienced problems like mine.

Of course, all that was empirically true. No exaggeration was required.

At least my wounds seemed to be healing at a faster rate than a normal mortal's. The swelling in my nose had subsided. My ribs still ached, but I no longer felt as if someone were knitting a sweater inside my chest with hot needles.

Accelerated healing was the *least* Zeus could do for me. I was a god of medicinal arts, after all. Zeus probably just wanted me to get well quickly so I could endure more pain, but I was grateful nonetheless.

I wondered if I should start a small fire in Percy Jackson's sink, perhaps burn some bandages in thanks, but I decided that might strain the Jacksons' hospitality.

I examined the black T-shirt Percy had given me. Emblazoned on the front was Led Zeppelin's logo for their record label: winged Icarus falling from the sky. I had no problem with Led Zeppelin. I had inspired all their best songs. But I had a sneaking suspicion that Percy had given me this shirt as a joke—the fall from the sky. Yes, ha-ha. I didn't need to be a god of poetry to spot the metaphor. I decided not to comment on it. I wouldn't give him the satisfaction.

I took a deep breath. Then I did my usual motivational speech in the mirror: "You are gorgeous and people love you!"

I went out to face the world.

Percy was sitting on his bed, staring at the trail of blood droplets I had made across his carpet.

"Sorry about that," I said.

Percy spread his hands. "Actually, I was thinking about the last time I had a nosebleed."

"Oh . . ."

The memory came back to me, though hazy and incomplete. Athens. The Acropolis. We gods had battled side by side with Percy Jackson and his comrades. We defeated an army of giants, but a drop of Percy's blood hit the earth and awakened the Earth Mother Gaea, who had not been in a good mood.

That's when Zeus turned on me. He'd accused me of starting the whole thing, just because Gaea had duped one of my progeny, a boy named Octavian, into plunging the Roman and Greek demigod camps into a civil war that almost destroyed human civilization. I ask you: How was that my fault?

Regardless, Zeus had held *me* responsible for Octavian's delusions of grandeur. Zeus seemed to consider egotism a trait the boy had inherited from me. Which is ridiculous. I am much too self-aware to be egotistical.

"What happened to you, man?" Percy's voice stirred me from my reverie. "The war ended in August. It's January."

"It is?" I suppose the wintry weather should have been a clue, but I hadn't given it much thought.

"Last I saw you," Percy said, "Zeus was chewing you out at the Acropolis. Then *bam*—he vaporized you. Nobody's seen or heard from you for six months."

I tried to recall, but my memories of godhood were getting fuzzier rather than clearer. What had happened in the last six months? Had I been in some kind of stasis? Had Zeus taken that long to decide what to do with me? Perhaps there was a reason he'd waited until this moment to hurl me to earth.

Father's voice still rang in my ears: *Your fault. Your punishment.* My shame felt fresh and raw, as if the conversation had just happened, but I could not be sure.

After being alive for so many millennia, I had trouble keeping track of time even in the best of circumstances. I would hear a song on Spotify and think, Oh, that's new! Then I'd realize it was Mozart's Piano Concerto no. 20 in D Minor from two hundred years ago. Or I'd wonder why Herodotus the historian wasn't in my contacts list. Then I'd remember Herodotus didn't have a smartphone, because he had been dead since the Iron Age.

It's very irritating how quickly you mortals die.

"I—I don't know where I've been," I admitted. "I have some memory gaps."

Percy winced. "I hate memory gaps. Last year I lost an entire semester thanks to Hera."

"Ah, yes." I couldn't quite remember what Percy Jackson was talking about. During the war with Gaea, I had been focused mostly on my own fabulous exploits. But I suppose he and his friends had undergone a few minor hardships.

"Well, never fear," I said. "There are always new opportunities to win fame! That's why I've come to you for help!"

He gave me that confusing expression again: as if he wanted to kick me, when I was sure he must be struggling to contain his gratitude.

"Look, man—"

"Would you please refrain from calling me *man?*" I asked. "It is a painful reminder that I am a man."

"Okay . . . Apollo, I'm fine with driving you and Meg to camp if that's what you want. I never turn away a demigod who needs help—"

"Wonderful! Do you have something besides the Prius? A Maserati, perhaps? I'd settle for a Lamborghini."

"*But,*" Percy continued, "I can't get involved in another Big Prophecy or whatever. I've made promises."

I stared at him, not quite comprehending. "Promises?"

Percy laced his fingers. They were long and nimble. He would have made an excellent musician. "I lost most of my junior year because of the war with Gaea. I've spent this entire fall playing catch-up with my classes. If I want to go to college with Annabeth next fall, I have to stay out of trouble and get my diploma."

"Annabeth." I tried to place the name. "She's the blond scary one?"

"That's her. I promised her *specifically* that I wouldn't get myself killed while she's gone."

"Gone?"

Percy waved vaguely toward the north. "She's in Boston for a few weeks. Some family emergency. The point is—"

"You're saying you cannot offer me your undivided ser-vice to restore me to my throne?"

"Um . . . yeah." He pointed at the bedroom doorway. "Besides, my mom's pregnant. I'm going to have a baby sis-ter. I'd like to be around to get to know her."

"Well, I understand that. I remember when Artemis was born—"

"Aren't you twins?"

"I've always regarded her as my little sister."

Percy's mouth twitched. "Anyway, my mom's got that going on, and her first novel is going to be published this spring as well, so I'd like to stay alive long enough to—"

"Wonderful!" I said. "Remind her to burn the proper sacrifices. Calliope is quite touchy when novelists forget to thank her."

"Okay. But what I'm saying . . . I can't go off on another world-stomping quest. I can't do that to my family."

Percy glanced toward his window. On the sill was a pot-ted plant with delicate silver leaves—possibly moonlace. "I've already given my mom enough heart attacks for one lifetime. She's just about forgiven me for disappearing last year, but I swore to her and Paul that I wouldn't do any-thing like that again."

"Paul?"

"My stepdad. He's at a teacher in-service today. He's a good guy."

"I see." In truth, I didn't see. I wanted to get back to talking about my problems. I was impatient with Percy for turning the conversation to himself. Sadly, I have found this sort of self-centeredness common among demigods.

"You *do* understand that I must find a way to return to Olympus," I said. "This will probably involve many harrowing trials with a high chance of death. Can you turn down such glory?"

"Yeah, I'm pretty sure I can. Sorry."

I pursed my lips. It always disappointed me when mortals put themselves first and failed to see the big picture—the importance of putting *me* first—but I had to remind myself that this young man had helped me out on many previous occasions. He had earned my goodwill.

"I understand," I said with incredible generosity. "You will at least escort us to Camp Half-Blood?"

"That I can do." Percy reached into his hoodie pocket and pulled out a ballpoint pen. For a moment I thought he wanted my autograph. I can't tell you how often that happens. Then I remembered the pen was the disguised form of his sword, Riptide.

He smiled, and some of that old demigod mischief twinkled in his eyes. "Let's see if Meg's ready for a field trip."

5

Seven-layer dip
Chocolate chip cookies in blue
I love this woman

SALLY JACKSON was a witch to rival Circe. She had transformed Meg from a street urchin into a shockingly pretty young girl. Meg's dark pageboy hair was glossy and brushed. Her round face was scrubbed clean of grime. Her cat-eye glasses had been polished so the rhinestones sparkled. She had evidently insisted on keeping her old red sneakers, but she wore new black leggings and a knee-length frock of shifting green hues.

Mrs. Jackson had figured out how to keep Meg's old look but tweak it to be more complementary. Meg now had an elfish springtime aura that reminded me very much of a dryad. In fact . . .

A sudden wave of emotion overwhelmed me. I choked back a sob.

Meg pouted. "Do I look that bad?"

"No, no," I managed. "It's just . . ."

I wanted to say: *You remind me of someone.* But I didn't dare open that line of conversation. Only two mortals *ever* had broken my heart. Even after so many centuries, I couldn't think of her, couldn't say her name without falling into despair.

Don't misunderstand me. I felt no attraction to Meg. I was sixteen (or four thousand plus, depending on how you looked at it). She was a very young twelve. But the way she appeared now, Meg McCaffrey might have been the daughter of my former love . . . if my former love had lived long enough to have children.

It was too painful. I looked away.

"Well," Sally Jackson said with forced cheerfulness, "how about I make some lunch while you three . . . talk."

She gave Percy a worried glance, then headed to the kitchen, her hands protectively over her pregnant belly.

Meg sat on the edge of the sofa. "Percy, your mom is so normal."

"Thanks, I guess." He picked up a stack of test preparation manuals from the coffee table and chucked them aside.

"I see you like to study," I said. "Well done."

Percy snorted. "I *hate* to study. I've been guaranteed admission with a full scholarship to New Rome University, but they're still requiring me to pass all my high school courses and score well on the SAT. Can you believe that? Not to mention I have to pass the DSTOMP."

"The what?" Meg asked.

"An exam for Roman demigods," I told her. "The Demigod Standard Test of Mad Powers."

Percy frowned. "That's what it stands for?"

"I should know. I wrote the music and poetry analysis sections."

"I will never forgive you for that," Percy said.

Meg swung her feet. "So you're really a demigod? Like me?"

"Afraid so." Percy sank into the armchair, leaving me to take the sofa next to Meg. "My dad is the godly one—Poseidon. What about your parents?"

Meg's legs went still. She studied her chewed cuticles, the matching crescent rings glinting on her middle fingers. "Never knew them . . . much."

Percy hesitated. "Foster home? Stepparents?"

I thought of a certain plant, the Mimosa pudica, which the god Pan created. As soon as its leaves are touched, the plant closes up defensively. Meg seemed to be playing mimosa, folding inward under Percy's questions.

Percy raised his hands. "Sorry. Didn't mean to pry." He gave me an inquisitive look. "So how did you guys meet?"

I told him the story. I may have exaggerated my brave defense against Cade and Mikey—just for narrative effect, you understand.

As I finished, Sally Jackson returned. She set down a bowl of tortilla chips and a casserole dish filled with elaborate dip in multicolored strata, like sedimentary rock.

"I'll be back with the sandwiches," she said. "But I had some leftover seven-layer dip."

"Yum." Percy dug in with a tortilla chip. "She's kinda famous for this, guys."

Sally ruffled his hair. "There's guacamole, sour cream, refried beans, salsa—"

"Seven layers?" I looked up in wonder. "You knew seven is my sacred number? You invented this for *me*?"

Sally wiped her hands on her apron. "Well, actually, I can't take credit—"

"You are too modest!" I tried some of the dip. It tasted almost as good as ambrosia nachos. "You will have immortal fame for this, Sally Jackson!"

"That's sweet." She pointed to the kitchen. "I'll be right back."

Soon we were plowing through turkey sandwiches, chips and dip, and banana smoothies. Meg ate like a chipmunk, shoving more food in her mouth than she could possibly chew. My belly was full. I had never been so happy. I had a strange desire to fire up an Xbox and play *Call of Duty*.

"Percy," I said, "your mom is awesome."

"I know, right?" He finished his smoothie. "So back to your story . . . you have to be Meg's servant now? You guys barely know each other."

"*Barely* is generous," I said. "Nevertheless, yes. My fate is now linked with young McCaffrey."

"We are *cooperating*," Meg said. She seemed to savor that word.

From his pocket, Percy fished his ballpoint pen. He tapped it thoughtfully against his knee. "And this whole turning-into-a-mortal thing . . . you've done it twice before?"

"Not by choice," I assured him. "The first time, we had a little rebellion in Olympus. We tried to overthrow Zeus."

Percy winced. "I'm guessing that didn't go well."

"I got most of the blame, naturally. Oh, and your father, Poseidon. We were both cast down to earth as mortals, forced to serve Laomedon, the king of Troy. He was a harsh master. He even refused to pay us for our work!"

Meg nearly choked on her sandwich. "I have to pay you?"

I had a terrifying image of Meg McCaffrey trying to pay me in bottle caps, marbles, and pieces of colored string.

"Never fear," I told her. "I won't be presenting you with a bill. But as I was saying, the second time I became mortal, Zeus got mad because I killed some of his Cyclopes."

Percy frowned. "Dude, not cool. My brother is a Cyclops."

"These were wicked Cyclopes! They made the lightning bolt that killed one of my sons!"

Meg bounced on the arm of the sofa. "Percy's brother is a Cyclops? That's crazy!"

I took a deep breath, trying to find my happy place. "At any rate, I was bound to Admetus, the king of Thessaly. He was a kind master. I liked him so much, I made all his cows have twin calves."

"Can I have baby cows?" Meg asked.

"Well, Meg," I said, "first you would have to have some mommy cows. You see—"

"Guys," Percy interrupted. "So, just to recap, you have to be Meg's servant for . . . ?"

"Some unknown amount of time," I said. "Probably a year. Possibly more."

"And during that time—"

"I will undoubtedly face many trials and hardships."

"Like getting me my cows," Meg said.

I gritted my teeth. "What those trials will be, I do not yet know. But if I suffer through them and prove I am worthy, Zeus will forgive me and allow me to become a god again."

Percy did not look convinced—probably because I did not sound convincing. I *had* to believe my mortal punishment was temporary, as it had been the last two times. Yet Zeus had created a strict rule for baseball and prison sentences: *Three strikes, you're out.* I could only hope this would not apply to me.

"I need time to get my bearings," I said. "Once we get to Camp Half-Blood, I can consult with Chiron. I can figure out which of my godly powers remain with me in this mortal form."

"If any," Percy said.

"Let's think positive."

Percy sat back in his armchair. "Any idea what kind of spirits are following you?"

"Shiny blobs," Meg said. "They were shiny and sort of . . . blobby."

Percy nodded gravely. "Those are the worst kind."

"It hardly matters," I said. "Whatever they are, we have to flee. Once we reach camp, the magical borders will protect me."

"And me?" Meg asked.

"Oh, yes. You, too."

Percy frowned. "Apollo, if you're really mortal, like, one hundred percent mortal, can you even get *in* to Camp Half-Blood?"

The seven-layer dip began to churn in my stomach. "Please don't say that. Of course I'll get in. I *have* to."

"But you could get hurt in battle now . . ." Percy mused. "Then again, maybe monsters would ignore you because you're not important?"

"Stop!" My hands trembled. Being a mortal was traumatic enough. The thought of being barred from camp, of being *unimportant* . . . No. That simply could not be.

"I'm sure I've retained some powers," I said. "I'm still gorgeous, for instance, if I could just get rid of this acne and lose some flab. I must have other abilities!"

Percy turned to Meg. "What about you? I hear you throw a mean garbage bag. Any other skills we should know about? Summoning lightning? Making toilets explode?"

Meg smiled hesitantly. "That's not a power."

"Sure it is," Percy said. "Some of the best demigods have gotten their start by blowing up toilets."

Meg giggled.

I did not like the way she was grinning at Percy. I didn't want the girl to develop a crush. We might never get out of here. As much as I enjoyed Sally Jackson's cooking—the divine smell of baking cookies was even now wafting from the kitchen—I needed to make haste to camp.

"Ahem." I rubbed my hands. "How soon can we leave?"

Percy glanced at the wall clock. "Right now, I guess. If you're being followed, I'd rather have monsters on our trail than sniffing around the apartment."

"Good man," I said.

Percy gestured with distaste at his test manuals. "I just have to be back tonight. Got a lot of studying. The first two times I took the SAT—ugh. If it wasn't for Annabeth helping me out—"

"Who's that?" Meg asked.

"My girlfriend."

Meg frowned. I was glad there were no garbage bags nearby for her to throw.

"So take a break!" I urged. "Your brain will be refreshed after an easy drive to Long Island."

"Huh," Percy said. "There's a lazy kind of logic to that. Okay. Let's do it."

He rose just as Sally Jackson walked in with a plate of fresh-baked chocolate chip cookies. For some reason, the cookies were blue, but they smelled heavenly—and I should know. I'm from heaven.

"Mom, don't freak," Percy said.

Sally sighed. "I hate it when you say that."

"I'm just going to take these two to camp. That's all. I'll be right back."

"I think I've heard that before."

"I *promise*."

Sally looked at me, then Meg. Her expression softened, her innate kindness perhaps overweighing her concern. "All right. Be careful. It was lovely meeting you both. Please try not to die."

Percy kissed her on the cheek. He reached for the cookies, but she moved the plate away.

"Oh, no," she said. "Apollo and Meg can have one, but I'm keeping the rest hostage until you're back safely. And hurry, dear. It would be a shame if Paul ate them all when he gets home."

Percy's expression turned grim. He faced us. "You hear that, guys? A batch of cookies is depending on me. If you get me killed on the way to camp, I am going be ticked off."

6

Aquaman driving

Couldn't possibly be worse

Oh, wait, now it is

MUCH TO MY DISAPPOINTMENT, the Jacksons did not have a spare bow or quiver to lend me.

"I suck at archery," Percy explained.

"Yes, but *I* don't," I said. "This is why you should always plan for *my* needs."

Sally lent Meg and me some proper winter fleece jackets, however. Mine was blue, with the word BLOFIS written inside the neckline. Perhaps that was an arcane ward against evil spirits. Hecate would have known. Sorcery really wasn't my thing.

Once we reached the Prius, Meg called shotgun, which was yet another example of my unfair existence. Gods do not ride in the back. I again suggested following them in a Maserati or a Lamborghini, but Percy admitted he had neither. The Prius was the only car his family owned.

I mean . . . wow. Just *wow*.

Sitting in the backseat, I quickly became carsick. I was used to driving my sun chariot across the sky, where every lane was the fast lane. I was not used to the Long Island

Expressway. Believe me, even at midday in the middle of January, there is nothing *express* about your expressways.

Percy braked and lurched forward. I sorely wished I could launch a fireball in front of us and melt cars to make way for our clearly more important journey.

"Doesn't your Prius have flamethrowers?" I demanded. "Lasers? At least some Hephaestian bumper blades? What sort of cheap economy vehicle is this?"

Percy glanced in the rearview mirror. "You have rides like that on Mount Olympus?"

"We don't have traffic jams," I said. "That, I can promise you."

Meg tugged at her crescent moon rings. Again I wondered if she had some connection to Artemis. The moon was my sister's symbol. Perhaps Artemis had sent Meg to look after me?

Yet that didn't seem right. Artemis had trouble sharing anything with me—demigods, arrows, nations, birthday parties. It's a twin thing. Also, Meg McCaffrey did not strike me as one of my sister's followers. Meg had another sort of aura . . . one I would have been able to recognize easily if I were a god. But, no. I had to rely on mortal intuition, which was like trying to pick up sewing needles while wearing oven mitts.

Meg turned and gazed out the rear windshield, probably checking for any shiny blobs pursuing us. "At least we're not being—"

"Don't say it," Percy warned.

Meg huffed. "You don't know what I was going to—"

"You were going to say, 'At least we're not being followed,'" Percy said. "That'll jinx us. Immediately we'll
notice that we *are* being followed. Then we'll end up in a
big battle that totals my family car and probably destroys
the whole freeway. Then we'll have to run all the way to
camp."

Meg's eyes widened. "You can tell the future?"

"Don't need to." Percy changed lanes to one that was
crawling slightly less slowly. "I've just done this a lot.
Besides"—he shot me an accusing look—"nobody can tell
the future anymore. The Oracle isn't working."

"What Oracle?" Meg asked.

Neither of us answered. For a moment, I was too stunned
to speak. And believe me, I have to be *very* stunned for that
to happen.

"It *still* isn't working?" I said in a small voice.

"You didn't know?" Percy asked. "I mean, sure, you've
been out of it for six months, but this happened on your
watch."

That was unjust. I had been busy hiding from Zeus's
wrath at the time, which was a perfectly legitimate excuse.
How was I to know that Gaea would take advantage of the
chaos of war and raise my oldest, greatest enemy from the
depths of Tartarus so he could take possession of his old lair
in the cave of Delphi and cut off the source of my prophetic
power?

Oh, yes, I hear you critics out there: *You're the god of
prophecy, Apollo. How could you not know that would happen?*

The next sound you hear will be me blowing you a giant
Meg-McCaffrey-quality raspberry.

I swallowed back the taste of fear and seven-layer dip. "I just . . . I assumed—I hoped this would be taken care of by now."

"You mean by demigods," Percy said, "going on a big quest to reclaim the Oracle of Delphi?"

"Exactly!" I knew Percy would understand. "I suppose Chiron just forgot. I'll remind him when we get to camp, and he can dispatch some of you talented fodder—I mean heroes—"

"Well, here's the thing," Percy said. "To go on a quest, we need a prophecy, right? Those are the rules. If there's no Oracle, there *are* no prophecies, so we're stuck in a—"

"A Catch-88." I sighed.

Meg threw a piece of lint at me. "It's a Catch-22."

"No," I explained patiently. "This is a Catch-88, which is four times as bad."

I felt as if I were floating in a warm bath and someone had pulled out the stopper. The water swirled around me, tugging me downward. Soon I would be left shivering and exposed, or else I would be sucked down the drain into the sewers of hopelessness. (Don't laugh. That's a perfectly fine metaphor. Also, when you're a god, you can get sucked down a drain quite easily—if you're caught off guard and relaxed, and you happen to change form at the wrong moment. Once I woke up in a sewage treatment facility in Biloxi, but that's another story.)

I was beginning to see what was in store for me during my mortal sojourn. The Oracle was held by hostile forces. My adversary lay coiled and waiting, growing stronger every day on the magical fumes of the Delphic caverns. And I was a weak mortal bound to an untrained demigod who threw garbage and chewed her cuticles.

No. Zeus could not *possibly* expect me to fix this. Not in my present condition.

And yet . . . *someone* had sent those thugs to intercept me in the alley. Someone had known where I would land.

Nobody can tell the future anymore, Percy had said.

But that wasn't quite true.

"Hey, you two." Meg hit us both with pieces of lint. Where was she finding this lint?

I realized I'd been ignoring her. It had felt good while it lasted.

"Yes, sorry, Meg," I said. "You see, the Oracle of Delphi is an ancient—"

"I don't care about that," she said. "There are three shiny blobs now."

"What?" Percy asked.

She pointed behind us. "Look."

Weaving through the traffic, closing in on us rapidly, were three glittery, vaguely humanoid apparitions—like billowing plumes from smoke grenades touched by King Midas.

"Just once I'd like an easy commute," Percy grumbled. "Everybody, hold on. We're going cross-country."

Percy's definition of *cross-country* was different from mine.

I envisioned crossing an actual countryside. Instead, Percy shot down the nearest exit ramp, wove across the parking lot of a shopping mall, then blasted through the drive-through of a Mexican restaurant without even ordering anything. We swerved into an industrial area of dilapidated warehouses, the smoking apparitions still closing in behind us.

My knuckles turned white on my seat belt's shoulder strap. "Is your plan to avoid a fight by dying in a traffic accident?" I demanded.

"Ha-ha." Percy yanked the wheel to the right. We sped north, the warehouses giving way to a hodgepodge of apartment buildings and abandoned strip malls. "I'm getting us to the beach. I fight better near water."

"Because Poseidon?" Meg asked, steadying herself against the door handle.

"Yep," Percy agreed. "That pretty much describes my entire life: *Because Poseidon*."

Meg bounced up and down with excitement, which seemed pointless to me, since we were already bouncing quite a lot.

"You're gonna be like Aquaman?" she asked. "Get the fish to fight for you?"

"Thanks," Percy said. "I haven't heard enough Aquaman jokes for one lifetime."

"I wasn't joking!" Meg protested.

I glanced out the rear window. The three glittering plumes were still gaining. One of them passed through a middle-aged man crossing the street. The mortal pedestrian instantly collapsed.

"Ah, I know these spirits!" I cried. "They are . . . um . . ."
My brain clouded over.

"What?" Percy demanded. "They are what?"

"I've forgotten! I *hate* being mortal! Four thousand years

of knowledge, the secrets of the universe, a sea of wisdom—lost, because I can't contain it all in this teacup of a head!"

"Hold on!" Percy flew through a railroad crossing and the Prius went airborne. Meg yelped as her head hit the ceiling. Then she began giggling uncontrollably.

The landscape opened into actual countryside—fallow fields, dormant vineyards, orchards of bare fruit trees.

"Just another mile or so to the beach," Percy said. "Plus we're almost to the western edge of camp. We can do it. We can do it."

Actually, we couldn't. One of the shiny smoke clouds pulled a dirty trick, pluming from the pavement directly in front of us.

Instinctively, Percy swerved.

The Prius went off the road, straight through a barbed wire fence and into an orchard. Percy managed to avoid hitting any of the trees, but the car skidded in the icy mud and wedged itself between two trunks. Miraculously, the air bags did not deploy.

Percy popped his seat belt. "You guys okay?"

Meg shoved against her passenger-side door. "Won't open. Get me out of here!"

Percy tried his own door. It was firmly jammed against the side of a peach tree.

"Back here," I said. "Climb over!"

I kicked my door open and staggered out, my legs feeling like worn shock absorbers.

The three smoky figures had stopped at the edge of the orchard. Now they advanced slowly, taking on solid shapes.

THE HIDDEN ORACLE   51

They grew arms and legs. Their faces formed eyes and wide, hungry mouths.

I knew instinctively that I had dealt with these spirits before. I couldn't remember what they were, but I had dispelled them many times, swatting them into oblivion with no more effort than I would a swarm of gnats.

Unfortunately, I wasn't a god now. I was a panicky sixteen-year-old. My palms sweated. My teeth chattered. My only coherent thought was: *YIKES!*

Percy and Meg struggled to get out of the Prius. They needed time, which meant I had to run interference.

"STOP!" I bellowed at the spirits. "I am the god Apollo!"

To my pleasant surprise, the three spirits stopped. They hovered in place about forty feet away.

I heard Meg grunt as she tumbled out of the backseat. Percy scrambled after her.

I advanced toward the spirits, the frosty mud crunching under my shoes. My breath steamed in the cold air. I raised my hand in an ancient three-fingered gesture for warding off evil.

"Leave us or be destroyed!" I told the spirits. "BLOFIS!"

The smoky shapes trembled. My hopes lifted. I waited for them to dissipate or flee in terror.

Instead, they solidified into ghoulish corpses with yellow eyes. Their clothes were tattered rags, their limbs covered with gaping wounds and running sores.

"Oh, dear." My Adam's apple dropped into my chest like a billiard ball. "I remember now."

Percy and Meg stepped to either side of me. With a

metallic *shink*, Percy's pen grew into a blade of glowing Celestial bronze.

"Remember what?" he asked. "How to kill these things?"

"No," I said. "I remember what they are: *nosoi*, plague spirits. Also . . . they can't be killed."

7

Tag with plague spirits
You're it, and you're infectious
Have fun with that, LOL

"NOSOI?" PERCY PLANTED HIS FEET in a fighting stance. "You know, I keep thinking, *I have now killed every single thing in Greek mythology.* But the list never seems to end."

"You haven't killed me yet," I noted.

"Don't tempt me."

The three nosoi shuffled forward. Their cadaverous mouths gaped. Their tongues lolled. Their eyes glistened with a film of yellow mucus.

"These creatures are *not* myths," I said. "Of course, most things in those old myths are not myths. Except for that story about how I flayed the satyr Marsyas alive. That was a total lie."

Percy glanced at me. "You did *what?*"

"Guys." Meg picked up a dead tree branch. "Could we talk about that later?"

The middle plague spirit spoke. "Apollooooo . . ." His voice gurgled like a seal with bronchitis. "We have coooome to—"

"Let me stop you right there." I crossed my arms and feigned arrogant indifference. (Difficult for me, but I managed.) "You've come to take your revenge on me, eh?" I looked at my demigod friends. "You see, nosoi are the spirits of disease. Once I was born, spreading illnesses became part of my job. I use plague arrows to strike down naughty populations with smallpox, athlete's foot, that sort of thing."

"Gross," Meg said.

"Somebody's got to do it!" I said. "Better a god, regulated by the Council of Olympus and with the proper health permits, than a horde of uncontrolled spirits like *these*."

The spirit on the left gurgled. "We're trying to have a moooment here. Stop interrupting! We wish to be free, uncontroooolled—"

"Yes, I know. You'll destroy me. Then you'll spread every known malady across the world. You've been wanting to do that ever since Pandora let you out of that jar. But you can't. I will strike you down!"

Perhaps you are wondering how I could act so confident and calm. In fact, I was terrified. My sixteen-year-old mortal instincts were screaming, *RUN!* My knees were knocking together, and my right eye had developed a nasty twitch. But the secret to dealing with plague spirits was to keep talking so as to appear in charge and unafraid. I trusted that this would allow my demigod companions time to come up with a clever plan to save me. I certainly *hoped* Meg and Percy were working on such a plan.

The spirit on the right bared his rotten teeth. "What will you strike us down with? Where is your booow?"

"It appears to be missing," I agreed. "But is it really? What if it's cleverly hidden under this Led Zeppelin T-shirt, and I am about to whip it out and shoot you all?"

The nosoi shuffled nervously.

"Yooou lie," said the one in the middle.

Percy cleared his throat. "Um, hey, Apollo . . ."

Finally! I thought.

"I know what you're going to say," I told him. "You and Meg have come up with a clever plan to hold off these spirits while I run away to camp. I hate to see you sacrifice yourselves, but—"

"That's not what I was going to say." Percy raised his blade. "I was going to ask what happens if I just slice and dice these mouth-breathers with Celestial bronze."

The middle spirit chortled, his yellow eyes gleaming. "A sword is such a small weapon. It does not have the pooooetry of a good epidemic."

"Stop right there!" I said. "You can't claim both my plagues *and* my poetry!"

"You are right," said the spirit. "Enough woooooords."

The three corpses shambled forward. I thrust out my arms, hoping to blast them to dust. Nothing happened.

"This is insufferable!" I complained. "How do demigods do it without an auto-win power?"

Meg jabbed her tree branch into the nearest spirit's chest. The branch stuck. Glittering smoke began swirling down the length of the wood.

"Let go!" I warned. "Don't let the nosoi touch you!"

Meg released the branch and scampered away.

Meanwhile, Percy Jackson charged into battle. He swung his sword, dodging the spirits' attempts to snare him, but his efforts were futile. Whenever his blade connected with the nosoi, their bodies simply dissolved into glittery mist, then resolidified.

A spirit lunged to grab him. From the ground, Meg scooped up a frozen black peach and threw it with such force it embedded itself in the spirit's forehead, knocking him down.

"We gotta run," Meg decided.

"Yeah." Percy backtracked toward us. "I like that idea."

I knew running would not help. If it were possible to run from disease spirits, the medieval Europeans would've put on their track shoes and escaped the Black Death. (And FYI, the Black Death was *not* my fault. I took one century off to lie around the beach in Cabo, and came back and found that the nosoi had gotten loose and a third of the continent was dead. *Gods*, I was so irritated.)

But I was too terrified to argue. Meg and Percy sprinted off through the orchard, and I followed.

Percy pointed to a line of hills about a mile ahead. "That's the western border of camp. If we can just get there . . ."

We passed an irrigation tank on a tractor-trailer. With a casual flick of his hand, Percy caused the side of the tank to rupture. A wall of water crashed into the three nosoi behind us.

"That was good." Meg grinned, skipping along in her new green dress. "We're going to make it!"

No, I thought, we're not.

My chest ached. Each breath was a ragged wheeze. I resented that these two demigods could carry on a conversation while running for their lives while I, the immortal Apollo, was reduced to gasping like a catfish.

"We can't—" I gulped. "They'll just—"

Before I could finish, three glittering pillars of smoke plumed from the ground in front of us. Two of the nosoi solidified into cadavers—one with a peach for a third eye, the other with a tree branch sticking out of his chest.

The third spirit . . . Well, Percy didn't see it in time. He ran straight into the plume of smoke.

"Don't breathe!" I warned him.

Percy's eyes bugged out as if to say, *Seriously?* He fell to his knees, clawing at his throat. As a son of Poseidon, he could probably breathe underwater, but holding one's breath for an indeterminate amount of time was a different matter altogether.

Meg picked up another withered peach from the field, but it would offer her little defense against the forces of darkness.

I tried to figure out how to help Percy—because I am all about helping—but the branch-impaled nosos charged at me. I turned and fled, running face-first into a tree. I'd like to tell you that was part of my plan, but even I, with all my poetic skill, cannot put a positive spin on it.

I found myself flat on my back, spots dancing in my eyes, the cadaverous visage of the plague spirit looming over me.

"Which fatal illness shall I use to kill the great Apolloooo?" the spirit gurgled. "Anthrax? Perhaps eboooola . . ."

"Hangnails," I suggested, trying to squirm away from my tormentor. "I live in fear of hangnails."

"I have the answer!" the spirit cried, rudely ignoring me. "Let's try this!"

He dissolved into smoke and settled over me like a glittering blanket.

8

Peaches in combat
I am hanging it up now
My brain exploded

I WILL NOT SAY my life passed before my eyes.

I wish it had. That would've taken several months, giving me time to figure out an escape plan.

Instead, my regrets passed before my eyes. Despite being a gloriously perfect being, I do have a few regrets. I remembered that day at Abbey Road Studios, when my envy led me to set rancor in the hearts of John and Paul and break up the Beatles. I remembered Achilles falling on the plains of Troy, cut down by an unworthy archer because of my wrath.

I saw Hyacinthus, his bronze shoulders and dark ringlets gleaming in the sunlight. Standing on the sideline of the discus field, he gave me a brilliant smile. *Even you can't throw that far*, he teased.

Watch me, I said. I threw the discus, then stared in horror as a gust of wind made it veer, inexplicably, toward Hyacinthus's handsome face.

And of course I saw *her*—the other love of my life—her fair skin transforming into bark, her hair sprouting green leaves, her eyes hardening into rivulets of sap.

Those memories brought back so much pain, you might think I would welcome the glittering plague mist descending over me.

Yet my new mortal self rebelled. I was too young to die! I hadn't even had my first kiss! (Yes, my godly catalogue of exes was filled with more beautiful people than a Kardashian party guest list, but none of that seemed real to me.)

If I'm being totally honest, I have to confess something else: all gods fear death, even when we are *not* encased in mortal forms.

That may seem silly. We are immortal. But as you've seen, immortality can be taken away. (In my case, *three stinking times*.)

Gods know about fading. They know about being forgotten over the centuries. The idea of ceasing to exist altogether terrifies us. In fact . . . well, Zeus would not like me sharing this information—and if you tell anyone I will deny I ever said it—but the truth is we gods are a little in awe of you mortals. You spend your whole lives knowing you will die. No matter how many friends and relatives you have, your puny existence will quickly be forgotten. How do you cope with it? Why are you not running around constantly screaming and pulling your hair out? Your bravery, I must admit, is quite admirable.

Now where was I?

Right. I was dying.

I rolled around in the mud, holding my breath. I tried to brush off the disease cloud, but it was not as easy as swatting a fly or an uppity mortal.

I caught a glimpse of Meg, playing a deadly game of tag

with the third nosos, trying to keep a peach tree between herself and the spirit. She yelled something to me, but her voice seemed tinny and far away.

Somewhere to my left, the ground shook. A miniature geyser erupted from the field. Percy crawled toward it desperately. He thrust his face in the water, washing away the smoke.

My eyesight began to dim.

Percy struggled to his feet. He ripped out the source of the geyser—an irrigation pipe—and turned the water on me.

Normally I do not like being doused. Every time I go camping with Artemis, she likes to wake me up with a bucket of ice-cold water. But in this case, I didn't mind.

The water disrupted the smoke, allowing me to roll away and gasp for air. Nearby, our two gaseous enemies re-formed as dripping wet corpses, their yellow eyes glowing with annoyance.

Meg yelled again. This time I understood her words. "GET DOWN!"

I found this inconsiderate, since I'd only just gotten up. All around the orchard, the frozen blackened remnants of the harvest were beginning to levitate.

Believe me, in four thousand years I have seen some strange things. I have seen the dreaming face of Ouranos etched in stars across the heavens, and the full fury of Typhon as he raged across the earth. I've seen men turn into snakes, ants turn into men, and otherwise rational people dance the macarena.

But never before had I seen an uprising of frozen fruit.

Percy and I hit the ground as peaches shot around

the orchard, ricocheting off trees like eight balls, ripping through the nosoi's cadaverous bodies. If I had been standing up, I would have been killed, but Meg simply stood there, unfazed and unhurt, as frozen dead fruit zinged around her.

All three nosoi collapsed, riddled with holes. Every piece of fruit dropped to the ground.

Percy looked up, his eyes red and puffy. "Whah jus happened?"

He sounded congested, which meant he hadn't completely escaped the effects of the plague cloud, but at least he wasn't dead. That was generally a good sign.

"I don't know," I admitted. "Meg, is it safe?"

She was staring in amazement at the carnage of fruit, mangled corpses, and broken tree limbs. "I—I'm not sure."

"How'd you do thah?" Percy snuffled.

Meg looked horrified. "I didn't! I just knew it would happen."

One of the cadavers began to stir. It got up, wobbling on its heavily perforated legs.

"But you *did* doooo it," the spirit growled. "Yooou are strong, child."

The other two corpses rose.

"Not strong enough," said the second nosos. "We will finish you now."

The third spirit bared his rotten teeth. "Your guardian would be sooooo disappointed."

Guardian? Perhaps the spirit meant me. When in doubt, I usually assumed the conversation was about me.

Meg looked as if she'd been punched in the gut. Her

face paled. Her arms trembled. She stamped her foot and yelled, "NO!"

More peaches swirled into the air. This time the fruit blurred together in a fructose dust devil, until standing in front of Meg was a creature like a pudgy human toddler wearing only a linen diaper. Protruding from his back were wings made of leafy branches. His babyish face might have been cute except for the glowing green eyes and pointy fangs. The creature snarled and snapped at the air.

"Oh, no." Percy shook his head. "I hate these things."

The three nosoi also did not look pleased. They edged away from the snarling baby.

"Wh-what is it?" Meg asked.

I stared at her in disbelief. She had to be the cause of this fruit-based strangeness, but she looked as shocked as we were. Unfortunately, if Meg didn't know how she had summoned this creature, she would not know how to make it go away, and like Percy Jackson, I was no fan of *karpoi*.

"It's a grain spirit," I said, trying to keep the panic out of my voice. "I've never seen a peach karpos before, but if it's as vicious as other types . . ."

I was about to say, *we're doomed*, but that seemed both obvious and depressing.

The peach baby turned toward the nosoi. For a moment, I feared he would make some hellish alliance—an axis of evil between illnesses and fruits.

The middle corpse, the one with the peach in his forehead, inched backward. "Do not interfere," he warned the karpos. "We will not allooow—"

The peach baby launched himself at the nosos and bit his head off.

That is not a figure of speech. The karpos's fanged mouth unhinged, expanding to an unbelievable circumference, then closed around the cadaver's head, and chomped it off in one bite.

Oh, dear . . . I hope you weren't eating dinner as you read that.

In a matter of seconds, the nosos had been torn to shreds and devoured.

Understandably, the other two nosoi retreated, but the karpos crouched and sprang. He landed on the second corpse and proceeded to rip it into plague-flavored Cream of Wheat.

The last spirit dissolved into glittering smoke and tried to fly away, but the peach baby spread his leafy wings and launched himself in pursuit. He opened his mouth and inhaled the sickness, snapping and swallowing until every wisp of smoke was gone.

He landed in front of Meg and belched. His green eyes gleamed. He did not appear even slightly sick, which I suppose wasn't surprising, since human diseases don't infect fruit trees. Instead, even after eating three whole nosoi, the little fellow looked hungry.

He howled and beat his small chest. "Peaches!"

Slowly, Percy raised his sword. His nose was still red and runny, and his face was puffy. "Meg, don move," he snuffled. "I'm gonna—"

"No!" she said. "Don't hurt him."

She put her hand tentatively on the creature's curly head. "You saved us," she told the karpos. "Thank you."

I started mentally preparing a list of herbal remedies for regenerating severed limbs, but to my surprise, the peach baby did not bite off Meg's hand. Instead he hugged Meg's leg and glared at us as if daring us to approach.

"Peaches," he growled.

"He likes you," Percy noted. "Um . . . why?"

"I don't know," Meg said. "Honestly, I didn't summon him!"

I was certain Meg *had* summoned him, intentionally or unintentionally. I also had some ideas now about her godly parentage, and some questions about this "guardian" that the spirits had mentioned, but I decided it would be better to interrogate her when she did not have a snarling carnivorous toddler wrapped around her leg.

"Well, whatever the case," I said, "we owe the karpos our lives. This brings to mind an expression I coined ages ago: *A peach a day keeps the plague spirits away!*"

Percy sneezed. "I thought it was apples and doctors."

The karpos hissed.

"Or peaches," Percy said. "Peaches work too."

"Peaches," agreed the karpos.

Percy wiped his nose. "Not criticizing, but why is he grooting?"

Meg frowned. "Grooting?"

"Yeah, like thah character in the movie . . . only saying one thing over and over."

"I'm afraid I haven't seen that movie," I said. "But this

karpos does seem to have a very . . . targeted vocabulary."

"Maybe Peaches is his name." Meg stroked the karpos's curly brown hair, which elicited a demonic purring from the creature's throat. "That's what I'll call him."

"Whoa, you are not adopting thah—" Percy sneezed with such force, another irrigation pipe exploded behind him, sending up a row of tiny geysers. "Ugh. Sick."

"You're lucky," I said. "Your trick with the water diluted the spirit's power. Instead of getting a deadly illness, you got a head cold."

"I hate head colds." His green irises looked like they were sinking in a sea of bloodshot. "Neither of you got sick?"

Meg shook her head.

"I have an excellent constitution," I said. "No doubt that's what saved me."

"And the fact thah I hosed the smoke off of you," Percy said.

"Well, yes."

Percy stared at me as if waiting for something. After an awkward moment, it occurred to me that if he was a god and I was a worshipper, he might expect gratitude.

"Ah . . . thank you," I said.

He nodded. "No problem."

I relaxed a little. If he had demanded a sacrifice, like a white bull or a fatted calf, I'm not sure what I would've done.

"Can we go now?" Meg asked.

"An excellent idea," I said. "Though I'm afraid Percy is in no condition—"

"I can drive you the rest of the way," he said. "If we can get my car out from between those trees. . . ." He glanced in that direction and his expression turned even more miserable. "Aw, Hades no. . . ."

A police cruiser was pulling over on the side of the road. I imagined the officers' eyes tracing the tire ruts in the mud, which led to the plowed-down fence and continued to the blue Toyota Prius wedged between two peach trees. The cruiser's roof lights flashed on.

"Great," Percy muttered. "If they tow the Prius, I'm dead. My mom and Paul *need* thah car."

"Go talk to the officers," I said. "You won't be any use to us anyway in your current state."

"Yeah, we'll be fine," Meg said. "You said the camp is right over those hills?"

"Right, but . . ." Percy scowled, probably trying to think straight through the effects of his cold. "Most people enter camp from the east, where Half-Blood Hill is. The western border is wilder—hills and woods, all heavily enchanted. If you're not careful, you can get lost. . . ." He sneezed again. "I'm still not even sure Apollo can get *in* if he's fully mortal."

"I'll get in." I tried to exude confidence. I had no alternative. If I was unable to enter Camp Half-Blood . . . No. I'd already been attacked twice on my first day as a mortal. There was no plan B that would keep me alive.

The police car's doors opened.

"Go," I urged Percy. "We'll find our way through the woods. You explain to the police that you're sick and you lost control of the car. They'll go easy on you."

Percy laughed. "Yeah. Cops love me almost as much as teachers do." He glanced at Meg. "You sure you're okay with the baby fruit demon?"

Peaches growled.

"All good," Meg promised. "Go home. Rest. Get lots of fluids."

Percy's mouth twitched. "You're telling a son of Poseidon to get lots of fluids? Okay, just try to survive until the weekend, will you? I'll come to camp and check on you guys if I can. Be careful and—CHOOOO!"

Muttering unhappily, he touched the cap of his pen to his sword, turning it back into a simple ballpoint. A wise precaution before approaching law enforcement. He trudged down the hill, sneezing and sniffling.

"Officer?" he called. "Sorry, I'm up here. Can you tell me where Manhattan is?"

Meg turned to me. "Ready?"

I was soaking wet and shivering. I was having the worst day in the history of days. I was stuck with a scary girl and an even scarier peach baby. I was by no means ready for anything. But I also desperately wanted to reach camp. I might find some friendly faces there—perhaps even jubilant worshippers who would bring me peeled grapes, Oreos, and other holy offerings.

"Sure," I said. "Let's go."

Peaches the karpos grunted. He gestured for us to follow, then scampered toward the hills. Maybe he knew the way. Maybe he just wanted to lead us to a grisly death.

Meg skipped after him, swinging from tree branches and cartwheeling through the mud as the mood took her.

You might've thought we'd just finished a nice picnic rather than a battle with plague-ridden cadavers.

I turned my face to the sky. "Are you sure, Zeus? It's not too late to tell me this was an elaborate prank and recall me to Olympus. I've learned my lesson. I promise."

The gray winter clouds did not respond. With a sigh, I jogged after Meg and her homicidal new minion.

9

A walk through the woods
Voices driving me bonkers
I hate spaghetti

I SIGHED WITH RELIEF. "This should be easy."

Granted, I'd said the same thing before I fought Poseidon in hand-to-hand combat, and that had *not* turned out to be easy. Nevertheless, our path into Camp Half-Blood looked straightforward enough. For starters, I was pleased I could *see* the camp, since it was normally shielded from mortal eyes. This boded well for me getting in.

From where we stood at the top of a hill, the entire valley spread out below us: roughly three square miles of woods, meadows, and strawberry fields bordered by Long Island Sound to the north and rolling hills on the other three sides. Just below us, a dense forest of evergreens covered the western third of the vale.

Beyond that, the buildings of Camp Half-Blood gleamed in the wintry light: the amphitheater, the sword-fighting stadium, the open-air dining pavilion with its white marble columns. A trireme floated in the canoe lake. Twenty cabins lined the central green where the communal hearth fire glowed cheerfully.

At the edge of the strawberry fields stood the Big House:

a four-story Victorian painted sky blue with white trim. My friend Chiron would be inside, probably having tea by the fireplace. I would find sanctuary at last.

My gaze rose to the far end of the valley. There, on the tallest hill, the Athena Parthenos shone in all its gold-and-alabaster glory. Once, the massive statue had graced the Parthenon in Greece. Now it presided over Camp Half-Blood, protecting the valley from intruders. Even from here I could feel its power, like the subsonic thrum of a mighty engine. Old Gray Eyes was on the lookout for threats, being her usual vigilant, no-fun, all-business self.

Personally, I would have installed a more interesting statue—of myself, for instance. Still, the panorama of Camp Half-Blood was an impressive sight. My mood always improved when I saw the place—a small reminder of the good old days when mortals knew how to build temples and do proper burnt sacrifices. Ah, everything was better in ancient Greece! Well, except for a few small improvements modern humans had made—the Internet, chocolate croissants, life expectancy.

Meg's mouth hung open. "How come I've never heard about this place? Do you need tickets?"

I chuckled. I always enjoyed the chance to enlighten a clueless mortal. "You see, Meg, magical borders camouflage the valley. From the outside, most humans would spy nothing here except boring farmland. If they approached, they would get turned around and find themselves wandering out again. Believe me, I tried to get a pizza delivered to camp once. It was quite annoying."

"You ordered a pizza?"

"Never mind," I said. "As for tickets . . . it's true the camp doesn't let in just anybody, but you're in luck. I know the management."

Peaches growled. He sniffed the ground, then chomped a mouthful of dirt and spit it out.

"He doesn't like the taste of this place," Meg said.

"Yes, well . . ." I frowned at the karpos. "Perhaps we can find him some potting soil or fertilizer when we arrive. I'll convince the demigods to let him in, but it would be helpful if he doesn't bite their heads off—at least not right away."

Peaches muttered something about peaches.

"Something doesn't feel right." Meg bit her nails. "Those woods . . . Percy said they were wild and enchanted and stuff."

I, too, felt as if something was amiss, but I chalked this up to my general dislike of forests. For reasons I'd rather not go into, I find them . . . uncomfortable places. Nevertheless, with our goal in sight, my usual optimism was returning.

"Don't worry," I assured Meg. "You're traveling with a god!"

"Ex-god."

"I wish you wouldn't keep harping on that. Anyway, the campers are very friendly. They'll welcome us with tears of joy. And wait until you see the orientation video!"

"The what?"

"I directed it myself! Now, come along. The woods can't be that bad."

———

The woods were that bad.

As soon as we entered their shadows, the trees seemed to crowd us. Trunks closed ranks, blocking old paths and opening new ones. Roots writhed across the forest floor, making an obstacle course of bumps, knots, and loops. It was like trying to walk across a giant bowl of spaghetti.

The thought of spaghetti made me hungry. It had only been a few hours since Sally Jackson's seven-layer dip and sandwiches, but my mortal stomach was already clenching and squelching for food. The sounds were quite annoying, especially while walking through dark scary woods. Even the karpos Peaches was starting to smell good to me, giving me visions of cobbler and ice cream.

As I said earlier, I was generally not a fan of the woods. I tried to convince myself that the trees were not watching me, scowling and whispering among themselves. They were just trees. Even if they had dryad spirits, those dryads couldn't possibly hold me responsible for what had happened thousands of years ago on a different continent.

Why not? I asked myself. *You still hold yourself responsible.*

I told myself to stuff a sock in it.

We hiked for hours . . . much longer than it should have taken to reach the Big House. Normally I could navigate by the sun—which shouldn't be a surprise, since I spent millennia driving it across the sky—but under the canopy of trees, the light was diffuse, the shadows confusing.

After we passed the same boulder for the third time, I stopped and admitted the obvious. "I have no idea where we are."

Meg plopped herself down onto a fallen log. In the green light, she looked more like a dryad than ever, though tree spirits do not often wear red sneakers and hand-me-down fleece jackets.

"Don't you have any wilderness skills?" she asked. "Reading moss on the sides of trees? Following tracks?"

"That's more my sister's thing," I said.

"Maybe Peaches can help." Meg turned to her karpos. "Hey, can you find us a way out of the woods?"

For the past few miles, the karpos had been muttering nervously, cutting his eyes from side to side. Now he sniffed the air, his nostrils quivering. He tilted his head.

His face flushed bright green. He emitted a distressed bark, then dissolved in a swirl of leaves.

Meg shot to her feet. "Where'd he go?"

I scanned the woods. I suspected Peaches had done the intelligent thing. He'd sensed danger approaching and abandoned us. I didn't want to suggest that to Meg, though. She'd already become quite fond of the karpos. (Ridiculous, getting attached to a small dangerous creature. Then again, we gods got attached to humans, so I had no room to criticize.)

"Perhaps he went scouting," I suggested. "Perhaps we should—"

APOLLO.

The voice reverberated in my head, as if someone had installed Bose speakers behind my eyes. It was not the voice of my conscience. My conscience was not female, and it was not that loud. Yet something about the woman's tone was eerily familiar.

"What's wrong?" Meg asked.

The air turned sickly sweet. The trees loomed over me like trigger hairs of a Venus flytrap.

A bead of sweat trickled down the side of my face.

"We can't stay here," I said. "Attend me, mortal."

"Excuse me?" Meg said.

"Uh, I mean come on!"

We ran, stumbling over tree roots, fleeing blindly through a maze of branches and boulders. We reached a clear stream over a bed of gravel. I barely slowed down. I waded in, sinking shin-deep into the ice-cold water.

The voice spoke again: *FIND ME*.

This time it was so loud, it stabbed through my forehead like a railroad spike. I stumbled, falling to my knees.

"Hey!" Meg gripped my arm. "Get up!"

"You didn't hear that?"

"Hear what?"

THE FALL OF THE SUN, the voice boomed. *THE FINAL VERSE*.

I collapsed face-first into the stream.

"Apollo!" Meg rolled me over, her voice tight with alarm. "Come on! I can't carry you!"

Yet she tried. She dragged me across the river, scolding me and cursing until, with her help, I managed to crawl to shore.

I lay on my back, staring wildly at the forest canopy. My soaked clothes were so cold they burned. My body trembled like an open E string on an electric bass.

Meg tugged off my wet winter coat. Her own coat was much too small for me, but she draped the warm dry fleece over my shoulders. "Keep yourself together," she ordered. "Don't go crazy on me."

My own laughter sounded brittle. "But I—I heard—"

THE FIRES WILL CONSUME ME. MAKE HASTE!

The voice splintered into a chorus of angry whispers. Shadows grew longer and darker. Steam rose from my clothes, smelling like the volcanic fumes of Delphi.

Part of me wanted to curl into a ball and die. Part of me wanted to get up and run wildly after the voices—to find their source—but I suspected that if I tried, my sanity would be lost forever.

Meg was saying something. She shook my shoulders. She put her face nose-to-nose with mine so my own derelict reflection stared back at me from the lenses of her cat-eye glasses. She slapped me, *hard*, and I managed to decipher her words: "GET UP!"

Somehow I did. Then I doubled over and retched.

I hadn't vomited in centuries. I'd forgotten how unpleasant it was.

The next thing I knew, we were staggering along, Meg bearing most of my weight. The voices whispered and argued, tearing off little pieces of my mind and carrying them away into the forest. Soon I wouldn't have much left.

There was no point. I might as well wander off into the forest and go insane. The idea struck me as funny. I began to giggle.

Meg forced me to keep walking. I couldn't understand her words, but her tone was insistent and stubborn, with just enough anger to outweigh her own terror.

In my fractured mental state, I thought the trees were

parting for us, grudgingly opening a path straight out of the woods. I saw a bonfire in the distance, and the open meadows of Camp Half-Blood.

It occurred to me that Meg was talking to the trees, telling them to get out of the way. The idea was ridiculous, and at the moment it seemed hilarious. Judging from the steam billowing from my clothes, I guessed I was running a fever of about a hundred and six.

I was laughing hysterically as we stumbled out of the forest, straight toward the campfire where a dozen teenagers sat making s'mores. When they saw us, they rose. In their jeans and winter coats, with assorted weapons at their sides, they were the dourest bunch of marshmallow roasters I had ever seen.

I grinned. "Oh, hi! I'm Apollo!"

My eyes rolled up in my head, and I passed out.

10

My bus is in flames
My son is older than me
Please, Zeus, make it stop

I DREAMED I WAS DRIVING the sun chariot across the sky. I had the top down in Maserati mode. I was cruising along, honking at jet planes to get out of my way, enjoying the smell of cold stratosphere, and bopping to my favorite jam: Alabama Shakes' "Rise to the Sun."

I was thinking about transforming the Spyder into a Google self-driving car. I wanted to get out my lute and play a scorching solo that would make Brittany Howard proud.

Then a woman appeared in my passenger seat. "You've got to hurry, man."

I almost jumped out of the sun.

My guest was dressed like a Libyan queen of old. (I should know. I dated a few of them.) Her gown swirled with red, black, and gold floral designs. Her long dark hair was crowned with a tiara that looked like a curved miniature ladder—two gold rails lined with rungs of silver. Her face was mature but stately, the way a benevolent queen should look.

So definitely not Hera, then. Besides, Hera would never smile at me so kindly. Also . . . this woman wore a large metal peace symbol around her neck, which did not seem like Hera's style.

Still, I felt I should know her. Despite the elder-hippie vibe, she was so attractive that I assumed we must be related.

"Who are you?" I asked.

Her eyes flashed a dangerous shade of gold, like a feline predator's. "Follow the voices."

A lump swelled in my throat. I tried to think straight, but my brain felt like it had been recently run through a Vitamix. "I heard you in the woods. . . . Were you—were you speaking a prophecy?"

"Find the gates." She grabbed my wrist. "You've gotta find them first, you dig?"

"But—"

The woman burst into flames. I pulled back my singed wrist and grabbed the wheel as the sun chariot plunged into a nosedive. The Maserati morphed into a school bus—a mode I only used when I had to transport a large number of people. Smoke filled the cabin.

Somewhere behind me, a nasal voice said, "By all means, find the gates."

I glanced in the rearview mirror. Through the smoke, I saw a portly man in a mauve suit. He lounged across the backseat, where the troublemakers normally sat. Hermes was fond of that seat—but this man was not Hermes.

He had a weak jawline, an overlarge nose, and a beard that wrapped around his double chin like a helmet strap. His hair was curly and dark like mine, except not as fashionably tousled or luxuriant. His lip curled as if he smelled something unpleasant. Perhaps it was the burning seats of the bus.

"Who are you?" I yelled, desperately trying to pull the chariot out of its dive. "Why are you on my bus?"

The man smiled, which made his face even uglier. "My own forefather does not recognize me? I'm hurt!"

I tried to place him. My cursed mortal brain was too small, too inflexible. It had jettisoned four thousand years of memories like so much ballast.

"I—I don't," I said. "I'm sorry."

The man laughed as flames licked at his purple sleeves. "You're not sorry *yet*, but you will be. Find me the gates. Lead me to the Oracle. I'll enjoy burning it down!"

Fire consumed me as the sun chariot careened toward the earth. I gripped the wheel and stared in horror as a massive bronze face loomed outside the windshield. It was the face of the man in purple, fashioned from an expanse of metal larger than my bus. As we hurtled toward it, the features shifted and became my own.

Then I woke, shivering and sweating.

"Easy." Someone's hand rested on my shoulder. "Don't try to sit up."

Naturally I tried to sit up.

My bedside attendant was a young man about my age—my *mortal* age—with shaggy blond hair and blue eyes. He wore doctor's scrubs with an open ski jacket, the words OKEMO MOUNTAIN stitched on the pocket. His face had a skier's tan. I felt I should know him. (I'd been having that sensation a lot since my fall from Olympus.)

I was lying in a cot in the middle of a cabin. On either

side, bunk beds lined the walls. Rough cedar beams ribbed the ceiling. The white plaster walls were bare except for a few hooks for coats and weapons.

It could have been a modest abode in almost any age— ancient Athens, medieval France, the farmlands of Iowa. It smelled of clean linen and dried sage. The only decorations were some flowerpots on the windowsill, where cheerful yellow blooms were thriving despite the cold weather outside.

"Those flowers . . ." My voice was hoarse, as if I'd inhaled the smoke from my dream. "Those are from Delos, my sacred island."

"Yep," said the young man. "They only grow in and around Cabin Seven—*your* cabin. Do you know who I am?"

I studied his face. The calmness of his eyes, the smile resting easily on his lips, the way his hair curled around his ears . . . I had a vague memory of a woman, an alt-country singer named Naomi Solace, whom I'd met in Austin. I blushed thinking about her even now. To my teenaged self, our romance felt like something that I'd watched in a movie a long ago time—a movie my parents wouldn't have allowed me to see.

But this boy was definitely Naomi's son.

Which meant he was *my* son too.

Which felt very, very strange.

"You're Will Solace," I said. "My, ah . . . erm—"

"Yeah," Will agreed. "It's awkward."

My frontal lobe did a one-eighty inside my skull. I listed sideways.

"Whoa, there." Will steadied me. "I tried to heal you, but honestly, I don't understand what's wrong. You've got blood, not ichor. You're recovering quickly from your injuries, but your vital signs are completely human."

"Don't remind me."

"Yeah, well . . ." He put his hand on my forehead and frowned in concentration. His fingers trembled slightly. "I didn't *know* any of that until I tried to give you nectar. Your lips started steaming. I almost killed you."

"Ah . . ." I ran my tongue across my bottom lip, which felt heavy and numb. I wondered if that explained my dream about smoke and fire. I hoped so. "I guess Meg forgot to tell you about my condition."

"I guess she did." Will took my wrist and checked my pulse. "You seem to be about my age, fifteen or so. Your heart rate is back to normal. Ribs are mending. Nose is swollen, but not broken."

"And I have acne," I lamented. "And flab."

Will tilted his head. "You're mortal, and *that's* what you're worried about?"

"You're right. I'm powerless. Weaker even than you puny demigods!"

"Gee, thanks. . . ."

I got the feeling that he almost said *Dad* but managed to stop himself.

It was difficult to think of this young man as my son. He was so poised, so unassuming, so free of acne. He also didn't appear to be awestruck in my presence. In fact, the corner of his mouth had started twitching.

"Are—are you amused?" I demanded.

Will shrugged. "Well, it's either find this funny or freak out. My dad, the god Apollo, is a fifteen-year-old—"

"*Sixteen,*" I corrected. "Let's go with sixteen."

"A sixteen-year-old mortal, lying in a cot in my cabin, and with all my healing arts—which I got from *you*—I still can't figure out how to fix you."

"There is no fixing this," I said miserably. "I am cast out of Olympus. My fate is tied to a girl named Meg. It could not be worse!"

Will laughed, which I thought took a great deal of gall. "Meg seems cool. She's already poked Connor Stoll in the eyes and kicked Sherman Yang in the crotch."

"She did *what?*"

"She'll get along just fine here. She's waiting for you outside—along with most of the campers." Will's smile faded. "Just so you're prepared, they're asking a lot of questions. Everybody is wondering if your arrival, your *mortal* situation, has anything to do with what's been going on at camp."

I frowned. "What has been going on at camp?"

The cabin door opened. Two more demigods stepped inside. One was a tall boy of about thirteen, his skin burnished bronze and his cornrows woven like DNA helixes. In his black wool peacoat and black jeans, he looked as if he'd stepped from the deck of an eighteenth-century whaling vessel. The other newcomer was a younger girl in olive camouflage. She had a full quiver on her shoulder, and her short ginger hair was dyed with a shock of bright green, which seemed to defeat the point of wearing camouflage.

I smiled, delighted that I actually remembered their names.

"Austin," I said. "And Kayla, isn't it?"

Rather than falling to their knees and blubbering gratefully, they gave each other a nervous glance.

"So it's really you," Kayla said.

Austin frowned. "Meg told us you were beaten up by a couple of thugs. She said you had no powers and you went hysterical out in the woods."

My mouth tasted like burnt school bus upholstery. "Meg talks too much."

"But you're mortal?" Kayla asked. "As in completely mortal? Does that mean I'm going to lose my archery skills? I can't even qualify for the Olympics until I'm sixteen!"

"And if I lose my music . . ." Austin shook his head. "No, man, that's wrong. My last video got, like, five hundred thousand views in a week. What am I supposed to do?"

It warmed my heart that my children had the right priorities: their skills, their images, their views on YouTube. Say what you will about gods being absentee parents; our children inherit many of our finest personality traits.

"My problems should not affect you," I promised. "If Zeus went around retroactively yanking my divine power out of all my descendants, half the medical schools in the country would be empty. The Rock and Roll Hall of Fame would disappear. The Tarot-card reading industry would collapse overnight!"

Austin's shoulders relaxed. "That's a relief."

"So if you die while you're mortal," Kayla said, "we won't disappear?"

"Guys," Will interrupted, "why don't you run to the Big House and tell Chiron that our . . . our *patient* is conscious. I'll bring him along in a minute. And, uh, see if you can disperse the crowd outside, okay? I don't want everybody rushing Apollo at once."

Kayla and Austin nodded sagely. As my children, they no doubt understood the importance of controlling the paparazzi.

As soon as they were gone, Will gave me an apologetic smile. "They're in shock. We all are. It'll take some time to get used to . . . whatever this is."

"You do not seem shocked," I said.

Will laughed under his breath. "I'm terrified. But one thing you learn as head counselor: you have to keep it together for everyone else. Let's get you on your feet."

It was not easy. I fell twice. My head spun, and my eyes felt as if they were being microwaved in their sockets. Recent dreams continued to churn in my brain like river silt, muddying my thoughts—the woman with the crown and the peace symbol, the man in the purple suit. *Lead me to the Oracle. I'll enjoy burning it down!*

The cabin began to feel stifling. I was anxious to get some fresh air.

One thing my sister, Artemis, and I agree on: every worthwhile pursuit is better outdoors than indoors. Music is best played under the dome of heaven. Poetry should be shared in the *agora*. Archery is definitely easier outside, as I can attest after that one time I tried target practice in my father's throne room. And driving the sun . . . well, that's not really an indoor sport either.

Leaning on Will for support, I stepped outside. Kayla and Austin had succeeded in shooing the crowd away. The only one waiting for me—oh, joy and happiness—was my young overlord, Meg, who had apparently now gained fame at camp as Crotchkicker McCaffrey.

She still wore Sally Jackson's hand-me-down green dress, though it was a bit dirtier now. Her leggings were ripped and torn. On her bicep, a line of butterfly bandages closed a nasty cut she must have gotten in the woods.

She took one look at me, scrunched up her face, and stuck out her tongue. "You look *yuck*."

"And you, Meg," I said, "are as charming as ever."

She adjusted her glasses until they were just crooked enough to be annoying. "Thought you were going to die."

"Glad to disappoint you."

"Nah." She shrugged. "You still owe me a year of service. We're bound, whether you like it or not!"

I sighed. It was ever so wonderful to be back in Meg's company.

"I suppose I should thank you. . . ." I had a hazy memory of my delirium in the forest, Meg carrying me along, the trees seeming to part before us. "How did you get us out of the woods?"

Her expression turned guarded. "Dunno. Luck." She jabbed a thumb at Will Solace. "From what he's been telling me, it's a good thing we got out before nightfall."

"Why?"

Will started to answer, then apparently thought better of it. "I should let Chiron explain. Come on."

I rarely visited Camp Half-Blood in winter. The last time had been three years ago, when a girl named Thalia Grace crash-landed my bus in the canoe lake.

I expected the camp to be sparsely populated. I knew

most demigods only came for the summer, leaving a small core of year-rounders during the school term—those who for various reasons found camp the only safe place they could live.

Still, I was struck by how few demigods I saw. If Cabin Seven was any indication, each god's cabin could hold beds for about twenty campers. That meant a maximum capacity of four hundred demigods—enough for several phalanxes or one really amazing yacht party.

Yet, as we walked across camp, I saw no more than a dozen people. In the fading light of sunset, a lone girl was scaling the climbing wall as lava flowed down either side. At the lake, a crew of three checked the rigging on the trireme.

Some campers had found reasons to be outside just so they could gawk at me. Over by the hearth, one young man sat polishing his shield, watching me in its reflective surface. Another fellow glared at me as he spliced barbed wire outside the Ares cabin. From the awkward way he walked, I assumed he was Sherman Yang of the recently kicked crotch.

In the doorway of the Hermes cabin, two girls giggled and whispered as I passed. Normally this sort of attention wouldn't have fazed me. My magnetism was understandably irresistible. But now my face burned. Me—the manly paragon of romance—reduced to a gawky, inexperienced boy!

I would have screamed at the heavens for this unfairness, but that would've been super-embarrassing.

We made our way through the fallow strawberry fields. Up on Half-Blood Hill, the Golden Fleece glinted in the lowest branch of a tall pine tree. Whiffs of steam rose from the head of Peleus, the guardian dragon coiled around the base of the trunk. Next to the tree, the Athena Parthenos looked angry red in the sunset. Or perhaps she just wasn't happy to see me. (Athena had never gotten over our little tiff during the Trojan War.)

Halfway down the hillside, I spotted the Oracle's cave, its entrance shrouded by thick burgundy curtains. The torches on either side stood unlit—usually a sign that my prophetess, Rachel Dare, was not in residence. I wasn't sure whether to be disappointed or relieved.

Even when she was not channeling prophecies, Rachel was a wise young lady. I had hoped to consult her about my problems. On the other hand, since her prophetic power had apparently stopped working (which I suppose in some *small* part was my fault), I wasn't sure Rachel would want to see me. She would expect explanations from her Main Man, and while I had invented *mansplaining* and was its foremost practitioner, I had no answers to give her.

The dream of the flaming bus stayed with me: the groovy crowned woman urging me to find the gates, the ugly mauve-suited man threatening to burn the Oracle.

Well . . . the cave was right there. I wasn't sure why the woman in the crown was having such trouble finding it, or why the ugly man would be so intent on burning its "gates," which amounted to nothing more than purple curtains.

Unless the dream was referring to something other than the Oracle of Delphi. . . .

I rubbed my throbbing temples. I kept reaching for memories that weren't there, trying to plunge into my vast lake of knowledge only to find it had been reduced to a kiddie pool. You simply can't do much with a kiddie pool brain.

On the porch of the Big House, a dark-haired young man was waiting for us. He wore faded black trousers, a Ramones T-shirt (bonus points for musical taste), and a black leather bomber jacket. At his side hung a Stygian iron sword.

"I remember you," I said. "Is it Nicholas, son of Hades?"

"Nico di Angelo." He studied me, his eyes sharp and colorless, like broken glass. "So it's true. You're completely mortal. There's an aura of death around you—a thick possibility of death."

Meg snorted. "Sounds like a weather forecast."

I did not find this amusing. Being face-to-face with a son of Hades, I recalled the many mortals I had sent to the Underworld with my plague arrows. It had always seemed like good clean fun—meting out richly deserved punishments for wicked deeds. Now, I began to understand the terror in my victims' eyes. I did not want an aura of death hanging over me. I definitely did not want to stand in judgment before Nico di Angelo's father.

Will put his hand on Nico's shoulder. "Nico, we need to have another talk about your people skills."

"Hey, I'm just stating the obvious. If this *is* Apollo, and he dies, we're all in trouble."

Will turned to me. "I apologize for my boyfriend."

Nico rolled his eyes. "Could you not—"

"Would you prefer *special guy*?" Will asked. "Or *significant other*?"

"Significant *annoyance*, in your case," Nico grumbled.

"Oh, I'll get you for that."

Meg wiped her dripping nose. "You guys fight a lot. I thought we were going to see a centaur."

"And here I am." The screen door opened. Chiron trotted out, ducking his head to avoid the doorframe.

From the waist up, he looked every bit the professor he often pretended to be in the mortal world. His brown wool jacket had patches on the elbows. His plaid dress shirt did not quite match his green tie. His beard was neatly trimmed, but his hair would have failed the tidiness inspection required for a proper rat's nest.

From the waist down, he was a white stallion.

My old friend smiled, though his eyes were stormy and distracted. "Apollo, it's good you are here. We need to talk about the disappearances."

11

Check your spam folder
The prophecies might be there
No? Well, I'm stumped. Bye

MEG GAWKED. "He—he really *is* a centaur."

"Well spotted," I said. "I suppose the lower body of a horse is what gave him away?"

She punched me in the arm.

"Chiron," I said, "this is Meg McCaffrey, my new master and wellspring of aggravation. You were saying something about disappearances?"

Chiron's tail flicked. His hooves clopped on the planks of the porch.

He was immortal, yet his visible age seemed to vary from century to century. I did not remember his whiskers ever being so gray, or the lines around his eyes so pronounced. Whatever was happening at camp must not have been helping his stress levels.

"Welcome, Meg." Chiron tried for a friendly tone, which I thought quite heroic, seeing as . . . well, *Meg*. "I understand you showed great bravery in the woods. You brought Apollo here despite many dangers. I'm glad to have you at Camp Half-Blood."

"Thanks," said Meg. "You're really tall. Don't you hit your head on light fixtures?"

Chiron chuckled. "Sometimes. If I want to be closer to human size, I have a magical wheelchair that allows me to compact my lower half into . . . Actually, that's not important now."

"Disappearances," I prompted. "What has disappeared?"

"Not *what*, but *who*," Chiron said. "Let's talk inside. Will, Nico, could you please tell the other campers we'll gather for dinner in one hour? I'll give everyone an update, then. In the meantime, no one should roam the camp alone. Use the buddy system."

"Understood." Will looked at Nico. "Will you be my buddy?"

"You are a dork," Nico announced.

The two of them strolled off bickering.

At this point, you may be wondering how I felt seeing my son with Nico di Angelo. I'll admit I did not understand Will's attraction to a child of Hades, but if the dark foreboding type was what made Will happy . . .

Oh. Perhaps some of you are wondering how I felt seeing him with a boyfriend rather than a girlfriend. If that's the case, *please*. We gods are not hung up about such things. I myself have had . . . let's see, thirty-three mortal girlfriends and eleven mortal boyfriends? I've lost count. My two greatest loves were, of course, Daphne and Hyacinthus, but when you're a god as popular as I am—

Hold on. Did I just tell you who I liked? I did, didn't I? Gods of Olympus, forget I mentioned their names! I am so embarrassed. Please don't say anything. In this mortal life, I've never been in love with *anyone*!

I am so confused.

Chiron led us into the living room, where comfy leather couches made a V facing the stone fireplace. Above the mantel, a stuffed leopard head was snoring contentedly.

"Is it alive?" Meg asked.

"Quite." Chiron trotted over to his wheelchair. "That's Seymour. If we speak quietly, we should be able to avoid waking him."

Meg immediately began exploring the living room. Knowing her, she was searching for small objects to throw at the leopard to wake him up.

Chiron settled into his wheelchair. He placed his rear legs into the false compartment of the seat, then backed up, magically compacting his equine hindquarters until he looked like a man sitting down. To complete the illusion, hinged front panels swung closed, giving him fake human legs. Normally those legs were fitted with slacks and loafers to augment his "professor" disguise, but today it seemed Chiron was going for a different look.

"That's new," I said.

Chiron glanced down at his shapely female mannequin legs, dressed in fishnet stockings and red sequined high heels. He sighed heavily. "I see the Hermes cabin have been watching *Rocky Horror Picture Show* again. I will have to have a chat with them."

Rocky Horror Picture Show brought back fond memories. I used to cosplay as Rocky at the midnight showings, because, naturally, the character's perfect physique was based on my own.

"Let me guess," I said. "Connor and Travis Stoll are the pranksters?"

From a nearby basket, Chiron grabbed a flannel blanket and spread it over his fake legs, though the ruby shoes still peeked out at the bottom. "Actually, Travis went off to college last autumn, which has mellowed Connor quite a bit."

Meg looked over from the old *Pac-Man* arcade game. "I poked that guy Connor in the eyes."

Chiron winced. "That's nice, dear. . . . At any rate, we have Julia Feingold and Alice Miyazawa now. They have taken up pranking duty. You'll meet them soon enough."

I recalled the girls who had been giggling at me from the Hermes cabin doorway. I felt myself blushing all over again.

Chiron gestured toward the couches. "Please sit."

Meg moved on from *Pac-Man* (having given the game twenty seconds of her time) and began literally climbing the wall. Dormant grapevines festooned the dining area— no doubt the work of my old friend Dionysus. Meg scaled one of the thicker trunks, trying to reach the Gorgon-hair chandelier.

"Ah, Meg," I said, "perhaps you should watch the orientation film while Chiron and I talk?"

"I know plenty," she said. "I talked to the campers while you were passed out. 'Safe place for modern demigods.' Blah, blah, blah."

"Oh, but the film is very good," I urged. "I shot it on a

tight budget in the 1950s, but some of the camera work was revolutionary. You should really—"

The grapevine peeled away from the wall. Meg crashed to the floor. She popped up completely unscathed, then spotted a platter of cookies on the sideboard. "Are those free?"

"Yes, child," Chiron said. "Bring the tea as well, would you?"

So we were stuck with Meg, who draped her legs over the couch's armrest, chomped on cookies, and threw crumbs at Seymour's snoring head whenever Chiron wasn't looking.

Chiron poured me a cup of Darjeeling. "I'm sorry Mr. D is not here to welcome you."

"Mr. Dee?" Meg asked.

"Dionysus," I explained. "The god of wine. Also the director of this camp."

Chiron handed me my tea. "After the battle with Gaea, I thought Mr. D might return to camp, but he never did. I hope he's all right."

The old centaur looked at me expectantly, but I had nothing to share. The last six months were a complete void; I had no idea what the other Olympians might be up to.

"I don't know anything," I admitted. I hadn't said those words very often in the last four millennia. They tasted bad. I sipped my tea, but that was no less bitter. "I'm a bit behind on the news. I was hoping you could fill me in."

Chiron did a poor job hiding his disappointment. "I see. . . ."

I realized he had been hoping for help and guidance—the

exact same things I needed from *him*. As a god, I was used to lesser beings relying on me—praying for this and pleading for that. But now that I was mortal, being relied upon was a little terrifying.

"So what is your crisis?" I asked. "You have the same look Cassandra had in Troy, or Jim Bowie at the Alamo—as if you're under siege."

Chiron did not dispute the comparison. He cupped his hands around his tea.

"You know that during the war with Gaea, the Oracle of Delphi stopped receiving prophecies. In fact, all known methods of divining the future suddenly failed."

"Because the original cave of Delphi was retaken," I said with a sigh, trying not to feel picked on.

Meg bounced a chocolate chip off Seymour the leopard's nose. "Oracle of Delphi. Percy mentioned that."

"Percy Jackson?" Chiron sat up. "Percy was with you?"

"For a time." I recounted our battle in the peach orchard and Percy's return to New York. "He said he would drive out this weekend if he could."

Chiron looked disheartened, as if my company alone wasn't good enough. Can you imagine?

"At any rate," he continued, "we hoped that once the war was over, the Oracle might start working again. When it did not . . . Rachel became concerned."

"Who's Rachel?" Meg asked.

"Rachel Dare," I said. "The Oracle."

"Thought the Oracle was a place."

"It is."

"Then Rachel is a place, and she stopped working?"

Had I still been a god, I would have turned her into a blue-belly lizard and released her into the wilderness never to be seen again. The thought soothed me.

"The original Delphi was a place in Greece," I told her. "A cavern filled with volcanic fumes, where people would come to receive guidance from my priestess, the Pythia."

"*Pythia.*" Meg giggled. "That's a funny word."

"Yes. Ha-ha. So the Oracle is both a place and a person. When the Greek gods relocated to America back in . . . what was it, Chiron, 1860?"

Chiron seesawed his hand. "More or less."

"I brought the Oracle here to continue speaking prophecies on my behalf. The power has passed down from priestess to priestess over the years. Rachel Dare is the present Oracle."

From the cookie platter, Meg plucked the only Oreo, which I had been hoping to have myself. "Mm-kay. Is it too late to watch that movie?"

"Yes," I snapped. "Now, the way I gained possession of the Oracle of Delphi in the first place was by killing this monster called Python who lived in the depths of the cavern."

"A python like the snake," Meg said.

"Yes and no. The snake species is named after Python the monster, who is also rather snaky, but who is much bigger and scarier and devours small girls who talk too much. At any rate, last August, while I was . . . indisposed, my ancient foe Python was released from Tartarus. He reclaimed the cave of Delphi. That's why the Oracle stopped working."

"But if the Oracle is in America now, why does it matter if some snake monster takes over its old cave?"

That was about the longest sentence I had yet heard her speak. She'd probably done it just to spite me.

"It's too much to explain," I said. "You'll just have to—"

"Meg." Chiron gave her one of his heroically tolerant smiles. "The original site of the Oracle is like the deepest taproot of a tree. The branches and leaves of prophecy may extend across the world, and Rachel Dare may be our loftiest branch, but if the taproot is strangled, the whole tree is endangered. With Python back in residence at his old lair, the spirit of the Oracle has been completely blocked."

"Oh." Meg made a face at me. "Why didn't you just say so?"

Before I could strangle her like the annoying taproot she was, Chiron refilled my teacup.

"The larger problem," he said, "is that we have no other source of prophecies."

"Who cares?" Meg asked. "So you don't know the future. Nobody knows the future."

"*Who cares?!*" I shouted. "Meg McCaffrey, prophecies are the catalysts for every important event—every quest or battle, disaster or miracle, birth or death. Prophecies don't simply foretell the future. They shape it! They *allow* the future to happen."

"I don't get it."

Chiron cleared his throat. "Imagine prophecies are flower seeds. With the right seeds, you can grow any garden you desire. Without seeds, no growth is possible."

THE HIDDEN ORACLE   99

"Oh." Meg nodded. "That would suck."

I found it strange that Meg, a street urchin and Dumpster warrior, would relate so well to garden metaphors, but Chiron was an excellent teacher. He had picked up on something about the girl . . . an impression that had been lurking in the back of my mind as well. I hoped I was wrong about what it meant, but with my luck, I would be right. I usually was.

"So where is Rachel Dare?" I asked. "Perhaps if I spoke with her . . . ?"

Chiron set down his tea. "Rachel planned to visit us during her winter vacation, but she never did. It might not mean anything. . . ."

I leaned forward. It was not unheard of for Rachel Dare to be late. She was artistic, unpredictable, impulsive, and rule-averse—all qualities I dearly admired. But it wasn't like her not to show up at all.

"Or?" I asked.

"Or it might be part of the larger problem," Chiron said. "Prophecies are not the only things that have failed. Travel and communication have become difficult in the last few months. We haven't heard from our friends at Camp Jupiter in weeks. No new demigods have arrived. Satyrs aren't reporting from the field. Iris messages no longer work."

"Iris what?" Meg asked.

"Two-way visions," I said. "A form of communication overseen by the rainbow goddess. Iris has always been flighty. . . ."

"Except that normal human communications are also on the fritz," Chiron said. "Of course, phones have always been dangerous for demigods—"

"Yeah, they attract monsters," Meg agreed. "I haven't used a phone in *forever*."

"A wise move," Chiron said. "But recently our phones have stopped working altogether. Mobile, landline, Internet . . . it doesn't seem to matter. Even the archaic form of communication known as *e-mail* is strangely unreliable. The messages simply don't arrive."

"Did you look in the junk folder?" I offered.

"I fear the problem is more complicated," Chiron said. "We have no communication with the outside world. We are alone and understaffed. You are the first newcomers in almost two months."

I frowned. "Percy Jackson mentioned nothing of this."

"I doubt Percy is even aware," Chiron said. "He's been busy with school. Winter is normally our quietest time. For a while, I was able to convince myself that the communication failures were nothing but an inconvenient happenstance. Then the disappearances started."

In the fireplace, a log slipped from the andiron. I may or may not have jumped in my seat.

"The disappearances, yes." I wiped drops of tea from my pants and tried to ignore Meg's snickering. "Tell me about those."

"Three in the last month," Chiron said. "First it was Cecil Markowitz from the Hermes cabin. One morning his bunk was simply empty. He didn't say anything about wanting to leave. No one saw him go. And in the past few weeks, no one has seen or heard from him."

"Children of Hermes do tend to sneak around," I offered.

"At first, that's what we thought," said Chiron. "But a

week later, Ellis Wakefield disappeared from the Ares cabin. Same story: empty bunk, no signs that he had either left on his own *or* was . . . ah, taken. Ellis was an impetuous young man. It was conceivable he might have charged off on some ill-advised adventure, but it made me uneasy. Then this morning we realized a third camper had vanished: Miranda Gardiner, head of the Demeter cabin. That was the worst news of all."

Meg swung her feet off the armrest. "Why is that the worst?"

"Miranda is one of our senior counselors," Chiron said. "She would never leave on her own without notice. She is too smart to be tricked away from camp, and too powerful to be forced. Yet something happened to her . . . something I can't explain."

The old centaur faced me. "Something is very wrong, Apollo. These problems may not be as alarming as the rise of Kronos or the awakening of Gaea, but in a way I find them even more unsettling, because I have never seen anything like this before."

I recalled my dream of the burning sun bus. I thought of the voices I'd heard in the woods, urging me to wander off and find their source.

"These demigods . . ." I said. "Before they disappeared, did they act unusual in any way? Did they report . . . hearing things?"

Chiron raised an eyebrow. "Not that I am aware of. Why?"

I was reluctant to say more. I didn't want to cause a panic without knowing what we were facing. When mortals panic, it can be an ugly scene, especially if they expect *me* to fix the problem.

Also, I will admit I felt a bit impatient. We had not yet addressed the most important issues—*mine*.

"It seems to me," I said, "that our first priority is to bend all the camp's resources to helping me regain my divine state. Then I can assist you with these other problems."

Chiron stroked his beard. "But what if the problems are connected, my friend? What if the only way to restore you to Olympus is by reclaiming the Oracle of Delphi, thus freeing the power of prophecy? What if Delphi is the key to it all?"

I had forgotten about Chiron's tendency to lay out obvious and logical conclusions that I tried to avoid thinking about. It was an infuriating habit.

"In my present state, that's impossible." I pointed at Meg. "Right now, my job is to serve this demigod, probably for a year. After I've done whatever tasks she assigns me, Zeus will judge that my sentence has been served, and I can once again become a god."

Meg pulled apart a Fig Newton. "I could order you to go to this Delphi place."

"No!" My voice cracked in midshriek. "You should assign me *easy* tasks—like starting a rock band, or just hanging out. Yes, hanging out is good."

Meg looked unconvinced. "Hanging out isn't a task."

"It is if you do it right. Camp Half-Blood can protect me while I hang out. After my year of servitude is up, I'll become a god. *Then* we can talk about how to restore Delphi."

Preferably, I thought, by ordering some demigods to undertake the quest for me.

"Apollo," Chiron said, "if demigods keep disappearing, we may not have a year. We may not have the strength to protect you. And, forgive me, but Delphi *is* your responsibility."

I tossed up my hands. "*I* wasn't the one who opened the Doors of Death and let Python out! Blame Gaea! Blame Zeus for his bad judgment! When the giants started to wake, I drew up a very clear *Twenty-Point Plan of Action to Protect Apollo and Also You Other Gods*, but he didn't even read it!"

Meg tossed half of her cookie at Seymour's head. "I still think it's your fault. Hey, look! He's awake!"

She said this as if the leopard had decided to wake up on his own rather than being beaned in the eye with a Fig Newton.

"*RARR*," Seymour complained.

Chiron wheeled his chair back from the table. "My dear, in that jar on the mantel, you'll find some Snausages. Why don't you feed him dinner? Apollo and I will wait on the porch."

We left Meg happily making three-point shots into Seymour's mouth with the treats.

Once Chiron and I reached the porch, he turned his wheelchair to face me. "She's an interesting demigod."

"*Interesting* is such a nonjudgmental term."

"She really summoned a karpos?"

"Well . . . the spirit appeared when she was in trouble. Whether she consciously summoned it, I don't know. She named him Peaches."

Chiron scratched his beard. "I have not seen a demigod with the power to summon grain spirits in a very long time. You know what it means?"

My feet began to quake. "I have my suspicions. I'm trying to stay positive."

"She guided you out of the woods," Chiron noted. "Without her—"

"Yes," I said. "Don't remind me."

It occurred to me that I'd seen that keen look in Chiron's eyes before—when he'd assessed Achilles's sword technique and Ajax's skill with a spear. It was the look of a seasoned coach scouting new talent. I'd never dreamed the centaur would look at *me* that way, as if I had something to prove to him, as if my mettle were untested. I felt so . . . so *objectified*.

"Tell me," Chiron said, "what did you hear in the woods?"

I silently cursed my big mouth. I should not have asked whether the missing demigods had heard anything strange.

I decided it was fruitless to hold back now. Chiron was more perceptive than your average horse-man. I told him what I'd experienced in the forest, and afterward in my dream.

His hands curled into his lap blanket. The bottom of it rose higher above his red sequined pumps. He looked about as worried as it is possible for a man to look while wearing fishnet stockings.

"We will have to warn the campers to stay away from the forest," he decided. "I do not understand what is happening, but I still maintain it *must* be connected to Delphi, and your present . . . ah, situation. The Oracle must be lib-erated from the monster Python. We must find a way."

I translated that easily enough: *I* must find a way.

Chiron must have read my desolate expression.

"Come, come, old friend," he said. "You have done it before. Perhaps you are not a god now, but the first time you killed Python it was no challenge at all! Hundreds of story-books have praised the way you easily slew your enemy."

"Yes," I muttered. "Hundreds of storybooks."

I recalled some of those stories: I had killed Python without breaking a sweat. I flew to the mouth of the cave, called him out, unleashed an arrow, and *BOOM!*—one dead giant snake monster. I became Lord of Delphi, and we all lived happily ever after.

How did storytellers get the idea that I vanquished Python so quickly?

All right . . . possibly it's because I told them so. Still, the truth was rather different. For centuries after our battle, I had bad dreams about my old foe.

Now I was almost grateful for my imperfect memory. I could not recollect all of the nightmarish details of my fight with Python, but I *did* know he had been no pushover. I had needed all my godly strength, my divine powers, and the world's most deadly bow.

What chance would I have as a sixteen-year-old mortal with acne, hand-me-down clothes, and the nom de guerre Lester Papadopoulos? I was not going to charge off to Greece and get myself killed, thank you very much, especially not without my sun chariot or the ability to teleport. I'm sorry; gods do *not* fly commercial.

I tried to figure out how to explain this to Chiron in a calm, diplomatic way that did not involve stomping my feet or screaming. I was saved from the effort by the sound of a conch horn in the distance.

"That means dinner." The centaur forced a smile. "We will talk more later, eh? For now, let's celebrate your arrival."

12

Ode to a hot dog
With bug juice and tater chips
I got nothing, man

I WAS NOT IN THE MOOD TO CELEBRATE.

Especially sitting at a picnic table eating mortal food. With mortals.

The dining pavilion was pleasant enough. Even in winter, the camp's magical borders shielded us from the worst of the elements. Sitting outdoors in the warmth of the torches and braziers, I felt only slightly chilly. Long Island Sound glittered in the light of the moon. (Hello, Artemis. Don't bother to say hi.) On Half-Blood Hill, the Athena Parthenos glowed like the world's largest nightlight. Even the woods did not seem so creepy with the pine trees blanketed in soft silvery fog.

My dinner, however, was less than poetic. It consisted of hot dogs, potato chips, and a red liquid I was told was bug juice. I did not know why humans consumed bug juice, or from which type of bug it had been extracted, but it was the tastiest part of the meal, which was disconcerting.

I sat at the Apollo table with my children Austin, Kayla, and Will, plus Nico di Angelo. I could see no difference between my table and any of the other gods' tables. Mine should have been shinier and more elegant. It should have played music or recited poetry upon command. Instead it was just a slab of stone with benches on either side. I found the seating uncomfortable, though my offspring didn't seem to mind.

Austin and Kayla peppered me with questions about Olympus, the war with Gaea, and what it felt like to be a god and then a human. I knew they did not mean to be rude. As my children, they were inherently inclined to the utmost grace. However, their questions were painful reminders of my fallen status.

Besides, as the hours passed, I remembered less and less about my divine life. It was alarming how fast my cosmically perfect neurons had deteriorated. Once, each memory had been like a high-definition audio file. Now those recordings were on wax cylinders. And believe me, I remember wax cylinders. They did not last long in the sun chariot.

Will and Nico sat shoulder to shoulder, bantering good-naturedly. They were so cute together it made me feel desolate. It jogged my memories of those few short golden months I'd shared with Hyacinthus before the jealousy, before the horrible accident . . .

"Nico," I said at last, "shouldn't you be sitting at the Hades table?"

He shrugged. "Technically, yes. But if I sit alone at my table, strange things happen. Cracks open in the floor. Zombies crawl out and start roaming around. It's a mood disorder. I can't control it. That's what I told Chiron."

"And is it true?" I asked.

Nico smiled thinly. "I have a note from my doctor."

Will raised his hand. "I'm his doctor."

"Chiron decided it wasn't worth arguing about," Nico said. "As long as I sit at a table with other people, like . . . oh, these guys for instance . . . the zombies stay away. Everybody's happier."

Will nodded serenely. "It's the strangest thing. Not that Nico would ever misuse his powers to get what he wants."

"Of course not," Nico agreed.

I glanced across the dining pavilion. As per camp tradition, Meg had been placed with the children of Hermes, since her godly parentage had not yet been determined. Meg didn't seem to mind. She was busy re-creating the Coney Island Hot Dog Eating Contest all by herself. The other two girls, Julia and Alice, watched her with a mixture of fascination and horror.

Across the table from her sat an older skinny boy with curly brown hair—Connor Stoll, I deduced, though I'd never been able to tell him apart from his older brother, Travis. Despite the darkness, Connor wore sunglasses, no doubt to protect his eyes from a repeat poking. I also noted that he wisely kept his hands away from Meg's mouth.

In the entire pavilion, I counted nineteen campers. Most sat alone at their respective tables—Sherman Yang for Ares; a girl I did not know for Aphrodite; another girl for Demeter. At the Nike table, two dark-haired young ladies who were obviously twins conversed over a war map. Chiron himself, again in full centaur form, stood at the head table, sipping his bug juice as he chatted with two satyrs, but their mood was subdued. The goat-men kept glancing at me, then eating their silverware, as satyrs tend to do when nervous. Half a dozen gorgeous dryads moved between the tables, offering food and drink, but I was so preoccupied I couldn't fully appreciate their beauty. Even more tragic: I felt too embarrassed to flirt with them. What was *wrong* with me?

I studied the campers, hoping to spot some potential servants . . . I mean new friends. Gods always like to keep a few strong veteran demigods handy to throw into battle, send on dangerous quests, or pick the lint off our togas. Unfortunately, no one at dinner jumped out at me as a likely minion. I longed for a bigger pool of talent.

"Where are the . . . others?" I asked Will.

I wanted to say *the A-List*, but I thought that might be taken the wrong way.

Will took a bite of his pizza. "Were you looking for somebody in particular?"

"What about the ones who went on that quest with the boat?"

Will and Nico exchanged a look that might have meant, *Here we go.* I suppose they got asked a lot about the seven legendary demigods who had fought side by side with the gods against Gaea's giants. It pained me that I had not gotten to see those heroes again. After any major battle, I liked to get a group photo—along with exclusive rights to compose epic ballads about their exploits.

"Well," Nico started, "you saw Percy. He and Annabeth

are spending their senior year in New York. Hazel and Frank are at Camp Jupiter doing the Twelfth Legion thing."

"Ah, yes." I tried to bring up a clear mental picture of Camp Jupiter, the Roman enclave near Berkeley, California, but the details were hazy. I could only remember my conversations with Octavian, the way he'd turned my head with his flattery and promises. That stupid boy . . . it was his fault I was here.

A voice whispered in the back of my mind. This time I thought it might be my conscience: *Who was the stupid boy? It wasn't Octavian.*

"Shut up," I murmured.

"What?" Nico asked.

"Nothing. Continue."

"Jason and Piper are spending the school year in Los Angeles with Piper's dad. They took Coach Hedge, Mellie, and Little Chuck with them."

"Uh-huh." I did not know those last three names, so I decided they probably weren't important. "And the seventh hero . . . Leo Valdez?"

Nico raised his eyebrows. "You remember his name?"

"Of course! He invented the Valdezinator. Oh, what a musical instrument! I barely had time to master its major scales before Zeus zapped me at the Parthenon. If anyone could help me, it would be Leo Valdez."

Nico's expression tightened with annoyance. "Well, Leo isn't here. He died. Then he came back to life. And if I see him again, I'll kill him."

Will elbowed him. "No, you won't." He turned to me.

"During the fight with Gaea, Leo and his bronze dragon, Festus, disappeared in a midair fiery explosion."

I shivered. After so many centuries driving the sun chariot, the term *midair fiery explosion* did not sit well with me.

I tried to remember the last time I'd seen Leo Valdez on Delos, when he'd traded the Valdezinator for information. . . .

"He was looking for the physician's cure," I recalled, "the way to bring someone back from the dead. I suppose he planned all along to sacrifice himself?"

"Yep," Will said. "He got rid of Gaea in the explosion, but we all assumed he died too."

"Because he *did*," Nico said.

"Then, a few days later," Will continued, "this scroll came fluttering into camp on the wind. . . ."

"I still have it." Nico rummaged through the pockets of his bomber jacket. "I look at it whenever I want to get angry."

He produced a thick parchment scroll. As soon as he spread it on the table, a flickering hologram appeared above the surface: Leo Valdez, looking impish as usual with his dark wispy hair, his mischievous grin, and his diminutive stature. (Of course, the hologram was only three inches tall, but even in real life Leo was not much more imposing.) His jeans, blue work shirt, and tool belt were speckled with machine oil.

"Hey, guys!" Leo spread his arms for a hug. "Sorry to leave you like that. Bad news: I died. Good news: I got better! I had to go rescue Calypso. We're both fine now. We're taking Festus to—" The image guttered like a flame in a strong breeze, disrupting Leo's voice. "Back as soon as—" Static. "Cook tacos when—" More static. "¡Vaya con queso! Love ya!" The image winked out.

"That's all we got," Nico complained. "And that was in August. We have no idea what he was planning, where he is now, or whether he's still safe. Jason and Piper spent most of September looking for him until Chiron finally insisted they go start their school year."

"Well," I said, "it sounds like Leo was planning to cook tacos. Perhaps that took longer than he anticipated. And *vaya con queso* . . . I believe he is admonishing us to go *with cheese*, which is always sound advice."

This did not seem to reassure Nico.

"I don't like being in the dark," he muttered.

An odd complaint for a child of Hades, but I understood what he meant. I, too, was curious to know the fate of Leo Valdez. Once upon a time, I could have divined his whereabouts as easily as you might check a Facebook timeline, but now I could only stare at the sky and wonder when a small impish demigod might appear with a bronze dragon and a plate of tacos.

And if Calypso was involved . . . that complicated things. The sorceress and I had a rocky history, but even I had to admit she was beguiling. If she'd captured Leo's heart, it was entirely possible he had gotten sidetracked. Odysseus spent seven years with her before returning home.

Whatever the case, it seemed unlikely that Valdez would be back in time to help me. My quest to master the Valdezinator's arpeggios would have to wait.

Kayla and Austin had been very quiet, following our

conversation with wonder and amazement. (My words have that effect on people.)

Now Kayla scooted toward me. "What did you guys talk about in the Big House? Chiron told you about the disappearances . . . ?"

"Yes." I tried to avoid looking in the direction of the woods. "We discussed the situation."

"And?" Austin spread his fingers on the table. "What's going on?"

I didn't want to talk about it. I didn't want them to see my fear.

I wished my head would stop pounding. On Olympus, headaches were so much easier to cure. Hephaestus simply split one's skull open and extracted whatever newborn god or goddess happened to be banging around in there. In the mortal world, my options were more limited.

"I need time to think about it," I said. "Perhaps in the morning I'll have some of my godly powers back."

Austin leaned forward. In the torchlight, his cornrows seemed to twist into new DNA patterns. "Is that how it works? Your strength comes back over time?"

"I—I think so." I tried to remember my years of servitude with Admetus and Laomedon, but I could barely conjure their names and faces. My contracting memory terrified me. It made each moment of the present balloon in size and importance, reminding me that time for mortals was limited.

"I have to get stronger," I decided. "I *must.*"

Kayla squeezed my hand. Her archer's fingers were rough

and calloused. "It's okay, Apollo . . . Dad. We'll help you."

Austin nodded. "Kayla's right. We're in this together. If anybody gives you trouble, Kayla will shoot them. Then I'll curse them so bad they'll be speaking in rhyming couplets for weeks."

My eyes watered. Not so long ago—like this morning, for instance—the idea of these young demigods being able to help me would have struck me as ridiculous. Now their kindness moved me more than a hundred sacrificial bulls. I couldn't recall the last time someone had cared about me enough to curse my enemies with rhyming couplets.

"Thank you," I managed.

I could not add *my children*. It didn't seem right. These demigods were my protectors and my family, but for the present I could not think of myself as their father. A father should do more—a father should give more to his children than he takes. I have to admit that this was a novel idea for me. It made me feel even worse than before.

"Hey . . ." Will patted my shoulder. "It's not so bad. At least with everybody being on high alert, we might not have to do Harley's obstacle course tomorrow."

Kayla muttered an ancient Greek curse. If I had been a *proper* godly father, I would have washed her mouth out with olive oil.

"I forgot all about that," she said. "They'll *have* to cancel it, won't they?"

I frowned. "What obstacle course? Chiron mentioned nothing about this."

I wanted to object that my entire day had been an

obstacle course. Surely they couldn't expect me to do their camp activities as well. Before I could say as much, one of the satyrs blew a conch horn at the head table.

Chiron raised his arms for attention.

"Campers!" His voice filled the pavilion. He could be quite impressive when he wanted to be. "I have a few announcements, including news about tomorrow's three-legged death race!"

13

Three-legged death race
Five terrible syllables
Oh, gods. Please not Meg

IT WAS ALL HARLEY'S FAULT.

After addressing the disappearance of Miranda Gardiner—"As a precautionary measure, please stay away from the woods until we know more"—Chiron called forward the young son of Hephaestus to explain how the three-legged death race would work. It quickly became apparent that Harley had masterminded the whole project. And, really, the idea was so horrifying, it could only have sprung from the mind of an eight-year-old boy.

I confess I lost track of the specifics after he explained the exploding chain-saw Frisbees.

"And they'll be like, ZOOM!" He bounced up and down with excitement. "And then BUZZ! And POW!" He pantomimed all sorts of chaos with his hands. "You have to be really quick or you'll die, and it's awesome!"

The other campers grumbled and shifted on their benches.

Chiron raised his hand for silence. "Now, I know there were problems last time," he said, "but fortunately our healers in the Apollo cabin were able to reattach Paolo's arms."

At a table in back, a muscular teen boy rose and began ranting in what I thought was Portuguese. He wore a white tank top over his dark chest, and I could see faint white scars around the tops of his biceps. Cursing rapidly, he pointed at Harley, the Apollo cabin, and pretty much everyone else.

"Ah, thank you, Paolo," Chiron said, clearly baffled. "I'm glad you are feeling better."

Austin leaned toward me and whispered, "Paolo understands English okay, but he only speaks Portuguese. At least, that's what he claims. None of us can understand a word he says."

I didn't understand Portuguese either. Athena had been lecturing us for years about how Mount Olympus might migrate to Brazil someday, and we should all be prepared for the possibility. She'd even bought the gods Berlitz Portuguese DVDs for Saturnalia presents, but what does Athena know?

"Paolo seems agitated," I noted.

Will shrugged. "He's lucky he's a fast healer—son of Hebe, goddess of youth, and all that."

"You're staring," Nico noted.

"I am not," Will said. "I am merely assessing how well Paolo's arms are functioning after surgery."

"Hmph."

Paolo finally sat down. Chiron went through a long list of other injuries they had experienced during the first three-legged death race, all of which he hoped to avoid this time: second-degree burns, burst eardrums, a pulled groin, and two cases of chronic Irish step dancing.

The lone demigod at the Athena table raised his hand.

"Chiron, just going to throw this out there. . . . We've had three campers disappear. Is it really wise to be running a dangerous obstacle course?"

Chiron gave him a pained smile. "An excellent question, Malcolm, but this course will not take you into the woods, which we believe is the most hazardous area. The satyrs, dryads, and I will continue to investigate the disappearances. We will not rest until our missing campers are found. In the meantime, however, this three-legged race can foster important team-building skills. It also expands our understanding of the Labyrinth."

The word smacked me in the face like Ares's body odor. I turned to Austin. "The Labyrinth? As in *Daedalus's* Labyrinth?"

Austin nodded, his fingers worrying the ceramic camp beads around his neck. I had a sudden memory of his mother, Latricia—the way she used to fiddle with her cowry necklace when she lectured at Oberlin. Even *I* learned things from Latricia Lake's music theory class, though I had found her distractingly beautiful.

"During the war with Gaea," Austin said, "the maze reopened. We've been trying to map it ever since."

"That's impossible," I said. "Also insane. The Labyrinth is a malevolent sentient creation! It can't be mapped or trusted."

As usual, I could only draw on random bits and pieces of my memories, but I was fairly certain I spoke the truth. I remembered Daedalus. Back in the old days, the king of Crete had ordered him to build a maze to contain the monstrous Minotaur. But, oh no, a simple maze wasn't *good* enough for a brilliant inventor like Daedalus. He had to make his Labyrinth self-aware and self-expanding. Over the centuries, it had honeycombed under the planet's surface like an invasive root system.

Stupid brilliant inventors.

"It's different now," Austin told me. "Since Daedalus died . . . I don't know. It's hard to describe. Doesn't feel so evil. Not quite as deadly."

"Oh, that's hugely reassuring. So of course you decided to do three-legged races through it."

Will coughed. "The other thing, Dad . . . Nobody wants to disappoint Harley."

I glanced at the head table. Chiron was still holding forth about the virtues of team building while Harley bounced up and down. I could see why the other campers might adopt the boy as their unofficial mascot. He was a cute little pip-squeak, even if he was scarily buff for an eight-year-old. His grin was infectious. His enthusiasm seemed to lift the mood of the entire group. Still, I recognized the mad gleam in his eyes. It was the same look his father, Hephaestus, got whenever he invented some automaton that would later go berserk and start destroying cities.

"Also keep in mind," Chiron was saying, "that none of the unfortunate disappearances has been linked to the Labyrinth. Remain with your partner and you should be safe . . . at least, as safe as one can be in a three-legged death race."

"Yeah," Harley said. "Nobody has even *died* yet." He sounded disappointed, as if he wanted us to try harder.

"In the face of a crisis," Chiron said, "it's important to

stick to our regular activities. We must stay alert and in top condition. Our missing campers would expect no less from us. Now, as to the teams for the race, you will be allowed to choose your partner—"

There followed a sort of piranha attack of campers lunging toward each other to grab their preferred teammate. Before I could contemplate my options, Meg McCaffrey pointed at me from across the pavilion, her expression exactly like Uncle Sam's in the recruitment poster.

Of course, I thought. Why should my luck improve now?

Chiron struck his hoof against the floor. "All right, everyone, settle down! The race will be tomorrow afternoon. Thank you, Harley, for your hard work on the . . . um, various lethal surprises in store."

"BLAM!" Harley ran back to the Hephaestus table to join his older sister, Nyssa.

"This brings us to our other news," Chiron said. "As you may have heard, two special newcomers joined us today. First, please welcome the god Apollo!"

Normally this was my cue to stand up, spread my arms, and grin as radiant light shone around me. The adoring crowd would applaud and toss flowers and chocolate bonbons at my feet.

This time I received no applause—just nervous looks. I had a strange, uncharacteristic impulse to slide lower in my seat and pull my coat over my head. I restrained myself through heroic effort.

Chiron struggled to maintain his smile. "Now, I know this is unusual," he said, "but gods *do* become mortal from time to time. You should not be overly alarmed. Apollo's presence among us could be a good omen, a chance for us to . . ." He seemed to lose track of his own argument. "Ah . . . do something good. I'm sure the best course of action will become clear in time. For now, please make Apollo feel at home. Treat him as you would any other new camper."

At the Hermes table, Connor Stoll raised his hand. "Does that mean the Ares cabin should stick Apollo's head in a toilet?"

At the Ares table, Sherman Yang snorted. "We don't do that to everyone, Connor. Just the newbies who deserve it."

Sherman glanced at Meg, who was obliviously finishing her last hot dog. The wispy black whiskers at the sides of her mouth were now frosted with mustard.

Connor Stoll grinned back at Sherman—a conspiratorial look if ever I saw one. That's when I noticed the open backpack at Connor's feet. Peeking from the top was something that looked like a net.

The implication sank in: two boys whom Meg had humiliated, preparing for payback. I didn't have to be Nemesis to understand the allure of revenge. Still . . . I felt an odd desire to warn Meg.

I tried to catch her eye, but she remained focused on her dinner.

"Thank you, Sherman," Chiron continued. "It's good to know you won't be giving the god of archery a swirly. As for the rest of you, we will keep you posted on our guest's situation. I'm sending two of our finest satyrs, Millard and Herbert"—he gestured to the satyrs on his left—"to hand-deliver a message to Rachel Dare in New York. With any luck, she will be able to join us soon and help determine how we can best assist Apollo."

There was some grumbling about this. I caught the words *Oracle* and *prophecies*. At a nearby table, a girl muttered to herself in Italian: *The blind leading the blind*.

I glared at her, but the young lady was quite beautiful. She was perhaps two years older than I (mortally speaking), with dark pixie hair and devastatingly fierce almond eyes. I may have blushed.

I turned back to my tablemates. "Um . . . yes, satyrs. Why not send that other satyr, the friend of Percy's?"

"Grover?" Nico asked. "He's in California. The whole Council of Cloven Elders is out there, meeting about the drought."

"Oh." My spirits fell. I remembered Grover as being quite resourceful, but if he was dealing with California's natural disasters, he was unlikely to be back anytime in the next decade.

"Finally," Chiron said, "we welcome a new demigod to camp—Meg McCaffrey!"

She wiped her mouth and stood.

Next to her, Alice Miyazawa said, "Stand up, Meg."

Julia Feingold laughed.

At the Ares table, Sherman Yang rose. "Now *this* one—this one deserves a special welcome. What do you think, Connor?"

Connor reached into his backpack. "I think maybe the canoe lake."

I started to say, "Meg—"

Then all Hades broke loose.

Sherman Yang strode toward Meg. Connor Stoll pulled out a golden net and threw it over her head. Meg yelped and tried to squirm free, while some of the campers chanted, "Dunk—her! Dunk—her!" Chiron did his best to shout them down: "Now, demigods, wait a moment!"

A guttural howl interrupted the proceedings. From the top of the colonnade, a blur of chubby flesh, leafy wings, and linen diaper hurtled downward and landed on Sherman Yang's back, knocking him face-first into the stone floor. Peaches the karpos stood and wailed, beating his chest. His eyes glowed green with anger. He launched himself at Connor Stoll, locked his plump legs around the demigod's neck, and began pulling out Connor's hair with his claws.

"Get it off!" Connor wailed, thrashing blindly around the pavilion. "Get it off!"

Slowly the other demigods overcame their shock. Several drew swords.

"*C'è un karpos!*" yelled the Italian girl.

"Kill it!" said Alice Miyazawa.

"No!" I cried.

Normally such a command from me would've initiated a prison lockdown situation, with all the mortals dropping to their bellies to await my further orders. Alas, now I was a mere mortal with a squeaky adolescent voice.

I watched in horror as my own daughter Kayla nocked an arrow in her bow.

"Peaches, get off him!" Meg screamed. She untangled herself from the net, threw it down, then ran toward Connor.

The karpos hopped off Connor's neck. He landed at

Meg's feet, baring his fangs and hissing at the other campers who had formed a loose semicircle with weapons drawn.

"Meg, get out of the way," said Nico di Angelo. "That thing is dangerous."

"No!" Meg's voice was shrill. "Don't kill him!"

Sherman Yang rolled over, groaning. His face looked worse than it probably was—a gash on the forehead can produce a shocking amount of blood—but the sight steeled the resolve of the other campers. Kayla drew her bow. Julia Feingold unsheathed a dagger.

"Wait!" I pleaded.

What happened next, a lesser mind could never have processed.

Julia charged. Kayla shot her arrow.

Meg thrust out her hands and faint gold light flashed between her fingers. Suddenly young McCaffrey was holding two swords—each a curved blade in the old Thracian style, *siccae* made from Imperial gold. I had not seen such weapons since the fall of the Rome. They seemed to have appeared from nowhere, but my long experience with magic items told me they must have been summoned from the crescent rings Meg always wore.

Both her blades whirled. Meg simultaneously sliced Kayla's arrow out of the air and disarmed Julia, sending her dagger skittering across the floor.

"What the Hades?" Connor demanded. His hair had been pulled out in chunks so he looked like an abused doll. "Who *is* this kid?"

Peaches crouched at Meg's side, snarling, as Meg fended off the confused and enraged demigods with her two swords.

My vision must have been better than the average mortal's, because I saw the glowing sign first—a light shining above Meg's head.

When I recognized the symbol, my heart turned to lead. I hated what I saw, but I thought I should point it out. "Look."

The others seemed confused. Then the glow became brighter: a holographic golden sickle with a few sheaves of wheat, rotating just above Meg McCaffrey.

A boy in the crowd gasped. "She's a communist!"

A girl who'd been sitting at Cabin Four's table gave him a disgusted sneer. "No, Damien, that's my *mom's* symbol." Her face went slack as the truth sank in. "Uh, which means . . . it's *her* mom's symbol."

My head spun. I did not want this knowledge. I did not want to serve a demigod with Meg's parentage. But now I understood the crescents on Meg's rings. They were not moons; they were sickle blades. As the only Olympian present, I felt I should make her title official.

"My friend is no longer unclaimed," I announced.

The other demigods knelt in respect, some more reluctantly than others.

"Ladies and gentlemen," I said, my voice as bitter as Chiron's tea, "please give it up for Meg McCaffrey, daughter of Demeter."

14

You've got to be kid—
Well, crud, what just happened there?
I ran out of syl—

NO ONE KNEW WHAT TO MAKE OF MEG.

I couldn't blame them.

The girl made even less sense to me now that I knew who her mother was.

I'd had my suspicions, yes, but I'd hoped to be proven wrong. Being right so much of the time was a terrible burden.

Why would I dread a child of Demeter?

Good question.

Over the past day, I had been doing my best to piece together my remembrances of the goddess. Once Demeter had been my favorite aunt. That first generation of gods could be a stuffy bunch (I'm looking at you, Hera, Hades, Dad), but Demeter had always been a kind and loving presence—except when she was destroying mankind through pestilence and famine, but everyone has their bad days.

Then I made the mistake of dating one of her daughters. I think her name was Chrysothemis, but you'll have to excuse me if I'm wrong. Even when I was a god, I had trouble remembering the names of all my exes. The young woman sang a harvest song at one of my Delphic festivals. Her voice was so beautiful, I fell in love. True, I fell in love with each year's winner and the runners-up, but what can I say? I'm a sucker for a melodious voice.

Demeter did not approve. Ever since her daughter Persephone had been kidnapped by Hades, she'd been a little touchy about her children dating gods.

At any rate, she and I had words. We reduced a few mountains to rubble. We laid waste to a few city-states. You know how family arguments can get. Finally we settled into an uneasy truce, but since then I'd made a point to steer clear of Demeter's children.

Now here I was—a servant to Meg McCaffrey, the most ragamuffin daughter of Demeter ever to swing a sickle.

I wondered who Meg's father had been to attract the attention of the goddess. Demeter rarely fell in love with mortals. Meg was unusually powerful, too. Most children of Demeter could do little more than make crops grow and keep bacterial fungi at bay. Dual-wielding golden blades and summoning karpoi—that was top-shelf stuff.

All of this went through my mind as Chiron dispersed the crowd, urging everyone to put away their weapons. Since head counselor Miranda Gardiner was missing, Chiron asked Billie Ng, the only other camper from Demeter, to escort Meg to Cabin Four. The two girls made a quick retreat, Peaches bouncing along excitedly behind them. Meg shot me a worried look.

Not sure what else to do, I gave her two thumbs-up. "See you tomorrow!"

She seemed less than encouraged as she disappeared in the darkness.

Will Solace tended to Sherman Yang's head injuries. Kayla and Austin stood over Connor, debating the need for a hair graft. This left me alone to make my way back to the Me cabin.

I lay on my sick cot in the middle of the room and stared at the ceiling beams. I thought again about what a depressingly simple, utterly mortal place this was. How did my children stand it? Why did they not keep a blazing altar, and decorate the walls with hammered gold reliefs celebrating my glory?

When I heard Will and the others coming back, I closed my eyes and pretended to be asleep. I could not face their questions or kindnesses, their attempts to make me feel at home when I clearly did not belong.

As they came in the door, they got quiet.

"Is he okay?" whispered Kayla.

Austin said, "Would you be, if you were him?"

A moment of silence.

"Try to get some sleep, guys," Will advised.

"This is crazy weird," Kayla said. "He looks so . . . human."

"We'll watch out for him," Austin said. "We're all he's got now."

I held back a sob. I couldn't bear their concern. Not being able to reassure them, or even disagree with them, made me feel very small.

A blanket was draped over me.

Will said, "Sleep well, Apollo."

Perhaps it was his persuasive voice, or the fact that I was more exhausted than I had been in centuries. Immediately, I drifted into unconsciousness.

Thank the remaining eleven Olympians, I had no dreams.

I woke in the morning feeling strangely refreshed. My chest no longer hurt. My nose no longer felt like a water balloon attached to my face. With the help of my offspring (*cabin mates*—I will call them cabin mates), I managed to master the arcane mysteries of the shower, the toilet, and the sink. The toothbrush was a shock. The last time I was mortal, there had been no such thing. And under-arm deodorant—what a ghastly idea that I should need enchanted salve to keep my armpits from producing stench!

When I was done with my morning ablutions and dressed in clean clothes from the camp store—sneakers, jeans, an orange Camp Half-Blood T-shirt, and a comfy winter coat of flannel wool—I felt almost optimistic. Perhaps I could survive this human experience.

I perked up even more when I discovered bacon.

Oh, gods—bacon! I promised myself that once I achieved immortality again, I would assemble the Nine Muses and together we would create an ode, a hymnal to the power of bacon, which would move the heavens to tears and cause rapture across the universe.

Bacon is good.

Yes—that may be the title of the song: "Bacon Is Good."

Seating for breakfast was less formal than dinner. We filled our trays at a buffet line and were allowed to sit wher-ever we wished. I found this delightful. (Oh, what a sad commentary on my new mortal mind that I, who once dictated the course of nations, should get excited about open seating.) I took my tray and found Meg, who was sitting by herself on the edge of the pavilion's retaining wall, dangling her feet over the side and watching the waves at the beach.

"How are you?" I asked.

Meg nibbled on a waffle. "Yeah. Great."

"You are a powerful demigod, daughter of Demeter."

"Mm-hm."

If I could trust my understanding of human responses, Meg did not seem thrilled.

"Your cabin mate, Billie . . . Is she nice?"

"Sure. All good."

"And Peaches?"

She looked at me sideways. "Disappeared overnight. Guess he only shows up when I'm in danger."

"Well, that's an appropriate time for him to show up."

"Ap-pro-pri-ate." Meg touched a waffle square for each syllable. "Sherman Yang had to get seven stitches."

I glanced over at Sherman, who sat at a safe distance across the pavilion, glaring daggers at Meg. A nasty red zigzag ran down the side of his face.

"I wouldn't worry," I told Meg. "Ares's children like scars. Besides, Sherman wears the Frankenstein look rather well."

The corner of her mouth twitched, but her gaze remained far away. "Our cabin has a grass floor—like, *green* grass. There's a huge oak tree in the middle, holding up the ceiling."

"Is that bad?"

"I have allergies."

"Ah . . ." I tried to imagine the tree in her cabin. Once upon a time, Demeter had had a sacred grove of oaks. I remembered she'd gotten quite angry when a mortal prince tried to cut it down.

A sacred grove . . .

Suddenly the bacon in my stomach expanded, wrapping around my organs.

Meg gripped my arm. Her voice was a distant buzz. I only heard the last, most important word: "—Apollo?"

I stirred. "What?"

"You blanked out." She scowled. "I said your name six times."

"You did?"

"Yeah. Where did you go?"

I could not explain. I felt as if I'd been standing on the deck of a ship when an enormous, dark, and dangerous shape passed beneath the hull—a shape almost discernible, then simply gone.

"I—I don't know. Something about trees. . . ."

"Trees," Meg said.

"It's probably nothing."

It *wasn't* nothing. I couldn't shake the image from my dreams: the crowned woman urging me to find the gates. That woman wasn't Demeter—at least, I didn't think so. But the idea of sacred trees stirred a memory within me . . . something very old, even by *my* standards.

I didn't want to talk about this with Meg, not until I'd had time to reflect. She had enough to worry about. Besides, after last night, my new young master made me more apprehensive than ever.

I glanced at the rings on her middle fingers. "So yesterday . . . those swords. And don't do that thing."

Meg's eyebrows furrowed. "What thing?"

"That thing where you shut down and refuse to talk. Your face turns to cement."

She gave me a furious pout. "It does not. I've got swords. I fight with them. So what?"

"So it might have been nice to know that earlier, when we were in combat with plague spirits."

"You said it yourself: those spirits couldn't be killed."

"You're sidestepping." I knew this because it was a tactic I had mastered centuries ago. "The style you fight in, with two curved blades, is the style of a *dimachaerus*, a gladiator from the late Roman Empire. Even back then, it was rare—possibly the most difficult fighting style to master, and one of the most deadly."

Meg shrugged. It was an eloquent shrug, but it did not offer much in the way of explanation.

"Your swords are Imperial gold," I said. "That would indicate *Roman* training, and mark you as a good prospect for Camp Jupiter. Yet your mother is Demeter, the goddess in her Greek form, not Ceres."

"How do you know?"

"Aside from the fact that I was a god? Demeter claimed you here at Camp Half-Blood. That was no accident. Also, her older Greek form is much more powerful. You, Meg, are powerful."

Her expression turned so guarded I expected Peaches to hurtle from the sky and start pulling out chunks of my hair.

"I never met my mom," she said. "I didn't know who she was."

"Then where did you get the swords? Your father?"

Meg tore her waffle into tiny pieces. "No. . . . My step-dad raised me. He gave me these rings."

"Your stepfather. Your stepfather gave you rings that turn into Imperial golden swords. What sort of man—"

"A good man," she snapped.

I noted the steel in Meg's voice and let the subject rest. I sensed a great tragedy in her past. Also, I feared that if I pressed my questions, I might find those golden blades at my neck.

"I'm sorry," I said.

"Mm-hm." Meg tossed a piece of waffle into the air. Out of nowhere, one of the camp's cleaning harpies swooped down like a two-hundred-pound kamikaze chicken, snatched up the food, and flew away.

Meg continued as if nothing had happened. "Let's just get through today. We've got the race after lunch."

A shiver ran down my neck. The last thing I wanted was to be strapped to Meg McCaffrey in the Labyrinth, but I managed to avoid screaming.

"Don't worry about the race," I said. "I have a plan for how to win it."

She raised an eyebrow. "Yeah?"

"Or rather, I *will* have a plan by this afternoon. All I need is a little time—"

Behind us, the conch horn blew.

"Morning boot camp!" Sherman Yang bellowed. "Let's go, you special snowflakes! I want you all in tears by lunchtime!"

15

Practice makes perfect
Ha, ha, ha, I don't think so
Ignore my sobbing

I WISHED I HAD A DOCTOR'S NOTE. I wanted to be excused from PE.

Honestly, I will never understand you mortals. You try to maintain good physical shape with push-ups, sit-ups, five-mile runs, obstacle courses, and other hard work that involves sweating. All the while, you know it is a losing battle. Eventually your weak, limited-use bodies will deteriorate and fail, giving you wrinkles, sagging parts, and old-person breath.

It's horrific! If I want to change shape, or age, or gender, or species, I simply wish it to happen and—*ka-bam!*—I am a young, large, female three-toed sloth. No amount of push-ups will accomplish that. I simply don't see the logic in your constant struggles. Exercise is nothing more than a depressing reminder that one is not a god.

By the end of Sherman Yang's boot camp, I was gasping and drenched in sweat. My muscles felt like quivering columns of gelatinous dessert.

I did *not* feel like a special snowflake (though my

mother, Leto, always assured me I was one), and I was sorely tempted to accuse Sherman of not treating me as such.

I grumbled about this to Will. I asked where the old head counselor of Ares had gone. Clarisse La Rue I could at least charm with my dazzling smile. Alas, Will reported she was attending the University of Arizona. Oh, why does college have to happen to perfectly good people?

After the torture, I staggered back to my cabin and took another shower.

Showers are good. Perhaps not as good as bacon, but good.

My second morning session was painful for a different reason. I was assigned to music lessons in the amphitheater with a satyr named Woodrow.

Woodrow seemed nervous to have me join his little class. Perhaps he had heard the legend about my skinning the satyr Marsyas alive after he challenged me to a music contest. (As I said, the flaying part was *totally* untrue, but rumors do have amazing staying power, especially when I may have been guilty of spreading them.)

Using his panpipe, Woodrow reviewed the minor scales. Austin had no problem with these, even though he was challenging himself by playing the violin, which was not his instrument. Valentina Diaz, a daughter of Aphrodite, did her best to throttle a clarinet, producing sounds like a basset hound whimpering in a thunderstorm. Damien White, son of Nemesis, lived up to his namesake by wreaking vengeance on an acoustic guitar. He played with such force that he broke the D string.

"You killed it!" said Chiara Benvenuti. She was the pretty Italian girl I'd noticed the night before—a child of Tyche, goddess of good fortune. "I needed to use that guitar!"

"Shut up, Lucky," Damien muttered. "In the *real* world, accidents happen. Strings snap sometimes."

Chiara unleashed some rapid-fire Italian that I decided not to translate.

"May I?" I reached for the guitar.

Damien reluctantly handed it over. I leaned toward the guitar case by Woodrow's feet. The satyr leaped several inches into the air.

Austin laughed. "Relax, Woodrow. He's just getting another string."

I'll admit I found the satyr's reaction gratifying. If I could still scare satyrs, perhaps there was hope for me reclaiming some of my former glory. From here I could work my way up to scaring farm animals, then demigods, monsters, and minor deities.

In a matter of seconds, I had replaced the string. It felt good to do something so familiar and simple. I adjusted the pitch, but stopped when I realized Valentina was sobbing.

"That was so beautiful!" She wiped a tear from her cheek. "What was that song?"

I blinked. "It's called tuning."

"Yeah, Valentina, control yourself," Damien chided, though his eyes were red. "It wasn't *that* beautiful."

"No." Chiara sniffled. "It wasn't."

Only Austin seemed unaffected. His eyes shone with what looked like pride, though I didn't understand why he would feel that way.

I played a C minor scale. The B string was flat. It's *always* the B string. Three thousand years since I invented the guitar (during a wild party with the Hittites—long story), and I still couldn't figure out how to make a B string that stays in tune.

I ran through the other scales, delighted that I still remembered them.

"Now this is a Lydian progression," I said. "It starts on the fourth of the major scale. They say it's called Lydian after the old kingdom of Lydia, but actually, I named it for an old girlfriend of mine, Lydia. She was the fourth woman I dated that year, so . . ."

I looked up mid-arpeggio. Damien and Chiara were weeping in each other's arms, hitting each other weakly and cursing, "I hate you. I hate you."

Valentina lay on the amphitheater bench, silently shaking. Woodrow was pulling apart his panpipes.

"I'm worthless!" he sobbed. "Worthless!"

Even Austin had a tear in his eye. He gave me a thumbs-up.

I was thrilled that some of my old skill remained intact, but I imagined Chiron would be annoyed if I drove the entire music class into major depression.

I pulled the D string slightly sharp—a trick I used to use to keep my adoring fans from exploding in rapture at my concerts. (And I mean literally exploding. Some of those gigs at the Fillmore in the 1960s . . . well, I'll spare you the gruesome details.)

I strummed a chord that was intentionally out of tune. To me it sounded awful, but the campers stirred from their misery. They sat up, wiped their tears, and watched in fascination as I played a simple one-four-five progression.

"Yeah, man." Austin brought his violin to his chin and began to improvise. His resin bow danced across the strings. He and I locked eyes, and for a moment we were more than family. We became part of the music, communicating on a level only gods and musicians will ever understand.

Woodrow broke the spell.

"That's amazing," the satyr sobbed. "You two should be teaching the class. What was I thinking? Please don't flay me!"

"My dear satyr," I said, "I would never—"

Suddenly, my fingers spasmed. I dropped the guitar in surprise. The instrument tumbled down the stone steps of the amphitheater, clanging and *sproinging*.

Austin lowered his bow. "You okay?"

"I . . . yes, of course."

But I was not okay. For a few moments, I had experienced the bliss of my formerly easy talent. Yet, clearly, my new mortal fingers were not up to the task. My hand muscles were sore. Red lines dug into my finger pads where I had touched the fret board. I had overextended myself in other ways, too. My lungs felt shriveled, drained of oxygen, even though I had done no singing.

"I'm . . . tired," I said, dismayed.

"Well, yeah." Valentina nodded. "The way you were playing was *unreal*!"

"It's okay, Apollo," Austin said. "You'll get stronger. When demigods use their powers, especially at first, they get tired quickly."

"But I'm not . . ."

I couldn't finish the sentence. I wasn't a demigod. I wasn't a god. I wasn't even myself. How could I ever play music again, knowing that I was a flawed instrument? Each note would bring me nothing but pain and exhaustion. My B string would *never* be in tune.

My misery must have shown on my face.

Damien White balled his fists. "Don't you worry, Apollo. It's not your fault. I'll make that stupid guitar pay for this!"

I didn't try to stop him as he marched down the stairs. Part of me took perverse satisfaction in the way he stomped the guitar until it was reduced to kindling and wires.

Chiara huffed. "*Idiota!* Now I'll never get my turn!"

Woodrow winced. "Well, um . . . thanks, everyone! Good class!"

Archery was an even bigger travesty.

If I ever become a god again (no, not if; *when, when*), my first act will be to wipe the memories of everyone who saw me embarrass myself in that class. I hit one bull's-eye. *One*. The grouping on my other shots was abysmal. Two arrows actually hit *outside* the black ring at a mere one hundred yards. I threw down my bow and wept with shame.

Kayla was our class instructor, but her patience and kindness only made me feel worse. She scooped up my bow and offered it back to me.

"Apollo," she said, "those shots were fantastic. A little more practice and—"

"I'm the god of archery!" I wailed. "I don't practice!"

Next to me, the daughters of Nike snickered.

They had the insufferably appropriate names Holly and Laurel Victor. They reminded me of the gorgeous, ferociously athletic African nymphs Athena used to hang out with at Lake Tritonis.

"Hey, ex-god," Holly said, nocking an arrow, "practice is the only way to improve." She scored a seven on the red ring, but she did not seem at all discouraged.

"For *you*, maybe," I said. "You're a mortal!"

Her sister, Laurel, snorted. "So are you now. Suck it up. Winners don't complain." She shot her arrow, which landed next to her sister's but just inside the red ring. "That's why I'm better than Holly. She's always complaining."

"Yeah, right," Holly growled. "The only thing I complain about is how lame *you* are."

"Oh, yeah?" said Laurel. "Let's go. Right now. Best two out of three shots. The loser scrubs the toilets for a month."

"You're on!"

Just like that, they forgot about me. They definitely would've made excellent Tritonian nymphs.

Kayla took me by the arm and led me downrange. "Those two, I swear. We made them Nike co-counselors so they'd compete with each other. If we hadn't, they would've taken over the camp by now and proclaimed a dictatorship."

I suppose she was trying to cheer me up, but I was not consoled.

I stared at my fingers, now blistered from archery as well as sore from guitar. Impossible. Agonizing.

"I can't do this, Kayla," I muttered. "I'm too old to be sixteen again!"

Kayla cupped her hand over mine. Beneath the green

shock of her hair, she had a ginger complexion—like cream painted over copper, the auburn sheen peeking through in the freckles of her face and arms. She reminded me very much of her father, the Canadian archery coach Darren Knowles.

I mean her *other* father. And, yes, of course it's possible for a demigod child to spring from such a relationship. Why not? Zeus gave birth to Dionysus out of his own thigh. Athena once had a child who was created from a handkerchief. Why should such things surprise you? We gods are capable of infinite marvels.

Kayla took a deep breath, as if preparing for an important shot. "You can do it, Dad. You're already good. *Very* good. You've just got to adjust your expectations. Be patient; be brave. You'll get better."

I was tempted to laugh. How could I get used to being merely *good*? Why would I strain myself to get better when before I had been *divine*?

"No," I said bitterly. "No, it is too painful. I swear upon the River Styx—until I am a god again, I will not use a bow or a musical instrument!"

Go ahead and chide me. I know it was a foolish oath, spoken in a moment of misery and self-pity. And it was binding. An oath sworn on the River Styx can have terrible consequences if broken.

But I didn't care. Zeus had cursed me with mortality. I was not going to pretend that everything was normal. I would not be Apollo until I was *really* Apollo. For now, I was just a stupid young man named Lester Papadopoulos. Maybe I would waste my time on skills I didn't care about—like sword fighting or badminton—but I would *not* sully the memory of my once-perfect music and archery.

Kayla stared at me in horror. "Dad, you don't mean it."

"I do!"

"Take it back! You can't . . ." She glanced over my shoulder. "What is he doing?"

I followed her gaze.

Sherman Yang was walking slowly, trancelike, into the woods.

It would have been foolhardy to run after him, straight into the most dangerous part of camp.

So that's exactly what Kayla and I did.

We almost didn't make it. As soon as we reached the tree line, the forest darkened. The temperature dropped. The horizon stretched out as if bent through a magnifying glass.

A woman whispered in my ear. This time I knew the voice well. It had never stopped haunting me. *You did this to me. Come. Chase me again.*

Fear rolled through my stomach.

I imagined the branches turning to arms; the leaves undulated like green hands.

Daphne, I thought.

Even after so many centuries, the guilt was overwhelming. I could not look at a tree without thinking of her. Forests made me nervous. The life force of each tree seemed to bear down on me with righteous hatred, accusing me of so many crimes. . . . I wanted to fall to my knees. I wanted to beg forgiveness. But this was not the time.

I couldn't allow the woods to confuse me again. I would not let anyone else fall into its trap.

Kayla didn't seem affected. I grabbed her hand to make sure we stayed together. We only had to go a few steps, but it felt like a boot camp run before we reached Sherman Yang.

"Sherman." I grabbed his arm.

He tried to shake me off. Fortunately, he was sluggish and dazed, or I would have ended up with scars of my own. Kayla helped me turn him around.

His eyes twitched as if he were in some sort of half-conscious REM sleep. "No. Ellis. Got to find him. Miranda. My girl."

I glanced at Kayla for explanation.

"Ellis is from the Ares cabin," she said. "He's one of the missing."

"Yes, but Miranda, his girl?"

"Sherman and she started dating about a week ago."

"Ah."

Sherman struggled to free himself. "Find her."

"Miranda is right over here, my friend," I lied. "We'll take you there."

He stopped fighting. His eyes rolled until only the whites were visible. "Over . . . here?"

"Yes."

"Ellis?"

"Yes, it's me," I said. "I'm Ellis."

"I love you, man," Sherman sobbed.

Still, it took all our strength to lead him out of the trees. I was reminded of the time Hephaestus and I had to wrestle the god Hypnos back to bed after he sleepwalked into Artemis's private chambers on Mount Olympus. It's a wonder any of us escaped without silver arrows pincushioning our posteriors.

We led Sherman to the archery range. Between one step and the next, he blinked his eyes and became his normal self. He noticed our hands on his arms and shook us off.

"What is this?" he demanded.

"You were walking into the woods," I said.

He gave us his drill sergeant glower. "No, I wasn't."

Kayla reached for him, then obviously thought better about it. Archery would be difficult with broken fingers. "Sherman, you were in some kind of trance. You were muttering about Ellis and Miranda."

Along Sherman's cheek, his zigzag scar darkened to bronze. "I don't remember that."

"Although you didn't mention the other missing camper," I added helpfully. "Cecil?"

"Why would I mention Cecil?" Sherman growled. "I can't stand the guy. And why should I believe you?"

"The woods had you," I said. "The trees were pulling you in."

Sherman studied the forest, but the trees looked normal again. The lengthening shadows and swaying green hands were gone.

"Look," Sherman said, "I have a head injury, thanks to your annoying friend Meg. If I was acting strange, *that's* why."

Kayla frowned. "But—"

"Enough!" Sherman snapped. "If either of you mention this, I'll make you eat your quivers. I don't need people questioning my self-control. Besides, I've got the race to think about."

He brushed past us.

"Sherman," I called.

He turned, his fists clenched.

"The last thing you remember," I said, "before you found yourself with us . . . what were you thinking about?"

For a microsecond, the dazed look passed across his face again. "About Miranda and Ellis . . . like you said. I was thinking . . . I wanted to know where they were."

"You were asking a question, then." A blanket of dread settled over me. "You wanted information."

"I . . ."

At the dining pavilion, the conch horn blew.

Sherman's expression hardened. "Doesn't matter. Drop it. We've got lunch now. Then I'm going to destroy you all in the three-legged death race."

As threats went, I had heard worse, but Sherman made it sound intimidating enough. He marched off toward the pavilion.

Kayla turned to me. "What just happened?"

"I think I understand now," I said. "I know why those campers went missing."

16

Tied to McCaffrey
We might end up in Lima
Harley is evil

NOTE TO SELF: trying to reveal important information just before a three-legged death race is not a good idea.

No one would listen to me.

Despite last night's grumbling and complaining, the campers were now buzzing with excitement. They spent their lunch hour frantically cleaning weapons, lacing armor straps, and whispering among one another to form secret alliances. Many tried to convince Harley, the course architect, to share hints about the best strategies.

Harley loved the attention. By the end of lunch, his table was piled high with offerings (read: bribes)—chocolate bars, peanut butter cups, gummy bears, and Hot Wheels. Harley would have made an excellent god. He took the gifts, mumbled a few pleasantries, but told his worshippers nothing helpful.

I tried to speak with Chiron about the dangers of the woods, but he was so frantic with last-minute race preparations that I almost got trampled just standing near him. He trotted nervously around the pavilion with a team of satyr and dryad referees in tow, comparing maps and issuing orders.

"The teams will be almost impossible to track," he murmured, his face buried in a Labyrinth schematic. "And we don't have any coverage in grid D."

"But, Chiron," I said, "if I could just—"

"The test group this morning ended up in Peru," he told the satyrs. "We can't have that happen again."

"About the woods," I said.

"Yes, I'm sorry, Apollo. I understand you are concerned—"

"The woods are actually speaking," I said. "You remember the old—"

A dryad ran up to Chiron with her dress billowing smoke. "The flares are exploding!"

"Ye gods!" Chiron said. "Those were for emergencies!"

He galloped over my feet, followed by his mob of assistants.

And so it went. When one is a god, the world hangs on your every word. When one is sixteen . . . not so much.

I tried to talk to Harley, hoping he might postpone the race, but the boy brushed me off with a simple "Nah."

As was so often the case with Hephaestus's children, Harley was tinkering with some mechanical device, moving the springs and gears around. I didn't really care what it was, but I asked Harley about it, hoping to win the boy's goodwill.

"It's a beacon," he said, adjusting a knob. "For lost people."

"You mean the teams in the Labyrinth?"

"No. You guys are on your own. This is for Leo."

"Leo Valdez."

Harley squinted at the device. "Sometimes, if you can't find your way back, a beacon can help. Just got to find the right frequency."

"And . . . how long have you been working on this?"

"Since he disappeared. Now I gotta concentrate. Can't stop the race." He turned his back on me and walked off.

I stared after him in amazement. For six months, the boy had been working on a beacon to help his missing brother Leo. I wondered if anyone would work so hard to bring me back home to Olympus. I very much doubted it.

I stood forlornly in a corner of the pavilion and ate a sandwich. I watched the sun wane in the winter sky and I thought about my chariot, my poor horses stuck in their stables with no one to take them out for a ride.

Of course, even without my help, other forces would keep the cosmos chugging along. Many different belief systems powered the revolution of the planets and stars. Wolves would still chase Sol across the sky. Ra would continue his daily journey in his sun barque. Tonatiuh would keep running on his surplus blood from human sacrifices back in the Aztec days. And that other thing—science—would still generate gravity and quantum physics and whatever.

Nevertheless, I felt like I wasn't doing my part, standing around waiting for a three-legged race.

Even Kayla and Austin were too distracted to talk with me. Kayla had told Austin about our experience rescuing

Sherman Yang from the woods, but Austin was more interested in swabbing out his saxophone.

"We can tell Chiron at dinner," he mumbled with a
reed in his mouth. "Nobody's going to listen until the race is
over, and we'll be staying out of the woods anyway. Besides,
if I can play the right tune in the Labyrinth . . ." He got a
gleam in his eyes. "Ooh. Come here, Kayla. I have an idea."

He steered her away and left me alone again.

I understood Austin's enthusiasm, of course. His saxophone skills were so formidable, I was certain he would
become the foremost jazz instrumentalist of his generation, and if you think it's easy to get half a million views
on YouTube playing jazz saxophone, think again. Still, his
musical career was not going to happen if the force in the
woods destroyed us all.

As a last resort (a *very* last resort), I sought out Meg
McCaffrey.

I spotted her at one of the braziers, talking with Julia
Feingold and Alice Miyazawa. Or rather, the Hermes
girls were talking while Meg devoured a cheeseburger. I
marveled that Demeter—the queen of grains, fruits, and
vegetables—could have a daughter who was such an unre-
pentant carnivore.

Then again, Persephone was the same way. You'll hear
stories about the goddess of springtime being all sweetness
and daffodils and nibbling on pomegranate seeds, but I'm
telling you, that girl was frightening when she attacked a
mound of pork spareribs.

I strode over to Meg's side. The Hermes girls stepped

back as if I were a snake handler. I found this reaction pleasing.

"Hello," I said. "What are we talking about?"

Meg wiped her mouth on the back of her hand. "These two wanna know our plans for the race."

"I'm sure they do." I plucked a small magnetic listening device from Meg's coat sleeve and tossed it back to Alice.

Alice smiled sheepishly. "Can't blame us for trying."

"No, of course not," I said. "In the same spirit, I hope you won't mind what I did to your shoes. Have a good race!"

The girls shuffled off nervously, checking the soles of their sneakers.

Meg looked at me with something resembling respect. "What did you do to them?"

"Nothing," I said. "Half the trick to being a god is knowing how to bluff."

She snorted. "So what's our top secret plan? Wait. Let me guess. You don't have one."

"You're learning. Honestly, I meant to come up with one, but I got sidetracked. We have a problem."

"Sure do." From her coat pocket, she pulled two loops of bronze, like resistance bands of braided metal. "You've seen these? They wrap around our legs. Once they're on, they *stay* on until the race is over. No way to get them off. I *hate* restraints."

"I agree." I was tempted to add *especially when I am tied to a small child named Meg*, but my natural diplomacy won out. "However, I was referring to a different problem."

I told her about the incident during archery, when Sherman had almost been lured into the forest.

Meg removed her cat-eye glasses. Without the lenses, her dark irises looked softer and warmer, like tiny plots of planting soil. "You think something in the woods is calling to people?"

"I think something in the woods is *answering* people. In ancient times, there was an Oracle—"

"Yeah, you told me. Delphi."

"No. Another Oracle, even older than Delphi. It involved trees. An entire grove of talking trees."

"Talking trees." Meg's mouth twitched. "What was that Oracle called?"

"I—I can't remember." I ground my teeth. "I *should* know. I should be able to tell you instantly! But the information . . . It's almost as if it is eluding me on purpose."

"That happens sometimes," Meg said. "You'll think of it."

"But it *never* happens to me! Stupid human brain! At any rate, I believe this grove is somewhere in those woods. I don't know how or why. The whispering voices, though . . . they are from this hidden Oracle. The sacred trees are trying to speak prophecies, reaching out to those with burning questions, luring them in."

Meg put her glasses back on. "You know that sounds crazy, right?"

I steadied my breathing. I had to remind myself that I was no longer a god. I had to put up with insults from mortals without being able to blast them to ashes.

"Just be on guard," I said.

"But the race doesn't even go through the woods."

"Nevertheless . . . we are not safe. If you can summon your friend Peaches, I would welcome his company."

"I told you, he sort of pops up when he feels like it. I can't—"

Chiron blew a hunting horn so loudly my vision doubled. Another pledge to myself: once I became a god again, I would descend upon this camp and take away all their horns.

"Demigods!" said the centaur. "Tie your legs together and follow me to your starting positions!"

We gathered in a meadow about a hundred yards from the Big House. Making it *that* far without a single life-threatening incident was a minor miracle. With my left leg bound to Meg's right, I felt the way I used to in Leto's womb just before my sister and I were born. And, yes, I remember that quite well. Artemis was always shoving me aside, elbowing me in the ribs and generally being a womb hog.

I said a silent prayer that if I got through this race alive, I would sacrifice a bull to myself and possibly even build myself a new temple. I am a sucker for bulls and temples.

The satyrs directed us to spread out across the meadow.

"Where is the starting line?" Holly Victor demanded, shoving her shoulder ahead of her sister's. "I want to be the closest."

"*I* want to be closest," Laurel corrected. "You can be *second* closest."

"Not to worry!" Woodrow the satyr sounded very worried. "We'll explain everything in a moment. As soon as I, um, know what to explain."

Will Solace sighed. He was, of course, tied to Nico. He

propped his elbow on Nico's shoulder as if the son of Hades were a convenient shelf. "I miss Grover. He used to organize things like this so well."

"I'd settle for Coach Hedge." Nico pushed Will's arm off. "Besides, don't talk about Grover too loudly. Juniper's right over there."

He pointed to one of the dryads—a pretty girl dressed in pale green.

"Grover's girlfriend," Will explained to me. "She misses him. A lot."

"Okay, everybody!" Woodrow shouted. "Spread out a little bit more, please! We want you to have plenty of room so, you know, if you die, you won't take down all the other teams too!"

Will sighed. "I am *so* excited."

He and Nico loped off. Julia and Alice from the Hermes cabin checked their shoes one more time, then glared at me. Connor Stoll was paired with Paolo Montes, the Brazilian son of Hebe, and neither of them seemed happy about it.

Perhaps Connor looked glum because his mangled scalp was covered in so much medicinal salve his head looked like it had been coughed up by a cat. Or perhaps he just missed his brother Travis.

As soon as Artemis and I were born, we couldn't *wait* to get some distance between us. We staked out our own territories and that was that. But I would've given anything to see her just then. I was sure Zeus had threatened her with severe punishment if she tried to help me during my time as a mortal, but she could have at least sent me a care package from Olympus—a decent toga, some magical acne cream, and maybe a dozen cranberry ambrosia scones from the Scylla Cafe. They made *excellent* scones.

I scanned the other teams. Kayla and Austin were bound together, looking like a deadly pair of street performers with her bow and his saxophone. Chiara, the cute girl from Tyche, was stuck with her nemesis, Damien White, son of . . . well, Nemesis. Billie Ng from Demeter was leg-tied with Valentina Diaz, who was hastily checking her makeup in the reflective surface of Billie's silver coat. Valentina didn't seem to notice that two twigs were sprouting from her hair like tiny deer antlers.

I decided the biggest threat would be Malcolm Pace. You can never be too careful with children of Athena. Surprisingly, though, he'd paired himself with Sherman Yang. That didn't seem like a natural partnership, unless Malcolm had some sort of plan. Those Athena children *always* had a plan. It rarely included letting me win.

The only demigods not participating were Harley and Nyssa, who had set up the course.

Once the satyrs judged we had all spread out sufficiently and our leg bindings had been double-checked, Harley clapped for our attention.

"Okay!" He bounced up and down eagerly, reminding me of the Roman children who used to cheer for executions at the Colosseum. "Here's the deal. Each team has to find three golden apples, then get back to this meadow alive."

Grumbling broke out among the demigods.

"Golden apples," I said. "I *hate* golden apples. They bring nothing but trouble."

Meg shrugged. "I like apples."

I remembered the rotten one she'd used to break Cade's nose in the alley. I wondered if perhaps she could use golden apples with the same deadly skill. Perhaps we stood a chance after all.

Laurel Victor raised her hand. "You mean the first team back wins?"

"*Any* team that gets back alive wins!" Harley said.

"That's ridiculous!" Holly said. "There can only be one winner. First team back wins!"

Harley shrugged. "Have it your way. My only rules are stay alive, and don't kill each other."

"*O quê?*" Paolo started complaining so loudly in Portuguese that Connor had to cover his left ear.

"Now, now!" Chiron called. His saddlebags were overflowing with extra first-aid kits and emergency flares. "We won't need any *help* making this a dangerous challenge. Let's have a good clean three-legged death race. And another thing, campers, given the problems our test group had this morning, please repeat after me: *Do not end up in Peru.*"

"Do not end up in Peru," everyone chanted.

Sherman Yang cracked his knuckles. "So where *is* the starting line?"

"There is no starting line," Harley said with glee. "You're all starting from right where you are."

The campers looked around in confusion. Suddenly the

meadow shook. Dark lines etched across the grass, forming a giant green checkerboard.

"Have fun!" Harley squealed.

The ground opened beneath our feet, and we fell into the Labyrinth.

17

Bowling balls of death
Rolling toward my enemies
I'll trade you problems

AT LEAST WE DID NOT LAND IN PERU.

My feet hit stone, jarring my ankles. We stumbled against a wall, but Meg provided me with a convenient cushion.

We found ourselves in a dark tunnel braced with oaken beams. The hole we'd fallen through was gone, replaced by an earthen ceiling. I saw no sign of the other teams, but from somewhere above I could vaguely hear Harley chanting, "Go! Go! Go!"

"When I get my powers back," I said, "I will turn Harley into a constellation called the Ankle Biter. At least constellations are silent."

Meg pointed down the corridor. "Look."

As my eyes adjusted, I realized the tunnel's dim light emanated from a glowing piece of fruit about thirty yards away.

"A golden apple," I said.

Meg lurched forward, pulling me with her.

"Wait!" I said. "There might be traps!"

As if to illustrate my point, Connor and Paolo emerged

from the darkness at the other end of the corridor. Paolo scooped up the golden apple and shouted, *"BRASIL!"*

Connor grinned at us. "Too slow, suckers!"

The ceiling opened above them, showering them with iron orbs the size of cantaloupes.

Connor yelped, "Run!"

He and Paolo executed an awkward one-eighty and hobbled away, hotly pursued by a rolling herd of cannon-balls with sparking fuses.

The sounds quickly faded. Without the glowing apple, we were left in total darkness.

"Great." Meg's voice echoed. "Now what?"

"I suggest we go the other direction."

That was easier said than done. Being blind seemed to bother Meg more than it did me. Thanks to my mortal body, I already felt crippled and deprived of my senses. Besides, I often relied on more than sight. Music required keen hearing. Archery required a sensitive touch and the ability to feel the direction of the wind. (Okay, sight was also helpful, but you get the idea.)

We shuffled ahead, our arms extended in front of us. I listened for suspicious clicks, snaps, or creaks that might indicate an incoming flock of explosions, but I suspected that if I *did* hear any warning signs, it would be too late.

Eventually Meg and I learned to walk with our bound legs in synchronicity. It wasn't easy. I had a flawless sense of rhythm. Meg was always a quarter beat slow or fast, which kept us veering left or right and running into walls.

We lumbered along for what might have been minutes or days. In the Labyrinth, time was deceptive.

I remembered what Austin had told me about the Labyrinth feeling different since the death of its creator. I was beginning to understand what he meant. The air seemed fresher, as if the maze hadn't been chewing up quite so many bodies. The walls didn't radiate the same malignant heat. As far as I could tell, they weren't oozing blood or slime, either, which was a definite improvement. In the old days, you couldn't take a step inside Daedalus's Labyrinth without sensing its all-consuming desire: *I will destroy your mind and your body.* Now the atmosphere was sleepier, the message not quite as virulent: *Hey, if you die in here, that's cool.*

"I never liked Daedalus," I muttered. "That old rascal didn't know when to stop. He always had to have the latest tech, the most recent updates. I *told* him not to make his maze self-aware. 'A.I. will destroy us, man,' I said. But noooo. He *had* to give the Labyrinth a malevolent consciousness."

"I don't know what you're talking about," Meg said. "But maybe you shouldn't bad-mouth the maze while we're inside it."

Once, I stopped when I heard the sound of Austin's saxophone. It was faint, echoing through so many corridors I couldn't pinpoint where it was coming from. Then it was gone. I hoped he and Kayla had found their three apples and escaped safely.

Finally, Meg and I reached a Y in the corridor. I could tell this from the flow of the air and the temperature differential against my face.

"Why'd we stop?" Meg asked.

"Shh." I listened intently.

From the right-hand corridor came a faint whining sound like a table saw. The left-hand corridor was quiet, but it exuded a faint odor that was unpleasantly familiar . . . not sulfur, exactly, but a vaporous mix of minerals from deep in the earth.

"I don't hear anything," Meg complained.

"A sawing noise to the right," I told her. "To the left, a bad smell."

"I choose the bad smell."

"Of course you do."

Meg blew me one of her trademark raspberries, then hobbled to the left, pulling me along with her.

The bronze bands around my leg began to chafe. I could feel Meg's pulse through her femoral artery, messing up my rhythm. Whenever I get nervous (which doesn't happen often), I like to hum a song to calm myself—usually Ravel's *Boléro* or the ancient Greek "Song of Seikilos." But with Meg's pulse throwing me off, the only tune I could conjure was the "Chicken Dance." That was not soothing.

We edged forward. The smell of volcanic fumes intensified. My pulse lost its perfect rhythm. My heart knocked against my chest with every *cluck, cluck, cluck, cluck* of the "Chicken Dance." I feared I knew where we were. I told myself it wasn't possible. We couldn't have walked halfway around the world. But this was the Labyrinth. Down here, distance was meaningless. The maze knew how to exploit its victims' weaknesses. Worse: it had a vicious sense of humor.

"I see light!" Meg said.

She was right. The absolute darkness had changed to

murky gray. Up ahead, the tunnel ended, joining with a narrow, lengthwise cavern like a volcanic vent. It looked as if a colossal claw had slashed across the corridor and left a wound in the earth. I had seen creatures with claws that big down in Tartarus. I did not fancy seeing them again.

"We should turn around," I said.

"That's stupid," Meg said. "Don't you see the golden glow? There's an apple in there."

All I saw were swirling plumes of ash and gas. "The glow could be lava," I said. "Or radiation. Or eyes. Glowing eyes are *never* good."

"It's an apple," Meg insisted. "I can smell apple."

"Oh, *now* you develop keen senses?"

Meg forged onward, giving me little choice but to go with. For a small girl, she was quite good at throwing her weight around. At the end of the tunnel, we found ourselves on a narrow ledge. The cliff wall opposite was only ten feet away, but the crevasse seemed to plunge downward forever. Perhaps a hundred feet above us, the jagged vent opened into a bigger chamber.

A painfully large ice cube seemed to be working its way down my throat. I had never seen this place from below, but I knew exactly where we were. We stood at the *omphalus*—the navel of the ancient world.

"You're shaking," Meg said.

I tried to cover her mouth with my hand, but she promptly bit it.

"Don't touch me," she snarled.

"*Please* be quiet."

"Why?"

"Because right above us—" My voice cracked. "Delphi. The chamber of the Oracle."

Meg's nose quivered like a rabbit's. "That's impossible."

"No, it's not," I whispered. "And if this is Delphi, that means . . ."

From overhead came a hiss so loud, it sounded as if the entire ocean had hit a frying pan and evaporated into a massive steam cloud. The ledge shook. Pebbles rained down. Above, a monstrous body slid across the crevasse, completely covering the opening. The smell of molting snakeskin seared my nostrils.

"Python." My voice was now an octave higher than Meg's. "He is here."

18

The Beast is calling
Tell him I'm not here. Let's hide
Where? In garbage. Natch

HAD I EVER BEEN SO TERRIFIED?

Perhaps when Typhon raged across the earth, scattering the gods before him. Perhaps when Gaea unleashed her giants to tear down Olympus. Or perhaps when I accidentally saw Ares naked in the gymnasium. That had been enough to turn my hair white for a century.

But I had been a god all of those times. Now I was a weak, tiny mortal cowering in the darkness. I could only pray my old enemy would not sense my presence. For once in my long glorious life, I wanted to be invisible.

Oh, why had the Labyrinth brought me here?

As soon as I thought this, I chided myself: Of *course* it would bring me where I least wanted to be. Austin had been wrong about the maze. It was still evil, designed to kill. It was just a little subtler about its homicides now.

Meg seemed oblivious to our danger. Even with an immortal monster a hundred feet above us, she had the nerve to stay on task. She elbowed me and pointed to a tiny ledge on the opposite wall, where a golden apple glowed cheerfully.

Had Harley *placed* it there? I couldn't imagine. More likely the boy had simply rolled golden apples down various corridors, trusting that they would find the most dangerous spots to roost. I was really starting to dislike that boy.

Meg whispered, "Easy jump."

I gave her a look that under different circumstances would've incinerated her. "Too dangerous."

"Apple," she hissed.

"Monster!" I hissed back.

"One."

"No!"

"Two."

"No!"

"Three." She jumped.

Which meant that I also jumped. We made the ledge, though our heels sent a spray of rubble into the chasm. Only my natural coordination and grace saved us from toppling backward to our deaths. Meg snatched up the apple.

Above us, the monster rumbled, "Who approaches?"

His voice . . . Gods above, I remembered that voice— deep and gruff, as if he breathed xenon rather than air. For all I knew, he did. Python could certainly *produce* his share of unhealthy gasses.

The monster shifted his weight. More gravel spilled into the crevasse.

I stood absolutely still, pressed against the cold face of the rock. My eardrums pulsed with every beat of my heart. I wished I could stop Meg from breathing. I wished I could stop the rhinestones on her eyeglasses from glittering.

Python had heard us. I prayed to all the gods that the monster would decide the noise was nothing. All he had to do was breathe down into the crevasse and he would kill us. There was no escaping his poisonous belch—not from this distance, not for a mortal.

Then, from the cavern above, came another voice, smaller and much closer to human. "Hello, my reptilian friend."

I nearly wept with relief. I had no idea who this newcomer was, or why he had been so foolish as to announce his presence to Python, but I always appreciated it when humans sacrificed themselves to save me. Common courtesy was not dead after all!

Python's harsh laugh shook my teeth. "Well, I was wondering if you would make the trip, Monsieur Beast."

"Don't call me that," the man snapped. "And the commute was quite easy now that the Labyrinth is back in service."

"I'm so pleased." Python's tone was dry as basalt.

I couldn't tell much about the man's voice, muffled as it was by several tons of reptile flesh, but he sounded calmer and more in control than I would have been talking to Python. I had heard the term *Beast* used to describe someone before, but as usual, my mortal brainpower failed me.

If only I'd been able to retain just the *important* information! Instead, I could tell you what I had for dessert the first time I dined with King Minos. (Spice cake.) I could tell you what color *chitons* the sons of Niobe were wearing when I slew them. (A very unflattering shade of orange.)

But I couldn't remember something as basic as whether this Beast was a wrestler, a movie star, or a politician. Possibly all three?

Next to me, in the glow of the apple, Meg seemed to have turned to bronze. Her eyes were wide with fear. A little late for that, but at least she was quiet. If I didn't know better, I might have thought the man's voice terrified her more than the monster's.

"So, Python," the man continued, "any prophetic words to share with me?"

"In time . . . my lord."

The last words were spoken with amusement, but I'm not sure anyone else would've recognized it. Aside from myself, few had been on the receiving end of Python's sarcasm and lived to tell the tale.

"I need more than your assurances," the man said. "Before we proceed, we must have *all* the Oracles under our control."

All the Oracles. Those words almost sent me off the cliff, but somehow I retained my balance.

"In time," Python said, "as we agreed. We have come this far by biding our time, yes? You did not reveal your hand when the Titans stormed New York. I did not march to war with Gaea's giants. We both realized the time for victory was not yet right. You must remain patient for a while longer."

"Don't lecture me, snake. While you slumbered, I built an empire. I have spent centuries—"

"Yes, yes." The monster exhaled, causing a tremor along

the cliff face. "And if you ever want your empire to come out of the shadows, you need to deliver on *your* side of the bargain first. When will you destroy Apollo?"

I stifled a yelp. I should not have been surprised that they were talking about me. For millennia, I had assumed that *everyone* talked about me all the time. I was so interesting they simply couldn't help it. But this business about destroying me—I didn't like that.

Meg looked more terrified than I'd ever seen her. I wanted to think she was worried for my sake, but I had a feeling she was equally concerned about herself. Again, those mixed-up demigod priorities.

The man stepped closer to the chasm. His voice became clearer and louder. "Don't worry about Apollo. He is exactly where I need him to be. He will serve our purpose, and once he is no longer useful . . ."

He did not bother finishing the statement. I was afraid it did not end with *we will give him a nice present and send him on his way.* With a chill, I recognized the voice from my dream. It was the nasal sneer of the man in the purple suit. I also had a feeling I'd heard him sing before, years and years ago, but that didn't make sense. . . . Why would I suffer through a concert given by an ugly purple-suited man who called himself the Beast? I was not even a *fan* of death metal polka!

Python shifted his bulk, showering us with more rubble. "And how exactly will you convince him to serve our purpose?"

The Beast chuckled. "I have well-placed help within

the camp who will steer Apollo toward us. Also, I have upped the stakes. Apollo will have no choice. He and the girl will open the gates."

A whiff of Python vapor floated across my nose—enough to make me dizzy, hopefully not enough to kill me.

"I trust you are right," said the monster. "Your judgment in the past has been . . . questionable. I wonder if you have chosen the right tools for this job. Have you learned from your past mistakes?"

The man snarled so deeply I could almost believe he was turning into a beast. I'd seen that happen enough times. Next to me, Meg whimpered.

"Listen here, you overgrown reptile," the man said, "my only mistake was not burning my enemies fast enough, often enough. I assure you, I am stronger than ever. My organization is everywhere. My colleagues stand ready. When we control all four Oracles, we will control fate itself!"

"And what a glorious day that will be." Python's voice was jagged with contempt. "But beforehand, you must destroy the *fifth* Oracle, yes? That is the only one I *cannot* control. You must set flame to the grove of—"

"Dodona," I said.

The word leaped unbidden from my mouth and echoed through the chasm. Of all the stupid times to retrieve a piece of information, of all the stupid times to say it aloud . . . oh, the body of Lester Papadopoulos was a terrible place to live.

Above us, the conversation stopped.

Meg hissed at me, "You idiot."

The Beast said, "What was that sound?"

Rather than answer, *Oh, that's just us*, we did something

even more foolish. One of us, Meg or me—personally, I blame her—must have slipped on a pebble. We toppled off the ledge and fell into the sulfurous clouds below.

SQUISH.

The Labyrinth most definitely had a sense of humor. Instead of allowing us to smash into a rock floor and die, the maze dropped us into a mound of wet, full garbage bags.

If you're keeping score, that was the *second* time since becoming mortal that I had crash-landed in garbage, which was two times more than any god should endure.

We tumbled down the pile in a frenzy of three-legged flailing. We landed at the bottom, covered with muck, but, miraculously, still alive.

Meg sat up, glazed in a layer of coffee grounds.

I pulled a banana peel off my head and flicked it aside. "Is there some reason you keep landing us in trash heaps?"

"Me? You're the one who lost his balance!" Meg wiped her face without much luck. In her other hand, she clutched the golden apple with trembling fingers.

"Are you all right?" I asked.

"Fine," she snapped.

Clearly that was not true. She looked as if she'd just gone through Hades's haunted house. (Pro tip: DO NOT.) Her face was pallid. She had bit her lip so hard, her teeth were pink with blood. I also detected the faint smell of urine, meaning one of us had gotten scared enough to lose bladder control, and I was seventy-five percent sure it wasn't me.

"That man upstairs," I said. "You recognized his voice?"

"Shut up. That's an order!"

I attempted to reply. To my consternation, I found that I couldn't. My voice had heeded Meg's command all on its own, which did not bode well. I decided to file away my questions about the Beast for later.

I scanned our surroundings. Garbage chutes lined the walls on all four sides of the dismal little basement. As I watched, another bag of refuse slid down the right-hand chute and hit the pile. The smell was so strong, it could have burned paint off the walls, if the gray cinder blocks had been painted. Still, it was better than smelling the fumes of Python. The only visible exit was a metal door marked with a biohazard sign.

"Where are we?" Meg asked.

I glared at her, waiting.

"You can talk now," she added.

"This is going to shock you," I said, "but it appears we are in a garbage room."

"But where?"

"Could be anywhere. The Labyrinth intersects with subterranean places all around the world."

"Like Delphi." Meg glowered at me as if our little Greek excursion had been my fault and not . . . well, only indirectly my fault.

"That was unexpected," I agreed. "We need to speak with Chiron."

"What is Dodona?"

"I—I'll explain it all later." I didn't want Meg to shut me up again. I also didn't want to talk about Dodona while trapped in the Labyrinth. My skin was crawling, and I didn't think it was just because I was covered in sticky soda syrup. "First, we need to get out of here."

Meg glanced behind me. "Well, it wasn't a total waste." She reached into the garbage and pulled out a second piece of glowing fruit. "Only one more apple to go."

"Perfect." The last thing I cared about was finishing Harley's ridiculous race, but at least it would get Meg moving. "Now, why don't we see what fabulous biohazards await us behind that door?"

19

They have gone missing?
No, no, no, no, no, no, no
No, et cetera

THE ONLY BIOHAZARDS we encountered were vegan cupcakes.

After navigating several torchlit corridors, we burst into a crowded modern bakery that, according to the menu board, had the dubious name THE LEVEL TEN VEGAN. Our garbage/volcanic gas stench quickly dispersed the customers, driving most toward the exit, and causing many non-dairy gluten-free baked goods to be trampled. We ducked behind the counter, charged through the kitchen doors, and found ourselves in a subterranean amphitheater that looked centuries old.

Tiers of stone seats ringed a sandy pit about the right size for a gladiator fight. Hanging from the ceiling were dozens of thick iron chains. I wondered what ghastly spectacles might have been staged here, but we didn't stay very long.

We limped out the opposite side, back into the Labyrinth's twisting corridors.

By this point, we had perfected the art of three-legged

running. Whenever I started to tire, I imagined Python behind us, spewing poisonous gas.

At last we turned a corner, and Meg shouted, "There!"

In the middle of the corridor sat a third golden apple.

This time I was too exhausted to care about traps. We loped forward until Meg scooped up the fruit.

In front of us, the ceiling lowered, forming a ramp. Fresh air filled my lungs. We climbed to the top, but instead of feeling elated, my insides turned as cold as the garbage juice on my skin. We were back in the woods.

"Not here," I muttered. "Gods, no."

Meg hopped us in a full circle. "Maybe it's a different forest."

But it wasn't. I could feel the resentful stare of the trees, the horizon stretching out in all directions. Voices began to whisper, waking to our presence.

"Hurry," I said.

As if on cue, the bands around our legs sprang loose. We ran.

Even with her arms full of apples, Meg was faster. She veered between trees, zigzagging left and right as if following a course only she could see. My legs ached and my chest burned, but I didn't dare fall behind.

Up ahead, flickering points of light resolved into torches. At last we burst out of the woods, right into a crowd of campers and satyrs.

Chiron galloped over. "Thank the gods!"

"You're welcome," I gasped, mostly out of habit. "Chiron . . . we have to talk."

In the torchlight, the centaur's face seemed carved from shadow. "Yes, we do, my friend. But first, I fear one more team is still missing . . . your children, Kayla and Austin."

Chiron forced us to take showers and change clothes. Otherwise I would have plunged straight back into the woods.

By the time I was done, Kayla and Austin still had not returned.

Chiron had sent search parties of dryads into the forest, on the assumption that they would be safe in their home territory, but he adamantly refused to let demigods join the hunt.

"We cannot risk anyone else," he said. "Kayla, Austin, and—and the other missing . . . They would not want that."

Five campers had now disappeared. I harbored no illusions that Kayla and Austin would return on their own. The Beast's words still echoed in my ears: *I have upped the stakes. Apollo will have no choice.*

Somehow he had targeted my children. He was inviting me to look for them, and to find the gates of this hidden Oracle. There was still so much I did not understand—how the ancient grove of Dodona had relocated here, what sort of "gates" it might have, why the Beast thought I could open them, and how he'd snared Austin and Kayla. But there was one thing I did know: the Beast was right. I had no choice. I had to find my children . . . my *friends*.

I would have ignored Chiron's warning and run into the forest except for Will's panicked shout: "Apollo, I need you!"

At the far end of the field, he had set up an impromptu hospital where half a dozen campers lay injured on stretchers. He was frantically tending to Paolo Montes while Nico held down the screaming patient.

I ran to Will's side and winced at what I saw.

Paolo had managed to get one of his legs sawed off.

"I got it reattached," Will told me, his voice shaky with exhaustion. His scrubs were speckled with blood. "I need somebody to keep him stable."

I pointed to the woods. "But—"

"I know!" Will snapped. "Don't you think I want to be out there searching too? We're shorthanded for healers. There's some salve and nectar in that pack. Go!"

I was stunned by his tone. I realized he was just as concerned about Kayla and Austin as I was. The only difference: Will knew his duty. He had to heal the injured first. And he needed my help.

"Y-yes," I said. "Yes, of course."

I grabbed the supply pack and took charge of Paolo, who had conveniently passed out from the pain.

Will changed his surgical gloves and glared at the woods. "We *will* find them. We *have* to."

Nico di Angelo gave him a canteen. "Drink. Right now, this is where you need to be."

I could tell the son of Hades was angry too. Around his feet, the grass steamed and withered.

Will sighed. "You're right. But that doesn't make me feel better. I have to set Valentina's broken arm now. You want to assist?"

"Sounds gruesome," Nico said. "Let's go."

I tended to Paolo Montes until I was sure he was out of danger, then asked two satyrs to carry his stretcher to the Hebe cabin.

I did what I could to nurse the others. Chiara had a mild concussion. Billie Ng had come down with a case of Irish step dancing. Holly and Laurel needed pieces of shrapnel removed from their backs, thanks to a close encounter with an exploding chain-saw Frisbee.

The Victor twins had placed in first, predictably, but they also demanded to know which of them had the *most* pieces of shrapnel extracted, so they could have bragging rights. I told them to be quiet or I would never allow them to wear laurel wreaths again. (As the guy who held the patent on laurel wreaths, that was my prerogative.)

I found my mortal healing skills were passable. Will Solace far outshone me, but that didn't bother me as much as my failures with archery and music had. I suppose I was used to being second in healing. My son Asclepius had become the god of medicine by the time he was fifteen, and I couldn't have been happier for him. It left me time for my other interests. Besides, it's every god's dream to have a child who grows up to be a doctor.

As I was washing up from the shrapnel extraction, Harley shuffled over, fiddling with his beacon device. His eyes were puffy from crying.

"It's my fault," he muttered. "I got them lost. I . . . I'm sorry."

He was shaking. I realized the little boy was terrified of what I might do.

For the past two days, I had yearned to cause fear in mortals again. My stomach had boiled with resentment and bitterness. I wanted someone to blame for my predicament, for the disappearances, for my own powerlessness to fix things.

Looking at Harley, my anger evaporated. I felt hollow, silly, ashamed of myself. Yes, me, Apollo . . . ashamed. Truly, it was an event so unprecedented, it should have ripped apart the cosmos.

"It's all right," I told him.

He sniffled. "The racecourse went into the woods. It shouldn't have done that. They got lost and . . . and—"

"Harley"—I placed my hands over his—"may I see your beacon?"

He blinked the tears away. I guess he was afraid I might smash his gadget, but he let me take it.

"I'm not an inventor," I said, turning the gears as gently as possible. "I don't have your father's skills. But I *do* know music. I believe automatons prefer a frequency of E at 329.6 hertz. It resonates best with Celestial bronze. If you adjust your signal—"

"Festus might hear it?" Harley's eyes widened. "Really?"

"I don't know," I admitted. "Just as you could not have known what the Labyrinth would do today. But that doesn't mean we should stop trying. Never stop inventing, son of Hephaestus."

I gave him back his beacon. For a count of three, Harley stared at me in disbelief. Then he hugged me so hard he nearly rebroke my ribs, and he dashed away.

I tended to the last of the injured while the harpies

cleaned the area, picking up bandages, torn clothing, and damaged weapons. They gathered the golden apples in a basket and promised to bake us some lovely glowing apple turnovers for breakfast.

At Chiron's urging, the remaining campers dispersed back to their cabins. He promised them we would determine what to do in the morning, but I had no intention of waiting.

As soon as we were alone, I turned to Chiron and Meg.

"I'm going after Kayla and Austin," I told them. "You can join me or not."

Chiron's expression tightened. "My friend, you're exhausted and unprepared. Go back to your cabin. It will serve no purpose—"

"No." I waved him off, as I once might have done when I was a god. The gesture probably looked petulant coming from a sixteen-year-old nobody, but I didn't care. "I have to do this."

The centaur lowered his head. "I should have listened to you before the race. You tried to warn me. What—what did you discover?"

The question stopped my momentum like a seat belt.

After rescuing Sherman Yang, after listening to Python in the Labyrinth, I had felt certain I knew the answers. I had remembered the name *Dodona*, the stories about talking trees . . .

Now my mind was once again a bowl of fuzzy mortal soup. I couldn't recall what I'd been so excited about, or what I had intended to do about it.

Perhaps exhaustion and stress had taken their toll. Or

maybe Zeus was manipulating my brain—allowing me tantalizing glimpses of the truth, then snatching them away, turning my aha! moments into huh? moments.

I howled in frustration. "I don't remember!"

Meg and Chiron exchanged nervous glances.

"You're not going," Meg told me firmly.

"*What?* You can't—"

"That's an order," she said. "No going into the woods until I say so."

The command sent a shudder from the base of my skull to my heels.

I dug my fingernails into my palms. "Meg McCaffrey, if my children die because you wouldn't let me—"

"Like Chiron said, you'd just get yourself killed. We'll wait for daylight."

I thought how satisfying it would be to drop Meg from the sun chariot at high noon. Then again, some small rational part of me realized she might be right. I was in no condition to launch a one-man rescue operation. That just made me angrier.

Chiron's tail swished from side to side. "Well, then . . . I will see you both in the morning. We *will* find a solution. I promise you that."

He gave me one last look, as if worried I might start running in circles and baying at the moon. Then he trotted back toward the Big House.

I scowled at Meg. "I'm staying out here tonight, in case Kayla and Austin come back. Unless you want to forbid me from doing that, *too.*"

She only shrugged. Even her *shrugs* were annoying.

I stormed off to the Me cabin and grabbed a few supplies: a flashlight, two blankets, a canteen of water. As an afterthought, I took a few books from Will Solace's bookshelf. No surprise, he kept reference materials about me to share with new campers. I thought perhaps the books might help jog my memories. Failing that, they'd make good tinder for a fire.

When I returned to the edge of the woods, Meg was still there.

I hadn't expected her to keep vigil with me. Being Meg, she had apparently decided it would be the best way to irritate me.

She sat next to me on my blanket and began eating a golden apple, which she had hidden in her coat. Winter mist drifted through the trees. The night breeze rippled through the grass, making patterns like waves.

Under different circumstances, I might have written a poem about it. In my present state of mind, I could only have managed a funeral dirge, and I did not want to think about death.

I tried to stay mad at Meg, but I couldn't manage it. I supposed she'd had my best interests at heart . . . or at least, she wasn't ready to see her new godly servant get himself killed.

She didn't try to console me. She asked me no questions. She amused herself by picking up small rocks and tossing them into the woods. That, I didn't mind. I happily would've given her a catapult if I had one.

As the night wore on, I read about myself in Will's books.

Normally this would have been a happy task. I am, after all, a fascinating subject. This time, however, I gained no satisfaction from my glorious exploits. They all seemed like exaggerations, lies, and . . . well, myths. Unfortunately, I found a chapter about Oracles. Those few pages stirred my memory, confirming my worst suspicions.

I was too angry to be terrified. I stared at the woods and dared the whispering voices to disturb me. I thought, *Come on, then. Take me, too.* The trees remained silent. Kayla and Austin did not return.

Toward dawn, it started to snow. Only then did Meg speak. "We should go inside."

"And abandon them?"

"Don't be stupid." Snow salted the hood of her winter coat. Her face was hidden except for the tip of her nose and the glint of rhinestones on her glasses. "You'll freeze out here."

I noticed she didn't complain about the cold herself. I wondered if she even felt uncomfortable, or if the power of Demeter kept her safe through the winter like a leafless tree or a dormant seed in the earth.

"They were my children." It hurt me to use the past tense, but Kayla and Austin felt irretrievably lost. "I should've done more to protect them. I should have antici-pated that my enemies would target them to hurt me."

Meg chucked another rock at the trees. "You've had a lot of children. You take the blame every time one of them gets in trouble?"

The answer was no. Over the millennia, I had barely managed to remember my children's names. If I sent them an occasional birthday card or a magic flute, I felt really good about myself. Sometimes I wouldn't realize one of them had died until decades later. During the French Revolution, I got worried about my boy Louis XIV, the Sun King, then went down to check on him and found out he had died seventy-five years earlier.

Now, though, I had a mortal conscience. My sense of guilt seemed to have expanded as my life span contracted. I couldn't explain that to Meg. She would never understand. She'd probably just throw a rock at me.

"It's my fault Python retook Delphi," I said. "If I had killed him the moment he reappeared, while I was still a god, he would never have become so powerful. He would never have made an alliance with this . . . this *Beast*."

Meg lowered her face.

"You know him," I guessed. "In the Labyrinth, when you heard the Beast's voice, you were terrified."

I was worried she might order me to shut up again. Instead, she silently traced the crescents on her gold rings.

"Meg, he wants to *destroy* me," I said. "Somehow, he's behind these disappearances. The more we understand about this man—"

"He lives in New York."

I waited. It was difficult to glean much information from the top of Meg's hood.

"All right," I said. "That narrows it down to eight and a half million people. What else?"

Meg picked at the calluses on her fingers. "If you're a demigod on the streets, you hear about the Beast. He takes people like me."

A snowflake melted on the back of my neck. "Takes people . . . why?"

"To train," Meg said. "To use like . . . servants, soldiers. I don't know."

"And you've met him."

"Please don't ask me—"

"Meg."

"He killed my dad."

Her words were quiet, but they hit me harder than a rock in the face. "Meg, I—I'm sorry. How . . . ?"

"I refused to work for him," she said. "My dad tried to . . ." She closed her fists. "I was really small. I hardly remember it. I got away. Otherwise, the Beast would've killed me, too. My stepdad took me in. He was good to me. You asked why he trained me to fight? Why he gave me the rings? He wanted me to be safe, to be able to protect myself."

"From the Beast."

Her hood dipped. "Being a good demigod, training hard . . . that's the only way to keep the Beast away. Now you know."

In fact, I had more questions than ever, but I sensed that Meg was in no mood for further sharing. I remembered her expression as we stood on that ledge under the chamber of Delphi—her look of absolute terror when she recognized the Beast's voice. Not all monsters were three-ton reptiles with poisonous breath. Many wore human faces.

I peered into the woods. Somewhere in there, five demigods were being used as bait, including two of my children. The Beast wanted me to search for them, and I would. But I would *not* let him use me.

I have well-placed help within the camp, the Beast had said. That bothered me.

I knew from experience that any demigod could be turned against Olympus. I had been at the banquet table when Tantalus tried to poison the gods by feeding us his chopped-up son in a stew. I'd watched as King Mithridates sided with the Persians and massacred every Roman in Anatolia. I'd witnessed Queen Clytemnestra turn homicidal, killing her husband Agamemnon just because he made one little human sacrifice to me. Demigods are an unpredictable bunch.

I glanced at Meg. I wondered if she could be lying to me—if she was some sort of spy. It seemed unlikely. She was too contrary, impetuous, and annoying to be an effective mole. Besides, she was technically my master. She could order me to do almost any task and I would have to obey. If she was out to destroy me, I was already as good as dead.

Perhaps Damien White . . . a son of Nemesis was a natural choice for backstabbing duty. Or Connor Stoll, Alice, or Julia . . . a child of Hermes had recently betrayed the gods by working for Kronos. They might do so again. Maybe that pretty Chiara, daughter of Tyche, was in league with the Beast. Children of luck were natural gamblers. The truth was, I had no idea.

The sky turned from black to gray. I became aware of a distant *thump, thump, thump*—a quick, relentless pulse that got louder and louder. At first, I feared it might be the blood in my head. Could human brains explode from too many worrisome thoughts? Then I realized the noise was mechanical, coming from the west. It was the distinctly modern sound of rotor blades cutting the air.

Meg lifted her head. "Is that a helicopter?"

I got to my feet.

The machine appeared—a dark red Bell 412 cutting north along the coastline. (Riding the skies as often as I do, I know my flying machines.) Painted on the helicopter's side was a bright green logo with the letters D.E.

Despite my misery, a small bit of hope kindled inside me. The satyrs Millard and Herbert must have succeeded in delivering their message.

"That," I told Meg, "is Rachel Elizabeth Dare. Let's go see what the Oracle of Delphi has to say."

20

Don't paint over gods
If you're redecorating
That's, like, common sense

RACHEL ELIZABETH DARE was one of my favorite mortals. As soon as she'd become the Oracle two summers ago, she'd brought new vigor and excitement to the job.

Of course, the previous Oracle had been a withered corpse, so perhaps the bar was low. Regardless, I was elated as the Dare Enterprises helicopter descended just beyond the eastern hills, outside the camp's boundary. I wondered what Rachel had told her father—a fabulously wealthy real estate magnate—to convince him she needed to borrow a helicopter. I knew Rachel could be quite convincing.

I jogged across the valley with Meg in tow. I could already imagine the way Rachel would look as she came over the summit: her frizzy red hair, her vivacious smile, her paint-spattered blouse, and jeans covered with doodles. I needed her humor, wisdom, and resilience. The Oracle would cheer us all up. Most importantly, she would cheer *me* up.

I was not prepared for the reality. (Which again, was a stunning surprise. Normally, reality prepares itself for *me*.)

Rachel met us on the hill near the entrance to her cave. Only later would I realize Chiron's two satyr messengers were not with her, and I would wonder what had happened to them.

Miss Dare looked thinner and older—less like a high school girl and more like a young farmer's wife from ancient times, weathered from hard work and gaunt from shortage of food. Her red hair had lost its vibrancy. It framed her face in a curtain of dark copper. Her freckles had faded to watermarks. Her green eyes did not sparkle. And she was wearing a dress—a white cotton frock with a white shawl, and a patina-green jacket. Rachel *never* wore dresses.

"Rachel?" I didn't trust myself to say any more. She was not the same person.

Then I remembered that I wasn't either.

She studied my new mortal form. Her shoulders slumped. "So it's true."

From below us came the voices of other campers. No doubt woken by the sound of the helicopter, they were emerging from their cabins and gathering at the base of the hill. None tried to climb toward us, though. Perhaps they sensed that all was not right.

The helicopter rose from behind Half-Blood Hill. It veered toward Long Island Sound, passing so close to the Athena Parthenos that I thought its landing skids might clip the goddess's winged helmet.

I turned to Meg. "Would you tell the others that Rachel needs some space? Fetch Chiron. He should come up. The rest should wait."

It wasn't like Meg to take orders from me. I half expected her to kick me. Instead, she glanced nervously at Rachel, turned, and trudged down the hill.

"A friend of yours?" Rachel asked.

"Long story."

"Yes," she said. "I have a story like that, too."

"Shall we talk in your cave?"

Rachel pursed her lips. "You won't like it. But yes, that's probably the safest place."

The cave was not as cozy as I remembered.

The sofas were overturned. The coffee table had a broken leg. The floor was strewn with easels and canvases. Even Rachel's tripod stool, the throne of prophecy itself, lay on its side on a pile of paint-splattered drop cloths.

Most disturbing was the state of the walls. Ever since taking up residence, Rachel had been painting them, like her cave-dwelling ancestors of old. She had spent hours on elaborate murals of events from the past, images from the future she'd seen in prophecies, favorite quotes from books and music, and abstract designs so good they would have given M. C. Escher vertigo. The art made the cave feel like a mixture of art studio, psychedelic hangout, and graffiti-covered highway underpass. I loved it.

But most of the images had been blotted out with a sloppy coat of white paint. Nearby, a roller was stuck in an encrusted tray. Clearly Rachel had defaced her own work months ago and hadn't been back since.

She waved listlessly at the wreckage. "I got frustrated."

"Your art . . ." I gaped at the field of white. "There was a lovely portrait of me—right there."

I get offended whenever art is damaged, especially if that art features me.

Rachel looked ashamed. "I—I thought a blank canvas might help me think." Her tone made it obvious that the whitewashing had accomplished nothing. I could have told her as much.

The two of us did our best to clean up. We hauled the sofas back into place to form a sitting area. Rachel left the tripod stool where it lay.

A few minutes later, Meg returned. Chiron followed in full centaur form, ducking his head to fit through the entrance. They found us sitting at the wobbly coffee table like civilized cave people, sharing lukewarm Arizona tea and stale crackers from the Oracle's larder.

"Rachel." Chiron sighed with relief. "Where are Millard and Herbert?"

She bowed her head. "They arrived at my house badly wounded. They . . . they didn't make it."

Perhaps it was the morning light behind him, but I fancied I could see new gray whiskers growing in Chiron's beard. The centaur trotted over and lowered himself to the ground, folding his legs underneath himself. Meg joined me on the couch.

Rachel leaned forward and steepled her fingers, as she did when she spoke a prophecy. I half hoped the spirit of Delphi would possess her, but there was no smoke, no hissing, no raspy voice of divine possession. It was a bit disappointing.

"You first," she told us. "Tell me what's been going on here."

We brought her up to speed on the disappearances and my misadventures with Meg. I explained about the three-legged race and our side trip to Delphi.

Chiron blanched. "I did not know this. You went to Delphi?"

Rachel stared at me in disbelief. "*The* Delphi. You saw Python and you . . ."

I got the feeling she wanted to say *and you didn't kill him?* But she restrained herself.

I felt like standing with my face against the wall. Perhaps Rachel could blot me out with white paint. Disappearing would've been less painful than facing my failures.

"At present," I said, "I cannot defeat Python. I am much too weak. And . . . well, the Catch-88."

Chiron sipped his Arizona tea. "Apollo means that we cannot send a quest without a prophecy, and we cannot get a prophecy without an Oracle."

Rachel stared at her overturned tripod stool. "And this man . . . the Beast. What do you know about him?"

"Not much." I explained what I had seen in my dream, and what Meg and I had overheard in the Labyrinth. "The Beast apparently has a reputation for snatching up young demigods in New York. Meg says . . ." I faltered when I saw her expression, clearly cautioning me to stay away from her personal history. "Um, she's had some experience with the Beast."

Chiron raised his brows. "Can you tell us anything that might help, dear?"

Meg sank into the sofa's cushions. "I've crossed paths with him. He's—he's scary. The memory is blurry."

"Blurry," Chiron repeated.

Meg became very interested in the cracker crumbs on her dress.

Rachel gave me a quizzical look. I shook my head, trying my best to impart a warning: *Trauma. Don't ask. Might get attacked by a peach baby.*

Rachel seemed to get the message. "That's all right, Meg," she said. "I have some information that may help."

She fished her phone from her coat pocket. "Don't touch this. You guys have probably figured it out, but phones are going even more haywire than usual around demigods. I'm not technically one of you, and even *I* can't place calls. I was able to take a couple of pictures, though." She turned the screen toward us. "Chiron, you recognize this place?"

The nighttime shot showed the upper floors of a glass residential tower. Judging from the background, it was somewhere in downtown Manhattan.

"That is the building you described last summer," Chiron said, "where you parleyed with the Romans."

"Yeah," Rachel said. "Something didn't feel right about that place. I got to thinking . . . how did the Romans take over such prime Manhattan real estate on such short notice? Who owns it? I tried to contact Reyna, to see if she could tell me anything, but—"

"Communication problems?" Chiron guessed.

"Exactly. I even sent physical mail to Camp Jupiter's drop box in Berkeley. No response. So I asked my dad's real estate lawyers to do some digging."

Meg peeked over the top of her glasses. "Your dad has lawyers? And a helicopter?"

"Several helicopters." Rachel sighed. "He's annoying. Anyway, that building is owned by a shell corporation, which is owned by another shell corporation, blah, blah, blah. The mother company is something called Triumvirate Holdings."

I felt a trickle like white paint rolling down my back. "*Triumvirate* . . ."

Meg made a sour face. "What does that mean?"

"A triumvirate is a ruling council of three," I said. "At least, that's what it meant in ancient Rome."

"Which is interesting," Rachel said, "because of this next shot." She tapped her screen. The new photo zoomed in on the building's penthouse terrace, where three shadowy figures stood talking together—men in business suits, illuminated only by the light from inside the apartment. I couldn't see their faces.

"These are the owners of Triumvirate Holdings," Rachel said. "Just getting this *one* picture wasn't easy." She blew a frizzy strand of hair out of her face. "I've spent the last two months investigating them, and I don't even know their names. I don't know where they live or where they came from. But I can tell you they own so much property and have so much money, they make my dad's company look like a kid's lemonade stand."

I stared at the picture of the three shadowy figures. I could almost imagine that the one on the left was the Beast. His slouching posture and the over-large shape of his head reminded me of the man in purple from my dream.

"The Beast said that his organization was everywhere," I recalled. "He mentioned he had colleagues."

Chiron's tail flicked, sending a paintbrush skidding across the cave floor. "Adult demigods? I can't imagine they would be Greek, but perhaps Roman? If they helped Octavian with his war—"

"Oh, they helped," Rachel said. "I found a paper trail—not much, but you remember those siege weapons Octavian built to destroy Camp Half-Blood?"

"No," said Meg.

I would have ignored her, but Rachel was a more generous soul.

She smiled patiently. "Sorry, Meg. You seem so at home here, I forgot you were new. Basically, the Roman demigods attacked this camp with giant catapulty things called onagers. It was all a big misunderstanding. Anyway, the weapons were paid for by Triumvirate Holdings."

Chiron frowned. "That is not good."

"I found something even more disturbing," Rachel continued. "You remember before that, during the Titan War, Luke Castellan mentioned he had backers in the mortal world? They had enough money to buy a cruise ship, helicopters, weapons. They even hired mortal mercenaries."

"Don't remember that, either," Meg said.

I rolled my eyes. "Meg, we can't stop and explain every major war to you! Luke Castellan was a child of Hermes. He betrayed this camp and allied himself with the Titans. They attacked New York. Big battle. I saved the day. Et cetera."

Chiron coughed. "At any rate, I do remember Luke

claiming that he had lots of supporters. We never found out exactly who they were."

"Now we know," Rachel said. "That cruise ship, the *Princess Andromeda*, was property of Triumvirate Holdings."

A cold sense of unease gripped me. I felt I should know something about this, but my mortal brain was betraying me again. I was more certain than ever that Zeus was toying with me, keeping my vision and memory limited. I remembered some assurances Octavian had given me, though—how easy it would be to win his little war, to raise new temples to me, how much support he had.

Rachel's phone screen went dark—much like my brain—but the grainy photo remained burned into my retinas.

"These men . . ." I picked up an empty tube of burnt sienna paint. "I'm afraid they are not modern demigods."

Rachel frowned. "You think they're ancient demigods who came through the Doors of Death—like Medea, or Midas? The thing is, Triumvirate Holdings has been around since way before Gaea started to wake. Decades, at least."

"Centuries," I said. "The Beast said that he'd been building his empire for centuries."

The cave became so silent, I imagined the hiss of Python, the soft exhale of fumes from deep in the earth. I wished we had some background music to drown it out . . . jazz or classical. I would have settled for death metal polka.

Rachel shook her head. "Then who—?"

"I don't know," I admitted. "But the Beast . . . in my dream, he called me his forefather. He assumed I would recognize him. And if my godly memory was intact, I think

I would. His demeanor, his accent, his facial structure—I have met him before, just not in modern times."

Meg had grown very quiet. I got the distinct impression she was trying to disappear into the couch cushions. Normally, this would not have bothered me, but after our experience in the Labyrinth, I felt guilty every time I mentioned the Beast. My pesky mortal conscience must have been acting up.

"The name Triumvirate . . ." I tapped my forehead, trying to shake loose information that was no longer there. "The last triumvirate I dealt with included Lepidus, Marc Antony, and my son, the *original* Octavian. A triumvirate is a very Roman concept . . . like patriotism, skullduggery, and assassination."

Chiron stroked his beard. "You think these men are ancient Romans? How is that possible? Hades is quite good at tracking down escaped spirits from the Underworld. He would not allow three men from ancient times to run amok in the modern world for centuries."

"Again, I do not know." Saying this so often offended my divine sensibilities. I decided that when I returned to Olympus, I would have to gargle the bad taste out of my mouth with Tabasco-flavored nectar. "But it seems these men have been plotting against us for a very long time. They funded Luke Castellan's war. They supplied aid to Camp Jupiter when the Romans attacked Camp Half-Blood. And despite those two wars, the Triumvirate is still out there—still plotting. What if this company is the root cause of . . . well, everything?"

Chiron looked at me as if I were digging his grave. "That is a very troubling thought. Could three men be so powerful?"

I spread my hands. "You've lived long enough to know, my friend. Gods, monsters, Titans . . . these are always dangerous. But the greatest threat to demigods has always been other demigods. Whoever this Triumvirate is, we must stop them before they take control of the Oracles."

Rachel sat up straight. "Excuse me? Oracles plural?"

"Ah . . . didn't I tell you about them when I was a god?"

Her eyes regained some of their dark green intensity. I feared she was envisioning ways she might inflict pain upon me with her art supplies.

"No," she said levelly, "you did not tell me about them."

"Oh . . . well, my mortal memory has been faulty, you see. I had to read some books in order to—"

"Oracles," she repeated. "Plural."

I took a deep breath. I wanted to assure her that those other Oracles didn't mean a thing to me! Rachel was special! Unfortunately, I doubted she was in a place where she could hear that right now. I decided it was best to speak plainly.

"In ancient times," I said, "there were many Oracles. Of course Delphi was the most famous, but there were four others of comparable power."

Chiron shook his head. "But those were destroyed ages ago."

"So I thought," I agreed. "Now I am not so sure. I believe Triumvirate Holdings wants to control *all* the ancient Oracles. And I believe the most ancient Oracle of all, the Grove of Dodona, is right here at Camp Half-Blood."

21

Up in my business
Always burning Oracles
Romans gonna hate

I WAS A DRAMATIC GOD.

I thought my last statement was a great line. I expected gasps, perhaps some organ music in the background. Maybe the lights would go out just before I could say more. Moments later, I would be found dead with a knife in my back. That would be exciting!

Wait. I'm mortal. Murder would kill me. Never mind.

At any rate, none of that happened. My three companions just stared at me.

"Four other Oracles," Rachel said. "You mean you have four other Pythias—"

"No, my dear. There is only one Pythia—*you*. Delphi is absolutely unique."

Rachel still looked like she wanted to jam a number ten bristle paintbrush up my nose. "So these other four *non-unique* Oracles . . ."

"Well, one was the Sybil of Cumae." I wiped the sweat off my palms. (Why did mortal palms sweat?) "You know, she wrote the Sibylline Books—those prophecies that Ella the harpy memorized."

Meg looked back and forth between us. "A harpy . . . like those chicken ladies who clean up after lunch?"

Chiron smiled. "Ella is a very special harpy, Meg. Years ago, she somehow came across a copy of the prophetic books, which we thought were burned before the Fall of Rome. Right now, our friends at Camp Jupiter are trying to reconstruct them based on Ella's recollections."

Rachel crossed her arms. "And the other three Oracles? I'm sure none of them was a beautiful young priestess whom you praised for her . . . what was it? . . . 'scintillating conversation'?"

"Ah . . ." I wasn't sure why, but it felt like my acne was turning into live insects and crawling across my face. "Well, according to my extensive research—"

"Some books he flipped through last night," Meg clarified.

"Ahem! There was an Oracle at Erythaea, and another at the Cave of Trophonius."

"Goodness," Chiron said. "I'd forgotten about those two."

I shrugged. I remembered almost nothing about them either. They had been some of my less successful prophetic franchises.

"And the fifth," I said, "was the Grove of Dodona."

"A grove," Meg said. "Like trees."

"Yes, Meg, like trees. Groves are typically composed of trees, rather than, say, Fudgsicles. Dodona was a stand of sacred oaks planted by the Mother Goddess in the first days of the world. They were ancient even when the Olympians were born."

"The Mother Goddess?" Rachel shivered in her patina jacket. "Please tell me you don't mean Gaea."

"No, thankfully. I mean Rhea, Queen of the Titans, the mother of the first generation of Olympian gods. Her sacred trees could actually speak. Sometimes they issued prophecies."

"The voices in the woods," Meg guessed.

"Exactly. I believe the Grove of Dodona has regrown itself here in the woods at camp. In my dreams, I saw a crowned woman imploring me to find her Oracle. I believe it was Rhea, though I still don't understand why she was wearing a peace symbol or using the term *dig it*."

"A peace symbol?" Chiron asked.

"A large brass one," I confirmed.

Rachel drummed her fingers on the couch's armrest. "If Rhea is a Titan, isn't she evil?"

"Not all Titans were bad," I said. "Rhea was a gentle soul. She sided with the gods in their first great war. I think she wants us to succeed. She doesn't want her grove in the hands of our enemies."

Chiron's tail twitched. "My friend, Rhea has not been seen for millennia. Her grove was burned in the ancient times. Emperor Theodosius ordered the last oak cut down in—"

"I know." I got a stabbing pain right between my eyes, as I always did when someone mentioned Theodosius. I now recalled that the bully had closed all the ancient temples across the empire, basically evicting us Olympian gods. I used to have an archery target with his face on it. "Nevertheless, many things from the old days have survived or regenerated.

The Labyrinth has rebuilt itself. Why couldn't a grove of sacred trees spring up again right here in this valley?"

Meg pushed herself deeper into the cushions. "This is all weird." Leave it to the young McCaffrey to summarize our conversation so effectively. "So if the tree voices are sacred and stuff, why are they making people get lost?"

"For once, you ask a good question." I hoped such praise wouldn't go to Meg's head. "In the old days, the priests of Dodona would take care of the trees, pruning them, watering them, and channeling their voices by hanging wind chimes in their branches."

"How would that help?" Meg asked.

"I don't know. I'm not a tree priest. But with proper care, these trees could divine the future."

Rachel smoothed her skirt. "And without proper care?"

"The voices were unfocused," I said. "A wild choir of disharmony." I paused, quite pleased with that line. I was hoping someone might write it down for posterity, but no one did. "Untended, the grove could most definitely drive mortals to madness."

Chiron furrowed his brow. "So our missing campers are wandering in the trees, perhaps already insane from the voices."

"Or they're dead," Meg added.

"No." I could not abide that thought. "No, they are still alive. The Beast is using them, trying to bait me."

"How can you be sure?" Rachel asked. "And why? If Python already controls Delphi, why are these other Oracles so important?"

I gazed at the wall formerly graced by my picture. Alas,

no answers magically appeared in the whitewashed space. "I'm not sure. I believe our enemies want to cut us off from every possible source of prophecy. Without a way to see and direct our fates, we will wither and die—gods and mortals alike, anyone who opposes the Triumvirate."

Meg turned upside down on the sofa and kicked off her red shoes. "They're strangling our taproots." She wriggled her toes to demonstrate.

I looked back at Rachel, hoping she would excuse my street urchin overlord's bad manners. "As for why the Grove of Dodona is so important, Python mentioned that it was the one Oracle he could not control. I don't understand exactly why—perhaps because Dodona is the only Oracle that has no connection with me. Its power comes from Rhea. So if the grove is working, and it is free of Python's influence, and it is here at Camp Half-Blood—"

"It could provide us with prophecies." Chiron's eyes gleamed. "It could give us a chance against our enemies."

I gave Rachel an apologetic smile. "Of course, we'd rather have our beloved Oracle of Delphi working again. And we will, eventually. But for now, the Grove of Dodona could be our best hope."

Meg's hair swept the floor. Her face was now the color of one of my sacred cattle. "Aren't prophecies all twisted and mysterious and murky, and people die trying to escape them?"

"Meg," I said, "you can't trust those reviews on RateMyOracle.com. The hotness factor for the Sibyl of Cumae, for instance, is *completely* off. I remember *that* quite clearly."

Rachel put her chin on her fist. "Really? Do tell."

"Uh, what I meant to say: the Grove of Dodona is a benevolent force. It has helped heroes before. The masthead of the original *Argo*, for instance, was carved from a branch of the sacred trees. It could speak to the Argonauts and give them guidance."

"Mm." Chiron nodded. "And that's why our mysterious Beast wants the grove burned."

"Apparently," I said. "And that's why we have to save it."

Meg rolled backward off the couch. Her legs knocked over the three-legged coffee table, spilling our Arizona tea and crackers. "Oops."

I ground my mortal teeth, which would not last a year if I kept hanging around Meg. Rachel and Chiron wisely ignored my young friend's display of Megness.

"Apollo . . ." The old centaur watched a waterfall of tea trickling from the edge of the table. "If you are right about Dodona, how do we proceed? We are already shorthanded. If we send search teams into the woods, we have no guarantee they'll come back."

Meg brushed the hair out of her eyes. "We'll go. Just Apollo and me."

My tongue attempted to hide in the depths of my throat. "We—we will?"

"You said you gotta do a bunch of trials or whatever to prove you're worthy, right? This'll be the first one."

Part of me knew she was right, but the remnants of my godly self rebelled at the idea. I never did my own dirty work. I would rather have picked a nice group of heroes and sent them to their deaths—or, you know, glorious success.

Yet Rhea had been clear in my dream: finding the Oracle was my job. And thanks to the cruelty of Zeus, where I went, Meg went. For all I knew, Zeus was aware of the Beast and his plans, and he had sent me here specifically to deal with the situation . . . a thought that did not make me any more likely to get him a nice tie for Father's Day.

I also remembered the other part of my dream: the Beast in his mauve suit, encouraging me to find the Oracle so he could burn it down. There was still too much I didn't understand, but I had to act. Austin and Kayla were depending on me.

Rachel put her hand on my knee, which made me flinch. Surprisingly, she did not inflict any pain. Her gaze was more earnest than angry. "Apollo, you have to try. If we can get a glimpse of the future . . . well, it may be the only way to get things back to normal." She looked longingly at the blank walls of her cave. "I'd like to have a future again."

Chiron shifted his forelegs. "What do you need from us, old friend? How can we help?"

I glanced at Meg. Sadly, I could tell that we were in agreement. We were stuck with each other. We couldn't risk anyone else.

"Meg is right," I said. "We have to do this ourselves. We should leave immediately, but—"

"We've been up all night," Meg said. "We need some sleep."

Wonderful, I thought. Now Meg is finishing my sentences.

This time I could not argue with her logic. Despite my fervor to rush into the woods and save my children, I had to proceed cautiously. I could not mess up this rescue. And I was increasingly certain that the Beast would keep his captives alive for now. He needed them to lure me into his trap.

Chiron rose on his front hooves. "This evening, then. Rest and prepare, my heroes. I fear you will need all your strength and wits for what comes next."

22

Armed to the eyeballs:
A combat ukulele
Magic Brazil scarf

SUN GODS ARE NOT GOOD at sleeping during the day, but somehow I managed a fitful nap.

When I woke in the late afternoon, I found the camp in a state of agitation.

Kayla and Austin's disappearance had been the tipping point. The other campers were now so rattled, no one could maintain a normal schedule. I suppose a single demigod disappearing every few weeks felt like a normal casualty rate. But a pair of demigods disappearing in the middle of a camp-sanctioned activity—that meant no one was safe.

Word must have spread of our conference in the cave. The Victor twins had stuffed wads of cotton in their ears to foil the oracular voices. Julia and Alice had climbed to the top of the lava wall and were using binoculars to scan the woods, no doubt hoping to spot the Grove of Dodona, but I doubted they could see the trees for the forest.

Everywhere I went, people were unhappy to see me. Damien and Chiara sat together at the canoe dock, glowering in my direction. Sherman Yang waved me away when

I tried to talk with him. He was busy decorating the Ares cabin with frag grenades and brightly decorated claymores. If it had been Saturnalia, he definitely would have won the prize for most violent holiday decorations.

Even the Athena Parthenos stared down at me accusingly from the top of the hill as if to say, *This is all your fault.*

She was right. If I hadn't let Python take over Delphi, if I'd paid more attention to the other ancient Oracles, if I hadn't lost my divinity—

Stop it, Apollo, I scolded myself. *You're beautiful and everyone loves you.*

But it was becoming increasingly difficult to believe that. My father, Zeus, did not love me. The demigods at Camp Half-Blood did not love me. Python and the Beast and his comrades at Triumvirate Holdings did not love me. It was almost enough to make me question my self-worth.

No, no. That was crazy talk.

Chiron and Rachel were nowhere to be seen. Nyssa Barrera informed me that they were hoping against hope to use the camp's sole Internet connection, in Chiron's office, to access more information about Triumvirate Holdings. Harley was with them for tech support. They were presently on hold with Comcast customer service and might not emerge for hours, if indeed they survived the ordeal at all.

I found Meg at the armory, browsing for battle supplies. She had strapped a leather cuirass over her green dress and greaves over orange leggings, so she looked like a kindergartener reluctantly stuffed into combat gear by her parents.

"Perhaps a shield?" I suggested.

"Nuh-uh." She showed me her rings. "I always use two

swords. Plus I need a free hand for slapping when you act stupid."

I had the uncomfortable sense she was serious.

From the weapon rack, she pulled out a long bow and offered it to me.

I recoiled. "No."

"It's your best weapon. You're Apollo."

I swallowed back the tang of mortal bile. "I swore an oath. I'm not the god of archery or music anymore. I won't use a bow or a musical instrument until I can use them *properly*."

"Stupid oath." She didn't slap me, but she looked like she wanted to. "What will you do, just stand around and cheer while I fight?"

That had indeed been my plan, but now I felt silly admitting it. I scanned the weapon display and grabbed a sword. Even without drawing it, I could tell it would be too heavy and awkward for me to use, but I strapped the scabbard around my waist.

"There," I said. "Happy?"

Meg did not appear happy. Nevertheless, she returned the bow to its place.

"Fine," she said. "But you'd better have my back."

I had never understood that expression. It made me think of the KICK ME signs Artemis used to tape to my toga during festival days. Still, I nodded. "Your back shall be had."

We reached the edge of the woods and found a small going-away party waiting for us: Will and Nico, Paolo Montes, Malcolm Pace, and Billie Ng, all with grim faces.

"Be careful," Will told me. "And here."

Before I could object, he placed a ukulele in my hands.

I tried to give it back. "I can't. I made an oath—"

"Yeah, I know. That was stupid of you. But it's a combat ukulele. You can fight with it if you need to."

I looked more closely at the instrument. It was made from Celestial bronze—thin sheets of metal acid-etched to resemble the grain of blond oak wood. The instrument weighed next to nothing, yet I imagined it was almost indestructible.

"The work of Hephaestus?" I asked.

Will shook his head. "The work of Harley. He wanted you to have it. Just sling it over your back. For me and Harley. It'll make us both feel better."

I decided I was obliged to honor the request, though my possession of a ukulele had rarely made anyone feel better. Don't ask me why. When I was a god, I used to do an absolutely blistering ukulele version of "Satisfaction."

Nico handed me some ambrosia wrapped in a napkin.

"I can't eat this," I reminded him.

"It's not for you." He glanced at Meg, his eyes full of misgiving. I remembered that the son of Hades had his own ways of sensing the future—futures that involved the possibility of death. I shivered and tucked the ambrosia into my coat pocket. As aggravating as Meg could be, I was deeply unsettled by the idea that she might come to harm. I decided that I could not allow that to happen.

Malcolm was showing Meg a parchment map, pointing out various places in the woods that we should avoid. Paolo— looking completely healed from his leg surgery—stood next

THE HIDDEN ORACLE   211

to him, carefully and earnestly providing Portuguese commentary that no one could understand.

When they were finished with the map, Billie Ng approached Meg.

Billie was a wisp of a girl. She compensated for her diminutive stature with the fashion sense of a K-Pop idol. Her winter coat was the color of aluminum foil. Her bobbed hair was aquamarine and her makeup gold. I completely approved. In fact, I thought I could rock that look myself if I could just get my acne under control.

Billie gave Meg a flashlight and a small packet of flower seeds.

"Just in case," Billie said.

Meg seemed quite overwhelmed. She gave Billie a fierce hug.

I didn't understand the purpose of the seeds, but it was comforting to know that in a dire emergency I could hit people with my ukulele while Meg planted geraniums.

Malcolm Pace gave me his parchment map. "When in doubt, veer to the right. That usually works in the woods, though I don't know why."

Paolo offered me a green-and-gold scarf—a bandana version of the Brazilian flag. He said something that, of course, I could not understand.

Nico smirked. "That's Paolo's good-luck bandana. I think he wants you to wear it. He believes it will make you invincible."

I found this dubious, since Paolo was prone to serious injury, but as a god, I had learned never to turn down offerings. "Thank you."

Paolo gripped my shoulders and kissed my cheeks. I may have blushed. He was quite handsome when he wasn't bleeding out from dismemberment.

I rested my hand on Will's shoulder. "Don't worry. We'll be back by dawn."

His mouth trembled ever so slightly. "How can you be sure?"

"I'm the sun god," I said, trying to muster more confidence than I felt. "I *always* return at dawn."

Of course it rained. Why would it not?

Up in Mount Olympus, Zeus must have been having a good laugh at my expense. Camp Half-Blood was supposed to be protected from severe weather, but no doubt my father had told Aeolus to pull out all the stops on his winds. My jilted ex-girlfriends among the air nymphs were probably enjoying their moment of payback.

The rain was just on the edge of sleet—liquid enough to soak my clothes, icy enough to slam against my exposed face like glass shards.

We stumbled along, lurching from tree to tree to find any shelter we could. Patches of old snow crunched under my feet. My ukulele got heavier as its sound hole filled with rain. Meg's flashlight beam cut across the storm like a cone of yellow static.

I led the way, not because I had any destination in mind, but because I was angry. I was tired of being cold and soaked. I was tired of being picked on. Mortals often talk about the whole world being against them, but that is ridiculous. Mortals aren't that important. In my case, the whole world really *was* against me. I refused to surrender to such abuse. I would do something about it! I just wasn't quite sure what.

From time to time we heard monsters in the distance—the roar of a drakon, the harmonized howl of a two-headed wolf—but nothing showed itself. On a night like this, any self-respecting monster would've remained in its lair, warm and cozy.

After what seemed like hours, Meg stifled a scream. I heroically leaped to her side, my hand on my sword. (I would have drawn it, but it was really heavy and got stuck in the scabbard.) At Meg's feet, wedged in the mud, was a glistening black shell the size of a boulder. It was cracked down the middle, the edges splattered with a foul gooey substance.

"I almost stepped on that." Meg covered her mouth as if she might be sick.

I inched closer. The shell was the crushed carapace of a giant insect. Nearby, camouflaged among the tree roots, lay one of the beast's dismembered legs.

"It's a *myrmeke*," I said. "Or it was."

Behind her rain-splattered glasses, Meg's eyes were impossible to read. "A *murr-murr-key*?"

"A giant ant. There must be a colony somewhere in the woods."

Meg gagged. "I hate bugs."

That made sense for a daughter of the agriculture goddess, but to me the dead ant didn't seem any grosser than the piles of garbage in which we often swam.

"Well, don't worry," I said. "This one is dead. Whatever killed it must've had powerful jaws to crack that shell."

"Not comforting. Are—are these things dangerous?"

I laughed. "Oh, yes. They range in size from as small as dogs to larger than grizzly bears. One time I watched a colony of myrmekes attack a Greek army in India. It was hilarious. They spit acid that can melt through bronze armor and—"

"Apollo."

My smile faded. I reminded myself I was no longer a spectator. These ants could kill us. Easily. And Meg was scared.

"Right," I said. "Well, the rain should keep the myrmekes in their tunnels. Just don't make yourself an attractive target. They like bright, shiny things."

"Like flashlights?"

"Um . . ."

Meg handed me the flashlight. "Lead on, Apollo."

I thought that was unfair, but we forged ahead.

After another hour or so (surely the woods weren't this big), the rain tapered off, leaving the ground steaming.

The air got warmer. The humidity approached bath-house levels. Thick white vapor curled off the tree branches.

"What's going on?" Meg wiped her face. "Feels like a tropical rain forest now."

I had no answer. Then, up ahead, I heard a massive flushing sound—like water being forced through pipes . . . or fissures.

I couldn't help but smile. "A geyser."

"A geyser," Meg repeated. "Like Old Faithful?"

"This is excellent news. Perhaps we can get directions. Our lost demigods might have even found sanctuary there!"

"With the geysers," Meg said.

"No, my ridiculous girl," I said. "With the geyser *gods*. Assuming they're in a good mood, this could be great."

"And if they're in a bad mood?"

"Then we'll cheer them up before they can boil us. Follow me!"

23

Scale of one to ten

How would you rate your demise?

Thanks for your input

WAS I RECKLESS to rush toward such volatile nature gods?

Please. Second-guessing myself is not in my nature. It's a trait I've never needed.

True, my memories about the *palikoi* were a little hazy. As I recalled, the geyser gods in ancient Sicily used to give refuge to runaway slaves, so they must be kindly spirits. Perhaps they would also give refuge to lost demigods, or at least notice when five of them wandered through their territory, muttering incoherently. Besides, I was Apollo! The palikoi would be honored to meet a major Olympian such as myself! The fact that geysers often blew their tops, spewing columns of scalding hot water hundreds of feet in the air, wasn't going to stop me from making some new fans . . . I mean *friends*.

The clearing opened before us like an oven door. A wall of heat billowed through the trees and washed over my face. I could feel my pores opening to drink in the moisture, which would hopefully help my spotty complexion.

The scene before us had no business being in a Long

Island winter. Glistening vines wreathed the tree branches. Tropical flowers bloomed from the forest floor. A red parrot sat on a banana tree heavy with green bunches.

In the midst of the glade stood two geysers—twin holes in the ground, ringed with a figure eight of gray mud pots. The craters bubbled and hissed, but they were not spewing at the moment. I decided to take that as a good omen.

Meg's boots squished in the mud. "Is it safe?"

"Definitely not," I said. "We'll need an offering. Perhaps your packet of seeds?"

Meg punched my arm. "Those are magic. For life-and-death emergencies. What about your ukulele? You're not going to play it anyway."

"A man of honor *never* surrenders his ukulele." I perked up. "But wait. You've given me an idea. I will offer the geyser gods a poem! I can still do that. It doesn't count as music."

Meg frowned. "Uh, I don't know if—"

"Don't be envious, Meg. I will make up a poem for you later. This will surely please the geyser gods!" I walked forward, spread my arms, and began to improvise:

> "Oh, geyser, my geyser,
> Let us spew then, you and I,
> Upon this midnight dreary, while we ponder
> Whose woods are these?
> For we have not gone gentle into this good night,
> But have wandered lonely as clouds.
> We seek to know for whom the bell tolls,
> So I hope, springs eternal,
> That the time has come to talk of many things!"

I don't wish to brag, but I thought it was rather good, even if I did recycle a few bits from my earlier works. Unlike my music and archery, my godly skills with poetry seemed to be completely intact.

I glanced at Meg, hoping to see shining admiration on her face. It was high time the girl started to appreciate me. Instead, her mouth hung open, aghast.

"What?" I demanded. "Did you fail poetry appreciation in school? That was first-rate stuff!"

Meg pointed toward the geysers. I realized she was not looking at me at all.

"Well," said a raspy voice, "you got my attention."

One of the palikoi hovered over his geyser. His lower half was nothing but steam. From the waist up, he was perhaps twice the size of a human, with muscular arms the color of caldera mud, chalk-white eyes, and hair like cappuccino foam, as if he had shampooed vigorously and left it sudsy. His massive chest was stuffed into a baby-blue polo shirt with a logo of trees embroidered on the chest pocket.

"O Great Palikos!" I said. "We beseech you—"

"What was that?" the spirit interrupted. "That stuff you were saying?"

"Poetry!" I said. "For you!"

He tapped his mud-gray chin. "No. That wasn't poetry."

I couldn't believe it. Did *no one* appreciate the beauty of language anymore? "My good spirit," I said. "Poetry doesn't have to rhyme, you know."

"I'm not talking about rhyming. I'm talking about getting your message across. We do a lot of market research, and that would *not* fly for our campaign. Now, the Oscar

Meyer Weiner song—*that* is poetry. The ad is fifty years old and people are still singing it. Do you think you could give us some poetry like that?"

I glanced at Meg to be sure I was not imagining this conversation.

"Listen here," I told the geyser god, "I've been the lord of poetry for four thousand years. I ought to know good poetry—"

The palikos waved his hands. "Let's start over. I'll run through our spiel, and maybe you can advise me. Hi, I'm Pete. Welcome to the Woods at Camp Half-Blood! Would you be willing to take a short customer satisfaction survey after this encounter? Your feedback is important."

"Um—"

"Great. Thanks."

Pete fished around in his vaporous region where his pockets would be. He produced a glossy brochure and began to read. "The Woods are your one-stop destination for . . . Hmm, it says *fun*. I thought we changed that to *exhilaration*. See, you've got to choose your words with care. If Paulie were here . . ." Pete sighed. "Well, he's better with the showmanship. Anyway, welcome to the Woods at Camp Half-Blood!"

"You already said that," I noted.

"Oh, right." Pete produced a red pen and began to edit.

"Hey." Meg shouldered past me. She had been speechless with awe for about twelve seconds, which must've been a new record. "Mr. Steamy Mud, have you seen any lost demigods?"

"Mr. Steamy Mud!" Pete slapped his brochure. "*That* is

effective branding! And great point about lost demigods. We can't have our guests wandering around aimlessly. We should be handing out maps at the entrance to the woods. So many wonderful things to see in here, and no one even knows about them. I'll talk to Paulie when he gets back."

Meg took off her fogged-up glasses. "Who's Paulie?"

Pete gestured at the second geyser. "My partner. Maybe we could add a map to this brochure if—"

"So *have* you seen any lost demigods?" I asked.

"What?" Pete tried to mark his brochure, but the steam had made it so soggy, his red pen went right through the paper. "Oh, no. Not recently. But we should have better signage. For instance, did you even know these geysers were here?"

"No," I admitted.

"Well, there you go! Double geysers—the only ones on Long Island!—and no one even knows about us. No outreach. No word-of-mouth. This is why we convinced the board of directors to hire us!"

Meg and I looked at each other. I could tell that for once we were on the same wavelength: utter confusion.

"Sorry," I said. "Are you telling me the forest has a board of directors?"

"Well, of course," Pete said. "The dryads, the other nature spirits, the sentient monsters . . . I mean, *somebody* has to think about property values and services and public relations. It wasn't easy getting the board to hire us for marketing, either. If we mess up this job . . . oh, man."

Meg squished her shoes in the mud. "Can we go? I don't understand what this guy's talking about."

"And that's the problem!" Pete moaned. "How do we write clear ad copy that conveys the right image of the Woods? For instance, palikoi like Paulie and me used to be famous! Major tourist destinations! People would come to us to make binding oaths. Runaway slaves would seek us out for shelter. We'd get sacrifices, offerings, prayers . . . It was great. Now, nothing."

I heaved a sigh. "I know how you feel."

"Guys," Meg said, "we're looking for missing demigods."

"Right," I agreed. "O, Great . . . Pete, do you have any idea where our lost friends might have gone? Perhaps you know of some secret locations within the woods?"

Pete's chalk-white eyes brightened. "Did you know the children of Hephaestus have a hidden workshop to the north called Bunker Nine?"

"I did, actually," I said.

"Oh." A puff of steam escaped Pete's left nostril. "Well, did you know the Labyrinth has rebuilt itself? There is an entrance right here in the woods—"

"We know," Meg said.

Pete looked crestfallen.

"But perhaps," I said, "that's because your marketing campaign is working."

"Do you think so?" Pete's foamy hair began to swirl. "Yes. Yes, that may be true! Did you happen to see our spot-lights, too? Those were my idea."

"Spotlights?" Meg asked.

Twin beams of red light blasted from the geysers and swept across the sky. Lit from beneath, Pete looked like the world's scariest teller of ghost stories.

"Unfortunately, they attracted the wrong kind of attention." Pete sighed. "Paulie doesn't let me use them often. He suggested advertising on a blimp instead, or perhaps a giant inflatable King Kong—"

"That's cool," Meg interrupted. "But can you tell us anything about a secret grove with whispering trees?"

I had to admit, Meg was good at getting us back on topic. As a poet, I did not cultivate directness. But as an archer, I could appreciate the value of a straight shot.

"Oh." Pete floated lower in his cloud of steam, the spotlight turning him the color of cherry soda. "I'm not supposed to talk about the grove."

My once-godly ears tingled. I resisted the urge to scream, *AHA!* "Why can't you talk about the grove, Pete?"

The spirit fiddled with his soggy brochure. "Paulie said it would scare away tourists. 'Talk about the dragons,' he told me. 'Talk about the wolves and serpents and ancient killing machines. But don't mention the grove.'"

"Ancient killing machines?" Meg asked.

"Yeah," Pete said halfheartedly. "We're marketing them as fun family entertainment. But the grove . . . Paulie said that was our worst problem. The neighborhood isn't even *zoned* for an Oracle. Paulie went there to see if maybe we could relocate it, but—"

"He didn't come back," I guessed.

Pete nodded miserably. "How am I supposed to run the marketing campaign all by myself? Sure, I can use robo-calls for the phone surveys, but a lot of networking has to be done face-to-face, and Paulie was always better with that stuff." Pete's voice broke into a sad hiss. "I miss him."

"Maybe we could find him," Meg suggested, "and bring him back."

Pete shook his head. "Paulie made me promise not to follow him and not to tell anybody else where the grove is. He's pretty good at resisting those weird voices, but you guys wouldn't stand a chance."

I was tempted to agree. Finding ancient killing machines sounded much more reasonable. Then I pictured Kayla and Austin wandering through the ancient grove, slowly going mad. They needed me, which meant I needed their location.

"Sorry, Pete." I gave him my most critical stare—the one I used to crush aspiring singers during Broadway auditions. "I'm just not buying it."

Mud bubbled around Pete's caldera. "Wh-what do you mean?"

"I don't think this grove exists," I said. "And if it does, I don't think you know its location."

Pete's geyser rumbled. Steam swirled in his spotlight beam. "I—I *do* know! Of course it exists!"

"Oh, really? Then why aren't there billboards about it all over the place? And a dedicated Web site? Why haven't I seen a groveofdodona hashtag on social media?"

Pete glowered. "I suggested all that! Paulie shot me down!"

"So do some outreach!" I demanded. "Sell us on your product! Show us where this grove is!"

"I can't. The only entrance . . ." He glanced over my shoulder and his face went slack. "Ah, spew." His spotlights shut off.

I turned. Meg made a squelching sound even louder than her shoes in the mud.

It took a moment for my vision to adjust, but at the edge of the clearing stood three black ants the size of Sherman tanks.

"Pete," I said, trying to remain calm, "when you said your spotlights attracted the wrong kind of attention—"

"I meant the myrmekes," he said. "I hope this won't affect your online review of the Woods at Camp Half-Blood."

24

Breaking my promise
Spectacularly failing
I blame Neil Diamond

MYRMEKES SHOULD BE high on your list of monsters not to fight.

They attack in groups. They spit acid. Their pincers can snap through Celestial bronze.

Also, they are ugly.

The three soldier ants advanced, their ten-foot-long antennae waving and bobbing in a mesmerizing way, trying to distract me from the true danger of their mandibles.

Their beaked heads reminded me of chickens—chickens with dark flat eyes and black armored faces. Each of their six legs would have made a fine construction winch. Their oversize abdomens throbbed and pulsed like noses sniffing for food.

I silently cursed Zeus for inventing ants. The way I heard it, he got upset with some greedy man who was always stealing from his neighbors' crops, so Zeus turned him into the first ant—a species that does nothing but scavenge, steal, and breed. Ares liked to joke that if Zeus wanted such a species, he could've just left humans the way they were. I used to laugh. Now that I am one of you, I no longer find it funny.

The ants stepped toward us, their antennae twitching. I imagined their train of thought was something like *Shiny? Tasty? Defenseless?*

"No sudden movements," I told Meg, who did not seem inclined to move at all. In fact, she looked petrified.

"Oh, Pete?" I called. "How do you deal with myrmekes invading your territory?"

"By hiding," he said, and disappeared into the geyser.

"Not helpful," I grumbled.

"Can we dive in?" Meg asked.

"Only if you fancy boiling to death in a pit of scalding water."

The tank bugs clacked their mandibles and edged closer.

"I have an idea." I unslung my ukulele.

"I thought you swore not to play," Meg said.

"I did. But if I throw this shiny object to one side, the ants might—"

I was about to say *the ants might follow it and leave us alone.*

I neglected to consider that, in my hands, the ukulele made me look shinier and tastier. Before I could throw the instrument, the soldier ants surged toward us. I stumbled back, only remembering the geyser behind me when my shoulder blades began to blister, filling the air with Apollo-scented steam.

"Hey, bugs!" Meg's scimitars flashed in her hands, making her the new shiniest thing in the clearing.

Can we take a moment to appreciate that Meg did this

on purpose? Terrified of insects, she could have fled and left me to be devoured. Instead, she chose to risk her life by distracting three tank-size ants. Throwing garbage at street thugs was one thing. But this . . . this was an entirely new level of foolishness. If I lived, I might have to nominate Meg McCaffrey for Best Sacrifice at the next Demi Awards.

Two of the ants charged at Meg. The third stayed on me, though he turned his head long enough for me to sprint to one side.

Meg ran between her opponents, her golden blades severing a leg from each. Their mandibles snapped at empty air. The soldier bugs wobbled on their five remaining legs, tried to turn, and bonked heads.

Meanwhile, the third ant charged me. In a panic, I threw my combat ukulele. It bounced off the ant's forehead with a dissonant *twang*.

I tugged my sword free of its scabbard. I've always hated swords. Such inelegant weapons, and they require you to be in close combat. How unwise, when you can shoot your enemies with an arrow from across the world!

The ant spat acid, and I tried to swat away the goop.

Perhaps that wasn't the brightest idea. I often got sword fighting and tennis confused. At least some of the acid splattered the ant's eyes, which bought me a few seconds. I valiantly retreated, raising my sword only to find that the blade had been eaten away, leaving me nothing but a steaming hilt.

"Oh, Meg?" I called helplessly.

She was otherwise occupied. Her swords whirled in golden arcs of destruction, lopping off leg segments, slicing antennae. I had never seen a dimachaerus fight with such skill, and I had seen all the best gladiators in combat. Unfortunately, her blades only sparked off the ants' thick main carapaces. Glancing blows and dismemberment did not faze them at all. As good as Meg was, the ants had more legs, more weight, more ferocity, and slightly more acid-spitting ability.

My own opponent snapped at me. I managed to avoid its mandibles, but its armored face bashed the side of my head. I staggered and fell. One ear canal seemed to fill with molten iron.

My vision clouded. Across the clearing, the other ants flanked Meg, using their acid to herd her toward the woods. She dove behind a tree and came up with only one of her blades. She tried to stab the closest ant but was driven back by acid cross fire. Her leggings were smoking, peppered with holes. Her face was tight with pain.

"Peaches," I muttered to myself. "Where is that stupid diaper demon when we need him?"

The karpos did not appear. Perhaps the presence of the geyser gods or some other force in the woods kept him away. Perhaps the board of directors had a rule against pets.

The third ant loomed over me, its mandibles foaming with green saliva. Its breath smelled worse than Hephaestus's work shirts.

My next decision I could blame on my head injury. I could tell you I wasn't thinking clearly, but that isn't true. I was desperate. I was terrified. I wanted to help Meg. Mostly I wanted to save myself. I saw no other option, so I dove for my ukulele.

I know. I promised on the River Styx not to play music until I was a god once more. But even such a dire oath can seem unimportant when a giant ant is about to melt your face off.

I grabbed the instrument, rolled onto my back, and belted out "Sweet Caroline."

Even without my oath, I would only have done something like that in the most extreme emergency. When I sing that song, the chances of mutually assured destruction are too great. But I saw no other choice. I gave it my utmost effort, channeling all the saccharine schmaltz I could muster from the 1970s.

The giant ant shook its head. Its antennae quivered. I got to my feet as the monster crawled drunkenly toward me. I put my back to the geyser and launched into the chorus.

The *Dah! Dah! Dah!* did the trick. Blinded by disgust and rage, the ant charged. I rolled aside as the monster's momentum carried it forward, straight into the muddy cauldron.

Believe me, the only thing that smells *worse* than Hephaestus's work shirts is a myrmeke boiling in its own shell.

Somewhere behind me, Meg screamed. I turned in time to see her second sword fly from her hand. She collapsed as one of the myrmekes caught her in its mandibles.

"NO!" I shrieked.

The ant did not snap her in half. It simply held her—limp and unconscious.

"Meg!" I yelled again. I strummed the ukulele desperately. "Sweet Caroline!"

But my voice was gone. Defeating one ant had taken all my energy. (I don't think I have ever written a sadder sentence than that.) I tried to run to Meg's aid, but I stumbled and fell. The world turned pale yellow. I hunched on all fours and vomited.

I have a concussion, I thought, but I had no idea what to do about it. It seemed like ages since I had been a god of healing.

I may have lain in the mud for minutes or hours while my brain slowly gyrated inside my skull. By the time I managed to stand, the two ants were gone.

There was no sign of Meg McCaffrey.

25

I'm on a roll now
Boiling, burning, throwing up
Lions? Hey, why not?

I STUMBLED THROUGH the glade, shouting Meg's name. I knew it was pointless, but yelling felt good. I looked for signs of broken branches or trampled ground. Surely two tank-size ants would leave a trail I could follow. But I was not Artemis; I did not have my sister's skill with tracking. I had no idea which direction they'd taken my friend.

I retrieved Meg's swords from the mud. Instantly, they changed into gold rings—so small, so easily lost, like a mortal life. I may have cried. I tried to break my ridiculous combat ukulele, but the Celestial bronze instrument defied my attempts. Finally, I yanked off the A string, threaded it through Meg's rings, and tied them around my neck.

"Meg, I will find you," I muttered.

Her abduction was my fault. I was sure of this. By playing music and saving myself, I had broken my oath on the River Styx. Instead of punishing me directly, Zeus or the Fates or all the gods together had visited their wrath upon Meg McCaffrey.

How could I have been so foolish? Whenever I angered

the other gods, those closest to me were struck down. I'd lost Daphne because of one careless comment to Eros. I'd lost the beautiful Hyacinthus because of a quarrel with Zephyros. Now my broken oath would cost Meg her life.

No, I told myself. *I won't allow it.*

I was so nauseous, I could barely walk. Someone seemed to be inflating a balloon inside my brain. Yet I managed to stumble to the rim of Pete's geyser.

"Pete!" I shouted. "Show yourself, you cowardly tele-marketer!"

Water shot skyward with a sound like the blast of an organ's lowest pipe. In the swirling steam, the palikos appeared, his mud-gray face hardening with anger.

"You call me a TELEMARKETER?" he demanded. "We run a full-service PR firm!"

I doubled over and vomited in his crater, which I thought an appropriate response.

"Stop that!" Pete complained.

"I need to find Meg." I wiped my mouth with a shaky hand. "What would the myrmekes do with her?"

"I don't know!"

"Tell me or I will *not* complete your customer service survey."

Pete gasped. "That's terrible! Your feedback is import-ant!" He floated down to my side. "Oh, dear . . . your head doesn't look good. You've got a big gash on your scalp, and there's blood. That must be why you're not thinking clearly."

"I don't care!" I yelled, which only made the pounding in my head worse. "Where is the myrmekes' nest?"

Pete wrung his steamy hands. "Well, that's what we were talking about earlier. That's where Paulie went. The nest is the only entrance."

"To what?"

"To the Grove of Dodona."

My stomach solidified into a pack of ice, which was unfair, because I needed one for my head. "The ant nest . . . is the way to the grove?"

"Look, you need medical attention. I *told* Paulie we should have a first-aid station for visitors." He fished around in his nonexistent pockets. "Let me just mark the location of the Apollo cabin—"

"If you pull out a brochure," I warned, "I will make you eat it. Now, explain how the nest leads to the grove."

Pete's face turned yellow, or perhaps that was just my vision getting worse. "Paulie didn't tell me everything. There's this thicket of woods that's grown so dense, nobody can get in. I mean, even from above, the branches are like . . ." He laced his muddy fingers, then caused them to liquefy and melt into one another, which made his point quite well.

"Anyway"—he pulled his hands apart—"the grove is in there. It could have been slumbering for centuries. Nobody on the board of directors even knew about it. Then, all of a sudden, the trees started whispering. Paulie figured those darned ants must have burrowed into the grove from underneath, and that's what woke it up."

I tried to make sense of that. It was difficult with a swollen brain. "Which way is the nest?"

"North of here," Pete said. "Half a mile. But, man, you are in no shape—"

"I must! Meg needs me!"

Pete grabbed my arm. His grip was like a warm wet tourniquet. "She's got time. If they carried her off in one piece, that means she's not dead yet."

"She will be soon enough!"

"Nah. Before Paulie . . . before he disappeared, he went into that nest a few times looking for the tunnel to the grove. He told me those myrmekes like to goop up their victims and let them, um, ripen until they're soft enough for the hatchlings to eat."

I made an un-godlike squeak. If there had been anything left in my stomach, I would have lost it. "How long does she have?"

"Twenty-four hours, give or take. Then she'll start to . . . um, soften."

It was difficult to imagine Meg McCaffrey softening under any circumstances, but I pictured her alone and scared, encased in insect goop, tucked in some larder of carcasses in the ants' nest. For a girl who hated bugs— Oh, Demeter had been right to hate me and keep her children away from me. I was a terrible god!

"Go get some help," Pete urged. "The Apollo cabin can heal that head wound. You're not doing your friend any favors by charging after her and getting yourself killed."

"Why do you care what happens to us?"

The geyser god looked offended. "Visitor satisfaction is always our top priority! Besides, if you find Paulie while you're in there . . ."

I tried to stay angry at the palikos, but the loneliness and worry on his face mirrored my own feelings. "Did Paulie explain how to navigate the ants' nest?"

Pete shook his head. "Like I said, he didn't want me to follow him. The myrmekes are dangerous enough. And if those other guys are still wandering around—"

"Other guys?"

Pete frowned. "Didn't I mention that? Yeah. Paulie saw three humans, heavily armed. They were looking for the grove too."

My left leg started thumping nervously, as if it missed its three-legged race partner. "How did Paulie know what they were looking for?"

"He heard them talking in Latin."

"*Latin?* Were they campers?"

Pete spread his hands. "I—I don't think so. Paulie described them like they were adults. He said one of them was the leader. The other two addressed him as *imperator*."

The entire planet seemed to tilt. "Imperator."

"Yeah, you know, like in Rome—"

"Yes, I know." Suddenly, too many things made sense. Pieces of the puzzle flew together, forming one huge picture that smacked me in the face. The Beast . . . Triumvirate Holdings . . . adult demigods completely off the radar.

It was all I could do to avoid pitching forward into the geyser. Meg needed me more than ever. But I would have to do this right. I would have to be careful—even more careful than when I gave the fiery horses of the sun their yearly vaccinations.

"Pete," I said, "do you still oversee sacred oaths?"

"Well, yes, but—"

"Then hear my solemn oath!"

"Uh, the thing is, you've got this aura around you like you just *broke* a sacred oath, maybe one you swore on the River Styx? And if you break *another* oath with me—"

"I swear that I will save Meg McCaffrey. I will use every means at my disposal to bring her safely from the ants' lair, and this oath supersedes any previous oath I have made. This I swear upon your sacred and extremely hot waters!"

Pete winced. "Well, okay. It's done now. But keep in mind that if you don't keep that oath, if Meg dies, even if it's not your fault . . . you'll face the consequences."

"I am already cursed for breaking my earlier oath! What does it matter?"

"Yeah, but see, those River Styx oaths can take *years* to destroy you. They're like cancer. My oaths . . ." Pete shrugged. "If you break it, there's nothing I can do to stop your punishment. Wherever you are, a geyser will instantly blast through the ground at your feet and boil you alive."

"Ah . . ." I tried to stop my knees from knocking. "Yes, of course I knew that. I stand by my oath."

"You've got no choice now."

"Right. I think I'll—I'll go get healed."

I staggered off.

"Camp is the other direction," Pete said.

I changed course.

"Remember to complete our survey online!" Pete called after me. "Just curious, on a scale of one to ten, how would you rate your overall satisfaction with the Woods at Camp Half-Blood?"

I didn't reply. As I stumbled into the darkness, I was too busy contemplating, on a scale of one to ten, the pain I might have to endure in the near future.

I didn't have the strength to make it back to camp. The farther I walked, the clearer that became. My joints were pudding. I felt like a marionette, and as much as I'd enjoyed controlling mortals from above in the past, I did not relish being on the other end of the strings.

My defenses were at level zero. The smallest hellhound or dragon could have easily made a meal of the great Apollo. If an irritated badger had taken issue with me, I would have been doomed.

I leaned against a tree to catch my breath. The tree seemed to push me away, whispering in a voice I remembered so well: *Keep moving, Apollo. You can't rest here.*

"I loved you," I muttered.

Part of me knew I was delirious—imagining things only because of my concussion—but I swore I could see the face of my beloved Daphne rising from each tree trunk I passed, her features floating under the bark like a mirage of wood— her slightly crooked nose, her offset green eyes, those lips I had never kissed but never stopped dreaming of.

You loved every pretty girl, she scolded. *And every pretty boy, for that matter.*

"Not like you," I cried. "You were my first true love. Oh, Daphne!"

Wear my crown, she said. *And repent.*

I remembered chasing her—her lilac scent on the breeze, her lithe form flitting through the dappled light of the forest.

I pursued her for what seemed like years. Perhaps it was.

For centuries afterward, I blamed Eros.

In a moment of recklessness, I had ridiculed Eros's archery skills. Out of spite, he struck me with a golden arrow. He bent all my love toward the beautiful Daphne, but that was not the worst of it. He also struck Daphne's heart with a lead arrow, leeching all possible affection she might have had for me.

What people do not understand: Eros's arrows can't summon emotion from nothing. They can only cultivate potential that is already there. Daphne and I could have been a perfect pair. She was my true love. She could have loved me back. Yet thanks to Eros, my love-o-meter was cranked to one hundred percent, while Daphne's feelings turned to pure hate (which is, of course, only the flip side of love). Nothing is more tragic than loving someone to the depths of your soul and knowing they cannot and will not ever love you back.

The stories say I chased her on a whim, that she was just another pretty dress. The stories are wrong. When she begged Gaea to turn her into a laurel tree in order to escape me, part of my heart hardened into bark as well. I invented the laurel wreath to commemorate my failure—to punish myself for the fate of my greatest love. Every time some hero wins the laurels, I am reminded of the girl I can never win.

After Daphne, I swore I would never marry. Sometimes I claimed that was because I couldn't decide between the Nine Muses. A convenient story. The Nine Muses were my constant companions, all of them beautiful in their own way. But they never possessed my heart like Daphne did.

Only one other person ever affected me so deeply—the perfect Hyacinthus—and he, too, was taken from me.

All these thoughts rambled through my bruised brain. I staggered from tree to tree, leaning against them, grabbing their lowest branches like handrails.

You cannot die here, Daphne whispered. *You have work to do. You made an oath.*

Yes, my oath. Meg needed me. I had to . . .

I fell face forward in the icy mulch.

How long I lay there, I'm not sure.

A warm snout breathed in my ear. A rough tongue lapped my face. I thought I was dead and Cerberus had found me at the gates of the Underworld.

Then the beast pushed me over onto my back. Dark tree branches laced the sky. I was still in the forest. The golden visage of a lion appeared above me, his amber eyes beautiful and deadly. He licked my face, perhaps trying to decide if I would make a good supper.

"*Ptfh.*" I spat mane fur out of my mouth.

"Wake up," said a woman's voice, somewhere to my right. It wasn't Daphne, but it was vaguely familiar.

I managed to raise my head. Nearby, a second lion sat at the feet of a woman with tinted glasses and a silver-and-gold tiara in her braided hair. Her batik dress swirled with images of fern fronds. Her arms and hands were covered in henna tattoos. She looked different than she had in my dream, but I recognized her.

"Rhea," I croaked.

She inclined her head. "Peace, Apollo. I don't want to bum you out, but we need to talk."

26

Imperators here?
Gag me with a peace symbol
Not groovy, Mama

MY HEAD WOUND MUST have tasted like Wagyu beef.

The lion kept licking the side of my face, making my hair stickier and wetter. Strangely, this seemed to clear my thoughts. Perhaps lion saliva had curative properties. I guess I should have known that, being a god of healing, but you'll have to excuse me if I haven't done trial-and-error experiments with the drool of every single animal.

With difficulty, I sat up and faced the Titan queen.

Rhea leaned against the side of a VW safari van painted with swirling black frond designs like those on her dress. I seemed to recall that the black fern was one of Rhea's symbols, but I couldn't remember why. Among the gods, Rhea had always been something of a mystery. Even Zeus, who knew her best, did not often speak of her.

Her turret crown circled her brow like a glittering railroad track. When she looked down at me, her tinted glasses changed from orange to purple. A macramé belt cinched her waist, and on a chain around her neck hung her brass peace symbol.

She smiled. "Glad you're awake. I was worried, man."

I really wished people would stop calling me *man*. "Why are you . . . Where have you been all these centuries?"

"Upstate." She scratched her lion's ears. "After Woodstock, I stuck around, started a pottery studio."

"You . . . what?"

She tilted her head. "Was that last week or last millennium? I've lost track."

"I—I believe you're describing the 1960s. That was last century."

"Oh, bummer." Rhea sighed. "I get mixed up after so many years."

"I sympathize."

"After I left Kronos . . . well, that man was so square, you could cut yourself on his corners, you know what I mean? He was the ultimate 1950s dad—wanted us to be Ozzie and Harriet or Lucy and Ricky or something."

"He—he swallowed his children alive."

"Yeah." Rhea brushed her hair from her face. "That was some bad karma. Anyway, I left him. Back then divorce wasn't cool. You just didn't do it. But me? I burned my *apodesmos* and got liberated. I raised Zeus in a commune with a bunch of naiads and *kouretes*. Lots of wheat germ and nectar. The kid grew up with a strong Aquarian vibe."

I was fairly sure Rhea was misremembering her centuries, but I thought it would be impolite to keep pointing that out.

"You remind me of Iris," I said. "She went organic vegan several decades ago."

Rhea made a face—just a ripple of disapproval before

regaining her karmic balance. "Iris is a good soul. I dig her. But you know, these younger goddesses, they weren't around to fight the revolution. They don't get what it was like when your old man was eating your children and you couldn't get a real job and the Titan chauvinists just wanted you to stay home and cook and clean and have more Olympian babies. And speaking of Iris . . ."

Rhea touched her forehead. "Wait, *were* we speaking of Iris? Or did I just have a flashback?"

"I honestly don't know."

"Oh, I remember now. She's a messenger of the gods, right? Along with Hermes and that other groovy liberated chick . . . Joan of Arc?"

"Er, I'm not sure about that last one."

"Well, anyway, the communication lines are down, man. Nothing works. Rainbow messages, flying scrolls, Hermes Express . . . it's all going haywire."

"We know this. But we don't know why."

"It's *them*. They're doing it."

"Who?"

She glanced to either side. "The Man, man. Big Brother. The suits. The imperators."

I had been hoping she would say something else: giants, Titans, ancient killing machines, aliens. I would've rather tangled with Tartarus or Ouranos or Primordial Chaos itself. I had hoped Pete the geyser misunderstood what his brother told him about the imperator in the ants' nest.

Now that I had confirmation, I wanted to steal Rhea's safari van and drive to some commune far, far upstate.

"Triumvirate Holdings," I said.

"Yeah," Rhea agreed. "That's their new military-industrial complex. It's bumming me out in a big way."

The lion stopped licking my face, probably because my blood had turned bitter. "How is this possible? How have they come back?"

"They never went away," Rhea said. "They did it to themselves, you know. Wanted to make themselves gods. That never works out well. Ever since the old days they've been hiding out, influencing history from behind the curtains. They're stuck in a kind of twilight life. They can't die; they can't really live."

"But how could we not *know* about this?" I demanded. "We are gods!"

Rhea's laugh reminded me of a piglet with asthma. "Apollo, Grandson, beautiful child . . . Has being a god ever stopped someone from being stupid?"

She had a point. Not about me personally, of course, but the stories I could tell you about the *other* Olympians . . .

"The emperors of Rome." I tried to come to terms with the idea. "They can't *all* be immortal."

"No," Rhea said. "Just the worst of them, the most notorious. They live in human memory, man. That's what keeps them alive. Same as us, really. They're tied to the course of Western civilization, even though that whole concept is imperialist Eurocentric propaganda, man. Like my guru would tell you—"

"Rhea"—I put my hands against my throbbing temples—"can we stick to one problem at a time?"

"Yeah, okay. I didn't mean to blow your mind."

"But how can they affect our lines of communication? How can they be so powerful?"

"They've had centuries, Apollo. *Centuries*. All that time, plotting and making war, building up their capitalist empire, waiting for this moment when you are mortal, when the Oracles are vulnerable for a hostile takeover. It's just evil. They have no chill whatsoever."

"I thought that was a more modern term."

"Evil?"

"No. *Chill*. Never mind. The Beast . . . he is the leader?"

"Afraid so. He's as twisted as the others, but he's the smartest and the most stable—in a sociopathic homicidal way. You know who he is—who he was, right?"

Unfortunately, I did. I remembered where I had seen his smirking ugly face. I could hear his nasal voice echoing through the arena, ordering the execution of hundreds while the crowds cheered. I wanted to ask Rhea who his two compatriots were in the Triumvirate, but I decided I could not bear the information at present. None of the options were good, and knowing their names might bring me more despair than I could handle.

"It's true, then," I said. "The other Oracles still exist. The emperors hold them all?"

"They're working on it. Python has Delphi—that's the biggest problem. But you won't have the strength to take him head-on. You've got to pry their fingers off the minor Oracles first, loosen their power. To do that, you need a new source of prophecy for this camp—an Oracle that is older and independent."

"Dodona," I said. "Your whispering grove."

"Right on," Rhea said. "I thought the grove was gone forever. But then—I don't know how—the oak trees regrew themselves in the heart of these woods. You have to find the grove and protect it."

"I'm working on that." I touched the sticky wound on the side of my face. "But my friend Meg—"

"Yeah. You had some setbacks. But there are always setbacks, Apollo. When Lizzy Stanton and I hosted the first women's rights convention in Woodstock—"

"I think you mean Seneca Falls?"

Rhea frowned. "Wasn't that in the '60s?"

"The '40s," I said. "The 1840s, if memory serves."

"So . . . Jimi Hendrix wasn't there?"

"Doubtful."

Rhea fiddled with her peace symbol. "Then who set that guitar on fire? Ah, never mind. The point is, you have to persevere. Sometimes change takes centuries."

"Except that I'm mortal now," I said. "I don't *have* centuries."

"But you have willpower," Rhea said. "You have mortal drive and urgency. Those are things the gods often lack."

At her side, her lion roared.

"I've gotta split," Rhea said. "If the imperators track me down—bad scene, man. I've been off the grid too long. I'm not going to get sucked into that patriarchal institutional oppression again. Just find Dodona. That's your first trial."

"And if the Beast finds the grove first?"

"Oh, he's already found the gates, but he'll never get through them without you and the girl."

"I—I don't understand."

"That's cool. Just breathe. Find your center. Enlightenment has to come from *within*."

It was very much like a line I would've given my worshippers. I was tempted to choke Rhea with her macramé
belt, but I doubted I would have the strength. Also, she had
two lions. "But what do I do? How do I save Meg?"

"First, get healed. Rest up. Then . . . well, how you save
Meg is up to you. The journey is greater than the destination, you know?"

She held out her hand. Draped on her fingers was a
set of wind chimes—a collection of hollow brass tubes and
medallions engraved with ancient Greek and Cretan symbols. "Hang these in the largest ancient oak. That will help
you focus the voices of the Oracle. If you get a prophecy,
groovy. It'll only be the beginning, but without Dodona,
nothing else will be possible. The emperors will suffocate
our future and divide up the world. Only when you have
defeated Python can you reclaim your rightful place on
Olympus. My kid, Zeus . . . he's got this whole 'tough love'
disciplinarian hang-up, you dig? Taking back Delphi is the
only way you're going to get on his good side."

"I—I was afraid you would say that."

"There's one other thing," she warned. "The Beast is
planning some kind of attack on your camp. I don't know
what it is, but it's going to be big. Like, even worse than
napalm. You have to warn your friends."

The nearest lion nudged me. I wrapped my arms around
his neck and allowed him to pull me to my feet. I managed
to remain standing, but only because my legs locked up in

complete fright. For the first time, I understood the trials that awaited me. I knew the enemies I must face. I would need more than wind chimes and enlightenment. I'd need a miracle. And as a god, I can tell you that those are never distributed lightly.

"Good luck, Apollo." The Titan queen placed the wind chimes in my hands. "I've got to check my kiln before my pots crack. Keep on trucking, and save those trees!"

The woods dissolved. I found myself standing in the central green at Camp Half-Blood, face-to-face with Chiara Benvenuti, who jumped back in alarm. "Apollo?"

I smiled. "Hey, girl." My eyes rolled up in my head and, for the second time that week, I charmingly passed out in front of her.

27

I apologize
For pretty much everything
Wow, I'm a good guy

"WAKE," SAID A VOICE.

I opened my eyes and saw a ghost—his face just as precious to me as Daphne's. I knew his copper skin, his kind smile, the dark curls of his hair, and those eyes as purple as senatorial robes.

"Hyacinthus," I sobbed. "I'm so sorry . . ."

He turned his face toward the sunlight, revealing the ugly dent above his left ear where the discus had struck him. My own wounded face throbbed in sympathy.

"Seek the caverns," he said. "Near the springs of blue. Oh, Apollo . . . your sanity will be taken away, but do not . . ."

His image faded and began to retreat. I rose from my sickbed. I rushed after him and grabbed his shoulders. "Do not *what*? Please don't leave me again!"

My vision cleared. I found myself by the window in Cabin Seven, holding a ceramic pot of purple and red hyacinths. Nearby, looking very concerned, Will and Nico stood as if ready to catch me.

"He's talking to the flowers," Nico noted. "Is that normal?"

"Apollo," Will said, "you had a concussion. I healed you, but—"

"These hyacinths," I demanded. "Have they always been here?"

Will frowned. "Honestly, I don't know where they came from, but . . ." He took the flowerpot from my hands and set it back on the windowsill. "Let's worry about you, okay?"

Usually that would've been excellent advice, but now I could only stare at the hyacinths and wonder if they were some sort of message. How cruel to see them—the flowers that I had created to honor my fallen love, with their plumes stained red like his blood or hued violet like his eyes. They bloomed so cheerfully in the window, reminding me of the joy I had lost.

Nico rested his hand on Will's shoulder. "Apollo, we were worried. Will was especially."

Seeing them together, supporting each other, made my heart feel even heavier. During my delirium, both of my great loves had visited me. Now, once again, I was devastatingly alone.

Still, I had a task to complete. A friend needed my help.

"Meg is in trouble," I said. "How long was I unconscious?"

Will and Nico glanced at each other.

"It's about noon now," Will said. "You showed up on the green around six this morning. When Meg didn't return with you, we wanted to search the woods for her, but Chiron wouldn't let us."

"Chiron was absolutely correct," I said. "I won't allow any others to put themselves at risk. But I must hurry. Meg has until tonight at the latest."

"Then what happens?" Nico asked.

I couldn't say it. I couldn't even *think* about it without losing my nerve. I looked down. Aside from Paolo's Brazilian-flag bandana and my ukulele-string necklace, I was wearing only my boxer shorts. My offensive flabbiness was on display for everyone to see, but I no longer cared about that. (Well, not much, anyway.) "I have to get dressed."

I staggered back to my cot. I fumbled through my meager supplies and found Percy Jackson's Led Zeppelin T-shirt. I tugged it on. It seemed more appropriate than ever.

Will hovered nearby. "Look, Apollo, I don't think you're back to a hundred percent."

"I'll be fine." I pulled on my jeans. "I have to save Meg."

"Let us help you," Nico said. "Tell us where she is and I can shadow-travel—"

"No!" I snapped. "No, you have to stay here and protect the camp."

Will's expression reminded me very much of his mother, Naomi—that look of trepidation she got just before she went onstage. "Protect the camp from what?"

"I—I'm not sure. You must tell Chiron the emperors have returned. Or rather, they never went away. They've been plotting, building their resources for centuries."

Nico's eyes glinted warily. "When you say emperors—"

"I mean the Roman ones."

Will stepped back. "You're saying the emperors of ancient Rome are alive? *How?* The Doors of Death?"

"No." I could barely speak through the taste of bile. "The emperors made themselves gods. They had their own temples and altars. They encouraged the people to worship them."

"But that was just propaganda," Nico said. "They weren't really divine."

I laughed mirthlessly. "Gods are sustained by worship, son of Hades. They continue to exist because of the collective memories of a culture. It's true for the Olympians; it's also true for the emperors. Somehow, the most powerful of them have survived. All these centuries, they have clung to half-life, hiding, waiting to reclaim their power."

Will shook his head. "That's impossible. How—?"

"I don't know!" I tried to steady my breathing. "Tell Rachel the men behind Triumvirate Holdings are former emperors of Rome. They've been plotting against us all this time, and we gods have been blind. *Blind.*"

I pulled on my coat. The ambrosia Nico had given me yesterday was still in the left pocket. In the right pocket, Rhea's wind chimes clanked, though I had no idea how they'd gotten there.

"The Beast is planning some sort of attack on the camp," I said. "I don't know what, and I don't know when, but tell Chiron you must be prepared. I have to go."

"Wait!" Will said as I reached the door. "Who is the Beast? Which emperor are we dealing with?"

"The worst of my descendants." My fingers dug into the doorframe. "The Christians called him the Beast because he burned them alive. Our enemy is Emperor Nero."

———

They must have been too stunned to follow me.

I ran toward the armory. Several campers gave me strange looks. Some called after me, offering help, but I ignored them. I could only think about Meg alone in the myrmekes' lair, and the visions I'd had of Daphne, Rhea, and Hyacinthus—all of them urging me onward, telling me to do the impossible in this inadequate mortal form.

When I reached the armory, I scanned the rack of bows. My hand trembling, I picked out the weapon Meg had tried to give me the day before. It was carved from mountain laurel wood. The bitter irony appealed to me.

I had sworn not to use a bow until I was a god again. But I had also sworn not to play music, and I had already broken that part of the oath in the most egregious, Neil-Diamondy way possible.

The curse of the River Styx could kill me in its slow cancerous way, or Zeus could strike me down. But my oath to save Meg McCaffrey had to come first.

I turned my face to the sky. "If you want to punish me, Father, be my guest, but have the courage to hurt *me* directly, not my mortal companion. BE A MAN!"

To my surprise, the skies remained silent. Lightning did not vaporize me. Perhaps Zeus was too taken aback to react, but I knew he would never overlook such an insult.

To Tartarus with him. I had work to do.

I grabbed a quiver and stuffed it with all the extra arrows I could find. Then I ran for the woods, Meg's two rings jangling on my makeshift necklace. Too late, I realized I had forgotten my combat ukulele, but I had no time to turn back. My singing voice would have to be enough.

I'm not sure how I found the nest.

Perhaps the forest simply allowed me to reach it, knowing that I was marching to my death. I've found that when one is searching for danger, it's never hard to find.

Soon I was crouched behind a fallen tree, studying the myrmekes' lair in the clearing ahead. To call the place an anthill would be like calling Versailles Palace a single-family home. Earthen ramparts rose almost to the tops of the surrounding trees—a hundred feet at least. The circumference could have accommodated a Roman hippodrome. A steady stream of soldiers and drones swarmed in and out of the mound. Some carried fallen trees. One, inexplicably, was dragging a 1967 Chevy Impala.

How many ants would I be facing? I had no idea. After you reach the number *impossible*, there's no point in counting.

I nocked an arrow and stepped into the clearing.

When the nearest myrmeke spotted me, he dropped his Chevy. He watched me approach, his antennae bobbing. I ignored him and strolled past, heading for the nearest tunnel entrance. That confused him even more.

Several other ants gathered to watch.

I've learned that if you act like you are supposed to be somewhere, most people (or ants) will not confront you. Normally, acting confident isn't a problem for me. Gods are allowed to be anywhere. It was a bit tougher for Lester Papadopoulos, dork teen extraordinaire, but I made it all the way to the nest without being challenged.

I plunged inside and began to sing.

This time I needed no ukulele. I needed no muse for

my inspiration. I remembered Daphne's face in the trees. I remembered Hyacinthus turning away, his death wound glistening on his scalp. My voice filled with anguish. I sang of heartbreak. Rather than collapsing under my own despair, I projected it outward.

The tunnels amplified my voice, carrying it through the nest, making the entire hill my musical instrument.

Each time I passed an ant, it curled its legs and touched its forehead to the floor, its antennae quivering from the vibrations of my voice.

Had I been a god, the song would have been stronger, but this was enough. I was impressed by how much sorrow a human voice could convey.

I wandered deeper into the hill. I had no idea where I was going until I spotted a geranium blooming from the tunnel floor.

My song faltered.

Meg. She must have regained consciousness. She had dropped one of her emergency seeds to leave me a trail. The geranium's purple flowers all faced a smaller tunnel leading off to the left.

"Clever girl," I said, choosing that tunnel.

A clattering sound alerted me to the approaching myrmeke.

I turned and raised my bow. Freed from the enchantment of my voice, the insect charged, its mouth foaming with acid. I drew and fired. The arrow embedded itself up to the fletching in the ant's forehead.

The creature dropped, its back legs twitching in death throes. I tried to retrieve my arrow, but the shaft snapped in my hand, the broken end covered in steaming corrosive goo. So much for reusing ammunition.

I called, "MEG!"

The only answer was the clattering of more giant ants moving in my direction. I began to sing again. Now, though, I had higher hopes of finding Meg, which made it difficult to summon the proper amount of melancholy. The ants I encountered were no longer catatonic. They moved slowly and unsteadily, but they still attacked. I was forced to shoot one after another.

I passed a cave filled with glittering treasure, but I was not interested in shiny things at the moment. I kept moving.

At the next intersection, another geranium sprouted from the floor, all its flowers facing right. I turned that direction, calling Meg's name again, then returning to my song.

As my spirits lifted, my song became less effective and the ants more aggressive. After a dozen kills, my quiver was growing dangerously light.

I had to reach deeper into my feelings of despair. I had to get the blues, good and proper.

For the first time in four thousand years, I sang of my own faults.

I poured out my guilt about Daphne's death. My boastfulness, envy, and desire had caused her destruction. When she ran from me, I should have let her go. Instead, I chased her relentlessly. I wanted her, and I intended to have her. Because of that, I had left Daphne no choice. To escape me, she sacrificed her life and turned into a tree, leaving my heart scarred forever. . . . But it was my fault. I apologized in song. I begged Daphne's forgiveness.

I sang of Hyacinthus, the most handsome of men. The West Wind Zephyros had also loved him, but I refused to share even a moment of Hyacinthus's time. In my jealousy, I threatened Zephyros. I dared him, *dared* him to interfere.

I sang of the day Hyacinthus and I played discus in the fields, and how the West Wind blew my disc off course—right into the side of Hyacinthus's head.

To keep Hyacinthus in the sunlight where he belonged, I created hyacinth flowers from his blood. I held Zephyros accountable, but my own petty greed had caused Hyacinthus's death. I poured out my sorrow. I took all the blame.

I sang of my failures, my eternal heartbreak and loneliness. I was the worst of the gods, the most guilt-ridden and unfocused. I couldn't commit myself to one lover. I couldn't even choose what to be the god of. I kept shifting from one skill to another—distracted and dissatisfied.

My golden life was a sham. My coolness was pretense. My heart was a lump of petrified wood.

All around me, myrmekes collapsed. The nest itself trembled with grief.

I found a third geranium, then a fourth.

Finally, pausing between verses, I heard a small voice up ahead: the sound of a girl crying.

"Meg!" I gave up on my song and ran.

She lay in the middle of a cavernous food larder, just as I had imagined. Around her were stacked the carcasses of animals—cows, deer, horses—all sheathed in hardened goop and slowly decaying. The smell hit my nasal passages like an avalanche.

Meg was also enveloped, but she was fighting back with the power of geraniums. Patches of leaves sprouted from the thinnest parts of her cocoon. A frilly collar of flowers kept the goo away from her face. She had even managed to free one of her arms, thanks to an explosion of pink geraniums at her left armpit.

Her eyes were puffy from crying. I assumed she was frightened, possibly in pain, but when I knelt next to her, her first words were, "I'm so sorry."

I brushed a tear from the tip of her nose. "Why, dear Meg? You did nothing wrong. I failed *you*."

A sob caught in her throat. "You don't understand. That song you were singing. Oh, gods . . . Apollo, if I'd known—"

"Hush, now." My throat was so raw I could barely talk. The song had almost destroyed my voice. "You're just reacting to the grief in the music. Let's get you free."

I was considering how to do that when Meg's eyes widened. She made a whimpering sound.

The hairs on the nape of my neck came to attention. "There are ants behind me, aren't there?" I asked.

Meg nodded.

I turned as four of them entered the cavern. I reached for my quiver. I had one arrow left.

28

Parenting advice:
Mamas, don't let your larvae
Grow up to be ants

MEG THRASHED IN HER GOO CASE. "Get me out of here!"

"I don't have a blade!" My fingers crept to the ukulele string around my neck. "Actually I have *your* blades, I mean your rings—"

"You don't need to cut me out. When the ant dumped me here, I dropped the packet of seeds. It should be close."

She was right. I spotted the crumpled pouch near her feet.

I inched toward it, keeping one eye on the ants. They stood together at the entrance as if hesitant to come closer. Perhaps the trail of dead ants leading to this room had given them pause.

"Nice ants," I said. "Excellent calm ants."

I crouched and scooped up the packet. A quick glance inside told me half a dozen seeds remained. "Now what, Meg?"

"Throw them on the goo," Meg said.

I gestured to the geraniums bursting from her neck and armpit. "How many seeds did that?"

"One."

"Then this many will choke you to death. I've turned too many people I cared about into flowers, Meg. I won't—"

"JUST DO IT!"

The ants did not like her tone. They advanced, snapping their mandibles. I shook the geranium seeds over Meg's cocoon, then nocked my arrow. Killing one ant would do no good if the other three tore us apart, so I chose a different target. I shot the roof of the cavern, just above the ants' heads.

It was a desperate idea, but I'd had success bringing down buildings with arrows before. In 464 BCE, I caused an earthquake that wiped out most of Sparta by hitting a fault line at the right angle. (I never liked the Spartans much.)

This time, I had less luck. The arrow embedded itself in the packed earth with a dull *thunk*. The ants took another step forward, acid dripping from their mouths. Behind me, Meg struggled to free herself from her cocoon, which was now covered in a shag carpet of purple flowers.

She needed more time.

Out of ideas, I tugged my Brazilian-flag handkerchief from my neck and waved it like a maniac, trying to channel my inner Paolo.

"BACK, FOUL ANTS!" I yelled. *"BRASIL!"*

The ants wavered—perhaps because of the bright colors, or my voice, or my sudden insane confidence. While they hesitated, cracks spread across the roof from my arrow's impact site, and then thousands of tons of earth collapsed on top of the myrmekes.

When the dust cleared, half the room was gone, along with the ants.

I looked at my handkerchief. "I'll be Styxed. It *does* have magic power. I can never tell Paolo about this or he'll be insufferable."

"Over here!" Meg yelled.

I turned. Another myrmeke was crawling over a pile of carcasses—apparently from a second exit I had failed to notice behind the disgusting food stores.

Before I could think what to do, Meg roared and burst from her cage, spraying geraniums in every direction. She shouted, "My rings!"

I yanked them from my neck and tossed them through the air. As soon as Meg caught them, two golden scimitars flashed into her hands.

The myrmeke barely had time to think *Uh-oh* before Meg charged. She sliced off his armored head. His body collapsed in a steaming heap.

Meg turned to me. Her face was a tempest of guilt, misery, and bitterness. I was afraid she might use her swords on me.

"Apollo, I . . ." Her voice broke.

I supposed she was still suffering from the effects of my song. She was shaken to her core. I made a mental note never again to sing so honestly when a mortal might be listening.

"It's all right, Meg," I said. "I should be apologizing to you. I got you into this mess."

Meg shook her head. "You don't understand. I—"

An enraged shriek echoed through the chamber, shaking the compromised ceiling and raining clods of dirt on our heads. The tone of the scream reminded me of Hera whenever she stormed through the hallways of Olympus, yelling at me for leaving the godly toilet seat up.

"That's the queen ant," I guessed. "We need to leave."

Meg pointed her sword toward the room's only remaining exit. "But the sound came from there. We'll be walking in her direction."

"Exactly. So perhaps we should hold off on making amends with each other, eh? We might still get each other killed."

We found the queen ant.

Hooray.

All corridors must have led to the queen. They radiated from her chamber like spikes on a morning star. Her Majesty was three times the size of her largest soldiers—a towering mass of black chitin and barbed appendages, with diaphanous oval wings folded against her back. Her eyes were glassy swimming pools of onyx. Her abdomen was a pulsing translucent sac filled with glowing eggs. The sight of it made me regret ever inventing gel capsule medications.

Her swollen abdomen might slow her down in a fight, but she was so large, she could intercept us before we reached the nearest exit. Those mandibles would snap us in half like dried twigs.

"Meg," I said, "how do you feel about dual-wielding scimitars against this lady?"

Meg looked appalled. "She's a mother giving birth."

"Yes . . . and she's an insect, which you hate. And her children were ripening you up for dinner."

Meg frowned. "Still . . . I don't feel right about it."

The queen hissed—a dry spraying noise. I imagined she would have already hosed us down with acid if she weren't worried about the long-term effects of corrosives on her larvae. Queen ants can't be too careful these days.

"You have another idea?" I asked Meg. "Preferably one that does not involve dying?"

She pointed to a tunnel directly behind the queen's clutch of eggs. "We need to go that way. It leads to the grove."

"How can you be sure?"

Meg tilted her head. "Trees. It's like . . . I can hear them growing."

That reminded me of something the Muses once told me—how they could actually hear the ink drying on new pages of poetry. I suppose it made sense that a daughter of Demeter could hear the growth of plants. Also, it didn't surprise me that the tunnel we needed was the most dangerous one to reach.

"Sing," Meg told me. "Sing like you did before."

"I—I can't. My voice is almost gone."

Besides, I thought, I don't want to risk losing you again.

I had freed Meg, so perhaps I'd fulfilled my oath to Pete the geyser god. Still, by singing and practicing archery, I had broken my oath upon the River Styx not once but twice. More singing would only make me *more* of a scofflaw.

Whatever cosmic punishments awaited me, I did not want them to fall on Meg.

Her Majesty snapped at us—a warning shot, telling us to back off. A few feet closer and my head would have rolled in the dirt.

I burst into song—or rather, I did the best I could with the raspy voice that remained. I began to rap. I started with the rhythm *boom chicka chicka*. I busted out some footwork the Nine Muses and I had been working on just before the war with Gaea.

The queen arched her back. I don't think she had expected to be rapped to today.

I gave Meg a look that clearly meant *Help me out!*

She shook her head. Give the girl two swords and she was a maniac. Ask her to lay down a simple beat and she suddenly got stage fright.

Fine, I thought. I'll do it by myself.

I launched into "Dance" by Nas, which I have to say was one of the most moving odes to mothers that I ever inspired an artist to write. (You're welcome, Nas.) I took some liberties with the lyrics. I may have changed *angel* to *brood mother* and *woman* to *insect*. But the sentiment remained. I serenaded the pregnant queen, channeling my love for my own dear mother, Leto. When I sang that I could only wish to marry a woman (or insect) so fine someday, my heartbreak was real. I would never have such a partner. It was not in my destiny.

The queen's antennae quivered. Her head seesawed back and forth. Eggs kept extruding from her abdomen, which made it difficult for me to concentrate, but I persevered.

When I was done, I dropped to one knee and held up my arms in tribute, waiting for the queen's verdict. Either she would kill me or she would not. I was spent. I had poured everything into that song and could not rap another line.

Next to me, Meg stood very still, gripping her swords.

Her Majesty shuddered. She threw back her head and wailed—a sound more brokenhearted than angry.

She leaned down and gently nudged my chest, pushing me in the direction of the tunnel we needed.

"Thank you," I croaked. "I—I'm sorry about the ants I killed."

The queen purred and clicked, extruding a few more eggs as if to say, *Don't worry; I can always make more.*

I stroked the queen ant's forehead. "May I call you Mama?"

Her mouth frothed in a pleased sort of way.

"Apollo," Meg urged, "let's go before she changes her mind."

I was not sure Mama *would* change her mind. I got the feeling she had accepted my fealty and adopted us into her brood. But Meg was right; we needed to hurry. Mama watched as we edged around her clutch of eggs.

We plunged into the tunnel and saw the glow of day-light above us.

29

Nightmares of torches
And a man in purple clothes
But that's not the worst

I HAD NEVER BEEN SO HAPPY to see a killing field.

We emerged into a glade littered with bones. Most were from forest animals. A few appeared human. I guessed we had found the myrmekes' dumping site, and they apparently didn't get regular garbage pickup.

The clearing was hemmed with trees so thick and tangled that traveling through them would've been impossible. Over our heads, the branches wove together in a leafy dome that let in sunlight but not much else. Anyone flying above the forest would never have realized this open space existed under the canopy.

At the far end of the glade stood a row of objects like football tackle dummies—six white cocoons staked on tall wooden poles, flanking a pair of enormous oaks. Each tree was at least eighty feet tall. They had grown so close together that their massive trunks appeared to have fused. I had the distinct impression I was looking at a set of living doors.

"It's a gateway," I said. "To the Grove of Dodona."

Meg's blades retracted, once again becoming gold rings on her middle fingers. "Aren't we *in* the grove?"

"No . . ." I stared across the clearing at the white cocoon Popsicles. They were too far away to make out clearly, but something about them seemed familiar in an evil, unwelcome sort of way. I wanted to get closer. I also wanted to keep my distance.

"I think this is more of an antechamber," I said. "The grove itself is behind those trees."

Meg gazed warily across the field. "I don't hear any voices."

It was true. The forest was absolutely quiet. The trees seemed to be holding their breath.

"The grove knows we are here," I guessed. "It's waiting to see what we'll do."

"We'd better do something, then." Meg didn't sound any more excited than I was, but she marched forward, bones crunching under her feet.

I wished I had more than a bow, an empty quiver, and a hoarse voice to defend myself with, but I followed, trying not to trip over rib cages and deer antlers. About halfway across the glade, Meg let out a sharp exhale.

She was staring at the posts on either side of the tree gates.

At first I couldn't process what I was seeing. Each stake was about the height of a crucifix—the kind Romans used to set up along the roadside to advertise the fates of criminals. (Personally, I find modern billboards much more tasteful.) The upper half of each post was wrapped in thick lumpy wads of white cloth, and sticking out from the top of each cocoon was something that looked like a human head.

My stomach somersaulted. They *were* human heads. Arrayed in front of us were the missing demigods, all tightly bound. I watched, petrified, until I discerned the slightest expansions and contractions in the wrappings around their chests. They were still breathing. Unconscious, not dead. Thank the gods.

On the left were three teenagers I didn't know, though I assumed they must be Cecil, Ellis, and Miranda. On the right side was an emaciated man with gray skin and white hair—no doubt the geyser god Paulie. Next to him hung my children . . . Austin and Kayla.

I shook so violently, the bones around my feet clattered. I recognized the smell coming from the prisoners' wrappings—sulfur, oil, powdered lime, and liquid Greek fire, the most dangerous substance ever created. Rage and disgust fought in my throat, vying for the right to make me throw up.

"Oh, monstrous," I said. "We need to free them immediately."

"Wh-what's wrong with them?" Meg stammered.

I dared not put it into words. I had seen this form of execution once before, at the hands of the Beast, and I never wished to see it again.

I ran to Austin's stake. With all my strength I tried to push it over, but it wouldn't budge. The base was sunk too deep in the earth. I tore at the cloth bindings but only managed to coat my hands in sulfurous resin. The wadding was stickier and harder than myrmekes' goo.

"Meg, your swords!" I wasn't sure they would do any good either, but I could think of nothing else to try.

Then from above us came a familiar snarl.

The branches rustled. Peaches the karpos dropped from the canopy, landing with a somersault at Meg's feet. He looked like he'd been through quite an ordeal to get here. His arms were sliced up and dripping peach nectar. His legs were dotted with bruises. His diaper sagged dangerously.

"Thank the gods!" I said. That was not my usual reaction when I saw the grain spirit, but his teeth and claws might be just the things to free the demigods. "Meg, hurry! Order your friend to—"

"Apollo." Her voice was heavy. She pointed to the tunnel from which we'd come.

Emerging from the ants' nest were two of the largest humans I had ever seen. Each was seven feet tall and perhaps three hundred pounds of pure muscle stuffed into horsehide armor. Their blond hair glinted like silver floss. Jeweled rings glittered in their beards. Each man carried an oval shield and a spear, though I doubted they needed weapons to kill. They looked like they could crack open cannonballs with their bare hands.

I recognized them from their tattoos and the circular designs on their shields. Such warriors weren't easy to forget.

"*Germani.*" Instinctively, I moved in front of Meg. The elite imperial bodyguards had been cold-blooded death reapers in ancient Rome. I doubted they'd gotten any sweeter over the centuries.

The two men glared at me. They had serpent tattoos curling around their necks, just like the ruffians who had jumped me in New York. The Germani parted, and their master climbed from the tunnel.

Nero hadn't changed much in one thousand nine hundred and some-odd years. He appeared to be no more than thirty, but it was a *hard* thirty, his face haggard and his belly distended from too much partying. His mouth was fixed in a permanent sneer. His curly hair extended into a wrap-around neck beard. His chin was so weak, I was tempted to create a GoFundMe campaign to buy him a better jaw.

He tried to compensate for his ugliness with an expensive Italian suit of purple wool, his gray shirt open to display gold chains. His shoes were hand-tooled leather, not the sort of thing to wear while stomping around in an ant pile. Then again, Nero had always had expensive, impractical tastes. That was perhaps the only thing I admired about him.

"Emperor Nero," I said. "The Beast."

He curled his lip. "Nero will do. It's good to see you, my honored ancestor. I'm sorry I've been so lax about my offerings during the past few millennia, but"—he shrugged—"I haven't needed you. I've done rather well on my own."

My fists clenched. I wanted to strike down this pot-bellied emperor with a bolt of white-hot power, except that I had no bolts of white-hot power. I had no arrows. I had no singing voice left. Against Nero and his seven-foot-tall bodyguards, I had a Brazilian handkerchief, a packet of ambrosia, and some brass wind chimes.

"It's me you want," I said. "Cut these demigods down from their stakes. Let them leave with Meg. They've done nothing to you."

Nero chuckled. "I'll be happy to let them go once we've

come to an agreement. As for Meg . . ." He smiled at her. "How are you, my dear?"

Meg said nothing. Her face was as hard and gray as a geyser god's. At her feet, Peaches snarled and rustled his leafy wings.

One of Nero's guards said something in his ear.

The Emperor nodded. "Soon."

He turned his attention back to me. "But where are my manners? Allow me to introduce my right hand, Vincius, and my left hand, Garius."

The bodyguards pointed across to each other.

"Ah, sorry," Nero corrected. "My right hand, Garius, and my left hand, Vincius. Those are the Romanized versions of their Batavi names, which I can't pronounce. Usually I just call them Vince and Gary. Say hello, boys."

Vince and Gary glowered at me.

"They have serpent tattoos," I noted, "like those street thugs you sent to attack me."

Nero shrugged. "I have many servants. Cade and Mikey are quite low on the pay scale. Their only job was to rattle you a bit, welcome you to my city."

"*Your* city." I found it just like Nero to go claiming major metropolitan areas that clearly belonged to me. "And these two gentlemen . . . they are actually Germani from the ancient times? How?"

Nero made a snide little barking sound in the back of his nose. I'd forgotten how much I hated his laugh.

"Lord Apollo, please," he said. "Even before Gaea commandeered the Doors of Death, souls escaped from Erebos all the time. It was quite easy for a god-emperor such as myself to call back my followers."

"A god-emperor?" I growled. "You mean a delusional ex-emperor."

Nero arched his eyebrows. "What made *you* a god, Apollo . . . back when you were one? Wasn't it the power of your name, your sway over those who believed in you? I am no different." He glanced to his left. "Vince, fall on your spear, please."

Without hesitation, Vince planted the butt of his spear against the ground. He braced the point under his rib cage.

"Stop," Nero said. "I changed my mind."

Vince betrayed no relief. In fact, his eyes tightened with faint disappointment. He brought his spear back to his side.

Nero grinned at me. "You see? I hold the power of life and death over my worshippers, like any proper god should."

I felt like I'd swallowed some gel capsule larvae. "The Germani were always crazy, much like you."

Nero put his hand to his chest. "I'm hurt! My barbarian friends are loyal subjects of the Julian dynasty! And, of course, we are all descended from you, Lord Apollo."

I didn't need the reminder. I'd been so proud of my son, the original Octavian, later Caesar Augustus. After his death, his descendants became increasingly arrogant and unstable (which I blamed on their mortal DNA; they certainly didn't get those qualities from me). Nero had been the last of the Julian line. I had not wept when he died. Now here he was, as grotesque and chinless as ever.

Meg stood at my shoulder. "Wh-what do you want, Nero?"

Considering she was facing the man who killed her father, she sounded remarkably calm. I was grateful for her strength. It gave me hope to have a skilled dimachaerus and a ravenous peach baby at my side. Still, I did not like our odds against two Germani.

Nero's eyes gleamed. "Straight to the point. I've always admired that about you, Meg. Really, it's simple. You and Apollo will open the gates of Dodona for me. Then these six"—he gestured to the staked prisoners—"will be released."

I shook my head. "You'll destroy the grove. Then you'll kill us."

The emperor made that horrible bark again. "Not unless you force me to. I'm a reasonable god-emperor, Apollo! I'd much rather have the Grove of Dodona under my control if it can be managed, but I certainly can't allow *you* to use it. You had your chance at being the guardian of the Oracles. You failed miserably. Now it's my responsibility. Mine . . . and my partners'."

"The two other emperors," I said. "Who are they?"

Nero shrugged. "Good Romans—men who, like me, have the willpower to do what is needed."

"Triumvirates have never worked. They always lead to civil war."

He smiled as if that idea did not bother him. "The three of us have come to an agreement. We have divided up the new empire . . . by which I mean North America. Once we have the Oracles, we'll expand and do what Romans have always done best—conquer the world."

I could only stare at him. "You truly learned nothing from your previous reign."

"Oh, but I did! I've had centuries to reflect, plan, and prepare. Do you have any idea how annoying it is to be a god-emperor, unable to die but unable to fully live? There was a period of about three hundred years during the Middle Ages when my name was almost forgotten. I was little more than a mirage! Thank goodness for the Renaissance, when our Classical greatness was remembered. And then came the Internet. Oh, gods, I *love* the Internet! It is impossible for me to fade completely now. I am immortal on Wikipedia!"

I winced. I was now fully convinced of Nero's insanity. Wikipedia was always getting stuff wrong about me.

He rolled his hand. "Yes, yes. You think I am crazy. I could explain my plans and prove otherwise, but I have a lot on my plate today. I need you and Meg to open those gates. They've resisted my best efforts, but together you two can do it. Apollo, you have an affinity with Oracles. Meg has a way with trees. Get to it. Please and thank you."

"We would rather die," I said. "Wouldn't we, Meg?"

No response.

I glanced over. A silvery streak glistened on Meg's cheek. At first I thought one of her rhinestones had melted. Then I realized she was crying.

"Meg?"

Nero clasped his hands as if in prayer. "Oh, my. It seems we've had a slight miscommunication. You see, Apollo, Meg brought you here, just as I asked her to. Well done, my sweet."

Meg wiped her face. "I—I didn't mean . . ."

My heart compressed to the size of a pebble. "Meg, no. I can't believe—"

I reached for her. Peaches snarled and inserted himself between us. I realized the karpos was not here to protect us from Nero. He was defending Meg from *me*.

"Meg?" I said. "This man killed your father! He's a murderer!"

She stared at the ground. When she spoke, her voice was even more tortured than mine was when I sang in the anthill. "The *Beast* killed my father. This is Nero. He's—he's my stepfather."

I could not fully grasp this before Nero spread his arms.

"That's right, my darling," he said. "And you've done a wonderful job. Come to Papa."

30

I school McCaffrey
Yo, girl, your stepdad is wack
Why won't she listen?

I HAD BEEN BETRAYED BEFORE.

The memories came flooding back to me in a painful tide. Once, my former girlfriend Cyrene took up with Ares just to get back at me. Another time, Artemis shot me in the groin because I was flirting with her Hunters. In 1928, Alexander Fleming failed to give me credit for inspiring his discovery of penicillin. I mean, *ouch*. That stung.

But I couldn't remember *ever* being so wrong about someone as I had been about Meg. Well . . . at least not since Irving Berlin. *"Alexander's Ragtime Band"*? I remember telling him. *You'll never make it big with a corny song like that!*

"Meg, we are friends." My voice sounded petulant even to myself. "How could you do this to me?"

Meg looked down at her red sneakers—the primary-colored shoes of a traitor. "I tried to tell you, to warn you."

"She has a good heart." Nero smiled. "But, Apollo, you and Meg have been friends for just a few days—and only because I *asked* Meg to befriend you. I have been Meg's stepfather, protector, and caretaker for years. She is a member of the Imperial Household."

I stared at my beloved Dumpster waif. Yes, somehow over the past week she had become beloved to me. I could not imagine her as Imperial *anything*—definitely not as a part of Nero's entourage.

"I risked my life for you," I said in amazement. "And that actually *means* something, because I can die!"

Nero clapped politely. "We're all impressed, Apollo. Now, if you'd open the gates. They've defied me for too long."

I tried to glare at Meg, but my heart wasn't in it. I felt too hurt and vulnerable. We gods do not like feeling vulnerable. Besides, Meg wasn't even looking at me.

In a daze, I turned to the oak tree gates. I saw now that their fused trunks were marred from Nero's previous efforts—chain-saw scars, burn marks, bites from ax blades, even some bullet holes. All these had barely chipped the outer bark. The most damaged area was an inch-deep impression in the shape of a human hand, where the wood had bubbled and peeled away. I glanced at the unconscious face of Paulie the geyser god, strung up and bound with the five demigods.

"Nero, what have you done?"

"Oh, a number of things! We found a way into this antechamber weeks ago. The Labyrinth has a convenient opening in the myrmekes' nest. But getting through these gates—"

"You forced the palikos to help you?" I had to restrain myself from throwing my wind chimes at the emperor. "You used a nature spirit to destroy nature? Meg, how can you tolerate this?"

Peaches growled. For once I had the feeling that the grain spirit might be in agreement with me. Meg's expression was as closed up as the gates. She stared intently at the bones littering the field.

"Come now," Nero said. "Meg knows there are good nature spirits, and bad ones. This geyser god was annoying. He kept asking us to fill out surveys. Besides, he shouldn't have ventured so far from his source of power. He was quite easy to capture. His steam, as you can see, didn't do us much good anyway."

"And the five demigods?" I demanded. "Did you 'use' them, too?"

"Of course. I didn't plan on luring them here, but every time we attacked the gates, the grove started wailing. I suppose it was calling for help, and the demigods couldn't resist. The first to wander in was this one." He pointed to Cecil Markowitz. "The last two were your own children—Austin and Kayla, yes? They showed up after we forced Paulie to steam-broil the trees. I guess the grove was quite nervous about that attempt. We got two demigods for the price of one!"

I lost control. I let out a guttural howl and charged the emperor, intending to wring his hairy excuse for a neck. The Germani would have killed me before I ever got that far, but I was saved the indignity. I tripped over a human pelvis and belly-surfed through the bones.

"Apollo!" Meg ran toward me.

I rolled over and kicked at her like a fussy child. "I don't need *your* help! Don't you understand who your protector is? He's a monster! He's the emperor who—"

"Don't say it," Nero warned. "If you say 'who fiddled while Rome burned,' I will have Vince and Gary flay you for a set of hide armor. You know as well as I do, Apollo, we didn't *have* fiddles back then. And I did *not* start the Great Fire of Rome."

I struggled to my feet. "But you profited from it."

Facing Nero, I remembered all the tawdry details of his rule—the extravagance and cruelty that had made him so embarrassing to me, his forefather. Nero was that relative you never wanted to invite to Lupercalia dinner.

"Meg," I said, "your stepfather watched as seventy percent of Rome was destroyed. Tens of thousands died."

"I was thirty miles away in Antium!" Nero snarled. "I rushed back to the city and personally led the fire brigades!"

"Only when the fire threatened your palace."

Nero rolled his eyes. "I can't help it if I arrived just in time to save the most important building!"

Meg cupped her hands over her ears. "Stop arguing. Please."

I didn't stop. Talking seemed better than my other options, like helping Nero or dying.

"After the Great Fire," I told her, "instead of rebuilding the houses on Palatine Hill, Nero leveled the neighborhood and built a new palace—the Domus Aurea."

Nero got a dreamy look on his face. "Ah, yes . . . the House of Gold. It was beautiful, Meg! I had my own lake, three hundred rooms, frescoes of gold, mosaics done in pearls and diamonds—I could finally live like a human being!"

"You had the nerve to put a hundred-foot-tall bronze statue in your front lawn!" I said. "A statue of yourself as

Sol-Apollo, the sun god. In other words, you claimed to be *me*."

"Indeed," Nero agreed. "Even after I died, that statue lived on. I understand it became famous as the Colossus of Nero! They moved it to the gladiators' amphitheater and everyone began calling the theater after the statue—*the Colosseum*." Nero puffed up his chest. "Yes . . . the statue was the perfect choice."

His tone sounded even more sinister than usual.

"What are you talking about?" I demanded.

"Hmm? Oh, nothing." He checked his watch . . . a mauve-and-gold Rolex. "The point is, I had style! The people loved me!"

I shook my head. "They turned against you. The people of Rome were sure you'd started the Great Fire, so you scapegoated the Christians."

I was aware that this arguing was pointless. If Meg had hidden her true identity all this time, I doubted I could change her mind now. But perhaps I could stall long enough for the cavalry to arrive. If only I *had* a cavalry.

Nero waved dismissively. "But the Christians were terrorists, you see. Perhaps they didn't start the fire, but they were causing all sorts of other trouble. I recognized that before anyone else!"

"He fed them to the lions," I told Meg. "He burned them as human torches, the way he will burn these six."

Meg's face turned green. She gazed at the unconscious prisoners on the stakes. "Nero, you wouldn't—"

"They will be released," Nero promised, "as long as Apollo cooperates."

"Meg, you can't trust him," I said. "The last time he did this, he strung up Christians all over his backyard and burned them to illuminate his garden party. I was there. I remember the screaming."

Meg clutched her stomach.

"My dear, don't believe his stories!" Nero said. "That was just propaganda invented by my enemies."

Meg studied the face of Paulie the geyser god. "Nero . . . you didn't say anything about making them into torches."

"They won't burn," he said, straining to soften his voice. "It won't come to that. The Beast will not have to act."

"You see, Meg?" I wagged a finger at the emperor. "It's never a good sign when someone starts referring to himself in the third person. Zeus used to scold me about that constantly!"

Vince and Gary stepped forward, their knuckles whitening on their spears.

"I would be careful," Nero warned. "My Germani are sensitive about insults to the Imperial person. Now, as much as I love talking about myself, we're on a schedule." He checked his watch again. "You'll open the gates. Then Meg will see if she can use the trees to interpret the future. If so, wonderful! If not . . . well, we'll burn that bridge when we come to it."

"Meg," I said, "he's a madman."

At her feet, Peaches hissed protectively.

Meg's chin quivered. "Nero cared about me, Apollo. He gave me a home. He taught me to fight."

"You said he killed your father!"

"No!" She shook her head adamantly, a look of panic in her eyes. "No, that's not what I said. The *Beast* killed him."

"But—"

Nero snorted. "Oh, Apollo . . . you understand so little. Meg's father was weak. She doesn't even remember him. He couldn't protect her. *I* raised her. I kept her alive."

My heart sank even further. I did not understand everything Meg had been through, or what she was feeling now, but I knew Nero. I saw how easily he could have twisted a scared child's understanding of the world—a little girl all alone, yearning for safety and acceptance after her father's murder, even if that acceptance came from her father's killer. "Meg . . . I am so sorry."

Another tear traced her cheek.

"She doesn't NEED sympathy." Nero's voice turned as hard as bronze. "Now, my dear, if you would be so kind, open the gates. If Apollo objects, remind him that he is bound to follow your orders."

Meg swallowed. "Apollo, don't make it harder. Please . . . help me open the gates."

I shook my head. "Not by choice."

"Then I—I command you. Help me. Now."

31

Listen to the trees
The trees know what is up, yo
They know all the things

MEG'S RESOLVE may have been wavering, but Peaches's was not.

When I hesitated to follow Meg's orders, the grain spirit bared his fangs and hissed, "Peaches," as if that was a new torture technique.

"Fine," I told Meg, my voice turning bitter. The truth was, I had no choice. I could feel Meg's command sinking into my muscles, compelling me to obey.

I faced the fused oaks and put my hands against their trunks. I felt no oracular power within. I heard no voices—just heavy stubborn silence. The only message the trees seemed to be sending was: GO AWAY.

"If we do this," I told Meg, "Nero will destroy the grove."

"He won't."

"He has to. He can't control Dodona. Its power is too ancient. He can't let anyone else use it."

Meg placed her hands against the trees, just below mine. "Concentrate. Open them. Please. You don't want to anger the Beast."

She said this in a low voice—again speaking as if the

Beast was someone I had not yet met . . . a boogeyman lurking under the bed, not a man in a purple suit standing a few feet away.

I could not refuse Meg's orders, but perhaps I should have protested more vigorously. Meg might have backed down if I called her bluff. But then Nero or Peaches or the Germani would have just killed me. I will confess to you: I was afraid of dying. Courageously, nobly, handsomely afraid, true. But afraid nonetheless.

I closed my eyes. I sensed the trees' implacable resistance, their mistrust of outsiders. I knew that if I forced open these gates, the grove would be destroyed. Yet I reached out with all my willpower and sought the voice of prophecy, drawing it to me.

I thought of Rhea, Queen of the Titans, who had first planted this grove. Despite being a child of Gaea and Ouranos, despite being married to the cannibal king Kronos, Rhea had managed to cultivate wisdom and kindness. She had given birth to a new, better breed of immortals. (If I do say so myself.) She represented the best of the ancient times.

True, she had withdrawn from the world and started a pottery studio in Woodstock, but she still cared about Dodona. She had sent me here to open the grove, to share its power. She was not the kind of goddess who believed in closed gates or NO TRESPASSING signs. I began to hum softly "This Land Is Your Land."

The bark grew warm under my fingertips. The tree roots trembled.

I glanced at Meg. She was deep in concentration, leaning against the trunks as if trying to push them over.

Everything about her was familiar: her ratty pageboy hair, her glittering cat-eye glasses, her runny nose and chewed cuticles and faint scent of apple pie.

But she was someone I didn't know at all: stepdaughter to the immortal crazy Nero. A member of the Imperial Household. What did that even *mean*? I pictured the Brady Bunch in purple togas, lined up on the family staircase with Nero at the bottom in Alice's maid uniform. Having a vivid imagination is a terrible curse.

Unfortunately for the grove, Meg was also the daughter of Demeter. The trees responded to her power. The twin oaks rumbled. Their trunks began to move.

I wanted to stop, but I was caught up in the momentum. The grove seemed to be drawing on my power now. My hands stuck to the trees. The gates opened wider, forcibly spreading my arms. For a terrifying moment, I thought the trees might keep moving and rip me limb from limb. Then they stopped. The roots settled. The bark cooled and released me.

I stumbled back, exhausted. Meg remained, transfixed, in the newly opened gateway.

On the other side were . . . well, more trees. Despite the winter cold, the young oaks rose tall and green, growing in concentric circles around a slightly larger specimen in the center. Littering the ground were acorns glowing with a faint amber light. Around the grove stood a protective wall of trees even more formidable than the ones in the antechamber. Above, another tightly woven dome of branches guarded the place from aerial intruders.

Before I could warn her, Meg stepped across the

threshold. The voices exploded. Imagine forty nail guns firing into your brain from all directions at once. The words were babble, but they tore at my sanity, demanding my attention. I covered my ears. The noise just got louder and more persistent.

Peaches clawed frantically at the dirt, trying to bury his head. Vince and Gary writhed on the ground. Even the unconscious demigods thrashed and moaned on their stakes.

Nero reeled, his hand raised as if to block an intense light. "Meg, control the voices! Do it now!"

Meg didn't appear hurt by the noise, but she looked bewildered. "They're saying something . . ." She swept her hands through the air, pulling at invisible threads to untangle the pandemonium. "They're agitated. I can't— Wait . . ."

Suddenly the voices shut off, as if they'd made their point.

Meg turned toward Nero, her eyes wide. "It's true. The trees told me you mean to burn them."

The Germani groaned, half-conscious on the ground. Nero recovered more quickly. He raised a finger, admonishing, guiding. "Listen to me, Meg. I'd hoped the grove could be useful, but obviously it is fractured and confused. You can't believe what it says. It's the mouthpiece of a senile Titan queen. The grove must be razed. It's the only way, Meg. You understand that, don't you?"

He kicked Gary over onto his back and rifled through the bodyguard's pouches. Then Nero stood, triumphantly holding a box of matches.

"After the fire, we'll rebuild," he said. "It will be glorious!"

Meg stared at him as if noticing his horrendous neck beard for the first time. "Wh-what are you talking about?"

"He's going to burn and level Long Island," I said. "Then he'll make it his private domain, just like he did with Rome."

Nero laughed in exasperation. "Long Island is a mess anyway! No one will miss it. My new imperial complex will extend from Manhattan to Montauk—the greatest palace ever built! We'll have private rivers and lakes, one hundred miles of beachfront property, gardens big enough for their own zip codes. I'll build each member of my household a private skyscraper. Oh, Meg, imagine the parties we will have in our new Domus Aurea!"

The truth was a heavy thing. Meg's knees buckled under its weight.

"You can't." Her voice shook. "The woods— I'm the daughter of Demeter."

"You're *my* daughter," Nero corrected. "And I care for you deeply. Which is why you need to move aside. Quickly."

He set a match to the striking surface of the box. "As soon as I light these stakes, our human torches will send a wave of fire straight through that gateway. Nothing will be able to stop it. The entire forest will burn."

"Please!" Meg cried.

"Come along, dearest." Nero's frown hardened. "Apollo is of no use to us anymore. You don't want to wake the Beast, do you?"

He lit his match and stepped toward the nearest stake, where my son Austin was bound.

32

It takes a Village
People to protect your mind
"Y.M.C.A." Yeah

OH, THIS PART IS DIFFICULT TO TELL.

I am a natural storyteller. I have an infallible instinct for drama. I want to relate what *should* have happened: how I leaped forward shouting, "Nooooo!" and spun like an acrobat, knocking aside the lit match, then twisted in a series of blazing-fast Shaolin moves, cracking Nero's head and taking out his bodyguards before they could recover.

Ah, yes. That would have been perfect.

Alas, the truth constrains me.

Curse you, truth!

In fact, I spluttered something like, "Nuh-uh, dundoot!" I may have waved my Brazilian handkerchief with the hope that its magic would destroy my enemies.

The real hero was Peaches. The karpos must have sensed Meg's true feelings, or perhaps he just didn't like the idea of burning forests. He hurtled through the air, screaming his war cry (you guessed it), "Peaches!" He landed on Nero's arm, chomped the lit match from the emperor's hand, then landed a few feet away, wiping his tongue and crying, "Hat!

Hat!" (Which I assumed meant *hot* in the dialect of deciduous fruit.)

The scene might have been funny except that the Germani were now back on their feet, five demigods and a geyser spirit were still tied to highly flammable posts, and Nero still had a box of matches.

The emperor stared at his empty hand. "Meg . . . ?" His voice was as cold as an icicle. "What is the meaning of this?"

"P-Peaches, come here!" Meg's voice had turned brittle with fear.

The karpos bounded to her side. He hissed at me, Nero, and the Germani.

Meg took a shaky breath, clearly gathering her nerve. "Nero . . . Peaches is right. You—you can't burn these people alive."

Nero sighed. He looked at his bodyguards for moral support, but the Germani still appeared woozy. They were hitting the sides of their heads as if trying to clear water from their ears.

"Meg," said the emperor, "I am trying so hard to keep the Beast at bay. Why won't you help me? I know you are a good girl. I wouldn't have allowed you to roam around Manhattan so much on your own, playing the street waif, if I didn't know you could take care of yourself. But softness toward your enemies is not a virtue. You are my stepdaughter. Any of these demigods would kill you without hesitation given the chance."

"Meg, that's not true!" I said. "You've seen what Camp Half-Blood is like."

She studied me uneasily. "Even . . . even if it was true . . ." She turned to Nero. "You told me never to lower myself to my enemies' level."

"No, indeed." Nero's tone had frayed like a weathered rope. "We are better. We are stronger. We will build a glorious new world. But these nonsense-spewing trees stand in our way, Meg. Like any invasive weeds, they must be burned. And the only way to do that is with a true conflagration—flames stoked by blood. Let us do this together, and not involve the Beast, shall we?"

Finally, in my mind, something clicked. I remembered how my father used to punish me centuries ago, when I was a young god learning the ways of Olympus. Zeus used to say, *Don't get on the wrong side of my lightning bolts, boy.*

As if the lightning bolt had a mind of its own—as if Zeus had nothing to do with the punishments he meted out upon me.

Don't blame me, his tone implied. *It's the lightning bolt that seared every molecule in your body.* Many years later, when I killed the Cyclopes who made Zeus's lightning, it was no rash decision. I'd always *hated* those lightning bolts. It was easier than hating my father.

Nero took the same tone when he referred to himself as the Beast. He spoke of his anger and cruelty as if they were forces outside his control. If he flew into a rage . . . well, then he would hold *Meg* responsible.

The realization sickened me. Meg had been trained to regard her kindly stepfather Nero and the terrifying Beast as two separate people. I understood now why she preferred to spend her time in the alleys of New York. I understood why she had such quick mood changes, going from cartwheels to full shutdown in a matter of seconds. She never knew what might unleash the Beast.

She fixed her eyes on me. Her lips quivered. I could tell she wanted a way out—some eloquent argument that would mollify her stepfather and allow her to follow her conscience. But I was no longer a silver-tongued god. I could not outtalk an orator like Nero. And I would not play the Beast's blame game.

Instead, I took a page from Meg's book, which was always short and to the point.

"He's evil," I said. "You're good. You must make your own choice."

I could tell that this was not the news Meg wanted. Her mouth tightened. She drew back her shoulder blades as if preparing for a measles shot—something painful but necessary. She placed her hand on the karpos's curly scalp. "Peaches," she said in a small but firm voice, "get the matchbox."

The karpos sprang into action. Nero barely had time to blink before Peaches ripped the box from his hand and jumped back to Meg's side.

The Germani readied their spears. Nero raised his hand for restraint. He gave Meg a look that might have been heartbreak—if he had possessed a heart.

"I see you weren't ready for this assignment, my dear," he said. "It's my fault. Vince, Gary, detain Meg but don't hurt her. When we get home . . ." He shrugged, his expression full of regret. "As for Apollo and the little fruit demon, they will have to burn."

"No," Meg croaked. Then, at full volume, she shouted, "NO!" And the Grove of Dodona shouted with her.

The blast was so powerful, it knocked Nero and his guards off their feet. Peaches screamed and beat his head against the dirt.

This time, however, I was more prepared. As the trees' ear-splitting chorus reached its crescendo, I anchored my mind with the catchiest tune I could imagine. I hummed "Y.M.C.A.," which I used to perform with the Village People in my construction worker costume until the Indian chief and I got in a fight over— Never mind. That's not important.

"Meg!" I pulled the brass wind chimes from my pocket and tossed them to her. "Put these on the center tree! Y.M.C.A. Focus the grove's energy! Y.M.C.A."

I wasn't sure she could hear me. She raised the chimes and watched as they swayed and clanked, turning the noise from the trees into snatches of coherent speech: *Happiness approaches. The fall of the sun; the final verse. Would you like to hear our specials today?*

Meg's face went slack with surprise. She turned toward the grove and sprinted through the gateway. Peaches crawled after her, shaking his head.

I wanted to follow, but I couldn't leave Nero and his guards alone with six hostages. Still humming "Y.M.C.A.," I marched toward them.

The trees screamed louder than ever, but Nero rose to his knees. He pulled something from his coat pocket—a vial of liquid—and splashed it on the ground in front of him. I doubted that was a good thing, but I had more immediate concerns. Vince and Gary were getting up. Vince thrust his spear in my direction.

I was angry enough to be reckless. I grabbed the point of his weapon and yanked the spear up, smacking Vince under his chin. He fell, stunned, and I grabbed fistfuls of his hide armor.

He was easily twice my size. I didn't care. I lifted him off his feet. My arms sizzled with power. I felt invincibly strong—the way a god *should* feel. I had no idea why my strength had returned, but I decided this was not the moment to question my good luck. I spun Vince like a discus, tossing him skyward with such force that he punched a Germanus-shaped hole in the tree canopy and sailed out of sight.

Kudos to the Imperial Guard for having stupid amounts of courage. Despite my show of force, Gary charged me. With one hand, I snapped his spear. With the other, I punched a fist straight through his shield and hit his chest with enough might to fell a rhinoceros.

He collapsed in a heap.

I faced Nero. I could already feel my strength ebbing. My muscles were returning to their pathetic mortal flabbiness. I just hoped I'd have enough time to rip off Nero's head and stuff it down his mauve suit.

The emperor snarled. "You're a fool, Apollo. You *always* focus on the wrong thing." He glanced at his Rolex. "My wrecking crew will be here any minute. Once Camp Half-Blood is destroyed, I'll make it my new front lawn! Meanwhile, you'll be here . . . putting out fires."

From his vest pocket, he produced a silver cigarette lighter. Typical of Nero to keep several forms of fire-making close at hand. I looked at the glistening streaks of oil he had splashed on the ground. . . . Greek fire, of course.

"Don't," I said.

Nero grinned. "Good-bye, Apollo. Only eleven more Olympians to go."

He dropped the lighter.

I did not have the pleasure of tearing Nero's head off.

Could I have stopped him from fleeing? Possibly. But the flames were roaring between us, burning grass and bones, tree roots, and the earth itself. The blaze was too strong to stamp out, if Greek fire even *could* be stamped out, and it was rolling hungrily toward the six bound hostages.

I let Nero go. Somehow he hauled Gary to his feet and lugged the punch-drunk Germanus toward the ants' nest. Meanwhile, I ran to the stakes.

The closest was Austin's. I wrapped my arms around the base and pulled, completely disregarding proper heavy-lifting techniques. My muscles strained. My vision swam with the effort. I managed to raise the stake enough to topple it backward. Austin stirred and groaned.

I dragged him, cocoon and all, to the other side of the clearing, as far from the fire as possible. I would have brought him into the Grove of Dodona, but I had a feeling I wouldn't be doing him any favors by putting him in a dead-end clearing full of insane voices, in the direct path of approaching flames.

I ran back to the stakes. I repeated the process—uprooting Kayla, then Paulie the geyser god, then the others. By the time I pulled Miranda Gardiner to safety, the fire was a raging red tidal wave, only inches from the gates of the grove.

My divine strength was gone. Meg and Peaches were nowhere to be seen. I had bought a few minutes for the hostages, but the fire would eventually consume us all. I fell to my knees and sobbed.

"Help." I scanned the dark trees, tangled and foreboding. I did not expect any help. I was not even used to *asking* for help. I was Apollo. Mortals called to *me*! (Yes, occasionally I might have ordered demigods to run trivial errands for me, like starting wars or retrieving magic items from monsters' lairs, but those requests didn't count.)

"I can't do this alone." I imagined Daphne's face floating beneath the trunk of one tree, then another. Soon the woods would burn. I couldn't save them any more than I could save Meg or the lost demigods or myself. "I'm so sorry. Please . . . forgive me."

My head must have been spinning from smoke inhalation. I began to hallucinate. The shimmering forms of dryads emerged from their trees—a legion of Daphnes in green gossamer dresses. Their expressions were melancholy, as if they knew they were going to their deaths, yet they circled the fire. They raised their arms, and the earth erupted at their feet. A torrent of mud churned over the flames. The dryads drew the fire's heat into their bodies. Their skin charred black. Their faces hardened and cracked.

As soon as the last flames were snuffed out, the dryads crumbled to ash. I wished I could crumble with them. I wanted to cry, but the fire had seared all the moisture from my tear ducts. I had not asked for so many sacrifices. I had not expected it! I felt hollow, guilty, and ashamed.

Then it occurred to me how many times I *had* asked for sacrifices, how many heroes I had sent to their deaths. Had they been any less noble and courageous than these dryads? Yet I had felt no remorse when I sent them off on deadly tasks. I had used them and discarded them, laid waste to their lives to build my own glory. I was no less of a monster than Nero.

Wind blew through the clearing—an unseasonably warm gust that swirled up the ashes and carried them through the forest canopy into the sky. Only after the breeze calmed did I realize it must have been the West Wind, my old rival, offering me consolation. He had swept up the remains and taken them off to their next beautiful reincarnation. After all these centuries, Zephyros had accepted my apology.

I discovered I had some tears left after all.

Behind me, someone groaned. "Where am I?"

Austin was awake.

I crawled to his side, now weeping with relief, and kissed his face. "My beautiful son!"

He blinked at me in confusion. His cornrows were sprinkled with ashes like frost on a field. I suppose it took a moment for him to process why he was being fawned over by a grungy, half-deranged boy with acne.

"Ah, right . . . Apollo." He tried to move. "What the—?

Why am I wrapped in smelly bandages? Could you free me, maybe?"

I laughed hysterically, which I doubt helped Austin's peace of mind. I clawed at his bindings but made no progress. Then I remembered Gary's snapped spear. I retrieved the point and spent several minutes sawing Austin free.

Once pulled from the stake, he stumbled around, trying to shake the circulation back into his limbs. He took in the scene—the smoldering forest, the other prisoners. The Grove of Dodona had stopped its wild chorus of screaming. (When had that happened?) A radiant amber light now glowed from the gateway.

"What's going on?" Austin asked. "Also, where is my saxophone?"

Sensible questions. I wished I had sensible answers. All I knew was that Meg McCaffrey was still wandering in the grove, and I did not like the fact that the trees had gone silent.

I stared at my weak mortal arms. I wondered why I'd experienced a sudden surge of divine strength when facing the Germani. Had my emotions triggered it? Was it the first sign of my godly vigor returning for good? Or perhaps Zeus was just messing with me again—giving me a taste of my old power before yanking it away once more. *Remember this, kid? WELL, YOU CAN'T HAVE IT!*

I wished I could summon that strength again, but I would have to make do.

I handed Austin the broken spear. "Free the others. I'll be back."

Austin stared at me incredulously. "You're going in *there*? Is it safe?"

"I doubt it," I said.

Then I ran toward the Oracle.

33

Parting is sorrow
Nothing about it is sweet
Don't step on my face

THE TREES WERE using their inside voices.

As I stepped through the gateway, I realized they were still talking in conversational tones, babbling nonsensically like sleepwalkers at a cocktail party.

I scanned the grove. No sign of Meg. I called her name. The trees responded by raising their voices, driving me cross-eyed with dizziness.

I steadied myself on the nearest oak.

"Watch it, man," the tree said.

I lurched forward, the trees trading bits of verse as if playing a game of rhymes:

> *Caves of blue.*
> *Strike the hue.*
> *Westward, burning.*
> *Pages turning.*
> *Indiana.*
> *Ripe banana.*
> *Happiness approaches.*
> *Serpents and roaches.*

None of it made sense, but each line carried the weight of prophecy. I felt as if dozens of important statements, each vital to my survival, were being blended together, loaded in a shotgun, and fired at my face.

(Oh, that's a rather good image. I'll have to use it in a haiku.)

"Meg!" I called again.

Still no reply. The grove did not seem so large. How could she not hear me? How could I not see her?

I slogged along, humming a perfect A 440 hertz tone to keep myself focused. When I reached the second ring of trees, the oaks became more conversational.

"Hey, buddy, got a quarter?" one asked.

Another tried to tell me a joke about a penguin and a nun walking into a Shake Shack.

A third oak was giving its neighbor an infomercial sales pitch about a food processor. "And you won't believe what it does with pasta!"

"Wow!" said the other tree. "It makes pasta, too?"

"Fresh linguine in minutes!" the sales oak enthused.

I did not understand why an oak tree would want linguine, but I kept moving. I was afraid that if I listened too long, I would order the food processor for three easy installments of $39.99, and my sanity would be lost forever.

Finally, I reached the center of the grove. On the far side of the largest oak tree, Meg stood with her back to the trunk, her eyes closed tight. The wind chimes were still in her hand, but they hung forgotten at her side. The brass cylinders clanked, muted against her dress.

At her feet, Peaches rocked back and forth, giggling. "Apples? Peaches! Mangoes? Peaches!"

"Meg." I touched her shoulder.

She flinched. She focused on me as if I were a clever optical illusion. Her eyes simmered with fear. "It's too much," she said. "Too much."

The voices had her in their grip. It was bad enough for me to endure—like a hundred radio stations playing at once, forcibly splitting my brain into different channels. But I was used to prophecies. Meg, on the other hand, was a daughter of Demeter. The trees liked her. They were all trying to share with her, to get her attention at the same time. Soon they would permanently fracture her mind.

"The wind chimes," I said. "Hang them in the tree!"

I pointed to the lowest branch, well above our heads. Alone, neither of us could reach it, but if I gave Meg a boost . . .

Meg backed away, shaking her head. The voices of Dodona were so chaotic I wasn't sure she had heard me. If she had, she either didn't understand or didn't trust me.

I had to tamp down my feelings of betrayal. Meg was Nero's stepdaughter. She had been sent to lure me here, and our whole friendship was a lie. She had no right to mistrust *me*.

But I could not stay bitter. If I blamed her for the way Nero had twisted her emotions, I was no better than the Beast. Also, just because she had lied about being my friend did not mean I wasn't hers. She was in danger. I was not going to leave her to the madness of the grove's penguin jokes.

I crouched and laced my fingers to make a foothold. "Please."

To my left, Peaches rolled onto his back and wailed, "Linguine? Peaches!"

Meg grimaced. I could see from her eyes that she was deciding to cooperate with me—not because she trusted me, but because Peaches was suffering.

Just when I thought my feelings could not be hurt any worse. It was one thing to be betrayed. It was another thing to be considered less important than a diapered fruit spirit.

Nevertheless, I remained steady as Meg placed her left foot in my hands. With all my remaining strength, I hoisted her up. She stepped onto my shoulders, then planted one red sneaker on top of my head. I made a mental note to put a safety label on my scalp: WARNING, TOP STEP IS NOT FOR STANDING.

With my back against the oak, I could feel the voices of the grove coursing up its trunk and drumming through its bark. The central tree seemed to be one giant antenna for crazy talk.

My knees were about to buckle. Meg's treads were grinding into my forehead. The A 440 I had been humming rapidly deflated to a G sharp.

Finally, Meg tied the wind chimes to the branch. She jumped down as my legs collapsed, and we both ended up sprawled in the dirt.

The brass chimes swayed and clanged, picking notes out of the wind and making chords from the dissonance.

The grove hushed, as if the trees were listening and thinking, *Oooh, pretty.*

Then the ground trembled. The central oak shook with such energy, it rained acorns.

Meg got to her feet. She approached the tree and touched its trunk.

"Speak," she commanded.

A single voice boomed forth from the wind chimes, like a cheerleader screaming through a megaphone:

> There once was a god named Apollo
> Who plunged in a cave blue and hollow
> Upon a three-seater
> The bronze fire-eater
> Was forced death and madness to swallow

The wind chimes stilled. The grove settled into tranquility, as if satisfied with the death sentence it had given me.

Oh, the horror!

A sonnet I could have handled. A quatrain would have been cause for celebration. But only the deadliest prophecies are couched in the form of a limerick.

I stared at the wind chimes, hoping they would speak again and correct themselves. *Oops, our mistake! That prophecy was for a different Apollo!*

But my luck was not that good. I had been handed an edict worse than a thousand advertisements for pasta makers.

Peaches rose. He shook his head and hissed at the oak tree, which expressed my own sentiments perfectly. He hugged Meg's calf as if she were the only thing keeping him from falling off the world. The scene was almost sweet, except for the karpos's fangs and glowing eyes.

Meg regarded me warily. The lenses of her glasses were spiderwebbed with cracks.

"That prophecy," she said. "Did you understand it?"

I swallowed a mouthful of soot. "Perhaps. Some of it. We'll need to talk to Rachel—"

"There's no more *we*." Meg's tone was as acrid as the volcanic gas of Delphi. "Do what you need to do. That's my final order."

This hit me like a spear shaft to the chin, despite the fact that she had lied to me and betrayed me.

"Meg, you can't." I couldn't keep the shakiness out of my voice. "You claimed my service. Until my trials are over—"

"I release you."

"No!" I could not stand the idea of being abandoned. Not again. Not by this ragamuffin Dumpster queen whom I'd learned to care about so much. "You can't *possibly* believe in Nero now. You heard him explain his plans. He means to level this entire island! You saw what he tried to do to his hostages."

"He—he wouldn't have let them burn. He promised. He held back. You saw it. That wasn't the Beast."

My rib cage felt like an over-tightened harp. "Meg . . . Nero *is* the Beast. He killed your father."

"No! Nero is my stepfather. My dad . . . my dad unleashed the Beast. He made it angry."

"Meg—"

"Stop!" She covered her ears. "You don't know him. Nero is good to me. I can talk to him. I can make it okay."

Her denial was so complete, so irrational, I realized there was no way I could argue with her. She reminded me painfully of myself when I fell to earth—how I had refused to accept my new reality. Without Meg's help, I would've gotten myself killed. Now our roles were reversed.

I edged toward her, but Peaches's snarl stopped me in my tracks.

Meg backed away. "We're done."

"We can't be," I said. "We're bound, whether you like it or not."

It occurred to me that she'd said the exact same thing to me only a few days before.

She gave me one last look through her cracked lenses. I would have given anything for her to blow a raspberry. I wanted to walk the streets of Manhattan with her doing cartwheels in the intersections. I missed hobbling with her through the Labyrinth, our legs tied together. I would've settled for a good garbage fight in an alley. Instead, she turned and fled, with Peaches at her heels. It seemed to me that they dissolved into the trees, just the way Daphne had done long ago.

Above my head, a breeze made the wind chimes jingle. This time, no voices came from the trees. I didn't know how long Dodona would remain silent, but I didn't want to be here if the oaks decided to start telling jokes again.

I turned and saw something strange at my feet: an arrow with an oak shaft and green fletching.

There shouldn't have been an arrow. I hadn't brought any into the grove. But in my dazed state, I didn't question this. I did what any archer would do: I retrieved it, and returned it to my quiver.

34

Uber's got nothing
Lyft is weak. And taxis? Nah
My ride is da mom

AUSTIN HAD FREED THE OTHER PRISONERS.

They looked like they had been dipped in a vat of glue and cotton swabs, but otherwise they seemed remarkably undamaged. Ellis Wakefield staggered around with his fists clenched, looking for something to punch. Cecil Markowitz, son of Hermes, sat on the ground trying to clean his sneakers with a deer's thighbone. Austin—resourceful boy!—had produced a canteen of water and was washing the Greek fire off of Kayla's face. Miranda Gardiner, the head counselor of Demeter, knelt by the place where the dryads had sacrificed themselves. She wept silently.

Paulie the palikos floated toward me. Like his partner, Pete, his lower half was all steam. From the waist up he looked like a slimmer, more abused version of his geyser buddy. His mud skin was cracked like a parched riverbed. His face was withered, as if every bit of moisture had been squeezed out of him. Looking at the damage Nero had done to him, I added a few more items to a mental list I was preparing: *Ways to Torture an Emperor in the Fields of Punishment.*

"You saved me," Paulie said with amazement. "Bring it in!"

He threw his arms around me. His power was so diminished that his body heat did not kill me, but it did open up my sinuses quite well.

"You should get home," I said. "Pete is worried, and you need to regain your strength."

"Ah, man . . ." Paulie wiped a steaming tear from his face. "Yeah, I'm gone. But anything you ever need—a free steam cleaning, some PR work, a mud scrub, you name it."

As he dissolved into mist, I called after him. "And Paulie? I'd give the Woods at Camp Half-Blood a ten for customer satisfaction."

Paulie beamed with gratitude. He tried to hug me again, but he was already ninety percent steam. All I got was a humid waft of mud-scented air. Then he was gone.

The five demigods gathered around me.

Miranda looked past me at the Grove of Dodona. Her eyes were still puffy from crying, but she had beautiful irises the color of new foliage. "So, the voices I heard from that grove . . . It's really an Oracle? Those trees can give us prophecies?"

I shivered, thinking of the oak trees' limerick. "Perhaps."

"Can I see—?"

"No," I said. "Not until we understand the place better."

I had already lost one daughter of Demeter today. I didn't intend to lose another.

"I don't get it," Ellis grumbled. "You're Apollo? Like, *the* Apollo."

"I'm afraid so. It's a long story."

"Oh, gods . . ." Kayla scanned the clearing. "I thought I heard Meg's voice earlier. Did I dream that? Was she with you? Is she okay?"

The others looked at me for an explanation. Their expressions were so fragile and tentative, I decided I couldn't break down in front of them.

"She's . . . alive," I managed. "She had to leave."

"*What?*" Kayla asked. "Why?"

"Nero," I said. "She . . . she went after Nero."

"Hold up." Austin raised his fingers like goalposts. "When you say Nero . . ."

I did my best to explain how the mad emperor had captured them. They deserved to know. As I recounted the story, Nero's words kept replaying in my mind: My *wrecking crew will be here any minute. Once Camp Half-Blood is destroyed, I'll make it my new front lawn!*

I wanted to think this was just bluster. Nero had always loved threats and grandiose statements. Unlike me, he was a terrible poet. He used flowery language like . . . well, like every sentence was a pungent bouquet of metaphors. (Oh, that's another good one. Jotting that down.)

Why had he kept checking his watch? And what wrecking crew could he have been talking about? I had a flashback to my dream of the sun bus careening toward a giant bronze face.

I felt like I was free-falling again. Nero's plan became horribly clear. After dividing the few demigods defending the camp, he had meant to burn this grove. But that was only part of his attack. . . .

"Oh, gods," I said. "The Colossus."

The five demigods shifted uneasily.

"What Colossus?" Kayla asked. "You mean the Colossus of Rhodes?"

"No," I said. "The Colossus Neronis."

Cecil scratched his head. "The Colossus Neurotic?"

Ellis Wakefield snorted. "*You're* a Colossus Neurotic, Markowitz. Apollo's talking about the big replica of Nero that stood outside the amphitheater in Rome, right?"

"I'm afraid so," I said. "While we're standing here, Nero is going to try to destroy Camp Half-Blood. And the Colossus will be his wrecking crew."

Miranda flinched. "You mean a giant statue is about to stomp on *camp*? I thought the Colossus was destroyed centuries ago."

Ellis frowned. "Supposedly, so was the Athena Parthenos. Now it's sitting on top of Half-Blood Hill."

The others' expressions turned grim. When a child of Ares makes a valid point, you know the situation is serious.

"Speaking of Athena . . ." Austin picked some incendiary fluff off his shoulder. "Won't the statue protect us? I mean, that's what she's there for, right?"

"She will try," I guessed. "But you must understand, the Athena Parthenos draws her power from her followers. The more demigods under her care, the more formidable her magic. And right now—"

"The camp is practically empty," Miranda finished.

"Not only that," I said, "but the Athena Parthenos is roughly forty feet tall. If memory serves, Nero's Colossus was more than twice that."

Ellis grunted. "So they're not in the same weight class. It's an uneven match."

Cecil Markowitz stood a little straighter. "Guys . . . did you feel that?"

I thought he might be playing one of his Hermes pranks. Then the ground shook again, ever so slightly. From somewhere in the distance came a rumbling sound like a battleship scraping over a sandbar.

"Please tell me that was thunder," Kayla said.

Ellis cocked his head, listening. "It's a war machine. A big automaton wading ashore about half a klick from here. We need to get to camp right now."

No one argued with Ellis's assessment. I supposed he could distinguish between the sounds of war machines the same way I could pick out an off-tune violin in a Rachmaninoff symphony.

To their credit, the demigods rose to the challenge. Despite the fact that they'd been recently bound, doused in flammable substances, and staked like human tiki torches, they closed ranks and faced me with determination in their eyes.

"How do we get out of here?" Austin asked. "The myrmekes' lair?"

I felt suddenly suffocated, partly because I had five people looking at me as if I knew what to do. I didn't. In fact, if you want to know a secret, we gods usually don't. When confronted for answers, we usually say something Rhea-like: *You will have to find out for yourself!* Or *True wisdom must be earned!* But I didn't think that would fly in this situation.

Also, I had no desire to plunge back into the ants' nest.

Even if we made it through alive, it would take much too long. Then we would have to run perhaps half the length of the forest.

I stared at the Vince-shaped hole in the canopy. "I don't suppose any of you can fly?"

They shook their heads.

"I can cook," Cecil offered.

Ellis smacked him on the shoulder.

I looked back at the myrmekes' tunnel. The solution came to me like a voice whispering in my ear: *You know someone who can fly, stupid.*

It was a risky idea. Then again, rushing off to fight a giant automaton was also not the safest plan of action.

"I think there's a way," I said. "But I'll need your help."

Austin balled his fists. "Anything you need. We're ready to fight."

"Actually . . . I don't need you to fight. I need you to lay down a beat."

My next important discovery: Children of Hermes cannot rap. At all.

Bless his conniving little heart, Cecil Markowitz tried his best, but he kept throwing off my rhythm section with his spastic clapping and terrible air mic noises. After a few trial runs, I demoted him to dancer. His job would be to shimmy back and forth and wave his hands, which he did with the enthusiasm of a tent-revival preacher.

The others managed to keep up. They still looked like half-plucked, highly combustible chickens, but they bopped with the proper amount of soul.

I launched into "Dear Mama," my throat reinforced with water and cough drops from Kayla's belt pack. (Ingenious girl! Who brings cough drops on a three-legged death race?)

I sang directly into the mouth of the myrmekes' tunnel, trusting the acoustics to carry my message. We did not have to wait long. The earth began to rumble beneath our feet. I kept singing. I had warned my comrades not to stop laying down the righteous beat until the song was over.

Still, I almost lost it when the ground exploded. I had been watching the tunnel, but Mama did not use tunnels. She exited wherever she wanted—in this case, straight out of the earth twenty yards away, spraying dirt, grass, and small boulders in all directions. She scuttled forward, mandibles clacking, wings buzzing, dark Teflon eyes focused on me. Her abdomen was no longer swollen, so I assumed she had finished depositing her most recent batch of killer-ant larvae. I hoped this meant she would be in a good mood, not a hungry mood.

Behind her, two winged soldiers clambered out of the earth. I had not been expecting bonus ants. (Really, *bonus ants* is not a term most people would like to hear.) They flanked the queen, their antennae quivering.

I finished my ode, then dropped to one knee, spreading my arms as I had before.

"Mama," I said, "we need a ride."

My logic was this: Mothers were used to giving rides. With thousands upon thousands of offspring, I assumed the queen ant would be the ultimate soccer mom. And indeed, Mama grabbed me with her mandibles and tossed me over her head.

Despite what the demigods may tell you, I did not flail, scream, or land in a way that damaged my sensitive parts. I landed heroically, straddling the queen's neck, which was no larger than the back of an average warhorse. I shouted to my comrades, "Join me! It's perfectly safe!"

For some reason, they hesitated. The ants did not. The queen tossed Kayla just behind me. The soldier ants followed Mama's lead—snapping up two demigods each and throwing them aboard.

The three myrmekes revved their wings with a noise like radiator fan blades. Kayla grabbed my waist.

"Is this *really* safe?" she yelled.

"Perfectly!" I hoped I was right. "Perhaps even safer than the sun chariot!"

"Didn't the sun chariot almost destroy the world once?"

"Well, twice," I said. "Three times, if you count the day I let Thalia Grace drive, but—"

"Forget I asked!"

Mama launched herself into the sky. The canopy of twisted branches blocked our path, but Mama didn't pay any more attention to them than she had to the ton of solid earth she'd plowed through.

I yelled, "Duck!"

We flattened ourselves against Mama's armored head as she smashed through the trees, leaving a thousand wooden splinters embedded in my back. It felt so good to fly again, I didn't care. We soared above the woods and banked to the east.

For two or three seconds, I was exhilarated.

Then I heard the screaming from Camp Half-Blood.

35

Buck-naked statue
A Neurotic Colossus
Where art thy undies?

EVEN MY SUPERNATURAL POWERS of description fail me.

Imagine seeing yourself as a hundred-foot-tall bronze statue—a replica of your own magnificence, gleaming in the late afternoon light.

Now imagine that this ridiculously handsome statue is wading out of Long Island Sound onto the North Shore. In his hand is a ship's rudder—a blade the size of a stealth bomber, fixed to a fifty-foot-long pole—and Mr. Gorgeous is raising said rudder to smash the crud out of Camp Half-Blood.

This was the sight that greeted us as we flew in from the woods.

"How is that thing *alive?*" Kayla demanded. "What did Nero do—order it online?"

"The Triumvirate has vast resources," I told her. "They've had centuries to prepare. Once they reconstructed the statue, all they had to do was fill it with some animating magic—usually the harnessed life forces of wind or water spirits. I'm not sure. That's really more of Hephaestus's specialty."

"So how do we kill it?"

"I'm . . . I'm working on that."

All across the valley, campers screamed and ran for their weapons. Nico and Will were floundering in the lake, apparently having been capsized in the middle of a canoe ride. Chiron galloped through the dunes, harrying the Colossus with his arrows. Even by my standards, Chiron was a very fine archer. He targeted the statue's joints and seams, yet his shots did not seem to bother the automaton at all. Already dozens of missiles stuck from the Colossus's armpits and neck like unruly hair.

"More quivers!" Chiron shouted. "Quickly!"

Rachel Dare stumbled from the armory carrying half a dozen, and she ran to resupply him.

The Colossus brought down his rudder to smash the dining pavilion, but his blade bounced off the camp's magical barrier, sparking as if it had hit solid metal. Mr. Gorgeous took another step inland, but the barrier resisted him, pushing him back with the force of a wind tunnel.

On Half-Blood Hill, a silver aura surrounded the Athena Parthenos. I wasn't sure the demigods could see it, but every so often a beam of ultraviolet light shot from Athena's helmet like a search lamp, hitting the Colossus's chest and pushing back the invader. Next to her, in the tall pine tree, the Golden Fleece blazed with fiery energy. The dragon Peleus hissed and paced around the trunk, ready to defend his turf.

These were powerful forces, but I did not need godly sight to tell me that they would soon fail. The camp's defensive barriers were designed to turn away the occasional stray monster, to confuse mortals and prevent them from detecting the valley, and to provide a first line of defense against invading forces. A criminally beautiful hundred-foot-tall Celestial bronze giant was another thing entirely. Soon the Colossus would break through and destroy everything in its path.

"Apollo!" Kayla nudged me in the ribs. "What do we do?"

I stirred, again with the unpleasant realization that I was expected to have answers. My first instinct was to order a seasoned demigod to take charge. Wasn't it the weekend yet? Where was Percy Jackson? Or those Roman praetors Frank Zhang and Reyna Ramírez-Arellano? Yes, they would have done nicely.

My second instinct was to turn to Meg McCaffrey. How quickly I had grown used to her annoying yet strangely endearing presence! Alas, she was gone. Her absence felt like a Colossus stomping upon my heart. (This was an easy metaphor to summon, since the Colossus was presently stomping on a great many things.)

Flanking us on either side, the soldier ants flew in formation, awaiting the queen's orders. The demigods watched me anxiously, random bits of bandage fluff swirling from their bodies as we sped through the air.

I leaned forward and spoke to Mama in a soothing tone. "I know I cannot ask you to risk your life for us."

Mama hummed as if to say, *You're darn right!*

"Just give us one pass around that statue's head?" I asked. "Enough to distract it. Then set us down on the beach?"

She clicked her mandibles doubtfully.

"You're the best mama in the whole world," I added, "and you look lovely today."

That line always worked with Leto. It did the trick with Mama Ant, too. She twitched her antennae, perhaps sending a high-frequency signal to her soldiers, and all three ants banked hard to the right.

Below us, more campers joined the battle. Sherman Yang had harnessed two pegasi to a chariot and was now circling the statue's legs, while Julia and Alice threw electric javelins at the Colossus's knees. The missiles stuck in his joints, discharging tendrils of blue lightning, but the statue barely seemed to notice. Meanwhile, at his feet, Connor Stoll and Harley used twin flamethrowers to give the Colossus a molten pedicure, while the Nike twins manned a catapult, lobbing boulders at the Colossus's Celestial bronze crotch.

Malcolm Pace, a true child of Athena, was coordinating the attacks from a hastily organized command post on the green. He and Nyssa had spread war maps across a card table and were shouting targeting coordinates, while Chiara, Damien, Paolo, and Billie rushed to set up ballistae around the communal hearth.

Malcolm looked like the perfect battlefield commander, except for the fact that he'd forgotten his pants. His red briefs made quite a statement with his sword and leather cuirass.

Mama dove toward the Colossus, leaving my stomach at a higher altitude.

I had a moment to appreciate the statue's regal features, its metal brow rimmed with a spiky crown meant to represent the beams of the sun. The Colossus was supposed to be Nero as the sun god, but the emperor had wisely made the face resemble mine more closely than his. Only the line of its nose and its ghastly neck beard suggested Nero's trademark ugliness.

Also . . . did I mention that the hundred-foot statue was entirely nude? Well, of course it was. Gods are almost always depicted as nude, because we are flawless beings. Why would you cover up perfection? Still, it was a little disconcerting to see my buck-naked self stomping around, slamming a ship's rudder at Camp Half-Blood.

As we approached the Colossus, I bellowed loudly, "IMPOSTOR! I AM THE REAL APOLLO! YOU'RE UGLY!"

Oh, dear reader, it was hard to yell such words at my own handsome visage, but I did. Such was my courage.

The Colossus did not like being insulted. As Mama and her soldiers veered away, the statue swung its rudder upward.

Have you ever collided with a bomber? I had a sudden flashback to Dresden in 1945, when the planes were so thick in the air, I literally could not find a safe lane to drive in. The axle on the sun chariot was out of alignment for *weeks* after that.

I realized the ants were not fast enough fliers to escape the rudder's reach. I saw catastrophe approaching in slow motion. At the last possible moment, I yelled, "Dive!"

We plunged straight down. The rudder only clipped the ants' wings—but it was enough to send us spiraling toward the beach.

I was grateful for soft sand.

I ate quite a bit of it when we crash-landed.

By sheer luck, none of us died, though Kayla and Austin had to pull me to my feet.

"Are you okay?" Austin asked.

"Fine," I said. "We must hurry."

The Colossus stared down at us, perhaps trying to discern whether we were dying in agony yet or needed some additional pain. I had wanted to get his attention, and I had succeeded. Huzzah.

I glanced at Mama and her soldiers, who were shaking the sand off their carapaces. "Thank you. Now save yourselves. Fly!"

They did not need to be told twice. I suppose ants have a natural fear of large humanoids looming over them, about to squash them with a heavy foot. Mama and her guards buzzed into the sky.

Miranda looked after them. "I never thought I'd say this about bugs, but I'm going to miss those guys."

"Hey!" called Nico di Angelo. He and Will scrambled over the dunes, still dripping from their swim in the canoe lake.

"What's the plan?" Will seemed calm, but I knew him well enough by now to tell that inside he was as charged as a bare electrical wire.

BOOM.

The statue strode toward us. One more step, and it would be on top of us.

"Isn't there a control valve on its ankle?" Ellis asked. "If we can open it—"

"No," I said. "You're thinking of Talos. This is not Talos."

Nico brushed his dark wet hair from his forehead. "Then what?"

I had a lovely view of the Colossus's nose. Its nostrils were sealed with bronze . . . I supposed because Nero hadn't wanted his detractors trying to shoot arrows into his imperial noggin.

I yelped.

Kayla grabbed my arm. "Apollo, what's wrong?"

Arrows into the Colossus's head. Oh, gods, I had an idea that would never, ever work. However, it seemed better than our other option, which was to be crushed under a two-ton bronze foot.

"Will, Kayla, Austin," I said, "come with me."

"And Nico," said Nico. "I have a doctor's note."

"Fine!" I said. "Ellis, Cecil, Miranda—do whatever you can to keep the Colossus's attention."

The shadow of an enormous foot darkened the sand.

"Now!" I yelled. "Scatter!"

36

I love me some plague
When it's on the right arrow
Ka-bam! You dead, bro?

SCATTERING WAS THE EASY PART. They did that very well.

Miranda, Cecil, and Ellis ran in different directions, screaming insults at the Colossus and waving their arms. This bought the rest of us a few seconds as we sprinted for the dunes, but I suspected the Colossus would soon enough come after me. I was, after all, the most important and attractive target.

I pointed toward Sherman Yang's chariot, which was still circling the statue's legs in a vain attempt to electro-cute its kneecaps. "We need to commandeer that chariot!"

"How?" Kayla asked.

I was about to admit I had no idea when Nico di Angelo grabbed Will's hand and stepped into my shadow. Both boys evaporated. I had forgotten about the power of shadow-traveling—the way children of the Underworld could step into one shadow and appear from another, sometimes hun-dreds of miles away. Hades used to love sneaking up on me that way and yelling, "HI!" just as I shot an arrow of death.

He found it amusing if I missed my target and accidentally wiped out the wrong city.

Austin shuddered. "I hate it when Nico disappears like that. What's our plan?"

"You two are my backup," I said. "If I miss, if I die . . . it will be up to you."

"Whoa, whoa," Kayla said. "What do you mean *if you miss?*"

I drew my last arrow—the one I'd found in the grove. "I'm going to shoot that gorgeous gargantuan in the ear."

Austin and Kayla exchanged looks, perhaps wondering if I'd finally cracked under the strain of being mortal.

"A plague arrow," I explained. "I'm going to enchant an arrow with sickness, then shoot it into the statue's ear. Its head is hollow. The ears are the only openings. The arrow should release enough disease to kill the Colossus's animating power . . . or at least to disable it."

"How do you know it will work?" Kayla asked.

"I don't, but—"

Our conversation was ruined by a sudden heavy downpour of Colossus foot. We darted inland, barely avoiding being flattened.

Behind us, Miranda shouted, "Hey, ugly!"

I knew she wasn't talking to me, but I glanced back anyway. She raised her arms, causing ropes of sea grass to spring from the dunes and wrap around the statue's ankles. The Colossus broke through them easily, but they annoyed him enough to be a distraction. Watching Miranda face the statue made me heartsick for Meg all over again.

Meanwhile, Ellis and Cecil stood on either side of the Colossus, throwing rocks at his shins. From the camp, a volley of flaming ballista projectiles exploded against Mr. Gorgeous's naked backside, which made me clench in sympathy.

"You were saying?" Austin asked.

"Right." I twirled the arrow between my fingers. "I know what you're thinking. I don't have godly powers. It's doubtful I'll be able to cook up the Black Death or the Spanish Flu. But still, if I can make the shot from close range, straight into its head, I might be able to do some damage."

"And . . . if you fail?" Kayla asked. I noticed her quiver was also empty.

"I won't have the strength to try twice. You'll have to make another pass. Find an arrow, try to summon some sickness, make the shot while Austin holds the chariot steady."

I realized this was an impossible request, but they accepted it with grim silence. I wasn't sure whether to feel grateful or guilty. Back when I was a god, I would've taken it for granted that mortals had faith in me. Now . . . I was asking my children to risk their lives again, and I was not at all sure my plan would work.

I caught a flash of movement in the sky. This time, instead of a Colossus foot, it was Sherman Yang's chariot, minus Sherman Yang. Will brought the pegasi in for a landing, then dragged out a half-conscious Nico di Angelo.

"Where are the others?" Kayla asked. "Sherman and the Hermes girls?"

Will rolled his eyes. "Nico convinced them to disembark."

As if on cue, I heard Sherman screaming from somewhere far in the distance, "I'll get you, di Angelo!"

"You guys go," Will told me. "The chariot is only designed for three, and after that shadow-travel, Nico is going to pass out any second."

"No, I'm not," Nico complained, then passed out.

Will caught him in a fireman's carry and took him away. "Good luck! I'm going to get the Lord of Darkness here some Gatorade!"

Austin hopped in first and took the reins. As soon as Kayla and I were aboard, we shot skyward, the pegasi swerving and banking around the Colossus with expert skill. I began to feel a glimmer of hope. We might be able to outmaneuver this giant hunk of good-looking bronze.

"Now," I said, "if I can just enchant this arrow with a nice plague."

The arrow shuddered from its fletching to its point.

THOU SHALT NOT, it told me.

I try to avoid weapons that talk. I find them rude and distracting. Once, Artemis had a bow that could cuss like a Phoenician sailor. Another time, in a Stockholm tavern, I met this god who was smoking hot, except his talking sword just would *not* shut up.

But I digress.

I asked the obvious question. "Did you just speak to me?"

THE HIDDEN ORACLE 325

The arrow quivered. (Oh, dear. That was a horrible pun. My apologies.) *YEA, VERILY. PRITHEE, SHOOTING IS NOT MY PURPOSE.*

His voice was definitely male, sonorous and grave, like a bad Shakespearean actor's.

"But you're an arrow," I said. "Shooting you is the whole point." (Ah, I really must watch those puns.)

"Guys, hang on!" Austin shouted.

The chariot plunged to avoid the Colossus's swinging rudder. Without Austin's warning, I would have been left in midair still arguing with my projectile.

"So you're made from Dodona oak," I guessed. "Is that why you talk?"

FORSOOTH, said the arrow.

"Apollo!" Kayla said. "I'm not sure why you're talking to that arrow, but—"

From our right came a reverberating *WHANG!* like a snapped power line hitting a metal roof. In a flash of silver light, the camp's magical barriers collapsed. The Colossus lurched forward and brought his foot down on the dining pavilion, smashing it to rubble like so many children's blocks.

"But that just happened," Kayla said with a sigh.

The Colossus raised his rudder in triumph. He marched inland, ignoring the campers who were running around his feet. Valentina Diaz launched a ballista missile into his groin. (Again, I had to wince in sympathy.) Harley and Connor Stoll kept blowtorching his feet, to no effect. Nyssa, Malcolm, and Chiron hastily ran a trip line of steel cable across the statue's path, but they would never have time to anchor it properly.

I turned to Kayla. "You can't hear this arrow talking?"

Judging from her wide eyes, I guessed the answer was, *No, and does hallucinating run in the family?*

"Never mind." I looked at the arrow. "What would you suggest, O Wise Missile of Dodona? My quiver is empty."

The arrow's point dipped toward the statue's left arm. *LO, THE ARMPIT DOTH HOLD THE ARROWS THOU NEEDEST!*

Kayla yelled, "Colossus is heading for the cabins!"

"Armpit!" I told Austin. "Flieth—er, fly for the armpit!"

That wasn't an order one heard much in combat, but Austin spurred the pegasi into a steep ascent. We buzzed the forest of arrows sticking out of the Colossus's arm seam, but I completely overestimated my mortal hand-eye coordination. I lunged for the shafts and came up empty.

Kayla was more agile. She snagged a fistful but screamed when she yanked them free.

I pulled her to safety. Her hand was bleeding badly, cut from the high-speed grab.

"I'm fine!" Kayla yelped. Her fingers were clenched, splattering drops of red all over the chariot's floor. "Take the arrows."

I did. I tugged the Brazilian-flag bandana from around my neck and gave it to her. "Bind your hand," I ordered. "There's some ambrosia in my coat pocket."

"Don't worry about me." Kayla's face was as green as her hair. "Make the shot! Hurry!"

I inspected the arrows. My heart sank. Only one of the missiles was unbroken, and its shaft was warped. It would be almost impossible to shoot.

I looked again at the talking arrow.

THOU SHALT NOT THINKEST ABOUT IT, he intoned. ENCHANT THOU THE WARPED ARROW!

I tried. I opened my mouth, but the proper words of enchantment were gone from my mind. As I feared, Lester Papadopoulos simply did not possess the power. "I can't!"

I SHALT ASSIST, promised the Arrow of Dodona. STARTEST THOU: "PLAGUEY, PLAGUEY, PLAGUEY."

"The enchantment does not start plaguey, plaguey, plaguey!"

"Who are you talking to?" Austin demanded.

"My arrow! I—I need more time."

"We don't have more time!" Kayla pointed with her wrapped bloody hand.

The Colossus was only a few steps away from the central green. I wasn't sure the demigods even realized how much danger they were in. The Colossus could do much more than just flatten buildings. If he destroyed the central hearth, the sacred shrine of Hestia, he would extinguish the very soul of the camp. The valley would be cursed and uninhabitable for generations. Camp Half-Blood would cease to exist.

I realized I had failed. My plan would take much too long, if I could even remember how to make a plague arrow. This was my punishment for breaking an oath on the River Styx.

Then, from somewhere above us, a voice yelled, "Hey, Bronze Butt!"

Over the Colossus's head, a cloud of darkness formed like a cartoon dialogue bubble. Out of the shadows dropped a furry black monster dog—a hellhound—and astride his back was a young man with a glowing bronze sword.

The weekend was here. Percy Jackson had arrived.

37

Hey, look! It's Percy
Least he could do was help out
Taught him everything

I WAS TOO SURPRISED TO SPEAK. Otherwise I would have warned Percy what was about to happen.

Hellhounds are not fond of heights. When startled, they respond in a predictable way. The moment Percy's faithful pet landed on top of the moving Colossus, she yelped and proceeded to wee-wee on said Colossus's head. The statue froze and looked up, no doubt wondering what was trickling down his imperial sideburns.

Percy leaped heroically from his mount and slipped in hellhound pee. He nearly slid off the statue's brow. "What the—Mrs. O'Leary, jeez!"

The hellhound bayed in apology. Austin flew our chariot to within shouting distance. "Percy!"

The son of Poseidon frowned across at us. "All right, who unleashed the giant bronze guy? Apollo, did you do this?"

"I am offended!" I cried. "I am only indirectly responsible for this! Also, I have a plan to fix it."

"Oh, yeah?" Percy glanced back at the destroyed dining pavilion. "How's that going?"

With my usual levelheadedness, I stayed focused on the greater good. "If you could please just keep this Colossus from stomping the camp's hearth, that would be helpful. I need a few more minutes to enchant this arrow."

I held up the talking arrow by mistake, then held up the bent arrow.

Percy sighed. "Of course you do."

Mrs. O'Leary barked in alarm. The Colossus was raising his hand to swat the trespassing tinkler.

Percy grabbed one of the crown's sunray spikes. He sliced it off at the base, then jabbed it into the Colossus's forehead. I doubted the Colossus could feel pain, but it staggered, apparently surprised to suddenly have grown a unicorn horn.

Percy sliced off another one. "Hey, ugly!" he called down. "You don't need all these pointy things, do you? I'm going to take one to the beach. Mrs. O'Leary, fetch!"

Percy tossed the spike like a javelin.

The hellhound barked excitedly. She leaped off the Colossus's head, vaporized into shadow, and reappeared on the ground, bounding after her new bronze stick.

Percy raised his eyebrows at me. "Well? Start enchanting!"

He jumped from the statue's head to its shoulder. Then he leaped to the shaft of the rudder and slid down it like a fire pole all the way to the ground. If I had been at my usual level of godly athletic skill, I could've done something like that in my sleep, of course, but I had to admit Percy Jackson was moderately impressive.

"Hey, Bronze Butt!" he yelled again. "Come get me!"

The Colossus obliged, slowly turning and following Percy toward the beach.

I began to chant, invoking my old powers as the god of plagues. This time, the words came to me. I didn't know why. Perhaps Percy's arrival had given me new faith. Perhaps I simply didn't think about it too much. I've found that thinking often interferes with doing. It's one of those lessons that gods learn early in their careers.

I felt an itchy sensation of sickness curling from my fingers and into the projectile. I spoke of my own awesomeness and the various horrible diseases I had visited upon wicked populations in the past, because . . . well, I'm awesome. I could feel the magic taking hold, despite the Arrow of Dodona whispering to me like an annoying Elizabethan stagehand, SAYEST THOU: "PLAGUEY, PLAGUEY, PLAGUEY!"

Below, more demigods joined the parade to the beach. They ran ahead of the Colossus, jeering at him, throwing things, and calling him Bronze Butt. They made jokes about his new horn. They laughed at the hellhound pee trickling down his face. Normally I have zero tolerance for bullying, especially when the victim looks like me, but since the Colossus was ten stories tall and destroying their camp, I suppose the campers' rudeness was understandable.

I finished chanting. Odious green mist now wreathed the arrow. It smelled faintly of fast-food deep fryers—a good sign that it carried some sort of horrible malady.

"I'm ready!" I told Austin. "Get me next to its ear!"

"You got it!" Austin turned to say something else, and a wisp of green fog passed under his nose. His eyes watered. His nose swelled and began to run. He scrunched up his face and sneezed so hard he collapsed. He lay on the floor of the chariot, groaning and twitching.

"My boy!" I wanted to grab his shoulders and check on him, but since I had an arrow in each hand, that was inadvisable.

FIE! TOO STRONG IS THY PLAGUE. The Dodona arrow hummed with annoyance. *THY CHANTING SUCKETH.*

"Oh, no, no, no," I said. "Kayla, be careful. Don't breathe—"

"ACHOO!" Kayla crumpled next to her brother.

"What have I done?" I wailed.

METHINKS THOU HAST BLOWN IT, said the Dodona arrow, my source of infinite wisdom. *MOREO'ER, HIE! TAKEST THOU THE REINS.*

"Why?"

You would think a god who drove a chariot on a daily basis would not need to ask such a question. In my defense, I was distraught about my children lying half-conscious at my feet. I didn't consider that no one was driving. Without anyone at the reins, the pegasi panicked. To avoid running into the huge bronze Colossus directly in their path, they dove toward the earth.

Somehow, I managed to react appropriately. (Three cheers for reacting appropriately!) I thrust both arrows into my quiver, grabbed the reins, and was able to level our descent just enough to prevent a crash landing. We bounced off a dune and swerved to a stop in front of Chiron and a group of demigods. Our entrance might have looked dramatic if the centrifugal force hadn't thrown Kayla, Austin, and me from the chariot.

Did I mention I was grateful for soft sand?

The pegasi took off, dragging the battered chariot into the sky and leaving us stranded.

Chiron galloped to our side, a cluster of demigods in his wake. Percy Jackson ran toward us from the surf while Mrs. O'Leary kept the Colossus occupied with a game of keep-away. I doubt that would hold the statue's interest very long, once he realized there was a group of targets right behind him, just perfect for stomping.

"The plague arrow is ready!" I announced. "We need to shoot it into the Colossus's ear!"

My audience did not seem to take this as good news. Then I realized my chariot was gone. My bow was still in the chariot. And Kayla and Austin were quite obviously infected with whatever disease I had conjured up.

"Are they contagious?" Cecil asked.

"No!" I said. "Well . . . probably not. It's the fumes from the arrow—"

Everyone backed away from me.

"Cecil," Chiron said, "you and Harley take Kayla and Austin to the Apollo cabin for healing."

"But they *are* the Apollo cabin," Harley complained. "Besides, my flamethrower—"

"You can play with your flamethrower later," Chiron

promised. "Run along. There's a good boy. The rest of you, do what you can to keep the Colossus at the water's edge. Percy and I will assist Apollo."

Chiron said the word *assist* as if it meant *slap upside the head with extreme prejudice.*

Once the crowd had dispersed, Chiron gave me his bow. "Make the shot."

I stared at the massive composite recursive, which probably had a draw weight of a hundred pounds. "This is meant for the strength of a centaur, not a teen mortal!"

"You created the arrow," he said. "Only you can shoot it without succumbing to the disease. Only you can hit such a target."

"From *here*? It's impossible! Where is that flying boy, Jason Grace?"

Percy wiped the sweat and sand from his neck. "We're fresh out of flying boys. And all the pegasi have stampeded."

"Perhaps if we got some harpies and some kite string . . ." I said.

"Apollo," Chiron said, "you must do this. You are the lord of archery and illness."

"I'm not lord of anything!" I wailed. "I'm a stupid ugly mortal teenager! I'm *nobody*!"

The self-pity just came pouring out. I thought for sure the earth would split in two when I called myself a *nobody*. The cosmos would stop turning. Percy and Chiron would rush to reassure me.

None of that happened. Percy and Chiron just stared at me grimly.

Percy put his hand on my shoulder. "You're Apollo. We

need you. You can do this. Besides, if you don't, I will personally throw you off the top of the Empire State Building."

This was exactly the pep talk I needed—just the sort of thing Zeus used to say to me before my soccer matches. I squared my shoulders. "Right."

"We'll try to draw him into the water," Percy said. "I've got the advantage there. Good luck."

Percy accepted Chiron's hand and leaped onto the centaur's back. Together they galloped into the surf, Percy waving his sword and calling out various bronze-butt-themed insults to the Colossus.

I ran down the beach until I had a line of sight on the statue's left ear.

Looking up at that regal profile, I did not see Nero. I saw myself—a monument to my own conceit. Nero's pride was no more than a reflection of mine. I was the bigger fool. I was exactly the sort of person who would construct a hundred-foot-tall naked statue of myself in my front yard.

I pulled the plague arrow from my quiver and nocked it in the bowstring.

The demigods were getting very good at scattering. They continued to harry the Colossus from both sides while Percy and Chiron galloped through the tide, Mrs. O'Leary romping at their heels with her new bronze stick.

"Yo, ugly!" Percy shouted. "Over here!"

The Colossus's next step displaced several tons of salt water and made a crater large enough to swallow a pickup truck.

The Arrow of Dodona rattled in my quiver. *RELEASE THY BREATH,* he advised. *DROPETH THY SHOULDER.*

"I *have* shot a bow before," I grumbled.

MINDETH THY RIGHT ELBOW, the arrow said.

"Shut up."

AND TELLEST NOT THINE ARROW TO SHUT UP.

I drew the bow. My muscles burned as if boiling water was being poured over my shoulders. The plague arrow did not make me pass out, but its fumes were disorienting. The warp of the shaft made my calculations impossible. The wind was against me. The arc of the shot would be much too high.

Yet I aimed, exhaled, and released the bowstring.

The arrow twirled as it rocketed upward, losing force and drifting too far to the right. My heart sank. Surely the curse of the River Styx would deny me any chance at success.

Just as the projectile reached its apex and was about to fall back to earth, a gust of wind caught it . . . perhaps Zephyros looking kindly on my pitiful attempt. The arrow sailed into the Colossus's ear canal and rattled in his head with a *clink, clink, clink* like a pachinko machine.

The Colossus halted. He stared at the horizon as if confused. He looked at the sky, then arched his back and lurched forward, making a sound like a tornado ripping off the roof of a warehouse. Because his face had no other open orifices, the pressure of his sneeze forced geysers of motor oil out his ears, spraying the dunes with environmentally unfriendly sludge.

Sherman, Julia, and Alice stumbled over to me, covered head to toe with sand and oil.

"I appreciate you freeing Miranda and Ellis," Sherman snarled, "but I'm going to kill you later for taking my chariot. What did you do to that Colossus? What kind of plague makes you sneeze?"

"I'm afraid I—I summoned a rather benign illness. I believe I have given the Colossus a case of hay fever."

You know that horrible pause when you're waiting for someone to sneeze? The statue arched his back again, and everyone on the beach cringed in anticipation. The Colossus inhaled several cubic acres of air through his ear canals, preparing for his next blast.

I imagined the nightmare scenarios: The Colossus would ear-sneeze Percy Jackson into Connecticut, never to be seen again. The Colossus would clear his head and then stomp all of us flat. Hay fever could make a person cranky. I knew this because I *invented* hay fever. Still, I had never intended it to be a killing affliction. I certainly never anticipated facing the wrath of a towering metal automaton with extreme seasonal allergies. I cursed my shortsightedness! I cursed my mortality!

What I had *not* considered was the damage our demigods had already done to the Colossus's metal joints—in particular, his neck.

The Colossus rocked forward with a mighty *CHOOOOO!* I flinched and almost missed the moment of truth when the statue's head achieved first-stage separation from his body. It hurtled over Long Island Sound, the face

spinning in and out of view. It hit the water with a mighty
WHOOSH and bobbed for a moment. Then the air *blooped*
out of its neck hole and the gorgeous regal visage of yours
truly sank beneath the waves.

The statue's decapitated body tilted and swayed. If it
had fallen backward, it might have crushed even more of
the camp. Instead, it toppled forward. Percy yelped a curse
that would have made any Phoenician sailor proud. Chiron
and he raced sideways to avoid being crushed while Mrs.
O'Leary wisely dissolved into shadows. The Colossus hit
the water, sending forty-foot tidal waves to port and starboard. I had never before seen a centaur hang hooves on a
tubular crest, but Chiron acquitted himself well.

The roar of the statue's fall finally stopped echoing off
the hills.

Next to me, Alice Miyazawa whistled. "Well, that
de-escalated quickly."

Sherman Yang asked in a voice of childlike wonder:
"What the Hades just happened?"

"I believe," I said, "the Colossus sneezed his head off."

38

After the sneezing
Healing peeps, parsing limericks
Worst God Award? Me

THE PLAGUE SPREAD.

That was the price of our victory: a massive outbreak of hay fever. By nightfall, most of the campers were dizzy, groggy, and heavily congested, though I was pleased that none of them sneezed their heads off, because we were running low on bandages and duct tape.

Will Solace and I spent the evening caring for the wounded. Will took the lead, which was fine with me; I was exhausted. Mostly I splinted arms, distributed cold medicine and tissues, and tried to keep Harley from stealing the infirmary's entire supply of smiley-face stickers, which he plastered all over his flamethrower. I was grateful for the distraction, since it kept me from thinking too much about the day's painful events.

Sherman Yang graciously agreed not to kill Nico for tossing him out of his chariot, or me for damaging it, though I had the feeling the son of Ares was keeping his options open for later.

Chiron provided healing poultices for the most extreme cases of hay fever. This included Chiara Benvenuti, whose good luck had, for once, abandoned her. Strangely enough, Damien White got sick right after he learned that Chiara was sick. The two had cots next to each other in the infirmary, which I found a little suspicious, even though they kept sniping at each other whenever they knew they were being watched.

Percy Jackson spent several hours recruiting whales and hippocampi to help him haul away the Colossus. He decided it would be easiest to tow it underwater to Poseidon's palace, where it could be repurposed as garden statuary. I was not sure how I felt about that. I imagined Poseidon would replace the statue's gorgeous face with his own weathered, bearded mien. Still, I wanted the Colossus gone, and I doubted it would have fit in the camp's recycling bins.

Thanks to Will's healing and a hot dinner, the demigods I had rescued from the woods quickly got back to full strength. (Paolo claimed it was because he waved a Brazilian-flag bandana over them, and I was not about to argue.)

As for the camp itself, the damage might have been much worse. The canoe dock could be rebuilt. The Colossus's footstep craters could be repurposed as convenient foxholes or koi ponds.

The dining pavilion was a total loss, but Nyssa and Harley were confident that Annabeth Chase could redesign the place next time she was here. With luck, it would be rebuilt in time for the summer.

The only other major damage was to the Demeter cabin. I had not realized it during the battle, but the Colossus had managed to step on it before turning around for the beach.

In retrospect, its path of destruction appeared almost purposeful, as if the automaton had waded ashore, stomped Cabin Four, and headed back out to sea.

Given what had happened with Meg McCaffrey, I had a hard time not seeing this as a bad omen. Miranda Gardiner and Billie Ng were given temporary bunks in the Hermes cabin, but for a long time that night they sat stunned among the smashed ruins as daisies popped up all around them from the cold winter ground.

Despite my exhaustion, I slept fitfully. I did not mind Kayla and Austin's constant sneezing, or Will's gentle snoring. I did not even mind the hyacinths blooming on the windowsill, filling the room with their melancholy perfume. But I could not stop thinking of the dryads raising their arms to the flames in the woods, and about Nero, and Meg. The Arrow of Dodona stayed silent, hanging in my quiver on the wall, but I suspected it would have more annoying Shakespearean advice soon. I did not relish what it might telleth me about my future.

At sunrise, I rose quietly, took my bow and quiver and combat ukulele, and hiked to the summit of Half-Blood Hill. The guardian dragon, Peleus, did not recognize me. When I came too close to the Golden Fleece, he hissed, so I had to sit some distance away at the foot of the Athena Parthenos.

I didn't mind not being recognized. At the moment, I did not *want* to be Apollo. All the destruction I saw below me . . . it was my fault. I had been blind and complacent. I had allowed the emperors of Rome, including one of my own descendants, to rise to power in the shadows. I had let my once-great network of Oracles collapse until even Delphi was lost. I had almost caused the death of Camp Half-Blood itself.

And Meg McCaffrey . . . Oh, Meg, where were you?

Do what you need to do, she had told me. *That's my final order.*

Her order had been vague enough to allow me to pursue her. After all, we were bound together now. What I *needed to do* was to find her. I wondered if Meg had phrased her order that way on purpose, or if that was just wishful thinking on my part.

I gazed up at the serene alabaster face of Athena. In real life, she didn't look so pale and aloof—well, not most of the time, anyway. I pondered why the sculptor, Phidias, had chosen to make her look so unapproachable, and whether Athena approved. We gods often debated how much humans could change our very nature simply by the way they pictured us or imagined us. During the eighteenth century, for instance, I could not escape the white powdered wig, no matter how hard I tried. Among immortals, our reliance on humans was an uncomfortable subject.

Perhaps I deserved my present form. After my carelessness and foolishness, perhaps humanity *should* see me as nothing but Lester Papadopoulos.

I heaved a sigh. "Athena, what would you do in my place? Something wise and practical, I suppose."

Athena offered no response. She stared calmly at the horizon, taking the long view, as always.

I didn't need the wisdom goddess to tell me what I must do. I should leave Camp Half-Blood immediately, before the campers woke. They had taken me in to protect me, and I had nearly gotten them all killed. I couldn't bear to endanger them any longer.

But, oh, how I wanted to stay with Will, Kayla, Austin—my mortal children. I wanted to help Harley put smiley faces on his flamethrower. I wanted to flirt with Chiara and steal her away from Damien . . . or perhaps steal Damien away from Chiara, I wasn't sure yet. I wanted to improve my music and archery through that strange activity known as *practice*. I wanted to have a home.

Leave, I told myself. *Hurry*.

Because I was a coward, I waited too long. Below me, the cabin lights flickered on. Campers emerged from their doorways. Sherman Yang began his morning stretches. Harley jogged around the green, holding his Leo Valdez beacon high with the hope it would finally work.

At last, a pair of familiar figures spotted me. They approached from different directions—the Big House and Cabin Three—hiking up the hill to see me: Rachel Dare and Percy Jackson.

"I know what you're thinking," Rachel said. "Don't do it."

I feigned surprise. "Can you read my mind, Miss Dare?"

"I don't need to. I know you, Lord Apollo."

A week ago, the idea would have made me laugh. A mortal could not *know* me. I had lived for four millennia. Merely looking upon my true form would have vaporized any human. Now, though, Rachel's words seemed perfectly reasonable. With Lester Papadopoulos, what you saw was what you got. There really wasn't much to know.

"Don't call me *Lord*," I sighed. "I am just a mortal teen. I do not belong at this camp."

Percy sat next to me. He squinted at the sunrise, the sea breeze tousling his hair. "Yeah, I used to think I didn't belong here either."

"It's not the same," I said. "You humans change and grow and mature. Gods do not."

Percy faced me. "You sure about that? You seem pretty different."

I think he meant that as a compliment, but I didn't find his words reassuring. If I was becoming more fully human, that was hardly a cause for celebration. True, I had mustered a few godly powers at important moments—a burst of divine strength against the Germani, a hay fever arrow against the Colossus—but I could not rely on those abilities. I didn't even understand how I had summoned them. The fact that I had limits, and that I couldn't be sure where those limits *were* . . . Well, that made me feel much more like Lester Papadopoulos than Apollo.

"The other Oracles must be found and secured," I said. "I cannot do that unless I leave Camp Half-Blood. And I cannot risk anyone else's life."

Rachel sat on my other side. "You sound certain. Did you get a prophecy from the grove?"

I shuddered. "I fear so."

Rachel cupped her hands on her knees. "Kayla said you

were talking to an arrow yesterday. I'm guessing it's wood from Dodona?"

"Wait," Percy said. "You found a talking arrow that gave you a prophecy?"

"Don't be silly," I said. "The arrow talks, but I got the prophecy from the grove itself. The Arrow of Dodona just gives random advice. He's quite annoying."

The arrow buzzed in my quiver.

"At any rate," I continued, "I must leave the camp. The Triumvirate means to possess all the ancient Oracles. I have to stop them. Once I have defeated the former emperors . . . only then will I be able to face my old enemy Python and free the Oracle of Delphi. After that . . . if I survive . . . perhaps Zeus will restore me to Olympus."

Rachel tugged at a strand of her hair. "You know it's too dangerous to do all that alone, right?"

"Listen to her," Percy urged. "Chiron told me about Nero and this weird holding company of his."

"I appreciate the offer of assistance, but—"

"Whoa." Percy held up his hands. "Just to be clear, I'm not offering to go with you. I still have to finish my senior year, pass my DSTOMP and my SAT, and avoid getting killed by my girlfriend. But I'm sure we can get you some other helpers."

"I'll go," Rachel said.

I shook my head. "My enemies would *love* to capture someone as dear to me as the priestess of Delphi. Besides, I need you and Miranda Gardiner to stay here and study the Grove of Dodona. For now, it is our only source of prophecy. And since our communication problems have not gone away, learning to use the grove's power is all the more critical."

Rachel tried to hide it, but I could see her disappointment in the lines around her mouth. "What about Meg?" she asked. "You'll try to find her, won't you?"

She might as well have plunged the Arrow of Dodona into my chest. I gazed at the woods—that hazy green expanse that had swallowed young McCaffrey. For a brief moment, I felt like Nero. I wanted to burn the whole place down.

"I will try," I said, "but Meg doesn't want to be found. She's under the influence of her stepfather."

Percy traced his finger across the Athena Parthenos's big toe. "I've lost too many people to bad influence: Ethan Nakamura, Luke Castellan . . . We almost lost Nico, too. . . ." He shook his head. "No. No more. You can't give up on Meg. You guys are bound together. Besides, she's one of the good guys."

"I've known many of the good guys," I said. "Most of them got turned into beasts, or statues, or—or trees. . . ." My voice broke.

Rachel put her hand over mine. "Things can turn out differently, Apollo. That's the nice thing about being human. We only have one life, but we can choose what kind of story it's going to be."

That seemed hopelessly optimistic. I had spent too many centuries watching the same patterns of behavior be repeated over and over, all by humans who thought they were being terribly clever and doing something that had never been done before. They thought they were crafting

THE HIDDEN ORACLE 347

their own stories, but they were only tracing over the same old narratives, generation after generation.

Still . . . perhaps human persistence was an asset. They never seemed to give up hope. Every so often they *did* manage to surprise me. I never anticipated Alexander the Great, Robin Hood, or Billie Holiday. For that matter, I never anticipated Percy Jackson and Rachel Elizabeth Dare.

"I—I hope you're right," I said.

She patted my hand. "Tell me the prophecy you heard in the grove."

I took a shaky breath. I didn't want to speak the words. I was afraid they might wake the grove and drown us in a cacophony of prophecies, bad jokes, and infomercials. But I recited the lines:

> *"There once was a god named Apollo*
> *Who plunged in a cave blue and hollow*
> *Upon a three-seater*
> *The bronze fire-eater*
> *Was forced death and madness to swallow."*

Rachel covered her mouth. "A limerick?"

"I know!" I wailed. "I'm doomed!"

"Wait." Percy's eyes glittered. "Those lines . . . Do they mean what I think?"

"Well," I said, "I believe the blue cave refers to the Oracle of Trophonius. It was a . . . a very dangerous ancient Oracle."

"No," Percy said. "The *other* lines. *Three-seater, bronze fire-eater*, yadda yadda."

"Oh. I have no clue about those."

"Harley's beacon." Percy laughed, though I could not understand why he was so pleased. "He said you gave it a tuning adjustment? I guess that did the trick."

Rachel squinted at him. "Percy, what are you . . ." Her expression went slack. "Oh. *Oh*."

"Were there any other lines?" Percy urged. "Like, except for the limerick?"

"Several," I admitted. "Just bits and pieces I didn't understand. *The fall of the sun; the final verse.* Um, *Indiana, banana. Happiness approaches.* Something about *pages burning*."

Percy slapped his knee. "There you go. *Happiness approaches.* Happy is a name—well, the English version, anyway." He stood and scanned the horizon. His eyes fixed on something in the distance. A grin spread across his face. "Yep. Apollo, your escort is on the way."

I followed his gaze. Spiraling down from the clouds was a large winged creature that glinted of Celestial bronze. On its back were two human-size figures.

Their descent was silent, but in my mind a joyous fanfare of Valdezinator music proclaimed the good news.

Leo had returned.

39

Want to hit Leo?
That is understandable
Hunk Muffin earned it

THE DEMIGODS HAD TO TAKE NUMBERS.

Nico commandeered a dispenser from the snack bar and carried it around, yelling, "The line starts to the left! Orderly queue, guys!"

"Is this really necessary?" Leo asked.

"Yes," said Miranda Gardiner, who had drawn the first number. She punched Leo in the arm.

"Ow," said Leo.

"You're a jerk, and we all hate you," said Miranda. Then she hugged him and kissed his cheek. "If you ever disappear like that again, we'll line up to *kill you*."

"Okay, okay!"

Miranda had to move on, because the line was getting pretty long behind her. Percy and I sat at the picnic table with Leo and his companion—none other than the immortal sorceress Calypso. Even though Leo was the one getting punched by everyone in camp, I was reasonably sure he was the *least* uncomfortable one at the table.

When they first saw each other, Percy and Calypso had hugged awkwardly. I hadn't witnessed such a tense greeting since Patroclus met Achilles's war prize, Briseis. (Long story. Juicy gossip. Ask me later.) Calypso had never liked me, so she pointedly ignored me, but I kept waiting for her to yell "BOO!" and turn me into a tree frog. The suspense was killing me.

Percy hugged Leo and didn't even punch him. Still, the son of Poseidon looked disgruntled.

"I can't believe it," he said. "Six months—"

"I told you," Leo said. "We tried sending more holographic scrolls. We tried Iris messages, dream visions, phone calls. Nothing worked.— Ow! Hey, Alice, how you doing?— Anyway, we ran into one crisis after another."

Calypso nodded. "Albania was particularly difficult."

From down the line, Nico di Angelo yelled, "Please do not mention Albania! Okay, who's next, folks? One line."

Damien White punched Leo's arm and walked away grinning. I wasn't sure Damien even knew Leo. He simply couldn't turn down a chance to punch someone.

Leo rubbed his bicep. "Hey, no fair. That guy's getting back in the line. So, like I was saying, if Festus hadn't picked up on that homing beacon yesterday, we'd still be flying around, looking for a way out of the Sea of Monsters."

"Oh, I hate that place," Percy said. "There's this big Cyclops, Polyphemus—"

"I know, right?" Leo agreed. "What is up with that guy's *breath?*"

"Boys," Calypso said, "perhaps we should focus on the present?"

She did not look at me, but I got the impression she meant *this silly former god and his problems*.

"Yeah," Percy said. "So the communication issues . . . Rachel Dare thinks it's got something to do with this company, Triumvirate."

Rachel herself had gone to the Big House to fetch Chiron, but Percy did a reasonable job summarizing what she had found out about the emperors and their evil corporation. Of course, we didn't know very much. By the time six more people had punched Leo in the arm, Percy had brought Leo and Calypso up to speed.

Leo rubbed his new bruises. "Man, why does it not surprise me that modern corporations are run by zombie Roman emperors?"

"They are not zombies," I said. "And I'm not sure they run *all* corporations—"

Leo waved away my explanation. "But they're trying to take over the Oracles."

"Yes," I agreed.

"And that's bad."

"Very."

"So you need our help.— Ow! Hey, Sherman. Where'd you get the new scar, dude?"

While Sherman told Leo the story of Crotchkicker McCaffrey and the Demon Peach Baby, I glanced at Calypso.

She looked very different from what I remembered. Her hair was still long and caramel brown. Her almond-shaped eyes were still dark and intelligent. But now, instead of a *chiton* she wore modern jeans, a white blouse, and a shocking-pink ski jacket. She looked younger—about my mortal age. I wondered if she had been punished with mortality for leaving her enchanted island. If so, it didn't seem fair that she had retained her otherworldly beauty. She had neither flab nor acne.

As I watched, she stretched two fingers toward the opposite end of the picnic table, where a pitcher of lemonade sweated in the sunlight. I had seen her do this sort of thing before, willing her invisible aerial servants to whisk objects into her hands. This time, nothing happened.

A look of disappointment crossed her face. Then she realized I was watching. Her cheeks colored.

"Since leaving Ogygia, I have no powers," she admitted. "I am fully mortal. I keep hoping, but—"

"You want a drink?" Percy asked.

"I got it." Leo beat him to the pitcher.

I had not expected to feel sympathy for Calypso. We'd had harsh words in the past. A few millennia ago, I had opposed her petition for early release from Ogygia because of some . . . ah, drama between us. (Long story. Juicy gossip. Please *do not* ask me later.)

Still, as a fallen god, I understood how disconcerting it was to be without one's powers.

On the other hand, I was relieved. This meant she could not turn me into a tree frog or order her aerial servants to toss me off the Athena Parthenos.

"Here you go." Leo handed her a glass of lemonade. His expression seemed darker and more anxious, as if . . . Ah, of course. Leo had rescued Calypso from her prison island. In doing so, Calypso had lost her powers. Leo felt responsible.

Calypso smiled, though her eyes were still touched by melancholy. "Thank you, babe."

"*Babe?*" Percy asked.

Leo's expression brightened. "Yeah. She won't call me Hunk Muffin, though. I dunno why.— Ow!"

It was Harley's turn. The little boy punched Leo, then threw his arms around him and broke down sobbing.

"Hey, brother." Leo ruffled his hair and had the good sense to look ashamed. "You brought me home with that beacon of yours, H-Meister. You're a hero! You know I never would've left you hanging like that on purpose, don't you?"

Harley wailed and sniffled and nodded. Then he punched Leo again and ran away. Leo looked like he was about to get sick. Harley was quite strong.

"At any rate," Calypso said, "these problems with the Roman emperors—how can we help?"

I raised my eyebrows. "You *will* help me, then? Despite . . . ah, well, I always knew you were kindhearted and forgiving, Calypso. I meant to visit you at Ogygia more often—"

"Spare me." Calypso sipped her lemonade. "I'll help you if *Leo* decides to help you, and he seems to have some affection for you. Why, I can't imagine."

I let go of the breath I had been holding for . . . oh, an hour. "I'm grateful. Leo Valdez, you have always been a gentleman and a genius. After all, you created the Valdezinator."

Leo grinned. "I did, didn't I? I suppose that was pretty awesome. So where is this next Oracle you— Ow!"

Nyssa had made it to the front of the line. She slapped Leo, then berated him in rapid Spanish.

"Yeah, okay, okay." Leo rubbed his face. "Dang, *hermana*, I love you, too!"

He turned his attention back to me. "So this next Oracle, you said it was where?"

Percy tapped the picnic table. "Chiron and I were talking about this. He figures this triumvirate thingie . . . they probably divided America into three parts, with one emperor in charge of each. We know Nero is holed up in New York, so we're guessing this next Oracle is in the second dude's territory, maybe in the middle third of the U.S."

"Oh, the middle third of the U.S.!" Leo spread his arms. "Piece of torta, then. We'll just search the entire middle of the country!"

"Still with the sarcasm," Percy noted.

"Hey, man, I've sailed with the most sarcastic scalawags on the high seas."

The two gave each other a high five, though I did not quite understand why. I thought about a snippet of prophecy I'd heard in the grove: something about Indiana. It might be a place to start. . . .

The last person to come through the line was Chiron himself, pushed in his wheelchair by Rachel Dare. The old centaur gave Leo a warm, fatherly smile. "My boy, I am so pleased to have you back. And you freed Calypso, I see. Well done, and welcome, both of you!" Chiron spread his arms for a hug.

"Uh, thanks, Chiron." Leo leaned forward.

From underneath Chiron's lap blanket, his equine foreleg shot out and implanted a hoof in Leo's gut. Then, just as quickly, the leg disappeared. "Mr. Valdez," Chiron said in the same kindly tone, "if you ever pull a stunt like that again—"

"I got it, I got it!" Leo rubbed his stomach. "Dang, for a teacher, you got a heck of a high kick."

Rachel grinned and wheeled Chiron away. Calypso and Percy helped Leo to his feet.

"Yo, Nico," Leo called, "please tell me that's it for the physical abuse."

"For now." Nico smiled. "We're still trying to get in touch with the West Coast. You'll have a few dozen people out there who will definitely want to hit you."

Leo winced. "Yeah, that's something to look forward to. Well, I guess I'd better keep my strength up. Where do you guys eat lunch now that the Colossus stepped on the dining pavilion?"

Percy left that night just before dinner.

I expected a moving one-on-one farewell, during which he would ask my advice about test taking, being a hero, and living life in general. After he lent me his help in defeating the Colossus, it would have been the least I could do.

Instead, he seemed more interested in saying good-bye to Leo and Calypso. I wasn't part of their conversation, but the three of them seemed to reach some sort of mutual understanding. Percy and Leo embraced. Calypso even pecked Percy on the cheek. Then the son of Poseidon waded into Long Island Sound with his extremely large dog and they both disappeared underwater. Did Mrs. O'Leary swim? Did she travel through the shadows of whales? I did not know.

Like lunch, dinner was a casual affair. As darkness fell, we ate on picnic blankets around the hearth, which blazed with Hestia's warmth and kept away the winter chill. Festus the dragon sniffed around the perimeter of the cabins, occasionally blowing fire into the sky for no apparent reason.

"He got a little dinged up in Corsica," Leo explained. "Sometimes he spews randomly like that."

"He hasn't blowtorched anyone important yet," Calypso added, her eyebrow arched. "We'll see how he likes you."

Festus's red jewel eyes gleamed in the darkness. After driving the sun chariot for so long, I wasn't nervous about riding a metal dragon, but when I thought about what we'd be riding *toward*, geraniums bloomed in my stomach.

"I had planned to go alone," I told them. "The prophecy from Dodona speaks of the bronze fire-eater, but . . . it feels wrong for me to ask you to risk your lives. You have been through so much just to get here."

Calypso tilted her head. "Perhaps you *have* changed. That does not sound like the Apollo I remember. You definitely are not as handsome."

"I am still *quite* handsome," I protested. "I just need to clear up this acne."

She smirked. "So you haven't completely lost your big head."

"I beg your pardon?"

"Guys," Leo interrupted, "if we're going to travel together, let's try to keep it friendly." He pressed an ice pack to his bruised bicep. "Besides, we were planning to head west anyway. I got to find my peeps Jason and Piper and Frank and Hazel and . . . well, pretty much everybody at Camp Jupiter, I guess. It'll be fun."

"*Fun?*" I asked. "The Oracle of Trophonius will supposedly swallow me in death and madness. Even if I survive that, my other trials will no doubt be long, harrowing, and quite possibly fatal."

"Exactly," Leo said. "Fun. I don't know about calling the whole quest thing *Apollo's trials*, though. I think we should call it *Leo Valdez's Victory Lap World Tour*."

Calypso laughed and laced her fingers in Leo's. She may not have been immortal anymore, but she still had a grace and easiness about her that I could not fathom. Perhaps she missed her powers, but she seemed genuinely happy to be with Valdez—to be young and mortal, even if it meant she could die at any moment.

Unlike me, she had *chosen* to become mortal. She knew that leaving Ogygia was a risk, but she had done it willingly. I didn't know how she'd found the courage.

"Hey, man," Leo told me. "Don't look so glum. We'll find her."

I stirred. "What?"

"Your friend Meg. We'll find her. Don't worry."

A bubble of darkness burst inside me. For once, I hadn't been thinking of Meg. I'd been thinking about myself, and that made me feel guilty. Perhaps Calypso was right to question whether or not I'd changed.

I gazed at the silent forest. I remembered Meg dragging me to safety when I was cold and soaked and delirious. I remembered how fearlessly she fought the myrmekes, and how she'd ordered Peaches to extinguish the match when Nero wanted to burn his hostages, despite her fear of unleashing the Beast. I had to make her realize how evil Nero was. I had to find her. But how?

"Meg knows the prophecy," I said. "If she tells Nero, he will know our plans as well."

Calypso took a bite of her apple. "I missed the whole Roman Empire. How bad can one emperor be?"

"Bad," I assured her. "And he is allied with two others. We don't know which ones, but it's safe to assume they are equally cutthroat. They've had centuries to amass fortunes, acquire property, build armies . . . Who knows what they are capable of?"

"Eh," Leo said. "We took down Gaea in, like, forty seconds. This'll be easy squeezy."

I seemed to recall that the *lead-up* to the fight with Gaea had involved months of suffering and near misses with death. Leo, in fact, *had* died. I also wanted to remind him that the Triumvirate might well have orchestrated all our previous troubles with the Titans and giants, which would make them more powerful than anything Leo had ever faced.

I decided that mentioning these things might affect group morale.

"We'll succeed," Calypso said. "We must. So we will. I have been trapped on an island for thousands of years. I don't know how long this mortal life will be, but I intend to live fully and without fear."

"That's my *mamacita*," Leo said.

"What have I told you about calling me *mamacita*?"

Leo grinned sheepishly. "In the morning we'll start getting our supplies together. As soon as Festus gets a tune-up and an oil change, we'll be good to go."

I considered what supplies I would take with me. I had

depressingly little: some borrowed clothes, a bow, a ukulele, and an overly theatrical arrow.

But the real difficulty would be saying good-bye to Will, Austin, and Kayla. They had helped me so much, and they embraced me as family more than I had ever embraced *them*. Tears stung my eyes. Before I could start sobbing, Will Solace stepped into the light of the hearth. "Hey, everybody! We've started a bonfire in the amphitheater! Sing-along time. Come on!"

Groans were mixed in with the cheers, but most everyone got to their feet and ambled toward the bonfire now blazing in the distance, where Nico di Angelo stood silhouetted in the flames, preparing rows of marshmallows on what looked like femur bones.

"Aw, man." Leo winced. "I'm terrible at sing-alongs. I always clap and do the 'Old MacDonald' sounds at the wrong time. Can we skip this?"

"Oh, no." I rose to my feet, suddenly feeling better. Perhaps tomorrow I would weep and think about good-byes. Perhaps the day after that we would be flying toward our deaths. But tonight, I intended to enjoy my time with my family. What had Calypso said? *Live fully and without fear.* If she could do it, then so could the brilliant, fabulous Apollo. "Singing is good for the spirits. You should never miss an opportunity to sing."

Calypso smiled. "I can't believe I'm saying this, but for once I agree with Apollo. Come on, Leo. I'll teach you to harmonize."

Together, the three of us walked toward the sounds of laughter, music, and a warm, crackling fire.

GUIDE TO APOLLO-SPEAK

Achilles the best fighter of the Greeks who besieged Troy in the Trojan War; extraordinarily strong, courageous, and loyal, he had only one weak spot: his heel

Admetus the king of Pherae in Thessaly; Zeus punished Apollo by sending him to work for Admetus as a shepherd

Aeolus the Greek god of the winds

Agamemnon king of Mycenae; the leader of the Greeks in the Trojan War; courageous, but also arrogant and overly proud

agora Greek for *gathering place*; a central outdoor spot for athletic, artistic, spiritual, and political life in ancient Greek city-states

Ajax Greek hero with great strength and courage; fought in the Trojan War; used a large shield in battle

ambrosia food of the gods; has healing powers

amphitheater an oval or circular open-air space used for performances or sporting events, with spectator seating built in a semicircle around the stage

Aphrodite   the Greek goddess of love and beauty

apodesmos   a band of material that women in ancient Greece wore around the chest, particularly while participating in sports

Apollo   the Greek god of the sun, prophecy, music, and healing; the son of Zeus and Leto, and the twin of Artemis

Ares   the Greek god of war; the son of Zeus and Hera, and half brother to Athena

Argo   the ship used by a band of heroes who accompanied Jason on his quest to find the Golden Fleece

Argonauts   a band of heroes who sailed with Jason on the *Argo*, in search of the Golden Fleece

Artemis   the Greek goddess of the hunt and the moon; the daughter of Zeus and Leto, and the twin of Apollo

Asclepius   the god of medicine; son of Apollo; his temple was the healing center of ancient Greece

Athena   the Greek goddess of wisdom

Athena Parthenos   a giant statue of Athena; the most famous Greek statue of all time

ballista (**ballistae**, pl.)   a Roman missile siege weapon that launched a large projectile at a distant target

Batavi   an ancient tribe that lived in modern-day Germany; also an infantry unit in the Roman army with Germanic origins

Briseis   a princess captured by Achilles during the Trojan War, causing a feud between Achilles and Agamemnon that resulted in Achilles refusing to fight alongside the Greeks

Bunker Nine   a hidden workshop Leo Valdez discovered at Camp Half-Blood, filled with tools and weapons; it is at least two hundred years old and was used during the Demigod Civil War

Caesar Augustus   the founder and first emperor of the Roman Empire; adopted son and heir of Julius Caesar (*see also* Octavian)

Calliope   the muse of epic poetry; mother of several sons, including Orpheus

Calypso   the goddess nymph of the mythical island of Ogygia; a daughter of the Titan Atlas; she detained the hero Odysseus for many years

Camp Half-Blood   the training ground for Greek demigods, located in Long Island, New York

Camp Jupiter   the training ground for Roman demigods, located between the Oakland Hills and the Berkeley Hills, in California

Cassandra   the daughter of King Priam and Queen Hecuba; had the gift of prophecy, but was cursed by Apollo so that her predictions were never believed, including her warning about the Trojan Horse

catapult   a military machine used to hurl objects

Cave of Trophonius   a deep chasm home to the Oracle Trophonius; its extremely narrow entrance required a visitor to lie flat on his back before being sucked into the cave; called "The Cave of Nightmares" due to the terrifying accounts of its visitors

Celestial bronze   a rare metal deadly to monsters

centaur   a race of creatures that is half-human, half-horse

Ceres the Roman god of agriculture; Greek form: Demeter

Chiron a centaur; the camp activities director at Camp Half-Blood

chiton a Greek garment; a sleeveless piece of linen or wool secured at the shoulders by brooches and at the waist by a belt

Chrysothemis a daughter of Demeter who won Apollo's love during a music contest

Circe a Greek goddess of magic

Cloacina goddess of the Roman sewer system

Clytemnestra the daughter of the king and queen of Sparta; married and later murdered Agamemnon

Colosseum an elliptical amphitheater in the center of Rome, Italy, capable of seating fifty thousand spectators; used for gladiatorial contests and public spectacles such as mock sea battles, animal hunts, executions, reenactments of famous battles, and dramas

Colossus Neronis (Colossus of Nero) a gigantic bronze statue of Emperor Nero; was later transformed into the sun god with the addition of a sunray crown

Cretan of the island of Crete

Crommyon a village in ancient Greece where a giant wild sow wreaked havoc before it was killed by Theseus

cuirass leather or metal armor consisting of a breastplate and backplate worn by Greek and Roman soldiers; often highly ornamented and designed to mimic muscles

Cyclops (Cyclopes, pl.) a member of a primordial race of giants, each with a single eye in the middle of his or her forehead

Cyrene   a fierce huntress with whom Apollo fell in love
after he saw her wrestle a lion; Apollo later transformed
her into a nymph in order to extend her life

Daedalus   a skilled craftsman who created the Labyrinth
on Crete in which the Minotaur (part man, part bull)
was kept

Daphne   a beautiful naiad who attracted Apollo's attention; she was transformed into a laurel tree in order to
escape him

Demeter   the Greek goddess of agriculture; a daughter of
the Titans Rhea and Kronos; Roman form: Ceres

dimachaerus   a Roman gladiator trained to fight with two
swords at once

Dionysus   the Greek god of wine and revelry; the son of
Zeus; activities director at Camp Half-Blood

Domus Aurea   Emperor Nero's extravagant villa in the
heart of ancient Rome, built after the Great Fire of Rome

Doors of Death   the doorway to the House of Hades,
located in Tartarus; doors have two sides—one in the
mortal world, and one in the Underworld

drakon   a gigantic yellow-and-green serpentlike monster,
with frills around its neck, reptilian eyes, and huge talons; it spits poison

dryads   tree nymphs

Erebos   a place of darkness between earth and Hades

Eros   the Greek god of love

Erythaea   an island where the Cumaean Sibyl, a love
interest of Apollo, originally lived before he convinced
her to leave it by promising her a long life

Fields of Punishment   the section of the Underworld where people who were evil during their lives are sent to face eternal punishment for their crimes after death

Gaea   the Greek earth goddess; mother of Titans, giants, Cyclopes, and other monsters

Germani (Germanus, sing.)   tribal people who settled to the west of the Rhine river

Golden Fleece   this hide from a gold-haired winged ram was a symbol of authority and kingship; it was guarded by a dragon and fire-breathing bulls; Jason was tasked with obtaining it, resulting in an epic quest

Gorgons   three monstrous sisters (Stheno, Euryale, and Medusa) who have hair of living, venomous snakes; Medusa's eyes can turn the beholder to stone

Great Fire of Rome   a devastating fire that took place in 64 CE, lasting for six days; rumors indicated that Nero started the fire to clear space for the building of his villa, Domus Aurea, but he blamed the Christian community for the disaster

greaves   shin armor

Greek fire   an incendiary weapon used in naval battles because it can continue burning in water

Grove of Dodona   the site of the oldest Greek Oracle, second only to the Delphi; the rustling of trees in the grove provided answers to priests and priestesses who journeyed to the site

Hades   the Greek god of death and riches; ruler of the Underworld

harpy   a winged female creature that snatches things

Hebe the Greek goddess of youth; daughter of Zeus and Hera

Hecate goddess of magic and crossroads

Hephaestus the Greek god of fire and crafts and of blacksmiths; the son of Zeus and Hera, and married to Aphrodite

Hera the Greek goddess of marriage; Zeus's wife and sister

Hermes Greek god of travelers; guide to spirits of the dead; god of communication

Herodotus a Greek historian known as the "Father of History"

Hestia Greek goddess of the hearth

hippocampi (**hippocampus**, sing.) half-horse, half-fish creatures

hippodrome an oval stadium for horse and chariot races in ancient Greece

Hittites a group of people who lived in modern Turkey and Syria; often in conflict with Egyptians; known for their use of chariots as assault weapons

House of Hades a place in the Underworld where Hades, the Greek god of death, and his wife, Persephone, rule over the souls of the departed

Hunters of Artemis a group of maidens loyal to Artemis and gifted with hunting skills and eternal youth as long as they reject men for life

Hyacinthus a Greek hero and Apollo's lover, who died while trying to impress Apollo with his discus skills

Hypnos the Greek god of sleep

ichor the golden fluid that is the blood of gods and immortals

imperator a term for *commander* in the Roman Empire

Imperial gold a rare metal deadly to monsters, consecrated at the Pantheon; its existence was a closely guarded secret of the emperors

Iris the Greek goddess of the rainbow, and a messenger of the gods

Julian dynasty the time period measured from the battle of Actium (31 BCE) to the death of Nero (68 CE)

karpoi (*karpos*, sing.) grain spirits

kouretes armored dancers who guarded the infant Zeus from his father, Kronos

Kronos the youngest of the twelve Titans; the son of Ouranos and Gaea; the father of Zeus; he killed his father at his mother's bidding; Titan lord of fate, harvest, justice, and time; Roman form: Saturn

Labyrinth an underground maze originally built on the island of Crete by the craftsman Daedalus to hold the Minotaur

Laomedon a Trojan king whom Poseidon and Apollo were sent to serve after they offended Zeus

Lepidus a Roman patrician and military commander who was in a triumvirate with Octavian and Marc Antony

Leto mother of Artemis and Apollo with Zeus; goddess of motherhood

Lupercalia a pastoral festival, observed on February 13 through 15, to avert evil spirits and purify the city, releasing health and fertility

Lydia   a province in ancient Rome; the double ax origi-
nated there, along with the use of coins and retail shops

Marc Antony   a Roman politician and general; part of the
triumvirate, with Lepidus and Octavian, who together
tracked down and defeated Caesar's killers; had an
enduring affair with Cleopatra

Marsyas   a satyr who lost to Apollo after challenging him
in a musical contest, which led to Marsyas being flayed
alive

Medea   a follower of Hecate and one of the great sorcer-
esses of the ancient world

Midas   a king with the power to transform anything he
touched to gold; he selected Marsyas as the winner
in the musical contest between Apollo and Marsyas,
resulting in Apollo giving Midas the ears of a donkey

Minos   king of Crete; son of Zeus; every year he made King
Aegus pick seven boys and seven girls to be sent to the
Labyrinth, where they would be eaten by the Minotaur;
after his death he became a judge in the Underworld

Minotaur   the half-man, half-bull son of King Minos of
Crete; the Minotaur was kept in the Labyrinth, where he
killed people who were sent in; he was finally defeated
by Theseus

Mithridates   king of Pontus and Armenia Minor in northern Anatolia (now Turkey) from about 120 to 63 BCE;
one of the Roman Republic's most formidable and
successful enemies, who engaged three of the prominent generals from the late Roman Republic in the
Mithridatic Wars

Mount Olympus   home of the Twelve Olympians

myrmeke   a giant antlike creature that poisons and paralyzes its prey before eating it; known for protecting various metals, particularly gold

Nemesis   the Greek goddess of revenge

Nero   Roman emperor from 54 to 68 CE; the last in the Julian dynasty

New Rome   a community near Camp Jupiter where demigods can live together in peace, without interference from mortals or monsters

Nike   the Greek goddess of strength, speed, and victory

Nine Muses   Greek goddesses of literature, science, and the arts, who have inspired artists and writers for centuries

Niobe   daughter of Tantalus and Dione; suffered the loss of her six sons and six daughters, who were killed by Apollo and Artemis as a punishment for her pride

nosoi (*nosos*, sing.)   spirits of plague and disease

nymph   a female nature deity who animates nature

Octavian   the founder and first emperor of the Roman Empire; adopted son and heir of Julius Caesar (*see also* Caesar Augustus)

Odysseus   legendary Greek king of Ithaca and the hero of Homer's epic poem *The Odyssey*

Ogygia   the island home—and prison—of the nymph Calypso

omphalus   stones used to mark the center—or navel—of the world

Oracle of Delphi   a speaker of the prophecies of Apollo

Oracle of Trophonius a Greek who was transformed into an Oracle after his death; located at the Cave of Trophonius; known for terrifying those who seek him

Ouranos the Greek personification of the sky; father of the Titans

palikoi (*palikos*, sing.) twin sons of Zeus and Thaleia; the gods of geysers and thermal springs

Pan the Greek god of the wild; the son of Hermes

Pandora the first human woman created by the gods; endowed with a unique gift from each; released evil into the world by opening a jar

Parthenon a temple dedicated to the goddess Athena located at the Athenian Acropolis in Greece

Patroclus son of Menoetius; he shared a deep friendship with Achilles after being raised alongside him; he was killed while fighting in the Trojan War

pegasus (**pegasi**, pl.) a winged divine horse; sired by Poseidon, in his role as horse-god

Peleus father of Achilles; his wedding to the sea-nymph Thetis was well attended by the gods, and a disagreement between them at the event eventually lead to the Trojan War; the guardian dragon at Camp Half-Blood is named after him

Persephone the Greek queen of the Underworld; wife of Hades; daughter of Zeus and Demeter

phalanx (**phalanxes**, pl.) a compact body of heavily armed troops

Phidias a famous ancient Greek sculptor who created the Athena Parthenos and many others

Polyphemus   the gigantic one-eyed son of Poseidon and Thoosa; one of the Cyclopes

Poseidon   the Greek god of the sea; son of the Titans Kronos and Rhea, and brother of Zeus and Hades

praetor   an elected Roman magistrate and commander of the army

Primordial Chaos   the first thing ever to exist; a void from which the first gods were produced

Prometheus   the Titan who created humans and gifted them with fire stolen from Mount Olympus

Pythia   the name given to every Oracle of Delphi

Python   a monstrous serpent that Gaea appointed to guard the Oracle at Delphi

Rhea Silvia   the queen of the Titans, mother of Zeus

Riptide   the name of Percy Jackson's sword; *Anaklusmos* in Greek

River Styx   the river that forms the boundary between earth and the Underworld

Saturnalia   an ancient Roman festival celebrating Saturn (Kronos)

satyr   a Greek forest god, part goat and part man

shadow-travel   a form of transportation that allows creatures of the Underworld and children of Hades to use shadows to leap to any desired place on earth or in the Underworld, although it makes the user extremely fatigued

Sibyl   a prophetess

Sibylline Books   a collection of prophecies in rhyme written in Greek; Tarquinius Superbus, a king of Rome, bought them from a prophetess and consulted them in times of great danger

siccae   a short curved sword used for battle in ancient Rome

Sparta   a city-state in ancient Greece with military dominance

Stygian iron   a magical metal, forged in the River Styx, capable of absorbing the very essence of monsters and injuring mortals, gods, Titans, and giants; has a significant effect on ghosts and creatures from the Underworld

Talos   a giant mechanical man made of bronze and used on Crete to guard its shoreline from invaders

Tantalus   According to legend, this king was such a good friend of the gods that he was allowed to dine at their table—until he spilled their secrets on earth; he was sent to the Underworld, where his curse was to be stuck in a pool of water under a fruit tree, but never be able to drink or eat

Tartarus   husband of Gaea; spirit of the abyss; father of the giants; a region of the Underworld

Theodosius   the last to rule over the united Roman Empire; known for closing all ancient temples across the empire

Thracian   of Thrace, a region centered on the modern borders of Bulgaria, Greece, and Turkey

Titan War   the epic ten-year battle between the Titans and the Olympians that resulted in the Olympians taking the throne

Titans   a race of powerful Greek deities, descendants of Gaea and Ouranos, that ruled during the Golden Age and were overthrown by a race of younger gods, the Olympians

trireme   a Greek warship, having three tiers of oars on each side

triumvirate   a political alliance formed by three parties

Trojan War   According to legend, the Trojan War was waged against the city of Troy by the Achaeans (Greeks) after Paris of Troy took Helen from her husband, Menelaus, king of Sparta

Troy   a Roman city situated in modern-day Turkey; site of the Trojan War

Tyche   the Greek goddess of good fortune; daughter of Hermes and Aphrodite

Typhon   the most terrifying Greek monster; father of many famous monsters, including Cerberus, the vicious multi-headed dog tasked with guarding the entrance to the Underworld

Underworld   the kingdom of the dead, where souls go for eternity; ruled by Hades

Zephyros   the Greek god of the West Wind

Zeus   the Greek god of the sky and the king of the gods

Can't get enough of Apollo? Read the first chapter of
Book Two in the Trials of Apollo series,

THE DARK PROPHECY

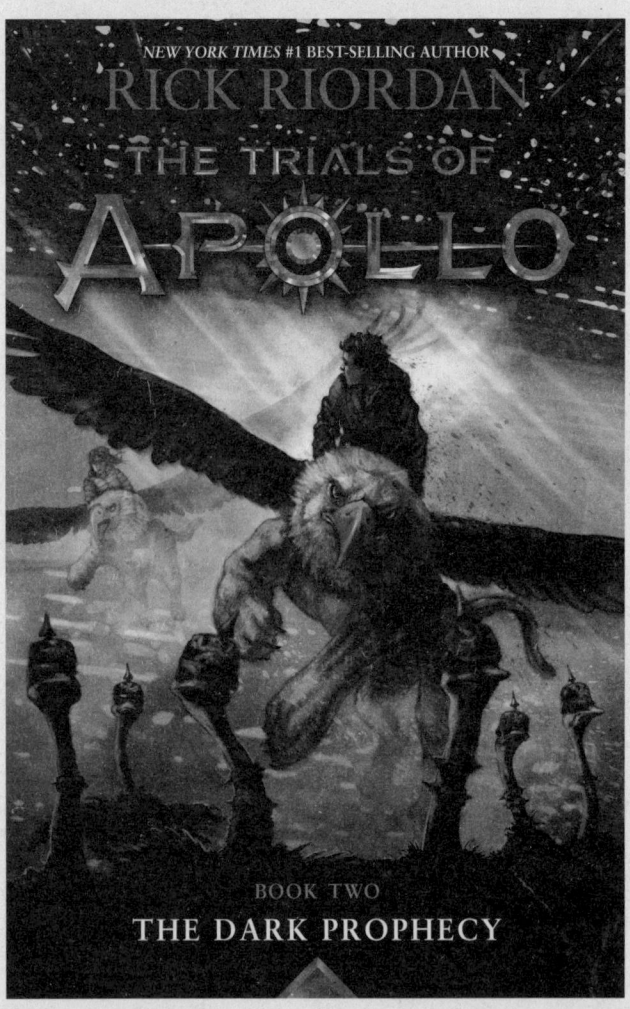

1

Lester (Apollo)
Still human; thanks for asking
Gods, I hate my life

WHEN OUR DRAGON declared war on Indiana, I knew it was going to be a bad day.

We'd been traveling west for six weeks, and Festus had never shown such hostility toward a state. New Jersey he ignored. Pennsylvania he seemed to enjoy, despite our battle with the Cyclops of Pittsburgh. Ohio he tolerated, even after our encounter with Potina, the Roman goddess of childhood drinks, who pursued us in the form of a giant red pitcher emblazoned with a smiley face.

Yet for some reason, Festus decided he did not like Indiana. He landed on the cupola of the Indiana Statehouse, flapped his metallic wings, and blew a cone of fire that incinerated the state flag right off the flagpole.

"Whoa, buddy!" Leo Valdez pulled the dragon's reins. "We've talked about this. No blowtorching public monuments!"

Behind him on the dragon's spine, Calypso gripped Festus's scales for balance. "Could we *please* get to the ground? *Gently* this time?"

For a formerly immortal sorceress who once controlled air spirits, Calypso was not a fan of flying. Cold wind blew her chestnut hair into my face, making me blink and spit.

That's right, dear reader.

I, the most important passenger, the youth who had once been the glorious god Apollo, was forced to sit in the back of the dragon. Oh, the indignities I had suffered since Zeus stripped me of my divine powers! It wasn't enough that I was now a sixteen-year-old mortal with the ghastly alias Lester Papadopoulos. It wasn't enough that I had to toil upon the earth doing (ugh) heroic quests until I could find a way back into my father's good graces, or that I had a case of acne which simply *would not* respond to over-the-counter zit medicine. Despite my New York State junior driver's license, Leo Valdez didn't trust me to operate his aerial bronze steed!

Festus's claws scrabbled for a hold on the green copper dome, which was much too small for a dragon his size. I had a flashback to the time I installed a life-size statue of the muse Calliope on my sun chariot and the extra weight of the hood ornament made me nosedive into China and create the Gobi Desert.

Leo glanced back, his face streaked with soot. "Apollo, you sense anything?"

"Why is it *my* job to sense things? Just because I used to be a god of prophecy—"

"You're the one who's been having visions," Calypso reminded me. "You said your friend Meg would be here."

Just hearing Meg's name gave me a twinge of pain. "That doesn't mean I can pinpoint her location with my mind! Zeus has revoked my access to GPS!"

"GPS?" Calypso asked.

"Godly positioning systems."

"That's not a real thing!"

"Guys, cool it." Leo patted the dragon's neck. "Apollo, just try, will you? Does this look like the city you dreamed about or not?"

I scanned the horizon.

Indiana was flat country—highways crisscrossing scrubby

brown plains, shadows of winter clouds floating above urban sprawl. Around us rose a meager cluster of downtown high-rises—stacks of stone and glass like layered wedges of black and white licorice. (Not the yummy kind of licorice, either; the nasty variety that sits for eons in your stepmother's candy bowl on the coffee table. And, no, Hera, why would I be talking about you?)

After falling to earth in New York City, I found Indianapolis desolate and uninspiring, as if one proper New York neighborhood—Midtown, perhaps—had been stretched out to encompass the entire area of Manhattan, then relieved of two-thirds of its population and vigorously power-washed.

I could think of no reason why an evil triumvirate of ancient Roman emperors would take interest in such a location. Nor could I imagine why Meg McCaffrey would be sent here to capture me. Yet my visions had been clear. I had seen this skyline. I had heard my old enemy Nero give orders to Meg: *Go west. Capture Apollo before he can find the next Oracle. If you cannot bring him to me alive, kill him.*

The truly sad thing about this? Meg was one of my better friends. She also happened to be my demigod master, thanks to Zeus's twisted sense of humor. As long as I remained mortal, Meg could order me to do anything, even kill myself. . . . No. Better not to think of such possibilities.

I shifted in my metal seat. After so many weeks of travel, I was tired and saddle sore. I wanted to find a safe place to rest. *This* was not such a city. Something about the landscape below made me as restless as Festus.

Alas, I was sure this was where we were meant to be. Despite the danger, if I had a chance of seeing Meg McCaffrey again, of prying her away from her villainous stepfather's grasp, I had to try.

"This is the spot," I said. "Before this dome collapses under us, I suggest we get to the ground."

Calypso grumbled in ancient Minoan, "I already *said* that."

"Well, excuse me, sorceress!" I replied in the same language. "Perhaps if *you* had helpful visions, I'd listen to you more often!"

Calypso called me a few names that reminded me how colorful the Minoan language had been before it went extinct.

"Hey, you two," Leo said. "No ancient dialects. Spanish or English, please. Or Machine."

Festus creaked in agreement.

"It's okay, boy," Leo said. "I'm sure they didn't mean to exclude us. Now let's fly down to street level, huh?"

Festus's ruby eyes glowed. His metal teeth spun like drill bits. I imagined him thinking, *Illinois is sounding pretty good right about now.*

But he flapped his wings and leaped from the dome. We hurtled downward, landing in front of the statehouse with enough force to crack the sidewalk. My eyeballs jiggled like water balloons.

Festus whipped his head from side to side, steam curling from his nostrils.

I saw no immediate threats. Cars drove leisurely down West Washington Street. Pedestrians strolled by: a middle-aged woman in a flowery dress, a heavyset policeman carrying a paper coffee cup labeled CAFÉ PATACHOU, a clean-cut man in a blue seersucker suit.

The man in blue waved politely as he passed. "Morning."

"'Sup, dude," Leo called.

Calypso tilted her head. "Why was he so friendly? Does he not *see* that we're sitting atop a fifty-ton metal dragon?"

Leo grinned. "It's the Mist, babe—messes with mortal eyes. Makes monsters look like stray dogs. Makes swords look like umbrellas. Makes me look even more handsome than usual!"

Calypso jabbed her thumbs into Leo's kidneys.

"Ow!" he complained.

"I know what the Mist is, *Leonidas*—"

"Hey, I told you never to call me that."

"—but the Mist must be very strong here if it can hide a monster of Festus's size at such close range. Apollo, don't you find that a little odd?"

I studied the passing pedestrians.

True, I had seen places where the Mist was particularly heavy. At Troy, the sky above the battlefield had been so thick with gods you couldn't turn your chariot without running into another deity, yet the Trojans and Greeks saw only hints of our presence. At Three Mile Island in 1979, the mortals somehow failed to realize that their partial nuclear meltdown was caused by an epic chainsaw fight between Ares and Hephaestus. (As I recall, Hephaestus had insulted Ares's bell-bottom jeans.)

Still, I did not think heavy Mist was the problem here. Something about these locals bothered me. Their faces were too placid. Their dazed smiles reminded me of ancient Athenians just before the Dionysus Festival—everyone in a good mood, distracted, thinking about the drunken riots and debauchery to come.

"We should get out of the public eye," I suggested. "Perhaps—"

Festus stumbled, shaking like a wet dog. From inside his chest came a noise like a loose bicycle chain.

"Aw, not again," Leo said. "Everybody off!"

Calypso and I quickly dismounted.

Leo ran in front of Festus and held out his arms in a classic dragon-wrangler's stance. "Hey, buddy, it's fine! I'm just going to switch you off for a while, okay? A little downtime to—"

Festus projectile-vomited a column of flames that engulfed

Leo. Fortunately, Valdez was fireproof. His clothes were not. From what Leo had told me, he could generally prevent his outfits from burning up simply by concentrating. If he were caught by surprise, however, it didn't always work.

When the flames dissipated, Leo stood before us wearing nothing but his asbestos boxer shorts, his magical tool belt, and a pair of smoking, partially melted sneakers.

"Dang it!" he complained. "Festus, it's cold out here!"

The dragon stumbled. Leo lunged and flipped the lever behind the dragon's left foreleg. Festus began to collapse. His wings, limbs, neck, and tail contracted into his body, his bronze plates overlapping and folding inward. In a matter of seconds, our robotic friend had been reduced to a large bronze suitcase.

That should have been physically impossible, of course, but like any decent god, demigod, or engineer, Leo Valdez refused to be stopped by the laws of physics.

He scowled at his new piece of luggage. "Man . . . I *thought* I fixed his gyro-capacitor. Guess we're stuck here until I can find a machine shop."

Calypso grimaced. Her pink ski jacket glistened with condensation from our flight through the clouds. "And if we find such a shop, how long will it take to repair Festus?"

Leo shrugged. "Twelve hours? Fifteen?" He pushed a button on the side of the suitcase. A handle popped up. "Also, if we see a men's clothing store, that might be good."

I imagined walking into a T.J. Maxx, Leo in boxer shorts and melted sneakers, rolling a bronze suitcase behind him. I did not relish the idea.

Then, from the direction of the sidewalk, a voice called, "Hello!"

The woman in the flowery dress had returned. At least she *looked* like the same woman. Either that or lots of ladies in Indianapolis wore purple-and-yellow honeysuckle-pattern dresses and had 1950s bouffant hairstyles.

She smiled vacantly. "Beautiful morning!"

It was in fact a miserable morning—cold and cloudy with a smell of impending snow—but I felt it would be rude to ignore her completely.

I gave her a little parade wave—the sort of gesture I used to give my worshippers when they came to grovel at my altar. To me, the message was clear enough: *I see you, puny mortal; now run along. The gods are talking.*

The woman did not take the hint. She strolled forward and planted herself in front of us. She wasn't particularly large, but something about her proportions seemed off. Her shoulders were too wide for her head. Her chest and belly protruded in a lumpy mass, as if she'd stuffed a sack of mangos down the front of her dress. With her spindly arms and legs, she reminded me of some sort of giant beetle. If she ever tipped over, I doubted she could easily get back up.

"Oh, my!" She gripped her purse with both hands. "Aren't you children *cute*!"

Her lipstick and eye shadow were both a violent shade of purple. I wondered if she was getting enough oxygen to her brain.

"Madam," I said, "we are not children." I could have added that I was over four thousand years old, and Calypso was even older, but I decided not to get into that. "Now, if you'll excuse us, we have a suitcase to repair and my friend is in dire need of a pair of pants."

I tried to step around her. She blocked my path.

"You can't go yet, dear! We haven't welcomed you to Indiana!" From her purse, she drew a smartphone. The screen glowed as if a call were already in progress.

"It's him, all right," she said into the phone. "Everybody, come on over. Apollo is here!"

My lungs shriveled in my chest.

In the old days, I would have expected to be recognized as soon as I arrived in a town. *Of course* the locals would rush to welcome me. They would sing and dance and throw flowers. They would immediately begin constructing a new temple.

But as Lester Papadopoulos, I did not warrant such treatment. I looked nothing like my former glorious self. The idea that the Indianans might recognize me despite my tangled hair, acne, and flab was both insulting and terrifying. What if they erected a statue of me in my present form—a giant golden Lester in the center of their city? The other gods would never let me hear the end of it!

"Madam," I said, "I'm afraid you have mistaken me—"

"Don't be modest!" The woman tossed her phone and purse aside. She grabbed my forearm with the strength of a weight-lifter. "Our master will be delighted to have you in custody. And please call me Nanette."

Calypso charged. Either she wished to defend me (unlikely), or she was not a fan of the name Nanette. She punched the woman in the face.

This by itself did not surprise me. Having lost her immortal powers, Calypso was in the process of trying to master other skills. So far, she'd failed at swords, polearms, shurikens, whips, and improvisational comedy. (I sympathized with her frustration.) Today, she'd decided to try fisticuffs.

What surprised me was the loud CRACK her fist made against Nanette's face—the sound of finger bones breaking.

"Ow!" Calypso stumbled away, clutching her hand.

Nanette's head slid backward. She released me to try to grab her own face, but it was too late. Her head toppled off her shoulders. It clanged against the pavement and rolled sideways, the eyes still blinking, the purple lips twitching. Its base was smooth stainless steel. Attached to it were ragged strips of duct tape stuck with hair and bobby pins.

"Holy Hephaestus!" Leo ran to Calypso's side. "Lady, you broke my girlfriend's hand with your face. What *are* you, an automaton?"

"No, dear," said decapitated Nanette. Her muffled voice didn't come from the stainless-steel head on the sidewalk. It emanated from somewhere inside her dress. Just above her collar, where her neck used to be, an outcropping of fine blond hair was tangled with bobby pins. "And I must say, hitting me wasn't very polite."

Belatedly, I realized the metal head had been a disguise. Just as satyrs covered their hooves with human shoes, this creature passed for mortal by pretending to have a human face. Its voice came from its gut area, which meant . . .

My knees trembled.

"A *blemmyae*," I said.

Nanette chuckled. Her bulging midsection writhed under the honeysuckle cloth. She ripped open her blouse—something a polite Midwesterner would never think of doing—and revealed her true face.

Where a woman's brassiere would have been, two enormous bulging eyes blinked at me. From her sternum protruded a large shiny nose. Across her abdomen curled a hideous mouth— glistening orange lips, teeth like a spread of blank white playing cards.

"Yes, dear," the face said. "And I'm arresting you in the name of the Triumvirate!"

Up and down Washington Street, pleasant-looking pedestrians turned and began marching in our direction.

Need even more Apollo? Read this bonus short story
by Rick Riordan:

"PERCY JACKSON
AND THE SINGER OF APOLLO"

I KNOW WHAT YOU'RE GOING TO ASK.

Percy Jackson, why are you hanging from a Times Square billboard without your pants on, about to fall to your death?

Good question. You can blame Apollo, god of music, archery, and poetry—also the god of making me do stupid quests.

This particular disaster started when I brought my friend Grover some aluminum cans for his birthday.

Perhaps I should mention . . . I'm a demigod. My dad, Poseidon, is the lord of the sea, which sounds cool, I guess, but mostly it means my life is filled with monster attacks and annoying Greek gods who tend to pop up on the subway or in the middle of math class or when I'm taking a shower. (Long story. Don't ask.)

I figured maybe I'd get a day off from the craziness for Grover's birthday, but of course I was wrong.

Grover and his girlfriend, Juniper, were spending the day in Prospect Park in Brooklyn, doing naturey stuff like dancing with the local tree nymphs and serenading the squirrels. Grover's a satyr. That's his idea of fun.

Juniper seemed to be having an especially good time. While Grover and I sat on the bench together, she frolicked across Long Meadow with the other nature spirits, her chlorophyll-tinted eyes glinting in the sunlight. Since she is a dryad, Juniper's life source is tied to a juniper bush back on Long Island, but Grover explained that she can take short trips away from home as long as she keeps a handful of fresh juniper berries in her pockets. I didn't want to ask what would happen if the berries got accidentally smashed.

Anyway, we hung out for a while, talking and enjoying the nice weather. I gave Grover his aluminum cans, which may sound like a lame gift, but that's his favorite snack.

He happily munched on the cans while the nymphs started discussing what party games we should play. Grover pulled a blindfold out of his pocket and suggested Pin the Tail on the Human, which made me kind of nervous since I was the only human.

Then, without warning, the sunlight brightened. The air turned uncomfortably hot. Twenty feet away, the grass hissed and a cloud of steam whooshed up like somebody had opened a big pressing machine at a Laundromat. The steam cleared, and standing in front of us was the god Apollo.

Gods can look like anything they want, but Apollo always seemed to go for that I-just-auditioned-for-a-boy-band look. Today he was rocking pencil-thin jeans, a white muscle shirt, and gilded Ray-Ban sunglasses. His wavy blond hair glistened with product. When he smiled the dryads squealed and giggled.

"Oh, no . . ." Grover murmured. "This can't be good."

"Percy Jackson!" Apollo beamed at me. "And, um, your goat friend—"

"His name is Grover," I said. "And we're kind of off duty, Lord Apollo. It's Grover's birthday."

"Happy birthday!" Apollo said. "I'm so glad you're taking the day off. That means you two have time to help me with a small problem!"

Naturally, the problem wasn't small.

Apollo led Grover and me away from the party so we could talk in private. Juniper didn't want to let Grover go, but she couldn't argue with a god. Grover promised to come back safely. I hoped it was a promise he'd be able to keep.

When we got to the edge of the woods, Apollo faced us. "Allow me to introduce the Chryseae Celedones."

The god snapped his fingers. More steam erupted from the ground, and three golden women appeared in front of us. When I say golden, I mean they were literally gold. Their metallic skin glittered. Their sleeveless gowns were made from enough gilded fabric to finance a bailout. Their golden hair was braided and piled on top of their heads in a sort of classical beehive hairdo. They were uniformly beautiful, and uniformly terrifying.

I'd seen living statues—automatons—many times before. Beautiful or not, they almost always tried to kill me.

"Uh . . ." I took a step back. "What did you say these were? Krissy Kelly something?"

"Chryseae Celedones," Apollo said. "Golden singers. They're my backup band!"

I glanced at Grover, wondering if this was some kind of joke.

Grover wasn't laughing. His mouth hung open in amazement, as if the golden ladies were the largest, tastiest aluminum cans he'd ever seen. "I—I didn't think they were real!"

Apollo smiled. "Well, it's been a few centuries since I brought them out. If they perform too often, you know, their novelty wears off. They used to live at my temple in Delphi. Man, they could rock that place. Now I only use them for special occasions."

Grover got teary-eyed. "You brought them out for my birthday?"

Apollo laughed. "No, fool! I've got a concert tonight on Mount Olympus. Everyone is going to be there! The Nine Muses are opening, and I'm performing a mix of old favorites and new material. I mean, it's not like I need the Celedones. My solo career has been great. But people will expect to hear some of my classic hits with the girls: 'Daphne on my Mind,' 'Stairway to Olympus,' 'Sweet Home Atlantis.' It's going to be awesome!"

I tried not to look nauseous. I'd heard Apollo's poetry before, and if his music was even half as bad, this concert was going to blow harder than Aeolus the wind god.

"Great," I said halfheartedly. "So what's the problem?"

Apollo's smile faded. "Listen."

He turned to his golden singers and raised his hands like a conductor. On cue, they sang in harmony: "Laaaa!"

It was only one chord, but it filled me with bliss. I suddenly couldn't remember where I was or what I was doing. If the golden singers had decided to tear me to pieces at that moment, I wouldn't have resisted, as long as they kept singing. Nothing mattered to me, except that sound.

Then the golden girls went silent. The feeling passed. Their faces returned to beautiful, impassive metal.

"That . . ." I swallowed. "That was amazing."

"Amazing?" Apollo wrinkled his nose. "There are only three of them! Their harmonies sound empty. I can't perform without the full quartet."

Grover was weeping with joy. "They're so beautiful. They're perfect!"

I was kind of glad Juniper wasn't within earshot, since she's the jealous type.

Apollo crossed his tan arms. "They're not perfect, Mr. Satyr. I need all four or the concert will be ruined. Unfortunately, my fourth Celedon went rogue this morning. I can't find her anywhere."

I looked at the three golden automatons, staring at Apollo, quietly waiting for orders. "Uh . . . how does a backup singer go rogue?"

Apollo made another conductor wave, and the singers sighed in three-part harmony. The sound was so mournful my heart sank into my gut. At that moment, I felt sure I'd never be happy again. Then, just as quickly, the feeling dissipated.

"They're out of warranty," the god explained. "Hephaestus made them for me back in the old days, and they worked fine . . . until the day after their two-thousand-year warranty expired. Then, naturally, WHAM! The fourth one goes haywire and runs off to the big city." He gestured in the general direction of Manhattan. "Of course I tried to complain to Hephaestus, but he's all, *Well, did you have my Protection Plus package?* And I'm like, *I didn't want your stupid extended warranty!* And he acts as if it's my fault the Celedon broke, and says if I'd bought the Plus package, I could've had a dedicated service hotline, but—"

"Whoa, whoa, whoa," I interrupted. I really didn't want to get in the middle of a god-versus-god argument. I'd been there too many times. "So if you know that your Celedon is in the city, why can't you just look for her yourself?"

"I don't have time! I have to practice. I have to write a set list and do a sound check! Besides, this is what heroes are for."

"Running the gods' errands," I muttered.

"Exactly." Apollo spread his hands. "I assume the missing Celedon is roaming the Theater District, looking for a suitable place to audition. Celedones have the usual starlet dreams— being discovered, headlining a Broadway musical, that sort of thing. Most of the time I can keep their ambitions under control. I mean, I can't have them upstaging me, can I? But I'm sure without me around she thinks she's the next Katy Perry. You two need to get her before she causes any problems. And hurry! The concert is tonight, and Manhattan is a large island."

Grover tugged his goatee. "So . . . you want us to find her, while you do sound checks?"

"Think of it as a favor," Apollo said. "Not just for me, but for all those mortals in Manhattan."

"Oh." Grover's voice got very small. "Oh, no . . ."

"What?" I demanded. "What *oh, no?*"

Years ago, Grover created a magic empathy link between us (another long story) and we could sense each other's emotions. It wasn't exactly mind reading, but I could tell he was terrified.

"Percy," he said, "if that Celedon starts singing in public, in the middle of afternoon rush hour—"

"She'll cause no end of havoc," Apollo said. "She might sing a love song, or a lullaby, or a patriotic war tune, and whatever the mortals hear . . ."

I shuddered. One sigh from the golden girls had plunged me into despair, even with Apollo controlling their power. I imagined a rogue Celedon busting into song in a crowded city—putting people to sleep, or making them fall in love, or urging them to fight.

"She has to be stopped," I agreed. "But why us?"

"I like you!" Apollo grinned. "You've faced the Sirens before. This isn't too different. Just put some wax in your ears. Besides, your friend Grover here is a satyr. He has natural resistance to magical music. Plus he can play the lyre."

"What lyre?" I asked.

Apollo snapped his fingers. Suddenly Grover was holding the weirdest musical instrument I'd ever seen. The base was a hollowed-out tortoise shell, which made me feel really bad for the tortoise. Two polished wooden arms stuck out one side like bull's horns, with a bar across the top and seven strings stretching from the bar to the base of the shell. It looked like a combination harp, banjo, and dead turtle.

"Oh!" Grover almost dropped the lyre. "I couldn't! This is your—"

"Yes," Apollo agreed cheerfully. "That's my own personal lyre. Of course if you damage it, I'll incinerate you, but I'm sure you'll be careful! You can play the lyre, can't you?"

"Um . . . ." Grover plucked a few notes that sounded like a funeral dirge.

"Keep practicing," Apollo said. "You'll need the lyre's magic to capture the Celedon. Have Percy distract her while you play."

"Distract her," I repeated.

This quest was sounding worse and worse. I didn't see how a tortoiseshell harp could defeat a golden automaton, but Apollo clapped me on the shoulder like everything was settled.

"Excellent!" he said. "I'll meet you at the Empire State Building at sunset. Bring me the Celedon. One way or another I'll persuade Hephaestus to fix her. Just don't be late! I can't keep my audience waiting. And remember, not a scratch on that lyre."

Then the sun god and his golden backup singers disappeared in a cloud of steam.

"Happy birthday to me," Grover whimpered, and plucked a sour note on the harp.

We caught the subway to Times Square. We figured that would be a good place to start looking. It was in the middle of the Theater District and full of weird street performers and about a billion tourists, so it was the natural place for a golden diva to get some attention for herself.

Grover hadn't bothered disguising himself. His white T-shirt read WHAT WOULD PAN DO? The tips of his horns stuck out from his curly hair. Usually he wore jeans over his shaggy legs and specially fitted shoes over his hooves, but today from the waist down he was au naturel goat.

I doubted it would matter. Most mortals can't see through the Mist, which hides the true appearance of monsters. Even without Grover's normal disguise, people would have to look really closely to notice he was a satyr, and even then they probably wouldn't bat an eye. This was New York, after all.

As we pushed through the crowd, I kept searching for the glint of gold, hoping to spot the rogue Celedon, but the square was packed as usual. A guy wearing only his underwear and a guitar was having his picture taken with some tourists. Cops hung out on the street corners, looking bored. At Broadway and West Forty-Ninth, the intersection was blocked and a crew of roadies was setting up some sort of stage. Preachers, ticket scalpers, and hawkers shouted over each other, trying to get attention. Music blasted from dozens of loudspeakers, but I didn't hear any magical singing.

Grover had given me a ball of warm wax to stuff in my ears whenever necessary. He said he always kept some handy, like chewing gum, which didn't make me anxious to use it.

He bumped into a pretzel vendor's cart and lurched back, hugging Apollo's lyre protectively.

"You know how to use that thing?" I asked. "I mean, what kind of magic does it do?"

Grover's eyes widened. "You don't know? Apollo built the walls of Troy just by playing this harp. With the right song, it can create almost anything!"

"Like a cage for the Celedon?" I asked.

"Uh . . . yeah!"

He didn't sound too confident, and I wasn't sure I wanted him playing Guitar Hero with a godly tortoise banjo. Sure, Grover could do some magic with his reed pipes. On a good day, he could make plants grow and tangle his enemies. On a bad day, he could only remember Justin Bieber songs, which didn't do anything except give me a headache.

I tried to think of a plan. I wished my girlfriend, Annabeth, was here. She was more of the planning type. Unfortunately, she was off in San Francisco visiting her dad.

Grover grabbed my arm. "There."

I followed his gaze. Across the square, at the outdoor stage, workers scurried around, installing lights on the scaffolding, setting up microphone stands, and plugging in giant speakers. Probably they were prepping for a Broadway musical preview or something.

Then I saw her—a golden lady making her way toward the platform. She climbed over the police barricades that cordoned off the intersection, squeezed between workers who completely ignored her, and headed for the steps, stage right. She glanced at the crowd in Times Square and smiled, as if imagining their wild applause. Then she headed for the center microphone.

"Oh, gods!" Grover yelped. "If that sound system is on . . ."

I stuffed wax in my ears as we ran for the stage.

Fighting automatons is bad enough. Fighting one in a crowd of mortals is a recipe for disaster. I didn't want to worry about the mortals' safety and mine and figure out how to capture the Celedon. I needed a way to evacuate Times Square without causing a stampede.

As we wove through the crowd, I grabbed the nearest cop by the shoulder.

"Hey!" I told him. "Presidential motorcade coming! You guys better clear the streets!"

I pointed down Seventh Avenue. Of course there was no motorcade, but I did my best to imagine one.

See, some demigods can actually control the Mist. They can make people see what they want them to see. I wasn't very good at it, but it was worth a shot. Presidential visits are common enough, with the United Nations in town and all, so I figured the cop might buy it.

Apparently he did. He glanced toward my imaginary line of limos, made a disgusted face, and said something into his two-way radio. With the wax in my ears, I couldn't hear what, but all the other cops in the square started herding the crowd toward the side streets.

Unfortunately, the Celedon had reached center stage.

We were still fifty feet away when she grabbed the mike and tapped it. BOOM, BOOM, BOOM echoed through the streets.

"Grover," I yelled, "you'd better start playing that lyre."

If he responded, I didn't hear it. I sprinted to the stage. The workers were too busy arguing with the cops to try stopping me. I bounded up the steps, pulled my pen from my pocket and uncapped it. My sword, Riptide, sprang into existence, though I wasn't sure it would help me. Apollo wouldn't be happy with me if I decapitated his backup singer.

I was twenty feet from the Celedon when a lot of things happened at once.

The golden singer belted out a note so powerful I could hear it through the wax plugs. Her voice was heartbreakingly sad, filled with longing. Even muffled through the wax, it made me want to break down and cry—which is what several thousand people around Times Square did. Cars stopped. Police and tourists fell to their knees, weeping, hugging each other in consolation.

Then I became aware of a different sound—Grover, frantically strumming his lyre. I couldn't exactly hear it, but I could feel the tremor of magic rippling through the air, shaking the stage under my feet. Thanks to the empathy link, I caught flashes of Grover's thoughts. He was singing about walls, trying to summon a box around the Celedon.

The good news: it sort of worked. A brick wall erupted from the stage between me and the Celedon, knocking over the mic stand and interrupting her song. The bad news: by the time I figured out what was going on, I couldn't stop my momentum. I ran straight into the wall, which wasn't mortared, so I promptly collapsed on top of the Celedon along with about a thousand bricks.

My eyes watered. My nose felt broken. Before I could regain my bearings, the Celedon struggled out of the pile of bricks and pushed me off. She raised her arms in triumph as if the whole thing had been a planned stunt.

She sang, "Ta-daaaaah!"

She was no longer amplified, but her voice carried. The mortals stopped sobbing and rose to their feet, clapping and cheering for the Celedon.

"Grover!" I yelled, not sure if he could hear me. "Play something else!"

I picked up my sword and struggled to my feet. I tackled the golden lady, but it was like tackling a lamppost. She ignored me and launched into song.

As I wrestled her, trying to pull her off balance, the temperature on stage began to rise. The Celedon's lyrics were in ancient Greek, but I caught a few of the words: Apollo, sunlight, golden fire. It was some kind of ode to the god. Her metal skin grew hot. I smelled something burning and realized it was my shirt.

I stumbled away from her, my clothes smoldering. The wax had melted out of my ears so I could hear her song clearly. All around Times Square, people started dropping from the heat.

Over at the barricades, Grover played wildly on the lyre, but he was too anxious to focus. Random bricks fell from the sky. One of the monitor speakers on stage morphed into a chicken. A plate of enchiladas appeared at the Celedon's feet.

"Not helpful!" I shouted through the pain of the rising heat. "Sing about cages! Or gags!"

The air felt like a blast furnace. If the Celedon kept this up, Midtown would burst into flames. I couldn't afford to play nice anymore. As the Celedon started her next verse, I lunged at her with my sword.

She lurched away with surprising speed. The tip of my blade missed her face by an inch. I'd managed to stop her singing, and she was not happy about it. She glared at me with outrage, then focused on my blade. Fear flickered across her metallic face. Most magical beings knew enough to respect Celestial bronze, since it could vaporize them on contact.

"Surrender and I won't hurt you," I said. "We just want to take you back to Apollo."

She spread her arms. I was afraid she was going to sing again, but instead the Celedon changed form. Her arms grew into golden feathery wings. Her face elongated, growing a beak. Her body shrank until I was staring at a plump metal bird about the size of a quail. Before I could react, the Celedon launched herself into the air and flew straight for the top of the nearest building.

Grover stumbled onto the stage next to me. All across Times Square, the mortals who had collapsed from the heat were starting to recover. The pavement still steamed. Police started shouting orders, making a serious effort now to clear the area. Nobody paid us any attention.

I watched the golden bird spiral up until she disappeared over the highest billboard on the Times Tower. You've probably seen the building in pictures: the tall skinny one that's stacked with glowing advertisements and Jumbotron screens.

To be completely honest, I didn't feel so great. I had molten wax oozing out of my ears. I'd been charbroiled medium rare.

My face felt like it had just been rammed into a brick wall . . .
because it had. I had the coppery taste of blood in my mouth,
and I was really starting to hate music. And quails.

I turned to Grover. "Did you know she could morph into a
bird?"

"Uh, yeah. . . . But I kind of forgot."

"Great." I nudged the enchilada plate at my feet. "Could you
try to summon something more helpful next time?"

"Sorry," he murmured. "I get hungry when I get nervous. So
what do we do now?"

I started up at the top of the Times Tower. "The golden girl
wins round one. Time for round two."

You're probably wondering why I didn't put more wax in my
ears. For one thing, I didn't have any. For another thing, wax
melting out of my ears hurts. And maybe part of me was thinking: Hey, I'm a demigod. This time I'm prepared. I can face the
music, literally.

Grover assured me he had the lyre figured out. No more
enchiladas or bricks falling from the sky. I just had to find the
Celedon, catch her by surprise, and distract her by . . . well, I
hadn't figured out that part yet.

We took the elevator to the top floor and found stairs to the
roof. I wished I could fly, but that wasn't one of my powers, and
my pegasus friend Blackjack hadn't been answering my calls for
help lately. (He gets a little distracted in the springtime when
he's searching the skies for cute lady pegasi.)

Once we made it to the roof, the Celedon was easy to find.
She was in human form, standing at the edge of the building
with her arms spread, serenading Times Square with her own
rendition of "New York, New York."

I really hate that song. I don't know anybody who's actually from New York who doesn't hate that song, but hearing her sing it made me hate it a whole lot more.

Anyway, she had her back to us, so we had an advantage. I was tempted to sneak up behind her and push her off, but she was so strong I hadn't been able to budge her before. Besides, she'd probably just turn into a bird and . . . Hmm. A bird.

An idea formed in my mind. Yes, I do get ideas sometimes.

"Grover," I said, "can you use the lyre to summon a birdcage? Like a really strong one, made from Celestial bronze?"

He pursed his lips. "I suppose, but birds shouldn't be caged, Percy. They should be free! They should fly and—" He looked at the Celedon. "Oh, you mean—"

"Yeah."

"I'll try."

"Good," I said. "Just wait for my cue. Do you still have that blindfold from Pin the Tail on the Human?"

He handed me the strip of cloth. I shrank my sword to ballpoint-pen form and slipped it in the pocket of my jeans. I'd need both hands free for this. I crept up on the Celedon, who was now belting out the final chorus.

Even though she was facing the other way, her music filled me with the urge to dance (which, believe me, you never want to see). I forced myself to keep going, but fighting her magic was like pushing my way through a row of heavy drapes.

My plan was simple: gag the Celedon. She would turn back into a bird and try to escape. I would grab her and shove her into a birdcage. What could go wrong?

On the last line of "New York, New York," I jumped on her back, locking my legs around her waist and yanking the blindfold across her mouth like a horse's bridle.

Her grand finale was cut short with a "New Yor—urff!"

"Grover, now!" I yelled.

The Celedon stumbled forward. I had a dizzying view of the chaos below in Times Square—cops trying to clear the crowd, lines of tourists doing impromptu high-kick routines like the Radio City Rockettes. The electronic billboards down the side of the Times Tower looked like a very steep, psychedelic water-slide, with nothing but hard pavement at the bottom.

The Celedon staggered backward, flailing and mumbling through the gag.

Grover desperately strummed his lyre. The strings sent powerful magic vibrations through the air, but Grover's voice quivered with uncertainty.

"Um, birds!" he warbled. "La, la, la! Birds in cages! Very strong cages! Birds!"

He wasn't going to win any Grammys with those lyrics, and I was losing my grip. The Celedon was strong. I'd ridden a Minotaur before, and the golden lady was at least that hard to hold on to.

The Celedon spun around, trying to throw me. She clamped her hands around my forearms and squeezed. Pain shot up to my shoulders.

I yelled, "Grover, hurry!" But with my teeth clenched, the words came out more like, "Grr—huh."

"Birds in cages!" Grover strummed another chord. "La, la, la, cages!"

Amazingly, a birdcage shimmered into being at the edge of the roof. I was too busy getting tossed around to have a good look, but Grover seemed to have done a good job. The cage was just large enough for a parrot, or a fat quail, and the bars glowed faintly . . . Celestial bronze.

Now if I could just get the Celedon into bird form. Unfortunately, she wasn't cooperating. She spun hard, breaking my grip and shoving me over the side of the building.

I tried not to panic. Sadly, this wasn't the first time I'd been thrown off a skyscraper.

I'd like to tell you that I did some cool acrobatic move, grabbed the edge of a billboard, and vaulted back up to the roof in a perfect triple flip.

Nope. As I bounced off the first Jumbotron screen, a metal strut somehow snagged my belt and stopped me from falling. It also gave me the ultimate wedgie of all time. Then, as if that wasn't bad enough, my momentum spun me upside down and I peeled right out of my pants.

I plummeted headfirst toward Times Square, grabbing wildly for anything to slow me down. Luckily, the top of the next billboard had a rung across it, maybe for extremely brave maintenance workers to latch their harnesses onto.

I managed to catch it and flipped right side up. My arms were nearly yanked out of their sockets, but somehow I kept my grip. And that's how I ended up hanging from a billboard over Times Square without my pants.

To answer your next question: Boxers. Plain blue boxers. No smiley faces. No hearts.

Laugh all you want. They're more comfortable than briefs.

The Celedon smiled at me from the top of the roof, about twenty feet above. Just below her, my jeans hung from the metal strut, blowing in the wind like they were waving me good-bye. I couldn't see Grover. His music had stopped.

My grip weakened. The pavement was maybe seven hundred feet down, which would make for a very long scream as I fell to my death. The glowing screen of the Jumbotron was slowly cooking my stomach.

As I was dangling there, the Celedon began a special serenade just for me. She sang about letting go, laying down my troubles, resting by the banks of a river. I don't remember the exact lyrics, but you get the idea.

It was all I could do to hold on. I didn't want to drop, but the Celedon's music washed over me, dismantling my resolve. I imagined that I would float down safely. I would land on the banks of a lazy river, where I could have a nice relaxing picnic with my girlfriend.

Annabeth.

I remembered the time I'd saved Annabeth from the Sirens in the Sea of Monsters. I'd held her while she cried and struggled, trying to swim to her death because she thought she would reach some beautiful promised land.

Now I imagined she was holding me back. I could hear what she'd say: *It's a trick, Seaweed Brain! You've got to trick her back or you'll die. And if you die, I'll never forgive you!*

That broke the Celedon's spell. Annabeth's anger was way scarier than most monsters, but don't tell her I said that.

I looked up at my jeans, dangling uselessly above. My sword was in pen form in one of the pockets, where it did me no good. Grover had started to sing about birds again, but it wasn't helping. Apparently the Celedon only turned into bird form when she was startled.

Wait. . . .

Out of desperation, I formed Stupid Plan Version 2.0.

"Hey!" I called up. "You really are amazing, Miss Celedon! Before I die, can I have your autograph?"

The Celedon halted midsong. She looked surprised, then smiled with pleasure.

"Grover!" I called. "Come over here!"

The lyre music stopped. Grover's head poked over the side. "Oh, Percy . . . I—I'm sorry—"

"It's okay!" I faked a smile, using our empathy link to tell him how I really felt. I couldn't send complete thoughts, but I tried to get the general point across: He needed to be ready. He needed to be quick. I hoped he was a good catch.

"Do you have a pen and paper?" I asked him. "I want to get this lady's autograph before I die."

Grover blinked. "Uh . . . jeez. No. But isn't there a pen in the pocket of your jeans?"

Best. Satyr. Ever. He totally got the plan.

"You're right!" I gazed up at the Celedon imploringly. "Please? Last request? Could you just fish the pen out of my jeans and sign them? Then I can die happy."

Golden statues can't blush, but the Celedon looked extremely flattered. She reached down, retrieved my jeans, and pulled out the pen.

I caught my breath. I'd never seen Riptide in the hands of a monster before. If this went wrong, if she realized it was a trick, she could kill Grover. Celestial bronze blades work just fine on satyrs.

She examined the pen like she'd never used one before.

"You have to take the cap off," I said helpfully. My fingers were beginning to slip.

She laid the jeans on the ledge, next to the birdcage. She uncapped the pen and Riptide sprang to life.

If I hadn't been about to die, it would've been the funniest thing I'd ever seen. You know those gag cans of candy with the coiled-up toy snake inside?

It was like watching somebody open one of those, except replace the toy snake with a three-foot-long blade.

The Celestial sword shot to full length and the Celedon thrust it away, leaping backward with a not-very-musical shriek. She turned into a bird, but Grover was ready. He dropped Apollo's lyre and caught the fat golden quail in both hands.

Grover stuffed her in the cage and slammed the door shut. The Celedon went crazy, squawking and flapping, but she didn't have room to turn back to human form, and in bird form—thank the gods—she didn't seem to have any magic in her voice.

"Good job!" I called up to Grover.

He looked sick. "I think I scratched Apollo's lyre. And I just caged a bird. This is the worst birthday ever."

"By the way," I reminded him, "I'm about to fall to my death here."

"Ah!" Grover snatched up the lyre and played a quick tune. Now that he wasn't in danger and the monster was caged, he seemed to have no problem using the harp's magic. Typical. He summoned a rope and threw it down to me. Somehow he managed to pull me to the top, where I collapsed.

Below us, Times Square was still in complete chaos. Tourists wandered around in a daze. The cops were breaking up the last of the high-kick dance routines. A few cars were on fire, and the outdoor stage had been reduced to a pile of kindling, bricks, and broken sound equipment.

Across the Hudson River, the sun was going down. All I wanted to do was lie there on the roof and enjoy the feeling of not being dead. But our job wasn't done yet.

"We've got to get the Celedon back to Apollo," I said.

"Yeah," Grover agreed. "But, uh . . . maybe put your pants on first?"

Apollo was waiting for us in the lobby of the Empire State Building. His three golden singers paced nervously behind him.

When he saw us, he brightened—literally. A glowing aura appeared around his head.

"Excellent!" He took the birdcage. "I'll get Hephaestus to fix her up, and this time I'm not taking any excuses about expired warranties. My show starts in half an hour!"

"You're welcome," I said.

Apollo accepted the lyre from Grover. The god's expression turned dangerously stormy. "You scratched it."

Grover whimpered. "Lord Apollo—"

"It was the only way to catch the Celedon," I interceded. "Besides, it'll buff out. Get Hephaestus to do it. He owes you, right?"

For a second, I thought Apollo might blast us both to ashes, but finally he just grunted. "I suppose you're right. Well, good job, you two! As your reward, you're invited to watch me perform on Mount Olympus!"

Grover and I glanced at each other. Insulting a god was dangerous, but the last thing I wanted to do was hear more music.

"We aren't worthy," I lied. "We'd love to, really, but you know, we'd probably explode or something if we heard your godly music at full volume."

Apollo nodded thoughtfully. "You're right. It might distract from my performance if you exploded. How considerate of you." He grinned. "Well, I'm off, then. Happy birthday, Percy!"

"It's Grover's birthday," I corrected, but Apollo and his singers had already disappeared in a flash of golden light.

"So much for a day off," I said, turning back to Grover.

"Back to Prospect Park?" he suggested. "Juniper must be worried to death."

"Yeah," I agreed. "And I'm really hungry."

Grover nodded enthusiastically. "If we leave now, we can pick up Juniper and reach Camp Half-Blood in time for the sing-along. They have s'mores!"

I winced. "No sing-along, please. But I'll go for the s'mores."

"Deal!" Grover said.

I clapped him on the shoulder. "Come on, G-man. Your birthday might turn out okay after all."

FROM *NEW YORK TIMES* BEST-SELLING AUTHOR
RICK RIORDAN

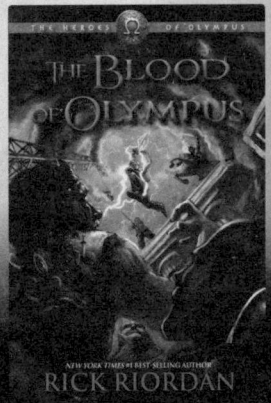

THE GREEKS AREN'T
THE *ONLY* GODS IN TOWN.

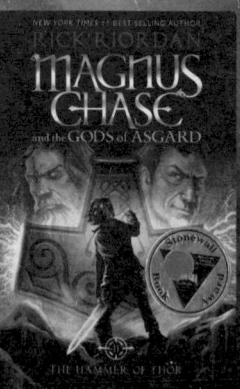

MAGNUS CHASE

and the GODS of ASGARD

THE SWORD OF SUMMER

RICK RIORDAN

MAGNUS CHASE
and the GODS of ASGARD

THE SWORD OF SUMMER

Disney • HYPERION

Los Angeles   New York

First Hardcover Edition, October 2015
First Paperback Edition, April 2017
7 9 10 8 6

FAC-025438-19221

Printed in the United States of America

This book is set in New Baskerville FS/Fontspring
Designed by Joann Hill

Library of Congress Control Number for the Hardcover Edition: 2015018467
ISBN 978-1-4231-6337-4

Visit www.DisneyBooks.com
Follow @ReadRiordan

To Cassandra Clare
Thanks for letting me share the excellent name Magnus

CONTENTS

MAGNUS CHASE

and the GODS of ASGARD

I

THE SWORD OF SUMMER

Good Morning! You're Going to Die

YEAH, I KNOW. You guys are going to read about how I died in agony, and you're going be like, "Wow! That sounds cool, Magnus! Can I die in agony too?"

No. Just no.

Don't go jumping off any rooftops. Don't run into the highway or set yourself on fire. It doesn't work that way. You will not end up where I ended up.

Besides, you wouldn't want to deal with my situation. Unless you've got some crazy desire to see undead warriors hacking one another to pieces, swords flying up giants' noses, and dark elves in snappy outfits, you shouldn't even *think* about finding the wolf-headed doors.

My name is Magnus Chase. I'm sixteen years old. This is the story of how my life went downhill after I got myself killed.

My day started out normal enough. I was sleeping on the sidewalk under a bridge in the Public Garden when a guy kicked me awake and said, "They're after you."

By the way, I've been homeless for the past two years.

Some of you may think, *Aw, how sad.* Others may think, *Ha, ha, loser!* But if you saw me on the street, ninety-nine percent of you would walk right past like I'm invisible. You'd pray, *Don't let him ask me for money.* You'd wonder if I'm older than I look, because surely a teenager wouldn't be wrapped in a stinky old sleeping bag, stuck outside in the middle of a Boston winter. *Somebody should help that poor boy!*

Then you'd keep walking.

Whatever. I don't need your sympathy. I'm used to being laughed at. I'm definitely used to being ignored. Let's move on.

The bum who woke me was a guy called Blitz. As usual, he looked like he'd been running through a dirty hurricane. His wiry black hair was full of paper scraps and twigs. His face was the color of saddle leather, and was flecked with ice. His beard curled in all directions. Snow caked the bottom of his trench coat where it dragged around his feet—Blitz being about five feet five—and his eyes were so dilated, the irises were all pupil. His permanently alarmed expression made him look like he might start screaming any second.

I blinked the gunk out of my eyes. My mouth tasted like day-old hamburger. My sleeping bag was warm, and I really didn't want to get out of it.

"Who's after me?"

"Not sure." Blitz rubbed his nose, which had been broken so many times it zigzagged like a lightning bolt. "They're handing out flyers with your name and picture."

I cursed. Random police and park rangers I could deal with. Truant officers, community service volunteers, drunken college kids, addicts looking to roll somebody small and weak— all those would've been as easy to wake up to as pancakes and orange juice.

But when somebody knew my name and my face—that was

bad. That meant they were targeting me specifically. Maybe the folks at the shelter were mad at me for breaking their stereo. (Those Christmas carols had been driving me crazy.) Maybe a security camera caught that last bit of pickpocketing I did in the Theater District. (Hey, I needed money for pizza.) Or maybe, unlikely as it seemed, the police were still looking for me, wanting to ask questions about my mom's murder. . . .

I packed my stuff, which took about three seconds. The sleeping bag rolled up tight and fit in my backpack with my toothbrush and a change of socks and underwear. Except for the clothes on my back, that's all I owned. With the backpack over my shoulder and the hood of my jacket pulled low, I could blend in with pedestrian traffic pretty well. Boston was full of college kids. Some of them were even more scraggly and younger-looking than me.

I turned to Blitz. "Where'd you see these people with the flyers?"

"Beacon Street. They're coming this way. Middle-aged white guy and a teenage girl, probably his daughter."

I frowned. "That makes no sense. Who—"

"I don't know, kid, but I gotta go." Blitz squinted at the sunrise, which was turning the skyscraper windows orange. For reasons I'd never quite understood, Blitz hated the daylight. Maybe he was the world's shortest, stoutest homeless vampire. "You should go see Hearth. He's hanging out in Copley Square."

I tried not to feel irritated. The local street people jokingly called Hearth and Blitz my mom and dad because one or the other always seemed to be hovering around me.

"I appreciate it," I said. "I'll be fine."

Blitz chewed his thumbnail. "I dunno, kid. Not today. You gotta be extra careful."

"Why?"

He glanced over my shoulder. "They're coming."

I didn't see anybody. When I turned back, Blitz was gone.

I hated it when he did that. Just— *Poof.* The guy was like a ninja. A homeless vampire ninja.

Now I had a choice: go to Copley Square and hang out with Hearth, or head toward Beacon Street and try to spot the people who were looking for me.

Blitz's description of them made me curious. A middle-aged white guy and a teenage girl searching for me at sunrise on a bitter-cold morning. Why? Who were they?

I crept along the edge of the pond. Almost nobody took the lower trail under the bridge. I could hug the side of the hill and spot anyone approaching on the higher path without them seeing me.

Snow coated the ground. The sky was eye-achingly blue. The bare tree branches looked like they'd been dipped in glass. The wind cut through my layers of clothes, but I didn't mind the cold. My mom used to joke that I was half polar bear.

Dammit, Magnus, I chided myself.

After two years, my memories of her were still a minefield. I stumbled over one, and instantly my composure was blown to bits.

I tried to focus.

The man and the girl were coming this way. The man's sandy hair grew over his collar—not like an intentional style, but like he couldn't be bothered to cut it. His baffled expression reminded me of a substitute teacher's: *I know I was hit by a spit wad, but I have no idea where it came from.* His dress shoes were totally wrong for a Boston winter. His socks were different shades of brown. His tie looked like it had been tied while he spun around in total darkness.

The girl was definitely his daughter. Her hair was just as thick and wavy, though lighter blond. She was dressed more sensibly in snow boots, jeans, and a parka, with an orange T-shirt peeking out at the neckline. Her expression was more determined, angry. She gripped a sheaf of flyers like they were essays she'd been graded on unfairly.

If she was looking for me, I did not want to be found. She was scary.

I didn't recognize her or her dad, but something tugged at the back of my skull . . . like a magnet trying to pull out a very old memory.

Father and daughter stopped where the path forked. They looked around as if just now realizing they were standing in the middle of a deserted park at no-thank-you o'clock in the dead of winter.

"Unbelievable," said the girl. "I want to strangle him."

Assuming she meant me, I hunkered down a little more.

Her dad sighed. "We should probably avoid killing him. He *is* your uncle."

"But *two years*?" the girl demanded. "Dad, how could he not tell us for *two years*?"

"I can't explain Randolph's actions. I never could, Annabeth."

I inhaled so sharply, I was afraid they would hear me. A scab was ripped off my brain, exposing raw memories from when I was six years old.

Annabeth. Which meant the sandy-haired man was . . . *Uncle Frederick?*

I flashed back to the last family Thanksgiving we'd shared: Annabeth and me hiding in the library at Uncle Randolph's town house, playing with dominoes while the adults yelled at each other downstairs.

You're lucky you live with your momma. Annabeth stacked another domino on her miniature building. It was amazingly good, with columns in front like a temple. *I'm going to run away.*

I had no doubt she meant it. I was in awe of her confidence.

Then Uncle Frederick appeared in the doorway. His fists were clenched. His grim expression was at odds with the smiling reindeer on his sweater. *Annabeth, we're leaving.*

Annabeth looked at me. Her gray eyes were a little too fierce for a first grader's. *Be safe, Magnus.*

With a flick of her finger, she knocked over her domino temple.

That was the last time I'd seen her.

Afterward, my mom had been adamant: *We're staying away from your uncles. Especially Randolph. I won't give him what he wants. Ever.*

She wouldn't explain what Randolph wanted, or what she and Frederick and Randolph had argued about.

You have to trust me, Magnus. Being around them . . . it's too dangerous.

I trusted my mom. Even after her death, I hadn't had any contact with my relatives.

Now, suddenly, they were looking for me.

Randolph lived in town, but as far as I knew, Frederick and Annabeth still lived in Virginia. Yet here they were, passing out flyers with my name and photo on them. Where had they even *gotten* a photo of me?

My head buzzed so badly, I missed some of their conversation.

"—to find Magnus," Uncle Frederick was saying. He checked his smartphone. "Randolph is at the city shelter in the South End. He says no luck. We should try the youth shelter across the park."

"How do we even know Magnus is alive?" Annabeth asked miserably. "Missing for *two years*? He could be frozen in a ditch somewhere!"

Part of me was tempted to jump out of my hiding place and shout, *TA-DA!*

Even though it had been ten years since I'd seen Annabeth, I didn't like seeing her distressed. But after so long on the streets, I'd learned the hard way: you never walk into a situation until you understand what's going on.

"Randolph is sure Magnus is alive," said Uncle Frederick. "He's somewhere in Boston. If his life is truly in danger . . ."

They set off toward Charles Street, their voices carried away by the wind.

I was shivering now, but it wasn't from the cold. I wanted to run after Frederick, tackle him, and demand to hear what was going on. How did Randolph know I was still in town? Why were they looking for me? How was my life in danger now more than on any other day?

But I didn't follow them.

I remembered the last thing my mom ever told me. I'd been reluctant to use the fire escape, reluctant to leave her, but she'd gripped my arms and made me look at her. *Magnus, run. Hide. Don't trust anyone. I'll find you. Whatever you do, don't go to Randolph for help.*

Then, before I'd made it out the window, the door of our apartment had burst into splinters. Two pairs of glowing blue eyes had emerged from the darkness. . . .

I shook off the memory and watched Uncle Frederick and Annabeth walk away, veering east toward the Common.

Uncle Randolph . . . For some reason, he'd contacted Frederick and Annabeth. He'd gotten them to Boston. All this time, Frederick and Annabeth hadn't known that my mom was dead and I was missing. It seemed impossible, but if it were true, why would Randolph tell them about it now?

Without confronting him directly, I could think of only one way to get answers. His town house was in Back Bay, an easy walk from here. According to Frederick, Randolph wasn't home. He was somewhere in the South End, looking for me.

Since nothing started a day better than a little breaking and entering, I decided to pay his place a visit.

TWO

The Man with the Metal Bra

THE FAMILY MANSION SUCKED.

Oh, sure, *you* wouldn't think so. You'd see the massive six-story brownstone with gargoyles on the corners of the roof, stained glass transom windows, marble front steps, and all the other blah, blah, blah, rich-people-live-here details, and you'd wonder why I'm sleeping on the streets.

Two words: *Uncle Randolph.*

It was *his* house. As the oldest son, he'd inherited it from my grandparents, who died before I was born. I never knew much about the family soap opera, but there was a lot of bad blood between the three kids: Randolph, Frederick, and my mom. After the Great Thanksgiving Schism, we never visited the ancestral homestead again. Our apartment was, like, half a mile away, but Randolph might as well have lived on Mars.

My mom only mentioned him if we happened to be driving past the brownstone. Then she would point it out the way you might point out a dangerous cliff. *See? There it is. Avoid it.*

After I started living on the streets, I would sometimes walk by at night. I'd peer in the windows and see glowing display cases of antique swords and axes, creepy helmets with facemasks staring at me from the walls, statues silhouetted in the upstairs windows like petrified ghosts.

Several times I considered breaking in to poke around, but I'd never been tempted to knock on the door. *Please, Uncle Randolph, I know you hated my mother and haven't seen me in ten years; I know you care more about your rusty old collectibles than you do about your family; but may I live in your fine house and eat your leftover crusts of bread?*

No thanks. I'd rather be on the street, eating day-old falafel from the food court.

Still . . . I figured it would be simple enough to break in, look around, and see if I could find answers about what was going on. While I was there, maybe I could grab some stuff to pawn.

Sorry if that offends your sense of right and wrong.

Oh, wait. No, I'm not.

I don't steal from just anybody. I choose obnoxious jerks who have too much already. If you're driving a new BMW and you park it in a handicapped spot without a disabled placard, then yeah, I've got no problem jimmying your window and taking some change from your cup holder. If you're coming out of Barneys with your bag of silk handkerchiefs, so busy talking on your phone and pushing people out of your way that you're not paying attention, I am there for you, ready to pickpocket your wallet. If you can afford five thousand dollars to blow your nose, you can afford to buy me dinner.

I am judge, jury, and thief. And as far as obnoxious jerks went, I figured I couldn't do better than Uncle Randolph.

The house fronted Commonwealth Avenue. I headed around back to the poetically named Public Alley 429. Randolph's parking spot was empty. Stairs led down to the basement entrance. If there was a security system, I couldn't spot it. The door was a simple latch lock without even a dead-bolt. *Come on, Randolph. At least make it a challenge.*

Two minutes later I was inside.

In the kitchen, I helped myself to some sliced turkey, crackers, and milk from the carton. No falafel. Dammit. Now I was really in the mood for some, but I found a chocolate bar and stuffed it in my coat pocket for later. (Chocolate must be savored, not rushed.) Then I headed upstairs into a mausoleum of mahogany furniture, oriental rugs, oil paintings, marble tiled floors, and crystal chandeliers. . . . It was just embarrassing. Who lives like this?

At age six, I couldn't appreciate how expensive all this stuff was, but my general impression of the mansion was the same: dark, oppressive, creepy. It was hard to imagine my mom growing up here. It was easy to understand why she'd become a fan of the great outdoors.

Our apartment over the Korean BBQ joint in Allston had been cozy enough, but Mom never liked being inside. She always said her real home was the Blue Hills. We used to go hiking and camping there in all kinds of weather—fresh air, no walls or ceilings, no company but the ducks, geese, and squirrels.

This brownstone, by comparison, felt like a prison. As I stood alone in the foyer, my skin crawled with invisible beetles.

I climbed to the second floor. The library smelled of lemon polish and leather, just like I remembered. Along one wall was a lit glass case full of Randolph's rusty Viking helmets and corroded ax blades. My mom once told me that Randolph taught history at Harvard before some big disgrace got him fired. She wouldn't go into details, but clearly the guy was still an artifact nut.

You're smarter than either of your uncles, Magnus, my mom once told me. *With your grades, you could easily get into Harvard.*

That had been back when she was still alive, I was still in school, and I might have had a future that extended past finding my next meal.

In one corner of Randolph's office sat a big slab of rock like a tombstone, the front chiseled and painted with elaborate red swirly designs. In the center was a crude drawing of a snarling beast—maybe a lion or a wolf.

I shuddered. Let's not think about *wolves.*

I approached Randolph's desk. I'd been hoping for a computer, or a notepad with helpful information—anything to explain why they were looking for me. Instead, spread across the desk were pieces of parchment as thin and yellow as onionskin. They looked like maps a school kid in medieval times had made for social studies: faint sketches of a coastline, various points labeled in an alphabet I didn't know. Sitting on top of them, like a paperweight, was a leather pouch.

My breath caught. I recognized that pouch. I untied the drawstring and grabbed one of the dominoes . . . except it wasn't a domino. My six-year-old self had assumed that's what Annabeth and I had been playing with. Over the years, the memory had reinforced itself. But instead of dots, these stones were painted with red symbols.

The one in my hand was shaped like a tree branch or a deformed *F*:

ᚠ

My heart pounded. I wasn't sure why. I wondered if coming here had been such a good idea. The walls felt like they were closing in. On the big rock in the corner, the drawing of the beast seemed to sneer at me, its red outline glistening like fresh blood.

I moved to the window. I thought it might help to look outside. Along the center of the avenue stretched the Commonwealth Mall—a ribbon of parkland covered in snow. The bare trees were strung with white Christmas lights. At the end of the block, inside an iron fence, the bronze statue of Leif Erikson stood on his pedestal, his hand cupped over his eyes. Leif gazed toward the Charlesgate overpass as if to say *Look, I discovered a highway!*

My mom and I used to joke about Leif. His armor was on the skimpy side: a short skirt and a breastplate that looked like a Viking bra.

I had no clue why that statue was in the middle of Boston, but I figured it couldn't be a coincidence that Uncle Randolph grew up to study Vikings. He'd lived here his whole life. He'd probably looked at Leif every day out the window. Maybe as a child Randolph had thought, *Someday, I want to study Vikings. Men who wear metal bras are cool!*

My eyes drifted to the base of the statue. Somebody was standing there . . . looking up at me.

You know how when you see somebody out of context and it takes you a second to recognize them? In Leif Erikson's shadow stood a tall pale man in a black leather jacket, black motorcycle pants, and pointy-toed boots. His short spiky hair was so blond it was almost white. His only dash of color was a striped red-and-white scarf wrapped around his neck and spilling off his shoulders like a melted candy cane.

If I didn't know him, I might've guessed he was cosplaying

some anime character. But I *did* know him. It was Hearth, my fellow homeless dude and surrogate "mom."

I was a little creeped out, a little offended. Had he seen me on the street and followed me? I didn't need some fairy god-stalker looking after me.

I spread my hands: *What are you doing here?*

Hearth made a gesture like he was plucking something from his cupped hand and throwing it away. After two years of hanging around him, I was getting pretty good at reading sign language.

He was saying *GET OUT.*

He didn't look alarmed, but it was hard to tell with Hearth. He never showed much emotion. Whenever we hung out, he mostly just stared at me with those pale gray eyes like he was waiting for me to explode.

I lost valuable seconds trying to figure out what he meant, why he was here when he was supposed to be in Copley Square.

He gestured again: both hands pointing forward with two fingers, dipping up and down twice. *Hurry.*

"Why?" I said aloud.

Behind me, a deep voice said, "Hello, Magnus."

I nearly jumped out of my shoes. Standing in the library doorway was a barrel-chested man with a trim white beard and a skullcap of gray hair. He wore a beige cashmere overcoat over a dark wool suit. His gloved hands gripped the handle of a polished wooden cane with an iron tip. Last time I'd seen him his hair had been black, but I knew that voice.

"Randolph."

He inclined his head a millimeter. "What a pleasant

surprise. I'm glad you're here." He sounded neither surprised nor glad. "We don't have much time."

The food and milk started to churn in my stomach. "M-much time . . . before what?"

His brow furrowed. His nose wrinkled as if he detected a mildly unpleasant odor. "You're sixteen today, aren't you? They'll be coming to kill you."

THREE

Don't Accept Rides from Strange Relatives

WELL, HAPPY BIRTHDAY TO ME!

Was it January 13? Honestly, I had no idea. Time flies when you're sleeping under bridges and eating from Dumpsters.

So I was officially sixteen. For my present, I got cornered by Uncle Freaky, who announced that I was marked for assassination.

"Who—" I started to ask. "You know what? Never mind. Nice seeing you, Randolph. I'll be going now."

Randolph remained in the doorway, blocking my exit. He pointed the iron tip of his cane at me. I swear I could feel it pushing against my sternum from across the room.

"Magnus, we need to talk. I don't want them to get to you. Not after what happened to your mother. . . ."

A punch in the face would've been less painful.

Memories from that night spun through my head like a sickening kaleidoscope: our apartment building shuddering, a scream from the floor below, my mother—who'd been tense and paranoid all day—dragging me toward the fire escape, telling me to run. The door splintered and burst. From the hallway, two beasts emerged, their pelts the color of dirty snow, their eyes glowing blue. My fingers slipped off the fire escape railing and I fell, landing in a pile of garbage bags in the alley. Moments later, the windows of our apartment exploded, belching fire.

My mom had told me to run. I did. She'd promised to find me. She never did. Later, on the news, I heard that her body had been recovered from the fire. The police were searching for me. They had questions: signs of arson; my record of disciplinary problems at school; neighbors' reports of shouting and a loud crash from our apartment just before the explosion; the fact that I'd run from the scene. None of the reports mentioned wolves with glowing eyes.

Ever since that night I'd been hiding, living under the radar, too busy surviving to grieve properly for my mom, wondering if I'd hallucinated those beasts . . . but I knew I hadn't.

Now, after all this time, Uncle Randolph wanted to help me.

I gripped the little domino stone so tightly, it cut into my palm. "You don't know what happened to my mom. You never cared about either of us."

Randolph lowered his cane. He leaned on it heavily and stared at the carpet. I could almost believe I'd hurt his feelings.

"I pleaded with your mother," he said. "I wanted her to bring you here—to live where I could protect you. She refused. After she died . . ." He shook his head. "Magnus, you have no idea how long I've looked for you, or how much danger you're in."

"I'm fine," I snapped, though my heart was thumping against my ribs. "I've been taking care of myself pretty well."

"Perhaps, but those days are over." The certainty in Randolph's voice gave me a chill. "You're sixteen now, the age of manhood. You escaped them once, the night your mother died. They won't let you escape again. This is our last chance. Let me help you, or you won't live through the day."

The low winter light shifted across the stained glass transom, washing Randolph's face in changing colors, chameleon-style.

I shouldn't have come here. Stupid, stupid, stupid. Over and over, my mom had given me one clear message: *Don't go to Randolph.* Yet here I was.

The longer I listened to him, the more terrified I got, and the more desperately I wanted to hear what he had to say.

"I don't need your help." I set the strange little domino on the desk. "I don't want—"

"I know about the wolves."

That stopped me.

"I know what you saw," he continued. "I know who sent the creatures. Regardless of what the police think, I know how your mother really died."

"How—"

"Magnus, there's so much I need to tell you about your parents, about your inheritance. . . . About your father."

An ice-cold wire threaded its way down my spine. "You knew my father?"

I didn't want to give Randolph any leverage. Living on the street had taught me how dangerous leverage could be. But he had me hooked. I *needed* to hear this information. Judging from the appraising gleam in his eyes, he knew it.

"Yes, Magnus. Your father's identity, your mother's murder, the reason she refused my help . . . it's all connected." He gestured toward his display of Viking goodies. "My whole life, I've been working toward one goal. I've been trying to solve a historical mystery. Until recently, I didn't see the whole picture. Now I do. It's all been leading to *this* day, your sixteenth birthday."

I backed up to the window, as far as I could get from Uncle Randolph. "Look, I don't understand ninety percent of what you're saying, but if you can tell me about my dad—"

The building rattled like a volley of cannons had gone off in the distance—a *rumble* so low I felt it in my teeth.

"They'll be here soon," Randolph warned. "We're running out of time."

"Who are *they*?"

Randolph limped forward, relying on his cane. His right knee didn't seem to work. "I'm asking a lot, Magnus. You have no reason to trust me. But you need to come with me *right now*. I know where your birthright is." He pointed to the old maps on the desk. "Together, we can retrieve what is yours. It's the only thing that might protect you."

I glanced over my shoulder, out the window. Down in the Commonwealth Mall, Hearth had disappeared. I should have done the same. Looking at Uncle Randolph, I tried to see any resemblance to my mother, anything that might inspire me to trust him. I found nothing. His imposing bulk, his intense dark eyes, his humorless face and stiff manner . . . he was the exact opposite of my mom.

"My car is out back," he said.

"M-maybe we should wait for Annabeth and Uncle Frederick."

Randolph grimaced. "They don't believe me. They *never* believed me. Out of desperation, as a last resort, I brought them to Boston to help me look for you, but now that you're here—"

The building shook again. This time the *boom* felt closer and stronger. I wanted to believe it was from construction nearby, or a military ceremony, or anything easily explainable. But my gut told me otherwise. The noise sounded like the fall of a gargantuan foot—like the noise that had shaken our apartment two years ago.

"Please, Magnus." Randolph's voice quavered. "I lost my *own* family to those monsters. I lost my wife, my daughters."

"You—you had a family? My mom never said anything—"

"No, she wouldn't have. But your mother . . . Natalie was my only sister. I loved her. I hated to lose her. I can't lose you, too. Come with me. Your father left something for you to find—something that will change the worlds."

Too many questions crowded my brain. I didn't like the crazy light in Randolph's eyes. I didn't like the way he said *worlds*, plural. And I didn't believe he'd been trying to find me since my mom died. I had my antenna up constantly. If Randolph had been asking about me by name, one of my street friends would've tipped me off, like Blitz had done this morning with Annabeth and Frederick.

Something had changed—something that made Randolph decide I was worth looking for.

"What if I just run?" I asked. "Will you try to stop me?"

"If you run, they'll find you. They'll kill you."

My throat felt like it was full of cotton balls. I didn't trust Randolph. Unfortunately, I believed he was in earnest about people trying to kill me. His voice had the ring of truth.

"Well, then," I said, "let's go for a ride."

FOUR

Seriously, the Dude Cannot Drive

YOU'VE HEARD ABOUT bad Boston drivers? That's my Uncle Randolph.

The dude gunned his BMW 528i (of course it *had* to be a BMW) and shot down Commonwealth Avenue, ignoring the lights, honking at other cars, weaving randomly from lane to lane.

"You missed a pedestrian," I said. "You want to go back and hit her?"

Randolph was too distracted to answer. He kept glancing at the sky as if looking for storm clouds. He gunned the BMW through the intersection at Exeter.

"So," I said, "where are we going?"

"The bridge."

That explained everything. There were, like, twenty bridges in the Boston area.

I ran my hand along the heated leather seat. It had been maybe six months since I'd ridden in a car. The last time it had been a social worker's Toyota. Before that, a police cruiser. Both times I'd used a fake name. Both times I'd escaped, but over the past two years I'd come to equate cars with holding cells. I wasn't sure my luck had changed any today.

I waited for Randolph to answer any of the nagging little

questions I had, like, oh: Who's my dad? Who murdered my mom? How did you lose your wife and kids? Are you presently hallucinating? Did you really have to wear that clove-scented cologne?

But he was too busy causing traffic havoc.

Finally, just to make small talk, I asked, "So who's trying to kill me?"

He turned right on Arlington. We skirted the Public Garden, past the equestrian statue of George Washington, the rows of gaslight lampposts and snow-covered hedges. I was tempted to bail out of the car, run back to the swan pond, and hide in my sleeping bag.

"Magnus," said Randolph, "I've made my life's work studying the Norse exploration of North America."

"Wow, thanks," I said. "That really answered my question."

Suddenly, Randolph *did* remind me of my mom. He gave me the same exasperated scowl, the same look over the top of his glasses, like *Please, kid, cut the sarcasm.* The similarity made my chest ache.

"Fine," I said. "I'll humor you. Norse exploration. You mean the Vikings."

Randolph winced. "Well . . . *Viking* means *raider.* It's more of a job description. Not all Norse people were Vikings. But, yes, those guys."

"The statue of Leif Erikson . . . Does that mean the Vikings—er, the Norse—discovered Boston? I thought the Pilgrims did that."

"I could give you a three-hour lecture on that topic alone."

"Please don't."

"Suffice it to say, the Norse explored North America and even built settlements around the year 1000, almost five hundred years before Christopher Columbus. Scholars agree on that."

"That's a relief. I hate it when scholars disagree."

"But no one is sure how far south the Norse sailed. Did they make it to what is now the United States? That statue of Leif Erikson . . . that was the pet project of a wishful thinker in the 1800s, a man named Eben Horsford. He was convinced that Boston was the lost Norse settlement of Norumbega, their farthest point of exploration. He had an instinct, a gut feeling, but no real proof. Most historians wrote him off as a crackpot."

He looked at me meaningfully.

"Let me guess . . . you don't think he's a crackpot." I resisted the urge to say *Takes one to believe one.*

"Those maps on my desk," Randolph said. "*They* are the proof. My colleagues call them forgeries, but they're not. I staked my reputation on it!"

And that's why you got fired from Harvard, I thought.

"The Norse explorers did make it this far," he continued. "They were searching for something . . . and they found it here. One of their ships sank nearby. For years I thought the shipwreck was in Massachusetts Bay. I sacrificed everything to find it. I bought my own boat, took my wife, my children on expeditions. The last time . . ." His voice broke. "The storm came out of nowhere, the fires . . ."

He didn't seem anxious to share more, but I got the general idea: he'd lost his family at sea. He really *had* staked everything on his crazy theory about Vikings in Boston.

I felt bad for the guy, sure. I also didn't want to be his next casualty.

We stopped at the corner of Boylston and Charles.

"Maybe I'll just get out here." I tried the handle. The door was locked from the driver's side.

"Magnus, listen. It's no accident you were born in Boston. Your father wanted you to find what he lost two thousand years ago."

My feet got jumpy. "Did you just say . . . two thousand years?"

"Give or take."

I considered screaming and pounding on the window. Would anybody help me? If I could get out of the car, maybe I could find Uncle Frederick and Annabeth, assuming they were any less insane than Randolph.

We turned onto Charles Street, heading north between the Public Garden and the Common. Randolph could've been taking me anywhere—Cambridge, the North End, or some out-of-the-way body dump.

I tried to keep calm. "Two thousand years . . . that's a longer lifespan than your average dad."

Randolph's face reminded me of the Man in the Moon from old black-and-white cartoons: pale and rotund, pitted and scarred, with a secretive smile that wasn't very friendly. "Magnus, what do you know about Norse mythology?"

This just gets better and better, I thought.

"Uh, not much. My mom had a picture book she used to read me when I was little. And weren't there a couple of movies about Thor?"

Randolph shook his head in disgust. "Those movies . . .

ridiculously inaccurate. The real gods of Asgard—Thor, Loki, Odin, and the rest—are much more powerful, much more terrifying than anything Hollywood could concoct."

"But . . . they're myths. They're not real."

Randolph gave me a sort of a pitying look. "Myths are simply stories about truths we've forgotten."

"So, look, I just remembered I have an appointment down the street—"

"A millennium ago, Norse explorers came to this land." Randolph drove us past the Cheers bar on Beacon Street, where bundled-up tourists were taking photos of themselves in front of the sign. I spotted a crumpled flyer skittering across the sidewalk: it had the word MISSING and an old picture of me. One of the tourists stepped on it.

"The captain of these explorers," Randolph continued, "was a son of the god Skirnir."

"A son of a god. Really, anywhere around here is good. I can walk."

"This man carried a very special item," Randolph said, "something that once belonged to your father. When the Norse ship went down in a storm, that item was lost. But you—you have the ability to find it."

I tried the door again. Still locked.

The really bad part? The more Randolph talked, the less I could convince myself that he was nuts. His story seeped into my mind—storms, wolves, gods, Asgard. The words clicked into place like pieces of a puzzle I'd never had the courage to finish. I was starting to believe him, and that scared the baked beans out of me.

Randolph whipped around the access road for Storrow

Drive. He parked at a meter on Cambridge Street. To the north, past the elevated tracks of the Mass General T station, rose the stone towers of the Longfellow Bridge.

"That's where we're going?" I asked.

Randolph fished for quarters in his cup holder. "All these years, it was so much closer than I realized. I just needed *you*!"

"I'm definitely feeling the love."

"You are sixteen today." Randolph's eyes danced with excitement. "It's the perfect day for you to reclaim your birthright. But it's also what your enemies have been waiting for. We have to find it first."

"But—"

"Trust me a little while longer, Magnus. Once we have the weapon—"

"Weapon? Now my birthright is a *weapon*?"

"Once you have it in your possession, you'll be much safer. I can explain everything to you. I can help you train for what's to come."

He opened his car door. Before he could get out, I grabbed his wrist.

I usually avoid touching people. Physical contact creeps me out. But I needed his full attention.

"Give me one answer," I said. "One *clear* answer, without the rambling and the history lectures. You said you knew my dad. Who is he?"

Randolph placed his hand over mine, which made me squirm. His palm was too rough and calloused for a history professor's. "On my life, Magnus, I swear this is the truth: your father is a Norse god. Now, hurry. We're in a twenty-minute parking spot."

FIVE

I've Always Wanted
to Destroy a Bridge

"YOU CAN'T DROP a bombshell like that and walk away!" I yelled as Randolph walked away.

Despite his cane and his stiff leg, the guy could really move. He was like an Olympic gold medalist in hobbling. He forged ahead, climbing the sidewalk of the Longfellow Bridge as I jogged after him, the wind screaming in my ears.

The morning commuters were coming in from Cambridge. A single line of cars was backed up the length of the span, barely moving. You'd think my uncle and I would be the only ones dumb enough to walk across the bridge in subzero weather, but this being Boston, half a dozen runners were chugging along, looking like emaciated seals in their Lycra bodysuits. A mom with two kids bundled in a stroller was walking on the opposite sidewalk. Her kids looked about as happy as I felt.

My uncle was still fifteen feet ahead of me.

"Randolph!" I called. "I'm talking to you!"

"The drift of the river," he muttered. "The landfill on the banks . . . allowing for a thousand years of shifting tidal patterns—"

"Yo!" I caught the sleeve of his cashmere coat. "Rewind to the part about a Norse god being my pappy."

Randolph scanned our surroundings. We'd stopped at

one of the bridge's main towers—a cone of granite rising fifty feet above us. People said the towers looked like giant salt and pepper shakers, but I'd always thought they looked like Daleks from *Doctor Who*. (So I'm a nerd. Sue me. And, yes, even homeless kids watch TV sometimes—in shelter rec rooms, on public library computers. . . . We have our ways.)

A hundred feet below us, the Charles River glistened steel gray, its surface mottled with patches of snow and ice like the skin of a massive python.

Randolph leaned so far over the railing it made me jittery.

"The irony," he muttered. "Here, of all places . . ."

"So, anyway," I said, "about my father . . ."

Randolph gripped my shoulder. "Look down there, Magnus. What do you see?"

Cautiously I glanced over the side. "Water."

"No, the carved ornamentation, just below us."

I looked again. About halfway down the side of the pier, a shelf of granite jutted over the water like a theater seating box with a pointy tip. "It looks like a nose."

"No, it's . . . Well, from this angle, it *does* sort of look like a nose. But it's the prow of a Viking longship. See? The other pier has one too. The poet Longfellow, for whom the bridge was named—he was fascinated by the Norse. Wrote poems about their gods. Like Eben Horsford, Longfellow believed the Vikings had explored Boston. Hence the designs on the bridge."

"You should give tours," I said. "All the rabid Longfellow fans would pay big bucks."

"Don't you see?" Randolph still had his hand on my shoulder, which wasn't making me any less anxious. "So many people over the centuries have known. They've *felt* it instinctively, even if they had no proof. This area wasn't just *visited* by the Vikings. It was *sacred* to them! Right below us—somewhere near these decorative longships—is the wreck of an *actual* longship, holding a cargo of incalculable value."

"I still see water. And I still want to hear about Dad."

"Magnus, the Norse explorers came here searching for the axis of the worlds, the very trunk of the tree. They found it—"

A low *boom* echoed across the river. The bridge shook. About a mile away, amid the thicket of chimneys and steeples of Back Bay, a column of oily black smoke mushroomed skyward.

I steadied myself against the railing. "Um, wasn't that close to your house?"

Randolph's expression hardened. His stubbly beard glistened silver in the sunlight.

"We're out of time. Magnus, extend your hand over the water. The sword is down there. Call it. Focus on it as if it's the most important thing in the world—the thing you want the most."

"A sword? I—look, Randolph, I can tell you're having a hard day, but—"

"DO IT."

The sternness in his voice made me flinch. Randolph *had* to be insane, talking about gods and swords and ancient shipwrecks. Yet the column of smoke over Back Bay was very real. Sirens wailed in the distance. On the bridge, drivers stuck their heads out their windows to gawk, holding up smartphones and taking pictures.

And as much as I wanted to deny it, Randolph's words

resonated with me. For the first time, I felt like my body was humming at the right frequency, like I'd finally been tuned to match the crappy soundtrack of my life.

I stretched my hand out over the river.

Nothing happened.

Of course nothing happened, I chided myself. *What were you expecting?*

The bridge shook more violently. Down the sidewalk, a jogger stumbled. From behind me came the *crunch* of one car rear-ending another. Horns blared.

Above the rooftops of Back Bay, a second column of smoke billowed. Ash and orange cinders sprayed upward as if the explosion were volcanic, spewing from the ground.

"That—that was a lot closer," I noted. "It's like something is zeroing in on us."

I really hoped Randolph would say *Nah, of course not. Don't be silly!*

He seemed to get older before my eyes. His wrinkles darkened. His shoulders slumped. He leaned heavily on his cane. "Please, not again," he muttered to himself. "Not like last time."

"*Last* time?" Then I remembered what he'd said about losing his wife and daughters—a storm out of nowhere, fires.

Randolph locked eyes with me. "Try again, Magnus. Please."

I thrust my hand toward the river. I imagined I was reaching for my mom, trying to pull her from the past—trying to save her from the wolves and the burning apartment. I reached for answers that might explain why I'd lost her, why my whole life since then had been nothing but a downhill spiral of *suck*.

Directly below me, the surface of the water began to steam.

Ice melted. Snow evaporated, leaving a hole in the shape of a hand—*my* hand, twenty times larger.

I didn't know what I was doing. I'd had the same feeling when my mom first taught me to ride a bike. *Don't think about what you're doing, Magnus. Don't hesitate, or you'll fall. Just keep going.*

I swept my hand back and forth. A hundred feet below, the steaming hand mirrored my movements, clearing the surface of the Charles. Suddenly I stopped. A pinpoint of warmth hit the center of my palm as if I'd intercepted a beam of sunlight.

Something was down there . . . a heat source buried deep in the frigid mud of the river bottom. I closed my fingers and pulled.

A dome of water swelled and ruptured like a dry-ice bubble. An object resembling a lead pipe shot upward and landed in my hand.

It looked nothing like a sword. I held it by one end, but there was no hilt. If it had ever had a point or a sharp edge, it didn't now. The thing was about the right size for a blade, but it was so pitted and corroded, so encrusted with barnacles and glistening with mud and slime, I couldn't even be sure it was metal. In short, it was the saddest, flimsiest, most disgusting piece of scrap I'd ever magically pulled from a river.

"At last!" Randolph lifted his eyes to the heavens. I got the feeling that, if not for his bum knee, he might've knelt on the pavement and offered a prayer to the nonexistent Norse gods.

"Yeah." I hefted my new prize. "I feel safer already."

"You can renew it!" Randolph said. "Just try!"

I turned the blade. I was surprised that it hadn't already disintegrated in my hand.

"I dunno, Randolph. This thing looks *way* past renewing. I'm not even sure it can be recycled."

If I sound unimpressed or ungrateful, don't get me wrong. The way I'd pulled the sword out of the river was so cool it freaked me out. I'd always wanted a superpower. I just hadn't expected mine to entail retrieving garbage from river bottoms. The community service volunteers were going to love me.

"Concentrate, Magnus!" Randolph said. "Quickly, before—"

Fifty feet away, the center of the bridge erupted in flames. The shockwave pushed me against the rail. The right side of my face felt sunburned. Pedestrians screamed. Cars swerved and crashed into one another.

For some stupid reason, I ran toward the explosion. It was like I couldn't help myself. Randolph shuffled after me, calling my name, but his voice seemed far away, unimportant.

Fire danced across the roofs of cars. Windows shattered from the heat, spraying the street with glass gravel. Drivers scrambled out of their vehicles and fled.

It looked like a meteor had hit the bridge. A ten-foot-diameter circle of asphalt was charred and steaming. In the center of the impact zone stood a human-size figure: a dark man in a dark suit.

When I say dark, I mean his skin was the purest, most beautiful shade of black I'd ever seen. Squid ink at midnight would not have been so black. His clothes were the same: a well-tailored jacket and slacks, a crisp dress shirt and tie—all cut from the fabric of a neutron star. His face was inhumanly handsome, chiseled obsidian. His long hair was combed back in an immaculate oil slick. His pupils glowed like tiny rings of lava.

I thought, *If Satan were real, he would look like this guy.*

Then I thought, *No, Satan would be a schlub next to this guy. This guy is like Satan's fashion consultant.*

Those red eyes locked on to me.

"Magnus Chase." His voice was deep and resonant, his accent vaguely German or Scandinavian. "You have brought me a gift."

An abandoned Toyota Corolla stood between us. Satan's fashion consultant walked straight through it, melting a path down the middle of the chassis like a blowtorch through wax.

The sizzling halves of the Corolla collapsed behind him, the wheels melted to puddles.

"I will make you a gift as well." The dark man extended his hand. Smoke curled off his sleeve and ebony fingers. "Give me the sword and I will spare your life."

SIX

Make Way for Ducklings, or They Will Smack You Upside the Head

I'D SEEN SOME WEIRD STUFF IN MY LIFE.

I once watched a crowd of people wearing nothing but Speedos and Santa hats jog down Boylston in the middle of winter. I met a guy who could play the harmonica with his nose, a drum set with his feet, a guitar with his hands, and a xylophone with his butt all at the same time. I knew a woman who'd adopted a grocery cart and named it Clarence. Then there was the dude who claimed to be from Alpha Centauri and had philosophical conversations with Canada geese.

So a well-dressed Satanic male model who could melt cars . . . why not? My brain just kind of expanded to accommodate the weirdness.

The dark man waited, his hand outstretched. The air around him rippled with heat.

About a hundred feet down the span, a Red Line commuter train ground to a halt. The conductor gawked at the chaos in front of her. Two joggers tried to pull a guy from a half-crushed Prius. The lady with the double stroller was unfastening her screaming kids, the stroller's wheels having melted into ovals. Standing next to her, instead of helping, one idiot held up his smartphone and tried to film the destruction.

His hand was shaking so badly I doubted he was getting a very good picture.

Now at my shoulder, Randolph said, "The sword, Magnus. Use it!"

I got the uncomfortable impression my big burly uncle was hiding behind me.

The dark man chuckled. "Professor Chase . . . I admire your persistence. I thought our last encounter would've broken your spirit. But here you are, ready to sacrifice another family member!"

"Be quiet, Surt!" Randolph's voice was shrill. "Magnus has the sword! Go back to the fires from whence you came."

Surt didn't seem intimidated, though personally I found the word *whence* very intimidating.

Fire Dude studied me like I was as barnacle-encrusted as the sword. "Give it here, boy, or I will show you the power of Muspell. I will incinerate this bridge and everyone on it."

Surt raised his arms. Flames slithered between his fingers. At his feet, the pavement bubbled. More windshields shattered. The train tracks groaned. The Red Line conductor yelled frantically into her walkie-talkie. The pedestrian with the smartphone fainted. The mom collapsed over the stroller, her kids still crying inside. Randolph grunted and staggered backward.

Surt's heat didn't make me pass out. It just made me angry. I didn't know who this fiery jack-hole was, but I knew a bully when I met one. First rule of the streets: Never let a bully take your stuff.

I pointed my once-might-have-been-a-sword at Surt. "Cool

down, man. I have a corroded piece of metal and I'm not afraid to use it."

Surt sneered. "Just like your father, you are no fighter."

I clenched my teeth. *Okay,* I thought, *time to ruin this guy's outfit.*

But before I could take action, something whizzed past my ear and smacked Surt in the forehead.

Had it been a *real* arrow, Surt would've been in trouble. Fortunately for him, it was a plastic toy projectile with a pink heart for a point—a Valentine's Day novelty, I guessed. It hit Surt between the eyes with a cheerful *squeak*, fell to his feet, and promptly melted.

Surt blinked. He looked as confused as I was.

Behind me a familiar voice shouted, "Run, kid!"

Charging up the bridge came my buddies Blitz and Hearth. Well . . . I say *charging.* That implies it was impressive. It really wasn't. For some reason, Blitz had donned a broad-brimmed hat and sunglasses along with his black trench coat, so he looked like a grungy, very short Italian priest. In his gloved hands he wielded a fearsome wooden dowel with a bright yellow traffic sign that read: MAKE WAY FOR DUCKLINGS.

Hearth's red-striped scarf trailed behind him like limp wings. He nocked another arrow in his pink plastic Cupid's bow and fired at Surt.

Bless their demented little hearts, I understood where they'd gotten the ridiculous weapons: the toy store on Charles Street. I panhandled in front of that place sometimes, and they had that stuff in their window display. Somehow, Blitz and Hearth must've followed me here. In their rush, they'd done a smash-and-grab of the nearest deadly objects. Being crazed homeless guys, they hadn't chosen very well.

Dumb and pointless? You bet. But it warmed my heart that they wanted to look out for me.

"We'll cover you!" Blitz charged by me. "Run!"

Surt hadn't been expecting an attack by lightly armed bums. He stood there while Blitz smacked him across the head with the MAKE WAY FOR DUCKLINGS sign. Hearth's next squeaky arrow misfired and hit me in the butt.

"Hey!" I complained.

Being deaf, Hearth couldn't hear me. He ran past me and into battle, thwacking Surt in the chest with his plastic bow.

Uncle Randolph grabbed my arm. He was wheezing badly. "Magnus, we have to go. NOW!"

Maybe I should have run, but I stood there frozen, watching my only two friends attack the dark lord of fire with cheap plastic toys.

Finally Surt tired of the game. He backhanded Hearth and sent him flying across the pavement. He kicked Blitz in the chest so hard the little guy stumbled backward and landed on his butt right in front of me.

"Enough." Surt extended his arm. From his open palm, fire spiraled and elongated until he was holding a curved sword made entirely of white flame. "I am annoyed now. You will all die."

"Gods' galoshes!" Blitz stammered. "That's not just any fire giant. That's the Black One!"

As opposed to the Yellow One? I wanted to ask, but the sight of the flaming sword kind of stifled my will to joke.

Around Surt, flames began to swirl. The firestorm spiraled outward, melting cars to slag heaps, liquefying the pavement, popping rivets from the bridge like champagne corks.

I'd only *thought* it was warm before. Now Surt was really turning up the temperature.

Hearth slumped against the railing about thirty feet away. The unconscious pedestrians and trapped motorists wouldn't last long either. Even if the flames didn't touch them, they'd die from asphyxiation or heat stroke. But for some reason, the heat still didn't bother me.

Randolph stumbled, hanging off my arm with his full weight. "I—I . . . hum, umm . . ."

"Blitz," I said, "get my uncle out of here. Drag him if you have to."

Blitz's sunglasses were steaming. The brim of his hat was beginning to smolder. "Kid, you can't fight that guy. That's Surt, the Black One himself!"

"You said that already."

"But Hearth and me—we're supposed to protect *you!*"

I wanted to snap *And you're doing a great job with the MAKE WAY FOR DUCKLINGS sign!* But what could I expect from a couple of homeless dudes? They weren't exactly commandos. They were just my friends. There was no way I'd let them die defending me. As for Uncle Randolph . . . I hardly knew the guy. I didn't much like him. But he was family. He'd said he couldn't stand to lose another family member. Yeah, well neither could I. This time I wasn't going to run away.

"Go," I told Blitz. "I'll get Hearth."

Somehow Blitz managed to hold up my uncle. Together they stumbled off.

Surt laughed. "The sword will be mine, boy. You cannot change fate. I will reduce your world to cinders!"

I turned to face him. "You're starting to aggravate me. I have to kill you now."

I walked into the wall of flames.

You Look Great
Without a Nose, Really

WOW, MAGNUS, you're probably thinking. *That was . . . stupid!*

Thanks. I have my moments.

Normally I don't go stepping into walls of flame. But I had a feeling it wouldn't hurt me. I know that sounds weird, but so far I hadn't passed out. The heat didn't feel so bad, even though the pavement was turning to sludge at my feet.

Extreme temperatures have never bothered me. I don't know why. Some people are double-jointed. Some people can wiggle their ears. I can sleep outside in the winter without freezing to death or hold matches under my hand without getting burned. I'd won some bets that way in the homeless shelters, but I'd never thought of my tolerance as something special . . . *magical.* I'd definitely never tested its limits.

I walked through the curtain of fire and smacked Surt in the head with my rusty sword. Because, you know, I always try to keep my promises.

The blade didn't seem to hurt him, but the swirling flames died. Surt stared at me for a millisecond, completely shocked. Then he punched me in the gut.

I'd been punched before, just not by a fiery heavyweight whose ring name was the Black One.

I folded like a deck chair. My vision blurred and tripled. When I regained my focus, I was on my knees, staring at a puddle of regurgitated milk, turkey, and crackers steaming on the asphalt.

Surt could have taken my head off with his fiery sword, but I guess he didn't feel I was worth it. He paced in front of me, making *tsk-tsk* sounds.

"Feeble," he said. "A soft little boy. Give me the blade of your own free will, Vanir-spawn. I promise you a quick death."

Vanir-spawn?

I knew a lot of good insults, but I'd never heard that one.

The corroded sword was still in my hand. I felt my pulse against the metal as if the sword itself had developed a heartbeat. Resonating up the blade, all the way to my ears, was a faint hum like a car engine turning over.

You can renew it, Randolph had told me.

I could almost believe the old weapon was stirring, waking up. Not fast enough, though. Surt kicked me in the ribs and sent me sprawling.

I lay flat on my back, staring at the smoke in the winter sky. Surt must have kicked me hard enough to trigger a near-death hallucination. A hundred feet up, I saw a girl in armor on a horse made of mist, circling like a vulture over the battle. She held a spear made of pure light. Her chain mail shone like silvered glass. She wore a conical steel helmet over a green head wrap, sort of like a medieval knight. Her face was beautiful but stern. Our eyes met for a fraction of a second.

If you're real, I thought, *help.*

She dissolved into smoke.

"The sword," Surt demanded, his obsidian face looming over me. "It's worth more to me freely surrendered, but if I must, I will pry it from your dead fingers."

In the distance, sirens wailed. I wondered why emergency crews hadn't shown up already. Then I remembered the other two giant explosions in Boston. Had Surt caused them, too? Or brought along some fiery friends?

At the edge of the bridge, Hearth staggered to his feet. A few unconscious pedestrians had started to stir. I couldn't see Randolph and Blitz anywhere. Hopefully they were out of danger by now.

If I could keep Burning Man occupied, maybe the rest of the bystanders would have time to clear out too.

Somehow I managed to stand.

I looked at the sword and . . . yeah, I was definitely hallucinating.

Instead of a corroded piece of junk, I held an actual weapon. The leather-wrapped grip felt warm and comfortable in my hand. The pommel, a simple polished steel oval, helped counterweight the thirty-inch blade, which was double-edged and rounded at the tip, more for hacking than for stabbing. Down the center of the blade, a wide groove was emblazoned with Viking runes—the same kind I'd seen in Randolph's office. They shimmered in a lighter shade of silver, as if they'd been inlaid while the blade was forged.

The sword was definitely humming now, almost like a human voice trying to find the right pitch.

Surt stepped back. His lava-red eyes flickered nervously. "You don't know what you have there, boy. You won't live long enough to find out."

He swung his scimitar.

I'd had no experience with swords, unless you count watching *The Princess Bride* twenty-six times as a kid. Surt would've cut me in half—but my weapon had other ideas.

Ever held a spinning top on the tip of your finger? You can feel it moving under its own power, tilting in all directions. The sword was like that. It swung itself, blocking Surt's fiery blade. Then it spun in an arc, dragging my arm along with it, and hacked into Surt's right leg.

The Black One screamed. The wound in his thigh smoldered, setting his pants on fire. His blood sizzled and glowed like the flow from a volcano. His fiery blade dissipated.

Before he could recover, my sword leaped upward and slashed his face. With a howl, Surt stumbled back, cupping his hands over his nose.

To my left, someone screamed—the mother with the two kids.

Hearth was trying to help her extract her toddlers from the stroller, which was now smoking and about to combust.

"Hearth!" I yelled, before remembering that was no good.

With Surt still distracted, I limped over to Hearth and pointed down the bridge. "Go! Get the kids out of here!"

He could read lips just fine, but he didn't like my message. He shook his head adamantly, hoisting one of the toddlers into his arms.

The mom was cradling the other kid.

"Leave now," I told her. "My friend will help you."

The mom didn't hesitate. Hearth gave me one last look: *This is not a good idea.* Then he followed her, the little kid bouncing up and down in his arms crying, "Ah! Ah! Ah!"

Other innocent people were still stuck on the bridge:
drivers trapped in their cars, pedestrians wandering around
in a daze, their clothes steaming and their skin lobster red.
Emergency sirens were closer now, but I didn't see how the
police or paramedics could help if Surt was still storming
around being all fiery and stuff.

"Boy!" The Black One sounded like he was gargling with
syrup.

He took his hands from his face, and I saw why. My self-
guided sword had taken off his nose. Molten blood streamed
down his cheeks, splattering on the pavement in sizzling
droplets. His pants had burned off, leaving him in a pair of
flame-patterned red boxers. Between that and the newly sawed-
off snout, he looked like a diabolical version of Porky Pig.

"I have tolerated you long enough," he gargled.

"I was just thinking the same thing about you." I raised the
sword. "You want this? Come and get it."

In retrospect, that was a pretty stupid thing to say.

Above me, I caught a glimpse of the weird gray apparition—
a girl on a horse, circling like a vulture, watching.

Instead of charging, Surt bent down and scooped asphalt
from the road with his bare hands. He molded it into a red-
hot sphere of steaming gunk and pitched it toward me like a
fastball.

Another game I'm not good at: baseball. I swung the
sword, hoping to knock away the projectile. I missed. The
asphalt cannonball plowed into my gut and embedded itself—
burning, searing, destroying.

I couldn't breathe. The pain was so intense I felt every cell
in my body explode in a chain reaction.

Despite that, a strange sort of calm fell over me: I was dying. I wasn't coming back from this. Part of me thought, *All right. Make it count.*

My vision dimmed. The sword hummed and tugged at my hand, but I could barely feel my arms.

Surt studied me, a smile on his ruined face.

He wants the sword, I told myself. *He can't have it. If I'm going out, he's going with me.*

Weakly, I raised my free hand. I flipped him a gesture that he wouldn't need to know sign language to understand.

He roared and charged.

Just as he reached me, my sword leaped up and ran him through. I used the last of my strength to grapple him as his momentum carried us both over the railing.

"No!" He fought to free himself, bursting into flames, kicking and gouging, but I held on as we plummeted toward the Charles River, my sword still embedded in his stomach, my own organs burning away from the molten tar in my gut. The sky flashed in and out of view. I caught a glimpse of the smoky apparition—the girl on the horse diving toward me at a full gallop, her hand outstretched.

FLOOM! I hit the water.

Then I died. The end.

EIGHT

Mind the Gap, and Also the Hairy Guy with the Ax

BACK IN SCHOOL, I loved ending stories that way.

It's the perfect conclusion, isn't it? *Billy went to school. He had a good day. Then he died. The end.*

It doesn't leave you hanging. It wraps everything up nice and neat.

Except in my case, it didn't.

Maybe you're thinking, *Oh, Magnus, you didn't really die. Otherwise you couldn't be narrating this story. You just came close. Then you were miraculously rescued, blah, blah, blah.*

Nope. I actually died. One hundred percent: guts impaled, vital organs burned, head smacked into a frozen river from forty feet up, every bone in my body broken, lungs filled with ice water.

The medical term for that is *dead.*

Gee, Magnus, what did it feel like?

It hurt. A lot. Thanks for asking.

I started to dream, which was weird—not only because I was dead, but because I never dream. People have tried to argue with me about that. They say everybody dreams and I just don't remember mine. But I'm telling you, I always slept like the dead. Until I *was* dead. Then I dreamed like a normal person.

I was hiking with my mom in the Blue Hills. I was maybe ten years old. It was a warm summer day, with a cool breeze through the pines. We stopped at Houghton's Pond to skip stones across the water. I managed three skips. My mom managed four. She always won. Neither of us cared. She would laugh and hug me and that was enough for me.

It's hard to describe her. To really understand Natalie Chase, you had to meet her. She used to joke that her role model was Tinker Bell from *Peter Pan*. If you can imagine Tinker Bell at age thirty-something, minus the wings, wearing flannel, denim, and Doc Martens, you've got a pretty good picture of my mom. She was a petite lady with delicate features, short blond pixie hair, and leaf-green eyes that sparkled with humor. Whenever she read me stories, I used to gaze at the spray of freckles across her nose and try to count them.

She radiated joy. That's the only way I can put it. She loved life. Her enthusiasm was infectious. She was the kindest, most easygoing person I ever knew . . . until the weeks leading up to her death.

In the dream, that was still years in the future. We stood together at the pond. She took a deep breath, inhaling the scent of warm pine needles.

"This is where I met your father," she told me. "On a summer day just like this."

The comment surprised me. She rarely talked about my dad. I'd never met him, never even seen pictures of him. That might sound strange, but my mom didn't make a big deal out of their relationship, so neither did I.

She was clear that my dad hadn't abandoned us. He'd just moved on. She wasn't bitter. She had fond memories of their brief time together. After it ended, she found out she was pregnant with me, and she was elated. Ever since, it had been just the two of us. We didn't need anyone else.

"You met him at the pond?" I asked. "Was he good at skipping stones?"

She laughed. "Oh, yeah. He *destroyed* me at stone skipping. That first day . . . it was perfect. Well, except for one thing." She pulled me close and kissed my forehead. "I didn't have *you* yet, pumpkin."

Okay, yes. My mom called me *pumpkin*. Go ahead and laugh. As I got older, it embarrassed me, but that was while she was still alive. Now I'd give anything to hear her call me pumpkin again.

"What was my dad like?" I asked. It felt strange to say *my dad*. How can somebody be *yours* if you never met him? "What happened to him?"

My mom spread her arms to the sunlight. "That's why I bring you here, Magnus. Can't you feel it? He's all around us."

I didn't know what she meant. Usually she didn't talk in metaphors. My mom was about as literal and down-to-earth as you could get.

She ruffled my hair. "Come on, I'll race you to the beach."

My dream shifted. I found myself standing in Uncle Randolph's library. In front of me, lounging sideways across the desk, was a man I'd never seen before. He was walking his fingers across the collection of old maps.

"Death was an interesting choice, Magnus."

The man grinned. His clothes looked fresh from the store: blinding white sneakers, crisp new jeans, and a Red Sox home jersey. His feathery hair was a mix of red, brown, and yellow, tousled in a fashionable *I-just-got-out-of-bed-and-I-look-this-good* sort of way. His face was shockingly handsome. He could've done ads for aftershave in men's magazines, but his scars ruined the perfection. Burn tissue splashed across the bridge of his nose and his cheekbones, like impact lines on the moon's surface. His lips were marred by a row of welts all the way around his mouth—maybe piercing holes that had closed over. But why would anyone have that many mouth piercings?

I wasn't sure what to say to the scarred hallucination, but since my mom's words were still lingering in my head, I asked, "Are you my father?"

The hallucination raised his eyebrows. He threw back his head and laughed.

"Oh, I *like* you! We'll have fun. No, Magnus Chase, I'm not your father, but I'm definitely on your side." He traced his finger under the Red Sox logo on his jersey. "You'll meet *my* son soon enough. Until then, a little advice: Don't trust appearances. Don't trust your comrades' motives. Oh, and"— he lunged forward and grabbed my wrist—"tell the All-Father I said hello."

I tried to break free. His grip was like steel. The dream changed. Suddenly I was flying through cold gray fog.

"Stop struggling!" said a female voice.

Holding my wrist was the girl I'd seen circling the bridge. She charged through the air on her nebulous horse, pulling me along at her side like I was a sack of laundry. Her blazing spear was strapped across her back. Her chain mail armor glinted in the gray light.

She tightened her grip. "Do you *want* to fall into the Gap?"

I got a feeling she wasn't talking about the clothing store.

Looking below me, I saw nothing—just endless gray. I decided I did not want to fall into it.

I tried to speak. I couldn't. I shook my head weakly.

"Then stop struggling," she ordered.

Beneath her helmet, a few wisps of dark hair had escaped her green headscarf. Her eyes were the color of redwood bark.

"Don't make me regret this," she said.

My consciousness faded.

I awoke gasping, every muscle in my body tingling with alarm.

I sat up and grabbed my gut, expecting to find a burning hole where my intestines used to be. No smoldering asphalt was embedded there. I felt no pain. The strange sword was gone. My clothes looked perfectly fine—not wet or burned or torn.

In fact, my clothes looked *too* fine. The same stuff I'd been wearing for weeks—my only pair of jeans, my layers of shirts, my jacket—didn't smell. They'd seemingly been washed, dried, and put back on me while I was unconscious, which was an unsettling idea. They even had a warm lemony scent that reminded me of the good old days when my mom did my laundry. My shoes were like new, as shiny as when I dug them out of the Dumpster behind Marathon Sports.

Even weirder: *I* was clean. My hands weren't caked with grime. My skin felt freshly scrubbed. I ran my fingers through my hair and found no tangles, no twigs, no pieces of litter.

Slowly I got to my feet. There wasn't a scratch on me. I bounced on my heels. I felt like I could run a mile. I breathed in the smell of chimney fires and an approaching snowstorm. I almost laughed with relief. Somehow I'd survived!

Except . . . that wasn't possible.

Where was I?

Gradually my senses expanded. I was standing in the entry courtyard of an opulent town house, the kind you might see on Beacon Hill—eight stories of imposing white limestone and gray marble jutting into the winter sky. The double front doors were dark heavy wood bound with iron. In the center of each was a life-size wolf's-head doorknocker.

Wolves . . . that alone was enough to make me hate the place.

I turned to look for a street exit. There wasn't one, just a fifteen-foot-tall white limestone wall surrounding the courtyard. How could you not have a front gate?

I couldn't see much over the wall, but I was obviously still in Boston. I recognized some of the surrounding buildings. In the distance rose the towers of Downtown Crossing. I was probably on Beacon Street, just across from the Common. But how had I gotten here?

In one corner of the courtyard stood a tall birch tree with pure white bark. I thought about climbing it to get over the wall, but the lowest branches were out of reach. Then I realized the tree was in full leaf, which shouldn't have been possible in the winter. Not only that: its leaves glittered gold as if someone had painted them with twenty-four-karat gilt.

Next to the tree, a bronze plaque was affixed to the wall. I hadn't really noticed it earlier, since half the buildings in Boston had historic markers, but now I looked closer. The inscriptions were in two languages. One was the Norse alphabet I'd seen earlier. The other was English:

WELCOME TO THE GROVE OF GLASIR.

NO SOLICITING. NO LOITERING.

HOTEL DELIVERIES: PLEASE USE THE NIFLHEIM ENTRANCE.

Okay . . . I'd exceeded my daily quota of bizarre. I had to
get out of here. I had to get over that wall, find out what had
happened to Blitz and Hearth—and maybe Uncle Randolph if
I was feeling generous—then possibly hitchhike to Guatemala.
I was *done* with this town.

Then the double doors swung inward with a groan. Blinding golden light spilled out.

A burly man appeared on the stoop. He wore a doorman's
uniform: top hat, white gloves, and a dark green jacket with
tails and the interlocking letters HV embroidered on the lapel,
but there was no way this guy was an actual doorman. His
warty face was smeared with ashes. His beard hadn't been
trimmed in decades. His eyes were bloodshot and murderous,
and a double-bladed ax hung at his side. His name tag read:
HUNDING, SAXONY, VALUED TEAM MEMBER SINCE 749 C.E.

"S-s-sorry," I stammered. "I must . . . um, wrong house."

The man scowled. He shuffled closer and sniffed me. He
smelled like turpentine and burning meat. "Wrong house? I
don't think so. You're checking in."

"Uh . . . what?"

"You're dead, aren't you?" the man said. "Follow me. I'll
show you to registration."

NINE

You Totally Want
the Minibar Key

WOULD IT SURPRISE you to learn that the place was bigger on the inside?

The foyer alone could've been the world's largest hunting lodge—a space twice as big as the mansion appeared on the outside. An acre of hardwood floor was covered with exotic animal skins: zebra, lion, and a forty-foot-long reptile that I wouldn't want to have met when it was alive. Against the right wall, a fire crackled in a bedroom-size hearth. In front of it, a few high-school-age guys in fluffy green bathrobes lounged on overstuffed leather couches, laughing and drinking from silver goblets. Over the mantel hung the stuffed head of a wolf.

Oh, joy, I thought with a shudder. *More wolves.*

Columns made from rough-hewn tree trunks held up the ceiling, which was lined with spears for rafters. Polished shields gleamed on the walls. Light seemed to radiate from everywhere—a warm golden glow that hurt my eyes like a summer afternoon after a dark theater.

In the middle of the foyer, a freestanding display board announced:

TODAY'S ACTIVITIES

SINGLE COMBAT TO THE DEATH!—OSLO ROOM, 10 A.M.

GROUP COMBAT TO THE DEATH!—STOCKHOLM ROOM, 11 A.M.

BUFFET LUNCH TO THE DEATH!—DINING HALL, 12 P.M.

FULL ARMY COMBAT TO THE DEATH!—MAIN COURTYARD, 1 P.M.

BIKRAM YOGA TO THE DEATH!—COPENHAGEN ROOM,

BRING YOUR OWN MAT, 4 P.M.

The doorman Hunding said something, but my head was ringing so badly I missed it.

"Sorry," I said, "what?"

"Luggage," he repeated. "Do you have any?"

"Um . . ." I reached for my shoulder strap. My backpack had apparently not been resurrected with me. "No."

Hunding grunted. "No one brings luggage anymore. Don't they put *anything* on your funeral pyre?"

"My what?"

"Never mind." He scowled toward the far corner of the room, where an overturned boat's keel served as the reception desk. "Guess there's no putting it off. Come on."

The man behind the keel apparently used the same barber as Hunding. His beard was so big it had its own zip code. His hair looked like a buzzard that had exploded on a windshield. He was dressed in a forest green pinstriped suit. His name tag read: HELGI, MANAGER, EAST GOTHLAND, VALUED TEAM MEMBER SINCE 749 C.E.

"Welcome!" Helgi glanced up from his computer screen. "Checking in?"

"Uh—"

"You realize check-in time is three P.M.," he said. "If you die earlier in the day, I can't guarantee your room will be ready."

"I can just go back to being alive," I offered.

"No, no." He tapped on his keyboard. "Ah, here we are." He grinned, revealing exactly three teeth. "We've upgraded you to a suite."

Next to me, Hunding muttered under his breath, "Everyone is upgraded to a suite. All we *have* are suites."

"Hunding . . ." warned the manager.

"Sorry, sir."

"You don't want me to use the stick."

Hunding winced. "No, sir."

I looked back and forth between them, checking their name tags.

"You guys started working here the same year," I noted. "749 . . . what is C.E.?"

"Common Era," said the manager. "What you might call A.D."

"Then why don't you just say A.D.?"

"Because Anno Domini, *in the Year of Our Lord*, is fine for Christians, but Thor gets a little upset. He still holds a grudge that Jesus never showed up for that duel he challenged him to."

"Say what now?"

"It's not important," Helgi said. "How many keys would you like? Is one sufficient?"

"I still don't get where I am. If you guys have been here since 749, that's over a thousand years."

"Don't remind me," Hunding grumbled.

"But that's impossible. And . . . and you said I'm dead? I don't feel dead. I feel fine."

"Sir," Helgi said, "all this will be explained tonight at dinner. That's when new guests are formally welcomed."

"Valhalla." The word surfaced from the depths of my

brain—a half-remembered story my mom had read me when I was little. "The *HV* on your lapel. The *V* stands for *Valhalla*?"

Helgi's eyes made it clear I was straining his patience. "Yes, sir. The Hotel Valhalla. Congratulations. You've been chosen to join the hosts of Odin. I look forward to hearing about your brave exploits at dinner."

My legs buckled. I leaned on the desk for support. I'd been trying to convince myself this was all a mistake—some elaborate theme hotel where I'd been mistaken for a guest. Now I wasn't so sure.

"Dead," I mumbled. "You mean I'm actually . . . I'm actually—"

"Here is your room key." Helgi handed me a stone engraved with a single Viking rune, like the stones in Uncle Randolph's library. "Would you like the minibar key?"

"Uh—"

"He wants the minibar key," Hunding answered for me. "Kid, you want the minibar key. It's going to be a long stay."

My mouth tasted like copper. "How long?"

"Forever," Helgi said, "or at least until Ragnarok. Hunding will now show you to your room. Enjoy your afterlife. Next!"

TEN

My Room Does Not Suck

I WASN'T PAYING the closest attention as Hunding guided me through the hotel. I felt as if I'd been spun around fifty times then released into the middle of a circus and told to have fun.

Each hall we walked through seemed bigger than the one before. Most of the hotel guests looked like they were in high school, though some looked slightly older. Guys and girls sat together in small groups, lounging in front of fire-places, chatting in many different languages, eating snacks or playing board games like chess and Scrabble and something that involved real daggers and a blowtorch. Peeking into side lounges, I spotted pool tables, pinball machines, an old-fashioned video arcade, and something that looked like an iron maiden from a torture chamber.

Staff members in dark green shirts moved among the guests, bringing platters of food and pitchers of drink. As far as I could tell, all the servers were buff female warriors with shields on their backs and swords or axes on their belts, which is not something you see a lot in the service industry.

One heavily armed waitress passed me with a steaming plate of egg rolls. My stomach rumbled.

"How can I be hungry if I'm dead?" I asked Hunding. "*None* of these people look dead."

Hunding shrugged. "Well, there's dead and then there's dead. Think of Valhalla more like . . . an upgrade. You're one of the *einherjar* now."

He pronounced the word like *in-HAIR-yar*.

"Einherjar," I repeated. "Just rolls right off the tongue."

"Yeah. Singular: *einherji*." He said it like *in-HAIR-yee*. "We're the chosen of Odin, soldiers in his eternal army. The word *einherjar* is usually translated as *lone warriors*, but that doesn't really capture the meaning. It's more like . . . the *once warriors*—the warriors who fought bravely in the last life and will fight bravely again on the Day of Doom. Duck."

"The Day of Doom Duck?"

"No, duck!"

Hunding pushed me down as a spear flew past. It impaled a guy sitting on the nearest sofa, killing him instantly. Drinks, dice, and Monopoly money flew everywhere. The people he'd been playing with rose to their feet, looking mildly annoyed, and glared in the direction the spear had come from.

"I saw that, John Red Hand!" Hunding yelled. "The lounge is a *No Impaling* area!"

From the billiard room, somebody laughed and called back in . . . Swedish? He didn't sound very remorseful.

"Anyway." Hunding resumed walking as if nothing had happened. "The elevators are right over here."

"Wait," I said. "That guy was just murdered with a spear. Aren't you going to *do* anything?"

"Oh, the wolves will clean up."

My pulse went into double time. "Wolves?"

Sure enough, while the other Monopoly players were sorting their pieces, a pair of gray wolves bounded into the lounge, grabbed the dead man by his legs, and dragged him away, the spear still sticking out of his chest. The trail of blood evaporated instantly. The perforated sofa mended itself.

I cowered behind the nearest potted plant. I don't care how that sounds. My fear simply took control. These wolves didn't have glowing blue eyes like the animals that had attacked my apartment, but still I wished I'd ended up in an afterlife where the mascot was a gerbil.

"Aren't there any rules against killing?" I asked in a small voice.

Hunding raised a bushy eyebrow. "That was just a bit of fun, boy. The victim will be fine by dinner." He pulled me out of my hiding place. "Come on."

Before I could ask more about the "bit of fun," we reached an elevator. Its cage door was made out of spears. Overlapping gold shields lined the walls. The control panel had so many buttons, it stretched from floor to ceiling. The highest number was 540. Hunding pressed 19.

"How can this place have five hundred and forty floors?" I said. "It would be the tallest building in the world."

"If it only existed in one world, yes. But it connects with all the Nine Worlds. You just came through the Midgard entrance. Most mortals do."

"Midgard . . ." I vaguely remembered something about the Vikings believing in nine different worlds. Randolph had used the term *worlds* too. But it had been a long time since my mom read me those Norse bedtime stories. "You mean, like, the world of humans."

"Aye." Hunding took a breath and recited, *"Five hundred and forty floors has Valhalla; five hundred and forty doors leading out into the Nine Worlds."* He grinned. "You never know when or where we'll have to march off to war."

"How often has that happened?"

"Well, never. But still . . . it could happen at any time. I, for one, can't wait! Finally, Helgi will have to stop punishing me."

"The manager? What's he punishing you for?"

Hunding's expression soured. "Long story. He and I—"

The elevator's spear-cage door rolled open.

"Forget it." Hunding clapped me on the back. "You'll like floor nineteen. Good hallmates!"

I'd always thought of hotel corridors as dark, depressing, and claustrophobic. Floor nineteen? Not so much. The vaulted ceiling was twenty feet tall, lined with—you guessed it—more spears for rafters. Valhalla had apparently gotten a good deal at the Spear Wholesale Warehouse. Torches burned in iron sconces, but they didn't seem to make any smoke. They just cast warm orange light across the wall displays of swords, shields, and tapestries. The hall was so wide you could've played a regulation soccer game, no problem. The bloodred carpet had tree branch designs that moved as if swaying in the wind.

Set about fifty feet apart, each guest room door was rough-hewn oak bound in iron. I didn't see any doorknobs or locks. In the center of each door, a plate-size iron circle was inscribed with a name surrounded by a ring of Viking runes.

The first read HALFBORN GUNDERSON. Behind that door I heard shouting and metal clanging like a sword fight was in progress.

The next read MALLORY KEEN. Behind that door, silence.

Then: THOMAS JEFFERSON, JR. The popping of gunfire came from inside, though it sounded more like a video game than the actual thing. (Yes, I've heard both.)

The fourth door was simply marked X. In front, a room-service cart sat in the hallway with the severed head of a pig on a silver platter. The pig's ears and nose looked slightly nibbled.

Now, I'm not a food critic. Being homeless, I could never afford to be. But I draw the line at pig heads.

We'd almost reached the T at the end of the hall when a large black bird shot around the corner and zipped past me, almost clipping my ear. I watched the bird disappear down the hall—a raven, with a notepad and a pen in its talons.

"What was that?" I asked.

"A raven," Hunding said, which I found very helpful.

Finally we stopped at a door inscribed MAGNUS CHASE.

Seeing my name written in iron, inscribed with runes, I started to tremble. My last hope that this might be a mistake, birthday prank, or cosmic mix-up finally evaporated. The hotel was expecting me. They'd spelled my name right and everything.

For the record, Magnus means *great*. My mom named me that because our family was descended from Swedish kings or something a billion years ago. Also, she said I was the great-est thing that ever happened to her. I know. One, two, three: *Awwwwww.* It was an annoying name to have. People tended to spell it Mangus, rhymes with Angus. I always corrected them: *No, it's Magnus, rhymes with swag-ness.* At which point they would stare at me blankly.

Anyway, there was my name on the door. Once I went

through, I would be checked in. According to the manager, I'd have a new home until doomsday.

"Go ahead." Hunding pointed at the runestone key in my hand. The symbol looked sort of like an infinity sign or a sideways hourglass:

ᛞ

"It's *dagaz*," Hunding said. "Nothing to be afraid of. It symbolizes new beginnings, transformations. It also opens your door. Only you have access."

I swallowed. "What if, for instance, the staff wants to get in?"

"Oh, we use the staff key." Hunding patted the ax on his belt. I couldn't tell if he was kidding.

I held up the runestone. I didn't want to try it, but I also didn't want to stay in the hallway until I got impaled by a random spear or injured by a raven hit-and-run. Instinctively, I touched the stone to the matching dagaz mark on the door. The ring of runes glowed green. The door swung open.

I stepped inside, and my jaw hit the floor.

The suite was nicer than any place I'd ever lived, nicer than any place I'd ever visited, including Uncle Randolph's mansion.

In a trance, I moved to the middle of the suite, where a central atrium was open to the sky. My shoes sank into the thick green grass. Four large oak trees ringed the garden like pillars. The lower branches spread into the room across the ceiling, interweaving with the rafters. The taller branches grew up through the opening of the atrium, making a lacy canopy. Sunlight warmed my face. A pleasant breeze wafted through the room, bringing the smell of jasmine.

"How?" I stared at Hunding. "Hundreds of floors are above us, but that's open sky. And it's the middle of winter. How can it feel sunny and warm?"

Hunding shrugged. "I don't know—magic. But this is *your* afterlife, boy. You've earned some perks, eh?"

Had I? I didn't feel particularly perk-worthy.

I turned in a slow circle. The suite was shaped like a cross, with four sections radiating from the central atrium. Each wing was as large as my old apartment. One was the entry hall where we'd come in. The next was a bedroom with a king-size bed. Despite its size, the room was spare and simple: a beige comforter and fluffy-looking pillows on the bed, beige walls with no artwork or mirrors or other decoration. Heavy brown curtains could be drawn to close off the space.

I remembered when I was a kid, how my mom used to make my room as no-frills as possible. I'd always found it hard to sleep indoors unless I had total darkness and nothing to distract me. Looking at this bedroom, I felt like somebody had reached into my mind and pulled out exactly what I needed to be comfortable.

The wing to the left was a dressing area/bathroom tiled in black and beige, my favorite colors. The perks included a sauna, a hot tub, a walk-in closet, a walk-in shower, and a walk-in toilet. (Just kidding on that last one, but it *was* a fancy throne, suitable for the honored dead.)

The suite's fourth wing was a full kitchen and living room. At one end of the living room, a big leather couch faced a plasma-screen TV with about six different game systems stacked in the media cabinet. On the other side, two recliners sat in front of a crackling fireplace and a wall of books.

Yes, I like to read. I'm weird that way. Even after dropping out of school, I spent a lot of time in the Boston Public Library, learning random stuff just to pass the time in a warm, safe place. For two years I had missed my old book collection; I never seriously thought I would have one again.

I walked over to check out the titles on the shelves. Then I noticed the picture framed in silver on the fireplace mantel.

Something like a bubble of helium made its way up my esophagus. "No way . . ."

I picked up the photo. It showed me, at age eight, and my mom at the summit of Mount Washington in New Hampshire. That had been one of the best trips of my life. We'd asked a park ranger to take the photo. In the shot, I was grinning (which I don't do much anymore), showing off my missing two front teeth. My mom knelt behind me with her arms wrapped around my chest, her green eyes crinkling at the corners, her freckles dark from the sun, her blond hair swept sideways by the wind.

"This is impossible," I murmured. "There was only one copy of this picture. It burned in the fire . . ." I turned to Hunding, who was wiping his eyes. "You okay?"

He cleared his throat. "Fine! Of course I'm fine. The hotel likes to provide you with keepsakes, reminders of your old life. Photographs . . ." Under his beard, his mouth might have been quivering. "Back when I died, they didn't have photographs. It's just . . . you're lucky."

No one had called me *lucky* in a very long time. The idea shook me out of my daze. I'd been without my mom for two years. I'd been dead, or *upgraded*, for only a few hours. This bellhop from Saxony had been here since 749 C.E. I wondered how he had died, and what family he'd left behind. Twelve hundred years later, he was still getting teary-eyed about them, which seemed like a cruel way to spend an afterlife.

Hunding straightened and wiped his nose. "Enough of that! If you have any questions, call the front desk. I look forward to hearing about your brave exploits tonight at dinner."

"My . . . brave exploits?"

"Now, don't be modest. You wouldn't have been chosen unless you did something heroic."

"But—"

"Been a pleasure serving you, sir, and welcome to the Hotel Valhalla."

He held out his palm. It took me a second to realize he wanted a tip.

"Oh, um . . ." I dug into my jacket pockets, not expecting to find anything. Miraculously, the chocolate bar I'd swiped from Uncle Randolph's house was still there, undamaged from its trip through the Great Beyond. I gave it to Hunding. "Sorry, that's all I have."

His eyes turned the size of drink coasters. "Gods of Asgard! Thank you, kid!" He sniffed the chocolate and held it up like a holy chalice. "Wow! Okay, you need anything, you let me know. Your Valkyrie will come get you right before dinner. Wow!"

"My Valkyrie? Wait. I don't have a Valkyrie."

Hunding laughed, his eyes still fixed on the chocolate bar. "Yeah, if I had *your* Valkyrie, I'd say the same thing. She's caused her share of trouble."

"What do mean?"

"See you tonight, kid!" Hunding headed for the door. "I got things to eat—I mean *do*. Try not to kill yourself before dinner!"

Pleased to Meet You. I Will Now Crush Your Windpipe

I COLLAPSED ON THE GRASS.

Gazing up through the tree branches at the blue sky, I had trouble breathing. I hadn't had an asthma attack in years, but I remembered all the nights my mom had held me while I wheezed, feeling like an invisible belt was tightening around my chest. Maybe you're wondering why my mom would take me camping and climbing mountains if I had asthma, but being outside always helped.

Lying in the middle of the atrium, I breathed in the fresh air and hoped my lungs would settle down.

Unfortunately, I was pretty sure this wasn't an asthma attack. This was a complete nervous breakdown. What shook me wasn't just the fact that I was dead, stuck in a bizarre Viking afterlife where people ordered pig heads from the room service menu and impaled each other in the lobby.

The way my life had gone so far, I could accept that. Of *course* I'd end up in Valhalla on my sixteenth birthday. Just my luck.

What really hit me: for the first time since my mom died, I was in a comfortable place, alone and safe (as far as I could tell at the moment). Shelters didn't count. Soup kitchens and

rooftops and sleeping bags under bridges didn't count. I'd
always slept with one eye open. I could never relax. Now, I was
free to think.

And thinking wasn't a good thing.

I'd never had the luxury of grieving properly for my mom.
I'd never had time to sit and feel sorry for myself. In a way,
that had been as helpful to me as the survival skills my mom
had taught me—how to navigate, how to camp, how to make
a fire.

All those trips to the parks, the mountains, the lakes. As
long as her old beat-up Subaru was working, we'd spend every
weekend out of town, exploring the wilderness.

What are we running from? I asked her one Friday, a few
months before she died. I was annoyed. I wanted to crash at
home for once. I didn't understand her frantic rush to pack
and leave.

She'd smiled, but she seemed more preoccupied than
usual. *We have to make the most of our time, Magnus.*

Had my mom been deliberately preparing me to survive
on my own? Almost as if she'd known what would happen to
her . . . but that wasn't possible. Then again, having a Norse
god for a dad wasn't possible either.

My breathing still rattled, but I got up and paced around my
new room. In the photo on the mantel, eight-year-old Magnus
grinned at me with his tangled hair and his missing teeth. That
kid was so clueless, so unappreciative of what he had.

I scanned the bookshelves: my favorite fantasy and horror
authors from when I was younger—Stephen King, Darren Shan,
Neal Shusterman, Michael Grant, Joe Hill; my favorite graphic
novel series—Scott Pilgrim, Sandman, Watchmen, Saga; plus

a lot of books I'd been meaning to read at the library. (Pro homeless tip: public libraries are safe havens. They have bathrooms. They hardly ever kick out kids who are reading as long as you don't smell too bad or cause a scene.)

I pulled down the illustrated children's book of Norse myths my mom read to me when I was little. Inside were simplistic pictures of happy smiling Viking gods, rainbows, flowers, and pretty girls with blond hair. And sentences like *The gods dwelt in a wonderful and beautiful realm!* There was nothing about the Black One Surt who burned baby carriages and threw molten asphalt, nothing about wolves that murdered people's mothers and made apartments explode. That made me angry.

On the coffee table was a leather-bound notebook titled GUEST SERVICES. I flipped through it. The room service menu went on for ten pages. The TV channel list was almost as long, and the hotel map was so convoluted, divided into so many subsections, I couldn't make sense of it. There were no clearly marked emergency doors labeled: EXIT HERE TO RETURN TO YOUR OLD LIFE!

I threw the guest services book into the fireplace.

As it burned, a new copy appeared on the coffee table. Stupid magical hotel wouldn't even allow me to properly vandalize things.

In a rage, I flipped the sofa. I didn't expect it to go far, but it cartwheeled across the room and smashed into the far wall.

I stared at the trail of dislodged cushions, the upside-down sofa, the cracked plaster and leather skid marks on the wall. How had I done that?

The sofa didn't magically right itself. It stayed where I'd thrown it. The anger drained out of me. I'd probably just made extra work for some poor staff member like Hunding. That didn't seem fair.

I paced some more, thinking about the dark fiery guy on the bridge and why he'd wanted the sword. I hoped Surt had died with me—more *permanently* than I had—but I wasn't optimistic. As long as Blitz and Hearth had gotten away safely. (Oh, yeah. Randolph, too, I guess.)

And the sword itself . . . where was it? Back on the river bottom? Valhalla could resurrect me with a chocolate bar in my pocket, but not a sword in my hand. That was messed up.

In the old stories, Valhalla was for heroes who died in battle. I remembered that much. I definitely didn't feel like a hero. I'd gotten my butt kicked and my guts cannonballed. By stabbing Surt and toppling off the bridge, I'd simply failed in the most productive way possible. A brave death? Not so much.

I froze.

An idea struck me with the force of a sledgehammer.

My mom . . . If anyone had died bravely, *she* had. To protect me from—

Just then someone knocked on my door.

It swung open and a girl stepped inside . . . the same girl who had circled over the battle on the bridge, then pulled me through the gray void.

She had ditched her helmet, chain mail, and glowing spear. Her green headscarf was now around her neck, letting her long brown hair spill freely over her shoulders. Her white dress was embroidered with Viking runes around the collar and cuffs. From her golden belt hung a set of old-fashioned keys and a single-bladed ax. She looked like the maid of honor at someone's Mortal Kombat wedding.

She glanced at the overturned sofa. "Did the furniture offend you?"

"You're real," I noted.

She patted her own arms. "Yes, it appears I am."

"My mother," I said.

"No," she said, "I'm not your mother."

"I mean, is she here in Valhalla?"

The girl's mouth formed a silent *Oh*. She gazed over my shoulder as if considering her answer. "I'm sorry. Natalie Chase is not among the Chosen."

"But *she* was the brave one. She sacrificed herself for me."

"I believe you." The girl examined her key ring. "But I would know if she were here. We Valkyries are not allowed to choose everyone who dies bravely. There are . . . many factors, many different afterlives."

"Then where is she? I want to be there. I'm no hero!"

She surged toward me, pushing me against the wall as easily as I'd flipped the sofa. She pressed her forearm against my throat.

"Don't say that," the girl hissed. "DO—NOT—SAY—THAT! Especially not tonight at dinner."

Her breath smelled like spearmint. Her eyes were somehow dark and bright at the same time. They reminded me of a fossil my mom used to have—a cross section of a nautilus-like sea animal called an ammonite. It seemed to glow from within, as if it had absorbed millions of years of memories while lying under the earth. The girl's eyes had that same sort of luster.

"You don't understand," I croaked. "I have to—"

She pushed harder against my windpipe. "What do you think I don't understand? Grieving for your mother? Being judged unfairly? Being somewhere you don't want to be, forced to deal with people you'd rather not deal with?"

I didn't know how to respond to that, especially since I couldn't breathe.

She stepped away. As I choked and gagged, she paced the foyer, glaring at nothing in particular. Her ax and keys swung on her belt.

I rubbed my bruised neck.

Stupid, Magnus, I told myself. *New place: learn the rules.*

I couldn't start whining and making demands. I had to set aside the question of my mother. If she were anywhere, I'd figure that out later. Right now, being in this hotel was no different than walking into an unfamiliar youth shelter, alley encampment, or church basement soup kitchen. Every place had rules. I had to learn the power structure, the pecking order, the no-nos that would get me stabbed or rolled. I had to survive . . . even if I was already dead.

"Sorry," I said. My throat felt like I'd swallowed a live rodent with lots of claws. "But why do you care if I'm a hero or not?"

She smacked her forehead. "Wow, okay. Maybe because I *brought* you here? Maybe because my career is on the line? One more slipup and—" She caught herself. "Never mind. When you're introduced, go along with what I say. Keep your mouth shut, nod your head, and try to look brave. Don't make me regret bringing you here."

"All right. But for the record, I didn't ask for your help."

"Odin's Eye! You were *dying*! Your other options were Helheim or Ginnungagap or . . ." She shuddered. "Let's just say there are worse places to spend your afterlife in than Valhalla.

I saw what you did on the bridge. Whether you recognize it or not, you acted bravely. You sacrificed yourself to save a lot of people."

Her words sounded like a compliment. Her tone sounded like she was calling me an idiot.

She marched over and poked me in the chest. "You have potential, Magnus Chase. *Don't* prove me wrong or—"

From the wall speakers, a horn blast sounded so loudly it rattled the picture on the mantel.

"What's that?" I asked. "An air raid?"

"Dinner." The girl straightened. She took a deep breath and extended her hand. "Let's start again. Hi, I'm Samirah al-Abbas."

I blinked. "Don't take this the wrong way, but that doesn't sound like a very Viking-ish name."

She smiled tightly. "You can call me Sam. Everyone does. I'll be your Valkyrie this evening. Pleased to meet you properly."

She shook my hand, her grip so tight my finger bones popped. "I will now escort you to dinner." She forced a smile. "If you embarrass me, I'll be the first to kill you."

TWELVE

At Least I'm Not on Goat-Chasing Duty

IN THE HALLWAY, my neighbors were starting to emerge. Thomas Jefferson, Jr. looked about my age. He had short curly hair, a lanky frame, and a rifle slung over one shoulder. His blue woolen coat had brass buttons and chevrons on the sleeve—a U.S. Army Civil War uniform, I guessed. He nodded and smiled. "How you doing?"

"Um, dead, apparently," I said.

He laughed. "Yeah. You'll get used to it. Call me T.J."

"Magnus," I said.

"Come on." Sam pulled me along.

We passed a girl who must've been Mallory Keen. She had frizzy red hair, green eyes, and a serrated knife, which she was shaking in the face of a six-foot-seven guy outside the door marked X.

"Again with the pig's head?" Mallory Keen spoke in a faint Irish brogue. "X, do you think I want to see a severed pig's head every time I step out my front door?"

"I could not eat anymore," X rumbled. "The pig head does not fit in my refrigerator."

Personally, I would not have antagonized the guy. He was built like a bomb containment chamber. If you happened to have a live grenade, I was pretty sure you could safely dispose of it simply by asking X to swallow it. His skin was the color of a shark's belly, rippling with muscles and stippled with warts. There were so many welts on his face it was hard to tell which one was his nose.

We walked past, X and Mallory too busy arguing to pay us any attention.

When we were out of earshot, I asked Sam, "What's the deal with the big gray dude?"

Sam put her finger to her lips. "X is a half-troll. He's a little sensitive about that."

"A half-troll. That's an actual thing?"

"Of course," she said. "And he deserves to be here as much as you."

"Hey, no doubt. Just asking."

The defensiveness in her voice made me wonder what the story was.

As we passed the door for HALFBORN GUNDERSON, an ax blade split the wood from the inside. Muffled laughter came from the room.

Sam ushered me onto the elevator. She pushed away several other einherjar who were trying to get on. "Next car, guys."

The spear-cage door slid shut. Sam inserted one of her keys into an override slot on the panel. She pressed a red rune and the elevator descended. "I'll take you into the dining hall before the main doors open. That way you can get the lay of the land."

"Uh . . . sure. Thanks."

Nordic easy listening music started playing from the ceiling.

Congratulations, Magnus! I thought. *Welcome to warrior paradise, where you can listen to Frank Sinatra in Norwegian FOREVER!*

I tried to think of something to say, preferably something that would not make Sam crush my windpipe.

"So . . . everybody on floor nineteen looks about my age," I noted. "Or—our age. Does Valhalla only take teenagers?"

Samirah shook her head. "The einherjar are grouped by the age they were when they died. You're in the youngest tier, which goes up to about age nineteen. Most of the time, you won't even see the other two tiers—adults and seniors. It's better that way. The adults . . . well, they don't take teens seriously, even if the teens have been here hundreds of years longer."

"Typical," I said.

"As for the senior warriors, they don't always mix well. Imagine a really violent retirement home."

"Sounds like some shelters I've been in."

"Shelters?"

"Forget it. So you're a Valkyrie. You chose all the people in the hotel?"

"Yes," she said. "I personally chose everyone in this hotel."

"Ha, ha. You know what I meant. Your . . . sisterhood or whatever."

"That's right. Valkyries are responsible for choosing the einherjar. Each warrior here died a valiant death. Each had a belief in honor, or some connection to the Norse gods that made him or her eligible for Valhalla."

I thought about what Uncle Randolph had told me, how the sword had been a birthright from my father. "A connection . . . like being the child of a god?"

I was afraid Sam might laugh at me, but she nodded gravely. "Many einherjar are demigods. Many are regular mortals. You're chosen for Valhalla because of your courage and honor, not your heritage. At least, that's how it's supposed to be. . . ."

I couldn't decide if her tone was wistful or resentful.

"And you?" I asked. "How did you become a Valkyrie? Did you die a noble death?"

She laughed. "Not yet. I'm still among the living."

"How does that work exactly?"

"Well, I live a double life. Tonight, I'll escort you to dinner. Then I have to rush home and finish my calculus homework."

"You're not joking, are you?"

"I never joke about calculus homework."

The elevator doors opened. We stepped into a room the size of a concert arena.

My mouth dropped. "Holy—"

"Welcome," Samirah said, "to the Feast Hall of the Slain."

Tiers of long tables like stadium seating curved downward from the nosebleed section. In the center of the room, instead of a basketball court, a tree rose taller than the Statue of Liberty. Its lowest branches were maybe a hundred feet up. Its canopy spread over the entire hall, scraping against the domed ceiling and sprouting through a massive opening at the top. Above, stars glittered in the night sky.

My first question probably wasn't the most important. "Why is there a goat in the tree?"

In fact, a lot of animals skittered among the branches. I couldn't tell what most of them were, but wobbling along the lowest branch was a very fat shaggy goat. Its swollen udders

rained milk like leaky showerheads. Below, on the dining-
hall floor, a team of four stocky warriors carried a big golden
bucket on poles set across their shoulders. They shuffled back
and forth, trying to stay under the goat so they could catch
the streams of milk. Judging by how soaked the warriors were,
they missed a lot.

"The goat is Heidrun," Sam told me. "Her milk is brewed
to make the mead of Valhalla. It's good stuff. You'll see."

"And the guys chasing her around?"

"Yeah, that's a thankless job. Behave yourself, or you might
get assigned to vat duty."

"Uh . . . couldn't they just, I don't know, bring the goat
down here?"

"She's a free-range goat. Her mead tastes better that way."

"Of course it does," I said. "And . . . all the other animals?
I see squirrels and possums and—"

"Sugar gliders and sloths," Sam offered. "Those are cute."

"Okay. But you guys eat dinner here? That can't be hygienic
with all the animal droppings."

"The animals in the Tree of Laeradr are well-behaved."

"The Tree of . . . Lay-rah-dur. You named your tree."

"Most important things have names." She frowned at me.
"Who are you again?"

"Very funny."

"Some of the animals are immortal and have particular
jobs. I can't spot him right now, but somewhere up there is a
stag named Eikthrymir. We call him Ike for short. You see that
waterfall?"

It was hard to miss. From somewhere high in the tree,
water ran down grooves in the bark and formed one powerful

torrent that cascaded off a branch in a roaring white curtain. It crashed into a pond the size of an Olympic pool between two of the tree's roots.

"The stag's horns spray water nonstop," Sam said. "It flows down the branches into that lake. From there, it goes underground and feeds every river in every world."

"So . . . *all* water is stag-horn runoff? I'm pretty sure that's not what they taught me in earth science."

"It's not all from Ike's horns. There's also snowmelt, rainwater, pollutants, and trace amounts of fluoride and jotun spit."

"Jotun?"

"You know, giants."

She didn't appear to be kidding, though it was hard to be sure. Her face was full of tense humor—her eyes darting and alert, her lips pressed together like she was either suppressing a laugh or expecting an attack. I could imagine her doing stand-up comedy, though maybe not with the ax at her side. Her features also seemed strangely familiar—the line of her nose, the curve of her jaw, the subtle streaks of red and copper in her dark hair.

"Have we met before?" I asked. "I mean . . . before you chose my soul for Valhalla?"

"I doubt it," she said.

"But you're mortal? You live in Boston?"

"Dorchester. I'm a sophomore at King Academy. I live with my grandparents and spend most of my time finding excuses to cover for my Valkyrie activities. Tonight, Jid and Bibi think I'm tutoring a group of elementary students in math. Any other questions?"

Her eyes sent the opposite message: *Enough with the personal stuff.*

I wondered why she lived with her grandparents. Then I remembered what she'd said earlier, about understanding what it was like to grieve for a mother.

"No more questions," I decided. "My head would explode."

"That would be messy," Sam said. "Let's get your seat before—"

Around the perimeter of the room, a hundred doors burst open. The armies of Valhalla swarmed in.

"Dinner is served," Sam said.

THIRTEEN

Phil the Potato
Meets His Doom

WE WERE SWEPT UP in a tidal wave of hungry warriors. Einherjar poured in from every direction, pushing, joking, and laughing as they headed for their seats.

"Hold on," Sam told me.

She grabbed my wrist and we flew into the air Peter Pan–style.

I yelped. "A little warning?"

"I *said* hold on."

We skimmed above the heads of the warriors. Nobody paid us much attention except for one guy I accidentally kicked in the face. Other Valkyries were also zipping around—some escorting warriors, some carrying platters of food and pitchers of drink.

We headed toward what was obviously the head table—where the home team would've sat if this were a Celtics game. A dozen grim-looking dudes were taking their seats in front of golden plates and jewel-encrusted goblets. In the place of honor stood an empty wooden throne with a high back, where two ravens perched, grooming their feathers.

Sam landed us at the table to the left. Twelve other people were just getting seated—two girls and four guys in regular street clothes; six Valkyries dressed more or less like Sam.

"Other newcomers?" I asked.

Sam nodded, her eyebrows furrowed. "Seven in one night is a lot."

"Is that good or bad?"

"More heroes dying means more bad things are stirring in the world. Which means . . ." She pursed her lips. "Never mind. Let's get seated."

Before we could, a tall Valkyrie stepped in our path. "Samirah al-Abbas, what have you brought us tonight—another half-troll? Perhaps a spy from your father?"

The girl looked about eighteen. She was big enough to play power forward, with snow-blond hair in braids down either shoulder. Over her green dress she wore a bandolier of ball-peen hammers, which struck me as an odd choice of weapon. Maybe Valhalla had a lot of loose nails. Around her neck hung a golden amulet shaped like a hammer. Her eyes were as pale blue and cold as a winter sky.

"Gunilla"—Sam's voice tightened—"this is Magnus Chase."

I held out my hand. "Gorilla? Pleased to meet you."

The girl's nostrils flared. "It is *Gunilla*, captain of the Valkyries. And you, newcomer—"

The foghorn I'd heard earlier echoed through the hall. This time I could see the source. Near the base of the tree, two guys held a black-and-white animal horn the size of a canoe while a third guy blew into it.

Thousands of warriors took their seats. Gorilla gave me one last stink-eye, then spun on her heel and marched off to the head table.

"Be careful," Sam warned me. "Gunilla is powerful."

"Also kind of a butt."

The corner of Sam's mouth twitched. "That, too."

She looked shaken, her knuckles white on the haft of her ax. I wondered what Gunilla had meant by *a spy from your father*, but since my windpipe was still sore from the last time I made Sam angry, I decided not to ask.

I sat at the end of the table next to Sam, so I didn't get to talk to the other newbies. Meanwhile, hundreds of Valkyries flew around the room, distributing food and drink. Whenever a Valkyrie's pitcher was empty, she would swoop over the golden vat now bubbling over a large fire, fill her pitcher with yummy goat's milk mead, and continue serving. The main course came from a roasting pit at the other end of the room. Rotating on a hundred-foot-long spit was the carcass of an animal. I wasn't sure what it had been when it was alive, but it was easily the size of a blue whale.

A Valkyrie flew past, depositing a platter of food and a goblet in front of me. I couldn't tell what the slices of meat were, but they smelled great, drizzled in gravy with potatoes on the side and thick slices of bread with butter. It had been a while since I'd had a hot meal, but I still hesitated.

"What kind of animal am I eating?"

Sam wiped her mouth with the back of her hand. "It's named Saehrimnir."

"Okay, first of all, who names their dinner? I don't want to know my dinner's name. This potato—is this potato named Steve?"

She rolled her eyes. "No, stupid. That's Phil. The *bread* is Steve."

I stared at her.

"Kidding," she said. "Saehrimnir is the magical beast of

Valhalla. Every day they kill it and cook it for dinner. Every morning it's resurrected alive and well."

"That must suck for the animal. But is it like a cow or a pig or—"

"It's whatever you want it to be. My portion is beef. Different sections of the animal are chicken or pork. I don't do pork, but some of the guys here love it."

"What if I'm a vegetarian? What if I want falafel?"

Sam became very still. "Was that some sort of joke?"

"Why would it be a joke? I like falafel."

Her shoulders relaxed. "Well, if you want falafel, just ask for the left flank. That part is tofu and bean curd. They can spice it to taste like just about anything."

"You have a magic animal whose left flank is made of tofu."

"This is Valhalla, paradise for warriors in the service of Odin. Your food will taste perfect, whatever you choose."

My stomach was getting impatient, so I dug in. The barbecue had just the right mix of spicy and sweet. The bread was like a warm cloud with a buttery crust. Even Phil the potato tasted great.

Not being a huge fan of free-range goat milk, I was reluctant to try the mead, but the stuff in my goblet looked more like sparkling cider.

I took a sip. Sweet, but not too sweet. Cold and smooth, with undercurrents I couldn't quite identify. Was that blackberry? Or honey? Or vanilla? I drained my glass.

Suddenly, my senses were on fire. It wasn't like alcohol (and, yes, I've tried alcohol, thrown up, tried alcohol again, thrown up). The mead didn't make me giddy, dopey, or nauseous. It was more like iced espresso without the bitter taste. It woke me up, filling me with a warm sense of confidence, but with no edginess or racing heartbeat.

"This stuff is good," I admitted.

A Valkyrie swooped in, refilled my cup, and flew away.

I glanced at Sam, who was brushing bread crumbs off of her scarf. "Do you ever do serving duty?"

"Yeah, sure. We take turns. It's an honor to serve the einherjar." She didn't even sound sarcastic.

"How many Valkyries are there?"

"Several thousand?"

"How many einherjar?"

Sam puffed her cheeks. "Tens of thousands? Like I said, this is just the first dinner. There are two other shifts for the older warriors. Valhalla has five hundred and forty doors. Each one is supposed to accommodate eight hundred warriors exiting for battle at once. That would mean four hundred and thirty-two thousand einherjar."

"That's a lot of tofu."

She shrugged. "Personally, I think the number is exaggerated, but only Odin knows for sure. We'll need a big army when Ragnarok rolls around."

"Ragnarok," I said.

"Doomsday," Sam said. "When the Nine Worlds are destroyed in a great conflagration and the armies of gods and giants meet in battle for the last time."

"Oh. *That* Ragnarok."

I scanned the sea of teenaged fighters. I remembered my first day of public high school in Allston, a few months before my mom died and my life turned to Dumpster sludge. The school had had around two thousand kids. Between classes, the halls were sheer chaos. The cafeteria was like a piranha tank. But it was nothing compared to Valhalla.

I pointed toward the head table. "What about the fancy dudes? Most of them look older."

"I wouldn't call them *fancy dudes*," Sam said. "Those are the thanes, the lords of Valhalla. Each one was personally invited by Odin to sit at his table."

"So the empty throne—"

"Is for Odin. Yes. He . . . well, it's been a while since he's shown up for dinner, but his ravens watch everything and report back to him."

Those ravens made me nervous with their beady black eyes. I got the feeling they were taking a particular interest in me.

Sam pointed to the right of the throne. "There's Erik Bloodax. And that's Erik the Red."

"A lot of Eriks."

"There's Leif Erikson."

"Whoa . . . but he's not wearing a metal bra."

"I'm going to ignore that comment. Over there is Snorri. Then our charming friend Gunilla. Then Lord Nelson and Davy Crockett."

"Davy . . . wait, *seriously?*"

"At the end is Helgi the hotel manager. You probably met him."

Helgi seemed to be having a good time, laughing with Davy Crockett and chugging mead. Behind his chair, the bellhop Hunding stood, looking miserable, carefully peeling grapes and handing them to Helgi one at a time.

"What's the deal with the manager and Hunding?"

Sam made a sour face. "Ancestral feud when they were alive. When they died, both made it to Valhalla, but Odin honored Helgi more. He put Helgi in charge of the hotel. Helgi's first order was that his enemy Hunding would be his servant and do his menial tasks for all time."

"That doesn't seem like much of a paradise for Hunding."

Sam hesitated. In a quieter voice, she said, "Even in Valhalla, there's a pecking order. You don't want to be at the bottom. Remember, when the ceremony begins—"

At the high table, the thanes began banging their cups on the table in unison. All around the hall, the einherjar joined in until the Hall of the Slain thundered with a metal heartbeat.

Helgi stood and raised his goblet. The noise died down.

"Warriors!" The manager's voice filled the hall. He looked so regal it was hard to believe he was the same guy who a few hours ago had offered me a suite upgrade and a minibar key. "Seven new fallen have joined us today! That would be reason enough to celebrate, but we also have a special treat for you. Thanks to Valkyrie Captain Gunilla, today, for the first time, we will not just *hear* about our newcomers' worthy deeds, we will be able to *see* them!"

Next to me, Sam made a choking sound. "No," she muttered. "No, no, no . . ."

"Let the presentation of the dead commence!" Helgi bellowed.

Ten thousand warriors turned and looked expectantly in my direction.

FOURTEEN

Four Million Channels and There's Still Nothing On Except Valkyrie Vision

HOORAY FOR GOING LAST.

I was relieved when the presentations started with einher-jar at the other end of the table . . . until I saw what the *other* newbies had done to get into Valhalla.

Helgi called, "Lars Ahlstrom!"

A heavyset blond guy rose with his Valkyrie. Lars was so nervous he knocked over his goblet, splashing magic mead all over his crotch. A wave of laughter rippled through the hall.

Helgi smiled. "As many of you know, Captain Gunilla has been phasing in new equipment over the past few months. She's been fitting her Valkyries' armor with cameras to keep everyone accountable—and hopefully to keep *us* entertained!"

The warriors cheered and banged their mugs, drowning out the sound of Sam cursing next to me.

Helgi raised his goblet. "I present to you, Valkyrie Vision!"

Around the tree trunk, a ring of giant holographic screens flickered to life, floating in midair. The video was choppy, apparently taken from a camera on the shoulder of a Valkyrie. We were high in the air, circling over the scene of a sinking ferry in a gray sea. Half the lifeboats dangled sideways from their cables. Passengers jumped overboard, some without life vests. The Valkyrie swooped in closer. The video's focus sharpened.

Lars Ahlstrom scrambled along the tilting deck, a fire extinguisher in his hands. The door to the inside lounge was blocked by a large metal container. Lars struggled to move it, but it was too heavy. Inside the lounge, a dozen people were trapped, banging desperately on the windows.

Lars shouted something to them in . . . Swedish? Norwegian? The meaning was clear: *GET BACK!*

As soon as they did, Lars smashed the extinguisher against the window. On the third try, it shattered. Despite the cold, Lars stripped off his coat and laid it across the broken glass.

He stayed at the window until the last passengers were safely out. They ran for the lifeboats. Lars picked up the fire extinguisher again and started to follow, but the ship lurched violently. His head slammed into the wall and he slid down, unconscious.

His body began to glow. The Valkyrie's arm appeared in the frame, reaching out. A shimmering golden apparition rose from Lars's body—his soul, I guessed. Golden Lars took the Valkyrie's hand, and the video screens went dark.

All around the feast hall, warriors cheered.

At the head table, the thanes debated among themselves. I was close enough to hear some of it. One guy—Lord Nelson?—questioned whether a fire extinguisher could count as a weapon.

I leaned toward Sam. "Why does that matter?"

She tore her bread into smaller and smaller pieces. "To get into Valhalla, a warrior must die in battle with a weapon in his or her hand. That's the only way."

"So," I whispered, "anyone could get into Valhalla if they just grabbed a sword and died?"

She snorted. "Of course not. We can't have kids taking up weapons and dying on purpose. There's nothing heroic about suicide. The sacrifice, the bravery has to be unplanned—a genuine heroic response to a crisis. It has to come from the heart, without any thought of reward."

"So . . . what if the thanes decide that a newbie shouldn't have been picked? Does he go back to being alive?" I tried not to sound too hopeful.

Sam wouldn't meet my eyes. "Once you're an einherji, there's no going back. You might get the worst work assignments. You might have a hard time earning respect. But you stay in Valhalla. If the thanes rule the death unworthy . . . well, the Valkyrie takes the punishment for that."

"Oh." Suddenly I understood why all the Valkyries at our table looked a little tense.

The thanes took a vote among themselves. They agreed unanimously that the fire extinguisher could count as a weapon and Lars's death could be seen as in combat.

"What greater enemy is there than the sea?" said Helgi. "We find Lars Ahlstrom worthy of Valhalla!"

More applause. Lars almost fainted. His Valkyrie held him up while smiling and waving at the crowd.

When the noise died down, Helgi continued. "Lars Ahlstrom, do you know your parentage?"

"I—" The newcomer's voice cracked. "I never knew my father."

Helgi nodded. "That is not uncommon. We will seek wisdom from the runes, unless the All-Father wishes to intercede."

Everyone turned toward the unoccupied throne. The

ravens ruffled their feathers and squawked. The throne remained empty.

Helgi didn't look surprised, but his shoulders slumped with disappointment. He motioned toward the fire pit. From a cluster of servers and cooks, a lady in a green hooded robe shuffled forward. Her face was hidden in the shadows of her cowl, but judging from her stooped posture and her gnarled hands, she must have been ancient.

I murmured to Sam, "Who's the Wicked Witch?"

"A *vala*. A seer. She can cast spells, read the future, and . . . other stuff."

The vala approached our table. She stopped in front of Lars Ahlstrom and pulled a leather pouch from the folds of her robe. She plucked out a handful of runestones like the ones in Uncle Randolph's study.

"And the runes?" I whispered to Sam. "What are they for?"

"They're the old Viking alphabet," she said, "but each letter also symbolizes something powerful—a god, a type of magic, a force of nature. They're like the genetic code of the universe. The vala can read the stones to see your fate. The greatest sorcerers, like Odin, don't even need to use the stones. They can manipulate reality simply by speaking the name of a rune."

I made a mental note to avoid Odin. I didn't need my reality manipulated any further.

In front of our table, the vala muttered something under her breath. She cast the stones at her feet. They landed on the dirt floor—some faceup, some facedown. One rune in particular seemed to catch everyone's attention. The holographic screens projected its image to everyone in the hall.

The mark meant nothing to me, but hundreds of warriors shouted with approval.

"Thor!" they cried. Then they started to chant, "THOR, THOR, THOR!"

Sam grunted. "As if we need another child of Thor."

"Why? What's wrong with them?"

"Nothing. They're great. Gunilla over there . . . she's a daughter of Thor."

"Oh."

The Valkyrie captain was smiling, which was even scarier than her scowl.

As the chanting subsided, the vala raised her withered arms. "Lars, son of Thor, rejoice! The runes say you shall fight well at Ragnarok. And tomorrow, in your first combat, you shall prove your valor and be decapitated!"

The audience cheered and laughed. Lars suddenly looked very pale. That just made the warriors laugh harder, as if decapitation were a hazing ritual no worse than a wedgie. The vala gathered her runes and retreated while Lars's Valkyrie helped him back into his seat.

The ceremony continued. Next up was a newcomer named Dede. She'd saved a bunch of kids at her village school when a warlord's soldiers had tried to kidnap them. She'd flirted with one of the soldiers, tricked him into letting her hold his assault rifle, then turned it on the warlord's men. She was killed, but her selfless act gave the other kids time to get away. The video was pretty violent. The Vikings loved it. Dede got a standing ovation.

The vala read the runes. She confirmed that Dede's parents were regular mortals, but nobody seemed to mind that. According to Dede's fortune, she would fight valiantly at Ragnarok. Over the next week she would lose her arms several times in combat. Within a hundred years she would rise to the thanes' table.

"Oooooo!" the crowd murmured appreciatively.

The other four newcomers were equally impressive. They'd all saved people. They'd sacrificed their lives bravely. Two were mortals. One was a son of Odin, which caused a minor commotion.

Sam leaned toward me. "Like I said, Odin has not been seen in quite a while. We welcome any sign that he still moves among mortals."

The last newcomer was a daughter of Heimdall. I wasn't sure who that was, but the Vikings seemed impressed.

My head was swimming from too much information. My senses were on fire from too much mead. I didn't even realize we'd reached the end of the table until Helgi called my name.

"Magnus Chase!" he bellowed. "Rise and impress us with your courage!"

FIFTEEN

My Blooper Video Goes Viral

MY COURAGE IMPRESSED NO ONE.

I squirmed in my seat as the video played. The einherjar watched the screens in shocked silence. Then the mumbling and grumbling began, punctuated by bursts of incredulous laughter.

Valkyrie Vision showed only portions of what had happened. I saw myself on the bridge, facing Surt as he summoned a fiery tornado. The camera zoomed in on me threatening him with my corroded piece of metal. Then Hearth and Blitz appeared. Blitz hit the Black One with his MAKE WAY FOR DUCK-LINGS sign. Hearth's squeaky toy arrow hit me in the butt. Surt punched me. Surt kicked me in the ribs. I puked and squirmed in agony.

The video fast-forwarded to me backing up against the bridge railing. Surt threw his fiery asphalt cannonball. I swung my sword and missed. In the feast hall, thousands of warriors grunted "Ooooo!" as the chunk of pavement hit me in the gut. Surt charged, and we both went over the side, grappling as we fell.

Just before we hit the water, the video froze and zoomed in. The sword was now sticking out of Surt's gut, but my hands weren't on the grip. They were wrapped around Surt's big neck.

An uncomfortable murmur spread through the room.

"No," I said. "No, that's not how— Someone edited that. It's like a blooper reel."

Sam's face had turned to stone. At the thanes' table, Captain Gunilla smirked. *Her cameras,* I realized, *her editing.*

For some reason, Gunilla wanted to disgrace Sam by making me look like an idiot . . . which, granted, wasn't a difficult task.

Helgi set down his goblet. "Samirah al-Abbas . . . explain."

Sam touched the edge of her scarf. I had a feeling she wanted to pull it over her head and hope the room disappeared. I couldn't blame her.

"Magnus Chase died bravely," she said. "He stood alone against Surt."

More uneasy murmuring.

One of the thanes stood. "You say that was Surt. A fire jotun, certainly, but if you are suggesting it was the Lord of Muspellheim himself—"

"I know what I saw, Erik Bloodax. This one"—Sam gestured at me like I was a prize specimen—"saved many lives on that bridge. The video does not show the whole story. Magnus Chase acted like a hero. He deserves to be among the fallen."

Another thane rose. "He didn't actually die with the sword in his hand."

"Lord Ottar"—Sam's voice sounded strained—"the thanes have looked past such a technicality before. Whether or not Magnus gripped the sword at the moment of death, he died bravely in combat. That is the spirit of Odin's law."

Lord Ottar sniffed. "Thank you, Samirah al-Abbas, daughter of Loki, for teaching us the spirit of Odin's law."

The tension level in the hall went up about thirty notches. Sam's hand drifted toward her ax. I doubted anyone but me could see how her fingers twitched.

Loki . . . I knew *that* name—Norse mythology's big villain, born of giants. He was the archenemy of the gods. If Sam was his daughter, why was she here? How had she become a Valkyrie?

I happened to meet Gunilla's eyes. The captain was obviously loving this drama. She could barely suppress a smile. If she was Thor's kid, that explained why she hated Sam. In the old stories, Thor and Loki were always trying to melt each other's faces.

The thanes debated among themselves.

Finally, Helgi the manager spoke. "Samirah, we're not seeing any heroism in this boy's death. We see a dwarf and an elf with toy weapons—"

"A dwarf and an elf?" I asked, but Helgi ignored me.

"—we see a fire jotun who fell off a bridge and took the boy with him. That's an unusual situation, a son of Muspell crossing into Midgard, but it has happened before."

"Shoot," muttered a thane with bushy sideburns. "Y'all should've seen the big ol' fire jotun Santa Anna had with him at the Alamo. I tell you—"

"Yes, thank you, Lord Crockett." Helgi cleared his throat. "As I was saying, we see very little evidence that Magnus Chase was a worthy choice for Valhalla."

"My lords"—Sam spoke slowly and carefully, like she was addressing children—"the video is not accurate."

Helgi laughed. "Are you suggesting we shouldn't trust our own eyes?"

"I'm suggesting that you hear the story from my point of view. It has always been our tradition to *tell* of the hero's deeds."

Gunilla stood. "Pardon me, my lords, but Samirah is correct. Perhaps we should let the daughter of Loki speak."

The crowd booed and hissed. Some called, "No! No!"

Helgi gestured for silence. "Gunilla, you do your sisterhood credit by defending a fellow Valkyrie, but Loki has always been a master of smooth, honeyed words. Personally, I would rather trust what I see than have it *spun* for me in some clever explanation."

Warriors applauded.

Gunilla shrugged like, *Oh, well, I tried!* and sank back into her chair.

"Magnus Chase!" Helgi called. "Do you know your parentage?"

I counted to five. My first inclination was to yell, *No, but your dad was apparently a jackass!*

"I don't know my father," I admitted. "But, look, about that video—"

"Perhaps you have potential we do not recognize," Helgi said. "Perhaps you are a son of Odin or Thor or some other noble war god, and your presence brings us honor. We will seek wisdom from the runes, unless the All-Father would intercede?"

He glanced at the throne, which remained empty. The ravens studied me with dark hungry eyes.

"Very well," Helgi said. "Bring forth the vala and—"

Between the roots of the tree, where the waterfall hit the dark lake, a massive bubble erupted. *BLOOP!* On the surface of the water stood three women shrouded in white.

Except for the crackle of cooking fire and the sound of the waterfall, the hall was silent. Thousands of warriors watched, frozen in amazement, as the three white women glided across the floor, heading toward me.

"Sam?" I whispered. "Sam, what's going on?"

Her hand fell from her ax.

"The Norns," she said. "The Norns themselves have come to read your fate."

SIXTEEN

Norns. Why Did It Have to Be Norns?

I REALLY WISHED someone had warned me I was going to die. Like, *Hey, you're diving off a bridge tomorrow and becoming an undead Viking, so go read up on Valhalla.*

I felt seriously unprepared.

I remembered hearing about Norns, the ladies who controlled mortal destinies, but I didn't know their names or their motivation or the proper etiquette for meeting them. Was I supposed to bow? Offer them gifts? Run away screaming?

Next to me, Sam muttered, "This is bad. The Norns only show up in extreme cases."

I didn't want to be an extreme case. I wanted to be an easy case: *Hey, good job. You're a hero. Have a cookie.*

Or even better: *Oops. This was all a mistake. You can go back to your regularly scheduled life.*

Not that my regularly scheduled life was so great, but it beat getting judged unworthy by twelve bearded guys named Erik.

As the Norns got closer, I realized how big they were—at least nine feet tall each. Under their hoods, their faces were beautiful but unnerving—blank white, even their eyes. Trailing behind them came a sheet of fog like a bridal train. They stopped twenty feet in front of my table and turned up their palms. Their skin was like sculpted snow.

Magnus Chase. I couldn't tell which Norn had spoken. The soft disembodied voice resonated through the hall, seeping into my head, turning my skull into an icebox. *Harbinger of the Wolf.*

The crowd stirred uneasily. I'd seen the word *harbinger* somewhere before, maybe in a fantasy novel, but I couldn't remember what it meant. I didn't like the sound of it. I liked the sound of *wolf* even less.

I'd just about decided that running away screaming was my smartest option. Then, in the hands of the middle Norn, fog collected, solidifying into half a dozen runestones. She threw them into the air. They floated above her, each rune expanding into a luminous white symbol as big as a poster board.

I couldn't read runes, but I recognized the one in the center. It was the same symbol I'd picked from the pouch in Uncle Randolph's office:

Fehu, announced the cold voice. *The rune of Frey.*

Thousands of warriors shifted in their seats, clanking restlessly in their armor.

Frey . . . Who was Frey? My mind felt coated with frost. My thoughts were sluggish.

The Norns spoke together, three ghostly voices chanting in unison, shaking leaves from the giant tree:

> *Wrongly chosen, wrongly slain,*
> *A hero Valhalla cannot contain.*
> *Nine days hence the sun must go east,*
> *Ere Sword of Summer unbinds the beast.*

The glowing runes dissolved. The three Norns bowed to me. They melted into the fog and disappeared.

I glanced at Sam. "How often does that happen?"

She looked like she'd been smacked between the eyes with one of Gunilla's hammers. "No. Choosing you *couldn't* have been a mistake. I was told . . . I was promised—"

"Someone *told* you to pick me up?"

Instead of answering, she murmured under her breath—as if running calculations for a rocket that had gone off course.

At the thanes' table, the lords conferred. All around the hall, thousands of einherjar studied me. My stomach folded itself into various origami shapes.

Finally, Helgi faced me. "Magnus Chase, son of Frey, your destiny is troubling. The lords of Valhalla must think on this further. For the time being, you shall be welcomed as a comrade. You are one of the einherjar now. That cannot be reversed, even if it was a mistake."

He scowled at Sam. "Samirah al-Abbas, the Norns themselves have pronounced your judgment in error. Do you have any defense?"

Sam's eyes widened as if she'd just realized something. "The son of Frey . . ." She looked around the room desperately. "Einherjar, don't you see? This is the son of Frey! Surt himself was on that bridge! That means the sword . . ." She turned to the thanes' table. "Gunilla, you *must* see what that means. We have to find that sword! A quest, immediately—"

Helgi banged his fist on the table. "Enough! Samirah, you stand in judgment for a grave mistake. It is not your place to tell us what to do. It is *definitely* not your place to order a quest!"

"I did not make a mistake," Sam said. "I did as I was ordered! I—"

"Ordered?" Helgi narrowed his eyes. "Ordered by whom?"

Sam's mouth shut. She seemed to deflate.

Helgi nodded grimly. "I see. Captain Gunilla, before I announce the thanes' judgment on this Valkyrie, do you wish to speak?"

Gunilla stirred. The gleam in her eyes was gone. She looked like someone who'd gotten in line for the merry-go-round and unexpectedly found herself trapped on a roller coaster.

"I—" She shook her head. "No, my lord. I—I have nothing to add."

"Very well," said Helgi. "Samirah al-Abbas, for your poor judgment with this einherji Magnus Chase, and for your past mistakes, the thanes rule that you be expelled from the sisterhood of Valkyries. You are hereby stripped of your powers and privileges. Return to Midgard in disgrace!"

Sam grabbed my arm. "Magnus, listen to me. You have to find the sword. You have to stop them—"

Like a camera flash: a burst of light and Sam was gone. Her half-eaten meal and the bread crumbs around her seat were the only signs she'd ever existed.

"So concludes our feast," Helgi announced. "I will see you all tomorrow on the field of battle! Sleep well, and dream of glorious death!"

SEVENTEEN

I Did Not Ask for Biceps

I DIDN'T SLEEP MUCH. I definitely didn't dream of glorious death. Been there, done that, got the afterlife.

While I was at dinner, my sofa had been put back and repaired. I sat on it and thumbed through my old children's book of Norse mythology, but it didn't have much about Frey. One tiny picture showed a blond guy in a tunic frolicking in the woods, a blond lady at his side, a couple of cats playing at their feet.

Frey was the god of spring and summer! read the caption. *He was the god of wealth, abundance, and fertility. His twin sister, Freya, the goddess of love, was very pretty! She had cats!*

I tossed the book aside. Great. My dad was a D-list god who frolicked in the woods. He was probably eliminated early last season on *Dancing with the Asgardians.*

Did it crush me to learn this? Not really. You might not believe it, but my dad's identity had never been a big deal to me. It wasn't like I ever felt incomplete—like if only I knew my dad, my life would make sense. I knew who I was. I was Natalie Chase's son. As for life making sense . . . I'd seen too much weirdness to expect that.

Still, I had a lot of items on my *I-don't-get-it* list. At the very top: How could a homeless kid have a dad who was the god of abundance and wealth? Talk about a cruel joke.

Also, why would I get targeted by a big bad dude like Surt? If he was the lord of Muspellheim, High King Roasty Toasty, shouldn't he pick on more interesting heroes, like the children of Thor? At least their dad had a movie franchise. Frey didn't even have his own cats. He had to borrow his sister's.

And the Sword of Summer . . . assuming that was the blade I had pulled from the Charles River, how had it ended up there? Why was it so important? Uncle Randolph had been searching for it for years. Sam's last words to me were about finding the sword again. If it had belonged to my dad, and my dad was an immortal god, why had he allowed his weapon to sit at the bottom of a river for a thousand years?

I stared at the empty fireplace. The Norns' words kept playing in my head, though I wanted to forget them.

Harbinger of the Wolf. I remembered what a harbinger was now: something that signaled the arrival of a powerful force, like a doorman announcing the president, or a red sky before a hurricane. I did not want to be the harbinger of the wolf. I'd seen enough wolves to last me an eternal lifetime. I wanted to be the harbinger of ice cream, or falafel.

Wrongly chosen, wrongly slain.

A little late to announce that now. I was a freaking ein-herji. My name was on the door. I had a key to the minibar.

A hero Valhalla cannot contain.

I liked this line better. Maybe it meant I could bust out of here. Or I guessed it could mean that the thanes would vaporize me in a burst of light or feed me to their magical goat.

> *Nine days hence the sun must go east,*
> *Ere Sword of Summer unbinds the beast.*

Those lines bothered me the most. Last I checked, the sun moved east to west. And who was the beast? I was betting a wolf, because it's always a stinking wolf. If the sword was supposed to let loose a wolf, the sword should've stayed lost.

Some memory nagged at me . . . a bound wolf. I stared at the children's book of mythology, half tempted to pick it up again. But I was already unsettled enough.

Magnus, listen to me, Sam had said. *You have to find the sword. You have to stop them.*

I felt bad about Samirah al-Abbas. I was still miffed at her for bringing me here, especially if it had been a mistake, but I didn't want to see her kicked out of the Valkyries because some doctored video made me look like a doofus. (Okay, *more* of a doofus than usual.)

I decided I should sleep. I didn't feel tired, but if I stayed awake thinking any longer, my brain would overheat.

I tried the bed. Too soft. I ended up in the atrium, sprawled on the grass, gazing at the stars through the tree branches.

At some point, I must have fallen asleep.

A sharp sound startled me awake—a branch cracking. Someone cursed.

Above me, the sky was turning gray in the predawn light. A few leaves helicoptered through the air. Branches bobbed as if something heavy had just scrambled through them.

I lay still, listening, watching. Nothing. Had I imagined
that voice?

Over in the foyer, a piece of paper slid under my doorway.

I sat up groggily.

Maybe the management was giving me the bill and letting
me check out. I staggered toward the door.

My hand trembled as I picked up the paper, but it wasn't a
bill. It was a handwritten note in really nice cursive:

> *Hi, neighbor.*
> *Join us in lounge 19 for breakfast. Down the hall*
> *to the left. Bring your weapons and armor.*
> *T.J.*

T.J. . . . Thomas Jefferson, Jr., the guy across the hall.

After the fiasco last night, I didn't know why he'd want to
invite me to breakfast. I also didn't understand why I needed
weapons and armor. Maybe Viking bagels fought back.

I was tempted to barricade my door and hide in my room.
Perhaps everyone would leave me alone. Maybe once all the
warriors were busy with their Bikram yoga to the death, I
could sneak out and find an exit to Boston.

On the other hand, I wanted answers. I couldn't shake the
idea that if this was a place for the brave dead, my mom might
be here somewhere. Or someone might know which afterlife
she *had* gone to. At least this guy T.J. seemed friendly. I could
hang with him for a while and see what he could tell me.

I trudged to the bathroom.

I was afraid the toilet would be some Viking death machine
with ax blades and a flush-operated crossbow, but it worked

like a normal one. It definitely wasn't any scarier than the public restrooms in the Common.

The medicine cabinet was stocked with all my usual toiletries . . . or at least the toiletries I *used* to like when I had a home.

And the shower . . . I tried to remember the last time I'd had a leisurely hot shower. Sure, I'd arrived in Valhalla feeling magically dry-cleaned, but after a bad night's sleep in the atrium, I was ready for a good old-fashioned scrub down.

I peeled off my layers of shirts and almost screamed.

What was wrong with my chest? Why did my arms look that way? What were those weird bulgy areas?

Usually I avoided looking at my reflection. I wasn't somebody I wanted to see on a regular basis. But now I faced the mirror.

My hair was the same, a bit less grimy and tangled, but still hanging to my jawline in a curtain of dirty blond, parted in the middle.

You look like Kurt Cobain, my mom used to tease me. *I loved Kurt Cobain, except for the fact that he died.*

Well, guess what, Mom? I thought. *I have that in common with him too now!*

My eyes were gray—more like my cousin Annabeth's than my mom's. They had a haunted, scary emptiness to them, but that was normal. The look had served me well on the streets.

My upper body, however, I hardly recognized. Ever since my bad asthma days when I was little, I'd always been on the scrawny side. Even with all the hiking and camping, I'd had a concave chest, sticking-out ribs, and skin so pale you could trace the road map of blue veins.

Now . . . those strange new bulgy areas looked suspiciously like muscles.

Don't get me wrong. It wasn't as dramatic as turning into Captain America. I was still lean and pale, but my arms had definition. My chest didn't look like it would collapse in the next strong wind. My skin was smoother, less translucent. All the rashes and nicks and bites that came from living on the street had disappeared. Even the scar on my left palm, where I'd cut myself on a hunting knife at age ten, had vanished.

I remembered how strong I'd felt when I first arrived at Valhalla, how I'd tossed my sofa across the room last night. I hadn't really stopped to think about it.

What had Hunding called Valhalla . . . *an upgrade*?

I made a fist.

I'm not sure what came over me. I guess when I realized that even my body wasn't my own, the anger, fear, and uncertainty of the last twenty-four hours reached critical mass. I'd been plucked out of my life. I'd been threatened, humiliated, and forcibly upgraded. I hadn't asked for a suite. I hadn't asked for biceps.

I hit the wall. Literally.

My fist went straight through the tile, the drywall, and a two-by-four stud. I pulled out my hand. I wriggled my fingers. Nothing felt broken.

I regarded the fist-shaped hole I'd made above the towel bar. "Yep," I grumbled. "Housekeeping loves me."

The shower helped calm me down. Afterward, wrapped in a fluffy HV-embroidered bathrobe, I padded to the closet to search for clothes. Inside were three sets of blue jeans, three green T-shirts (all marked PROPERTY OF HOTEL VALHALLA), underwear, socks, a pair of good running shoes, and a sheathed sword. Leaning against the ironing board was a circular green shield with the golden rune of Frey painted in the middle.

Okay, then. I guess I knew what I was wearing today.

I spent ten minutes trying to figure out how to position the sword's sheath on my belt. I was left-handed. Did that mean the sword went on the right? Were left-handed swords different from right-handed ones?

I attempted to draw the blade and just about ripped my pants off. Oh, yeah, I was going to be a hit on the battlefield.

I practiced swinging the sword. I wondered if it would start humming and guiding my hand, the way the sword on the bridge had done when I faced Surt. But no. This blade seemed to be a regular piece of non-humming metal with no cruise-control feature. I managed to sheathe it without losing any fingers. I slung the shield across my back, the way the warriors at dinner last night had been wearing theirs. The strap dug into my neck and made me want to gag.

I looked in the mirror again.

"You, sir," I muttered, "look like a huge dork."

My reflection did not argue.

I went out to find breakfast and kill it with my sword.

I Do Mighty Combat
with Eggs

"THERE HE IS." T.J. rose and grabbed my hand. "Sit. Join us. You made quite a first impression last night!"

He was dressed the same as yesterday: a blue wool army jacket over a green hotel T-shirt, jeans, and leather boots.

With him sat the half-troll X, the redhead Mallory Keen, and a guy I guessed was Halfborn Gunderson, who looked like Robinson Crusoe on steroids. His shirt was a patchwork of animal pelts. His hide pants were in tatters. Even by Viking standards his beard was wild, decorated with most of a cheese omelet.

My four hallmates made room for me at the table, which felt pretty good.

Compared to the main feast hall, lounge nineteen was downright intimate. Scattered around the room were a dozen tables, most unoccupied. In one corner, a fireplace crackled in front of a beat-up sofa. Along the other wall, a buffet table was laden with every kind of breakfast food imaginable (and a few kinds I had *never* imagined).

T.J. and company had parked themselves in front of a big picture window overlooking a vast field of ice and swirling snow. It made no sense, considering that it was summer in my atrium right down the hall, but I'd already learned that the hotel's geography was wack.

"That's Niflheim," T.J. explained, "the realm of ice. The view changes daily, cycling through the Nine Worlds."

"The Nine Worlds . . ." I stared at my scrambled eggs, wondering which solar system they'd come from. "I keep hearing about nine worlds. Hard to believe."

Mallory Keen blew powdered sugar off her doughnut. "Believe it, newbie. I've visited six of them so far."

"Five here." Halfborn grinned, showing me the rest of his cheese omelet. " 'Course, Midgard hardly counts. That's the human world. Been to Alfheim, Nidavellir, Jotunheim—"

"Disney World," X said.

Mallory sighed. With her red hair, green eyes, and powdered sugar around her mouth, she reminded me of a reverse-color-scheme Joker. "For the last time, you numbskull, Disney World is not one of the nine."

"Why is it called a world, then?" X nodded smugly, the argument won, and went back to his meal, sucking meat from the shell of a large crustacean.

T.J. pushed his empty plate away. "Magnus, I don't know if it helps, but the Nine Worlds aren't really separate planets. They're more like . . . different dimensions, different layers of reality, all connected by the World Tree."

"Thanks," I said. "That's much more confusing."

He laughed. "Yeah, I guess it is."

"The World Tree is the tree in the feast hall?"

"Nah," Mallory said. "The World Tree is *much* bigger. You'll see, sooner or later."

That sounded ominous. I tried to concentrate on my food, but it was difficult with X right next to me demolishing a slimy mutant crab.

I pointed at T.J.'s jacket. "That's a Civil War uniform?"

"Private in the Fifty-Fourth Massachusetts, my friend. I'm a Boston boy, same as you. I just got here a little earlier."

I did the calculations. "You died in battle a hundred and fifty years ago?"

T.J. beamed. "The assault on Fort Wagner, South Carolina. My dad was Tyr, god of courage, law, and trial by combat. My mom was a runaway slave."

I tried to fit that into my new worldview: a teenager from the 1860s, the son of a former slave and a Norse god, who was now having breakfast with me in an extra-dimensional hotel.

X belched, which put things in perspective.

"Gods of Asgard!" Mallory complained. "That smell!"

"Sorry," X grunted.

"Is your name really X?" I asked.

"No. My real name is—" The half-troll said something that started with *K*s and went on for about thirty seconds.

Halfborn wiped his hands on his pelt shirt. "You see? Nobody can pronounce that. We call him X."

"X," agreed X.

"He's another one of Sam al-Abbas's acquisitions," T.J. said. "X stumbled across a dogfight . . . one of those illegal ones in, where, Chicago?"

"Chee-cah-go," affirmed X.

"He saw what was going on and went nuts. Started smashing up the place, walloping the bettors, freeing the animals."

"Dogs should fight for themselves," X said. "Not for greedy

humans. They should be wild and free. They should not be kept in cages."

I didn't want to argue with the big guy, but I wasn't sure I liked the idea of wild dogs fighting for themselves. That sounded a lot like wolves—an animal I refused to harbinge.

"Anyway," T.J. said, "it turned into a full-scale battle: X against a bunch of gangsters with automatic weapons. They finally killed him, but X took down a lot of scumbags and freed a lot of dogs. That was what . . . a month ago?"

X grunted and continued sucking his shellfish.

T.J. spread his hands. "Samirah judged him worthy and brought him here. She got some flak for that decision."

Mallory snorted. "That's putting it mildly. A troll in Valhalla. Who could possibly object?"

"Half-troll," X corrected. "That is my *better* half, Mallory Keen."

"She didn't mean anything, X," T.J. said. "It's just that prejudice dies hard. When I got here in 1863, I wasn't exactly welcomed with open arms, either."

Mallory rolled her eyes. "Then you won them over with your dazzling personality. I swear, you lot are giving floor nineteen a bad name. And now we have Magnus."

Halfborn leaned toward me. "Don't mind Mallory. She's a sweetheart, once you get past the fact that she's a horrible person."

"Shut up, Halfborn."

The big guy chuckled. "She's just grumpy because she died trying to disarm a car bomb with her face."

Mallory's ears turned as red as hummingbird juice. "I didn't—it wasn't— Argh!"

"Magnus, don't worry about that mess last night," continued Halfborn. "Folks will forget about it in a few decades.
Believe me, I've seen it all. I died during the Viking invasion
of East Anglia, fought under the banner of Ivar the Boneless. I
took twenty arrows in the chest protecting my thane!"

"Ouch," I said.

Halfborn shrugged. "I've been here for . . . oh, going on
twelve hundred years now."

I stared at him. Despite his bulk and his beard, Halfborn
looked maybe eighteen, tops. "How do you stand it without
going crazy? And why do they call you Halfborn?"

His smile faded. "Second question first . . . when I was
born, I was so big, strong, and ugly that my mother said I
looked like I'd been half born, half carved from rock. The
name stuck."

"And you're still ugly," Mallory muttered.

"As for how to avoid going crazy here . . . Some do lose it,
Magnus. Waiting for Ragnarok is hard. The trick is to keep
busy. There's plenty to do here. Me, I've learned a dozen languages, including English. I earned a doctorate in Germanic
literature, and I learned to knit."

T.J. nodded. "That's why I invited you to breakfast,
Magnus."

"To learn knitting?"

"To keep active! Spending too much time alone in your
room can be dangerous. If you isolate yourself, you start to
fade. Some of the old-timers . . ." He cleared his throat. "It
doesn't matter. You're here! Just keep showing up every morning until Doomsday, and you'll be fine."

I stared out the window at the swirling snow. I thought about Sam's warning to find the sword, the Norns chanting that something bad would happen in nine days. "You said you've visited the other worlds. That means you can leave the hotel."

The group exchanged uneasy glances.

"Yes," Halfborn said. "But our main job is to wait for Ragnarok. Train, train, train."

"I rode the train at Disney World," said X.

Maybe he meant it as a jest. The half-troll seemed to have two facial expressions: wet cement and dry cement.

"Occasionally," said T.J., "einherjar are sent into the Nine Worlds on missions."

"Tracking down monsters," Mallory offered. "Killing giants who cross into Midgard. Stopping witches and wights. And of course, dealing with rogues—"

"Wights? Rogues?" I asked.

"Point is," said Halfborn, "we only leave Valhalla under orders from Odin or the thanes."

"But, hypothetically," I said, "I could go back to earth, Midgard, whatever—"

"Hypothetically, yes," T.J. said. "Look, I know that business with the Norns must be driving you bonkers, but we don't know what the prophecy means. Give the thanes some time to decide what to do. You can't rush off and do something stupid."

"Gods forbid," said Mallory. "We *never* do anything stupid. Like that late-night pizza run to Santarpio's. That never happened."

"Shut up, woman," Halfborn growled.

"*Woman?*" Mallory reached for the knife at her belt. "Watch your words, you overgrown Swedish hamster."

"Hold on," I said. "You guys know how to sneak out of—"

T.J. coughed loudly. "Sorry, I didn't hear that. I'm sure you weren't asking about anything against the rules. Magnus, first of all: if you returned to Midgard so soon, how would you explain it to those who knew you? Everyone thinks you're dead. Usually, *if* we go back, we wait until everyone we knew is dead. It's easier all the way around. Besides, it takes a while, sometimes years, for your einherji strength to develop fully."

I tried to imagine waiting here for years. I didn't have many friends or relatives to go back to. Still, I didn't want to be stuck here—learning new languages, knitting sweaters—for ages. After seeing my cousin Annabeth, I kind of wanted to reconnect with her before she died. And if Samirah was right about my mom not being in Valhalla . . . I wanted to find her, wherever she was.

"But it's possible to leave without permission," I persisted. "Maybe not forever, just for a while."

T.J. shifted uncomfortably. "Valhalla has doors into every world. The hotel is designed that way. Most exits are guarded, but . . . well, there are a lot of ways to Boston, since Boston is the center of Midgard."

I glanced around the table. Nobody was laughing. "It is?"

"Sure," T.J. said. "It's right at the trunk of the World Tree, the easiest spot from which to access the other worlds. Why do you think Boston is called the Hub of the Universe?"

"Wishful thinking?"

"No. Mortals have always known there was something about that location, even if they couldn't put their finger on what it was. The Vikings searched for the center of the world for years. They knew the entrance to Asgard was in the west. That's one reason they kept exploring into North America. When they met the Native Americans—"

"We called them the skraelings," Halfborn said. "Vicious fighters. I liked them."

"—the natives had all sorts of stories about how strong the spirit world was in this area. Later, when the Puritans settled, well . . . John Winthrop's vision of a shining 'City on a Hill'? That wasn't just a metaphor. He had a vision of Asgard, a glimpse into the other worlds. And the Salem witch trials? Hysteria caused by magic seeping into Midgard. Edgar Allan Poe was born in Boston. It's no accident his most famous poem was about a raven, one of Odin's sacred animals."

"Enough." Mallory gave me a disgusted look. "T.J. will take forever when answering a yes/no question. The answer is yes, Magnus. It is possible to leave, with or without permission."

X cracked a crab claw. "You would not be immortal."

"Yeah," T.J. said. "That's the second big problem. In Valhalla, you can't die—not permanently. You'll just keep getting resurrected. It's part of the training."

I remembered the guy who had gotten impaled in the lobby and dragged off by wolves. Hunding had said he would be fine again by dinner.

"But outside of Valhalla?"

"Out in the Nine Worlds," T.J. said, "you're still an einherji. You're faster and stronger and tougher than any regular mortal. But if you die out there, you stay dead. Your soul might go to Helheim. Or you might simply dissolve into the primordial void—Ginnungagap. Hard to know. It's not worth the risk."

"Unless . . ." Halfborn picked some egg out of his beard. "Unless he really *did* find the sword of Frey, and the legends are true—"

"It's Magnus's first day," T.J. said. "Let's not go into that. He's already freaked out enough."

"Freak me out more," I said. "What legends exactly?"

In the hallway, a horn blasted. At the other tables, einherjar started to get up and clear their plates.

Halfborn rubbed his hands eagerly. "Talking will have to wait. It's battle time!"

"Battle time," X agreed.

T.J. grimaced. "Magnus, we should probably warn you about the first day initiation. Don't be discouraged if—"

"Oh, shush," said Mallory. "Don't spoil the surprise!" She gave me a powdered sugar smile. "I can't wait to see the new boy get dismembered!"

NINETEEN

Do Not Call Me Beantown. Like, *Ever*

I TOLD MY NEW FRIENDS I was allergic to dismember-ment. They just laughed and herded me toward the combat arena. This is why I don't like making new friends.

The battlefield was so huge I couldn't process what I was seeing.

Back in the good old days when I was a street kid, I used to sleep on rooftops in the summertime. I could see the entire cityscape of Boston from Fenway Park to Bunker Hill. Valhalla's battlefield was bigger than that. It offered maybe three square miles of interesting places to die, all contained within the hotel like an interior courtyard.

On all four sides rose the walls of the building—cliffs of white marble and gold-railed balconies, some hung with ban-ners, some decorated with shields, some fitted with catapults. The upper floors seemed to dissolve in the hazy glow of the sky, as blank white as a fluorescent light.

In the center of the field loomed a few craggy hills. Clumps of forest marbled the landscape. The outer rim was mostly rolling pastures, with a river as wide as the Charles snaking through. Several villages dotted the riverbank, maybe for those who preferred their warfare urban.

From hundreds of doors in the walls around the field,

battalions of warriors were streaming in, their weapons and armor glinting in the harsh light. Some einherjar wore full plate mail like medieval knights. Others wore chain mail shirts, breeches, and combat boots. A few sported camo fatigues and AK-47s. One guy wore nothing but a Speedo. He'd painted himself blue and was armed only with a baseball bat. Across his chest were the words COME AT ME, BRO.

"I feel underdressed," I said.

X cracked his knuckles. "Armor does not make victory. Neither do weapons."

Easy for him to say. He was larger than some sovereign nations.

Halfborn Gunderson was also taking the minimalist approach. He'd stripped down to nothing but his leggings, though he did sport a pair of vicious-looking double-bladed axes. Standing next to anyone else, Halfborn would've looked massive. Next to X, he looked like a toddler . . . with a beard, abs, and axes.

T.J. fastened his bayonet to his rifle. "Magnus, if you want more than the basic equipment, you'll have to capture it or trade for it. The hotel armories take red gold, or they work on a barter system."

"Is that how you got your rifle?"

"Nah, this is the weapon I died with. I hardly ever fire it. Bullets don't have much effect on einherjar. Those guys out there with the assault rifles? That's all flash and noise. They're the least dangerous people on the field. But this bayonet? It's bone steel, a gift from my father. Bone steel works just fine."

"Bone steel."

"Yeah. You'll learn."

My sword hand was already sweating. My shield felt much too flimsy. "So which groups are we fighting against?"

Halfborn clapped me on the back. "All of them! Vikings fight in small groups, my friend. We are your shield brothers."

"And shield sister," Mallory said. "Though some of us are shield idiots."

Halfborn ignored her. "Stick with us, Magnus, and . . . well, you won't do fine. You'll get killed quickly. But stick with us anyway. We'll wade into battle and slaughter as many as possible!"

"That's your plan?"

Halfborn tilted his head. "Why would I have a plan?"

"Oh, sometimes we do," said T.J. "Wednesdays are siege warfare. That's more complicated. Thursdays they bring out the dragons."

Mallory drew her sword and serrated dagger. "Today is free-for-all combat. I love Tuesdays."

From a thousand different balconies, horns blasted. The einherjar charged into battle.

Until that morning, I'd never understood the term *bloodbath*. Within a few minutes, we were literally slipping in the stuff.

We'd just stepped onto the field when an ax flew out of nowhere and stuck in my shield, the blade going right through the wood above my arm.

Mallory yelled and threw her knife, which sank into the ax thrower's chest. He fell to his knees, laughing. "Good one!" Then he collapsed, dead.

Halfborn waded through enemies, his axes whirling, chopping off heads and limbs until he looked like he'd been playing

paintball with only red paint. It was disgusting. And horrifying. And the most disturbing part? The einherjar treated it
like a game. They killed with glee. They died as if someone
had just taken down their avatar in *Call of Duty*. I'd never liked
that game.

"Ah, that sucks," one guy muttered as he studied the four
arrows in his chest.

Another yelled, "I'll get you tomorrow, Trixie!" before falling sideways, a spear stuck through his gut.

T.J. sang "The Battle Hymn of the Republic" while he
stabbed and parried with his bayonet.

X smashed through one group after another. A dozen
arrows now stuck out of his back like porcupine quills, but
they didn't seem to bother him. Every time his fist connected,
an einherji turned two-dimensional.

As for me, I shuffled along in abject terror, my shield
raised, my sword dragging. I'd been told that death here
wasn't permanent, but I had a hard time believing it. A bunch
of warriors with sharp pointy objects were trying to kill me. I
didn't want to be killed.

I managed to parry a sword strike. I deflected a spear with
my shield. I had a clear opening to stab one girl whose guard
was down, but I just couldn't make myself do it.

That was a mistake. Her ax bit into my thigh. Pain flared
all the way up to my neck.

Mallory cut the girl down. "Come on, Chase, keep moving!
You'll get used to the pain after a while."

"Great." I grimaced. "Something to look forward to."

T.J. jabbed his bayonet through the faceplate of a medieval

knight. "Let's take that hill!" He pointed to a nearby ridge at the edge of the woods.

"Why?" I yelled.

"Because it's a hill!"

"He loves taking hills," Mallory grumbled. "It's a Civil War thing."

We waded through the battle, heading for the high ground. My thigh still hurt, but the bleeding had stopped. Was that normal?

T.J. raised his rifle. He yelled, "Charge!" just as a javelin ran him through from behind.

"T.J.!" I yelled.

He caught my eye, managed a weak smile, then face-planted in the mud.

"For Frigg's sake!" Mallory cursed. "Come on, newbie."

She grabbed my arm and pulled me along. More javelins sailed over my head.

"You guys do this every *day*?" I demanded.

"No. Like we told you—Thursdays are dragons."

"But—"

"Hey, Beantown, the whole point is to get used to the horrors of battle. You think this is bad? Wait until we actually have to fight at Ragnarok."

"Why am *I* Beantown? T.J.'s from Boston. Why isn't *he* Beantown?"

"Because T.J. is slightly less annoying."

We reached the edge of the woods. X and Halfborn guarded our backs, slowing down the pursuing horde. And the enemies *were* a horde now. All the scattered groups within sight had stopped fighting one another and were after us. Some pointed at me. Some called my name, and not in a friendly way.

"Yeah, they've spotted you." Mallory sighed. "When I said I wanted to see you eviscerated, I didn't mean I wanted to be standing *next* to you. Oh, well."

I almost asked why everyone was after me. But I got it. I was a newbie. Of *course* the other einherjar would gang up on me and the other newcomers. Lars Ahlstrom was probably already decapitated. Dede might be running around with her arms cut off. The veteran einherjar would make this as painful and terrifying for us as possible to see how we handled ourselves. That made me angry.

We climbed the hill, weaving from tree to tree for cover. Halfborn threw himself into a group of twenty guys who were following us. He destroyed them all. He came up laughing, an insane light in his eyes. He was bleeding from a dozen wounds. A dagger stuck out of his chest, right over his heart.

"How is he not dead yet?" I asked.

"He's a berserker." Mallory glanced back, her expression a mix of disdain and exasperation and something else . . . admiration? "That idiot will keep fighting until he is literally hacked to pieces."

Something clicked in my head. Mallory *liked* Halfborn. You don't call somebody an idiot that many times unless you're really into them. Under different circumstances, I might have teased her, but while she was distracted there was a wet *thwack*. An arrow sprouted from her neck.

She scowled at me as if to say, *Totally your fault*.

She collapsed. I knelt at her side, putting my hand on her neck. I could feel the life seeping out of her. I could sense the severed artery, the fading heartbeat, all the damage that had to be mended. My fingers seemed to grow warmer. If I had a little more time—

"Look out!" shouted X.

I raised my shield. A sword clanged against it. I pushed back, knocking the attacker downhill. My arms ached. My head was throbbing, but somehow I got to my feet.

Halfborn was forty yards away, surrounded by a mob of warriors all jabbing him with spears, shooting him full of arrows. Somehow he kept fighting, but even *he* wouldn't be able to stand much longer.

X ripped a guy's AK-47 out of his hands and smacked him over the head with it.

"Go, Magnus Beantown," said the half-troll. "Take the crest for floor nineteen!"

"My nickname will not be Beantown," I muttered. "I refuse."

I stumbled uphill until I reached the summit. I put my back against a big oak tree while X smashed and backhanded and head-butted Vikings into oblivion.

An arrow hit my shoulder, pinning me to the tree. The pain almost made me black out, but I snapped the shaft and pulled myself free. The bleeding stopped instantly. I felt the wound closing as if somebody had filled it with hot wax.

A shadow passed over me—something large and dark hurtling from the sky. It took me a millisecond to realize it was a boulder, probably shot from a balcony catapult. It took me another millisecond to realize where it would land.

Too late. Before I could shout a warning to X, the half-troll and a dozen other einherjar disappeared under a twenty-ton chunk of limestone, the side of which was painted: WITH LOVE FROM FLOOR 63.

A hundred warriors stared at the rock. Leaves and broken twigs fluttered around them. Then the einherjar all turned toward me.

Another arrow hit me in the chest. I screamed, more in rage than in pain, and pulled it out.

"Wow," one of the Vikings commented. "He's a fast healer."

"Try a spear," someone suggested. "Try *two* spears."

They spoke as if I wasn't worth addressing—as if I were a cornered animal they could experiment with.

Twenty or thirty einherjar raised their weapons. The anger inside me exploded. I shouted, expelling energy like the shockwave from a bomb. Bowstrings snapped. Swords fell out of their owners' hands. Spears and guns and axes went flying into the trees.

As quickly as it started, the surge of power shut off. All around me, a hundred einherjar had been stripped of their weapons.

The blue-painted guy stood in the front row, his baseball bat at his feet. He stared at me in shock. "What just happened?"

The warrior next to him had an eye patch and red leather armor decorated with silver curlicues. Cautiously, he crouched and retrieved his fallen ax.

"*Alf seidr*," said Eye Patch. "Nicely done, son of Frey. I haven't seen a trick like that in centuries. But bone steel is better."

My eyes crossed as his ax blade spun toward my face. Then everything went dark.

TWENTY

Come to the Dark Side. We Have Pop-Tarts

A FAMILIAR VOICE SAID, "Dead again, eh?"

I opened my eyes. I was standing in a pavilion ringed with gray stone columns. Outside was nothing but empty sky. The air was thin. Cold wind whipped across the marble floor, stirring the fire in the central hearth, making the flames gutter in the braziers on either side of the tall dais. Three steps led up to a double throne—a loveseat of white wood carved with intricate shapes of animals, birds, and tree branches. The seat itself was lined with ermine. Sprawling across it, eating Pop-Tarts from a silver wrapper, was the man in the Red Sox jersey.

"Welcome to Hlidskjalf." He grinned, his scarred lips like the sides of a zipper. "The High Seat of Odin."

"You're not Odin," I said, using process of elimination. "You're Loki."

Sox Man chuckled. "Nothing escapes your keen intellect."

"First, what are we doing here? Second, why is Odin's throne named Lid Scalp?"

"*Hlidskjalf.* Put an *h* at the beginning and an *f* at the end. On that first letter you have to sound like you're hawking spit."

"On further reflection, I don't care."

"You should. This is where it all started. That's the answer to your second question—why we're here." He patted the seat next to him. "Join me. Have a Pop-Tart."

"Uh, no thanks."

"Your loss." He broke off the edge of a pastry and tossed it into his mouth. "This purple icing . . . I don't know what flavor it's supposed to be, but it is *insanely* good."

My pulse throbbed in my neck, which was strange since I was dreaming, and probably also dead.

Loki's eyes unnerved me. They had that same intense glow as Sam's, but Sam kept the flames under control. Loki's gaze flitted restlessly like the fire in the hearth, pushed by the wind, looking for anything it could set ablaze.

"Frey once sat here." He stroked the ermine fur. "Do you know the story?"

"No, but . . . isn't it illegal for anyone to sit there except Odin?"

"Oh, yes. Well, Odin and Frigg, the king and queen. They can sit here and see anywhere in the Nine Worlds. They merely have to concentrate and they will find whatever they are looking for. But if anyone else sits here . . ." He made *tsk-tsk* sounds. "The throne's magic can be a terrible curse. *I* certainly would never risk it if this weren't an illusion. But your father did. It was his one moment of rebellion." Loki took another bite of purple Pop-Tart. "I always admired him for that."

"And?"

"And instead of seeing what he was looking for, he saw what he most desired. It ruined his life. It's the reason he lost his sword. He—" Loki winced. "Excuse me."

He turned his head, his features contorting like he was about to sneeze. Then he let loose a scream of agony. When he faced me again, wisps of steam rose from the scar tissue across the bridge of his nose.

"Sorry," he said. "Every so often the poison splashes in my eyes."

"The poison." I remembered a fragment of a myth. "You killed somebody. The gods captured you and tied you up. There was something about poison. Where are you now, really?"

He gave me that twisted grin. "Right where I always am. The gods had me, ah, properly restrained. But that's not important. I can still send out splinters of my essence from time to time—like I'm doing now, to speak with my favorite friends!"

"Just because you're wearing a Sox jersey does not mean we're friends."

"I'm hurt!" His eyes sparkled. "My daughter Samirah saw something in you. We could help each other."

"You ordered her to take me to Valhalla?"

"Oh, no. That wasn't my idea. You, Magnus Chase, are of interest to many different parties. Some of them are not as charming or helpful as I."

"How about being charming and helpful to your daughter? She got kicked out of the Valkyries for choosing me."

His smile faded. "That's the gods for you. They banished me, too, and how many times did I save their hides? Don't worry about Samirah. She is strong. She'll be fine. I'm more worried about *you*."

Cold wind blew through the pavilion, so strong it pushed me a few inches across the polished stone floor.

Loki crumpled his Pop-Tart wrapper. "You'll be waking up soon. Before you go, some advice."

"I don't suppose I can refuse."

"The Sword of Summer," Loki said. "When your father sat on this throne, what he saw doomed him. He gave his sword away. It passed to his servant and messenger, Skirnir."

For a moment I was back on the Longfellow Bridge, the sword humming in my hand as if trying to speak.

"Uncle Randolph mentioned Skirnir," I said. "His descendant was in that shipwreck."

Loki pantomimed wild applause. "And there the sword lay for a thousand years, waiting for someone to reclaim it—someone who had the right to wield the blade."

"Me."

"Ah, but you aren't the only one who can use the sword. We know what will happen at Ragnarok. The Norns have told us our fates. Frey . . . poor Frey, because of the choices he made, will die at the hands of Surt. The lord of the fire giants will cut him down with his own lost sword."

A spike of pain hit me between the eyes, right about where the einherji's ax had killed me. "That's why Surt wants the sword. So he'll be ready for Ragnarok."

"Not only that. He'll use the sword to set in motion a chain of events to hasten Doomsday. In eight days, unless you stop him, he will cut loose my son, the Wolf."

"Your son . . . ?" My arms were evaporating. My eyesight grew hazy. Too many questions crowded into my head. "Wait . . . aren't you destined to fight against the gods at Ragnarok too?"

"Yes, but that was the *gods'* choice, not mine. The thing about fate, Magnus: even if we can't change the big picture, our choices can alter the details. *That's* how we rebel against destiny, how we make our mark. What will you choose to do?"

His image flickered. For a moment I saw him spread-eagle on a slab of stone, his wrists and ankles tied with slimy ropes, his body writhing in pain. Then I saw him in a hospital bed, a female doctor leaning over him, her hand resting gently on his forehead. She looked like an older version of Sam—curls of dark hair escaping from a scarlet headscarf, her mouth set tight with concern.

Loki appeared on the throne again, brushing Pop-Tart crumbs from his Red Sox jersey. "I won't tell you what to do, Magnus. That's the difference between me and the other gods. I'll only ask you this question: when you get a chance to sit on Odin's throne—and that day is coming—will you search for your heart's desire, knowing it may doom you as it doomed your father? Think on that, son of Frey. Perhaps we'll speak again, if you survive the next eight days."

My dream changed. Loki vanished. The braziers burst, showering hot coals across the dais, and the High Seat of Odin erupted in flames. The clouds turned into rolling banks of volcanic ash. Above the burning throne, two glowing red eyes appeared in the smoke.

YOU. The voice of Surt washed over me like a flamethrower. *YOU HAVE ONLY DELAYED ME. YOU HAVE EARNED A MORE PAINFUL, MORE PERMANENT DEATH.*

I tried to speak. The heat sucked the oxygen from my lungs. My lips cracked and blistered.

Surt laughed. *THE WOLF THINKS YOU MAY STILL BE USEFUL. I DO NOT. WHEN WE MEET AGAIN, YOU WILL BURN, SON OF FREY. YOU AND YOUR FRIENDS WILL BE MY TINDER. YOU WILL START THE FIRE THAT BURNS THE NINE WORLDS.*

The smoke thickened. I couldn't breathe, couldn't see.

My eyes flew open. I bolted upright, gasping for air. I was in bed in my hotel room. Surt was gone. I touched my face, but it wasn't burned. No ax was embedded there. All my battle-field wounds had vanished.

Still, my whole body was buzzing with alarm. I felt like I'd fallen asleep on active train tracks and the Acela Express had just roared past.

The dream was already erasing itself. I struggled to hold on to the specifics: the throne of Odin; Loki and Pop-Tarts; *my son, the Wolf*; Surt promising to burn the Nine Worlds. Trying to make sense of it was even more painful than getting an ax in my face.

Someone knocked on my door.

Thinking it might be one of my hallmates, I leaped out of bed and ran to answer. I threw open the door, found myself face-to-face with the Valkyrie Gunilla, and only then realized I was wearing nothing but underwear.

Her face turned magenta. Her jaw muscles knotted. "Oh."

"Captain Gorilla," I said. "What an honor."

She recovered quickly, glaring at me like she was trying to activate her freeze-ray vision. "Magnus Chase. I, um—you resurrected with incredible speed."

From her tone, I guessed that she hadn't expected to find me here. But then why had she knocked?

"I wasn't timing my resurrection," I said. "Was it fast?"

"Very." She glanced past me, maybe looking for something. "We have a few hours before dinner. Perhaps I could give you a tour of the hotel, since your own Valkyrie has been dismissed."

"You mean since you *got* her dismissed."

Gunilla turned up her palms. "I don't control the Norns. They decide all our fates."

"That's convenient." I remembered what Loki had said: *Our choices can alter the details. That's how we rebel against destiny.* "What about me? Have you—I mean *the Norns*—decided my fate?"

Gunilla scowled. Her posture was stiff and uneasy. Something was bothering her—maybe even scaring her.

"The thanes are discussing your situation now." She unhooked the key ring from her belt. "Take a tour with me. We can talk. If I understand you better, I may be able to speak to the thanes on your behalf. Unless, of course, you want to take your chances without my help. You might get lucky. The thanes might sentence you to bellhop duty for a few centuries. Or washing dishes in the kitchen."

The last thing I wanted was quality time with Gunilla. On the other hand, a tour of the hotel might show me some important features—like the exits. Also, after the dream I'd just had, I didn't want to be alone.

Besides, I could imagine how many dirty dishes would need washing after three rounds of dinner in the feast hall.

"I'll take the tour," I said. "But I should probably put some clothes on first."

TWENTY-ONE

Gunilla Gets Blowtorched and It's Not Funny. Okay, It's a Little Bit Funny

THE MAIN THING I discovered: Valhalla needed GPS. Even Gunilla got turned around in the endless corridors, banquet halls, gardens, and lounges.

At one point we were riding in a service elevator when Gunilla said, "Here's the food court."

The doors opened and a wall of flames engulfed us both.

My heart leaped into my throat. I thought Surt had found me. Gunilla screamed and staggered backward. I smashed random buttons until the doors shut. Then I did my best to put out the burning hem of Gunilla's dress.

"You okay?" My pulse was still racing. Gunilla's arms were covered with patches of steaming red skin.

"My skin will heal," Gunilla said. "My pride may not. That—that was Muspellheim, not the food court."

I wondered if Surt had engineered our little detour somehow, or if elevator doors in Valhalla often opened into the world of fire. I wasn't sure which possibility was more disturbing.

The tightness in Gunilla's voice told me how much pain she was in. I remembered standing over Mallory Keen when she fell in battle—the way I'd been able to sense the damage and how it could be mended if I'd had more time.

I knelt next to the Valkyrie. "May I?"

"What are you—"

I touched her forearm.

My fingers began to steam, drawing the heat from her skin. The redness faded. Her burns disappeared. Even the singed tip of her nose healed.

Gunilla stared at me as if I'd sprouted horns. "How did you . . . ? You weren't burned, either. How?"

"I don't know." My head spun with exhaustion. "Good luck? Healthy living?"

I tried to stand and promptly collapsed.

"Whoa, son of Frey." Gunilla grabbed my arm.

The elevator doors opened again. This time we really were at a food court. The smells of lemon chicken and pizza wafted in.

"Let's keep walking," Gunilla said. "Clear your head."

We got some strange looks as we stumbled through the dining area, me leaning against the Valkyrie captain for support, Gunilla's dress still smoking and tattered.

We turned into a corridor lined with conference rooms. Inside one, a guy in studded leather armor was giving a PowerPoint presentation to a dozen warriors, explaining the weaknesses of mountain trolls.

A few doors down, Valkyries in glittering party hats socialized over cake and ice cream. The birthday candle was shaped like the number 500.

"I think I'm okay now," I told Gunilla. "Thanks."

I wobbled a few steps on my own but managed to stay upright.

"Your healing abilities are remarkable," Gunilla said. "Frey is the god of abundance and fertility, growth and vitality—I guess that explains it. Still, I've never seen an einherji who can heal himself so quickly, much less heal others."

"Your guess is as good as mine," I said. "Normally I have trouble just opening Band-Aids."

"And your immunity to fire?"

I concentrated on the carpet designs, keeping one foot in front of the other. I could walk now, but healing Gunilla's burns had left me feeling like I'd just had a bad case of pneumonia.

"I don't think it's fire immunity," I said. "I've burned myself before. I just . . . I have a high tolerance for extreme temperatures. Cold. Heat. The same thing happened on the Longfellow Bridge when I walked into the flames . . ." My voice faltered. I remembered that Gunilla had edited that video and made me look like a fool. "But you know all about that."

Gunilla didn't seem to notice the sarcasm. She absently stroked one of the hammers in her bandolier as if it were a kitten. "Perhaps. . . . In the beginning of creation, only two worlds existed: Muspellheim and Niflheim, fire and ice. Life rose between those extremes. Frey is the god of moderate climes and the growing season. He represents the middle ground. Perhaps that's why you can resist heat and cold." She shook her head. "I don't know, Magnus Chase. It has been a long time since I met a child of Frey."

"Why? Are we not allowed in Valhalla?"

"Oh, we have some children of Frey from the old days. The kings of Sweden were his descendants, for instance. But we haven't seen a new one in Valhalla for centuries. Frey is Vanir, for one thing."

"Is that bad? Surt called me *Vanir-spawn*."

"That wasn't Surt."

I thought about my dream: those glowing eyes in the smoke. "It *was* Surt."

Gunilla looked like she wanted to argue, but she let it drop. "Whatever the case, the gods are divided into two tribes. The Aesir are mostly gods of war: Odin, Thor, Tyr, and the rest. The Vanir are more like the gods of nature: Frey, Freya, their father, Njord. That's an oversimplification, but anyway—long ago, the two tribes had a war. They almost destroyed the Nine Worlds. They finally settled their differences. They intermarried. They joined forces against the giants. But still they're different clans. Some Vanir have palaces in Asgard, the seat of the Aesir gods, but the Vanir also have their own world, Vanaheim. When a child of the Vanir dies bravely, they don't usually go to Valhalla. More often they go to the Vanir afterlife, overseen by the goddess Freya."

It took me a minute to digest all that. Clans of gods. Wars. Whatever. But that last part, *the Vanir afterlife* . . . "You're telling me there's another place like Valhalla, except for Vanir children, and I'm not there? What if that's where my mom went? What if I was supposed to—"

Gunilla took my arm. Her blue eyes were intense with anger. "That's right, Magnus. Think about what Samirah al-Abbas has done. I'm not saying *all* children of the Vanir go to Folkvanger—"

"You put them in a Volkswagen?"

"*Folkvanger.* It's the name of Freya's hall for the slain."

"Oh."

"My point is, you could have gone there. It would've been more likely. Half the honored dead go to Odin. Half go to

Freya. That was part of the agreement that ended the gods' war eons ago. So why did Samirah bring you here? *Wrongly chosen, wrongly slain.* She's the daughter of Loki, the father of evil. She cannot be trusted."

I wasn't sure how to answer. I hadn't known Samirah all that long, but she seemed pretty nice. Of course, so did her dad, Loki. . . .

"You may not believe this," Gunilla said, "but I'm giving you the benefit of the doubt. I think you may be innocent of Samirah's plans."

"What plans?"

She laughed bitterly. "To hasten Doomsday, of course. To bring the war before we are ready. That's what Loki wants."

I was tempted to protest that Loki had told me otherwise. He seemed more interested in *stopping* Surt from getting my dad's sword. . . . But I decided it wouldn't be wise to tell Gunilla I'd been having chats with the father of evil.

"If you hate Sam so much," I said, "why did you let her be a Valkyrie in the first place?"

"That wasn't my choice. I oversee the Valkyries, but Odin picks them. Samirah al-Abbas was the last Valkyrie he chose, two years ago, under what were . . . unusual circumstances. The All-Father has not appeared in Valhalla since."

"You think Sam killed him?"

I meant it as a joke, but Gunilla actually seemed to consider it. "I think Samirah should never have been chosen as a Valkyrie. I think she's working for her father as a spy and a saboteur. Getting her kicked out of Valhalla was the best thing I ever did."

"Wow."

"Magnus, you don't know her. There was another child of Loki here once. He—he wasn't what he seemed. He—" She stopped herself, looking like someone had just stepped on her heart. "Never mind. I swore to myself I wouldn't be fooled again. I intend to delay Ragnarok for as long as possible."

The edge of fear had crept back into her voice. She didn't sound much like the daughter of a war god.

"Why delay?" I asked. "Isn't Ragnarok what you're all training for? It's like your big graduation party."

"You don't understand," she said. "Come. There's something I need to show you. We will go through the gift shop."

When she said *gift shop*, I imagined a glorified closet selling cheap Valhalla souvenirs. Instead, it was a five-level department store combined with a convention center trade show. We passed through a supermarket, a clothing boutique with the latest in Viking fashions, and an IKEA outlet (naturally).

Most of the showroom floor was a maze of stalls, kiosks, and workshops. Bearded guys in leather aprons stood outside their forges offering free samples of arrowheads. There were specialized merchants for shields, spears, crossbows, helmets, and drinking cups (lots and lots of drinking cups). Several of the larger booths had full-size boats for sale.

I patted the hull of a sixty-foot warship. "I don't think this would fit in my bathtub."

"We have several lakes and rivers in Valhalla," Gunilla said. "There's also the Whitewater Rafting Experience on floor twelve. All einherjar should know how to fight at sea as well as on land."

I pointed to a riding ring where a dozen horses were tethered. "And those? You can ride a horse through the hallways?"

"Of course," said Gunilla. "We're pet-friendly. But notice, Magnus—the lack of weapons. The scarcity of armor."

"You're kidding, right? This place has *thousands* of weapons for sale."

"Not enough," Gunilla said. "Not for Ragnarok."

She led me down the Nordic Knickknacks aisle to a big iron door marked: AUTHORIZED PERSONNEL ONLY.

She slipped one of her keys into the lock. "I don't show this to many people. It's too disturbing."

"Not another wall of fire, is it?"

"Worse."

Behind the door was a set of stairs. Then another set of stairs. Then another set of stairs. By the time we reached the top, I'd lost count of how many flights. My upgraded einherji legs felt like overcooked linguine.

At last we stepped out onto a narrow balcony.

"This," Gunilla said, "is my favorite view."

I couldn't answer. I was too busy trying not to die from vertigo.

The balcony ringed the opening in the roof above the Hall of the Slain. The tree Laeradr's topmost branches stretched upward, making a green dome the size of Spaceship Earth at Epcot Center. Inside, far below, hotel staff scurried around the tables like termites, getting things ready for dinner.

From the outer edge of the balcony, the roofline of Valhalla sloped away—a thatch-work of gold shields blazing red in the evening sun. I felt like I was standing on the surface of a metal planet.

"Why don't you show this to people?" I asked. "It's . . . well, intimidating, but it's also beautiful."

"Over here." Gunilla pulled me to a spot where I could gaze down between two sections of roof.

My eyeballs felt like they were going to implode. I flashed back to a presentation my sixth grade science teacher once gave about the size of the universe. He explained how vast the earth was, then described how that was nothing compared to the solar system, which in turn was nothing compared to the galaxy, et cetera, et cetera, until I felt as significant as a speck on the underarm of a flea.

Stretching out around Valhalla, gleaming to the horizon, was a city of palaces, each as big and impressive as the hotel.

"Asgard," Gunilla said. "The realm of the gods."

I saw roofs made entirely of silver ingots, hammered bronze doors big enough to fly a B-1 bomber through, sturdy stone towers that pierced the clouds. Streets were paved in gold. Each garden was as vast as Boston Harbor. And circling the edge of the city were white ramparts that made the Great Wall of China look like a baby fence.

At the very edge of my vision, the city's widest avenue ran through a gateway in the walls. On the far side, the pavement dissolved into multicolored light—a roadway of prismatic fire.

"The Bifrost," Gunilla said. "The rainbow bridge leading from Asgard to Midgard."

I'd heard about the Bifrost Bridge. In my children's myth book, it was a seven-color pastel arc with happy bunny rabbits dancing around the base. *This* bridge had no happy bunnies. It was terrifying. It was a rainbow in the way a nuclear explosion was a mushroom.

"Only the gods may cross over," Gunilla said. "Anyone else would burn the moment they set foot on it."

"But . . . we're *in* Asgard?"

"Of course. Valhalla is one of Odin's halls. That's why, within the hotel, the einherjar are immortal."

"So you can go down there and see the gods, sell Girl Scout cookies door-to-door or whatever?"

Gunilla curled her lip. "Even gazing upon Asgard, you have no sense of reverence."

"Not really, no."

"Without the express permission of Odin, we aren't allowed to visit the city of the gods, at least not until the day of Ragnarok, when we will defend the gates."

"But you can fly."

"It's forbidden to go there. If I tried, I would fall from the sky. You're missing the point, Magnus. Look at the city again. What do you notice?"

I scanned the neighborhood, trying to see past all the silver and gold and the scary huge architecture. In one window, rich drapes hung in tatters. Along the streets, fire braziers stood empty and cold. The statues in one garden were completely overgrown with thorn bushes. The streets were deserted. No fires burned in any of the windows.

"Where is everybody?" I asked.

"Exactly. I would not be selling many Girl Scout cookies."

"You mean the gods are *gone*?"

Gunilla turned toward me, her string of hammers glinting orange in the sunset. "Some may be slumbering. Some are roaming the Nine Worlds. Some still appear from time to time. The fact is, we don't know what's going on. I've been in

Valhalla five hundred years, and I have never seen the gods so quiet, so inactive. The last two years . . ."

She plucked a leaf from a low-hanging branch of Laeradr. "Two years ago, something changed. The Valkyries and thanes all felt it. The barriers between the Nine Worlds began to weaken. Frost giants and fire giants raided Midgard more frequently. Monsters from Helheim broke into the worlds of the living. The gods grew distant and silent. This was around the time when Samirah became a Valkyrie—the last time we saw Odin. It was also when your mother died."

A raven circled overhead. Two more joined it. I thought about my mom—how she used to joke that birds of prey were stalking us when we went hiking. *They think we're dead. Quick, start dancing!*

At the moment I wasn't tempted to dance. I wanted to borrow Gunilla's hammers and knock the birds out of the sky.

"You think there's a connection between those things?" I asked.

"All I know . . . we are poorly prepared for Ragnarok. Then *you* arrive. The Norns issue dire warnings, calling you the Harbinger of the Wolf. That's not good, Magnus. Samirah al-Abbas may have been watching you for years, waiting for the right moment to insert you into Valhalla."

"*Insert* me?"

"Those two friends of yours on the bridge, the ones who had been monitoring you since you became homeless, perhaps they were working with her."

"You mean Blitz and Hearth? They're homeless guys."

"Are they? Don't you find it strange they looked after you so carefully?"

I wanted to tell her to go to Helheim, but Blitz and Hearth *had* always seemed a little . . . unusual. Then again, when you live on the streets, the definition of normal gets a little fuzzy.

Gunilla took my arm. "Magnus, I didn't believe it at first, but if that *was* Surt on the bridge, if you *did* find the Sword of Summer . . . then you're being used by the forces of evil. If Samirah al-Abbas wants you to retrieve the sword, then that's exactly what you *cannot* do. Stay in Valhalla. Let the thanes deal with this prophecy. Swear you'll do this, and I will speak to the thanes on your behalf. I'll convince them that you can be trusted."

"Do I detect an *or else*?"

"Only this: by tomorrow morning, the thanes will announce their decision regarding your fate. If we *cannot* trust you, then we will have to take precautions. We must know whose side you're on."

I looked down at the empty golden streets. I thought about Sam al-Abbas dragging me through the cold void, putting her career on the line because she thought I was brave. *You have potential, Magnus Chase. Don't prove me wrong.* Then she'd been vaporized in the feast hall thanks to Gunilla's edited blooper reel.

I pulled my arm away. "You said Frey is about the middle ground between fire and ice. Maybe this isn't about choosing sides. Maybe I don't want to pick an extreme."

Gunilla's expression rolled shut like a storm window. "I can be a powerful enemy, Magnus Chase. I will warn you one time: if you follow the plans of Loki, if you seek to hasten Ragnarok, I will destroy you."

I tried to meet her eyes, and to ignore my lungs flopping around in my chest. "I'll keep that in mind."

Below us, the dinner horn echoed through the feast hall.

"The tour is over," Gunilla announced. "From this point on, Magnus Chase, I will guide you no more."

She leaped over the side of the balcony and flew down through the branches, leaving me to find my own way back. Without GPS.

TWENTY-TWO

My Friends
Fall Out of a Tree

FORTUNATELY, a friendly berserker found me wandering through the spa on the hundred and twelfth floor. He'd just gotten the gentleman's pedicure ("Just Because You Kill People Doesn't Mean Your Feet Should!") and was happy to lead me back to the elevators.

By the time I reached the feast hall, dinner was under way. I navigated toward X—who was hard to miss even in the huge crowd—and joined my hallmates from floor nineteen.

We traded stories about the morning's battle.

"I hear you used alf seidr!" Halfborn said. "Impressive!"

I'd almost forgotten about the energy blast that had knocked everybody's weapons away. "Yeah, uh . . . what exactly is *alf seidr*?"

"Elf magic," Mallory said. "Sneaky Vanir-style witchcraft unfit for a true warrior." She punched me in the arm. "I like you better already."

I tried for a smile, though I wasn't sure how I'd managed to wield elf magic. As far as I knew, I was not an elf. I thought about the way I resisted extreme temperatures, and the way I'd healed Gunilla in the elevator . . . was that alf seidr too? Maybe it came from being a son of Frey, though I didn't understand how the powers were related.

T.J. complimented me on taking the crest of the hill. X complimented me on staying alive longer than five minutes.

It was good to feel like part of the group, but I didn't pay much attention to their conversation. My head was still buzzing from the tour with Gunilla, and the dream of Loki at the throne of Odin.

At the head table, Gunilla occasionally murmured something to Helgi, and the manager would scowl in my direction. I kept waiting for him to call me up and put me on grape-peeling duty with Hunding, but I guess he was contemplating some better punishment.

Tomorrow morning, Gunilla had warned, *we will have to take precautions.*

At the end of dinner, a couple of newbies were welcomed to Valhalla. Their videos were suitably heroic. No Norns showed up. No Valkyries got banished in disgrace. No butts were shot with squeaky arrows.

As the crowds filed out of the feast hall, T.J. clapped me on the shoulder. "Get some rest. Another glorious death tomorrow!"

"Yippee," I said.

Back in my room, I couldn't sleep. I spent hours pacing around like a zoo animal. I didn't want to wait for the thanes' judgment in the morning. I'd seen how wisely they judged when they exiled Sam.

But what choice did I have? Sneak around the hotel randomly opening doors, hoping to find one that led back to Boston? Even if I succeeded, there was no guarantee I'd be allowed to go back to my luxurious life as a homeless kid. Gunilla or Surt or some other Norse nasty might track me down again.

We must know whose side you are on, Gunilla had said.

I was on *my* side. I didn't want to get wrapped up in some Viking Doomsday, but something told me it was too late. My mom had died two years ago, around the same time a bunch of other bad stuff was breaking loose in the Nine Worlds. With my luck, there was a connection. If I wanted justice for my mother—if I wanted to find out what had happened to her—I couldn't go back to hiding under a bridge.

I also couldn't keep hanging out in Valhalla, taking Swedish lessons and watching PowerPoint presentations on killing trolls.

At about five in the morning, I finally gave up on sleeping. I went to the restroom to wash my face. Clean towels hung on the rod. The hole in the wall had been repaired. I wondered if it had been done by magic or if some poor schmuck had had to fix it as a punishment from the thanes. Maybe tomorrow I'd be the one plastering drywall.

I walked to the atrium and stared at the stars through the trees. I wondered what sky I was looking at—what world, what constellations.

The branches rustled. Something dark and man-shaped toppled out of the tree. He landed at my feet with a nasty crunch.

"OW!" he wailed. "Stupid gravity!"

My old buddy Blitz lay on his back, moaning and cradling his left arm.

A second person dropped lightly to the grass—Hearth, dressed in his usual black leather clothes and candy-striped scarf. He signed: *Hi.*

I stared at them. "What are you—how did you—?" I started to grin. I'd never been happier to see anyone.

"Arm!" Blitz yelped. "Broken!"

"Right." I knelt, trying to focus. "I might be able to heal this."

"Might?"

"Wait . . . did you get a makeover?"

"You're asking about my *wardrobe*?"

"Well, yeah." I'd never seen Blitz look so nice.

His chaotic hair had been washed and combed back. His beard was trimmed. His Cro-Magnon unibrow had been plucked and waxed. Only his zigzag nose had not been cosmetically corrected.

As for the clothes, he'd apparently robbed several high-end boutiques on Newbury Street. His boots were alligator leather. His black wool suit was tailored to fit his stocky five-feet-five frame and looked lovely with his dark skin tone. Under the jacket, he was rocking a charcoal paisley vest with a gold watch chain, a turquoise dress shirt, and a bolo tie. He looked like a very short, well-groomed African American cowboy hit man.

Hearth clapped to get my attention. He signed: *Arm. Fix?*

"Right. Sorry." I placed my hand gently on Blitz's forearm. I could feel the fracture under the skin. I willed it to mend. *Click.* Blitz yelped as the bone moved back into place.

"Try it now," I said.

Blitz moved the arm. His expression changed from pain to surprise. "That actually worked!"

Hearth looked even more shocked. He signed, *Magic? How?*

"I've been wondering that myself," I said. "Guys, don't take this the wrong way, because I'm really glad to see you. But why are you falling out of my trees?"

"Kid," Blitz said, "for the past twenty-four hours we've been climbing all over the World Tree looking for you. We thought we found you last night, but—"

"I think you might have," I said. "Just before dawn I heard somebody moving in the branches."

Blitz turned to Hearth. "I *told* you that was the right room!"

Hearth rolled his eyes and signed too fast for me to read.

"Oh, please," Blitz said. "Your idea, my idea—it doesn't matter. The point is, we're here, and Magnus is alive! Well . . . technically he's dead. But he's alive. Which means the boss might not kill us!"

"The boss?" I asked.

Blitz developed a tic in his eye. "Yeah. We have a confession to make."

"You're not really homeless," I said. "Last night, one of the thanes saw you guys on video and—"

Video? Hearth signed.

"Yeah. Valkyrie Vision. Anyway, this thane called you a dwarf and an elf. I'm guessing"—I pointed at Blitz—"you're the dwarf?"

"Typical," Blitz grumbled. "Assume I'm the dwarf because I'm short."

"So you're not the dwarf?"

He sighed. "No. I'm the dwarf."

"And you . . ." I looked at Hearth, but I couldn't even make myself say it. I'd hung out with this guy for two years. He'd taught me curses in sign language. We'd eaten burritos out of trash cans together. What kind of elf does that?

E-L-F. Hearth signed the individual letters. *Sometimes spelled A-L-F.*

"But . . . you guys don't look that different from humans."

"Actually," Blitz said, "humans don't look that different from dwarves and elves."

"I can't believe I'm having this conversation, but you're not *that* short. Like, for a dwarf. You could pass for a regular short human."

"Which I've been doing," Blitz said, "for two years now. Dwarves come in different sizes, just like humans. I happen to be a *svartalf.*"

"A fart elf?"

"Gah! Clean your ears, kid. A *svartalf.* It means *dark elf.* I'm from *Svartalfheim.*"

"Um, I thought you just said you're a dwarf."

"Dark elves aren't actually elves, kid. It's . . . what do you call it? A misnomer. We're a subset of dwarves."

"Well, that certainly clears things up."

Hearth developed a faint smile, which for him was the equivalent of rolling on the floor laughing. He signed, *Fart elf.*

Blitz pointedly ignored him. "Svartalfs tend to be taller than your average Nidavellir dwarves. Plus we're devilishly handsome. But that's not important right now. Hearthstone and I are here to help you."

"Hearthstone?"

Hearth nodded. *My full name. He is B-L-I-T-Z-E-N.*

"Kid, we don't have much time. We've been watching you for the last two years, trying to keep you safe."

"For your boss."

"That's right."

"And who is your boss?"

"That's . . . classified. But he's one of the good guys. He's the head of our organization, dedicated to delaying Ragnarok as long as possible. And you, my friend, have been his most important project."

"So, just taking a wild guess here . . . you're not working for Loki?"

Blitzen looked outraged. Hearth signed one of those curses he'd taught me.

"That was uncalled for, kid." Blitzen sounded genuinely hurt. "I dressed up like a homeless person every day for two years for you. I let my personal hygiene go to Helheim. You know how long I had to stay in the bubble bath every morning to get the *smell* out?"

"Sorry. So . . . were you working with Samirah, the Valkyrie?"

Another curse sign from Hearthstone. *The one who took you? No. She made things hard for us.*

Actually the literal signs were more like: *HER. TOOK. YOU. MADE. DIFFICULT. US.* But I'd gotten fairly good at interpreting.

"You weren't supposed to die, kid," said Blitzen. "Our job was to protect you. But now . . . well, you're an einherji. Maybe we can still make this work. We've got to get you out of here. We have to find that sword."

"Let's go, then," I said.

"Now, don't argue," Blitzen said. "I know you're in warriors' paradise and it's all very new and exciting—"

"Blitz, I said sure."

The dwarf blinked. "But I had this whole speech prepared."

"No need. I trust you."

The strange thing? I was telling the truth.

Maybe Blitzen and Hearthstone were professional stalkers who'd been keeping an eye on me for a top-secret anti-Ragnarok organization. Maybe their idea of protecting me involved attacking the lord of the fire giants with cheap plastic toys. Maybe they weren't even the same species as me.

But they'd stuck by me while I was homeless. They were my best friends. Yes . . . that's how messed up my life was.

"Well, then." Blitzen brushed the grass from his paisley vest. "We'll just climb back into the World Tree before—"

From somewhere above, an explosive *yap!* reverberated through the room. It sounded like a rabid six-thousand-pound Boston terrier choking on a mammoth bone.

Hearthstone's eyes widened. The sound was so loud he'd probably felt the vibrations through his shoes.

"Gods almighty!" Blitzen grabbed my arm. Together with Hearthstone, he pulled me away from the atrium. "Kid, please tell me you know another way out of this hotel. Because we *aren't* using the tree."

Another *yap* shook the room. Broken branches tumbled to the floor.

"Wh-what's up there?" I asked, my knees shaking. I thought about the Norns' prophecy, naming me a harbinger of evil. "Is it—the Wolf?"

"Oh, much worse," Blitzen said. "It's the Squirrel."

TWENTY-THREE

I Recycle Myself

WHEN SOMEONE SAYS, *It's the Squirrel*, you don't ask questions. You run. The barking alone was enough to scare the mead out of me.

I grabbed my hotel-issued sword on the way out. Since I was wearing green silk Valhalla pajamas, I doubted I would need it. If I had to fight anyone, they would die laughing before I ever drew the blade.

We burst into the hallway to find T.J. and Mallory already standing there, bleary-eyed and hastily dressed.

"What was that sound?" Mallory scowled at me. "Why do you have a dwarf and an elf in your room?"

"SQUIRREL!" Blitzen yelled, slamming my door shut.

Hearth said the same thing in sign language—a gesture that looked disturbingly like a set of mandibles rending flesh.

T.J. looked like he'd been slapped across the face. "Magnus, what have you done?"

"I need to leave the hotel. *Now.* Please don't stop us."

Mallory cursed in what was maybe Gaelic. Our little hallway group was a veritable United Nations of Cussing.

"We won't stop you," she said. "This is going to get us laundry duty for a decade, but we'll help you."

I stared at her. "Why? You've known me less than a day."

"Long enough to know you're an idiot," she grumbled.

"What she's trying to say," T.J. offered, "is that hallmates always protect each other. We'll cover your escape."

The door of my room shook. Cracks spiderwebbed from the nameplate. A decorative spear fell off the wall of the corridor.

"X!" T.J. called. "Help!"

The half-troll's door exploded off its hinges. X lumbered into the hallway as if he'd been standing just inside, waiting for the call. "Yes?"

T.J. pointed. "Magnus's door. Squirrel."

"Okay."

X marched over and shoved his back against my door. It shuddered again, but X held firm. Enraged barking echoed from inside.

Halfborn Gunderson stumbled out of his room wearing nothing but smiley-face boxers, double-bladed axes in his hands.

"What's going on?" He glowered at Blitz and Hearth. "Should I kill the dwarf and the elf?"

"No!" Blitzen yelped. "Don't kill the dwarf and the elf!"

"They're with me," I said. "We're leaving."

"Squirrel," T.J. explained.

Halfborn's shaggy eyebrows achieved orbit. "Squirrel as in *squirrel* squirrel?"

"*Squirrel* squirrel," Mallory agreed. "And I'm surrounded by moron morons."

A raven soared down the hall. It landed on the nearest light fixture and squawked at me accusingly.

"Well, that's great," Mallory said. "The ravens have sensed your friends' intrusion. That means the Valkyries won't be far behind."

From the direction of the elevator banks, half a dozen howls pierced the air.

"And those would be Odin's wolves," Halfborn said. "Very friendly unless you're trespassing or leaving the hotel without permission, in which case they'll tear you apart."

An unmanly sob started to build in my throat. I could accept being killed by a squirrel, or an army of Valkyries, or even another ax in my face, but not wolves. My legs threatened to give out beneath me.

"Blitz and Hearth"—my voice trembled—"is there any alarm you guys *failed* to set off?"

Not fair, Hearth signed. *We avoided the tree mines.*

"*Tree* mines?" I wasn't sure I'd understood him correctly.

Halfborn Gunderson hefted his ax. "I'll slow down the wolves. Good luck, Magnus!"

He charged down the hall screaming, "DEATH!" while the smiley faces rippled on his boxer shorts.

Mallory's face turned red—with embarrassment or delight, I couldn't tell. "I'll stay with X in case the squirrel breaks through," she said. "T.J., you take them to recycling."

"Yeah."

"*Recycling?*" Blitz asked.

Mallory drew her sword. "Magnus, I can't say it's been a pleasure. You're a true pain in the *nári*. Now get out of here."

The door of my room shuddered again. Plaster rained from the ceiling.

"The squirrel is strong," X grunted. "Hurry."

T.J. fixed his bayonet. "Let's go."

He led us down the corridor, his blue Union jacket over his pj's. I got a feeling he probably slept in that jacket. Behind us, wolves howled and Halfborn Gunderson bellowed in Old Norse.

As we ran, a few einherjar opened their doors to see what was going on. When they spotted T.J. with his bayonet, they ducked back inside.

Left, right, right, left—I lost track of the turns. Another raven shot past, cawing angrily. I tried to swat it.

"Don't," T.J. warned. "They're sacred to Odin."

We were just passing a T in the hallway when a voice shouted, "MAGNUS!"

I made the mistake of looking.

To our left, fifty feet away, Gunilla stood in full armor, a hammer in either hand. "Take another step," she snarled, "and I will destroy you."

T.J. glanced at me. "You three keep going. Next right, there's a chute marked 'recycling.' Jump in."

"But—"

"No time." T.J. grinned. "Go kill some rebs for me—or monsters—or whatever."

He pointed his rifle at the Valkyrie, shouted, "Fifty-Fourth Massachusetts!" and charged.

Hearth grabbed my arm and pulled me along. Blitz found the recycling chute and yanked it open. "GO, GO!"

Hearthstone dove in headfirst.

"You next, kid," said the dwarf.

I hesitated. The smell coming out of the chute reminded me of my Dumpster-diving days. Suddenly the comforts of the Hotel Valhalla didn't seem so bad.

Then more wolves howled, closer this time, and I recycled myself.

TWENTY-FOUR

You Had One Job

TURNS OUT VALHALLA had been sending its recycling to home plate at Fenway, which could explain any problems the Red Sox were having with their offensive lineup.

Hearthstone was just getting to his feet when I landed on top of him and knocked him flat. Before I could extricate myself, Blitzen plowed into my chest. I pushed him off and rolled away just in case anyone else decided to drop out of the sky.

I struggled to my feet. "Why are we in Fenway Park?"

"Don't ask me." Blitzen sighed dismally. His nice wool suit looked like it had passed through the digestive tract of a snail. "The doors in and out of Valhalla are notoriously wonky. At least we're in Midgard."

Rows of red bleachers stood empty and silent, uncomfortably similar to the Feast Hall of the Slain before the einherjar marched in. The field was covered in a patchwork of frozen tarps that crunched under my feet.

It must have been around six in the morning. The eastern sky was just starting to turn gray. My breath steamed in the air.

"What were we running from?" I asked. "What kind of mutant squirrel—"

"Ratatosk," Blitz said. "The bane of the World Tree. Anyone

who dares climb Yggdrasil's branches sooner or later has to deal with that monster. Count yourself lucky we escaped."

Hearthstone pointed toward the dawn. He signed: *Sun. Bad for Blitzen.*

Blitz squinted. "You're right. After that business on the bridge, I can't stand any more direct exposure."

"What do you mean?" I looked more closely at his face. "Are you turning gray?"

Blitzen looked away, but there was no doubt. His cheeks had lightened to the color of wet clay. "Kid, you may have noticed I never hung around with you much during the day?"

"I . . . yeah. It was like Hearth took the day shift. You took the night shift."

"Exactly. Dwarves are subterranean creatures. Sunlight is deadly to us. Mind you, not as deadly as it is to *trolls*. I can stand a little bit, but if I'm out for too long I start to . . . uh, petrify."

I remembered the fight on Longfellow Bridge, how Blitzen had been wearing a broad-brimmed hat, coat, gloves, and sunglasses—a strange fashion statement, especially with the MAKE WAY FOR DUCKLINGS sign. "If you cover up, will you be okay?"

"It helps. Thick clothing, sunscreen, et cetera. But at the moment"—he gestured to his clothes—"I'm not prepared. I dropped my supply pack somewhere in the World Tree."

Hearthstone signed: *After bridge, his legs turned to stone. No walking until night.*

A lump formed in my throat. Blitz and Hearth's attempt to protect me on the Longfellow Bridge had been pretty ridiculous, but they'd *tried.* Just by being out in the daytime, Blitzen had risked his life.

As many questions as I had, as messed up as my life (death?) was at the moment, knowing that Blitzen was in danger again for my sake readjusted my priorities.

"Let's get you someplace dark," I said.

The easiest option was the Green Monster—the famous home-run-blocking four-story wall along the left outfield. I'd been behind it once before on a school trip—first grade, maybe? I remembered there were service doors under the scoreboard.

I found one unlocked, and we slipped inside.

There wasn't much to see—just metal scaffolding, stacks of green number cards hanging on the wall, and the stadium's concrete ribs tattooed with a hundred years of graffiti. The space had one important requirement, though: it was dark.

Blitzen sat on a pile of mats and pulled off his boots. Acorns spilled out. His socks were gray paisley, matching his vest.

The socks amazed me as much as anything I'd encountered in Valhalla. "Blitz, what's with the outfit? You look so . . . spiffy."

He puffed up his chest. "Thank you, Magnus. It hasn't been easy dressing like a bum the last two years. No offense, of course."

"Of course."

"This is how I usually dress. I take my appearance very seriously. I'll admit I'm a bit of a clotheshorse."

Hearth made a sound between a sneeze and a snort. He signed: *A bit?*

"Oh, be quiet," Blitz grumbled. "Who bought you that scarf, eh?" He turned to me for support. "I told Hearth he needed a splash of color. The black clothes. The platinum blond hair. The red-striped scarf makes a bold statement, don't you think?"

"Uh . . . sure," I said. "As long as *I* don't have to wear it. Or the paisley socks."

"Don't be silly. Patterned fabric would look terrible on you." Blitz frowned at his boot. "What were we talking about again?"

"How about why you've been watching me for the last two years?"

Hearth signed: *Told you. The boss.*

"Not Loki," I said. "Odin, then?"

Blitz laughed. "No. The Capo is even smarter than Odin. He likes to work behind the scenes, stay anonymous. He assigned us to watch you and, uh"—he cleared his throat—"keep you alive."

"Ah."

"Yeah." Blitzen shook the acorns out of his other boot. "We had one job. We failed. 'Keep him alive,' said the Capo. 'Watch him. Protect him if needed, but don't interfere with his choices. He's important to the plan.'"

"The plan."

"The Capo knows stuff. The future, for instance. He does his best to nudge events in the right direction, keep the Nine Worlds from spiraling into chaos and exploding."

"That sounds like a good plan."

"He told us you were the son of Frey. He didn't go into details, but he was very insistent: you were important, had to be protected. When you died . . . well, I'm just glad we found you in Valhalla. Maybe all isn't lost. Now we've got to report to the Capo and get new orders."

Hearthstone signed: *And hope he doesn't kill us.*

"That, too." Blitzen didn't sound optimistic. "The thing is, Magnus, until we talk to the boss, I can't really go into many details."

"Even though I'm important to the plan."

That's why *we can't,* Hearth signed.

"What about what happened after I fell off the bridge? Can you tell me that?"

Blitz picked a leaf out of his beard. "Well, Surt disappeared into the water with you."

"It *was* Surt."

"Oh, yeah. And I gotta say, nice job with that. A mortal taking down the lord of the fire giants? Even if you died doing it, that was impressive."

"So . . . I killed him?"

No such luck, Hearth signed.

"Yeah," Blitz agreed. "But fire giants don't do well in icy water. I imagine the impact shocked him right back to Muspellheim. And cutting off his nose . . . that was brilliant. It'll take him a while to regain enough strength to travel between worlds."

A few days, Hearth guessed.

"Maybe longer," Blitz said.

I looked back and forth between them, two nonhumans discussing the mechanics of traveling between worlds the way somebody else might debate how long it would take to fix a carburetor.

"You guys got away okay, obviously," I said. "What about Randolph?"

Hearthstone wrinkled his nose. *Your uncle. Annoying, but fine.*

"Kid, you saved lives," Blitzen said. "There were a lot of injuries, a lot of damage, but no mortals died—um, except you. The last time Surt visited Midgard, it didn't go so well."

Great Chicago Fire, Hearth signed.

"Yeah," said Blitz. "Anyway, the Boston explosions made national news. The humans are still investigating. They're speculating the damage was caused by meteor strikes."

I remember thinking that myself at first. And later wondering whether Surt had been responsible for them all. "But dozens of people saw Surt on the bridge! At least one guy caught him on video."

Blitz shrugged. "You'd be amazed what mortals *don't* see. Not just humans. Dwarves and elves are just as bad. Besides, giants are experts at glamour."

"*Glamour.* I'm guessing you don't mean fashion."

"No. Giants are *horrible* at fashion. I mean glamour like illusions. Giants are magic by nature. They can manipulate your senses without even trying. One time a giant made Hearthstone think I was a warthog, and Hearth almost killed me."

No more about the warthog! Hearthstone pleaded.

"So, anyway," Blitz said, "you fell in the river and died. The emergency services retrieved your body, but—"

"My body . . ."

Hearthstone pulled a newspaper clipping from his jacket pocket and handed it to me.

I read my own obituary. There was my class picture from fifth grade—my hair in my eyes, my uncomfortable *why-am-I-here* smile, my ratty DROPKICK MURPHYS T-shirt. The obituary didn't say much. Nothing about my two-year disappearance, my homelessness, my mom's death. Just: *Untimely demise. Survived by two uncles and a cousin. Private service to be held*.

"But my body is here," I said, touching my chest. "I *have* a body."

"A new and improved body," Blitz agreed, squeezing my biceps in admiration. "They retrieved your *old* body. Hearth and I did our own search of the river. There was no sign of Surt. Worse . . . there was no sign of the sword. If it's not at the bottom of the river again—"

"Could Randolph have found it?" I asked.

Hearthstone shook his head. *We watched him. Doesn't have it.*

"Then Surt has the sword," I guessed.

Blitz shuddered. "Let's not assume that. There's still a chance it's with your old body."

"Why would it be?"

Blitz pointed to Hearth. "Ask him. He's the expert at magic."

Hard to explain in signs, Hearth gestured. *A magic sword stays with you. You claimed it.*

"But . . . I didn't."

You summoned it, Hearth signed. *Held it first, before Surt. Hope that means Surt didn't get it. Don't know why the sword didn't go to Valhalla.*

"I wasn't holding the sword when I hit the river," I said. "It slipped out of my hand."

"Ah." Blitz nodded. "That might be why. Still, the sword would traditionally go into your grave, or get burned on your pyre. So there's a decent chance it will materialize next to your dead body. We need to look in your coffin."

My skin crawled. "You want me to go to my own funeral?"

Hearth signed: *No. We go before.*

"According to your obituary notice," Blitz said, "your body is at the funeral home today for viewing hours. The service isn't until tonight. If you go now, you should have the place to yourself. The building isn't open yet, and you won't exactly have mourners lining up outside."

"Thanks a lot."

Blitzen tugged on his boots. "I'll go talk to the boss. On the way, I'll pop by Svartalfheim and pick up some proper anti-sunlight supplies."

"You'll pop by the world of the dark elves?"

"Yeah. It's not as hard as it sounds. I've had a lot of practice, and Boston is at the center of Yggdrasil. Slipping between worlds is easy here. One time Hearth and I stepped off a curb in Kendall Square and fell into Niflheim by accident."

That was cold, Hearth signed.

"While I'm gone," Blitz said, "Hearthstone will take you to the funeral home. I'll meet you . . . where?"

Arlington—nearest T stop, Hearth signed.

"Good." Blitzen stood. "Get that sword, kid . . . and be careful. Outside Valhalla, you can die like anybody else. The last thing we need to explain to the boss is *two* Magnus Chase corpses."

TWENTY-FIVE

My Funeral Director Dresses Me Funny

ONE GOOD THING about being homeless: I knew where to find free clothes. Hearth and I raided a charity drop box on Charlesgate so I wouldn't have to walk around town in my pj's. Soon I was resplendent in stonewashed jeans, a hunting jacket, and a T-shirt peppered with holes. I looked more like Kurt Cobain than ever, except I doubt Cobain ever wore a shirt that read: WIGGLES ROCK & ROLL PRESCHOOL TOUR! The really disturbing thing was that they made shirts like that in my size.

I held up my hotel-issued sword. "Hearth, what about this? I doubt the cops will like me walking around with a three-foot blade."

Glamour, Hearth signed. *Attach it to your belt.*

As soon as I did, the weapon shrank and melted into a simple loop of chain, which was only slightly less fashionable than the Wiggles T-shirt.

"Great," I said. "Now my humiliation is complete."

Still a sword, Hearth signed. *Mortals are not good at seeing magical things. Between Ice and Fire is Mist, G-i-n-n-u-n-g-a-g-a-p. Obscures appearances. Hard to explain in signs.*

"Okay." I remembered what Gunilla had told me about the worlds forming between ice and fire, and how Frey represented the temperate zone between. Apparently, though, Frey's children didn't inherit an innate understanding of what the heck that meant.

I read my obituary again for the address of the funeral home. "Let's go pay our respects to me."

It was a long, cold walk. The temperature didn't bother me, but Hearth shivered in his leather jacket. His lips were cracked and peeling. His nose was runny. From all the fantasy books and movies I had devoured in middle school, I'd gotten an impression of elves as noble creatures of unearthly beauty. Hearthstone looked more like an anemic college kid who hadn't eaten in a few weeks.

Still . . . I began to notice non-human details about him. His pupils were strangely reflective, like a cat's. Under his translucent skin, his veins were more green than blue. And despite his disheveled appearance, he didn't reek like a normal homeless person—body odor, alcohol, stale grease. He smelled more like pine needles and woodsmoke. How had I not realized that before?

I wanted to ask him about elves, but walking and talking in sign language don't mix. Nor could Hearth read lips very well on the move. I kind of liked that, actually. You couldn't multitask while talking to him. The dialogue required one hundred percent focus. If all conversations were like that, I imagined people wouldn't say so much stupid garbage.

We were passing Copley Square when he pulled me into the doorway of an office building.

Gómez, he signed. *Wait.*

Gómez was a beat cop who knew us by sight. He didn't

know my real name, but if he'd seen a recent picture of me on the news, I would have a hard time explaining why I wasn't dead. Also, Gómez wasn't the friendliest guy.

I tapped Hearth's shoulder for attention. "What's it like . . . where you're from?"

Hearth's expression turned guarded. *Alfheim not so different. Only brighter. No night.*

"No night . . . like *ever*?"

No night. The first time I saw a sunset . . .

He hesitated, then splayed both hands in front of his chest like he was having a heart attack: the sign for *scared*.

I tried to imagine living in a world where it was always daytime, then watching the sun disappear in a wash of blood-colored light on the horizon.

"That would be freaky," I decided. "But don't elves have stuff *humans* would be scared of? Like . . . alf seidr?"

A light kindled in Hearth's eyes. *How do you know that term?*

"Uh . . . yesterday on the battlefield, somebody said I did it." I told him about the blast that had knocked everyone's weapons away. "And when I healed Blitz's arm, or walked into that wall of flames on the Longfellow Bridge . . . I wondered if it was all the same kind of magic."

Hearth seemed to take longer than usual to process my words.

Not sure. His gestures were smaller, more careful. *Alf seidr can be many things—usually peaceful magic. Healing. Growing. Stopping violence. It cannot be learned. Not like rune magic. You have alf seidr in your blood, or you do not. You are son of Frey. Maybe have some of his abilities.*

"Frey is an elf?"

Hearth shook his head. *Frey is the lord of Alfheim, our patron god. Vanir are close to elves. Vanir were the source of all alf seidr.*

"Past tense? Don't elves still talk to trees and speak with birds and stuff?"

Hearth grunted with irritation. He peeked around the corner to check on our neighborhood policeman.

Alfheim not like that, he signed. *Not for centuries. Almost no one is born with alf seidr. No one practices magic. Most elves think Midgard is a myth. Humans live in castles and wear plate mail and tights.*

"Maybe a thousand years ago."

Hearth nodded. *Back then, our worlds interacted more. Now, both worlds have changed. Elves spend most of their time staring at screens, watching funny pixie videos when they are supposed to be working.*

I wasn't sure I'd interpreted his signs correctly—*pixie videos?*—but Alfheim sounded depressingly like Midgard.

"So you don't know any more about magic than I do," I said.

I don't know what it looked like in the old days. But I am trying to learn. I have given up everything to try.

"What do you mean?"

He glanced around the corner again. *Gómez is gone. Come on.*

I wasn't sure if he'd missed my question or he'd just chosen to ignore it.

The funeral home was near Washington and Charles, tucked in a row of Bay Village town houses that seemed lost among the newer concrete and glass skyscrapers. A sign on the awning read: TWINING & SONS MEMORIAL SERVICES.

A display by the door listed upcoming viewings. The top

one read: MAGNUS CHASE. The date was today, starting at ten
A.M. The door was locked. The lights were off.

"Early for my own funeral," I said. "Typical."

My hands were shaking. The idea of seeing my dead self
was more unnerving than actually dying. "So do we break in?"

I'll try something, Hearth signed.

From his coat, he pulled a leather pouch. The contents
clattered with a familiar sound.

"Runestones," I guessed. "You know how to use them?"

He shrugged like, *We're about to find out.* He took one stone
and tapped it against the door handle. The lock clicked. The
door swung open.

"Nice," I said. "Would that work on any door?"

Hearth put away the pouch. I couldn't quite read his
expression—a mixture of sadness and wariness.

I'm learning, he signed. *Only tried that once before, when I met
Blitz.*

"How did you two—"

Hearth cut me off with a wave. *Blitz saved my life. Long story.
You go inside. I will stand guard here. Dead human bodies . . .* He
shuddered and shook his head.

So much for my elfish backup.

Inside, the funeral home smelled of moldering bouquets.
The threadbare red carpet and dark wood paneling made the
whole place feel like one giant coffin. I crept down the hallway
and peeked into the first room.

It was a set up like a chapel: three stained glass windows
on the back wall, rows of folding chairs facing an open coffin
on a dais. I hated this already. I'd been raised nonreligious. I'd
always considered myself an atheist.

So, of course, my punishment was to find out I was the son of a Norse deity, go to a Viking afterlife, and have an open-coffin memorial in a cheesy uni-faith chapel. If there was an Almighty God up there, a head honcho of the universe, He was totally laughing at me right now.

At the entrance of the room was a poster-size portrait of me, wreathed in black crepe paper. They'd chosen the same goofy fifth grade picture from my elementary school year-book. Next to it, on a small table, was a guest book.

I was tempted to pick up the pen and write the first entry: *Thanks for coming to my funeral!—Magnus.*

Who would be here, anyway? Uncle Randolph? Maybe Frederick and Annabeth, if they were still in town. My old classmates from two years ago? Yeah, right. If the funeral home offered snacks, some of my homeless buddies might show up, but the only ones I really cared about were Blitzen and Hearthstone.

I realized I was procrastinating. I wasn't sure how long I'd been standing in the chapel doorway. I forced myself down the aisle.

When I saw my own face in the coffin, I nearly threw up.

Not because I'm *that* ugly, but because . . . well, you know how weird it is to hear your own voice on a recording? And how irritating it can be to see yourself in a photo if you don't think you look good? Okay, imagine seeing your actual body lying right in front of you. It was so real, and yet so *not* me.

My hair was shellacked to the sides of my head. My face was caked with makeup, probably to cover cuts and bruises. My mouth was fixed in a weird little smile that I never would've made in real life. I was dressed in a cheap-looking blue suit with a blue tie. I hated blue. My hands were clasped over my stomach, hiding the place where I'd been impaled by a molten piece of asphalt.

"No, no, no." I gripped the sides of the coffin.

The *wrongness* of it made me feel like my guts were burning all over again.

I'd always had an image of what would happen to my body after death. This wasn't it. My mom and I had a pact—which sounds creepy, but it really wasn't. She made me promise that when she died, I'd have her cremated. I'd scatter her ashes in the woods of the Blue Hills. If I died first, she promised she would do the same for me. Neither of us liked the idea of being embalmed, turned into some chemically stabilized exhibition, then buried in a box. We wanted to be in the sunshine and the fresh air and just kind of dissolve.

I hadn't been able to keep my promise to my mother. Now I was getting exactly the kind of funeral I didn't want.

My eyes watered. "I'm sorry, Mom."

I wanted to push over the coffin. I wanted to torch this place. But I had a job to do. *The sword.*

If it was in the coffin, it wasn't in plain sight. I held my breath and slipped my hand along the inside lining like I was searching for loose change. Nothing.

Thinking the sword might be hidden by a glamour, I stretched my arm over the coffin, trying to sense the blade's presence like I'd done on the Longfellow Bridge. No heat. No humming.

The only other option was to check under the body.

I looked down at Magnus 1.0. "Sorry, man."

I tried to tell myself the corpse was an inanimate object like a scarecrow. Not a real person. Certainly not me.

I rolled him to one side. He was heavier than I would've thought.

Nothing underneath but safety pins holding the coat in place. A label on the white lining read, 50% SATIN, 50% POLYESTER, PRODUCT OF TAIWAN.

I lowered the body back into place. Dead Magnus's hair was all messed up now. The left side bloomed like a bird-of-paradise flower. My hands had come unclasped so I appeared to be giving everybody the finger.

"Much better," I decided. "At least that looks like me."

Behind me, a broken voice said, "Magnus?"

I almost jumped out of my Wiggles shirt.

Standing in the doorway was my cousin Annabeth.

TWENTY-SIX

Hey, I Know You're Dead, But Call Me Maybe

EVEN IF I HADN'T seen her in the park two days before, I would've recognized her up close. Her wavy blond hair hadn't changed since childhood. Her gray eyes had the same determined look—like she'd chosen a target in the distance and was going to march over and destroy it. She was better dressed than me—orange North Face ski jacket, black jeans, lace-up winter boots—but if people saw us together they would've mistaken us for brother and sister.

She stared at me, then at the coffin. Slowly her expression changed from shock to cold calculation.

"I knew it," she said. "I *knew* you weren't dead."

She tackled me in a hug. As I may have mentioned, I'm not a big fan of physical contact, but after all I'd been through, a hug from Annabeth was enough to make me crumble.

"Yeah . . . um . . ." My voice turned ragged. I extracted myself as gently as I could and blinked tears out of my eyes. "It's really good to see you."

She wrinkled her nose at the corpse. "Are you going to make me ask? I thought you were dead, you butt."

I couldn't help smiling. It had been ten years since she'd called me a butt. We were overdue. "Hard to explain."

"I guessed that much. The body is fake? You're trying to convince everyone you died?"

"Uh . . . not exactly. It's best if people think I'm dead, though. Because . . ." *Because I* am *dead,* I thought. *Because I went to Valhalla, and now I'm back with a dwarf and an elf!* How could I say that?

I glanced at the chapel doorway. "Wait . . . Did you pass an el—a guy on the way in? My friend was supposed to be keeping watch."

"No. Nobody was out there. The front door was unlocked."

My equilibrium tilted. "I should check—"

"Whoa. Not until I get some answers."

"I— Honestly, I don't know where to start. I'm in kind of a dangerous situation. I don't want to get you involved."

"Too late." She crossed her arms. "And I know a lot about dangerous situations."

Somehow, I believed her. Here I was, a reborn superwarrior from Valhalla, and Annabeth still intimidated me. The way she held herself, her steely confidence—I could tell she'd overcome some hard stuff, the same way I could tell which guys in the shelters were the most dangerous. I couldn't just blow her off. But I also didn't want to drag her into my mess.

"Randolph almost got killed on that bridge," I said. "I don't want anything to happen to you."

She laughed without humor. "Randolph—I swear, I'm going to shove that cane of his . . . Never mind. He wouldn't explain why he took you to the bridge. He kept talking about how you were in danger because of your birthday. He said he was trying to help. Something about our family history—"

"He told me about my father."

Annabeth's eyes darkened. "You never knew your dad."

"Yeah. But apparently . . ." I shook my head. "Look, it would sound crazy. Just . . . there's a connection between what happened on the bridge and what happened to my mom two years ago, and—and who my father is."

Annabeth's expression transformed. She looked as if she'd opened a window expecting to see a swimming pool and instead found the Pacific Ocean.

"Magnus . . . oh, gods."

Gods, I noted. *Plural.*

She paced in front of my coffin, her hands tented like she was praying. "I should've known. Randolph kept rambling about how our family was special, how we attracted attention. But I had no idea you . . ." She froze, then grabbed my shoulders. "I'm so sorry I didn't know sooner. I could've helped you."

"Um, I'm not sure—"

"My dad's flying back to California tonight after the funeral," she continued. "I was going to catch the train for New York, but school can wait. I *get* it now. I can help you. I know a place where you'll be safe."

I pulled away.

I wasn't sure what Annabeth knew, or what she thought she knew. Maybe she'd gotten mixed up with the Nine Worlds somehow. Maybe she was talking about something totally different. But every nerve in my body tingled with warning when I thought about telling her the truth.

I appreciated her offer of help. I could tell it was genuine. Still . . . those words: *I know a place where you'll be safe.* Nothing activated the flight instincts of a homeless kid faster than hearing that.

I was trying to figure out how to explain that when Hearthstone stumbled into the chapel doorway. His left eye was swollen shut. He gesticulated so frantically I could barely read the signs: *HURRY. DANGER.*

Annabeth turned, following my gaze. "Who—"

"That's my friend," I said. "I really have to go. Listen, Annabeth . . ." I took her hands. "I have to do this by myself. It's like . . . like a personal—"

"Quest?"

"I was going to say pain in the—yeah, *quest* works. If you really want to help me, please, just pretend you didn't see me. Later, after I'm done, I'll find you. I'll explain everything, I promise. Right now, I have to go."

She took a shaky breath. "Magnus, I probably *could* help. But . . ." She reached into her coat pocket and pulled out a folded piece of paper. "Recently I learned the hard way that sometimes I have to step back and let other people do their own quests, even people I care about. At least take this."

I unfolded the paper. It was one of the MISSING flyers she and Uncle Frederick had been handing out.

"The second number is my phone. Call me. Let me know when you're okay, or if you change your mind and—"

"I'll call." I kissed her cheek. "You're the best."

She sighed. "You're still a butt."

"I know. Thanks. Bye."

I ran to Hearthstone, who was bouncing up and down with impatience. "What happened?" I demanded. "Where were you?"

He was already running. I followed him out of the funeral home, north on Arlington. Even pouring on the speed with my upgraded einherji legs, I could barely keep up. Elves, I discovered, could run fast when they wanted to.

We reached the stairs to the T stop just as Blitzen was coming up. I recognized the wide-brimmed hat and coat from the Longfellow Bridge. He'd added larger sunglasses, a ski mask, leather gloves, and a scarf. In one hand he carried a black canvas bag. I guessed he was going for that *Invisible-Man-Goes-Bowling* look.

"Whoa, whoa, whoa!" Blitz grabbed Hearth to keep him from tumbling into traffic. "What happened to your eye? Did you guys find the sword?"

"No sword," I gasped. "Hearth's eye—I don't know—something about danger."

Hearth clapped for our attention.

Knocked out, he signed. *Girl jumped from second story of funeral home. Landed on me. I woke up in alley.*

"A girl in the funeral home?" I scowled. "You don't mean Annabeth? She's my cousin."

He shook his head. *Not her. Other girl. She was–* His hands froze when he noticed Blitz's bag.

Hearth stepped back, shaking his head in disbelief. *You brought him?* He spelled it out: H-I-M, so I knew I hadn't misunderstood.

Blitz hefted the bag. His face was impossible to read, swaddled in anti-sunlight protection, but his voice was heavy. "Yeah. Capo's orders. First things first. Magnus, your cousin was at the funeral home?"

"It's okay." I resisted the urge to ask why there was a *him* in the bowling bag. "Annabeth won't say anything."

"But . . . *another* girl was there?"

"I didn't see her. I guess she heard me coming in and went upstairs."

The dwarf turned to Hearth. "At which point, she jumped from the second-floor window, knocked *you* out, and got away?"

Hearth nodded. *She had to be looking for the sword.*

"You think she found it?" Blitz asked.

Hearth shook his head.

"How can you be sure?" I asked.

Because she's right there.

Hearth pointed across Boylston. A quarter mile down Arlington Street, walking at a fast clip, was a girl in a brown peacoat and a green headscarf. I recognized that scarf.

Hearth's swollen eye had been compliments of Samirah al-Abbas, my ex-Valkyrie.

TWENTY-SEVEN

Let's Play Frisbee with Bladed Weapons!

AT THE NORTH END of the park, Sam crossed Beacon Street, heading for the footbridge over Storrow Drive.

"Where's she going?" I asked.

"The river, obviously," Blitz said. "She checked out your body at the funeral home—"

"Can we please not phrase it that way?"

"She didn't find the sword. Now she's checking the river."

Sam climbed the spiral ramp of the footbridge. She glanced back in our direction and we had to hide behind a pile of dirty snow. During the summer tourist season, it would've been easier to follow her without attracting attention. Now, the sidewalks were mostly empty.

Blitzen adjusted his dark glasses. "I don't like it. *Best* case scenario, the Valkyries sent her, but—"

"No," I said. "She was kicked out of the Valkyries."

I told them the story as we crouched behind our snowbank.

Hearth looked aghast. His swollen eye had turned the color of Kermit the Frog. *Daughter of Loki?* he signed. *She's working for her dad.*

"I don't know," I said. "I can't quite believe that."

Because she saved you?

I wasn't sure. Maybe I didn't want to believe she was playing for Team Evil. Maybe Loki's words had wormed their way into my head: *I'm definitely on your side!*

I pointed at Hearth's eye and signed *P* for *Permission?* I touched his eyelid. A spark of warmth passed through my fingertip. The bruising faded.

Blitz chuckled. "You're getting good at that, Magnus."

Hearthstone grabbed my hand. He studied my fingertips as if looking for residual magic.

"Whatever." I pulled my hand away, a little embarrassed. The last thing I wanted to be was Magnus Chase, Viking Paramedic. "We're losing Sam. Let's go."

Sam headed downstream on the Esplanade jogging trail. We crossed the footbridge. Beneath us, cars edged along bumper to bumper, honking incessantly. Judging from all the construction vehicles and flashing lights on the Longfellow Bridge, the traffic was probably my fault. My battle with Surt had completely closed the span.

We lost sight of Sam as we took the spiral ramp to the Esplanade. We walked past the playground. I figured we would spot her somewhere down the path, but she had disappeared.

"Well, that's just great," I said.

Blitz limped into the shadow of the closed concession stand. He looked like he was having trouble carrying his bowling bag.

"You okay?" I asked.

"Legs are just slightly petrified. **Nothing to worry about.**"

"That sounds like something to worry about."

Hearth paced. *Wish I had a bow. I could have shot her.*

Blitzen shook his head. "Stick to magic, my friend."

Hearth's gestures were sharp with irritation. *Can't read your lips. The beard is bad enough. The ski mask—impossible.*

Blitz set down the bowling bag, then signed while he spoke. "Hearth is very good with runes. He knows more rune magic than any living mortal."

"Mortal like human?" I asked.

Blitz snorted. "Kid, humans aren't the only mortal species. I meant humans, dwarves, *or* elves. You can't count giants—they're weird. Or the gods, obviously. Or the soothsayers who live in Valhalla. I never understood *what* they were. But among the three mortal species, Hearthstone is the best magician! Well, he's also the *only* magician, as far as I know. He's the first person in centuries to dedicate his life to magic."

I'm blushing, Hearthstone signed, clearly not blushing.

"My point is, you've got real talent," Blitz told him. "But still you want to be an archer!"

Elves were great archers! Hearth protested.

"A thousand years ago!" Blitzen chopped his hand twice between his opposite thumb and forefinger, the sign for *annoyed.* "Hearth is a romantic. He longs for the old days. He's the sort of elf who goes to Renaissance festivals."

Hearth grunted. *I went* one *time.*

"Guys," I said, "we have to find Sam."

No point, Hearth signed. *She'll search the river. Let her waste her time. We already looked.*

"What if we missed the sword?" Blitz asked. "What if she's got another way to find it?"

"It's not in the river," I said.

Blitz and Hearth both stared at me.

"You sure about that?" Blitz asked.

"I . . . Yeah. Don't ask me how, but now that I'm closer to the water . . ." I stared out over the Charles, its rippling gray lines etched with ice. "I feel the same as when I stood over my coffin. There's a kind of hollowness—like when you rattle a can and you can tell there's nothing inside. I just know—the sword isn't anywhere close."

"Rattling a can . . ." Blitzen mused. "Okay. I don't suppose you could direct us toward the cans we *should* be rattling?"

"That would be good," said Samirah al-Abbas.

She charged from behind the concession building and kicked me in the chest, propelling me backward into a tree. My lungs imploded like paper sacks. By the time I could see straight again, Blitzen was slumped against the wall. Hearth's bag of runestones had scattered across the pavement, and Sam was swinging her ax at him.

"Stop it!" I meant to yell, but it came out as more of a wheeze.

Hearth dodged the ax and tried to tackle her. Sam judo-flipped him over her knee. Hearth landed flat on his back.

Blitzen tried to get up. His hat was tilted sideways. His glasses had been knocked off, and the skin around his eyes was turning gray in the daylight.

Sam turned to ax-smack him. Anger roared through me. I reached for the chain on my belt. Instantly, it was a sword again. I pulled the blade and sent it spinning like a Frisbee. It clanged against Sam's ax, knocking the weapon from her hand, almost taking off her face in the process.

She stared at me in disbelief. "What the Helheim?"

"You started it!"

Hearth grabbed her ankle. Sam kicked him away.

"And stop kicking my elf!" I said.

Sam pushed back her headscarf, letting her dark hair sweep her shoulders. She crouched in a wrestler's stance, ready to take us all on. "So help me, Magnus, if I had my full powers, I would rip your soul from your body for all the trouble you've caused me."

"That's nice," I said. "Or you could tell us what you're doing here. Maybe we could help each other."

Blitzen snatched up his sunglasses. "Help *her*? Why would we help *her*? She knocked out Hearth at the funeral home! My eyes feel like chunks of quartz!"

"Well, maybe if you hadn't been stalking me," Sam said.

"Bah!" Blitzen readjusted his hat. "Nobody was stalking you, Valkyrie! We're looking for the same thing—the sword!"

Still lying on the ground, Hearth signed, *Somebody please kill her.*

"What's he doing?" Sam demanded. "Is he making rude elf gestures at me?"

"It's ASL," I said. "American Sign Language."

"*Alf* Sign Language," Blitz corrected.

"Anyway"—I raised my palms—"can we call a truce and talk? We can always go back to killing each other later."

Sam paced, muttering under her breath. She retrieved her ax and my sword.

Nice job, Magnus, I told myself. *Now she has all the weapons.*

She tossed the sword back to me. "I should never have chosen you for Valhalla."

Blitzen snorted. "On that, at least, we agree. If you hadn't interfered on the bridge—"

"*Interfered?*" Sam demanded. "Magnus was already dead

when I chose him! You and the elf weren't doing him any good with your plastic sign and your squeaky arrows!"

Blitz stood straight, which didn't make him much taller. "I'll have you know my friend is a great rune caster."

"Really?" Samirah asked. "I didn't see him using magic on the bridge against Surt."

Hearthstone looked offended. *Would have. Got sidetracked.*

"Exactly," Blitz said. "And as for me, I have *many* skills, Valkyrie."

"For instance?"

"For instance, I could fix your disgraceful outfit. *No one* wears a brown peacoat with a green headscarf."

"A dwarf in sunglasses and a ski mask is giving me fashion advice."

"I have daylight issues!"

"Guys," I said, "stop, please. Thank you."

I helped Hearthstone to his feet. He scowled at Sam and began collecting his runestones.

"Okay," I said. "Sam, why are you looking for the sword?"

"Because it's my only chance! Because—" Her voice cracked. All the rage seemed to ebb out of her. "Because I honored your stupid bravery. I rewarded you with Valhalla. And it cost me *everything*. If I can find the sword, *maybe* the thanes will reinstate me. I can convince them that . . . that I'm not—"

"The daughter of Loki?" Blitzen asked, but his voice had lost some of its edge.

Sam lowered her ax. "I can't do anything about that. But I'm *not* working for my father. I'm loyal to Odin."

Hearthstone glanced at me skeptically, like, *Are you buying this?*

"I trust her," I said.

Blitz grunted. "Is this another rattle-the-can instinct?"

"Maybe," I said. "Look, we all want to find this sword, right? We want to keep it away from Surt."

"Assuming Surt doesn't already have it," Sam said. "Assuming we can figure out what's going on. Assuming the Norns' prophecy for you isn't as bad as it sounds—"

"One way to find out." Blitz held up the bowling ball bag.

Sam stepped away. "What's in there?"

Hearth made a claw and tapped it twice on his shoulder—the sign for *boss*.

"Answers," Blitz said, "whether we want them or not. Let's confer with the Capo."

TWENTY-EIGHT

Talk to the Face, 'Cause That's Pretty Much All He's Got

BLITZ LED US down the Esplanade, where a pier extended into an icy lagoon. At the base of the dock, a candy-striped pole listed sideways.

"This is where they do gondola rides in the summer," I said. "I don't think you're going to find one now."

"We just need water." Blitz sat on the dock and unzipped the bowling bag.

"Oh, gods." Sam peered inside. "Is that human hair?"

"Hair, yes," Blitz said. "Human, no."

"You mean . . ." She pressed her hand to her stomach. "You're not serious. You work for *him*? You brought *him* here?"

"He insisted." Blitz pushed down the sides of the bag, revealing . . . yep, a severed head. The most messed-up thing about that? After two days in Valhalla, I wasn't even surprised.

The beheaded man's face was shriveled like a month-old apple. Tufts of rust-colored hair clung to his scalp. His closed eyes were sunken and dark. His bearded jaw protruded bulldog-style, revealing a crooked row of bottom teeth.

Blitz unceremoniously shoved the head in the water, bag and all.

"Dude," I said, "the state river authority isn't going to like that."

The head bobbed on the surface of the lagoon. The water around it bubbled and swirled. The man's face inflated, his wrinkles softening, his skin turning pink. He opened his eyes.

Sam and Hearth both knelt. Sam elbowed me to take a knee.

"Lord Mimir," Sam said. "You honor us."

The head opened his mouth and spewed water. More came out of his nostrils, his ears, his tear ducts. He reminded me of a catfish dragged from the bottom of a lake.

"Man, I hate—" The head coughed more water. His eyes turned from chalk white to blue. "I hate traveling in that bag."

Blitzen bowed. "Sorry, Capo. It was that or the fish tank. And the fish tank breaks easily."

The head gurgled. He scanned the faces on the dock until he found me. "Son of Frey, I've come a long way to speak with you. Hope you appreciate it."

"You're the mysterious classified boss," I said. "Hearth and Blitz have been watching me for two years . . . because they got orders from a severed head?"

"Show some respect, boyo." Mimir's voice reminded me of the longshoremen down at the Union Hall—their lungs half nicotine, half seawater.

Hearth frowned at me. *Told you C-A-P-O. Capo means head. Why surprised?*

"I am Mimir," said the head. "Once I was mighty among the Aesir. Then came the war with the Vanir. Now I got my own operation."

His face was so ugly it was hard to tell whether he was giving me an ugly look.

"Did Frey cut off your head?" I asked. "Is that why you're mad at me?"

Mimir huffed. "I'm not mad. You'll know when I'm mad."

I wondered what that meant. Maybe he would gurgle more threateningly.

"Your dad was part of the reason I lost my head, though," said Mimir. "See, as part of the truce to end the war, the two godly tribes exchanged hostages. Your father, Frey, and *his* father, Njord, came to live in Asgard. The god Honir and I—we were sent to live in Vanaheim."

"I'm guessing that didn't go well."

More water spouted from Mimir's ears. "Your father made me look bad! He was this great general among the Vanir—all golden and shiny and handsome. He and Njord got all kinds of respect in Asgard. As for me and Honir—the Vanir weren't so impressed."

"No kidding."

"Well, Honir was never very, how you say, charismatic. The Vanir would ask his opinions on important business. He'd mumble, 'Yeah, whatever. It's all good.' Me, I tried to pull my weight. I told the Vanir they should be getting into casinos."

"Casinos."

"Yeah, busloads of retirees coming to Vanaheim. Easy money. And the Vanir had all these dragons. I told them, race-tracks. In the sky. With dragons. They'd make a killing."

I looked at Blitz and Hearth. They seemed resigned, like they'd heard this story many times before.

"So anyway," said Mimir, "the Vanir didn't like my worthy counsel. They felt cheated in the hostage swap. As a protest, they cut off my head and sent it to Odin."

"Shocking. When they could've had casinos."

Sam coughed loudly. "Of course, great Mimir, both Aesir and Vanir honor you now. Magnus didn't mean to insult you. He is not so stupid."

She glared at me like, *You are so stupid.*

Around Mimir's head, the water bubbled faster. It trickled from his pores and streamed from his eyes. "Forget about it, son of Frey. I don't hold a grudge. Besides, when Odin received my severed head, he didn't take revenge. See, the All-Father was smart. He knew the Vanir and Aesir had to unite against our common enemy, the Triads."

"Uh . . ." Blitz adjusted his hat. "I think you mean the giants, boss."

"Right. Those guys. So Odin carried me to a hidden cave in Jotunheim where this magical spring feeds the roots of Yggdrasil. He placed my head in the well. The water brought me back to life, and I soaked in all the knowledge of the World Tree. My wisdom increased a thousandfold."

"But . . . you're still a severed head."

Mimir made a sideways nod. "It's not so bad. I operate across the Nine Worlds—loans, protection, pachinko machines—"

"Pachinko."

"Pachinko is huge. Plus I'm always working to delay Ragnarok. Ragnarok would be bad for business."

"Right." I decided to sit down, because it seemed like this could take a while. Once I did it, Sam and Hearth followed my example. Chickens.

"Also," Mimir said, "Odin visits me for advice from time to time. I'm his consigliere. I guard the well of knowledge.

Sometimes I let travelers drink from its waters, though that kind of intel never comes without a price."

The word *price* settled over the dock like a heavy blanket. Blitzen sat so still I was afraid he'd turned to stone. Hearthstone studied the grain of the planks. I began to understand how my friends had gotten involved with Mimir. They'd drunk from his waters (gross), and paid the price by watching me for the past two years. I wondered if what they'd learned had been worth it.

"So, Great and Well-Connected Mimir," I said, "what do you want with me?"

Mimir spit out a minnow. "I don't have to tell you, boyo. You already know."

I wanted to disagree, but the longer I listened to Mimir, the more I felt like I was breathing pure oxygen. I don't know why. The Capo wasn't exactly inspiring. Yet being around him, my mind seemed to function better, weaving together bits and pieces of weirdness I'd experienced over the last few days into one strangely cohesive picture.

An illustration from my old children's book of Norse myths came back to me—a tale so terrifying, even in its watered-down kiddie version, that I had buried it in my memory for years.

"The Wolf," I said. "Surt wants to free Fenris Wolf."

I was hoping somebody would contradict me. Hearth lowered his head. Sam closed her eyes like she was praying.

"Fenris," said Blitzen. "There's a name I was hoping never to hear again."

Mimir kept crying ice water. His lips curled in a faint smile. "There you go, son of Frey. Now tell me: What do you know about Fenris Wolf?"

I buttoned my hunting jacket. The wind off the river seemed cold even to me. "Correct me if I'm wrong. I'd *love* to be wrong. Ages ago, Loki had an affair with a giantess. They had three monstrous kids."

"I was *not* one of them," Sam muttered. "I've heard all the jokes."

Hearthstone winced, like he'd been wondering about that.

"One," I said, "was a huge snake."

"Jormungand," Sam said. "The World Serpent, which Odin threw into the sea."

"The second was Hel," I continued. "She became, like, the goddess of the dishonorable dead."

"And the third," Blitzen said, "was Fenris Wolf."

His tone was bitter, full of pain.

"Blitz," I said, "you sound like you know him."

"Every dwarf knows of Fenris. That was the first time the Aesir came to us for help. Fenris grew so savage he would've devoured the gods. They tried to tie him up, but he broke every chain."

"I remember," I said. "Finally the dwarves made a rope strong enough to hold him."

"Ever since," Blitzen said, "the children of Fenris have been enemies of the dwarves." He looked up, his dark shades reflecting my face. "You're not the only one who's lost family to wolves, kid."

I had a strange urge to hug him. Suddenly I didn't feel so bad about all the time he'd spent watching me. We were brothers in something more than homelessness. Still . . . I resisted the impulse. Whenever I'm tempted to hug a dwarf, that's usually a sign I need to move along.

"On Ragnarok," I said, "the Day of Doom, one of the first things that's supposed to happen is Fenris gets freed."

Sam nodded. "The old stories don't say how that happens—"

"But one way," Blitz said, "would be to cut him loose. The rope Gleipnir is unbreakable, but . . ."

Frey's sword, Hearth signed, *is the sharpest blade in the Nine Worlds.*

"Surt wants to free the Wolf with my father's sword." I looked at Mimir. "How are we doing so far?"

"Not bad," the head burbled. "Which brings us to your task."

"Stop Surt," I said. "Find the sword before he does . . . assuming he hasn't got it already."

"He doesn't," Mimir said. "Believe me, an event like that would make the Nine Worlds tremble. I'd taste fear in the waters of Yggdrasil."

"Yuck," I said.

"You have no idea," said Mimir. "But you must hurry."

"The Norns' prophecy. Nine days hence, blah, blah, blah."

Water bubbled out of Mimir's ears. "I'm pretty sure they didn't say *blah, blah, blah.* However, you're correct. The island where the gods imprisoned Fenris is only accessible on the first full moon of each year. That's now seven days hence."

"Who makes up these rules?" I asked.

"*I* made up that rule," Mimir said. "So shut up. Find the sword. Reach the island before Surt does."

Sam raised her hand. "Um, Lord Mimir, I understand finding the sword. But why take it to the island? Isn't that where Surt *wants* the sword?"

"See, Miss al-Abbas . . . this is why I'm the boss and you're not. Yeah, bringing the sword to the island is dangerous. Yeah, Surt could use it to free the Wolf. But Surt is gonna find a way to free Fenris with or without it. I did mention I can see the future, right? The only person who might be able to stop Surt is Magnus Chase—assuming he can find the sword and learn to wield it properly."

I'd shut up for almost a whole minute, so I figured I could raise my hand. "Lord Mister Bubbles—"

"Mimir."

"If this sword is such a big deal, why did everybody let it sit on the bottom of the Charles River for a thousand years?"

Mimir sighed foam. "My regular minions never ask so many questions."

Blitz coughed. "Actually, we do, boss. You just ignore us."

"To answer your question, Magnus Chase, the sword can only be found by a descendant of Frey upon reaching the age of maturity. Others have tried, failed, and died. Right now, you're the only living descendant of Frey."

"The only one . . . in the world?"

"In the *Nine* Worlds. Frey doesn't get out much anymore. Your mother—she must've been really something to attract his attention. Anyway, a lot of people in the Nine Worlds—gods, giants, bookies, you name it—have been waiting for you to turn sixteen. Some wanted you killed so you couldn't find the sword. Some wanted you to succeed."

Hot pins pressed against the base of my neck. The idea of a bunch of gods peering through their Asgardian telescopes, watching me grow up, creeped me out. My mom must have known all along. She'd done her best to keep me safe, to teach me survival skills. The night the wolves attacked our apartment, she'd given her life to save me.

I met the Capo's watery eyes. "And you?" I asked. "What do you want?"

"You're a risky bet, Magnus. A lot of possible fates intersect in your life. You could deal the forces of evil a great setback and delay Ragnarok for generations. Or, if you fail, you could hasten the Day of Doom."

I tried to swallow. "Hasten it, like, by how much?"

"How does next week work for you?"

"Oh."

"I decided to take the bet," Mimir said. "After the children of Fenris killed your mother, I sent Blitz and Hearth to guard you. You probably don't realize how many times they've saved your life."

Hearth held up seven fingers.

I shuddered, but mostly from the mention of Fenris's two children, the wolves with blue eyes. . . .

"To succeed," said Mimir, "you're gonna need this team. Hearthstone here—he's dedicated his life to rune magic. Without him, you'll fail. You'll also need an able dwarf like Blitzen who understands dwarven crafting. You might need to strengthen the Wolf's bindings, or even replace them."

Blitz shifted. "Uh, boss . . . my crafting skills are, well, you know—"

"Don't give me that," said Mimir. "No dwarf has a stouter heart. No dwarf has traveled farther in the Nine Worlds or has more of a desire to keep Fenris chained. Also, you're in my service. You'll do what I say."

"Ah." Blitzen nodded. "When you put it that way . . ."

"What about me, Lord Mimir?" asked Sam. "What's my part in your plan?"

Mimir frowned. Around his beard, the water bubbled a darker shade of green. "You weren't part of the plan at all. There's a cloud around your fate, Miss al-Abbas. Taking Magnus to Valhalla—I didn't see that coming. It wasn't supposed to happen."

Sam looked away, her lips pressed tight with anger.

"Sam's got a part to play," I said. "I'm sure of it."

"Do not patronize me, Magnus. I chose you because—" She stopped herself. "It was supposed to happen."

I remembered what she'd said in the feast hall: *I was told . . . I was promised.* By whom? I decided not to ask that in front of the Capo.

Mimir studied her. "I hope you're right, Miss al-Abbas. When Magnus first took the sword from the river, he couldn't control it very well. Maybe now that he's an einherji, he'll have the strength, in which case you've saved the day. Or maybe you've completely messed up his destiny."

"We're going to succeed," I insisted. "Just two questions: Where is the sword, and where is the island?"

Mimir nodded, which made him look like an oversize fishing bobber. "Well, that's the trick, isn't it? To find that kinda information, I'd have to tear the veils between the worlds, grease a lot of palms, see into the realms of the other gods."

"Couldn't we just drink your magic well water?"

"You could," he agreed. "But it would cost you. Are you and Samirah al-Abbas ready to be bound to my service?"

Hearth's face froze in apprehension. From the tension in

Blitz's shoulders, I guessed he was trying very hard not to leap to his feet and scream, *Don't do it!*

"You couldn't make an exception?" I asked the Capo. "Seeing as how you *want* this job done?"

"No can do, boyo. I'm not being greedy. It's just, well, you get what you pay for. Something comes cheap, it ain't worth much. That's true for knowledge especially. You can pay for a shortcut, get the information right now, or you'll have to find it on your own, the hard way."

Sam crossed her arms. "Apologies, Lord Mimir. I may be kicked out of the Valkyries, but I still consider myself bound to Odin's service. I can't take on another master. Magnus can make his own choice, but—"

"We'll figure it out on our own," I agreed.

Mimir made a low sloshing sound. He looked almost impressed. "Interesting choice. Good luck, then. If you succeed, you'll have a house account at all my pachinko parlors. If you fail . . . I'll see you next week for Doomsday."

The god's head swirled and disappeared into the icy water of the lagoon.

"He flushed himself," I said.

Hearth looked even paler than usual. *What now?*

My stomach rumbled. I hadn't eaten anything since last night, and apparently my system had gotten spoiled after a couple of all-you-can-eat Viking buffets.

"Now," I said, "I'm thinking lunch."

TWENTY-NINE

We Are Falafel-Jacked by an Eagle

WE DIDN'T TALK MUCH as we headed back through the park. The air smelled of incoming snow. The wind picked up and howled like wolves, or maybe I just had wolves on the brain.

Blitz limped along, zigzagging from shadow to shadow as best he could. Hearth's brightly striped scarf didn't match his grim expression. I wanted to ask him more about rune magic now that I knew he was the best (and only) mortal practitioner. Maybe there was a rune that could make wolves explode, preferably from a safe distance. But Hearth kept his hands shoved in his pockets—the sign language equivalent of *I don't want to talk.*

We were passing my old sleeping spot under the footbridge when Sam grumbled, "Mimir. I should've known he was involved."

I glanced over. "A few minutes ago, you were all, *Lord Mimir, you honor us; we're not worthy.*"

"Of *course* I showed respect when he was right in front of me! He's one of the oldest gods. But he's unpredictable. It's never been clear whose side he's on."

Blitzen jumped to the shade of a willow tree, alarming several ducks. "The Capo is on the side of everybody in the world who doesn't want to die. Isn't that enough?"

Sam laughed. "I suppose you two work for him of your own free will? You didn't drink from his well and pay the price?"

Neither Blitz nor Hearth responded.

"That's what I thought," Sam said. "I'm not part of Mimir's plan because I would never blindly go along with it and drink his magical knowledge Kool-Aid."

"It doesn't taste like Kool-Aid," Blitz objected. "It's more like root beer with a hint of clove."

Sam turned to me. "I'm telling you, this doesn't add up. Finding the Sword of Summer—I get that. But taking it to the very place where Surt wants to use it? Unwise."

"Yeah, but if *I* have the sword—"

"Magnus, the sword is *destined* to fall into Surt's hands sooner or later. At Ragnarok, your father will die because he gave his sword away. Surt will kill him with it. That's what most of the stories say, anyway."

I got claustrophobic just thinking about it. How could anybody, even a god, avoid going crazy if he knew centuries in advance exactly how he was going to die?

"Why does Surt hate Frey so much?" I asked. "Couldn't he pick on a big strong war god?"

Blitzen frowned. "Kid, Surt wants death and destruction. He wants fire to run rampant across the Nine Worlds. A war god can't stop that. Frey can. He's the god of the growing season—the god of health and new life. He keeps the extremes in check, both fire and ice. There's nothing Surt hates worse than being restrained. Frey is his natural enemy."

And by extension, I thought, *Surt hates me.*

"If Frey knew what his fate would be," I said, "why did he give up his blade in the first place?"

Blitz grunted. "Love. Why else?"

"Love?"

"Ugh," Sam said. "I *hate* that story. Where are you taking us for lunch, Magnus?"

Part of me wanted to hear the story. Part of me remembered my conversation with Loki: *Will you search for your heart's desire, knowing it may doom you as it doomed your father?*

A lot of Norse stories seemed to have the same message: Knowing things wasn't always worth the price. Unfortunately for me, I'd always been the curious type.

"It's . . . uh, just up ahead," I said. "Come on."

The food court at the Transportation Building wasn't Valhalla, but if you were homeless in Boston, it was pretty close. The indoor atrium was warm, open to the public, and never crowded. It was only halfheartedly patrolled by private security. As long as you had a drink cup or a plate of half-eaten food, you could sit at the tables for a long time before anybody made you move.

On the way in, Blitzen and Hearthstone started toward the garbage cans to check for lunch leavings, but I stopped them.

"Guys, no," I said. "We're eating actual meals today. My treat."

Hearth raised an eyebrow. He signed, *You have money?*

"He's got that friend here," Blitzen recalled. "The falafel guy."

Sam froze in her tracks. "What?"

She looked around as if just realizing where we were.

"It's cool," I promised. "I know a guy at Fadlan's Falafel. You'll thank me for it. Stuff is amazing—"

"No—I—oh, gods—" She hastily put her scarf over her hair. "Maybe I'll wait outside—I can't—"

"Nonsense." Blitz hooked his arm through hers. "They might serve more food if we've got a pretty woman with us!"

Sam clearly wanted to bolt, but she allowed Hearth and Blitz to steer her into the food court. I guess I should've paid more attention to how uncomfortable she was acting, but once you put me within a hundred feet of Fadlan's Falafel, I get tunnel vision.

Over the past two years, I'd struck up a friendship with the manager, Abdel. I think he saw me as his community service project. The shop always had surplus food—slightly out-of-date pita bread, day-old shawarma, kibbeh that had been sitting under the heat lamps a little too long. Abdel couldn't legally sell the stuff, but it still tasted perfectly fine. Instead of throwing it out, Abdel gave it to me. Whenever I came around, I could count on a falafel flatbread sandwich or something just as tasty. In return, I made sure the other homeless folks in the atrium stayed polite and cleaned up after themselves so Abdel's paying customers weren't scared away.

In Boston, you couldn't walk a block without stumbling into some icon of liberty—the Freedom Trail, the Old North Church, the Bunker Hill Monument, whatever—but to me, liberty tasted like Fadlan's Falafel. That stuff had kept me alive and independent ever since my mom died.

I didn't want to overwhelm Abdel with too many people, so I sent Blitz and Hearth to grab a table while I escorted Sam to get the food. The whole way, she dragged her feet, turning aside, fiddling with her headscarf as if she wanted to disappear inside it.

"What's the matter with you?" I asked.

"Maybe he's not there," she muttered. "Maybe you can say I'm your tutor."

I didn't know what she was talking about. I bellied up to the counter while Sam hung back, doing her best to hide behind a potted ficus tree.

"Is Abdel here?" I asked the guy at the register.

He started to say something, but then Abdel's son Amir came out from the back, grinning and wiping his hands on his apron. "Jimmy, how's it going?"

I relaxed. If Abdel wasn't around, Amir was the next best thing. He was eighteen or nineteen, trim and good-looking, with slick dark hair, an Arabic tattoo on his biceps, and a smile so brilliant, it could've sold truckloads of teeth whitener. Like everybody at Fadlan's Falafel, he knew me as "Jimmy."

"Yeah, I'm good," I said. "How's your pop?"

"He's at the Somerville location today. Can I get you some food?"

"Man, you're the best."

Amir laughed. "No biggie." He glanced over my shoulder and did a double take. "And there's Samirah! What are you doing here?"

She shuffled forward. "Hi, Amir. I am . . . tutoring Ma— Jimmy. I am tutoring Jimmy."

"Oh, yeah?" Amir leaned on the counter, which made his arm muscles flex. The dude worked full-time at his dad's various shops, yet he somehow managed to avoid getting even a speck of grease on his white T-shirt. "Don't you have school?"

"Um, yes, but I get credit for tutoring off campus. Jimmy and . . . his classmates." She pointed toward Blitz and Hearth,

who were having a rapid-fire argument in sign language, tracing circles in the air. "Geometry," Samirah said. "They're
hopeless with geometry."

"Hopeless," I agreed. "But food helps us study."

Amir's eyes crinkled. "I've got you covered. Glad to see
you're okay, Jimmy. That bridge accident the other day—the
paper had this picture of a kid who died? Looked a lot like
you. Different name, but we were worried."

I'd been so focused on falafel that I'd forgotten to think
about them making that connection. "Ah, yeah, I saw that. I'm
good. Just studying geometry. With my tutor."

"Okay!" Amir smiled at Sam. The awkwardness was so
thick you could've cut it with a broadsword. "Well, Samirah,
say hi to Jid and Bibi for me. You guys go ahead and sit. I'll
bring out some food in a sec."

Sam muttered something that might have been *Thanks a
lot* or *Kill me now*. Then we joined Blitz and Hearth at the table.

"What was that about?" I asked her. "How do you know
Amir?"

She pulled her scarf a little lower over her forehead.
"Don't sit too close to me. Try to look like we're talking about
geometry."

"Triangles," I said. "Quadrilaterals. Also, why are you
embarrassed? Amir is awesome. If you know the Fadlan family, you're like a rock star to me."

"He's my cousin," she blurted. "Second cousin, twice
removed. Or something."

I looked at Hearth. He was scowling at the floor. Blitz had
taken off his ski mask and glasses, I guess because the interior light didn't bother him as much, and was now sullenly

spinning a plastic fork on the table. Apparently I'd missed a good argument between him and Hearth.

"Okay," I said. "But why so nervous?"

"Can you drop it?" she said.

I raised my hands. "Fine. Let's all start over. Hi, everybody. I'm Magnus, and I'm an einherji. If we're not going to study geometry, could we talk about how we're going to find the Sword of Summer?"

Nobody answered.

A pigeon waddled past, pecking at crumbs.

I glanced back at the falafel shop. For some reason, Amir had rolled down the steel curtain. I'd never seen him close the shop during lunch hour. I wondered if Sam had somehow offended him and he'd cut off my falafel allowance.

If so, I was going to go berserker.

"What happened to our food?" I wondered.

At my feet, a small voice croaked, "I can help with both those questions."

I looked down. My week had been so wack I didn't even flinch when I realized who had spoken.

"Guys," I said, "this pigeon wants to help."

The pigeon fluttered onto our table. Hearth nearly fell out of his chair. Blitz snatched up a fork.

"Service here can be a little slow," said the pigeon. "But I can speed up your order. I can also tell you where to find the sword."

Sam reached for her ax. "That's not a pigeon."

The bird regarded her with a beady orange eye. "Maybe not. But if you kill me, you'll never get your lunch. You'll also never find the sword or see your intended again."

Samirah's eyes looked like they were going to shoot across the atrium.

"What is he talking about?" I said. "Intended *what*?"

The bird cooed. "If you ever want Fadlan's Falafel to open again—"

"Okay, that's a declaration of war." I considered grabbing for the bird, but even with my einherji reflexes, I doubted I could catch it. "What did you do? What's happened to Amir?"

"Nothing yet!" said the pigeon. "I'll bring you your lunch. All I want is first pick of the food."

"Uh-huh," I said. "And assuming I believe you, what would you want in exchange for information about the sword?"

"A favor. It's negotiable. Now, does that falafel shop stay closed forever, or do we have a deal?"

Blitzen shook his head. "Don't do it, Magnus."

Hearth signed, *Pigeons cannot be trusted.*

Sam met my eyes. Her expression was pleading—almost frantic. Either she liked falafel even more than I did, or she was worried about something else.

"Fine," I said. "Bring us our lunch."

Immediately the shop's steel curtain rolled up. The cashier stood like a statue, the phone to his ear. Then he unfroze, glanced over his shoulder, and shouted an order to the cook as if nothing had happened. The pigeon took off and sped toward the shop, disappearing behind the counter. The cashier didn't seem to notice.

A moment later, a much larger bird shot out of the kitchen—a bald eagle with a tray in his claws. He landed in the middle of our table.

"You're an eagle now?" I asked.

"Yeah," he said in the same croaky voice. "I like to mix it up. Here's your food."

It was everything I could've asked for: steaming squares of spiced ground beef kibbeh; a stack of lamb kebabs with mint yogurt dip; four fresh slabs of pita bread filled with deep-fried nuggets of chickpea goodness, drizzled in tahini sauce and garnished with pickle wedges.

"Oh, Helheim yes." I reached for the tray, but the eagle pecked at my hand.

"Now, now," he chided. "I get first pick."

Ever seen an eagle eat falafel?

That horrifying image now haunts my nightmares.

Faster than I could blink, the eagle struck, vacuuming up everything but a single wedge of pickle.

"Hey!" I yelled.

Sam rose, hefting her ax. "He's a giant. He's got to be!"

"We had a deal." The eagle belched. "Now about the sword—"

I let loose a guttural roar—the cry of a man who has been deprived of his rightful kibbeh. I drew my sword and smacked the eagle with the flat of the blade.

It wasn't the most rational move, but I was hungry. I was angry. I hated being taken advantage of, and I didn't particularly like bald eagles.

The blade hit the bird's back and stuck there like superglue. I tried to pull it away, but it wouldn't move. My hands were grafted to the sword grip.

"Okay, then," the eagle squawked, "we can play it that way."

He took off through the food court at sixty miles an hour, dragging me along behind him.

THIRTY

An Apple a Day
Will Get You Killed

ADD TO MY LIST of Least Favorite Activities: eagle surfing.

The stupid bird shouldn't have been able to take off with a more-or-less-full-grown Magnus in tow. Yet he did.

Behind me, Blitz and Sam yelled helpful stuff like "Hey! Stop!" as the eagle dragged me through tables, chairs, and potted plants, then blasted through the double glass doors and soared over Charles Street.

A guy having lunch in the tenth-floor condo across the street spewed Cheetos when I shot past. I left a nice footprint on his window.

"Let me go!" I yelled at the eagle.

The bird cackled as he pulled me along a rooftop. "You sure about that? Heads up!"

I twisted, barely avoiding a face-first encounter with an industrial AC unit. I plowed through a brick chimney, using my chest as a battering ram. Then the eagle plummeted down the other side of the building.

"So!" the eagle said. "You ready to negotiate that favor?"

"With a mutant pigeon who steals falafel?" I yelled. "No thanks!"

"Suit yourself." The eagle veered, slamming me into a fire

escape. I felt my ribs crack, like vials of acid breaking inside my chest. My empty stomach tried unsuccessfully to hurl.

We climbed above one of the churches on Boylston and circled the steeple. I had an addled thought about Paul Revere and the whole *One if by land, two if by sea* thing.

And if you see a dude being dragged by a giant eagle, uh, I don't even know how many lights that is.

I tried to heal my ribs through willpower, but I couldn't concentrate. The pain was too intense. I kept running into walls and kicking out windows.

"All I want," the eagle said, "is a favor for a favor. I'll tell you how to get the sword, but you have to get me something while you're at it. Nothing much. Just an apple. One apple."

"What's the catch?"

"The catch is that if you don't agree . . . oh, look! Pigeon spikes!"

Ahead of us, the edge of a hotel roof bristled with steel like a miniature line of World War I barbed wire. The spikes were there to discourage roosting birds, but they'd also do a great job shredding my soft underbelly.

Fear got the best of me. I don't like pointy objects. My gut was still sensitive from my recent death by molten asphalt.

"Fine!" I yelled. "No spikes!"

"Say: *By my troth, I agree to your terms.*"

"I don't even know what that means!"

"Say it!"

"By my troth, I agree to your terms! Yes, apples! No, spikes!"

The eagle climbed, narrowly clearing the roof. The tips

of my shoes twanged against the barbs. We circled Copley Square and landed on the roof of the Boston Public Library.

The sword came free of the eagle's back. My hands unglued themselves, which was great, except that I now had nothing to hold on to. The red curved clay tiles were almost impossible to stand on. The roof slanted precariously. Eighty feet below me stretched a wide expanse of pavement-flavored death.

I crouched to avoid falling. Carefully, I sheathed my sword, which melted back into a length of chain.

"Ow," I said.

My ribs ached. My arms had been pulled half out of their sockets. My chest felt like it had been permanently tattooed with a brick wall design.

To my left, the eagle perched on a lightning-rod spire, lording over the decorative bronze griffins around the base.

I'd never thought of eagles as having expressions, but this one definitely looked smug.

"I'm glad you saw reason!" he said. "Though, honestly, I enjoyed our little flight through the city. It's good to speak with you alone."

"I'm blushing," I grumbled. "Oh, no, wait. That's the blood all over my face."

"Here's the information you need," the eagle continued. "When your sword fell in the river, the current carried it downstream. It was claimed by the goddess Ran. Lots of valuable things end up in her net."

"Ran?"

The eagle clicked his beak. "Sea goddess. Has a net. Try to keep up."

"Where do I find her? And please don't say 'the sea.'"

"She could be anywhere, so you'll have to get her attention. The way to do that: I know this guy, Harald. He's got a boat at the Fish Pier, does deep-sea excursions. Tell him Big Boy sent you."

"Big Boy."

"One of my many names. Harald will know what you mean. Convince him to take you fishing in Massachusetts Bay. If you cause enough of a ruckus out there, you'll attract Ran's attention. Then you can negotiate. Ask her for the sword and one of Idun's apples."

"Eden."

"Are you just going to repeat every name I give you? It's I-D-U-N. She distributes the apples of immortality that keep the gods young and spry. Ran is sure to have one lying around, because seriously, once you see her, you'll be able to tell she's not good about remembering to eat her apples. When you have the apple, bring it back here. Give it to me, and I'll release you from your vow."

"Two questions. Are you insane?"

"No."

"Second question: How is fishing in the bay going to create a ruckus that attracts a sea goddess?"

"That depends on what you fish for. Tell Harald you need the special bait. He'll understand. If he protests, tell him Big Boy insists."

"I have no idea what that means," I confessed. "Assuming I meet Ran, how am I supposed to bargain with her?"

"That's three questions. Also, that's your problem."

"Last question."

"This is four now."

"What's to keep me from getting the sword and not bringing you an apple?"

"Well, you swore by your troth," said the eagle. "Your troth is your word, your faith, your honor, your soul. It's a binding oath, especially for an einherji. Unless you want to spontaneously combust and find yourself trapped forever in the icy darkness of Helheim . . ."

I chewed my lip. "I guess I'll keep my promise."

"Excellent!" The eagle flapped his wings. "Here come your friends, which is my cue to leave. I'll see you when you have my fresh produce!"

The eagle soared away and disappeared behind the glass walls of the Hancock Tower, leaving me to find my own way off the roof.

Down in Copley Square, Blitzen, Hearthstone, and Sam were just running onto the frozen lawn. Sam saw me first. She stopped in her tracks and pointed.

I waved.

I couldn't see her expression, but she spread her arms like, *What the heck are you doing up there?*

With some difficulty, I got to my feet. Thanks to my ValhallaCare health plan, my injuries were already starting to mend, but I still felt sore and stiff. I picked my way to the edge of the roof and peered over. Magnus 1.0 never would've considered it, but now I plotted a series of ten-foot jumps—to that window ledge, that flagpole, the top of that light fixture, then the front steps—and I thought, *Yeah, no problem.*

In a matter of seconds, I'd safely reached the ground. My friends met me at the sidewalk.

"What was *that* about?" Blitzen demanded. "Was he a giant?"

"Dunno," I said. "His name is Big Boy, and he likes apples."

I told them the story.

Hearthstone smacked his forehead. He signed: *You swore by your troth?*

"Well, it was either that or get shredded by pigeon spikes, so yeah."

Sam stared at the sky, maybe hoping to see an eagle she could hit with her ax. "This will end badly. Deals with giants always do."

"At least Magnus found out where the sword is," Blitzen said. "Besides, Ran's a goddess. She'll be on our side, right?"

Sam snorted. "I guess you haven't heard the stories about her that *I* have. But at this point, we don't have much choice. Let's find Harald."

THIRTY-ONE

Go Smelly or Go Home

I'D NEVER BEEN SCARED of boats until I saw Harald's.

Painted on the prow was HARALD'S DEEP-SEA EXCURSIONS AND DEATH WISHES, which seemed like a lot of verbiage for a twenty-foot-long dinghy. The deck was a mess of ropes, buckets, and tackle boxes. Nets and buoys festooned the sides like Christmas decorations. The hull had once been green but had faded to the color of well-chewed spearmint gum.

Nearby on the dock sat Harald himself, in splattered yellow coveralls and a T-shirt so grungy, my donation box Wiggles shirt would've been an upgrade. He was a sumo-size guy with arms as thick as the rotating meat spits back at Fadlan's Falafel. (Yes, I was still thinking about food.)

The weirdest thing about him was his hair. His shaggy locks, his beard, even his fuzzy forearms glistened whitish blue, as if he'd been caught outside overnight and glazed with frost.

As we approached, he looked up from the rope he was coiling. "Well, now. A dwarf, an elf, and two humans walk onto my pier . . . Sounds like the beginning of a joke."

"I hope not," I said. "We want to rent your boat for a fishing expedition. We'll need the special bait."

Harald snorted. "You four on one of *my* expeditions? I don't think so."

"Big Boy sent us."

Harald furrowed his brow, causing light snow to fall across his cheeks. "Big Boy, eh? What does he want with the likes of you?"

Sam stepped forward. "None of your concern." From her coat pocket she pulled a large coin and tossed it to Harald. "One red gold now; five more when we finish. Will you rent us the boat or not?"

I leaned toward her. "What is red gold?"

"The currency of Asgard and Valhalla," she said. "Widely accepted in the other realms."

Harald sniffed the coin. Its gold surface glowed so warmly it seemed to be on fire. "You have giantish blood, girl? I can see it in your eyes."

"That's also none of your concern."

"Humph. The payment is sufficient, but my boat is small. Two passengers maximum. I'll take you and the human boy, but the dwarf and the elf—forget it."

Blitzen cracked his knuckles inside his leather gloves. "Look here, Frosty—"

"HUR! Never call a frost giant *Frosty*. We hate that. Besides, you look half petrified already, dwarf. I don't need another anchor. As for elves, they are creatures of air and light. They're useless aboard a ship. Two passengers only. That's the deal. Take it or leave it."

I glanced at my friends. "Guys, sidebar please."

I led them down the dock, out of earshot from Harald. "That dude is a frost giant?"

Hearthstone signed: *Icy hair. Ugly. Big. Yes.*

"But . . . I mean, he's large, but he's not *giant*."

Sam's expression made me suspect she was not the most patient geometry tutor. "Magnus, giants aren't necessarily enormous. Some are. Some can *grow* to enormous size if they feel like it. But they're even more varied than humans. Many look like regular people. Some can change shape into eagles or pigeons or almost anything."

"But what's a frost giant doing on the docks in Boston? Can we trust him?"

"First answer," Blitzen said, "frost giants are all over the place, especially in the north of Midgard. As for trusting him— absolutely not. He might take you two straight to Jotunheim and throw you in a dungeon, or he might use you for bait. You have to insist that Hearth and I go with you."

Hearth tapped Blitz's shoulder.

Giant is right, he signed. *I told you—too much daylight. You are turning to stone. Too stubborn to admit.*

"Nah, I'm fine."

Hearth looked around the dock. He spotted a metal pail, picked it up, and slammed it over Blitz's head. Blitz didn't react, but the pail crumpled into the shape of his skull.

"Okay," Blitz admitted, "maybe I'm petrifying a little, but—"

"Get out of the light for a while," I told him. "We'll be fine. Hearth, can you find him a nice underground lair or something?"

Hearth nodded. *We will try to find out more about Fenris and his chains. Meet you tonight. Back at library?*

"Sounds good," I said. "Sam, let's go fishing."

We returned to Harald, who was fashioning his rope into a lovely noose.

"Okay," I told him, "two passengers. We need to fish as far

out in Massachusetts Bay as possible, and we need the special bait."

Harald gave me a twisted grin. His teeth might have been cut from the same fuzzy brown cord he was coiling. "By all means, little human." He pointed to a sliding door on the side of the warehouse. "Pick your own bait . . . if you can carry it."

When Sam and I opened the door, I almost passed out from the stench.

Sam gagged. "Odin's Eye, I have smelled less fragrant battlefields."

Inside the storage room, hanging from meat hooks, was an impressive collection of rotting carcasses. The smallest was a five-foot-long shrimp. The largest was a severed bull's head the size of a Fiat.

I covered my nose with my jacket sleeve. That didn't help. I felt like somebody had filled a grenade with rotten egg, rusty metal, and raw onion, then tossed it into my sinus cavity.

"It hurts to breathe," I said. "Which of these tasty morsels do you think is the special bait?"

Sam pointed at the bull's head. "Go big or go home?"

"She said to the homeless kid." I forced myself to study the bull's head—its curved black horns, its lolling pink tongue like a hairy air mattress, its white steaming fur, and the glistening slime craters of its nostrils. "How is it possible that a bull grew that large?"

"It's probably from Jotunheim," Sam said. "Their cattle get pretty big."

"You don't say. Any idea what we're supposed to be fishing for?"

"There are lots of sea monsters in the deep. As long as it's not . . ." A shadow crossed her face. "Never mind. Probably just a sea monster."

"Just a sea monster," I said. "That's a relief."

I was tempted to take the jumbo shrimp and get out of there, but I had a feeling we'd need bigger bait if we were going to cause a ruckus that would attract a sea goddess.

"The bull's head it is," I decided.

Sam hefted her ax. "I'm not sure it'll even fit on Harald's boat, but—"

She threw her ax at the meat hook chain, which broke with a snap. The bull's head crashed to the floor like a large, disgusting piñata. The ax flew back to Sam's hand.

Together we gripped the meat hook and dragged the bull's head out of the storage locker. Even with help, I shouldn't have been able to move it, but my einherji strength was up to the task.

Die painfully. Go to Valhalla. Gain the ability to drag rancid, colossal severed heads across a dock. Hooray.

When we got to the boat, I yanked the chain with all my strength. The bull's head toppled off the pier and smashed onto the deck. The S.S. *Harald* almost capsized, but somehow it stayed afloat. The bull's head took up the back half of the ship. Its tongue hung over the stern. Its left eye rolled up in its head so it looked seasick.

Harald rose from his bait bucket. If he was at all surprised or annoyed that I'd dropped a five-hundred-pound cow head on his boat, he didn't show it.

"An ambitious choice of bait." Harald gazed across the harbor. The sky was darkening. Light sleet needled the surface of the water. "Let's get going, then. Lovely afternoon to fish."

THIRTY-TWO

My Years of Playing Bassmasters 2000 Really Pay Off

IT WAS A TERRIBLE AFTERNOON TO FISH.

The sea heaved and so did I, right over the side several times. The cold didn't bother me, but the sleet stung my face. The rocking of the deck made my legs feel like Slinkys. Harald the frost giant stood at the wheel, singing in a guttural language I assumed was Jotunese.

Sam didn't seem to mind the rough seas. She leaned against the bow rail and stared into the gray, her scarf rippling around her neck like gills.

"What's with the scarf anyway?" I asked. "Sometimes you cover your head. Sometimes you don't."

She laid her fingers protectively over the green silk. "It's a hijab. I wear it when I want to, or when I think I need to. Like when I take my grandmother to mosque on Friday, or—"

"Or when you see Amir?"

She muttered under her breath. "I almost thought you were going to let that go."

"The pigeon said Amir is your intended. Like . . . *engaged*? What are you, like, sixteen?"

"Magnus—"

"I'm just saying, if this is one of those forced arranged

marriages, that's messed up. You're a Valkyrie. You should be able to—"

"Magnus, shut it. Please."

The boat hit a swell, spraying us with saltwater buckshot.

Samirah gripped the rail. "My grandparents are old-fashioned. They were raised in Baghdad, but fled to the U.S. when Saddam Hussein was in power."

"And . . . ?"

"They've known the Fadlans since forever. They're good people. Distant kin. Successful, kind—"

"I know. Abdel is awesome. Amir seems cool. But a forced marriage if you don't love the guy—"

"Ugh! You don't get it. I've been in love with Amir since I was twelve."

The boat groaned as it dipped between the waves. Harald kept singing his Jotunese version of "Ninety-Nine Bottles of Beer."

"Oh," I said.

"Not that it's any of your business," Samirah said.

"Yeah. No."

"But sometimes when a family tries to find a good match, they actually *care* what the girl thinks."

"Okay."

"I didn't realize until I was older . . . After my mom died, my grandparents took me in but, well, my mom wasn't married when she had me. That's still a big deal for my grandparents' generation."

"Yeah." I decided not to add: *Plus the fact that your dad was Loki, the father of evil.*

Sam seemed to read my thoughts. "She was a doctor, my mom. She found Loki in the emergency room. He was . . . I don't know . . . he'd used up too much of his power trying to appear in Midgard in physical form. He got trapped somehow, divided between worlds. His manifestation in Boston was in agony, weak and helpless."

"She cured him?"

Sam brushed a droplet of seawater from her wrist. "In a way. She was kind to him. She stayed by his side. Loki can be very charming when he wants to be."

"I know." I blinked. "I mean . . . from the stories. You've met him in person?"

She shot me a dark look. "I don't approve of my father. He may be charismatic, but he's also a liar, a thief, a murderer. He's visited me several times. I refused to talk to him, which drives him nuts. He likes to be noticed. He's not exactly low-key."

"I get it," I said. "Loki. Low-key."

She rolled her eyes. "Anyway, my mom mostly raised me by herself. She was headstrong, unconventional. When she died . . . Well, in the local community, I was damaged goods, a bastard child. My grandparents were lucky, *very* lucky, to get the Fadlans' blessing for me to marry Amir. I won't really bring anything to the marriage. I'm not rich or respectable or—"

"Come on," I said. "You're smart. You're tough. You're an honest-to-Frigg Valkyrie. And I can't believe I'm finding reasons to support your arranged marriage. . . ."

Her dark hair whipped around her, collecting flecks of ice.

"The Valkyrie thing is a problem," she said. "My family . . . well, we're a little different. We have a long, long history with the Norse gods."

"How?"

She waved away the question like, *Too much to explain.*

"Still," she said, "if anyone found out about my other life . . . I don't think Mr. Fadlan would be okay with his eldest son marrying a girl who moonlights as a soul collector for pagan gods."

"Ah. When you put it that way . . ."

"I cover for my absences as best I can."

"Math tutoring."

"And some simple Valkyrie glamours. But a good Muslim girl is not supposed to hang out on her own with strange guys."

"Strange guys. Thanks."

I had a sudden image of Sam sitting in English class when her phone started to buzz. The screen flashed: ODIN CALLING. She dashed to the restroom, changed into her Super Valkyrie costume, and flew out the nearest window.

"When you got kicked out of Valhalla . . . uh, I mean, I'm sorry about that. But didn't you think, *Hey, maybe this is a good thing. I can have a normal life now*?"

"No. That's the problem. I want *both*. I want to marry Amir when the time comes. But also, all my life, I've wanted to fly."

"Flying like *airplanes* or flying like *zooming around on a magic horse*?"

"Both. When I was six, I started drawing pictures of airplanes. I wanted to be a pilot. How many Arab American female pilots do you know?"

"You would be the first," I admitted.

"I *like* that idea. Ask me any question about airplanes. I can answer it."

"So when you became a Valkyrie—"

"It was a total rush. A dream come true, being able to take off at a moment's notice. Besides, I felt like I was doing some good. I could find honorable, brave people who died protecting others, and I could bring them to Valhalla. You don't know how much I miss that."

I could hear the pain in her voice. *Honorable brave people . . .* She was including me in that group. After all the trouble she'd gotten into for my sake, I wanted to tell her that it would be all right. We would figure out a way so she could have both her lives.

But I couldn't even promise we'd live through this boat trip.

From the wheelhouse, Harald bellowed, "Mortals, you should bait your hooks! We're getting close to good fishing!"

Sam shook her head. "No. Go farther out!"

Harald scowled. "Not safe! Any farther—"

"You want your gold or not?"

Harald muttered something that was probably inappropriate in Jotunese. He gunned the motor.

I looked at Sam. "How do you know we need to go farther?"

"I can sense it," she said. "One of the advantages of my father's blood, I guess. I can usually tell where the biggest monsters are lurking."

"Joy and happiness."

I peered into the gloom. I thought about Ginnungagap, the primordial mist between ice and fire. We seemed to be sailing right into it. Any moment the sea might dissolve and we'd fall into oblivion. I hoped I was wrong. Sam's grandparents would probably be ticked off if she didn't get home in time for dinner.

The boat shuddered. The sea darkened.

"There," Sam said. "Did you feel it? We've passed from Midgard into Jotunheim waters."

I pointed off the port bow. A few hundred yards away, a granite spire jutted out of the fog. "But that's Graves Light. We're not too far from the harbor."

Sam grabbed one of the giant's fishing poles, which looked more appropriate for heavyweight pole-vaulting. "The worlds overlap, Magnus, especially near Boston. Go get the bait."

Harald slowed the engines when he saw me coming aft.

"Too dangerous to fish here," he warned. "Besides, I doubt you'll be able to cast that bait."

"Shut up, Harald." I grabbed the chain and dragged the bull's head forward, almost knocking the captain overboard with one of its horns.

When I got back to Sam, we examined the meat hook, which was embedded pretty well in the bull's skull.

"That should work for a fishing hook," Sam decided. "Let's get this chain tied on."

We spent a few minutes attaching the chain to the fishing line—a thin braided steel cable that made the reel weigh about three hundred pounds.

Together, Sam and I rolled the bull's head off the front of the boat. It sank slowly into the icy froth, the bull's dead eye staring at me as it submerged, like, *Not cool, man!*

Harald lumbered over carrying a large chair. He sunk its four feet into anchor holes on the deck. Then he lashed the seat in place with steel cables.

"If I were you, human," he said, "I'd buckle up."

With its leather harnesses, the seat looked a little too

much like an electric chair to me, but Sam held the fishing
pole while I strapped myself in.

"So why am *I* in the chair?" I asked.

"Your promise," she reminded me. "You swore by your
troth."

"Troth sucks." From the giant's supply kit, I pulled some
leather gloves that were only four sizes too big and put them on.

Sam handed me the pole, and then found gloves for herself.

I had a disjointed memory from when I was ten years old,
watching *Jaws* with my mom because she insisted. She warned
me it was superscary, but the whole time I was either bored
at the slow pace or laughing at the schlocky-looking rubber
shark.

"Please let me catch a rubber shark," I muttered now.

Harald cut the engines. Suddenly it was freakishly quiet.
The wind died. The sleet against the deck sounded like sand
hitting glass. The waves calmed as if the sea was holding its
breath.

Sam stood at the rail, feeding out cable as the bull's head
sank into the depths. Finally the line went slack.

"Did we hit bottom?" I asked.

Sam bit her lip. "I don't know. I think—"

The line sprang taut with a sound like a hammer on a saw
blade. Sam let go to avoid being catapulted into space. The
pole was nearly ripped out of my hands, taking my fingers
with it, but somehow I held on.

The chair groaned. The leather straps dug into my collar-
bones. The entire boat leaned forward into the waves with
timbers creaking and rivets popping.

"Ymir's Blood!" Harald yelled. "We're breaking apart!"

"Give it more line!" Sam grabbed a bucket. She poured water on the cable, which steamed as it raced off the prow.

I gritted my teeth. My arm muscles felt like warm bread dough. Just when I was sure I couldn't hold on any longer, the pulling stopped. The line hummed with tension, laser-dotting on the gray water about a hundred yards starboard.

"What's going on?" I asked. "Is it resting?"

Harald cursed. "I don't like this. Sea monsters don't act this way. Even the biggest catches—"

"Reel it in," Sam said. "Now!"

I turned the handle. It was like arm-wrestling the Terminator. The rod bent. The cable creaked. Sam pulled the line, keeping it clear of the rail, but even with her help I could barely make any progress.

My shoulders went numb. My lower back spasmed. Despite the cold, I was soaked with sweat and shivering with exhaustion. I felt like I was reeling in a sunken battleship.

From time to time, Sam yelled encouraging things like, "No, you idiot! Pull!"

Finally, in front of the boat, the sea darkened in a fifty-foot-diameter oval. The waves sloshed and boiled.

Up in the wheelhouse, Harald must have had a better view of whatever was coming to the surface. He screamed in a very ungiantish voice, "Cut the line!"

"No," Sam said. "It's too late for that."

Harald snatched up a knife. He threw it at the cable, but Sam deflected the blade with her ax.

"Back off, giant!" she yelled.

"But you can't bring that thing up!" Harald wailed. "It's the—"

"Yes, I know!"

The rod began slipping from my hands. "Help!"

Sam lunged and grabbed the fishing pole. She wedged herself next to me in the chair to assist, but I was too tired and terrified to feel embarrassed.

"We may all die," she muttered, "but this will *definitely* get Ran's attention."

"Why?" I asked. "What is that thing?"

Our catch broke the surface and opened its eyes.

"Meet my older brother," Sam said, "the World Serpent."

THIRTY-THREE

Sam's Brother Wakes Up Kinda Cranky

WHEN I SAY the serpent opened his eyes, I mean he switched on green spotlights the size of trampolines. His irises glowed so intensely I was pretty sure everything I saw for the rest of my life would be tinted the color of lime Jell-O.

The good news: the rest of my life didn't look like it was going to be very long.

The monster's ridged forehead and tapered snout made him look more like an eel than a snake. His hide glistened in a camouflage patchwork of green, brown, and yellow. (Here I am calmly describing him. At the time the only thought in my mind was: YIKES! HUGE SNAKE!)

He opened his mouth and hissed—the stench of rancid bull's head and poison so strong my clothes smoked. He may not have used mouthwash, but obviously the World Serpent cared about flossing. His teeth gleamed in rows of perfect white triangles. His pink maw was big enough to swallow Harald's boat and a dozen of Harald's closest friends' boats.

My meat hook was embedded in the back of his mouth, right where the hangy-down uvula thing would be in a human mouth. The serpent didn't seem too happy about that.

He shook back and forth, raking the steel line across his teeth. My fishing pole whipped sideways. The boat seesawed port to starboard, planks cracking and popping, but somehow we stayed afloat. My line didn't break.

"Sam?" I said in a small voice. "Why hasn't he killed us yet?"

She pressed so close to me I could feel her shivering. "I think he's studying us, maybe even trying to talk to us."

"What is he saying?"

Sam gulped. "My guess? *How dare you?*"

The serpent hissed, spitting globs of poison that sizzled against the deck.

Behind us, Harald whimpered, "Drop the pole, you fools! You'll get us all killed!"

I tried to meet the serpent's gaze. "Hey, Mr. Jormungand. Can I call you Mr. J? Look, sorry to bother you. Nothing personal. We're just using you to get somebody's attention."

Mr. J didn't like that. His head surged out of the water, towering above us, then crashed down again off the bow, triggering a forty-foot-tall ring of waves.

Sam and I were definitely sitting in the splash zone. I ate salt water for lunch. My lungs discovered they could not in fact breathe the stuff. My eyes got a thorough power washing. But, incredibly, the boat didn't capsize. When the rocking and sloshing subsided, I found myself still alive, still holding the fishing pole with my line still attached to the World Serpent's mouth. The monster stared at me like, *Why are you not dead?*

Out of the corner of my eye, I saw the tsunami crash against the Graves, washing all the way up to the base of the lighthouse. I wondered if I'd just flooded Boston.

I remembered why Jormungand was called the World Serpent. Supposedly his body was so long it wrapped around the earth, stretching across the sea floor like a monstrous telecommunication cable. Most of the time he kept his tail in his mouth—Hey, I used a pacifier until I was almost two, so I can't judge—but apparently he'd decided our bull's-head bait was worth the switch.

The point being: if the World Serpent was shaking, the whole world might be shaking with him.

"So," I said to nobody in particular, "what now?"

"Magnus," Sam said in a strangled tone, "try not to panic. But look off the starboard side."

I couldn't imagine what would be more panic-inducing than Mr. J until I saw the woman in the whirlpool.

Compared to the serpent, she was tiny—only about ten feet tall. From the waist up, she wore a blouse of silver chain mail encrusted with barnacles. She might have once been beautiful, but her pearlescent skin was withered, her seaweed-green eyes were milky with cataracts, and her rippling blond hair was shot through with gray like blight in a wheat field.

From the waist down, things got weird. Spinning around her like a dancer's skirt, a waterspout swirled within a silver fishing net a hundred yards in diameter. Trapped in its weave was a kaleidoscope of ice floe, dead fish, plastic garbage bags, car tires, grocery carts, and other assorted flotsam. As the woman floated toward us, the edge of her net *thwapped* against our hull and scraped against the World Serpent's neck.

She spoke in a deep baritone. "Who dares interrupt my scavenging?"

Harald the frost giant screamed. He was a champion screamer. He scrambled to the bow and threw a bunch of gold coins over the side. Then he turned to Sam. "Quick, girl, your payment to me! Give it to Ran!"

Sam frowned, but she tossed another five coins overboard.

Instead of sinking, the red gold swirled into Ran's net and joined the floating merry-go-round of debris.

"O, Great Ran!" Harald wailed. "Please don't kill me! Here, take my anchor! Take these humans! You can even have my lunch box!"

"Silence!" The goddess shooed away the frost giant, who did his best to cower, grovel, and retreat all at the same time.

"I'll just be belowdecks," he sobbed. "Praying."

Ran regarded me as if deciding whether I was large enough to filet. "Release Jormungand, mortal! The last thing I need today is a world-flooding event."

The World Serpent hissed in agreement.

Ran turned on him. "And you shut up, you overgrown moray. All your writhing is stirring up the silt. I can't see a thing down there. How many times have I told you not to bite at any old rancid bull's head? Rancid bulls' heads are not native to these waters!"

The World Serpent snarled petulantly, tugging at the steel cable in his mouth.

"O, Great Ran," I said, "I am Magnus Chase. This is Sam al-Abbas. We've come to bargain with you. Also, just wondering . . . why can't you cut the fishing line yourself?"

Ran let loose a torrent of Norse curses that literally steamed in the air. Now that she was closer, I could see stranger things swirling in her net—ghostly bearded faces, gasping and terrified as they tried to reach the surface; hands clawing at the ropes.

"Worthless einherji," said the goddess, "you know full well what you have done."

"I do?" I asked.

"You are Vanir-spawn! A child of Njord?" Ran sniffed the air. "No, your scent is fainter. Perhaps a grandchild."

Sam's eyes widened. "Right! Magnus, you're the son of Frey, son of Njord—god of ships, sailors, and fishermen. That's why our boat didn't capsize. That's why you were able to catch the serpent!" She looked at Ran. "Um, which, of course, we already knew."

Ran snarled. "Once brought to the surface, the World Serpent is not simply bound by your fishing line. He is connected to you by fate! *You* must now decide, and quickly, whether to cut him loose and return him to his slumber, or let him awaken fully and destroy your world!"

In the back of my neck, something snapped like a rusty spring—probably the last bit of my courage. I looked at the World Serpent. For the first time, I noticed that his glowing green peepers were covered by a thin translucent membrane—a second set of eyelids.

"You mean he's only partially awake?"

"If he were fully awake," said the goddess, "your entire Eastern Seaboard would already be underwater."

"Ah." I had to resist the urge the throw away the fishing pole, undo my safety harness, and run around the deck screaming like a little Harald.

"I will release him," I said. "But first, great Ran, you have to promise to negotiate with us in good faith. We want to barter."

"Barter with you?" Ran's skirts swirled faster. Ice and plastic crackled. Shopping carts plowed into one another. "By rights, Magnus Chase, you should *belong* to me! You died of drowning. Drowned souls are *my* property."

"Actually," Sam said, "he died in combat, so he belongs to Odin."

"Technicalities!" Ran snapped.

The faces in Ran's net gaped and gasped, pleading for help. Sam had told me, *There are worse places to spend your afterlife in than Valhalla.* Imagining myself tangled in that silvery web, I was suddenly grateful to my Valkyrie.

"Well, okay then," I said. "I guess I can just let Mr. J wake up fully. I didn't have any plans for tonight."

"No!" Ran hissed. "Do you have any idea how hard it is to scavenge along the seafloor when Jormungand gets agitated? Let him go!"

"And you promise to negotiate in good faith?" I asked.

"Yes. Fine. I am in no mood for Ragnarok today."

"Say, 'By my troth—'"

"I am a goddess! I know better than to swear by my troth!"

I glanced at Sam, who shrugged. She handed me her ax, and I cut the fishing line.

Jormungand sank beneath the waves, glaring at me through a bubbling green cloud of poison as he descended, as if to say, *NEXT TIME, LITTLE MORTAL.*

Ran's swirling skirts slowed to the speed of a tropical storm. "Very well, einherji. I promised to barter in good faith. What do you want?"

"The Sword of Summer," I said. "I had it with me when I hit the Charles River."

Ran's eyes glistened. "Oh, yes. I could give you the sword. But in exchange, I would want something valuable. I'm thinking . . . your soul."

THIRTY-FOUR

My Sword Almost
Ends Up on eBay

"I'M THINKING NOT," I REPLIED.

Ran made a rumbling sound like a whale with heartburn. "You—the grandson of that meddler, Njord—come here asking to barter, disturbing the World Serpent, interrupting my scavenging, and you won't even agree to a reasonable offer? The Sword of Summer is the greatest artifact to come into my nets in ages. Your soul is a small price to pay in exchange!"

"Lady Ran." Sam took back her ax and slipped down from the fishing chair. "Magnus has already been claimed by Odin. He is einherji. That cannot be changed."

"Besides," I said, "you don't want my soul. It's really small. I don't use it much. I doubt it even works anymore."

The goddess's watery skirts swirled. Trapped souls clawed for the surface. Plastic garbage bags popped like Bubble Wrap. The smell of dead fish almost made me nostalgic for the bull's head.

"What do you offer me, then?" Ran demanded. "What could possibly be worth that sword?"

Good question, I thought.

I stared into the goddess's nets and an idea began to form.

"You said you were scavenging," I recalled. "What for?"

The goddess's expression softened. Her eyes shone a greedier shade of green. "Many things. Coins. Souls. Lost valuables of every description. Just before you woke the serpent, I had my eye on a Chevy Malibu radial hubcap that was worth forty dollars *easy*. Just sitting there at the bottom of the harbor. But now"—she threw up her hands—"gone."

"You collect stuff." I corrected myself: "I mean . . . wonderful treasures."

Sam squinted at me, clearly wondering if I'd lost my mind, but I was starting to understand what made Ran tick—what she cared about most.

The goddess stretched her fingers toward the horizon. "Have you heard of the Pacific garbage patch?"

"*I* have, Lady Ran," Sam said. "It's a floating collection of rubbish the size of Texas. It sounds terrible."

"It is amazing," said the goddess. "The first time I saw it, I was overwhelmed! It put my own collection to shame. For centuries, all shipwrecks of the northern seas have been mine to claim. Anything lost in the depths comes to me. But when I saw the wonders of the garbage patch, I realized how puny my efforts had been. Ever since, I've spent all my time scavenging the seafloor, looking for additions to my net. I would not have found your sword if I hadn't been so quick!"

I nodded with sympathy. Now I could fit this Norse goddess into the Magnus Chase worldview. Ran was a bag lady. I could work with a bag lady.

I peered overboard at the floating junk. A silver teaspoon balanced on an island of Styrofoam. A bicycle wheel spun past, shredding the ghostly head of a lost soul.

"Lady Ran," I said, "your husband, Aegir, is the lord of the sea, right? You share a golden palace with him at the bottom of the ocean?"

The goddess scowled. "What is your point?"

"Well . . . what does your husband think of your collection?"

"Aegir." Ran spat. "The great stirrer of sea storms! These days the only thing he wants to do is brew his mead. He's *always* been a brewer, but lately it's ridiculous. He spends all his time at the hops shop, or going on brewery tours with his buddies. And don't get me started on the flannel shirt, rolled-up skinny jeans, glasses, and the way he trims his beard. He's always talking about microbrews. He has a cauldron a mile wide! How can he *microbrew*?"

"Right," I said. "That must be annoying. He doesn't appreciate how important your treasures are."

"He has his lifestyle," Ran said. "I have mine!"

Sam looked bewildered, but all of this made total sense to me. I knew a bag lady in Charlestown whose husband had left her a six-million-dollar mansion on Beacon Hill, but sitting at home alone had made her feel suffocated, lonely, and unhappy. So instead she lived out on the streets, pushing her shopping cart, collecting plastic lawn ornaments and aluminum cans. *That* made her feel complete.

Ran frowned. "What were we talking about again?"

"The Sword of Summer," I said. "And what I could offer you in return."

"Yes!"

"What I'm offering," I said, "is to let you keep your collection."

Frost spread down the ropes of the net. Ran's tone turned dangerous. "Are you threatening to take my stuff?"

"Oh, no. I would never do that. I understand how valuable—"

"Because this whirling plastic sunflower ornament right here? They don't make these anymore! It's easily worth ten dollars."

"Right. But if you don't give me the Sword of Summer, Surt and his fire giants will come looking for it. And *they* won't show you such respect."

Ran scoffed. "The sons of Muspell cannot touch me. My realm is deadly to them."

"But Surt has many allies," Sam said, picking up on the idea. "They would annoy you, harass you, take your . . . treasures. They'll do anything to retrieve that sword. Once they have it, they'll start Ragnarok. Then there will be no more scavenging. The oceans will boil. Your collection will be destroyed."

"No!" shrieked the goddess.

"Yes," I said. "But if you give us the sword, Surt won't have any reason to bother you. We'll keep it safe."

Ran scowled at her nets, studying the patterns of glittering trash. "And how, son of Frey, will the sword be safer with you than with me? You cannot return it to your father. Frey gave up his rights to use the weapon when he gifted it to Skirnir."

For the millionth time, I wanted to find my frolicking summer-god dad and smack him. Why had he given away his weapon in the first place? For love? Weren't gods supposed to be smarter than that? Then again, Ran collected hubcaps, and Aegir was into microbrewing.

"I'll wield it myself," I said. "Or I'll take it back to Valhalla for safekeeping."

"In other words, you don't know." The goddess arched her kelpy eyebrows at Sam. "And you, daughter of Loki, why are you siding with the gods of Asgard? Your father is no friend of theirs—not anymore."

"I'm not my father," Sam said. "I'm a—I was a Valkyrie."

"Ah, yes. The girl who dreamed of flying. But the thanes of Valhalla expelled you. Why do you still try to earn their favor? You don't need them to fly. You know very well that with your father's blood—"

"Give us the sword, Lady Ran." Sam's voice hardened. "It's the only way to delay Ragnarok."

The goddess smiled sourly. "You even sound like Loki. He was such a persuasive speaker—one moment flattering, the next moment threatening. Once, he actually convinced me to lend him my net! That led to all sorts of trouble. Loki figured out the secrets of net weaving. The gods learned how, then the humans. Pretty soon *everyone* had nets. My trademark item! I won't be so easily convinced again. I'll keep the sword and take my chances with Surt."

I unstrapped myself from the fishing chair. I moved to the tip of the bow and locked eyes with the goddess. I didn't normally shake down bag ladies, but I had to make Ran take me seriously. I lifted the chain from my belt. The silver links glinted in the fading light.

"This chain is also a sword," I said. "An authentic blade from Valhalla. How many of those do you have in your net?"

Ran started to reach for the chain, then caught herself.

"Yes . . . I can see the sword through the glamour. But why would I trade—"

"A new sword for an old one," I offered. "This blade is shinier, only used once in combat. You could get twenty bucks for it, no problem. The Sword of Summer, however, has no resale value."

"Mmm, true, but—"

"The other option," I said, "is I *take* the Sword of Summer. It belongs to me."

Ran growled. Her fingernails stretched into jagged points like shark's teeth. "You dare threaten me, mortal?"

"Just telling the truth," I said, trying to stay calm. "I can sense the sword within your nets." (Total lie.) "I pulled it from the depths once before. I can do it again. The sword is the sharpest weapon in the Nine Worlds. Do you really want it cutting through your net, spilling all your stuff and freeing all those trapped souls? If they got away, do you think they'd fight *for* you or against you?"

Her gaze wavered. "You would not dare."

"Trade me a sword for a sword," I said. "And throw in one of Idun's apples for our trouble."

Ran hissed. "You said nothing about an apple!"

"That's an easy request," I said. "I know you've got an extra apple of immortality swirling around in there somewhere. Then we'll go in peace. We'll stop Ragnarok and let you go back to your scavenging. Otherwise"—I shrugged—"you'll find out what the son of Frey can do with his father's sword."

I was pretty sure the goddess would laugh in my face, capsize the boat, and add our drowned souls to her collection. But I stared her down like I had nothing to lose.

After a count of twenty—long enough for a bead of sweat to trickle down my neck and freeze at my collar—Ran snarled, "Very well."

She flicked her hand. The Sword of Summer came flying out of the water and landed in my grip. Immediately it began to hum, agitating every molecule in my body.

I tossed my chain overboard. "Now the apple."

A piece of fruit shot out from the net. It would've beaned Sam between the eyes if not for her fast reflexes. The apple didn't look like much—just a shriveled Golden Delicious—but Sam held it gingerly, as if it were radioactive. She slipped it into her coat pocket.

"Go now, as you promised," Ran said. "But I tell you this, son of Frey: your high-handed bargaining will cost you dearly. You have made an enemy of Ran. My husband, Aegir, lord of the waves, will also hear about this, if I can ever get him out of the hops shop. For your sake, I hope you're not planning any more sea voyages. Next time, your kinship with Njord will not save you. Cross my waters again and I will personally drag your soul to the bottom."

"Well," I said, "that's something to look forward to."

Ran spun. Her form blurred into a misty funnel cloud, her nets wrapping around her like twirled spaghetti. She sank into the depths and was gone.

Sam shuddered. "That was interesting."

Behind us, a ladder creaked. Harald's head popped up from below.

"Interesting?" he demanded. "Did you say it was *interesting*?"

He climbed out, glowering at us, his fists balled, his icy blue beard dripping. "World Serpent fishing—that's one thing.

But antagonizing Ran? I never would have taken you aboard if I had known, no matter what Big Boy said! I have to make a living on the ocean! I should throw you overboard—"

"I'll double your price," Sam said. "Ten red gold. Just get us back to dock."

Harald blinked. "Okay." He headed for the wheelhouse.

I studied the Sword of Summer. Now that I had it, I wasn't sure what to do with it. The steel glowed with its own light, silvery runes burning along the flat of the blade. The sword radiated warmth, heating the air around me, melting the frost on the railings, filling me with the same sense of quiet power I felt when I healed someone. It wasn't so much like holding a weapon . . . more like holding open a door to a different time, walking with my mom in the Blue Hills, feeling the sunlight on my face.

Sam reached over. Still wearing her oversize leather gloves, she brushed a tear from my cheek.

I hadn't realized I was crying.

"Sorry," I said, my voice hoarse.

Sam studied me with concern. "Could you really have summoned the sword from Ran?"

"I don't know."

"In that case, you're insane. But I'm impressed."

I lowered the blade. It kept humming as if trying to tell me something.

"What did Ran mean?" I asked. "She said you didn't need to be a Valkyrie to fly. Something about your father's blood?"

Sam's expression closed up faster than Ran's nets. "It's not important."

"You sure about that?"

She hung her ax on her belt. She looked everywhere but my eyes. "As sure as you could summon that sword."

The outboard engines rumbled. The ship began to turn.

"I'll be at the wheel with Harald," Sam said, apparently anxious to put some distance between us. "I'll make sure he takes us to Boston and not Jotunheim."

THIRTY-FIVE

Thou Shalt Not Poop on the Head of Art

AFTER GIVING ME the slightly shriveled apple of immortality, Sam left me at the docks. Not that she wanted to, she said, but her grandparents were going to murder her, and she didn't want to be any later for that. We made plans to meet the next morning at the Public Garden.

I made my way toward Copley Square. I felt a little self-conscious walking the streets with a glowing broadsword, so I had a conversation with my weapon. (Because that wasn't crazy at all.)

"Could you do a glamour and turn into something smaller?" I asked it. "Preferably not a chain, since it's no longer the 1990s?"

The sword didn't reply (duh), but I imagined it was humming at a more interrogative pitch, like, *Such as what?*

"I dunno. Something pocket-size and innocuous. A pen, maybe?"

The sword pulsed, almost like it was laughing. I imagined it saying, *A pen sword. That is the stupidest thing I've ever heard.*

"You have a better idea?" I asked it.

The sword shrank in my hand, melting into a runestone on a gold chain. The small white stone was emblazoned with a black symbol:

"The rune of Frey," I said. "I'm not really a jewelry guy, but okay."

I fastened the chain around my neck. I discovered the stone was attached magnetically to its bail, so I could easily pull it off the chain. As soon as I did, the stone grew into a sword. If I wanted it back in pendant form, all I had to do was picture that. The sword shrank into a stone, and I could reattach it to the necklace.

"Cool," I admitted.

Perhaps the sword really *had* heard my request. Perhaps I'd somehow created the glamour by myself. Or maybe I was hallucinating and wearing a huge sword around my neck.

I doubted anyone would look twice at my new medallion. They'd see the ᚠ and assume it stood for ᚠailure.

By the time I reached Copley Square it was fully dark out. No sign of Blitz or Hearthstone, which made me apprehensive. The library had closed for the night. I wondered if Big Boy expected me to meet him on the roof, but I wasn't about to climb the walls of the library.

It had been a long day. Einherji superwarrior strength or not, I was exhausted and shaking from hunger. If Big Boy wanted the apple, he would have to come get it. Otherwise I'd eat it myself.

I sat on the front steps of the library, the stone swaying under me like I was still on Harald's ship. To either side of me, a bronze lady statue reclined on a marble throne. I remembered that one symbolized Art and the other Science, but to me they both looked ready for Recess. They leaned on their armrests, metal shawls covering their heads, glancing in my direction like, *Tough week, huh?*

This was the first time I'd been alone and not in imminent danger since . . . the funeral home? Did it count as being alone if you were staring at your own dead body?

My memorial service had probably happened by now. I imagined my coffin being lowered into an icy grave; Uncle Randolph leaning on his cane, frowning resentfully; Uncle Frederick looking baffled and distressed in his mismatched clothes; and Annabeth . . . I couldn't imagine what she was feeling.

She'd rushed to Boston to find me. She'd learned I was dead. Then she learned I *wasn't* dead, but she still had to attend my funeral and not tell anyone she'd seen me.

I believed she would keep her promise, but our meeting had unsettled me. Some of the things she'd said: *I can help you. I know a place where you'll be safe.*

I pulled the battered flyer from my coat pocket. MISSING! MAGNUS CHASE, 16 YEARS OLD. PLEASE CALL. I studied Annabeth's phone number, committing it to memory. I owed her an explanation, but not yet. I'd already gotten Hearthstone knocked unconscious, Blitzen half petrified, and Sam kicked out of the Valkyries. I couldn't risk dragging anyone else into my problems.

According to the Norns, Fenris Wolf would be unleashed seven days from now unless I stopped it from happening. Ragnarok would begin. Surt would consume the Nine Worlds in fire. I would never find my mom or get justice for her murder.

Despite all that, every time I thought about facing a wolf—facing *the* Wolf, Fenris himself—I wanted to curl up in my old sleeping bag, stick my fingers in my ears, and hum, *La, la, la, it's not happening.*

A shadow swooped over my head. Big Boy the eagle landed on the bronze statue to my left and promptly decorated her head with eagle droppings.

"Dude," I said, "you just pooped on Art."

"Did I?" Big Boy lifted his tail feathers. "Ah, well. I imagine she's used to it. I see you survived your fishing expedition!"

"Surprised?" I asked.

"Yes, actually. Do you have my apple?"

I pulled it from my pocket and tossed it over. Big Boy caught it in his left claw and began to eat. "Ah, that's the stuff!"

I'd seen some strange things recently, but an eagle eating an apple atop the poopy head of Art was definitely in the top twenty.

"So will you tell me who you are, now?" I asked.

Big Boy burped. "I suppose you've earned it. I'll confess: I'm not really an eagle."

"I'm shocked. Shocked, I tell you."

He snapped off another chunk of apple. "Also, I doubt you'll make many friends among the gods when they learn you've assisted me."

"Wonderful," I said. "I'm already on Ran and Aegir's naughty list."

"Oh, those two aren't properly *gods*. They are neither Aesir nor Vanir. I think they're more giantish, though of course the line between giant and god has always been blurred. Our clans have intermarried so many times over the years."

"*Our clans.* Meaning . . ."

The eagle grew. Shadows folded around him, adding to his

size like a snowball gathering mass. His shape resolved into a huge old man lounging in the lap of Art. He wore iron-shod boots, leather britches, and a tunic of eagle feathers that was probably not in compliance with the Endangered Species Act. His hair was gray, his face weathered with age. On one forearm he wore a gold bracer encrusted with bloodstones—the sort of armband worn by the thanes in Valhalla.

"You're a lord?" I asked.

"A king, in fact." Big Boy took another bite of apple. Immediately his hair darkened and some of his wrinkles faded. "Utgard-Loki at your service!"

I curled my fingers around my sword pendant. "Loki as in *Loki* Loki?"

The giant king made a sour face. "You have no idea how many times I get that question. *Are you the 'famous' Loki?*" He put *famous* in air quotes. "Ugh! I was named Loki before *he* ever came along. It's a popular name among giants! At any rate—no, Magnus Chase, I am not related to the *famous* Loki. I am Utgard-Loki, meaning Loki of the Outlands, king of the mountain giants. I've been watching you for years."

"I get that a lot."

"Well, you're much more interesting than those dense children of Thor who usually challenge me. You'll make a wonderful enemy!"

Pressure built in my ear canals. "We're enemies now?"

"Oh, there's no need to draw your sword just yet. Nice pendant, though. Someday we'll find ourselves on opposite sides. That can't be helped. But for the present, I'm happy to observe. I hope you'll learn to use the sword without getting yourself killed. That would be amusing. Surt, the old bag of smoke, deserves to be humiliated."

"Well, I'm always happy to amuse you."

The giant popped the rest of the apple in his mouth and swallowed it whole. He now looked about twenty-five, with coal-black hair, his handsome angular face free of wrinkles.

"Speaking of Surt," he said, "the fire lord will never let you keep that sword. You have . . . probably until morning before he realizes that you've found it."

My hand dropped from my pendant. My arms felt like wet sandbags. "I impaled Surt, cut off his nose, and dropped him in an icy river. That didn't even slow him down?"

"Oh, it did! Right now he's nothing but a seething noseless ball of fire, raging down in Muspellheim. He'll have to conserve all his power to manifest again on the day of the full moon."

"When he tries to free the Wolf." Maybe I shouldn't have been chatting about that with a self-declared enemy, but something told me Utgard-Loki already knew.

The giant nodded. "Surt is more anxious than anyone for Ragnarok to start. He knows he'll get to consume the Nine Worlds in flames, and that's what he's been waiting for since the dawn of time. Me, I like the way things are! I'm having fun. But fire giants . . . ah, there's no reasoning with them. It's all burn, burn, burn. Anyway, the good news is that Surt won't be able to kill you personally until the full moon. He's much too weak. The bad news: he has lots of minions."

"I hate minions."

"Surt's not the only one after you. Your former comrades

from Valhalla have been searching. They're not pleased that you left without permission."

I thought about Captain Gunilla and her bandolier of hammers. I imagined one spinning toward my face. "Well, that's just perfect."

"If I were you, Magnus, I'd get out of Midgard by dawn. That should throw your pursuers off your trail, at least temporarily."

"Leave the earth. Simple as that."

"I knew you were a quick learner." Utgard-Loki slid off the statue's lap. Standing up, he was easily twelve feet tall. "We'll meet again, Magnus Chase. Someday you'll need a favor only Utgard-Loki can grant. But for now . . . your friends would like a word. Farewell!"

Shadows funneled around him. Utgard-Loki was gone. In his place stood Blitzen and Hearthstone.

Hearth leaped away from me like a startled cat.

Blitzen dropped his duffel bag. "Heimdall's Horn, kid! Where did you come from?"

"Where did I— I've been here for almost an hour. I was talking to a giant."

Hearth crept toward me. He poked me in the chest to see if I was real.

We have been here for hours, he signed. *Waiting for you. We talked to giant. You just appeared.*

A sick feeling rose in my chest. "Maybe we should compare notes."

I told them what had happened since we parted ways: Harald's boat; Mr. J and Bag Lady Ran (which would make an awesome name for a rapper duo); and my conversation with Utgard-Loki.

"Ah. Not good." Blitzen stroked his beard. He'd dispensed with the anti-sun gear and was now wearing an eggplant-purple three-piece suit with a mauve dress shirt and a green carnation in the lapel. "The giant told us some of the same things, but . . . the giant did not tell us his own name."

Hearth signed, *Surprise,* opening his pinched fingers on either side of his eyes, which in this context I took to mean *YIKES!*

Utgard-Loki. He spelled out the name. *Most powerful sorcerer of Jotunheim. Can make any illusion.*

"We were lucky," Blitz said. "Utgard-Loki could've tricked us into seeing or doing *anything.* He could've made us walk off a roof, accidentally kill each other, or even eat steak tartare. In fact"—Blitz narrowed his eyes—"we could still be in an illusion. Any of us might be giants."

Blitzen punched Hearthstone in the arm.

OUCH! Hearth signed. He stepped on the dwarf's toes.

"Or maybe not," Blitzen decided. "Still, this is very bad. Magnus, you've given an apple of immortality to a giant king."

"And . . . what does that mean, exactly?"

Blitz fiddled with his carnation. "To be honest, I'm not sure. I've never understood how those apples work. I imagine it will make Utgard-Loki stronger as well as younger. And make no mistake, when Ragnarok comes, he won't be on our side."

Hearthstone signed: *Wish I'd known it was Utgard-Loki. I could have asked about magic.*

"Hmph," Blitz said. "You know plenty. Besides, you can't

trust a giant to give you straight answers. Right now, you two need sleep. Elves can't stay awake very long without sunlight. And Magnus looks like he's going to fall over."

Blitz was right. I was starting to see double Blitzens and double Hearthstones, and I didn't think it had anything to do with illusions.

We made camp in the library doorway, just like old times except with better supplies. Blitz pulled three down sleeping bags out of his duffel, along with a fresh change of clothes for me and some sandwiches, which I ate too fast to taste. Hearth collapsed in his bag and immediately began snoring.

"Rest," Blitz told me. "I'll keep watch. Tomorrow, we visit my kin."

"The dwarf world?" My thoughts were getting fuzzy. "Your home?"

"My home." Blitzen sounded uneasy. "Some of the research Hearth and I did today—it's looking like we'll need more information about the rope that bound Fenris. We can only get that in Nidavellir." He focused on the chain around my neck. "Can I see it? The sword?"

I pulled off the pendant and set the sword between us, its light making Blitz's face glitter like a vein of copper in the dark.

"Breathtaking," he murmured. "Bone steel . . . or something even more exotic."

"Bone steel . . . T.J. in Valhalla mentioned that."

Blitz didn't touch the blade, but he passed his hand over it reverently. "To make steel, iron is smelted with carbon. Most swordsmiths use coal, but you can also use bones—the bones of enemies, or monsters, or ancestors."

"Oh . . ." I stared at the blade, wondering if my great-great-grandparents might be in there somewhere.

"Forged correctly," Blitz said, "bone steel can cut down supernatural creatures, even giants and gods. Of course, you have to quench the blade in blood to harden it, preferably the blood of whatever type of creature you want the sword to be most lethal against."

The sandwiches weren't sitting so well in my stomach. "This blade was made like that?"

"I don't know," Blitz admitted. "The sword of Frey is Vanir work, which is a mystery to me. It might be closer to Hearth's elf magic."

My spirits sank. I'd had this idea that dwarves were good with weapon crafting. In the back of my mind, I'd been hoping Blitzen could tell me something about the blade's secrets.

I glanced at Hearth, still snoring peacefully. "You said Hearth knew a lot of magic. I'm not criticizing. I've just never seen him cast any . . . well, except maybe opening one door. What else can he do?"

Blitz set his hand protectively next to Hearth's feet. "Magic drains him. He's careful about using it. Also his family . . ."

He took a deep breath. "Modern elves don't approve of magic. His parents shamed Hearthstone pretty badly. It still makes him self-conscious about casting magic in front of others. Hearthstone wasn't the son his parents wanted, between the magic and the, you know . . ." Blitz tapped his own earlobes.

I felt like saying something rude about Hearthstone's parents in sign language. "It's not his fault he's deaf."

"Elves." Blitz shrugged. "They have a low tolerance for

anything that isn't perfect—music, art, appearances. Their own children."

I wanted to protest how messed up that was. Then I thought about humans, and I decided we weren't much better.

"Get some sleep, kid," Blitz urged. "Big day tomorrow. To keep Fenris Wolf bound, we're going to need help from a certain dwarf . . . and that help isn't going to come cheap. We'll need you at full strength when we jump to Nidavellir."

"Jump . . ." I said. "What do you mean *jump*?"

He gave me a worried look, as if I might be getting another funeral very soon. "In the morning, you're going to try climbing the World Tree."

THIRTY-SIX

Duck!

CALL ME CRAZY.

I was expecting the World Tree to be a tree. Not a row of bronze ducks.

"Behold!" Blitzen said. "The nexus of the universe!"

Hearthstone knelt reverently.

I glanced at Sam, who had joined us after a daring escape from first period physics. She wasn't laughing.

"So . . ." I said, "I'm just going to point out that this is the *Make Way for Ducklings* statue."

"Do you think it's a coincidence?" Blitzen demanded. "Nine Worlds? Nine ducks? The symbolism screams *portal*! This spot is the crux of creation, the center of the tree, the easiest place to jump from one duck—I mean one world—to another."

"If you say so." I'd passed these bronze ducks a thousand times. I'd never considered them much of a nexus. I hadn't read the children's book they were based on, but I gathered it was about a mama duck and her babies crossing a street in Boston, so they put a sculpture of it in the Public Garden.

In the summer, little kids would sit on Mrs. Mallard and get their pictures taken. At Christmas, the ducks got little Santa hats. At the moment they were naked and alone, buried up to their necks in fresh snowfall.

Hearthstone passed his hands over the statues like he was testing a stovetop for heat.

He glanced at Blitz and shook his head.

"As I feared," Blitz said. "Hearth and I have been traveling too much. We won't be able to activate the ducks. Magnus, we'll need you."

I waited for an explanation, but Blitz just studied the sculptures. He was testing out a new hat this morning—a pith helmet with dark netting that draped to his shoulders. According to Blitz, the net fabric was his own design. It blocked ninety-eight percent of the sunlight, allowing us to see his face while not covering up his fashionable outfit. It made him look like a beekeeper in mourning.

"Okay, I'll bite," I said. "How do I activate ducks?"

Sam scanned our surroundings. She didn't look like she'd slept much. Her eyes were puffy. Her hands were raw and blistered from our fishing expedition. She'd changed into a black wool trench coat, but otherwise she was dressed the same as yesterday: green hijab, ax, shield, jeans, winter boots—all the accoutrements of a fashionable ex-Valkyrie.

"However you do it," she said, "do it quickly. I don't like how close we are to the gates of Valhalla."

"But I don't know how," I protested. "Don't you guys go world-jumping all the time?"

Hearth signed, *Too much.*

"Kid," Blitz said, "the more frequently you travel between the worlds, the harder it gets. It's kind of like overheating an engine. At some point, you have to stop and let the engine cool down. Besides, jumping randomly from one world to another is one thing. Traveling on a quest—that's different. We can't be sure where exactly we need to go."

I turned to Sam. "What about you?"

"When I was a Valkyrie, it would've been no problem. But now?" She shook her head. "You're a child of Frey. Your father is the god of growth and fertility. You should be able to coax Yggdrasil's branches close enough to let us jump on. Besides, it's your quest. You have the best chance of navigating. Just use the sculpture as a point of focus. Find us the quickest path."

She would've had better luck explaining calculus to me.

I felt stupid, but I knelt next to the sculpture. I touched the duckling at the end of the line. Cold crept up my arm. I sensed ice, fog, and darkness—somewhere harsh and unwelcoming.

"This," I decided, "is the quickest way to Niflheim."

"Excellent," Blitz said. "Let's not go there."

I was just reaching for the next duck when someone yelled, "MAGNUS CHASE!"

Two hundred yards away, on the opposite side of Charles Street, Captain Gunilla stood flanked by two other Valkyries. Behind them was a line of einherjar. I couldn't make out their expressions, but the gray looming mass of X the half-troll was unmistakable. Gunilla had drafted my own hallmates to fight against me.

My fingers twitched with anger. I wanted to get a meat hook and go fishing with Gunilla as bait. I reached for my pendant.

"Magnus, no," Sam said. "Concentrate on the ducks. We have to change worlds *now*."

On either side of Gunilla, the Valkyries slung glowing

spears from their backs. They yelled at the einherjar to ready
their weapons. Gunilla pulled two of her hammers and threw
them in our direction.

Sam deflected one with her shield. She knocked the other
aside with her ax, spinning the hammer into the nearest willow tree, where it embedded itself up to the handle. Across the
street, all three Valkyries rose into the air.

"I can't fight them all," Sam warned. "It's leave now or be
captured."

My anger turned to panic. I looked at the row of bronze
ducks, but my concentration was shattered. "I—I need more
time."

"We don't *have* time!" Sam deflected another hammer.
The force of the blow cracked her shield down the middle.

"Hearth." Blitzen nudged the elf's arm. "Now would be
good."

A frown tugged at the corners of Hearthstone's mouth. He
reached into his pouch and pulled out a runestone. He cupped
it in his hands and muttered to it silently, as if speaking to a
captured bird. He threw the stone into the air.

It exploded above us, creating a rune of burning golden
light:

Between Gunilla's hunting party and us, distance seemed
to elongate. The Valkyries flew toward us at top speed; my einherjar comrades drew their weapons and charged; but they
made no progress.

It reminded me of those cheap 1970s cartoons where a
character runs but the scenery behind him just keeps repeating

itself. Charles Street spiraled around our pursuers like a giant hamster wheel. For the first time, I got what Sam had told me about runes being able to change reality.

"*Raidho*," Blitzen said appreciatively. "It stands for the wheel, the journey. Hearthstone has bought you some time."

Only seconds, Hearth signed. *Hurry.*

He promptly collapsed into Sam's arms.

I ran my hands quickly across the bronze ducks. At the fourth one, I stopped. I felt warmth, safety . . . a sense of rightness.

"This one," I said.

"Well, open it!" Blitzen shouted.

I rose to my feet. Not sure what I was doing, I pulled my pendant from its chain. The Sword of Summer appeared in my hands. Its blade purred like a demented cat. I tapped it against the bronze duck and sliced upward.

The air parted like a curtain. Stretching in front of me, instead of a sidewalk, was an expanse of tree branches. The nearest one, as wide as Beacon Street, ran directly under us, maybe three feet down, suspended over a gray void. Unfortunately, the cut I'd made in the fabric of Midgard was already closing.

"Hurry!" I said. "Jump!"

Blitzen didn't hesitate. He leaped through the rift.

Over on Charles Street, Gunilla screamed in outrage. She and her Valkyries were still flying full-tilt on their cartoon hamster wheel, the einherjar stumbling along behind them.

"You are doomed, Magnus Chase!" Gunilla shouted. "We will pursue you to the ends of—"

With a loud *POP*, Hearth's spell broke. The einherjar fell

face-first in the street. The three Valkyries shot over our heads. Judging from the sound of breaking glass, they must have hit a building over on Arlington Street.

I didn't wait for my old hallmates to recover their senses.

I grabbed Hearth's left arm while Sam took his right. Together, we leaped into the World Tree.

THIRTY-SEVEN

I Am Trash-Talked by a Squirrel

I ALWAYS LIKED CLIMBING TREES.

My mom had been pretty understanding about that. She'd only get nervous if I got above twenty feet. Then a little tension crept into her voice. "Pumpkin, that branch may not hold you. Could you come down a little?"

On the World Tree, *every* branch would hold me. The biggest ones were wider than Interstate 93. The smallest were as large as your average redwood. As for Yggdrasil's trunk, it was so immense it just didn't compute. Each crevice in its surface seemed to lead to a different world, as if someone had wrapped tree bark around a column of television monitors glowing with a million different movies.

The wind roared, ripping at my new denim jacket. Beyond the tree's canopy I saw nothing but a hazy white glow. Below was no ground—just more branches crisscrossing the void. The tree had to be rooted somewhere, but I felt woozy and unbalanced—as if Yggdrasil and everything it contained, including my world, was free-floating in primordial mist—the Ginnungagap.

If I fell here, in the best-case scenario I'd hit another branch and break my neck. Worst-case scenario, I'd keep falling forever into the Great White Nothingness.

I must've been leaning forward, because Blitzen grabbed my arm. "Careful kid. First time in the tree will make you dizzy."

"Yeah, I noticed."

Hearthstone still sagged between Sam and me. He tried to find his footing, but his ankles kept bending in odd directions.

Sam stumbled. Her broken shield slipped from her grip and somersaulted into the abyss.

She crouched, a look of barely controlled panic in her eyes. "I liked Yggdrasil a lot better when I could fly."

"What about Gunilla and the others?" I asked. "Will they be able to follow us?"

"Not easily," Sam said. "They can open another portal, but it won't necessarily lead to the same branch of the tree. Still, we should keep moving. Being on Yggdrasil is not good for your sanity."

Hearthstone managed to stand on his own. He signed: *I'm okay. Let's go.* Though his hands were so shaky it looked more like: *You are a rabbit tunnel.*

We moved farther along the branch.

The Sword of Summer hummed in my hand, tugging me along like it knew where we were going. I hoped it did, anyway.

Hostile winds buffeted us from side to side. Branches swayed, throwing deep pools of shadow and brilliant patches of light across our path. A leaf the size of a canoe fluttered by.

"Stay focused," Blitzen told me. "That feeling you had when you opened the portal? Look for it again. Find us an exit."

After walking about a quarter of a mile, we found a smaller branch crossing directly under ours. My sword hummed louder, tugging to the right.

I looked at my friends. "I think we need to take this exit."

Changing branches might sound easy, but it involved sliding down ten feet from one curved surface to another, with the wind howling and the branches swaying apart. Amazingly, we managed it without anyone getting crushed or falling into oblivion.

Navigating the narrower branch was worse. It bobbed more violently under our feet. At one point I got flattened by a leaf—like a green tarp dropping on top of me out of nowhere. At another point I looked down and realized I was standing over a crack in the bark. Half a mile down, *inside* the branch, I could see a snow-capped mountain range, as if I were standing in a glass-bottom airplane.

We picked our way through a maze of lichen patches that looked like hills of burned marshmallows. I made the mistake of touching one. My hand sunk up to my wrist and I almost couldn't pull it free.

Finally the lichen dispersed into smaller clumps like burned marshmallow sofas. We followed our branch until it split into half a dozen unclimbable twigs. The Sword of Summer seemed to go to sleep in my hand.

"Well?" Sam asked.

I peered over the side. About thirty feet below us, a larger branch swayed. In the middle of that branch, a hot-tub-size knothole glowed with soft warm light.

"That's it," I said. "That's our way out."

Blitzen scowled. "You sure? Nidavellir isn't warm and glowy."

"I'm just telling you—the sword seems to think that's our destination."

Sam whistled silently. "Quite a jump. If we miss the hole . . ."

Hearthstone spelled out, *S-P-L-A-T*.

A gust of wind hit us, and Hearth stumbled. Before I could catch him, he fell backward into a clump of lichen. His legs were promptly swallowed in the marshmallow gunk.

"Hearth!" Blitzen scrambled to his side. He pulled at Hearth's arms, but the mucky lichen held on to his legs like a needy toddler.

"We can cut him out," said Sam. "Your sword, my ax. It'll take time. We'll have to be careful of his legs. But it could be worse."

Naturally, things got worse. From somewhere above us came an explosive *YARK!*

Blitzen crouched under his pith helmet. "Ratatosk! That damnable squirrel *always* appears at the worst time. Hurry with those blades!"

Sam cut into the lichen with her ax, but her blade stuck. "This is like cutting through melting tires! It's not going to be quick."

GO! Hearth signed. *Leave me.*

"Not an option," I said.

YAAAAARRRRK! The sound was much louder this time. A dozen branches above us, a large shadow passed across the leaves.

I hefted my sword. "We'll fight the squirrel. We can do that, right?"

Sam looked at me like I was mad. "Ratatosk is invulnerable. There is no fighting him. Our options are running, hiding, or dying."

"We can't run," I said. "And I've already died twice this week."

"So we hide." Sam unwrapped her hijab. "At least, Hearth and I do. I can cover two people, no more. You and Blitz run— find the dwarves. We'll meet up with you later."

"*What?*" I wondered if Utgard-Loki was messing with her brain somehow. "Sam, you can't hide under a green piece of silk! The squirrel can't be that stupid . . ."

She shook out the fabric. It grew to the size of a twin sheet, the colors rippling until the hijab was exactly the same brown and yellow and white of the lichen patch.

She's right, Hearth signed. *GO.*

Sam crouched next to him and pulled the hijab over them both, and they vanished, blending perfectly against the lichen.

"Magnus." Blitz tugged at my arm. "It's now or never." He pointed to the branch below. The knothole was closing.

At that moment, Ratatosk broke through foliage above. If you can imagine a Sherman tank covered in red fur, barreling down the side of a tree . . . well, the squirrel was *way* scarier than that. His front teeth were twin wedges of white enamel terror. His claws were scimitars. His eyes were sulfur yellow, burning with fury.

YARK! The squirrel's battle cry pierced my eardrums. A thousand insults were packed into that one sound, all of them invading my brain, drowning out any rational thought.

You have failed.

No one likes you.

You are dead.

Your dwarf's pith helmet is stupid.

You could not save your mother.

I fell to my knees. A sob built in my chest. I probably would have died then and there if Blitz hadn't hauled me up with all his dwarven strength and slapped me across the face.

I couldn't hear him, but I read his lips well enough: "NOW, KID!"

Gripping my hand in rough calloused fingers, he jumped off the branch, dragging me with him into the wind.

THIRTY-EIGHT

I Break Down in a Volkswagen

I STOOD IN A SUNLIT meadow with no memory of how I got there.

In the distance, wildflowers dusted rolling green hills. The breeze smelled of lavender. The light was warm and rich as if the air had turned to butter.

My thoughts moved sluggishly. Light . . . sunlight was bad for dwarves. I was pretty sure I'd been traveling with a dwarf—someone who had slapped me and saved my life.

"Blitz?"

He stood to my left, holding his pith helmet at his side.

"Blitz, your hat!"

I was afraid he'd already become stone.

Then he turned. His eyes were stormy and distant. "It's okay, kid. This isn't regular sunlight. We're not on Midgard anymore."

He sounded like he was talking through wax paper. The squirrel's yap had left a crackling in my ears and some corrosive thoughts rattling around in my brain.

"Ratatosk . . ." I couldn't finish the sentence. Just saying his name made me want to curl up in the fetal position.

"Yeah," Blitz said. "His bark is literally worse than his bite. He . . ." Blitz looked down, blinking rapidly. "He's the most destructive creature in the World Tree. He spends his time running up and down the trunk, carrying insults from the eagle who lives at the top to Nidhogg, the dragon who lives at the roots."

I gazed toward the hills. Faint sounds of music seemed to be coming from that direction, or maybe it was the static in my ears. "Why would a squirrel do that?"

"To damage the tree," Blitz said. "Ratatosk keeps the eagle and the dragon whipped into a frenzy. He tells them lies, rumors, nasty gossip about each other. His words can . . . well, you know what his words can do. The dragon Nidhogg is always chewing on the roots of the World Tree, trying to kill it. The eagle flaps his wings and creates windstorms that rip the branches and cause devastation throughout the Nine Worlds. Ratatosk makes sure the two monsters stay angry and in competition with each other, to see which one can destroy their end of Yggdrasil faster."

"But that's . . . crazy. The squirrel *lives* in the tree."

Blitz grimaced. "We all do, kid. People have destructive impulses. Some of us want to see the world in ruins just for the fun of it . . . even if we're ruined along with it."

Ratatosk's chatter echoed in my head: *You have failed. You could not save your mother.* The squirrel had driven me to despair, but I could see how his bark might stir up other emotions—hatred, bitterness, self-loathing.

"How did you keep your wits?" I asked Blitz. "When the squirrel barked, what did you hear?"

Blitz ran his fingers across the brim of his pith helmet, pinching the edge of the black veil. "Nothing I don't tell myself all the time, kid. We should get going."

He trudged off toward the hills. Despite his short stride, I had to power walk to keep up.

We crossed a stream where a picturesque little frog sat on a lily pad. Doves and falcons spiraled through the air like they were playing tag. I half expected a chorus line of fuzzy animals to pop out of the wildflowers and launch into a Disney musical number.

"I'm guessing this is not Nidavellir," I said as we climbed the hill.

Blitzen snorted. "No. Much worse."

"Alfheim?"

"Worse." Blitzen stopped just short of the crest and took a deep breath. "Come on. Let's get this over with."

At the top of the hill I froze. "Whoa."

Down the other side, green fields stretched to the horizon. Meadows were strewn with picnic blankets. Crowds of people were hanging out—eating, laughing, chatting, playing music, flying kites, tossing beach balls. It was the world's largest, most laid-back outdoor concert, minus the concert. Some folks were dressed in various bits of armor. Most had weapons, but they didn't seem very interested in using them.

In the shade of an oak tree, a couple of young ladies were sword fighting, but after crossing blades a few times, they got bored, dropped their weapons, and started chatting. Another guy lounged in a lawn chair, flirting with the girl on his left while he casually parried attacks from the guy standing on his right.

Blitz pointed to the crest of the next hill about half a mile away, where a strange palace gleamed. It looked like an upside-down Noah's Ark made of gold and silver.

"Sessrumnir," said Blitzen. "The Hall of Many Seats. If we're lucky, maybe she won't be home."

"Who?"

Instead of answering, he waded into the crowd.

We hadn't gone twenty feet before a guy on a nearby picnic blanket called, "Hey, Blitzen! What's up, dude?"

Blitzen ground his teeth so hard I could hear them popping. "Hello, Miles."

"Yeah, I'm good!" Miles raised his sword absently as another guy in beach trunks and a muscle shirt charged toward him with a battle-ax.

The attacker screamed, "DIE! Ha, ha, just kidding." Then he walked away eating a chocolate bar.

"So, Blitz," Miles said, "what brings you to Casa de Awesome?"

"Nice seeing you, Miles." Blitzen grabbed my arm and led me onward.

"Okay, cool!" Miles called after us. "Keep in touch!"

"Who was that?" I asked.

"Nobody."

"How do you know him?"

"I don't."

As we made our way toward the upside-down ark mansion, more people stopped and said hello to Blitzen. A few greeted me and complimented me on my sword, or my hair, or my shoes. One girl said, "Oh, nice ears!" Which didn't even make sense.

"Everybody is so—"

"Stupid?" Blitzen offered.

"I was going to say *mellow*."

He grunted. "This is Folkvanger, the Field of the Army . . . or you could translate it as the People's Battlefield."

"So this is Volkswagen." I scanned the crowds, wondering if I would spot my mother, but I couldn't imagine her in a place like this. There was too much lounging around, not enough action. My mom would've rousted these warriors to their feet, led them on a ten-mile hike, then insisted they set up their own campsites if they wanted any dinner. "They don't seem like much of an army."

"Yeah, well," Blitz said, "these fallen are just as powerful as the einherjar, but they have a different attitude. This realm is one little subsection of Vanaheim—sort of the Vanir gods' flipside version of Valhalla."

I tried to picture myself spending eternity here. Valhalla had its good points, but as far as I'd seen it didn't have picnics or beach balls, and I definitely wouldn't describe it as mellow. Still . . . I wasn't sure I liked Folkvanger any better.

"So half the worthy dead go here," I remembered, "half go to Valhalla. How do they pick who goes where? Is it a coin toss?"

"That would make more sense, actually."

"But I was trying to get us to Nidavellir. Why did we come here?"

Blitzen stared at the mansion atop the hill. "You were looking for the path we needed for our quest. That path led us through Folkvanger. Unfortunately, I think I know why. Let's go pay our respects before I lose my nerve."

As we approached the gates, I realized Sessrumnir wasn't just built to look like an upside-down ship. It actually *was* an upside-down ship. The rows of tall windows were oar slots. The sloping walls of the hull were made from clinkered gold planks riveted with silver nails. The main entrance had a long awning that would've served as a gangplank.

"Why is it a boat?" I asked.

"What?" Blitzen fiddled nervously with his carnation. "Not so unusual. Your Norse ancestors made lots of buildings by turning their ships upside down. In the case of Sessrumnir, when the Day of Doom comes around, they'll just flip the palace over and *voilà*, it's a vessel big enough for all the warriors of Folkvanger to sail nobly to their deaths. Sort of like we're doing now."

He led me inside.

I'd been expecting a gloomy interior like the hold of a ship, but the Hall of Many Seats was more like a cathedral. The ceiling rose all the way to the keel. The oar-hole windows crosshatched the air with bars of light. The entire space was open, no separate rooms or partitions—just clusters of sofas, comfy chairs, throw pillows, and freestanding hammocks, most of which were occupied by snoring warriors. I hoped the half million inhabitants of Folkvanger liked one another's company, because there was *no* privacy. Me being me, the main thing I wondered was where they all went to the bathroom.

Down the center of the hall ran an aisle of Persian carpets, flanked by braziers with glowing spheres of gold light. At the far end stood a throne on a raised dais.

Blitz marched in that direction, ignoring the warriors who greeted him with "Dude!" and "Sup, Dwarf Man!" and "Welcome home!"

Welcome home?

In front of the dais, a cozy fire crackled in the hearth. Piles of jewelry and precious gems glittered here and there as if somebody had swept them up just to get them off the floor. On either side of the steps lounged a calico house cat the size of a saber-toothed tiger.

The throne was carved from wood as soft and buttery as the light—linden wood, maybe. The back was draped with a cloak of downy feathers like on the underside of a falcon. In the throne itself sat the most beautiful woman I'd ever seen.

She looked maybe twenty years old, surrounded by an aura of golden radiance that made me realize what Blitzen meant earlier when he'd said the daylight here wasn't normal. The entire realm of Folkvanger was warm and bright, not because of the sun, but because it basked in this woman's power.

Her blond hair fell across her shoulder in a single long plait. Her white halter top showed off her tan shoulders and smooth midriff. Her knee-length skirt was belted with a gold braid holding a sheathed knife and a ring of keys. Around her neck was a dazzling piece of jewelry—a lacework collar of gold and gems, like Ran's net in miniature, except with rubies and diamonds instead of sailors' souls and hubcaps.

The woman fixed me with her sky-blue eyes. When she smiled, heat traveled from the tips of my ears right down to my toes. I would have done anything to make her keep smiling at me. If she'd told me to jump off the World Tree into oblivion, I would've done it in a second.

I remembered her picture from my old children's mythology book, and realized how ridiculously it undersold her beauty.

The goddess of love was very pretty! She had cats!

I knelt before my aunt, the twin sister of my father. "Freya."

"My dear Magnus," she said, "how nice to meet you in person!" She turned to Blitzen, who was glowering at his boots.

"And how are you, Blitzen?" asked the goddess.

Blitzen sighed. "I'm fine, Mom."

Freya Is Pretty! She Has Cats!

"MOM?" I WAS SO STARTLED I wasn't sure I'd said it aloud. "Wait . . . You, Blitzen. *Mom?*"

Blitzen kicked me in the shin.

Freya continued smiling. "I suppose my son didn't tell you? He's quite modest. Blitzen dear, you look very nice, but could you straighten your collar?"

Blitzen did, muttering under his breath, "Been a little busy running for my life."

"And, dear," Freya said, "are you sure about the vest?"

"Yes, Mom," Blitz grumbled, "I'm sure about the vest. Vests are making a comeback."

"Well, I suppose you know best." Freya winked at me. "Blitzen is a *genius* with fabrics and fashion. The other dwarves don't appreciate his expertise, but I think it's marvelous. He wants to open his own—"

"Anyway," Blitzen said, a little too loudly, "we're on this quest. . . ."

Freya clapped. "I know! It's very exciting. You're trying to get to Nidavellir to find out more about the rope Gleipnir. And so, naturally, the World Tree directed you first to me."

One of her cats clawed at a Persian rug, ripping several

thousand dollars of weaving into fluff. I tried not to imagine what the cat could do to me.

"So, Lady Freya," I said, "can you help us?"

"Of course!" said the goddess. "More importantly, you can help *me*."

"Here we go," said Blitzen.

"Son, be polite. First, Magnus, how are you faring with your sword?"

I missed a beat.

I guess I still didn't think of the Sword of Summer as *mine*. I pulled off the pendant and the blade took shape in my hand. In Freya's presence, it was silent and still like it was playing dead. Maybe it was afraid of cats.

"I haven't had much time to use it," I said. "Just got it back from Ran."

"Yes, I know." Freya's nose wrinkled with the slightest hint of distaste. "And you delivered an apple to Utgard-Loki in exchange. Perhaps not the wisest move, but I won't criticize your choices."

"You just did," Blitzen said.

The goddess ignored his comment. "At least you didn't promise *me* to Utgard-Loki. Usually when giants make demands, they want apples *and* my hand in marriage." She flipped her braid over her shoulder. "It gets very tiresome."

I had a hard time looking at Freya without staring. There really wasn't anything safe to focus on—her eyes, her lips, her belly button. I silently scolded myself, *This is Blitzen's mom! This is my aunt!*

I decided to focus on her left eyebrow. There was nothing entrancing about a left eyebrow.

"So anyway," I said, "I haven't really killed anything yet with the eyebrow—I mean the sword."

Freya sat forward. "*Killed* anything with it? Oh, dear, that's the least of its powers. Your first task is to befriend the sword. Have you done this?"

I imagined the sword and me sitting side by side in a movie theater, a tub of popcorn between us. I imagined dragging the sword on a leash, taking it for a walk through the park. "How do I befriend a sword?"

"Ah . . . well, if you have to ask—"

"Look, Aunt Freya," I said, "couldn't I just give the sword to you for safekeeping? It's a Vanir weapon. You're Frey's sister. You've got a few hundred thousand well-armed, laid-back warriors to guard it from Surt—"

"Oh, no," she said sadly. "The sword is already in your hands, Magnus. You summoned it from the river. You have laid claim to it. The best we can hope for is that *Sumarbrander*, the Sword of Summer, will allow you to use it. Keeping it from Surt is *your* job now, as long as you manage to stay alive."

"I hate my job."

Blitz elbowed me. "Don't say that, kid. You'll offend the blade."

I looked down at the gleaming runes on the blade. "I'm sorry, long sharp piece of metal. Did that hurt your feelings? Also, if you *allow* people to wield you, why would you allow an evil fire giant to do so? Why wouldn't you want to go back to Frey, or at least his lovely sister here?"

The sword did not reply.

"Magnus," said the goddess, "this is no jesting matter. The sword is fated to belong to Surt, sooner or later. You know this. The sword cannot escape its destiny any more than you can escape yours."

I envisioned Loki chuckling as he lounged on the High Seat of Odin. *Our choices can alter the details.* That's *how we rebel against destiny.*

"Besides," Freya said, "the sword would never allow me to use it. Sumarbrander holds me partially responsible for its loss. . . . It resents me almost as much as it resents Frey."

Maybe it was my imagination, but the sword seemed to become colder and heavier.

"But it's Frey's sword," I protested.

Blitzen grunted. "It *was*. I told you, kid, he gave it away for love."

The calico cat on Freya's right rolled over and stretched. Its spotted tummy was pretty cute, except for the fact that I kept imagining how many warriors it could comfortably digest.

"When Frey sat on Odin's throne," continued the goddess, "he did so for *my* sake. It was a dark time for me. I was wandering the Nine Worlds, grieving and bereft. Frey hoped that by sitting in the throne, he might find me. Instead, the throne showed him his heart's desire—a frost giantess, Gerd. He fell madly in love with her."

I stared at Freya's eyebrow. Her story wasn't helping my opinion of my dad.

"He fell in love at first sight . . . with a frost giantess."

"Oh, she was beautiful," Freya said. "Silver to Frey's gold, cold to his warmth, winter to his summer. You've heard that opposites attract? She was his perfect match. But she was a giant. She would never agree to marry a Vanir. Her family would not allow it. Knowing this, Frey fell into despair. Crops stopped growing. Summer lost its warmth. Finally, Frey's servant and best friend came to ask him what was wrong."

"Skirnir," I said. "The dude who got the sword."

Freya frowned. "Yes. *Him*."

Blitzen took a step back, like he was afraid his mom might explode. For the first time, I realized how scary the goddess could look—beautiful, yes, but also terrifying and powerful. I imagined her armed with a shield and spear, riding with the Valkyries. If I saw her on the battlefield, I would run the other direction.

"Skirnir promised he could deliver Gerd within nine days," said the goddess. "All he required was a small fee for his services—the Sword of Summer. Frey was so love-stricken that he asked no questions. The sword . . . I can only imagine how it felt when it was betrayed by its master. It allowed Skirnir to wield it, though not happily."

Freya sighed. "That is why the sword will never allow Frey to use it again. And that is why, at Ragnarok, Frey is fated to die because he does not have his weapon."

I wasn't sure what to say. *Bummer* didn't seem to cover it. I remembered Loki's warning about sitting on Odin's throne, looking for my heart's desire. What would I look for? My mother's whereabouts. Would I give up a sword to find her? Of course. Would I risk getting killed or even hastening Doomsday? Yes. So maybe I couldn't judge my father.

Blitz gripped my arm. "Don't look so glum, kid. I have faith in you."

Freya's expression softened. "Yes, Magnus. You *will* learn to use the sword—and I don't mean just swinging it like a brute. Once you discover its full abilities, you will be formidable indeed."

"I don't suppose it comes with a user's manual?"

Freya laughed gently. "I'm sorry I didn't get you in Folkvanger, Magnus. You would've been a good addition to my followers. But Valhalla called you first. It was meant to be."

I wanted to argue that the Norns, the einherjar, and the captain of the Valkyries didn't seem to think so.

Thinking about Gunilla made me remember our flight into the World Tree, and Sam and Hearthstone hiding under a veil from a murderous squirrel. "Our friends . . . we got separated from them on Yggdrasil. Freya, do you know if they made it here safely?"

Freya peered into the distance. "They are not in Folkvanger. I see them . . . Yes. Wait. Lost them again. Ah!" She winced. "That was a close call, but they're fine for the moment. A resourceful pair. I sense they will not come here. You must continue on and meet them in Nidavellir. Which brings us to your quest."

"And how we can help you," Blitz said.

"Exactly, darling. Your need brought you here. *Need* speaks strongly when you travel the World Tree. After all, that's how my poor son found himself being a bondservant to Mimir."

"We're not having this discussion again," Blitz said.

Freya turned over her lovely hands. "Fine. Moving along. As you well know, the dwarves created the rope Gleipnir, which bound Fenris Wolf. . . ."

"Yes, Mom," Blitz said, rolling his eyes. "Everyone learns that nursery rhyme in kindergarten."

I squinted at him. "Nursery rhyme?"

" '*Gleipnir, Gleipnir, strong and stout, wrapped the Wolf around the snout.*' Humans don't learn that one?"

"Um . . . I don't think so."

"At any rate," said the goddess, "the dwarves will be able to tell you more about how the rope was made, and how it might be replaced."

"Replaced?" I willed the sword back into pendant form. Even so, hanging around my neck, it seemed to weigh a hundred pounds. "I thought the idea was to keep the rope from getting cut in the first place."

"Ah . . ." Freya tapped her lips. "Magnus, I don't want to discourage you, but I'd say there is a good chance, perhaps a seventy-five percent chance, that even if you keep the sword from Surt, the fire giant will still find a way to free Fenris Wolf. In such a case, you must be prepared with a replacement rope."

My tongue felt almost as heavy as my sword pendant. "Yeah, that's not at all discouraging. The last time the Wolf was free, didn't it take all the gods working together to bind him?"

Freya nodded. "It took three tries and much trickery. Poor Tyr lost his hand. But don't worry. The Wolf will never fall for the hand-in-the-mouth trick again. If it comes to that, you will have to find another way to bind him."

I bet Miles out in the People's Battlefield didn't have these sorts of problems. I wondered if he'd be interested in trading places for a while, going after Fenris Wolf while I played volleyball. "Freya, can you at least tell us where the Wolf *is*?"

"On Lyngvi—the Isle of Heather." The goddess tapped her chin. "Let's see, today is Thor's Day the sixteenth."

"You mean Thursday?"

"That's what I said. The island will rise on the full moon six days from now, on the twenty-second, which is Woden's Day."

"Wednesday?" I asked.

"That's what I said. So you should have plenty of time to get my earrings before you seek out the Wolf. Unfortunately, the island's location shifts every year as the branches of Yggdrasil sway in the winds of the void. The dwarves should be able to help you locate it. Blitzen's father knew the way. Others might as well."

At the mention of his father, Blitz's face clouded over. Very carefully, he took the carnation from his vest and tossed it into the hearth fire. "And what do you want, Mother? What's your part in this?"

"Oh, my needs are simple." Her fingers fluttered over her golden lace collar. "I want you to commission some earrings to match my necklace Brisingamen. Something nice. Not too flashy, but noticeable. Blitzen, you have excellent taste. I trust you."

Blitzen glared at the nearest pile of riches, which contained dozens, maybe hundreds of earrings. "You know who I have to talk to in Nidavellir. Only one dwarf has the skill to replace the rope Gleipnir."

"Yes," Freya agreed. "Fortunately, he's also an excellent jeweler, so he will be able to accommodate both our requests."

"Unfortunately," said Blitzen, "this particular dwarf wants me dead."

Freya waved aside his objection. "Oh, he can't possibly. Not after all this time."

"Dwarves have very long memories, Mother."

"Well, generous payment will soften his attitude. I can help with that." She called across the hall, "Dmitri? I need you!"

From one of the sofa clusters, three guys scrambled to their feet, grabbed their musical instruments, and hustled over. They wore matching Hawaiian shirts, Bermuda shorts, and sandals. Their hair was greased back in pompadours. The first guy had a guitar. The second had bongos. The third had a triangle.

The guy with the guitar bowed to Freya. "At your service, my lady!"

Freya gave me a conspiratorial smile, as if she had some wonderful secret to share. "Magnus, meet Dmitri and the Do-Runs, the best band you've never heard of. They died in 1963, just as they were about to get their big break. So sad! They valiantly swerved their car off Route One to spare a busload of schoolchildren from a terrible collision. In honor of their selfless deaths, I brought them here to Folkvanger."

"And we're very grateful, my lady," said Dmitri. "Being your house band has been a sweet gig!"

"Dmitri, I need to cry," she said. "Could you please play the one about my lost husband? I love that song."

"I hate that song," Blitzen mumbled under his breath.

The trio hummed. Dmitri strummed a chord.

I whispered to Blitzen, "Why does your mom need to cry?"

He turned toward me and made a finger-down-the-throat gesture. "Just watch. You'll see."

Dmitri began to sing:

> "Oh, Odur! Od, Od, Odur,
> Where is that Odur; where is my love?"

The other two musicians harmonized on the chorus:

> *"Od wanders far, my Odur is missing,*
> *How odd it is, not to be kissing*
> *My Odur! My sweet Od Odur!"*

Triangle.

Bongo solo.

Blitzen whispered, "Her godly husband was an Aesir named Odur, Od for short."

I wasn't sure which name was worse.

"He disappeared?" I guessed.

"Two thousand years ago," Blitzen said. "Freya went looking for him, disappeared herself for almost a century while she searched. She never found him, but that's why Frey sat in Odin's chair in the first place—to look for his sister."

The goddess leaned forward and cupped her face in her hands. She drew a shaky breath. When she looked up again, she was weeping—but her tears were small pellets of red gold. She wept until her hands were full of glittering droplets.

"Oh, Odur!" she sobbed. "Why did you leave me? I miss you still!"

She sniffled and nodded to the musicians. "Thank you, Dmitri. That's enough."

Dmitri and his friends bowed. Then the best band I wished I'd never heard of shuffled away.

Freya raised her cupped hands. Out of nowhere, a leather pouch appeared, hovering above her lap. Freya spilled her tears into the bag.

"Here, my son." Freya passed the pouch to Blitzen. "That

should be enough payment if Eitri Junior is at all reasonable."

Blitzen stared glumly at the pouch of tears. "The only problem is, he's *not*."

"You will succeed!" Freya said. "The fate of my earrings is in your hands!"

I scratched the back of my neck. "Uh, Lady Freya . . . thanks for the tears and all, but couldn't you just go to Nidavellir and pick out your own earrings? I mean, isn't shopping half the fun?"

Blitzen shot me a warning look.

Freya's blue eyes turned a few degrees colder. Her fingertips traced the filigree of her necklace. "No, Magnus, I *can't* just go shopping in Nidavellir. You *know* what happened when I bought Brisingamen from the dwarves. Do you want that to happen again?"

Actually, I had no idea what she was talking about, but she didn't wait for an answer.

"Every time I go to Nidavellir, I get myself in trouble," she said. "It's not my fault! The dwarves *know* my weakness for beautiful jewelry. Believe me, it's *much* better that I send you. Now, if you'll excuse me, it's time for our evening luau with optional combat. Good-bye, Magnus. Good-bye, my darling Blitzen!"

The floor opened beneath us, and we fell into darkness.

FORTY

My Friend Evolved from a— Nope. I Can't Say It

I DON'T REMEMBER LANDING.

I found myself on a dark street on a cold, cloudy night. Three-story clapboard row houses edged the sidewalk. At the end of the block, a tavern's grimy windows glowed with neon drink signs.

"This is Southie," I said. "Around D Street."

Blitzen shook his head. "This is Nidavellir, kid. It looks like South Boston . . . or rather, South Boston looks like *it*. I told you, Boston is the nexus. The Nine Worlds blend together there and affect one another. Southie has a definite dwarvish feeling to it."

"I thought Nidavellir would be underground. With claustrophobic tunnels and—"

"Kid, that's a cavern ceiling above your head. It's just a long way up and hidden by air pollution. We don't have daytime here. It's this dark all the time."

I stared into the murky clouds. After being in Freya's realm, the world of the dwarves seemed oppressive, but it also seemed more familiar, more . . . genuine. I guess no true Bostonian would trust a place that was sunny and pleasant all the time. But a gritty, perpetually cold and gloomy neighborhood? Throw in a couple of Dunkin' Donuts locations, and I'm right at home.

Blitz wrapped his pith helmet in its dark netting. The

whole thing collapsed into a small black handkerchief, which he tucked into his coat pocket. "We should get going."

"We're not going to talk about what happened up there in Volkswagen?"

"What's there to say?"

"For one thing, we're cousins."

Blitz shrugged. "I'm happy to be your cousin, kid, but children of the gods don't put much stock in that sort of connection. Godly family lines are so tangled—thinking about it will drive you crazy. Everybody's related to everybody."

"But you're a demigod," I said. "That's a good thing, right?"

"I hate the word *demigod*. I prefer *born with a target on my back*."

"Come on, Blitz. Freya is your mom. That's important information you kinda forgot to mention."

"Freya is my mother," he agreed. "A lot of svartalfs are descended from Freya. Down here, it's not such a big deal. She mentioned how she got Brisingamen? A few millennia ago she was strolling through Nidavellir—who knows why—and she came across these four dwarves who were crafting the necklace. She was obsessed. She had to have it. The dwarves said sure, for the right price. Freya had to marry each of them, one after the other, for one day each."

"She . . ." I wanted to say, *Gross, she married four dwarves?* Then I remembered who was telling the story. "Oh."

"Yeah." Blitz sounded miserable. "She had four dwarvish children, one for each marriage."

I frowned. "Wait. If she was married for one day to each dwarf and a pregnancy lasts . . . the math doesn't work out on that."

"Don't ask me. Goddesses live by their own rules. Anyway, she got the necklace. She was ashamed of herself for marrying dwarves. Tried to keep it a secret. But the thing is, she *loved* dwarven jewelry. She kept coming back to Nidavellir to pick out new pieces, and every time . . ."

"Wow."

Blitzen's shoulders slumped. "That's the main difference between dark elves and regular dwarves. The svartalfs are taller and generally more handsome because we have Vanir blood. We're descended from Freya. You say I'm a demigod. I say I'm a receipt. My dad crafted a pair of earrings for Freya. She married him for a day. She couldn't resist his craftsmanship. He couldn't resist her beauty. Now she sends me to purchase a new pair of earrings because she's tired of the old ones and Asgard forbid she find herself saddled with another little Blitzen."

The bitterness in his voice could've melted iron plating. I wanted to tell him I understood how he felt, but I wasn't sure I did. Even if I never knew my dad, I'd had my mom. That had always been enough for me. For Blitzen . . . not so much. I wasn't sure what had happened to his father, but I remembered what he'd told me at the Esplanade lagoon: *You're not the only one who's lost family to the wolves, kid.*

"Come on," he told me. "If we stand in the street any longer, we'll get mugged for this bag of tears. Dwarves can smell red gold a mile away." He pointed to the bar on the corner. "I'll buy you a drink at Nabbi's Tavern."

Nabbi's restored my faith in dwarves, because it was in fact a claustrophobic tunnel. The ceiling was a low-clearance hazard. The walls were papered with old fight posters like DONNER

THE DESTROYER VS. MINI-MURDER, ONE NIGHT ONLY! featuring pictures of muscular snarling dwarves in wrestling masks.

Mismatched tables and chairs were occupied by a dozen mismatched dwarves—some svartalfs like Blitzen who could easily have passed for human, some much shorter guys who could have easily passed for garden gnomes. A few of the patrons glanced at us, but nobody seemed shocked that I was a human . . . if they even realized. The idea that I could pass for a dwarf was pretty disturbing.

The most unreal thing about the bar was Taylor Swift's "Blank Space" blasting from the speakers.

"Dwarves like human music?" I asked Blitzen.

"You mean humans like *our* music."

"But . . ." I had a sudden image of Taylor Swift's mom and Freya having a girls' night out in Nidavellir. "Never mind."

As we made our way toward the bar, I realized that the furniture wasn't just mismatched. Every single table and chair was unique—apparently handcrafted from various metals, with different designs and upholstery. One table was shaped like a bronze wagon wheel with a glass top. Another had a tin and brass chessboard hammered into the surface. Some chairs had wheels. Others had adjustable booster seats. Some had massage controls or propellers on the back.

Over by the left wall, three dwarves were playing darts. The board's rings rotated and blew steam. One dwarf tossed his dart, which buzzed toward the target like a tiny drone. While it was still in flight, another dwarf took a shot. His dart rocketed toward the drone dart and exploded, knocking it out of the air.

The first dwarf just grunted. "Nice shot."

Finally we reached the polished oak bar, where Nabbi himself was waiting. I could tell who he was because of my highly trained deductive mind, and also because his stained yellow apron read HI! I'M NABBI.

I thought he was the tallest dwarf I'd met so far until I realized he was standing on a catwalk behind the counter. Nabbi was actually only two feet tall, including the shock of black hair that stuck up from his scalp like a sea urchin. His clean-shaven face made me appreciate why dwarves wear beards. Without one, Nabbi was gods-awful ugly. He had no chin to speak of. His mouth puckered sourly.

He scowled at us like we'd tracked in mud.

"Greetings, Blitzen, son of Freya," he said. "No explosions in my bar this time, I hope?"

Blitzen bowed. "Greetings, Nabbi, son of Loretta. To be fair, I wasn't the one who brought the grenades. Also, this is my friend Magnus, son of—"

"Um. Son of Natalie."

Nabbi nodded to me. His busy eyebrows were fascinating. They seemed to move like live caterpillars.

I reached for a bar stool, but Blitzen stopped me.

"Nabbi," he said formally, "may my friend use this stool? What is its name and history?"

"That stool is Rear-Rester," said Nabbi. "Crafted by Gonda. Once it held the tush of the master smith Alviss. Use it in comfort, Magnus, son of Natalie. And Blitzen, you may sit on Keister-Home, famed among stools, made by yours truly. It survived the Great Bar Fight of 4109 A.M.!"

"My thanks." Blitzen climbed on his stool, which was pol-ished oak with a velvet-padded seat. "A fine Keister-Home it is!"

Nabbi looked at me expectantly. I tried my stool, which was hard steel with no cushion. It wasn't much of a Rear-Rester. It was more of a Magnus Mangler, but I tried for a smile. "Yep, that's a nice stool all right!"

Blitzen rapped his knuckles on the bar. "Mead for me, Nabbi. And for my friend—"

"Uh, soda or something?" I wasn't sure I wanted to be walking around Dwarven Southie with a mead buzz.

Nabbi filled two mugs and set them in front of us. Blitzen's goblet was gold on the inside, silver on the outside, decorated with images of dancing dwarf women.

"That cup is Golden Bowl," said Nabbi. "Made by my father, Darbi. And this one"—he nudged my pewter tankard—"is Boom Daddy, made by yours truly. Always ask for a refill before you reach the bottom of the cup. Otherwise"—he splayed his fingers—"boom, Daddy!"

I really hoped he was kidding, but I decided to take small sips.

Blitz drank his mead. "Mmm. A fine cup for quaffing! And now that we are past the formalities, Nabbi . . . we need to speak with Junior."

A vein throbbed in Nabbi's left temple. "Do you have a death wish?"

Blitz reached into his pouch. He slid a single gold tear across the counter. "This one is for you," he said in a low voice. "Just for making the call. Tell Junior we have more. All we want is a chance to barter."

After my experience with Ran, the word *barter* made me

even more uncomfortable than Rear-Rester. Nabbi looked back and forth between Blitzen and the tear, his expression vacillating between apprehension and greed. Finally the greed won. The barkeep snatched the drop of gold.

"I'll make the call. Enjoy your drinks." He climbed off his catwalk and disappeared into the kitchen.

I turned to Blitz. "A few questions."

He chuckled. "Only a few?"

"What does 4109 A.M. mean? Is it the time, or—"

"Dwarves count years from the creation of our species," Blitz said. "A.M. is *After Maggots*."

I decided my ears must still be defective from Ratatosk's barking. "Say what?"

"The creation of the world . . . Come on, you know the story. The gods killed the largest of the giants, Ymir, and used his flesh to create Midgard. Nidavellir developed *under* Midgard, where maggots ate into the giant's dead flesh and created tunnels. Some of those maggots evolved, with a little help from the gods, into dwarves."

Blitzen looked proud of this historical tidbit. I decided to do my best to erase it from my long-term memory.

"Different question," I said. "Why does my goblet have a name?"

"Dwarves are craftsmen," said Blitzen. "We're serious about the things we make. You humans—you make a thousand crappy chairs that all look alike and all break within a year. When *we* make a chair, we make one chair to last a lifetime, a chair unlike any other in the world. Cups, furniture, weapons . . . every crafted item has a soul and a name. You can't appreciate something unless it's good enough for a name."

I studied my tankard, which was painstakingly engraved with runes and wave designs. I wished it had a different name—like *No Way Will I Explode*—but I had to admit it was a nice cup.

"And calling Nabbi son of Loretta?" I asked. "Or me the son of Natalie?"

"Dwarves are matriarchal. We trace our lineage through our mothers. Again, it makes much more sense than your patrilineal way. After all, one can only be born from a single biological mother. Unless you are the god Heimdall. He had nine biological mothers. But that's another story."

Synapses melted in my brain. "Let's move along. Freya's tears . . . red gold? Sam told me that's the currency of Asgard."

"Yes. But Freya's tears are one hundred percent pure. The finest red gold in creation. For the pouch of tears we're carrying, most dwarves would give their right eyeballs."

"So this guy Junior—he'll bargain with us?"

"Either that," Blitz said, "or he'll chop us into small pieces. You want some nachos while we wait?"

Blitz Makes a Bad Deal

I HAD TO HAND IT TO NABBI. He served good near-death nachos.

I was halfway through my plate of guacamole-enhanced tastiness when Junior showed up. On first sight, I wondered if it would be faster just to drain Boom Daddy and go boom, because I didn't like our chances of bartering with the old dwarf.

Junior looked about two hundred years old. Scraps of gray hair clung to his liver-spotted head. His beard gave *scraggly* a bad name. His malicious brown eyes flitted around the bar as if he were thinking, *I hate that. I hate that. And I* really *hate that.* He wasn't physically intimidating, shuffling along with his gold-plated walker, but he was flanked by a pair of dwarven bodyguards, each so burly that they could've been used as NFL tackle dummies.

The other customers got up and quietly left, like in a scene from an old Western. Blitzen and I both stood.

"Junior." Blitz bowed. "Thank you for meeting with us."

"Some nerve," Junior snarled.

"Would you like my seat?" Blitzen offered. "It is Keister-Home, made by—"

"No, thanks," Junior said. "I'll stand, compliments of my

walker, Granny Shuffler, famous among geriatric products, made by Nurse Bambi, my private assistant."

I bit the inside of my cheek. I doubted that laughing would be good diplomacy.

"This is Magnus, son of Natalie," Blitzen said.

The old dwarf glared at me. "I know who he is. Found the Sword of Summer. You couldn't wait until after I died? I'm too old for this Ragnarok nonsense."

"My bad," I said. "I should have checked with you before I got attacked by Surt and sent to Valhalla."

Blitzen coughed. The bodyguards appraised me like I might have just made their day more interesting.

Junior cackled. "I like you. You're rude. Let's see this blade, then."

I showed him my magic pendant trick. In the dim neon lights of the barroom, the blade's runes glowed orange and green.

The old dwarf sucked his teeth. "That's Frey's blade, all right. Bad news."

"Then, perhaps," Blitzen said, "you'll be willing to help us?"

"*Help you?*" Junior wheezed. "Your father was my nemesis! *You* besmirched my reputation. And you want my help. You've got iron guts, Blitzen, I'll give you that."

The tendons in Blitz's neck looked like they might bust his well-starched collar. "This isn't about our family feud, Junior. This is about the rope. It's about securing Fenris Wolf."

"Oh, of course it is." Junior sneered at his bodyguards. "The fact that *my father*, Eitri Senior, was the only dwarf talented enough to *make* Gleipnir, and your father, Bilì, spent his life questioning the quality of the rope—that has nothing to do with it!"

Blitzen clenched his pouch of red gold tears. I was afraid he might smack Junior upside the head with it. "The Sword of Summer is right here. In just six Midgardian nights, Surt is planning to free the Wolf. We're going to do our best to stop him, but you *know* the rope Gleipnir is beyond its expiration date. We need information about the Wolf's bindings. More importantly, we need a replacement rope just in case. Only you have the talent to make one."

Junior cupped his ear. "Say that last part again."

"You're talented, you crusty old—" Blitzen stopped. "Only you have the skill to make a new rope."

"True." Junior smirked. "It so happens I *have* a replacement rope already made. Not because of any problems with Gleipnir, mind you, or because of any of your family's scandalous accusations about its quality—just because I like to be prepared. Unlike *your* father, I might add, going off alone to check on Fenris Wolf like an idiot and getting himself killed."

I had to step in front of Blitzen to keep him from attacking the old dwarf.

"Okay, then!" I said. "Guys, this isn't the time. Junior, if you've got a new rope, that's great. Let's talk price. And, um, we'll also need a nice set of earrings."

"Heh." Junior wiped his mouth. "Of *course* you will. For Blitzen's mother, no doubt. What are you offering in payment?"

"Blitzen," I said, "show him."

Blitz's eyes still danced with rage, but he opened the pouch and spilled some red gold tears into his palm.

"Huh," said Junior. "An acceptable price . . . or it *would* be, if it wasn't from Blitzen. I'll sell you what you want for that pouch of tears, but first my family's honor must be satisfied.

It's high time we settled this feud. What do you say, son of Freya? A contest—you and me. The traditional rules, the traditional wager."

Blitzen backed into the bar. He squirmed so badly I could almost believe he had evolved from maggots. (ERASE. *Bad,* long-term memory. ERASE!)

"Junior," he said, "you know I don't—I couldn't possibly—"

"Shall we say tomorrow at mossglow?" Junior asked. "The panel of judges can be headed by a neutral party—perhaps Nabbi, who I'm sure is not eavesdropping behind the bar right now."

Something banged against the catwalk. From below the counter, Nabbi's muffled voice said, "I would be honored."

"There you are, then!" Junior smiled. "Well, Blitzen? I have challenged you according to our ancient customs. Will you defend the honor of your family?"

"I . . ." Blitzen hung his head. "Where should we meet?"

"The forges in Kenning Square," Junior said. "Oh, this will be amusing. Come on, boys. I have to tell Nurse Bambi about it!"

The old dwarf shuffled out with his bodyguards in tow. As soon as they were gone, Blitzen collapsed on Keister-Home and drained Golden Bowl.

Nabbi emerged from behind the counter. His caterpillar eyebrows wriggled with concern as he refilled Blitz's goblet. "This one's on the house, Blitzen. It's been nice knowing you."

He went back to the kitchen, leaving Blitz and me alone with Taylor Swift singing "I Know Places." The lyrics took on a whole new meaning in a subterranean dwarf world.

"Are you going to explain what just happened?" I asked Blitz. "What is this contest at mossglow? Also, what is mossglow?"

"Mossglow . . ." Blitzen stared into his cup. "Dwarf version of dawn, when the moss begins to glow. As for the contest . . ." He swallowed back a sob. "It's nothing. I'm sure you'll be able to continue the quest without me."

Just then the barroom doors burst open. Sam and Hearthstone tumbled inside like they'd been pushed from a moving car.

"They're alive!" I jumped up. "Blitz, look!"

Hearthstone was so excited he couldn't even sign. He rushed over and almost tackled Blitzen off his stool.

"Hey, buddy." Blitz patted his back absently. "Yeah, I'm glad to see you, too."

Sam didn't hug me, but she managed a smile. She was scratched up and covered with leaves and twigs, but she didn't look badly hurt. "Magnus, glad you haven't died yet. I want to be there for that."

"Thanks, al-Abbas. What happened to you guys?"

She shrugged. "We hid under the hijab as long as we could."

With all the other stuff going on, I'd forgotten about the scarf. "Yeah, what was that about? You've got an invisibility hijab?"

"It doesn't make me invisible. It's just camouflage. All Valkyries are given swan cloaks to help us hide when necessary. I just made mine a hijab."

"But you weren't a swan. You were tree moss."

"It can do different things. Anyway, we waited until the squirrel left. The barking left me in bad shape, but, thankfully, Hearth wasn't affected. We climbed Yggdrasil for a while—"

A moose tried to eat us, Hearth signed.

"Excuse me?" I asked. "A moose?"

Hearth grunted in exasperation. He spelled out: *D-E-E-R. Same sign for both animals.*

"Oh, that's much better," I said. "A deer tried to eat you."

"Yes," Sam agreed. "Dvalinn or maybe Duneyrr—one of the stags that roam the World Tree. We got away, took a wrong turn into Alfheim . . ."

Hearthstone shuddered, then simply signed, *Hate.*

"And here we are." Sam eyed Blitzen, whose expression was still blank with shock. "So . . . what's going on?"

I told them about our visit with Freya, then our conversation with Junior. Hearthstone steadied himself on the bar. He spelled with one hand: *M-a-k-i-n-g?* Then he shook his head vehemently.

"What do you mean, *making*?" I asked.

"A making," Blitz muttered into his goblet, "is the dwarven contest. It tests our crafting skills."

Sam tapped her fingers on her ax. "Judging from your expression, I'm guessing you don't trust your skills."

"I am rubbish at crafting," Blitzen said.

Not true, Hearth protested.

"Hearthstone," Blitzen said, "even if I was *excellent* at crafting, Junior is the most skilled dwarf alive. He'll destroy me."

"Come on," I said. "You'll do fine. And if you lose, we'll find another way to get that rope."

Blitzen looked at me mournfully. "It's worse than that, kid. If I lose, I pay the traditional price: my head."

FORTY-TWO

We Have a Pre-decapitation Party, with Egg Rolls

CRASHING AT BLITZEN'S apartment was the high point of our trip. Not that that was saying much.

Blitz rented the third floor of a row house across the street from Svartalf Mart (yes, that's a real thing). Considering the fact that he was due to be decapitated the next day, he was a good host. He apologized for not cleaning up (though the place looked spotless to me), microwaved some egg rolls, and brought out a liter of Diet Sergeant Pepper and a six-pack of Fjalar's Foaming Mead, each bottle uniquely handcrafted in a different color of glass.

His furniture was spare but stylish: an L-shaped sofa and two space-age armchairs. They probably had names and were famous among living-room furniture, but Blitzen didn't introduce them. Neatly arranged on the coffee table was a spread of dwarf men's fashion and interior design magazines.

While Sam and Hearth sat with Blitz, trying to console him, I paced the room. I felt angry and guilty that I'd put Blitzen in such a tight spot. He'd already risked enough for me. He'd spent two years on the streets watching out for me when he could've been here, kicking back with egg rolls and foaming mead. He'd tried to protect me by attacking the lord of the fire giants with a toy sign. Now he was going to lose his head in a craft-off with an evil senior citizen.

Also . . . the dwarven philosophy of crafting had unsettled me. In Midgard, most things were breakable, replaceable junk. I'd *lived* off that junk for the last two years—picking through what people discarded, finding bits I could use or sell or at least make a fire with.

I wondered what it would be like living in Nidavellir, where every item was crafted to be a lifetime work of art—right down to your cup or your chair. It might get annoying to have to recite the deeds of your shoes before you put them on in the morning, but at least you'd know they were amazing shoes.

I wondered about the Sword of Summer. Freya had told me to befriend it. She'd implied that the weapon had thoughts and feelings.

Every crafted item has a soul, Blitz had told me.

Maybe I hadn't properly introduced myself. Maybe I needed to treat the sword like another companion. . . .

"Blitz, you must have a specialty," Samirah was saying. "What did you study in trade school?"

"Fashion." Blitzen sniffled. "I designed my own degree program. But clothing isn't a recognized craft. They'll expect me to hammer molten ingots or tinker with machinery! I'm no good at that!"

You are, Hearth signed.

"Not under pressure," Blitz said.

"I don't get it," I said. "Why does the loser have to die? How do they decide the winner?"

Blitzen stared at the cover of *Dwarf Quarterly—New Looks for Spring! 100 Uses for Warg Leather!* "Each contestant makes three items. They can be anything. At the end of the day, the judges rate each item according to its usefulness, beauty, quality, whatever. They can assign points any way they wish. The contestant with the most overall points wins. The other guy dies."

"You must not have a lot of competitions," I said, "if the loser always gets decapitated."

"That's the traditional wager," Blitz said. "Most people don't insist on it anymore. Junior is old-fashioned. Also, he hates me."

"Something about Fenris Wolf and your dad?"

Hearth shook his head to shut me up, but Blitzen patted his knee. "It's okay, buddy. They deserve to know."

Blitz leaned back on the sofa. He seemed suddenly calmer about his impending doom, which I found unsettling. I kind of wanted him to be punching walls.

"I told you dwarven items are made for life?" he said. "Well . . . *lifetime* for a dwarf can mean hundreds of years."

I studied Blitz's beard, wondering if he dyed out the gray whiskers. "How old are you?"

"Twenty," Blitz said. "But Junior . . . he's going on five hundred. His dad, Eitri, was one of the most famous craftsmen in dwarven history. He lived over a thousand years, made some of the gods' most important items."

Samirah nibbled on an egg roll. "Even *I've* heard of him. He's in the old stories. He made Thor's hammer."

Blitz nodded. "Anyway, the rope Gleipnir . . . you could argue it was his most important work, even more than Thor's hammer. The rope keeps Fenris Wolf from getting free and starting Doomsday."

"I'm with you so far," I said.

"The thing is—the rope was a rush job. The gods were clamoring for help. They'd already tried to bind Fenris with two massive chains. They knew their window of opportunity was closing. The Wolf was getting stronger and wilder by the day. Pretty soon he'd be uncontrollable. So Eitri . . . well, he did his best. Obviously, the rope has held together this long. But a thousand years is a long time, even for a dwarven rope, especially when the strongest wolf in the universe is straining against it day and night. My dad, Bilì, was a great rope maker. He spent years trying to convince Junior that Gleipnir needed to be replaced. Junior wouldn't hear of it. Junior said he went to the Wolf's island from time to time to inspect the rope, and he swore that Gleipnir was fine. He thought my dad was just insulting his family's reputation. Finally my dad . . ."

Blitz's voice cracked.

Hearthstone signed, *You don't have to tell.*

"I'm okay." Blitzen cleared his throat. "Junior used all his influence to turn people against my dad. Our family lost business. Nobody would buy Bilì's crafts. Finally Dad went to the island of Lyngvi himself. He wanted to check the rope, prove that it needed replacing. He never came back. Months later a dwarf patrol found . . ." He looked down and shook his head.

Hearthstone signed: *Clothes. Ripped. Washed up on shore.*

Either Samirah was catching on to sign language or she got the general idea. She put her fingertips to her mouth. "Blitz, I'm so sorry."

"Well"—he shrugged listlessly—"now you know. Junior

is still holding a grudge. My dad's death wasn't enough. He wants to shame and kill *me*, too."

I set my drink on the coffee table. "Blitz, I think I speak for all of us when I say that Junior can shove his Granny Shuffler—"

"Magnus . . ." Sam warned.

"What? That old dwarf needs to be decapitated in the worst way. What can we do to help Blitz win the contest?"

"I appreciate it, kid." Blitz struggled to his feet. "But there's nothing. I . . . if you'll excuse me . . ."

He staggered to his bedroom and shut the door behind him.

Samirah pursed her lips. She still had a twig of Yggdrasil sticking out of her coat pocket. "Is there any chance Junior isn't *that* good? He's very old now, isn't he?"

Hearthstone unwrapped his scarf and threw it on the couch. He wasn't doing well in the darkness of Nidavellir. The green veins on his neck stood out more than usual. His hair floated with static, like plant tendrils searching for sunlight.

Junior is very good. He made a sign like ripping a piece of paper in half and throwing away the pieces: *Hopeless.*

I felt like throwing bottles of Fjalar's Foaming Mead out the window. "But Blitz *can* craft, right? Or were you just being encouraging?"

Hearth rose. He walked to a sideboard along the dining room wall. I hadn't paid the table much attention, but Hearth pressed something on its surface—a hidden switch, I guess—and the tabletop opened like a clamshell. The underside of the top section was one big light panel. It flickered to life, glowing warm and golden.

"A tanning bed." As soon as I said that, the truth sank in. "When you first came to Nidavellir, Blitzen saved your life. That's how. He made a way for you to get sunlight."

Hearth nodded. *First time I used runes for magic. Mistake. I dropped into Nidavellir. Almost died. Blitzen—he can craft. Kind and smart. But no good under pressure. Contests . . . no.*

Sam hugged her knees. "So what do we do? Do you have any magic that will help?"

Hearth hesitated. *Some. Will use before contest. Not enough.*

I translated for Sam and then asked, "What can I do?"

Protect him, Hearth signed. *Junior will try to s-a-b-o-t-a-g-e.*

"Sabotage?" I frowned. "Isn't that cheating?"

"I've heard about this," Sam said. "In dwarven contests, you can mess with your competitor as long as you aren't caught. The interference has to look like an accident, or at least something the judges can't trace back to you. But it sounds like Junior doesn't need to cheat to win."

He will cheat. Hearth made a sign like a hook swinging into a latch. *Spite.*

"Okay," I said. "I'll keep Blitz safe."

Still not enough. Hearth peered at Sam. *Only way to win— mess with Junior.*

When I told Sam what he'd signed, she turned as gray as a dwarf in sunlight. "No." She wagged her finger at Hearth. "No, absolutely not. I *told* you."

Blitz will die, Hearth signed. *You did it before.*

"What's he talking about?" I asked. "What did you do before?"

She got to her feet. The tension in the room was suddenly at DEFCON Two. "Hearthstone, you said you wouldn't mention it. You promised." She faced me, her expression shutting down any further questions. "Excuse me. I need some air."

She stormed out of the apartment.

I stared at Hearthstone. "What was that?"

His shoulders slumped. His face was empty, drained of hope. He signed, *A mistake.* Then he climbed onto his sun bed and turned toward the light, his body casting a wolf-shaped shadow across the floor.

FORTY-THREE

Let the Crafting of Decorative Metal Waterfowl Begin

KENNING SQUARE looked like a basketball court without the baskets. A chain-link fence bordered a stretch of cracked asphalt. Along one side stood a row of stone pillars carved like totem poles with dragon heads, centipedes, and troll faces. Along the other side, bleachers were packed with dwarf spectators. On the court, where the free-throw lines would've been, two open-air blacksmith shops were ready for action. Each had a forge with bellows to stoke the fire, an assortment of anvils, a few sturdy tables, and racks of tools that looked like torture equipment.

The crowd seemed prepared for a long day. They'd brought coolers, blankets, and picnic baskets. A few enterprising dwarves had parked their food trucks nearby. The sign for IRI'S HANDCRAFTED CONFECTIONS showed a waffle cone topped with a three-story ice-cream palace. BUMBURR'S BREAKFAST BURRITOS had a line twenty dwarves long, which made me sorry I'd eaten stale doughnuts at Blitz's place.

As we approached the court, the crowd gave Blitzen a smattering of applause. Sam was nowhere to be seen. She'd never come back to the apartment the previous night. I wasn't sure whether to be worried or angry.

Junior was waiting, leaning on his gold-plated walker. His

two bodyguards stood behind him, dressed like their boss in overalls and leather gauntlets.

"Well, well, Blitzen." The old dwarf sneered. "Mossglow started ten minutes ago. Were you getting your beauty sleep?"

Blitzen looked like he hadn't slept at all. His eyes were sunken and bloodshot. He'd spent the past hour worrying about what to wear, finally deciding on gray slacks, a white dress shirt with black suspenders, pointy black shoes, and a porkpie hat. He might not win for his crafting, but he would definitely get the vote for best-dressed blacksmith.

He glanced around distractedly. "Get started?"

The crowd cheered. Hearthstone accompanied Blitzen to the forge. After a night on Blitzen's tanning bed, the elf's face had a rosy sheen as if he'd been infused with paprika. Before we left the apartment, he'd cast a rune on Blitz to help him feel rested and focused, which had left Hearth exhausted and unfocused. Nevertheless, Hearth stoked the forge while Blitzen puttered around his workstation, staring in confusion at the racks of tools and baskets of metal ore.

Meanwhile Junior scooted around on his walker, barking at one of his bodyguards to fetch him a lump of iron and a sack of bone chips. The other bodyguard stood watch, scanning for anything that might disrupt his boss's work.

I tried to do the same for Blitz, but I doubted I looked as intimidating as a muscular dwarf in overalls. (And, yes, that was depressing.)

After about an hour, my initial adrenaline rush wore off. I began to realize why the spectators had brought picnic lunches. Crafting was not a fast-moving sport. Every once in a while the crowd would clap or murmur approvingly when

Junior struck a good hit with his hammer, or plunged a piece of metal into the cooling vat with a satisfying hiss. Nabbi and two other judges paced back and forth between the work-stations, scribbling notes on their clipboards. But for me, most of the morning was spent with the Sword of Summer in my hand, trying not to look like a fool.

A couple of times I had to do my job. Once a dart shot out of nowhere, heading for Blitzen. The Sword of Summer leaped into action. Before I even knew what was happening, the blade sliced the dart out of the air. The crowd applauded, which would have been gratifying if I'd actually done anything.

A little later, a random dwarf charged me from the side-lines, swinging an ax and screaming, "BLOOD!" I hit him in the head with the hilt of my sword. He collapsed. More polite applause. A couple of bystanders hauled the dwarf away by his ankles.

Junior was busy hammering out a red-hot iron cylinder the size of a shotgun barrel. He'd already crafted a dozen smaller mechanisms that I guessed would fit together with the cylin-der, but I couldn't tell what the final product was supposed to be. The old dwarf's walker didn't slow him down at all. He had some trouble shuffling around, but he could stand in one place just fine. Despite his age, his arm muscles were ripped from a lifetime swinging hammers at anvils.

Meanwhile, Blitzen hunched over his worktable with a pair of needle-nose pliers, connecting thin sheets of curved metal into some kind of figurine. Hearthstone stood nearby, drenched with sweat from working the bellows.

I tried not to worry about how exhausted Hearth looked,

or where Sam was, or how many times Blitzen dropped his tools and wept over his project.

Finally Nabbi yelled, "Ten minutes until mid-morning break!"

Blitzen sobbed. He attached another sheet of metal to his project, which was starting to resemble a duck.

Most of the crowd focused on the other workstation, where Junior was attaching various mechanisms to the cylinder. He hobbled to the forge and reheated the whole contraption until it was glowing red.

Carefully, he set the cylinder against the anvil, holding it steady with his tongs. He raised his hammer.

Just as he struck, something went wrong. Junior screamed. The hammer went askew, flattening the cylinder and sending attachments flying everywhere. Junior staggered backward, his hands cupped over his face.

His bodyguards rushed to his aid, crying, "What? What is it?"

I couldn't hear the whole conversation, but apparently some kind of insect had bitten Junior between the eyes.

"Did you get it?" asked one of the guards.

"No! The little pest flew off! Quick, before the cylinder cools—"

"Time!" shouted Nabbi.

Junior stomped his foot and cursed. He glared at his ruined project and yelled at his bodyguards.

I went to check on Blitzen, who sat slumped on his anvil. His porkpie hat was pushed back on his head. His left suspender had snapped.

"How you doing, champ?" I asked.

"Horrible." He gestured at his project. "I made a duck."

"Yeah . . ." I searched for a compliment. "It's a really nice duck. That's the bill, right? And those are the wings?"

Hearthstone sat next to us on the asphalt. *Ducks,* he signed. *Always ducks.*

"I'm sorry," Blitz moaned. "When I'm stressed, I default to waterfowl. I don't know why."

"No worries," I said. "Junior had a setback. His first project is pretty much ruined."

Blitz tried to brush the cinders off his white shirt. "It doesn't matter. Junior's first item is always his warm-up. He's got two more chances to destroy me."

"Hey, none of that." I rummaged through our supply bag and handed out canteens of water and some peanut butter crackers.

Hearthstone ate like a starving elf. Then he sat back and shone a flashlight on his face, trying to absorb the rays. Blitzen barely sipped his water.

"I never wanted this," Blitz murmured. "Crafting contests, magic items. All I ever wanted was to design quality clothing and sell it at reasonable prices in my own store."

I stared at his sweat-stained collar and thought about what Freya had said: *Blitzen is a genius at fabrics and fashion. The other dwarves don't appreciate his expertise, but I think it's marvelous.*

"That's your dream," I realized. "That's why you drank from Mimir's Well—to find out how to open a clothing shop?"

Blitzen scowled. "It was more than that. I wanted to follow my dream. I wanted other dwarves to stop laughing at me. I wanted to avenge my father's death and restore the family's honor! But those things didn't go together. I went to Mimir for advice."

"And . . . what did he say?"

Blitzen shrugged helplessly. "Four years of service—that was the price for drinking from his well. He said the cost of knowledge was also the answer. By serving him, I would get what I wanted. Except I didn't. Now I'm going to die."

No, Hearth signed. *Someday you will get your dream.*

"How, exactly?" Blitzen asked. "It's a little hard to cut and sew fabric when you're decapitated."

"That's not going to happen," I said.

In my chest, several ideas started to smelt together into a usable molten ingot—unless that sensation was just the peanut butter crackers. I thought about my sword that could turn into a pendant, and Sam's hijab that was magical high-tech camouflage. "Blitz, your next two items are going to be awesome."

"How do you know? I might panic and make more ducks!"

"You want to make clothing, right? So make clothing."

"Kid, this is a *forge*, not a haberdashery. Besides, fashion is not a recognized craft."

"What about armor?"

Blitz hesitated. "Well, yeah, but—"

"What about fashionable clothing that doubles as armor?"

Blitz's mouth fell open. "Balder's Bling . . . Kid, you may be on to something!" He shot to his feet and began hurrying around the workspace, gathering tools.

Hearth beamed at me—literally, since he still had the flashlight aimed at his face. He tapped his free hand to his head—the sign for *genius.*

When Nabbi called time, I took over at the bellows to give

Hearth a rest. He stood guard. Stoking the fire was about as fun as riding a stationary bike inside a baking oven.

After a while, Blitzen took me off the bellows and had me assist with the crafting. I was hopeless at it, but being forced to give me directions seemed to increase Blitz's confidence. "No, put that here. No, the big tongs! Hold it steady, kid! That's not steady!"

I lost track of time. I didn't pay much attention to what Blitz was making—something small, woven from chain. Instead I kept thinking about the Sword of Summer, now back in pendant form around my neck.

I remembered walking from the docks to Copley Square, half delirious with hunger and exhaustion, and the imaginary conversation I'd had with the blade. I considered how the sword either hummed or stayed silent, either guided my hand or lay heavy and inert. If it had a soul and emotions—then I hadn't given it enough credit. I'd been treating it like a dangerous object. I should be treating it like a person.

"Thanks," I said under my breath, trying not to feel ridiculous. "When you cut that dart out of the air earlier, you saved my friend. I should've thanked you sooner."

The pendant seemed to grow warmer, though standing next to the forge, it was hard to be sure.

"Sumarbrander," I said. "Is that what you like to be called? Sorry I've been ignoring you."

Hmmm, the pendant hummed skeptically.

"You're much more than a sword," I said. "You're not just for slashing at things. You—"

From across the courtyard, Nabbi yelled, "Ten minutes until lunch break!"

"Oh, gods," Blitzen muttered. "I can't— Kid, quick! Hand me that texturing hammer."

His hands flew, snatching up various tools, making minor adjustments to his creation. It didn't look like much—just a flat narrow length of chain mail—but Blitz worked as if his life depended on it, which it did.

He folded and crimped the chain mail into its final shape, then soldered the seam.

"It's a necktie!" I realized. "Blitzen, I actually recognize what you made!"

"Thank you. Shut up." He raised his soldering gun and announced, "Done!" just as a crash reverberated from Junior's workstation.

"GAAHHH!" screamed the old dwarf.

The entire crowd surged to their feet.

Junior was on his butt, cradling his face in his hands. On his worktable sat a flattened, misshapen lump of cooling iron.

His bodyguards rushed to help him.

"Damnable insect!" Junior howled. He was bleeding from the bridge of his nose. He looked at his palms but apparently found no squashed bug. "I hit it this time, I'm sure! Where is it?"

Nabbi and the other judges frowned in our direction, as if we somehow might have orchestrated a kamikaze insect attack. I guess we looked clueless enough to convince them otherwise.

"Time for lunch," Nabbi announced. "One more item shall be made this afternoon!"

We ate quickly, because Blitz was raring to get back to work.

"I've got the hang of it now," he said. "I've *got* it. Kid, I owe you big-time."

I glanced over at Junior's workstation. His bodyguards were glaring at me, cracking their knuckles.

"Let's just get through the contest," I said. "I wish Sam was here. We may need to fight our way out."

Hearth gave me a curious look when I mentioned Sam.

"What?" I asked.

He shook his head and went back to eating his watercress sandwich.

The afternoon session went quickly. I was so busy on guard duty I barely had time to think. Junior must have hired some extra saboteurs, because every half hour or so I had to deal with a new threat: a spear thrown from the audience, a rotten apple aimed at Blitzen's head, a steam-powered predator drone, and a pair of dwarves in green Spandex jumpsuits, wielding baseball bats. (The less said about that, the better.) Each time, the Sword of Summer guided my hand and neutralized the threat. Each time, I remembered to thank the sword.

I could almost discern its voice now: *Yeah, okay. Mmm-hmm. I suppose.* Like it was slowly warming up to me, getting over its resentment at being ignored.

Hearthstone rushed around the workstation, bringing Blitz extra materials and tools. Blitz was weaving a larger, more complicated piece of metal fabric. Whatever it was, he seemed pleased.

Finally, he set down his bezel roller and shouted, "Success!"

At the same moment, Junior suffered his most spectacular fail. His bodyguards had been standing close, ready for another kamikaze insect attack, but it made no difference. As Junior brought down his hammer for a masterstroke, a dark speck zipped out of the sky. The horsefly bit Junior on the face so hard he spun sideways under the momentum of his hammer. Wailing and staggering, he knocked both his guards unconscious, destroyed the contents of two worktables, and swept his third invention into the forge before he collapsed on the asphalt.

It shouldn't have been funny—an old dwarf getting humiliated like that. Except that it was, kind of. Probably because that old dwarf was a spiteful, nasty piece of work.

In the midst of the commotion, Nabbi rang a hand bell. "The contest has ended!" he announced. "Time for judging the items . . . and killing the loser!"

FORTY-FOUR

Junior Wins a Bag of Tears

SAM PICKED THAT MOMENT TO SHOW UP.

She shouldered through the crowd, her headscarf pulled low over her face. Her jacket was dusted with ash, as if she'd spent the night in a chimney.

I wanted to yell at her for being gone so long, but my anger evaporated when I noticed her black eye and swollen lip.

"What happened?" I asked. "Are you okay?"

"Little scuffle," she said. "No worries. Let's watch the judging."

Spectators gathered around two tables on the sideline, where Junior's and Blitzen's crafts were on display. Blitzen stood with his hands clasped behind his back, looking confident despite his snapped suspenders, his grease-stained shirt, and his sweat-soaked porkpie hat.

Junior's face was a bloody mess. He could barely hold himself up on his walker. The murderous gleam in his eyes made him look like a serial killer exhausted after a hard day's work.

Nabbi and the other judges circled the tables, inspecting the crafted items and jotting notes on their clipboards.

At last Nabbi faced the audience. He arched his wriggly eyebrows and tried for a smile.

"Well, then!" he said. "Thank you all for attending this

contest, sponsored by Nabbi's Tavern, famous among taverns, built by Nabbi and home to Nabbi's Stout, the only mead you'll ever need. Now our contestants will tell us about their first items. Blitzen, son of Freya!"

Blitz gestured to his metal sculpture. "It's a duck."

Nabbi blinked. "And . . . what does it do?"

"When I press its back . . ." Blitzen did so. The duck swelled to three times its size, like a frightened pufferfish. "It turns into a larger duck."

The second judge scratched his beard. "That's it?"

"Well, yes," Blitz said. "I call it the Expando-Duck. It's perfect if you need a small metal duck. Or a larger metal duck."

The third judge turned to his colleagues. "Garden knick-knack, perhaps? Conversation piece? Decoy?"

Nabbi coughed. "Yes, thank you, Blitzen. And now you, Eitri Junior, son of Edna. What is your first creation?"

Junior wiped the blood out of his eyes. He held up his flat-tened iron cylinder, with several springs and latches dangling from it. "This is a self-guiding troll-seeking missile! If it were undamaged, it could destroy any troll at a distance of half a mile. And it's reusable!"

The crowd murmured appreciatively.

"Um, but does it work?" asked the second judge.

"No!" Junior said. "It was ruined on the final hammer stroke. But if it *did* work—"

"But it doesn't," observed the third judge. "So what is it at the moment?"

"It's a useless metal cylinder!" Junior snarled. "Which isn't my fault!"

The judges conferred and scribbled some notes.

"So, in the first round," Nabbi summed up, "we have an expandable duck versus a useless metal cylinder. Our contestants are running very close indeed. Blitzen, what is your second item?"

Blitzen proudly held up his chain mail neckware. "The bulletproof tie!"

The judges lowered their clipboards in perfect synchronicity.

"What?" asked Nabbi.

"Oh, come now!" Blitz turned to the audience. "How many of you have been in the embarrassing situation of wearing a bulletproof vest without a matching bulletproof tie?"

In the back of the crowd, one dwarf raised his hand.

"Exactly!" Blitzen said. "Not only is this accessory fashionable, but it will stop anything up to a 30-06 round. It can also be worn as a cravat."

The judges frowned and took notes, but a few audience members seemed impressed. They examined their shirts, maybe thinking how underdressed they felt without a chain mail neckpiece.

"Junior?" asked Nabbi. "What is your second work of craftsmanship?"

"The Goblet of Infinity!" Junior gestured to a misshapen hunk of iron. "It holds a limitless amount of any liquid—great for road trips through waterless wastelands."

"Uh . . ." Nabbi pointed with his pen. "It looks a bit crushed."

"Stupid horsefly again!" Junior protested. "It bit me right between the eyes! Not *my* fault if an insect turned my brilliant invention into a slag heap."

"Slag heap," Nabbi repeated, jotting on his clipboard. "And Blitzen, your final item?"

Blitzen held up a glittering length of woven metal fabric. "The chain mail vest! For use with a three-piece suit of chain mail. Or, if you want to dress it down, you can wear it with jeans and a nice shirt."

And a shield, Hearthstone offered.

"Yes, and a shield," Blitzen said.

The third judge leaned forward, squinting. "I suppose it would offer some minor protection. If you were stabbed in the back at a disco, for instance."

The second judge jotted something down. "Does it have any magic abilities?"

"Well, no," Blitz said. "But it's reversible: silver on the outside, gold on the inside. Depending on what jewelry you're wearing, or what color armor—"

"I see." Nabbi made a note on his clipboard and turned to Junior. "And your final item, sir?"

Junior's fists trembled with rage. "This is unfair! I have never lost a contest. All of you know my skills. This meddler, this *poseur* Blitzen has somehow managed to ruin my—"

"Eitri Junior, son of Edna," interrupted Nabbi, "what is your third item?"

He waved impatiently at the furnace. "My third item is in there! It doesn't *matter* what it was, because it's now boiling sludge!"

The judges circled up and conferred. The crowd shifted restlessly.

Nabbi faced the audience. "Judging has been difficult. We have weighed the merits of Junior's boiling sludge, slag heap, and useless metal cylinder against the chain mail vest, bullet-proof tie, and Expando-Duck. It was a close call. However, we judge the winner of this contest to be Blitzen, son of Freya!"

Spectators applauded. Some gasped in disbelief. A female dwarf in a nurse's outfit, possibly Bambi, famous among dwarf nurses, passed out cold.

Hearthstone jumped up and down and made the ends of his scarf do the wave. I looked for Sam, but she was hanging back at the edges of the crowd.

Junior scowled at his fists as if deciding whether to hit himself. "Fine," he growled. "Take my head! I don't want to live in a world where Blitzen wins crafting contests!"

"Junior, I don't want to kill you," Blitzen said. Despite his win, he didn't sound proud or gloating. He looked tired, maybe even sad.

Junior blinked. "You—you don't?"

"No. Just give me the earrings and the rope as you promised. Oh, and a public admission that my father was right about Gleipnir all along. You should have replaced it centuries ago."

"Never!" Junior shrieked. "You impugn my father's reputation! I cannot—"

"Okay, I'll get my ax," Blitzen said in a resigned tone. "I'm afraid the blade is a little dull. . . ."

Junior gulped. He looked longingly at the bulletproof necktie. "Very well. Perhaps . . . perhaps Bili had a point. The rope needed replacement."

"And you were wrong to tarnish his reputation."

The old dwarf's facial muscles convulsed, but he managed to get out the words. "And I was . . . wrong. Yes."

Blitzen gazed up into the gloom, whispering something

under his breath. I wasn't a good lip-reader, but I was pretty sure he said, *I love you, Dad. Good-bye.*

He refocused on Junior. "Now, about the items you promised . . ."

Junior snapped his fingers. One of his bodyguards wobbled over, his head newly bandaged from his recent encounter with a hammer. He handed Blitzen a small velvet box.

"Earrings for your mother," Junior said.

Blitz opened the box. Inside were two tiny cats made from gold filigree like Brisingamen. As I watched, the cats stretched, blinking their emerald eyes and flicking their diamond tails.

Blitz snapped the box shut. "Adequate. And the rope?"

The bodyguard tossed him a ball of silk kite string.

"You're joking," I said. "That's supposed to bind Fenris Wolf?"

Junior glowered at me. "Boy, your ignorance is breathtaking. Gleipnir was just as thin and light, but its paradox ingredients gave it great strength. This rope is the same, only better!"

"Paradox ingredients?"

Blitz held up the end of the rope and whistled appreciatively. "He means things that aren't supposed to exist. Paradox ingredients are very difficult to craft with, very dangerous. Gleipnir contained the footfall of a cat, the spittle of a bird, the breath of a fish, the beard of a woman."

"Dunno if that last one is a paradox," I said. "Crazy Alice in Chinatown has a pretty good beard."

Junior huffed. "The point is, this rope is even better! I call it Andskoti, the Adversary. It is woven with the most powerful paradoxes in the Nine Worlds—Wi-Fi with no lag, a politician's sincerity, a printer that prints, healthy deep-fried food, and an interesting grammar lecture!"

"Okay, yeah," I admitted. "Those things don't exist."

Blitz stuffed the rope in his backpack. He took out his pouch of tears and handed it to the old dwarf. "Thank you, Junior. I consider our bargain complete, but I would ask one more thing. Where is the island of Fenris Wolf?"

Junior hefted his payment. "If I could tell you, Blitzen, I would. I'd be happy to see you ripped apart by the Wolf like your father was! Alas, I don't know."

"But—"

"Yes, I said I checked on the rope from time to time. I lied! The truth is, very few gods or dwarves know where the Wolf's island appears. Most of them are sworn to secrecy. How your father found the place, I really don't know, but if you want to find it, the best person to ask is Thor. He knows, and he has a big mouth."

"Thor," I said. "Where do we find Thor?"

"I have no idea," Junior admitted.

Hearthstone signed, *Sam might. She knows a lot about the gods.*

"Yeah." I turned. "Sam, get over here! Why are you lurking?"

The crowd parted around her.

As soon as Junior saw her, he made a strangled squawk. "You! It was you!"

Sam tried to cover her busted lip. "Sorry? Have we met?"

"Oh, don't play innocent with me." Junior scooted forward on his walker, his flushed scalp turning his gray hair pink. "I've seen shape-shifters before. That scarf is the same color as the horsefly's wings. And that black eye is from when I swatted you! You're in league with Blitzen! Friends, colleagues, honest dwarves—kill these cheaters!"

I was proud that the four of us responded as a team. In perfect unison, like a well-oiled combat machine, we turned and ran for our lives.

FORTY-FIVE

I Get to Know Jack

I'M PRETTY GOOD at multitasking, so I figured I could flee in terror and argue at the same time.

"A horsefly?" I yelled at Sam. "You can turn into a horsefly?"

She ducked as a steam-powered dart buzzed over her head. "Now is not the time!"

"Oh, excuse me. I should wait for the designated talk-about-turning-into-horseflies time."

Hearthstone and Blitzen led the way. Behind us, a mob of thirty dwarves was closing fast. I didn't like their murderous expressions or their fine assortment of handcrafted weapons.

"This way!" Blitzen ducked down an alley.

Unfortunately, Hearthstone wasn't watching. The elf barreled straight ahead.

"Mother!" Blitz cursed—at least, I thought it was a curse until Sam and I reached the corner and faltered.

A few steps down the alley, Blitz was trapped in a net of light. He squirmed and cussed as the glowing web lifted him into the air. "It's my mother!" he yelped. "She wants her damnable earrings. Go! Catch up with Hearthstone! I'll meet you—"

POP! Our dwarf disappeared in a flash.

I glanced at Sam. "Did that just happen?"

"We've got other problems." She pulled out her ax.

The mob had caught up with us. They fanned out in an angry semicircle of beards, scowls, baseball bats, and broadswords. I wasn't sure what they were waiting for. Then I heard Junior's voice somewhere behind them. "Hold on!" he wheezed. "I—" *Wheeze.* "Kill—" *Wheeze.* "First!"

The mob parted. Flanked by his bodyguards, the old dwarf pushed his walker toward us.

He eyed me, then Sam.

"Where are Blitzen and the elf?" Junior muttered. "Well, no matter. We'll find them. You, boy, I don't care about so much. Run now and I might let you live. The girl is obviously a daughter of Loki. She bit me and ruined my crafting! She dies."

I pulled off my pendant. The Sword of Summer grew to full length. The crowd of dwarves edged backward. I guess they knew a dangerous blade when they saw one.

"I'm not going anywhere," I said. "You'll have to take on both of us."

The sword hummed for attention.

"Correction," I said. "You'll have to take on all *three* of us. This is Sumarbrander, the Sword of Summer, crafted by . . . actually I'm not sure, but it is definitely famous among swords, and it is about to kick your collective butts."

"Thank you," said the sword.

Sam made a squeaking noise. The dwarves' shocked expressions told me I hadn't imagined hearing the sword's voice.

I held up the blade. "You can talk? I mean . . . of course you can talk. You have many, uh, incredible abilities."

"That's what I've been saying." The sword's voice was definitely male. It emanated from the runes along the blade, which vibrated and glowed with every word like the lights on a stereo equalizer.

I gave the dwarves an arrogant look, like, *Yeah, that's right. I've got a talking disco sword and you don't.*

"Sumarbrander," I said, "how do you feel about taking on this mob?"

"Sure," said the sword. "You want them dead or . . . ?"

The mob shuffled backward in alarm.

"Nah," I decided. "Just make them go away."

"You're no fun," the sword said. "Okay, then, let go."

I hesitated. I didn't particularly want to hold a flashing talking humming sword, but dropping my weapon didn't seem like the natural first step toward victory.

Junior must've sensed my reluctance.

"We can take him!" he yelled. "He's one boy with a sword he doesn't know how to use!"

Sam snarled. "And a former Valkyrie with an ax she very much *does* know how to use."

"Bah!" Junior said. "Let's get 'em, boys! Granny Shuffler, activate!"

Rows of dagger blades extended from the front of his walker. Two miniature rocket engines fired in the back, propelling Junior toward us at a mind-boggling one mile an hour. His comrades roared and charged.

I let go of my sword. It hovered in the air for a split second. Then it flew into action. Faster than you could say *son of Edna*, every dwarf was disarmed. Their weapons were cut in half, split down the middle, knocked to the ground, or diced into hors d'oeuvre-size cubes. The daggers and rockets were sheared off Junior's walker. The severed ends of thirty beards fluttered to the pavement, leaving thirty shocked dwarves with fifty percent less facial hair.

The Sword of Summer hovered between the mob and me.

"Anybody want more?" the sword asked.

The dwarves turned and fled.

Junior yelled over his shoulder as he hobbled away, following his bodyguards, who were already a block ahead of him. "This isn't over, boy! I'll be back with reinforcements!"

Sam lowered her ax. "That was . . . Wow."

"Yeah," I agreed. "Thank you, Sumarbrander."

"*De nada*," said the sword. "But you know, Sumarbrander is a really long name, and I've never liked it much."

"Okay." I wasn't sure where to look when addressing the sword—the glowing runes? The tip of the blade? "What would you like us to call you?"

The sword hummed thoughtfully. "What is your name?"

"Magnus."

"That's a good name. Call me Magnus."

"You can't be Magnus. *I'm* Magnus."

"Then what is her name?"

"Sam. You can't be Sam, either. It would be too confusing."

The blade swished from side to side. "Well, what *is* a good name? Something that fits my personality and my many talents."

"But I don't really know you as well as I'd like to." I looked at Samirah, who just shook her head like, *Hey, it's your disco sword.*

"Honestly," I said. "I don't know jack—"

"Jack!" the sword cried. "Perfect!"

The thing about talking swords . . . it's hard to tell when they're kidding. They have no facial expressions. Or faces.

"So . . . you want me to call you Jack."

"It is a noble name," said the sword. "Fit for kings and sharp carving implements!"

"Okay," I said. "Well, then, Jack, thanks for the save. You mind if . . . ?" I reached for the hilt, but Jack floated away from me.

"I wouldn't do that yet," he warned. "The price of my amazing abilities: as soon as you sheathe me, or turn me into a pendant, or whatever, you will feel just as exhausted as if you had performed all my actions yourself."

My shoulder muscles tightened. I considered how tired I would feel if I had just destroyed all those weapons and cut all those beards. "Oh. I didn't notice that earlier."

"Because you hadn't used me for anything amazing yet."

"Right."

In the distance, an air raid horn howled. I doubted they got many air raids in an underground world, so I figured the alarm had to do with us.

"We need to go," Sam urged. "We have to find Hearthstone. I doubt Junior was joking about reinforcements."

Finding Hearthstone was the easy part. Two blocks away, we ran into him as he was coming back to find us.

What the H-e-l-h-e-i-m? he signed. *Where is Blitzen?*

I told him about Freya's gold net. "We'll find him. Right now, Junior is calling up the Dwarven National Guard."

Your sword is floating, Hearth noted.

"Your elf is deaf," Jack noted.

I turned to the sword. "I know that. Sorry, introductions. Jack, Hearth. Hearth, Jack."

Hearth signed, *Is it talking? I don't read sword lips.*

"What is he saying?" Jack asked. "I don't read elf hands."

"Guys." Sam pointed behind us. A few blocks away, an iron-plated vehicle with caterpillar treads and a mounted turret was turning slowly onto our street.

"That's a tank," I said. "Junior has a *tank*?"

"We should leave," Jack said. "I am awesome, but if I try to destroy a tank, the strain might kill you."

"Yeah," I agreed. "How do we get out of Nidavellir?"

Hearthstone clapped for my attention. *This way.*

We sprinted after him, zigzagging through alleys, knocking over carefully handcrafted garbage cans that probably had names and souls.

From somewhere behind us, a deep *BOOM!* rattled windows and made pebbles rain from above.

"Is the tank shaking the *sky*?" I yelled. "That *can't* be good."

Hearthstone led us down another street of clapboard row houses. Dwarves sat on stoops, clapping and cheering as we ran by. A few of them recorded videos of us on uniquely crafted smartphones. I figured our attempted getaway would go viral on the Dwarven Internet, famous among Internets.

Finally we reached what would've been the southern edge of South Boston. On the far side of the avenue, instead of the M Street Beach, the ground dropped off into a chasm.

"Oh, this is very helpful," Sam said.

Behind us in the gloom, Junior's voice shouted, "Bazookas, take the right flank!"

Hearthstone led us to the rim of the canyon. Far below, a river roared.

He signed: *We jump in.*

"Are you serious?" I asked.

Blitzen and I did this before. River washes out of Nidavellir.

"To where?"

Depends, Hearthstone signed.

"That's not reassuring," said Sam.

Hearthstone pointed back toward the avenue. The dwarven mob was gathering, tanks and jeeps and RPGs and a whole bunch of really angry geriatric dwarves in armor-plated walkers.

"We jump," I decided.

Jack the Sword hovered next to me. "Better hold me now, boss. Otherwise I might get lost again."

"But you said the exhaustion—"

"Might make you pass out," the sword agreed. "On the bright side, it looks like you're going to die anyway."

He had a point. (Oh, sorry. That was bad.) I took the sword and willed it back into pendant form. I just had time to attach it to the chain before my legs buckled.

Sam caught me. "Hearthstone! Take his other arm!"

As my vision went dark, Sam and Hearth helped me leap off the cliff. Because, you know, what are friends for?

FORTY-SIX

Aboard the Good Ship *Toenail*

I KNEW I WAS IN TROUBLE when I woke up dreaming.

I found myself standing next to Loki on the deck of a massive ship.

"There you are!" said Loki. "I was starting to wonder."

"How . . . ?" I noticed his outfit. "What are you wearing?"

"You like it?" His scarred lips twisted into a grin. His white admiral's jacket gleamed with medals, but Loki wasn't exactly wearing it regulation-style. It was open over a black T-shirt featuring Jack Nicholson's face from *The Shining*. The caption read: HEEEERE'S LOKI!

"Where are we?" I asked.

Loki polished his medals with his coat sleeve. "Well, neither of us is *here*, of course. I'm still tied up on a stone slab with snake poison dripping in my face. You're dying on the banks of a river in Jotunheim."

"I'm what?"

"Whether you live or not, this may be our last chance to talk. I wanted you to see this—*Naglfar*, the Ship of Nails! It's almost complete."

The ship came into clearer focus—a Viking longship larger than an aircraft carrier. The main deck could've accommodated the Boston Marathon. Giant shields lined the railings.

Fore and aft rose thirty-foot-tall figureheads shaped like snarling wolves. Naturally, they had to be wolves.

I peered over the side between two shields. A hundred feet down, braided iron cables moored the ship to a dock. The gray sea churned with ice.

I ran my hand along the railing. The surface was bumpy and prickly—enameled with white and gray ridges like fish scales or pearl shavings. At first glance, I'd assumed the deck was made of steel, but now I realized the whole ship was constructed of this weird translucent material—not metal, not wood, but something strangely familiar.

"What is this?" I asked Loki. "I don't see any wood or nails. Why is it called the Ship of Nails?"

Loki chuckled. "Not *carpentry* nails, Magnus. *Naglfar* is made from the fingernails and toenails of dead men."

The deck seemed to pitch beneath me. I wasn't sure if it was possible to puke in a dream, but I was tempted. It wasn't just the obvious grossness of standing on a ship made of nail clippings that made me nauseated—it was the sheer *volume* of the material. How many corpses had had to contribute their nails to make a ship this size?

Once I managed to steady my breathing, I faced Loki. "Why?"

Even with the ruined lips and scarred face, Loki's grin was so infectious, I almost smiled back—*almost*.

"Amazingly disgusting, isn't it?" he said. "Back in the old days, your ancestors knew that nail clippings carried part of your spirit, your essence . . . your DNA, you'd call it now. Throughout their lives, mortals were careful to burn any clippings they made. When they died, their nails would be trimmed and the clippings destroyed so the material wouldn't contribute to this great ship. But sometimes"—Loki shrugged—"as you can see, the proper precautions weren't taken."

"You've built yourself a battleship out of toenails."

"Well, the ship is building *itself*. And, technically, *Naglfar* belongs to Surt and the fire giants, but when Ragnarok comes, I will guide this ship out of the harbor. We'll have an army of giants led by Captain Hrym, plus hundreds of thousands of dishonored dead from Helheim—all those who were careless or unlucky enough to die without a sword in their hand, a proper burial, and a decent post-mortem mani-pedi. We'll sail to Asgard and destroy the gods. It'll be awesome."

I looked aft, expecting to see an army gathering on the shore, but the mist was so thick I couldn't see the end of the dock. Despite my usual resistance to cold, the damp air soaked into my bones and made my teeth chatter.

"Why are you showing me this?" I asked.

"Because I like you, Magnus. You've got a sense of humor. You've got *zing*. So rare in a demigod! Even rarer among the einherjar. I'm glad my daughter found you."

"Samirah . . . that's how she can turn into a horsefly. She's a shape-shifter like you."

"Oh, she's Daddy's girl, all right. She doesn't like to admit it, but she's inherited a lot of things from me: my abilities, my dashing good looks, my keen intellect. She can spot talent too. After all, she chose you, my friend."

I clutched my stomach. "I don't feel so good."

"Duh! You're on the verge of death. Personally, I hope you wake up, because if you kick the bucket now, your death will be meaningless and nothing you've done will matter."

"Thanks for the pep talk."

"Listen—I brought you here for some perspective. When Ragnarok comes, *all* bonds will break, not just the ropes binding Fenris. The moorings of this ship—*snap*. The bindings that hold me captive—*snap*. Whether or not you keep that sword out of Surt's hands, it's only a matter of time. One bond will snap and they'll all start going—unraveling like one huge tapestry."

"You're trying to discourage me? I thought you wanted Ragnarok delayed."

"Oh, I do!" He put up his hands. His wrists were raw and bleeding, as if he'd been handcuffed too tightly. "I'm totally on your side, Magnus! Look at the figureheads. The wolves' snouts aren't finished yet. Is there anything more embarrassing than sailing into battle with half-finished figureheads?"

"So what do you want?"

"The same thing I've always wanted," Loki said. "To help you fight your fate. Which of the gods besides me has bothered to speak to you as a friend and an equal?"

His eyes were like Sam's—bright and intense, the color of burning—but there was something harder and more calculating about Loki's gaze—something that didn't jibe with his friendly smile. I remembered how Sam had described him: *a liar, a thief, a murderer.*

"We're friends now?" I asked. "Equals?"

"We could be," he said. "In fact, I have an idea. Forget going to Fenris's island. Forget facing Surt. I know a place where the sword will be safe."

"With you?"

Loki laughed. "Don't tempt me, kid. No, no. I was thinking about your Uncle Randolph. He understands the value of the sword. He's spent his life looking for it, preparing to study it. You might not know it, but his house is *heavily* fortified with magic. If you took the sword to him . . . well, the old man can't use it himself. But he would store it away. It would be out of Surt's hands. And that's what matters, eh? It would buy us all some time."

I wanted to laugh in Loki's face and tell him no. I figured he was trying to trick me. Yet I couldn't see his angle.

"You think it's a trap," Loki said. "I get that. But you must have wondered why Mimir told you to take the blade to the Wolf's island—the very place where Surt *wants* to use it. What's the sense in that? What if Mimir is playing you? I mean, come on. That old severed head runs a pachinko racket! If you don't bring the sword to the island, Surt won't be able get his hands on it. Why take the risk?"

I struggled to clear my thoughts. "You're—you're a smooth talker. You'd make a good used car salesman."

Loki winked. "I think the term is *pre-owned*. You've got to make a choice soon, Magnus. We may not be able to speak again. If you want a gesture of good faith, however, I can sweeten the deal. My daughter Hel and I . . . we've been talking."

My heart jackknifed. "Talking about . . ."

"I'll let her tell you. But now . . ." He tilted his head, listening. "Yes, we don't have much time. You might be waking up."

"Why were you bound?" The question forced itself out before I realized I was thinking it. "I remember you killed somebody. . . ."

His smile hardened. The angry lines around his eyes made him look ten years older.

"You know how to ruin a conversation," Loki said. "I killed Balder, the god of light—the handsome, perfect, *incredibly* annoying son of Odin and Frigg." He stepped toward me and poked my chest, emphasizing each word. "And—I'd—do—it—again."

In the back of my brain, my common sense yelled, *DROP IT!* But as you have probably figured out by now, I don't listen to my common sense much.

"Why did you kill him?"

Loki barked a laugh. His breath smelled of almonds, like cyanide. "Did I mention he was annoying? Frigg was *so* worried about him. The poor baby had been having bad dreams about his own doom. Welcome to *reality*, Balder! We *all* have bad dreams. But Frigg couldn't stand the idea that her precious angel might bruise his little foot. She exacted promises from everything in creation that nothing would hurt her beautiful son—people, gods, trees, rocks. . . . Can you imagine exacting a promise from a rock? Frigg managed it. Afterward, the gods had a party to celebrate. They started throwing things at Balder just for laughs. Arrows, swords, boulders, each other . . . nothing would hurt him. It was as if the idiot was surrounded by a force field. Well . . . *I'm sorry.* The thought of Mr. Perfect also being Mr. Invulnerable made me sick."

I blinked, trying to get the sting out of my eyes. Loki's voice was so full of hatred it seemed to make the air burn. "You found a way to kill him."

"Mistletoe!" Loki's smile brightened. "Can you imagine? Frigg forgot one tiny little plant. I fashioned a dart from the stuff, gave it to Balder's blind brother, a god named Hod. I didn't want him to miss the fun of chucking deadly objects at

Balder, so I guided Hod's hand and . . . well, Frigg's worst fears came true. Balder *deserved* it."

"For being too handsome and popular."

"Yes!"

"For being loved."

"Exactly!" Loki leaned forward until we were almost nose-to-nose. "Don't tell me *you* haven't done the same kinds of things. Those cars you broke into, those people you stole from . . . you picked people you didn't like, eh? You picked the rich handsome stuck-up snobs who *annoyed* you."

My teeth chattered harder. "I never *killed* anyone."

"Oh, please." Loki stepped back, examining me with a look of disappointment. "It's only a matter of degree. So I killed a god. Big deal! He went to Helheim and became an honored guest in my daughter's palace. And *my* punishment? You want to know *my* punishment?"

"You were tied on a stone slab," I said. "With poison from a snake dripping on your face. I know."

"*Do* you?" Loki pulled back his cuffs, showing me the raw scars on his wrists. "The gods were not content to punish me with eternal torture. They took out their wrath upon my two favorite sons—Vali and Narvi. They turned Vali into a wolf and watched with amusement while he disemboweled his brother Narvi. Then they shot and gutted the wolf. The gods took my innocent sons' own entrails . . ." Loki's voice cracked with grief. "Well, Magnus Chase, let's just say I was not bound with *ropes*."

Something in my chest curled up and died—possibly my hope that there was any kind of justice in the universe. "Gods."

Loki nodded. "Yes, Magnus. The *gods*. Think about that when you meet Thor."

"I'm meeting Thor?"

"I'm afraid so. The gods don't even *pretend* to deal in good and evil, Magnus. It's not the Aesir way. Might makes right. So tell me . . . do you really want to charge into battle on their behalf?"

The ship trembled under my feet. Fog rolled across the deck.

"Time for you to go," Loki said. "Remember what I said. Oh, and have fun getting mouth-to-mouth from a goat."

"Wait . . . what?"

Loki wiggled his fingers, his eyes full of malicious glee. Then the ship dissolved into gray nothingness.

FORTY-SEVEN

I Psychoanalyze a Goat

AS LOKI HAD PROMISED, I woke up with a goat in my face.

Confession time: My only previous experience with kissing had been with Jackie Molotov in seventh grade, behind the bleachers at a school dance. Yes, I know that's lame, seeing as how I was now sixteen. But during the past few years I'd been a little busy, living on the street and whatnot. Anyway, with apologies to Jackie, getting mouth-to-mouth from a goat reminded me of her.

I rolled over and puked into the river conveniently located right next to me. My bones felt as if they'd been broken and mended with duct tape. My mouth tasted like chewed grass and old nickels.

"Oh, you're alive," said the goat. He sounded mildly disappointed.

I sat up and groaned. The goat's horns curved outward like the top half of an hourglass. Sticker burrs matted his shaggy brown fur.

A lot of questions crowded into my head: *Where am I? Why are you a talking goat? Why does your breath smell so bad? Have you been eating spare change?*

The first question that came out was: "Where are my friends?"

"The elf and girl?" asked the goat. "Oh, they're dead."

My heart threatened to exit via my throat. "What? No!"

The goat gestured with his horns. A few yards to my right, Hearthstone and Sam lay crumpled on the rocky beach.

I scrambled over. I placed my hands on their throats and almost passed out again, from relief this time.

"They're not dead," I told the goat. "They both have pulses."

"Oh." The goat sighed. "Well, give them a few more hours and they'll probably be dead."

"What is *wrong* with you?"

"Everything," said the goat. "My whole life is one big—"

"Never mind," I said. "Just be quiet."

The goat brayed. "Sure, I understand. You don't want to know my problems. No one does. I'll be over here, weeping or whatever. Just ignore me."

Keeping my hands against Sam's and Hearthstone's carotid arteries, I sent warmth through my fingertips into their circulatory systems.

Sam was easy to heal. Her heart was strong. She responded almost immediately, her eyes fluttering open, her lungs gasping for air. She curled sideways and began vomiting, which I took as a good sign.

Hearthstone, though . . . something was wrong beyond the water in his lungs and the cold in his limbs. Right at his core, a dense knot of dark emotion sapped his will to live. The pain was so intense it threw me back to the night of my mother's death. I remembered my hands slipping from the fire escape, the windows of our apartment exploding above me.

Hearthstone's grief was even worse than that. I didn't

know exactly what he had suffered, but his despair almost overwhelmed me. I grasped for a happy memory—my mom and me picking wild blueberries on Hancock Hill, the air so clear I could see Quincy Bay glittering on the horizon. I sent a flood of warmth into Hearthstone's chest.

His eyes flew open.

He stared at me, uncomprehending. Then he pointed at my face and gestured weakly—the sign for light.

"What do you mean?" I asked.

Sam groaned. She rose on one arm and squinted at me. "Magnus . . . why are you glowing?"

I looked at my hands. Sure enough, I seemed to have been dipped in Folkvanger light. The warm buttery aura was starting to fade, but I could feel residual power tingling along my arm hairs.

"Apparently," I said, "if I heal too much at once, I glow."

Sam winced. "Well, thanks for healing us. But try not to self-combust. How is Hearth?"

I helped him sit up. "How you feeling, buddy?"

He made a circle with his thumb and middle finger, then flicked it upward, the sign for *terrible*.

No surprise. Given the depth of pain I'd felt within him, I was surprised he wasn't constantly screaming.

"Hearth . . ." I started to say, "when I healed you, I—"

He put his hands over mine—a sign language version of *hush*.

Maybe we had some residual connection from the healing magic, but when I met Hearthstone's eyes, I could tell what he was thinking. His message was an almost audible voice in my head—like when Jack the sword had started to speak.

Later, Hearth told me. *Thank you . . . brother.*

I was too startled to reply.

The goat plodded over. "You really should take better care of your elf. They need lots of sunshine—not this weak Jotunheim light. And you can't overwater them by drowning them in rivers."

Hearthstone frowned. He signed, *The goat is speaking?*

I tried to clear my head. "Uh, yeah, he is."

"I also read sign language," said the goat. "My name is Tanngnjóstr, which means Teeth Grinder, because . . . well, it's a nervous habit of mine. But nobody calls me Tanngnjóstr. It's a horrible name. Just call me Otis."

Sam struggled to her feet. Her hijab had come undone and now hung around her neck like a gunslinger's bandanna. "So, Otis, what brings you here to this place that is . . . wherever we are?"

Otis sighed. "I got lost. Which is typical. I was trying to find my way back to camp when I found you all instead. I suppose you'll kill me and eat me for dinner now."

I frowned at Sam. "Were you planning to kill the goat?"

"No. Were you?"

I looked at Otis. "We weren't planning to kill you."

"It's okay if you want to," Otis said. "I'm used to it. My master kills me all the time."

"He . . . does?" I asked.

"Oh, sure. I'm basically a talking meal on four hooves. My therapist says that's why I'm so down all the time, but I don't know. I think it goes way back to when I was a kid—"

"Sorry. Wait. Who is your master?"

Hearthstone spelled out, *T-H-O-R. D-U-H.*

"That's right," said the goat. "Although his last name is not *Duh*. You haven't seen him, have you?"

"No . . ." I thought about my dream. I could still smell the bitter almonds on Loki's breath. *The gods don't even pretend to deal in good and evil, Magnus. Think about that when you meet Thor.*

Junior had told us to seek out Thor. The river had somehow brought us to where we needed to be. Only now, I wasn't sure I wanted to be here.

Sam readjusted her headscarf. "I'm not a big fan of Thor, but if he can give us directions to Lyngvi, we need to talk to him."

"Except the goat is lost," I said. "So how do we find Thor?"

Hearthstone pointed to my pendant. *Ask Jack.*

Instead of spelling the name, he made the sign for *jack-in-the-box,* which looked like a finger rabbit popping up from behind his hand. Sometimes sign language can be a little too literal.

I pulled off the pendant. The sword grew to full length and began to hum.

"Hey," said Jack, the runes glowing along his blade, "glad you survived! Oh, is that Otis? Cool! Thor must be around here somewhere."

Otis bleated. "You have a talking sword? I've never been killed by a talking sword before. That's fine. If you could just make a clean cut right across the throat—"

"Otis!" Jack said. "Don't you know me? I'm Frey's Sword, Sumarbrander. We met at that party at Bilskirner—the one where you were playing tug-of-war with Loki?"

"Oh . . ." Otis shook his horns. "Yes. That was embarrassing."

"Jack," I said, "we're looking for Thor. Any chance you can point us in the right direction?"

"Easy McSqueezy." The sword tugged at my arm. "I'm reading a big concentration of hot air and thunder that way!"

Sam and I helped Hearthstone to his feet. He wasn't looking too good. His lips were pale green. He wobbled like he'd just gotten off a Tilt-a-Whirl.

"Otis," Sam said, "can our friend ride you? It might be quicker."

"Sure," the goat said. "Ride me, kill me, whatever. But I should warn you, this is Jotunheim. If we go the wrong way, we'll run across giants. Then we'll all be butchered and put in a stew pot."

"We won't go the wrong way," I promised. "Will we, Jack?"

"Hmm?" said the sword. "Oh, no. Probably not. Like, a sixty percent chance we'll live."

"Jack. . . ."

"Kidding," he said. "Jeez, so uptight."

He pointed upstream and led us through the foggy morning, with spotty snow flurries and a forty percent chance of death.

FORTY-EIGHT

Hearthstone Passes Out
Even More than Jason Grace
(Though I Have No Idea
Who That Is)

JOTUNHEIM LOOKED a lot like Vermont, just with fewer signs offering maple syrup products. Snow dusted the dark mountains. Waist-high drifts choked the valleys. Pine trees bristled with icicles. Jack hovered in front, guiding us along the river as it zigzagged through canyons blanketed in subzero shadows. We climbed trails next to half-frozen waterfalls, my sweat chilling instantly against my skin.

In other words, it was a huge amount of fun.

Sam and I stayed close to Hearthstone. I hoped my residual aura of Frey-glow might do him some good, but he still looked pretty weak. The best we could do was keep him from sliding off the goat.

"Hang in there," I told him.

He signed something—maybe *sorry*—but his gesture was so listless I wasn't sure.

"Just rest," I said.

He grunted in frustration. He groped through his bag of runes, pulled one out, and placed it in my hands. He pointed to the stone, then to himself, as if to say *This is me*.

The rune was one I didn't know:

Sam frowned when she saw it. "That's *perthro*."

"What does it mean?" I asked.

She glanced cautiously at Hearth. "Are you trying to explain what happened to you? You want Magnus to know?"

Hearthstone took a deep breath, like he was preparing for a sprint. He signed: *Magnus–felt–pain*.

I closed my fingers around the stone. "Yeah. . . . When I healed you, there was something dark—"

Hearth pointed again at the stone. He looked at Sam.

"You want me to tell him?" she asked. "You sure?"

He nodded, then rested his head against the goat's back and closed his eyes.

We walked for about twenty yards before Sam said anything.

"When Hearth and I were in Alfheim," she started, "he told me part of his story. I don't know all the details, but . . . his parents . . ." She struggled to find words.

Otis the goat bleated. "Go on. I love depressing stories."

"Be quiet," Sam ordered.

"I'll just be quiet, then," the goat agreed.

I studied Hearthstone's face. He looked so peaceful asleep. "Blitzen told me a little bit," I said. "Hearth's parents never accepted him, because he was deaf."

"It was worse than that," Sam said. "They were . . . not good people."

Some of Loki's acidic tone crept into her voice, as if she were imagining Hearth's parents on the receiving end of mistletoe darts. "Hearth had a brother—Andiron—who died very young. It wasn't Hearthstone's fault, but his parents took out their bitterness on him. They always told him the wrong brother had died. To them, Hearth was a disappointment, a disabled elf, a punishment from the gods. He could do no right."

I clenched the runestone. "He still carries all that pain inside. Gods . . ."

Sam laid her hand on Hearth's ankle. "He couldn't tell me the details of how he grew up, but I—I got the feeling it was worse than you can imagine."

I looked at the rune. "No wonder he daydreamed about working magic. But this symbol . . . ?"

"Perthro symbolizes an empty cup lying sideways," Sam said. "It could be spilled drink, or a cup waiting to be filled, or a cup for throwing dice, like fate."

"I don't understand."

Sam brushed some goat hair from Hearthstone's pants cuff. "I think . . . I think perthro is the rune Hearthstone personally relates to. When he went to Mimir and drank from the well, Hearthstone was offered a choice between two futures. If he took the first path, Mimir would grant him speech and hearing and send him back to Alfheim to live a normal life, but he would have to give up his dream of magic. If he chose the second path—"

"He'd learn magic," I guessed, "but he would stay the way he is—deaf and dumb, hated by his own parents. What kind of messed-up choice is that? I should've stepped on Mimir's face when I had the chance."

Sam shook her head. "Mimir just presented the choices. Magic and normal life are mutually exclusive. Only people who have known great pain have the capacity to learn magic. They have to be like hollow cups. Even Odin . . . he gave up an eye to drink from Mimir's well, but that was just the beginning. In order to learn the runes, Odin fashioned a noose and hanged himself from a branch of the World Tree for nine days."

My stomach checked to see if it had anything left to retch. It settled for dry spasms. "That's . . . not right."

"But it was necessary," Sam said. "Odin pierced his side with his own spear and hung there in pain, without food or water, until the runes revealed themselves. The pain made him hollow . . . a receptacle for magic."

I looked at Hearthstone. I wasn't sure whether to hug him or wake him up and scold him. How could anyone willingly choose to hold on to that much pain? What kind of magic could possibly be worth the cost?

"I've done magic," I said. "Healing, walking into flames, blasting weapons out of people's hands. But I've never suffered like Hearth has."

Samirah pursed her lips. "That's different, Magnus. You were born with your magic—an inheritance from your father. You can't choose your abilities or change them. Alf seidr is innate. It's also lesser magic compared to what the runes can do."

"Lesser?" I didn't want to argue about whose magic was more impressive, but most of the things I'd seen Hearthstone do had been pretty . . . subtle.

"I told you back in Valhalla," Sam said, "the runes are

the secret language of the universe. Learning them, you can recode reality. The only limits on your magic are your strength and your imagination."

"So why don't more people learn runes?"

"That's what I've been telling you. It requires incredible sacrifice. Most people would die before they got as far as Hearthstone has."

I tucked Hearthstone's scarf around his neck. I understood now why he'd been willing to risk rune magic. To a guy with his troubled past, recoding reality must have sounded pretty good. I also thought about the message he'd whispered into my mind. He'd called me *brother*. After everything Hearthstone had been through with his own brother's death . . . that could not have been easy.

"So Hearth made himself an empty cup," I said. "Like perthro."

"Trying to fill himself with the power of magic," Sam agreed. "I don't know all the meanings of perthro, Magnus. But I do know one thing—Hearthstone cast it when we were falling from the cliff into the river."

I tried to remember, but I'd been overwhelmed with exhaustion as soon as I gripped the sword. "What did it do?"

"It got us *here*," Sam said. "And it left Hearthstone like that." She nodded to his snoring form. "I can't be sure, but I think perthro is his . . . what do Christians call it? A 'Hail Mary pass.' He was throwing that rune like you'd throw dice from a cup, turning our fate over to the gods."

My palm was now bruised from clenching the stone. I still wasn't sure why Hearthstone had given it to me, but I felt a strong instinct to keep it for him—if only temporarily. No one should carry that kind of fate alone. I slipped the rune into my pocket.

We trekked through the wilderness in silence for a while. At one point, Jack led us over the river on a fallen tree trunk. I couldn't help looking both ways for giant squirrels before crossing.

In places the snow was so deep we had to hop from boulder to boulder while Otis the goat speculated about which one of us would slip, fall, and die first.

"I wish you'd be quiet," I muttered. "I also wish we had snowshoes."

"You'd need Uller for that," said the goat.

"Who?"

"The god of snowshoes," said Otis. "He invented them. Also archery and . . . I don't know, other stuff."

I'd never heard of a snowshoe god. But I would've paid real money if the god of snowmobiles had come roaring out of the woods right then to give us a lift.

We kept trudging along.

Once, we spotted a stone house on the summit of a hill. The gray light and the mountains played tricks with my perception. I couldn't tell if the house was small and nearby, or massive and far away. I remembered what my friends had told me about giants—that they lived and breathed illusions.

"See that house?" Jack said. "Let's not go there."

I didn't argue.

Judging time was difficult, but by late afternoon the river had turned into a raging current. Cliffs rose along the opposite bank. In the distance, through the trees, I heard the roar of a waterfall.

"Oh, that's right," said Otis. "I remember now."

"You remember what?" I asked.

"Why I left. I was supposed to get help for my master."

Sam brushed a clump of snow off her shoulder. "Why would Thor need help?"

"The rapids," said Otis. "I guess we'd better hurry. I was supposed be quick, but I stood watching you guys for almost a day."

I flinched. "Wait . . . we were unconscious for *a whole day?*"

"At least," said Otis.

"He's right," Jack said. "According to my internal clock, it's Sunday the nineteenth. I warned you, once you took hold of me . . . well, we fought those dwarves on Friday. You slept all the way through Saturday."

Sam grimaced. "We've lost valuable time. The Wolf's island will appear in three more days, and we don't even know where Blitzen is."

"Probably my fault," Otis offered. "I should've saved you earlier, but giving a human mouth-to-mouth—I had to work up my nerve. My therapist gave me some breathing exercises—"

"Guys," Jack the sword interrupted, "we're close now. For real this time." He hovered off through the woods.

We followed the floating sword until the trees parted. In front of us stretched a beach of jagged black rocks and chunks of ice. On the opposite bank, sheer cliffs rose into the sky. The river had turned into full-on class five rapids—a combat zone of whitewater and half-submerged boulders. Upstream, the river was compressed between two skyscraper-size stone columns—man-made or natural, I couldn't tell. Their tops were lost in the clouds. From the fissure between them, the river blasted out in a vertical sheet—less like a waterfall and more like a dam splitting down the middle.

Suddenly Jotunheim did not seem like Vermont. It seemed more like the Himalayas—someplace not meant for mortals.

It was hard to focus on anything except the raging falls, but eventually I noticed a small campsite on the beach—a tent, a fire pit, and a second goat with dark fur pacing nervously on the shore. When the goat saw us, he came galloping over.

Otis turned to us and shouted over the roar of the river, "This is Marvin! He's my brother! His proper name is Tanngrisnr—Snarler—but—"

"Otis!" Marvin yelled. "Where have you been?"

"I forgot what I was doing," said Otis.

Marvin bleated in exasperation. His lips were curled in a permanent snarl, which—gee, I dunno—might have been how he got the name Snarler.

"This is the help you found?" Marvin fixed his yellow eyes on me. "Two scrawny humans and a dead elf?"

"He's not dead!" I yelled. "Where is Thor?"

"In the river!" Marvin pointed with his horns. "The god of thunder is about to drown, and if you don't figure out a way to help him, I'll kill you. By the way, nice to meet you."

FORTY-NINE

Well, There's Your Problem. You've Got a Sword Up Your Nose

I COULDN'T HELP IT.

When I heard the name Thor, I thought about the guy from the movies and comics—a big superhero from outer space, with bright Spandex tights, a red cape, goldilocks hair, and maybe a helmet with fluffy little dove wings.

In real life, Thor was scarier. And redder. And grungier.

Also, he could cuss like a drunken, creative sailor.

"Mother-grubbing scum bucket!" he yelled. (Or something along those lines. My brain may have filtered the actual language, as it would've made my ears bleed.) "Where is my backup?"

He stood chest-deep in the flood near the opposite side, clinging to a scrubby bush that grew from the cliff. The rock was so smooth and slick there were no other handholds. The bush looked like it was about to pull free of its roots. Any minute, Thor was going to get flushed downstream, where rows of jagged rocks shredded the current in a series of cataracts, perfect for making a Thor smoothie.

From this distance, through the spray of water and mist, I couldn't see much of the god himself: shoulder-length red hair, a curly red beard, and bodybuilder arms protruding from a sleeveless leather jerkin. He wore dark iron gauntlets that reminded me of robot hands, and a chain mail vest Blitzen would've found very trendy.

"Beard-burning son of a mud-lover!" roared the god. "Otis, is that you? Where's my artillery? My air support? Where the Helheim is my cavalry?"

"I'm here, boss!" Otis called. "I brought . . . two kids and a dead elf!"

"He's not dead," I said again.

"A half-dead elf," Otis corrected.

"What good is that?" Thor bellowed. "I need that giantess killed, and I need her killed NOW!"

"Giantess?" I asked.

Marvin head-butted me. "That one, stupid."

He nodded toward the waterfall. For a moment, the fog cleared from the tops of the cliffs, and I saw the problem.

Next to me, Sam made a sound like she was being garroted. "Holy Heimdall."

Those skyscraper-size pillars of rock were actually legs—*immense* legs so gray and rough they blended in with the surrounding cliffs. The rest of the woman was so tall she made Godzilla look like a toy poodle. She made the Sears Tower look like a traffic cone. Her thigh-length dress was stitched together from so many animal hides it probably represented the extinction of several dozen species. Her face, somewhere up there in the stratosphere, was as stony and grim as a Mount Rushmore president's, surrounded by a hurricane of long dark hair. She gripped the cliff tops on either side of the river as if straddling the torrent was hard even for her.

She looked down, smiling cruelly at the little speck of thunder god caught in the current, then squeezed her legs closer together. The waterfall sprayed out between her shins in a highly pressurized curtain of liquid force.

Thor tried to shout but got a mouthful of river. His head went under. The bush he was clinging to bent sideways, its roots snapping one after the other.

"She's going to wash him into oblivion!" Marvin said. "Do something, humans!"

Like what? I thought.

"He's a god," I said. "Can't he fly? Can't he zap her with lightning or—what about his hammer? Doesn't he have a hammer?"

Marvin snarled. He was very good at snarling. "Gee, why didn't *we* think of that? If Thor could do any of those things without losing his grip and getting instantly killed, don't you think he would've done it by now?"

I wanted to ask how a god could get killed, since they were supposed to be immortal. Then I thought about Mimir existing forever as a severed head, and Balder getting cut down by a mistletoe dart and spending eternity down in Hel World.

I looked at Sam.

She shrugged helplessly. "Against a giant that big, I have nothing."

Hearthstone mumbled in his sleep. His eyelids were starting to flutter, but he wasn't going to be casting magic anytime soon.

That left me only one friend to call on.

"Jack."

The sword hovered next to me. "Yeah?"

"You see that massive giantess blocking the river?"

"Technically speaking," Jack said, "I can't see anything, because I don't have eyes. But yes, I see the giant."

"You think you could fly up there and, I dunno, kill her?"

Jack hummed indignantly. "You want me to kill a two-thousand-foot-tall giantess?"

"Yeah."

"Well, here's the thing. You'd need to grab me and throw me like you've never thrown anything before. You'd need to *really* believe that killing this giantess is a worthy deed. And you'd need to be prepared for what will happen when you take hold of me again. How much energy would it take you, person-ally, to climb that two-thousand-foot-tall giant and kill her?"

The effort would probably destroy me, I thought. But I didn't see much choice.

We needed information from Thor. Sam and Hearthstone and two antisocial talking goats were depending on me.

"Let's do it." I grabbed the sword.

I tried to focus. I didn't care so much about saving Thor. I didn't even know the guy. Nor did I particularly care why a half-mile-tall giantess thought it was funny to stand in a river and spray a waterfall between her shins.

But I *did* care about Sam, Blitzen, and Hearthstone. They'd risked their lives to get me this far. No matter what Loki prom-ised, I had to find a way to stop Surt and keep Fenris Wolf chained. The Wolf had caused my mother's death. Mimir had said that Fenris sent his two children. . . . They were supposed to kill *me*. My mom had sacrificed her life to keep me alive. I had to make her sacrifice *mean* something.

The huge gray giantess represented everything that was in my way. She had to go.

With every bit of my strength, I threw the sword.

Jack sliced skyward like a rocket-powered boomerang.

What happened next . . . well, I wasn't sure I saw correctly. It was a long way up. But it looked like Jack flew into the giantess's left nostril.

The giantess arched her back. She made a face like she was going to sneeze. Her hands slipped from the cliff tops. Jack flew out of her right nostril as the giantess's knees buckled and she fell toward us.

"Timber!" Jack yelled, spiraling back to me.

"RUN!" I screamed.

Too late. The giantess face-planted in the river with a mighty *FLOOM!*

I have no memory of the wall of water that washed me into a tree, along with Sam, a half-asleep Hearthstone, and the two startled goats. Nevertheless, that's what must have happened. By sheer luck, none of us died.

The giantess's body had completely changed the topography. Where there had been a river, there was now a wide icy marsh, with water gurgling and spluttering around Dead Lady Island as it tried to find new ways to get downstream. The beach was six inches underwater. Thor's campsite had vanished. The god himself was nowhere to be seen.

"You killed Thor!" Otis bleated. "You dropped a giantess on him!"

The giantess's right arm twitched. I almost fell out of the tree. I was afraid Jack had only stunned her, but then Thor wriggled his way out of the giantess's armpit with much cursing and grunting.

Sam and I helped Hearthstone out of the tree as the god of thunder trudged across the giantess's back, jumped into the marsh, and waded toward us. His eyes were blue, rimmed with angry red. His expression was so fierce it would've sent wild boars running for their mommies.

Jack the sword appeared at my side, glistening with various types of goo typically found in a giant's nostril.

"So what do you think, *señor*?" His runes glowed. "You proud of me?"

"I'll answer that if I survive the next two minutes."

The angry god stopped in front of me. Water dripped from his red beard onto his extremely large chain-mail-clad chest. His pot-roast-size fists were clenched in their iron gauntlets.

"That"—he cracked a grin—"was amazing!"

He clapped me on the shoulder so hard he dislocated several joints. "Join me for dinner! We can kill Otis and Marvin!"

No Spoilers. Thor Is *Way* Behind on His Shows

YEP. WE KILLED THE GOATS.

Thor promised they would be resurrected good as new the next morning, so long as we didn't break any bones. Otis assured me frequent death was good for his exposure therapy. Marvin growled at me to get on with it and not be a weak-kneed wimp.

It was a lot easier killing Marvin.

After two years of homelessness, I thought I knew how tough it could be to keep myself fed, but let me tell you: killing and butchering an animal for my own supper was a new experience. You think it's gross to pull a half-eaten sandwich out of a trash bin? Try skinning a goat, cutting it into chunks, building a fire, then cooking the meat on a spit while attempting to ignore the goat heads staring at you from the scrap pile.

You might assume that kind of experience would turn me into a vegetarian. But nope. As soon as I smelled the cooking meat, my hunger took over. I forgot all about the horrors of goat slaughter. Those Otis-kebabs were the best things I ever tasted.

As we ate, Thor chatted about giants, Jotunheim, and his opinions of Midgard television shows, which, for some reason, he followed religiously. (Can I say a god did something religiously?)

"Giants!" He shook his head in disgust. "After all these centuries, you'd think they would learn to stop invading Midgard. But no! They're like the . . . what is it? The League of Assassins in *Arrow*! They just keep coming back! As if I would let anything happen to humans! You guys are my favorite species!"

He patted my cheek. Fortunately, he had taken off his iron gloves, or he would've broken my jaw. Unfortunately, he hadn't washed his hands after gutting the goats.

Hearthstone sat at the fire, nibbling on a piece of Marvin haunch. He was getting some of his strength back, though every time I looked at him I had to force myself not to sob. I wanted to hug the poor guy, bake him a batch of cookies, and tell him how sorry I was about his crappy childhood, but I knew he wouldn't want pity. He wouldn't want me to start treating him differently.

Still . . . the empty cup runestone weighed heavily in my coat pocket.

Sam stayed at the edge of the fire, as far from Thor as she could get. She said as little as possible and made no sudden movements, which meant that most of Thor's attention was on me.

Everything the thunder god did, he did with gusto. He loved cooking his goats. He loved eating and drinking mead. He loved telling stories. And he loved farting. Boy, did he love farting. When he got excited, sparks of electricity flew from his hands, his ears, and . . . well, I'll leave the rest to your imagination.

Unlike his movie version, there was nothing polished about

Thor. His face was handsome in a beat-up way, like he'd spent years in the boxing ring. His chain mail was filthy. His leather jerkin and trousers had worn to the color of dirty snow. Tattoos covered his muscular arms. On his left biceps, SIF was inscribed inside a heart. Around his right forearm coiled a stylized World Serpent. Across his knuckles on either hand, in block letters, were the names MAGNI and MODI. At first I was nervous about the name *Magni*, because it was so close to *Magnus*—the last thing I wanted was my name printed across the thunder god's fist—but Sam assured me, quietly, that it was a totally different name.

Thor regaled me with his theories about a hypothetical death match between Daryl from *The Walking Dead* and Mike from *Breaking Bad*. Back when I was hanging out on the sidewalks of Boston, I would've been happy to talk TV for hours just to pass the time, but now I had a quest looming. We'd lost a whole day to unconsciousness. Speculating on the new fall lineup wasn't going to mean much if the world was consumed in flames three days from now.

Still, Thor was having so much fun it was hard to change the subject.

"So what do you think?" he asked. "Best villain in an ongoing series?"

"Uh . . . wow, tough one." I pointed at his knuckles. "Who are Magni and Modi?"

"My sons!" Thor beamed. With the goat grease in his beard and the random electrical sparks flying from his fingers, I was worried he might set himself on fire. "I've got a lot of sons, of course, but they're my favorites."

"Yeah?" I asked. "How old are they?"

He frowned. "Ah, this is embarrassing, but I'm not sure. They might not even be born yet."

"How—?"

"Magnus," Sam interrupted, "Lord Thor's two sons Magni and Modi are fated to survive Ragnarok. Their names are spoken in the prophecies of the Norns."

"That's right!" Thor leaned toward Sam. "Who are you again?"

"Uh . . . Sam, my lord."

"You have a familiar aura, girl." The god furrowed his red eyebrows. "Why is that?"

"I was a Valkyrie . . . ?" Sam inched backward.

"Oh. Maybe that's it." Thor shrugged. "You'll have to excuse me. I've been on three thousand five hundred and six consecutive deployments to the eastern front, keeping the giants at bay. I get a little jumpy sometimes."

Hearthstone signed, *And gassy.*

Thor belched. "What did the elf say? I do not speak Gesticulation."

"Um, he was wondering how you keep current on television," I said, "seeing as you're out in the field so much."

Thor laughed. "I have to do *some*thing to keep myself sane!"

Hearthstone signed: *How's that working out for you?*

"The elf agrees!" Thor guessed. "I can watch my shows anywhere, or at least I *could*. Among its many other powers, my hammer Mjolnir got full bars of service and HD resolution in any of the Nine Worlds!"

"*Got*, past tense?" Sam asked.

Thor cleared his throat loudly. "But enough about

television! How's that goat meat? You didn't break any bones, did you?"

Sam and I exchanged looks. When we'd first introduced ourselves to the god, I'd found it strange that Thor didn't have his hammer. It was sort of his signature weapon. I'd figured maybe it was just in disguise, like my sword. Now I was starting to wonder. His piercing bloodshot gaze made me think it might be dangerous to ask, though.

"Uh, no, sir," I said. "We didn't break any bones. Just theoretically, what would happen if we did?"

"The goats would be resurrected with that damage," he said. "Which would take a long time to heal and be very annoying. Then I'd either have to kill you or make you my slave forever."

Hearthstone signed, *This god is a freak.*

"You're right, Mr. Elf," Thor said. "It is a fair and just punishment! That's how I got my regular manservant, Thjalfi." Thor shook his head. "Poor kid. These deployments were starting to get to him. I had to grant him a furlough. I really *could* use another slave . . ." He studied me appraisingly.

"So . . ." I set aside my goat meat. "How did you end up in the river, and why was that giantess trying to drown you?"

"Oh, her." Thor glowered at the neighborhood-size corpse in the middle of the icy swamp. "She's a daughter of Geirrod, one of my old enemies. I hate that guy. He's always sending his daughters to kill me." He gestured toward the cliffs. "I was heading to his fortress to see if— Well, no matter. Thank you for the assist. That was Frey's sword, wasn't it?"

"Yes. Jack's around here somewhere." I whistled. Jack came hovering over.

"Hello, Thor," said the sword. "Long time no see."

"Ha!" The god clapped his hands in delight. "I thought I recognized you. But isn't your name Sumarbrander? Why did the human call you Jorvik?"

"Jack," the sword corrected.

"Yak."

"No," the sword said patiently. "Jack, with the English *jay* sound."

"Okay, fine. Well, nice job with the giantess."

"You know what they say." Jack sounded smug. "The bigger they are, the easier it is to fly up their nasal cavity."

"True," Thor said. "But I thought you were lost. How did you come to be with these strange folk?"

He calls us *strange?* Hearthstone signed.

"Lord Thor," Sam said, "we actually came here looking for you. We need your help, as Magnus will now explain." She stared at me like, *If he knows what's good for him.*

I told Thor about the Norns' prophecy—nine days hence, sun going east, Surt explodes everything, Fenris Wolf, nasty teeth, eats world, et cetera.

Thor became agitated. Sparks flew from his elbows. He rose and paced around the fire, occasionally punching nearby trees.

"You want me to tell you where the island is," he deduced.

"That would be great," I said.

"But I can't," Thor muttered to himself. "I can't be sending random mortals on wolf-watching tours. Too dangerous. But Ragnarok. Not ready. No. Not unless—" He froze, then turned toward us with an eager gleam in his eyes. "Perhaps *that's* why you're here."

I do not like this, Hearthstone signed.

Thor nodded. "The elf agrees! You have come to assist me!"

"Exactly!" said Jack, humming with excitement. "Let's do it, whatever it is!"

I had a sudden desire to hide behind the goat carcasses. Anything the god of thunder and the Sword of Summer agreed on, I didn't want to be part of.

Sam placed her ax at her side, as if she anticipated needing it soon. "Let me guess, Lord Thor: you've lost your hammer again."

"Now, I did *not* say that!" Thor wagged a finger at her. "You did *not* hear that from me. Because if that were true, hypothetically speaking, and if word got out, the giants would invade Midgard immediately! You mortals don't realize how often I keep you safe. My reputation alone makes most giants too afraid to attack your world."

"Back up," I said. "What did Sam mean by *again*? You've lost your hammer before?"

"Once," Thor said. "Okay, twice. Three times if you count this time, which you shouldn't, because I am not admitting that the hammer is missing."

"Right . . ." I said. "So how did you lose it?"

"I don't know!" Thor started to pace again, his long red hair sparking and popping. "It was just like . . . *Poof!* I tried retracing my steps. I tried the Find My Hammer app, but it doesn't work!"

"Isn't your hammer the most powerful weapon in the universe?" I asked.

"Yes!"

"And I thought it was so heavy nobody except you could pick it up."

"True. Even *I* need my iron gloves of strength to lift it! But giants are tricky. They're big and strong and they have magic. With them, many impossible things are possible."

I thought about the eagle Big Boy and how easily he'd suckered me. "Yeah, I get it. Is that why you were going to A-Rod's?"

"Geirrod's," Thor corrected. "And, yes. He's a likely suspect. Even if he doesn't have it, he might know who does. Besides, without my hammer I can't watch my shows. I'm a season behind on *Sherlock* and it's killing me! I was ready to go to Geirrod's fortress myself, but I'm very glad you volunteered to go for me!"

We did? Hearthstone asked.

"That's the spirit, Mr. Elf! I'm glad you are ready to die for my cause!"

Really not, Hearth signed.

"Just go to Geirrod's fortress and check for my hammer. Of course it's important you don't let on that it is missing. If Geirrod *doesn't* have it, we don't want him to know that *I* don't have it. But, you know, if he doesn't have it, obviously ask him if he knows who does, without actually admitting that it's missing."

Samirah pressed her fingers to her temples. "I'm getting a headache. Lord Thor, how are we supposed to find your hammer if we can't mention—"

"You'll figure it out!" he said. "You humans are a clever bunch. Then, once you've determined the truth, I will know you are worthy of facing Fenris Wolf. I'll give you the location of his island and you can stop Ragnarok. You help me, I help you."

It sounded more like *You help me, then you help me some more,* but I doubted there was a polite way to decline without getting an iron gauntlet in my teeth.

Sam must have been thinking the same thing. Her face turned roughly the same shade of green as her hijab. "Lord Thor," she said, "invading a giant's fortress with only three people would be . . ."

Suicidal, Hearthstone suggested. *Stupid.*

"Difficult," Sam said.

Just then, a nearby pine tree shuddered. Blitzen dropped from the branches and landed waist-deep in a pile of slush.

Hearthstone scrambled over and helped him to his feet.

"Thanks, buddy," Blitz said. "Stupid tree travel. Where—?"

"Is this a friend of yours?" Thor raised one ironclad fist. "Or should I—"

"No! I mean, yes, he's a friend. Blitzen, Thor. Thor, Blitzen."

"*The* Thor?" Blitzen bowed so low it looked like he was trying to avoid an air strike. "Honored. Seriously. Hi. Wow."

"Well, then!" The thunder god grinned. "You have *four* people to storm the giant's citadel! Friend dwarf, help yourself to my goat meat and my fire. As for me, after being stuck in that river so long, I'm going to turn in early. In the morning, you all can set off to find my hammer, which of course is not officially missing!"

Thor tromped over to his bed of furs, threw himself down, and began snoring with as much gusto as he'd been farting.

Blitzen frowned at me. "What have you gotten us into?"

"Long story," I said. "Here, have some Marvin."

FIFTY-ONE

We Have the Talk-About-Turning-Into-Horseflies Chat

HEARTHSTONE WENT to sleep first, mostly because he was the only one who *could* sleep with Thor's snoring. Since the god had crashed outside, Hearthstone commandeered the two-man tent. He crawled inside and promptly collapsed.

The rest of us stayed up and talked around the campfire. At first I was worried we might wake Thor, but I soon realized we could've tap-danced around his head, banged gongs, shouted his name, and set off large explosions, and he would've slept right through it.

I wondered if that was how he had lost his hammer. The giants could've waited until he was asleep, backed up a couple of industrial cranes, and done the job easy.

As night fell, I was grateful for the fire. The darkness was more complete than in the wildest places my mom and I had ever camped. Wolves howled in the forest, which gave me a bad case of the shivers. Wind moaned through the canyons like a chorus of zombies.

I mentioned this to Blitzen, but he set me straight.

"No, kid," he said. "Norse zombies are called *draugr*. They move silently. You'd never hear them coming."

"Thanks," I said. "That's a huge relief."

Blitzen stirred his cup of goat stew, though he didn't seem

interested in tasting it. He'd changed into a blue wool suit with a cream-colored trench coat, perhaps so he could blend in with the Jotunheim snow in the most stylish way possible. He'd also brought each of us a new supply pack filled with fresh winter clothes, which of course he'd sized perfectly just by guessing. Sometimes it pays to have a friend who's a thoughtful clotheshorse.

Blitz explained how he'd delivered the earrings to his mother, then gotten detained in Folkvanger for various duties as Freya's representative: judging an oyster bake, refereeing a volleyball game, serving as guest of honor at the 678th annual ukulele festival.

"It was murder," he said. "Mom liked the earrings. Didn't ask how I got them. Didn't want to hear about the contest with Junior. She just said, 'Oh, don't you wish you could do work like this, Blitzen?'" From his coat pocket, he pulled the rope Andskoti. The ball of silk glowed silver like a miniature moon. "I hope this was worth it."

"Hey," I told him, "what you did in that contest? I've never seen *anybody* work that hard. You poured your heart and soul into that Expando-Duck. And the bulletproof tie? The chain mail vest? Just wait. We'll get you an endorsement deal with Thor, and you'll start a fashion trend."

"Magnus is right," Sam said. "Well, maybe not about the endorsement deal with Thor—but you have real talent, Blitzen. If Freya and the other dwarves don't see it, that's their problem. Without you, we never would've gotten this far."

"You mean you wouldn't have gotten kicked out of the Valkyries; Magnus wouldn't have died; we wouldn't have half the gods mad at us; fire giants and einherjar wouldn't be out to kill us; and we wouldn't be sitting in the wilderness of Jotunheim with a snoring god?"

"Exactly," Sam said. "Life is good."

Blitzen snorted, but I was happy to see a little spark of humor in his eyes. "Yeah, okay. I'm going to sleep. I'll need it if we're going to storm a giant's castle in the morning."

He crawled into the tent and muttered to Hearthstone, "Make some room, you tent hog!" Then he draped his overcoat across the elf, which I thought was kind of sweet.

Sam sat cross-legged in her jeans and new snow jacket, her hood pulled over her headscarf. Snow had started to fall—big fluffy flakes that dissolved and hissed in the flames.

"Speaking of the contest in Dwarfland," I said, "we never got to talk about the horsefly—"

"Hush." Sam glanced apprehensively at Thor. "Certain people aren't keen on my father, or my father's children."

"Certain people are snoring like a chain saw."

"Still . . ." She studied her hand as if making sure it hadn't changed. "I promised myself I wouldn't shape-shift, and in the last week I've done it twice. The first time . . . well, the stag was after us on the World Tree. I turned into a deer to distract it so Hearthstone could get away. I didn't think I had a choice."

I nodded. "And the second time, you turned into the horsefly to help Blitzen. Those are both great reasons. Besides, shape-shifting is an awesome power. Why wouldn't you want to use it?"

The firelight made her irises almost as red as Surt's. "Magnus, true shape-shifting isn't like my hijab's camouflage. Shape-shifting doesn't just change your appearance. It changes *you*. Every time I do it, I feel . . . I feel more of my father's nature trying to take hold of me. He's fluid, unpredictable, untrustworthy—I don't want to be like that."

I gestured at Thor. "You could have *him* for a dad—a farting giant with goat grease in his beard and tattoos on his knuckles. Then everybody in Valhalla would love you."

I could tell she was trying not to smile. "You are *very* bad. Thor is an important god."

"No doubt. So is Frey, supposedly, but I've never met him. At least your dad is kind of charming, and he has a sense of humor. He may be a sociopath, but—"

"Wait." Sam's voice tightened. "You talk as if you've met him."

"I . . . I kind of walked right into that, didn't I? Truth is, he's been in a few of my near-death experiences."

I told Sam about the dreams: Loki's warnings, his promises, his suggestion that I take the sword to my Uncle Randolph and forget about the quest.

Sam listened. I couldn't tell if she was angry or shocked or both.

"So," she said, "you didn't tell me this earlier because you didn't trust me?"

"Maybe at first. Later, I just—I wasn't sure what to do. Your dad is kind of unsettling."

She tossed a twig into the flames and watched it burn. "You can't do what my dad suggests, no matter what he promises. We have to face Surt. We'll need the sword."

I remembered my dream of the burning throne—the dark face floating in the smoke, the voice with the heat of a flamethrower. *YOU AND YOUR FRIENDS WILL BE MY TINDER. YOU WILL START THE FIRE THAT BURNS THE NINE WORLDS.*

I looked around for Jack, but I didn't see him. The sword had volunteered to hover the perimeter "on patrol," as he put it. He suggested I wait until the last possible minute to reclaim him, since once I did, I would pass out instantly from the strain of murdering a giantess by nostrilcide.

Snow continued to fall, steaming against the stones around the fire pit. I thought about our near-lunch in the food court of the Transportation Building, how nervous Sam had acted around Amir. That seemed like a thousand years ago.

"When we were on Harald's boat," I recalled, "you said your family had a long history with all the Norse god stuff. How? You said your grandparents came from Iraq . . . ?"

She threw another stick into the flames. "Vikings were traders, Magnus. They traveled everywhere. They got all the way to America. It shouldn't be a surprise they got to the Middle East, too. Arabic coins have been found in Norway. The best Viking swords were modeled after Damascus steel."

"But *your* family . . . You've got a more personal connection?"

She nodded. "Back in medieval times, some of the Vikings settled in Russia. They called themselves the Rus. That's where the word *Russian* comes from. Anyway, the Caliph—the big king down in Baghdad—he sent an ambassador north to find out more about the Vikings, set up trade routes with them, that kind of stuff. The ambassador's name was Ahmed ibn-Fadlan ibn-al-Abbas."

"Fadlan like Fadlan's Falafel. Al-Abbas like—"

"Right. Like me. Al-Abbas means *of the lion.* That's my branch of the clan. Anyway"—she pulled a sleeping bag out of her backpack—"this guy Ibn Fadlan kept a journal about his time with the Vikings. It's one of the only written sources about what the Norse were like back then. Ever since, my family and the Vikings have been intertwined. Over the centuries, my relatives have racked up a lot of weird encounters with . . . supernatural beings. Maybe that's why my mother wasn't too surprised when she found out who my dad really was." She spread out her sleeping bag next to the fire. "And that's why Samirah al-Abbas is fated never to have a normal life. The end."

"Normal life," I mused. "I don't even know what that means anymore."

She looked like she wanted to say something, then changed her mind. "I'm going to sleep."

I had a weird vision of our ancestors, medieval Chase and medieval al-Abbas, sitting around a campfire in Russia twelve hundred years ago, comparing notes on how the Norse gods had messed up their lives, maybe with Thor snoring on a bed of furs nearby. Sam's family might be intertwined with the gods, but as my Valkyrie she was also intertwined with *my* family now.

"We'll figure things out," I promised. "I don't know about *normal,* but I'll do everything I can to help you get what you want—a place in the Valkyries again, your marriage with Amir, a pilot's license. Whatever it takes."

She stared at me as if processing the words from another language.

"What?" I asked. "Do I have goat blood on my face?"

"No. Well, yes, you do have goat blood on your face. But that's not . . . I was just trying to remember the last time anybody said something that nice to me."

"If you want, I'll go back to insulting you tomorrow," I said. "For now, get some sleep. Sweet dreams."

Sam curled up by the fire. Snow settled lightly on the sleeve of her coat. "Thank you, Magnus. But no dreams, please. I don't want to dream in Jotunheim."

FIFTY-TWO

I Got the Horse Right Here. His Name Is Stanley

THOR WAS STILL SNORING like a defective wood chipper when we were ready to leave the next morning. That's really saying something, since I had slept forever. Jack the sword had not been kidding about the effect of killing the giantess. As soon as I'd reclaimed the sword after Sam fell asleep, I had passed out instantly.

At least I hadn't lost a full twenty-four hours this time. With Fenris Wolf appearing in only two more days, I couldn't afford any more long naps. I wondered if maybe, just maybe, I was growing more resilient as I became bonded to the sword. I hoped so, but I still felt like I'd been flattened under a rolling pin all night.

We packed up our gear and ate a cold breakfast of MORNING, MAGGOT! energy bars from Blitz's supply bags (yum). Then Hearthstone nestled the severed heads of the two still-dead goats in Thor's arms like teddy bears. Never let it be said that elves don't have a sense of humor.

I looked down at the drool turning to ice in Thor's beard. "And to think that the defense of Nine Worlds rests on this god."

"Let's get going," Blitzen muttered. "I don't want to be around when he wakes up with Otis and Marvin."

The dead giantess proved helpful. We climbed over her to cross the icy swamp. Then we discovered that we could scale her left foot to reach the first ledge in the side of the cliff.

Once we got that far, I stared up at the remaining five hundred meters of sheer icy rock. "Awesome. Now the real fun begins."

"Wish I could still fly," Sam murmured.

I imagined she *could* fly, with a little shape-shifting, but after our conversation last night, I decided against mentioning that.

Blitz handed his pack to Hearthstone, then wriggled his stubby fingers. "Don't worry, kids. You're climbing with a dwarf today."

I frowned. "You're a mountaineer now as well as a master of fashion?"

"I told you, kid, dwarves were formed from maggots that burrowed through Ymir's flesh."

"And you seem strangely proud of it."

"Rock to us is like . . . well, not rock." He punched the side of the cliff. Rather than breaking his fist, he left an indentation just the right size for a handhold. "I'm not saying it'll be fast or easy. It takes me a lot of effort to shape rock. But we can do it."

I glanced at Sam. "Did you know dwarves could punch through stone?"

"Nope. That's new to me."

Hearthstone signed, *Use the magic rope? Rather not fall to death.*

I shuddered. I couldn't think about the rope Andskoti without thinking about the Wolf, and I didn't like thinking about the Wolf. "We need that rope to bind Fenris, right? I don't want to do anything that might weaken it."

"Don't worry, kid." Blitz brought out the silken cord. "This rope can't be weakened. And Hearthstone's right. We might as well tie it to one another for safety."

"That way if we fall," Sam said, "we'll fall together."

"Sold," I said, trying to tamp down my anxiety. "I love dying with friends."

We got hitched (so to speak) and followed our intrepid rock-shaping, fashion-conscious guide up the side of Mount You-Gotta-Be-Kidding-Me.

I'd heard homeless military vets describe war as ninety-five percent boredom and five percent terror. Climbing the cliff was more like five percent terror and ninety-five percent excruciating pain. My arms shook. My legs wobbled. Every time I looked down I wanted to cry or throw up.

Despite the handholds and footholds Blitzen made, the wind almost knocked me off several times. There was nothing I could do except keep going.

I knew for certain that my Valhalla-enhanced strength was the only thing keeping me alive. Magnus 1.0 would have fallen to his death. I didn't understand how Hearthstone could manage, bringing up the end of the rope, but he did. And Sam ... . demigod or not, she didn't have the advantage of being an einherji. Yet she didn't complain, didn't waver, didn't slip—which was good, since she was climbing right above me.

Finally, as the sky began to darken, we reached the top. Down in the canyon we'd come from, the body of the giantess was so small it looked like a normal-sized body. The river glittered in the gloom. If Thor's camp was still there, I saw no sign of it.

In the other direction, Jotunheim spread out like an electron microscope landscape—impossibly jagged peaks, crystalline cliffs, ravines filled with ovoid clouds like floating bacteria.

The good news: I could see the giant's fortress. Across a mile-wide chasm, windows glowed red in the side of a mountain. Towers rose from the summit as if they'd been shaped from the rock dwarven-style rather than built.

The bad news: Did I mention the mile-wide chasm? The cliff top where we were standing was no more than a narrow plateau. The drop on the other side was just as precipitous as the one we'd climbed.

Considering it had taken us all day to get this far, I figured we'd reach the castle in another six months, easy. Unfortunately, it was Monday evening and the Wolf's island was supposed to rise on Wednesday.

"Let's camp here tonight," Blitzen said. "Maybe in the morning we'll see a better way across."

Despite our time crunch, nobody argued. We were all so tired we collapsed.

As is so often the case, in the fresh light of morning our situation looked much worse.

There were no stairs, no convenient zip lines, no direct commuter flights to Geirrod's fortress. I was about to risk an ax in the face by suggesting that Sam shape-shift—maybe change into a giant sugar glider and carry us across—when Hearthstone signed: *Have an idea.*

He pulled out a runestone:

$$\mathsf{M}$$

"M," I said.

He shook his head then spelled out the name: *E-H-W-A-Z*.

"Right," I said. "Because calling it *M* would be too easy."

Sam plucked the stone from Hearth's palm. "I know this one. It symbolizes a horse, right? The shape is like a saddle."

I squinted at the rune. The wind was so cold and harsh that I had a hard time thinking imaginatively, but the symbol still looked like an M to me. "How does this help us?"

Hearthstone signed: *Means horse, transportation. Maybe a way to go—* He pointed to the castle.

Blitzen tugged his beard. "Sounds like powerful magic. Have you tried it before?"

Hearthstone shook his head. *Don't worry. I can do it.*

"I know you can," said Blitz. "But you've already taxed yourself to the limit several times."

Be fine, Hearth insisted.

"I don't see that we have much choice," I said, "since we don't have anyone who can grow wings."

"I will push you off this mountain," Sam warned.

"All right," Blitzen decided, "let's try it. I mean the rune, not pushing Magnus off the mountain. Maybe Hearth can summon a helicopter."

"Geirrod would hear a helicopter," I said. "And probably throw rocks at us. And kill us."

"Well, then," Blitzen said, "perhaps a stealth helicopter. Hearthstone, do your stuff!"

Sam returned the stone. Hearth passed his hand over it, moving his lips as if imagining how the syllables might sound.

The runestone burst into dust. Hearthstone stared at the white powder trickling through his fingers.

"I'm guessing it wasn't supposed to do that?" I asked.

"Guys." Sam's voice was so small it was almost lost in the wind.

She pointed up, where a gray shape was hurtling out of the clouds. It moved so fast and blended with the sky so well, I didn't realize what the creature was until it was almost on top of us—a stallion twice the size of a normal horse, his coat rippling like liquid steel, his white mane billowing, his eyes glittering black.

The stallion had no wings, but he galloped through the air as easily as if he were running down a gentle slope. Only when he landed next to us did I notice he had four, five, six . . . *eight* legs—a pair in each place where a normal horse would have one, kind of like dual wheels on a pickup truck.

I turned to Hearthstone. "Dude, when you summon a horse, you don't mess around."

Hearthstone grinned. Then his eyes rolled up in his head and he fell forward. I managed to catch him and ease him to the ground while Blitzen and Sam moved warily around the stallion.

"It—it c-can't be," Blitzen stammered.

"One of Sleipnir's offspring?" Sam wondered. "Gods, what a magnificent animal."

The horse nuzzled her hand, clearly pleased with the compliment.

I moved toward him, fascinated by his intelligent eyes and

his regal stance. The stallion gave the word *horsepower* a new meaning. He radiated strength.

"Is somebody going to introduce me?" I asked.

Sam shook herself out of her reverie. "I . . . I don't know who he is. He looks like Sleipnir, Odin's steed, but this can't be him. Only Odin can summon him. I'm guessing this is one of Sleipnir's sons."

"Well, he's amazing." I extended my hand. The horse brushed his lips against my fingers. "He's friendly. And he's definitely big enough to carry us all across the chasm. Would you be okay with that, buddy?"

The horse nickered, like, *Uh, duh, that's why I'm here.*

"The eight legs are"—I was about to say weird but changed my mind—"awesome. How did that happen?"

Blitzen glanced at Sam. "Sleipnir was one of Loki's children. They tend to come out . . . interesting."

I smiled. "So this horse is your nephew, Sam?"

She glared at me. "Let's not go there."

"How did your dad father a horse?"

Blitzen coughed. "Actually, Loki was Sleipnir's mother."

"What—?"

"Let's *definitely* not go there," Sam warned.

I filed that away for later research. "Okay, Mr. Horse, since we don't know your name, I'm going to call you Stanley, because you look like a Stanley. That okay with you?"

The horse seemed to shrug, which was good enough for me.

We draped Hearthstone over Stanley's extra-long back like a sack of elfish potatoes. The rest of us climbed on.

"We're going to that castle over there, Stanley," I told the stallion. "Looking for a quiet entrance. That work for you?"

The horse whinnied. I was pretty sure he was warning me to hold on.

I wondered what exactly I should hold on *to*, since there were no reins and no saddle. Then the stallion pawed the rocks with his front four hooves, leaped off the side of the cliff, and plummeted straight down.

And we all died.

FIFTY-THREE

How to Kill Giants Politely

JUST KIDDING THIS TIME.

It only *felt* like we were going to die.

The horse must have enjoyed the feeling of free fall. I didn't. I grabbed his neck and screamed in terror (which was not very stealthy). Meanwhile, Blitzen grabbed my waist, and behind him Sam somehow stayed on board while managing to keep Hearthstone from slipping into oblivion.

The fall felt like hours, though it probably lasted only a second or two. During that time I thought of several more colorful names for Stanley. Finally he churned his eight legs like locomotive wheels. We leveled out and began to climb.

Stanley punched through a cloud, zigzagged along the face of the mountain, and landed on a window ledge near the top of the fortress. I dismounted, my legs shaking, then helped the others with Hearthstone.

The ledge was so wide, the four of us plus the horse could stand in one corner and seem no bigger than mice. The window had no glass (probably because there wasn't that much glass in the world), but Stanley had landed us behind a panel of gathered curtain, so nobody inside could've seen us, even if they were randomly scanning the window for mice.

"Thanks, buddy," I told Stanley. "That was horrifying. I mean, great."

Stanley nickered. He gave me an affectionate nip, then disappeared in a burst of dust. On the windowsill where he'd been standing was the ehwaz runestone.

"He seemed to like me," I noted.

Blitzen slid down next to Hearthstone and said, "Eep."

Only Sam didn't seem ruffled. In fact, she seemed exhilarated. Her eyes sparkled and she couldn't stop smiling. I guess she really *did* love flying, even if it was a near-death free fall on an eight-legged horse.

"Of course Stanley liked you." She picked up the runestone. "Horses are one of Frey's sacred animals."

"Huh." I thought about my experiences with the Boston mounted police that patrolled the Public Garden. The horses always seemed friendly, even if their riders weren't. One time, when a mounted officer had started to question me, his horse had suddenly taken off, galloping toward the nearest low-hanging tree branch.

"I've always liked horses," I said.

"Frey's temples kept their own herds," Sam told me. "No mortal was allowed to ride them without the god's permission."

"Well, I wish Stanley had asked my permission before leaving," I said. "We have no exit strategy, and Hearthstone doesn't look like he's going to be casting more spells anytime soon."

The elf had regained consciousness . . . sort of. He leaned against Blitz, giggling silently and making random signs like, *Butterfly. Pop. Yippee.* Blitzen clutched his stomach and stared into space as if he were thinking of interesting ways to die.

Sam and I crept to the edge of the curtain. We peeked around it and found we were at ceiling level of a stadium-size room. In the hearth burned a fire as big as an urban riot. The only exit was a closed wooden door on the far wall. In the center of the room, seated at a stone table, two giantesses were having dinner, ripping into a carcass that reminded me of the roast beast in Valhalla's dining hall.

The giantesses didn't look as tall as the dead one back in the river, though it was hard to be sure. In Jotunheim, proportions made no sense. My eyes felt like they were constantly adjusting to different funhouse mirrors.

Sam nudged my arm. "Look."

She pointed to a birdcage suspended from the ceiling, hanging just about eye-level to us. Inside the cage, waddling around on a bed of straw and looking miserable, was a white swan.

"That's a Valkyrie," Sam said.

"How can you be sure?"

"I just am. Not only that . . . I'm pretty sure it's Gunilla."

I shuddered. "What would she be doing here?"

"Looking for us. Valkyries are excellent trackers. I imagine she got here before we did and . . ." Sam mimed a hand snatching something out of the air.

"So . . . do we leave her?"

"For the giants to eat? Of course not."

"She set you up. She got you kicked out of the Valkyries."

"She's still my captain," Sam said. "She . . . well, she has her reasons for mistrusting me. A few centuries ago, there was a son of Loki who made it into Valhalla."

"He and Gunilla fell in love," I guessed. "I kind of got that impression when she was taking me on a tour of the hotel."

Sam nodded. "The son of Loki betrayed her. Turned out he *was* a spy for my dad. Broke her heart. Well . . . you get the picture. Anyway, I'm not going to leave her to die."

I sighed. "Okay."

I pulled off my pendant.

Jack the sword hummed to life.

"About time," he said. "What did I miss yesterday?"

"Bunch of climbing," I told him. "Now we're looking at two more giantesses. How do you feel about flying up their nostrils?"

The sword tugged at my hand, his blade peeking around the corner of the curtain. "Dude, we're on their windowsill. We've technically crossed the threshold of the giants' home."

"So?"

"So you have to follow the rules! Killing them in their home without provocation would be rude!"

"Right," I said. "We wouldn't want to kill them rudely."

"Hey, *señor*, guest rights and host rights are important magic protocols. They keep situations from escalating."

Blitzen groaned in the corner. "The sword has a point, kid. And, no, that wasn't a joke. We should go in, claim guest rights, and barter for what we need. If the giants try to kill us, *then* we can attack."

Hearthstone hiccupped, grinned, and signed: *Washing machine.*

Sam shook her head. "You two are in no condition to go anywhere. Blitz, stay here and watch Hearthstone. Magnus and

I will go in, find Thor's hammer, and free Gunilla. If things go wrong, it'll be up to you two to figure out how to rescue us."

"But—" Blitzen put his fist over his mouth and stifled an *urp*. "Yeah . . . okay. How are you guys going to get down there?"

Sam peered over the ledge. "We'll use your magic rope to reach the floor. Then we'll walk up to the giants and introduce ourselves."

"I hate this plan," I said. "Let's do it."

FIFTY-FOUR

Why You Should Not Use a Steak Knife as a Diving Board

RAPPELLING DOWN THE WALL was the easy part.

When we reached the bottom, I started having serious doubts. The giantesses were definitely smaller than their dead sister—maybe fifty feet tall. If I'd been asked to wrestle one of their big toes, I could've won no problem. Other than that, I didn't like my chances.

"I feel like Jack up the beanstalk," I muttered.

Sam laughed under her breath. "Where do you think that story comes from? It's a cultural memory—a watered-down account of what happens when humans blunder into Jotunheim."

"Super."

The sword buzzed in my hand. "Besides, you can't be Jack. I'm Jack."

I couldn't argue with that logic.

We navigated across the stone floor, through a wasteland of dust bunnies, food scraps, and grease puddles.

The fireplace was so hot my clothes steamed. My hair crackled. The smell of the giants' body odor—a combination of wet clay and sour meat—was almost as deadly as a sword flying up my nose.

We got within shouting distance of the dining table, but the two giantesses still hadn't noticed us. They both wore sandals, size 120 leather dresses, and Flintstones-style necklaces made from polished boulders. Their stringy black hair was woven into pigtails. Their gray faces were hideously painted with rouge and lipstick. I didn't have my fashion advisor Blitzen with me, but I guessed the giant sisters were dolled up for a girls' night out, even though it was barely lunchtime.

"Ready?" Sam asked me.

The answer was no, but I took a deep breath and yelled, "Hello!"

The giantesses kept chatting, banging their cups, and chomping their meat.

I tried again. "YO!"

The big ladies froze. They scanned the room. Finally the one on the left spotted us. She burst out laughing, spraying bits of mead and meat. "More humans! I don't believe it!"

The other giantess leaned over. "Is that another Valkyrie? And . . ." She sniffed the air. "The boy is an einherji. Perfect! I was just wondering what we'd have for dessert."

"We claim guest rights!" I yelled.

The giantess on the left made a sour face. "Now, why did you have to go and do that?"

"We want to barter." I pointed to the birdcage, now so far above us I could only see its rusted base hovering like a moon. "For that swan's freedom. And also . . . possibly, you know, if you have any stolen weapons lying around. Like, I don't know, a hammer or something."

"Smooth," Sam muttered.

The giantesses looked at each other like they were trying not to giggle. They'd obviously been hitting the mead pretty hard.

"Very well," said the giantess on the left. "I am Gjalp. This is my sister Griep. We agree to host you while we barter. What are your names?"

"I am Magnus, son of Natalie," I said. "And this is—"

"Samirah, daughter of Ayesha," said Sam.

"You are welcome in the house of our father, Geirrod," said Gjalp. "But I can barely hear you down there. Do you mind if I put you in a chair?"

"Uh, okay," I said.

The other sister, Griep, snatched us up like toys. She set us on an empty chair, its seat the size of a living room. The tabletop was still a good five feet above my head.

"Oh, dear," Griep said. "That's still too low. May I raise your chair for you?"

Sam started to say, "Magnus—"

I blurted out, "Sure."

With a shriek of glee, Griep picked up our chair and thrust it over her head. If not for the backrest, Sam and I would've been smashed flat against the ceiling. As it was, we got knocked off our feet and showered in plaster.

Griep put down the chair. It took a moment for my eyeballs to stop rattling. Then I saw the giantesses' scowling faces looming over us.

"It didn't work," Griep said, with obvious disappointment.

"Of course it didn't work," Gjalp growled. "You *never* do that trick right. I told you, it has to be something without a back, like a stool. And we should have installed those spikes in the ceiling."

"You were trying to kill us!" I said. "That can't be in the rules for good hosts."

"Kill you?" Gjalp looked offended. "That's an absolutely baseless accusation. My sister only did as you requested. She asked your permission to raise the chair."

"You just said it was a trick."

"Did I?" Gjalp blinked. Up close, her heavily mascaraed lashes looked like the obstacle course for a mud run. "Pretty sure I didn't."

I looked at the Sword of Summer, which was still in my hand. "Jack, have they broken the host rules yet? Because trying to kill us seems kinda borderline."

"Not unless they admit their intent," Jack said. "And they're saying it was an accident."

The giantesses both straightened.

"A talking sword?" Gjalp said. "Well now, that's interesting."

"You sure I can't raise your chair for you again?" Griep offered. "I could run to the kitchen and get a stool. It's no trouble."

"Honored hosts," Sam said, her voice shaky, "please put us gently and safely on the top of your table, so we may barter with you."

Griep muttered unhappily, but she did as Sam asked. The giantess deposited us next to her fork and knife, which were roughly the same size as me. Her mug would've made a fine water tower for a rural town. I just hoped it wasn't named Boom Daddy.

"So . . ." Griep plopped back in her chair. "You want freedom for the swan? You'll have to wait until our father gets home to negotiate terms. She is his prisoner, not ours."

"She's a Valkyrie, of course," Gjalp added. "Flew in our window last night. She refuses to show her true form. Thinks she can fool us by staying in that silly swan costume, but Dad is too clever for her."

"Bummer," I said. "Well, we tried."

"Magnus . . ." Sam chided. "Gracious hosts, will you at least consent not to kill the swan until we've had a chance to speak with Geirrod?"

Gjalp shrugged. "Like I said, her fate is up to Dad. He might let her go if you surrendered yourselves in exchange, but I don't know. We need *something* spicy for the stew tonight."

"Let's put a pin in that," I said.

"Which is only an expression," Sam added hastily. "By no means is my friend granting you permission to put a pin in anything, especially us."

"Nice save," I told her.

Sam gave me a *you're-such-an-idiot* look. I was getting used to that.

Gjalp crossed her arms, forming a new mesa against her chest. "You said you also wanted to barter for a stolen weapon?"

"Yeah," I said. "Something thunder-goddish, if you have it—not that any particular thunder god is missing any particular weapon."

Griep cackled. "Oh, we have something like that . . . something that belongs to Thor himself."

Since Thor wasn't there to creatively cuss, Sam did the honors, muttering a few comments that I doubted her grandparents would approve of.

"Those are just expressions," I added hastily. "In no way was my friend giving you permission to do . . . any of those rude and colorful things. Will you barter with us for the h—for the weapon you spoke of?"

"Of course!" Gjalp grinned. "In fact, I'd like to wrap up these negotiations quickly since my sister and I have an appointment—"

"With hot frost giant twins," Griep said.

"—so we'll make you a fair deal," Gjalp continued. "We'll give you Thor's weapon for that lovely talking sword. And we'll release the swan—I'm pretty sure Dad will be okay with that—as long as you give yourselves in exchange. You won't get a better deal than that."

"That's hardly a deal," Sam growled.

"Then you can refuse," Griep said, "and leave in peace. It's all the same to us."

Jack thrummed indignantly, his runes glowing. "Magnus, you'd never give me up, right? We're friends! You're not like your dad, gonna toss me aside as soon as you see something you like better?"

I thought about Loki's suggestion that I give the sword to my Uncle Randolph. At the time, I'd actually been tempted. Now, the idea seemed impossible—and only partly because the giantesses wanted to put us in a cage and have us for dinner. Jack had saved our lives at least twice now. I liked him, even if he did occasionally call me *señor*.

An alternative came to me. A bad idea, yes, but better than the giants' offer.

"Jack," I said, "hypothetically speaking, if I told these giantesses how we killed their sister, would that break the rules of guest etiquette?"

"*What?*" Gjalp cried.

Jack's runes glowed a more cheerful shade of red. "No etiquette problem there, my friend, because that happened before we were guests here."

"Okay." I smiled at the giantesses. "We killed your sister—big ugly lady, trying to block the river and drown Thor? Yeah. She's dead now."

"LIES!" Gjalp shot to her feet. "Puny humans! You could not possibly have killed our sister!"

"Actually, my sword flew up her nose and scrambled her brains."

Griep howled in outrage. "I should have crushed you like bugs! Curse my lack of a stool and strategically placed ceiling spikes!"

I'll admit, having two giantesses tower over me bellowing death threats was a wee bit unnerving.

But Sam kept her cool.

She pointed her ax accusingly at Griep. "So, you *were* trying to kill us just now!"

"Of course, you dolt!"

"Which violates the rules of hosts."

"Who cares?" Griep cried.

"Magnus's sword does," Sam said. "Jack, did you hear that?"

"I sure did. I'd like to point out, though, that the effort required to kill these two giantesses might be too much—"

"Do it!" I hurled the sword.

Jack spiraled upward, straight into Griep's right nostril and out her left. The giantess collapsed, shaking the room at 6.8 on the Richter scale.

Gjalp stifled a scream. She covered her nose and mouth and stumbled around as Jack tried in vain to stab his way through her fingers.

"Oh, this one is getting smart!" Jack yelled. "A little help over here?"

"Magnus!" Sam pushed the giantess's steak knife to the edge of the table until the blade extended like a diving board.

I got what she wanted me to do. It was stupid crazy, but I didn't give myself time to reflect. I ran full tilt at the knife and jumped toward the end of the blade.

Sam yelled, "Wait!"

By then I was already in midair. I landed on the knife, which catapulted upward as I dropped. The plan worked, sort of. I landed on the empty seat of the chair, which was not far enough down to kill me, but was enough to break my leg. Hooray! The pain drove a hot nail up the base of my spine.

Gjalp got it worse. The spinning steak knife hit her in the chest. It didn't impale her. It didn't even go through her dress, but the poke was enough to make her yell. She lowered her hands, grabbing instinctively for her chest, which allowed Jack full access to her nose.

A second later, Gjalp was lying dead on the floor next to her sister.

"Magnus!" Sam lowered herself off the table and dropped next to me on the chair. "You fool! I wanted you to help me throw a saltshaker on the blade! I didn't expect you to jump on it yourself!"

"You're welcome." I grimaced. "Also, *ow*."

"Is it broken?"

"Yeah. Don't worry, I'm a fast healer. Give me an hour—"

"I don't think we have—" Sam started to say.

From the next room, a deep voice boomed, "Girls, I'm home!"

FIFTY-FIVE

I'm Carried into Battle by the First Dwarven Airborne Division

THERE'S NEVER A GREAT TIME for Daddy Giant to come home.

But when you're sitting in his dining room with your leg broken, the corpses of two of his daughters sprawled nearby . . . that's an *especially* bad time. Sam and I stared at each other as the giant's footsteps echoed louder and louder in the next chamber.

Sam's expression said: *I got nothing.*

I, also, had nothing.

Which is exactly the sort of moment when you might welcome a dwarf, an elf, and a swan parachuting onto your chair. Blitzen and Hearth were lashed side-by-side in the harness, with Gunilla the waterfowl cradled in Hearthstone's arms. Blitzen pulled the steering toggles and executed a perfect landing. Behind him pooled the parachute—a swath of turquoise silk that exactly matched Blitz's suit. That was the only fact about his entrance that did *not* surprise me.

"How?" I asked.

Blitzen scoffed. "Why do you look so amazed? You distracted those giantesses long enough. I'd be a poor dwarf indeed if I couldn't rig a grappling hook, shoot a line from the window to the birdcage, shimmy across, free the swan, and use my emergency parachute to get down here."

Sam pinched her nose. "You've had an emergency parachute this entire time?"

"Don't be silly," Blitzen said. "Dwarves always carry emergency parachutes. Don't you?"

"We'll talk about this later," I said. "Right now—"

"Girls?" called the giant from the next room. His speech sounded a little slurred. "Wh-where are you?"

I snapped my fingers. "Come on, guys, options. Sam, can you and Gunilla camouflage us?"

"My hijab can only cover two people," Sam said. "And Gunilla . . . the fact that she's still a swan might indicate she's too weak to change back to normal."

The swan honked.

"I'll take that as a yes," Sam said. "It could be a few hours."

"Which we don't have." I looked at Hearth. "Runestones?"

No strength, he signed, though he hardly needed to tell me that. He was upright and conscious but still looked like he'd been run over by an eight-legged horse.

"Jack!" I called to the sword. "Where is Jack?"

From the table above us, the sword yelled, "Dude, what? I'm washing off in this goblet. Give a guy some privacy, huh?"

"Magnus," Sam said, "you can't ask him to kill three giants in a row. That much effort really *will* kill you."

In the next room, the footsteps got louder. The giant sounded like he was stumbling. "Gjalp? Griep? I swear—*HIC!*—if you're texting those frost giant boys again, I will wring your necks!"

"The floor," I decided. "Get me to the floor!"

Blitzen scooped me up, which almost made me black out from pain. He yelled, "Hang on!" and leaped from the chair, somehow managing to paraglide me down safely. By the time I regained my senses, Sam, Hearth, and his new pet swan were standing next to us, apparently having used the chair leg as a fire pole.

I shivered with nausea. My face was slick with sweat, and my broken leg felt like one enormous open blister, but we had no time for minor concerns like my unbearable pain. Across the threshold of the dining room door, the shadows of the giant's feet got closer and darker, though they did seem to be weaving back and forth.

"Blitzen, carry me under that door!" I said. "We have to intercept Geirrod."

"Excuse me?" asked the dwarf.

"You're strong! You're already holding me. Hurry!"

Grumbling, he jogged toward the door, every bounce sending a stab of pain into the base of my skull. The parachute slithered behind us. Sam and Hearth followed, the swan honking unhappily in Hearthstone's arms.

The doorknob started to turn. We ducked under the sill and charged out the other side, right between the giant's feet.

I yelled, "HI, HOW YA DOING!"

Geirrod stumbled back. I guess he hadn't been expecting to see a paratrooper dwarf carrying a human, followed by another human and an elf holding a swan.

I wasn't prepared for what I saw either.

For one thing, the room we entered was about half the size of the one we'd just left. By most standards, the hall would've been considered grand. The black marble floor gleamed. Rows of stone columns were interspersed with iron braziers filled with burning coals like dozens of barbecue grills. But the ceilings were only about twenty-five feet tall. Even the door we'd come through was smaller on this side, though that made no sense.

Squeezing back under the sill would be impossible. In fact, I didn't see how Gjalp or Griep could have fit through the doorway, unless they changed size as they moved from room to room.

Maybe that's what they did. Giants were shape-shifters. Magic and illusion were second nature to them. If I spent much more time here, I'd have to bring a large supply of motion sickness medicine and some 3-D glasses.

In front of us, Geirrod was still staggering around, sloshing mead from his drinking horn.

"Whoeryou?" he slurred.

"Guests!" I called. "We have claimed guest rights!"

I doubted those applied anymore, since we'd killed our hosts, but since my etiquette-minded sword was still in the next room, washing the nostril goo off his blade, nobody challenged me.

Geirrod frowned. He looked like he'd just come from a wild party at the Jotunheim Marquee, which was weird, since the day was young. Giants apparently partied 24/7.

He wore a rumpled mauve jacket, an untucked black dress shirt, striped slacks, and dress shoes that many patent leather animals had died to create. His dark hair was greased back but springing up in unruly cowlicks. His face had a three-day stubble. He reeked of fermented honey. The overall impression was less "fashionable nightclub dude" and more "well-dressed wino."

The weirdest thing about him was his size. I'm not going to say he was short. Twenty feet tall is still good if you're looking for somebody to play point in the NBA or change those hard-to-reach lightbulbs. But the guy was minuscule compared to his daughters, who were, of course, now dead.

Geirrod belched. Judging from his expression, he was making a mighty effort to form rational thoughts. "If you're guests . . . why have you got my swan? And where are my daughters?"

Sam forced a laugh. "Oh, those crazy girls? We were bartering with them for your swan."

"Yeah," I said. "Right now they're on the floor in the other room. They don't look so good." I mimed drinking from a bottle, which probably confused Hearthstone, as it looked like the sign for *I love you*.

Geirrod seemed to get my meaning. His shoulders relaxed, as if the idea of his daughters passing out drunk on the floor was nothing to be concerned about.

"Well, then," he said, "as long as they weren't—*HIC!*—entertaining those frost giant boys again."

"Nope, just us," I assured him.

Blitzen grunted as he shifted me in his arms. "Heavy."

Hearthstone, trying to keep up with the conversation, signed *I love you* at the giant.

"Oh, Great Geirrod!" Sam said. "We actually came here to bargain for Thor's weapon. Your daughters told us you have it."

Geirrod glanced to his right. Against the far wall, almost hidden behind a column, was a human-sized iron door.

"And the weapon is behind that door," I guessed.

Geirrod's eyes widened. "What sorcery is this? How did you know that?"

"We want to barter for the weapon," I repeated.

In Hearthstone's arms, Gunilla honked irritably.

"And also for the freedom of this swan," Sam added.

"Ha!" Geirrod sloshed more mead from his drinking horn. "I don't—*HIC!*—need anything you could offer. But perhaps you could—*BELCH*—earn the weapon and the golden goose."

"The swan," I corrected.

"Whatever," said the giant.

Blitzen whimpered, "Heavy. Very heavy."

The pain in my leg made it hard to think. Every time Blitzen moved I wanted to scream, but I tried to keep a clear head.

"What did you have in mind?" I asked the giant.

"Entertain me! Join me in a game!"

"Like . . . Words with Friends?"

"What? No! Like catch!" He gestured disdainfully toward the dining room. "I have only daughters. They never want to play catch with me. I like playing catch! Play catch with me."

I glanced at Sam. "I think he wants to play catch."

"Bad idea," she murmured.

"Survive ten minutes!" Geirrod said. "That's all I ask! Then I'll be—*HIC!*—happy."

"Survive?" I asked. "A game of catch?"

"Good, so you agree!" He stumbled to the nearest brazier and scooped up a red-hot coal the size of an easy chair. "Go long!"

FIFTY-SIX

Never Ask a Dwarf to "Go Long"

"RUN!" I TOLD BLITZEN. "Run, run, run!"

Blitzen, who was still trailing the parachute, only managed a dazed stumble. "Heavy, very heavy," he wheezed again.

We made it about twenty feet before Geirrod yelled, "CATCH!"

The four of us ducked behind the nearest column as a coal cannonball slammed against it, burning a hole straight through the stone and spraying ash and sparks over our heads. The column groaned. Cracks spread all the way up to the ceiling.

"Run more!" Sam yelped.

We shambled across the hall as Geirrod scooped coals and threw them with appalling accuracy. If he hadn't been drunk, we would've been in serious trouble.

The next salvo set Blitzen's parachute on fire. Sam was able to cut it off with her ax, but we lost valuable time. Another chunk of flaming apocalypse blasted a crater in the floor next to us, singeing Gunilla's wings and Hearthstone's scarf. Sparks flew into Blitzen's eyes.

"I'm blind!" he yelped.

"I'll direct you!" I shouted. "Left! Left! Your other left!"

Meanwhile, across the hall, Geirrod was having a grand

old time singing in Jotunese, staggering from brazier to brazier, occasionally dousing himself in mead. "Come on now, little guests! This is not how you play. You're supposed to catch the coals and throw them back!"

I looked around desperately for exits. There was one other door, on the wall directly across from the dining room, but it was too small to crawl under and too big to force open, not to mention barred with a tree-trunk beam across iron brackets.

For the first time since becoming an einherji, I was annoyed that my super-quick healing wasn't super quick enough. If we were going to die, I at least wanted to be standing on my own two feet.

I glanced at the ceiling. Above the last column Geirrod had hit, cracks spread across the roof. The column bowed, ready to snap. I remembered the first time my mom had made me set up our camping tent by myself. The poles had been a nightmare. Getting them to hold the roof required just the right balance of tension. But making them collapse . . . that was easy.

"I've got an idea," I said. "Blitzen, you're going to have to carry me a while longer, unless Sam—"

"Um, no," said Sam.

"I'm fine," Blitzen whimpered. "I'm just great. I can almost see again."

"Okay, everybody," I said. "We're going to run toward the giant."

I didn't need sign language to read Hearth's expression: *Are you crazy?* The swan gave me the same look.

"Just follow my lead," I said. "It'll be fun."

"Please," Sam begged, "don't let those words be carved on my tombstone."

I yelled at the giant, "Hey, Geirrod, you throw like a Folkvanger person!"

"What? BAH!" Geirrod turned to scoop up another coal.

"Straight at him," I told my friends. "Go!"

As the giant prepared to throw, I told Blitzen, "Right, go right!"

We all ducked behind the nearest pillar. Geirrod's coal bored straight through it, spewing cinders and sending more cracks up the ceiling.

"Now left," I told my friends. "Toward him and up another row."

"What are you—" Sam's eyes widened with understanding. "Oh, gods, you really *are* crazy."

"Got a better idea?"

"Sadly, no."

We ran across Geirrod's line of sight.

"Your daughters aren't drunk!" I shouted. "They're dead!"

"WHAT? NO!"

Another coal cannonball hurtled toward us, hitting the nearest column with such force, it collapsed into a pile of colossal stone Lifesavers.

The ceiling groaned. The cracks spread. We ran into the central aisle and I yelled, "MISSED AGAIN!"

Geirrod howled in fury. He tossed aside his drinking horn so he could scoop coals with both hands. Fortunately for us, his anger and his double-handed throwing made his aim terrible. We jogged around him, weaving from column to column as he splattered coal everywhere, tipping over braziers, breaking pillars.

I insulted Geirrod's suit, his haircut, his patent leather

shoes. Finally the giant tossed an entire brazier at us, taking out the last support pillar on his side of the room.

"Retreat!" I told Blitzen. "Go! NOW!"

Poor Blitzen huffed and wheezed. We ran for the far wall as Geirrod shouted, "Cowards! I will kill you!"

He easily could have run after us and caught us, but the giant's drunken mind was still thinking in terms of projectile weapons. He searched around him for more coals as the ceiling above him crumbled.

Too late, he realized what was happening. He looked up and screamed as half the room collapsed on top of him, burying Geirrod under a thousand tons of rock.

The next thing I knew, I was on the floor in a whiteout of dust and debris, trying my best to cough up my lungs.

Slowly the air cleared. A few feet away, Sam sat cross-legged, also hacking and gasping, looking like she'd been rolled in flour.

"Blitzen?" I called. "Hearth?"

I was so worried about them I forgot about my broken leg. I tried to stand and was surprised to find that I could. The leg still throbbed with agony, but it held my weight.

Blitzen came stumbling out of a dust cloud. "Present." he squeaked. His suit was ruined. His hair and beard had gone prematurely gray with plaster.

I tackled him in a hug. "You," I said, "are the strongest, most amazing dwarf ever."

"Okay, kid, okay." He patted my arm. "Where's Hearthstone? Hearth!"

In moments like that, we forgot that yelling Hearthstone's name wasn't really helpful.

"Here he is," Sam called, brushing some rubble off the fallen elf. "I think he's okay."

"Thank Odin!" Blitz started forward but almost fell.

"Whoa, there." I propped him against one of the remaining columns. "Just rest for a sec. I'll be right back."

I jogged over to Sam and helped her extract Hearthstone from the wreckage.

His hair was smoldering, but otherwise he looked all right. We pulled him to his feet. Immediately he started scolding me in sign language: *Stupid? Trying to kill us?*

It took me a second to realize he wasn't holding the swan.

"Wait," I said. "Where's Gunilla?"

Behind me, Blitzen yelped. I turned and discovered a hostage situation in progress.

"I'm right here," Gunilla snarled. She was back in human form, standing behind Blitzen, the point of her blazing spear pressed to his throat. "And the four of you are coming back to Valhalla as my prisoners."

FIFTY-SEVEN

Sam Hits the EJECT Button

GUNILLA JABBED HER spear tip against Blitz's jugular.

"No closer," she warned. "Rogues and liars, all of you. You've endangered Midgard and Asgard, roused the giants, caused chaos across the realms—"

"We also rescued you from a birdcage," I added.

"After luring me here in the first place!"

"Nobody lured you," I said. "Nobody asked you to hunt us."

"Gunilla." Samirah placed her ax on the floor. "Let the dwarf go, please."

"Urgh," Blitzen agreed.

The Valkyrie captain glanced at Hearthstone. "You, elf—don't even *think* about it. Put that bag of runestones on the floor or I will burn you to ashes."

I hadn't realized Hearthstone was about to make a move. He complied with Gunilla's order, though his eyes blazed. He looked like he wanted to do something much worse to Gunilla than put her in a magic hamster wheel.

Sam raised her palms. "We're not going to fight you. Please, release the dwarf. We all know what a Valkyrie spear can do."

I didn't, actually, but I tried to look as meek and harmless as possible. As exhausted as I felt, it wasn't hard.

Gunilla eyed me. "Where is your sword, Magnus?"

I gestured to the ruined end of the hall. "Last I checked, he was taking a bath in a goblet."

Gunilla considered that. It was the sort of statement that only made sense in the loony world of the Vikings. "Very well." She shoved Blitzen toward me.

She swept her spear forward, keeping us all within striking distance. The weapon's light was so intense I felt like it was baking my skin.

"We will return to Asgard as soon as my full strength returns," said Gunilla. "In the meantime, explain why you were asking the giants about Thor's weapon."

"Oh . . ." I remembered Thor being pretty specific about not telling anyone of his missing hammer. "Well—"

"A trick," Sam interrupted. "To confuse the giants."

Gunilla narrowed her eyes. "A dangerous trick. If the giants believed Thor had lost his hammer . . . the consequences would be unthinkable."

"Speaking of unthinkable," I said, "Surt is going to release Fenris Wolf tomorrow night."

"Tonight," Sam corrected.

My stomach dropped. "Isn't it Tuesday? Freya said the full moon was Wednesday—"

"Which technically starts at sundown on Tuesday," Sam said. "The full moon rises tonight."

"Well that's just wonderful," I said. "Why didn't you say so?"

"I thought you understood."

"Silence, both of you!" Gunilla ordered. "Magnus Chase, you've fallen for the lies of this daughter of Loki."

"You mean the full moon isn't tonight?"

"No, it's tonight. I meant—" Gunilla scowled. "Stop confusing me!"

Blitzen whimpered as she throttled him with her light spear. Hearthstone edged next to me, his fists clenched.

I raised my hands. "Gunilla, all I'm saying is, if you don't let us go so we can stop Surt—"

"I warned you," Gunilla said. "Listening to Samirah will only hasten Ragnarok. Feel fortunate *I* found you rather than the other Valkyries who are hunting you, or your former einherjar hallmates. They are anxious to prove their loyalty to Valhalla by killing you. I, at least, will make sure you get a proper trial before the thanes cast your soul into Ginnungagap!"

Samirah and I exchanged glances. We didn't have time to be captured and sent back to Asgard. I definitely didn't have time to get my soul cast into a place I couldn't even pronounce.

Hearthstone saved us. His face became transfixed with horror. He pointed behind Gunilla as if Geirrod was rising from the rubble. It was the oldest trick in the Nine Worlds, and it worked.

Gunilla glanced behind her. Sam lunged with blinding speed. Instead of trying to tackle the Valkyrie captain, she simply touched the golden bracer on Gunilla's arm.

The air hummed as if someone had turned on an industrial vacuum cleaner.

Gunilla shrieked. She stared at Sam in dismay. "What have you—"

The Valkyrie imploded. She collapsed into a pinpoint of light and was gone.

"Sam?" I couldn't believe what had happened. "You—you killed her?"

"Of course not!" Sam swatted my arm. (Thankfully, I did not implode.) "I just recalled her to Valhalla."

"The armband?" asked Blitzen.

Sam smiled modestly. "I didn't know if it would work. I guess my fingerprints haven't been de-registered from the Valkyrie database yet."

Hearthstone rolled his hand. *Explain.*

"Valkyrie armbands have an emergency evacuation feature," Sam said. "If a Valkyrie is wounded in battle and needs immediate attention, another Valkyrie can send her back to the Halls of Healing simply by touching her armband. She'll be instantly extracted, but it's powerful magic. One use and the armband melts."

I blinked. "So Gunilla got yanked to Valhalla."

"Yep. But I haven't bought us much time. She'll be back as soon as she gathers her strength. I imagine she'll bring reinforcements, too."

"Thor's hammer," I said. "The storage room."

We ran for the small iron door. I'd like to say I had carefully planned the ceiling's collapse to make sure the door didn't get buried in wreckage. In truth, I just got lucky.

Sam's ax cut through the lock in one swipe. Hearthstone yanked open the door. Inside was a closet, empty except for an iron pole the size of a broom handle leaning against the corner.

"Well," I said. "That's kind of anticlimactic."

Blitzen studied the iron pole. "I dunno, kid. See this runework? It isn't Mjolnir, but this staff was forged with powerful magic."

Sam's face fell. "Oh . . . Thor's weapon. Just not the *right* weapon."

"Mmm." Blitzen nodded sagely.

"Mmm," I agreed. "Would one of you tell me what you're talking about?"

"Kid, this is Thor's backup weapon," Blitz explained. "The staff was a gift from a friend of his—the giantess Grid."

"Three questions," I said. "First: Thor has a giantess friend?"

"Yes," Blitz said. "Not all giants are bad."

"Second: Do all giantess names begin with G?"

"No."

"Last question: Thor is a martial artist? Does he have, like, backup nunchuks, too?"

"Hey, kid, don't dis the staff. It may not be dwarven work like the hammer, but giant-forged iron is still powerful stuff. I hope we're able to pick it up and carry it back to Thor. I'm sure it's heavy and protected by enchantments."

"You needn't worry about that!" bellowed a voice above.

From one of the high windows, the god of thunder soared into the room on a chariot pulled by Otis and Marvin. My sword Jack floated along next to them.

Thor landed in front of us in all his grungy glory. "Good work, mortals!" He grinned. "You found the staff. That's better than nothing!"

"And, dude," said Jack, "I take one quick bath. I turn around and not only have you left the room, but you've collapsed the exit. What's a sword supposed to think?"

I bit back a comment. "Yeah. Sorry, Jack."

Thor reached out toward the supply closet. The iron rod flew into his hand. Thor executed a few thrusts, swipes, and baton twirls. "Yes, this will do nicely until I find that—ah, *other* weapon which is not officially missing. Thanks!"

I tried to resist the urge to smack him. "You have a flying chariot?"

"Of course!" He laughed. "Thor without his flying chariot would be like a dwarf without an emergency parachute!"

"*Thank* you," Blitz said.

"You could have flown us straight here," I noted. "You could have saved us a day and a half and several close calls with death. But you let us climb that cliff, navigate a chasm—"

"I would never deprive you of the chance to prove your heroism!" the thunder god said.

Blitzen whimpered.

Hearthstone signed, *I hate this god.*

"Exactly, Mr. Elf!" Thor said. "I gave you the opportunity to prove your mettle. You're quite welcome!"

Otis bleated and clopped his hooves. "Besides, the boss couldn't show up here without his hammer, especially since his daughter was stuck in that birdcage."

Sam flinched. "You *knew* about that?"

Thor scowled at his goat. "Otis, we need to have another talk about you keeping your snout shut."

"Sorry." Otis hung his horns. "Go ahead and kill me. It's fine."

Marvin nipped him. "Will you shut up? Every time you get killed, I get killed!"

Thor rolled his eyes at the ceiling. " 'What kind of animals would you like pulling your chariot, Thor?' my dad asked me. 'Goats,' I said. 'Flying re-consumable goats would be great.' I could've chosen dragons or lions, but noooo." He faced Sam.

"To answer your question, yes, I sensed Gunilla was here. I can usually tell when one of my children is nearby. I figured, if you could save her, that would be a nice bonus. But I also didn't want her learning about my missing hammer. That information is a bit sensitive. You should feel honored I told *you* about it, daughter of Loki."

Sam inched away. "You know about that? Listen, Lord Thor—"

"Girl, stop calling me *lord*. I'm a god of the common people, not a lord! And don't worry, I won't kill you. Not all of Loki's brood is evil. Even Loki himself . . ." He heaved a sigh. "I kind of miss the guy."

Sam looked at him sideways. "You do?"

"Oh, sure." Thor scratched his red beard. "Most of the time I wanted to kill him, like when he cut off all my wife's hair, or convinced me to wear a bridal gown."

"Do what now?" I asked.

"But Loki made life interesting," Thor continued. "People got the idea we were brothers, which isn't true. He was *Odin's* blood brother. Still, I understand how the rumor got started. I hate to admit it, but Loki and I made a good team."

"Like Marvin and me," Otis suggested. "My therapist says—"

"Shut up, you dolt!" said Marvin.

Thor twirled his iron staff. "At any rate, thanks for this. It will help until I can find that *other* item. And please, *DO NOT* mention my loss to anyone. Not even my children. *Especially* not them. Otherwise I'd have to kill you, and I might even feel bad about that."

"But what will you do without Mjolnir?" Sam asked. "How will you—"

"Watch television?" Thor shrugged. "I know . . . the screen size and resolution on the end of this staff are pitiful, but I will have to make do. As for you, the island of Lyngvi rises from the waves tonight. You must hurry! Good-bye, mortals, and—"

"Hold up," I said. "We need the location of the island."

Thor frowned. "Oh, right. I was supposed to give that to you. Well, all you have to do is seek out the dwarf brothers at the Long Wharf in Boston. They will take you to the island. Their boat usually leaves at sunset."

"Ah, dwarves." Blitz nodded approvingly. "We can trust them, then?"

"Oh, no," Thor said. "They'll try to kill you at the first opportunity, but they *do* know the way to the island."

"Lord Th— I mean, Thor," said Sam, "Won't you come with us? This is an important battle—the fire lord Surt, Fenris Wolf. Surely that's worthy of your attention."

Thor's right eye twitched. "That's a fine offer. Really. I'd love to, but I have another pressing appointment—"

"Game of Thrones," Marvin explained.

"Shut up!" Thor raised his staff over our heads. "Use your time well, heroes. Prepare for battle, and be at the Long Wharf by sundown!"

The room started to spin. Jack the sword flew into my hand, flooding me with exhaustion.

I braced myself against the nearest column. "Thor, where are you sending us?"

The thunder god chuckled. "Wherever you each need to go."

Jotunheim collapsed around me like a tent falling on my head.

FIFTY-EIGHT

What the Hel?

I STOOD ALONE in a snowstorm on Bunker Hill.

My exhaustion was gone. Jack had returned to pendant form around my neck. None of that made sense, but I didn't seem to be dreaming.

I felt like I was really in Charlestown, just across the river from Boston, standing right where my fourth grade school bus had dropped us off for a class trip. Gauzy curtains of snow swept across the brownstones. The park itself wasn't much more than a white field dotted with bare trees. In the center, a gray obelisk rose into the winter sky. After my time in Geirrod's fortress, the monument looked small and sad.

Thor had said I'd be sent where I needed to go. Why did I need to be here, and where were my friends?

A voice at my shoulder said, "Tragic, isn't it?"

I hardly flinched. I supposed I was getting used to strange Norse entities popping up in my personal space.

Standing next to me, gazing at the monument, was a woman with elven-pale skin and long dark hair. In profile, she looked heart-achingly beautiful, about twenty-five years old. Her ermine cloak shimmered like a snowdrift rippling in the wind.

Then she turned toward me, and my lungs flattened against the back of my rib cage.

The right side of the woman's face was a nightmare—withered skin, patches of blue ice covering decayed flesh, membrane-thin lips over rotten teeth, a milky white eye, and tufts of desiccated hair like black spiderwebs.

I tried to tell myself, *Okay, this isn't so bad. She's just like that guy Two-Face from Batman.* But Two-Face had always struck me as kind of comical, like, come on, nobody with that much facial damage could be alive.

The woman in front of me was *very* real. She looked like someone who'd been stuck halfway through a door when a devastating blizzard struck. Or worse . . . some hideous ghoul who'd tried to transform into a human, only to get interrupted in the middle of the process.

"You're Hel." My voice sounded like I was five years old again.

She lifted her skeletal right hand, brushing a tuft of hair behind her ear . . . or the stub of frostbitten flesh that might once have been an ear.

"I am Hel," she agreed. "Sometimes called Hela, though most mortals dare not speak my name at all. No jokes, Magnus Chase? *Who the Hel are you? What the Hel do you want? You look Hela bad.* I was expecting more bravado."

I was fresh out of bravado. The best I could manage was not running away shrieking. Wind gusted around Hel, lifting a few flakes of blackened skin from her zombie forearm and swirling them into the snow.

"Wh-what do you want?" I asked. "I'm already dead. I'm an einherji."

"I know that, young hero. I don't want your soul. I have plenty of those already. I called you here to talk."

"*You* brought me? I thought Thor—"

"Thor." The goddess scoffed. "If you want someone who can navigate one hundred and seventy channels of HD content, go to Thor. If you want someone who can accurately send people through the Nine Worlds, he's not your guy."

"So—"

"So I thought it was high time we talked. My father did mention I'd be seeking you out, yes? He gave you an exit strategy, Magnus: Surrender the sword to your uncle. Remove it from play. This is your last opportunity. Perhaps you can take a lesson from this place."

"Bunker Hill?"

She turned toward the monument so only her mortal side was visible. "Sad and meaningless. Another hopeless battle, like the one you're about to engage in. . . ."

Granted, my American history was a little rusty, but I was pretty sure they didn't build monuments at the site of sad and meaningless events.

"Wasn't Bunker Hill a victory? Americans holding off the British at the top of the hill? Don't fire until you see . . ."

She fixed me with her milky zombie gaze, and I couldn't make myself say *the whites of their eyes*.

"For every hero, a thousand cowards," said Hel. "For every brave death, a thousand senseless ones. For every einherji . . . a thousand souls who enter *my* realm."

She pointed with her withered hand. "Right over there, a British boy of your age died behind a hay bale, crying for his mother. He was the youngest of his regiment. His own commander shot him for cowardice. Do you think he appreciates this lovely monument? And there, at the top of the hill, after their ammunition ran out, your ancestors threw rocks at the British, fighting like cavemen. Some fled. Some stayed and were butchered with bayonets. Which were smarter?"

She smiled. I wasn't sure which side of her mouth was more ghastly—the living zombie, or the beautiful woman who was amused by massacres.

"No one ever said *the whites of their eyes*," she continued. "That's a myth, made up years later. This isn't even Bunker Hill. It's Breed's Hill. And though the battle was costly to the British, it was an American defeat, not a victory. Such is human memory . . . you forget the truth and believe what makes you feel better."

Snow melted against my neck, dampening my collar. "What's your point? I shouldn't fight? I should just let Surt free your brother the Big Bad Wolf?"

"I merely point out options," Hel said. "Did Bunker Hill really affect the outcome of your Revolution? If you face Surt tonight, will you delay Ragnarok or hasten it? Charging into battle is what the hero would do—the sort of person who ends up in Valhalla. But what of the millions of souls who lived more careful lives and died peacefully in their beds at an old age? They ended up in my realm. Were they not wiser? Do you really belong in Valhalla, Magnus?"

The words of the Norns seemed to spiral around me in the cold. *Wrongly chosen, wrongly slain; a hero Valhalla cannot contain.*

I thought about my hallmate T.J., still carrying his rifle and wearing his Civil War coat, charging up hills day after day in a series of endless battles, waiting for his final death at Ragnarok. I thought about Halfborn Gunderson, trying to stay sane by earning PhDs in literature when he wasn't going berserk and smashing skulls. Did I belong with those guys?

"Take the sword to your uncle," Hel urged. "Let events unfold without you. This is the safer course. If you do so . . . my father Loki has asked me to reward you."

The skin on my face burned. I had an irrational fear that I might be decaying from frostbite, becoming like Hel. "Reward me?"

"Helheim is not such a terrible place," said the goddess. "My hall has many fine chambers for my favored guests. A reunion could be arranged."

"A reunion . . ." I could barely speak the words. "With my mother? You have her?"

The goddess seemed to consider the question, tilting her head from the living side to the dead. "I *could* have her. The status of her soul, of everything that she was, is still in flux."

"How . . . ? I don't—"

"The prayers and wishes of the living often affect the dead, Magnus. Mortals have always known that." She bared her teeth—rotten on one side, pristine white on the other. "I cannot return Natalie Chase to life, but I can unite you both in Helheim if you wish it. I can bind your souls there so that you will never be separated. You could be a family again."

I tried to imagine that. My tongue froze in my mouth.

"You need not speak," Hel said. "Only give me an indication. Cry for your mother. Let your tears fall, and I will know you agree. But you must decide now. If you reject my offer, if you insist on fighting your own Bunker Hill tonight, I promise you will never see your mother again in this life or any other."

I thought about my mother skipping stones with me at Houghton's Pond, her green eyes sparkling with humor. She spread her arms in the sunlight, trying to explain what my father was like. *That's why I bring you here, Magnus. Can't you feel it? He's all around us.*

Then I imagined my mother in a cold dark palace, her soul bound for eternity. I remember my own corpse in the funeral home—an embalmed relic, dressed up for display. I thought about the faces of the drowned souls swirling in Ran's net.

"You are crying," Hel noted with satisfaction. "Then we have a deal?"

"You don't understand." I looked at the goddess. "I'm crying because I know what my mother would want. She'd want me to remember her as she was. That's the only monument she needs. She wouldn't want to be trapped, preserved, forced to live as a ghost in some cold storage underworld."

Hel scowled, the right side of her face wrinkling and crackling. "You dare?"

"You want bravado?" I pulled my pendant from its chain. Jack the sword stretched to full length, his blade steaming in the cold. "Leave me alone. Tell Loki we have no deal. If I see you again, I'll cut you right down the dotted line."

I raised my blade.

The goddess dissolved into snow. My surroundings faded. Suddenly I found myself balanced at the edge of a rooftop, five stories above a stretch of asphalt.

FIFTY-NINE

The Terror That Is Middle School

BEFORE I COULD plummet to my death, someone grabbed me and pulled me back.

"Whoa, there, cowboy," Sam said.

She was dressed in a new peacoat—navy blue this time, with dark jeans and boots. Blue wasn't my favorite color, but it made her look dignified and serious, like an air force officer. Her headscarf was freckled with snow. Her ax wasn't at her side; I guessed it was tucked in the backpack over her shoulder.

She didn't look surprised to see me. Then again, her expression was preoccupied, her gaze stuck somewhere in the distance.

My senses started to adjust. Jack was still in my hand. For some reason, I didn't feel any exhaustion from his recent slaying of the giant sisters.

Below us, the patch of asphalt was not exactly a playground—more like a holding area between school buildings. Inside the chain-link fence, a few dozen students huddled in cliques, chatting in doorways or pushing each other around the icy pavement. They looked like seventh graders, though it was hard to be sure with everybody in their dark winter coats.

I willed my sword back into pendant form and returned it to its chain. I figured I shouldn't be walking on the roof of a school with a broadsword.

"Where are we?" I asked Sam.

"My old stomping ground." Her voice had a bitter edge. "Malcolm X Middle School."

I tried to imagine Sam down in that courtyard, mingling with those cliques of girls, her headscarf the only splash of color in the crowd.

"Why did Thor send you back to middle school?" I asked. "That seems especially cruel."

She smirked. "He actually transported me home. I appeared in my bedroom, just in time for Jid and Bibi to barge in and demand to know where I'd been. That conversation was worse than middle school."

My heart sank. I'd been so focused on my own problems I'd forgotten that Sam was trying to balance a normal life on top of everything else. "What did you tell them?"

"That I'd been staying with friends. They'll assume I meant Marianne Shaw."

"Rather than three strange guys."

She hugged her arms. "I told Bibi I tried to text her, which is true. She'll assume it was her fault. Bibi is hopeless with phones. Actually, Jotunheim just has no reception. I—I try not to actually *lie*, but I hate misleading them. After everything they've done for me, they worry I'm going to get in trouble, turn out like my mom."

"You mean a successful doctor who liked to help people? Gee, that would be terrible."

She gave me an eye roll. "You know what I mean—a rebel,

an embarrassment. They locked me in my room, told me I was grounded until Doomsday. I didn't have the heart to tell them that might be tonight."

The wind picked up, spinning the old metal roof fans like pinwheels.

"How did you sneak out?" I asked.

"I didn't. I just appeared here." She gazed down into the courtyard. "Maybe I needed a reminder of how it all started."

My brain felt as rusty as the roof fans, but one thought gained traction and started to spin. "This is where you became a Valkyrie."

Sam nodded. "A frost giant . . . he'd gotten into the school somehow. Maybe looking for me, maybe hunting some other demigod. He wrecked a few classrooms, caused a panic. He didn't seem to care if there were mortal casualties. The school went on lockdown. They didn't know what they were dealing with. They thought some crazy human was making a scene. They called the police, but there was no time. . . ."

She slipped her hands into her coat pockets. "I taunted the giant—insulted his mom, that kind of thing. I lured him up here to the roof and . . ." She looked below us. "The giant couldn't fly. He landed right there on the asphalt and shattered into a million shards of ice."

She sounded strangely embarrassed.

"You took on a giant single-handedly," I said. "You saved your school."

"I suppose," she said. "The staff, the police . . . they never figured out what happened. They thought the guy must've fled the scene. In the confusion, nobody noticed what I'd done . . . except Odin. After the giant died, the All-Father appeared in front of me, right where you're standing. He offered me a job as a Valkyrie. I accepted."

After my conversation with Hel, I didn't think it was possible for me to feel worse. The loss of my mother still stung as painfully as the night she'd died. But Sam's story made me feel bad in a different way. Sam had brought me to Valhalla. She'd lost her place among the Valkyries because she believed I was a hero—a hero like *her*. And despite all that had happened since, she didn't seem to blame me.

"Do you regret it?" I asked. "Taking my soul when I fell?"

She laughed under her breath. "You don't get it, Magnus. I was *told* to bring you to Valhalla. And not by Loki. By Odin himself."

My pendant heated up against my collarbone. For an instant, I smelled warm roses and strawberries, as if I'd stepped through a pocket of summer.

"Odin," I said. "I thought he was missing . . . hadn't appeared since you became a Valkyrie."

"He told me to say nothing." Sam shivered. "I guess I failed in that, too. The night before your fight with Surt, Odin met me outside my grandparents' house. He was disguised as a homeless guy—a ratty beard, an old blue coat, a broad-brimmed hat. But I knew who he was. The eye patch, the voice. . . . He told me to watch for you, and if you fought well, to bring you to Valhalla."

Down in the courtyard, a period bell rang. The students headed inside, jostling and laughing. For them, it was a normal school day—the kind of day I could hardly remember.

"I was *wrongly chosen*," I said. "The Norns told me I wasn't supposed to be in Valhalla."

"Yet you were," Sam said. "Odin foresaw it. I don't know why the contradiction, but we have to finish this quest. We have to reach that island tonight."

I watched the snow erase footprints in the empty yard. Soon there'd be no more trace of the students than there was of the frost giant's impact from two years ago.

I wasn't sure what to think about Odin choosing me for Valhalla. I suppose I should've felt honored. The All-Father himself thought I was important. He had chosen me, no matter what the Norns said. But if that was true, why hadn't Odin bothered to meet me in person? Loki was bound on a slab for eternity. *He'd* found a way to talk to me. Mimir was a severed head. He'd made the trip. But the All-Father, the great sorcerer who could supposedly bend reality just by speaking a rune—he couldn't find the time for a quick check-in?

Hel's voice echoed in my head: *Do you really belong in Valhalla, Magnus?*

"I just came from Bunker Hill," I told Sam. "Hel offered me a reunion with my mother."

I managed to tell her the story.

Samirah reached out as if to touch my arm, then apparently changed her mind. "I'm so sorry, Magnus. But Hel lies. You can't trust her. She's just like my father, only colder. You made the right choice."

"Yeah . . . still. You ever do the right thing, and you *know* it's the right thing, but it leaves you feeling horrible?"

"You've just described most days of my life." Sam pulled up her hood. "When I became a Valkyrie . . . I'm still not sure why I fought that frost giant. The kids at Malcolm X were terrible to me. The usual garbage: they asked me if I was a terrorist.

They yanked off my hijab. They slipped disgusting notes and pictures into my locker. When that giant attacked . . . I could've pretended to be just another mortal and gotten myself to safety. But I didn't even think about running away. Why did I risk my life for those kids?"

I smiled.

"What?" she demanded.

"Somebody once told me that a hero's bravery has to be unplanned—a genuine response to a crisis. It has to come from the heart, without any thought of reward."

Sam huffed. "That somebody sounds pretty smug."

"Maybe you didn't need to come here," I decided. "Maybe *I* did. To understand why we're a good team."

"Oh?" She arched an eyebrow. "Are we a good team now?"

"We're about to find out." I gazed north into the snowstorm. Somewhere in that direction lay downtown Boston and Long Wharf. "Let's find Blitzen and Hearthstone. We've got a fire giant to extinguish."

SIXTY

A Lovely Homicidal
Sunset Cruise

BLITZ AND HEARTH were waiting for us outside the New England Aquarium.

Blitz had scored a new outfit, of course: olive-colored fatigues, a yellow ascot, and a matching yellow pith helmet with yellow sun-proof netting. "My wolf-hunting clothes!" he told us cheerfully.

He explained how Thor's magic had transported him where he most needed to be: the best department store in Nidavellir. He'd used his Svartalf Express Card to charge a number of expeditionary supplies, including several spare out-fits and a retractable bone steel harpoon.

"Not only that," Blitz said, "but the contest scandal with Junior? It backfired on the old maggot! Word got around about how badly he failed. Nobody is blaming me anymore, or the horsefly, or anything! People started talking about my stylish armor designs, and now they're clamoring for product. If I live through tonight, I might get to start my own clothing line after all!"

Sam and I both congratulated him, though living through the night did seem like a pretty big *if*. Nevertheless, Blitz was so happy, I didn't want to bring him down. He started bouncing on his heels, singing "Sharp Dressed Dwarf" under his breath.

As for Hearth, he'd done a different kind of shopping. He was now carrying a polished staff of white oak. At the top, the staff split into a Y like a slingshot. I got the feeling—I don't know how—that a piece was missing between the two prongs.

With his staff in hand, Hearth looked like a proper sword-and-sorcery elf—except that he was still wearing black jeans, a leather jacket over a HOUSE OF BLUES T-shirt, and a candy-striped scarf.

Hearth rested the staff in the crook of his arm and explained in signs how he'd ended up at Mimir's Well. The Capo had pronounced him a full master of alf seidr, ready to use a sorcerer's staff.

"Isn't that awesome?" Blitzen clapped him on the back. "I knew he could do it!"

Hearthstone pursed his lips. *I don't feel like a master.*

"I've got something that might help." I reached in my pocket and pulled out the runestone perthro. "A couple of hours ago I had a conversation with Hel. She reminded me of everything I've lost."

I told them what the half-zombie goddess had offered me.

"Ah, kid . . ." Blitzen shook his head. "Here I've been going on about my new clothing line, and you had to deal with *that*."

"It's okay," I assured him. Strangely, it *did* feel okay. "The thing is, when I appeared on Bunker Hill, I'd just used my sword to kill two giantesses. I should've passed out or died from exhaustion. I didn't. I think I know why."

I turned the runestone between my fingers. "The longer I'm with you guys, the easier it gets to use my sword, or heal, or do anything, really. I'm no magic expert, but I think . . . somehow, we're sharing the cost."

THE SWORD OF SUMMER

I held out the rune for Hearthstone. "I know what it feels like to be an empty cup, to have everything taken away from you. But you're not alone. However much magic you need to use, it's okay. We've got you. We're your family."

Hearth's eyes rimmed with green water. He signed to us, and this time I think he actually meant *I love you* and not *the giantesses are drunk.*

He took the rune and set it between the prongs of his new staff. The stone snapped into place the same way my pendant did on its chain. The symbol perthro glowed with a gentle gold light.

My sign, he announced. *My family's sign.*

Blitzen sniffled. "I like that. A family of four empty cups!"

Sam wiped her eyes. "Suddenly I feel thirsty."

"Al-Abbas," I said, "I nominate you for the role of annoying sister."

"Shut up, Magnus." She straightened her coat, shouldered her backpack, and took a deep breath. "All right. If we're done with the family bonding, I don't suppose anyone knows where we can find two dwarves with a boat?"

"I do." Blitzen fluffed his ascot. "Hearth and I scouted it out before you got here. Come on!"

He led the way down the pier. I think he just wanted us to appreciate how well he swaggered in his new yellow pith helmet.

At the end of Long Wharf, across from the closed-for-the-season kiosk for whale watching tours, another kiosk had been cobbled together from plywood scraps and cardboard appliance boxes. Above the service window, a sloppily finger-painted sign read: WOLF-WATCHING CRUISE. TONIGHT ONLY! ONE RED GOLD PER PERSON! CHILDREN UNDER FIVE FREE!

Sitting in the booth was a dwarf who was definitely less svartalf and more maggot. About two feet tall, he had so much facial hair it was impossible to tell if he had eyes or a mouth. He was dressed in a yellow rain slicker and a captain's hat, which no doubt protected him from the dim daylight and also made him look like the mascot for a gnomish lobster restaurant franchise.

"Hello, there!" said the dwarf. "Fjalar, at your service. Care to take the cruise? Lovely wolf-spotting weather!"

"Fjalar?" Blitzen's face sagged. "You wouldn't happen to have a brother named Gjalar?"

"Right over there."

I wasn't sure how I'd missed it, but docked a few feet away was a Viking longship fitted with an outboard motor. At the stern, chewing on a piece of jerky, sat another dwarf who looked exactly like Fjalar except he wore grease-stained coveralls and a floppy-brimmed felt hat.

"I can see you've heard about our exceptional service," Fjalar continued. "So can I put you down for four tickets? Once-a-year opportunity!"

"Excuse us a moment." Blitzen steered us out of earshot. "Those are Fjalar and Gjalar," he whispered. "They're notorious."

"Thor warned us," Sam said. "We don't have much choice."

"I know, but"—Blitzen wrung his hands—"Fjalar and Gjalar? They've been robbing and murdering people for over a thousand years! They'll try to kill us if we give them any opportunity."

"So basically," I summed up, "they're like pretty much everyone else we've met."

"They'll stab us in the back," Blitz fretted, "or strand us on a desert island, or shove us overboard into the mouth of a shark."

Hearth pointed to himself then tapped a finger to his palm. *I'm sold.*

We marched back to the kiosk.

I smiled at the homicidal lobster mascot. "We'd love four tickets, please."

SIXTY-ONE

Heather Is My New
Least Favorite Flower

I DIDN'T THINK anything could be worse than our fishing expedition with Harald. I was wrong.

As soon as we left the harbor, the sky darkened. The water turned as black as squid ink. Through the haze of snow, the shoreline of Boston morphed into something primeval—the way it might have looked when Skirnir's descendant first sailed his longship up the Charles.

Downtown was reduced to a few gray hills. The runways at Logan Airport turned to sheets of ice floating on open water. Islands sank and rose around us like a time-lapse video of the last two millennia.

It occurred to me that I might be looking at the future rather than the past—the way Boston would appear after Ragnarok. I decided to keep that thought to myself.

In the quiet of the bay, Gjalar's outboard motor made an obscene amount of noise—rattling, growling, and coughing smoke as our boat cut through the water. Any monsters within a five-mile radius would know where to find us.

At the prow, Fjalar kept watch, occasionally shouting warnings to his brother, "Rocks to port! Iceberg to starboard! Kraken at two o'clock!"

None of that helped calm my nerves. Surt had promised

we would meet tonight. He planned on burning my friends and me alive, and destroying the Nine Worlds. But in the back of my mind lurked an even deeper fear. I was about to meet the Wolf at last. That realization dredged up every nightmare I'd ever had about glowing blue eyes, white fangs, feral snarls in the darkness.

Sitting next to me, Sam kept her ax across her lap, where the dwarves could see it. Blitzen fussed with his yellow ascot, as if he could intimidate our hosts with his wardrobe. Hearthstone practiced making his new staff appear and disappear. If he did it right, the staff shot into his hand out of nowhere, like a bouquet of flowers spring-loaded in a magician's sleeve. If he did it wrong, he goosed Blitzen or whopped me upside the back of the head.

After a few hours and a dozen staff-induced concussions, the boat shuddered like we'd hit a crosscurrent. From the bow, Fjalar announced, "It won't be long now. We've entered Amsvartnir—Pitch-Black Bay."

"Gee"—I looked at the inky waves—"why do they call it that?"

The clouds broke. The full moon, pale and silver, peered down at us from a starless void. In front of us, fog and moon-light wove together, forming a coastline. I'd never hated the full moon so much.

"Lyngvi," Fjalar announced. "The Isle of Heather, prison of the Wolf."

The island looked like the caldera of an ancient volcano—a flattened cone maybe fifty feet above sea level. I'd always thought of heather as purple, but the rocky slopes were car-peted with ghostly white flowers.

"If that's heather," I said, "there sure is a lot of it."

Fjalar cackled. "It's a magical plant, my friend—used to ward off evil and keep ghosts at bay. What better prison for Fenris Wolf than an island entirely ringed with the stuff?"

Sam rose. "If Fenris is as big as I've heard, shouldn't we be able to see him by now?"

"Oh, no," Fjalar said. "You have to go ashore for that. Fenris lies bound in the center of the island like a runestone in a bowl."

I glanced at Hearthstone. I doubted he could read Fjalar's lips behind that bushy beard, but I didn't like the reference to a runestone in a bowl. I remembered the other meaning of perthro: a dice-rolling cup. I didn't want to run blindly into that caldera and hope for Yahtzee.

When we were about ten feet from the beach, the keel of the boat ground against a sandbar. The sound reminded me unpleasantly of the night my mother died—our apartment door creaking just before it burst open.

"Out you go!" Fjalar said cheerfully. "Enjoy your walking tour. Just head over the ridge there. I think you'll find the Wolf well worth the trip!"

Maybe it was my imagination, but my nostrils filled with the smell of smoke and wet animal fur. My new einherji heart was testing the limits of how fast it could beat.

If it hadn't been for my friends, I'm not sure I would've had the courage to disembark. Hearthstone leaped over the side first. Sam and Blitzen followed. Not wanting to be stuck on the boat with lobster dwarf and his jerky-eating brother, I swung my legs overboard. The waist-deep water was so cold I imagined I would be singing soprano for the rest of the week.

I slogged onto the beach, and a wolf's howl split my eardrums.

Now, sure . . . I'd been expecting a wolf. Ever since childhood, wolves had terrified me, so I'd tried my best to gather my courage. But Fenris's howl was unlike anything I'd ever heard—a note of pure rage so deep it seemed to shake me apart, breaking my molecules into random amino acids and icy Ginnungagap runoff.

Safe in their boat, the two dwarves cackled with glee.

"I should have mentioned," Fjalar called to us, "the ride back is a little more expensive. All your valuables, please. Gather them together in one of your bags. Toss them to me. Otherwise, we'll leave you here."

Blitzen cursed. "They'll leave us here anyway. That's what they do."

At the moment, heading inland to confront Fenris Wolf was very low on my wish list. At the top of my wish list was: *Cry and Plead for the Treacherous Dwarves to Take Me Back to Boston.*

My voice quavered, but I tried to act more courageous than I felt.

"Get lost," I told the dwarves. "We don't need you anymore."

Fjalar and Gjalar exchanged looks. Already their boat was drifting farther away.

"Didn't you hear the Wolf?" Fjalar spoke more slowly, as if he'd overestimated my intelligence. "You're stuck on that island. With Fenris. That's a bad thing."

"Yeah, we know," I said.

"The Wolf will eat you!" Fjalar cried. "Bound or not, he will *eat* you. At dawn the island will disappear and take you with it!"

"Thanks for the lift," I said. "Pleasant trip back."

Fjalar flung up his hands. "Idiots! Suit yourself. We'll collect your valuables from your skeletal remains next year! Come on, Gjalar, back to the docks. We might have time to pick up another load of tourists."

Gjalar revved the motor. The longship turned and disappeared into the darkness.

I faced my friends. I got the feeling they wouldn't mind another rousing speech like, *We're a family of empty cups and we will dominate!*

"Well," I said, "after running from an army of dwarves, facing a monster squirrel, killing three giant sisters, and butchering a pair of talking goats . . . how bad can Fenris Wolf be?"

"Very bad," Sam and Blitz said in unison.

Hearthstone made two *okay* signs, crossed them at the wrists, and flicked them apart—the sign for *awful.*

"Right." I pulled my sword from pendant form. The blade's glow made the heather look even paler and more ghostly. "Jack, you ready?"

"Dude," said the sword, "I was *forged* ready. Still, I get the feeling we're walking into a trap here."

"Show of hands," I asked my friends, "is anybody surprised by that?"

Nobody raised their hand.

"Okay, cool," said Jack. "As long as you realize you'll probably all die in agony and start Ragnarok, I'm down. Let's do this!"

The Small Bad Wolf

I REMEMBER THE FIRST TIME I saw Plymouth Rock.

My reaction was, "That's *it*?"

Same with the Liberty Bell in Philadelphia and the Empire State Building in New York—up close and personal, they seemed smaller than I'd imagined, not worth the hype.

That's how I felt when I saw Fenris Wolf.

I'd heard all these terrible stories about him: the gods were too scared to feed him; he could break the strongest chains; he'd eaten Tyr's hand; he was going to swallow the sun on Doomsday; he was going to devour Odin in a single bite. I expected a wolf bigger than King Kong with flame-thrower breath, death-ray eyes, and laser nostrils.

What I got instead was a Wolf the size of a wolf.

We stood at the top of the ledge, looking down into the valley where Fenris sat calmly on his haunches. He was larger than an average Labrador retriever, but definitely no bigger than me. His legs were long and muscular, built for running. His shaggy gray coat swirled with tufts of black. Nobody would've called him *cute*—not with those gleaming white fangs, or the bones littering the ground around his paws—but he was a handsome animal.

I'd been hoping to find the Wolf lying on his side, hog-tied and fastened to the ground with nails, staples, duct tape, and Krazy Glue. Instead, the golden rope Gleipnir restrained him more like the leg irons used to transport criminals. The glimmering cord was tied around all four of his ankle joints, allowing enough slack for the Wolf to shuffle around. Part of the rope had apparently once been tied around the Wolf's snout like a muzzle. That section now fell across his chest in a loose loop. The rope didn't even appear to be anchored to the ground. I wasn't sure what was keeping Fenris from leaving the island unless there was one of those doggy no-no invisible fences around the perimeter.

All in all, if I were the god Tyr, getting my hand bit off so the other gods would have time to bind the Wolf, I would've been pretty torqued off at this shoddy work. Didn't the Aesir have *one* decent god of knots?

I glanced at my friends. "Where's the real Fenris? That has to be a decoy, right?"

"No." Sam's knuckles whitened on the handle of her ax. "That's him. I can sense it."

The Wolf turned toward the sound of our voices. His eyes shone with a familiar blue light that sent a xylophone mallet down the back of my rib cage.

"Well." His voice was deep and rich. His black lips curled in a very human sneer. "Who do we have here? Have the gods sent me a snack?"

I revised my impression of the Wolf. Maybe his size was ordinary. Maybe he didn't sneeze laser beams. But his eyes were colder and more intelligent than any predator I'd ever encountered—animal or human. His snout quivered as if he could smell the fear on my breath. And his voice . . . his voice flowed over me like molasses, dangerously smooth and sweet. I remembered my first feast in Valhalla, when the thanes didn't want Sam to speak in her defense because they feared the silver tongue of Loki's children. Now I understood.

The last thing I wanted to do was approach the Wolf. Yet his tone said, *Come on down. We're all friends here.*

The entire caldera was maybe a hundred yards across, which meant the Wolf was much closer than I would've liked. The ground sloped gently, but the heather was slick under my feet. I was terrified I might slip and slide right between the Wolf's paws.

"I'm Magnus Chase." My voice was *not* as smooth as molasses. I forced myself to meet Fenris's gaze. "We have an appointment."

The Wolf bared his teeth. "We do indeed, son of Frey. Vanir-spawn have such an interesting scent. Normally I only get to devour the children of Thor, or Odin, or my old friend Tyr."

"Sorry to disappoint."

"Oh, not at all." The Wolf paced, the rope gleaming between his feet, barely slowing his gait. "I'm quite pleased. I've been waiting a long time for this."

On my left, Hearthstone banged his white oak staff against the rocks. The heather plants glowed brighter, a fine silvery mist rising from them like a lawn sprinkler system. With his free hand, Hearth signed to me, *Flowers make the prison. Stay within.*

Fenris Wolf chuckled. "The elf is wise. Not powerful enough—not *nearly* powerful enough to face me—but he is right about the heather. I can't stand the stuff. Funny, though . . .

how many brave mortals choose to leave its safety and come within my reach. They want to test their skill against me, or perhaps they simply want to make sure I am still bound." The Wolf leered at Blitzen. "Your father was one of those. A noble dwarf with the best of intentions. He approached me. He died. His bones are around here somewhere."

Blitzen let loose a guttural scream. Sam and I had to restrain him to keep him from charging the Wolf with his new harpoon.

"Quite sad, really," the Wolf mused. "Bilì was his name? He was right, of course. This ridiculous rope has been loosening for ages. At one time, I was completely unable to walk. After a few centuries, I managed to hobble. I still can't cross the heather. The farther I move from the center of the island, the more the rope tightens and the more pain I endure. But it's progress! The real breakthrough came . . . oh, a little over two years ago, when I finally managed to shake that cursed muzzle off my snout!"

Sam faltered. "Two years ago . . ."

The Wolf tilted his head. "That's right, little sister. Surely you knew. I began whispering in the dreams of Odin—what a fine idea it would be to make you, the daughter of Loki, a Valkyrie! What a fine way to turn a potential enemy into a valuable friend."

"No," Sam said. "Odin would never listen to you."

"Would he not?" The Wolf snarled with pleasure. "That's the wonderful thing about you so-called *good* folk. You hear what you want to believe. You think your conscience is whispering to you when it is, perhaps, the Wolf instead. Oh, you have done very well, little sister, bringing Magnus to me—"

"I didn't *bring* him to you!" Sam shouted. "And I'm not your little sister!"

"No? I smell the changeling blood in your veins. You could be powerful. You could make our father proud. Why do you fight it?"

The Wolf's teeth were as sharp as ever, his leer just as vicious, but his voice filled with sympathy, disappointment, melancholy. His tone said *I could help you. I am your brother.*

Sam took a step forward. I grabbed her arm.

"Fenris," I said, "you sent those wolves . . . the night my mother died."

"Of course."

"You wanted to kill me—"

"Now, why would I want that?" His blue eyes were worse than mirrors. They seemed to reflect back at me all my failures— my cowardice, my weakness, my selfishness in running away when my mother needed me most. "You were valuable to me, Magnus. But you needed . . . seasoning. Hardship is wonderful for cultivating power. And look! You have succeeded—the first child of Frey strong enough to find the Sword of Summer. You have brought me the means to escape these bonds at last."

The world spun beneath me. I felt like I was back on Stanley the horse—plummeting with no reins, no saddle, no control. All this time, I'd assumed Fenris wanted me dead. That's why his wolves had attacked our apartment. But his real target had been my mother. He'd killed her to affect me. That idea was even worse than believing my mom had died to protect me. She'd died so this monster could forge me into his harbinger— a demigod capable of attaining the Sword of Summer.

I was filled with so much rage I couldn't focus.

In my hand, the sword began to hum. I realized how long Jack had been silent. He pulled at my arm, tugging me forward.

"Jack," I muttered. "Jack, what are you—?"

The Wolf laughed. "You see? The Sword of Summer is destined to cut these bonds. You cannot stop it. The children of Frey have never been fighters, Magnus Chase. You can't hope to control the blade, much less fight me with it. Your usefulness is at an end. Surt will arrive soon. The blade will fly to his hands."

"Mistake . . ." Jack murmured, tugging to escape my grip. "Mistake to bring me here."

"Yes," the Wolf purred. "Yes, it was, my fine blade. Surt thinks all of this was *his* idea, you understand. He's an imperfect tool. Like most fire giants, he's a lot of hot air, more bluster than brains, but he will serve his purpose. He'll be very happy to take possession of you."

"Jack, you're my sword now," I said, though I could barely hold on with both hands.

"Cut the cord . . ." Jack hummed insistently. "Cut the cord."

"Do it, Magnus Chase," said Fenris. "Why wait for Surt? Cut me loose of your own free will and I will be grateful. Perhaps I would even spare you and your friends."

Blitzen growled even better than the Wolf. From his pack, he pulled out the new string, Andskoti. "I was ready to bind this mutt. Now I think I might just strangle him."

"I agree," Samirah said. "He dies."

I wanted more than anything to join them. I wanted to charge the beast and run him through. The Sword of Summer was supposed to be the sharpest blade in the Nine Worlds. Surely it could cut wolf hide.

I think we would've done it, but Hearthstone swept his

staff in front of us. The runestone perthro flared with gold light.

Look. The command was more a tremor than a sound. I turned and stared in amazement at Hearthstone.

The bones. He didn't use sign language. He didn't speak. His thought was simply *there*, clearing my mind like wind through fog.

I looked again at the skeletons littering the ground. All of them had been heroes—the children of Odin, Thor, or Tyr. Dwarves, humans, elves. They'd all been tricked, enraged, enchanted by Fenris. They'd all died.

Hearthstone was the only one of us who couldn't hear the Wolf's voice. He was the only one thinking clearly.

Suddenly the sword was easier to control. It didn't stop fighting me, but I felt the balance shift slightly in my favor.

"I'm not freeing you," I told the Wolf. "And I don't need to fight you. We'll wait for Surt. We'll stop him."

The Wolf sniffed the air. "Oh . . . too late for that. You don't need to fight me? Poor mortal . . . I don't need to fight you, either. There are others to do that for me. As I said, good folk are so easy to manipulate, so ready to do my work for me. Here are some now!"

Across the island, a voice yelled, "STOP!"

At the opposite side of the ridge stood our old friend Gunilla with a Valkyrie on either side of her. Fanning out to her left and right were my old hallmates: T.J., Halfborn, Mallory, and X the half-troll.

"Caught in the act of aiding the enemy," Gunilla said. "You've signed your own death warrants!"

I Hate Signing My Own Death Warrant

"WELL, WELL," said the Wolf. "I haven't had this much company since my binding party."

Gunilla gripped her spear. She didn't look at the Wolf, as if ignoring him might make him go away.

"Thomas Jefferson, Jr.," she said, "you and your hallmates take the prisoners. Go around the edges, obviously. Slow and careful."

T.J. didn't look happy about it, but he nodded. His army jacket was buttoned up tight. His bayonet gleamed in the moonlight. Mallory Keen gave me the stink eye, but that could have been her version of a happy greeting. The two of them went left, picking their way across the rim of the crater while the three Valkyries kept their spears pointed at Fenris.

X lumbered to the right, followed by Halfborn, who was twirling his battle-axes and whistling under his breath, as if this was a pleasant stroll through a field of fallen enemies.

"Sam," I muttered, "if we're taken—"

"I know."

"No one will be here to stop Surt."

"I know."

"We can take them," Blitz said. "They're not wearing armor, much less fashionable armor."

"No," I said. "These are my shield bro—my shield siblings. Let me try talking to them."

Hearth signed, *Crazy. You?*

The beauty of sign language: He could've meant *Are you crazy?* Or *I'm crazy. Just like you!* I decided to interpret it as a show of support.

Fenris Wolf sat on his haunches and tried to scratch his ear, which wasn't possible with the cord binding his legs.

He sniffed the air and grinned at me. "Interesting company you keep, Magnus Chase. Someone is hiding, but I can smell him. Which one is he, eh? Perhaps I will get a feast today after all!"

I glanced at Sam. She looked just as mystified as I felt.

"Sorry, fuzzball," I said. "No idea what you're talking about."

Fenris laughed. "We shall see. I wonder if he will dare to show his true face."

"Chase!" Gunilla plucked a hammer from her bandolier. "Do not speak with the Wolf again or I will cave in your skull."

"Gunilla," I said, "great to see you again too. Surt is on his way right now. We don't have time for this."

"Oh? Have you made common cause with the fire lord who killed you? Or perhaps that was part of the plan from the beginning—to get you into Valhalla."

Sam sighed. "For a child of Thor, you think too much."

"And you, daughter of Loki, listen too little. Jefferson, hurry it up!"

My hallmates got to either side of us.

Mallory made a *tsk-tsk* sound. "You led us on quite a chase, Chase."

"Clever," I said. "How long have you been waiting to use that line?"

Mallory smirked.

Next to her, X wiped beads of green sweat from his forehead. "Wolf's rope is loose. This is not good."

From across the valley, Gunilla yelled, "No fraternizing! I want them in chains!"

T.J. dangled four sets of handcuffs from his finger. "Here's the thing, Magnus: Gunilla made it clear that if we don't prove our loyalty to Valhalla by apprehending you, we will spend the next hundred years in the boiler room shoveling coal. So consider yourself under arrest, blah, blah, blah."

Halfborn grinned. "But the *other* thing is: we're Vikings. We're pretty bad at following orders. So consider yourself free again."

T.J. let the handcuffs slip from his finger. "Oops."

My spirits lifted. "You mean—"

"He means, you idiot," Mallory said, "that we're here to help."

"I love you guys."

"What do you need us to do?" T.J. asked.

Sam nodded to Blitzen. "Our dwarf has a rope to rebind the Wolf. If we can—"

"Enough!" Gunilla shouted. On either side, her Valkyrie lieutenants readied their spears. "I will take you *all* back in chains if I must!"

Fenris howled with pleasure. "That would be delightful to watch. Unfortunately, Valkyrie, you are too slow. My other friends have arrived, and they won't be taking any prisoners."

X gazed toward the south, his neck muscles rippling like freshly poured cement. "There."

At the same moment, Hearthstone pointed with his staff, the whole length of white oak suddenly burning with gold fire.

On the ridge to the right, between the Valkyries and us, a dozen fire giants marched into view. Each stood about ten feet tall. They wore leather scale armor, carried swords the size of plow blades, and had various axes and knives hanging from their belts. Their complexions were an assortment of volcanic colors—ash, lava, pumice, obsidian. The fields of heather may have been noxious to the Wolf, but the stuff didn't seem to bother the fire giants. Wherever they stepped, the plants burned and smoked.

In the middle of their line stood Satan's fashion consultant himself, the fire lord Surt, wearing a trim-cut three-piece suit of chain mail, a tie, and a dress shirt that appeared to be woven from flame—elegantly accessorized with a burning scimitar in his hand. He looked pretty good, despite the fact that his nose was still cut off. That fact, at least, made me happy.

Blitzen clenched his teeth. "That's my design. He *stole* my design."

"Magnus Chase!" Surt's voice boomed. "I see you have brought my new sword. Excellent!"

Jack almost leaped out of my hands. I must have looked ridiculous trying to keep him under control, like a fireman wrestling a high-pressure hose.

"My master . . ." Jack said. "He shall be my master."

Surt laughed. "Surrender the sword and I will kill you quickly." He sneered at Gunilla and her two lieutenants. "As for Odin's wenches, I make no promises."

Fenris Wolf rose and stretched. "Lord Surt, as much as I love posturing and threats, can we move things along? Moonlight is a-wasting."

"T.J.," I said.

"Yeah?"

"You asked how you could help. My friends and I need to rebind Fenris Wolf. Can you keep those fire giants busy?"

T.J. smiled. "I charged uphill against seventeen hundred Confederates. I think I can handle a dozen fire giants."

He called across the valley, "Captain Gunilla, are you with us? Because I'd rather not fight another Civil War."

Gunilla scanned the army of fire giants. Her expression soured, as if she found them even more repugnant than she found me. She raised her spear. "Death to Surt! Death to the enemies of Asgard!"

She and her lieutenants charged at the giants.

"I guess we're in business," T.J. said. "Fix bayonets!"

SIXTY-FOUR

Whose Idea Was It to Make This Wolf Un-killable?

VALHALLA'S DAILY COMBAT training finally made sense to me. After the terror and chaos of war in the hotel courtyard, I was more prepared to face Fenris Wolf and the fire giants, even if they didn't have AK-47s or chests painted with COME AT ME, BRO!

I was still having trouble controlling the sword, though. The only thing that helped: Jack now seemed divided between wanting to fly to Surt's hand or flying toward the Wolf. Lucky for me, I needed to approach the Wolf.

Sam knocked a giant's thrown ax out of the air. "Rebinding Fenris—any idea how we're doing that?"

"Yes," I said. "Maybe. Not really."

A fire giant charged in our direction. Blitzen was so angry—between the Wolf gloating about his dad's death and Surt stealing his fashion ideas—that he howled like Crazy Alice in Chinatown and rammed his harpoon right through the giant's gut. The fire giant stumbled off, belching flames and taking the harpoon with him.

Hearthstone pointed to the Wolf. *Idea,* he signed. *Follow me.*

"I thought we needed to stay in the heather," I recalled.

Hearthstone raised his staff. Across the ground at his feet, a rune spread like a shadow:

Heather bloomed around it, sprouting new tendrils.

"*Algiz*," Sam marveled. "The rune of shielding. I've never seen it used."

I felt as if I were seeing Hearthstone for the first time. He didn't stumble. He didn't faint. He strode confidently forward, the flowers expanding before him like an unrolling carpet. Not only was Hearth immune to the Wolf's voice, his rune magic was literally redrawing the boundaries of Fenris's prison.

We inched into the valley, following Hearthstone. On the right side of the island, my einherjar friends clashed with Surt's forces. Halfborn Gunderson buried his ax in the breast-plate of a giant. X picked up another fire-breather and tossed him off the side of the ridge. Mallory and T.J. fought back-to-back—jabbing and slashing and dodging blasts of flame.

Gunilla and her two Valkyrie lieutenants were fighting Surt himself. Between the shining white spears and the flaming sword, their combat was almost too bright to watch.

My friends fought valiantly, but they were outnumbered two-to-one. The fire giants didn't want to die. Even the one Blitzen had harpooned was still staggering around, trying to blowtorch the einherjar with his bad breath.

"We have to hurry," I said.

"Open to suggestions, kid," Blitzen said.

Fenris paced expectantly. He didn't seem concerned to see us shuffling toward him on a carpet of heather, collectively armed with an ax, a glowing white staff, an uncooperative sword, and a ball of string.

"By all means, come down," he said. "Bring that blade closer."

Blitzen huffed. "I'll tie him up. Hearth can guard me. Magnus and Sam—you two keep him from biting off my head for a few minutes."

"Terrible idea," Sam said.

"Got a better one?" Blitz asked.

"I do!" Fenris lunged. He could've torn my throat out, but that wasn't his plan. His front paws passed on either side of my sword. Jack cheerfully cooperated, slicing the rope in half.

Sam brought down her ax between the Wolf's ears, but Fenris leaped out of the way. His back legs were still hobbled, but his front paws were free. The Wolf's coat steamed from contact with the heather. Blisters swelled all over his legs, but he sounded too delighted to care.

"Oh, that's wonderful," he crowed. "Just the back legs now, please. Then we can get Ragnarok underway!"

All the rage that had built inside me for two years boiled to the surface.

"Blitz," I said, "do what you need to do. I'm going to knock this mutt's teeth out."

I ran at the Wolf—possibly my worst idea ever. Sam charged in next to me.

Fenris might have been the size of a normal wolf, but even with his back legs hobbled, his speed and strength were impossible to match.

As soon as I stepped from the edge of the heather, he became a blur of claws and teeth. I stumbled and fell, a line of deep cuts across my chest. Fenris would've torn me open if Sam's ax hadn't slammed him aside.

The Wolf snarled. "You can't hurt me. The *gods* couldn't hurt me. Don't you think they would've slit my throat if they could have? My destiny is fixed. Until Ragnarok, I am un-killable!"

"Must be nice." I stumbled to my feet. "But it won't keep me from trying."

Unfortunately, Jack wasn't helping. Every time I tried to attack, the sword turned and swerved, doing its best to cut the rope around the Wolf's back legs. My fight with the Wolf was more like a game of keep-away.

Blitzen lunged forward, the end of Andskoti tied in a noose. He tried to snare the Wolf's hindquarters, but he might as well have been moving in slow motion. Fenris stepped aside, dodging another strike from Sam's ax. The Wolf slashed Blitzen across the throat and the dwarf fell facedown. The string rolled away.

"NO!" I yelled.

I moved toward Blitzen, but Hearthstone was faster.

He slammed his staff across Fenris's skull. Golden fire blazed. The Wolf clambered away, whining in pain. A rune mark now steamed on his forehead—a simple arrow seared into the gray fur:

"*Tiwaz?*" The Wolf snarled. "You *dare* attack me with the rune of Tyr?" The Wolf lunged at Hearthstone but seemed to hit an invisible barrier. He stumbled and howled.

Sam appeared next to me. Her ax was gone. Her left eye was swollen shut and her hijab had been cut to shreds. "Hearth used the rune of sacrifice," she said, her voice quavering. "To save Blitz."

"What does that mean?" I asked.

Hearth collapsed to his knees, leaning against his staff. Still he managed to put himself between the dwarf and the Wolf.

"You sacrifice your strength to shield your friend?" The Wolf laughed. "Fine. Enjoy your spellwork. The dwarf is already dead. Your own rune magic has doomed you. You can watch while I deal with my other tasty prey."

He bared his fangs at us.

Across the field, the battle was not going well.

One of Gunilla's Valkyries sprawled lifeless on the rocks. The other one fell, her armor burning from Surt's sword. Gunilla faced the Fire Lord alone, swinging her spear like a whip of light, but she couldn't last. Her clothes smoldered. Her shield was charred and cracked.

The einherjar were surrounded. Halfborn had lost one of his axes. He was covered with so many burns and gashes I didn't understand how he could still be alive, but he just kept fighting, laughing as he charged the giants. Mallory was on one knee, cursing as she parried attacks from three giants at once. T.J. swung his rifle wildly. Even X looked tiny compared to the enemies now looming over him.

My head throbbed. I could feel my einherji powers at work, trying to close the cuts on my chest, but I knew Fenris could kill me faster than I could possibly heal.

The Wolf sniffed, no doubt smelling my weakness.

"Ah, well," he chuckled. "A good try, Magnus, but the sons of Frey never were fighters. All that's left for me to do now is devour my enemies. I love this part!"

SIXTY-FIVE

I Hate This Part

THE STRANGEST THINGS can save your life. Like lions. Or bulletproof ascots.

Fenris lunged at my face. I cleverly escaped by falling on my butt. A blurred shape launched itself at the Wolf and knocked him aside.

Two animals tumbled across the bone yard in a whirl of fangs and claws. When they separated, I realized Fenris was facing a she-lion with a swollen eye.

"Sam?" I yelped.

"Get the rope." She kept her gaze on her enemy. "I need to have a talk with my brother."

The fact that she could speak in lion form freaked me out even more than the fact that she had a lion form. Her lips moved in a very human way. Her eyes were the same color. Her voice was still Sam's voice.

Fenris's fur stood up on the back of his neck. "So you accept your birthright as you are about to die, little sister?"

"I accept who I am," Sam said. "But not the way you mean. I am Samirah al-Abbas. Samirah of the Lion." She leaped at the Wolf. They clawed, bit, kicked, and howled. I'd heard the term *fur flying*, but I'd never realized what a horrific thing it could be. The two beasts literally tried to tear each other apart. And one of those beasts was a friend of mine.

My first instinct was to charge into battle. But that wouldn't work.

Freya had told me that killing was the least of the sword's powers.

The sons of Frey have never been fighters, the Wolf had said.

So what *was* I?

Blitzen rolled over, groaning. Hearthstone frantically checked the dwarf's neck.

The ascot glittered. Somehow, it had turned from yellow silk to woven metal, saving Blitzen's throat in the process. It was honest-to-Frigg bulletproof neckwear.

I couldn't help grinning. Blitz was alive. He had played to his strength.

He wasn't a fighter. Neither was I. But there were other ways to win a battle.

I snatched up the ball of string. It felt like woven snow—impossibly soft and cold. In my other hand, the sword became still.

"What are we doing?" Jack asked.

"Figuring stuff out."

"Oh, cool." The blade quivered as if stretching after a nap. "How's that going?"

"Better." I stabbed the end of the blade into the ground. Jack did not try to fly away. "Surt may get you someday," I said, "but he doesn't understand your power. I do now. We're a team."

I looped the string's noose around Jack's hilt and pulled it tight. The battle seemed to fade around me. I stopped thinking about how to fight the Wolf. He couldn't be killed—at least not now, not by me.

Instead, I focused on the warmth I felt whenever I healed someone: the power of growth and life—the power of Frey. The Norns had told me nine days ago: *The sun must go east.*

This place was all about night, winter, and silver moonlight. I needed to be the summer sun.

Fenris Wolf noticed the change in the air. He swiped at Sam and sent her tumbling across the lawn of bones. His snout was shredded with claw marks. The rune of Tyr glistened ugly and black on his forehead.

"What are you up to, Magnus? None of that!" He lunged, but before he could reach me, he fell out of the air, twisting and howling in pain.

Light surrounded me—the same golden aura as when I'd healed Sam and Hearthstone in Jotunheim. It wasn't hot like the fires of Muspellheim. It wasn't particularly bright, but it obviously pained the Wolf. He snarled and paced, squinting at me like I'd become a spotlight.

"Stop that!" he howled. "Are you trying to *annoy* me to death?"

Sam the lion struggled to her feet. She had a nasty cut on her flank. Her face looked like she'd rear-ended a tractor-trailer. "Magnus, what are you doing?"

"Bringing the summer."

The cuts on my chest mended. My strength returned. My father was the god of light and warmth. Wolves were creatures of darkness. The power of Frey could constrain Fenris just as it constrained the extremes of fire and ice.

Sticking up from the ground, Jack hummed with satisfaction. "Summer. Yeah, I remember summer."

I rolled out Andskoti until it trailed Jack like a kite string.

I faced the Wolf. "An old dwarf once told me that the most powerful crafting materials are paradoxes. This rope is made of them. But I've got one more—the final paradox that will bind you: the Sword of Summer, a weapon that wasn't designed to be a weapon, a blade that is best used by letting go of it."

I willed Jack to fly, trusting he would do the rest.

He could have sliced the last of the Wolf's bonds. He could have flown across the battlefield straight into Surt's hands, but he didn't. He zipped under the Wolf's belly, threading the cord Andskoti around his legs faster than Fenris could react, binding him and toppling him.

Fenris's howl shook the island. "No! I will not—!"

The sword zipped around his snout. Jack tied off the rope in an aerial pirouette then floated back to me, his blade glowing with pride. "How'd I do, boss?"

"Jack," I said, "you are one awesome sword."

"Well, I *know* that," he said. "But how about that ropework, huh? That's a perfect stevedore's knot right there, and I don't even have hands."

Sam stumbled toward us. "You did it! You—ugh."

Her lion form melted into regular old Sam—badly injured, face battered, her side soaked with blood. Before she could fall, I grabbed her and dragged her away from the Wolf. Even fully bound, he thrashed and frothed at the mouth. I didn't want to be any closer to him than I had to be.

Hearthstone staggered after me, holding up Blitzen. The four of us fell together on a bed of heather.

"Alive," I said. "I wasn't expecting that."

Our moment of triumph lasted about . . . well, one moment. Then the sounds of battle became louder and clearer around us, as if a curtain had been ripped away. Hearthstone's shielding magic may have given us extra protection against the Wolf, but it had also sealed us off from the fight with the fire giants . . . and my einherjar friends weren't doing well.

"To the Valkyrie!" T.J. shouted. "Hurry!"

He stumbled across the ridge, bayoneting a fire giant and trying to reach Gunilla. All this time, while we'd been dealing with the Wolf, the Valkyrie captain had been holding off Surt. Now she was on the ground, her spear held weakly above her as Surt raised his scimitar.

Mallory staggered around weaponless, too far away and too bloodied to help. X was trying to dig his way out from beneath a pile of giant corpses. Halfborn Gunderson sat bloody and unmoving, his back propped against a rock.

I processed this in a split second. Just as quickly, I realized Hearth, Blitz, Sam, and I wouldn't be there in time to make a difference.

Nevertheless, I gripped my sword and rose. I staggered toward Gunilla. Our eyes met across the field, her last expression one of resignation and anger: *Make it count.*

The fire lord brought down his scimitar.

Sacrifices

I DON'T KNOW WHY IT BROKE ME SO BADLY.

I didn't even like Gunilla.

But when I saw Surt standing over her lifeless body, his eyes smoldering in triumph, I wanted to fall down in the pile of bones and stay there until Ragnarok.

Gunilla was dead. Her lieutenants were dead. I didn't even know their names, but they'd sacrificed their lives to buy me time. Halfborn was dead or dying. The other einherjar were not much better off. Sam and Blitz and Hearth were in no shape to fight.

And Surt was still on his feet, as strong as ever, his burning sword ready. Three of his fire giants were also still alive and armed.

After all we'd been through, the fire lord could kill me, take my sword, and cut the Wolf free.

Judging from the smile on his face, Surt expected to do just that.

"I am impressed," he admitted. "The Wolf told me you had potential. I don't think even Fenris expected you to do this well."

The Wolf thrashed in his new magic bonds.

A few feet from the fire lord, T.J. crouched, his bayonet

ready. He glanced at me, waiting for a sign. I knew he was
ready to charge one last time, distract the giants if it would
help me, but I couldn't let another person die.

"Go now," I told Surt. "Go back to Muspellheim."

The fire lord threw back his head and laughed. "Brave to
the end! I think not, Magnus Chase. I think you will burn."

He thrust out his hand. A column of fire shot toward me.

I stood my ground.

I imagined being with my mom in the Blue Hills on the
first day of spring, the sunlight warming my skin, gently thaw-
ing three months of cold and darkness out of my system.

My mom turned to me, her smile luminous: *This is where I
am, Magnus. In this moment. With you.*

A sense of serenity anchored me. I remembered my mom
once telling me how the town houses in Back Bay, like our
family's ancestral home, had been built on landfill. Every so
often, engineers had to sink new pylons beneath the foundations to keep the buildings from collapsing. I felt like I'd had
my pylons reinforced. I was solid.

Surt's flames rolled over me. They lost their intensity. They
were nothing but ghostly flickers of warm orange, as harmless
as butterflies.

At my feet, the heather began to bloom—white flowers
spreading across the landscape, reclaiming the trampled and
burned areas where Surt's warriors had walked, soaking up
the blood, covering the corpses of the fallen giants.

"The battle is over," I announced. "I consecrate this ground
in the name of Frey."

The words sent a shockwave in every direction. Swords,
daggers, and axes flew from the fire giants' hands. T.J.'s rifle

spun from his grasp. Even the weapons lying on the ground were expelled from the island, blasted into the darkness like shrapnel.

The only one left holding a weapon was me.

Without his flaming scimitar, Surt didn't look so confident. "Tricks and childish magic," he snarled. "You cannot defeat me, Magnus Chase. That sword will be mine!"

"Not today."

I threw the blade. It spiraled toward Surt, passing over the giant's head. Surt grabbed for it and missed.

"What was that?" The giant laughed. "An attack?"

"No," I said. "That was your exit."

Behind Surt, Jack slashed the air, ripping the fabric between the worlds. A zigzag of fire burned on the ridge. My ears popped. As if someone had shot out the window in an airplane's pressurized cabin, Surt and the other fire giants were sucked screaming into the rift, which closed behind them.

"Bye!" Jack called. "Catch you later!"

Except for the outraged snarling of the Wolf, the island was silent.

I stumbled across the field. I fell to my knees in front of Gunilla. I could tell immediately that the Valkyrie captain was gone. Her blue eyes stared into the dark. Her bandolier was empty of hammers. Her white spear lay broken across her chest.

My eyes stung. "I'm sorry."

For five hundred years she'd been in Valhalla, collecting the souls of the dead, preparing for the final battle. I remembered how she'd scolded me: *Even gazing upon Asgard, you have no sense of reverence.*

In death, her face seemed full of wonder and awe. I hoped she was gazing upon Asgard the way she wanted it to be—filled with Aesir, all the lights burning in her father's mansion.

"Magnus," called T.J., "we have to go."

He and Mallory were struggling to carry Halfborn Gunderson. X had managed to dig his way out from under the fire giant corpse pile and was now carrying the two other fallen Valkyries. Blitz and Hearthstone stumbled along together, Sam close behind.

I picked up the body of the Valkyrie captain. She was not light, and my strength was fading again.

"We have to hurry." T.J. spoke as gently as he could, but I heard the urgency in his tone.

The ground was shifting under my feet. I realized my glowing aura had done more than blind the Wolf. The sunlight had affected the texture of the island. The island was supposed to disappear at dawn. My magic had hastened the process, causing the ground to dissolve into spongy mist.

"Only seconds," Sam gasped. "Go."

The last thing I felt capable of was a burst of speed, but somehow, carrying Gunilla, I followed T.J. as he led the way to the shore.

SIXTY-SEVEN

One More, for a Friend

"WE'VE GOT A FREY BOAT!" YELLED T.J.

I had no idea what a Frey boat was. I didn't see any boat on the beach, but I was too stunned and exhausted to ask questions. I felt like the extremes of heat and cold I'd tolerated my entire life were now taking revenge. My forehead burned with fever. My eyes felt close to boiling. My chest felt like a block of ice.

I plodded along. The ground became softer under my feet. The beach sank. The waves rushed in. My arm muscles screamed under the weight of the Valkyrie captain.

I started veering sideways. Sam grabbed my arm. "Just a little farther, Magnus. Stay with me."

We got to the beach. T.J. pulled out a piece of cloth like a handkerchief and tossed it into the surf. Immediately the cloth expanded, unfolding. By the count of ten, a full-size Viking warship bobbed in the surf with two oversize oars, a figurehead carved like a wild boar, and a green sail emblazoned with the Hotel Valhalla logo. Along the side of the prow, lettered in white, were the words: HOTEL VALHALLA COURTESY VEHICLE.

"In!" T.J. jumped aboard first and reached out to take Gunilla from me.

The wet sand pulled at my feet, but somehow I managed

to get over the rail. Sam made sure everyone else got in safely. Then she climbed aboard.

A deep hum reverberated across the island, like a bass amp turned to maximum. The Isle of Heather sank beneath the black waves. The ship's sail tacked by itself. The oars began to row, and the ship turned west.

Blitzen and Hearthstone collapsed at the bow. They started arguing with each other about which of them had taken the stupider risks, but they were so tired the debate deteriorated into a halfhearted poking contest, like a couple of second graders.

Sam knelt next to Gunilla. She folded the Valkyrie captain's arms across her chest and gently closed Gunilla's blue eyes.

"The others?" I asked.

X lowered his head.

He had set the two Valkyries in the stern, but it was clear they were gone. He folded their arms like Gunilla's. "Brave warriors." He touched their foreheads with tenderness.

"I didn't know them," I said.

"Margaret and Irene." Sam's voice was unsteady. "They—they never liked me much, but . . . good Valkyries."

"Magnus," T.J. called from amidships, "we need you."

He and Mallory were kneeling next to Halfborn Gunderson, whose berserker strength had finally failed him. His chest was a nightmarish patchwork of cuts and burns. His left arm hung at an unnatural angle. His beard and hair were sprinkled with blood and small bits of heather.

"Good—fight," he wheezed.

"Don't talk, you big idiot!" Mallory sobbed. "How *dare* you get yourself hurt like this?"

He grinned sleepily. "Sorry . . . Mother."

"Hang in there," T.J. said. "We can get you back to Valhalla. Then if—if anything happens, you can be reborn."

I put my hand on Halfborn's shoulder. I sensed damage so severe I almost pulled away. It was like forcing myself to explore a bowl of glass shards.

"There's no time," I said. "We're losing him."

Mallory choked on tears. "Not an option. No. Halfborn Gunderson, I hate you so much."

He coughed. Blood flecked his lips. "I hate you too, Mallory Keen."

"Hold him still," I said. "I'll do what I can."

"Kid, think about this," Blitz said. "You're already weak."

"I have to." I extended my senses, taking in Halfborn's broken bones, his internal bleeding, his bruised organs. Fear washed over me. It was too much, too close to death. I needed help.

"Jack," I called.

The sword hovered to my side. "Boss?"

"Halfborn is dying. I'll need your strength to help heal him. You can do that?"

The sword hummed nervously. "Yeah. But boss, the second you take hold of me—"

"I know. I'll be even more exhausted."

"It's not just binding the Wolf," Jack warned. "I also helped with the aura of golden light, which was pretty cool if I do say so myself. And then there was the Peace of Frey."

"The peace . . ." I realized he meant the shockwave that had disarmed everyone, but I didn't have time to worry about that. "Fine. Yes. We have to act now."

I grabbed the sword. My eyesight dimmed. If I hadn't been sitting already, I would've fallen down. I fought against the nausea and dizziness and placed the sword flat against Halfborn's chest.

Warmth flooded through me. Light turned Halfborn's beard to red gold. I sent the last of my strength coursing through his veins, repairing damage, closing ruptures.

The next thing I remember, I was lying faceup on the deck, staring at a green sail rippling in the wind as my friends shook me and shouted my name.

Then I was standing in a sunlit meadow at the edge of a lake with blue sky above me. A warm breeze ruffled my hair.

Somewhere behind me, a man's voice said, "Welcome."

SIXTY-EIGHT

Don't Be a No-bro, Bro

HE LOOKED LIKE a Hollywood Viking. He looked more like Thor from the movies than Thor did.

Blond hair fell to his shoulders. His tan face, blue eyes, hawkish nose, and stubbly beard would've worked equally well on the red carpet or the beaches of Malibu.

He reclined on a throne of living tree branches, the seat draped with deer hide. Across his lap lay a sort of scepter—a stag's antler fitted with a leather grip.

When he smiled, I saw my own self-conscious smirk, the same crooked chin. He even had the same cowlick I always got above my right ear.

I understood why my mom would've fallen in love with him. It wasn't just because he was handsome, or because his faded jeans, flannel shirt, and hiking boots were exactly her style. He radiated warmth and tranquility. Every time I'd healed someone, every time I'd called on the power of Frey, I'd captured a fragment of this guy's aura.

"Dad," I said.

"Magnus." Frey rose. His eyes twinkled, but he didn't seem sure what to do with his arms. "I'm so glad to see you at last. I'd—I'd give you a hug, but I imagine that would not be welcome. I understand you need more time—"

I charged in and gave him a bear hug.

That wasn't like me. I'm not a hugger, especially not with strangers.

But he wasn't a stranger. I knew him as well as I knew my mother. For the first time, I understood why my mom had been so insistent on taking me hiking and camping. Every time we were in the woods on a summer day, every time the sun came out from behind the clouds, Frey had been there.

Maybe I should have resented him, but I didn't. After losing my mother, I didn't have patience for grudges. My years on the street had taught me that it was pointless to whine and moan about what you could've had—what you deserved, what was fair. I was just happy to have this moment.

He cupped his hand gently on the back of my head. He smelled of campfire smoke, pine needles, and toasted s'mores. Did they have s'mores in Vanaheim?

It occurred to me why I must be here. I was dead. Or at least dying again.

I pulled away. "My friends—"

"Are safe," Frey assured me. "You pushed yourself to the verge of death healing the berserker, but he will live. So will you. You have done well, Magnus."

His praise made me uncomfortable. "Three Valkyries died. I almost lost every friend I had. All I did was bind the Wolf with a new rope and send Surt back to Muspellheim—and Jack did all that work. It doesn't really change anything."

Frey laughed. "Magnus, you have changed *everything*. You, the wielder of the sword, are shaping the destiny of the Nine Worlds. As for the deaths of the Valkyries—that was a sacrifice they willingly made. Do not dishonor them by feeling guilt. You cannot prevent every death, any more than I can prevent each summer from becoming autumn . . . or any more than I can prevent my *own* fate at Ragnarok."

"Your fate . . ." I closed my fingers around the runestone, now back on its chain. "I have your sword. Couldn't you . . . ?"

Frey shook his head. "No, son. As your Aunt Freya told you, I can never wield the Sword of Summer again. Ask the sword, if you want to be sure."

I pulled off the pendant. Jack sprang to life, spewing a tirade of insults I can't really repeat.

"And another thing!" he yelled. "Giving me away so you could marry a giantess? Dude, what was *that*? Blades before babes, you know what I'm saying?"

Frey smiled sadly. "Hello, old friend."

"Oh, we're friends again?" the sword demanded. "Nah. Nuh-uh. We're done." Jack paused. "Your son's okay, though. I like him. As long as he's not planning to trade me for a giantess's hand in marriage."

"That's not on my to-do list," I promised.

"Then we're cool. But as for this sorry father of yours, this traitorous no-bro—"

I willed the sword back to pendant form. "No-bro?"

Frey shrugged. "I made my choice long ago. I surrendered the blade for the sake of love."

"But on Ragnarok, you'll die because you don't have it."

He held up the deer antler. "I will fight with this."

"An animal horn?"

"Knowing your fate is one thing. Accepting it is another. I

will do my duty. With this antler I will slay many giants, even Beli, one of their great generals. But you're right. It won't be enough to bring down Surt. In the end, I will die."

"How can you be so calm about it?"

"Magnus . . . even gods can't last forever. I don't expend my energy trying to fight the change of seasons. I focus on making sure the days I have, and the season I oversee, are as joyful, rich, and plentiful as possible." He touched my face. "But you already understand this. No child of Thor or Odin or even noble Tyr could have withstood Hel's promises, Loki's silver words. You did. Only a son of Frey, with the Sword of Summer, could choose to let go as you did."

"Letting go . . . My mom . . ."

"Yes." Frey retrieved something from his throne—a sealed ceramic jar about the size of a heart. He placed it in my hands. "You know what she would want?"

I couldn't speak. I nodded, hoping my expression told Frey how grateful I was.

"You, my son, will bring hope to the Nine Worlds. You have heard the term Indian summer? You will be our last such season—a chance for warmth, light, and growth before the long winter of Ragnarok."

"But . . ." I cleared my throat. "But no pressure."

Frey flashed his brilliant white teeth. "Exactly. Much needs to be done. The Aesir and Vanir are scattered. Loki grows stronger. Even in his bonds, he has played us against each other, distracted us, made us lose focus. I am guilty of becoming distracted as well. For too long I have been removed from the world of men. Only your mother managed to . . ." He focused on the jar in my hands. "Well, after my big speech

THE SWORD OF SUMMER

about not holding on to the past . . ." He smiled ruefully. "She was a vibrant soul. She would be proud of you."

"Dad . . ." I wasn't sure what else to say. Maybe I just wanted to try out the word again. I'd never had much experience using it. "I don't know if I'm up to this."

From the pocket of his flannel shirt, he pulled a tattered piece of paper—the MISSING flyer Annabeth and her dad had been distributing on the day I died. Frey handed it to me. "You will not be alone. For now, rest, my son. I promise it won't be another sixteen years before we meet again. In the meantime, you should call your cousin. You should talk. You will need her help before all is said and done."

That sounded ominous, but I didn't get the chance to ask about it. I blinked and Frey was gone. I was sitting in the longship again, holding the flyer and the ceramic jar. Next to me sat Halfborn Gunderson, sipping from a cup of mead.

"Well." He gave me a bloody grin. Most of his wounds had faded to scar tissue. "I owe you my life. How about I buy you dinner?"

I blinked and looked around us. Our ship had docked in Valhalla, on one of the rivers that ran through the lobby. How we'd gotten there, I had no idea. My other friends stood on the wharf, speaking with Helgi the hotel manager—grim faces all around as they regarded the off-loaded bodies of the three dead Valkyries.

"What's going on?" I asked.

Halfborn drained his cup. "We've been summoned to the feast hall to explain ourselves before the thanes and the host of einherjar. I hope they let us eat before they kill us again. I'm starving."

SIXTY-NINE

Oh . . . So *That's* Who Fenris Smelled in Chapter Sixty-Three

WE MUST HAVE LOST an entire day returning to Valhalla, because dinner was under way in the Feast Hall of the Slain. Valkyries flew around with mead pitchers. Einherjar threw bread and roasted Saehrimnir at each other. Clusters of musicians jammed out all over the room.

The fiesta slowly quieted as our procession made its way toward the thanes' table. An honor guard of Valkyries carried the bodies of Gunilla, Irene, and Margaret, covered with white linen, on stretchers. I had hoped the fallen might come back to life when they reached Valhalla. Couldn't Valkyries become einherjar? But it didn't happen.

Mallory, X, T.J., and Halfborn followed the litters. Sam, Blitzen, Hearth, and I brought up the caboose.

Warriors glared at us as we passed. The Valkyries' expressions were even worse. I was surprised we weren't killed before we reached the thanes. I suppose the crowd wanted to see us publicly humiliated. They didn't know what we'd done. They just knew we were escaped rogues brought back for judgment, following the bodies of three Valkyries. We weren't shackled, but I still shuffled along as if the rope Andskoti was wrapped around my ankles. I cradled the ceramic jar in the crook of my arm. Whatever else happened, I couldn't lose that.

We stopped in front of the thanes' table. Erik, Helgi, Leif, and all the other Eriks looked grim. Even my old buddy Hunding the bellhop stared at me with shock and disappointment, as if I'd taken away his chocolate.

Helgi finally spoke. "Explain."

I saw no reason to hold anything back. I didn't speak loudly, but my words echoed through the hall. When I got to the fight with Fenris, my voice failed me. Sam picked up the story.

When she was done, the thanes sat silently. I couldn't read their mood. Perhaps they were more unsure now than angry, but it didn't matter. Despite my talk with my father, I didn't feel proud of what we'd accomplished. I was only alive because the three Valkyries in front of me had kept the fire giants at bay while we chained the Wolf. No punishment from the thanes could make me feel worse than that.

Finally Helgi rose. "This is the most serious matter to come before this table in many years. If you speak truly, you have done deeds worthy of warriors. You have stopped Fenris Wolf from breaking free. You have sent Surt back to Muspellheim. But you acted as rogues—without the leave of the thanes, and in . . . questionable company." He glanced distastefully at Hearth, Blitz, and Sam. "Loyalty, Magnus Chase . . . loyalty to Valhalla is everything. The thanes must discuss all this in private before passing judgment, unless Odin wishes to intercede."

He glanced at the vacant wooden throne, which of course stayed empty. Perched on the backrest, the ravens fixed me with their glittering black eyes.

"Very well," Helgi sighed. "We—"

To my left, a booming voice said, "Odin wishes to intercede."

Nervous murmurs rippled through the feast hall. X raised his stone-gray face toward the thanes.

"X," T.J. whispered, "this is no time for jokes."

"Odin wishes to intercede," said the half-troll stubbornly.

His appearance changed. His huge trollish shape dropped away like camouflage fabric. In X's place stood a man who looked like a retired drill sergeant. He was barrel-chested, with massive arms stuffed in a short-sleeve Hotel Valhalla polo shirt. His gray hair was close-cropped, his beard cut square to accentuate his hardened weathered face. A black patch covered his left eye. His right eye was dark blue, the color of vein blood. At his side hung a sword so massive it made Jack the pendant tremble on his chain.

The man's name tag read: ODIN, ALL-FATHER, OWNER AND FOUNDER.

"Odin." Sam dropped to one knee.

The god smiled down at her. Then he gave me what I thought was a conspiratorial wink, though it was hard to tell, since he had only one eye.

His name rippled through the feast hall. The einherjar got to their feet. The thanes rose and bowed deeply.

Odin, formerly the half-troll known as X, marched around the table and took his place on the throne. The two ravens landed on his shoulders and pecked affectionately at his ears.

"Well!" Odin's voice boomed. "What does a god have to do to get a cup of mead around here?"

We Are Subjected to the PowerPoint of Doom

ODIN GOT HIS DRINK, offered some toasts, then began pacing in front of his throne, talking about where he'd been and what he'd been doing the past few decades. I was too shocked to register much of Odin's speech. I think most of the einherjar felt the same way.

The room only began to unfreeze when Odin summoned up the glowing Valkyrie-Vision screens. Einherjar blinked and stirred as if coming out of mass hypnosis.

"I am a seeker of knowledge!" Odin announced. "This has always been true. I hung from the World Tree for nine days and nights, racked with pain, in order to discover the secret of runes. I stood in line in a blizzard for six days to discover the sorcery of the smartphone."

"What?" I muttered.

Blitzen coughed. "Just roll with it."

"And more recently," Odin announced, "I endured seven weeks of motivational speaker training at a hotel in Peoria to discover . . . this!"

A clicker appeared in his hand. On all the magical screens, a PowerPoint title slide glowed, with a whirling emblem that read: ODIN'S PLAN: HOW TO HAVE A HIGHLY SUCCESSFUL AFTERLIFE!

"What is going on?" I whispered to Sam.

"Odin is always trying different things," she said. "Looking in new places for knowledge. He is very wise, but . . ."

Hearthstone signed as discreetly as possible: *This is why I work for Mimir.*

"So you see," Odin continued, pacing back and forth, his ravens flapping their wings for balance, "everything these heroes have done, they did with my knowledge and my permission. I have been with them the entire time—either in person or in spirit."

The screen changed. Odin started lecturing through some bullet points. My eyes kind of glazed over, but he talked about why he'd hidden in Valhalla as X the half-troll:

"To see how you would welcome such a warrior, and how you would carry out your duties when you didn't think I was around. You all need to work on your positive empowerment and self-actualization."

He explained why he'd chosen Samirah al-Abbas as a Valkyrie:

"If the daughter of Loki can show such bravery, why can't we all? Samirah demonstrates the seven heroic qualities I'll be highlighting in my upcoming book, *Seven Heroic Qualities*, which will be available in the Valhalla gift shop."

He explained why the Norns' prophecy didn't mean what we thought it did:

"*Wrongly chosen, wrongly slain,*" he recited. "Magnus Chase was wrongly chosen by *Loki*—who thought this boy could be easily influenced. Instead, Magnus Chase proved himself a true hero!"

Despite the compliment, I liked Odin better as a taciturn half-troll than as a motivational speaker. The dinner crowd didn't seem sure what to make of him either, though some of the thanes were dutifully taking notes.

"Which brings us to the *affirmations* portion of this presentation." Odin advanced his slide show. A photograph of Blitzen popped up. It had obviously been taken during the crafting contest with Junior. Sweat streamed down Blitzen's face. His expression was agonized, as if somebody had just dropped a hammer on his foot.

"Blitzen, son of Freya!" Odin said. "This noble dwarf won the rope Andskoti, which rebound Fenris Wolf. He followed his heart, mastered his fears, and served my old friend Mimir faithfully. For your heroism, Blitzen, you shall be released from Mimir's service and given funding to open the shop you have always wanted. Because I have to say . . ." Odin waved his hand over his hotel polo shirt. Suddenly he was wearing a chain mail vest. "I picked up your prototype after the contest, and it's a very fine fashion statement. Any warrior would be wise to acquire one!"

The einherjar murmured in approval. Some oohed and ahhed.

Blitzen bowed deeply. "Thank you, Lord Odin. I am— I can't begin to— Could I use that endorsement for my product line?"

Odin smiled benevolently. "Of course. And next we have Hearthstone the elf!"

Hearth's photo appeared on the screens. He was slumped in the window of Geirrod's palace. He had a silly grin on his face. His hands were making the sign for *washing machine*.

"This noble creature risked everything to rediscover rune magic. He is the first true sorcerer to appear from the mortal realms in centuries. Without him, the quest to restrain the Wolf would have failed many times over." Odin beamed down at the elf. "My friend, you also shall be released from Mimir's service. I will personally bring you to Asgard, where I will teach you the runes in a ninety-minute one-on-one free tutoring session, accompanied by a DVD and signed copy of my book *Rune Magic with the All-Father*."

Polite clapping.

Hearthstone looked stunned. He managed to sign, *Thank you*.

The screen changed. In Sam's photo, she was standing nervously at the counter of Fadlan's Falafel, her face turned aside, blushing furiously as Amir leaned toward her, grinning.

"Ooooooo," said the crowd of einherjar, followed by a fair amount of snickering.

"Kill me now," Sam muttered. "Please."

"Samirah al-Abbas!" Odin said. "I personally chose you to be a Valkyrie because of your courage, your resilience, your potential greatness. Many here mistrusted you, but you rose to the challenge. You followed my orders. You did your duty even when you were reviled and exiled. To you, I give a choice."

Odin regarded the fallen Valkyries who lay before the thanes' table. He allowed a respectful silence to fall across the room.

"Gunilla, Margaret, Irene—all knew the risks of being a Valkyrie. All gave their lives to make today's victory possible. In the end, they saw your true worth, and they fought at your side. I believe they would agree you should be reinstated as a Valkyrie."

Sam's knees almost gave out. She had to lean on Mallory Keen for support.

"I offer you a choice of jobs," Odin continued. "I need a

captain for my Valkyries. I can think of no one better than you. This would allow you more time to spend in the mortal world, perhaps a chance to rest after your harrowing quest. *Or*"—his blue eye gleamed—"you could choose a much more dangerous assignment, working directly for me as the need arises on other, shall we say, high-risk, high-reward missions."

Sam bowed. "All-Father, you honor me. I could never replace Gunilla. All I ask for is the chance to prove myself, as many times as necessary, until no one here has any doubt of my loyalties to Valhalla. I will take the more dangerous assignment. Command me, and I will not fail."

This went down pretty well with the crowd. The einherjar applauded. Some shouted approval. Even the other Valkyries regarded Sam with less hostile expressions.

"Very well," Odin said. "Once again, Samirah, you prove your wisdom. We will speak later of your duties. And now . . . Magnus Chase."

The screens changed. There I was: frozen mid-scream as I fell from the Longfellow Bridge. "Son of Frey, you retrieved the Sword of Summer. You kept it from the grip of Surt. You have proven yourself . . . well, perhaps not a great warrior—"

"Thanks," I muttered.

"—but certainly a great einherji. I think we are in agreement—all of us here at the thanes' table—that you, too, deserve a reward."

Odin glanced to his left and right. The thanes stirred, hastily muttering, "Yes. Um. Absolutely."

"I do not offer this lightly," Odin said. "But if you still feel that Valhalla is not your place, I will send you to Folkvanger, where your aunt holds court. As a child of the Vanir, perhaps that would be more to your liking. Or"—his blue eye seemed to pierce right through me—"if you wish, I will even allow you to return to the mortal world, and be released from your duties as an einherji."

The room filled with murmuring and tension. From the faces of the crowd, I could tell this was an unusual offer. Odin was taking a risk. If he set a precedent of letting einherjar return to the world, wouldn't others want to go too?

I looked at Sam and Blitzen and Hearthstone. I looked at my hallmates from floor nineteen—T.J., Halfborn, Mallory. For the first time in years, I didn't feel homeless.

I bowed to Odin. "Thank you, All-Father. But wherever these friends of mine are—that's my home. I am one of the einherjar. I am one of your warriors. That is reward enough."

The whole dining hall erupted in cheering. Goblets banged on tables. Swords clattered against shields. My friends surrounded me, hugging me and clapping me on the shoulders. Mallory kissed my cheek and said, "You are a *huge* idiot." Then she whispered in my ear, "Thank you."

Halfborn ruffled my hair. "We'll make you a warrior yet, Frey-son."

When the cheering died down, Odin raised his hand. His clicker elongated into a glowing white spear.

"By Gungnir, the hallowed weapon of the All-Father, I declare that these seven heroes shall have full rights of passage through the Nine Worlds, including Valhalla. Wherever they go, they shall go in my name, serving the will of Asgard. Let no one interfere on pain of death!" He lowered his spear. "Tonight, we feast in their honor. Tomorrow, our fallen comrades shall be given to water and flame!"

SEVENTY-ONE

We Burn a Swan Boat,
Which I'm Pretty Sure Is Illegal

THE FUNERAL was held on the pond in the Public Garden. Somehow, the einherjar had gotten possession of a swan boat—the kind that normally don't ply the waters during the winter. They'd modified the boat, turning it into a floating funeral pyre for the three Valkyries. The bodies were wrapped in white and laid on a bed of wood, with weapons and armor and gold heaped around them.

The pond was frozen over. There shouldn't have been any way to launch the boat, but the einherjar had brought along a friend—a fifteen-foot-tall giantess named Hyrokkin.

Despite the weather, Hyrokkin was dressed in cut-off shorts and an XXXXL T-shirt from the Boston Rowing Club. Before the ceremony, she stomped barefoot all over the pond, breaking the ice and scaring the ducks. Then she came back and waited respectfully at the shore, her shins glazed with freezing water, while einherjar came forward to say their good-byes to the fallen. Many left weapons, coins, or other keepsakes on the funeral pyres. Some spoke about how Gunilla, Margaret, or Irene had been responsible for bringing them to Valhalla.

Finally Helgi lit the fire. Hyrokkin pushed the boat into the pond.

There were no pedestrians in the Public Garden. Maybe

magic kept them away. If any had been around, maybe some glamour would've kept them from seeing the crowd of undead warriors watching a ship burn.

My eyes drifted to the spot under the bridge where two weeks ago I'd been alive, homeless, and miserable. Only now could I admit how terrified I'd felt all the time.

The boat roared into a column of fire, obscuring the bodies of the Valkyries. Then the flames vanished as if somebody had turned off the gas, leaving no trace of the boat—just a steaming circle in the pond.

Mourners turned and drifted through the park, heading toward the Hotel Valhalla on Beacon Street.

T.J. gripped my shoulder. "You coming, Magnus?"

"In a bit."

As my hallmates headed back home, I was happy to see Halfborn Gunderson slip his arm around Mallory Keen's waist. She didn't even cut his hand off for doing so.

Blitzen, Hearth, Sam, and I stayed behind, watching steam curl off the pond.

Finally Hearth signed: *I am going to Asgard. Thank you, Magnus.*

I'd seen the envious looks some of the einherjar had given him. For decades, maybe centuries, no mortal had been allowed to visit the city of the gods. Now Odin had agreed to teach an elf.

"That's awesome, man," I said. "But listen, don't forget to come back and visit, huh? You've got a family now."

Hearthstone smiled. He signed: *I hear you.*

"Oh, he'll visit, all right," Blitzen said. "He's promised to help me move into my new store. I'm not lugging all those boxes without some magic assistance!"

I felt happy for Blitz, though it was hard to think about yet another one of my friends going away. "I'm sure you'll have the best shop in Nidavellir."

Blitzen snorted. "Nidavellir? Bah. Dwarves don't deserve my fashion brilliance. That red gold from Odin will buy me a nice storefront on Newbury Street. *Blitzen's Best* will be open in the spring, so you have absolutely no excuse not to come by and get fitted for one of these." He brushed aside his overcoat, revealing a glittering, stylish bulletproof vest.

I couldn't help it. I gave Blitzen a hug.

"All right, kid, all right." He patted me on the back. "Let's not wrinkle the fabric."

Sam grinned. "Maybe you can make a new hijab for me. The old one got kind of ripped to shreds."

"I'll make it for you at cost, with more magical properties!" Blitzen promised. "And I have some ideas for colors."

"You're the expert," Sam said. "As for me, I've got to get home. I'm grounded. I have a pile of make-up work from school."

"And you have a boyfriend to deal with," I said.

She blushed, which was kind of cute. "He's not . . . All right, fine. Yes, I should probably deal with that, whatever that means." She poked me in the chest. "Thanks to you, I can fly again. That's the main thing. Try not to die too often until I see you again."

"When will that be?"

"Soon," Sam promised. "Odin wasn't kidding about the

high-risk assignments. The good news is"—she put a finger to her lips—"I can pick my own strike force. So all of you . . . consider yourselves warned."

I wanted to hug her, to tell her how much I appreciated everything she'd done, but I knew Sam wouldn't be comfortable with that. I settled for a smile. "Any time, al-Abbas. Now that Odin has given us permission to travel the worlds, maybe I can come visit you in Dorchester."

"That," she said, "is a truly mortifying idea. My grandparents would kill me. Amir would—"

"Okay, jeez," I said. "Just remember: you're not in this alone."

"Noted." She bumped me with her elbow. "And what about you, Magnus—back to Valhalla for the feast? Your hallmates have been singing your praises. I even heard a few Valkyries speculating that you might be made a thane one of these centuries."

I smiled, but I wasn't ready to think about *one of these centuries*. I gazed across the Public Garden. A taxi was just pulling up in front of the Cheers bar on the corner of Beacon and Brimmer. The ceramic jar weighed heavily inside my winter coat.

"First I have an appointment," I said. "I have to keep a promise."

I said good-bye to my friends. Then I went to meet my cousin.

SEVENTY-TWO

I Lose a Bet

"THIS IS WAY BETTER than the last memorial I attended," Annabeth said. "Yours."

We stood on a ridge in the Blue Hills, watching my mother's ashes drift across the snowy trees. Far below, the sun glittered on Houghton's Pond. The day was cold, but I didn't feel uncomfortable. I felt warm and calm—more *right* than I'd felt in years.

I tucked the empty ceramic jar under my arm.

"Thanks for coming with me," I said.

Annabeth's gray eyes studied me, the same way she seemed to study everything—assessing not just my appearance, but my composition, my stress points, my potential for renovation. This was a girl, after all, who had made Parthenon models out of runestones when she was six years old.

"Glad to," she said. "Your mom . . . from what I remember, she was great."

"She would've liked the fact that you're here."

Annabeth gazed across the tree line. Her face looked sun-burned from the wind. "They cremated you, too, you know. I mean that other body . . . whatever that was. Your ashes were placed in the family mausoleum. I didn't even know we *had* a family mausoleum."

I shuddered, imagining those ashes in a porcelain vase in a dank stone cubbyhole. Much better to be here, in the fresh air and the frigid sunlight.

"Pretending I was dead couldn't have been easy for you," I said.

She brushed a strand of hair from her face. "The service was harder on Randolph, I think. He seemed pretty shaken up, considering, you know . . ."

"That he never cared about me?"

"Or any of us. My dad, though . . . Magnus, that was difficult. He and I have had a rocky history, but I'm trying to be honest with him now. I don't like hiding things."

"Sorry." I spread my hands. "I thought it was better if I didn't drag you into my problems. For the last few days, I wasn't sure if I was going to make it. Some . . . some dangerous things were happening. It had to do with my father's, uh, side of the family."

"Magnus, I might understand more than you think I do."

I thought about that. Annabeth *did* seem more attuned, more grounded than most people I talked to—even most of the people in Valhalla. On the other hand, I didn't want to put her at risk, or threaten the tenuous relationship we were starting to reconstruct.

"I'm okay now," I assured her. "I'm staying with friends. It's a good place, but it's not the kind of arrangement most people would understand. Uncle Randolph can't know about it. I'd appreciate it if you didn't tell anyone, not even your dad."

"Hmm," she said. "I don't suppose I get details?"

I thought about what Frey had told me: *You should talk. You will need her help before all is said and done.* I remembered what Sam had said about her own family—how they'd attracted the attention of the gods for generations. Randolph had hinted that our family was the same way.

"I just don't want to put you in danger," I said. "I kind of hoped you could be my one connection to the regular world."

Annabeth stared at me. She snorted and began to laugh. "Wow. You have no idea how funny that is." She took a deep breath. "Magnus, if you had any clue about how weird my life is—"

"Okay, but being here with you?" I said. "This is the most *normal* I've felt in years. After all the crazy fighting between our parents, the stupid grudges and years of not speaking to each other, I was hoping we could make our generation of the family not so messed up."

Annabeth's expression turned serious. "*That* kind of normal I like." She extended her hand. "To us, the Chase cousins. Here's to being less messed up."

We shook on it.

"Now spill," she commanded. "Tell me what's been going on. I promise I won't tell. I might even be able to help. I also promise that whatever's been going on with you, my life is weirder. It'll make yours look downright suburban."

I considered everything I'd been through—death and resurrection, fishing for the World Serpent, fighting with giants, running from monster squirrels, binding a wolf on a disappearing island.

"How much you want to bet?" I said.

"Bring it on, cousin."

"Lunch?" I suggested. "I know a great falafel place."

"You've got a bet," she said. "Let's hear what you've been up to."

"Oh, no," I said. "Your story is so amazing? You go first."

RANDOLPH HADN'T SLEPT since his nephew's funeral service.

Every day he visited the mausoleum, hoping for some sign, some miracle. He cried real tears, but not for young Magnus. He wept for everything he'd lost—everything that might never be recovered now.

He came in the back door of the town house, his hands shaking so badly he could barely work the lock. He removed his snow boots and his heavy coat, then padded upstairs, going over what he'd said to Magnus on the bridge for the millionth time, wondering what he could have done differently.

He froze in the doorway of his office. A man in a priest's frock was sitting on his desk, dangling his feet.

"Visiting the gravesite again?" Loki grinned. "Honestly, I thought the service provided some excellent closure."

"You were the priest?" Randolph sighed. "Of course you were the priest."

Loki chuckled. *"A young life cut short, but let us celebrate his gifts and the impact he had upon us . . .* I was improvising, of course. But that's what I do best."

Randolph had seen the god of lies a dozen times before—when Loki had chosen to send his essence to Midgard—but it was always a shock—those brilliant eyes, the hair like flames, the ruined lips, and the scars across his nose. He was unnaturally handsome and unnaturally terrifying in equal measure.

"You've come to kill me, I expect." Randolph tried to remain calm, but his heartbeat still pulsed in his ears. "Why did you wait this long?"

Loki spread his hands magnanimously. "I didn't want to be hasty. I needed to see how things played out. It's true you failed. I could kill you, but you might still be useful. After all, I still have something you want."

The god rose from the desk and opened his hand. Above his palm, flames flickered, consolidating into the miniature shapes of a woman and two girls. They writhed in the fire, reaching out to Randolph, silently pleading.

Only Randolph's cane kept him from collapsing. "Please. I tried. I didn't—I didn't anticipate the dwarf and the elf. Or that cursed Valkyrie. You didn't tell me—"

"Randolph, my dear friend . . ." Loki closed his hand, extinguishing the fire. "I hope you're not making excuses?"

"No, but—"

"I'm the *master* of excuses. You'd have to try really hard to impress me. Just tell me, do you still want your family returned?"

"Of—of course."

"Oh, good. How nice. Because I'm not done with you. Nor am I done with that little boy, Magnus."

"But he has the sword. He stopped your plan."

"He stopped *one facet* of my plan. Yes, it was very educational." Loki stepped forward. He cupped his hand on

Randolph's cheek—an almost tender gesture. "I must say, your nephew is impressive. I don't see the family resemblance at all."

Randolph smelled the poison before he felt it. Acrid steam curled into his nostrils. The side of his face erupted in white-hot pain. He fell to his knees, his throat seizing up in shock. He tried to pull away, but Loki's hand stayed stuck in place.

"There, there," Loki said soothingly. "It's just a little taste of my life—the snake venom that is splashed in *my* face every day. Perhaps you can understand why it makes me a tad grumpy."

Randolph screamed until his throat was raw.

"I won't kill you, old friend," Loki said. "But I do punish failure. Absolutely!"

He took the hand away. Randolph crumpled, weeping, the smell of burned flesh in his nose.

"Why . . ." he croaked. "Why . . . ?"

Loki raised his eyebrows in mock surprise. "Why what— torture you? Continue to use you? Fight against the gods? It is my nature, Randolph! Now, don't fuss. I'm sure you'll find a way to explain the horrible hand-shaped scar on your face. I think it lends you a certain . . . *gravitas*. The Vikings will be most impressed."

Loki strolled to Randolph's display cases. He ran his fingers along Randolph's collection of trinkets and talismans. "Ragnarok has many triggers, my friend. The Sword of Summer is not the only weapon in play."

He plucked a necklace from the display. His eyes gleamed as the small silver hammer pendant swung between his fingers.

"Oh, yes, Randolph." Loki grinned. "You and I are going to have lots of fun."

GLOSSARY

AEGIR—lord of the waves

AESIR—gods of war, close to humans

ALF SEIDR—elf magic

ANDSKOTI—the Adversary, the new, magic-infused rope binding Fenris Wolf

BALDER—god of light; the second son of Odin and Frigg, and twin brother of Hod. Frigg made all earthly things swear to never harm her son, but she forgot about mistletoe. Loki tricked Hod into killing Balder with a dart made of mistletoe.

BIFROST—the rainbow bridge leading from Asgard to Midgard

DRAUGR—Norse zombies

EIKTHRYMIR—a stag in the Tree of Laeradr whose horns spray water nonstop that feeds every river in every world

EINHERJAR (EINHERJI, sing.)—great heroes who have died with bravery on Earth; soldiers in Odin's eternal army; they train in Valhalla for Ragnarok, when the bravest of them will join Odin against Loki and the giants in the battle at the end of the world

FENRIS WOLF—an invulnerable wolf born of Loki's affair with a giantess; his mighty strength strikes fear even in the gods, who keep him tied to a rock on an island. He is destined to break free on the day of Ragnarok.

FOLKVANGER—the Vanir afterlife for slain heroes, ruled by the goddess Freya

FREY—the god of spring and summer; the sun, the rain, and the harvest; abundance and fertility, growth and vitality. Frey is the twin brother of Freya and, like his sister, is associated with great beauty. He is lord of Alfheim.

FREYA—the goddess of love; twin sister of Frey; ruler of Folkvanger

FRIGG—goddess of marriage and motherhood; Odin's wife and the queen of Asgard; mother of Balder and Hod

GINNUNGAGAP—the primordial void; a mist that obscures appearances

GLEIPNIR—a rope made by dwarves to keep Fenris Wolf in bondage

HEIDRUN—the goat in the Tree of Laeradr whose milk is brewed for the magical mead of Valhalla

HEIMDALL—god of vigilance and the guardian of Bifrost, the gateway to Asgard

HEL—goddess of the dishonorable dead; born of Loki's affair with a giantess

HELHEIM—the underworld, ruled by Hel and inhabited by those who died in wickness, old age, or illness

HLIDSKJALF—the High Seat of Odin

HOD—Balder's blind brother

HONIR—an Aesir god who, along with Mimir, traded places with Vanir gods Frey and Njord at the end of the war between the Aesir and the Vanir

IDUN—she distributes the apples of immortality that keep the gods young and spry

JORMUNGAND—the World Serpent, born of Loki's affair with a giantess; his body is so long it wraps around the earth

JOTUN—giant

LOKI—god of mischief, magic, and artifice; the son of two giants; adept at magic and shape-shifting. He is alternately malicious and heroic to the Asgardian gods and to humankind. Because of his role in the death of Balder, Loki was chained by Odin to three giant boulders with a poisonous serpent coiled over his head. The venom of the snake occasionally irritates Loki's face, and his writhing is the cause of earthquakes.

LYNGVI—the Isle of Heather, where Fenris Wolf is bound; the island's location shifts every year as the branches of Yggdrasil sway in the winds of the void. It only surfaces during the first full moon of each year.

MAGNI AND MODI—Thor's favorite sons, fated to survive Ragnarok

MIMIR—an Aesir god who, along with Honir, traded places with Vanir gods Frey and Njord at the end of the war between the Aesir and the Vanir. When the Vanir didn't like his counsel, they cut off his head and sent it to Odin. Odin placed the head in a magical well, where the water brought it back to life, and Mimir soaked up all the knowledge of the World Tree.

MJOLNIR—Thor's hammer

MUSPELL—fire

NAGLFAR—the Ship of Nails

NARVI—one of Loki's sons, disemboweled by his brother Vali, who was turned into a wolf after Loki killed Balder

NIDHOGG—the dragon that lives at the bottom of the World Tree and chews on its roots

NJORD—god of ships, sailors, and fishermen; father of Frey and Freya

NORNS—three sisters who control the destinies of both gods and humans.

NORUMBEGA—a lost Norse settlement in their farthest point of exploration

ODIN—the "All-Father" and king of the gods; the god of war and death, but also poetry and wisdom. By trading one eye for a drink from the Well of Wisdom, Odin gained unparalleled knowledge. He has the ability to observe all the Nine Worlds from his throne in Asgard; in addition to his great hall, he also resides in Valhalla with the bravest of those slain in battle.

RAGNAROK—the Day of Doom or Judgment, when the bravest of the einherjar will join Odin against Loki and the giants in the battle at the end of the world

RAN—goddess of the sea; wife of Aegir

RATATOSK—an invulnerable squirrel that constantly runs up and down the World Tree carrying insults between the eagle that lives at the top and Nidhogg, the dragon that lives at the roots

RED GOLD—the currency of Asgard and Valhalla

SAEHRIMNIR—the magical beast of Valhalla; every day it is killed and cooked for dinner and every morning it is resurrected; it tastes like whatever the diner wants

SESSRUMNIR—the Hall of Many Seats, Freya's mansion in Folkvanger

SKIRNIR—a god; Frey's servant and messenger

SLEIPNIR—Odin's eight-legged steed; only Odin can summon him; one of Loki's children

SUMARBRANDER—the Sword of Summer

SURT—lord of Muspellheim

SVARTALF—dark elf, a subset of dwarves

THANE—a lord of Valhalla

THOR—god of thunder; son of Odin. Thunderstorms are the earthly effects of Thor's mighty chariot rides across the sky, and lightning is caused by hurling his great hammer, Mjolnir.

TREE OF LAERADR—a tree in the center of the Feast Hall of the Slain in Valhalla containing immortal animals that have particular jobs

TYR—god of courage, law, and trial by combat; he lost a hand to Fenris's bite when the Wolf was restrained by the gods

ULLER—the god of snowshoes and archery

UTGARD-LOKI—the most powerful sorcerer of Jotunheim; king of the mountain giants

VALA—a seer

VALHALLA—paradise for warriors in the service of Odin

VALI—Loki's son, who was turned into a wolf after Loki killed Balder; as a wolf he disemboweled his brother Narvi before he was gutted himself

VALKYRIE—Odin's handmaidens, who choose slain heroes to bring to Valhalla

VANIR—gods of nature; close to elves

YGGDRASIL—the World Tree

YMIR—the largest of the giants; father to both the giants and the gods. He was killed by Odin and his brothers, who used his flesh to create Midgard. This act was the genesis of the cosmic hatred between the gods and the giants.

THE NINE WORLDS

ASGARD—the home of the Aesir

VANAHEIM—the home of the Vanir

ALFHEIM—the home of the light elves

MIDGARD—the home of humans

JOTUNHEIM—the home of the giants

NIDAVELLIR—the home of the dwarves

NIFLHEIM—the world of ice, fog, and mist

MUSPELLHEIM—the home of the fire giants and demons

HELHEIM—the home of Hel and the dishonorable dead

RUNES (IN ORDER OF APPEARANCE)

DAGAZ—new beginnings, transformations

THURISAZ—the rune of Thor

FEHU—the rune of Frey

RAIDHO—the wheel, the journey

PERTHRO—the empty cup

EHWAZ—horse, transportation

ALGIZ—shielding

TIWAZ—the rune of Tyr

PRONUNCIATION GUIDE

AEGIR	*AY-gear*
AESIR	*AY-ser*
ALF SEIDR	*ALF SAY-der*
ALFHEIM	*ALF-haym*
ALICARL	*AL-ih-carrl*
ARGR	*ARR-ger*
ASGARD	*AZ-gahrrd*
BIFROST	*BEE-frrohst*
BILSKIRNIR	*BEEL-skeerr-neer*
DAGAZ	*DAH-gahz*
DRAUGR	*DRRAW-ger*
EINHERJAR/EINHERJI	*in-HAIRR-yar/in-HAIRR-yee*
EHWAZ	*AY-wahz*
FEHU	*FAY-hoo*
FENRIS	*FEHN-rrihss*
FOLKVANGER	*FOHK-vahn-ger*
FREY	*FRRAY*
FREYA	*FRRAY-uh*
FRIGG	*FRRIHG*
GAMALOST	*GA-ma-lohst*
GEBO	*GIH-bo*
GEIRROD	*GAR-rod*
GERD	*GAIRRD*
GINNUNGAGAP	*GEEN-un-guh-gahp*
GJALLAR	*gee-YALL-ar*
HAGALAZ	*HA-ga-lahts*

HEIDRUN	*HY-drrun*
HEIMDALL	*HAME-doll*
HEL	*HEHL*
HELGI	*HEL-ghee*
HELHEIM	*HEHL-haym*
HUGINN	*HOO-gihn*
HULDER	*HOOL-dihr*
HUNDING	*HOON-deeng*
HUSVAETTR	*HOOS-veht-tr*
ISA	*EES-ah*
JORMUNGAND	*YOHRR-mun-gand*
JOTUN	*YOH-toon*
JOTUNHEIM	*YOH-tuhn-haym*
LAERADR	*LAY-rrah-dur*
KENNING	*KEN-ning*
LINDWORM	*LIHND-wohrrm*
LOKI	*LOH-kee*
MEINFRETR	*MAYN-frih-ter*
MIDGARD	*MIHD-gahrrd*
MIMIR	*MEE-meer*
MJOLNIR	*MEE'OHL-neer*
MODI	*MOH-dee*
MORGEN-GIFU	*MORR-ghen-GIH-foo*
MUNDR	*MOON-der*
MUNINN	*MOON-in*
MUSPELL	*MOO-spel*
MUSPELLHEIM	*MOOS-pehl-haym*
NAGLFAR	*NAHG'L-fahr*
NARVI	*NAHRR-vee*
NIDAVELLIR	*Nee-duh-vehl-EER*

NIDHOGG	*NEED-hawg*
NIFLHEIM	*NIHF-uh-haym*
NØKK	*NAWK*
NORNS	*NOHRRNZ*
NORUMBEGA	*nohrr-uhm-BAY-guh*
ODIN	*OH-dihn*
OSTARA	*OH-starr-ah*
OTHALA	*OH-thal-ah*
PERTHRO	*PERR-thrroh*
RAGNAROK	*RAG-nuh-rrawk*
RAN	*RAN*
RATATOSK	*RAT-uh-tawsk*
SAEHRIMNIR	*SAY-h'rrihm-neer*
SAMIRAH AL-ABBAS	*sah-MEER-ah ahl-AH-bahss*
SIF	*SEEV*
SLEIPNIR	*SLAYP-neer*
SUMARBRANDER	*SOO-marr-brrand-der*
SVARTALF	*SVAHRR-tahlf*
SVARTALFHEIM	*SVAHRR-talhf-haym*
THINGVELLIR	*THING-vih-leer*
THURISAZ	*THOORR-ee-sahts*
THOR	*THORE*
THRYM	*THRRIMM*
THRYNGA	*THRRIN-gah*
TIWAZ	*TEE-vahz*
TYR	*TEER*
ULLER	*OO-lir*
URNES	*OORR-nis*
URUZ	*OORR-oots*
UTGARD-LOKI	*OOT-gahrrd-LOH-kee*

VALA	*VAL-uh*
VALHALLA	*Val-HAHL-uh*
VALKYRIE	*VAL-kerr-ee*
VANAHEIM	*VAN-uh-haym*
VANIR	*Vah-NEER*
VIDAR	*VEE-dar*
WERGILD	*WIRR-gild*
WIGHT	*WHITE*
YGGDRASIL	*IHG-drruh-sihl*

Before all Muspellheim breaks loose,
read the second book in the

MAGNUS CHASE

and the Gods of Asgard series:

THE HAMMER OF THOR

Could You Please
Stop Killing My Goat?

LESSON LEARNED: If you take a Valkyrie out for coffee, you'll get stuck with the check and a dead body.

I hadn't seen Samirah al-Abbas in almost six weeks, so when she called out of the blue and said we needed to talk about a matter of life and death, I agreed right away.

(Technically I'm already dead, which means the whole *life-and-death* thing didn't apply, but still . . . Sam sounded anxious.)

She hadn't yet arrived when I got to the Thinking Cup on Newbury Street. The place was packed as usual, so I queued up for coffee. A few seconds later, Sam flew in—literally—right over the heads of the café patrons.

Nobody batted an eye. Regular mortals aren't good at processing magical stuff, which is fortunate, because otherwise Bostonians would spend most of their time running around in a panic from giants, trolls, ogres, and *einherjar* with battle-axes and lattes.

Sam landed next to me in her school uniform—white sneakers, khaki slacks, and a long-sleeve navy shirt with the King Academy logo. A green hijab covered her hair. An ax hung from her belt. I was pretty sure the ax wasn't standard dress code.

As glad as I was to see her, I noted that the skin under her eyes was darker than usual. She was swaying on her feet.

"Hey," I said. "You look terrible."

"Nice to see you, too, Magnus."

"No, I mean . . . not terrible like *different than normal* terrible. Just terrible like exhausted."

"Should I get you a shovel so you can dig that hole a little deeper?"

I raised my hands in surrender. "Where have you been the last month and a half?"

Her shoulders tightened. "My workload this semester has been killing me. I'm tutoring kids after school. Then, as you might remember, there's my part-time job reaping souls of the dead and running top secret missions for Odin."

"You kids today and your busy schedules."

"On top of all that . . . there's flight school."

"Flight school?" We shuffled forward with the line. "Like *airplanes*?"

I knew Sam's goal was to become a professional pilot someday, but I hadn't realized she was already taking lessons. "You can *do* that at sixteen?"

Her eyes sparkled with excitement. "My grandparents could never have afforded it, but the Fadlans have this friend who runs a flight school. They finally convinced Jid and Bibi—"

"Ah." I grinned. "So the lessons were a gift from Amir."

Sam blushed. She's the only teenager I know who has a *betrothed*, and it's cute how flustered she gets when she talks about Amir Fadlan.

"Those lessons were the most thoughtful, the most considerate . . ." She sighed wistfully. "But enough of that. I didn't bring you here to talk about my schedule. We have an informant to meet."

"An informant?"

"This could be the break I've been waiting for. If his information is good—"

Sam's phone buzzed. She fished it out of her pocket, checked the screen, and cursed. "I have to go."

"You just got here."

"Valkyrie business. Possible code three-eight-one: heroic death in progress."

"You're making that up."

"I'm not."

"So . . . what, somebody thinks they're about to die and they text you *'Going down! Need Valkyrie ASAP!'* followed by a bunch of sad-face emojis?"

"I seem to recall taking *your* soul to Valhalla. You didn't text me."

"No, but I'm special."

"Just get a table outside," she said. "Meet my informant. I'll be back as soon as I can."

"I don't even know what your informant looks like."

"You'll recognize him when you see him," Sam promised. "Be brave. Also, get me a scone."

She flew out of the shop like Super Muslima, leaving me to pay for our order.

I got two large coffees and two scones and found a table outside.

Spring had arrived early in Boston. Patches of dirty snow still clung to the curbs like dental plaque, but the cherry trees popped with white and red buds. Flowery pastel clothing displays bloomed in the windows of high-end boutiques. Tourists strolled by enjoying the sunshine.

Sitting outside, comfortable in my freshly laundered jeans, T-shirt, and denim jacket, I realized this would be the first spring in three years that I hadn't been homeless.

Last March, I had been scrounging from Dumpsters. I'd been sleeping under a bridge in the Public Garden, hanging out with my buddies Hearth and Blitz, avoiding the cops and just trying to stay alive.

Then, two months ago, I died fighting a fire giant. I'd woken up in the Hotel Valhalla as one of Odin's *einherji* warriors.

Now I had clean clothes. I took a shower every day. I slept in a comfortable bed every night. I could sit at this café table, eating food I'd actually paid for, and not worry about when the staff would force me to move along.

Since my rebirth, I'd gotten used to a lot of weird stuff. I'd traveled the Nine Worlds meeting Norse gods, elves, dwarves, and a bunch of monsters with names I couldn't pronounce. I'd scored a magical sword that presently hung around my neck in the form of a runestone pendant. I'd even had a mind-melting conversation with my cousin Annabeth about the *Greek* gods who hung out in New York and made *her* life difficult. Apparently North America was lousy with ancient gods. We had a full-blown infestation.

All of that I'd learned to accept.

But being back in Boston on a nice spring day, hanging out like a regular mortal kid?

That felt strange.

I scanned the crowd of pedestrians, looking for Sam's

informant. *You'll recognize him when you see him,* she'd promised. I wondered what kind of information this guy had, and why Sam considered it life-and-death.

My gaze fixed on a storefront at the end of the block. Over the doorway, the brass-and-silver sign still gleamed proudly: BLITZEN'S BEST—but the shop was shuttered. The front door window was papered over on the inside, with a message hastily scrawled in red marker: *Closed for remodeling. Back soon!*

I'd been hoping to ask Samirah about that. I had no idea why my old friend Blitz had abruptly disappeared. One day a few weeks ago, I'd just walked by the shop and found it closed. Since then, there'd been no word from Blitzen or Hearthstone, which wasn't like them.

Thinking about this made me so preoccupied I almost didn't see our informant until he was right on top of me. But Sam was correct: he kind of stood out. It's not every day you see a goat in a trench coat.

A porkpie hat was wedged between his curly horns. A pair of sunglasses perched on his nose. His trench coat kept getting tangled in his back hooves.

Despite his clever disguise, I recognized him. I'd killed and eaten this particular goat on another world, which is the sort of bonding experience you don't forget.

"Otis," I said.

"*Shhh,*" he said. "I'm incognito. Call me . . . *Otis.*"

"I'm not sure that's how *incognito* works, but okay."

Otis, aka Otis, climbed into the chair I'd reserved for Sam. He sat on his back haunches and put his front hooves on the table. "Where is the Valkyrie? Is she incognito, too?" He peered at the nearest pastry bag as if Sam might be hiding inside.

"Samirah had to go reap a soul," I said. "She'll be back soon."

"It must be nice having a purpose in life." Otis sighed. "Well, thank you for the food."

"That's not for—"

Otis snapped up Sam's scone bag and began to eat it, paper and all.

At the table next to us, an older couple glanced at my goat friend and smiled. Maybe their mortal senses perceived him as a cute child or a funny pet dog.

"So." I had a hard time watching Otis devour the pastry, spraying crumbs across the lapels of his trench coat. "You had something to tell us?"

Otis belched. "It's about my master."

"Thor."

Otis flinched. "Yes, him."

If I worked for the thunder god, I too would have flinched when I heard Thor's name. Otis and his brother, Marvin, pulled the god's chariot. They also provided Thor with a never-ending supply of goat meat. Each night, Thor killed and ate them for dinner. Each morning, Thor resurrected them. This is why you should go to college, kids—so when you grow up you do not have to take a job as a magical goat.

"I finally have a lead," Otis said, "on that *certain object* my master is missing."

"You mean his ham—?"

"Don't say it aloud!" Otis warned. "But, yes . . . his *ham*."

I flashed back to January, when I'd first met the thunder god. Good times around the campfire, listening to Thor fart, talk about his favorite TV shows, fart, complain about his missing hammer, which he used to kill giants and stream his favorite TV shows, and fart.

"It's *still* missing?" I asked.

Otis clacked his front hooves on the tabletop. "Well, not *officially*, of course. If the giants knew for certain that Thor was without his you-know-what, they would invade the mortal worlds, destroy everything, and send me into a very deep funk. But unofficially . . . yes. We've been searching for months with no luck. Thor's enemies are getting bolder. They sense weakness. I told my therapist it reminds me of when I was a kid in the goat pen and the bullies were sizing me up." Otis got a faraway look in his yellow slit-pupil eyes. "I think that's when my traumatic stress started."

This was my cue to spend the next several hours talking to Otis about his feelings. Being a terrible person, I just said "I feel your pain" and moved on.

"Otis," I said, "the last time we saw you, we found Thor a nice iron staff to use as a backup weapon. He's not exactly defenseless."

"No, but the staff is not as good as the . . . *ham*. It doesn't inspire the same fear in the giants. Also, Thor gets cranky trying to watch his shows on the staff. The screen is tiny, and the resolution is terrible. I don't like it when Thor is cranky. It makes it hard for me to find my happy space."

A lot about this did not make sense: why Thor would have so much trouble locating his own hammer; how he could possibly have kept its loss a secret from the giants for so long; and the idea that Otis the goat would have a happy space.

"So Thor wants our help," I guessed.

"Not officially."

"Of course not. We'll all have to wear trench coats and glasses."

"That's an excellent idea," Otis said. "Anyway, I told the Valkyrie I would keep her updated since she is in charge of Odin's . . . you know, special missions. This is the first good lead I've gotten to the location of the *certain object*. My source is reliable. He's another goat who goes to the same psychiatrist. He overheard some talk in his barnyard."

"You want us to track down a lead based on barnyard gossip you heard in your psychiatrist's waiting room."

"That would be great." Otis leaned so far forward I was afraid he might fall out of his chair. "But you're going to have to be careful."

It took all my effort not to laugh. I'd played catch-the-lava-ball with fire giants. I'd eagle-skied over the rooftops of Boston. I'd pulled the World Serpent out of Massachusetts Bay and defeated Fenris Wolf with a ball of yarn. Now this goat was telling me to be careful.

"So where is the *ham*?" I asked. "Jotunheim? Niflheim? Thorfartheim?"

"You're teasing." Otis's sunglasses slipped sideways on his snout. "But the *ham* is in a different dangerous location. It's in Provincetown."

"Provincetown," I repeated. "On the tip of Cape Cod."

I had vague memories of the place. My mom had taken me there for a weekend one summer when I was about eight. I remembered beaches, saltwater taffy, lobster rolls, and a bunch of art galleries. The most dangerous thing we'd encountered was a seagull with irritable bowel syndrome.

Otis lowered his voice. "There is a barrow in Provincetown—a *wight's* barrow."

"Is that like a wheelbarrow?"

"No, no. A wight . . ." Otis shuddered. "Well, a wight is a powerful undead creature that likes to collect magical weapons. A wight's tomb is called a—a *barrow*. Sorry, I have a hard time talking about wights. They remind me of my father."

That raised another batch of questions about Otis's childhood, but I decided to leave them for his therapist.

"Are there a lot of lairs of undead Vikings in Provincetown?" I asked.

"Only one, as far as I know. But that's enough. If the *certain object* is there, it will be difficult to retrieve—underground, and guarded by powerful magic. You'll need your friends—the dwarf and the elf."

That would have been great, if I had any idea where those friends were. I hoped Sam knew more than I did.

"Why doesn't Thor go and check this barrow himself?" I asked. "Wait . . . let me guess. He doesn't want to draw attention. Or he wants us to have a chance to be heroes. Or it's hard work and he has some shows to catch up on."

"To be fair," Otis said, "the new season of *Jessica Jones* did just start streaming."

It's not the goat's fault, I told myself. *He does not deserve to be punched.*

"Fine," I said. "When Sam gets here, we'll talk strategy."

"I'm not sure I should wait with you." Otis licked a crumb

off his lapel. "I should have mentioned this earlier, but you see, someone . . . or *something* . . . has been stalking me."

The hairs on my neck tingled. "You think they followed you here?"

"I'm not sure," Otis said. "Hopefully my disguise threw them off."

Oh, great, I thought.

I scanned the street but saw no obvious lurkers. "Did you get a good look at this someone/something?"

"No," Otis admitted. "But Thor has all sorts of enemies who would want to stop us from getting his—his *ham* back. They would not want me sharing information with you, especially this last part. You have to warn Samirah that—"

THUNK.

Living in Valhalla, I was used to deadly weapons flying out of nowhere, but I was still surprised when an ax sprouted from Otis's furry chest.

I lunged across the table to help him. As the son of Frey, god of fertility and health, I can do some pretty awesome first aid magic given enough time. But as soon as I touched Otis, I sensed that it was too late. The ax had pierced his heart.

"Oh, dear." Otis coughed blood. "I'll just . . . die . . . now."

His head lolled backward. His porkpie hat rolled across the pavement. The lady sitting behind us screamed as if just now noticing that Otis was not a cute puppy dog. He was, in fact, a dead goat.

I scanned the rooftops across the street. Judging from the angle of the ax, it must have been thrown from somewhere up there . . . yes. I caught a flicker of movement just as the attacker ducked out of sight—a figure in black wearing some sort of metal helmet.

So much for a leisurely cup of coffee. I yanked the magical pendant from my neck chain and raced after the goat-assassin.

Follow fallen god Apollo on a hair-raising journey
to another Oracle in

THE TRIALS OF APOLLO
Book 2:

THE DARK PROPHECY

1

Lester (Apollo)
Still human; thanks for asking
Gods, I hate my life

WHEN OUR DRAGON declared war on Indiana, I knew it was going to be a bad day.

We'd been traveling west for six weeks, and Festus had never shown such hostility toward a state. New Jersey he ignored. Pennsylvania he seemed to enjoy, despite our battle with the Cyclopes of Pittsburgh. Ohio he tolerated, even after our encounter with Potina, the Roman goddess of childhood drinks, who pursued us in the form of a giant red pitcher emblazoned with a smiley face.

Yet for some reason, Festus decided he did not like Indiana. He landed on the cupola of the Indiana Statehouse, flapped his metallic wings, and blew a cone of fire that incinerated the state flag right off the flagpole.

"Whoa, buddy!" Leo Valdez pulled the dragon's reins. "We've talked about this. No blowtorching public monuments!"

Behind him on the dragon's spine, Calypso gripped Festus's scales for balance. "Could we *please* get to the ground? *Gently* this time?"

For a formerly immortal sorceress who once controlled

air spirits, Calypso was not a fan of flying. Cold wind blew her chestnut hair into my face, making me blink and spit.

That's right, dear reader.

I, the most important passenger, the youth who had once been the glorious god Apollo, was forced to sit in the back of the dragon. Oh, the indignities I had suffered since Zeus stripped me of my divine powers! It wasn't enough that I was now a sixteen-year-old mortal with the ghastly alias Lester Papadopoulos. It wasn't enough that I had to toil upon the earth doing (ugh) heroic quests until I could find a way back into my father's good graces, or that I had a case of acne which simply *would not* respond to over-the-counter zit medicine. Despite my New York State junior driver's license, Leo Valdez didn't trust me to operate his aerial bronze steed!

Festus's claws scrabbled for a hold on the green copper dome, which was much too small for a dragon his size. I had a flashback to the time I installed a life-size statue of the muse Calliope on my sun chariot and the extra weight of the hood ornament made me nosedive into China and create the Gobi Desert.

Leo glanced back, his face streaked with soot. "Apollo, you sense anything?"

"Why is it *my* job to sense things? Just because I used to be a god of prophecy—"

"You're the one who's been having visions," Calypso reminded me. "You said your friend Meg would be here."

Just hearing Meg's name gave me a twinge of pain. "That doesn't mean I can pinpoint her location with my mind! Zeus has revoked my access to GPS!"

"GPS?" Calypso asked.

"Godly positioning systems."

"That's not a real thing!"

"Guys, cool it." Leo patted the dragon's neck. "Apollo, just try, will you? Does this look like the city you dreamed about or not?"

I scanned the horizon.

Indiana was flat country—highways crisscrossing scrubby brown plains, shadows of winter clouds floating above urban sprawl. Around us rose a meager cluster of downtown high-rises—stacks of stone and glass like layered wedges of black and white licorice. (Not the yummy kind of licorice, either; the nasty variety that sits for eons in your stepmother's candy bowl on the coffee table. And, no, Hera, why would I be talking about you?)

After falling to earth in New York City, I found Indianapolis desolate and uninspiring, as if one proper New York neighborhood—Midtown, perhaps—had been stretched out to encompass the entire area of Manhattan, then relieved of two-thirds of its population and vigorously power-washed.

I could think of no reason why an evil triumvirate of ancient Roman emperors would take interest in such a location. Nor could I imagine why Meg McCaffrey would be sent here to capture me. Yet my visions had been clear. I had seen this skyline. I had heard my old enemy Nero give orders to Meg: Go west. Capture Apollo before he can find the next Oracle. If you cannot bring him to me alive, kill him.

The truly sad thing about this? Meg was one of my better friends. She also happened to be my demigod master, thanks to Zeus's twisted sense of humor. As long as I remained mortal, Meg could order me to do anything, even kill myself. . . . No. Better not to think of such possibilities.

I shifted in my metal seat. After so many weeks of travel, I was tired and saddle sore. I wanted to find a safe place to rest. *This* was not such a city. Something about the landscape below made me as restless as Festus.

Alas, I was sure this was where we were meant to be. Despite the danger, if I had a chance of seeing Meg McCaffrey again, of prying her away from her villainous stepfather's grasp, I had to try.

"This is the spot," I said. "Before this dome collapses under us, I suggest we get to the ground."

Calypso grumbled in ancient Minoan, "I already *said* that."

"Well, excuse me, sorceress!" I replied in the same language. "Perhaps if *you* had helpful visions, I'd listen to you more often!"

Calypso called me a few names that reminded me how colorful the Minoan language had been before it went extinct.

"Hey, you two," Leo said. "No ancient dialects. Spanish or English, please. Or machine."

Festus creaked in agreement.

"It's okay, boy," Leo said. "I'm sure they didn't mean to exclude us. Now let's fly down to street level, huh?"

Festus's ruby eyes glowed. His metal teeth spun like drill bits. I imagined him thinking, *Illinois is sounding pretty good right about now.*

But he flapped his wings and leaped from the dome. We

hurtled downward, landing in front of the statehouse with enough force to crack the sidewalk. My eyeballs jiggled like water balloons.

Festus whipped his head from side to side, steam curling from his nostrils.

I saw no immediate threats. Cars drove leisurely down West Washington Street. Pedestrians strolled by: a middle-aged woman in a flowery dress, a heavyset policeman carrying a paper coffee cup labeled CAFÉ PATACHOU, a clean-cut man in a blue seersucker suit.

The man in blue waved politely as he passed. "Morning."

"'Sup, dude," Leo called.

Calypso tilted her head. "Why was he so friendly? Does he not *see* that we're sitting atop a fifty-ton metal dragon?"

Leo grinned. "It's the Mist, babe—messes with mortal eyes. Makes monsters look like stray dogs. Makes swords look like umbrellas. Makes me look even more handsome than usual!"

Calypso jabbed her thumbs into Leo's kidneys.

"Ow!" he complained.

"I know what the Mist is, *Leonidas*—"

"Hey, I told you never to call me that."

"—but the Mist must be very strong here if it can hide a monster of Festus's size at such close range. Apollo, don't you find that a little odd?"

I studied the passing pedestrians.

True, I had seen places where the Mist was particularly heavy. At Troy, the sky above the battlefield had been so thick with gods you couldn't turn your chariot without running into another deity, yet the Trojans and Greeks saw only hints of our presence. At Three Mile Island in 1979, the mortals somehow failed to realize that their nuclear meltdown was caused by an epic chainsaw fight between Ares and Hephaestus. (As I recall, Hephaestus had insulted Ares's bell-bottom jeans.)

Still, I did not think heavy Mist was the problem here. Something about these locals bothered me. Their faces were too placid. Their dazed smiles reminded me of ancient Athenians just before the Dionysus Festival—everyone in a good mood, distracted, thinking about the drunken riots and debauchery to come.

"We should get out of the public eye," I suggested. "Perhaps—"

Festus stumbled, shaking like a wet dog. From inside his chest came a noise like a loose bicycle chain.

"Aw, not again," Leo said. "Everybody off!"

Calypso and I quickly dismounted.

Leo ran in front of Festus and held out his arms in a classic dragon-wrangler's stance. "Hey, buddy, it's fine! I'm just going to switch you off for a while, okay? A little downtime to—"

Festus projectile-vomited a column of flames that engulfed Leo. Fortunately, Valdez was fireproof. His clothes were not. From what Leo had told me, he could generally prevent his outfits from burning up simply by concentrating. If he were caught by surprise, however, it didn't always work.

When the flames dissipated, Leo stood before us wearing nothing but his asbestos boxer shorts, his magical tool belt, and a pair of smoking, partially melted sneakers.

"Dang it!" he complained. "Festus, it's cold out here!"

The dragon stumbled. Leo lunged and flipped the lever behind the dragon's left foreleg. Festus began to collapse. His wings, limbs, neck, and tail contracted into his body, his bronze plates overlapping and folding inward. In a matter of seconds, our robotic friend had been reduced to a large bronze suitcase.

That should have been physically impossible, of course, but like any decent god, demigod, or engineer, Leo Valdez refused to be stopped by the laws of physics.

He scowled at his new piece of luggage. "Man . . . I *thought* I fixed his gyro-capacitor. Guess we're stuck here until I can find a machine shop."

Calypso grimaced. Her pink ski jacket glistened with condensation from our flight through the clouds. "And if we find such a shop, how long will it take to repair Festus?"

Leo shrugged. "Twelve hours? Fifteen?" He pushed a button on the side of the suitcase. A handle popped up. "Also, if we see a men's clothing store, that might be good."

I imagined walking into a T.J. Maxx, Leo in boxer shorts and melted sneakers, rolling a bronze suitcase behind him. I did not relish the idea.

Then, from the direction of the sidewalk, a voice called, "Hello!"

The woman in the flowery dress had returned. At least she *looked* like the same woman. Either that or lots of ladies in Indianapolis wore purple-and-yellow honeysuckle-pattern dresses and had 1950s bouffant hairstyles.

She smiled vacantly. "Beautiful morning!"

It was in fact a miserable morning—cold and cloudy

with a smell of impending snow —but I felt it would be rude to ignore her completely.

I gave her a little parade wave—the sort of gesture I used to give my worshippers when they came to grovel at my altar. To me, the message was clear enough: *I see you, puny mortal; now run along. The gods are talking.*

The woman did not take the hint. She strolled forward and planted herself in front of us. She wasn't particularly large, but something about her proportions seemed off. Her shoulders were too wide for her head. Her chest and belly protruded in a lumpy mass, as if she'd stuffed a sack of mangos down the front of her dress. With her spindly arms and legs, she reminded me of some sort of giant beetle. If she ever tipped over, I doubted she could easily get back up.

"Oh, my!" She gripped her purse with both hands. "Aren't you children *cute!*"

Her lipstick and eye shadow were both a violent shade of purple. I wondered if she were getting enough oxygen to her brain.

"Madam," I said, "we are not children." I could have added that I was over four thousand years old, and Calypso was even older, but I decided not to get into that. "Now, if you'll excuse us, we have a suitcase to repair and my friend is in dire need of a pair of pants."

I tried to step around her. She blocked my path.

"You can't go yet, dear! We haven't welcomed you to Indiana!" From her purse, she drew a smartphone. The screen glowed as if a call were already in progress.

"It's him, all right," she said into the phone. "Everybody, come on over. Apollo is here!"

My lungs shriveled in my chest.

In the old days, I would have expected to be recognized as soon as I arrived in a town. *Of course* the locals would rush to welcome me. They would sing and dance and throw flowers. They would immediately begin constructing a new temple.

But as Lester Papadopoulos, I did not warrant such treatment. I looked nothing like my former glorious self. The idea that the Indianans might recognize me despite my tangled hair, acne, and flab was both insulting and ter-rifying. What if they erected a statue of me in my present form—a giant golden Lester in the center of their city? The other gods would never let me hear the end of it!

"Madam," I said, "I'm afraid you have mistaken me—"

"Don't be modest!" The woman tossed her phone and purse aside. She grabbed my forearm with the strength of a weightlifter. "Our master will be delighted to have you in custody. And please call me Nanette."

Calypso charged. Either she wished to defend me (unlikely), or she was not a fan of the name Nanette. She punched the woman in the face.

This by itself did not surprise me. Having lost her immortal powers, Calypso was in the process of trying to master other skills. So far, she'd failed at swords, polearms, shurikens, whips, and improvisational comedy. (I sympa-thized with her frustration.) Today, she'd decided to try fisticuffs.

What surprised me was the loud CRACK her fist made against Nanette's face—the sound of finger bones breaking.

"Ow!" Calypso stumbled away, clutching her hand.

Nanette's head slid backward. She released me to try to grab her own face, but it was too late. Her head toppled off her shoulders. It clanged against the pavement and rolled sideways, the eyes still blinking, the purple lips twitching. Its base was smooth stainless steel. Attached to it were ragged strips of duct tape stuck with hair and bobby pins.

"Holy Hephaestus!" Leo ran to Calypso's side. "Lady, you broke my girlfriend's hand with your face. What *are* you, an automaton?"

"No, dear," said decapitated Nanette. Her muffled voice didn't come from the stainless-steel head on the sidewalk. It emanated from somewhere inside her dress. Just above her collar, where her neck used to be, an outcropping of fine blond hair was tangled with bobby pins. "And I must say, hitting me wasn't very polite."

Belatedly, I realized the metal head had been a disguise. Just as satyrs covered their hooves with human shoes, this creature passed for mortal by pretending to have a human face. Its voice came from its gut area, which meant . . .

My knees trembled.

"A blemmyae," I said.

Nanette chuckled. Her bulging midsection writhed under the honeysuckle cloth. She ripped open her blouse—something a polite Midwesterner would never think of doing—and revealed her true face.

Where a woman's brassiere would have been, two enormous bulging eyes blinked at me. From her sternum protruded a large shiny nose. Across her abdomen curled a hideous mouth—glistening orange lips, teeth like a spread of blank white playing cards.

"Yes, dear," spoke the face. "And I'm arresting you in the name of the Triumvirate!"

Up and down Washington Street, pleasant-looking pedestrians turned and began marching in our direction.

THE RED PYRAMID

RICK RIORDAN

BOOK ONE

THE RED PYRAMID

Disney • Hyperion
Los Angeles New York

First Hardcover Edition, May 2010
First Paperback Edition, August 2011

3 5 7 9 10 8 6 4 2
FAC-025438-19221
Printed in the United States of America

This book is set in Goudy Old Style/Monotype
Designed by Joann Hill
Hieroglyph art by Michelle Gengaro-Kokmen

Library of Congress Control Number for Hardcover Edition: 2010549563
ISBN: 978-1-368-01358-1

Visit www.DisneyBooks.com
Follow @ReadRiordan

SUSTAINABLE
FORESTRY
INITIATIVE

Certified Chain of Custody
Promoting Sustainable Forestry

www.sfiprogram.org
SFI-01054

The SFI label applies to the text stock

To all my librarian friends, champions of books,
true magicians in the House of Life. Without you,
this writer would be lost in the Duat.

Contents

CONTENTS

WARNING

The following is a transcript of a digital recording. In certain places, the audio quality was poor, so some words and phrases represent the author's best guesses. Where possible, illustrations of important symbols mentioned in the recording have been added. Background noises such as scuffling, hitting, and cursing by the two speakers have not been transcribed. The author makes no claims for the authenticity of the recording. It seems impossible that the two young narrators are telling the truth, but you, the reader, must decide for yourself.

1. A Death at the Needle

C
A
R
T
E
R

WE ONLY HAVE A FEW HOURS, so listen carefully.

If you're hearing this story, you're already in danger. Sadie and I might be your only chance.

Go to the school. Find the locker. I won't tell you which school or which locker, because if you're the right person, you'll find it. The combination is 13/32/33. By the time you finish listening, you'll know what those numbers mean. Just remember the story we're about to tell you isn't complete yet. How it ends will depend on you.

The most important thing: when you open the package and find what's inside, *don't* keep it longer than a week. Sure, it'll be tempting. I mean, it will grant you almost unlimited power. But if you possess it too long, it will consume you. Learn its secrets quickly and pass it on. Hide it for the next person, the way Sadie and I did for you. Then be prepared for your life to get very interesting.

Okay, Sadie is telling me to stop stalling and get on with

the story. Fine. I guess it started in London, the night our dad blew up the British Museum.

My name is Carter Kane. I'm fourteen and my home is a suitcase.

You think I'm kidding? Since I was eight years old, my dad and I have traveled the world. I was born in L.A. but my dad's an archaeologist, so his work takes him all over. Mostly we go to Egypt, since that's his specialty. Go into a bookstore, find a book about Egypt, there's a pretty good chance it was written by Dr. Julius Kane. You want to know how Egyptians pulled the brains out of mummies, or built the pyramids, or cursed King Tut's tomb? My dad is your man. Of course, there are other reasons my dad moved around so much, but I didn't know his secret back then.

I didn't go to school. My dad homeschooled me, if you can call it "home" schooling when you don't have a home. He sort of taught me whatever he thought was important, so I learned a lot about Egypt and basketball stats and my dad's favorite musicians. I read a lot, too—pretty much anything I could get my hands on, from dad's history books to fantasy novels—because I spent a lot of time sitting around in hotels and airports and dig sites in foreign countries where I didn't know anybody. My dad was always telling me to put the book down and play some ball. You ever try to start a game of pick-up basketball in Aswan, Egypt? It's not easy.

Anyway, my dad trained me early to keep all my possessions in a single suitcase that fits in an airplane's overhead compart-ment. My dad packed the same way, except he was allowed an extra workbag for his archaeology tools. Rule number one: I was not allowed to look in his workbag. That's a rule I never broke until the day of the explosion.

It happened on Christmas Eve. We were in London for visitation day with my sister, Sadie.

See, Dad's only allowed two days a year with her—one in the winter, one in the summer—because our grandparents hate him. After our mom died, her parents (our grandparents) had this big court battle with Dad. After six lawyers, two fistfights, and a near fatal attack with a spatula (don't ask), they won the right to keep Sadie with them in England. She was only six, two years younger than me, and they couldn't keep us both—at least that was their excuse for not taking me. So Sadie was raised as a British schoolkid, and I traveled around with my dad. We only saw Sadie twice a year, which was fine with me.

[Shut up, Sadie. Yes—I'm getting to that part.]

So anyway, my dad and I had just flown into Heathrow after a couple of delays. It was a drizzly, cold afternoon. The whole taxi ride into the city, my dad seemed kind of nervous.

Now, my dad is a big guy. You wouldn't think anything could make him nervous. He has dark brown skin like mine, piercing brown eyes, a bald head, and a goatee, so he looks like a buff evil scientist. That afternoon he wore his cashmere winter coat and his best brown suit, the one he used for public lectures. Usually he exudes so much confidence that he dominates any room he walks into, but sometimes—like that afternoon—I saw another side to him that I didn't really understand. He kept looking over his shoulder like we were being hunted.

"Dad?" I said as we were getting off the A-40. "What's wrong?"

"No sign of them," he muttered. Then he must've realized he'd spoken aloud, because he looked at me kind of startled. "Nothing, Carter. Everything's fine."

Which bothered me because my dad's a terrible liar. I always knew when he was hiding something, but I also knew no amount of pestering would get the truth out of him. He was probably trying to protect me, though from what I didn't know. Sometimes I wondered if he had some dark secret in his past, some old enemy following him, maybe; but the idea seemed ridiculous. Dad was just an archaeologist.

The other thing that troubled me: Dad was clutching his workbag. Usually when he does that, it means we're in danger. Like the time gunmen stormed our hotel in Cairo. I heard shots coming from the lobby and ran downstairs to check on my dad. By the time I got there, he was just calmly zipping up his workbag while three unconscious gunmen hung by their feet from the chandelier, their robes falling over their heads so you could see their boxer shorts. Dad claimed not to have witnessed anything, and in the end the police blamed a freak chandelier malfunction.

Another time, we got caught in a riot in Paris. My dad found the nearest parked car, pushed me into the backseat, and told me to stay down. I pressed myself against the floorboards and kept my eyes shut tight. I could hear Dad in the driver's seat, rummaging in his bag, mumbling something to himself while the mob yelled and destroyed things outside. A few minutes later he told me it was safe to get up. Every other car on the block had been overturned and set on fire. Our car had been freshly washed and polished, and several twenty-euro notes had been tucked under the windshield wipers.

Anyway, I'd come to respect the bag. It was our good luck charm. But when my dad kept it close, it meant we were going to need good luck.

We drove through the city center, heading east toward my grandparents' flat. We passed the golden gates of Buckingham Palace, the big stone column in Trafalgar Square. London is a pretty cool place, but after you've traveled for so long, all cities start to blend together. Other kids I meet sometimes say, "Wow, you're so lucky you get to travel so much." But it's not like we spend our time sightseeing or have a lot of money to travel in style. We've stayed in some pretty rough places, and we hardly ever stay anywhere longer than a few days. Most of the time it feels like we're fugitives rather than tourists.

I mean, you wouldn't think my dad's work was dangerous. He does lectures on topics like "Can Egyptian Magic Really Kill You?" and "Favorite Punishments in the Egyptian Underworld" and other stuff most people wouldn't care about. But like I said, there's that other side to him. He's always very cautious, checking every hotel room before he lets me walk into it. He'll dart into a museum to see some artifacts, take a few notes, and rush out again like he's afraid to be caught on the security cameras.

One time when I was younger, we raced across the Charles de Gaulle airport to catch a last-minute flight, and Dad didn't relax until the plane was off the ground, I asked him point blank what he was running from, and he looked at me like I'd just pulled the pin out of a grenade. For a second I was scared he might actually tell me the truth. Then he said, "Carter, it's nothing." As if "nothing" were the most terrible thing in the world.

After that, I decided maybe it was better not to ask questions.

My grandparents, the Fausts, live in a housing development near Canary Wharf, right on the banks of the River Thames. The taxi let us off at the curb, and my dad asked the driver to wait.

We were halfway up the walk when Dad froze. He turned and looked behind us.

"What?" I asked.

Then I saw the man in the trench coat. He was across the street, leaning against a big dead tree. He was barrel shaped, with skin the color of roasted coffee. His coat and black pinstriped suit looked expensive. He had long braided hair and wore a black fedora pulled down low over his dark round glasses. He reminded me of a jazz musician, the kind my dad would always drag me to see in concert. Even though I couldn't see his eyes, I got the impression he was watching us. He might've been an old friend or colleague of Dad's. No matter where we went, Dad was always running into people he knew. But it did seem strange that the guy was waiting here, outside my grandparents'. And he didn't look happy.

"Carter," my dad said, "go on ahead."

"But—"

"Get your sister. I'll meet you back at the taxi."

He crossed the street toward the man in the trench coat, which left me with two choices: follow my dad and see what was going on, or do what I was told.

I decided on the slightly less dangerous path. I went to retrieve my sister.

Before I could even knock, Sadie opened the door.

"Late as usual," she said.

She was holding her cat, Muffin, who'd been a "going away" gift from Dad six years before. Muffin never seemed to get older or bigger. She had fuzzy yellow-and-black fur like a miniature leopard, alert yellow eyes, and pointy ears that were too tall for her head. A silver Egyptian pendant dangled from her collar. She didn't look anything like a muffin, but Sadie had been little when she named her, so I guess you have to cut her some slack.

Sadie hadn't changed much either since last summer.

[As I'm recording this, she's standing next to me, glaring, so I'd better be careful how I describe her.]

You would never guess she's my sister. First of all, she'd been living in England so long, she has a British accent. Second, she takes after our mom, who was white, so Sadie's skin is much lighter than mine. She has straight caramel-colored hair, not exactly blond but not brown, which she usually dyes with streaks of bright colors. That day it had red streaks down the left side. Her eyes are blue. I'm serious. *Blue* eyes, just like our mom's. She's only twelve, but she's exactly as tall as me, which

7

is really annoying. She was chewing gum as usual, dressed for her day out with Dad in battered jeans, a leather jacket, and combat boots, like she was going to a concert and was hoping to stomp on some people. She had headphones dangling around her neck in case we bored her.

[Okay, she didn't hit me, so I guess I did an okay job of describing her.]

"Our plane was late," I told her.

She popped a bubble, rubbed Muffin's head, and tossed the cat inside. "Gran, going out!"

From somewhere in the house, Grandma Faust said something I couldn't make out, probably "Don't let them in!"

Sadie closed the door and regarded me as if I were a dead mouse her cat had just dragged in. "So, here you are again."

"Yep."

"Come on, then." She sighed. "Let's get on with it."

That's the way she was. No "Hi, how you been the last six months? So glad to see you!" or anything. But that was okay with me. When you only see each other twice a year, it's like you're distant cousins rather than siblings. We had absolutely nothing in common except our parents.

We trudged down the steps. I was thinking how she smelled like a combination of old people's house and bubble gum when she stopped so abruptly, I ran into her.

"Who's that?" she asked.

I'd almost forgotten about the dude in the trench coat. He and my dad were standing across the street next to the big tree, having what looked like a serious argument. Dad's back was turned so I couldn't see his face, but he gestured with his hands like he does when he's agitated. The other guy scowled and shook his head.

"Dunno," I said. "He was there when we pulled up."

"He looks familiar." Sadie frowned like she was trying to remember. "Come on."

"Dad wants us to wait in the cab," I said, even though I knew it was no use. Sadie was already on the move.

Instead of going straight across the street, she dashed up the sidewalk for half a block, ducking behind cars, then crossed to the opposite side and crouched under a low stone wall. She started sneaking toward our dad. I didn't have much choice but to follow her example, even though it made me feel kind of stupid.

"Six years in England," I muttered, "and she thinks she's James Bond."

Sadie swatted me without looking back and kept creeping forward.

A couple more steps and we were right behind the big dead tree. I could hear my dad on the other side, saying, "—have to, Amos. You know it's the right thing."

"No," said the other man, who must've been Amos. His voice was deep and even—very insistent. His accent was American. "If I don't stop you, Julius, they will. The Per Ankh is shadowing you."

Sadie turned to me and mouthed the words "Per what?"

I shook my head, just as mystified. "Let's get out of here," I whispered, because I figured we'd be spotted any minute and get in serious trouble. Sadie, of course, ignored me.

"They don't know my plan," my father was saying. "By the time they figure it out—"

9

"And the children?" Amos asked. The hairs stood up on the back of my neck. "What about them?"

"I've made arrangements to protect them," my dad said. "Besides, if I don't do this, we're all in danger. Now, back off."

"I can't, Julius."

"Then it's a duel you want?" Dad's tone turned deadly serious. "You never could beat me, Amos."

I hadn't seen my dad get violent since the Great Spatula Incident, and I wasn't anxious to see a repeat of *that*, but the two men seemed to be edging toward a fight.

Before I could react, Sadie popped up and shouted, "Dad!"

He looked surprised when she tackle-hugged him, but not nearly as surprised as the other guy, Amos. He backed up so quickly, he tripped over his own trench coat.

He'd taken off his glasses. I couldn't help thinking that Sadie was right. He did look familiar—like a very distant memory.

"I—I must be going," he said. He straightened his fedora and lumbered down the road.

Our dad watched him go. He kept one arm protectively around Sadie and one hand inside the workbag slung over his shoulder. Finally, when Amos disappeared around the corner, Dad relaxed. He took his hand out of the bag and smiled at Sadie. "Hello, sweetheart."

Sadie pushed away from him and crossed her arms. "Oh, now it's *sweetheart*, is it? You're late. Visitation Day's nearly over! And what was that about? Who's Amos, and what's the Per Ankh?"

Dad stiffened. He glanced at me like he was wondering how much we'd overheard.

"It's nothing," he said, trying to sound upbeat. "I have a wonderful evening planned. Who'd like a private tour of the British Museum?"

Sadie slumped in the back of the taxi between Dad and me.

"I can't believe it," she grumbled. "One evening together, and you want to do research."

Dad tried for a smile. "Sweetheart, it'll be fun. The curator of the Egyptian collection personally invited—"

"Right, big surprise." Sadie blew a strand of red-streaked hair out of her face. "Christmas Eve, and we're going to see some moldy old relics from Egypt. Do you ever think about *anything* else?"

Dad didn't get mad. He never gets mad at Sadie. He just stared out the window at the darkening sky and the rain.

"Yes," he said quietly. "I do."

Whenever Dad got quiet like that and stared off into nowhere, I knew he was thinking about our mom. The last few months, it had been happening a lot. I'd walk into our hotel room and find him with his cell phone in his hands, Mom's picture smiling up at him from the screen—her hair tucked under a headscarf, her blue eyes startlingly bright against the desert backdrop.

Or we'd be at some dig site. I'd see Dad staring at the horizon, and I'd know he was remembering how he'd met her—two young scientists in the Valley of the Kings, on a dig to discover a lost tomb. Dad was an Egyptologist. Mom was an anthropologist looking for ancient DNA. He'd told me the story a thousand times.

Our taxi snaked its way along the banks of the Thames. Just past Waterloo Bridge, my dad tensed.

"Driver," he said. "Stop here a moment."

The cabbie pulled over on the Victoria Embankment.

"What is it, Dad?" I asked.

He got out of the cab like he hadn't heard me. When Sadie and I joined him on the sidewalk, he was staring up at Cleopatra's Needle.

In case you've never seen it: the Needle is an obelisk, not a needle, and it doesn't have anything to do with Cleopatra. I guess the British just thought the name sounded cool when they brought it to London. It's about seventy feet tall, which would've been really impressive back in Ancient Egypt, but on the Thames, with all the tall buildings around, it looks small and sad. You could drive right by it and not even realize you'd just passed something that was a thousand years older than the city of London.

"God." Sadie walked around in a frustrated circle. "Do we have to stop for *every* monument?"

My dad stared at the top of the obelisk. "I had to see it again," he murmured. "Where it happened..."

A freezing wind blew off the river. I wanted to get back in the cab, but my dad was really starting to worry me. I'd never seen him so distracted.

"What, Dad?" I asked. "What happened here?"

"The last place I saw her."

Sadie stopped pacing. She scowled at me uncertainly, then back at Dad. "Hang on. Do you mean Mum?"

Dad brushed Sadie's hair behind her ear, and she was so surprised, she didn't even push him away.

I felt like the rain had frozen me solid. Mom's death had always been a forbidden subject. I knew she'd died in an accident in London. I knew my grandparents blamed my dad. But no one would ever tell us the details. I'd given up asking my dad, partly because it made him so sad, partly because he absolutely refused to tell me anything. "When you're older" was all he would say, which was the most frustrating response ever.

"You're telling us she died here," I said. "At Cleopatra's Needle? What happened?"

He lowered his head.

"Dad!" Sadie protested. "I go past this *every* day, and you mean to say—all this time—and I didn't even *know*?"

"Do you still have your cat?" Dad asked her, which seemed like a really stupid question.

"Of course I've still got the cat!" she said. "What does that have to do with anything?"

"And your amulet?"

Sadie's hand went to her neck. When we were little, right before Sadie went to live with our grandparents, Dad had given us both Egyptian amulets. Mine was an Eye of Horus, which was a popular protection symbol in Ancient Egypt.

In fact my dad says the modern pharmacist's symbol, ℞, is a simplified version of the Eye of Horus, because medicine is supposed to protect you.

Anyway, I always wore my amulet under my shirt, but I figured Sadie would've lost hers or thrown it away.

To my surprise, she nodded. "'Course I have it, Dad, but don't change the subject. Gran's always going on about how you caused Mum's death. That's not true, is it?"

We waited. For once, Sadie and I wanted exactly the same thing—the truth.

"The night your mother died," my father started, "here at the Needle—"

A sudden flash illuminated the embankment. I turned, half blind, and just for a moment I glimpsed two figures: a tall pale man with a forked beard and wearing cream-colored robes, and a coppery-skinned girl in dark blue robes and a headscarf—the kind of clothes I'd seen hundreds of times in Egypt. They were just standing there side by side, not twenty feet away, watching us. Then the light faded. The figures melted into a fuzzy afterimage. When my eyes readjusted to the darkness, they were gone.

"Um . . ." Sadie said nervously. "Did you just see that?"

"Get in the cab," my dad said, pushing us toward the curb. "We're out of time."

From that point on, Dad clammed up.

"This isn't the place to talk," he said, glancing behind us. He'd promised the cabbie an extra ten pounds if he got us to the museum in under five minutes, and the cabbie was doing his best.

"Dad," I tried, "those people at the river—"

"And the other bloke, Amos," Sadie said. "Are they Egyptian police or something?"

"Look, both of you," Dad said, "I'm going to need your help tonight. I know it's hard, but you have to be patient. I'll explain everything, I promise, after we get to the museum. I'm going to make everything right again."

"What do you mean?" Sadie insisted. "Make *what* right?"

Dad's expression was more than sad. It was almost guilty. With a chill, I thought about what Sadie had said: about our grandparents blaming him for Mom's death. That *couldn't* be what he was talking about, could it?

The cabbie swerved onto Great Russell Street and screeched to a halt in front of the museum's main gates.

"Just follow my lead," Dad told us. "When we meet the curator, act normal."

I was thinking that Sadie never acted *normal*, but I decided not to say anything.

We climbed out of the cab. I got our luggage while Dad paid the driver with a big wad of cash. Then he did something strange. He threw a handful of small objects into the backseat—they looked like stones, but it was too dark for me to be sure. "Keep driving," he told the cabbie. "Take us to Chelsea."

That made no sense since we were already out of the cab, but the driver sped off. I glanced at Dad, then back at the cab, and before it turned the corner and disappeared in the dark, I caught a weird glimpse of three passengers in the backseat: a man and two kids.

I blinked. There was no way the cab could've picked up another fare so fast. "Dad—"

"London cabs don't stay empty very long," he said matter-of-factly. "Come along, kids."

He marched off through the wrought iron gates. For a second, Sadie and I hesitated.

"Carter, *what* is going on?"

I shook my head. "I'm not sure I want to know."

"Well, stay out here in the cold if you want, but *I'm* not leaving without an explanation." She turned and marched after our dad.

Looking back on it, I should've run. I should've dragged Sadie out of there and gotten as far away as possible. Instead I followed her through the gates.

2. An Explosion for Christmas

I'D BEEN TO THE BRITISH MUSEUM BEFORE. In fact I've been in more museums than I like to admit—it makes me sound like a total geek.

[That's Sadie in the background, yelling that I *am* a total geek. Thanks, Sis.]

Anyway, the museum was closed and completely dark, but the curator and two security guards were waiting for us on the front steps.

"Dr. Kane!" The curator was a greasy little dude in a cheap suit. I'd seen mummies with more hair and better teeth. He shook my dad's hand like he was meeting a rock star. "Your last paper on Imhotep—brilliant! I don't know how you translated those spells!"

"Im-ho-who?" Sadie muttered to me.

"Imhotep," I said. "High priest, architect. Some say he was a magician. Designed the first step pyramid. You know."

"Don't know," Sadie said. "Don't care. But thanks."

Dad expressed his gratitude to the curator for hosting us on a holiday. Then he put his hand on my shoulder. "Dr. Martin, I'd like you to meet Carter and Sadie."

"Ah! Your son, obviously, and—" The curator looked hesitantly at Sadie. "And this young lady?"

"My daughter," Dad said.

Dr. Martin's stare went temporarily blank. Doesn't matter how open-minded or polite people think they are, there's always that moment of confusion that flashes across their faces when they realize Sadie is part of our family. I hate it, but over the years I've come to expect it.

The curator regained his smile. "Yes, yes, of course. Right this way, Dr. Kane. We're very honored!"

The security guards locked the doors behind us. They took our luggage, then one of them reached for Dad's workbag.

"Ah, no," Dad said with a tight smile. "I'll keep this one."

The guards stayed in the foyer as we followed the curator into the Great Court. It was ominous at night. Dim light from the glass-domed ceiling cast crosshatched shadows across the walls like a giant spiderweb. Our footsteps clicked on the white marble floor.

"So," Dad said, "the stone."

"Yes!" the curator said. "Though I can't imagine what new information you could glean from it. It's been studied to death—our most famous artifact, of course."

"Of course," Dad said. "But you may be surprised."

"What's he on about now?" Sadie whispered to me.

I didn't answer. I had a sneaking suspicion what stone they

were talking about, but I couldn't figure out why Dad would drag us out on Christmas Eve to see it.

I wondered what he'd been about to tell us at Cleopatra's Needle—something about our mother and the night she died. And why did he keep glancing around as if he expected those strange people we'd seen at the Needle to pop up again? We were locked in a museum surrounded by guards and high-tech security. Nobody could bother us in here—I hoped.

We turned left into the Egyptian wing. The walls were lined with massive statues of the pharaohs and gods, but my dad bypassed them all and went straight for the main attraction in the middle of the room.

"Beautiful," my father murmured. "And it's not a replica?"

"No, no," the curator promised. "We don't always keep the actual stone on display, but for you—this is quite real."

We were staring at a slab of dark gray rock about three feet tall and two feet wide. It sat on a pedestal, encased in a glass box. The flat surface of the stone was chiseled with three distinct bands of writing. The top part was Ancient Egyptian picture writing: hieroglyphics. The middle section...I had to rack my brain to remember what my dad called it: *Demotic*, a kind of writing from the period when the Greeks controlled Egypt and a lot of Greek words got mixed into Egyptian. The last lines were in Greek.

"The Rosetta Stone," I said.

"Isn't that a computer program?" Sadie asked.

I wanted to tell her how stupid she was, but the curator cut me off with a nervous laugh. "Young lady, the Rosetta Stone was the key to deciphering hieroglyphics! It was discovered by Napoleon's army in 1799 and—"

"Oh, right," Sadie said. "I remember now."

I knew she was just saying that to shut him up, but my dad wouldn't let it go.

"Sadie," he said, "until this stone was discovered, regular mortals...er, I mean, no one had been able to read hieroglyphics for centuries. The written language of Egypt had been completely forgotten. Then an Englishman named Thomas Young proved that the Rosetta Stone's three languages all conveyed the same message. A Frenchman named Champollion took up the work and cracked the code of hieroglyphics."

Sadie chewed her gum, unimpressed. "What's it say, then?"

Dad shrugged. "Nothing important. It's basically a thank-you letter from some priests to King Ptolemy V. When it was first carved, the stone was no big deal. But over the centuries...over the centuries it has become a powerful symbol. Perhaps the most important connection between Ancient Egypt and the modern world. I was a fool not to realize its potential sooner."

He'd lost me, and apparently the curator too.

"Dr. Kane?" he asked. "Are you quite all right?"

Dad breathed deeply. "My apologies, Dr. Martin. I was just...thinking aloud. If I could have the glass removed? And if you could bring me the papers I asked for from your archives."

Dr. Martin nodded. He pressed a code into a small remote control, and the front of the glass box clicked open.

"It will take a few minutes to retrieve the notes," Dr. Martin said. "For anyone else, I would hesitate to grant unguarded access to the stone, as you've requested. I trust you'll be careful."

He glanced at us kids like we were troublemakers.

"We'll be careful," Dad promised.

As soon as Dr. Martin's steps receded, Dad turned to us with a frantic look in his eyes. "Children, this is very important. You have to stay out of this room."

He slipped his workbag off his shoulder and unzipped it just enough to pull out a bike chain and padlock. "Follow Dr. Martin. You'll find his office at the end of the Great Court on the left. There's only one entrance. Once he's inside, wrap this around the door handles and lock it tight. We need to delay him."

"You want us to lock him in?" Sadie asked, suddenly interested. "Brilliant!"

"Dad," I said, "what's going on?"

"We don't have time for explanations," he said. "This will be our only chance. They're coming."

"Who's coming?" Sadie asked.

He took Sadie by the shoulders. "Sweetheart, I love you. And I'm sorry . . . I'm sorry for many things, but there's no time now. If this works, I promise I'll make everything better for all of us. Carter, you're my brave man. You have to trust me. Remember, lock up Dr. Martin. Then stay out of this room!"

Chaining the curator's door was easy. But as soon as we'd finished, we looked back the way we'd come and saw blue light streaming from the Egyptian gallery, as if our dad had installed a giant glowing aquarium.

Sadie locked eyes with me. "Honestly, do you have *any* idea what he's up to?"

"None," I said. "But he's been acting strange lately. Thinking a lot about Mom. He keeps her picture..."

I didn't want to say more. Fortunately Sadie nodded like she understood.

"What's in his workbag?" she asked.

"I don't know. He told me never to look."

Sadie raised an eyebrow. "And you never did? God, that is so like you, Carter. You're hopeless."

I wanted to defend myself, but just then a tremor shook the floor.

Startled, Sadie grabbed my arm. "He told us to stay put. I suppose you're going to follow that order too?"

Actually, that order was sounding pretty good to me, but Sadie sprinted down the hall, and after a moment's hesitation, I ran after her.

When we reached the entrance of the Egyptian gallery, we stopped dead in our tracks. Our dad stood in front of the Rosetta Stone with his back to us. A blue circle glowed on the floor around him, as if someone had switched on hidden neon tubes in the floor.

My dad had thrown off his overcoat. His workbag lay open at his feet, revealing a wooden box about two feet long, painted with Egyptian images.

"What's he holding?" Sadie whispered to me. "Is that a boomerang?"

Sure enough, when Dad raised his hand, he was brandishing

a curved white stick. It did look like a boomerang. But instead of throwing the stick, he touched it to the Rosetta Stone. Sadie caught her breath. Dad was *writing* on the stone. Wherever the boomerang made contact, glowing blue lines appeared on the granite. Hieroglyphs.

It made no sense. How could he write glowing words with a stick? But the image was bright and clear: ram's horns above a box and an X.

"*Open,*" Sadie murmured. I stared at her, because it sounded like she had just translated the word, but that was impossible. I'd been hanging around Dad for years, and even I could read only a few hieroglyphs. They are seriously hard to learn.

Dad raised his arms. He chanted: "*Wo-seer, i-ei.*" And two more hieroglyphic symbols burned blue against the surface of the Rosetta Stone.

As stunned as I was, I recognized the first symbol. It was the name of the Egyptian god of the dead.

"Wo-seer," I whispered. I'd never heard it pronounced that way, but I knew what it meant. "Osiris."

"*Osiris, come,*" Sadie said, as if in a trance. Then her eyes widened. "No!" she shouted. "Dad, no!"

Our father turned in surprise. He started to say, "Children—" but it was too late. The ground rumbled. The blue light turned to searing white, and the Rosetta Stone exploded.

When I regained consciousness, the first thing I heard was laughter—horrible, gleeful laughter mixed with the blare of the museum's security alarms.

I felt like I'd just been run over by a tractor. I sat up, dazed, and spit a piece of Rosetta Stone out of my mouth. The gallery was in ruins. Waves of fire rippled in pools along the floor. Giant statues had toppled. Sarcophagi had been knocked off their pedestals. Pieces of the Rosetta Stone had exploded outward with such force that they'd embedded themselves in the columns, the walls, the other exhibits.

Sadie was passed out next to me, but she looked unharmed. I shook her shoulder, and she grunted. "Ugh."

In front of us, where the Rosetta Stone had been, stood a smoking, sheared-off pedestal. The floor was blackened in a starburst pattern, except for the glowing blue circle around our father.

He was facing our direction, but he didn't seem to be looking at us. A bloody cut ran across his scalp. He gripped the boomerang tightly.

I didn't understand what he was looking at. Then the horrible laughter echoed around the room again, and I realized it was coming from right in front of me.

Something stood between our father and us. At first, I could barely make it out—just a flicker of heat. But as I concentrated, it took on a vague form—the fiery outline of a man.

He was taller than Dad, and his laugh cut through me like a chainsaw.

"Well done," he said to my father. "Very well done, Julius."

"You were not summoned!" My father's voice trembled. He

held up the boomerang, but the fiery man flicked one finger, and the stick flew from Dad's hand, shattering against the wall.

"I am never summoned, Julius," the man purred. "But when you open a door, you must be prepared for guests to walk through."

"Back to the Duat!" my father roared. "I have the power of the Great King!"

"Oh, scary," the fiery man said with amusement. "And even if you knew how to use that power, which you do not, he was never my match. I am the strongest. Now you will share his fate."

I couldn't make sense of anything, but I knew that I had to help my dad. I tried to pick up the nearest chunk of stone, but I was so terrified my fingers felt frozen and numb. My hands were useless.

Dad shot me a silent look of warning: *Get out.* I realized he was intentionally keeping the fiery man's back to us, hoping Sadie and I would escape unnoticed.

Sadie was still groggy. I managed to drag her behind a column, into the shadows. When she started to protest, I clamped my hand over her mouth. That woke her up. She saw what was happening and stopped fighting.

Alarms blared. Fire circled around the doorways of the gallery. The guards had to be on their way, but I wasn't sure if that was a good thing for us.

Dad crouched to the floor, keeping his eyes on his enemy, and opened his painted wooden box. He brought out a small rod like a ruler. He muttered something under his breath and the rod elongated into a wooden staff as tall as he was.

Sadie made a squeaking sound. I couldn't believe my eyes either, but things only got weirder.

Dad threw his staff at the fiery man's feet, and it changed into an enormous serpent—ten feet long and as big around as I was—with coppery scales and glowing red eyes. It lunged at the fiery man, who effortlessly grabbed the serpent by its neck. The man's hand burst into white-hot flames, and the snake burned to ashes.

"An old trick, Julius," the fiery man chided.

My dad glanced at us, silently urging us again to run. Part of me refused to believe any of this was real. Maybe I was unconscious, having a nightmare. Next to me, Sadie picked up a chunk of stone.

"How many?" my dad asked quickly, trying to keep the fiery man's attention. "How many did I release?"

"Why, all five," the man said, as if explaining something to a child. "You should know we're a package deal, Julius. Soon I'll release even more, and they'll be very grateful. I shall be named king again."

"The Demon Days," my father said. "They'll stop you before it's too late."

The fiery man laughed. "You think the House can stop me? Those old fools can't even stop arguing among themselves. Now let the story be told anew. And this time you shall *never* rise!"

The fiery man waved his hand. The blue circle at Dad's feet went dark. Dad grabbed for his toolbox, but it skittered across the floor.

"Good-bye, Osiris," the fiery man said. With another flick of his hand, he conjured a glowing coffin around our dad. At first it was transparent, but as our father struggled and pounded on its sides, the coffin became more and more solid—a golden Egyptian sarcophagus inlaid with jewels. My dad caught my eyes one last time, and mouthed the word *Run!* before the coffin sank into the floor, as if the ground had turned to water.

"Dad!" I screamed.

Sadie threw her stone, but it sailed harmlessly through the fiery man's head.

He turned, and for one terrible moment, his face appeared in the flames. What I saw made no sense. It was as if someone had superimposed two different faces on top of each other—one almost human, with pale skin, cruel, angular features, and glowing red eyes, the other like an animal with dark fur and sharp fangs. Worse than a dog or a wolf or a lion—some animal I'd never seen before. Those red eyes stared at me, and I knew I was going to die.

Behind me, heavy footsteps echoed on the marble floor of the Great Court. Voices were barking orders. The security guards, maybe the police—but they'd never get here in time.

The fiery man lunged at us. A few inches from my face, something shoved him backward. The air sparked with electricity. The amulet around my neck grew uncomfortably hot.

The fiery man hissed, regarding me more carefully. "So . . . it's *you.*"

The building shook again. At the opposite end of the room, part of the wall exploded in a brilliant flash of light. Two people stepped through the gap—the man and the girl we'd seen at the Needle, their robes swirling around them. Both of them held staffs.

The fiery man snarled. He looked at me one last time and said, "Soon, boy."

Then the entire room erupted in flames. A blast of heat sucked all the air of out my lungs and I crumpled to the floor.

The last thing I remember, the man with the forked beard and the girl in blue were standing over me. I heard the security guards running and shouting, getting closer. The girl crouched over me and drew a long curved knife from her belt.

"We must act quickly," she told the man.

"Not yet," he said with some reluctance. His thick accent sounded French. "We must be sure before we destroy them."

I closed my eyes and drifted into unconsciousness.

3. Imprisoned with My Cat

S
A
D
I
E

[Give me the bloody mic.]

Hullo. Sadie here. My brother's a rubbish storyteller. Sorry about that. But now you've got me, so all is well.

Let's see. The explosion. Rosetta Stone in a billion pieces. Fiery evil bloke. Dad boxed in a coffin. Creepy Frenchman and Arab girl with the knife. Us passing out. Right.

So when I woke up, the police were rushing about as you might expect. They separated me from my brother. I didn't really mind that part. He's a pain anyway. But they locked me in the curator's office for *ages*. And yes, they used *our* bicycle chain to do it. Cretins.

I was shattered, of course. I'd just been knocked out by a fiery whatever-it-was. I'd watched my dad get packed in a sarcophagus and shot through the floor. I tried to tell the police about all that, but did they care? No.

Worst of all: I had a lingering chill, as if someone was pushing ice-cold needles into the back of my neck. It had started when I looked at those blue glowing words Dad had drawn on the Rosetta Stone and I *knew* what they meant. A family disease, perhaps? Can knowledge of boring Egyptian stuff be hereditary? With my luck.

Long after my gum had gone stale, a policewoman finally retrieved me from the curator's office. She asked me no questions. She just trundled me into a police car and took me home. Even then, I wasn't allowed to explain to Gran and Gramps. The policewoman just tossed me into my room and I waited. And waited.

I don't like waiting.

I paced the floor. My room was nothing posh, just an attic space with a window and a bed and a desk. There wasn't much to do. Muffin sniffed my legs and her tail puffed up like a bottlebrush. I suppose she doesn't fancy the smell of museums. She hissed and disappeared under the bed.

"Thanks a lot," I muttered.

I opened the door, but the policewoman was standing guard.

"The inspector will be with you in a moment," she told me. "Please stay inside."

I could see downstairs—just a glimpse of Gramps pacing the room, wringing his hands, while Carter and a police inspector talked on the sofa. I couldn't make out what they were saying.

"Could I just use the loo?" I asked the nice officer.

"No." She closed the door in my face. As if I might rig an explosion in the toilet. Honestly.

I dug out my iPod and scrolled through my playlist. Nothing struck me. I threw it on my bed in disgust. When I'm too distracted for music, that is a very sad thing. I wondered why Carter got to talk to the police first. It wasn't fair.

I fiddled with the necklace Dad had given me. I'd never been sure what the symbol meant. Carter's was obviously an eye, but mine looked a bit like an angel, or perhaps a killer alien robot.

Why on earth had Dad asked if I still had it? *Of course* I still had it. It was the only gift he'd ever given me. Well, apart from Muffin, and with the cat's attitude, I'm not sure I would call her a proper gift.

Dad had practically abandoned me at age six, after all. The necklace was my one link to him. On good days I would stare at it and remember him fondly. On bad days (which were much more frequent) I would fling it across the room and stomp on it and curse him for not being around, which I found quite therapeutic. But in the end, I always put it back on.

At any rate, during the weirdness at the museum—and I'm not making this up—the necklace got *hotter*. I nearly took it off, but I couldn't help wondering if it truly was protecting me somehow.

I'll make things right, Dad had said, with that guilty look he often gives me.

Well, colossal fail, Dad.

What had he been thinking? I wanted to believe it had all been a bad dream: the glowing hieroglyphs, the snake staff, the coffin. Things like that simply don't happen. But I knew better. I couldn't dream anything as horrifying as that fiery man's face when he'd turned on us. "Soon, boy," he'd told Carter, as if he intended to track us down. Just the idea made my hands tremble. I also couldn't help wondering about our stop at Cleopatra's Needle, how Dad had insisted on seeing it, as if he were steeling his courage, as if what he did at the British Museum had something to do with my mum.

My eyes wandered across my room and fixed on my desk.

No, I thought. *Not going to do it.*

But I walked over and opened the drawer. I shoved aside a few old mags, my stash of sweets, a stack of maths homework I'd forgotten to hand in, and a few pictures of me and my mates Liz and Emma trying on ridiculous hats in Camden Market. And there at the bottom of it all was the picture of Mum.

Gran and Gramps have loads of pictures. They keep a shrine to Ruby in the hall cupboard—Mum's childhood artwork, her O-level results, her graduation picture from university, her favorite jewelry. It's quite mental. I was determined not to be like them, living in the past. I barely remembered Mum, after all, and nothing could change the fact she was dead.

But I did keep the one picture. It was of Mum and me at our house in Los Angeles, just after I was born. She stood out on the balcony, the Pacific Ocean behind her, holding a wrinkled pudgy lump of baby that would some day grow up to be yours truly. Baby me was not much to look at, but Mum was gorgeous, even in shorts and a tattered T-shirt. Her eyes were deep blue. Her blond hair was clipped back. Her skin was perfect. Quite depressing compared to mine. People always say I look like her, but I couldn't even get the spot off my chin much less look so mature and beautiful.

[Stop smirking, Carter.]

The photo fascinated me because I hardly remembered our lives together at all. But the main reason I'd kept the photo was because of the symbol on Mum's T-shirt: one of those life symbols—an ankh.

My dead mother wearing the symbol for life. Nothing could've been sadder. But she smiled at the camera as if she knew a secret. As if my dad and she were sharing a private joke.

Something tugged at the back of my mind. That stocky man in the trench coat who'd been arguing with Dad across the street—he'd said something about the Per Ankh.

Had he meant *ankh* as in the symbol for life, and if so, what was a *per*? I supposed he didn't mean pear as in the fruit.

I had an eerie feeling that if I saw the words *Per Ankh* written in hieroglyphics, I would know what they meant.

I put down the picture of Mum. I picked up a pencil and turned over one of my old homework papers. I wondered what would happen if I tried to *draw* the words *Per Ankh*. Would the right design just occur to me?

As I touched pencil to paper, my bedroom door opened. "Miss Kane?"

I whirled and dropped the pencil.

A police inspector stood frowning in my doorway. "What are you doing?"

"Maths," I said.

My ceiling was quite low, so the inspector had to stoop to come in. He wore a lint-colored suit that matched his gray hair and his ashen face. "Now then, Sadie. I'm Chief Inspector Williams. Let's have a chat, shall we? Sit down."

I didn't sit, and neither did he, which must've annoyed him. It's hard to look in charge when you're hunched over like Quasimodo.

"Tell me everything, please," he said, "from the time your father came round to get you."

"I already told the police at the museum."

"Again, if you don't mind."

So I told him everything. Why not? His left eyebrow crept higher and higher as I told him the strange bits like the glowing letters and serpent staff.

"Well, Sadie," Inspector Williams said. "You've got quite an imagination."

"I'm not lying, Inspector. And I think your eyebrow is trying to escape."

He tried to look at his own eyebrows, then scowled. "Now, Sadie, I'm sure this is very hard on you. I understand you want to protect your father's reputation. But he's gone now—"

"You mean through the floor in a coffin," I insisted. "He's *not* dead."

Inspector Williams spread his hands. "Sadie, I'm very sorry. But we must find out why he did this act of ... well ..."

"Act of *what*?"

He cleared his throat uncomfortably. "Your father destroyed priceless artifacts and apparently killed himself in the process. We'd very much like to know why."

I stared at him. "Are you saying my father's a terrorist? Are you *mad*?"

"We've made calls to some of your father's associates. I understand his behavior had become erratic since your mother's death. He'd become withdrawn and obsessive in his studies, spending more and more time in Egypt—"

"He's a bloody Egyptologist! You should be looking for him, not asking stupid questions!"

"Sadie," he said, and I could hear in his voice that he was resisting the urge to strangle me. Strangely, I get this a lot from adults. "There are extremist groups in Egypt that object to Egyptian artifacts being kept in other countries' museums. These people might have approached your father. Perhaps in his state, your father became an easy target for them. If you've heard him mention any names—"

I stormed past him to the window. I was so angry I could hardly think. I refused to believe Dad was dead. No, no, no. And a terrorist? Please. Why did adults have to be so thick? They always say "tell the truth," and when you do, they don't believe you. What's the point?

I stared down at the dark street. Suddenly that cold tingly

feeling got worse than ever. I focused on the dead tree where I'd met Dad earlier. Standing there now, in the dim light of a streetlamp, looking up at me, was the pudgy bloke in the black trench coat and the round glasses and the fedora—the man Dad had called Amos.

I suppose I should've felt threatened by an odd man staring up at me in the dark of night. But his expression was full of concern. And he looked *so* familiar. It was driving me mad that I couldn't remember why.

Behind me, the inspector cleared his throat. "Sadie, no one blames you for the attack on the museum. We understand you were dragged into this against your will."

I turned from the window. "Against my will? I chained the curator in his office."

The inspector's eyebrow started to creep up again. "Be that as it may, surely you didn't understand what your father meant to do. Possibly your brother was involved?"

I snorted. "Carter? Please."

"So you are determined to protect him as well. You consider him a proper brother, do you?"

I couldn't believe it. I wanted to smack his face. "What's that supposed to mean? Because he doesn't *look* like me?"

The inspector blinked. "I only meant—"

"I *know* what you meant. Of course he's my brother!"

Inspector Williams held up his hands apologetically, but I was still seething. As much as Carter annoyed me, I hated it when people assumed we weren't related, or looked at my father askance when he said the three of us were a family— like we'd done something wrong. Stupid Dr. Martin at the

36

museum. Inspector Williams. It happened every time Dad and Carter and I were together. *Every* bloody time.

"I'm sorry, Sadie," the inspector said. "I only want to make sure we separate the innocent from the guilty. It will go much easier for everyone if you cooperate. Any information. Anything your father said. People he might've mentioned."

"Amos," I blurted out, just to see his reaction. "He met a man named Amos."

Inspector Williams sighed. "Sadie, he couldn't have done. Surely you know that. We spoke with Amos not one hour ago, on the phone from his home in New York."

"He isn't in New York!" I insisted. "He's right—"

I glanced out the window and Amos was gone. Bloody typical.

"That's not possible," I said.

"Exactly," the inspector said.

"But he was here!" I exclaimed. "Who *is* he? One of Dad's colleagues? How did you know to call him?"

"Really, Sadie. This acting must stop."

"*Acting?*"

The inspector studied me for a moment, then set his jaw as if he'd made a decision. "We've already had the truth from Carter. I didn't want to upset you, but he told us everything. He understands there's no point protecting your father now. You might as well help us, and there will be no charges against you."

"You shouldn't lie to children!" I yelled, hoping my voice carried all the way downstairs. "Carter would never say a word against Dad, and neither will I!"

The inspector didn't even have the decency to look embarrassed.

He crossed his arms. "I'm sorry you feel that way, Sadie. I'm afraid it's time we went downstairs . . . to discuss consequences with your grandparents."

4. Kidnapped by a Not-So-Stranger

I JUST LOVE FAMILY MEETINGS. Very cozy, with the Christmas garlands round the fireplace and a nice pot of tea and a detective from Scotland Yard ready to arrest you.

Carter slumped on the sofa, cradling Dad's workbag. I wondered why the police had let him keep it. It should have been evidence or something, but the inspector didn't seem to notice it at all.

Carter looked awful—I mean even worse than usual. Honestly, the boy had never been in a proper school, and he dressed like a junior professor, with his khaki trousers and a button-down shirt and loafers. He's not bad looking, I suppose. He's reasonably tall and fit and his hair isn't hopeless. He's got Dad's eyes, and my mates Liz and Emma have even told me from his picture that he's *hot*, which I must take with a grain of salt because (a) he's my brother, and (b) my mates are a bit crazed. When it came to clothes, Carter wouldn't have known *hot* if it bit him on the bum.

[Oh, don't look at me like that, Carter. You know it's *true*.]

At any rate, I shouldn't have been too hard on him. He was taking Dad's disappearance even worse than I was.

Gran and Gramps sat on either side of him, looking quite nervous. The pot of tea and a plate of biscuits sat on the table, but no one was having any. Chief Inspector Williams ordered me into the only free chair. Then he paced in front of the fireplace importantly. Two more police stood by the front door—the woman from earlier and a big bloke who kept eyeing the biscuits.

"Mr. and Mrs. Faust," Inspector Williams said, "I'm afraid we have two uncooperative children."

Gran fidgeted with the trim of her dress. It's hard to believe she's related to Mum. Gran is frail and colorless, like a stick person really, while Mum in the photos always looked so happy and full of life. "They're just children," she managed. "Surely you can't blame them."

"*Pah!*" Gramps said. "This is ridiculous, Inspector. They aren't responsible!"

Gramps is a former rugby player. He has beefy arms, a belly much too big for his shirt, and eyes sunk deep in his face, as if someone had punched them (well, actually Dad *had* punched them years ago, but that's another story). Gramps is quite scary looking. Usually people got out of his way, but Inspector Williams didn't seem impressed.

"Mr. Faust," he said, "what do you imagine the morning headlines will read? 'British Museum attacked. Rosetta Stone destroyed.' Your son-in-law—"

"*Former* son-in-law," Gramps corrected.

"—was most likely vaporized in the explosion, or he ran off, in which case—"

"He didn't run off!" I shouted.

"We need to know where he is," the inspector continued. "And the only witnesses, your grandchildren, refuse to tell me the truth."

"We *did* tell you the truth," Carter said. "Dad isn't dead. He sank through the floor."

Inspector Williams glanced at Gramps, as if to say, *There, you see?* Then he turned to Carter. "Young man, your father has committed a criminal act. He's left you behind to deal with the consequences—"

"That's not true!" I snapped, my voice trembling with rage. I couldn't believe Dad would intentionally leave us at the mercy of police, of course. But the idea of him abandoning me—well, as I might have mentioned, that's a bit of a sore point.

"Dear, please," Gran told me, "the inspector is only doing his job."

"Badly!" I said.

"Let's all have some tea," Gran suggested.

"No!" Carter and I yelled at once, which made me feel bad for Gran, as she practically wilted into the sofa.

"We *can* charge you," the inspector warned, turning on me. "We can and we will—"

He froze. Then he blinked several times, as if he'd forgotten what he was doing.

Gramps frowned. "*Er*, Inspector?"

"Yes..." Chief Inspector Williams murmured dreamily. He reached in his pocket and took out a little blue booklet—an American passport. He threw it in Carter's lap.

"You're being deported," the inspector announced. "You're to leave the country within twenty-four hours. If we need to question you further, you'll be contacted through the FBI."

Carter's mouth fell open. He looked at me, and I knew I wasn't imagining how odd this was. The inspector had completely changed direction. He'd been about to arrest us. I was sure of it. And then out of the blue, he was deporting Carter? Even the other police officers looked confused.

"Sir?" the policewoman asked. "Are you sure—"

"Quiet, Linley. The two of you may go."

The cops hesitated until Williams made a shooing motion with his hand. Then they left, closing the door behind them.

"Hold on," Carter said. "My father's disappeared, and you want me to leave the country?"

"Your father is either dead or a fugitive, son," the inspector said. "Deportation is the kindest option. It's already been arranged."

"With whom?" Gramps demanded. "Who authorized this?"

"With..." The inspector got that funny blank look again. "With the proper authorities. Believe me, it's better than prison."

Carter looked too devastated to speak, but before I could feel sorry for him, Inspector Williams turned to me. "You, too, miss."

He might as well have hit me with a sledgehammer.

"You're deporting *me?*" I asked. "I live here!"

"You're an American citizen. And under the circumstances, it's best for you to return home."

I just stared at him. I couldn't remember any home except this flat. My mates at school, my room, *everything* I knew was here. "Where am I supposed to go?"

"Inspector," Gran said, her voice trembling. "This isn't fair. I can't believe—"

"I'll give you some time to say good-bye," the inspector interrupted. Then he frowned as if baffled by his own actions. "I—I must be going."

This made no sense, and the inspector seemed to realize it, but he walked to the front door anyway. When he opened it, I almost jumped out of my chair, because the man in black, Amos, was standing there. He'd lost his trench coat and hat somewhere, but was still wearing the same pinstripe suit and round glasses. His braided hair glittered with gold beads.

I thought the inspector would say something, or express surprise, but he didn't even acknowledge Amos. He walked right past him and into the night.

Amos came inside and closed the door. Gran and Gramps stood up.

"You," Gramps growled. "I should've known. If I was younger, I would beat you to a pulp."

"Hello, Mr. and Mrs. Faust," Amos said. He looked at Carter and me as if we were problems to be solved. "It's time we had a talk."

Amos made himself right at home. He flopped onto the sofa and poured himself tea. He munched on a biscuit, which was quite dangerous, because Gran's biscuits are horrid.

I thought Gramps's head would explode. His face went bright red. He came up behind Amos and raised his hand as if he were about to smack him, but Amos kept munching his biscuit.

"Please, sit down," he told us.

And we all sat. It was the strangest thing—as if we'd been waiting for his order. Even Gramps dropped his hand and moved round the sofa. He sat next to Amos with a disgusted sigh.

Amos sipped his tea and regarded me with some displeasure. That wasn't fair, I thought. I didn't look *that* bad, considering what we'd been through. Then he looked at Carter and grunted.

"Terrible timing," he muttered. "But there's no other way. They'll have to come with me."

"Excuse me?" I said. "I'm not going anywhere with some strange man with biscuit on his face!"

He did in fact have biscuit crumbs on his face, but he apparently didn't care, as he didn't bother to check.

"I'm no stranger, Sadie," he said. "Don't you remember?"

It was creepy hearing him talk to me in such a familiar way. I felt I *should* know him. I looked at Carter, but he seemed just as mystified as I was.

"No, Amos," Gran said, trembling. "You can't take Sadie. We had an agreement."

"Julius broke that agreement tonight," Amos said. "You

44

know you can't care for Sadie anymore—not after what's happened. Their only chance is to come with me."

"Why should we go anywhere with you?" Carter asked. "You almost got in a fight with Dad!"

Amos looked at the workbag in Carter's lap. "I see you kept your father's bag. That's good. You'll need it. As for getting into fights, Julius and I did that quite a lot. If you didn't notice, Carter, I was trying to *stop* him from doing something rash. If he'd listened to me, we wouldn't be in this situation."

I had no idea what he was on about, but Gramps apparently understood.

"You and your superstitions!" he said. "I told you we want none of it."

Amos pointed to the back patio. Through the glass doors, you could see the lights shining on the Thames. It was quite a nice view at night, when you couldn't notice how run-down some of the buildings were.

"Superstition, is it?" Amos asked. "And yet you found a place to live on the *east* bank of the river."

Gramps turned even redder. "That was Ruby's idea. Thought it would protect us. But she was wrong about many things, wasn't she? She trusted Julius and you, for one!"

Amos looked unfazed. He smelled interesting—like old-timey spices, copal and amber, like the incense shops in Covent Garden.

He finished his tea and looked straight at Gran. "Mrs. Faust, you know what's begun. The police are the least of your worries."

Gran swallowed. "You...*you* changed that inspector's mind. You made him deport Sadie."

"It was that or see the children arrested," Amos said.

"Hang on," I said. "You *changed* Inspector Williams's mind? How?"

Amos shrugged. "It's not permanent. In fact we should get to New York in the next hour or so before Inspector Williams begins to wonder why he let you go."

Carter laughed incredulously. "You can't get to New York from London in a hour. Not even the fastest plane—"

"No," Amos agreed. "Not a plane." He turned back to Gran as if everything had been settled. "Mrs. Faust, Carter and Sadie have only one safe option. You know that. They'll come to the mansion in Brooklyn. I can protect them there."

"You've got a mansion," Carter said. "In Brooklyn."

Amos gave him an amused smile. "The family mansion. You'll be safe there."

"But our dad—"

"Is beyond your help for now," Amos said sadly. "I'm sorry, Carter. I'll explain later, but Julius would want you to be safe. For that, we must move quickly. I'm afraid I'm all you've got."

That was a bit harsh, I thought. Carter glanced at Gran and Gramps. Then he nodded glumly. He knew that they didn't want him around. He'd always reminded them of our dad. And yes, it was a stupid reason not to take in your grandson, but there you are.

"Well, Carter can do what he wants," I said. "But *I live here*. And I'm not going off with some stranger, am I?"

I looked at Gran for support, but she was staring at the lace doilies on the table as if they were suddenly quite interesting.

"Gramps, surely..."

But he wouldn't meet my eyes either. He turned to Amos. "You can get them out of the country?"

"Hang on!" I protested.

Amos stood and wiped the crumbs off his jacket. He walked to the patio doors and stared out at the river. "The police will be back soon. Tell them anything you like. They won't find us."

"You're going to *kidnap* us?" I asked, stunned. I looked at Carter. "Do you believe this?"

Carter shouldered the workbag. Then he stood like he was ready to go. Possibly he just wanted to be out of Gran and Gramps's flat. "How do you plan to get to New York in an hour?" he asked Amos. "You said, not a plane."

"No," Amos agreed. He put his finger to the window and traced something in the condensation—another bloody hieroglyph.

"A boat," I said—then realized I'd translated aloud, which I wasn't supposed to be able to do.

Amos peered at me over the top of his round glasses. "How did you—"

"I mean that last bit looks like a boat," I blurted out. "But that can't be what you mean. That's ridiculous."

"Look!" Carter cried.

I pressed in next to him at the patio doors. Down at the

quayside, a boat was docked. But not a regular boat, mind you. It was an Egyptian reed boat, with two torches burning in the front, and a big rudder in the back. A figure in a black trench coat and hat—possibly Amos's—stood at the tiller.

I'll admit, for once, I was at a loss for words.

"We're going in that," Carter said. "To Brooklyn."

"We'd better get started," Amos said.

I whirled back to my grandmother. "Gran, please!"

She brushed a tear from her cheek. "It's for the best, my dear. You should take Muffin."

"Ah, yes," Amos said. "We can't forget the cat."

He turned towards the stairs. As if on cue, Muffin raced down in a leopard-spotted streak and leaped into my arms. She *never* does that.

"Who are you?" I asked Amos. It was clear I was running out of options, but I at least wanted answers. "We can't just go off with some stranger."

"I'm not a stranger." Amos smiled at me. "I'm family."

And suddenly I remembered his face smiling down at me, saying, "Happy birthday, Sadie." A memory so distant, I'd almost forgotten.

"Uncle Amos?" I asked hazily.

"That's right, Sadie," he said. "I'm Julius's brother. Now come along. We have a long way to go."

5. We Meet the Monkey

It's Carter again. Sorry. We had to turn off the tape for a while because we were being followed by—well, we'll get to that later.

Sadie was telling you how we left London, right?

So anyway, we followed Amos down to the weird boat docked at the quayside. I cradled Dad's workbag under my arm. I still couldn't believe he was gone. I felt guilty leaving London without him, but I believed Amos about one thing: right now Dad was beyond our help. I didn't trust Amos, but I figured if I wanted to find out what had happened to Dad, I was going to have to go along with him. He was the only one who seemed to know anything.

Amos stepped aboard the reed boat. Sadie jumped right on, but I hesitated. I'd seen boats like this on the Nile before, and they never seemed very sturdy.

It was basically woven together from coils of plant fiber— like a giant floating rug. I figured the torches at the front couldn't be a good idea, because if we didn't sink, we'd burn. At the back, the tiller was manned by a little guy wearing Amos's black trench coat and hat. The hat was shoved down on his head so I couldn't see his face. His hands and feet were lost in the folds of the coat.

"How does this thing move?" I asked Amos. "You've got no sail."

"Trust me." Amos offered me a hand.

The night was cold, but when I stepped on board I suddenly felt warmer, as if the torchlight were casting a protective glow over us. In the middle of the boat was a hut made from woven mats. From Sadie's arms, Muffin sniffed at it and growled.

"Take a seat inside," Amos suggested. "The trip might be a little rough."

"I'll stand, thanks." Sadie nodded at the little guy in back. "Who's your driver?"

Amos acted as if he hadn't heard the question. "Hang on, everyone!" He nodded to the steersman, and the boat lurched forward.

The feeling was hard to describe. You know that tingle in the pit of your stomach when you're on a roller coaster and it goes into free fall? It was kind of like that, except we weren't falling, and the feeling didn't go away. The boat moved with astounding speed. The lights of the city blurred, then were swallowed in a thick fog. Strange sounds echoed in the dark: slithering and hissing, distant screams, voices whispering in languages I didn't understand.

The tingling turned to nausea. The sounds got louder, until I was about to scream myself. Then suddenly the boat slowed.

The noises stopped, and the fog dissipated. City lights came back, brighter than before.

Above us loomed a bridge, much taller than any bridge in London. My stomach did a slow roll. To the left, I saw a familiar skyline—the Chrysler Building, the Empire State Building.

"Impossible," I said. "That's New York."

Sadie looked as green as I felt. She was still cradling Muffin, whose eyes were closed. The cat seemed to be purring. "It can't be," Sadie said. "We only traveled a few minutes."

And yet here we were, sailing up the East River, right under the Williamsburg Bridge. We glided to a stop next to a small dock on the Brooklyn side of the river. In front of us was an industrial yard filled with piles of scrap metal and old construction equipment. In the center of it all, right at the water's edge, rose a huge factory warehouse heavily painted with graffiti, the windows boarded up.

"That is not a mansion," Sadie said. Her powers of perception are really amazing.

"Look again." Amos pointed to the top of the building.

"How . . . how did you . . ." My voice failed me. I wasn't sure why I hadn't seen it before, but now it was obvious: a five-story mansion perched on the roof of the warehouse, like another layer of a cake. "You couldn't build a mansion up there!"

"Long story," Amos said. "But we needed a private location."

"And is this the east shore?" Sadie asked. "You said something about that in London—my grandparents living on the east shore."

Amos smiled. "Yes. Very good, Sadie. In ancient times, the east bank of the Nile was always the side of the living, the side where the sun rises. The dead were buried west of the river. It was considered bad luck, even dangerous, to live there. The tradition is still strong among . . . our people."

"Our people?" I asked, but Sadie muscled in with another question.

"So you can't live in Manhattan?" she asked.

Amos's brow furrowed as he looked across at the Empire State Building. "Manhattan has other problems. Other gods. It's best we stay separate."

"Other *what?*" Sadie demanded.

"Nothing." Amos walked past us to the steersman. He plucked off the man's hat and coat—and there was no one underneath. The steersman simply wasn't there. Amos put on his fedora, folded his coat over his arm, then waved toward a metal staircase that wound all the way up the side of the warehouse to the mansion on the roof.

"All ashore," he said. "And welcome to the Twenty-first Nome."

"Gnome?" I asked, as we followed him up the stairs. "Like those little runty guys?"

"Heavens, no," Amos said. "I hate gnomes. They smell horrible."

"But you said—"

"*Nome*, n-o-m-e. As in a district, a region. The term is from ancient times, when Egypt was divided into forty-two provinces. Today, the system is a little different. We've gone global. The world is divided into three hundred and sixty

52

nomes. Egypt, of course, is the First. Greater New York is the Twenty-first."

Sadie glanced at me and twirled her finger around her temple.

"No, Sadie," Amos said without looking back. "I'm not crazy. There's much you need to learn."

We reached the top of the stairs. Looking up at the mansion, it was hard to understand what I was seeing. The house was at least fifty feet tall, built of enormous limestone blocks and steel-framed windows. There were hieroglyphs engraved around the windows, and the walls were lit up so the place looked like a cross between a modern museum and an ancient temple. But the weirdest thing was that if I glanced away, the whole building seemed to disappear. I tried it several times just to be sure. If I looked for the mansion from the corner of my eye, it wasn't there. I had to force my eyes to refocus on it, and even that took a lot of willpower.

Amos stopped before the entrance, which was the size of a garage door—a dark heavy square of timber with no visible handle or lock. "Carter, after you."

"Um, how do I—"

"How do you think?"

Great, another mystery. I was about to suggest we ram Amos's head against it and see if that worked. Then I looked at the door again, and I had the strangest feeling. I stretched out my arm. Slowly, without touching the door, I raised my hand and the door followed my movement—sliding upward until it disappeared into the ceiling.

Sadie looked stunned. "How…"

"I don't know," I admitted, a little embarrassed. "Motion sensor, maybe?"

"Interesting." Amos sounded a little troubled. "Not the way I would've done it, but very good. Remarkably good."

"Thanks, I think."

Sadie tried to go inside first, but as soon as she stepped on the threshold, Muffin wailed and almost clawed her way out of Sadie's arms.

Sadie stumbled backward. "What was that about, cat?"

"Oh, of course," Amos said. "My apologies." He put his hand on the cat's head and said, very formally, "You may enter."

"The cat needs permission?" I asked.

"Special circumstances," Amos said, which wasn't much of an explanation, but he walked inside without saying another word. We followed, and this time Muffin stayed quiet.

"Oh my god…" Sadie's jaw dropped. She craned her neck to look at the ceiling, and I thought the gum might fall out of her mouth.

"Yes," Amos said. "This is the Great Room."

I could see why he called it that. The cedar-beamed ceiling was four stories high, held up by carved stone pillars engraved with hieroglyphs. A weird assortment of musical instruments and Ancient Egyptian weapons decorated the walls. Three levels of balconies ringed the room, with rows of doors all looking out on the main area. The fireplace was big enough to park a car in, with a plasma-screen TV above the mantel and massive leather sofas on either side. On the floor was a snakeskin rug, except it was forty feet long and fifteen feet wide—bigger than any snake. Outside, through glass walls, I could see the terrace that wrapped around the house. It had a swimming pool, a dining area, and a blazing fire pit. And at the far end of the Great Room was a set of double doors marked with the Eye of Horus, and chained with half a dozen padlocks. I wondered what could possibly be behind them.

But the real showstopper was the statue in the center of the Great Room. It was thirty feet tall, made of black marble. I could tell it was of an Egyptian god because the figure had a human body and an animal's head—like a stork or a crane, with a long neck and a really long beak.

The god was dressed ancient-style in a kilt, sash, and neck collar. He held a scribe's stylus in one hand, and an open scroll in the other, as if he had just written the hieroglyphs inscribed there: an ankh—the Egyptian looped cross—with a rectangle traced around its top.

"That's it!" Sadie exclaimed. "Per Ankh."

I stared at her in disbelief. "All right, how can you read that?"

"I don't know," she said. "But it's obvious, isn't it? The top one is shaped like the floor plan of a house."

"How did you get that? It's just a box." The thing was, she

was right. I recognized the symbol, and it *was* supposed to be a simplified picture of a house with a doorway, but that wouldn't be obvious to most people, especially people named Sadie. Yet she looked absolutely positive.

"It's a house," she insisted. "And the bottom picture is the ankh, the symbol for life. Per Ankh—the House of Life."

"Very good, Sadie." Amos looked impressed. "And this is a statue of the only god still allowed in the House of Life—at least, normally. Do you recognize him, Carter?"

Just then it clicked: the bird was an ibis, an Egyptian river bird. "Thoth," I said. "The god of knowledge. He invented writing."

"Indeed," Amos said.

"Why the animal heads?" Sadie asked. "All those Egyptian gods have animal heads. They look so silly."

"They don't normally appear that way," Amos said. "Not in real life."

"Real life?" I asked. "Come on. You sound like you've met them in person."

Amos's expression didn't reassure me. He looked as if he were remembering something unpleasant. "The gods could appear in many forms—usually fully human or fully animal, but occasionally as a hybrid form like this. They are primal forces, you understand, a sort of bridge between humanity and nature. They are depicted with animal heads to show that they exist in two different worlds at once. Do you understand?"

"Not even a little," Sadie said.

"*Mmm.*" Amos didn't sound surprised. "Yes, we have much training to do. At any rate, the god before you, Thoth, founded the House of Life, for which this mansion is the re-gional headquarters. Or at least . . . it used to be. I'm the only member left in the Twenty-first Nome. Or I *was*, until you two came along."

"Hang on." I had so many questions I could hardly think where to start. "What *is* the House of Life? Why is Thoth the only god allowed here, and why are you—"

"Carter, I understand how you feel." Amos smiled sympa-thetically. "But these things are better discussed in daylight. You need to get some sleep, and I don't want you to have nightmares."

"You think I can sleep?"

"*Mrow.*" Muffin stretched in Sadie's arms and let loose a huge yawn.

Amos clapped his hands. "Khufu!"

I thought he'd sneezed, because Khufu is a weird name, but then a little dude about three feet tall with gold fur and a purple shirt came clambering down the stairs. It took me a second to realize it was a baboon wearing an L.A. Lakers jersey.

The baboon did a flip and landed in front of us. He showed off his fangs and made a sound that was half roar, half belch. His breath smelled like nacho-flavored Doritos.

All I could think to say was, "The Lakers are my home team!"

The baboon slapped his head with both hands and belched again.

"Oh, Khufu likes you," Amos said. "You'll get along famously."

"Right." Sadie looked dazed. "You've got a monkey butler. Why not?"

Muffin purred in Sadie's arms as if the baboon didn't bother her at all.

"*Agh!*" Khufu grunted at me.

Amos chuckled. "He wants to go one-on-one with you, Carter. To, ah, see your game."

I shifted from foot to foot. "Um, yeah. Sure. Maybe tomorrow. But how can you understand—"

"Carter, I'm afraid you'll have a lot to get used to," Amos said. "But if you're going to survive and save your father, you have to get some rest."

"Sorry," Sadie said, "did you say 'survive and save our father'? Could you expand on that?"

"Tomorrow," Amos said. "We'll begin your orientation in the morning. Khufu, show them to their rooms, please."

"*Agh-uhh!*" the baboon grunted. He turned and waddled up the stairs. Unfortunately, the Lakers jersey didn't completely cover his multicolored rear.

We were about to follow when Amos said, "Carter, the workbag, please. It's best if I lock it in the library."

I hesitated. I'd almost forgotten the bag on my shoulder, but it was all I had left of my father. I didn't even have our luggage because it was still locked up at the British Museum. Honestly, I'd been surprised that the police hadn't taken the workbag too, but none of them seemed to notice it.

"You'll get it back," Amos promised. "When the time is right."

He asked nicely enough, but something in his eyes told me that I really didn't have a choice.

I handed over the bag. Amos took it gingerly, as if it were full of explosives.

"See you in the morning." He turned and strode toward the chained-up doors. They unlatched themselves and opened just enough for Amos to slip through without showing us anything on the other side. Then the chains locked again behind him.

I looked at Sadie, unsure what to do. Staying by ourselves in the Great Room with the creepy statue of Thoth didn't seem like much fun, so we followed Khufu up the stairs.

Sadie and I got adjoining rooms on the third floor, and I've got to admit, they were way cooler than any place I'd ever stayed before.

I had my own kitchenette, fully stocked with my favorite snacks: ginger ale—[No, Sadie. It's not an old person's soda! Be quiet!]—Twix, and Skittles. It seemed impossible. How did Amos know what I liked? The TV, computer, and stereo system were totally high-tech. The bathroom was stocked with my regular brand of toothpaste, deodorant, everything. The king-size bed was awesome, too, though the pillow was a little strange. Instead of a cloth pillow, it was an ivory headrest like I'd seen in Egyptian tombs. It was decorated with lions and (of course) more hieroglyphs.

The room even had a deck that looked out on New York Harbor, with views of Manhattan and the Statue of Liberty in the distance, but the sliding glass doors were locked shut somehow. That was my first indication that something was wrong.

I turned to look for Khufu, but he was gone. The door to my room was shut. I tried to open it, but it was locked.

A muffled voice came from the next room. "Carter?"

"Sadie." I tried the door to her adjoining room, but it was locked too.

"We're prisoners," she said. "Do you think Amos...I mean, can we trust him?"

After all I'd seen today, I didn't trust *anything*, but I could hear the fear in Sadie's voice. It triggered an unfamiliar feeling in me, like I needed to reassure her. The idea seemed ridiculous. Sadie had always seemed so much braver than me—doing what she wanted, never caring about the consequences. I was the one who got scared. But right now, I felt like I needed to play a role I hadn't played in a long, long time: big brother.

"It'll be okay." I tried to sound confident. "Look, if Amos wanted to hurt us, he could've done it by now. Try to get some sleep."

"Carter?"

"Yeah?"

"It was magic, wasn't it? What happened to Dad at the museum. Amos's boat. This house. All of it's magic."

"I think so."

I could hear her sigh. "Good. At least I'm not going mad."

"Don't let the bedbugs bite," I called. And I realized I hadn't said that to Sadie since we had lived together in Los Angeles, when Mom was still alive.

"I miss Dad," she said. "I hardly ever saw him, I know, but...I miss him."

My eyes got a little teary, but I took a deep breath. I was *not* going to go all weak. Sadie needed me. Dad needed us.

"We'll find him," I told her. "Pleasant dreams."

I listened, but the only thing I heard was Muffin meowing and scampering around, exploring her new space. At least *she* didn't seem unhappy.

I got ready for bed and crawled in. The covers were comfortable and warm, but the pillow was just too weird. It gave me neck cramps, so I put it on the floor and went to sleep without it.

My first big mistake.

6. Breakfast with a Crocodile

How to describe it? Not a nightmare. It was much more real and frightening.

As I slept, I felt myself go weightless. I drifted up, turned, and saw my own sleeping form below.

I'm dying, I thought. But that wasn't it, either. I wasn't a ghost. I had a new shimmering golden form with wings instead of arms. I was some kind of bird. [No, Sadie, not a chicken. Will you let me tell the story, please?]

I knew I wasn't dreaming, because I don't dream in color. I certainly don't dream in all five senses. The room smelled faintly of jasmine. I could hear the carbonation bubbles pinging in the can of ginger ale I'd opened on my nightstand. I could feel a cold wind ruffling through my feathers, and I realized the windows were open. I didn't want to leave, but a strong current pulled me out of the room like a leaf in a storm.

The lights of the mansion faded below me. The skyline of New York blurred and disappeared. I shot through the mist and darkness, strange voices whispering all around me. My stomach tingled as it had earlier that night on Amos's barge. Then the mist cleared, and I was in a different place.

I floated above a barren mountain. Far below, a grid of city lights stretched across the valley floor. Definitely not New York. It was nighttime, but I could tell I was in the desert. The wind was so dry, the skin on my face was like paper. And I know that doesn't make sense, but my face felt like my normal face, as if that part of me hadn't transformed into a bird. [Fine, Sadie. Call me the Carter-headed chicken. Happy?]

Below me on a ridge stood two figures. They didn't seem to notice me, and I realized I wasn't glowing anymore. In fact I was pretty much invisible, floating in the darkness. I couldn't make out the two figures clearly, except to recognize that they weren't human. Staring harder, I could see that one was short, squat, and hairless, with slimy skin that glistened in the starlight—like an amphibian standing on its hind legs. The other was tall and scarecrow skinny, with rooster claws instead of feet. I couldn't see his face very well, but it looked red and moist and . . . well, let's just say I was glad I couldn't see it better.

"Where is he?" the toadie-looking one croaked nervously.

"Hasn't taken a permanent host yet," the rooster-footed guy chided. "He can only appear for a short time."

"You're sure this is the place?"

"Yes, fool! He'll be here as soon—"

A fiery form appeared on the ridge. The two creatures fell to the ground, groveling in the dirt, and I prayed like crazy that I really was invisible.

"My lord!" the toad said.

Even in the dark, the newcomer was hard to see—just the silhouette of a man outlined in flames.

"What do they call this place?" the man asked. And as soon as he spoke, I knew for sure he was the guy who'd attacked my dad at the British Museum. All the fear I'd felt at the museum came rushing back, paralyzing me. I remembered trying to pick up that stupid rock to throw, but I hadn't been able to do even that. I'd completely failed my dad.

"My lord," Rooster Foot said. "The mountain is called Camelback. The city is called Phoenix."

The fiery man laughed—a booming sound like thunder. "Phoenix. How appropriate! And the desert so much like home. All it needs now is to be scoured of life. The desert should be a sterile place, don't you think?"

"Oh yes, my lord," the toadie agreed. "But what of the other four?"

"One is already entombed," the fiery man said. "The second is weak. She will be easily manipulated. That leaves only two. And they will be dealt with soon enough."

"Er . . . how?" the toadie asked.

The fiery man glowed brighter. "You are an inquisitive little tadpole, aren't you?" He pointed at the toad and the poor creature's skin began to steam.

"No!" the toadie begged. "No-o-o-o!"

I could hardly watch. I don't want to describe it. But if you've heard what happens when cruel kids pour salt on snails, you'll have a pretty good idea of what happened to the toadie. Soon there was nothing left.

Rooster Foot took a nervous step back. I couldn't blame him.

"We will build my temple here," the fiery man said, as if nothing had happened. "This mountain shall serve as my place of worship. When it is complete, I will summon the greatest storm ever known. I will cleanse everything. *Everything.*"

"Yes, my lord," Rooster Foot agreed quickly. "And, ah, if I may suggest, my lord, to increase your power . . ." The creature bowed and scraped and moved forward, as if he wanted to whisper in the fiery man's ear.

Just when I thought Rooster Foot was going to become fried chicken for sure, he said something to the fiery dude that I couldn't make out, and the fiery dude burned brighter.

"Excellent! If you can do this, you will be rewarded. If not . . ."

"I understand, my lord."

"Go then," the fiery man said. "Unleash our forces. Start with the longnecks. That should soften them up. Collect the younglings and bring them to me. I want them alive, before they have time to learn their powers. Do not fail me."

"No, lord."

"Phoenix," the fiery man mused. "I like that very much." He swept his hand across the horizon, as if he were imagining the city in flames. "Soon I will rise from your ashes. It will be a lovely birthday present."

I woke with my heart pounding, back in my own body. I felt hot, as if the fiery guy were starting to burn me. Then I realized that there was a cat on my chest.

Muffin stared at me, her eyes half closed. *"Mrow."*

"How did you get in?" I muttered.

I sat up, and for a second I wasn't sure where I was. Some hotel in another city? I almost called for my dad...and then I remembered.

Yesterday. The museum. The sarcophagus.

It all crashed down on me so hard I could barely breathe.

Stop, I told myself. *You don't have time for grief.* And this is going to sound weird, but the voice in my head almost sounded like a different person—older, stronger. Either that was a good sign, or I was going crazy.

Remember what you saw, the voice said. *He's after you. You have to be ready.*

I shivered. I wanted to believe I'd just had a bad dream, but I knew better. I'd been through too much in the last day to doubt what I'd seen. Somehow, I'd actually left my body while I slept. I'd *been* to Phoenix—thousands of miles away. The fiery dude was there. I hadn't understood much of what he'd said, but he'd talked about sending his forces to capture the younglings. Gee, wonder who that could be?

Muffin jumped off the bed and sniffed at the ivory headrest, looking up at me as if she were trying to tell me something.

"You can have it," I told her. "It's uncomfortable."

She butted her head against it and stared at me accusingly. *"Mrow."*

"Whatever, cat."

I got up and showered. When I tried to get dressed, I found that my old clothes had disappeared in the night. Everything in the closet was my size, but way different than what I was used to—baggy drawstring pants and loose shirts, all plain white linen, and robes for cold weather, kind of what the *fellahin*, the peasants in Egypt, wear. It wasn't exactly my style.

Sadie likes to tell me that I don't *have* a style. She complains that I dress like I'm an old man—button-down shirt, slacks, dress shoes. Okay, maybe. But here's the thing. My dad had always drilled into my head that I had to dress my best.

I remember the first time he explained it to me. I was ten. We were on our way to the airport in Athens, and it was like 112 degrees outside, and I was complaining that I wanted to wear shorts and a T-shirt. Why couldn't I be comfortable? We weren't going anywhere important that day—just traveling.

My dad put his hand on my shoulder. "Carter, you're getting older. You're an African American man. People will judge you more harshly, and so you must always look impeccable."

"That isn't fair!" I insisted.

"Fairness does not mean everyone gets the same," Dad said. "Fairness means everyone gets what they need. And the only way to get what you need is to make it happen *yourself*. Do you understand?"

I told him I didn't. But still I did what he asked—like caring about Egypt, and basketball, and music. Like traveling with only one suitcase. I dressed the way Dad wanted me to, because Dad was usually right. In fact I'd never known him to be wrong...until the night at the British Museum.

Anyway, I put on the linen clothes from the closet. The slipper shoes were comfortable, though I doubted they'd be much good to run in.

The door to Sadie's room was open, but she wasn't there.

Thankfully my bedroom door wasn't locked anymore. Muffin joined me and we walked downstairs, passing a lot of unoccupied bedrooms on the way. The mansion could've easily slept a hundred people, but instead it felt empty and sad.

Down in the Great Room, Khufu the baboon sat on the sofa with a basketball between his legs and a chunk of strange-looking meat in his hands. It was covered in pink feathers. ESPN was on the television, and Khufu was watching highlights from the games the night before.

"Hey," I said, though I felt a little weird talking to him. "Lakers win?"

Khufu looked at me and patted his basketball like he wanted a game. "*Agh, agh.*"

He had a pink feather hanging from his chin, and the sight made my stomach do a slow roll.

"Um, yeah," I said. "We'll play later, okay?"

I could see Sadie and Amos out on the terrace, eating breakfast by the pool. It should've been freezing out there, but the fire pit was blazing, and neither Amos nor Sadie looked cold. I headed their way, then hesitated in front of the statue of Thoth. In the daylight, the bird-headed god didn't look quite so scary. Still, I could swear those beady eyes were watching me expectantly.

What had the fiery guy said last night? Something about catching us before we learned our powers. It sounded ridiculous, but for a moment I felt a surge of strength—like the night before when I'd opened the front door just by raising my hand. I felt like I could lift anything, even this thirty-foot-tall statue if I wanted to. In a kind of trance, I stepped forward.

Muffin meowed impatiently and butted my foot. The feeling dissolved.

"You're right," I told the cat. "Stupid idea."

Besides, I could smell breakfast now—French toast, bacon, hot chocolate—and I couldn't blame Muffin for being in a hurry. I followed her out to the terrace.

"Ah, Carter," Amos said. "Merry Christmas, my boy. Join us."

"About time," Sadie grumbled. "I've been up for ages."

But she held my eyes for a moment, like she was thinking the same thing I was: *Christmas*. We hadn't spent a Christmas morning together since Mom died. I wondered if Sadie remembered how we used to make god's-eye decorations out of yarn and Popsicle sticks.

Amos poured himself a cup of coffee. His clothes were similar to those he'd worn the day before, and I had to admit the guy had style. His tailored suit was made of blue wool, he wore a matching fedora, and his hair was freshly braided with dark blue lapis lazuli, one of the stones the Egyptians often used for jewelry. Even his glasses matched. The round lenses were tinted blue. A tenor sax rested on a stand near the fire pit, and I could totally picture him playing out here, serenading the East River.

As for Sadie, she was dressed in a white linen pajama outfit like me, but somehow she'd managed to keep her combat boots. She'd probably slept with them on. She looked pretty comical with the red-streaked hair and the outfit, but since I wasn't dressed any better, I could hardly make fun of her.

"Um . . . Amos?" I asked. "You didn't have any pet birds, did you? Khufu's eating something with pink feathers."

"Mmm." Amos sipped his coffee. "Sorry if that disturbed you. Khufu's very picky. He only eats foods that end in -o. Doritos, burritos, flamingos."

I blinked. "Did you say—"

"Carter," Sadie warned. She looked a little queasy, like she'd already had this conversation. "Don't ask."

"Okay," I said. "Not asking."

"Please, Carter, help yourself." Amos waved toward a buffet table piled high with food. "Then we can get started with the explanations."

I didn't see any flamingo on the buffet table, which was fine by me, but there was just about everything else. I snagged some pancakes with butter and syrup, some bacon, and a glass of OJ.

Then I noticed movement in the corner of my eye. I glanced at the swimming pool. Something long and pale was gliding just under the surface of the water.

I almost dropped my plate. "Is that—"

"A crocodile," Amos confirmed. "For good luck. He's albino, but please don't mention that. He's sensitive."

"His name is Philip of Macedonia," Sadie informed me.

I wasn't sure how Sadie was taking this all so calmly, but I figured if she wasn't freaking out, I shouldn't either.

"That's a long name," I said.

"He's a long crocodile," Sadie said. "Oh, and he likes bacon."

To prove her point, she tossed a piece of bacon over her shoulder. Philip lunged out of the water and snapped up the treat. His hide was pure white and his eyes were pink. His mouth was so big, he could've snapped up an entire pig.

"He's quite harmless to my friends," Amos assured me. "In the old days, no temple would be complete without a lake full of crocodiles. They are powerful magic creatures."

"Right," I said. "So the baboon, the crocodile . . . any other pets I should know about?"

Amos thought for a moment. "Visible ones? No, I think that's it."

I took a seat as far from the pool as possible. Muffin circled my legs and purred. I hoped she had enough sense to stay away from magic crocodiles named Philip.

"So, Amos," I said between bites of pancake. "Explanations."

"Yes," he agreed. "Where to start . . ."

"Our dad," Sadie suggested. "What happened to him?"

Amos took a deep breath. "Julius was attempting to summon a god. Unfortunately, it worked."

It was kind of hard to take Amos seriously, talking about summoning gods while he spread butter on a bagel.

"Any god in particular?" I asked casually. "Or did he just order a generic god?"

Sadie kicked me under the table. She was scowling, as if she actually believed what Amos was saying.

Amos took a bite of bagel. "There are many Egyptian gods, Carter. But your dad was after one in particular."

He looked at me meaningfully.

"Osiris," I remembered. "When Dad was standing in front

of the Rosetta Stone, he said, 'Osiris, come.' But Osiris is a legend. He's make-believe."

"I wish that were true." Amos stared across the East River at the Manhattan skyline, gleaming in the morning sun. "The Ancient Egyptians were not fools, Carter. They built the pyramids. They created the first great nation state. Their civilization lasted thousands of years."

"Yeah," I said. "And now they're gone."

Amos shook his head. "A legacy that powerful does not disappear. Next to the Egyptians, the Greeks and Romans were babies. Our modern nations like Great Britain and America? Blinks of an eye. The very oldest root of civilization, at least of Western civilization, is Egypt. Look at the pyramid on the dollar bill. Look at the Washington Monument—the world's largest Egyptian obelisk. Egypt is still very much alive. And so, unfortunately, are her gods."

"Come on," I argued. "I mean . . . even if I believe there's a real thing called magic. Believing in ancient gods is totally different. You're joking, right?"

But as I said it, I thought about the fiery guy in the museum, the way his face had shifted between human and animal. And the statue of Thoth—how its eyes had followed me.

"Carter," Amos said, "the Egyptians would not have been stupid enough to believe in imaginary gods. The beings they described in their myths are very, very real. In the old days, the priests of Egypt would call upon these gods to channel their power and perform great feats. That is the origin of what we now call magic. Like many things, magic was first invented by the Egyptians. Each temple had a branch of magicians called the House of Life. Their magicians were famed throughout the ancient world."

"And you're an Egyptian magician."

Amos nodded. "So was your father. You saw it for yourself last night."

I hesitated. It was hard to deny my dad had done some weird stuff at the museum—some stuff that looked like magic.

"But he's an archaeologist," I said stubbornly.

"That's his cover story. You'll remember that he specialized in translating ancient spells, which are very difficult to understand unless you work magic yourself. Our family, the Kane family, has been part of the House of Life almost since the beginning. And your mother's family is almost as ancient."

"The Fausts?" I tried to imagine Grandma and Grandpa Faust doing magic, but unless watching rugby on TV and burning cookies was magical, I couldn't see it.

"They had not practiced magic for many generations," Amos admitted. "Not until your mother came along. But yes, a very ancient bloodline."

Sadie shook her head in disbelief. "So now Mum was magic, too. Are you joking?"

"No jokes," Amos promised. "The two of you . . . you combine the blood of two ancient families, both of which have a long, complicated history with the gods. You are the most powerful Kane children to be born in many centuries."

I tried to let that sink in. At the moment, I didn't feel powerful. I felt queasy. "You're telling me our parents secretly worshipped animal-headed gods?" I asked.

"Not worshipped," Amos corrected. "By the end of the

ancient times, Egyptians had learned that their gods were not to be worshipped. They are powerful beings, primeval forces, but they are not divine in the sense one might think of God. They are created entities, like mortals, only much more powerful. We can respect them, fear them, use their power, or even fight them to keep them under control—"

"*Fight* gods?" Sadie interrupted.

"Constantly," Amos assured her. "But we don't worship them. Thoth taught us that."

I looked at Sadie for help. The old guy had to be crazy. But Sadie was looking like she believed every word.

"So . . ." I said. "Why did Dad break the Rosetta Stone?"

"Oh, I'm sure he didn't mean to break it," Amos said. "That would've horrified him. In fact, I imagine my brethren in London have repaired the damage by now. The curators will soon check their vaults and discover that the Rosetta Stone miraculously survived the explosion."

"But it was blown into a million pieces!" I said. "How could they repair it?"

Amos picked up a saucer and threw it onto the stone floor. The saucer shattered instantly.

"That was *to destroy*," Amos said. "I could've done it by magic—*ha-di*—but it's simpler just to smash it. And now . . ." Amos held out his hand. "Join. *Hi-nehm*."

A blue hieroglyphic symbol burned in the air above his palm.

The pieces of the saucer flew into his hand and reassembled like a puzzle, even the smallest bits of dust gluing themselves into place. Amos put the perfect saucer back on the table.

"Some trick," I managed. I tried to sound calm about it, but I was thinking of all the odd things that had happened to my dad and me over the years, like those gunmen in the Cairo hotel who'd ended up hanging by their feet from a chandelier. Was it possible my dad had made that happen with some kind of spell?

Amos poured milk in the saucer, and put it on the floor. Muffin came padding over. "At any rate, your father would never intentionally damage a relic. He simply didn't realize how much power the Rosetta Stone contained. You see, as Egypt faded, its magic collected and concentrated into its remaining relics. Most of these, of course, are still in Egypt. But you can find some in almost every major museum. A magician can use these artifacts as focal points to work more powerful spells."

"I don't get it," I said.

Amos spread his hands. "I'm sorry, Carter. It takes years of study to understand magic, and I'm trying to explain it to you in a single morning. The important thing is, for the past six years your father has been looking for a way to summon Osiris, and last night he thought he had found the right artifact to do it."

"Wait, why did he want Osiris?"

Sadie gave me a troubled look. "Carter, Osiris was the lord of the dead. Dad was talking about making things right. He was talking about Mum."

Suddenly the morning seemed colder. The fire pit sputtered in the wind coming off the river.

"He wanted to bring Mom back from the dead?" I said. "But that's crazy!"

Amos hesitated. "It would've been dangerous. Inadvisable. Foolish. But not crazy. Your father is a powerful magician. If, in fact, that is what he was after, he might have accomplished it, using the power of Osiris."

I stared at Sadie. "You're actually buying this?"

"You saw the magic at the museum. The fiery bloke. Dad summoned something from the stone."

"Yeah," I said, thinking of my dream. "But that wasn't Osiris, was it?"

"No," Amos said. "Your father got more than he bargained for. He did release the spirit of Osiris. In fact, I think he successfully joined with the god—"

"Joined with?"

Amos held up his hand. "Another long conversation. For now, let's just say he drew the power of Osiris into himself. But he never got the chance to use it because, according to what Sadie has told me, it appears that Julius released *five* gods from the Rosetta Stone. Five gods who were all trapped together."

I glanced at Sadie. "You told him everything?"

"He's going to help us, Carter."

I wasn't quite ready to trust this guy, even if he was our uncle, but I decided I didn't have much choice.

"Okay, yeah," I said. "The fiery guy said something like 'You released all five.' What did he mean?"

Amos sipped his coffee. The faraway look on his face re-minded me of my dad. "I don't want to scare you."

"Too late."

"The gods of Egypt are very dangerous. For the last two thousand years or so, we magicians have spent much of our time binding and banishing them whenever they appear. In fact, our most important law, issued by Chief Lector Iskandar in Roman times, forbids unleashing the gods or using their power. Your father broke that law once before."

Sadie's face paled. "Does this have something to do with Mum's death? Cleopatra's Needle in London?"

"It has *everything* to do with that, Sadie. Your parents... well, they thought they were doing something good. They took a terrible risk, and it cost your mother her life. Your father took the blame. He was exiled, I suppose you would say. Banished. He was forced to move around constantly because the House monitored his activities. They feared he would continue his ...research. As indeed he did."

I thought about the times Dad would look over his shoulder as he copied some ancient inscriptions, or wake me up at three or four in the morning and insist it was time to change hotels, or warn me not to look in his workbag or copy certain pictures from old temple walls—as if our lives depended on it.

"Is that why you never came round?" Sadie asked Amos. "Because Dad was banished?"

"The House forbade me to see him. I loved Julius. It hurt me to stay away from my brother, and from you children. But I could not see you—until last night, when I simply had no choice but to try to help. Julius has been obsessed with finding Osiris for years. He was consumed with grief because of what happened to your mother. When I learned that Julius was about to break the law again, to try to set things right, I had to stop him. A second offense would've meant a death sentence. Unfortunately, I failed. I should've known he was too stubborn."

I looked down at my plate. My food had gotten cold. Muffin leaped onto the table and rubbed against my hand. When I didn't object, she started eating my bacon.

"Last night at the museum," I said, "the girl with the knife, the man with the forked beard—they were magicians too? From the House of Life?"

"Yes," Amos said. "Keeping an eye on your father. You are fortunate they let you go."

"The girl wanted to kill us," I remembered. "But the guy with the beard said, *not yet.*"

"They don't kill unless it is absolutely necessary," Amos said. "They will wait to see if you are a threat."

"Why would we be a threat?" Sadie demanded. "We're children! The summoning wasn't our idea."

Amos pushed away his plate. "There is a reason you two were raised separately."

"Because the Fausts took Dad to court," I said matter-of-factly. "And Dad lost."

"It was much more than that," Amos said. "The House insisted you two be separated. Your father wanted to keep you both, even though he knew how dangerous it was."

Sadie looked like she'd been smacked between the eyes. "He did?"

"Of course. But the House intervened and made sure your grandparents got custody of you, Sadie. If you and Carter were raised together, you could become very powerful. Perhaps you have already sensed changes over the past day."

I thought about the surges of strength I'd been feeling, and the way Sadie suddenly seemed to know how to read Ancient Egyptian. Then I thought of something even further back.

"Your sixth birthday," I told Sadie.

"The cake," she said immediately, the memory passing between us like an electric spark.

At Sadie's sixth birthday party, the last one we'd shared as a family, Sadie and I had a huge argument. I don't remember what it was about. I think I wanted to blow out the candles for her. We started yelling. She grabbed my shirt. I pushed her. I remember Dad rushing toward us, trying to intervene, but before he could, Sadie's birthday cake exploded. Icing splattered the walls, our parents, the faces of Sadie's little six-year-old friends. Dad and Mom separated us. They sent me to my room. Later, they said we must've hit the cake by accident as we were fighting, but I knew we hadn't. Something much weirder had made it explode, as if it had responded to our anger. I remembered Sadie crying with a chunk of cake on her forehead, an upside-down candle stuck to the ceiling with its wick still burning, and an adult visitor, one of my parents' friends, his glasses speckled with white frosting.

I turned to Amos. "That was you. You were at Sadie's party."

"Vanilla icing," he recalled. "Very tasty. But it was clear even then that you two would be difficult to raise in the same household."

"And so . . ." I faltered. "What happens to us now?"

I didn't want to admit it, but I couldn't stand the thought of being separated from Sadie again. She wasn't much, but she was all I had.

"You must be trained properly," Amos said, "whether the House approves or not."

"Why wouldn't they approve?" I asked.

"I will explain everything, don't worry. But we must start your lessons if we are to stand any chance of finding your father and putting things right. Otherwise the entire world is in danger. If we only knew where—"

"Phoenix," I blurted out.

Amos stared at me. "What?"

"Last night I had . . . well, not a dream, exactly . . ." I felt stupid, but I told him what had happened while I slept.

Judging from Amos's expression, the news was even worse than I thought.

"You're *sure* he said 'birthday present'?" he asked.

"Yeah, but what does that mean?"

"And a permanent host," Amos said. "He didn't have one yet?"

"Well, that's what the rooster-footed guy said—"

"That was a demon," Amos said. "A minion of chaos. And if demons are coming through to the mortal world, we don't have much time. This is bad, very bad."

"If you live in Phoenix," I said.

"Carter, our enemy won't stop in Phoenix. If he's grown so powerful so fast...What did he say about the storm, exactly?"

"He said: 'I will summon the greatest storm ever known.'"

Amos scowled. "The last time he said that, he created the Sahara. A storm that large could destroy North America, generating enough chaos energy to give him an almost invincible form."

"What are you talking about? Who *is* this guy?"

Amos waved away the question. "More important right now: why didn't you sleep with the headrest?"

I shrugged. "It was uncomfortable." I looked at Sadie for support. "You didn't use it, did you?"

Sadie rolled her eyes. "Well, of course I did. It was *obviously* there for a reason."

Sometimes I really hate my sister. [Ow! That's my foot!]

"Carter," Amos said, "sleep is dangerous. It's a doorway into the Duat."

"Lovely," Sadie grumbled. "Another strange word."

"Ah...yes, sorry," Amos said. "The Duat is the world of spirits and magic. It exists beneath the waking world like a vast ocean, with many layers and regions. We submerged just under its surface last night to reach New York, because travel through the Duat is much faster. Carter, your consciousness also passed through its shallowest currents as you slept, which is how you witnessed what happened in Phoenix. Fortunately, you survived that experience. But the deeper you go into the Duat, the more horrible things you encounter, and the more difficult it is to return. There are entire realms filled with demons, palaces where the gods exist in their pure forms, so powerful their mere presence would burn a human to ashes. There are prisons that hold beings of unspeakable evil, and some chasms so deep and chaotic that not even the gods dare explore them. Now that your powers are stirring, you must not sleep without protection, or you leave yourself open to attacks from the Duat or . . . unintended journeys through it. The headrest is enchanted, to keep your consciousness anchored to your body."

"You mean I actually *did* . . ." My mouth tasted like metal. "Could he have killed me?"

Amos's expression was grave. "The fact that your soul can travel like that means you are progressing faster than I thought. Faster than should be possible. If the Red Lord had noticed you—"

"The Red Lord?" Sadie said. "That's the fiery bloke?"

Amos rose. "I must find out more. We can't simply wait for him to find you. And if he releases the storm on his birthday, at the height of his powers—"

"You mean you're going to Phoenix?" I could barely get the words out. "Amos, that fiery man defeated Dad like his magic was a joke! Now he's got demons, and he's getting stronger, and—you'll be killed!"

Amos gave me a dry smile, like he'd already weighed the dangers and didn't need a reminder. His expression reminded me painfully of Dad's. "Don't count your uncle out so quickly, Carter. I've got some magic of my own. Besides, I must see what is happening for myself if we're to have any chance at saving your father and stopping the Red Lord. I'll be quick and careful. Just stay here. Muffin will guard you."

I blinked. "The cat will guard us? You can't just leave us here! What about our training?"

"When I return," Amos promised. "Don't worry, the mansion is protected. Just do not leave. Do not be tricked into opening the door for anyone. And whatever happens, *do not* go into the library. I absolutely forbid it. I will be back by sunset."

Before we could protest, Amos walked calmly to the edge of the terrace and jumped.

"No!" Sadie screamed. We ran to the railing and looked over. Below was a hundred-foot drop into the East River. There was no sign of Amos. He'd simply vanished.

Philip of Macedonia splashed in his pool. Muffin jumped onto the railing and insisted we pet her.

We were alone in a strange mansion with a baboon, a crocodile, and a weird cat. And apparently, the entire world was in danger.

I looked at Sadie. "What do we do now?"

She crossed her arms. "Well, that's obvious, isn't it? We explore the library."

7. I Drop a Little Man on His Head

HONESTLY, CARTER IS SO THICK sometimes I can't believe we're related.

I mean when someone says *I forbid it*, that's a good sign it's worth doing. I made for the library straightaway.

"Hold on!" Carter cried. "You can't just—"

"Brother dear," I said, "did your soul leave your body again while Amos was talking, or did you actually *hear* him? Egyptian gods *real*. Red Lord *bad*. Red Lord's birthday: very soon, very bad. House of Life: fussy old magicians who hate our family because Dad was a bit of a rebel, whom by the way you could take a lesson from. Which leaves us—*just* us—with Dad missing, an evil god about to destroy the world, and an uncle who just jumped off the building—and I *can't* actually blame him." I took a breath. [Yes, Carter, I do have to breathe occasionally.] "Am I missing anything? Oh, yes, I also have a brother who is supposedly quite powerful from an ancient bloodline, blah, blah, et cetera, but is too afraid to visit a library. Now, coming or not?"

Carter blinked as if I'd just hit him, which I suppose I had in a way.

"I just..." He faltered. "I just think we should be careful."

I realized the poor boy was quite scared, which I couldn't hold against him, but it did startle me. Carter was my *big* brother, after all—older, more sophisticated, the one who traveled the world with Dad. Big brothers are the ones who are supposed to pull their punches. Little sisters—well, we should be able to hit as hard as we like, shouldn't we? But I realized that possibly, just possibly, I'd been a bit harsh with him.

"Look," I said. "We need to help Dad, yes? There's got to be some powerful stuff in that library, otherwise Amos wouldn't keep it locked up. You do want to help Dad?"

Carter shifted uncomfortably. "Yeah...of course."

Well, that was one problem sorted, so we headed for the library. But as soon as Khufu saw what we were up to, he scrambled off the sofa with his basketball and jumped in front of the library doors. Who knew baboons were so speedy? He barked at us, and I have to say baboons have *enormous* fangs. And they're not any prettier when they've been chewing up exotic pink birds.

Carter tried to reason with him. "Khufu, we're not going to steal anything. We just want—"

"*Agh!*" Khufu dribbled his basketball angrily.

"Carter," I said, "you're not helping. Look here, Khufu. I

have...ta-da!" I held up a little yellow box of cereal I'd taken from the buffet table. "Cheerios! Ends with an -o. Yumsies!"

"Aghhh!" Khufu grunted, more excited now than angry.

"Want it?" I coaxed. "Just take it to the couch and pretend you didn't see us, yes?"

I threw the cereal towards the couch, and the baboon lunged after it. He grabbed the box in midair and was so excited, he ran straight up the wall and sat on the fireplace mantel, where he began gingerly picking out Cheerios and eating them one at a time.

Carter looked at me with grudging admiration. "How did you—"

"Some of us think ahead. Now, let's open these doors."

That was not so easily done. They were made of thick wood laced with giant steel chains and padlocked. *Complete* overkill.

Carter stepped forward. He tried to raise the doors by lifting his hand, which had been quite impressive the night before, only now accomplished nothing.

He shook the chains the old-fashioned way, then yanked on the padlocks.

"No good," he said.

Ice needles tingled on the back of my neck. It was almost as if someone—or something—was whispering an idea in my head. "What was that word Amos used at breakfast with the saucer?"

"For 'join'?" Carter said. "*Hi-nehm* or something."

"No, the other one, for 'destroy'."

"Uh, *ha-di*. But you'd need to know magic and the hieroglyphics, wouldn't you? And even then—"

I raised my hand toward the door. I pointed with two fingers and my thumb—an odd gesture I'd never made before, like a make-believe gun except with the thumb parallel to the ground.

"*Ha-di!*"

Bright gold hieroglyphs burned against the largest padlock.

And the doors exploded. Carter hit the floor as chains shattered and splinters flew all over the Great Room. When the dust cleared, Carter got up, covered in wood shavings. I seemed to be fine. Muffin circled my feet, mewing contentedly, as if this were all very normal.

Carter stared at me. "How exactly—"

"Don't know," I admitted. "But the library's open."

"Think you overdid it a little? We're going to be in so much trouble—"

"We'll just figure out a way to zap the door back, won't we?"

"No more zapping, please," Carter said. "That explosion could've killed us."

"Oh, do you think if you tried that spell on a person—"

"No!" He stepped back nervously.

I felt gratified that I could make him squirm, but I tried not to smile. "Let's just explore the library, shall we?"

The truth was, I couldn't have *ha-di*-ed anyone. As soon as I stepped forward, I felt so faint that I almost collapsed.

Carter caught me as I stumbled. "You okay?"

"Fine," I managed, though I didn't feel fine. "I'm tired"—my stomach rumbled—"and famished."

"You just ate a huge breakfast."

It was true, but I felt as if I hadn't had food in weeks.

"Never mind," I told him. "I'll manage."

Carter studied me skeptically. "Those hieroglyphs you cre-ated were golden. Dad and Amos both used blue. Why?"

"Maybe everyone has his own color," I suggested. "Maybe you'll get hot pink."

"Very funny."

"Come on, pink wizard," I said. "Inside we go."

The library was so amazing, I almost forgot my dizziness. It was bigger than I'd imagined, a round chamber sunk deep into solid rock, like a giant well. This didn't make sense, as the mansion was sitting on top of a warehouse, but then again nothing else about the place was exactly normal.

From the platform where we stood, a staircase descended three stories to the bottom floor. The walls, floor, and domed ceiling were all decorated with multicolored pictures of people, gods, and monsters. I'd seen such illustrations in Dad's books (yes, all right, sometimes when I was in the Piccadilly book-shop I'd wander into the Egypt section and sneak a look at Dad's books, just to feel some connection to him, not because I wanted to read them) but the pictures in the books had always been faded and smudged. These in the library looked newly painted, making the entire room a work of art.

"It's beautiful," I said.

A blue starry sky glittered on the ceiling, but it wasn't a solid field of blue. Rather, the sky was painted in a strange swirling pattern. I realized it was shaped like a woman. She lay curled on her side—her body, arms, and legs dark blue and dotted with stars. Below, the library floor was done in a similar way, the green-and-brown earth shaped into a man's body, dotted with forests and hills and cities. A river snaked across his chest.

The library had no books. Not even bookshelves. Instead, the walls were honeycombed with round cubbyholes, each one holding a sort of plastic cylinder.

At each of the four compass points, a ceramic statue stood on a pedestal. The statues were half-size humans wearing kilts and sandals, with glossy black wedge-shaped haircuts and black eyeliner around their eyes.

[Carter says the eyeliner stuff is called kohl, as if it matters.]

At any rate, one statue held a stylus and scroll. Another held a box. Another held a short, hooked staff. The last was empty-handed.

"Sadie." Carter pointed to the center of the room. Sitting on a long stone table was Dad's workbag.

Carter started down the stairs, but I grabbed his arm. "Hang on. What about traps?"

He frowned. "Traps?"

"Didn't Egyptian tombs have traps?"

"Well...sometimes. But this isn't a tomb. Besides, more often they had curses, like the burning curse, the donkey curse—"

"Oh, lovely. That sounds so much better."

He trotted down the steps, which made me feel quite

ridiculous, as I'm usually the one to forge ahead. But I supposed if someone had to get cursed with a burning skin rash or attacked by a magical donkey, it was better Carter than me.

We made it to the middle of the room with no excitement. Carter opened the bag. Still no traps or curses. He brought out the strange box Dad had used in the British Museum.

It was made of wood, and about the right size to hold a loaf of French bread. The lid was decorated much like the library, with gods and monsters and sideways-walking people.

"How did the Egyptians move like that?" I wondered. "All sideways with their arms and legs out. It seems quite silly."

Carter gave me one of his *God, you're stupid* looks. "They didn't walk like that in real life, Sadie."

"Well, why are they painted like that, then?"

"They thought paintings were like magic. If you painted yourself, you had to show all your arms and legs. Otherwise, in the afterlife you might be reborn without all your pieces."

"Then why the sideways faces? They never look straight at you. Doesn't that mean they'll lose the other side of their face?"

Carter hesitated. "I think they were afraid the picture would be *too* human if it was looking right at you. It might try to *become* you."

"So is there anything they *weren't* afraid of?"

"Little sisters," Carter said. "If they talked too much, the Egyptians threw them to the crocodiles."

He had me for a second. I wasn't used to him displaying a sense of humor. Then I punched him. "Just open the bloody box."

The first thing he pulled out was a lump of white gunk.

"Wax," Carter pronounced.

"Fascinating." I picked up a wooden stylus and a palette with small indentations in its surface for ink, then a few glass jars of the ink itself—black, red, and gold. "And a prehistoric painting set."

Carter pulled out several lengths of brown twine, a small ebony cat statue, and a thick roll of paper. No, not paper. Papyrus. I remembered Dad explaining how the Egyptians made it from a river plant because they never invented paper. The stuff was so thick and rough, it made me wonder if the poor Egyptians had had to use toilet papyrus. If so, no wonder they walked sideways.

Finally I pulled out a wax figurine.

"*Ew,*" I said.

He was a tiny man, crudely fashioned, as if the maker had been in a hurry. His arms were crossed over his chest, his mouth was open, and his legs were cut off at the knees. A lock of human hair was wrapped round his waist.

Muffin jumped on the table and sniffed the little man. She seemed to think him quite interesting.

"There's nothing here," Carter said.

"What do you want?" I asked. "We've got wax, some toilet papyrus, an ugly statue—"

"Something to explain what happened to Dad. How do we get him back? Who was that fiery man he summoned?"

I held up the wax man. "You heard him, warty little troll. Tell us what you know."

I was just messing about. But the wax man became soft and warm like flesh. He said, "I answer the call."

I screamed and dropped him on his tiny head. Well, can you blame me?

"*Ow!*" he said.

Muffin came over to have a sniff, and the little man started cursing in another language, possibly Ancient Egyptian. When that didn't work, he screeched in English: "Go away! I'm not a mouse!"

I scooped up Muffin and put her on the floor.

Carter's face had gone as soft and waxy as the little man's. "What *are* you?" he asked.

"I'm a *shabti*, of course!" The figurine rubbed his dented head. He still looked quite lumpish, only now he was a living lump. "Master calls me Doughboy, though I find the name insulting. You may call me Supreme-Force-Who-Crushes-His-Enemies!"

"All right, Doughboy," I said.

He scowled at me, I think, though it was hard to tell with his mashed-up face.

"*You* weren't supposed to trigger me! Only the master does that."

"The master, meaning Dad," I guessed. "*Er*, Julius Kane?"

"That's him," Doughboy grumbled. "Are we done yet? Have I fulfilled my service?"

Carter stared at me blankly, but I thought I was beginning to understand.

"So, Doughboy," I told the lump. "You were triggered when I picked you up and gave you a direct order: *Tell us what you know.* Is that correct?"

Doughboy crossed his stubby arms. "You're just toying with me now. *Of course* that's correct. Only the master is supposed to be able to trigger me, by the way. I don't know how you did it, but he'll blast you to pieces when he finds out."

Carter cleared his throat. "Doughboy, the master is our dad, and he's missing. He's been magically sent away somehow and we need your help—"

"Master is gone?" Doughboy smiled so widely, I thought his wax face would split open. "Free at last! See you, suckers!"

He lunged for the end of the table but forgot he had no feet. He landed on his face, then began crawling toward the edge, dragging himself with his hands. "Free! Free!"

He fell off the table and onto the floor with a thud, but that didn't seem to discourage him. "Free! Free!"

He made it another centimeter or two before I picked him up and threw him in Dad's magic box. Doughboy tried to get out, but the box was just tall enough that he couldn't reach the rim. I wondered if it had been designed that way.

"Trapped!" he wailed. "Trapped!"

"Oh, shut up," I told him. "*I'm* the mistress now. And you'll answer my questions."

Carter raised his eyebrow. "How come *you* get to be in charge?"

"Because I was smart enough to activate him."

"You were just joking around!"

I ignored my brother, which is one of my many talents. "Now, Doughboy, first off, what's a *shabti*?"

"Will you let me out of the box if I tell you?"

"You *have* to tell me," I pointed out. "And no, I won't."

He sighed. "*Shabti* means *answerer,* as even the stupidest slave could tell you."

Carter snapped his fingers. "I remember now! The Egyptians made models out of wax or clay—servants to do every kind of job they could imagine in the afterlife. They were supposed to come to life when their master called, so the deceased person could, like, kick back and relax and let the *shabti* do all his work for eternity."

"First," Doughboy snipped, "that is typical of humans! Lazing around while we do all the work. Second, afterlife work is only *one* function of *shabti*. We are also used by magicians for a great number of things in *this* life, because magicians would be total incompetents without us. Third, if you know so much, why are you asking me?"

"Why did Dad cut off your legs," I wondered, "and leave you with a mouth?"

"I—" Doughboy clapped his little hands over his mouth. "Oh, very funny. Threaten the wax statue. Big bully! He cut my legs off so I wouldn't run away or come to life in perfect form and try to kill him, naturally. Magicians are very mean. They maim statues to control them. They are afraid of us!"

"Would you come to life and try to kill him, had he made you perfectly?"

"Probably," Doughboy admitted. "Are we done?"

"Not by half," I said. "What happened to our dad?"

Doughboy shrugged. "How should I know? But I see his wand and staff aren't in the box."

"No," Carter said. "The staff—the thing that turned into

a snake—it got incinerated. And the wand . . . is that the boomerang thing?"

"The *boomerang thing*?" Doughboy said. "Gods of Eternal Egypt, you're dense. Of course that's his wand."

"It got shattered," I said.

"Tell me how," Doughboy demanded.

Carter told him the story. I wasn't sure that was the best idea, but I supposed a ten-centimeter-tall statue couldn't do us *that* much harm.

"This is wonderful!" Doughboy cried.

"Why?" I asked. "Is Dad still alive?"

"No!" Doughboy said. "He's almost certainly dead. The five gods of the Demon Days released? Wonderful! And anyone who duels with the Red Lord—"

"Wait," I said. "I order you to tell me what happened."

"Ha!" Doughboy said. "I only have to tell you what I *know*. Making educated guesses is a completely different task. I declare my service fulfilled!"

With that, he turned back to lifeless wax.

"Wait!" I picked him up again and shook him. "Tell me your educated guesses!"

Nothing happened.

"Maybe he's got a timer," Carter said. "Like only once a day. Or maybe you broke him."

"Carter, make a *helpful* suggestion! What do we do now?"

He looked at the four ceramic statues on their pedestals. "Maybe—"

"Other *shabti*?"

"Worth a shot."

If the statues were *answerers*, they weren't very good at it. We tried holding them while giving them orders, though they were quite heavy. We tried pointing at them and shouting. We tried asking nicely. They gave us no answers at all.

I grew so frustrated I wanted to *ha-di* them into a million pieces, but I was still so hungry and tired, I had the feeling that spell would not be good for my health.

Finally we decided to check the cubbyholes round the walls. The plastic cylinders were the kind you might find at a drive-through bank—the kind that shoot up and down the pneumatic tubes. Inside each case was a papyrus scroll. Some looked new. Some looked thousands of years old. Each canister was labeled in hieroglyphs and (fortunately) in English.

"The Book of the Heavenly Cow," Carter read on one. "What kind of name is that? What've you got, *The Heavenly Badger*?"

"No," I said. *"The Book of Slaying Apophis."*

Muffin meowed in the corner. When I looked over, her tail was puffed up.

"What's wrong with her?" I asked.

"Apophis was a giant snake monster," Carter muttered. "He was bad news."

Muffin turned and raced up the stairs, back into the Great Room. Cats. No accounting for them.

Carter opened another scroll. "Sadie, look at this."

He'd found a papyrus that was quite long, and most of the text on it seemed to be lines of hieroglyphs.

"Can you read any of this?" Carter asked.

I frowned at the writing, and the odd thing was, I *couldn't* read it—except for one line at the top. "Only that bit where the title should be. It says...*Blood of the Great House*. What does that mean?"

"Great house," Carter mused. "What do the words sound like in Egyptian?"

"Per-roh. Oh, it's *pharaoh*, isn't it? But I thought a pharaoh was a king?"

"It is," Carter said. "The word literally means 'great house,' like the king's mansion. Sort of like referring to the president as 'the White House.' So here it probably means more like *Blood of the Pharaohs*, all of them, the whole lineage of all the dynasties, not just one guy."

"So why do I care about the pharaohs' blood, and why can't I read any of the rest?"

Carter stared at the lines. Suddenly his eyes widened. "They're names. Look, they're all written inside cartouches."

"Excuse me?" I asked, because *cartouche* sounded like a rather rude word, and I pride myself on knowing those.

"The circles," Carter explained. "They symbolize magic ropes. They're supposed to protect the holder of the name from evil magic." He eyed me. "And possibly also from other magicians reading their names."

"Oh, you're mental," I said. But I looked at the lines, and saw what he meant. All the other words were protected by cartouches, and I couldn't make sense of them.

97

"Sadie," Carter said, his voice urgent. He pointed to a cartouche at the very end of the list—the last entry in what looked to be a catalogue of thousands.

Inside the circle were two simple symbols, a basket and a wave.

"KN," Carter announced. "I know this one. It's our name, KANE."

"Missing a few letters, isn't it?"

Carter shook his head. "Egyptians usually didn't write vowels. Only consonants. You have to figure out the vowel sounds from context."

"They really *were* nutters. So that could be KON or IKON or KNEE or AKNE."

"It could be," Carter agreed. "But it's our name, Kane. I asked Dad to write it for me in hieroglyphs once, and that's how he did it. But why are we in this list? And what is 'blood of the pharaohs'?"

That icy tingle started on the back of my neck. I remembered what Amos had said, about both sides of our family being very ancient. Carter's eyes met mine, and judging from his expression, he was having the same thought.

"There's no way," I protested.

"Must be some kind of joke," he agreed. "Nobody keeps family records that far back."

I swallowed, my throat suddenly very dry. So many odd things had happened to us in the last day, but it was only when I saw our name in that book that I finally began to believe all

this mad Egyptian stuff was real. Gods, magicians, monsters…
and our family was tied into it.

Ever since breakfast, when it occurred to me that Dad had
been trying to bring Mum back from the dead, a horrible emotion had been trying to take hold of me. And it wasn't dread.
Yes, the whole idea was creepy, *much* creepier than the shrine
my grandparents kept in the hall cupboard to my dead mother.
And yes, I told you I try not to live in the past and nothing
could change the fact that my mum was gone. But I'm a liar.
The truth was, I'd had one dream ever since I was six: to see
my mum again. To actually get to know her, talk to her, go
shopping, do *anything.* Just be with her once so I could have a
better memory to hold on to. The feeling I was trying to shake
was *hope.* I knew I was setting myself up for a colossal hurt.
But if it really *were* possible to bring her back, then I would've
blown up any number of Rosetta Stones to make it happen.

"Let's keep looking," I said.

After a few more minutes, I found a picture of some of
animal-headed gods, five in a row, with a starry woman figure
arching over them protectively like an umbrella. Dad had released five gods. *Hmm.*

"Carter," I called. "What's this, then?"

He came to have a look and his eyes lit up.

"That's it!" he announced. "These five… and up here, their
mother, Nut."

I laughed. "A goddess named Nut? Is her last name Case?"

"Very funny," Carter said. "She was the goddess of the sky."

He pointed to the painted ceiling—the lady with the blue
star-spangled skin, same as in the scroll.

"So what about her?" I asked.

Carter knit his eyebrows. "Something about the Demon Days. It had to do with the birth of these five gods, but it's been a long time since Dad told me the story. This whole scroll is written in hieratic, I think. That's like hieroglyph cursive. Can you read it?"

I shook my head. Apparently, my particular brand of insanity only applied to regular hieroglyphs.

"I wish I could find the story in English," Carter said.

Just then there was a cracking noise behind us. The empty-handed clay statue hopped off his pedestal and marched towards us. Carter and I scrambled to get out of his way, but he walked straight past us, grabbed a cylinder from its cubbyhole and brought it to Carter.

"It's a retrieval *shabti*," I said. "A clay librarian!"

Carter swallowed nervously and took the cylinder. "*Um* ... thanks."

The statue marched back to his pedestal, jumped on, and hardened again into regular clay.

"I wonder..." I faced the *shabti*. "Sandwich and chips, please!"

Sadly, none of the statues jumped down to serve me. Perhaps food wasn't allowed in the library.

Carter uncapped the cylinder and unrolled the papyrus. He sighed with relief. "This version is in English."

As he scanned the text, his frown got deeper.

"You don't look happy," I noticed.

"Because I remember the story now. The five gods ... if Dad really released them, it isn't good news."

"Hang on," I said. "Start from the beginning."

Carter took a shaky breath. "Okay. So the sky goddess, Nut, was married to the earth god, Geb."

"That would be this chap on the floor?" I tapped my foot on the big green man with the river and hills and forests all over his body.

"Right," Carter said. "Anyway, Geb and Nut wanted to have kids, but the king of the gods, Ra—he was the sun god—heard this bad prophecy that a child of Nut—"

"Child of Nut," I snickered. "Sorry, go on."

"—a child of Geb and Nut would one day replace Ra as king. So when Ra learned that Nut was pregnant, Ra freaked out. He forbade Nut to give birth to her children on any day or night of the year."

I crossed my arms. "So what, she had to stay pregnant forever? That's awfully mean."

Carter shook his head. "Nut figured out a way. She set up a game of dice with the moon god, Khons. Every time Khons lost, he had to give Nut some of his moonlight. He lost so many times, Nut won enough moonlight to create five *new* days and tag them on to the end of the year."

"Oh, please," I said. "First, how can you gamble moonlight? And if you did, how could you make extra days out of it?"

"It's a story!" Carter protested. "Anyway, the Egyptian calendar had three hundred and sixty days in the year, just like the three hundred and sixty degrees in a circle. Nut created the five days and added them to the end of the year—days that were not part of the regular year."

"The Demon Days," I guessed. "So the myth explains why

a year has three hundred and sixty-five days. And I suppose she had her children—"

"During those five days," Carter agreed. "One kid per day."

"Again, how do you have five children in a row, each on a different day?"

"They're gods," Carter said. "They can do stuff like that."

"Makes as much sense as the name Nut. But please, go on."

"So when Ra found out, he was furious, but it was too late. The children were already born. Their names were Osiris—"

"The one Dad was after."

"Then Horus, Set, Isis, and, um…" Carter consulted his scroll. "Nephthys. I always forget that one."

"And the fiery man in the museum said, *you have released all five.*"

"Exactly. What if they were imprisoned together and Dad didn't realize it? They were born together, so maybe they had to be summoned back into the world together. The thing is, one of these guys, Set, was a really bad dude. Like, the villain of Egyptian mythology. The god of evil and chaos and desert storms."

I shivered. "Did he perhaps have something to do with fire?"

Carter pointed to one of the figures in the picture. The god had an animal head, but I couldn't quite make out which sort of animal: Dog? Anteater? Evil bunny rabbit? Whichever it was, his hair and his clothes were bright red.

"The Red Lord," I said.

"Sadie, there's more," Carter said. "Those five days—the Demon Days—were bad luck in Ancient Egypt. You had to be

careful, wear good luck charms, and not do anything important or dangerous on those days. And in the British Museum,
Dad told Set: *They'll stop you before the Demon Days are over*."

"Surely you don't think he meant *us*," I said. "*We're* supposed to stop this Set character?"

Carter nodded. "And if the last five days of *our* calendar
year still count as the Egyptian Demon Days—they'd start on
December 27, the day after tomorrow."

The *shabti* seemed to be staring at me expectantly, but I
had not the slightest idea what to do. Demon Days and evil
bunny gods—if I heard *one* more impossible thing, my head
would explode.

And the worst of it? The little insistent voice in the back
of my head saying: *It's not impossible. To save Dad, we must
defeat Set.*

As if that had been on my to-do list for Christmas hols.
See Dad—check. Develop strange powers—check. Defeat an
evil god of chaos—check. The whole idea was mad!

Suddenly there was a loud crash, as if something had
broken in the Great Room. Khufu began barking in alarm.

Carter and I locked eyes. Then we ran for the stairs.

8. Muffin Plays with Knives

OUR BABOON WAS GOING completely sky goddess—which is to say, *nuts.*

He swung from column to column, bouncing along the balconies, overturning pots and statues. Then he ran back to the terrace windows, stared outside for a moment, and proceeded to go berserk again.

Muffin was also at the window. She crouched on all fours with her tail twitching as if she were stalking a bird.

"Perhaps it's just a passing flamingo," I suggested hopefully, but I'm not sure Carter could hear me over the screaming baboon.

We ran to the glass doors. At first I didn't see any problem. Then water exploded from the pool, and my heart nearly jumped out of my chest. Two enormous creatures, most definitely not flamingos, were thrashing about with our crocodile, Philip of Macedonia.

I couldn't make out what they were, only that they were fighting Philip two against one. They disappeared under the boiling water, and Khufu ran screaming through the Great Room again, bonking himself on the head with his empty Cheerios box, which I must say was not particularly helpful.

"Longnecks," Carter said incredulously. "Sadie, did you *see* those things?"

I couldn't find an answer. Then one of the creatures was thrown out of the pool. It slammed into the doors right in front of us, and I jumped back in alarm. On the other side of the glass was the most terrifying animal I'd ever seen. Its body was like a leopard's—lean and sinewy, with golden spotted fur—but its neck was completely wrong. It was green and scaly and at least as long as the rest of its body. It had a cat's head, but no normal cat's. When it turned its glowing red eyes towards us, it howled, showing a forked tongue and fangs dripping with green venom.

I realized my legs were shaking and I was making a very undignified whimpering sound.

The cat-serpent jumped back into the pool to join its companion in beating up Philip, who spun and snapped but seemed unable to hurt his attackers.

"We have to help Philip!" I cried. "He'll be killed!"

I reached for the door handle, but Muffin growled at me.

Carter said, "Sadie, no! You heard Amos. We can't open the doors for any reason. The house is protected by magic. Philip will have to beat them on his own."

"But what if he can't? Philip!"

The old crocodile turned. For a second his pink reptilian eye focused on me as if he could sense my concern. Then the cat-snakes bit at his underbelly and Philip rose up so that only the tip of his tail still touched the water. His body began to glow. A low hum filled the air, like an airplane engine starting up. When Philip came down, he slammed into the terrace with all his might.

The entire house shook. Cracks appeared in the concrete terrace outside, and the swimming pool split right down the middle as the far end crumbled into empty space.

"No!" I cried.

But the edge of the terrace ripped free, plunging Philip and the monsters straight into the East River.

My whole body began to tremble. "He sacrificed himself. He killed the monsters."

"Sadie..." Carter's voice was faint. "What if he didn't? What if they come back?"

"Don't say that!"

"I—I recognized them, Sadie. Those creatures. Come on."

"Where?" I demanded, but he ran straight back to the library.

Carter marched up to the *shabti* who'd helped us before. "Bring me the...*gah*, what's it called?"

"What?" I asked.

"Something Dad showed me. It's a big stone plate or something. Had a picture of the first pharaoh, the guy who united Upper and Lower Egypt into one kingdom. His name..." His eyes lit up. "Narmer! Bring me the Narmer Plate!"

Nothing happened.

"No," Carter decided. "Not a plate. It was...one of those things that holds paint. A palette. Bring me the Narmer Palette!"

The empty-handed *shabti* didn't move, but across the room, the statue with the little hook came to life. He jumped off his pedestal and disappeared in a cloud of dust. A heartbeat later, he reappeared on the table. At his feet was a wedge of flat gray stone, shaped like a shield and about as long as my forearm.

"No!" Carter protested. "I meant a *picture* of it! Oh great, I think this is the *real* artifact. The *shabti* must've stolen it from the Cairo Museum. We've got to return—"

"Hang on," I said. "We might as well have a look."

The surface of the stone was carved with the picture of a man smashing another man in the face with what looked like a spoon.

"That's Narmer with the spoon," I guessed. "Angry because the other bloke stole his breakfast cereal?"

Carter shook his head. "He's conquering his enemies and uniting Egypt. See his hat? That's the crown of Lower Egypt, before the two countries united."

"The bit that looks like a bowling pin?"

"You're impossible," Carter grumbled.

"He looks like Dad, doesn't he?"

"Sadie, be serious!"

"I *am* serious. Look at his profile."

Carter decided to ignore me. He examined the stone like he was afraid to touch it. "I need to see the back but I don't want to turn it over. We might damage—"

I grabbed the stone and flipped it over.

"Sadie! You could've broken it!"

"That's what mend spells are for, yes?"

We examined the back of the stone, and I had to admit I was impressed by Carter's memory. Two cat-snake monsters stood in the center of the palette, their necks entwined. On either side, Egyptian men with ropes were trying to capture the creatures.

"They're called serpopards," Carter said. "Serpent leopards."

"Fascinating," I said. "But what *are* serpopards?"

"No one knows exactly. Dad thought they were creatures of chaos—very bad news, and they've been around forever. This stone is one of the oldest artifacts from Egypt. Those pictures were carved five thousand years ago."

"So why are five-thousand-year-old monsters attacking our house?"

"Last night, in Phoenix, the fiery man ordered his servants to capture us. He said to send the longnecks first."

I had a metallic taste in my mouth, and I wished I hadn't

chewed my last piece of gum. "Well…good thing they're at the bottom of the East River."

Just then Khufu rushed into the library, screaming and slapping his head.

"Suppose I shouldn't have said that," I muttered.

Carter told the *shabti* to return the Narmer Palette, and both statue and stone disappeared. Then we followed the baboon upstairs.

The serpopards were back, their fur wet and slimy from the river, and they weren't happy. They prowled the broken ledge of the terrace, their snake necks whipping round as they sniffed the doors, looking for a way in. They spit poison that steamed and bubbled on the glass. Their forked tongues darted in and out.

"*Agh, agh!*" Khufu picked up Muffin, who was sitting on the sofa, and offered me the cat.

"I really don't think that will help," I told him.

"AGH!" Khufu insisted.

Neither *Muffin* nor *cat* ended in *-o*, so I guessed Khufu was not trying to offer me a snack, but I didn't know what he was on about. I took the cat just to shut him up.

"*Mrow?*" Muffin looked up at me.

"It'll be all right," I promised, trying not to sound scared out of my mind. "The house is protected by magic."

"Sadie," Carter said. "They've found something."

The serpopards had converged at the left-hand door and were intently sniffing the handle.

"Isn't it locked?" I asked.

THE RED PYRAMID

Both monsters smashed their ugly faces against the glass. The door shuddered. Blue hieroglyphs glowed along the doorframe, but their light was faint.

"I don't like this," Carter murmured.

I prayed that the monsters would give up. Or that perhaps Philip of Macedonia would climb back to the terrace (do crocodiles climb?) and renew the fight.

Instead, the monsters smashed their heads against the glass again. This time a web of cracks appeared. The blue hieroglyphs flickered and died.

"AGH!" Khufu screamed. He waved his hand vaguely at the cat.

"Maybe if I try the *ha-di* spell," I said.

Carter shook his head. "You almost fainted after you blew up those doors. I don't want you passing out, or worse."

Carter once again surprised me. He tugged a strange sword from one of Amos's wall displays. The blade had an odd crescent-moon curve and looked horribly impractical.

"You can't be serious," I said.

"Unless—unless you've got a better idea," he stammered, his face beading with perspiration. "It's me, you, and the baboon against *those* things."

I'm sure Carter was trying to be brave in his own extremely unbrave way, but he was shaking worse than I was. If anyone was going to pass out, I feared it would be him, and I didn't fancy him doing that while holding a sharp object.

Then the serpopards struck a third time, and the door shattered. We backed up to the foot of Thoth's statue as the creatures stalked into the great room. Khufu threw his basketball, which bounced harmlessly off the first monster's head. Then he launched himself at the serpopard.

"Khufu, don't!" Carter yelled.

But the baboon sank his fangs into the monster's neck. The serpopard lashed around, trying to bite him. Khufu leaped off, but the monster was quick. It used its head like a bat and smacked poor Khufu in midair, sending him straight through the shattered door, over the broken terrace, and into the void.

I wanted to sob, but there wasn't time. The serpopards came toward us. We couldn't outrun them. Carter raised his sword. I pointed my hand at the first monster and tried to speak the *ha-di* spell, but my voice stuck in my throat.

"*Mrow!*" Muffin said, more insistently. Why was the cat still nestled in my arm and not running away in terror?

Then I remembered something Amos had said: *Muffin will protect you.* Was that what Khufu had been trying to remind me? It seemed impossible, but I stammered, "M-Muffin, I order you to protect us."

I tossed her on the floor. Just for a moment, the silver pendant on her collar seemed to gleam. Then the cat arched her back leisurely, sat down, and began licking a front paw. Well, really, what was I expecting—heroics?

The two red-eyed monsters bared their fangs. They raised their heads and prepared to strike—and an explosion of dry air blasted through the room. It was so powerful, it knocked Carter and me to the floor. The serpopards stumbled and backed away.

I staggered to my feet and realized that the center of the blast had been *Muffin*. My cat was no longer there. In her place was a woman—small and lithe like a gymnast. Her jet-black hair was tied in a ponytail. She wore a skintight leopard-skin jumpsuit and Muffin's pendant around her neck.

She turned and grinned at me, and her eyes were still Muffin's—yellow with black feline pupils. "About time," she chided.

The serpopards got over their shock and charged the cat woman. Their heads struck with lightning speed. They should've ripped her in two, but the cat lady leaped straight up, flipping three times, and landed above them, perched on the mantel.

She flexed her wrists, and two enormous knives shot from her sleeves into her hands. "*A-a-ah*, fun!"

The monsters charged. She launched herself between them, dancing and dodging with incredible grace, letting them lash at her futilely while she threaded their necks together. When she stepped away, the serpopards were hopelessly intertwined. The more they struggled, the tighter the knots became. They trampled back and forth, knocking over furniture and roaring in frustration.

"Poor things," the cat woman purred. "Let me help."

Her knives flashed, and the two monsters' heads thudded to the floor at her feet. Their bodies collapsed and dissolved into enormous piles of sand.

"So much for my playthings," the woman said sadly. "From sand they come, and to sand they return."

She turned towards us, and the knives shot back into her sleeves. "Carter, Sadie, we should leave. Worse will be coming."

Carter made a choking sound. "*Worse?* Who—how—what—"

"All in good time." The woman stretched her arms above her head with great satisfaction. "So good to be in human form again! Now, Sadie, can you open us a door through the Duat, please?"

I blinked. "Um...no. I mean—I don't know how."

The woman narrowed her eyes, clearly disappointed. "Shame. We'll need more power, then. An obelisk."

"But that's in London," I protested. "We can't—"

"There's a nearer one in Central Park. I try to avoid Manhattan, but this is an emergency. We'll just pop over and open a portal."

"A portal to where?" I demanded. "Who are you, and why are you my cat?"

The woman smiled. "For now, we just want a portal out of danger. As for my name, it's *not* Muffin, thank you very much. It's—"

"Bast," Carter interrupted. "Your pendant—it's the symbol of Bast, goddess of cats. I thought it was just decoration but ...that's you, isn't it?"

"Very good, Carter," Bast said. "Now come, while we can still make it out of here alive."

C
A
R
T
E
R

9. We Run from Four Guys in Skirts

So, yeah. Our cat was a goddess.

What else is new?

She didn't give us much time to talk about it. She ordered me to the library to grab my dad's magic kit, and when I came back she was arguing with Sadie about Khufu and Philip.

"We have to search for them!" Sadie insisted.

"They'll be fine," said Bast. "However, *we* will not be, unless we leave now."

I raised my hand. "*Um*, excuse me, Miss Goddess Lady? Amos told us the house was—"

"Safe?" Bast snorted. "Carter, the defenses were too easily breached. Someone *sabotaged* them."

"What do you mean? Who—"

"Only a magician of the House could've done it."

"Another magician?" I asked. "Why would another magician want to sabotage Amos's house?"

"Oh, Carter," Bast sighed. "So young, so innocent.

Magicians are devious creatures. Could be a million reasons why one would backstab another, but we don't have time to discuss it. Now, come on!"

She grabbed our arms and led us out the front door. She'd sheathed her knives, but she still had some wicked sharp claws for fingernails that hurt as they dug into my skin. As soon as we stepped outside, the cold wind stung my eyes. We climbed down a long flight of metal stairs into the industrial yard that surrounded the factory.

Dad's workbag was heavy on my shoulder. The curved sword I'd strapped across my back felt cold against my thin linen clothes. I'd started to sweat during the serpopard attack, and now my perspiration felt like it was turning to ice.

I looked around for more monsters, but the yard seemed abandoned. Old construction equipment lay in rusting heaps—a bulldozer, a crane with a wrecking ball, a couple of cement mixers. Piles of sheet metal and stacks of crates made a maze of obstacles between the house and the street a few hundred yards away.

We were about halfway across the yard when an old gray tomcat stepped in our path. One of his ears was torn. His left eye was swollen shut. Judging from his scars, he'd spent most of his life fighting.

Bast crouched and stared at the cat. He looked up at her calmly.

"Thank you," Bast said.

The old tomcat trotted off toward the river.

"What was that about?" Sadie asked.

"One of my subjects, offering help. He'll spread the news

about our predicament. Soon every cat in New York will be on alert."

"He was so battered," Sadie said. "If he's your subject, couldn't you heal him?"

"And take away his marks of honor? A cat's battle scars are part of his identity. I couldn't—" Suddenly Bast tensed. She dragged us behind a stack of crates.

"What is it?" I whispered.

She flexed her wrists and her knives slid into her hands. She peeped over the top of the crates, every muscle in her body trembling. I tried to see what she was looking at, but there was nothing except the old wrecking-ball crane.

Bast's mouth twitched with excitement. Her eyes were fixed on the huge metal ball. I'd seen kittens look like that when they stalked catnip toy mice, or pieces of string, or rubber balls. . . . Balls? No. Bast was an ancient goddess. Surely she wouldn't—

"This could be it." She shifted her weight. "Stay very *very* still."

"There's no one there," Sadie hissed.

I started to say, *"Um . . ."*

Bast lunged over the crates. She flew thirty feet through the air, knives flashing, and landed on the wrecking ball with such force that she broke the chain. The cat goddess and the huge metal sphere smashed into the dirt and went rolling across the yard.

"Rowww!" Bast wailed. The wrecking ball rolled straight over her, but she didn't appear hurt. She leaped off and pounced again. Her knives sliced through the metal like wet

clay. Within seconds, the wrecking ball was reduced to a mound of scraps.

Bast sheathed her blades. "Safe now!"

Sadie and I looked at each other.

"You saved us from a metal ball," Sadie said.

"You never know," Bast said. "It could've been hostile."

Just then a deep *boom!* shook the ground. I looked back at the mansion. Tendrils of blue fire curled from the top windows.

"Come on," Bast said. "Our time is up!"

I thought maybe she'd whisk us off by magic, or at least hail a taxi. Instead, Bast borrowed a silver Lexus convertible.

"Oh, yes," she purred. "I like this one! Come along, children."

"But this isn't yours," I pointed out.

"My dear, I'm a cat. Everything I *see* is mine." She touched the ignition and the keyhole sparked. The engine began to purr. [No, Sadie. Not like a cat, like an engine.]

"Bast," I said, "you can't just—"

Sadie elbowed me. "We'll work out how to return it later, Carter. Right now we've got an emergency."

She pointed back toward the mansion. Blue flames and smoke now billowed from every window. But that wasn't the scary part—coming down the stairs were four men carrying a large box, like an oversize coffin with long handles sticking out at both ends. The box was covered with a black shroud and looked big enough for at least two bodies. The four men wore only kilts and sandals. Their coppery skin glinted in the sun as if made of metal.

"Oh, that's bad," Bast said. "In the car, please."

I decided not to ask questions. Sadie beat me to the shotgun seat so I climbed in back. The four metallic guys with the box were racing across the yard, coming straight for us at an unbelievable speed. Before I even had my seat belt on, Bast hit the gas.

We tore through the streets of Brooklyn, weaving insanely through traffic, riding over sidewalks, narrowly missing pedestrians.

Bast drove with reflexes that were...well, catlike. Any human trying to drive so fast would've had a dozen wrecks, but she got us safely onto the Williamsburg Bridge.

I thought for sure we must've lost our pursuers, but when I looked back, the four copper men with the black box were weaving in and out of traffic. They appeared to be jogging at a normal pace, but they passed cars that were doing fifty. Their bodies blurred like choppy images in an old movie, as if they were out of sync with the regular stream of time.

"What are they?" I asked. "Shabti?"

"No, carriers." Bast glanced in the rearview mirror. "Summoned straight from the Duat. They'll stop at nothing to find their victims, throw them in the sedan—"

"The what?" Sadie interrupted.

"The large box," Bast said. "It's a kind of carriage. The carriers capture you, beat you senseless, throw you in, and carry you back to their master. They never lose their prey, and they never give up."

"But what do they want us for?"

"Trust me," Bast growled, "you don't want to know."

I thought about the fiery man last night in Phoenix—how he'd fried one of his servants into a grease spot. I was pretty sure I didn't want to meet him face-to-face again.

"Bast," I said, "if you're a goddess, can't you just snap your fingers and disintegrate those guys? Or wave your hand and teleport us away?"

"Wouldn't that be nice? But my power in this host is limited."

"You mean Muffin?" Sadie asked. "But you're not a cat anymore."

"She's still my host, Sadie, my anchor on this side of the Duat—and a very imperfect one. Your call for help allowed me to assume human shape, but that alone takes a great deal of power. Besides, even when I'm in a *powerful* host, Set's magic is stronger than mine."

"Could you please say something I actually understand?" I pleaded.

"Carter, we don't have time for a full discussion on gods and hosts and the limits of magic! We have to get you to safety."

Bast floored the accelerator and shot up the middle of the bridge. The four carriers with the sedan raced after us, blurring the air as they moved, but no cars swerved to avoid them. No one panicked or even looked at them.

"How can people not see them?" I said. "Don't they notice four copper men in skirts running up the bridge with a weird black box?"

Bast shrugged. "Cats can hear many sounds you can't.

Some animals see things in the ultraviolet spectrum that are invisible to humans. Magic is similar. Did you notice the mansion when you first arrived?"

"Well…no."

"And you are born to magic," Bast said. "Imagine how hard it would be for a regular mortal."

"Born to magic?" I remembered what Amos had said about our family being in the House of Life for a long time. "If magic, like, runs in the family, why haven't I ever been able to do it before?"

Bast smiled in the mirror. "Your sister understands."

Sadie's ears turned red. "No, I don't! I still can't believe you're a *goddess*. All these years, you've been eating crunchy treats, sleeping on my head—"

"I made a deal with your father," Bast said. "He let me remain in the world as long as I assumed a minor form, a normal housecat, so I could protect and watch over you. It was the least I could do after—" She stopped abruptly.

A horrible thought occurred to me. My stomach fluttered, and it had nothing to do with how fast we were going. "After our mom's death?" I guessed.

Bast stared straight ahead out the windshield.

"That's it, isn't it?" I said. "Dad and Mom did some kind of magic ritual at Cleopatra's Needle. Something went wrong. Our mom died and…and they released you?"

"That's not important right now," Bast said. "The point is I agreed to look after Sadie. And I will."

She was hiding something. I was sure of it, but her tone made it clear that the subject was closed.

"If you gods are so powerful and helpful," I said, "why does the House of Life forbid magicians from summoning you?"

Bast swerved into the fast lane. "Magicians are paranoid. Your best hope is to stay with me. We'll get as far away as possible from New York. Then we'll get help and challenge Set."

"What help?" Sadie asked.

Bast raised an eyebrow. "Why, we'll summon more gods, of course."

10. Bast Goes Green

[Sadie, stop it! Yeah, I'm getting to that part.] Sorry, she keeps trying to distract me by setting fire to my—never mind. Where was I?

We barreled off the Williamsburg Bridge into Manhattan and headed north on Clinton Street.

"They're still following," Sadie warned.

Sure enough, the carriers were only a block behind us, weaving around cars and trampling over sidewalk displays of tourist junk.

"We'll buy some time." Bast growled deep in her throat—a sound so low and powerful it made my teeth buzz. She yanked the wheel and swerved right onto East Houston.

I looked back. Just as the carriers turned the corner, a horde of cats materialized all around them. Some jumped from windows. Some ran from the sidewalks and alleys. Some crawled from the storm drains. All of them converged on the carriers in a wave of fur and claws—climbing up their copper legs, scratching their backs, clinging to their faces, and weighing down the sedan box. The carriers stumbled, dropping the box. They began blindly swatting at the cats. Two cars swerved to avoid the animals and collided, blocking the entire street, and the carriers went down under the mass of angry felines. We turned onto the FDR Drive, and the scene disappeared from view.

"Nice," I admitted.

"It won't hold them long," Bast said. "Now—Central Park!"

Bast ditched the Lexus at the Metropolitan Museum of Art.

"We'll run from here," she said. "It's just behind the museum."

When she said run, she meant it. Sadie and I had to sprint to keep up, and Bast wasn't even breaking a sweat. She didn't stop for little things like hot dog stands or parked cars. Anything under ten feet tall she leaped over with ease, leaving us to scramble around the obstacles as best we could.

We ran into the park on the East Drive. As soon as we turned north, the obelisk loomed above us. A little over seventy feet tall, it looked like an exact copy of the needle in London. It was tucked away on a grassy hill, so it actually felt isolated, which is hard to achieve in the center of New York. There was no one around except a couple of joggers farther down the path. I could hear the traffic behind us on Fifth Avenue, but even that seemed far away.

We stopped at the obelisk's base. Bast sniffed the air as if smelling for trouble. Once I was standing still, I realized just how cold I was. The sun was directly overhead, but the wind ripped right through my borrowed linen clothes.

"I wish I'd grabbed something warmer," I muttered. "A wool coat would be nice."

"No, it wouldn't," Bast said, scanning the horizon. "You're dressed for magic."

Sadie shivered. "We have to freeze to be magical?"

"Magicians avoid animal products," Bast said absently. "Fur, leather, wool, any of that. The residual life aura can interfere with spells."

"My boots seem all right," Sadie noted.

"Leather," Bast said with distaste. "You may have a higher tolerance, so a bit of leather won't bother your magic. I don't know. But linen clothing is always best, or cotton—plant material. At any rate, Sadie, I think we're clear for the moment. There's a window of auspicious time starting right now, at eleven thirty, but it won't last long. Get started."

Sadie blinked. "Me? Why me? You're the goddess!"

"I'm not good at portals," Bast said. "Cats are protectors. Just control your emotions. Panic or fear will kill a spell. We *have* to get out of here before Set summons the other gods to his cause."

I frowned. "You mean Set's got, like, other evil gods on speed dial?"

Bast glanced nervously toward the trees. "Evil and good may not be the best way to think of it, Carter. As a magician, you must think about chaos and order. *Those* are the two forces that control the universe. Set is all about chaos."

"But what about the other gods Dad released?" I persisted. "Aren't they good guys? Isis, Osiris, Horus, Nephthys—where are they?"

Bast fixed her eyes on me. "That's a good question, Carter."

A Siamese cat broke through the bushes and ran up to Bast. They looked at each other for a moment. Then the Siamese dashed away.

"The carriers are close," Bast announced. "And something else...something much stronger, closing in from the east. I think the carriers' master has grown impatient."

My heart did a flip. "*Set* is coming?"

"No," Bast said. "Perhaps a minion. Or an ally. My cats are having trouble describing what they're seeing, and I *don't* want to find out. Sadie, now is the time. Just concentrate on opening a gateway to the Duat. I'll keep off the attackers. Combat magic is my specialty."

"Like what you did in the mansion?" I asked.

Bast showed her pointed teeth. "No, that was just combat."

The woods rustled, and the carriers emerged. Their sedan chair's shroud had been shredded by cat claws. The carriers themselves were scratched and dented. One walked with a limp, his leg bent backward at the knee. Another had a car fender wrapped around his neck.

The four metal men carefully set down their sedan chair. They looked at us and drew golden metal clubs from their belts.

"Sadie, get to work," Bast ordered. "Carter, you're welcome to help me."

The cat goddess unsheathed her knives. Her body began

to glow with a green hue. An aura surrounded her, growing larger, like a bubble of energy, and lifting her off the ground. The aura took shape until Bast was encased in a holographic projection about four times her normal size. It was an image of the goddess in her ancient form—a twenty-foot-tall woman with the head of a cat. Floating in midair in the center of the hologram, Bast stepped forward. The giant cat goddess moved with her. It didn't seem possible that a see-through image could have substance, but its foot shook the ground. Bast raised her hand. The glowing green warrior did the same, unsheathing claws as long and sharp as rapiers. Bast swiped the sidewalk in front of her and shredded the pavement to concrete ribbons. She turned and smiled at me. The giant cat's head did likewise, baring horrible fangs that could've bitten me in half.

"*This*," Bast said, "is combat magic."

At first I was too stunned to do anything but watch as Bast launched her green war machine into the middle of the carriers.

She slashed one carrier to pieces with a single swipe, then stepped on another and flattened him into a metal pancake. The other two carriers attacked her holographic legs, but their metal clubs bounced harmlessly off the ghostly light with showers of sparks.

Meanwhile Sadie stood in front of the obelisk with her arms raised, shouting: "Open, you stupid piece of rock!"

Finally I drew my sword. My hands were shaking. I didn't want to charge into battle, but I felt like I should help. And if I *had* to fight, I figured having a twenty-foot-tall glowing cat warrior on my side was the way to do it. "Sadie, I—I'm going to help Bast. Keep trying!"

"I *am!*"

I ran forward just as Bast sliced the other two carriers apart like loaves of bread. With relief, I thought: *Well, that's it.*

Then all four carriers began to re-form. The flat one peeled himself off the pavement. The sliced ones' pieces clicked together like magnets, and the carriers stood up good as new.

"Carter, help me hack them apart!" Bast called. "They need to be in smaller pieces!"

I tried to stay out of Bast's way as she sliced and stomped. Then as soon as she disabled a carrier, I went to work chopping its remains into smaller pieces. They seemed more like Play-Doh than metal, because my blade mashed them up pretty easily.

Another few minutes and I was surrounded by piles of coppery rubble. Bast made a glowing fist and smashed the sedan into kindling.

"That wasn't so hard," I said. "What were we running for?"

Inside her glowing shell, Bast's face was coated with sweat. It hadn't occurred to me that a goddess could get tired, but her magic avatar must've taken a lot of effort.

"We're not safe yet," she warned. "Sadie, how's it coming?"

"It's not," Sadie complained. "Isn't there another way?"

Before Bast could answer, the bushes rustled with a new sound—like rain, except more *slithery*.

A chill ran up my back. "What...what is that?"

"No," Bast murmured. "It can't be. Not her."

Then the bushes exploded. A thousand brown creepy-crawlies poured from the woods in a carpet of grossness—all pincers and stinging tails.

I wanted to yell, "Scorpions!" But my voice wouldn't work. My legs started trembling. I *hate* scorpions. They're everywhere in Egypt. Many times I'd found them in my hotel bed or shower. Once I'd even found one in my sock.

"Sadie!" Bast called urgently.

"Nothing!" Sadie moaned.

The scorpions kept coming—thousands upon thousands. Out of the woods a woman appeared, walking fearlessly through the middle of the arachnids. She wore brown robes with gold jewelry glinting around her neck and arms. Her long black hair was cut Ancient Egyptian–style with a strange crown on top. Then I realized it wasn't a crown—she had a live, supersize scorpion nesting on her head. Millions of the little nasties swirled around her like she was the center of their storm.

"Serqet," Bast growled.

"The scorpion goddess," I guessed. Maybe that should've terrified me, but I was already pretty much at my maximum. "Can you take her?"

Bast's expression didn't reassure me.

"Carter, Sadie," she said, "this is going to get ugly. Get to the museum. Find the temple. It may protect you."

"What temple?" I asked.

"And what about you?" Sadie added.

"I'll be fine. I'll catch up." But when Bast looked at me, I could tell she wasn't sure. She was just buying us time.

"Go!" she ordered. She turned her giant green cat warrior to face the mass of scorpions.

Embarrassing truth? In the face of those scorpions, I didn't even pretend to be brave. I grabbed Sadie's arm and we ran.

11. We Meet the Human Flamethrower

RIGHT, I'M TAKING THE MICROPHONE. There is *no chance* Carter would tell this part properly, as it's about Zia. [Shut up, Carter. You know it's true.]

Oh, who is Zia? Sorry, getting ahead of myself.

We raced to the entrance of the museum, and I had no idea why, except that a giant glowing cat woman had told us to. Now, you must realize I was already devastated by every-thing that had happened. First, I'd lost my father. Second, my loving grandparents had kicked me out of the flat. Then I'd discovered I was apparently "blood of the pharaohs," born to a magical family, and all sorts of rubbish that sounded quite impressive but only brought me loads of trouble. And as soon as I'd found a new home—a mansion with proper breakfast and friendly pets and quite a nice room for me, by the way— Uncle Amos disappeared, my lovely new crocodile and baboon friends were tossed in a river, and the mansion was set on fire.

And if *that* wasn't enough, my faithful cat Muffin had decided to engage in a hopeless battle with a swarm of scorpions.

Do you call it a "swarm" for scorpions? A herd? A gaggle? Oh, never mind.

The point is I couldn't believe I'd been asked to open a magic doorway when clearly I had no such skill, and now my brother was dragging me away. I felt like an utter failure. [And no comments from you, Carter. As I recall, *you* weren't much help at the time, either.]

"We can't just leave Bast!" I shouted. "Look!"

Carter kept running, dragging me along, but I could see quite clearly what was happening back at the obelisk. A mass of scorpions had crawled up Bast's glowing green legs and were wriggling into the hologram like it was gelatin. Bast smashed hundreds of them with her feet and fists, but there were simply too many. Soon they were up to her waist, and her ghostly shell began to flicker. Meanwhile, the brown-robed goddess advanced slowly, and I had a feeling she would be worse than any number of scorpions.

Carter pulled me through a row of bushes and I lost sight of Bast. We burst onto Fifth Avenue, which seemed ridiculously normal after the magic battle. We ran down the sidewalk, shoved through a knot of pedestrians, and climbed the steps of the Met.

A banner above the entrance announced some sort of special Christmas event, which I suppose is why the museum was open on a holiday, but I didn't bother reading the details. We pushed straight inside.

What did it look like? Well, it was a museum: huge entry hall, lots of columns and so on. I can't claim I spent much time admiring the decor. I do remember it had queues for the ticket windows, because we ran right past them. There were also security guards, because they yelled at us as we dashed into the exhibits. By luck, we ended up in the Egyptian area, in front of a reconstructed tomb sort of place with narrow corridors. Carter probably could've told you what the structure was supposed to be, but honestly I didn't care.

"Come on," I said.

We slipped inside the exhibit, which proved quite enough to lose the security guards, or perhaps they had better things to do than pursue naughty children.

When we popped out again, we sneaked around until we were sure we weren't being followed. The Egypt wing wasn't crowded—just a few clumps of old people and a foreign tour group with a guide explaining a sarcophagus in French. *"Et voici la momie!"*

Strangely, no one seemed to notice the enormous sword on Carter's back, which surely must've been a security issue (and much more interesting than the exhibits). A few old people did give us odd looks, but I suspect that was because we were dressed in linen pajamas, drenched in sweat, and covered in grass and leaves. My hair was probably a nightmare as well.

I found an empty room and pulled Carter aside. The glass cases were full of *shabti*. A few days earlier I wouldn't have given them a second thought. Now, I kept glancing at the statues, sure they'd come to life any minute and try to bash me on the head.

"What now?" I asked Carter. "Did you see any temple?"

"No." He knit his eyebrows as if trying hard to remember. "I think there's a rebuilt temple down that hall . . . or is that in the Brooklyn Museum? Maybe the one in Munich? Sorry, I've been to so many museums with Dad that they all get mixed together."

I sighed in exasperation. "Poor boy, forced to travel the world, skip school, and spend time with Dad while I get a whole two days a year with him!"

"Hey!" Carter turned on me with surprising force. "You get a *home*! You get friends and a normal life and don't wake up each morning wondering what country you're in! You don't—"

The glass case next to us shattered, spraying glass at our feet.

Carter looked at me, bewildered. "Did we just—"

"Like my exploding birthday cake," I grumbled, trying not to let on how startled I was. "You need to control your temper."

"*Me?*"

Alarms began to blare. Red lights pulsed through the corridor. A garbled voice came on the loudspeaker and said something about proceeding calmly to the exits. The French tour group ran past us, screaming in panic, followed by a crowd of remarkably fast old people with walkers and canes.

"Let's finish arguing later, shall we?" I told Carter. "Come on!"

We ran down another corridor, and the sirens died as suddenly as they'd started. The blood-red lights kept pulsing in eerie silence. Then I heard it: the slithering, clacking sounds of scorpions.

"What about Bast?" My voice choked up. "Is she—"

"Don't think about it," Carter said, though, judging from his face, that's *exactly* what he was thinking about. "Keep moving!"

Soon we were hopelessly lost. As far as I could tell, the Egyptian part of the museum was designed to be as confusing as possible, with dead ends and halls that doubled back on themselves. We passed hieroglyphic scrolls, gold jewelry, sarcophagi, statues of pharaohs, and huge chunks of limestone. Why would someone display a rock? Aren't there enough of those in the world?

We saw no one, but the slithering sounds grew louder no matter which way we ran. Finally I rounded a corner and smacked straight into someone.

I yelped and scrambled backwards, only to stumble into Carter. We both fell on our bums in a most unflattering way. It's a miracle Carter didn't impale himself on his own sword.

At first I didn't recognize the girl standing in front of us, which seems strange, looking back on it. Perhaps she was using some sort of magic aura, or perhaps I just didn't want to believe it was *her*.

She looked a bit taller than me. Probably older, too, but not by much. Her black hair was trimmed along her jawline and longer in the front so that it swept over her eyes. She had caramel-colored skin and pretty, vaguely Arab features. Her eyes—lined in black kohl, Egyptian style—were a strange amber color that was either quite beautiful or a bit scary; I couldn't decide which. She had a backpack on her shoulder,

SADIE

and wore sandals and loose-fitting linen clothes like ours. She looked as if she were on her way to a martial arts class. God, now that I think of it, we probably looked the same way. How embarrassing.

I slowly began to realize I'd seen her before. She was the girl with the knife from the British Museum. Before I could say anything, Carter sprang to his feet. He moved in front of me and brandished his sword as if trying to *protect* me. Can you believe the nerve?

"Get—get back!" he stammered.

The girl reached into her sleeve and produced a curved white piece of ivory—an Egyptian wand.

She flicked it to one side, and Carter's sword flew out of his hands and clattered to the floor.

"Don't embarrass yourself," the girl said sternly. "Where is Amos?"

Carter looked too stunned to speak. The girl turned towards me. Her golden eyes were both beautiful *and* scary, I decided, and I didn't like her a bit.

"Well?" she demanded.

I didn't see why I needed to tell her a bloody thing, but an uncomfortable pressure started building in my chest, like a burp trying to get free. I heard myself say, "Amos is gone. He left this morning."

"And the cat demon?"

"That's *my* cat," I said. "And she's a goddess, not a demon. She saved us from the scorpions!"

Carter unfroze. He snatched up his sword and pointed it at the girl again. Full credit for persistence, I suppose.

"Who are you?" he demanded. "What do you want?"

"My name is Zia Rashid." She tilted her head as if listening.

Right on cue, the entire building rumbled. Dust sprinkled from the ceiling, and the slithering sounds of scorpions doubled in volume behind us.

"And right now," Zia continued, sounding a bit disappointed, "I must save your miserable lives. Let's go."

I suppose we could've refused, but our choices seemed to be Zia or the scorpions, so we ran after her.

She passed a case full of statues and casually tapped the glass with her wand. Tiny granite pharaohs and limestone gods stirred at her command. They hopped off their pedestals and crashed through the glass. Some wielded weapons. Others simply cracked their stone knuckles. They let us pass, but stared down the corridor behind us as if waiting for the enemy.

"Hurry," Zia told us. "These will only—"

"Buy us time," I guessed. "Yes, we've heard that before."

"You talk too much," Zia said without stopping.

I was about to make a withering retort. Honestly, I would've put her in her place quite properly. But just then we emerged into an enormous room and my voice abandoned me.

"Whoa," Carter said.

I couldn't help agreeing with him. The place was extremely *whoa*.

The room was the size of a football stadium. One wall was made completely of glass and looked out on the park. In the middle of the room, on a raised platform, an ancient building had been reconstructed. There was a freestanding stone gateway about eight meters tall, and behind that an open courtyard and square structure made of uneven sandstone blocks carved all over on the outside with images of gods and pharaohs and hieroglyphs. Flanking the building's entrance were two columns bathed in eerie light.

"An Egyptian temple," I guessed.

"The Temple of Dendur," Zia said. "Actually it was built by the Romans—"

"When they occupied Egypt," Carter said, like this was delightful information. "Augustus commissioned it."

"Yes," Zia said.

"Fascinating," I murmured. "Would you two like to be left alone with a history textbook?"

Zia scowled at me. "At any rate, the temple was dedicated to Isis, so it will have enough power to open a gate."

"To summon more gods?" I asked.

Zia's eyes flashed angrily. "Accuse me of that again, and I will cut out your tongue. I meant a gateway to get you out of here."

I felt completely lost, but I was getting used to that. We followed Zia up the steps and through the temple's stone gateway.

The courtyard was empty, abandoned by the fleeing museum visitors, which made it feel quite creepy. Giant carvings of gods stared down at me. Hieroglyphic inscriptions were everywhere, and I was afraid that if I concentrated too hard, I might be able to read them.

Zia stopped at the front steps of the temple. She held up her wand and wrote in the air. A familiar hieroglyph burned between the columns.

Open—the same symbol Dad had used at the Rosetta Stone. I waited for something to blow up, but the hieroglyph simply faded.

Zia opened her backpack. "We'll make our stand here until the gate can be opened."

"Why not just open it now?" Carter asked.

"Portals can only appear at auspicious moments," Zia said. "Sunrise, sunset, midnight, eclipses, astrological alignments, the exact time of a god's birth—"

"Oh, come on," I said. "How can you possibly know all that?"

"It takes years to memorize the complete calendar," Zia said. "But the next auspicious moment is easy: high noon. Ten and a half minutes from now."

She didn't check a watch. I wondered how she knew the time so precisely, but I decided it wasn't the most important question.

"Why should we trust you?" I asked. "As I recall, at the British Museum, you wanted to gut us with a knife."

"That would've been simpler." Zia sighed. "Unfortunately, my superiors think you might be *innocents*. So for now, I can't kill you. But I also can't allow you to fall into the hands of the Red Lord. And so...you can trust me."

"Well, I'm convinced," I said. "I feel all warm and fuzzy inside."

Zia reached in her bag and took out four little statues—animal-headed men, each about five centimeters tall. She handed them to me. "Put the Sons of Horus around us at the cardinal points."

"Excuse me?"

"North, south, east, west." She spoke slowly, as if I were an idiot.

"I know compass directions! But—"

"That's north." Zia pointed out the wall of glass. "Figure out the rest."

I did what she asked, though I didn't see how the little men would help. Meanwhile, Zia gave Carter a piece of chalk and told him to draw a circle around us, connecting the statues.

"Magic protection," Carter said. "Like what Dad did at the British Museum."

"Yes," I grumbled. "And we saw how well *that* worked."

Carter ignored me. What else is new? He was so eager to please Zia that he jumped right to the task of drawing his sidewalk art.

Then Zia took something else from her bag—a plain wooden rod like the one our dad had used in London. She spoke a word under her breath, and the rod expanded into a two-meter-long black staff topped with a carved lion's head. She twirled it around single-handedly like a baton—just showing off, I was sure—while holding the wand in her other hand.

Carter finished the chalk circle as the first scorpions appeared at the gallery's entrance.

"How much longer on that gate?" I asked, hoping I didn't sound as terrified as I felt.

"Stay inside the circle no matter what," Zia said. "When the gate opens, jump through. And keep behind me!"

She touched her wand to the chalk circle, spoke another word, and the circle began to glow dark red.

Hundreds of scorpions swarmed towards the temple, turning the floor into a living mass of claws and stingers. Then the woman in brown, Serqet, entered the gallery. She smiled at us coldly.

"Zia," I said, "that's a goddess. She defeated *Bast*. What chance do *you* have?"

Zia held up her staff and the carved lion's head burst into flames—a small red fireball so bright, it lit the entire room. "I am a scribe in the House of Life, Sadie Kane. I am trained to fight gods."

12. A Jump Through the Hourglass

WELL, THAT WAS ALL VERY IMPRESSIVE, I suppose. You should've seen Carter's face—he looked like an excited puppy. [Oh, stop shoving me. You did!]

But I felt much less sure of Miss Zia "I'm-So-Magical" Rashid when the army of scorpions scuttled towards us. I wouldn't have thought it possible so many scorpions existed in the world, much less in Manhattan. The glowing circle round us seemed like insignificant protection against the millions of arachnids crawling over one another, many layers deep, and the woman in brown, who was even more horrible.

From a distance she looked all right, but as she got closer I saw that Serqet's pale skin glistened like an insect shell. Her eyes were beady black. Her long, dark hair was unnaturally thick, as if made from a million bristling bug antennae. And when she opened her mouth, sideways mandibles snapped and retracted outside her regular human teeth.

The goddess stopped about twenty meters away, studying us. Her hateful black eyes fixed on Zia. "Give me the younglings."

Her voice was harsh and raspy, as if she hadn't spoken in centuries.

Zia crossed her staff and wand. "I am mistress of the elements, Scribe of the First Nome. Leave or be destroyed."

Serqet clicked her mandibles in a gruesome foamy grin. Some of her scorpions advanced, but when the first one touched the glowing lines of our protective circle, it sizzled and turned to ashes. Mark my words, *nothing* smells worse than burned scorpion.

The rest of the horrible things retreated, swirling round the goddess and crawling up her legs. With a shudder, I realized they were wriggling into her robes. After a few seconds, all the scorpions had disappeared into the brown folds of her clothes.

The air seemed to darken behind Serqet, as if she were casting an enormous shadow. Then the darkness rose up and took the form of a massive scorpion tail, arcing over Serqet's head. It lashed down at us at blazing speed, but Zia raised her wand and the sting glanced off the ivory tip with a hissing sound. Steam rolled off Zia's wand, smelling of sulfur.

Zia pointed her staff towards the goddess, engulfing her body in fire. Serqet screamed and staggered backwards, but the fire died almost instantly. It left Serqet's robes seared and smoking, but the goddess looked more enraged than hurt.

"Your days are past, magician. The House is weak. Lord Set will lay waste to this land."

Zia threw her wand like a boomerang. It smashed into the shadowy scorpion tail and exploded in a blinding flash of light. Serqet lurched back and averted her eyes, and as she did, Zia reached into her sleeve and brought out something small—something closed inside her fist.

The wand was a diversion, I thought. *A magician's sleight of hand.*

Then Zia did something reckless: she leaped out of the magic circle—the very thing she'd warned us not to do.

"Zia!" Carter called. "The gate!"

I glanced behind me, and my heart almost stopped. The space between the two columns at the temple's entrance was now a vertical tunnel of sand, as if I were looking into the funnel of an enormous sideways hourglass. I could feel it tugging at me, pulling me towards it with magical gravity.

"I'm not going in *there*," I insisted, but another flash of light brought my attention back to Zia.

She and the goddess were involved in a dangerous dance. Zia twirled and spun with her fiery staff, and everywhere she passed, she left a trail of flames burning in the air. I had to admit it: Zia was almost as graceful and impressive as Bast.

I had the oddest desire to help. I wanted—very badly, in fact—to step outside the circle and engage in combat. It was a completely mad urge, of course. What could I possibly have done? But still I felt I shouldn't—or *couldn't*—jump through the gate without helping Zia.

"Sadie!" Carter grabbed me and pulled me back. Without my even realizing it, my foot had almost stepped across the line of chalk. "What are you thinking?"

I didn't have an answer, but I stared at Zia and mumbled in a sort of trance, "She's going to use ribbons. They won't work."

"What?" Carter demanded. "Come on, we've got to go through the gate!"

Just then Zia opened her fist and small red tendrils of cloth fluttered into the air. *Ribbons.* How had I known? They zipped about like living things—like eels in water—and began to grow larger.

Serqet was still concentrating on the fire, trying to keep Zia from caging her. At first she didn't seem to notice the ribbons, which grew until they were several meters long. I counted five, six, seven of them in all. They zipped around, orbiting Serqet, ripping through her shadow scorpion as if it were a harmless illusion. Finally they wrapped around Serqet's body, pinning her arms and legs. She screamed as if the ribbons burned her. She dropped to her knees, and the shadow scorpion disintegrated into an inky haze.

Zia spun to a stop. She pointed her staff at the goddess's face. The ribbons began to glow, and the goddess hissed in pain, cursing in a language I didn't know.

"I bind you with the Seven Ribbons of Hathor," Zia said. "Release your host or your essence will burn forever."

"Your *death* will last forever!" Serqet snarled. "You have made an enemy of Set!"

Zia twisted her staff, and Serqet fell sideways, writhing and smoking.

"I will...not..." the goddess hissed. But then her black eyes turned milky white, and she lay still.

"The gate!" Carter warned. "Zia, come on! I think it's closing!"

He was right. The tunnel of sand seemed to be moving a bit more slowly. The tug of its magic did not feel as strong.

Zia approached the fallen goddess. She touched Serqet's forehead, and black smoke billowed from the goddess's mouth. Serqet transformed and shrank until we were looking at a completely different woman wrapped in red ribbons. She had pale skin and black hair, but otherwise she didn't look anything like Serqet. She looked, well, *human*.

"Who is that?" I asked.

"The host," Zia said. "Some poor mortal who—"

She looked up with a start. The black haze was no longer dissipating. It was getting thicker and darker again, swirling into a more solid form.

"Impossible," Zia said. "The ribbons are too powerful. Serqet *can't* re-form unless—"

"Well, she *is* re-forming," Carter yelled, "and our exit is closing! Let's go!"

I couldn't believe he was willing to jump into a churning wall of sand, but as I watched the black cloud take the shape of a two-story-tall scorpion—a very *angry* scorpion—I made my decision.

"Coming!" I yelled.

"Zia!" Carter yelled. "Now!"

"Perhaps you're right," the magician decided. She turned, and together we ran and plunged straight into the swirling vortex.

13. I Face the Killer Turkey

MY TURN.

First of all, Sadie's "puppy dog" comment was totally out of line. I was *not* starry-eyed about Zia. It's just that I don't meet a lot of people who can throw fireballs and battle gods. [Stop making faces at me, Sadie. You look like Khufu.]

Anyway, we plunged into the sand tunnel.

Everything went dark. My stomach tingled with that top-of-the-roller-coaster weightlessness as I hurtled forward. Hot winds whipped around me, and my skin burned.

Then I tumbled out onto a cold tile floor, and Sadie and Zia crashed on top of me.

"*Ow!*" I grumbled.

The first thing I noticed was the fine layer of sand covering my body like powdered sugar. Then my eyes adjusted to the harsh light. We were in a big building like a shopping mall, with crowds bustling around us.

No . . . not a mall. It was a two-level airport concourse, with shops, lots of windows, and polished steel columns. Outside, it was dark, so I knew we must be in a different time zone. Announcements echoed over the intercom in a language that sounded like Arabic.

Sadie spit sand out of her mouth. "Yuck!"

"Come on," Zia said. "We can't stay here."

I struggled to my feet. People were streaming past—some in Western clothes, some in robes and headscarves. A family arguing in German rushed by and almost ran over me with their suitcases.

Then I turned and saw something I recognized. In the middle of the concourse stood a life-size replica of an Ancient Egyptian boat made from glowing display cases—a sales counter for perfume and jewelry.

"This is the Cairo airport," I said.

"Yes," Zia said. "Now, let's go!"

"Why the rush? Can Serqet...can she follow us through that sand gate?"

Zia shook her head. "An artifact overheats whenever it creates a gate. It requires a twelve-hour cooldown before it can be used again. But we still have to worry about airport security. Unless you'd like to meet the Egyptian police, you'll come with me *now*."

She grabbed our arms and steered us through the crowd. We must've looked like beggars in our old-fashioned clothes, covered head-to-toe in sand. People gave us a wide berth, but nobody tried to stop us.

"Why are we here?" Sadie demanded.

"To see the ruins of Heliopolis," Zia said.

"Inside an *airport?*" Sadie asked.

I remembered something Dad had told me years ago, and my scalp tingled.

"Sadie, the ruins are *under* us." I looked at Zia. "That's right, isn't it?"

She nodded. "The ancient city was pillaged centuries ago. Some of its monuments were carted away, like Cleopatra's two needles. Most of its temples were broken down to make new buildings. What was left disappeared under Cairo's suburbs. The largest section is under this airport."

"And how does that help us?" Sadie asked.

Zia kicked open a maintenance door. On the other side was a broom closet. Zia muttered a command—*"Sahad"*—and the image of the closet shimmered and disappeared, revealing a set of stone steps leading down.

"Because not *all* Heliopolis is in ruins," Zia said. "Follow closely. And *touch nothing.*"

The stairs must've led down about seven million miles, because we descended *forever.* The passage had been made for miniature people, too. We had to crouch and crawl most of the way, and even so, I bonked my head on the ceiling a dozen times. The only light was from a ball of fire in Zia's palm, which made shadows dance across the walls.

I'd been in places like this before—tunnels inside pyramids, tombs my dad had excavated—but I've never liked them. Millions of tons of rock above me seemed to crush the air out of my lungs.

Finally we reached the bottom. The tunnel opened up, and

Zia stopped abruptly. After my eyes adjusted, I saw why. We were standing at the edge of a chasm.

A single wooden plank spanned the void. On the opposite ledge, two jackal-headed granite warriors flanked a doorway, their spears crossed over the entrance.

Sadie sighed. "Please, no more psychotic statues."

"Do not joke," Zia warned. "This is an entrance to the First Nome, the oldest branch of the House of Life, headquarters for all magicians. My job was to bring you here safely, but I cannot help you cross. Each magician must unbar the path for herself, and the challenge is different for each supplicant."

She looked at Sadie expectantly, which annoyed me. First Bast, now Zia—both of them treated Sadie like she should have some kind of superpowers. I mean, okay, so she'd been able to blast the library doors apart, but why didn't anyone look at *me* to do cool tricks?

Plus, I was still annoyed with Sadie for the comments she'd made at the museum in New York—how I had it so good traveling the world with Dad. She had no idea how often I wanted to complain about the constant traveling, how many days I wished I didn't have to get on a plane and could just be like a normal kid going to school and making friends. But I couldn't complain. *You always have to look impeccable,* Dad had told me. And he didn't just mean my clothes. He meant my attitude. With Mom gone, I was all he had. Dad needed me to be strong. Most days, I didn't mind. I loved my dad. But it was also hard.

Sadie didn't understand that. *She* had it easy. And now

she seemed to be getting all the attention, as if *she* were the special one. It wasn't fair.

Then I heard Dad's voice in my head: "Fairness means everyone gets what they need. And the only way to get what you need is to make it happen yourself."

I don't know what got into me, but I drew my sword and marched across the plank. It was like my legs were working by themselves, not waiting for my brain. Part of me thought: *This is a really bad idea.* But part of me answered: *No, we do not fear this.* And the voice didn't sound like mine.

"Carter!" Sadie cried.

I kept walking. I tried not to look down at the yawning void under my feet, but the sheer size of the chasm made me dizzy. I felt like one of those gyroscope toys, spinning and wobbling as I crossed the narrow plank.

As I got closer to the opposite side, the doorway between the two statues began to glow, like a curtain of red light.

I took a deep breath. Maybe the red light was a portal, like the gate of sand. If I just charged through fast enough....

Then the first dagger shot out of the tunnel.

My sword was in motion before I realized it. The dagger should've impaled me in the chest, but somehow I deflected it with my blade and sent it sailing into the abyss. Two more daggers shot out of the tunnel. I'd never had the best reflexes, but now they sped up. I ducked one dagger and hooked the other with the curved blade of my sword, turned the dagger and flung it back into the tunnel. *How the heck did I do that?*

I advanced to the end of the plank and slashed through

the red light, which flickered and died. I waited for the statues to come alive, but nothing happened. The only sound was a dagger clattering against the rocks in the chasm far below.

The doorway began to glow again. The red light coalesced into a strange form: a five-foot-tall bird with a man's head. I raised my sword, but Zia yelled, "Carter, no!"

The bird creature folded his wings. His eyes, lined with kohl, narrowed as they studied me. A black ornamental wig glistened on his head, and his face was etched with wrinkles. One of those fake braided pharaoh beards was stuck on his chin like a backward ponytail. He didn't look hostile, except for the red flickering light all around him, and the fact that from the neck down he was the world's largest killer turkey.

Then a chilling thought occurred to me: This was a bird with a human head, the same form I'd imagined taking when I slept in Amos's house, when my soul left my body and flew to Phoenix. I had no idea what that meant, but it scared me.

The bird creature scratched at the stone floor. Then, unexpectedly, he smiled.

"*Pari, niswa nafeer*," he told me, or at least that's what it sounded like.

Zia gasped. She and Sadie were standing behind me now, their faces pale. Apparently they'd managed to cross the chasm without my noticing.

Finally Zia seemed to collect herself. She bowed to the bird creature. Sadie followed her example.

The creature winked at me, as if we'd just shared a joke. Then he vanished. The red light faded. The statues retracted their arms, uncrossing their spears from the entrance.

"That's it?" I asked. "What did the turkey say?"

Zia looked at me with something like fear. "That was *not* a turkey, Carter. That was a *ba*."

I'd heard my dad use that word before, but I couldn't place it. "Another monster?"

"A human soul," Zia said. "In this case, a spirit of the dead. A magician from ancient times, come back to serve as a guardian. They watch the entrances of the House."

She studied my face as if I'd just developed some terrible rash.

"What?" I demanded. "Why are you looking at me that way?"

"Nothing," she said. "We must hurry."

She squeezed by me on the ledge and disappeared into the tunnel.

Sadie was staring at me too.

"All right," I said. "What did the bird guy say? You understood it?"

She nodded uneasily. "He mistook you for someone else. He must have bad eyesight."

"Because?"

"Because he said, 'Go forth, good king.'"

I was in a daze after that. We passed through the tunnel and entered a vast underground city of halls and chambers, but I only remember bits and pieces of it.

The ceilings soared to twenty or thirty feet, so it didn't feel like we were underground. Every chamber was lined with massive stone columns like the ones I'd seen in Egyptian ruins, but these were in perfect condition, brightly painted to resemble palm trees, with carved green fronds at the top, so I felt like I was walking through a petrified forest. Fires burned in copper braziers. They didn't seem to make any smoke, but the air smelled good, like a marketplace for spices—cinnamon, clove, nutmeg, and others I couldn't identify. The city smelled like Zia. I realized that this was her home.

We saw a few other people—mostly older men and women. Some wore linen robes, some modern clothes. One guy in a business suit walked past with a black leopard on a leash, as if that were completely normal. Another guy barked orders to a small army of brooms, mops, and buckets that were scuttling around, cleaning up the city.

"Like that cartoon," Sadie said. "Where Mickey Mouse tries to do magic and the brooms keep splitting and toting water."

"'The Sorcerer's Apprentice,'" Zia said. "You do know that was based on an Egyptian story, don't you?"

Sadie just stared back. I knew how she felt. It was too much to process.

We walked through a hall of jackal-headed statues, and I could swear their eyes watched us as we passed. A few minutes later, Zia led us through an open-air market—if you can call anything "open-air" underground—with dozens of stalls selling weird items like boomerang wands, animated clay dolls, parrots, cobras, papyrus scrolls, and hundreds of different glittering amulets.

Next we crossed a path of stones over a dark river teeming with fish. I thought they were perch until I saw their vicious teeth.

"Are those piranhas?" I asked.

"Tiger fish from the Nile," Zia said. "Like piranhas, except these can weigh up to sixteen pounds."

I watched my step more closely after that.

We turned a corner and passed an ornate building carved out of black rock. Seated pharaohs were chiseled into the walls, and the doorway was shaped like a coiled serpent.

"What's in there?" Sadie asked.

We peeked inside and saw rows of children—maybe two dozen in all, about six to ten years old or so—sitting cross-legged on cushions. They were hunched over brass bowls, peering intently into some sort of liquid and speaking under their breath. At first I thought it was a classroom, but there was no sign of a teacher, and the chamber was lit only by a few candles. Judging by the number of empty seats, the room was meant to hold twice as many kids.

"Our initiates," Zia said, "learning to scry. The First Nome must keep in contact with our brethren all over the world. We use our youngest as . . . operators, I suppose you would say."

"So you've got bases like this all over the world?"

"Most are much smaller, but yes."

I remembered what Amos had told us about the nomes. "Egypt is the First Nome. New York is the Twenty-first. What's the last one, the Three-hundred-and-sixtieth?"

"That would be Antarctica," Zia said. "A punishment assignment. Nothing there but a couple of cold magicians and some magic penguins."

"Magic penguins?"

154

"Don't ask."

Sadie pointed to the children inside. "How does it work? They see images in the water?"

"It's oil," Zia said. "But yes."

"So few," Sadie said. "Are these the only initiates in the whole city?"

"In the whole *world*," Zia corrected. "There were more before—" She stopped herself.

"Before what?" I asked.

"Nothing," Zia said darkly. "Initiates do our scrying because young minds are most receptive. Magicians begin training no later than the age of ten . . . with a few dangerous exceptions."

"You mean us," I said.

She glanced at me apprehensively, and I knew she was still thinking about what the bird spirit had called me: a *good king*. It seemed so unreal, like our family name in that *Blood of the Pharaohs* scroll. How could I be related to some ancient kings? And even if I was, *I* certainly wasn't a king. I had no kingdom. I didn't even have my single suitcase anymore.

"They'll be waiting for you," Zia said. "Come along."

We walked so far, my feet began to ache.

Finally we arrived at a crossroads. On the right was a massive set of bronze doors with fires blazing on either side; on the left, a twenty-foot-tall sphinx carved into the wall. A doorway nestled between its paws, but it was bricked in and covered in cobwebs.

"That looks like the Sphinx at Giza," I said.

"That's because we are directly under the *real* Sphinx," Zia said. "That tunnel leads straight up to it. Or it used to, before it was sealed."

"But..." I did some quick calculations in my head. "The Sphinx is, like, twenty miles from the Cairo Airport."

"Roughly."

"No way we've walked that far."

Zia actually smiled, and I couldn't help noticing how pretty her eyes were. "Distance changes in magic places, Carter. Surely you've learned that by now."

Sadie cleared her throat. "So why is the tunnel closed, then?"

"The Sphinx was too popular with archaeologists," Zia said. "They kept digging around. Finally, in the 1980s, they discovered the first part of the tunnel under the Sphinx."

"Dad told me about that!" I said. "But he said the tunnel was a dead end."

"It was when we got through with it. We couldn't let the archaeologists know how much they're missing. Egypt's leading archaeologist recently speculated that they've only discovered thirty percent of the ancient ruins in Egypt. In truth, they've only discovered one tenth, and not even the *interesting* tenth."

"What about King Tut's tomb?" I protested.

"That boy king?" Zia rolled her eyes. "*Boring.* You should see some of the *good* tombs."

I felt a little hurt. Dad had named me after Howard Carter, the guy who discovered King Tut's tomb, so I'd always felt a personal attachment to it. If that wasn't a "good" tomb, I wondered what was.

Zia turned to face the bronze doors.

"This is the Hall of Ages." She placed her palm against the seal, which bore the symbol of the House of Life.

The hieroglyphs began to glow, and the doors swung open.

Zia turned to us, her expression deadly serious. "You are about to meet the Chief Lector. Behave yourselves, unless you wish to be turned into insects."

14. A French Guy Almost Kills Us

THE LAST COUPLE OF DAYS I'd seen a lot of crazy things, but the Hall of Ages took the prize.

Double rows of stone pillars held up a ceiling so high, you could've parked a blimp under it with no trouble. A shimmering blue carpet that looked like water ran down the center of the hall, which was so long, I couldn't see the end even though it was brightly lit. Balls of fire floated around like helium basketballs, changing color whenever they bumped into one another. Millions of tiny hieroglyphic symbols also drifted through the air, randomly combining into words and then breaking apart.

I grabbed a pair of glowing red legs.

They walked across my palm before jumping off and dissolving.

But the weirdest things were the *displays*.

I don't know what else to call them. Between the columns on either side of us, images shifted, coming into focus and then blurring out again like holograms in a sandstorm.

"Come on," Zia told us. "And don't spend too much time looking."

It was impossible not to. The first twenty feet or so, the magical scenes cast a golden light across the hall. A blazing sun rose above an ocean. A mountain emerged from the water, and I had the feeling I was watching the beginning of the world. Giants strode across the Nile Valley: a man with black skin and the head of a jackal, a lioness with bloody fangs, a beautiful woman with wings of light.

Sadie stepped off the rug. In a trance, she reached toward the images.

"Stay on the carpet!" Zia grabbed Sadie's hand and pulled her back toward the center of the hall. "You are seeing the Age of the Gods. No mortal should dwell on these images."

"But..." Sadie blinked. "They're only pictures, aren't they?"

"Memories," Zia said, "so powerful they could destroy your mind."

"Oh," Sadie said in a small voice.

We kept walking. The images changed to silver. I saw armies clashing—Egyptians in kilts and sandals and leather armor, fighting with spears. A tall, dark-skinned man in red-and-white armor placed a double crown on his head: Narmer, the king who united Upper and Lower Egypt. Sadie was right: he did look a bit like Dad.

"This is the Old Kingdom," I guessed. "The first great age of Egypt."

Zia nodded. As we walked down the hall, we saw workers building the first step pyramid out of stone. Another few steps, and the biggest pyramid of all rose from the desert at Giza. Its outer layer of smooth white casing stones gleamed in the sun. Ten thousand workers gathered at its base and knelt before the pharaoh, who raised his hands to the sun, dedicating his own tomb.

"Khufu," I said.

"The baboon?" Sadie asked, suddenly interested.

"No, the pharaoh who built the Great Pyramid," I said. "It was the tallest structure in the world for almost four thousand years."

Another few steps, and the images turned from silver to coppery.

"The Middle Kingdom," Zia announced. "A bloody, chaotic time. And yet this is when the House of Life came to maturity."

The scenes shifted more rapidly. We watched armies fighting, temples being built, ships sailing on the Nile, and magicians throwing fire. Every step covered hundreds of years, and yet the hall still went on forever. For the first time I understood just how ancient Egypt was.

We crossed another threshold, and the light turned bronze.

"The New Kingdom," I guessed. "The last time Egypt was ruled by Egyptians."

Zia said nothing, but I watched scenes passing that my dad had described to me: Hatshepsut, the greatest female pharaoh, putting on a fake beard and ruling Egypt as a man; Ramesses the Great leading his chariots into battle.

I saw magicians dueling in a palace. A man in tattered robes, with a shaggy black beard and wild eyes, threw down his staff, which turned into a serpent and devoured a dozen other snakes.

I got a lump in my throat. "Is that—"

"Musa," Zia said. "Or Moshe, as his own people knew him. You call him Moses. The only foreigner ever to defeat the House in a magic duel."

I stared at her. "You're kidding, right?"

"We would not kid about such a thing."

The scene shifted again. I saw a man standing over a table of battle figurines: wooden toy ships, soldiers, and chariots. The man was dressed like a pharaoh, but his face looked oddly familiar. He looked up and seemed to smile right at me. With a chill, I realized he had the same face as the *ba,* the bird-faced spirit who'd challenged me on the bridge.

"Who is that?" I asked.

"Nectanebo II," Zia said. "The last native Egyptian king, and the last sorcerer pharaoh. He could move entire armies, create or destroy navies by moving pieces on his board, but in the end, it was not enough."

We stepped over another line and the images shimmered blue. "These are the Ptolemaic times," Zia said. "Alexander the Great conquered the known world, including Egypt. He set up his general Ptolemy as the new pharaoh, and founded a line of Greek kings to rule over Egypt."

The Ptolemaic section of the hall was shorter, and seemed sad compared to all the others. The temples were smaller. The kings and queens looked desperate, or lazy, or simply apathetic.

There were no great battles...except toward the end. I saw Romans march into the city of Alexandria. I saw a woman with dark hair and a white dress drop a snake into her blouse.

"Cleopatra," Zia said, "the seventh queen of that name. She tried to stand against the might of Rome, and she lost. When she took her life, the last line of pharaohs ended. Egypt, the great nation, faded. Our language was forgotten. The ancient rites were suppressed. The House of Life survived, but we were forced into hiding."

We passed into an area of red light, and history began to look familiar. I saw Arab armies riding into Egypt, then the Turks. Napoleon marched his army under the shadow of the pyramids. The British came and built the Suez Canal. Slowly Cairo grew into a modern city. And the old ruins faded farther and farther under the sands of the desert.

"Each year," Zia said, "the Hall of Ages grows longer to encompass our history. Up until the present."

I was so dazed I didn't even realize we'd reached the end of the hall until Sadie grabbed my arm.

In front of us stood a dais and on it an empty throne, a gilded wooden chair with a flail and a shepherd's crook carved in the back—the ancient symbols of the pharaoh.

On the step below the throne sat the oldest man I'd ever seen. His skin was like lunch-bag paper—brown, thin, and crinkled. White linen robes hung loosely off his small frame. A leopard skin was draped around his shoulders, and his hand shakily held a big wooden staff, which I was sure he was going to drop any minute. But weirdest of all, the glowing hiero-glyphs in the air seemed to be coming *from him*. Multicolored symbols popped up all around him and floated away as if he were some sort of magic bubble machine.

At first I wasn't sure he was even alive. His milky eyes stared into space. Then he focused on me, and electricity coursed through my body.

He wasn't just looking at me. He was scanning me—reading my entire being.

Hide, something inside me said.

I didn't know where the voice came from, but my stomach clenched. My whole body tensed as if I were bracing for a hit, and the electrical feeling subsided.

The old man raised an eyebrow as if I'd surprised him. He glanced behind him and said something in a language I didn't recognize.

A second man stepped out of the shadows. I wanted to yelp. He was the guy who'd been with Zia in the British Museum—the one with the cream-colored robes and the forked beard.

The bearded man glared at Sadie and me.

"I am Desjardins," he said with a French accent. "My master, Chief Lector Iskandar, welcomes you to the House of Life."

I couldn't think what to say to that, so of course I asked a stupid question. "He's really old. Why isn't he sitting on the throne?"

Desjardins' nostrils flared, but the old dude, Iskandar, just chuckled, and said something else in that other language.

Desjardins translated stiffly: "The master says thank you for noticing; he is in fact *really* old. But the throne is for the pharaoh. It has been vacant since the fall of Egypt to Rome. It is…*comment dit-on?* Symbolic. The Chief Lector's role is to serve and protect the pharaoh. Therefore he sits at the foot of the throne."

I looked at Iskandar a little nervously. I wondered how many years he'd been sitting on that step. "If you ... if he can understand English ... what language is he speaking?"

Desjardins sniffed. "The Chief Lector understands many things. But he prefers to speak Alexandrian Greek, his birth tongue."

Sadie cleared her throat. "Sorry, his *birth* tongue? Wasn't Alexander the Great way back in the blue section, thousands of years ago? You make it sound like Lord Salamander is—"

"Lord *Iskandar*," Desjardins hissed. "Show respect!"

Something clicked in my mind: back in Brooklyn, Amos had talked about the magicians' law against summoning gods—a law made in Roman times by the Chief Lector ... Iskandar. Surely it had to be a different guy. Maybe we were talking to Iskandar the XXVII or something.

The old man looked me in the eyes. He smiled, as if he knew exactly what I was thinking. He said something else in Greek, and Desjardins translated.

"The master says not to worry. You will not be held responsible for the past crimes of your family. At least, not until we have investigated you further."

"Gee ... thanks," I said.

"Do not mock our generosity, boy," Desjardins warned. "Your father broke our most important law twice: once at Cleopatra's Needle, when he tried to summon the gods and your mother died assisting him. Then again at the British

Museum, when your father was foolish enough to use the Rosetta Stone itself. Now your uncle too is missing—"

"You know what's happened to Amos?" Sadie blurted out.

Desjardins scowled. "Not yet," he admitted.

"You have to find him!" Sadie cried. "Don't you have some sort of GPS magic or—"

"We are searching," Desjardins said. "But you cannot worry about Amos. You must stay here. You must be . . . trained."

I got the impression he was going to say a different word, something not as nice as *trained*.

Iskandar spoke directly to me. His tone sounded kindly.

"The master warns that the Demon Days begin tomorrow at sunset," Desjardins translated. "You must be kept safe."

"But we have to find our dad!" I said. "Dangerous gods are on the loose out there. We saw Serqet. And Set!"

At these names, Iskandar's expression tightened. He turned and gave Desjardins what sounded like an order. Desjardins protested. Iskandar repeated his statement.

Desjardins clearly didn't like it, but he bowed to his master. Then he turned toward me. "The Chief Lector wishes to hear your story."

So I told him, with Sadie jumping in whenever I stopped to take a breath. The funny thing was, we both left out certain things without planning to. We didn't mention Sadie's magic abilities, or the encounter with the *ba* who'd called me a king. It was like I literally *couldn't* mention those things. Whenever I tried, the voice inside my head whispered, *Not that part. Be silent.*

When I was done, I glanced at Zia. She said nothing, but she was studying me with a troubled expression.

Iskandar traced a circle on the step with the butt of his staff. More hieroglyphs popped into the air and floated away.

After several seconds, Desjardins seemed to grow impatient. He stepped forward and glared at us. "You are lying. That could not have been Set. He would need a powerful host to remain in this world. *Very* powerful."

"Look, you," Sadie said. "I don't know what all this rubbish is about hosts, but I saw Set with my own eyes. You were there at the British Museum—you must have done, too. And if Carter saw him in Phoenix, Arizona, then..." She looked at me doubtfully. "Then he's probably not crazy."

"Thanks, Sis," I mumbled, but Sadie was just getting started.

"And as for Serqet, she's real too! Our friend, my cat, Bast, died protecting us!"

"So," Desjardins said coldly, "you admit to consorting with gods. That makes our investigation much easier. Bast is not your *friend*. The gods caused the downfall of Egypt. It is forbidden to call on their powers. Magicians are sworn to keep the gods from interfering in the mortal world. We must use all our power to fight them."

"Bast said you were paranoid," Sadie added.

The magician clenched his fists, and the air tingled with the weird smell of ozone, like during a thunderstorm. The hairs on my neck stood straight up. Before anything bad could happen, Zia stepped in front of us.

"Lord Desjardins," she pleaded, "there *was* something

strange. When I ensnared the scorpion goddess, she re-formed almost instantly. I could not return her to the Duat, even with the Seven Ribbons. I could only break her hold on the host for a moment. Perhaps the rumors of other escapes—"

"What other escapes?" I asked.

She glanced at me reluctantly. "Other gods, *many* of them, released since last night from artifacts all over the world. Like a chain reaction—"

"Zia!" Desjardins snapped. "That information is not for sharing."

"Look," I said, "lord, sir, whatever—Bast warned us this would happen. She said Set would release more gods."

"Master," Zia pleaded, "if Ma'at is weakening, if Set is increasing chaos, perhaps that is why I could not banish Serqet."

"Ridiculous," Desjardins said. "You are skilled, Zia, but perhaps you were not skilled enough for this encounter. And as for these two, the contamination must be contained."

Zia's face reddened. She turned her attention to Iskandar. "Master, please. Give me a chance with them."

"You forget your place," Desjardins snapped. "These two are guilty and must be destroyed."

My throat started closing up. I looked at Sadie. If we had to make a run for it down that long hall, I didn't like our chances....

The old man finally looked up. He smiled at Zia with true affection. For a second I wondered if she were his great-great-great-granddaughter or something. He spoke in Greek, and Zia bowed deeply.

Desjardins looked ready to explode. He swept his robes away from his feet and marched behind the throne.

"The Chief Lector will allow Zia to test you," he growled. "Meanwhile, I will seek out the truth—or the lies—in your story. You will be punished for the lies."

I turned to Iskandar and copied Zia's bow. Sadie did the same.

"Thank you, master," I said.

The old man studied me for a long time. Again I felt as if he were trying to burn into my soul—not in an angry way. More out of concern. Then he mumbled something, and I understood two words: *Nectanebo* and *ba*.

He opened his hand and a flood of glowing hieroglyphs poured out, swarming around the dais. There was a blinding flash of light, and when I could see again, the dais was empty. The two men were gone.

Zia turned toward us, her expression grim. "I will show you to your quarters. In the morning, your testing begins. We will see what magic you know, and how you know it."

I wasn't sure what she meant by that, but I exchanged an uneasy look with Sadie.

"Sounds fun," Sadie ventured. "And if we fail this test?"

Zia regarded her coldly. "This is not the sort of test you fail, Sadie Kane. You pass or you die."

15. A Godly Birthday Party

THEY TOOK CARTER TO A DIFFERENT dormitory, so I don't know how he slept. But *I* couldn't get a wink.

It would've been hard enough with Zia's comments about passing our tests or dying, but the girls' dormitory just wasn't as posh as Amos's mansion. The stone walls sweated moisture. Creepy pictures of Egyptian monsters danced across the ceiling in the torchlight. I got a floating cot to sleep in, and the other girls in training—*initiates*, Zia had called them—were much younger than me, so when the old dorm matron told them to go to sleep straightaway, they actually *obeyed*. The matron waved her hand and the torches went out. She shut the door behind her, and I could hear the sound of locks clicking.

Lovely. Imprisoned in a nursery school dungeon.

I stared into the dark until I heard the other girls snoring. A single thought kept bothering me: an urge I just couldn't shake. Finally I crept out of bed and tugged on my boots.

I felt my way to the door. I tugged at the handle. Locked, as I suspected. I was tempted to kick it till I remembered what Zia had done in the Cairo Airport broom closet.

I pressed my palm against the door and whispered, "*Sahad.*" Locks clicked. The door swung open. Handy trick.

Outside, the corridors were dark and empty. Apparently, there wasn't much nightlife in the First Nome. I sneaked through the city back the way we'd come and saw nothing but an occasional cobra slithering across the floor. After the last couple of days, that didn't even faze me. I thought about trying to find Carter, but I wasn't sure where they'd taken him, and honestly, I wanted to do this on my own.

After our last argument in New York, I wasn't sure how I felt about my brother. The idea that he could be jealous of *my* life while he got to travel the world with Dad—please! And he had the nerve to call my life *normal?* All right, I had a few mates at school like Liz and Emma, but my life was hardly easy. If Carter made a social faux pas or met people he didn't like, he could just move on! I had to stay put. I couldn't answer simple questions like "Where are your parents?" or "What does your family do?" or even "Where are you from?" without exposing just how odd my situation was. I was always the *different* girl. The mixed-race girl, the American who wasn't American, the girl whose mother had died, the girl with the absent father, the girl who made trouble in class, the girl who couldn't concentrate on her lessons. After a while one learns that blending in simply doesn't work. If people are going to single me out, I might as well give them something to stare at. Red stripes in my hair? Why not! Combat boots with the school uniform? Absolutely.

Headmaster says, "I'll have to call your parents, young lady." I say, "Good luck." Carter didn't know anything about my life.

But enough of that. The point was, I decided to do this particular bit of exploring alone, and after a few wrong turns, I found my way back to the Hall of Ages.

What was I up to, you may ask? I certainly didn't want to meet Monsieur Evil again or creepy old Lord Salamander.

But I *did* want to see those images—*memories*, Zia had called them.

I pushed open the bronze doors. Inside, the hall seemed deserted. No balls of fire floated around the ceiling. No glowing hieroglyphs. But images still shimmered between the columns, washing the hall with strange, multicolored light.

I took a few nervous steps.

I wanted another look at the Age of the Gods. On our first trip through the hall, something about those images had shaken me. I knew Carter thought I'd gone into a dangerous trance, and Zia had warned that the scenes would melt my brain; but I had a feeling she was just trying to scare me off. I felt a connection to those images, like there was an answer within—a vital piece of information I needed.

I stepped off the carpet and approached the curtain of golden light. I saw sand dunes shifting in the wind, storm clouds brewing, crocodiles sliding down the Nile. I saw a vast hall full of revelers. I touched the image.

And I was in the palace of the gods.

Huge beings swirled around me, changing shape from human to animal to pure energy. On a throne in the center of the room sat a muscular African man in rich black robes. He had a handsome face and warm brown eyes. His hands looked strong enough to crush rocks.

The other gods celebrated round him. Music played—a sound so powerful that the air burned. At the man's side stood a beautiful woman in white, her belly swollen as if she were a few months pregnant. Her form flickered; at times she seemed to have multicolored wings. Then she turned in my direction and I gasped. She had my mother's face.

She didn't seem to notice me. In fact, none of the gods did, until a voice behind me said, "Are you a ghost?"

I turned and saw a good-looking boy of about sixteen, dressed in black robes. His complexion was pale, but he had lovely brown eyes like the man on the throne. His black hair was long and tousled—rather wild, but it worked for me. He tilted his head, and it finally occurred to me that he'd asked me a question.

I tried to think of something to say. Excuse me? Hello? Marry me? Anything would've done. But all I could manage was a shake of the head.

"Not a ghost, eh?" he mused. "A *ba* then?" He gestured towards the throne. "Watch, but do not interfere."

Somehow I wasn't interested in watching the throne so much, but the boy in black dissolved into a shadow and disappeared, leaving me no further distraction.

"Isis," said the man on the throne.

The pregnant woman turned towards him and beamed. "My lord Osiris. Happy birthday."

"Thank you, my love. And soon we shall mark the birth

of our son—Horus, the great one! His new incarnation shall be his greatest yet. He shall bring peace and prosperity to the world."

Isis took her husband's hand. Music kept playing around them, gods celebrating, the very air swirling in a dance of creation.

Suddenly the palace doors blew open. A hot wind made the torches sputter.

A man strode into the hall. He was tall and strong, almost a twin to Osiris, but with dark red skin, blood-colored robes, and a pointed beard. He looked human, except when he smiled. Then his teeth turned to fangs. His face flickered—sometimes human, sometimes strangely wolflike. I had to stifle a scream, because I'd seen that wolfish face before.

The dancing stopped. The music died.

Osiris rose from his throne. "Set," he said in a dangerous tone. "Why have you come?"

Set laughed, and the tension in the room broke. Despite his cruel eyes, he had a wonderful laugh—nothing like the screeching he'd done at the British Museum. It was carefree and friendly, as if he couldn't possibly mean any harm.

"I come to celebrate my brother's birthday, of course!" he exclaimed. "And I bring entertainment!"

He gestured behind him. Four huge men with the heads of wolves marched into the room, carrying a jewel-encrusted golden coffin.

My heart began to race. It was the same box Set had used to imprison my dad at the British Museum.

No! I wanted to scream. *Don't trust him!*

But the assembled gods oohed and aahed, admiring the box, which was painted with gold and red hieroglyphs, trimmed with jade and opals. The wolf-men set down the box, and I saw it had no lid. The interior was lined with black linen.

"This sleeping casket," Set announced, "was made by my finest craftsmen, using the most expensive materials. Its value is beyond measure. The god who lies within, even for a night, will see his powers increase tenfold! His wisdom will never falter. His strength will never fail. It is a gift"—he smiled slyly at Osiris—"for the *one and only* god who fits within perfectly!"

I wouldn't have queued up first, but the gods surged forward. They pushed each other out of the way to get at the golden coffin. Some climbed in but were too short. Others were much too big. Even when they tried to change their shapes, the gods had no luck, as if the magic of the box were thwarting them. No one fit exactly. Gods grumbled and complained as others, anxious to try, pushed them to the floor.

Set turned to Osiris with a good-natured laugh. "Well, brother, we have no winner yet. Will you try? Only the best of the gods can succeed."

Osiris's eyes gleamed. Apparently he wasn't the god of brains, because he seemed completely taken in by the box's beauty. All the other gods looked at him expectantly, and I could see what he was thinking: if he fit in the box, what a brilliant birthday present. Even Set, his wicked brother, would have to admit that he was the rightful king of the gods.

Only Isis seemed troubled. She laid her hand on her husband's shoulder. "My lord, do not. Set does not bring presents."

"I am offended!" Set sounded genuinely hurt. "Can I not celebrate my brother's birthday? Are we so estranged that I cannot even apologize to the king?"

Osiris smiled at Isis. "My dear, it is only a game. Fear nothing."

He rose from his throne. The gods applauded as he approached the box.

"All hail Osiris!" Set cried.

The king of the gods lowered himself into the box, and when he glanced in my direction, just for a moment, he had my father's face.

No! I thought again. *Don't do it!*

But Osiris lay down. The coffin fit him exactly.

A cheer went up from the gods, but before Osiris could rise, Set clapped his hands. A golden lid materialized above the box and slammed down on top of it.

Osiris shouted in rage, but his cries were muffled.

Golden latches fastened around the lid. The other gods surged forward to intervene—even the boy in black I'd seen earlier reappeared—but Set was faster. He stamped his foot so hard, the stone floor trembled. The gods toppled over each other like dominoes. The wolf-men drew their spears, and the gods scrambled away in terror.

Set said a magic word, and a boiling cauldron appeared out of thin air. It poured its contents over the coffin—molten lead, coating the box, sealing it shut, probably heating the interior to a thousand degrees.

"Villain!" Isis wailed. She advanced on Set and began to speak a spell, but Set held up his hand. Isis rose from the floor, clawing at her mouth, her lips pressed as if an invisible force were suffocating her.

"Not today, lovely Isis," Set purred. "Today, I am king. And your child shall never be born!"

Suddenly, another goddess—a slender woman in a blue dress—charged out of the crowd. "Husband, no!"

She tackled Set, who momentarily lost his concentration. Isis fell to the floor, gasping. The other goddess yelled, "Flee!"

Isis turned and ran.

Set rose. I thought he would hit the goddess in blue, but he only snarled. "Foolish wife! Whose side are you on?"

He stamped his foot again, and the golden coffin sank into the floor.

Set raced after Isis. At the edge of the palace, Isis turned into a small bird of prey and soared into the air. Set sprouted demon's wings and launched himself in pursuit.

Then suddenly *I* was the bird. I was Isis, flying desperately over the Nile. I could sense Set behind me—closing. Closing.

You must escape, the voice of Isis said in my mind. *Avenge Osiris. Crown Horus king!*

Just when I thought my heart would burst, I felt a hand on my shoulder. The images evaporated.

The old master, Iskandar, stood next to me, his face pinched with concern. Glowing hieroglyphs danced round him.

"Forgive the interruption," he said in perfect English. "But you were almost dead."

That's when my knees turned to water, and I lost consciousness.

When I awoke, I was curled at Iskandar's feet on the steps below the empty throne. We were alone in the hall, which was mostly dark except for the light from the hieroglyphs that always seemed to glow around him.

"Welcome back," he said. "You're lucky you survived."

I wasn't so sure. My head felt like it had been boiled in oil.

"I'm sorry," I said. "I didn't mean to—"

"Look at the images? And yet you did. Your *ba* left your body and entered the past. Hadn't you been warned?"

"Yes," I admitted. "But...I was drawn to the pictures."

"*Mmm.*" Iskandar stared into space, as if remembering something from long ago. "They *are* hard to resist."

"You speak perfect English," I noticed.

Iskandar smiled. "How do you know I'm speaking English? Perhaps you are speaking Greek."

I hoped he was kidding, but I couldn't tell. He seemed so frail and warm, and yet...it was like sitting next to a nuclear reactor. I had a feeling he was full of more danger than I wanted to know.

"You're not really *that* old, are you?" I asked. "I mean, old enough to remember Ptolemaic times?"

"I am *exactly* that old, my dear. I was born in the reign of Cleopatra VII."

"Oh, please."

"I assure you, it's true. It was my sorrow to behold the last days of Egypt, before that foolhardy queen lost our kingdom to the Romans. I was the last magician to be trained before the House went underground. Many of our most powerful secrets were lost, including the spells my master used to extend my life.

Magicians these days still live long—sometimes centuries—but I have been alive for two millennia."

"So you're immortal?"

His chuckle turned into a racking cough. He doubled over and cupped his hands over his mouth. I wanted to help, but I wasn't sure how. The glowing hieroglyphs flickered and dimmed around him.

Finally the coughing subsided.

He took a shaky breath. "Hardly immortal, my dear. In fact . . ." His voice trailed off. "But never mind that. What did you see in your vision?"

I probably should've kept quiet. I didn't want to be turned into a bug for breaking any rules, and the vision had terrified me—especially the moment when I'd changed into the bird of prey. But Iskandar's kindly expression made it hard to hold back. I ended up telling him everything. Well, almost everything. I left out the bit about the good-looking boy, and yes, I know it was silly, but I was *embarrassed*. I reckoned that part could've been my own crazed imagination at work, as Ancient Egyptian gods could *not* have been that gorgeous.

Iskandar sat for a moment, tapping his staff against the steps. "You saw a very old event, Sadie—Set taking the throne of Egypt by force. He hid Osiris's coffin, you know, and Isis searched the entire world to find it."

"So she got him back eventually?"

"Not exactly. Osiris was resurrected—but only in the Underworld. He became the king of the dead. When their son, Horus, grew up, Horus challenged Set for the throne of Egypt and won after many hard battles. That is why Horus was called the Avenger. As I said—an old story, but one that the gods have repeated many times in our history."

"Repeated?"

"The gods follow patterns. In some ways they are quite predictable: acting out the same squabbles, the same jealousies down through the ages. Only the settings change, and the hosts."

There was that word again: *hosts*. I thought about the poor woman in the New York museum who'd turned into the goddess Serqet.

"In my vision," I said, "Isis and Osiris were married. Horus was about to be born as their son. But in another story Carter told me, all three of them were siblings, children of the sky goddess."

"Yes," Iskandar agreed. "This can be confusing for those who do not know the nature of gods. They cannot walk the earth in their pure form—at least, not for more than a few moments. They must have hosts."

"Humans, you mean."

"Or powerful objects, such as statues, amulets, monuments, certain models of cars. But they *prefer* human form. You see gods have great power, but only humans have creativity, the power to change history rather than simply repeat it. Humans can . . . how do you moderns say it . . . think outside the cup."

"The box," I suggested.

"Yes. The combination of human creativity and godly power can be quite formidable. At any rate, when Osiris and Isis first walked the earth, their hosts were brother and sister. But mortal hosts are not permanent. They die, they wear out.

Later in history, Osiris and Isis took new forms—humans who were husband and wife. Horus, who in one lifetime was their brother, was born into a new life as their son."

"That's confusing," I said. "And a little gross."

Iskandar shrugged. "The gods do not think of relationships the way we humans do. Their hosts are merely like changes of clothes. This is why the ancient stories seem so mixed up. Sometimes the gods are described as married, or siblings, or parent and child, depending on their hosts. The pharaoh himself was called a living god, you know. Egyptologists believe this was just a lot of propaganda, but in fact it was often literally true. The greatest of the pharaohs became hosts for gods, usually Horus. He gave them power and wisdom, and let them build Egypt into a mighty empire."

"But that's good, isn't it? Why is it against the law to host a god?"

Iskandar's face darkened. "Gods have different agendas than humans do, Sadie. They can overpower their hosts, literally burn them out. That is why so many hosts die young. Tutankhamen, poor boy, died at nineteen. Cleopatra VII was even worse. She tried to host the spirit of Isis without knowing what she was doing, and it shattered her mind. In the old days, the House of Life taught the use of divine magic. Initiates could study the path of Horus, or Isis, or Sekhmet, or any number of gods, learning to channel their powers. We had many more initiates back then."

Iskandar looked round the empty hall, as if imagining it filled with magicians. "Some adepts could call upon the gods only from time to time. Others attempted to host their spirits...with varying degrees of success. The ultimate goal was to become the 'eye' of the god—a perfect union of the two souls, mortal and immortal. Very few achieved this, even among the pharaohs, who were born to the task. Many destroyed themselves trying." He turned up his palm, which had the most deeply etched lifeline I'd ever seen. "When Egypt finally fell to the Romans, it became clear to us—to *me*—that mankind, our rulers, even the strongest magicians, no longer had the strength of will to master a god's power. The only ones who could..." His voice faltered.

"What?"

"Nothing, my dear. I talk too much. An old man's weakness."

"It's the blood of the pharaohs, isn't it?"

He fixed me in his gaze. His eyes no longer looked milky. They burned with intensity. "You are a remarkable young girl. You remind me of your mother."

My mouth fell open. "You knew her?"

"Of course. She trained here, as did your father. Your mother...well, aside from being a brilliant scientist, she had the gift of divination. One of the most difficult forms of magic, and she was the first in centuries to possess it."

"Divination?"

"Seeing the future. Tricky business, never perfect, but she saw things that made her seek advice from... *unconventional* places, things that made even *this* old man question some long-held beliefs..."

He drifted off into Memoryland again, which was infuriating enough when my grandparents did it, but when it's an all-powerful magician who has valuable information, it's enough to drive one mad.

"Iskandar?"

He looked at me with mild surprise, as if he'd forgotten I was there. "I'm sorry, Sadie. I should come to the point: you have a hard path ahead of you, but I'm convinced now it's a path you must take, for all our sakes. Your brother will need your guidance."

I was tempted to laugh. "Carter, need my guidance? For what? What path do you mean?"

"All in good time. Things must take their course."

Typical adult answer. I tried to bite back my frustration. "And what if *I* need guidance?"

"Zia," he said, without hesitation. "She is my best pupil, and she is wise. When the time comes, she will know how to help you."

"Right," I said, a bit disappointed. "Zia."

"For now you should rest, my dear. And it seems I, too, can rest at last." He sounded sad but relieved. I didn't know what he was talking about, but he didn't give me the chance to ask.

"I am sorry our time together was so brief," he said. "Sleep well, Sadie Kane."

"But—"

Iskandar touched my forehead. And I fell into a deep, dreamless sleep.

16. How Zia Lost Her Eyebrows

S A D I E

I WOKE TO A BUCKET OF ICE WATER IN MY FACE.

"Sadie! Get up," Zia said.

"God!" I yelled. "Was that *necessary?*"

"No," Zia admitted.

I wanted to strangle her, except I was dripping wet, shivering, and still disoriented. How long had I slept? It felt like only a few minutes, but the dormitory was empty. All the other cots were made. The girls must've already gone to their morning lessons.

Zia tossed me a towel and some fresh linen clothes. "We'll meet Carter in the cleansing room."

"I just *got* a bath, thanks very much. What I need is a proper breakfast."

"The cleansing prepares you for magic." Zia slung her bag of tricks over her shoulder and unfolded the long black staff she'd used in New York. "If you survive, we'll see about food."

I was tired of being reminded that I might die, but I got dressed and followed her out.

After another endless series of tunnels, we came to a chamber with a roaring waterfall. There was no ceiling, just a shaft above us that seemed to go up forever. Water fell from the darkness into a fountain, splashing over a five-meter-tall statue of that bird-headed god. What was his name—Tooth? No, Thoth. The water cascaded over his head, collected in his palms, then spilled out into the pool.

Carter stood beside the fountain. He was dressed in linen with Dad's workbag over one shoulder and his sword strapped to his back. His hair was rumpled, as if he hadn't slept well. At least he hadn't been doused in ice water. Seeing him, I felt a strange sense of relief. I thought about Iskandar's words last night: *Your brother will need your guidance.*

"What?" Carter asked. "You're staring at me funny."

"Nothing," I said quickly. "How'd you sleep?"

"Badly. I'll . . . I'll tell you about it later."

Was it my imagination, or did he frown in Zia's direction? *Hmm,* possible romantic trouble between Miss Magic and my brother? I made a mental note to interrogate him next time we were alone.

Zia went to a nearby cabinet. She brought out two ceramic cups, dipped them into the fountain, then offered them to us. "Drink."

I glanced at Carter. "After you."

"It's only water," Zia assured me, "but purified by contact with Thoth. It will focus your mind."

I didn't see how a statue could purify water. Then I

remembered what Iskandar had said, how gods could inhabit anything.

I took a drink. Immediately I felt like I'd had a good strong cup of Gran's tea. My brain buzzed. My eyesight sharpened. I felt so hyperactive, I almost didn't miss my chewing gum—almost.

Carter sipped from his cup. "Wow."

"Now the tattoos," Zia announced.

"Brilliant!" I said.

"On your tongue," she added.

"Excuse me?"

Zia stuck out her tongue. Right in the middle was a blue hieroglyph.

"Nith ith Naat," she tried to say with her tongue out. Then she realized her mistake and stuck her tongue back in. "I mean, this is Ma'at, the symbol of order and harmony. It will help you speak magic clearly. One mistake with a spell—"

"Let me guess," I said. "We'll die."

From her cabinet of horrors, Zia produced a fine-tipped paintbrush and a bowl of blue dye. "It doesn't hurt. And it's not permanent."

"How does it taste?" Carter wondered.

Zia smiled. "Stick out your tongue."

To answer Carter's question, the tattoo tasted like burning car tires.

"*Ugh.*" I spit a blue gob of "order and harmony" into the fountain. "Never mind breakfast. Lost my appetite."

Zia pulled a leather satchel out of the cabinet. "Carter will be allowed to keep your father's magic implements, plus a new staff and wand. Generally speaking, the wand is for defense, the staff is for offense, although, Carter, you may prefer to use your *khopesh*."

"*Khopesh?*"

"The curved sword," Zia said. "A favored weapon of the pharaoh's guard. It can be used in combat magic. As for Sadie, you will need a full kit."

"How come *he* gets Dad's kit?" I complained.

"He is the eldest," she said, as if that explained everything. Typical.

Zia tossed me the leather satchel. Inside was an ivory wand, a rod that I supposed turned into a staff, some paper, an ink set, a bit of twine, and a lovely chunk of wax. I was less than thrilled.

"What about a little wax man?" I asked. "I want a Doughboy."

"If you mean a figurine, you must make one yourself. You will be taught how, if you have the skill. We will determine your specialty later."

"Specialty?" Carter asked. "You mean like Nectanebo specialized in statues?"

Zia nodded. "Nectanebo was extremely skilled in statuary magic. He could make *shabti* so lifelike, they could pass for human. No one has ever been greater at statuary . . . except perhaps Iskandar. But there are many other disciplines: Healer. Amulet maker. Animal charmer. Elementalist. Combat magician. Necromancer."

"Diviner?" I asked.

Zia looked at me curiously. "Yes, although that is quite rare. Why do you—"

I cleared my throat. "So how do we know our specialty?"

"It will become clear soon enough," Zia promised, "but a good magician knows a bit of everything, which is why we start with a basic test. Let us go to the library."

The First Nome's library was like Amos's, but a hundred times bigger, with circular rooms lined with honeycomb shelves that seemed to go on forever, like the world's largest beehive. Clay *shabti* statues kept popping in and out, retrieving scroll canisters and disappearing, but we saw no other people.

Zia brought us to a wooden table and spread out a long, blank papyrus scroll. She picked up a stylus and dipped it in ink.

"The Egyptian word *shesh* means scribe or writer, but it can also mean magician. This is because magic, at its most basic, turns words into reality. You will create a scroll. Using your own magic, you will send power into the words on paper. When spoken, the words will unleash the magic."

She handed the stylus to Carter.

"I don't get it," he protested.

"A simple word," she suggested. "It can be anything."

"In English?"

Zia curled her lip. "If you must. Any language will work, but hieroglyphics are best. They are the language of creation, of magic, of Ma'at. You must be careful, however."

Before she could explain, Carter drew a simple hieroglyph of a bird.

The picture wriggled, peeled itself off the papyrus, and flew away. It splattered Carter's head with some hieroglyphic droppings on its way out. I couldn't help laughing at Carter's expression.

"A beginner's mistake," Zia said, scowling at me to be quiet. "If you use a symbol that stands for something alive, it is wise to write it only partially—leave off a wing, or the legs. Otherwise the magic you channel could make it come alive."

"And poop on its creator." Carter sighed, wiping off his hair with a bit of scrap papyrus. "That's why our father's wax statue, Doughboy, has no legs, right?"

"The same principle," Zia agreed. "Now, try again."

Carter stared at Zia's staff, which was covered in hieroglyphics. He picked the most obvious one and copied it on the papyrus—the symbol for fire.

Uh-oh, I thought. But the word did not come alive, which would've been rather exciting. It simply dissolved.

"Keep trying," Zia urged.

"Why am I so tired?" Carter wondered.

He definitely looked exhausted. His face was beaded with sweat.

"You're channeling magic from within," Zia said. "For me, fire is easy. But it may not be the most natural type of magic for you. Try something else. Summon . . . summon a sword."

Zia showed him how to form the hieroglyph, and Carter wrote it on the papyrus. Nothing happened.

"Speak it," Zia said.

"Sword," Carter said. The word glowed and vanished, and a butter knife lay on the papyrus.

I laughed. "Terrifying!"

Carter looked like he was about to pass out, but he managed

a grin. He picked up the knife and threatened to poke me with it.

"Very good for a first time," Zia said. "Remember, you are not creating the knife yourself. You are summoning it from Ma'at—the creative power of the universe. Hieroglyphs are the code we use. That's why they are called Divine Words. The more powerful the magician, the easier it becomes to control the language."

I caught my breath. "Those hieroglyphs floating in the Hall of Ages. They seemed to gather around Iskandar. Was he summoning them?"

"Not exactly," Zia said. "His presence is so strong, he makes the language of the universe visible simply by being in the room. No matter what our specialty, each magician's greatest hope is to become a speaker of the Divine Words—to know the language of creation so well that we can fashion reality simply by speaking, not even using a scroll."

"Like saying *shatter*," I ventured. "And having a door explode."

Zia scowled. "Yes, but such a thing would take years of practice."

"Really? Well—"

Out of the corner of my eye, I saw Carter shaking his head, silently warning me to shut up.

"*Um* . . ." I stammered. "Some day, I'll learn to do that."

Zia raised an eyebrow. "First, master the scroll."

I was getting tired of her attitude, so I picked up the stylus and wrote *Fire* in English.

Zia leaned forward and frowned. "You shouldn't—"

Before she could finish, a column of flame erupted in her face. I screamed, sure I'd done something horrible, but when the fire died Zia was still there, looking astonished, her eyebrows singed and her bangs smoldering.

"Oh, god," I said. "Sorry, sorry. Do I die now?"

For three heartbeats, Zia stared at me.

"Now," she announced. "I think you are ready to duel."

We used another magic gateway, which Zia summoned right on the library wall. We stepped into a circle of swirling sand and popped out the other side, covered in dust and grit, in the front of some ruins. The harsh sunlight almost blinded me.

"I hate portals," Carter muttered, brushing the sand out of his hair.

Then he looked around and his eyes widened. "This is Luxor! That's, like, hundreds of miles south of Cairo."

I sighed. "And that amazes you after teleporting from New York?"

He was too busy checking out our surroundings to answer.

I suppose the ruins were all right, though once you've seen one pile of crumbly Egyptian stuff, you've seen them all, I say. We stood on a wide avenue flanked by human-headed beasties, most of which were broken. The road went on behind us as far as I could see, but in front of us it ended at a temple much bigger than the one in the New York museum.

The walls were at least six stories high. Big stone pharaohs stood guard on either side of the entrance, and a single obelisk stood on the left-hand side. It looked as if one used to stand on the right as well, but it was now gone.

SADIE

"Luxor is a modern name," Zia said. "This was once the city of Thebes. This temple was one of the most important in Egypt. It is the best place for us to practice."

"Because it's already destroyed?" I asked.

Zia gave me one of her famous scowls. "No, Sadie—because it is still full of magic. And it was sacred to your family."

"Our family?" Carter asked.

Zia didn't explain, as usual. She just gestured for us to follow.

"I don't like those ugly sphinxes," I mumbled as we walked down the path.

"Those ugly sphinxes are creatures of law and order," Zia said, "protectors of Egypt. They are on *our* side."

"If you say so."

Carter nudged me as we passed the obelisk. "You know the missing one is in Paris."

I rolled my eyes. "Thank you, Mr. Wikipedia. I thought they were in New York and London."

"That's a different pair," Carter said, like I was supposed to care. "The other *Luxor* obelisk is in Paris."

"Wish I was in Paris," I said. "Lot better than this place."

We walked into a dusty courtyard surrounded by crumbling pillars and statues with various missing body parts. Still, I could tell the place had once been quite impressive.

"Where are the people?" I asked. "Middle of the day, winter holidays. Shouldn't there be loads of tourists?"

Zia made a distasteful expression. "Usually, yes. I have encouraged them to stay away for a few hours."

"How?"

191

"Common minds are easy to manipulate." She looked pointedly at me, and I remembered how she'd forced me to talk in the New York museum. Oh, yes, she was just *begging* for more scorched eyebrows.

"Now, to the duel." She summoned her staff and drew two circles in the sand about ten meters apart. She directed me to stand in one of them and Carter in the other.

"I've got to duel *him*?" I asked.

I found the idea preposterous. The only thing Carter had shown aptitude for was summoning butter knives and pooping birds. Well, all right, and that bit on the chasm bridge deflecting the daggers, but still—what if I hurt him? As annoying as Carter might be, I didn't want to accidentally summon that glyph I'd made in Amos's house and explode him to bits.

Perhaps Carter was thinking the same thing, because he'd started to sweat. "What if we do something wrong?" he asked.

"I will oversee the duel," Zia promised. "We will start slowly. The first magician to knock the other out of his or her circle wins."

"But we haven't been trained!" I protested.

"One learns by doing," Zia said. "This is not school, Sadie. You cannot learn magic by sitting at a desk and taking notes. You can only learn magic by doing magic."

"But—"

"Summon whatever power you can," Zia said. "Use whatever you have available. Begin!"

I looked at Carter doubtfully. *Use whatever I have?* I opened the leather satchel and looked inside. A lump of wax? Probably not. I drew the wand and rod. Immediately, the rod expanded until I was holding a two-meter-long white staff.

Carter drew his sword, though I couldn't imagine what he'd do with it. Rather hard to hit me from ten meters away.

I wanted this over, so I raised my staff like I'd seen Zia do. I thought the word *Fire*.

A small flame sputtered to life on the end of the staff. I willed it to get bigger. The fire momentarily brightened, but then my eyesight went fuzzy. The flame died. I fell to my knees, feeling as if I'd run a marathon.

"You okay?" Carter called.

"No," I complained.

"If she knocks herself out, do I win?" he asked.

"Shut up!" I said.

"Sadie, you must be careful," Zia called. "You drew from your own reserves, not from the staff. You can quickly deplete your magic."

I got shakily to my feet. "Explain?"

"A magician begins a duel full of magic, the way you might be full after a good meal—"

"Which I never got," I reminded her.

"Each time you do magic," Zia continued, "you expend energy. You can draw energy from *yourself*, but you must know your limits. Otherwise you could exhaust yourself, or worse."

I swallowed and looked at my smoldering staff. "How much worse?"

"You could literally burn up."

I hesitated, thinking how to ask my next question without saying too much. "But I've done magic before. Sometimes it doesn't exhaust me. Why?"

From around her neck, Zia unclasped an amulet. She threw it into the air, and with a flash it turned into a giant vulture. The massive black bird soared over the ruins. As soon as it was out of sight, Zia extended her hand and the amulet appeared in her palm.

"Magic can be drawn from many sources," she said. "It can be stored in scrolls, wands, or staffs. Amulets are especially powerful. Magic can also be drawn straight from Ma'at, using the Divine Words, but this is difficult. Or"—she locked eyes with me—"it can be summoned from the gods."

"Why are you looking at me?" I demanded. "*I* didn't summon any gods. They just seem to *find* me!"

She put on her necklace but said nothing.

"Hold on," Carter said. "You claimed this place was sacred to our family."

"It was," Zia agreed.

"But wasn't this . . ." Carter frowned. "Didn't the pharaohs have a yearly festival here or something?"

"Indeed," she said. "The pharaoh would walk down the processional path all the way from Karnak to Luxor. He would enter the temple and become one with the gods. Sometimes, this was purely ceremonial. Sometimes, with the great pharaohs like Ramesses, here—" Zia pointed to one of the huge crumbling statues.

"They actually hosted the gods," I interrupted, remembering what Iskandar had said.

Zia narrowed her eyes. "And yet you claim to know nothing of your family's past."

"Wait a second," Carter protested. "You're saying we're related to—"

"The gods choose their hosts carefully," Zia said. "They always prefer the blood of the pharaohs. When a magician has the blood of *two* royal families..."

I exchanged looks with Carter. Something Bast said came back to me: "Your family was born to magic." And Amos had told us that both sides of our family had a complicated history with the gods, and that Carter and I were the most powerful children to be born in centuries. A bad feeling settled over me, like an itchy blanket prickling against my skin.

"Our parents were from different royal lines," I said. "Dad ...he must've been descended from Narmer, the first pharaoh. I told you he looked like that picture!"

"That's not possible," Carter said. "That was five thousand years ago." But I could see his mind was racing. "Then the Fausts..." He turned to Zia. "Ramesses the Great built this courtyard. You're telling me our mom's family is descended from him?"

Zia sighed. "Don't tell me your parents kept this from you. Why do you think you are so dangerous to us?"

"You think we're hosting gods," I said, absolutely stunned. "That's what you're worried about—just because of something our great-times-a-thousand grandparents did? That's completely daft."

"Then prove it!" Zia said. "Duel, and show me how weak your magic is!"

She turned her back on us, as if we were completely unimportant.

Something inside me snapped. I'd had the worst two days ever. I'd lost my father, my home, and my cat, been attacked by monsters and had ice water dumped on my head. Now this *witch* was turning her back on me. She didn't want to train us. She wanted to see how dangerous we were.

Well, fine.

"Um, Sadie?" Carter called. He must've seen from my expression that I was beyond reason.

I focused on my staff. *Maybe not fire. Cats have always liked me. Maybe . . .*

I threw my staff straight at Zia. It hit the ground at her heels and immediately transformed into a snarling she-lion. Zia whirled in surprise, but then everything went wrong.

The lion turned and charged at Carter, as if she knew I was supposed to be dueling him.

I had a split second to think: *What have I done?*

Then the cat lunged . . . and Carter's form flickered. He rose off the ground, surrounded by a golden holographic shell like the one Bast had used, except that his giant image was a warrior with the head of a falcon. Carter swung his sword, and the falcon warrior did likewise, slicing the lion with a shimmering blade of energy. The cat dissolved in midair, and my staff clattered to the ground, cut neatly in half.

Carter's avatar shimmered, then disappeared. He dropped to the ground and grinned. "Fun."

He didn't even look tired. Once I got over my relief that

I hadn't killed him, I realized I didn't feel tired either. If anything, I had *more* energy.

I turned defiantly to Zia. "Well? Better, right?"

Her face was ashen. "The falcon. He—he summoned—"

Before she could finish, footsteps pounded on the stones.
A young initiate raced into the courtyard, looking panicked.
Tears streaked his dusty face. He said something to Zia in hurried Arabic. When Zia got his message, she sat down hard in
the sand. She covered her face and began to tremble.

Carter and I left our dueling circles and ran to her.

"Zia?" Carter said. "What's wrong?"

She took a deep breath, trying to gather her composure.
When she looked up, her eyes were red. She said something
to the adept, who nodded and ran back the way he'd come.

"News from the First Nome," she said shakily. "Iskandar..."
Her voice broke.

I felt as if a giant fist had punched me in the stomach. I
thought about Iskandar's strange words last night: *It seems I,
too, can rest at last.* "He's dead, isn't he? That's what he meant."

Zia stared at me. "What do you mean: 'That's what he
meant'?"

"I..." I was about to say that I'd spoken with Iskandar the
night before. Then I realized this might not be a good thing
to mention. "Nothing. How did it happen?"

"In his sleep," Zia said. "He—he had been ailing for years,
of course. But still..."

"It's okay," Carter said. "I know he was important to you."

She wiped at her tears, then rose unsteadily. "You don't

understand. Desjardins is next in line. As soon as he is named Chief Lector, he will order you executed."

"But we haven't done anything!" I said.

Zia's eyes flashed with anger. "You still don't realize how dangerous you are? You are hosting gods."

"Ridiculous," I insisted, but an uneasy feeling was building inside me. If it were true...no, it couldn't be! Besides, how could anyone, even a poxy old nutter like Desjardins, seriously execute children for something they weren't even aware of?

"He will order me to bring you in," Zia warned, "and I will have to obey."

"You can't!" Carter cried. "You *saw* what happened in the museum. We're not the problem. Set is. And if Desjardins isn't taking that seriously...well, maybe he's part of the problem too."

Zia gripped her staff. I was sure she was going to fry us with a fireball, but she hesitated.

"Zia." I decided to take a risk. "Iskandar talked with me last night. He caught me sneaking around the Hall of Ages."

She looked at me in shock. I reckoned I had only seconds before that shock turned to anger.

"He said you were his best pupil," I recalled. "He said you were wise. He also said Carter and I have a difficult path ahead of us, and you would know how to help us when the time came."

Her staff smoldered. Her eyes reminded me of glass about to shatter.

"Desjardins will kill us," I persisted. "Do you think that's what Iskandar had in mind?"

I counted to five, six, seven. Just when I was sure she was going to blast us, she lowered her staff. "Use the obelisk."

"What?" I asked.

"The obelisk at the entrance, fool! You have five minutes, perhaps less, before Desjardins sends orders for your execution. Flee, and destroy Set. The Demon Days begin at sundown. All portals will stop working. You need to get as close as possible to Set before that happens."

"Hold on," I said. "I meant you should come with us and help us! We can't even use an obelisk, much less destroy Set!"

"I cannot betray the House," she said. "You have four minutes now. If you can't operate the obelisk, you'll die."

That was enough incentive for me. I started to drag Carter off, but Zia called: "Sadie?"

When I looked back, Zia's eyes were full of bitterness.

"Desjardins will order me to hunt you down," she warned. "Do you understand?"

Unfortunately, I did. The next time we met, we would be enemies.

I grabbed Carter's hand and ran.

17. A Bad Trip to Paris

OKAY, BEFORE I GET TO THE demon fruit bats, I should back up.

The night before we fled Luxor, I didn't get much sleep—first because of an out-of-body experience, then a run-in with Zia. [Stop smirking, Sadie. It wasn't a *good* run-in.]

After lights out, I tried to sleep. Honest. I even used the stupid magic headrest they gave me instead of a pillow, but it didn't help. As soon as I managed to shut my eyes, my *ba* decided to take a little trip.

Just like before, I felt myself floating above my body, taking on a winged form. Then the current of the Duat swept me away at blurring speed. When my vision cleared, I found myself in a dark cavern. Uncle Amos was sneaking through it, finding his way with a faint blue light that flickered on the top of his staff. I wanted to call to him, but my voice didn't work. I'm not sure how he could miss me, floating a few feet away in glowing chicken form, but apparently I was invisible to him.

He stepped forward and the ground at his feet suddenly blazed to life with a red hieroglyph. Amos cried out, but his mouth froze half open. Coils of light wrapped around his legs like vines. Soon red tendrils completely entwined him, and Amos stood petrified, his unblinking eyes staring straight ahead.

I tried to fly to him, but I was stuck in place, floating helplessly, so I could only observe.

Laughter echoed through the cavern. A horde of *things* emerged from the darkness—toad creatures, animal-headed demons, and even stranger monsters half hidden in the gloom. They'd been lying in ambush, I realized—waiting for Amos. In front of them appeared a fiery silhouette—Set, but his form was much clearer now, and this time it wasn't human. His body was emaciated, slimy, and black, and his head was that of a feral beast.

"*Bon soir*, Amos," Set said. "How nice of you to come. We're going to have so much fun!"

I sat bolt upright in bed, back in my own body, with my heart pounding.

Amos had been captured. I knew it for certain. And even worse…Set had known somehow that Amos was coming. I thought back to something Bast had said, about how the serpopards had broken in to the mansion. She'd said the defenses had been sabotaged, and only a magician of the House could've done it. A horrible suspicion started building inside me.

I stared into the dark for a long time, listening to the little kid next to me mumbling spells in his sleep. When I couldn't stand it any longer, I opened the door with a push of my mind, the way I'd done at Amos's mansion, and I sneaked out.

I was wandering through the empty marketplace, thinking about Dad and Amos, replaying the events over and over, trying to figure out what I could've done differently to save them, when I spotted Zia.

She was hurrying across the courtyard as if she were being chased, but what really caught my attention was the shimmering black cloud around her, as if someone had wrapped her in a glittery shadow. She came to a section of blank wall and waved her hand. Suddenly a doorway appeared. Zia glanced nervously behind her and ducked inside.

Of course I followed.

I moved quietly up to the doorway. I could hear Zia's voice inside, but I couldn't make out what she was saying. Then the doorway began to solidify, turning back into a wall, and I made a split-second decision. I jumped through.

Inside, Zia was alone with her back to me. She was kneeling at a stone altar, chanting something under her breath. The walls were decorated with Ancient Egyptian drawings and modern photographs.

The glittery shadow no longer surrounded Zia, but something even stranger was happening. I'd been planning to tell Zia about my nightmare, but that went completely out of my thoughts when I saw what she was doing. She cupped her palms, the way you might hold a bird, and a glowing blue sphere appeared, about the size of a golf ball. Still chanting, she raised her hands. The sphere flew up, straight through the ceiling, and vanished.

Some instinct told me this was *not* something I was supposed to see.

I thought about backing out of the room. Only problem: the door was gone. No other exits. It was only a matter of time before— *Uh-oh*.

Maybe I'd made a noise. Maybe her magical senses had kicked in. But faster than I could react, Zia pulled her wand and turned on me, flames flickering down the edge of the boomerang.

"Hi," I said nervously.

Her expression turned from anger to surprise, then back to anger. "Carter, what are you doing here?"

"Just walking around. I saw you in the courtyard, so—"

"What do you mean you *saw* me?"

"Well... you were running, and you had this black shimmery stuff around you, and—"

"You *saw* that? Impossible."

"Why? What was it?"

She dropped her wand and the fire died. "I don't appreciate being followed, Carter."

"Sorry. I thought you might be in trouble."

She started to say something, but apparently changed her mind. "In trouble... that's true enough."

She sat down heavily and sighed. In the candlelight, her amber eyes looked dark and sad.

She stared at the photos behind the altar, and I realized she was in some of them. There she was as a little girl, standing barefoot outside a mud-brick house, squinting resentfully at the camera as if she didn't want her picture taken. Next to that, a wider shot showed a whole village on the Nile—the kind of place my dad took me to sometimes, where nothing had changed much in the last two thousand years. A crowd of villagers grinned and waved at the camera as if they were celebrating, and above them little Zia rode on the shoulders of a man who must've been her father. Another photo was a family shot: Zia holding hands with her mother and father. They could've been any *fellahin* family anywhere in Egypt, but her dad had especially kindly, twinkling eyes—I thought he must have a good sense of humor. Her mom's face was unveiled, and she laughed as if her husband had just cracked a joke.

"Your folks look cool," I said. "Is that home?"

Zia seemed like she wanted to get angry, but she kept her emotions under control. Or maybe she just didn't have the energy. "It *was* my home. The village no longer exists."

I waited, not sure I dared to ask. We locked eyes, and I could tell she was deciding how much to tell me.

"My father was a farmer," she said, "but he also worked for archaeologists. In his spare time he'd scour the desert for artifacts and new sites where they might want to dig."

I nodded. What Zia described was pretty common. Egyptians have been making extra money that way for centuries.

"One night when I was eight, my father found a statue," she said. "Small but very rare: a statue of a monster, carved from red stone. It had been buried in a pit with a lot of other statues that were all smashed. But somehow this one survived. He brought it home. He didn't know... He didn't realize magicians imprison monsters and spirits inside such statues, and break them to destroy their essence. My father brought the unbroken statue into our village, and...and accidentally unleashed..."

Her voice faltered. She stared at the picture of her father smiling and holding her hand.

"Zia, I'm sorry."

She knit her eyebrows. "Iskandar found me. He and the other magicians destroyed the monster...but not in time. They found me curled in a fire pit under some reeds where my mother had hidden me. I was the only survivor."

I tried to imagine how Zia would've looked when Iskandar found her—a little girl who'd lost everything, alone in the ruins of her village. It was hard to picture her that way.

"So this room is a shrine to your family," I guessed. "You come here to remember them."

Zia looked at me blankly. "That's the problem, Carter. I *can't* remember. Iskandar tells me about my past. He gave me these pictures, explained what happened. But...I have no memory at all."

I was about to say, "You were only eight." Then I realized I'd been the same age when my mom died, when Sadie and I were split up. I remembered all of that so clearly. I could still see our house in Los Angeles and the way the stars looked at night from our back porch overlooking the ocean. My dad would tell us wild stories about the constellations. Then every night before bed, Sadie and I would cuddle up with Mom on the sofa, fighting for her attention, and she'd tell us not to believe a word of Dad's stories. She'd explain the science behind the stars, talk about physics and chemistry as if we were her college students. Looking back on it, I wondered if she'd been trying to warn us: Don't believe in those gods and myths. They're too dangerous.

I remembered our last trip to London as a family, how nervous Mom and Dad seemed on the plane. I remembered our dad coming back to our grandparents' flat after Mom had died, and telling us there had been an accident. Even before he explained, I knew it was bad, because I'd never seen my dad cry before.

The little details that *did* fade drove me crazy—like the smell of Mom's perfume, or the way her voice sounded. The older I got, the harder I held on to those things. I couldn't imagine not remembering anything. How could Zia stand it?

"Maybe..." I struggled to find the right words. "Maybe you just—"

She held up her hand. "Carter, believe me. I've tried to remember. It's no use. Iskandar is the only family I've ever had."

"What about friends?"

Zia stared at me as if I'd used a foreign term. I realized I hadn't seen anyone close to our age in the First Nome. Everyone was either much younger or much older.

"I don't have time for friends," she said. "Besides, when initiates turn thirteen, they're assigned to other nomes around the world. I am the only one who stayed here. I like being alone. It's fine."

The hairs stood up on the back of my neck. I'd said almost the same thing, many times, when people asked me what it was like being homeschooled by my dad. Didn't I miss having friends? Didn't I want a normal life? "I like being alone. It's fine."

I tried to picture Zia going to a regular public high school, learning a locker combination, hanging out in the cafeteria. I couldn't picture it. I imagined she would be as lost as I would.

"Tell you what," I said. "After the testing, after the Demon Days, when things settle down—"

"Things won't settle down."

"—I'm going to take you to the mall."

She blinked. "The mall? For what reason?"

"To hang out," I said. "We'll get some hamburgers. See a movie."

Zia hesitated. "Is this what you'd call a 'date'?"

My expression must've been priceless, because Zia actually cracked a smile. "You look like a cow hit with a shovel."

"I didn't mean...I just meant..."

She laughed, and suddenly it was easier to imagine her as a regular high school kid.

"I will look forward to this *mall*, Carter," she said. "You are either a very interesting person...or a very dangerous one."

"Let's go with interesting."

She waved her hand, and the door reappeared. "Go now. And be careful. The next time you sneak up on me, you might not be so fortunate."

At the doorway, I turned. "Zia, what was that black shimmery stuff?"

Her smile faded. "An invisibility spell. Only very powerful magicians are able to see through it. *You* should not have."

She stared at me for answers, but I didn't have any.

"Maybe it was...wearing off or something," I managed. "And, can I ask, the blue sphere?"

She frowned. "The what?"

"The thing you released that went into the ceiling."

She looked mystified. "I...I don't know what you mean. Perhaps the candlelight was playing tricks on your eyes."

Awkward silence. Either she was lying to me, or I was going crazy, or...I didn't know what. I realized I hadn't told her about my vision of Amos and Set, but I felt that I'd already pushed her as far as I could for one night.

"Okay," I said. "Good night."

I made my way back to the dorm, but I didn't get to sleep again for a long time.

Fast-forward to Luxor. Maybe now you understand why I didn't want to leave Zia behind, and why I didn't believe Zia would actually hurt us.

On the other hand, I knew she wasn't lying about Desjardins. That guy wouldn't think twice about turning us into escargots. And the fact that Set had spoken French in my dream—"*Bon soir*, Amos." Was that just a coincidence... or was something a *lot* worse going on?

Anyway, when Sadie tugged on my arm, I followed.

We ran out of the temple and headed for the obelisk. But naturally, it wasn't that simple. We're the Kane family. Nothing is *ever* that simple.

Just as we reached the obelisk, I heard the *slish*-ing sound of a magic portal. About a hundred yards down the path, a bald magician in white robes stepped out of a whirling sand vortex.

"Hurry," I told Sadie. I grabbed the staff-rod from my bag

and threw it to her. "Since I cut yours in half. I'll stick with the sword."

"But I don't know what I'm doing!" she protested, searching the obelisk's base as if she hoped to find a secret switch.

The magician regained his balance and spit the sand out of his mouth. Then he spotted us. "Stop!"

"Yeah," I muttered. "That's gonna happen."

"Paris." Sadie turned to me. "You said the other obelisk is in Paris, right?"

"Right. *Um*, not to rush you, but . . ."

The magician raised his staff and started chanting.

I fumbled for the hilt of my sword. My legs felt like they were turning to butter. I wondered if I could pull off that hawk warrior thing again. That had been cool, but it had also been just a duel. And the test at the chasm bridge, when I'd deflected those daggers—that hadn't seemed like *me*. Every time I'd drawn this sword so far, I'd had help: Zia had been there, or Bast. I'd never felt completely alone. This time, it was just me. I was crazy to think I could hold off a full-fledged magician. I was no warrior. Everything I knew about swords came from reading books—the history of Alexander the Great, *The Three Musketeers*—as if that could help! With Sadie occupied at the obelisk, I was on my own.

No you're not, said a voice inside me.

Great, I thought. *I'm on my own* and *going crazy*.

At the far end of the avenue, the magician called out: "Serve the House of Life!"

But I got the feeling he wasn't talking to me.

The air between us began to shimmer. Waves of heat flowed from the double lines of sphinxes, making them look as if they were moving. Then I realized they *were* moving. Each one cracked down the middle, and ghostly apparitions appeared from the stone like locusts breaking out of their shells. Not all of them were in good shape. The spirit creatures from broken statues had missing heads or feet. Some limped along on only three legs. But at least a dozen attack sphinxes were in perfect condition, and they all came toward us—each one the size of a Doberman, made of milky white smoke and hot vapor. So much for the sphinxes being on *our* side.

"Soon!" I warned Sadie.

"Paris!" she called, and raised her staff and wand. "I want to go there *now*. Two tickets. First-class would be nice!"

The sphinxes advanced. The nearest one launched itself toward me, and with sheer luck I managed to slice it in half. The monster evaporated into smoke, but it let out a blast of heat so intense I thought my face was going to melt right off.

Two more sphinx ghosts loped toward me. A dozen more were only a few steps behind. I could feel my pulse pounding in my neck.

Suddenly the ground shook. The sky darkened, and Sadie yelled, "Yes!"

The obelisk glowed with purple light, humming with power. Sadie touched the stone and yelped. She was sucked inside and disappeared.

"Sadie!" I yelled.

In my moment of distraction, two of the sphinxes slammed

into me, knocking me to the ground. My sword skittered away. My rib cage went *crack!* and my chest erupted in pain. The heat coming off the creatures was unbearable—it was like being crushed under a hot oven.

I stretched out my fingers toward the obelisk. Just a few inches too far. I could hear the other sphinxes coming, the magician chanting, "Hold him! Hold him!"

With my last bit of strength, I lurched toward the obelisk, every nerve in my body screaming with pain. My fingertips touched the base, and the world went black.

Suddenly I was lying on cold, wet stone. I was in the middle of a huge public plaza. Rain was pouring down, and the chilly air told me I was no longer in Egypt. Sadie was somewhere close by, yelling in alarm.

The bad news: I'd brought the two sphinxes with me. One jumped off me and bounded after Sadie. The other was still on my chest, glaring down at me, its back steaming in the rain, its smoky white eyes inches from my face.

I tried to remember the Egyptian word for *fire*. Maybe if I could set the monster ablaze . . . but my mind was too full of panic. I heard an explosion off to my right, in the direction Sadie had run. I hoped she'd gotten away, but I couldn't be sure.

The sphinx opened its mouth and formed smoky fangs that had no business on an Ancient Egyptian king. It was about to chomp my face when a dark form loomed up behind it and shouted, *"Mange des muffins!"*

Slice!

The sphinx dissolved into smoke.

I tried to rise but couldn't. Sadie stumbled over. "Carter! Oh god, are you okay?"

I blinked at the other person—the one who had saved me: a tall, thin figure in a black, hooded raincoat. What had she yelled: *Eat muffins?* What kind of battle cry was that?

She threw off her coat, and a woman in a leopard-skin acrobatic suit grinned down at me, showing off her fangs and her lamplike yellow eyes.

"Miss me?" asked Bast.

18. When Fruit Bats Go Bad

WE HUDDLED UNDER THE EAVES of a big white government building and watched the rain pour down on the Place de la Concorde. It was a miserable day to be in Paris. The winter skies were heavy and low, and the cold, wet air soaked right into my bones. There were no tourists, no foot traffic. Everyone with any sense was inside by a fire enjoying a hot drink.

To our right, the River Seine wound sluggishly through the city. Across the enormous plaza, the gardens of the Tuileries were shrouded in a soupy haze.

The Egyptian obelisk rose up lonely and dark in the middle of the square. We waited for more enemies to pop out of it, but none came. I remembered what Zia had said about artifacts needing a twelve-hour cooldown before they could be used again. I hoped she was right.

"Hold still," Bast told me.

I winced as she pressed her hand against my chest. She whispered something in Egyptian, and the pain slowly subsided.

"Broken rib," she announced. "Better now, but you should rest for at least a few minutes."

"What about the magicians?"

"I wouldn't worry about them just yet. The House will assume you teleported somewhere else."

"Why?"

"Paris is the Fourteenth Nome—Desjardins' headquarters. You would be insane trying to hide in his home territory."

"Great." I sighed.

"And your amulets *do* shield you," Bast added. "I could find Sadie anywhere because of my promise to protect her. But the amulets will keep you veiled from the eyes of Set and from other magicians."

I thought about the dark room in the First Nome with all the children looking into bowls of oil. Were they looking for us right now? The thought was creepy.

I tried to sit up and winced again.

"Stay still," Bast ordered. "Really, Carter, you should learn to fall like a cat."

"I'll work on that," I promised. "How are you even alive? Is it that 'nine lives' thing?"

"Oh, that's just a silly legend. I'm *immortal*."

"But the scorpions!" Sadie scrunched in closer, shivering and drawing Bast's raincoat around her shoulders. "We saw them overwhelm you!"

Bast made a purring sound. "Dear Sadie, you do care! I must say I've worked for *many* children of the pharaohs, but you two—" She looked genuinely touched. "Well, I'm sorry if I worried you. It's true the scorpions reduced my power to almost nothing. I held them off as long as I could. Then I had just enough energy to revert to Muffin's form and slip into the Duat."

"I thought you weren't good at portals," I said.

"Well, first off, Carter, there are many ways in and out of the Duat. It has many different regions and layers—the Abyss, the River of Night, the Land of the Dead, the Land of Demons—"

"Sounds lovely," Sadie muttered.

"Anyway, portals are like doors. They pass through the Duat to connect one part of the mortal world to another. And yes, I'm not good at those. But I *am* a creature of the Duat. If I'm on my own, slipping into the nearest layer for a quick escape is relatively easy."

"And if they'd killed you?" I asked. "I mean, killed Muffin?"

"That would've banished me deep into the Duat. It would've been rather like putting my feet in concrete and dropping me into the middle of the sea. It would've taken years, perhaps centuries, before I would've been strong enough to return to the mortal world. Fortunately, that didn't happen. I came back straightaway, but by the time I got to the museum, the magicians had already captured you."

"We weren't exactly *captured*," I said.

"Really, Carter? How long were you in the First Nome before they decided to kill you?"

"Um, about twenty-four hours."

Bast whistled. "They've gotten friendlier! They used to blast godlings to dust in the first few minutes."

"We're *not*—wait, what did you call us?"

Sadie answered, sounding as if in a trance: "'Godlings.' That's what we are, aren't we? That's why Zia was so frightened of us, why Desjardins wants to kill us."

Bast patted Sadie's knee. "You always were bright, dear."

"Hold on," I said. "You mean hosts for *gods*? That's not possible. I think I'd know if..."

Then I thought about the voice in my head, warning me to hide when I met Iskandar. I thought about all the things I was suddenly able to do—like fight with a sword and summon a magical shell of armor. Those were not things I'd covered in home school.

"Carter," Sadie said. "When the Rosetta Stone shattered, it let out five gods, right? Dad joined with Osiris. Amos told us that. Set... I don't know. He got away somehow. But you and I—"

"The amulets protected us." I clutched the Eye of Horus around my neck. "Dad said they would."

"*If* we had stayed out of the room, as Dad told us to," Sadie recalled. "But we were there, watching. We wanted to help him. We practically *asked* for power, Carter."

Bast nodded. "That makes all the difference. An invitation."

"And since then..." Sadie looked at me tentatively, almost daring me to make fun of her. "I've had this feeling. Like a voice inside me...."

By now the cold rain had soaked right through my clothes. If Sadie hadn't said something, maybe I could've denied what was happening a little longer. But I thought about what Amos had said about our family having a long history with the gods. I thought about what Zia had told us about our lineage: "The gods choose their hosts carefully. They always prefer the blood of the pharaohs."

"Okay," I admitted. "I've been hearing a voice too. So either we're both going crazy—"

"The amulet." Sadie pulled it from her shirt collar and held it for Bast to see. "It's the symbol of a goddess, isn't it?"

I hadn't seen her amulet in a long time. It was different from mine. It reminded me of an ankh, or maybe some kind of fancy tie.

"That is a *tyet*," Bast said. "A magic knot. And yes, it is often called—"

"The Knot of Isis," Sadie said. I didn't see how she could know that, but she looked absolutely certain. "In the Hall of Ages, I saw an image of Isis, and then I *was* Isis, trying to get away from Set, and—oh, god. That's it, isn't it? I'm her."

She grabbed her shirt like she physically wanted to pull the goddess away from her. All I could do was stare. My sister, with her ratty red-highlighted hair and her linen pajamas and her combat boots—how could she possibly worry about being possessed by a *goddess*? What goddess would want her, except maybe the goddess of chewing gum?

But then . . . I'd been hearing a voice inside me too. A voice that was definitely not mine. I looked at my amulet, the Eye of Horus. I thought about the myths I knew—how Horus, the son of Osiris, had to avenge his father by defeating Set. And at Luxor I'd summoned an avatar with the head of a falcon.

I was afraid to try it, but I thought: *Horus?*

Well, it's about time, the other voice said. *Hello, Carter.*

"Oh, no," I said, panic rising in my chest. "No, no, no. Somebody get a can opener. I've got a god stuck in my head."

Bast's eyes lit up. "You communicated with Horus directly? That's excellent progress!"

"Progress?" I banged my palms against my head. "Get him out!"

Calm down, Horus said.

"Don't tell me to calm down!"

Bast frowned. "I didn't."

"Talking to him!" I pointed at my forehead.

"This is awful," Sadie wailed. "How do I get rid of her?"

Bast sniffed. "First off, Sadie, you don't have *all* of her. Gods are very powerful. We can exist in many places at once. But yes, part of Isis's spirit now resides inside you. Just as Carter now carries the spirit of Horus. And frankly, you both should feel honored."

"Right, very honored," I said. "Always wanted to be possessed!"

Bast rolled her eyes. "Please, Carter, it's *not* possession. Besides, you and Horus want the same thing—to defeat Set, just as Horus did millennia ago, when Set first killed Osiris. If you don't, your father is doomed, and Set will become king of the earth."

I glanced at Sadie, but she was no help. She ripped the amulet off her neck and threw it down. "Isis got in through the amulet, didn't she? Well, I'll just—"

"I really wouldn't do that," Bast warned.

But Sadie pulled out her wand and smashed the amulet. Blue sparks shot up from the ivory boomerang. Sadie yelped and dropped her wand, which was now smoking. Her hand was covered in black scorch marks. The amulet was fine. *"Ow!"* she said.

Bast sighed. She put her hand on Sadie's, and the burn marks faded. "I *did* tell you. Isis channeled her power through the amulet, yes, but she's not there now. She's in *you*. And even so, magical amulets are practically indestructible."

"So what are we supposed to do?" Sadie said.

"Well, for starters," Bast said, "Carter must use the power of Horus to defeat Set."

"Oh, is that all?" I said. "All by myself?"

"No, no. Sadie can help."

"Oh, super."

"I'll guide you as much as possible," Bast promised, "but in the end, the two of you must fight. Only Horus and Isis can defeat Set and avenge the death of Osiris. That's the way it was before. That's the way it must be now."

"Then we get our dad back?" I asked.

Bast's smile wavered. "If all goes well."

She wasn't telling us everything. No surprise. But my brain was too fuzzy to figure out what I was missing.

I looked down at my hands. They didn't seem any different—no stronger, no godlier. "If I've got the powers of a god, then why am I so..."

"Lame?" Sadie offered.

"Shut up," I said. "Why can't I use my powers better?"

"Takes practice," Bast said. "Unless you wish to give over

control to Horus. Then he would use your form, and you would not have to worry."

I could, a voice said inside me. *Let me fight Set. You can trust me.*

Yeah, right, I told him. *How can I be sure you wouldn't get me killed and just move on to some other host? How can I be sure you're not influencing my thoughts right now?*

I would not do that, the voice said. *I chose you because of your potential, Carter, and because we have the same goal. Upon my honor, if you let me control—*

"No," I said.

I realized I'd spoke aloud; Sadie and Bast were both looking at me.

"I mean I'm not giving up control," I said. "This is *our* fight. Our dad's locked in a coffin. Our uncle's been captured."

"Captured?" Sadie asked. I realized with a shock that I hadn't told her about my last little *ba* trip. There just hadn't been time.

When I gave her the details, she looked stricken. "God, no."

"Yeah," I agreed. "And Set spoke in French—'*Bon soir.*' Sadie, what you said about Set getting away—maybe he didn't. If he was looking for a powerful host—"

"Desjardins," Sadie finished.

Bast growled deep in her throat. "Desjardins was in London the night your father broke the Rosetta Stone, wasn't he? Desjardins has always been full of anger, full of ambition. In many ways, he would be the perfect host for Set. If Set managed to possess Desjardins' body, that would mean the

Red Lord now controls the man who is Chief Lector of the House.... By Ra's throne, Carter, I hope you're wrong. The two of you will have to learn to use the power of the gods quickly. Whatever Set is planning, he'll do it on his birthday, when he's strongest. That's the third Demon Day—three days from now."

"But I've already used Isis's powers, haven't I?" Sadie asked. "I've summoned hieroglyphs. I activated the obelisk at Luxor. Was that her or me?"

"Both, dear," Bast said. "You and Carter have great abilities on your own, but the power of the gods has hastened your development, and given you an extra reservoir to draw on. What would've taken you years to learn, you've accomplished in days. The more you channel the power of the gods, the more powerful you will become."

"And the more dangerous it gets," I guessed. "The magicians told us hosting the gods can burn you out, kill you, drive you crazy."

Bast fixed her eyes on me. Just for a second they were the eyes of a predator—ancient, powerful, dangerous. "Not everyone can host a god, Carter. That's true. But *you* two are *both* blood of the pharaohs. You combine *two* ancient bloodlines. That's very rare, very powerful. And besides, if you think you can survive *without* the power of the gods, think again. Don't repeat your mother's—" She stopped herself.

"What?" Sadie demanded. "What about our mother?"

"I shouldn't have said that."

"Tell us, cat!" Sadie said.

I was afraid Bast might unsheathe her knives. Instead she

leaned against the wall and stared out at the rain. "When your parents released me from Cleopatra's Needle ... there was much more energy than they expected. Your father spoke the actual summoning spell, and the blast would've killed him instantly, but your mother threw up a shield. In that split second, I offered her my help. I offered to merge our spirits and help protect them. But she would not accept my help. She chose to tap her own reservoir...."

"Her own magic," Sadie murmured.

Bast nodded sadly. "When a magician commits herself to a spell, there is no turning back. If she overreaches her power ... well, your mother used her last bit of energy protecting your father. To save him, she sacrificed herself. She literally—"

"Burned up," I said. "That's what Zia warned us about."

The rain kept pouring down. I realized I was shivering.

Sadie wiped a tear from her cheek. She picked up her amulet and glared at it resentfully. "We've got to save Dad. If he's really got the spirit of Osiris..."

She didn't finish, but I knew what she was thinking. I thought about Mom when I was little, her arm around my shoulders as we stood on the back deck of our house in L.A. She'd pointed out the stars to me: Polaris, Orion's Belt, Sirius. Then she'd smile at me, and I'd feel like I was more important than any constellation in the sky. My mom had sacrificed herself to save Dad's life. She'd used so much magic, she literally burned up. How could I ever be that brave? Yet I had to try to save Dad. Otherwise I'd feel like Mom's sacrifice had been for nothing. And maybe if we could rescue Dad, he could set things right, even bring back our mom.

Is that possible? I asked Horus, but his voice was silent.

"All right," I decided. "So how do we stop Set?"

Bast thought for a moment, then smiled. I got the feeling that whatever she was about to suggest, I wasn't going to like it. "There *might* be a way without completely giving yourself over to the gods. There's a book by Thoth—one of the rare spell books written by the god of wisdom himself. The one I'm thinking of details a way to overcome Set. It is the prized possession of a certain magician. All we need to do is sneak into his fortress, steal it, and leave before sunset, while we can still create a portal to the United States."

"Perfect," Sadie said.

"Hold up," I said. "Which magician? And where's the fortress?"

Bast stared at me as if I were a bit slow. "Why, I think we already discussed him. Desjardins. His house is right here in Paris."

Once I saw Desjardins' house, I hated him even more. It was a huge mansion on the other side of the Tuileries, on the rue des Pyramides.

"Pyramids Road?" Sadie said. "Obvious, much?"

"Maybe he couldn't find a place on Stupid Evil Magician Street," I suggested.

The house was spectacular. The spikes atop its wrought iron fence were gilded. Even in the winter rain, the front garden was bursting with flowers. Five stories of white marble walls and black-shuttered windows loomed before us, the whole thing topped off by a roof garden. I'd seen royal palaces smaller than this place.

I pointed to the front door, which was painted bright red. "Isn't red a bad color in Egypt? The color of Set?"

Bast scratched her chin. "Now that you mention it, yes. It's the color of chaos and destruction."

"I thought black was the evil color," Sadie said.

"No, dear. As usual, modern folk have it backward. Black is the color of good soil, like the soil of the Nile. You can grow food in black soil. Food is good. Therefore black is good. Red is the color of desert sand. Nothing grows in the desert. Therefore red is evil." She frowned. "It *is* strange that Desjardins has a red door."

"Well, I'm excited," Sadie grumbled. "Let's go knock."

"There will be guards," Bast said. "And traps. And alarms. You can bet the house is heavily charmed to keep out gods."

"Magicians can do that?" I asked. I imagined a big can of pesticide labeled *God-Away*.

"Alas, yes," Bast said. "I will not be able to cross the threshold uninvited. You, however—"

"I thought we're gods too," Sadie said.

"That's the beauty of it," Bast said. "As hosts, you are still quite human. I have taken full possession of Muffin, so I am pretty much *me*—a goddess. But you are still—well, yourselves. Clear?"

"No," I said.

"I suggest you turn into birds," Bast said. "You can fly to the roof garden and make your way in. Plus, I like birds."

"First problem," I said, "we don't know how to turn into birds."

"Easily fixed! And a good test at channeling godly power.

Both Isis and Horus have bird forms. Simply imagine your-selves as birds, and birds you shall become."

"Just like that," Sadie said. "You won't pounce on us?"

Bast looked offended. "Perish the thought!"

I wished she hadn't used the word *perish*.

"Okay," I said. "Here goes."

I thought: *You in there, Horus?*

What? he said testily.

Bird form, please.

Oh, I see. You don't trust me. But now you need my help.

Man, come on. Just do the falcon thing.

Would you settle for an emu?

I decided talking wasn't going to help, so I closed my eyes and imagined I was a falcon. Right away, my skin began to burn. I had trouble breathing. I opened my eyes and gasped.

I was really, really short—eye-level with Bast's shins. I was covered in feathers, and my feet had turned into wicked claws, kind of like my *ba* form, but this was real flesh and blood. My clothes and bag were gone, as if they'd melted into my feathers. My eyesight had completely changed, too. I could see a hundred and eighty degrees around, and the detail was incredible. Every leaf on every tree popped out. I spotted a cockroach a hundred yards away, scurrying into a sewer drain. I could see every pore on Bast's face, now looming above me and grinning.

"Better late than never," she said. "Took you almost ten minutes."

Huh? The change had seemed instantaneous. Then I looked next to me and saw a beautiful gray bird of prey, a little bit smaller than me, with black-tipped wings and golden eyes. I'm not sure how, but I knew it was a kite—like the *bird* kite, not the kind with a string.

The kite let out a chirping sound—"*Ha, ha, ha.*" Sadie was laughing at me.

I opened my own beak, but no sound came out.

"Oh, you two look delicious," Bast said, licking her lips. "No, no—*er,* I mean wonderful. Now, off you go!"

I spread my majestic wings. I had really done it! I was a noble falcon, lord of the sky. I launched myself off the sidewalk and flew straight into the fence.

"*Ha—ha—ha,*" Sadie chirped behind me.

Bast crouched down and began making weird chittering noises. *Uh-oh.* She was imitating birds. I'd seen enough cats do this when they were stalking. Suddenly my own obituary flashed in my head: *Carter Kane, 14, died tragically in Paris when he was eaten by his sister's cat, Muffin.*

I spread my wings, kicked off with my feet, and with three strong flaps, I was soaring through the rain. Sadie was right behind me. Together we spiraled up into the air.

I have to admit: it felt amazing. Ever since I was a little kid, I'd had dreams in which I was flying, and I always hated waking up. Now it wasn't a dream or even a *ba* trip. It was one hundred percent real. I sailed on the cold air currents above the rooftops of Paris. I could see the river, the Louvre Museum, the gardens and palaces. And a mouse—yum.

Hang on, Carter, I thought. *Not hunting mice.* I zeroed in on Desjardins' mansion, tucked in my wings, and shot downward.

I saw the rooftop garden, the double glass doors leading

inside, and the voice inside me said: *Don't stop. It's an illusion. You've got to punch through their magic barriers.*

It was a crazy thought. I was plummeting so fast I would smack against the glass and become a feathery pancake, but I didn't slow down.

I rammed straight into the doors—and sailed through them as if they didn't exist. I spread my wings and landed on a table. Sadie sailed in right behind me.

We were alone in the middle of a library. So far, so good.

I closed my eyes and thought about returning to my normal form. When I opened my eyes again, I was regular old Carter, sitting on a table in my regular clothes, my workbag back on my shoulder.

Sadie was still a kite.

"You can turn back now," I told her.

She tilted her head and regarded me quizzically. She let out a frustrated croak.

I cracked a smile. "You can't, can you? You're stuck?"

She pecked my hand with her extremely sharp beak.

"Ow!" I complained. "It's not my fault. Keep trying."

She closed her eyes and ruffled her feathers until she looked like she was going to explode, but she stayed a kite.

"Don't worry," I said, trying to keep a straight face. "Bast will help once we get out of here."

"Ha—ha—ha."

"Just keep watch. I'm going to look around."

The room was huge—more like a traditional library than a magician's lair. The furniture was dark mahogany. Every wall was covered with floor-to-ceiling bookcases. Books overflowed onto the floor. Some were stacked on tables or stuffed into smaller shelves. A big easy chair by the window looked like the kind of place Sherlock Holmes would sit smoking a pipe.

Every step I took, the floorboards creaked, which made me wince. I couldn't hear anyone else in the house, but I didn't want to take any chances.

Aside from the glass doors to the rooftop, the only other exit was a solid wooden door that locked from the inside. I turned the deadbolt. Then I wedged a chair up under the handle. I doubted that would keep magicians out for very long, but it might buy me a few seconds if things went bad.

I searched the bookshelves for what seemed like ages. All different types of books were jammed together—nothing alphabetized, nothing numbered. Most of the titles weren't in English. None were in hieroglyphics. I was hoping for something with big gold lettering that said *The Book of Thoth*, but no such luck.

"What would a *Book of Thoth* even look like?" I wondered.

Sadie turned her head and glared at me. I was pretty sure she was telling me to hurry up.

I wished there were *shabti* to fetch things, like the ones in Amos's library, but I didn't see any. Or maybe . . .

I slung Dad's bag off my shoulder. I set his magic box on the table and slid open the top. The little wax figure was still there, right where I'd left him. I picked him up and said, "Doughboy, help me find *The Book of Thoth* in this library."

His waxy eyes opened immediately. "And why should I help you?"

"Because you have no choice."

"I hate that argument! Fine—hold me up. I can't see the shelves."

I walked him around the room, showing him the books. I felt pretty stupid giving the wax doll a tour, but probably not as stupid as Sadie felt. She was still in bird form, scuttling back and forth on the table and snapping her beak in frustration as she tried to change back.

"Hold it!" Doughboy announced. "This one is ancient— right here."

I pulled down a thin volume bound in linen. It was so tiny, I would've missed it, but sure enough, the front cover was inscribed in hieroglyphics. I brought it over to the table and carefully opened it. It was more like a map than a book, unfolding into four parts until I was looking at a wide, long papyrus scroll with writing so old I could barely make out the characters.

I glanced at Sadie. "I bet you could read this to me if you weren't a bird."

She tried to peck me again, but I moved my hand.

"Doughboy," I said. "What is this scroll?"

"A spell lost in time!" he pronounced. "Ancient words of tremendous power!"

"Well?" I demanded. "Does it tell how to defeat Set?"

"Better! The title reads: *The Book of Summoning Fruit Bats*!"

I stared at him. "Are you serious?"

"Would I joke about such a thing?"

"Who would want to summon fruit bats?"

"*Ha—ha—ha*," Sadie croaked.

I pushed the scroll away and we went back to searching.

After about ten minutes, Doughboy squealed with delight. "Oh, look! I remember this painting."

It was a small oil portrait in a gilded frame, hanging on the end of a bookshelf. It must've been important, because it was bordered by little silk curtains. A light shone upon the portrait dude's face so he seemed about to tell a ghost story.

"Isn't that the guy who plays Wolverine?" I asked, because he had some serious jowl hair going on.

"You disgust me!" Doughboy said. "That is Jean-François Champollion."

It took me a second, but I remembered the name. "The guy who deciphered hieroglyphics from the Rosetta Stone."

"Of course. Desjardins' great uncle."

I looked at Champollion's picture again, and I could see the resemblance. They had the same fierce black eyes. "Great uncle? But wouldn't that make Desjardins—"

"About two hundred years old," Doughboy confirmed. "Still a youngster. You know that when Champollion first deciphered hieroglyphics, he fell into a coma for five days? He became the first man outside the House of Life to ever unleash their magic, and it almost killed him. Naturally, that got the attention of the First Nome. Champollion died before he could join the House of Life, but the Chief Lector accepted his descendants for training. Desjardins is very proud of his family ... but a little sensitive too, because he's such a newcomer."

"That's why he didn't get along with our family," I guessed. "We're like ... ancient."

Doughboy cackled. "And your father breaking the Rosetta Stone? Desjardins would've viewed that as an insult to his family honor! Oh, you should've seen the arguments Master Julius and Desjardins had in this room."

"You've been here before?"

"Many times! I've been everywhere. I'm all-knowing."

I tried to imagine Dad and Desjardins having an argument in here. It wasn't hard. If Desjardins hated our family, and if gods tended to find hosts who shared their goals, then it made total sense that Set would try to merge with him. Both wanted power, both were resentful and angry, both wanted to smash Sadie and me to a pulp. And if Set was now secretly controlling the Chief Lector...A drop of sweat trickled down the side of my face. I wanted to get out of this mansion.

Suddenly there was a banging sound below us, like someone closing a door downstairs.

"Show me where *The Book of Thoth* is," I ordered Doughboy. "Quick!"

As we moved down the shelves, Doughboy grew so warm in my hands, I was afraid he would melt. He kept a running commentary on the books.

"Ah, *Mastery of the Five Elements!*"

"Is that the one we want?" I asked.

"No, but a good one. How to tame the five essential elements of the universe—earth, air, water, fire, and cheese!"

"Cheese?"

He scratched his wax head. "I'm pretty sure that's the fifth, yes. But moving right along!"

We turned to the next shelf. "No," he announced. "No. Boring. Boring. Oh, Clive Cussler! No. No."

I was about to give up hope when he said, "There."

I froze. "Where—here?"

"The blue book with the gold trim," he said. "The one that's—"

I pulled it out, and the entire room began to shake.

"—trapped," Doughboy continued.

Sadie squawked urgently. I turned and saw her take flight. Something small and black swooped down from the ceiling. Sadie clashed with it in midair, and the black thing disappeared down her throat.

Before I could even register how gross that was, alarms blared downstairs. More black forms dropped from the ceiling and seemed to multiply in the air, swirling into a funnel cloud of fur and wings.

"There's your answer," Doughboy told me. "*Desjardins* would want to summon fruit bats. You mess with the wrong books, you trigger a plague of fruit bats. That's the trap!"

The things were on me like I was a ripe mango—diving at my face, clawing at my arms. I clutched the book and ran to the table, but I could hardly see. "Sadie, get out of here!" I yelled.

"*SAW!*" she cried, which I hoped meant yes.

I found Dad's workbag and shoved the book and Doughboy inside. The library door rattled. Voices yelled in French.

Horus, bird time! I thought desperately. *And no emu, please!*

I ran for the glass doors. At the last second, I found myself flying—once again a falcon, bursting into the cold rain. I knew with the senses of a predator that I was being followed by approximately four thousand angry fruit bats.

But falcons are wicked fast. Once outside, I raced north,

hoping to draw the bats away from Sadie and Bast. I outdistanced the bats easily but let them keep close enough that they wouldn't give up. Then, with a burst of speed, I turned in a tight circle and shot back toward Sadie and Bast in a hundred-mile-an-hour dive.

Bast looked up in surprise as I plummeted to the sidewalk, tumbling over myself as I turned back into a human. Sadie caught my arm, and only then did I realize she was back to normal as well.

"That was awful!" she announced.

"Exit strategy, quick!" I pointed at the sky, where an angry black cloud of fruit bats was getting closer and closer.

"The Louvre." Bast grabbed our hands. "It's got the closest portal."

Three blocks away. We'd never make it.

Then the red door of Desjardins' house blasted open, but we didn't wait to see what came out of it. We ran for our lives down the rue des Pyramides.

19. A Picnic in the Sky

[Right, Carter. Give me the mic.]

So I'd been to the Louvre once before on holiday, but I hadn't been chased by vicious fruit bats. I would've been terrified, except I was too busy being angry with Carter. I couldn't believe the way he'd treated my bird problem. Honestly, I thought I would be a kite *forever*, suffocating inside a little feathery prison. And he had the nerve to make fun!

I promised myself I'd get revenge, but for the time being we had enough worries staying alive.

We raced along in the cold rain. It was all I could do to avoid slipping on the slick pavements. I glanced back and saw two figures chasing us—men with shaved heads and goatees and black raincoats. They might've passed for normal mortals except they each carried a glowing staff. Not a good sign.

The bats were literally at our heels. One nipped my leg. Another buzzed my hair. I had to force myself to keep running.

My stomach still felt queasy from eating one of the little pests when I was a kite—and no, that had *not* been my idea. Totally a defensive instinct!

"Sadie," Bast called as we ran. "You'll have only seconds to open the portal."

"Where is it?" I yelled.

We dashed across the rue de Rivoli into a wide plaza surrounded by the wings of the Louvre. Bast made straight for the glass pyramid at the entrance, glowing in the dusk.

"You can't be serious," I said. "That isn't a *real* pyramid."

"Of course it's real," Bast said. "The *shape* gives a pyramid its power. It is a ramp to the heavens."

The bats were all around us now—biting our arms, flying around our feet. As their numbers increased, it got harder to see or move.

Carter reached for his sword, then apparently remembered it wasn't there anymore. He'd lost it at Luxor. He swore and rummaged around in his workbag.

"Don't slow down!" Bast warned.

Carter pulled out his wand. In total frustration, he threw it at a bat. I thought this a pointless gesture, but the wand glowed white-hot and thumped the bat solidly on the head, knocking it out of the air. The wand ricocheted through the swarm, thumping six, seven, eight of the little monsters before returning to Carter's hand.

"Not bad," I said. "Keep it up!"

We arrived at the base of the pyramid. The plaza was thankfully empty. The last thing I wanted was my embarrassing death by fruit bats posted on YouTube.

"One minute until sundown," Bast warned. "Our last chance for summoning is *now*."

She unsheathed her knives and started slicing bats out of the air, trying to keep them away from me. Carter's wand flew wildly, knocking fruit bats every which way. I faced the pyramid and tried to think of a portal, the way I'd done at Luxor, but it was almost impossible to concentrate.

Where do you wish to go? Isis said in my mind.

God, I don't care! America!

I realized I was crying. I hated to, but shock and fear were starting to overwhelm me. Where did I want to go? Home, of course! Back to my flat in London—back to my own room, my grandparents, my mates at school and my *old life*. But I couldn't. I had to think about my father and our mission. We had to get to Set.

America, I thought. *Now!*

My burst of emotion must've had some effect. The pyramid trembled. Its glass walls shimmered and the top of the structure began to glow.

A swirling sand vortex appeared, all right. Only one problem: it was hovering above the very top of the pyramid.

"Climb!" Bast said. Easy for her—she was a cat.

"The side is too steep!" Carter objected.

He'd done a good job with the bats. Dazed heaps littered the pavement, but more still flew round us, biting every bit of exposed skin, and the magicians were closing in.

"I'll toss you," Bast said.

"Excuse me?" Carter protested, but she picked him up by his collar and pants and tossed him up the side of the pyramid.

He skittered to the top in a very undignified manner and slipped straight through the portal.

"Now you, Sadie," Bast said. "Come on!"

Before I could move, a man's voice yelled, "Stop!"

Stupidly, I froze. The voice was so powerful, it was hard not to.

The two magicians were approaching. The taller one spoke in perfect English: "Surrender, Miss Kane, and return our master's property."

"Sadie, don't listen," Bast warned. "Come here."

"The cat goddess deceives you," the magician said. "She abandoned her post. She endangered us all. She will lead you to ruin."

I could tell he meant it. He was absolutely convinced of what he said.

I turned to Bast. Her expression had changed. She looked wounded, even grief-stricken.

"What does he mean?" I said. "What did you do wrong?"

"We have to leave," she warned. "Or they will kill us."

I looked at the portal. Carter was already through. That decided it. I wasn't going to be separated from him. As annoying as he was, Carter was the only person I had left. (How is that for depressing?)

"Toss me," I said.

Bast grabbed me. "See you in America." Then she chucked me up the side of the pyramid.

I heard the magician roar, "Surrender!" And an explosion rattled the glass next to my head. Then I plunged into the hot vortex of sand.

I woke in a small room with industrial carpeting, gray walls, and metal-framed windows. I felt as if I were inside a high-tech refrigerator. I sat up groggily and discovered I was coated in cold, wet sand.

"*Ugh*," I said. "Where are we?"

Carter and Bast stood by the window. Apparently they'd been conscious for a while, because they'd both brushed themselves off.

"You've got to see this view," Carter said.

I got shakily to my feet and nearly fell down again when I saw how high we were.

An entire city spread out below us—I mean *far* below, well over a hundred meters. I could almost believe we were still in Paris, because a river curved off to our left, and the land was mostly flat. There were white government buildings clustered around networks of parks and circular roads, all spread out under a winter sky. But the light was wrong. It was still afternoon here, so we must've traveled west. And as my eyes made their way to the other end of a long rectangular green space, I found myself staring at a mansion that looked oddly familiar.

"Is that ... the White House?"

Carter nodded. "You got us to America, all right. Washington, D.C."

"But we're sky high!"

Bast chuckled. "You didn't specify any particular American city, did you?"

"Well ... no."

"So you got the default portal for the U.S.—the largest single source of Egyptian power in North America."

I stared at her uncomprehendingly.

"The biggest obelisk ever constructed," she said. "The Washington Monument."

I had another moment of vertigo and moved away from the window. Carter grabbed my shoulder and helped me sit down.

"You should rest," he said. "You passed out for ... how long, Bast?"

"Two hours and thirty-two minutes," she said. "I'm sorry, Sadie. Opening more than one portal a day *is* extremely taxing, even with Isis helping."

Carter frowned. "But we need her to do it again, right? It's not sunset here yet. We can still use portals. Let's open one and get to Arizona. That's where Set is."

Bast pursed her lips. "Sadie can't summon another portal. It would overextend her powers. I don't have the talent. And you, Carter ... well, your abilities lie elsewhere. No offense."

"Oh, no," he grumbled. "I'm sure you'll call me next time you need to boomerang some fruit bats."

"Besides," Bast said, "when a portal is used, it needs time to cool down. No one will be able to use the Washington Monument—"

"For another twelve hours." Carter cursed. "I forgot about that."

Bast nodded. "And by then, the Demon Days will have begun."

"So we need another way to Arizona," Carter said.

I suppose he didn't mean to make me feel guilty, but I did. I hadn't thought things through, and now we were stuck in Washington.

I glanced at Bast out the corner of my eye. I wanted to ask her what the men at the Louvre had meant about her leading us to ruin, but I was afraid to. I wanted to believe she was on our side. Perhaps if I gave her a chance, she'd volunteer the information.

"At least those magicians can't follow us," I prompted.

Bast hesitated. "Not through the portal, no. But there are other magicians in America. And worse...Set's minions."

My heart climbed into my throat. The House of Life was scary enough, but when I remembered Set, and what his minions had done to Amos's house...

"What about Thoth's spellbook?" I said. "Did we at least find a way to fight Set?"

Carter pointed to the corner of the room. Spread out on Bast's raincoat was Dad's magic toolbox and the blue book we'd stolen from Desjardins.

"Maybe you can make sense of it," Carter said. "Bast and I couldn't read it. Even Doughboy was stumped."

I picked up the book, which was actually a scroll folded into sections. The papyrus was so brittle, I was afraid to touch it. Hieroglyphs and illustrations crowded the page, but I couldn't make sense of them. My ability to read the language seemed to be switched off.

Isis? I asked. *A little help?*

Her voice was silent. Maybe I'd worn her out. Or maybe

she was cross with me for not letting her take over my body, the way Horus had asked Carter to do. Selfish of me, I know.

I closed the book in frustration. "All that work for nothing."

"Now, now," Bast said. "It's not so bad."

"Right," I said. "We're stuck in Washington, D.C. We have two days to make it to Arizona and stop a god we don't know how to stop. And if we can't, we'll never see our dad or Amos again, and the world might end."

"That's the spirit!" Bast said brightly. "Now, let's have a picnic."

She snapped her fingers. The air shimmered, and a pile of Friskies cans and two jugs of milk appeared on the carpet.

"*Um*," Carter said, "can you conjure any people food?"

Bast blinked. "Well, no accounting for taste."

The air shimmered again. A plate of grilled cheese sandwiches and crisps appeared, along with a six-pack of Coke.

"Yum," I said.

Carter muttered something under his breath. I suppose grilled cheese wasn't his favorite, but he picked up a sandwich.

"We should leave soon," he said between bites. "I mean... tourists and all."

Bast shook her head. "The Washington Monument closes at six o'clock. The tourists are gone now. We might as well stay the night. If we must travel during the Demon Days, best to do it in daylight hours."

We all must've been exhausted, because we didn't talk again until we'd finished our food. I ate three sandwiches and drank two Cokes. Bast made the whole place smell like fish

Friskies, then started licking her hand as if preparing for a cat bath.

"Could you not do that?" I asked. "It's disturbing."

"Oh." She smiled. "Sorry."

I closed my eyes and leaned against the wall. It felt good to rest, but I realized the room wasn't actually quiet. The entire building seemed to be humming ever so slightly, sending a tremble through my skull that made my teeth buzz. I opened my eyes and sat up. I could still feel it.

"What is that?" I asked. "The wind?"

"Magic energy," Bast said. "I told you, this is a powerful monument."

"But it's modern. Like the Louvre pyramid. Why is it magic?"

"The Ancient Egyptians were excellent builders, Sadie. They picked shapes—obelisks, pyramids—that were charged with symbolic magic. An obelisk represents a sunbeam frozen in stone—a life-giving ray from the original king of the gods, Ra. It doesn't matter *when* the structure was built: it is still Egyptian. That's why any obelisk can be used for opening gates to the Duat, or releasing great beings of power—"

"Or trapping them," I said. "The way you were trapped in Cleopatra's Needle."

Her expression darkened. "I wasn't actually trapped *in* the obelisk. My prison was a magically created abyss deep in the Duat, and the obelisk was the door your parents used to release me. But, yes. All symbols of Egypt are concentrated nodes of magic power. So an obelisk can definitely be used to imprison gods."

An idea was nagging at the back of my mind, but I couldn't quite pin it down. Something about my mother, and Cleopatra's Needle, and my father's last promise in the British Museum: *I'll put things right.*

Then I thought back to the Louvre, and the comment the magician had made. Bast looked so cross at the moment I was almost afraid to ask, but it was the only way I'd get an answer. "The magician said you abandoned your post. What did he mean?"

Carter frowned. "When was this?"

I told him what had happened after Bast chucked him through the portal.

Bast stacked her empty Friskies cans. She didn't look eager to reply.

"When I was imprisoned," she said at last, "I—I wasn't alone. I was locked inside with a ... creature of chaos."

"Is that bad?" I asked.

Judging from Bast's expression, the answer was yes. "Magicians often do this—lock a god up together with a monster so we have no time to try escaping our prison. For eons, I fought this monster. When your parents released me—".

"The monster got out?"

Bast hesitated a little too long for my taste.

"No. My enemy couldn't have escaped." She took a deep breath. "Your mother's final act of magic sealed that gate. The enemy was still inside. But that's what the magician meant. As far as he was concerned, my 'post' was battling that monster forever."

It had the ring of truth, as if she were sharing a painful

memory, but it didn't explain the other bit the magician had said: *She endangered us all.* I was getting up the nerve to ask exactly what the monster had been, when Bast stood up.

"I should go scout," she said abruptly. "I'll be back."

We listened to her footsteps echo down the stairwell.

"She's hiding something," Carter said.

"Work that out yourself, did you?" I asked.

He looked away, and immediately I felt bad.

"I'm sorry," I said. "It's just . . . what are we going to do?"

"Rescue Dad. What else can we do?" He picked up his wand and turned it in his fingers. "Do you think he really meant to . . . you know, bring Mom back?"

I wanted to say yes. More than anything, I wanted to believe that was possible. But I found myself shaking my head. Something about it didn't seem right. "Iskandar told me something about Mum," I said. "She was a diviner. She could see the future. He said she made him rethink some old ideas."

It was my first chance to tell Carter about my conversation with the old magician, so I gave him the details.

Carter knit his eyebrows. "You think that has something to do with why Mom died—she saw something in the future?"

"I don't know." I tried to think back to when I was six, but my memory was frustratingly fuzzy. "When they took us to England the last time, did she and Dad seem like they were in a hurry—like they were doing something really important?"

"Definitely."

"Would you say freeing Bast was really important? I mean—I love her, of course—but *worth dying for* important?"

Carter hesitated. "Probably not."

"Well, there you are. I think Dad and Mum were up to something bigger, something they didn't complete. Possibly that's what Dad was after at the British Museum—completing the task, whatever it was. *Making things right.* And this whole business about our family going back a billion years to some god-hosting pharaohs—why didn't anyone *tell* us? Why didn't Dad?"

Carter didn't answer for a long time.

"Maybe Dad was protecting us," he said. "The House of Life doesn't trust our family, especially after what Dad and Mom did. Amos said we were raised apart for a reason, so we wouldn't, like, trigger each other's magic."

"Bloody awful reason to keep us apart," I muttered.

Carter looked at me strangely, and I realized what I'd said might have been construed as a compliment.

"I just mean they should've been honest," I rushed on. "Not that I *wanted* more time with my annoying brother, of course."

He nodded seriously. "Of course."

We sat listening to the magic hum of the obelisk. I tried to remember the last time Carter and I had simply spent time like this together, talking.

"Is your, *um*..." I tapped the side of my head. "Your *friend* being any help?"

"Not much," he admitted. "Yours?"

I shook my head. "Carter, are you scared?"

"A little." He dug his wand into the carpet. "No, a lot."

I looked at the blue book we'd stolen—pages full of wonderful secrets I couldn't read. "What if we can't do it?"

"I don't know," he said. "That book about mastering the element of cheese would've been more helpful."

"Or summoning fruit bats."

"Please, not the fruit bats."

We shared a weary smile, and it felt rather good. But it changed nothing. We were still in serious trouble with no clear plan.

"Why don't you sleep on it?" he suggested. "You used a lot of energy today. I'll keep watch until Bast gets back."

He actually sounded concerned for me. How cute.

I didn't want to sleep. I didn't want to miss anything. But I realized my eyelids *were* incredibly heavy.

"All right, then," I said. "Don't let the bedbugs bite."

I lay down to sleep, but my soul—my *ba*—had other ideas.

20. I Visit the Star-Spangled Goddess

I HADN'T REALIZED HOW UNSETTLING it would be. Carter had explained how his *ba* left his body while he slept, but having it happen to me was another thing altogether. It was much worse than my vision in the Hall of Ages.

There I was, floating in the air as a glowing birdlike spirit. And there was my body below me, fast asleep. Just trying to describe it gives me a headache.

My first thought as I gazed down on my sleeping form: *God, I look awful.* Bad enough looking in a mirror or seeing pictures of myself on my friends' Web pages. Seeing myself in person was simply *wrong.* My hair was a rat's nest, the linen pajamas were not in the least flattering, and the spot on my chin was *enormous.*

My second thought as I examined the strange shimmering form of my *ba: This won't do at all.* I didn't care if I was invisible to the mortal eye or not. After my bad experience as a kite, I simply refused to go about as a glowing Sadie-headed chicken. That's fine for Carter, but I have standards.

I could feel the currents of the Duat tugging at me, trying to pull my *ba* to wherever souls go when they have visions, but I wasn't ready. I concentrated hard, and imagined my normal appearance (well, all right, perhaps my appearance as I'd *like* it to be, a bit better than normal). And *voilà*, my *ba* morphed into a human form, still see-through and glowing, mind you, but more like a proper ghost.

Well, at least that's sorted, I thought. And I allowed the currents to sweep me away. The world melted to black.

At first, I was nowhere—just a dark void. Then a young man stepped out of the shadows.

"You again," he said.

I stammered. "*Uh . . .*"

Honestly, you know me well enough by now. That's *not* like me. But this was the boy I'd seen in my Hall of Ages vision—the very handsome boy with the black robes and tousled hair. His dark brown eyes had the most unnerving effect on me, and I was *very* glad I'd changed out of my glowing chicken outfit.

I tried again, and managed three entire words. "What are you . . ."

"Doing here?" he said, gallantly finishing my sentence. "Spirit travel and death are very similar."

"Not sure what that means," I said. "Should I be worried?"

He tilted his head as if considering the question. "Not this trip. She only wants to talk to you. Go ahead."

He waved his hand and a doorway opened in the darkness. I was pulled towards it.

"See you again?" I asked.

But the boy was gone.

I found myself standing in a luxury flat in the middle of the sky. It had no walls, no ceiling, and a see-through floor looking straight down at city lights from the height of an airplane. Clouds drifted below my feet. The air should've been freezing cold and too thin to breathe, but I felt warm and comfortable.

Black leather sofas made a U round a glass coffee table on a blood-red rug. A fire burned in a slate fireplace. Bookshelves and paintings hovered in the air where the walls should've been. A black granite bar stood in the corner, and in the shadows behind it, a woman was making tea.

"Hello, my child," she said.

She stepped into the light, and I gasped. She wore an Egyptian kilt from the waist down. From the waist up, she wore only a bikini top, and her skin... her skin was dark blue, covered with stars. I don't mean *painted* stars. She had the entire cosmos living on her skin: gleaming constellations, galaxies too bright to look at, glowing nebulae of pink and blue dust. Her features seemed to disappear into the stars that shifted across her face. Her hair was long and as black as midnight.

"You're the Nut," I said. Then I realized maybe that had come out wrong. "I mean... the sky goddess."

The goddess smiled. Her bright white teeth were like a new galaxy bursting into existence. "Nut is fine. And believe me, I've heard all the jokes about my name."

She poured a second cup from her teapot. "Let's sit and talk. Care for some *sahlab*?"

"Uh, it's not tea?"

"No, an Egyptian drink. You've heard of hot chocolate? This is rather like hot vanilla."

I would've preferred tea, as I hadn't had a proper cup in ages. But I supposed one didn't turn down a goddess. "Um... yeah. Thanks."

We sat together on the sofa. To my surprise, my glowing spirity hands had no trouble holding a teacup, and I could drink quite easily. The *sahlab* was sweet and tasty, with just a hint of cinnamon and coconut. It warmed me up nicely and filled the air with the smell of vanilla. For the first time in days I felt safe. Then I remembered I was only here in spirit.

Nut set down her cup. "I suppose you're wondering why I've brought you here."

"Where exactly is 'here'? And, ah, who's your doorman?"

I hoped she'd drop some information about the boy in black, but she only smiled. "I must keep my secrets, dear. I can't have the House of Life trying to find me. Let's just say I've built this home with a nice city view."

"Is that..." I gestured to her starry blue skin. "*Um*... are you inside a human host?"

"No, dear. The sky itself is my body. This is merely a manifestation."

"But I thought—"

"Gods need a physical host outside the Duat? It's somewhat easier for me, being a spirit of the air. I was one of the few gods who was never imprisoned, because the House of Life could never catch me. I'm used to being... *free-form*." Suddenly Nut and the entire apartment flickered. I felt like I would drop through the floor. Then the sofa became stable again.

"Please don't do that again," I begged.

"My apologies," Nut said. "The point is, each god is different. But all my brethren are free now, all finding places in this modern world of yours. They won't be imprisoned again."

"The magicians won't like that."

"No," Nut agreed. "That's the first reason you are here. A battle between the gods and the House of Life would serve only chaos. You must make the magicians understand this."

"They won't listen to me. They think I'm a godling."

"You *are* a godling, dear." She touched my hair gently, and I felt Isis stirring within me, struggling to speak using my voice.

"I'm Sadie Kane," I said. "I didn't ask for Isis to hitch a ride."

"The gods have known your family for generations, Sadie. In the olden days, we worked together for the benefit of Egypt."

"The magicians said that gods caused the fall of the empire."

"That is a long and pointless debate," Nut said, and I could hear an edge of anger in her voice. "All empires fall. But *the idea* of Egypt is eternal—the triumph of civilization, the forces of Ma'at overcoming the forces of chaos. That battle is fought generation after generation. Now it's your turn."

"I know, I know," I said. "We have to defeat Set."

"But is it that simple, Sadie? Set is my son, too. In the old days, he was Ra's strongest lieutenant. He protected the sun god's boat from the serpent Apophis. Now *there* was evil. Apophis was the embodiment of chaos. He hated Creation from the moment the first mountain appeared out of the sea. He hated the gods, mortals, and everything they built. And yet Set fought against him. Set was one of us."

"Then he turned evil?"

Nut shrugged. "Set has always been Set, for better or worse. But he is still part of our family. It is difficult to lose any member of your family . . . is it not?"

My throat tightened. "That's hardly fair."

"Don't speak to me of fairness," Nut said. "For five thousand years, I have been kept apart from my husband, Geb."

I vaguely remembered Carter saying something about this, but it seemed different listening to her now, hearing the pain in her voice.

"What happened?" I asked.

"Punishment for bearing my children," she said bitterly. "I disobeyed Ra's wishes, and so he ordered my own father, Shu—"

"Hang on," I said. "Shoe?"

"S-h-u," she said. "The god of the wind."

"Oh." I wished these gods had names that weren't common household objects. "Go on, please."

"Ra ordered my father, Shu, to keep us apart, forever. I am exiled to the sky, while my beloved Geb cannot leave the ground."

"What happens if you try?"

Nut closed her eyes and spread her hands. A hole opened where she was sitting, and she fell through the air. Instantly, the clouds below us flickered with lightning. Winds raged across the flat, throwing books off the shelves, ripping away paintings and flinging them into the void. My teacup leaped out of my hand. I grabbed the sofa to avoid getting blown away myself.

Below me, lightning struck Nut's form. The wind pushed her violently upward, shooting past me. Then the winds died. Nut settled back onto the couch. She waved her hand and the flat repaired itself. Everything returned to normal.

"*That* happens," she said sadly.

"Oh."

She gazed at the city lights far below. "It has given me appreciation for my children, even Set. He has done horrible things, yes. It is his nature. But he is still my son, and still one of the gods. He acts his part. Perhaps the way to defeat him is not the way you would imagine."

"Hints, please?"

"Seek out Thoth. He has found a new home in Memphis."

"Memphis . . . Egypt?"

Nut smiled. "Memphis, Tennessee. Although the old bird probably *thinks* it is Egypt. He so rarely takes his beak out of his books, I doubt he would know the difference. You will find him there. He can advise you. Be wary, though: Thoth often asks for favors. He is sometimes hard to predict."

"Getting used to that," I said. "How are we supposed to get there?"

"I am goddess of the sky. I can guarantee you safe travel as far as Memphis." She waved her hand, and a folder appeared in my lap. Inside were three plane tickets—Washington to Memphis, first-class.

I raised my eyebrow. "I suppose you get a lot of frequent flyer miles?"

"Something like that," Nut agreed. "But as you get closer

to Set, you will be beyond my help. And I cannot protect you on the ground. Which reminds me: You need to wake up soon. Set's minion is closing in on your hideout."

I sat up straight. "How soon?"

"Minutes."

"Send my spirit back, then!" I pinched my ghostly arm, which hurt just like it would on my normal arm, but nothing happened.

"Soon, Sadie," Nut promised. "But two more things you must know. I had five children during the Demon Days. If your father released all of them, you should consider: Where is the fifth?"

I racked my brain trying to remember the names of all of Nut's five children. Bit difficult without my brother, the Human Wikipedia, around to keep track of such trivia for me. There was Osiris, the king, and Isis, his queen; Set, the evil god, and Horus, the avenger. But the fifth child of Nut, the one Carter said he could never remember... Then I recalled my vision in the Hall of Ages—Osiris's birthday and the woman in blue who'd helped Isis escape Set. "You mean Nephthys, Set's wife?"

"Consider it," Nut said again. "And lastly... a favor."

She opened her hand and produced an envelope sealed with red wax. "If you see Geb... will you give him this?"

I'd been asked to pass notes before, but never between gods. Honestly, Nut's anguished expression was no different than those of my love-struck friends back at school. I wondered if she'd ever written on her notebook: GEB + NUT = TRUE LOVE or MRS. GEB.

"Least I can do," I promised. "Now, about sending me back…"

"Safe travels, Sadie," the goddess said. "And Isis, restrain yourself."

The spirit of Isis rumbled inside me, as if I'd eaten a bad curry.

"Wait," I said, "what do you mean restrain—"

Before I could finish, my vision went black.

I snapped awake, back in my own body at the Washington Monument. "Leave now!"

Carter and Bast jumped in surprise. They were already awake, packing their things.

"What's wrong?" Carter asked.

I told them about my vision while I frantically searched my pockets. Nothing. I checked my magician's bag. Tucked inside with my wand and rod were three plane tickets and a sealed envelope.

Bast examined the tickets. "Excellent! First class serves salmon."

"But what about Set's minion?" I asked.

Carter glanced out the window. His eyes widened. "Yeah, *um*…it's here."

21. Aunt Kitty to the Rescue

I'D SEEN PICTURES OF THE CREATURE BEFORE, but pictures didn't come close to capturing how horrible it was in real life.

"The Set animal," Bast said, confirming my fear.

Far below, the creature prowled the base of the monument, leaving tracks in the new-fallen snow. I had trouble judging its size, but it must've been at least as big as a horse, with legs just as long. It had an unnaturally lean, muscled body with shiny reddish gray fur. You could almost mistake it for a huge greyhound—except for the tail and the head. The tail was reptilian, forked at the end with triangular points, like squid tentacles. It lashed around as if it had a mind of its own.

The creature's head was the strangest part. Its oversize ears stuck straight up like rabbit ears, but they were shaped more like ice cream cones, curled inward and wider on the top than the bottom. They could rotate almost three hundred and sixty degrees, so they could hear anything. The creature's snout was long and curved like an anteater's—only anteaters don't have razor-sharp teeth.

"Its eyes are glowing," I said. "That can't be good."

"How can you see that far?" Sadie demanded.

She stood next to me, squinting at the tiny figure in the snow, and I realized she had a point. The animal was at least five hundred feet below us. How was I able to see its eyes?

"You still have the sight of the falcon," Bast guessed. "And you're right, Carter. The glowing eyes mean the creature has caught our scent."

I looked at her and almost jumped out of my skin. Her hair was sticking straight up all over her head, like she'd stuck her finger in a light socket.

"*Um*, Bast?" I asked.

"What?"

Sadie and I exchanged looks. She mouthed the word *scared*. Then I remembered how Muffin's tail would always poof up when something startled her.

"Nothing," I said, though if the Set animal was so dangerous that it gave our goddess light-socket hair, that had to be a very bad sign. "How do we get out of here?"

"You don't understand," Bast said. "The Set animal is the perfect hunter. If it has our scent, there is no stopping it."

"Why is it called the 'Set animal'?" Sadie asked nervously. "Doesn't it have a name?"

"If it did," Bast said, "you would not want to speak it. It is merely known as the Set animal—the Red Lord's symbolic creature. It shares his strength, cunning . . . and his evil nature."

"Lovely," Sadie said.

The animal sniffed at the monument and recoiled, snarling.

"It doesn't seem to like the obelisk," I noticed.

"No," Bast said. "Too much Ma'at energy. But that won't hold it back for long."

As if on cue, the Set animal leaped onto the side of the monument. It began climbing like a lion scaling a tree, digging its claws into the stone.

"That's messed up," I said. "Elevator or stairs?"

"Both are too slow," Bast said. "Back away from the window."

She unsheathed her knives and sliced through the glass. She punched out the window, setting off alarm bells. Freezing air blasted into the observation room.

"You'll need to fly," Bast yelled over the wind. "It's the only way."

"No!" Sadie's face went pale. "Not the kite again."

"Sadie, it's okay," I said.

She shook her head, terrified.

I grabbed her hand. "I'll stay with you. I'll make sure you turn back."

"The Set animal is halfway up," Bast warned. "We're running out of time."

Sadie glanced at Bast. "What about you? You can't fly."

"I'll jump," she said. "Cats always land on their feet."

"It's over a hundred meters!" Sadie cried.

"A hundred and seventy," Bast said. "I'll distract the Set animal, buy you some time."

"You'll be killed." Sadie's voice sounded close to breaking. "Please, I can't lose you too."

Bast looked a little surprised. Then she smiled and put her hand on Sadie's shoulder. "I'll be fine, dear. Meet me at Reagan National, terminal A. Be ready to run."

Before I could argue, Bast jumped out the window. My heart just about stopped. She plummeted straight toward the pavement. I was sure she'd die, but as she fell she spread her arms and legs and seemed to relax.

She hurtled straight past the Set animal, which let out a horrible scream like a wounded man on a battlefield, then turned and leaped after her.

Bast hit the ground with both feet and took off running. She must've been doing sixty miles an hour, easy. The Set animal wasn't as agile. It crashed so hard, the pavement cracked. It stumbled for a few steps but didn't appear hurt. Then it loped after Bast and was soon gaining on her.

"She won't make it," Sadie fretted.

"Never bet against a cat," I said. "We've got to do our part. Ready?"

She took a deep breath. "All right. Before I change my mind."

Instantly, a black-winged kite appeared in front of me, flapping its wings to keep its balance in the intense wind. I willed myself to become a falcon. It was even easier than before.

A moment later, we soared into the cold morning air over Washington, D.C.

Finding the airport was easy. Reagan National was so close, I could see the planes landing across the Potomac.

The hard part was remembering what I was doing. Every

time I saw a mouse or a squirrel, I instinctively veered toward it. A couple of times I caught myself about to dive, and I had to fight the urge. Once I looked over and realized I was a mile away from Sadie, who was off doing her own hunting. I had to force myself to fly next to her and get her attention.

It takes willpower to stay human, the voice of Horus warned. *The more time you spend as a bird of prey, the more you think like one.*

Now you tell me, I thought.

I could help, he urged. *Give me control.*

Not today, bird-head.

Finally, I steered Sadie toward the airport, and we started hunting for a place to change back to human form. We landed at the top of a parking garage.

I willed myself to turn human. Nothing happened.

Panic started building in my throat. I closed my eyes and pictured my dad's face. I thought about how much I missed him, how much I needed to find him.

When I opened my eyes, I was back to normal. Unfortunately, Sadie was still a kite. She flapped around me and cawed frantically. *"Ha—ha—ha!"* There was a wild look in her eyes, and this time I understood how scared she was. Bird form had been hard enough for her to break out of the first time. If the second time took even more energy, she could be in serious trouble.

"It's all right." I crouched down, careful to move slowly. "Sadie, don't force it. You have to relax."

"Ha!" She tucked in her wings. Her chest was heaving.

"Listen, it helped me to focus on Dad. Remember what's

important to you. Close your eyes and think about your human life."

She closed her eyes, but almost instantly cried out in frustration and flapped her wings.

"Stop," I said. "Don't fly away!"

She tilted her head and gurgled in a pleading way. I started talking to her the way I would to a scared animal. I wasn't really paying attention to the words. I was just trying to keep my tone calm. But after a minute I realized I was telling her about my travels with Dad, and the memories that had helped me get out of bird form. I told her about the time Dad and I got stuck in the Venice airport and I ate so many cannoli, I got sick. I told her about the time in Egypt when I found the scorpion in my sock, and Dad managed to kill it with a TV remote control. I told her how we'd gotten separated once in the London Underground and how scared I was until Dad finally found me. I told her some pretty embarrassing stories that I'd never shared with anyone, because who could I share them with? And it seemed to me that Sadie listened. At least she stopped flapping her wings. Her breathing slowed. She became very still, and her eyes didn't look so panicked.

"Okay, Sadie," I said at last. "I've got an idea. Here's what we're going to do."

I took Dad's magic box out of its leather bag. I wrapped the bag around my forearm and tied it with the straps as best I could. "Hop on."

Sadie flew up and perched at my wrist. Even with my makeshift armguard, her sharp talons dug into my skin.

"We'll get you out of this," I said. "Keep trying. Relax, and focus on your human life. You'll figure it out, Sadie. I know you will. I'll carry you until then."

"*Ha.*"

"Come on," I said. "Let's find Bast."

With my sister perched on my arm, I walked to the elevator. A businessman with a rolling suitcase was waiting by the doors. His eyes widened when he saw me. I must've looked pretty strange—a tall black kid in dirty, ragged Egyptian clothes, with a weird box tucked under one arm and a bird of prey perched on the other.

"How's it going?" I said.

"I'll take the stairs." He hurried off.

The elevator took me to the ground level. Sadie and I crossed to the departures curb. I looked around desperately, hoping to see Bast, but instead I caught the attention of a curbside policeman. The guy frowned and started lumbering in my direction.

"Stay calm," I told Sadie. Resisting the urge to run, I turned and walked through the revolving doors.

Here's the thing—I always get a little edgy around police. I remember when I was like seven or eight and still a cute little kid, it wasn't a problem; but as soon as I hit eleven, I started to get the Look, like *What's that kid doing here? Is he going to steal something?* I mean it's ridiculous, but it's a fact. I'm not saying it happens with *every* police officer, but when it doesn't happen—let's just say it's a pleasant surprise.

This was not one of the pleasant times. I knew the cop was going to follow me, and I knew I had to act calm and walk like I had a purpose... which is not easy with a kite on your arm.

Christmas vacation, so the airport was pretty full—mostly families standing in line at the ticket counters, kids arguing and parents labeling luggage. I wondered what that would be like: a normal family trip, no magic problems or monsters chasing you.

Stop it, I told myself. *You've got work to do.*

But I didn't know where to go. Would Bast be inside security? Outside? The crowds parted as I walked through the terminal. People stared at Sadie. I knew I couldn't wander around looking lost. It was only a matter of time before the cops—

"Young man."

I turned. It was the police officer from outside. Sadie squawked, and the cop backed up, resting his hand on his nightstick.

"You can't have pets in here," he told me.

"I have tickets...." I tried to reach my pockets. Then I remembered that Bast had our tickets.

The cop scowled. "You'd better come with me."

Suddenly a woman's voice called: "There you are, Carter!"

Bast was hurrying over, pushing her way through the crowd. I'd never been happier to see an Egyptian god in my life.

Somehow she'd managed to change clothes. She wore a rose-colored pantsuit, lots of gold jewelry, and a cashmere coat, so she looked like a wealthy businesswoman. Ignoring the cop, she sized up my appearance and wrinkled her nose. "Carter, I *told* you not to wear those horrible falconry clothes. Honestly, you look like you've been sleeping in the wild!"

She took out a handkerchief and made a big production of wiping my face, while the policeman stared.

"*Uh*, ma'am," he finally managed. "Is this your—"

"Nephew," Bast lied. "I'm so sorry, officer. We're heading to Memphis for a falconry competition. I hope he hasn't caused any problems. We're going to miss our flight!"

"*Um*, the falcon can't fly..."

Bast giggled. "Well, of course it can fly, officer. It's a bird!"

His face reddened. "I mean on a plane."

"Oh! We have the paperwork." To my amazement, she pulled out an envelope and handed it to the cop, along with our tickets.

"I see," the cop said. He looked our tickets over. "You bought...a first class ticket for your falcon."

"It's a black kite, actually," Bast said. "But yes, it's a very temperamental bird. A prizewinner, you know. Give it a coach seat and try to offer it pretzels, and I won't be held responsible for the consequences. No, we *always* fly first class, don't we, Carter?"

"*Um*, yeah...Aunt Kitty."

She flashed me a look that said: *I'll get you for that.* Then she went back to smiling at the cop, who handed back our tickets and Sadie's "paperwork."

"Well, if you'll excuse us, officer. That's a very handsome uniform, by the way. Do you work out?" Before he could respond, Bast grabbed my arm and hurried me toward the security checkpoint. "Don't look back," she said under her breath.

As soon as we turned the corner, Bast pulled me aside by the vending machines.

"The Set animal is close," she said. "We've got a few minutes at best. What's wrong with Sadie?"

"She can't…" I stammered. "I don't know exactly."

"Well, we'll have to figure it out on the plane."

"How did you change clothes?" I asked. "And the document for the bird…"

She waved her hand dismissively. "Oh, mortal minds are weak. That 'document' is an empty ticket sleeve. And my clothes haven't really changed. It's just a glamour."

I looked at her more closely, and I saw she was right. Her new clothes flickered like a mirage over her usual leopard-skin bodysuit. As soon as she pointed it out, the magic seemed flimsy and obvious.

"We'll try to make it to the gate before the Set animal," she said. "It will be easier if you stow your things in the Duat."

"What?"

"You don't really want to tote that box around under your arm, do you? Use the Duat as a storage bin."

"How?"

Bast rolled her eyes. "Honestly, what do they teach magicians these days?"

"We had about twenty seconds of training!"

"Just imagine a space in the air, like a shelf or a treasure chest—"

"A locker?" I asked. "I've never had a school locker."

"Fine. Give it a combination lock—anything you want. Imagine opening the locker with your combination. Then shove the box inside. When you need it again, just call it to mind, and it will appear."

I was skeptical, but I imagined a locker. I gave it a combination: 13/32/33—retired numbers for the Lakers, obviously:

Chamberlain, Johnson, Abdul-Jabbar. I held out my dad's magic box and let it go, sure it would smash to the floor. Instead, the box disappeared.

"Cool," I said. "Are you sure I can get it back?"

"No," Bast said. "Now, come on!"

22. Leroy Meets the Locker of Doom

I'D NEVER GONE THROUGH SECURITY with a live bird of prey before. I thought it would cause a holdup, but instead the guards moved us into a special line. They checked our paperwork. Bast smiled a lot, flirted with the guards and told them they must be working out, and they waved us through. Bast's knives didn't set off the alarms, so maybe she'd stored them in the Duat. The guards didn't even try to put Sadie through the X-ray machine.

I was retrieving my shoes when I heard a scream from the other side of security.

Bast cursed in Egyptian. "We were too slow."

I looked back and saw the Set animal charging through the terminal, knocking passengers out of its way. Its weird rabbit ears swiveled back and forth. Foam dripped from its curved, toothy snout, and its forked tail lashed around, looking for something to sting.

"Moose!" a lady screamed. "Rabid moose!"

Everyone started screaming, running in different directions and blocking the Set animal's path.

"Moose?" I wondered.

Bast shrugged. "No telling what mortals will perceive. Now the idea will spread by power of suggestion."

Sure enough, more passengers started yelling "Moose!" and running around as the Set animal plowed through the lines and got tangled up in the stanchions. TSA officers surged forward, but the Set animal tossed them aside like rag dolls.

"Come on!" Bast told me.

"I can't just let it hurt these people."

"We can't stop it!"

But I didn't move. I wanted to believe Horus was giving me courage, or that maybe the past few days had finally woken up some dormant bravery gene I'd inherited from my parents. But the truth was scarier. This time, nobody was making me take a stand. I *wanted* to do it.

People were in trouble because of us. I *had* to fix it. I felt the same kind of instinct I felt when Sadie needed my help, like it was time for me to step up. And yes, it terrified me. But it also felt *right*.

"Go to the gate," I told Bast. "Take Sadie. I'll meet you there."

"What? Carter—"

"Go!" I imagined opening my invisible locker: 13/32/33. I reached out my hand, but not for my dad's magic box. I concentrated on something I'd lost in Luxor. It *had* to be there. For a moment, I felt nothing. Then my hand closed around a hard leather grip, and I pulled my sword out of nowhere.

Bast's eyes widened. "Impressive."

"Get moving," I said. "It's my turn to run interference."

"You realize it'll kill you."

"Thanks for the vote of confidence. Now, scat!"

Bast took off at top speed, Sadie flapping to stay balanced on her arm.

A shot rang out. I turned and saw the Set animal plow into a cop who'd just fired at its head to no effect. The poor cop flew backward and toppled over the metal detector gate.

"Hey, moose!" I screamed.

The Set animal locked its glowing eyes on me.

Well done! Horus said. *We will die with honor!*

Shut up, I thought.

I glanced behind me to make sure Bast and Sadie were out of sight. Then I approached the creature.

"So you've got no name?" I asked. "They couldn't think of one ugly enough?"

The creature snarled, stepping over the unconscious policeman.

"*Set animal* is too hard to say," I decided. "I'll call you Leroy."

Apparently, Leroy didn't like his name. He lunged.

I dodged his claws and managed to smack him in the snout with the flat of my blade, but that barely fazed him. Leroy backed up and charged again, slavering, baring his fangs. I slashed at his neck, but Leroy was too smart. He darted to the left and sank his teeth into my free arm. If it hadn't been for my makeshift leather armguard, I would've been minus one arm. As it was, Leroy's fangs still bit clear through the leather. Red-hot pain shot up my arm.

I yelled, and a primal surge of power coursed through my body. I felt myself rising off the ground and the golden aura of the hawk warrior forming around me. The Set animal's jaws were pried open so fast that it yelped and let go of my arm. I stood, now encased in a magical barrier twice my normal size, and kicked Leroy into the wall.

Good! said Horus. *Now dispatch the beast to the netherworld!*

Quiet, man. I'm doing all the work.

I was vaguely aware of security guards trying to regroup, yelling into their walkie-talkies and calling for help. Travelers were still screaming and running around. I heard a little girl shout: "Chicken man, get the moose!"

You know how hard it is to feel like an extreme falcon-headed combat machine when somebody calls you "chicken man"?

I raised my sword, which was now at the center of a ten-foot-long energy blade.

Leroy shook the dust off his cone-shaped ears, and came at me again. My armored form might've been powerful, but it was also clumsy and slow; moving it around felt like moving through Jell-O. Leroy dodged my sword strike and landed on my chest, knocking me down. He was a lot heavier than he looked. His tail and claws raked against my armor. I caught his neck in my glowing fists and tried to keep his fangs away from my face, but everywhere he drooled, my magical shield hissed and steamed. I could feel my wounded arm going numb.

Alarms blared. More passengers crowded toward the

checkpoint to see what was happening. I had to end this soon—before I passed out from pain or more mortals got hurt.

I felt my strength fading, my shield flickering. Leroy's fangs were an inch from my face, and Horus was offering no words of encouragement.

Then I thought about my invisible locker in the Duat. I wondered if other things could be put in there too... large, evil things.

I closed my hands around Leroy's throat and wedged my knee against his rib cage. Then I imagined an opening in the Duat—in the air right above me: 13/32/33. I imagined my locker opening as wide as it could go.

With my last bit of strength, I pushed Leroy straight up. He flew toward the ceiling, his eyes widening with surprise as he passed through an unseen rift and disappeared.

"Where'd it go?" someone yelled.

"Hey, kid!" another guy called. "You okay?"

My energy shield was gone. I wanted to pass out, but I had to leave before the security guys came out of their shock and arrested me for moose fighting. I got to my feet and threw my sword at the ceiling. It disappeared into the Duat. Then I wrapped the torn leather around my bleeding arm as best I could and ran for the gates.

I reached our flight just as they were closing the door.

Apparently, word of the chicken man incident hadn't spread quite yet. The gate agent gestured back toward the checkpoint as she took my ticket. "What's all the noise up there?"

"A moose got through security," I said. "It's under control now." Before she could ask questions, I raced down the jetway.

I collapsed into my seat across the aisle from Bast. Sadie, still in kite form, was pacing in the window seat next to me.

Bast let out a huge sigh of relief. "Carter, you made it! But you're hurt. What happened?"

I told her.

Bast's eyes widened. "You put the Set animal in your locker? Do you know how much strength that requires?"

"Yeah," I said. "I was there."

The flight attendant started making her announcements. Apparently, the security incident hadn't affected our flight. The plane pushed back from the gate on time.

I doubled forward in pain, and only then did Bast notice how bad my arm was. Her expression turned grim.

"Hold still." She whispered something in Egyptian, and my eyes began to feel heavy.

"You'll need sleep to heal that wound," she said.

"But if Leroy comes back—"

"Who?"

"Nothing."

Bast studied me as if seeing me for the first time. "That was extraordinarily brave, Carter. Facing the Set monster—you have more tomcat in you than I realized."

"*Um*—thanks?"

She smiled and touched my forehead. "We'll be in the air soon, my tomcat. Sleep."

I couldn't really object. Exhaustion washed over me, and I closed my eyes.

Naturally my soul decided to take a trip.

I was in *ba* form, circling above Phoenix. It was a brilliant winter morning. The cool desert air felt good under my wings. The city looked different in the daylight—a vast grid of beige and green squares dotted with palm trees and swimming pools. Stark mountains rose up here and there like chunks of the moon. The most prominent mountain was right below me—a long ridge with two distinct peaks. What had Set's minion called it on my first soul visit? Camelback Mountain.

Its foothills were crowded with luxury homes, but the top was barren. Something caught my attention: a crevice between two large boulders, and a shimmer of heat coming from deep within the mountain—something that no human eye would've noticed.

I folded my wings and dove toward the crevice.

Hot air vented out with such force that I had to push my way through. About fifty feet down, the crevice opened up, and I found myself in a place that simply couldn't exist.

The entire inside of the mountain had been hollowed out. In the middle of the cavern, a giant pyramid was under construction. The air rang with the sound of pickaxes. Hordes of demons cut blood-red limestone into blocks and hauled it to the middle of the cave, where more swarms of demons used ropes and ramps to hoist the blocks into place, the way my dad said the Giza pyramids were built. But the Giza pyramids had taken, like, twenty years each to complete. This pyramid was already halfway done.

There was something odd about it, too—and not just the

blood-red color. When I looked at it I felt a familiar tingle, as if the whole structure were humming with a tone...no, a *voice* I almost recognized.

I spotted a smaller shape floating in the air above the pyramid—a reed barge like Uncle Amos's riverboat. On it stood two figures. One was a tall demon in leather armor. The other was a burly man in red combat fatigues.

I circled closer, trying to stay in the shadows because I wasn't sure I was really invisible. I landed on the top of the mast. It was a tricky maneuver, but neither of the boat's occupants looked up.

"How much longer?" asked the man in red.

He had Set's voice, but he looked completely different than he had in my last vision. He wasn't a slimy black thing, and he wasn't on fire—except for the scary mixture of hatred and amusement burning in his eyes. He had a big thick body like a linebacker's, with meaty hands and a brutish face. His short bristly hair and trimmed goatee were as red as his combat fatigues. I'd never seen camouflage that color before. Maybe he was planning on hiding out in a volcano.

Next to him, the demon bowed and scraped. It was the weird rooster-footed guy I'd seen before. He was at least seven feet tall and scarecrow thin, with bird talons for feet. And unfortunately, this time I could see his face. It was almost too hideous to describe. You know those anatomy exhibits where they show dead bodies without skin? Imagine one of those faces alive, only with solid black eyes and fangs.

"We're making excellent progress, master!" the demon

promised. "We conjured a hundred more demons today. With luck, we will be done at sunset on your birthday!"

"That is unacceptable, Face of Horror," Set said calmly.

The servant flinched. I guessed his name was Face of Horror. I wondered how long it had taken his mom to think of that. *Bob? No. Sam? No. How about Face of Horror?*

"B-but, master," Face stammered. "I thought—"

"Do not think, demon. Our enemies are more resourceful than I imagined. They have temporarily disabled my favorite pet and are now speeding toward us. We must finish before they arrive. *Sunrise* on my birthday, Face of Horror. No later. It will be the dawn of my new kingdom. I will scour all life from this continent, and this pyramid shall stand as a monument to my power—the final and eternal tomb of Osiris!"

My heart almost stopped. I looked down at the pyramid again, and I realized why it felt so familiar. It had an energy to it—*my father's* energy. I can't explain how, but I knew his sarcophagus lay hidden somewhere inside that pyramid.

Set smiled cruelly, as if he would be just as happy to have Face obey him or to rip Face to pieces. "You understand my order?"

"Yes, lord!" Face of Horror shifted his bird feet, as if building up his courage. "But may I ask, lord...why stop there?"

Set's nostrils flared. "You are one sentence away from destruction, Face of Horror. Choose your next words carefully."

The demon ran his black tongue across his teeth. "Well, my lord, is the annihilation of only one god worthy of your glorious self? What if we could create even more chaos energy—to feed your pyramid for all time and make you the eternal lord of all worlds?"

A hungry light danced in Set's eyes. "'Lord of all worlds' ... that has a nice ring to it. And how would you accomplish this, puny demon?"

"Oh, not I, my lord. I am an insignificant worm. But if we were to capture the others: Nephthys—"

Set kicked Face in the chest, and the demon collapsed, wheezing. "I told you never to speak her name."

"Yes, master," Face panted. "Sorry, master. But if we were to capture her, and the others... think on the power you could consume. With the right plan..."

Set began nodding, warming to the idea. "I think it's time we put Amos Kane to use."

I tensed. Was Amos here?

"Brilliant, master. A brilliant plan."

"Yes, I'm glad I thought of it. Soon, Face of Horror, *very* soon, Horus, Isis, and my treacherous wife will bow at my feet—and Amos will help. We'll have a nice little family reunion."

Set looked up—straight at me, as if he'd known I was there all along, and gave me that rip-you-to-pieces smile. "Isn't that right, boy?"

I wanted to spread my wings and fly. I had to get out of the cavern and warn Sadie. But my wings wouldn't work. I sat there paralyzed as Set reached out to grab me.

23. Professor Thoth's Final Exam

SADIE HERE. SORRY FOR THE DELAY, though I don't suppose you'd notice on a recording. My nimble-fingered brother dropped the microphone into a pit full of...oh, never mind. Back to the story.

Carter woke with such a start, he banged his knees against the drinks tray, which was quite funny.

"Sleep well?" I asked.

He blinked at me in confusion. "You're human."

"How kind of you to notice."

I took another bite of my pizza. I'd never eaten pizza from a china plate or had a Coke in a glass (with ice no less—Americans are so odd) but I was enjoying first class.

"I changed back an hour ago." I cleared my throat. "It—ah—was helpful, what you said, about focusing on what's important."

Awkward saying even that much, as I remembered everything he'd told me while I was in kite form about his travels

277

with Dad—how he'd gotten lost in the Underground, gotten sick in Venice, squealed like a baby when he'd found a scorpion in his sock. So much ammunition to tease him with, but oddly I wasn't tempted. The way he'd poured out his soul... Perhaps he thought I didn't understand him in kite form—but he'd been so honest, so unguarded, and he'd done it all to calm me down. If he hadn't given me something to focus on, I'd probably still be hunting field mice over the Potomac.

Carter had spoken about Dad as if their travels together had been a great thing, yes, but also quite a chore, with Carter always struggling to please and be on his best behavior, with no one to relax with, or talk to. Dad *was,* I had to admit, quite a presence. You'd be hard-pressed *not* to want his approval. (No doubt that's where I get my own stunningly charismatic personality.) I saw him only twice a year, and even so I had to prepare myself mentally for the experience. For the first time, I began to wonder if Carter really had the better end of the bargain. Would I trade my life for his?

I also decided not to tell him what had finally changed me back to human. I hadn't focused on Dad at all. I'd imagined Mum alive, imagined us walking down Oxford Street together, gazing in the shop windows and talking and laughing—the kind of ordinary day we'd never gotten to share. An impossible wish, I know. But it had been powerful enough to remind me of who I was.

Didn't say any of that, but Carter studied my face, and I sensed that he picked up my thoughts a little too well.

I took a sip of Coke. "You missed lunch, by the way."

"You didn't try to wake me?"

On the other side of the aisle, Bast burped. She'd just finished off her plate of salmon and was looking quite satisfied. "I could summon more Friskies," she offered. "Or cheese sandwiches."

"No thanks," Carter muttered. He looked devastated.

"God, Carter," I said. "If it's that important to you, I've got some pizza left—"

"It's not that," he said. And he told us how his *ba* had almost been captured by Set.

The news gave me trouble breathing. I felt as if I were stuck in kite form again, unable to think clearly. Dad trapped in a red pyramid? Poor Amos used as some sort of pawn? I looked at Bast for some kind of reassurance. "Isn't there anything we can do?"

Her expression was grim. "Sadie, I don't know. Set will be most powerful on his birthday, and sunrise is the most auspicious moment for magic. If he's able to generate one great explosion of storm energy at sunrise on that day—using not only his own magic, but augmenting it with the power of other gods he's managed to enslave . . . the amount of chaos he could unleash is almost unimaginable." She shuddered. "Carter, you say a simple demon gave him this idea?"

"Sounded like it," Carter said. "Or he tweaked the original plan, anyway."

She shook her head. "This is not like Set."

I coughed. "What do you mean? It's *exactly* like him."

"No," Bast insisted. "This is horrendous, even for him. Set wishes to be king, but such an explosion might leave him nothing to rule. It's almost as if . . ." She stopped herself, the thought seemingly too disturbing. "I don't understand it, but we'll be landing soon. You'll have to ask Thoth."

"You make it sound like you're not coming," I said.

"Thoth and I don't get along very well. Your chances of surviving might be better—"

The seat belt light came on. The captain announced we'd started our descent into Memphis. I peered out the window and saw a vast brown river cutting across the landscape—a river larger than any I'd ever seen. It reminded me uncomfortably of a giant snake.

The flight attendant came by and pointed to my lunch plate. "Finished, dear?"

"It seems so," I told her gloomily.

Memphis hadn't gotten word that it was winter. The trees were green and the sky was a brilliant blue.

We'd insisted Bast not "borrow" a car this time, so she agreed to rent one as long as she got a convertible. I didn't ask where she got the money, but soon we were cruising through the mostly deserted streets of Memphis with our BMW's top down.

I remember only snapshots of the city. We passed through one neighborhood that might've been a set from *Gone with the Wind*—big white mansions on enormous lawns shaded by cypress trees, although the plastic Santa Claus displays on the rooftops rather ruined the effect. On the next block, we almost got killed by an old woman driving a Cadillac out of a church parking lot. Bast swerved and honked her horn, and the woman just smiled and waved. Southern hospitality, I suppose.

After a few more blocks, the houses turned to rundown shacks. I spotted two African American boys wearing jeans and muscle shirts, sitting on their front porch, strumming acoustic guitars and singing. They sounded so good, I was tempted to stop.

On the next corner stood a cinder block restaurant with a hand-painted sign that read CHICKEN & WAFFLES. There was a queue of twenty people outside.

"You Americans have the strangest taste. What planet is this?" I asked.

Carter shook his head. "And where would Thoth be?"

Bast sniffed the air and turned left onto a street called Poplar. "We're getting close. If I know Thoth, he'll find a center of learning. A library, perhaps, or a cache of books in a magician's tomb."

"Don't have a lot of those in Tennessee," Carter guessed.

Then I spotted a sign and grinned broadly. "The University of Memphis, perhaps?"

"Well done, Sadie!" Bast purred.

Carter scowled at me. The poor boy gets jealous, you know.

A few minutes later, we were strolling through the campus of a small college: red brick buildings and wide courtyards. It was eerily quiet, except for the sound of a ball echoing on concrete.

As soon as Carter heard it, he perked up. "Basketball."

"Oh, please," I said. "We need to find Thoth."

But Carter followed the sound of the ball, and we followed him. He rounded the corner of a building and froze. "Let's ask them."

I didn't understand what he was on about. Then I turned the corner and yelped. On the basketball court, five players were in the middle of an intense game. They wore an assortment of jerseys from different American teams, and they all seemed keen to win—grunting and snarling at each other, stealing the ball and pushing.

Oh... and the players were all baboons.

"The sacred animal of Thoth," Bast said. "We must be in the right place."

One of the baboons had lustrous golden hair much lighter than the others, and a more, er, colorful bottom. He wore a purple jersey that seemed oddly familiar.

"Is that... a Lakers jersey?" I asked, hesitant to even name Carter's silly obsession.

He nodded, and we both grinned.

"Khufu!" we yelled.

True, we hardly knew the baboon. We'd spent less than a day with him, and our time at Amos's mansion seemed like ages ago, but still I felt like we'd recovered a long-lost friend.

Khufu jumped into my arms and barked at me. *"Agh! Agh!"* He picked through my hair, looking for bugs, I suppose [No comments from you, Carter!], and dropped to the ground, slapping the pavement to show how pleased he was.

Bast laughed. "He says you smell like flamingos."

"You speak Baboon?" Carter asked.

The goddess shrugged. "He also wants to know where you've been."

"Where *we've* been?" I said. "Well, first off, tell him I've spent the better part of the day as a kite, which is *not* a flamingo and does not end in *-o*, so it shouldn't be on his diet. Secondly—"

"Hold on." Bast turned to Khufu and said, *"Agh!"* Then she looked back at me. "All right, go ahead."

I blinked. "Okay . . . *um*, and secondly, where has *he* been?"

She relayed this in a single grunt.

Khufu snorted and grabbed the basketball, which sent his baboon friends into a frenzy of barking and scratching and snarling.

"He dove into the river and swam back," Bast translated, "but when he returned, the house was destroyed and we were gone. He waited a day for Amos to return, but he never did. So Khufu made his way to Thoth. Baboons are under his protection, after all."

"Why is that?" Carter asked. "I mean, no offense, but Thoth is the god of knowledge, right?"

"Baboons are very wise animals," Bast said.

"Agh!" Khufu picked his nose, then turned his Technicolor bum our direction. He threw his friends the ball. They began to fight over it, showing one another their fangs and slapping their heads.

"Wise?" I asked.

"Well, they're not *cats*, mind you," Bast added. "But, yes, wise. Khufu says that as soon as Carter keeps his promise, he'll take you to the professor."

I blinked. "The prof— Oh, you mean . . . right."

"What promise?" Carter asked.

The corner of Bast's mouth twitched. "Apparently, you promised to show him your basketball skills."

Carter's eyes widened in alarm. "We don't have time!"

"Oh, it's fine," Bast promised. "It's best that I go now."

"But where, Bast?" I asked, as I wasn't anxious to be separated from her again. "How will we find you?"

The look in her eyes changed to something like guilt, as if she'd just caused a horrible accident. "I'll find you when you get out, if you get out...."

"What do you mean *if*?" Carter asked, but Bast had already turned into Muffin and raced off.

Khufu barked at Carter most insistently. He tugged his hand, pulling him onto the court. The baboons immediately broke into two teams. Half took off their jerseys. Half left them on. Carter, sadly, was on the no-jersey team, and Khufu helped him pull his shirt off, exposing his bony chest. The teams began to play.

Now, I know nothing about basketball. But I'm fairly sure one isn't supposed to trip over one's shoes, or catch a pass with one's forehead, or dribble (is that the word?) with both hands as if petting a possibly rabid dog. But that is exactly the way Carter played. The baboons simply ran him over, quite literally. They scored basket after basket as Carter staggered back and forth, getting hit with the ball whenever it came close to him, tripping over monkey limbs until he was so dizzy he turned in a circle and fell over. The baboons stopped playing and watched him in disbelief. Carter lay in the middle of the court, covered in sweat and panting. The other baboons looked at Khufu. It was quite obvious what they were thinking: *Who invited this human?* Khufu covered his eyes in shame.

"Carter," I said with glee, "all that talk about basketball and the Lakers, and you're absolute *rubbish*! Beaten by monkeys!"

He groaned miserably. "It was . . . it was Dad's favorite game."

I stared at him. Dad's favorite game. God, why hadn't that occurred to me?

Apparently he took my gobsmacked expression as further criticism.

"I . . . I can tell you any NBA stat you want," he said a bit desperately. "Rebounds, assists, free throw percentages."

The other baboons went back to their game, ignoring Carter and Khufu both. Khufu let out a disgusted noise, half gag and half bark.

I understood the sentiment, but I came forward and offered Carter my hand. "Come on, then. It doesn't matter."

"If I had better shoes," he suggested. "Or if I wasn't so tired—"

"Carter," I said with a smirk. "It *doesn't* matter. And I'll not breathe a word to Dad when we save him."

He looked at me with obvious gratitude. (Well, I am rather wonderful, after all.) Then he took my hand, and I hoisted him up.

"Now for god's sake, put on your shirt," I said. "And Khufu, it's time you took us to the professor."

Khufu led us into a deserted science building. The air in the hallways smelled of vinegar, and the empty classroom labs looked like something from an American high school, not the sort of place a god would hang out. We climbed the stairs and found a row of professors' offices. Most of the doors were closed. One had been left open, revealing a space no bigger than a broom closet stuffed with books, a tiny desk, and one chair. I wondered if that professor had done something bad to get such a small office.

"*Agh!*" Khufu stopped in front of a polished mahogany door, much nicer than the others. A newly stenciled name glistened on the glass: DR. THOTH.

Without knocking, Khufu opened the door and waddled inside.

"After you, chicken man," I said to Carter. (And yes, I'm sure he was regretting telling me about that particular incident. After all, I couldn't *completely* stop teasing him. I have a reputation to maintain.)

I expected another broom closet. Instead, the office was impossibly big.

The ceiling rose at least ten meters, with one side of the office all windows, looking out over the Memphis skyline. Metal stairs led up to a loft dominated by an enormous telescope, and from somewhere up there came the sound of an electric guitar being strummed quite badly. The other walls of the office were crammed with bookshelves. Worktables overflowed with weird bits and bobs—chemistry sets, half-assembled computers, stuffed animals with electrical wires sticking out of their heads. The room smelled strongly of cooked beef, but with a smokier, tangier scent than I'd ever smelled.

Strangest of all, right in front of us, half a dozen longnecked birds—ibises—sat behind desks like receptionists, typing on laptop computers with their beaks.

Carter and I looked at each other. For once I was at a loss for words.

"*Agh!*" Khufu called out.

Up in the loft, the strumming stopped. A lanky man in his twenties stood up, electric guitar in hand. He had an unruly mane of blond hair like Khufu's, and he wore a stained white lab coat over faded jeans and a black T-shirt. At first I thought blood was trickling from the corner of his mouth. Then I realized it was some sort of meat sauce.

"Fascinating." He broke into a wide grin. "I've discovered something, Khufu. This is *not* Memphis, Egypt."

Khufu gave me a sideways look, and I could swear his expression meant, *Duh.*

"I've also discovered a new form of magic called blues music," the man continued. "And barbecue. Yes, you must try barbecue."

Khufu looked unimpressed. He climbed to the top of a bookshelf, grabbed a box of Cheerios, and began to munch.

The guitar man slid down the banister with perfect balance and landed in front of us. "Isis and Horus," he said. "I see you've found new bodies."

His eyes were a dozen colors, shifting like a kaleidoscope, with hypnotic effect.

I managed to stutter, "*Um*, we're not—"

"Oh, I see," he said. "Trying to share the body, eh? Don't think I'm fooled for a minute, Isis. I know you're in charge."

"But she's not!" I protested. "My name is Sadie Kane. I assume you're Thoth?"

He raised an eyebrow. "You claim not to know me? Of course I'm Thoth. Also called Djehuti. Also called—"

I stifled a laugh. "Ja-hooty?"

Thoth looked offended. "In Ancient Egyptian, it's a perfectly fine name. The Greeks called me Thoth. Then later they confused me with their god Hermes. Even had the nerve to rename my sacred city Hermopolis, though we're nothing alike. Believe me, if you've ever met Hermes—"

"*Agh!*" Khufu yelled through a mouthful of Cheerios.

"You're right," Thoth agreed. "I'm getting off track. So you claim to be Sadie Kane. And..." He swung a finger toward Carter, who was watching the ibises type on their laptops. "I suppose you're not Horus."

"Carter Kane," said Carter, still distracted by the ibises' screens. "What *is* that?"

Thoth brightened. "Yes, they're called computers. Marvelous, aren't they? Apparently—"

"No, I mean what are the birds typing?" Carter squinted and read from the screen. "'A Short Treatise on the Evolution of Yaks'?"

"My scholarly essays," Thoth explained. "I try to keep several projects going at once. For instance, did you know this university does not offer majors in astrology or leechcraft? Shocking! I intend to change that. I'm renovating new headquarters right now down by the river. Soon Memphis will be a true center of learning!"

"That's brilliant," I said halfheartedly. "We need help defeating Set."

The ibises stopped typing and stared at me.

Thoth wiped the barbecue sauce off his mouth. "You have the nerve to ask this after last time?"

"Last time?" I repeated.

"I have the account here somewhere...." Thoth patted the pockets of his lab coat. He pulled out a rumpled piece of paper and read it. "No, grocery list."

He tossed it over his shoulder. As soon as the paper hit the floor, it became a loaf of wheat bread, a jug of milk, and a six-pack of Mountain Dew.

Thoth checked his sleeves. I realized the stains on his coat were smeared words, printed in every language. The stains moved and changed, forming hieroglyphs, English letters, Demotic symbols. He brushed a stain off his lapel and seven letters fluttered to the floor, forming a word: *crawdad*. The word morphed into a slimy crustacean, like a shrimp, which wiggled its legs for only a moment before an ibis snapped it up.

"Ah, never mind," Thoth said at last. "I'll just tell you the short version: To avenge his father, Osiris, Horus challenged Set to a duel. The winner would become king of the gods."

"Horus won," Carter said.

"You do remember!"

"No, I read about it."

"And do you remember that without my help, Isis and you both would've died? Oh, I tried to mediate a solution to prevent the battle. That is one of my jobs, you know: to keep balance between order and chaos. But no-o-o, Isis convinced me to help your side because Set was getting too powerful. And the battle almost destroyed the world."

He complains too much, Isis said inside my head. *It wasn't so bad.*

"No?" Thoth demanded, and I got the feeling he could hear her voice as well as I could. "Set stabbed out Horus's eye."

"Ouch." Carter blinked.

"Yes, and I replaced it with a new eye made of moonlight. The Eye of Horus—your famous symbol. That was *me*, thank you very much. And when you cut off Isis's head—"

"Hold up." Carter glanced at me. "I cut off her *head?*"

I got better, Isis assured me.

"Only because I healed you, Isis!" Thoth said. "And yes, Carter, Horus, whatever you call yourself, you were so mad, you cut off her head. You were reckless, you see—about to charge Set while you were still weak, and Isis tried to stop you. That made you so angry you took your sword— Well, the point is, you almost destroyed each other before you could defeat Set. If you start another fight with the Red Lord, beware. He will use chaos to turn you against each other."

We'll defeat him again, Isis promised. *Thoth is just jealous.*

"Shut up," Thoth and I said at the same time.

He looked at me with surprise. "So, Sadie . . . you *are* trying to stay in control. It won't last. You may be blood of the pharaohs, but Isis is a deceptive, power-hungry—"

"I can contain her," I said, and I had to use all my will to keep Isis from blurting out a string of insults.

Thoth fingered the frets of his guitar. "Don't be so sure. Isis probably told you she helped defeat Set. Did she also tell you she was the reason Set got out of control in the first place? She exiled our first king."

"You mean Ra?" Carter said. "Didn't he get old and decide to leave the earth?"

Thoth snorted. "He was old, yes, but he was *forced* to leave. Isis got tired of waiting for him to retire. She wanted her husband, Osiris, to become king. She also wanted more power. So one day, while Ra was napping, Isis secretly collected a bit of the sun god's drool."

"*Eww,*" I said. "Since when does drool make you powerful?"

Thoth scowled at me accusingly. "You mixed the spit with clay to create a poisonous snake. That night, the serpent slipped into Ra's bedroom and bit him on the ankle. No amount of magic, even mine, could heal him. He would've died—"

"Gods can die?" Carter asked.

"Oh, yes," Thoth said. "Of course most of the time we rise again from the Duat—eventually. But this poison ate away at Ra's very being. Isis, of course, acted innocent. She cried to see Ra in pain. She tried to help with her magic. Finally she told Ra there was only one way to save him: Ra must tell her his secret name."

"Secret name?" I asked. "Like Bruce Wayne?"

"Everything in Creation has a secret name," Thoth said. "Even gods. To know a being's secret name is to have power over that creature. Isis promised that with Ra's secret name, she could heal him. Ra was in so much pain, he agreed. And Isis healed him."

"But it gave her power over him," Carter guessed.

"Extreme power," Thoth agreed. "She forced Ra to retreat into the heavens, opening the way for her beloved, Osiris, to become the new king of the gods. Set had been an important lieutenant to Ra, but he could not bear to see his brother Osiris become king. This made Set and Osiris enemies, and here we are five millennia later, still fighting that war, all because of Isis."

"But that's not my fault!" I said. "I would never do something like that."

"Wouldn't you?" Thoth asked. "Wouldn't you do anything to save your family, even if it upset the balance of the cosmos?"

His kaleidoscope eyes locked on mine, and I felt a surge of defiance. Well, why shouldn't I help my family? Who was this nutter in a lab coat telling me what I could and couldn't do?

Then I realized I didn't know who was thinking that: Isis or me. Panic started building in my chest. If I couldn't tell my own thoughts from those of Isis, how long before I went completely mad?

"No, Thoth," I croaked. "You have to believe me. I'm in control—me, Sadie—and I need your help. Set has our father."

I let it spill out, then—everything from the British Museum to Carter's vision of the red pyramid. Thoth listened without comment, but I could swear new stains developed on his lab coat as I talked, as if some of my words were being added to the mix.

"Just look at something for us," I finished. "Carter, hand him the book."

Carter rummaged through his bag and brought out the

book we'd stolen in Paris. "You wrote this, right?" he said. "It tells how to defeat Set."

Thoth unfolded the papyrus pages. "Oh, dear. I hate reading my old work. Look at this sentence. I'd never write it that way now." He patted his lab coat pockets. "Red pen—does anyone have one?"

Isis chafed against my willpower, insisting that we blast some sense into Thoth. *One fireball*, she pleaded. *Just one enormous magical fireball, please?*

I can't say I wasn't tempted, but I kept her under control.

"Look, Thoth," I said. "Ja-hooty, whatever. Set is about to destroy North America at the very least, possibly the world. Millions of people will die. You said you care about balance. Will you help us or not?"

For a moment, the only sounds were ibis beaks tapping on keyboards.

"You *are* in trouble," Thoth agreed. "So let me ask, why do you think your father put you in this position? Why did he release the gods?"

I almost said, *To bring back Mum*. But I didn't believe that anymore.

"My mum saw the future," I guessed. "Something bad was coming. I think she and Dad were trying to stop it. They thought the only way was to release the gods."

"Even though using the power of the gods is incredibly dangerous for mortals," Thoth pressed, "and against the law of the House of Life—a law that I convinced Iskandar to make, by the way."

I remembered something the old Chief Lector had told me

in the Hall of Ages. "Gods have great power, but only humans have creativity." "I think my mum convinced Iskandar that the rule was wrong. Maybe he couldn't admit it publicly, but she made him change his mind. Whatever is coming—it's so bad, gods and mortals are going to need each other."

"And what is coming?" Thoth asked. "The rise of Set?" His tone was coy, like a teacher trying a trick question.

"Maybe," I said carefully, "but I don't know."

Up on the bookshelf, Khufu belched. He bared his fangs in a messy grin.

"You have a point, Khufu," Thoth mused. "She does not sound like Isis. Isis would never admit she doesn't know something."

I had to clamp a mental hand over Isis's mouth.

Thoth tossed the book back to Carter. "Let's see if you act as well as you talk. I will explain the spell book, provided you prove to me that you truly have control of your gods, that you're not simply repeating the same old patterns."

"A test?" Carter said. "We accept."

"Now, hang on," I protested. Maybe being homeschooled, Carter didn't realize that "test" is normally a bad thing.

"Wonderful," Thoth said. "There is an item of power I require from a magician's tomb. Bring it to me."

"Which magician's tomb?" I asked.

But Thoth took a piece of chalk from his lab coat and scribbled something in the air. A doorway opened in front of him.

"How did you do that?" I asked. "Bast said we can't summon portals during the Demon Days."

"Mortals can't," Thoth agreed. "But a god of magic can. If you succeed, we'll have barbecue."

The doorway pulled us into a black void, and Thoth's office disappeared.

24. I Blow Up Some
Blue Suede Shoes

"Where are we?" I asked.

We stood on a deserted avenue outside the gates of a large estate. We still seemed to be in Memphis—at least the trees, the weather, the afternoon light were all the same.

The estate must've been several acres at least. The white metal gates were done in fancy designs of silhouetted guitar players and musical notes. Beyond them, the driveway curved through the trees up to a two-story house with a white-columned portico.

"Oh, no," Carter said. "I recognize those gates."

"What? Why?"

"Dad brought me here once. A great magician's tomb… Thoth has got to be kidding."

"Carter, what are you talking about? Is someone buried here?"

He nodded. "This is Graceland. Home to the most famous musician in the world."

"Michael Jackson lived here?"

"No, dummy," Carter said. "Elvis Presley."

I wasn't sure whether to laugh or curse. "Elvis Presley. You mean white suits with rhinestones, big slick hair, Gran's record collection—*that* Elvis?"

Carter looked around nervously. He drew his sword, even though we seemed to be totally alone. "This is where he lived and died. He's buried in back of the mansion."

I stared up at the house. "You're telling me Elvis was a magician?"

"Don't know." Carter gripped his sword. "Thoth did say something about music being a kind of magic. But something's not right. Why are we the only ones here? There's usually a mob of tourists."

"Christmas holidays?"

"But no security?"

I shrugged. "Maybe it's like what Zia did at Luxor. Maybe Thoth cleared everyone out."

"Maybe." But I could tell Carter was still uneasy. He pushed the gates, and they opened easily. "Not right," he muttered.

"No," I agreed. "But let's go pay our respects."

As we walked up the drive, I couldn't help thinking that the home of "the King" wasn't very impressive. Compared to some of the rich and famous homes I'd seen on TV, Elvis's place looked awfully small. It was just two stories high, with that white-columned portico and brick walls. Ridiculous plaster lions flanked the steps. Perhaps things were simpler back in Elvis's day, or maybe he spent all his money on rhinestone suits.

We stopped at the foot of the steps.

"So Dad brought you here?" I asked.

"Yeah." Carter eyed the lions as if expecting them to attack. "Dad loves blues and jazz, mostly, but he said Elvis was important because he took African American music and made it popular for white people. He helped invent rock and roll. Anyway, Dad and I were in town for a symposium or something. I don't remember. Dad insisted I come here."

"Lucky you." And yes, perhaps I was beginning to understand that Carter's life with Dad hadn't been all glamour and holiday, but still I couldn't help being a bit jealous. Not that I'd ever wanted to see Graceland, of course, but Dad had never insisted on taking me anywhere—at least until the British Museum trip when he disappeared. I hadn't even known Dad was an Elvis fan, which was rather horrifying.

We walked up the steps. The front door swung open all by itself.

"I don't like that," Carter said.

I turned to look behind us, and my blood went ice cold. I grabbed my brother's arm. "*Um*, Carter, speaking of things we don't like . . ."

Coming up the driveway were two magicians brandishing staffs and wands.

"Inside," Carter said. "Quick!"

I didn't have much time to admire the house. There was a dining room to our left and a living room–music room to our right, with a piano and a stained glass archway decorated with peacocks. All the furniture was roped off. The house smelled like old people.

"Item of power," I said. "Where?"

"I don't know," Carter snapped. "They didn't have 'items of power' listed on the tour!"

I glanced out the window. Our enemies were getting close. The bloke in front wore jeans, a black sleeveless shirt, boots, and a battered cowboy hat. He looked more like an outlaw than a magician. His friend was similarly dressed but much heftier, with tattooed arms, a bald head, and a scraggly beard. When they were ten meters away, the man with the cowboy hat lowered his staff, which morphed into a shotgun.

"Oh, please!" I yelled, and pushed Carter into the living room.

The blast shattered Elvis's front door and set my ears ringing. We scrambled to our feet and ran deeper into the house. We passed through an old-fashioned kitchen, then into the strangest den I'd ever seen. The back wall was made of vine-covered bricks, with a waterfall trickling down the side. The carpet was green shag (floor *and* ceiling, mind you) and the furniture was carved with creepy animal shapes. Just in case all that wasn't dreadful enough, plaster monkeys and stuffed lions had been strategically placed around the room. Despite the danger we were in, the place was so horrid, I just had to stop and marvel.

"God," I said. "Did Elvis have *no* taste?"

"The Jungle Room," Carter said. "He decorated it like this to annoy his dad."

"I can respect that."

Another shotgun blast roared through the house.

"Split up," Carter said.

"Bad idea!" I could hear the magicians tromping through the rooms, smashing things as they came closer.

"I'll distract them," Carter said. "You search. The trophy room is through there."

"Carter!"

But the fool ran off to protect me. I *hate* it when he does that. I should have followed him, or run the other way, but I stood frozen in shock as he turned the corner with his sword raised, his body beginning to glow with a golden light...and everything went wrong.

Blam! An emerald flash brought Carter to his knees. For a heartbeat, I thought he'd been hit with the shotgun, and I had to stifle a scream. But immediately, Carter collapsed and began to shrink, clothes, sword and all—melting into a tiny sliver of green.

The lizard that used to be my brother raced toward me, climbed up my leg and into my palm, where it looked at me desperately.

From around the corner, a gruff voice said, "Split up and find the sister. She'll be somewhere close."

"Oh, Carter," I whispered fondly to the lizard. "I will *so* kill you for this."

I stuffed him in my pocket and ran.

The two magicians continued to smash and crash their way through Graceland, knocking over furniture and blasting things to bits. Apparently they were not Elvis fans.

I ducked under some ropes, crept through a hallway, and found the trophy room. Amazingly, it was full of trophies. Gold records crowded the walls. Rhinestone Elvis jumpsuits glittered in four glass cases. The room was dimly lit, probably to keep the jumpsuits from blinding visitors, and music played softly from overhead speakers: Elvis warning everyone not to step on his blue suede shoes.

I scanned the room but found nothing that looked magical. The suits? I hoped Thoth did not expect me to wear one. The gold records? Lovely Frisbees, but no.

"Jerrod!" a voice called to my right. A magician was coming down the hallway. I darted toward the other exit, but a voice just outside it called back, "Yeah, I'm over here."

I was surrounded.

"Carter," I whispered. "Curse your lizard brain."

He fluttered nervously in my pocket but was no help.

I fumbled through my magician's bag and grasped my wand. Should I try drawing a magic circle? No time, and I didn't want to duel toe-to-toe with two older magicians. I had to stay mobile. I took out my rod and willed it into a full-length staff. I could set it on fire, or turn it into a lion, but what good would that do? My hands started to tremble. I wanted to crawl into a ball and hide beneath Elvis's gold record collection.

Let me take over, Isis said. *I can turn our enemies to dust.*

No, I told her.

You will get us both killed.

I could feel her pressing against my will, trying to bust out. I could taste her anger with these magicians. How dare they challenge us? With a word, we could destroy them.

No, I thought again. Then I remembered something Zia had said: *Use whatever you have available.* The room was dimly lit . . . perhaps if I could make it darker.

"Darkness," I whispered. I felt a tugging sensation in my stomach, and the lights flickered off. The music stopped. The light continued to dim—even the sunlight faded from the windows until the entire room went black.

Somewhere to my left, the first magician sighed in exasperation. "Jerrod!"

"Wasn't me, Wayne!" Jerrod insisted. "You always blame me!"

Wayne muttered something in Egyptian, still moving towards me. I needed a distraction.

I closed my eyes and imagined my surroundings. Although it was pitch-black, I could still sense Jerrod in the hallway to my left, stumbling through the darkness. I sensed Wayne on the other side of the wall to the right, only a few steps from the doorway. And I could visualize the four glass display cases with Elvis's suits.

They're tossing your house, I thought. *Defend it!*

A stronger pull in my gut, as if I were lifting a heavy weight—then the display cases blew open. I heard the shuffling of stiff cloth, like sails in the wind, and was dimly aware of four pale white shapes in motion—two heading to either door.

Wayne yelled first as the empty Elvis suits tackled him. His shotgun lit up the dark. Then to my left, Jerrod shouted in surprise. A heavy *clump!* told me he'd been knocked over. I decided to go in Jerrod's direction—better an off-balance bloke than one with a shotgun. I slipped through the doorway and down a hall, leaving Jerrod scuffling behind me and yelling, "Get off! Get off!"

Take him while he's down, Isis urged. *Burn him to ashes!*

Part of me knew she had a point: if I left Jerrod in one piece, he would be up in no time and after me again; but it didn't seem right to hurt him, especially while he was being tackled by Elvis suits. I found a door and burst outside into the afternoon sunlight.

I was in the backyard of Graceland. A large fountain gurgled nearby, ringed by grave markers. One had a glass-encased flame at the top and was heaped with flowers. I took a wild guess: it must be Elvis's.

A magician's tomb.

Of course. We'd been searching the house, but the item of power would be at his gravesite. But what exactly *was* the item?

Before I could approach the grave, the door burst open. The big bald man with the straggly beard stumbled out. A tattered Elvis suit had its sleeves wrapped around his neck like it was getting a piggyback ride.

"Well, well." The magician threw off the jumpsuit. His voice confirmed for me that he was the one called Jerrod. "You're just a little girl. You've caused us a lot of trouble, missy."

He lowered his staff and fired a shot of green light. I raised my wand and deflected the bolt of energy straight up. I heard a surprised coo—the cry of a pigeon—and a newly made lizard fell out of the sky at my feet.

"Sorry," I told it.

Jerrod snarled and threw down his staff. Apparently, he specialized in lizards, because the staff morphed into a komodo dragon the size of a London taxicab.

The monster charged me with unnatural speed. It opened

its jaws and would've bitten me in half, but I just had time to wedge my staff in its mouth.

Jerrod laughed. "Nice try, girl!"

I felt the dragon's jaws pressing on the staff. It was only a matter of seconds before the wood snapped, and then I'd be a komodo dragon's snack. *A little help*, I told Isis. Carefully, very carefully, I tapped in to her strength. Doing so without letting her take over was like riding a surfboard over a tidal wave, trying desperately to stay on my feet. I felt five thousand years of experience, knowledge, and power course through me. She offered me options, and I selected the simplest. I channeled power through my staff and felt it grow hot in my hands, glowing white. The dragon hissed and gurgled as my staff elongated, forcing the creature's jaws open wider, wider, and then: *boom!*

The dragon shattered into kindling and sent the splintered remains of Jerrod's staff raining down around me.

Jerrod had only a moment to look stunned before I threw my wand and whapped him solidly on the forehead. His eyes crossed, and he collapsed on the pavement. My wand returned to my hand.

That would've been a lovely happy ending...except I'd forgotten about Wayne. The cowboy-hatted magician stumbled out the door, almost tripping over his friend, but he recovered with lightning speed.

He shouted, "Wind!" and my staff flew out of my hands and into his.

He smiled cruelly. "Well fought, darlin'. But elemental magic is always quickest."

He struck the ends of both staffs, his and mine, against the pavement. A wave rippled over the dirt and pavement as if the ground had become liquid, knocking me off my feet and sending my wand flying. I scrambled backwards on hands and knees, but I could hear Wayne chanting, summoning fire from the staffs.

Rope, Isis said. *Every magician carries rope.*

Panic had made my mind go blank, but my hand instinctively went for my magic bag. I pulled out a small bit of twine. Hardly a rope, but it triggered a memory—something Zia had done in the New York museum. I threw the twine at Wayne and yelled a word Isis suggested: *"Tas!"*

A golden hieroglyph burned in the air over Wayne's head:

The twine whipped toward him like an angry snake, growing longer and thicker as it flew. Wayne's eyes widened. He stumbled back and sent jets of flame shooting from both staffs, but the rope was too quick. It lashed round his ankles and toppled him sideways, wrapping round his whole body until he was encased in a twine cocoon from chin to toes. He struggled and screamed and called me quite a few unflattering names.

I got up unsteadily. Jerrod was still out cold. I retrieved my staff, which had fallen next to Wayne. He continued straining against the twine and cursing in Egyptian, which sounded strange with an American Southern accent.

Finish him, Isis warned. *He can still speak. He will not rest until he destroys you.*

"Fire!" Wayne screamed. "Water! Cheese!"

Even the cheese command did not work. I reckoned his rage was throwing his magic off balance, making it impossible to focus, but I knew he would recover soon.

"Silence," I said.

Wayne's voice abruptly stopped working. He kept screaming, but no sound came out.

"I'm not your enemy," I told him. "But I can't have you killing me, either."

Something wriggled in my pocket, and I remembered Carter. I took him out. He looked okay, except of course for the fact he was still a lizard.

"I'll try to change you back," I told him. "Hopefully I don't make things worse."

He made a little croak that didn't convey much confidence.

I closed my eyes and imagined Carter as he should be: a tall boy of fourteen, badly dressed, very human, very annoying. Carter began to feel heavy in my hands. I put him down and watched as the lizard grew into a vaguely human blob. By the count of three, my brother was lying on his stomach, his sword and pack next to him on the lawn.

He spit grass out of his mouth. "How'd you do that?"

"I don't know," I admitted. "You just seemed...wrong."

"Thanks a lot." He got up and checked to make sure he had all his fingers. Then he saw the two magicians and his mouth fell open. "What did you do to them?"

"Just tied one up. Knocked one out. Magic."

"No, I mean..." He faltered, searching for words, then gave up and pointed.

I looked at the magicians and yelped. Wayne wasn't moving. His eyes and mouth were open, but he wasn't blinking or breathing. Next to him, Jerrod looked just as frozen. As we watched, their mouths began to glow as if they'd swallowed matches. Two tiny yellow orbs of fire popped out from between their lips and shot into the air, disappearing in the sunlight.

"What—what was that?" I asked. "Are they dead?"

Carter approached them cautiously and put his hand on Wayne's neck. "It doesn't even feel like skin. More like rock."

"No, they were human! I didn't turn them to rock!"

Carter felt Jerrod's forehead where I'd whacked him with my wand. "It's cracked."

"What?"

Carter picked up his sword. Before I could even scream, he brought the hilt down on Jerrod's face and the magician's head cracked into shards like a flowerpot.

"They're made of clay," Carter said. "They're both *shabti*."

He kicked Wayne's arm and I heard it crunch under the twine.

"But they were casting spells," I said. "And talking. They were *real*."

As we watched, the *shabti* crumbled to dust, leaving nothing behind but my bit of twine, two staffs, and some grungy clothes.

"Thoth was testing us," Carter said. "Those balls of fire, though…" He frowned as if trying to recall something important.

"Probably the magic that animated them," I guessed. "Flying back to their master—like a recording of what they did?"

It sounded like a solid theory to me, but Carter seemed awfully troubled. He pointed to the blasted back door of Graceland. "Is the whole house like that?"

"Worse." I looked at the ruined Elvis jumpsuit under Jerrod's clothes and scattered rhinestones. Maybe Elvis had no taste, but I still felt bad about trashing the King's palace. If the place had been important to Dad...Suddenly an idea perked me up. "What was it Amos said, when he repaired that saucer?"

Carter frowned. "This is a whole house, Sadie. Not a saucer."

"Got it," I said. "*Hi-nehm!*"

A gold hieroglyphic symbol flickered to life in my palm.

I held it up and blew it towards the house. The entire outline of Graceland began to glow. The pieces of the door flew back into place and mended themselves. The tattered bits of Elvis clothing disappeared.

"Wow," Carter said. "Do you think the inside is fixed too?"

"I—" My vision blurred, and my knees buckled. I would've knocked my head on the pavement if Carter hadn't caught me.

"It's okay," he said. "You did a lot of magic, Sadie. That was amazing."

"But we haven't even found the item Thoth sent us for."

"Yeah," Carter said. "Maybe we have."

He pointed to Elvis's grave, and I saw it clearly: a memento left behind by some adoring fan—a necklace with a silver loop-topped cross, just like the one on Mum's T-shirt in my old photograph.

"An ankh," I said. "The Egyptian symbol for eternal life."

Carter picked it up. There was a small papyrus scroll attached to the chain.

"What's this?" he murmured, and unrolled the sheet. He stared at it so hard I thought he'd burn a hole in it.

"What?" I looked over his shoulder.

The painting looked quite ancient. It showed a golden, spotted cat holding a knife in one paw and chopping the head off a snake.

Beneath it, in black marker, someone had written: *Keep up the fight!*

"That's vandalism, isn't it?" I asked. "Marking up an ancient drawing like that? Rather an odd thing to leave for Elvis."

Carter didn't seem to hear. "I've seen this picture before. It's in a lot of tombs. Don't know why it never occurred to me..."

I studied the picture more closely. Something about it did seem rather familiar.

"You know what it means?" I asked.

"It's the Cat of Ra, fighting the sun god's main enemy, Apophis."

"The snake," I said.

"Yeah, Apophis was—"

"The embodiment of chaos," I said, remembering what Nut had said.

Carter looked impressed, as well he should have. "Exactly. Apophis was even worse than Set. The Egyptians thought Doomsday would come when Apophis ate the sun and destroyed all of Creation."

"But...the cat killed it," I said hopefully.

"The cat had to kill it over and over again," Carter said. "Like what Thoth said about repeating patterns. The thing is ...I asked Dad one time if the cat had a name. And he said nobody knows for sure, but most people assume it's Sekhmet, this fierce lion goddess. She was called the Eye of Ra because she did his dirty work. He saw an enemy; she killed it."

"Fine. So?"

"So the cat doesn't look like Sekhmet. It just occurred to me..."

I finally saw it, and a shiver went down my back. "The Cat of Ra looks exactly like Muffin. It's Bast."

Just then the ground rumbled. The memorial fountain began to glow, and a dark doorway opened.

"Come on," I said. "I've got some questions for Thoth. And then I'm going to punch him in the beak."

25. We Win an All-Expenses-Paid Trip to Death

BEING TURNED INTO A LIZARD can really mess up your day. As we stepped through the doorway, I tried to hide it, but I was feeling pretty bad.

You're probably thinking: *Hey, you already turned into a falcon. What's the big deal?* But someone else *forcing* you into another form—that's totally different. Imagine yourself in a trash compactor, your entire body smashed into a shape smaller than your hand. It's painful and it's humiliating. Your enemy pictures you as a stupid harmless lizard, then imposes their will on you, overpowering your thoughts until you have to be what *they* want you to be. I guess it could've been worse. He could've pictured me as a fruit bat, but still...

Of course I felt grateful to Sadie for saving me, but I also felt like a complete loser. It was bad enough that I'd embarrassed myself on the basketball court with a troop of baboons. But I'd also totally failed in battle. Maybe I'd done okay with

Leroy, the airport monster, but faced with a couple of magicians (even clay ones), I got turned into a reptile in the first two seconds. How would I stand a chance against Set?

I was shaken out of those thoughts when we emerged from the portal, because we were definitely not in Thoth's office.

In front of us loomed a life-size glass-and-metal pyramid, almost as big as the ones at Giza. The skyline of downtown Memphis rose up in the distance. At our backs were the banks of the Mississippi River.

The sun was setting, turning the river and the pyramid to gold. On the pyramid's front steps, next to a twenty-foot-tall pharaoh statue labeled RAMESSES THE GREAT, Thoth had set out a picnic with barbecued ribs and brisket, bread and pickles, the works. He was playing his guitar with a portable amp. Khufu stood nearby, covering his ears.

"Oh, good." Thoth strummed a chord that sounded like the death cry of a sick donkey. "You lived."

I stared up at the pyramid in amazement. "Where did this come from? You didn't just...build it, did you?" I remembered my *ba* trip to Set's red pyramid, and suddenly pictured gods building monuments all over the U.S.

Thoth chuckled. "I didn't have to build it. The people of Memphis did that. Humans never really forget Egypt, you know. Every time they build a city on the banks of a river, they remember their heritage, buried deep in their subconscious. This is the Pyramid Arena—sixth largest pyramid in the world. It used to be a sports arena for...what is that game you like, Khufu?"

"*Agh!*" Khufu said indignantly. And I swear he gave me a dirty look.

"Yes, basketball," Thoth said. "But the arena fell on hard times. It's been abandoned for years. Well, no longer. I'm moving in. You do have the ankh?"

For a moment, I wondered if it had been such a good idea helping Thoth, but we needed him. I tossed him the necklace.

"Excellent," he said. "An ankh from the tomb of Elvis. Powerful magic!"

Sadie clenched her fists. "We almost died getting that. You tricked us."

"Not a trick," he insisted. "A test."

"Those *things*," Sadie said, "the *shabti*—"

"Yes, my best work in centuries. A shame to break them, but I couldn't have you beating up on *real* magicians, could I? *Shabti* make excellent stunt doubles."

"So you saw the whole thing," I muttered.

"Oh, yes." Thoth held out his hand. Two little fires danced across his palm—the magic essences we'd seen escape from the *shabti*'s mouths. "These are . . . recording devices, I suppose you'd say. I got a full report. You defeated the *shabti* without killing. I must admit I'm impressed, Sadie. You controlled your magic and controlled Isis. And you, Carter, did well turning into a lizard."

I thought he was teasing me. Then I realized there was genuine sympathy in his eyes, as if my failure had also been some kind of test.

"You will find worse enemies ahead, Carter," he warned.

"Even now, the House of Life sends its best against you. But you will also find friends where you least expect them."

I didn't know why, but I got the feeling he was talking about Zia...or maybe that was just wishful thinking.

Thoth stood and handed Khufu his guitar. He tossed the ankh at the statue of Ramesses, and the necklace fastened itself around the pharaoh's neck.

"There you are, Ramesses," Thoth said to the statue. "Here's to our new life."

The statue glowed faintly, as if the sunset had just gotten ten times brighter. Then the glow spread to the entire pyramid before slowly fading.

"Oh, yes," Thoth mused. "I think I'll be happy here. Next time you children visit me, I'll have a much bigger laboratory."

Scary thought, but I tried to stay focused.

"That's not all we found," I said. "You need to explain *this*."

I held out the painting of the cat and the snake.

"It's a cat and a snake," Thoth said.

"Thank you, god of wisdom. You placed it for us to find, didn't you? You're trying to give us some kind of clue."

"Who, me?"

Just kill him, Horus said.

Shut up, I said.

At least kill the guitar.

"The cat is Bast," I said, trying to ignore my inner psycho falcon. "Does this have something to do with why our parents released the gods?"

Thoth gestured toward the picnic plates. "Did I mention we have barbecue?"

Sadie stomped her foot. "We had a deal, Ja-hooty!"

"You know . . . I like that name," Thoth mused, "but not so much when *you* say it. I believe our deal was that I would explain how to use the spell book. May I?"

He held out his hand. Reluctantly I dug the magic book out of my bag and handed it over.

Thoth unfolded the pages. "Ah, this takes me back. So many formulae. In the old days, we believed in ritual. A good spell might take weeks to prepare, with exotic ingredients from all over the world."

"We don't have weeks," I said.

"Rush, rush, rush." Thoth sighed.

"*Agh*," Khufu agreed, sniffing the guitar.

Thoth closed the book and handed it back to me. "Well, it's an incantation for destroying Set."

"We *know* that," Sadie said. "Will it destroy him forever?"

"No, no. But it will destroy his form in this world, banishing him deep into the Duat and reducing his power so he will not be able to appear again for a long, long time. Centuries, most likely."

"Sounds good," I said. "How do we read it?"

Thoth stared at me like the answer should be obvious. "You cannot read it now because the words can only be spoken in Set's presence. Once before him, Sadie should open the book and recite the incantation. She'll know what to do when the time comes."

"Right," Sadie said. "And Set will just stand there calmly while I read him to death."

Thoth shrugged. "I did not say it would be easy. You'll also require two ingredients for the spell to work—a verbal ingredient, Set's secret name—"

"*What?*" I protested. "How are we supposed to get that?"

"With difficulty, I'd imagine. You can't simply read a secret name from a book. The name must come from the owner's own lips, in his own pronunciation, to give you power over him."

"Great," I said. "So we just force Set to tell us."

"Or trick him," Thoth said. "Or convince him."

"Isn't there any other way?" Sadie asked.

Thoth brushed an ink splotch off his lab coat. A hieroglyph turned into a moth and fluttered away. "I suppose . . . yes. You could ask the person closest to Set's heart—the person who loves him most. She would also have the ability to speak the name."

"But nobody loves Set!" Sadie said.

"His wife," I guessed. "That other goddess, Nephthys."

Thoth nodded. "She's a river goddess. Perhaps you could find her in a river."

"This just gets better and better," I muttered.

Sadie frowned at Thoth. "You said there was another ingredient?"

"A physical ingredient," Thoth agreed, "a feather of truth."

"A what?" Sadie asked.

But I knew what he was talking about, and my heart sank. "You mean from the Land of the Dead."

Thoth beamed. "Exactly."

"Wait," Sadie said. "What is he talking about?"

I tried to conceal my fear. "When you died in Ancient

Egypt, you had to take a journey to the Land of the Dead," I explained. "A really *dangerous* journey. Finally, you made it to the Hall of Judgment, where your life was weighed on the Scales of Anubis: your heart on one side, the feather of truth on the other. If you passed the test, you were blessed with eternal happiness. If you failed, a monster ate your heart and you ceased to exist."

"Ammit the Devourer," Thoth said wistfully. "Cute little thing."

Sadie blinked. "So we're supposed to get a feather from this Hall of Judgment *how*, exactly?"

"Perhaps Anubis will be in a good mood," Thoth suggested. "It happens every thousand years or so."

"But how do we even get to the Land of the Dead?" I asked. "I mean . . . without dying."

Thoth gazed at the western horizon, where the sunset was turning blood-red. "Down the river at night, I should think. That's how most people pass into the Land of the Dead. I would take a boat. You'll find Anubis at the end of the river—" He pointed north, then changed his mind and pointed south. "Forgot, rivers flow south here. Everything is backward."

"*Agh!*" Khufu ran his fingers down the frets of the guitar and ripped out a massive rock 'n' roll riff. Then he belched as if nothing had happened and set down the guitar. Sadie and I just stared at him, but Thoth nodded as if the baboon had said something profound.

"Are you sure, Khufu?" Thoth asked.

Khufu grunted.

"Very well." Thoth sighed. "Khufu says he would like to go

317

with you. I told him he could stay here and type my doctoral thesis on quantum physics, but he's not interested."

"Can't imagine why," Sadie said. "Glad to have Khufu along, but where do we find a boat?"

"You are the blood of pharaohs," Thoth said. "Pharaohs always have access to a boat. Just make sure you use it wisely."

He nodded toward the river. Churning toward the shore was an old-fashioned paddlewheel steamboat with smoke billowing from its stacks.

"I wish you a good journey," Thoth said. "Until we meet again."

"We're supposed to take *that*?" I asked. But when I turned to look at Thoth, he was gone, and he'd taken the barbecue with him.

"Wonderful," Sadie muttered.

"*Agh!*" Khufu agreed. He took our hands and led us down to the shore.

26. Aboard the *Egyptian Queen*

AS FAR AS RIDES TO THE Land of Death go, the boat was pretty cool. It had multiple decks with ornate railings painted black and green. The side paddlewheels churned the river into froth, and along the paddlewheel housings the name of the boat glittered in gold letters: EGYPTIAN QUEEN.

At first glance, you'd think the boat was just a tourist attraction: one of those floating casinos or cruise boats for old people. But if you looked closer you started noticing strange little details. The boat's name was written in Demotic and in hieroglyphics underneath the English. Sparkly smoke billowed from the stacks as if the engines were burning gold. Orbs of multicolored fire flitted around the decks. And on the prow of the ship, two painted eyes moved and blinked, scanning the river for trouble.

"That's odd," Sadie remarked.

I nodded. "I've seen eyes painted on boats before. They still do that all over the Mediterranean. But usually they don't move."

"What? No, not the stupid eyes. That lady on the highest deck. Isn't that..." Sadie broke into a grin. "Bast!"

Sure enough, our favorite feline was leaning out the window of the pilot's house. I was about to wave to her, when I noticed the creature standing next to Bast, gripping the wheel. He had a human body and was dressed in the white uniform of a boat captain. But instead of a head, a double-bladed axe sprouted from his collar. And I'm not talking about a *small* axe for chopping wood. I'm talking *battle*-axe: twin crescent-shaped iron blades, one in front where his face should be, one in the back, the edges splattered with suspicious-looking dried red splotches.

The ship pulled up to the dock. Balls of fire began zipping around—lowering the gangplank, tying off ropes, and basically doing crew-type stuff. How they did it without hands, and without setting everything on fire, I don't know, but it wasn't the strangest thing I'd seen that week.

Bast climbed down from the wheelhouse. She hugged us as we came aboard—even Khufu, who tried to return the favor by grooming her for lice.

"I'm glad you survived!" Bast told us. "What happened?"

We gave her the basics and her hair poofed out again. "Elvis? *Gah!* Thoth is getting cruel in his old age. Well, I can't say I'm glad to be on this boat again. I *hate* the water, but I suppose—"

"You've been on this boat before?" I asked.

Bast's smile wavered. "A million questions as usual, but let's eat first. The captain is waiting."

I wasn't anxious to meet a giant axe, and I wasn't

enthusiastic about another one of Bast's grilled-cheese-and-Friskies dinners, but we followed her inside the boat.

The dining parlor was lavishly decorated in Egyptian style. Colorful murals depicting the gods covered the walls. Gilded columns supported the ceiling. A long dining table was laden with every kind of food you could want—sandwiches, pizzas, hamburgers, Mexican food, you name it. It *way* made up for missing Thoth's barbecue. On a side table stood an ice chest, a line of golden goblets, and a soda dispenser with about twenty different choices. The mahogany chairs were carved to look like baboons, which reminded me a little too much of Graceland's Jungle Room, but Khufu thought they were okay. He barked at his chair just to show it who was top monkey, then sat on its lap. He picked an avocado from a basket of fruit and started peeling it.

Across the room, a door opened, and the axe dude came in. He had to duck to avoid cleaving the doorframe.

"Lord and Lady Kane," the captain said, bowing. His voice was a quivery hum that resonated along his front blade. I saw a video one time of a guy playing music by hitting a saw with a hammer, and that's sort of the way the captain sounded. "It is an honor to have you aboard."

"'Lady Kane,'" Sadie mused. "I like that."

"I am Bloodstained Blade," the captain said. "What are your orders?"

Sadie raised an eyebrow at Bast. "He takes orders from us?"

"Within reason," Bast said. "He is bound to your family. Your father..." She cleared her throat. "Well, he and your mother summoned this boat."

The axe demon made a disapproving hum. "You haven't told them, goddess?"

"I'm getting to it," Bast grumbled.

"Told us what?" I asked.

"Just details." She rushed on. "The boat can be summoned once a year, and only in times of great need. You'll need to give the captain your orders now. He must have clear directions if we're to proceed, ah, *safely*."

I wondered what was bothering Bast, but the axe dude was waiting for orders, and the flecks of dried blood on his blades told me I'd better not keep him in suspense.

"We need to visit the Hall of Judgment," I told him. "Take us to the Land of the Dead."

Bloodstained Blade hummed thoughtfully. "I will make the arrangements, Lord Kane, but it will take time."

"We don't have a lot of that." I turned to Sadie. "It's . . . what, the evening of the twenty-seventh?"

She nodded in agreement. "Day after tomorrow, at sunrise, Set completes his pyramid and destroys the world unless we stop him. So, yes, Captain Very Large Blade, or whatever it is, I'd say we're in a bit of a rush."

"We will, of course, do our best," said Bloodstained Blade, though his voice sounded a little, well, sharp. "The crew will prepare your staterooms. Will you dine while you wait?"

I looked at the table laden with food and realized how hungry I was. I hadn't eaten since we were in the Washington Monument. "Yeah. *Um*, thanks, BSB."

The captain bowed again, which made him look a little too much like a guillotine. Then he left us to our dinner.

At first, I was too busy eating to talk. I inhaled a roast beef sandwich, a couple of pieces of cherry pie with ice cream, and three glasses of ginger ale before I finally came up for air.

Sadie didn't eat as much. Then again she'd had lunch on the plane. She settled for a cheese-and-cucumber sandwich and one of those weird British drinks she likes—a Ribena. Khufu carefully picked out everything that ended with *-o*— Doritos, Oreos, and some chunks of meat. Buffalo? Armadillo? I was scared to even guess.

The balls of fire floated attentively around the room, refilling our goblets and clearing away our plates as we finished.

After so many days spent running for our lives, it felt good to just sit at a dinner table and relax. The captain's informing us that he couldn't transport us instantly to the Land of the Dead was the best news I'd had in a long time.

"*Agh!*" Khufu wiped his mouth and grabbed one of the balls of fire. He fashioned it into a glowing basketball and snorted at me.

For once I was pretty sure what he'd said in Baboon. It wasn't an invitation. It meant something like: "I'm going to play basketball by myself now. I will not invite you because your lack of skill would make me throw up."

"No problem, man," I said, though my face felt hot with embarrassment. "Have fun."

Khufu snorted again, then loped off with the ball under his arm. I wondered if he'd find a court somewhere on board.

At the far end of the table, Bast pushed her plate away. She'd hardly touched her tuna Friskies.

"Not hungry?" I asked.

"*Hmm?* Oh...I suppose not." She turned her goblet listlessly. She was wearing an expression I didn't associate with cats: guilt.

Sadie and I locked eyes. We had a brief, silent exchange, something like:

You ask her.

No, you.

Of course Sadie's better at giving dirty looks, so I lost the contest.

"Bast?" I said. "What did the captain want you to tell us?"

She hesitated. "Oh, that? You shouldn't listen to demons. Bloodstained Blade is bound by magic to serve, but if he ever got loose, he'd use that axe on all of us, believe me."

"You're changing the subject," I said.

Bast traced her finger across the table, drawing hieroglyphs in the condensation ring from her goblet. "The truth? I haven't been on board since the night your mother died. Your parents had docked this boat on the Thames. After the...accident, your father brought me here. This is where we made our deal."

I realized she meant *right* here, at this table. My father had sat here in despair after Mom's death—with no one to console him except the cat goddess, an axe demon, and a bunch of floating lights.

I studied Bast's face in the dim light. I thought about the painting we'd found at Graceland. Even in human form, Bast looked so much like that cat—a cat drawn by some artist thousands of years ago.

"It wasn't just a chaos monster, was it?" I asked.

Bast eyed me. "What do you mean?"

"The thing you were fighting when our parents released you from the obelisk. It wasn't just a chaos monster. You were fighting Apophis."

All around the parlor, the servant fires dimmed. One dropped a plate and fluttered nervously.

"Don't say the Serpent's name," Bast warned. "Especially as we head into the night. Night is his realm."

"It's true, then." Sadie shook her head in dismay. "Why didn't you say anything? Why did you lie to us?"

Bast dropped her gaze. Sitting in the shadows, she looked weary and frail. Her face was etched with the traces of old battle scars.

"I was the Eye of Ra." She spoke quietly. "The sun god's champion, the instrument of his will. Do you have any idea what an honor it was?"

She extended her claws and studied them. "When people see pictures of Ra's warrior cat, they assume it's Sekhmet, the lioness. And she *was* his first champion, it's true. But she was too violent, too out of control. Eventually Sekhmet was forced to step down, and Ra chose *me* as his fighter: little Bast."

"Why do you sound ashamed?" Sadie asked. "You said it's an honor."

"At first I was proud, Sadie. I fought the Serpent for ages. Cats and snakes are mortal enemies. I did my job well. But then Ra withdrew to the heavens. He bound me to the Serpent with his last spell. He cast us both into that abyss, where I was charged to fight the Serpent and keep it down forever."

A realization crept over me. "So you *weren't* a minor prisoner. You were imprisoned longer than any of the other gods."

She closed her eyes. "I still remember Ra's words: 'My loyal cat. This is your greatest duty.' And I was proud to do it... for centuries. Then millennia. Can you imagine what it was like? Knives against fangs, slashing and thrashing, a never-ending war in the darkness. Our life forces grew weaker, my enemy's and mine, and I began to realize that was Ra's plan. The Serpent and I would rip each other to nothingness, and the world would be safe. Only in this way could Ra withdraw in peace of mind, knowing chaos would not overcome Ma'at. I would have done my duty, too. I had no choice. Until your parents—"

"Gave you an escape route," I said. "And you took it."

Bast looked up miserably. "I am the queen of cats. I have many strengths. But to be honest, Carter... cats are not very brave."

"And Ap—your enemy?"

"He stayed trapped in the abyss. Your father and I were sure of it. The Serpent was already greatly weakened from eons of fighting with me, and when your mother used her own life force to close the abyss, well... she worked a powerful feat of magic. There should've been no way for the Serpent to break through that kind of seal. But as the years have gone by... we became less and less sure the prison would hold him. If some-how he managed to escape and regain his strength, I cannot imagine what would happen. And it would be my fault."

I tried to imagine the serpent, Apophis—a creature of chaos even worse than Set. I pictured Bast with her knives, locked in combat with that monster for eons. Maybe I should've been angry at Bast for not telling us the truth earlier. Instead, I felt sorry for her. She'd been put in the same position we were now in—forced to do a job that was way too big for her.

"So why did my parents release you?" I asked. "Did they say?"

She nodded slowly. "I was losing my fight. Your father told me that your mother had foreseen...horrible things if the Serpent overcame me. They had to free me, give me time to heal. They said it was the first step in restoring the gods. I don't pretend to understand their whole plan. I was relieved to take your father's offer. I convinced myself I was doing the right thing for the gods. But it does not change the fact that I was a coward. I failed in my duty."

"It isn't your fault," I told her. "It wasn't fair of Ra to ask of you."

"Carter's right," Sadie said. "That's too much sacrifice for one person—one cat goddess, whatever."

"It was my king's will," Bast said. "The pharaoh can command his subjects for the good of the kingdom—even to lay down their lives—and they must obey. Horus knows this. He was the pharaoh many times."

She speaks truly, Horus said.

"Then you had a stupid king," I said.

The boat shuddered as if we'd ground the keel over a sandbar.

"Be careful, Carter," Bast warned. "Ma'at, the order of creation, hinges on loyalty to the rightful king. If you question it, you'll fall under the influence of chaos."

I felt so frustrated, I wanted to break something. I wanted to yell that order didn't seem much better than chaos if you had to get yourself killed for it.

You are being childish, Horus scolded. *You are a servant of Ma'at. These thoughts are unworthy.*

My eyes stung. "Then maybe *I'm* unworthy."

"Carter?" Sadie asked.

"Nothing," I said. "I'm going to bed."

I stormed off. One of the flickering lights joined me, guiding me upstairs to my quarters. The stateroom was probably very nice. I didn't pay attention. I just fell on the bed and passed out.

I seriously needed an extra-strength magic pillow, because my *ba* refused to stay put. [And no, Sadie, I don't think wrapping my head in duct tape would've worked either.]

My spirit floated up to the steamboat's wheelhouse, but it wasn't Bloodstained Blade at the wheel. Instead, a young man in leather armor navigated the boat. His eyes were outlined with kohl, and his head was bald except for a braided ponytail. The guy definitely worked out, because his arms were ripped. A sword like mine was strapped to his belt.

"The river is treacherous," he told me in a familiar voice. "A pilot cannot get distracted. He must always be alert for sandbars and hidden snags. That's why boats are painted with my eyes, you know—to see the dangers."

"The Eyes of Horus," I said. "You."

The falcon god glanced at me, and I saw that his eyes were two different colors—one blazing yellow like the sun, the other reflective silver like the moon. The effect was so disorienting, I had to look away. And when I did, I noticed that Horus's shadow didn't match his form. Stretched across the wheelhouse was the silhouette of a giant falcon.

"You wonder if order is better than chaos," he said. "You become distracted from our real enemy: Set. You should be taught a lesson."

I was about to say, *No really, that's okay*.

But immediately my *ba* was whisked away. Suddenly, I was on board an airplane—a big international aircraft like planes my dad and I had taken a million times. Zia Rashid, Desjardins, and two other magicians were scrunched up in a middle row, surrounded by families with screaming children. Zia didn't seem to mind. She meditated calmly with her eyes closed, while Desjardins and the other two men looked so uncomfortable, I almost wanted to laugh.

The plane rocked back and forth. Desjardins spilled wine all over his lap. The seat belt light blinked on, and a voice crackled over the intercom: "This is the captain. It looks like we'll be experiencing some minor turbulence as we make our descent into Dallas, so I'm going to ask the flight attendants—"

Boom! A blast rattled the windows—lightning followed immediately by thunder.

Zia's eyes snapped open. "The Red Lord."

The passengers screamed as the plane plummeted several hundred feet.

"*Il commence!*" Desjardins shouted over the noise. "Quickly!"

As the plane shook, passengers shrieked and grabbed

their seats. Desjardins got up and opened the overhead compartment.

"Sir!" a flight attendant yelled. "Sir, sit down!"

Desjardins ignored the attendant. He grabbed four familiar bags—magical tool kits—and threw them to his colleagues.

Then things really went wrong. A horrible shudder passed through the cabin and the plane lurched sideways. Outside the right-hand windows, I saw the plane's wing get sheared off by a five-hundred-mile-an-hour wind.

The cabin devolved into chaos—drinks, books, and shoes flying everywhere, oxygen masks dropping and tangling, people screaming for their lives.

"Protect the innocents!" Desjardins ordered.

The plane began to shake and cracks appeared in the windows and walls. The passengers went silent, slumping into unconsciousness as the air pressure dropped. The four magicians raised their wands as the airplane broke to pieces.

For a moment, the magicians floated in a maelstrom of storm clouds, chunks of fuselage, luggage, and spinning passengers still strapped to their seats. Then a white glow expanded around them, a bubble of power that slowed the breakup of the plane and kept the pieces swirling in a tight orbit. Desjardins reached out his hand and the edge of a cloud stretched toward him—a tendril of cottony white mist, like a safety line. The other magicians did likewise, and the storm bent to their will. White vapor wrapped around them and began to send out more tendrils, like funnel clouds, which snatched pieces of the plane and pulled them back together.

A child fell past Zia, but she pointed her staff and murmured a spell. A cloud enveloped the little girl and brought her back. Soon the four magicians were reassembling the plane around them, sealing the breaches with cloudy cobwebs until the entire cabin was encased in a glowing cocoon of vapor. Outside, the storm raged and thunder boomed, but the passengers slept soundly in their seats.

"Zia!" Desjardins shouted. "We can't hold this for long."

Zia ran past him up the aisle to the flight deck. Somehow the front of the plane had survived the breakup intact. The door was armored and locked, but Zia's staff flared, and the door melted like wax. She stepped through and found three unconscious pilots. The view through the window was enough to make me sick. Through the spiraling clouds, the ground was coming up fast—*very* fast.

Zia slammed her wand against the controls. Red energy surged through the displays. Dials spun, meters blinked, and the altimeter leveled out. The plane's nose came up, its speed dropping. As I watched, Zia glided the plane toward a cow pasture and landed it without even a bump. Then her eyes rolled back in her head, and she collapsed.

Desjardins found her and gathered her in his arms. "Quickly," he told his colleagues, "the mortals will wake soon."

They dragged Zia out of the cockpit, and my *ba* was swept away through a blur of images.

I saw Phoenix again—or at least *some* of the city. A massive red sandstorm churned across the valley, swallowing buildings and mountains. In the harsh, hot wind, I heard Set laughing, reveling in his power.

Then I saw Brooklyn: Amos's ruined house on the East

331

River and a winter storm raging overhead, howling winds slamming the city with sleet and hail.

And then I saw a place I didn't recognize: a river winding through a desert canyon. The sky was a blanket of pitch-black clouds, and the river's surface seemed to boil. Something was moving under the water, something huge, evil, and powerful—and I knew it was waiting for me.

This is only the beginning, Horus warned me. *Set will destroy everyone you care about. Believe me, I know.*

The river became a marsh of tall reeds. The sun blazed overhead. Snakes and crocodiles slid through the water. At the water's edge sat a thatched hut. Outside it, a woman and a child of about ten stood examining a battered sarcophagus. I could tell the coffin had once been a work of art—gold encrusted with gems—but now it was dented and black with grime.

The woman ran her hands over the coffin's lid.

"Finally." She had my mother's face—blue eyes and caramel-colored hair—but she glowed with magical radiance, and I knew I was looking at the goddess Isis.

She turned to the boy. "We have searched so long, my son. Finally we have retrieved him. I will use my magic and give him life again!"

"Papa?" The boy gazed wide-eyed at the box. "He's really inside?"

"Yes, Horus. And now—"

Suddenly their hut erupted into flames. The god Set stepped from the inferno—a mighty red-skinned warrior with smoldering black eyes. He wore the double crown of Egypt and the robes of a pharaoh. In his hands, an iron staff smoldered.

"Found the coffin, did you?" he said. "Good for you!"

Isis reached toward the sky. She summoned lightning against the god of chaos, but Set's rod absorbed the attack and reflected it back at her. Arcs of electricity blasted the goddess and sent her sprawling.

"Mother!" The boy drew a knife and charged Set. "I'll kill you!"

Set bellowed with laughter. He easily sidestepped the boy and kicked him into the dirt.

"You have spirit, nephew," Set admitted. "But you won't live long enough to challenge me. As for your father, I'll just have to dispose of him more permanently."

Set slammed his iron staff against the coffin's lid.

Isis screamed as the coffin shattered like ice.

"Make a wish." Set blew with all his might, and the shards of coffin flew into the sky, scattering in all directions. "Poor Osiris—he's gone to pieces, scattered all over Egypt now. And as for you, sister Isis—run! That's what you do best!"

Set lunged forward. Isis grabbed her son's hand and they both turned into birds, flying for their lives.

The scene faded, and I was back in the steamboat's wheel-house. The sun rose in fast-forward as towns and barges sped past and the banks of the Mississippi blurred into a play of light and shadow.

"He destroyed my father," Horus told me. "He will do the same to yours."

"No," I said.

Horus fixed me with those strange eyes—one blazing gold, one full-moon silver. "My mother and Aunt Nephthys spent years searching for the pieces of the coffin and Father's body. When they collected all fourteen, my cousin Anubis helped bind my father back together with mummy wrappings, but still Mother's magic could not bring him back to life fully. Osiris became an undead god, a half-living shadow of my father, fit to rule only in the Duat. But his loss gave me anger. Anger gave me the strength to defeat Set and take the throne for myself. You must do the same."

"I don't want a throne," I said. "I want my dad."

"Don't deceive yourself. Set is merely toying with you. He will bring you to despair, and your sorrow will make you weak."

"I have to save my dad!"

"That is not your mission," Horus chided. "The world is at stake. Now, wake!"

Sadie was shaking my arm. She and Bast stood over me, looking concerned.

"What?" I asked.

"We're here," Sadie said nervously. She'd changed into a fresh linen outfit, black this time, which matched her combat boots. She'd even managed to redye her hair so the streaks were blue.

I sat up and realized I felt rested for the first time in a week. My soul may have been traveling, but at least my body had gotten some sleep. I glanced out the stateroom window. It was pitch-black outside.

"How long was I out?" I demanded.

"We've sailed down most of the Mississippi and into the Duat," Bast said. "Now we approach the First Cataract."

"The First Cataract?" I asked.

"The entrance," Bast said grimly, "to the Land of the Dead."

S
A
D
I
E

27. A Demon with Free Samples

ME? I SLEPT LIKE THE DEAD, which I hoped wasn't a sign of things to come.

I could tell Carter's soul had been wandering through some frightening places, but he wouldn't talk about them.

"Did you see Zia?" I asked. He looked so rattled I thought his face would fall off. "Knew it," I said.

We followed Bast up to the wheelhouse, where Bloodstained Blade was studying a map while Khufu manned—*er*, babooned—the wheel.

"The baboon is driving," I noted. "Should I be worried?"

"Quiet, please, Lady Kane." Bloodstained Blade ran his fingers over a long stretch of papyrus map. "This is delicate work. Two degrees to starboard, Khufu."

"*Agh!*" Khufu said.

The sky was already dark, but as we chugged along, the stars disappeared. The river turned the color of blood. Darkness swallowed the horizon, and along the riverbanks, the lights of towns changed to flickering fires, then winked out completely.

Now our only lights were the multicolored servant fires and the glittering smoke that bloomed from the smokestacks, washing us all in a weird metallic glow.

"Should be just ahead," the captain announced. In the dim light, his red-flecked axe blade looked scarier than ever.

"What's that map?" I asked.

"*Spells of Coming Forth by Day*," he said. "Don't worry. It's a good copy."

I looked at Carter for a translation.

"Most people call it *The Book of the Dead*," he told me. "Rich Egyptians were always buried with a copy, so they could have directions through the Duat to the Land of the Dead. It's like an *Idiot's Guide to the Afterlife*."

The captain hummed indignantly. "I am no idiot, Lord Kane."

"No, no, I just meant..." Carter's voice faltered. "*Uh*, what is *that?*"

Ahead of us, crags of rock jutted from the river like fangs, turning the water into a boiling mass of rapids.

"The First Cataract," Bloodstained Blade announced. "Hold on."

Khufu pushed the wheel to the left, and the steamboat skidded sideways, shooting between two rocky spires with only centimeters to spare. I'm not much of a screamer, but I'll readily admit that I screamed my head off. [And don't look at me like that, Carter. You weren't much better.]

We dropped over a stretch of white water—or red

water—and swerved to avoid a rock the size of Paddington Station. The steamboat made two more suicidal turns between boulders, did a three-sixty spin round a swirling vortex, launched over a ten-meter waterfall, and came crashing down so hard, my ears popped like a gunshot.

We continued downstream as if nothing had happened, the roar of the rapids fading behind us.

"I don't like cataracts," I decided. "Are there more?"

"Not as large, thankfully," said Bast, who was also looking seasick. "We've crossed over into—"

"The Land of the Dead," Carter finished.

He pointed to the shore, which was shrouded in mist. Strange things lurked in the darkness: flickering ghost lights, giant faces made of fog, hulking shadows that seemed unconnected to anything physical. Along the riverbanks, old bones dragged themselves through the mud, linking with other bones in random patterns.

"I'm guessing this isn't the Mississippi," I said.

"The River of Night," Bloodstained Blade hummed. "It is every river and no river—the shadow of the Mississippi, the Nile, the Thames. It flows throughout the Duat, with many branches and tributaries."

"Clears that right up," I muttered.

The scenes got stranger. We saw ghost villages from ancient times—little clusters of reed huts made of flickering smoke. We saw vast temples crumbling and reconstructing themselves over and over again like a looped video. And everywhere, ghosts turned their faces towards our boat as we passed. Smoky hands reached out. Shades silently called to us, then turned away in despair as we passed.

"The lost and confused," Bast said. "Spirits who never found their way to the Hall of Judgment."

"Why are they so sad?" I asked.

"Well, they're dead," Carter speculated.

"No, it's more than that," I said. "It's like they're . . . expecting someone."

"Ra," Bast said. "For eons, Ra's glorious sun boat would travel this route each night, fighting off the forces of Apophis." She looked round nervously as if remembering old ambushes. "It was dangerous: every night, a fight for existence. But as he passed, Ra would bring sunlight and warmth to the Duat, and these lost spirits would rejoice, remembering the world of the living."

"But that's a legend," Carter said. "The earth revolves around the sun. The sun never actually descends under the earth."

"Have you learned nothing of Egypt?" Bast asked. "Conflicting stories can be equally true. The sun is a ball of fire in space, yes. But its image you see as it crosses the sky, the life-giving warmth and light it brings to the earth—that was embodied by Ra. The sun was his throne, his source of power, his very spirit. But now Ra has retreated into the heavens. He sleeps, and the sun is just the sun. Ra's boat no longer travels on its cycle through the Duat. He no longer lights the dark, and the dead feel his absence most keenly."

"Indeed," Bloodstained Blade said, though he didn't sound

very upset about it. "Legend says the world will end when Ra gets too tired to continue living in his weakened state. Apophis will swallow the sun. Darkness will reign. Chaos will overcome Ma'at, and the Serpent will reign forever."

Part of me thought this was absurd. The planets would not simply stop spinning. The sun would not cease to rise.

On the other hand, here I was riding a boat through the Land of the Dead with a demon and a god. If Apophis was real too, I didn't fancy meeting him.

And to be honest, I felt guilty. If the story Thoth told me was true, Isis had *caused* Ra to retreat into the heavens with that secret name business. Which meant, in a ridiculous, maddening way, the end of the world would be my fault. Bloody typical. I wanted to punch myself to get even with Isis, but I suspected it would hurt.

"Ra should wake up and smell the *sahlab*," I said. "He should come back."

Bast laughed without humor. "And the world should be young again, Sadie. I wish it could be so...."

Khufu grunted and gestured ahead. He gave the captain back the wheel and ran out of the wheelhouse and down the stairs.

"The baboon is right," said Bloodstained Blade. "You should get to the prow. A challenge will be coming soon."

"What sort of challenge?" I asked.

"It's hard to tell," Bloodstained Blade said, and I thought I detected smug satisfaction in his voice. "I wish you luck, Lady Kane."

"Why me?" I grumbled.

Bast, Carter, and I stood at the prow of the boat, watching the river appear out of the darkness. Below us, the boat's painted eyes glowed faintly in the dark, sweeping beams of light across the red water. Khufu had climbed to the top of the gangplank, which stood straight up when retracted, and cupped his hand over his eyes like a sailor in a crow's-nest.

But all that vigilance didn't do much good. With the dark and the mist, our visibility was nil. Massive rocks, broken pillars, and crumbling statues of pharaohs loomed out of nowhere, and Bloodstained Blade yanked the wheel to avoid them, forcing us to grab hold of the rails. Occasionally we'd see long slimy lines cutting through the surface of the water, like tentacles, or the backs of submerged creatures—I really didn't want to know.

"Mortal souls are always challenged," Bast told me. "You must prove your worth to enter the Land of the Dead."

"Like it's such a big treat?"

I'm not sure how long I stared into the darkness, but after a good while a reddish smudge appeared in the distance, as if the sky were becoming lighter.

"Is that my imagination, or—"

"Our destination," Bast said. "Strange, we really should've been challenged by now—"

The boat shuddered, and the water began to boil. A giant figure erupted from the river. I could see him only from the waist up, but he towered several meters over the boat. His body was humanoid—bare-chested and hairy with purplish skin. A rope belt was tied around his waist, festooned with leather pouches, severed demon heads, and other charming bits and bobs. His head was a strange combination of lion and human, with gold eyes and a black mane done in dreadlocks. His blood-splattered mouth was feline, with bristly whiskers and razor-sharp fangs. He roared, scaring Khufu right off the gangplank. The poor baboon did a flying leap into Carter's arms, which knocked them both to the deck.

"You *had* to say something," I told Bast weakly. "This a relative of yours, I hope?"

Bast shook her head. "I cannot help you with this, Sadie. *You* are the mortals. You must deal with the challenge."

"Oh, thanks for that."

"I am Shezmu!" the bloody lion man said.

I wanted to say, "Yes, you certainly are." But I decided to keep my mouth shut.

He turned his golden eyes on Carter and tilted his head. His nostrils quivered. "I smell the blood of pharaohs. A tasty treat...or do you dare to name me?"

"N-name you?" Carter sputtered. "Do you mean your secret name?"

The demon laughed. He grabbed a nearby spire of rock, which crumpled like old plaster in his fist.

I looked desperately at Carter. "You don't happen to have his secret name lying around somewhere?"

"It may be in *The Book of the Dead*," Carter said. "I forgot to check."

"Well?" I said.

"Keep him busy," Carter replied, and scrambled off to the wheelhouse.

Keep a demon busy, I thought. *Right. Maybe he fancies a game of tiddlywinks.*

"Do you give up?" Shezmu bellowed.

"No!" I yelled. "No, we don't give up. We will name you. Just…Gosh, you're quite well muscled, aren't you? Do you work out?"

I glanced at Bast, who nodded approval.

Shezmu rumbled with pride and flexed his mighty arms. Never fails with men, does it? Even if they're twenty meters tall and lion-headed.

"I am Shezmu!" he bellowed.

"Yes, you might've mentioned that already," I said. "I'm wondering, *um*, what sort of titles you've earned over the years, eh? Lord of this and that?"

"I am Osiris's royal executioner!" he yelled, smashing a fist into the water and rocking our boat. "I am the Lord of Blood and Wine!"

"Brilliant," I said, trying not to get sick. "Er, how are blood and wine connected, exactly?"

"*Garrr!*" He leaned forward and bared his fangs, which were not any prettier up close. His mane was matted with nasty bits of dead fish and river moss. "Lord Osiris lets me behead the wicked! I crush them in my wine press, and make wine for the dead!"

I made a mental note never to drink the wine of the dead.

You're doing well. Isis's voice gave me a start. She'd been quiet so long, I'd almost forgotten her. *Ask him about his other duties.*

"And what are your other duties…O powerful wine demon guy?"

"I am Lord of..." He flexed his muscles for maximum effect. "Perfume!"

He grinned at me, apparently waiting for terror to set it.

"Oh, my!" I said. "That must make your enemies tremble."

"Ha, ha, ha! Yes! Would you like to try a free sample?" He ripped a slimy leather pouch off his belt, and brought out a clay pot filled with sweet-smelling yellow powder. "I call this ...Eternity!"

"Lovely," I gagged. I glanced behind me, wondering where Carter had gone to, but there was no sign of him.

Keep him talking, Isis urged.

"And, *um*...perfume is part of your job because...wait, I've got it, you squeeze it out of plants, like you squeeze wine..."

"Or blood!" Shezmu added.

"Well, naturally," I said. "The blood goes without saying."

"Blood!" he said.

Khufu yelped and covered his eyes.

"So you serve Osiris?" I asked the demon.

"Yes! At least..." He hesitated, snarling in doubt. "I did. Osiris's throne is empty. But he will return. He will!"

"Of course," I said. "And so your friends call you what... Shezzy? Bloodsiekins?"

"I have no friends! But if I did, they would call me Slaughterer of Souls, Fierce of Face! But I don't have any friends, so my name is not in danger. Ha, ha, ha!"

I looked at Bast, wondering if I'd just gotten as lucky as I thought. Bast beamed at me.

Carter came stumbling down the stairs, holding *The Book*

of the Dead. "I've got it! Somewhere here. Can't read this part, but—"

"Name me or be eaten!" Shezmu bellowed.

"I name you!" I shouted back. "Shezmu, Slaughterer of Souls, Fierce of Face!"

"*GAAAAHHHHH!*" He writhed in pain. "How do they always know?"

"Let us pass!" I commanded. "Oh, and one more thing... my brother wants a free sample."

I just had time to step away, and Carter just had time to look confused before the demon blew yellow dust all over him. Then Shezmu sank under the waves.

"What a nice fellow," I said.

"*Pah!*" Carter spit perfume. He looked like a piece of breaded fish. "What was *that* for?"

"You smell lovely," I assured him. "What's next, then?"

I was feeling very pleased with myself until our boat rounded a bend in the river. Suddenly the reddish glow on the horizon became a blaze of light. Up in the wheelhouse, the captain rang the alarm bell.

Ahead of us, the river was on fire, rushing through a steaming stretch of rapids towards what looked like a bubbling volcanic crater.

"The Lake of Fire," Bast said. "This is where it gets interesting."

28. I Have a Date with the God of Toilet Paper

BAST HAD AN INTERESTING DEFINITION of *interesting*: a boiling lake several miles wide that smelled like burning petrol and rotten meat. Our steamboat stopped short where the river met the lake, because a giant metal gate blocked our path. It was a bronze disk like a shield, easily as wide as our boat, half submerged in the river. I wasn't sure how it avoided melting in the heat, but it made going forward impossible. On either bank of the river, facing the disk, was a giant bronze baboon with its arms raised.

"What is this?" I asked.

"The Gates of the West," Bast said. "Ra's sunboat would pass through and be renewed in the fires of the lake, then pass through to the other side and rise through the Gates of the East for a new day."

Looking up at the huge baboons, I wondered if Khufu had some sort of secret baboon code that would get us in. But instead he barked at the statues and cowered heroically behind my legs.

"How do we get past?" I wondered.

"Perhaps," a new voice said, "you should ask me."

The air shimmered. Carter backed up quickly, and Bast hissed.

In front of me appeared a glowing bird spirit: a *ba*. It had the usual combination of human head and killer turkey body, with its wings tucked back and its entire form glowing, but something about this *ba* was different. I realized I knew the spirit's face—an old bald man with brown, papery skin, milky eyes, and a kindly smile.

"Iskandar?" I managed.

"Hello, my dear." The old magician's voice echoed as if from the bottom of a well.

"But…" I found myself tearing up. "You're really dead, then?"

He chuckled. "Last I checked."

"But *why?* I didn't make you—"

"No, my dear. It wasn't your fault. It was simply the right time."

"It was horrible timing!" My surprise and sadness abruptly turned to anger. "You *left* us before we got trained or anything, and now Desjardins is after us and—"

"My dear, look how far you've come. Look how well you have done. You didn't need me, nor would more training have helped. My brethren would have found out the truth about you soon enough. They are excellent at sniffing out godlings, I fear, and they would not have understood."

"You knew, didn't you? You knew we were possessed by gods."

"*Hosts* of the gods."

"Whatever! You knew."

"After our second meeting, yes. My only regret is that I did not realize it sooner. I could not protect you and your brother as much as—"

"As much as who?"

Iskandar's eyes became sad and distant. "I made choices, Sadie. Some seemed wise at the time. Some, in retrospect..."

"Your decision to forbid the gods. My mum convinced you it was a bad idea, didn't she?"

His spectral wings fluttered. "You must understand, Sadie. When Egypt fell to the Romans, my spirit was crushed. Thousands of years of Egyptian power and tradition toppled by that foolish Queen Cleopatra, who thought she could host a goddess. The blood of the pharaohs seemed weak and diluted—lost forever. At the time I blamed everyone—the gods who used men to act out their petty quarrels, the Ptolemaic rulers who had driven Egypt into the ground, my own brethren in the House for becoming weak and greedy and corrupt. I communed with Thoth, and we agreed: the gods must be put away, banished. The magicians must find their way without them. The new rules kept the House of Life intact for another two thousand years. At the time, it was the right choice."

"And now?" I asked.

Iskandar's glow dimmed. "Your mother foresaw a great imbalance. She foresaw the day—very soon—when Ma'at would be destroyed, and chaos would reclaim all of Creation. She insisted that only the gods and the House together could prevail. The old way—the path of the gods—would have to be reestablished. I was a foolish old man. I knew in my heart she was right, but I refused to believe ... and your parents took it upon themselves to act. They sacrificed themselves trying to put things right, because I was too stubborn to change. For that, I am truly sorry."

As much as I tried, I found it hard to stay angry at the old turkey. It's a rare thing when an adult admits they are wrong to a child—especially a wise, two-thousand-year-old adult. You rather have to cherish those moments.

"I forgive you, Iskandar," I said. "Honestly. But Set is about to destroy North America with a giant red pyramid. What do I *do* about it?"

"That, my dear, I can't answer. Your choice ..." He tilted his head back toward the lake, as if hearing a voice. "Our time is at an end. I must do my job as gatekeeper, and decide whether or not to grant you access to the Lake of Fire."

"But I've got more questions!"

"And I wish we had more time," Iskandar said. "You have a strong spirit, Sadie Kane. Someday, you will make an excellent guardian *ba*."

"Thanks," I muttered. "Can't wait to be poultry forever."

"I can only tell you this: your choice approaches. Don't let your feelings blind you to what is best, as I did."

"What choice? Best for whom?"

"That's the key, isn't it? Your father—your family—the gods—the world. Ma'at and Isfet, order and chaos, are about to collide more violently than they have in eons. You and your brother will be instrumental in balancing those forces, or destroying everything. That, also, your mother foresaw."

349

"Hang on. What do you—"

"Until we meet again, Sadie. Perhaps some day, we will have a chance to talk further. But for now, pass through! My job is to assess your courage—and you have that in abundance."

I wanted to argue that no, in fact, I didn't. I wanted Iskandar to stay and tell me exactly what my mother had foreseen in my future. But his spirit faded, leaving the deck quiet and still. Only then did I realize that no one else on board had said a thing.

I turned to face Carter. "Leave everything to me, eh?"

He was staring into space, not even blinking. Khufu still clung to my legs, absolutely petrified. Bast's face was frozen in mid-hiss.

"*Um*, guys?" I snapped my fingers, and they all unfroze.

"*Ba!*" Bast hissed. Then she looked around and scowled. "Wait, I thought I saw . . . what just happened?"

I wondered how powerful a magician had to be to stop time, to freeze even a goddess. Some day, Iskandar was going to teach me that trick, dead or no.

"Yeah," I said. "I reckon there was a *ba*. Gone now."

The baboon statues began to rumble and grind as their arms lowered. The bronze sun disk in the middle of the river sank below the surface, clearing the way into the lake. The boat shot forward, straight into the flames and the boiling red waves. Through the shimmering heat, I could just make out an island in the middle of the lake. On it rose a glittering black temple that looked not at all friendly.

"The Hall of Judgment," I guessed.

Bast nodded. "Times like this, I'm glad I don't have a mortal soul."

As we docked at the island, Bloodstained Blade came down to say good-bye.

"I hope to see you again, Lord and Lady Kane," he hummed. "Your rooms will be waiting aboard the *Egyptian Queen*. Unless, of course, you see fit to release me from service."

Behind his back, Bast shook her head adamantly.

"*Um*, we'll keep you around," I told the captain. "Thanks for everything."

"As you wish," the captain said. If axes could frown, I'm sure he would have.

"Stay sharp," Carter told him, and with Bast and Khufu, we walked down the gangplank. Instead of pulling away, the ship simply sank into the boiling lava and disappeared.

I scowled at Carter. "'Stay sharp?'"

"I thought it was funny."

"You're hopeless."

We walked up the steps of the black temple. A forest of stone pillars held up the ceiling. Every surface was carved with hieroglyphs and images, but there was no color—just black on black. Haze from the lake drifted through the temple, and despite reed torches that burned on each pillar, it was impossible to see very far through the gloom.

"Stay alert," Bast warned, sniffing the air. "He's close."

"Who?" I asked.

"The Dog," Bast said with disdain.

There was a snarling noise, and a huge black shape leaped out of the mist. It tackled Bast, who rolled over and wailed in feline outrage, then raced off, leaving us alone with the beast. I suppose she had warned us that she wasn't brave.

The new animal was sleek and black, like the Set animal we'd seen in Washington, D.C., but more obviously canine, graceful and rather cute, actually. A jackal, I realized, with a golden collar around its neck.

Then it morphed into a young man, and my heart almost stopped. He was the boy from my dreams, quite literally—the guy in black I'd seen twice before in my *ba* visions.

In person, if possible, Anubis was even more drop-dead gorgeous. [Oh...ha, ha. I didn't catch the pun, but thank you, Carter. God of the dead, drop-dead gorgeous. Yes, hilarious. Now, may I continue?]

He had a pale complexion, tousled black hair, and rich brown eyes like melted chocolate. He was dressed in black jeans, combat boots (like mine!), a ripped T-shirt, and a black leather jacket that suited him quite nicely. He was long and lean like a jackal. His ears, like a jackal's, stuck out a bit (which I found cute), and he wore a gold chain around his neck.

Now, please understand, I am *not* boy crazy. I'm not! I'd spent most of the school term making fun of Liz and Emma, who were, and I was very glad they weren't with me just then, because they would've teased me to no end.

The boy in black stood and brushed off his jacket. "I'm *not* a dog," he grumbled.

"No," I agreed. "You're..."

No doubt I would've said *delicious* or something equally embarrassing, but Carter saved me.

"You're Anubis?" he asked. "We've come for the feather of truth."

Anubis frowned. He locked his very nice eyes with mine. "You're not dead."

"No," I said. "Though we're trying awfully hard."

"I don't deal with the living," he said firmly. Then he looked at Khufu and Carter. "However, you travel with a baboon. That shows good taste. I won't kill you until you've had a chance to explain. Why did Bast bring you here?"

"Actually," Carter said, "Thoth sent us."

Carter started to tell him the story, but Khufu broke in impatiently. *"Agh! Agh!"*

Baboon-speak must have been quite efficient, because Anubis nodded as if he'd just gotten the whole tale. "I see."

He scowled at Carter. "So you're Horus. And you're..." His finger drifted towards me.

"I'm—I'm, *um*—" I stammered. Quite unlike me to be tongue-tied, I'll admit, but looking at Anubis, I felt as if I'd just gotten a large shot of Novocain from the dentist. Carter looked at me as if I'd gone daft.

"I'm not Isis," I managed. "I mean, Isis is milling about inside, but I'm not her. She's just...visiting."

Anubis tilted his head. "And the two of you intend to challenge Set?"

"That's the general idea," Carter agreed. "Will you help?"

Anubis glowered. I remembered Thoth saying Anubis was

only in a good mood once an eon or so. I had the feeling this was not one of those days.

"No," he said flatly. "I'll show you why."

He turned into a jackal and sped back the way he'd come. Carter and I exchanged looks. Not knowing what else to do, we ran after Anubis, deeper into the gloom.

In the center of the temple was a large circular chamber that seemed to be two places at once. On the one hand, it was a great hall with blazing braziers and an empty throne at the far end. The center of the room was dominated by a set of scales—a black iron T with ropes linked to two golden dishes, each big enough to hold a person—but the scales were broken. One of the golden dishes was bent into a V, as if something very heavy had jumped up and down on it. The other dish was hanging by a single rope.

Curled at the base of the scales, fast asleep, was the oddest monster I'd seen yet. It had the head of crocodile with a lion's mane. The front half of its body was lion, but the back end was sleek, brown, and fat—a hippo, I decided. The odd bit was, the animal was tiny—I mean, no larger than an average poodle, which I suppose made him a hippodoodle.

So that was the hall, at least *one* layer of it. But at the same time, I seemed to be standing in a ghostly graveyard—like a three-dimensional projection superimposed on the room. In some places, the marble floor gave way to patches of mud and moss-covered paving stones. Lines of aboveground tombs like miniature row houses radiated from the center of the chamber in a wheel-spokes pattern. Many of the tombs had cracked open. Some were bricked up, others ringed with iron fences. Around the edges of the chamber, the black pillars shifted form, sometimes changing into ancient cypress trees. I felt as if I were stepping between two different worlds, and I couldn't tell which one was real.

Khufu loped straight over to the broken scales and climbed to the top, making himself right at home. He paid no attention to the hippodoodle.

The jackal trotted to the steps of the throne and changed back into Anubis.

"Welcome," he said, "to the last room you will ever see."

Carter looked around in awe. "The Hall of Judgment." He focused on the hippodoodle and frowned. "Is that..."

"Ammit the Devourer," Anubis said. "Look upon him and tremble."

Ammit apparently heard his name in his sleep. He made a yipping sound and turned on his back. His lion and hippo legs twitched. I wondered if netherworld monsters dreamed of chasing rabbits.

"I always pictured him...bigger," Carter admitted.

Anubis gave Carter a harsh look. "Ammit only has to be big enough to eat the hearts of the wicked. Trust me, he does his job well. Or...he *did* it well, anyway."

Up on the scales, Khufu grunted. He almost lost his balance on the central beam, and the dented saucer clanged against the floor.

"Why are the scales broken?" I asked.

Anubis frowned. "Ma'at is weakening. I've tried to fix them, but..." He spread his hands helplessly.

I pointed to the ghostly rows of tombs. "Is that why the, ah, graveyard is butting in?"

Carter looked at me strangely. "What graveyard?"

"The tombs," I said. "The trees."

"What are you talking about?"

"He can't see them," Anubis said. "But you, Sadie—you're perceptive. What do you hear?"

At first I didn't know what he meant. All I heard was the blood rushing through my ears, and the distant rumble and crackle of the Lake of Fire. (And Khufu scratching himself and grunting, but that was nothing new.)

Then I closed my eyes, and I heard another distant sound—music that triggered my earliest memories, my father smiling as he danced me round our house in Los Angeles.

"Jazz," I said.

I opened my eyes, and the Hall of Judgment was gone. Or not *gone*, but faded. I could still see the broken scales and the empty throne. But no black columns, no roar of fire. Even Carter, Khufu, and Ammit had disappeared.

The cemetery was *very* real. Cracked paving stones wobbled under my feet. The humid night air smelled of spices and fish stew and old mildewed places. I might've been back in England—a churchyard in some corner of London, perhaps—but the writing on the graves was in French, and the air was much too mild for an English winter. The trees hung low and lush, covered with Spanish moss.

And there was music. Just outside the cemetery's fence, a jazz band paraded down the street in somber black suits and brightly colored party hats. Saxophonists bobbed up and down. Cornets and clarinets wailed. Drummers grinned and swayed, their sticks flashing. And behind them, carrying flowers and torches, a crowd of revelers in funeral clothes danced round an old-fashioned black hearse as it drove along.

"Where *are* we?" I said, marveling.

Anubis jumped from the top of a tomb and landed next to me. He breathed in the graveyard air, and his features relaxed. I found myself studying his mouth, the curve of his lower lip.

"New Orleans," he said.

"Sorry?"

"The Drowned City," he said. "In the French Quarter, on the west side of the river—the shore of the dead. I love it here. That's why the Hall of Judgment often connects to this part of the mortal world."

The jazz procession made its way down the street, drawing more onlookers into the party.

"What are they celebrating?"

"A funeral," Anubis said. "They've just put the deceased in his tomb. Now they're 'cutting the body loose.' The mourners celebrate the dead one's life with song and dance as they escort the empty hearse away from the cemetery. Very Egyptian, this ritual."

"How do you know so much?"

"I'm the god of funerals. I know every death custom in the world—how to die properly, how to prepare the body and soul for the afterlife. I live for death."

"You must be fun at parties," I said. "Why have you brought me here?"

"To talk." He spread his hands, and the nearest tomb

rumbled. A long white ribbon shot out of a crack in the wall. The ribbon just kept coming, weaving itself into some kind of shape next to Anubis, and my first thought was, *My god, he's got a magic roll of toilet paper.*

Then I realized it was cloth, a length of white linen wrappings—*mummy* wrappings. The cloth twisted itself into the form of a bench, and Anubis sat down.

"I don't like Horus." He gestured for me to join him. "He's loud and arrogant and thinks he's better than me. But Isis always treated me like a son."

I crossed my arms. "You're *not* my son. And I told you I'm *not* Isis."

Anubis tilted his head. "No. You don't act like a godling. You remind me of your mother."

That hit me like a bucket of cold water (and sadly, I knew exactly what *that* felt like, thanks to Zia). "You've met my mother?"

Anubis blinked, as if realizing he'd done something wrong. "I—I know all the dead, but each spirit's path is secret. I should not have spoken."

"You can't just say something like that and then clam up! Is she in the Egyptian afterlife? Did she pass your little Hall of Judgment?"

Anubis glanced uneasily at the golden scales, which shimmered like a mirage in the graveyard. "It is not *my* hall. I merely oversee it until Lord Osiris returns. I'm sorry if I upset you, but I can't say anything more. I don't know why I said anything at all. It's just . . . your soul has a similar glow. A strong glow."

"How flattering," I grumbled. "My soul glows."

"I'm sorry," he said again. "Please, sit."

I had no interest in letting the matter drop, or sitting with him on a bunch of mummy wrappings, but my direct approach to information gathering didn't seem to be working. I plopped down on the bench and tried to look as annoyed as possible.

"So." I gave him a sulky glare. "What's *that* form, then? Are you a godling?"

He frowned and put his hand to his chest. "You mean, am I inhabiting a human body? No, I can inhabit any graveyard, any place of death or mourning. This is my natural appearance."

"Oh." Part of me had hoped there was an actual boy sitting next to me—someone who just happened to be hosting a god. But I should've known that was too good to be true. I felt disappointed. Then I felt angry with myself for feeling disappointed.

It's not like there was any potential, Sadie, I chided myself. *He's the bloody god of funerals. He's like five thousand years old.*

"So," I said, "if you can't tell me anything useful, at least help me. We need a feather of truth."

He shook his head. "You don't know what you're asking. The feather of truth is too dangerous. Giving it to a mortal would be against the rules of Osiris."

"But Osiris isn't here." I pointed at the empty throne. "That's his seat, isn't it? Do you see Osiris?"

Anubis eyed the throne. He ran his fingers along his gold chain as if it were getting tighter. "It's true that I've waited here for ages, keeping my station. I was not imprisoned like the rest. I don't know why... but I did the best I could. When

I heard the five had been released, I hoped Lord Osiris would return, but ..." He shook his head dejectedly. "Why would he neglect his duties?"

"Probably because he's trapped inside my dad."

Anubis stared at me. "The baboon did not explain this."

"Well, I can't explain as well as a baboon. But basically my dad wanted to release some gods for reasons I don't quite ... Maybe he thought, *I'll just pop down to the British Museum and blow up the Rosetta Stone!* And he released Osiris, but he also got Set and the rest of that lot."

"So Set imprisoned your father while he was hosting Osiris," Anubis said, "which means Osiris has also been trapped by my—" He stopped himself. "By Set."

Interesting, I thought.

"You understand, then," I said. "You've got to help us."

Anubis hesitated, then shook his head. "I can't. I'll get in trouble."

I just stared at him and laughed. I couldn't help it, he sounded so ridiculous. "You'll get in *trouble*? How old are you, sixteen? You're a god!"

It was hard to tell in the dark, but I could swear he blushed. "You don't understand. The feather cannot abide the smallest lie. If I gave it to you, and you spoke a single untruth while you carried it, or acted in a way that was not truthful, you would burn to ashes."

"You're assuming I'm a liar."

He blinked. "No, I simply—"

"You've never told a lie? What were you about to say just now—about Set? He's your father, I'm guessing. Is that it?"

Anubis closed his mouth, then opened it again. He looked as if he wanted to get angry but couldn't quite remember how. "Are you always this infuriating?"

"Usually more," I admitted.

"Why hasn't your family married you off to someone far, far away?"

He asked as if it were an honest question, and now it was my turn to be flabbergasted. "Excuse me, death boy! But I'm twelve! Well...almost thirteen, and a very mature almost thirteen, but that's *not* the point. We don't 'marry off' girls in my family, and you may know everything about funerals, but apparently you aren't very up to speed on courtship rituals!"

Anubis looked mystified. "Apparently not."

"Right! Wait—what were we talking about? Oh, thought you could distract me, eh? I remember. Set's your father, yes? Tell the truth."

Anubis gazed across the graveyard. The sound of the jazz funeral was fading into the streets of the French Quarter.

"Yes," he said. "At least, that's what the legends say. I've never met him. My mother, Nephthys, gave me to Osiris when I was a child."

"She...gave you away?"

"She said she didn't want me to know my father. But in truth, I'm not sure she knew what to do with me. I wasn't like my cousin Horus. I wasn't a warrior. I was a...*different* child."

He sounded so bitter, I didn't know what to say. I mean, I'd asked for the truth, but usually you don't actually *get* it, especially from guys. I also knew something about being the different child—and feeling like my parents had given me away.

"Maybe your mum was trying to protect you," I said. "Your dad being Lord of Evil, and all."

"Maybe," he said halfheartedly. "Osiris took me under his wing. He made me the Lord of Funerals, the Keeper of the Ways of Death. It's a good job, but... you asked how old I am. The truth is I don't know. Years don't pass in the Land of the Dead. I still feel quite young, but the world has gotten old around me. And Osiris has been gone so long... He's the only family I had."

Looking at Anubis in the dim light of the graveyard, I saw a lonely teenage guy. I tried to remind myself that he was a god, thousands of years old, probably able to control vast powers *well* beyond magic toilet paper, but I still felt sorry for him.

"Help us rescue my dad," I said. "We'll send Set back to the Duat, and Osiris will be free. We'll all be happy."

Anubis shook his head again. "I told you—"

"Your scales are broken," I noticed. "That's because Osiris isn't here, I'm guessing. What happens to all the souls that come for judgment?"

I knew I'd hit a nerve. Anubis shifted uncomfortably on the bench. "It increases chaos. The souls become confused. Some cannot go to the afterlife. Some manage, but they must find other ways. I try to help, but... the Hall of Judgment is also called the Hall of Ma'at. It is meant to be the center of order, a stable foundation. Without Osiris, it is falling into disrepair, crumbling."

"Then what are you waiting for? Give us the feather. Unless you're afraid your dad will ground you."

His eyes flashed with irritation. For a moment I thought

he was planning *my* funeral, but he simply sighed in exasperation. "I do a ceremony called the opening of the mouth. It lets the soul of the dead person come forth. For you, Sadie Kane, I would invent a new ceremony: the closing of the mouth."

"Ha, ha. Are you going to give me the feather or not?"

He opened his hand. There was a burst of light, and a glowing feather floated above his palm—a snowy plume like a writing quill. "For Osiris's sake—but I will insist on several conditions. First, only you may handle it."

"Well, of course. You don't think I'd let Carter—"

"Also, you must listen to my mother, Nephthys. Khufu told me you were looking for her. If you manage to find her, listen to her."

"Easy," I said, though the request did leave me strangely uncomfortable. Why would Anubis ask something like that?

"And before you go," Anubis continued, "you must answer three questions for me as you hold the feather of truth, to prove that you are honest."

My mouth suddenly felt dry. "Um . . . what sort of questions?"

"Any that I want. And remember, the slightest lie will destroy you."

"Give me the bloody feather."

As he handed it to me, the feather stopped glowing, but it felt warmer and heavier than a feather should.

"It's the tail feather from a *bennu*," Anubis explained, "what you'd call a phoenix. It weighs exactly the same as a human soul. Are you ready?"

"No," I said, which must've been truthful, as I didn't burn up. "Does that count as one question?"

Anubis actually smiled, which was quite dazzling. "I suppose it does. You bargain like a Phoenician sea trader, Sadie Kane. Second question, then: Would you give your life for your brother?"

"Yes," I said immediately.

(I know. It surprised me too. But holding the feather forced me to be truthful. Obviously it didn't make me any wiser.)

Anubis nodded, apparently not surprised. "Final question: If it means saving the world, are you prepared to lose your father?"

"That's not a fair question!"

"Answer it honestly."

How could I answer something like that? It wasn't a simple yes/no.

Of course I knew the "right" answer. The heroine is supposed to refuse to sacrifice her father. Then she boldly goes off and saves her dad *and* the world, right? But what if it really *was* one or the other? The whole world was an awfully large place: Gran and Gramps, Carter, Uncle Amos, Bast, Khufu, Liz and Emma, everyone I'd ever known. What would my dad say if I chose him instead?

"If...if there really was no other way," I said, "no other way *at all*— Oh, come off. It's a ridiculous question."

The feather began to glow.

"All right," I relented. "If I had to, then I suppose...I suppose I would save the world."

Horrible guilt crushed down on me. What kind of daughter was I? I clutched the *tyet* amulet on my necklace—my one remembrance of Dad. I know some of you lot will be thinking:

You hardly ever saw your dad. You barely knew him. Why would you care so much?

But that didn't make him any less my dad, did it? Or the thought of losing him forever any less horrible. And the thought of failing him, of *willingly* choosing to let him die even to save the world—what sort of awful person was I?

I could barely meet Anubis's eyes, but when I did, his expression softened.

"I believe you, Sadie."

"Oh, really. I'm holding the bloody feather of truth, and you believe me. Well, thanks."

"The truth is harsh," Anubis said. "Spirits come to the Hall of Judgment all the time, and they *cannot* let go of their lies. They deny their faults, their true feelings, their mistakes... right up until Ammit devours their souls for eternity. It takes strength and courage to admit the truth."

"Yeah. I feel so strong and courageous. Thanks."

Anubis stood. "I should leave you now. You're running out of time. In just over twenty-four hours, the sun will rise on Set's birthday, and he will complete his pyramid—unless you stop him. Perhaps when next we meet—"

"You'll be just as annoying?" I guessed.

He fixed me with those warm brown eyes. "Or perhaps you could bring me up to speed on modern courtship rituals."

I sat there stunned until he gave me a glimpse of a smile—just enough to let me know he was teasing. Then he disappeared.

"Oh, very funny!" I yelled. The scales and the throne vanished. The linen bench unraveled and dumped me in the middle of the graveyard. Carter and Khufu appeared next to me, but I just kept yelling at the spot where Anubis had stood, calling him some choice names.

"What's going on?" Carter demanded. "Where are we?"

"He's horrible!" I growled. "Self-important, sarcastic, incredibly hot, insufferable—"

"*Agh!*" Khufu complained.

"Yeah," Carter agreed. "Did you get the feather or not?"

I held out my hand, and there it was—a glowing white plume floating above my fingers. I closed my fist and it disappeared again.

"Whoa," Carter said. "But what about Anubis? How did you—"

"Let's find Bast and get out of here," I interrupted. "We've got work to do."

And I marched out of the graveyard before he could ask me more questions, because I was in *no* mood to tell the truth.

29. Zia Sets a Rendezvous

C A R T E R

[Yeah, thanks a lot, Sadie. You get to tell the part about the Land of the Dead. I get to describe Interstate 10 through Texas.]

Long story short: It took forever and was totally boring, unless your idea of fun is watching cows graze.

We left New Orleans about 1 A.M. on December twenty-eighth, the day before Set planned to destroy the world. Bast had "borrowed" an RV—a FEMA leftover from Hurricane Katrina. At first Bast suggested taking a plane, but after I told her about my dream of the magicians on the exploding flight, we agreed planes might not be a good idea. The sky goddess Nut had promised us safe air travel as far as Memphis, but I didn't want to press our luck the closer we got to Set.

"Set is not our only problem," Bast said. "If your vision is correct, the magicians are closing in on us. And not just *any* magicians—Desjardins himself."

"And Zia," Sadie put in, just to annoy me.

In the end, we decided it was safer to drive, even though it was slower. With luck, we'd make Phoenix just in time to challenge Set. As for the House of Life, all we could do was hope to avoid them while we did our job. Maybe once we dealt with Set, the magicians would decide we were cool. Maybe . . .

I kept thinking about Desjardins, wondering if he really could be a host for Set. A day ago, it had made perfect sense. Desjardins wanted to crush the Kane family. He'd hated our dad, and he hated us. He'd probably been waiting for decades, even centuries, for Iskandar to die, so he could become Chief Lector. Power, anger, arrogance, ambition: Desjardins had it all. If Set was looking for a soulmate, literally, he couldn't do much better. And if Set could start a war between the gods and magicians by controlling the Chief Lector, the only winner would be the forces of chaos. Besides, Desjardins was an easy guy to hate. *Somebody* had sabotaged Amos's house and alerted Set that Amos was coming.

But the way Desjardins saved all those people on the plane—that just didn't seem like something the Lord of Evil would do.

Bast and Khufu took turns driving while Sadie and I dozed off and on. I didn't know baboons could drive recreational vehicles, but Khufu did okay. When I woke up around dawn, he was navigating through early morning rush hour in Houston, baring his fangs and barking a lot, and none of the other drivers seemed to notice anything out of the ordinary.

For breakfast, Sadie, Bast, and I sat in the RV's kitchen while the cabinets banged open and the dishes clinked and miles and miles of nothing went by outside. Bast had snagged us some snacks and drinks (and Friskies, of course) from a New Orleans all-night convenience store before we left, but nobody seemed very hungry. I could tell Bast was anxious. She'd already shredded most of the RV's upholstery, and was now using the kitchen table as a scratching post.

As for Sadie, she kept opening and closing her hand, staring at the feather of truth as if it were a phone she wished would ring. Ever since her disappearance in the Hall of Judgment, she'd been acting all distant and quiet. Not that I'm complaining, but it wasn't like her.

"What happened with Anubis?" I asked her for the millionth time.

She glared at me, ready to bite my head off. Then she apparently decided I wasn't worth the effort. She fixed her eyes on the glowing feather that hovered over her palm.

"We talked," she said carefully. "He asked me some questions."

"What kind of questions?"

"Carter, don't ask. Please."

Please? Okay, that really wasn't like Sadie.

I looked at Bast, but she wasn't any help. She was slowly gouging the Formica to bits with her claws.

"What's wrong?" I asked her.

She kept her eyes on the table. "In the Land of the Dead, I abandoned you. *Again.*"

"Anubis startled you," I said. "It's no big deal."

Bast gave me the big yellow eyes, and I got the feeling I'd only made things worse.

"I made a promise to your father, Carter. In exchange for

my freedom, he gave me a job even more important than fighting the Serpent: protecting Sadie—and if it ever became necessary, protecting *both* of you."

Sadie flushed. "Bast, that's . . . I mean, thank you and all, but we're hardly more important than fighting . . . you know, *him*."

"You don't understand," Bast said. "The two of you are not just blood of the pharaohs. You're the most powerful royal children to be born in centuries. You're the only chance we have of reconciling the gods and the House of Life, of relearning the old ways before it's too late. If you could learn the path of the gods, you could find others with royal blood and teach *them*. You could revitalize the House of Life. What your parents did—*everything* they did, was to prepare the way for you."

Sadie and I were silent. I mean, what do you say to something like that? I guessed I'd always felt like my parents loved me, but willing to *die* for me? Believing it was necessary so Sadie and I could do some amazing world-saving stuff? I didn't ask for that.

"They didn't want to leave you alone," Bast said, reading my expression. "They didn't plan on it, but they knew releasing the gods would be dangerous. Believe me, they understood how special you are. At first I was protecting you two because I promised. Now even if I hadn't promised, I would. You two are like kittens to me. I won't fail you again."

I'll admit I got a lump in my throat. I'd never been called someone's kitten before.

Sadie sniffled. She brushed something from under her eye. "You're not going to wash us, are you?"

It was good to see Bast smile again. "I'll try to resist. And by the way, Sadie, I'm proud of you. Dealing with Anubis on your own—those death gods can be nasty customers."

Sadie shrugged. She seemed strangely uncomfortable. "Well, I wouldn't call him *nasty*. I mean, he looked hardly more than a teenager."

"What are you talking about?" I said. "He had the head of a jackal."

"No, when he turned human."

"Sadie..." I was starting to get worried about her now. "When Anubis turned human he *still* had the head of a jackal. He was huge and terrifying and, yeah, pretty nasty. Why, what did he look like to you?"

Her cheeks reddened. "He looked...like a mortal guy."

"Probably a glamour," Bast said.

"No," Sadie insisted. "It couldn't have been."

"Well, it's not important," I said. "We got the feather."

Sadie fidgeted, as if it was *very* important. But then she closed her fist, and the feather of truth disappeared. "It won't do us any good without the secret name of Set."

"I'm working on that." Bast's gaze shifted around the room—she seemed afraid of being overheard. "I've got a plan. But it's dangerous."

I sat forward. "What is it?"

"We'll have to make a stop. I'd rather not jinx us until we get closer, but it's on our way. Shouldn't cause much of a delay."

I tried to calculate. "This is the morning of the second Demon Day?"

Bast nodded. "The day Horus was born."

"And Set's birthday is tomorrow, the third Demon Day. That means we have about twenty-four hours until he destroys North America."

"And if he gets his hands on us," Sadie added, "he'll ramp up his power even more."

"It'll be enough time," Bast said. "It's roughly twenty-four hours driving from New Orleans to Phoenix, and we've already been on the road over five hours. If we don't have any more nasty surprises—"

"Like the kind we have every day?"

"Yes," Bast admitted. "Like those."

I took a shaky breath. Twenty-four hours and it would be over, one way or the other. We'd save Dad and stop Set, or everything would've been for nothing—not just what Sadie and I had done, but all our parents' sacrifices too. Suddenly I felt like I was underground again, in one of those tunnels in the First Nome, with a million tons of rock over my head. One little shift in the ground, and everything would come crashing down.

"Well," I said. "If you need me, I'll be outside, playing with sharp objects."

I grabbed my sword and headed for the back of the RV.

I'd never seen a mobile home with a porch before. The sign on the back door warned me not to use it while the vehicle was in motion, but I did anyway.

It wasn't the best place to practice swordplay. It was too small, and two chairs took up most of the space. The cold wind whipped around me, and every bump in the road threw me off balance. But it was the only place I could go to be alone. I needed to clear my thoughts.

I practiced summoning my sword from the Duat and putting it back. Soon I could do it almost every time, as long as I kept my focus. Then I practiced some moves—blocks, jabs, and strikes—until Horus couldn't resist offering his advice.

Lift the blade higher, he coached. *More of an arc, Carter. The blade is designed to hook an enemy's weapon.*

Shut up, I grumbled. *Where were you when I needed help on the basketball court?* But I tried holding the sword his way and found he was right.

The highway wound through long stretches of empty scrubland. Once in a while we'd pass a rancher's truck or a family SUV, and the driver would get wide-eyed when he saw me: a black kid swinging a sword on the back of an RV. I'd just smile and wave, and Khufu's driving soon left them in the dust.

After an hour of practice, my shirt was stuck to my chest with cold sweat. My breathing was heavy. I decided to sit and take a break.

"It approaches," Horus told me. His voice sounded more substantial, no longer in my head. I looked next to me and saw him shimmering in a golden aura, sitting back in the other deck chair in his leather armor with his sandaled feet up on the railing. His sword, a ghostly copy of *my* sword, was propped next to him.

"What's approaching?" I asked. "The fight with Set?"

"That, of course," Horus said. "But there is another challenge before that, Carter. Be prepared."

"Great. As if I didn't have enough challenges already."

Horus's silver-and-gold eyes glittered. "When I was growing up, Set tried to kill me many times. My mother and I fled from place to place, hiding from him until I was old enough to face him. The Red Lord will send the same forces against you. The next will come—"

"At a river," I guessed, remembering my last soul trip. "Something bad is going is happen at a river. But what's the challenge?"

"You must beware—" Horus's image began to fade, and the god frowned. "What's this? Someone is trying to—a different force—"

He was replaced by the glowing image of Zia Rashid.

"Zia!" I stood up, suddenly conscious of the fact that I was sweaty and gross and looked like I'd just been dragged through the Land of the Dead.

"Carter?" Her image flickered. She was clutching her staff, and wore a gray coat wrapped over her robes as if she were standing somewhere cold. Her short black hair danced around her face. "Thank Thoth I found you."

"How did you get here?"

"No time! Listen: we're coming after you. Desjardins, me, and two others. We don't know exactly where you are. Desjardins' tracking spells are having trouble finding you, but he knows we're getting close. And he knows where you're going—Phoenix."

My mind started racing. "So he finally believes Set is free? You're coming to help us?"

Zia shook her head. "He's coming to stop you."

"*Stop* us? Zia, Set's about to blow up the continent! My

dad—" My voice cracked. I hated how scared and powerless I sounded. "My dad's in trouble."

Zia reached out a shimmering hand, but it was just an image. Our fingers couldn't touch. "Carter, I'm sorry. You have to see Desjardins' point of view. The House of Life has been trying to keep the gods locked up for centuries to prevent something like *this* from happening. Now that you've unleashed them—"

"It wasn't *my* idea!"

"I know, but you're trying to fight Set with divine magic. Gods can't be controlled. You could end up doing even more damage. If you let the House of Life handle this—"

"Set is too strong," I said. "And I *can* control Horus. I can do this."

Zia shook her head. "It will get harder as you get closer to Set. You have no idea."

"And you do?"

Zia glanced nervously to her left. Her image turned fuzzy, like a bad television signal. "We don't have much time. Mel will be out of the restroom soon."

"You've got a magician named Mel?"

"Just listen. Desjardins is splitting us into two teams. The plan is for us to cut you off on either side and intercept you. If *my* team reaches you first, I think I can keep Mel from attacking long enough for us all to talk. Then maybe we can figure out how to approach Desjardins, to convince him we have to cooperate."

"Don't take this the wrong way, but why should I trust you?"

She pursed her lips, looking genuinely hurt. Part of me felt guilty, while part of me worried this was some kind of trick.

"Carter...I have something to tell you. Something that might help, but it has to be said in person."

"Tell me now."

"Thoth's beak! You are impossibly stubborn."

"Yeah, it's a gift."

We locked eyes. Her image was fading, but I didn't want her to go. I wanted to talk longer.

"If you won't trust me, I'll have to trust you," Zia said. "I will arrange to be in Las Cruces, New Mexico, tonight. If you choose to meet me, perhaps we can convince Mel. Then together, we'll convince Desjardins. Will you come?"

I wanted to promise, just to see her, but I imagined myself trying to convince Sadie or Bast that this was a good idea. "I don't know, Zia."

"Just think about it," she pleaded. "And Carter, don't trust Amos. If you see him—" Her eyes widened. "Mel's here!" she whispered.

Zia slashed her staff in front of her, and her image vanished.

30. Bast Keeps a Promise

HOURS LATER, I WOKE UP ON THE RV's couch with Bast shaking my arm.

"We're here," she announced.

I had no idea how long I'd been asleep. At some point, the flat landscape and complete boredom had zonked me out, and I'd started having bad dreams about tiny magicians flying around in my hair, trying to shave me bald. Somewhere in there, I'd had a nightmare about Amos too, but it was fuzzy. I still didn't understand why Zia would mention him.

I blinked the sleep out of my eyes and realized my head was in Khufu's lap. The baboon was foraging my scalp for munchies.

"Dude." I sat up groggily. "Not cool."

"But he gave you a lovely hairdo," Sadie said.

"*Agh-agh!*" Khufu agreed.

Bast opened the door of the trailer. "Come on," she said. "We'll have to walk from here."

When I got to the door I almost had a heart attack. We

were parked on a mountain road so narrow, the RV would've toppled over if I'd sneezed wrong.

For a second, I was afraid we were already in Phoenix, because the landscape looked similar. The sun was just setting on the horizon. Rugged mountain ranges stretched out on either side, and the desert floor between them seemed to go on forever. In a valley to our left lay a colorless city—hardly any trees or grass, just sand, gravel, and buildings. The city was much smaller than Phoenix, though, and a large river traced its southern edge, glinting red in the fading light. The river curved around the base of the mountains below us before snaking off to the north.

"We're on the moon," Sadie murmured.

"El Paso, Texas," Bast corrected. "And that's the Rio Grande." She took a big breath of the cool dry air. "A river civilization in the desert. Very much like Egypt, actually! *Er*, except for the fact that Mexico is next door. I think this is the best spot to summon Nephthys."

"You really think she'll tell us Set's secret name?" Sadie asked.

Bast considered. "Nephthys is unpredictable, but she has sided against her husband before. We can hope."

That didn't sound very promising. I stared at the river far below. "Why did you park us on the mountain? Why not closer?"

Bast shrugged, as if this hadn't occurred to her. "Cats like to get as high up as possible. In case we have to pounce on something."

"Great," I said. "So if we have to pounce, we're all set."

"It's not so bad," Bast said. "We just climb our way down to the river through a few miles of sand, cacti, and rattlesnakes, looking out for the Border Patrol, human traffickers, magicians, and demons—and summon Nephthys."

Sadie whistled. "Well, I'm excited!"

"*Agh*," Khufu agreed miserably. He sniffed the air and snarled.

"He smells trouble," Bast translated. "Something bad is about to happen."

"Even *I* could smell that," I grumbled, and we followed Bast down the mountain.

Yes, Horus said. *I remember this place.*

It's El Paso, I told him. *Unless you went out for Mexican food, you've never been here.*

I remember it well, he insisted. *The marsh, the desert.*

I stopped and looked around. Suddenly I remembered this place, too. About fifty yards in front of us, the river spread out into a swampy area—a web of slow-moving tributaries cutting a shallow depression through the desert. Marsh grass grew tall along the banks. There must've been some kind of surveillance, its being an international border and all, but I couldn't spot any.

I'd been here in *ba* form. I could picture a hut right there in the marsh, Isis and young Horus hiding from Set. And just downriver—that's where I'd sensed something dark moving under the water, waiting for me.

I caught Bast's arm when she was a few steps from the bank. "Stay away from the water."

She frowned. "Carter, I'm a *cat*. I'm not going for a swim. But if you want to summon a river goddess, you really need to do it at the riverbank."

She made it sound so logical that I felt stupid, but I couldn't help it. Something bad was about to happen.

What is it? I asked Horus. *What's the challenge?*

But my ride-along god was unnervingly silent, as if waiting.

Sadie tossed a rock into the murky brown water. It sank with a loud *ker-plunk!*

"Seems quite safe to me," she said, and trudged down to the banks.

Khufu followed hesitantly. When he reached the water, he sniffed at it and snarled.

"See?" I said. "Even Khufu doesn't like it."

"It's probably ancestral memory," Bast said. "The river was a dangerous place in Egypt. Snakes, hippos, all kinds of problems."

"Hippos?"

"Don't take it lightly," Bast warned. "Hippos can be *deadly*."

"Was that what attacked Horus?" I asked. "I mean in the old days, when Set was looking for him?"

"Haven't heard that story," Bast said. "Usually you hear that Set used scorpions first. Then later, crocodiles."

"Crocodiles," I said, and a chill went down my back.

Is that it? I asked Horus. But again he didn't answer. "Bast, does the Rio Grande have crocodiles?"

"I very much doubt it." She knelt by the water. "Now, Sadie, if you'd do the honors?"

"How?"

"Just ask for Nephthys to appear. She was Isis's sister. If she's anywhere on this side of the Duat, she should hear your voice."

Sadie looked doubtful, but she knelt next to Bast and touched the water. Her fingertips caused ripples that seemed much too large, rings of force emanating all the way across the river.

"Hullo, Nephthys?" she said. "Anyone home?"

I heard a splash downriver, and turned to see a family of immigrants crossing midstream. I'd heard stories about how thousands of people cross the border from Mexico illegally each year, looking for work and a better life, but it was startling to actually see them in front of me—a man and a woman hurrying along, carrying a little girl between them. They were dressed in ragged clothes and looked poorer than the poorest Egyptian peasants I'd ever seen. I stared at them for a few seconds, but they didn't appear to be any kind of supernatural threat. The man gave me a wary look and we seemed to come to a silent understanding: we both had enough problems without bothering each other.

Meanwhile Bast and Sadie stayed focused on the water, watching the ripples spread out from Sadie's fingers.

Bast tilted her head, listening intently. "What's she saying?"

"I can't make it out," Sadie whispered. "Very faint."

"You can actually hear something?" I asked.

"*Shhh*," they both said at once.

"*'Caged'*..." Sadie said. "No, what is that word in English?"

"Sheltered," Bast suggested. "She is sheltered far away. A *sleeping host*. What is *that* supposed to mean?"

I didn't know what they were talking about. I couldn't hear a thing.

Khufu tugged at my hand and pointed downriver. "*Agh.*"

The immigrant family had disappeared. It seemed impossible they could cross the river so quickly. I scanned both banks—no sign of them—but the water was more turbulent where they'd been standing, as if someone had stirred it with a giant spoon. My throat tightened.

"*Um*, Bast—"

"Carter, we can barely hear Nephthys," she said. "Please."

I gritted my teeth. "Fine. Khufu and I are going to check something—"

"*Shh!*" Sadie said again.

I nodded to Khufu, and we started down the riverbank. Khufu hid behind my legs and growled at the river.

I looked back, but Bast and Sadie seemed fine. They were still staring at the water as if it were some amazing Internet video.

Finally we got to the place where I'd seen the family, but the water had calmed. Khufu slapped the ground and did a handstand, which meant he was either break dancing or really nervous.

"What is it?" I asked, my heart pounding.

"*Agh, agh, agh!*" he complained. That was probably an entire lecture in Baboon, but I had no idea what he was saying.

"Well, I don't see any other way," I said. "If that family got pulled into the water or something . . . I have to find them. I'm going in."

"*Agh!*" He backed away from the water.

"Khufu, those people had a little girl. If they need help, I can't just walk away. Stay here and watch my back."

Khufu grunted and slapped his own face in protest as I stepped into the water. It was colder and swifter than I'd imagined. I concentrated, and summoned my sword and wand out of the Duat. Maybe it was my imagination, but that seemed to make the river run even faster.

I was midstream when Khufu barked urgently. He was jumping around on the riverbank, pointing frantically at a nearby clump of reeds.

The family was huddled inside, trembling with fear, their eyes wide. My first thought: *Why are they hiding from me?*

"I won't hurt you," I promised. They stared at me blankly, and I wished I could speak Spanish.

Then the water churned around me, and I realized they weren't scared of me. My next thought: *Man, I'm stupid.*

Horus's voice yelled: *Jump!*

I sprang out of the water as if shot from a cannon—twenty, thirty feet into the air. No way I should've been able to do that, but it was a good thing, because a monster erupted from the river beneath me.

At first all I saw were hundreds of teeth—a pink maw three times as big as me. Somehow I managed to flip and land on my feet in the shallows. I was facing a crocodile as long as our

RV—and that was just the half sticking out of the water. Its gray-green skin was ridged with thick plates like a camouflage suit of armor, and its eyes were the color of moldy milk.

The family screamed and started scrambling up the banks. That caught the crocodile's attention. He instinctively turned toward the louder, more interesting prey. I'd always thought of crocodiles as slow animals, but when it charged the immigrants, I'd never seen anything move so fast.

Use the distraction, Horus urged. *Get behind it and strike.*

Instead I yelled, "Sadie, Bast, help!" and I threw my wand.

Bad throw. The wand hit the river right in front of the croc, then skipped off the water like a stone, smacked the croc between the eyes, and shot back into my hand.

I doubt I did any damage, but the croc glanced over at me, annoyed.

Or you can smack it with a stick, Horus muttered.

I charged forward, yelling to keep the croc's attention. Out of the corner of my eye, I could see the family scrambling to safety. Khufu ran along behind them, waving his arms and barking to herd them out of harm's way. I wasn't sure if they were running from the croc or the crazy monkey, but as long as they kept running, I didn't care.

I couldn't see what was happening with Bast and Sadie. I heard shouting and splashing behind me, but before I could look, the crocodile lunged.

I ducked to the left, slashing with my sword. The blade just bounced off the croc's hide. The monster thrashed sideways, and its snout would've bashed my head in; but I instinctively raised my wand and the croc slammed into a wall of force, bouncing off as if I were protected by a giant invisible energy bubble.

I tried to summon the falcon warrior, but it was too hard to concentrate with a six-ton reptile trying to bite me in half.

Then I heard Bast scream, "NO!" and I knew immediately, without even looking, that something was wrong with Sadie.

Desperation and rage turned my nerves to steel. I thrust out my wand and the wall of energy surged outward, slamming into the crocodile so hard, it went flying through the air, tumbling out of the river and onto the Mexican shore. While it was on its back, flailing and off balance, I leaped, raising my sword, which was now glowing in my hands, and drove the blade into the monster's belly. I held on while the crocodile thrashed, slowly disintegrating from its snout to the tip of its tail, until I stood in the middle of a giant pile of wet sand.

I turned and saw Bast battling a crocodile just as big as mine. The crocodile lunged, and Bast dropped beneath it, raking her knives across its throat. The croc melted into the river until it was only a smoky cloud of sand, but the damage had been done: Sadie lay in a crumpled heap on the riverbank.

By the time I got there, Khufu and Bast were already at her side. Blood trickled from Sadie's scalp. Her face was a nasty shade of yellow.

"What happened?" I asked.

"It came out of nowhere," Bast said miserably. "Its tail hit Sadie and sent her flying. She never had a chance. Is she . . . ?"

Khufu put his hand on Sadie's forehead and made popping noises with his mouth.

Bast sighed with relief. "Khufu says she'll live, but we have to get her out of here. Those crocodiles could mean..."

Her voice trailed off. In the middle of the river, the water was boiling. Rising from it was a figure so horrible, I knew we were doomed.

"Could mean *that*," Bast said grimly.

To start with, the guy was twenty feet tall—and I don't mean with a glowing avatar. He was all flesh and blood. His chest and arms were human, but he had light green skin, and his waist was wrapped in a green armored kilt like reptile hide. He had the head of a crocodile, a massive mouth filled with white crooked teeth, and eyes that glistened with green mucus (yeah, I know—real attractive). His black hair hung in plaits down to his shoulders, and bull's horns curved from his head. If that wasn't weird enough, he appeared to be sweating at an unbelievable rate—oily water poured off him in torrents and pooled in the river.

He raised his staff—a length of green wood as big as a telephone pole.

Bast yelled, "Move!" and pulled me back as the crocodile man smashed a five-foot-deep trench in the riverbank where I'd been standing.

He bellowed: "Horus!"

The last thing I wanted to do was say, *Here!* But Horus spoke urgently in my mind: *Face him down. Sobek only understands strength. Do not let him grasp you, or he will pull you down and drown you.*

I swallowed my fear and yelled, "Sobek! You, uh, weakling! How the heck are ya?"

Sobek bared his teeth. Maybe it was his version of a friendly smile. Probably not.

"That form does not serve you, falcon god," he said. "I will snap you in half."

Next to me, Bast slipped her knives from her sleeves. "Don't let him grasp you," she warned.

"Already got the memo," I told her. I was conscious of Khufu off to my right, slowly lugging Sadie uphill. I had to keep this green guy distracted, at least until they were safe. "Sobek, god of . . . I'm guessing crocodiles! Leave us in peace or we'll destroy you!"

Good, Horus said. *"Destroy" is good.*

Sobek roared with laughter. "Your sense of humor has improved, Horus. You and your kitty will destroy me?" He turned his mucus-filmed eyes on Bast. "What brings you to my realm, cat goddess? I thought you didn't like the *water*!"

On the last word, he aimed his staff and shot forth a torrent of green water. Bast was too quick. She jumped and came down behind Sobek with her avatar fully formed—a massive, glowing cat-headed warrior. "Traitor!" Bast yelled. "Why do you side with chaos? Your duty is to the king!"

"What king?" Sobek roared. "Ra? Ra is gone. Osiris is dead *again,* the weakling! And this boy child cannot restore the empire. There was a time I supported Horus, yes. But he has no strength in this form. He has no followers. Set offers power. Set offers fresh meat. I think I will start with godling flesh!"

He turned on me and swung his staff. I rolled away from his strike, but his free hand shot out and grabbed me around the waist. I just wasn't quick enough. Bast tensed, preparing to launch herself at the enemy, but before she could, Sobek dropped his staff, grasped me with both massive hands, and dragged me into the water. The next thing I knew I was drowning in the cold green murk. I couldn't see or breathe. I sank into the depths as Sobek's hands crushed the air out of my lungs.

Now or never! Horus said. *Let me take control.*

No, I replied. *I'll die first.*

I found the thought strangely calming. If I was already dead, there was no point in being afraid. I might as well go down fighting.

I focused my power and felt strength coursing through my body. I flexed my arms and felt Sobek's grip weaken. I summoned the avatar of the hawk warrior and was instantly encased in a glowing golden form as large as Sobek. I could just see him in the dark water, his slimy eyes wide with surprise.

I broke his grip and head-butted him, breaking off a few of his teeth. Then I shot out of the water and landed on the riverbank next to Bast, who was so startled, she almost slashed me.

"Thank Ra!" she exclaimed.

"Yeah, I'm alive."

"No, I almost jumped in after you. I hate the water!"

Then Sobek exploded out of the river, roaring in rage. Green blood oozed from one of his nostrils.

"You cannot defeat me!" He held out his arms, which were raining perspiration. "I am lord of the water! My sweat creates the rivers of the world!"

Eww. I decided not to swim in rivers anymore. I glanced

back, looking for Khufu and Sadie, but they were nowhere in sight. Hopefully Khufu had gotten Sadie to safety, or at least found a good place to hide.

Sobek charged, and he brought the river with him. A massive wave smashed into me, toppling me to the ground, but Bast jumped and came down on Sobek's back in full avatar form. The weight hardly seemed to bother him. He tried to grab her without any luck. She slashed repeatedly at his arms, back and neck, but his green skin seemed to heal as quickly as she could cut him.

I struggled to my feet, which in avatar form is like trying to get up with a mattress strapped to your chest. Sobek finally managed to grab Bast and throw her off. She tumbled to a stop without getting hurt, but her blue aura was flickering. She was losing power.

We played tag team with the crocodile god—stabbing and slashing—but the more we wounded him, the more enraged and powerful he seemed to get.

"More minions!" he shouted. "Come to me!"

That couldn't be good. Another round of giant crocs and we'd be dead.

Why don't we get minions? I complained to Horus, but he didn't answer. I could feel him struggling to channel his power through me, trying to keep up our combat magic.

Sobek's fist smashed into Bast, and she went flying again. This time when she hit the ground, her avatar flickered off completely.

I charged, trying to draw Sobek's attention. Unfortunately,

it worked. Sobek turned and blasted me with water. While I was blind, he slapped me so hard I flew across the riverbank, tumbling through the reeds.

My avatar collapsed. I sat up groggily and found Khufu and Sadie right next to me, Sadie still passed out and bleeding, Khufu desperately murmuring in Baboon and stroking her forehead.

Sobek stepped out of the water and grinned at me. Far downstream in the dim evening light, about a quarter of a mile away, I could see two wake lines in the river, coming toward us fast—Sobek's reinforcements.

From the river, Bast yelled, "Carter, hurry! Get Sadie out of here!"

Her face went pale with strain, and her cat warrior avatar appeared around her one more time. It was weak, though—barely substantial.

"Don't!" I called. "You'll die!"

I tried to summon the falcon warrior, but the effort made my insides burn with pain. I was out of power, and Horus's spirit was slumbering, completely spent.

"Go!" Bast yelled. "And tell your father I kept my promise."

"NO!"

She leaped at Sobek. The two grappled—Bast slashing furiously across his face while Sobek howled in pain. The two gods toppled into the water, and down they went.

I ran to the riverbank. The river bubbled and frothed. Then a green explosion lit the entire length of the Rio Grande, and a small black-and-gold creature shot out of the river as if it had been tossed. It landed on the grass at my feet—a wet, unconscious, half-dead cat.

"Bast?" I picked up the cat gingerly. It wore Bast's collar, but as I watched, the talisman of the goddess crumbled to dust. It wasn't Bast anymore. Only Muffin.

Tears stung my eyes. Sobek had been defeated, forced back to the Duat or something, but there were still two wake lines coming toward us in the river, close enough now that I could see the monsters' green backs and beady eyes.

I cradled the cat against my chest and turned toward Khufu. "Come on, we have to—"

I froze, because standing right behind Khufu and my sister, glaring at me, was a different crocodile—one that was pure white.

We're dead, I thought. And then, *Wait . . . a white crocodile?*

It opened its mouth and lunged—straight over me. I turned and saw it slam into the two other crocodiles—the giant green ones that had been about to kill me.

"Philip?" I said in amazement, as the crocodiles thrashed and fought.

"Yes," said a man's voice.

I turned again and saw the impossible. Uncle Amos was kneeling next to Sadie, frowning as he examined her head wound. He looked up at me urgently. "Philip will keep Sobek's minions busy, but not for long. Follow me now, and we have a slim chance of surviving!"

31. I Deliver a Love Note

I'M GLAD CARTER TOLD THAT LAST BIT—partly because I was unconscious when it happened, partly because I can't talk about what Bast did without going to pieces.

Ah, but more on that later.

I woke feeling as if someone had overinflated my head. My eyes weren't seeing the same things. Out my left, I saw a baboon bum, out my right, my long-lost uncle Amos. Naturally, I decided to focus on the right.

"Amos?"

He laid a cool cloth on my forehead. "Rest, child. You had quite a concussion."

That at least I could believe.

As my eyes began to focus, I saw we were outside under a starry night sky. I was lying on a blanket on what felt like soft sand. Khufu stood next to me, his colorful side a bit too close to my face. He was stirring a pot over a small fire, and whatever he was cooking smelled like burning tar. Carter sat nearby at

the top of a sand dune, looking despondent and holding...
was that Muffin in his lap?

Amos appeared much as he had when we last saw him,
ages ago. He wore his blue suit with matching coat and fedora.
His long hair was neatly braided, and his round glasses glinted
in the sun. He appeared fresh and rested—not like someone
who'd been the prisoner of Set.

"How did you—"

"Get away from Set?" His expression darkened. "I was a fool
to go looking for him, Sadie. I had no idea how powerful he'd
become. His spirit is tied to the red pyramid."

"So...he doesn't *have* a human host?"

Amos shook his head. "He doesn't need one as long as he
has the pyramid. As it gets closer to completion, he gets stronger and stronger. I sneaked into his lair under the mountain
and walked right into a trap. I'm ashamed to say he took me
without a fight."

He gestured at his suit, showing off how perfectly fine he
was. "Not a scratch. Just—*bam*. I was frozen like a statue. Set
stood me outside his pyramid like a trophy and let his demons
laugh and mock me as they passed by."

"Did you see Dad?" I asked.

His shoulders slumped. "I heard the demons talking. The
coffin is inside the pyramid. They're planning to use Osiris's
power to augment the storm. When Set unleashes it at
sunrise—and it will be *quite* an explosion—Osiris and your
father will be obliterated. Osiris will be exiled so deep into the
Duat he may never rise again."

My head began to throb. I couldn't believe we had so

little time, and if Amos couldn't save Dad, how could Carter and I?

"But you got away," I said, grasping for any good news. "So there must be weaknesses in his defenses or—"

"The magic that froze me eventually began to weaken. I concentrated my energy and worked my way out of the binding. It took many hours, but finally I broke free. I sneaked out at midday, when the demons were sleeping. It was much too easy."

"It doesn't sound easy," I said.

Amos shook his head, obviously troubled. "Set allowed me to escape. I don't know why, but I shouldn't be alive. It's a trick of some sort. I'm afraid..." Whatever he was going to say, he changed his mind. "At any rate, my first thought was to find you, so I summoned my boat."

He gestured behind him. I managed to lift my head and saw we were in a strange desert of white dunes that stretched as far as I could see in the starlight. The sand under my fingers was so fine and white, it might've been sugar. Amos's boat, the same one that had carried us from the Thames to Brooklyn, was beached at the top of a nearby dune, canted at a precarious angle as if it had been thrown there.

"There's a supply locker aboard," Amos offered, "if you'd like fresh clothes."

"But where are we?"

"White Sands," Carter told me. "In New Mexico. It's a government range for testing missiles. Amos said no one would look for us here, so we gave you some time to heal. It's about seven in the evening, still the twenty-eighth. Twelve hours or so until Set... you know."

"But..." Too many questions swam round in my mind. The last thing I remembered, I'd been at the river talking to Nephthys. Her voice had seemed to come from the other side of the world. She'd spoken faintly through the current—so hard to understand, yet quite insistent. She'd told me she was sheltered far away in a sleeping host, which I couldn't make sense of. She'd said she could not appear in person, but that she would send a message. Then the water had started to boil.

"We were attacked." Carter stroked Muffin's head, and I finally noticed that the amulet—*Bast's* amulet—was missing. "Sadie, I've got some bad news."

He told me what had happened, and I closed my eyes. I started to weep. Embarrassing, yes, but I couldn't help it. Over the last few days, I'd lost everything—my home, my ordinary life, my father. I'd been almost killed half a dozen times. My mother's death, which I'd never gotten over to begin with, hurt like a reopened wound. And now Bast was gone too?

When Anubis had questioned me in the Underworld, he'd wanted to know what I would sacrifice to save the world.

What haven't I sacrificed already? I wanted to scream. *What have I got left?*

Carter came over and gave me Muffin, who purred in my arms, but it wasn't the same. It wasn't Bast.

"She'll come back, won't she?" I looked at Amos imploringly. "I mean she's immortal, isn't she?"

Amos tugged at the rim of his hat. "Sadie...I just don't know. It seems she sacrificed herself to defeat Sobek. Bast forced him back to the Duat at the expense of her own life force. She even spared Muffin, her host, probably with the last shred of her power. If that's true, it would be very difficult for Bast to come back. Perhaps some day, in a few hundred years—"

"No, not a few hundred years! I can't—" My voice broke.

Carter put his hand on my shoulder, and I knew he understood. We *couldn't* lose anyone else. We just couldn't.

"Rest now," Amos said. "We can spare another hour, but then we'll have to get moving."

Khufu offered me a bowl of his concoction. The chunky liquid looked like soup that had died long ago. I glanced at Amos, hoping he'd give me a pass, but he nodded encouragingly.

Just my luck, on top of everything else I had to take baboon medicine.

I sipped the brew, which tasted almost as bad as it smelled, and immediately my eyelids felt heavy. I closed my eyes and slept.

And just when I thought I had this soul-leaving-the-body business sorted, my soul decided to break the rules. Well, it is *my* soul after all, so I suppose that makes sense.

As my *ba* left my body, it kept its human form, which was better than the winged poultry look, but it kept growing and growing until I towered above White Sands. I'd been told many times that I have a lot of spirit (usually not as a compliment), but this was absurd. My *ba* was as tall as the Washington Monument.

To the south, past miles and miles of desert, steam rose from the Rio Grande—the battle site where Bast and Sobek had perished. Even as tall as I was, I shouldn't have been able to see all the way to Texas, especially at night, but somehow I could. To the north, even farther away, I saw a distant red glow and I knew it was the aura of Set. His power was growing as his pyramid neared completion.

I looked down. Next to my foot was a tiny cluster of specks—our camp. Miniature Carter, Amos, and Khufu sat talking round the cooking fire. Amos's boat was no larger than my little toe. My own sleeping form lay curled in a blanket, so small I could've crushed myself with one misstep.

I was enormous, and the world was small.

"That's how gods see things," a voice told me.

I looked around but saw nothing, just the vast expanse of rolling white dunes. Then, in front of me, the dunes shifted. I thought it was the wind, until an entire dune rolled sideways like a wave. Another moved, and another. I realized I was looking at a human form—an enormous man lying in the fetal position. He got up, shaking white sand everywhere. I knelt down and cupped my hands over my companions to keep them from getting buried. Oddly, they didn't seem to notice, as if the disruption were no more than a sprinkle of rain.

The man rose to his full height—at least a head taller than my own giant form. His body was made of sand that curtained off his arms and chest like waterfalls of sugar. The sand shifted across his face until he formed a vague smile.

"Sadie Kane," he said. "I have been waiting for you."

"Geb." Don't ask me how, but I knew instantly that this was the god of the earth. Maybe the sand body was a giveaway. "I have something for you."

It didn't make sense that my *ba* would have the envelope,

but I reached into my shimmering ghostly pocket and pulled out the note from Nut.

"Your wife misses you," I said.

Geb took the note gingerly. He held it to his face and seemed to sniff it. Then he opened the envelope. Instead of a letter, fireworks burst out. A new constellation blazed in the night sky above us—the face of Nut, formed by a thousand stars. The wind rose quickly and ripped the image apart, but Geb sighed contentedly. He closed the envelope and tucked it inside his sandy chest as if there were a pocket right where his heart should be.

"I owe you thanks, Sadie Kane," Geb said. "It has been many millennia since I saw the face of my beloved. Ask me a favor that the earth can grant, and it shall be yours."

"Save my father," I said immediately.

Geb's face rippled with surprise. "*Hmm*, what a loyal daughter! Isis could learn a thing from you. Alas, I cannot. Your father's path is twined with that of Osiris, and matters between the gods cannot be solved by the earth."

"Then I don't suppose you could collapse Set's mountain and destroy his pyramid?" I asked.

Geb's laughter was like the world's largest sand shaker. "I cannot intervene so directly between my children. Set is my son too."

I almost stamped my foot in frustration. Then I remembered I was giant and might smash the whole camp. Could a *ba* do that? Better not to find out. "Well, your favors aren't very useful, then."

Geb shrugged, sloughing off a few tons of sand from his

shoulders. "Perhaps some advice to help you achieve what you desire. Go to the place of the crosses."

"And where is that?"

"Close," he promised. "And, Sadie Kane, you are right. You have lost too much. Your family has suffered. I know what that is like. Just remember, a parent would do anything to save his children. I gave up my happiness, my wife—I took on the curse of Ra so that my children could be born." He looked up at the sky wistfully. "And while I miss my beloved more each millennium, I know neither of us would change our choice. I have five children whom I love."

"Even Set?" I asked incredulously. "He's about to destroy millions of people."

"Set is more than he appears," Geb said. "He is our flesh and blood."

"Not mine."

"No?" Geb shifted, lowering himself. I thought he was crouching, until I realized he was melting into the dunes. "Think on it, Sadie Kane, and proceed with care. Danger awaits you at the place of crosses, but you will also find what you need most."

"Could you be a little more vague?" I grumbled.

But Geb was gone, leaving only a taller than normal dune in the sands; and my *ba* sank back into my body.

32. The Place of Crosses

I WOKE WITH MUFFIN SNUGGLED on my head, purring and chewing my hair. For a moment, I thought I was home. I used to wake with Muffin on my head all the time. Then I remembered I *had* no home, and Bast was gone. My eyes started tearing up again.

No, Isis's voice chided. *We must stay focused.*

For once, the goddess was right. I sat up and brushed the white sand off my face. Muffin meowed in protest, then waddled two steps and decided she could settle for my warm place on the blanket.

"Good, you're up," Amos said. "We were about to wake you."

It was still dark. Carter stood on the deck of the boat, pulling on a new linen coat from Amos's supply locker. Khufu loped over to me and made a purring sound at the cat. To my surprise, Muffin leaped into his arms.

400

"I've asked Khufu to take the cat back to Brooklyn," Amos said. "This is no place for her."

Khufu grunted, clearly unhappy with his assignment.

"I know, my old friend," Amos said. His voice had a hard edge; he seemed to be asserting himself as the alpha baboon. "It is for the best."

"*Agh*," Khufu said, not meeting Amos's eyes.

Unease crept over me. I remembered what Amos said: that his release might have been a trick of Set's. And Carter's vision: Set was *hoping* that Amos would lead us to the mountain so we could be captured. What if Set was influencing Amos somehow? I didn't like the idea of sending Khufu away.

On the other hand, I didn't see much choice but to accept Amos's help. And seeing Khufu there, holding Muffin, I couldn't bear the idea of putting either of them in danger. Maybe Amos had a point.

"Can he travel safely?" I asked. "Out here all by himself?"

"Oh, yes," Amos promised. "Khufu—and all baboons—have their own brand of magic. He'll be fine. And just in case..."

He brought out a wax figurine of a crocodile. "This will help if the need arises."

I coughed. "A crocodile? After what we just—"

"It's Philip of Macedonia," Amos explained.

"Philip is wax?"

"Of course," Amos said. "Real crocodiles are much too difficult to keep. And I *did* tell you he's magic."

Amos tossed the figurine to Khufu, who sniffed it, then

stuffed it into a pouch with his cooking supplies. Khufu gave me one last nervous look, glanced fearfully at Amos, then ambled over the dune with his bag in one arm and Muffin in the other.

I didn't see how they would survive out here, magic or no. I waited for Khufu to appear on the crest of the next dune, but he never did. He simply vanished.

"Now, then," Amos said. "From what Carter has told me, Set means to unleash his destruction tomorrow at sunrise. That gives us very little time. What Carter would *not* explain is how you plan to destroy Set."

I glanced at Carter and saw warning in his eyes. I understood immediately, and felt a flush of gratitude. Perhaps the boy wasn't completely thick. He shared my concerns about Amos.

"It's best we keep that to ourselves," I told Amos flatly. "You said so yourself. What if Set attached a magic listening device to you or something?"

Amos's jaw tightened. "You're right," he said grudgingly. "I can't trust myself. It's just...so frustrating."

He sounded truly anguished, which made me feel guilty. I was tempted to change my mind and tell him our plan, but one look at Carter and I kept my resolve.

"We should head to Phoenix," I said. "Perhaps along the way..."

I slipped my hand into my pocket. Nut's letter was gone. I wanted to tell Carter about my talk with the earth god, Geb, but I didn't know if it was safe in front of Amos. Carter and I had been a team for so many days now, I realized that I resented Amos's presence a little. I didn't want to confide in anyone else. God, I can't believe I just said that.

Carter spoke up. "We should stop in Las Cruces."

I'm not sure who was more surprised: Amos or me.

"That's near here," Amos said slowly. "But..." He picked up a handful of sand, murmured a spell, and threw the sand into the air. Instead of scattering, the grains floated and formed a wavering arrow, pointing southwest toward a line of rugged mountains that made a dark silhouette against the horizon.

"As I thought," Amos said, and the sand fell to the earth. "Las Cruces is out of our way by forty miles—over those mountains. Phoenix is northwest."

"Forty miles isn't so bad," I said. "Las Cruces..." The name seemed strangely familiar to me, but I couldn't decide why. "Carter, why there?"

"I just..." He looked so uncomfortable I knew it must have something to do with Zia. "I had a vision."

"A vision of loveliness?" I ventured.

He looked like he was trying to swallow a golf ball, which confirmed my suspicions. "I just think we should go there," he said. "We might find something important."

"Too risky," Amos said. "I can't allow it with the House of Life on your trail. We should stay in the wilderness, away from cities."

Then suddenly: *click*. My brain had one of those amazing moments when it actually works correctly.

"No, Carter's right," I said. "We have to go there."

It was my brother's turn to look surprised. "I am? We do?"

"Yes." I took the plunge and told them about my talk with Geb.

Amos brushed some sand off his jacket. "That's interesting, Sadie. But I don't see how Las Cruces comes into play."

"Because it's Spanish, isn't it?" I said. "Las Cruces. *The crosses*. Just as Geb told me."

Amos hesitated, then nodded reluctantly. "Get in the boat."

"A bit short on water for a boat ride, aren't we?" I asked.

But I followed him on board. Amos took off his coat and uttered a magic word. Instantly, the coat came to life, drifted to the stern and grasped the tiller.

Amos smiled at me, and some of that old twinkle came back into his eyes. "Who needs water?"

The boat shuddered and lifted into the sky.

If Amos ever got tired of being a magician, he could've gotten a job as a sky boat tour operator. The vista coming over the mountains was quite stunning.

At first, the desert had seemed barren and ugly to me compared to the lush greens of England, but I was starting to appreciate that the desert had its own stark beauty, especially at night. The mountains rose like dark islands in a sea of lights. I'd never seen so many stars above us, and the dry wind smelled of sage and pine. Las Cruces spread out in the valley below—a glowing patchwork of streets and neighborhoods.

As we got closer, I saw that most of the town was nothing very remarkable. It might've been Manchester or Swindon or any place, really, but Amos aimed our ship toward the south of the city, to an area that was obviously much older—with adobe buildings and tree-lined streets.

As we descended, I began to get nervous.

"Won't they notice us in a flying boat?" I asked. "I mean, I know magic is hard to see, but—"

"This is New Mexico," Amos said. "They see UFOs here all the time."

And with that, we landed on the roof of a small church.

It was like dropping back in time, or onto a Wild West film set. The town square was lined with stucco buildings like an Indian pueblo. The streets were brightly lit and crowded—it looked like a festival—with stall vendors selling strings of red peppers, Indian blankets, and other curios. An old stagecoach was parked next to a clump of cacti. In the plaza's bandstand, men with large guitars and loud voices played mariachi music.

"This is the historic area," Amos said. "I believe they call it Mesilla."

"Have a lot of Egyptian stuff here, do they?" I asked dubiously.

"Oh, the ancient cultures of Mexico have a lot in common with Egypt," Amos said, retrieving his coat from the tiller. "But that's a talk for another day."

"Thank god," I muttered. Then I sniffed the air and smelled something strange but wonderful—like baking bread and melting butter, only spicer, yummier. "I—am—*starving*."

It didn't take long, walking the plaza, to discover handmade tortillas. God, they were good. I suppose London has Mexican restaurants. We've got everything else. But I'd never been to one, and I doubt the tortillas would've tasted this heavenly.

A large woman in a white dress rolled out balls of dough in her flour-caked hands, flattened and baked the tortillas on a hot skillet, and handed them to us on paper napkins. They didn't need butter or jam or anything. They were so delicate, they just melted in my mouth. I made Amos pay for about a dozen, just for me.

Carter was enjoying himself too until he tried the red-chili tamales at another booth. I thought his face would explode. "Hot!" he announced. "Drink!"

"Eat more tortilla," Amos advised, trying not to laugh. "Bread cuts the heat better than water."

I tried the tamales myself and found they were excellent, not nearly as hot as a good curry, so Carter was just being a wimp, as usual.

Soon we'd eaten our fill and began wandering the streets, looking for . . . well, I wasn't sure, exactly. Time was a-wasting. The sun was going down, and I knew this would be the last night for all of us unless we stopped Set, but I had no idea why Geb had sent me here. *You will also find what you need most.* What did that mean?

I scanned the crowds and caught a glimpse of a tall young guy with dark hair. A thrill went up my spine—*Anubis?* What if he was following me, making sure I was safe? What if *he* was what I needed most?

Wonderful thought, except it wasn't Anubis. I scolded myself for thinking I could have luck that good. Besides, Carter had seen Anubis as a jackal-headed monster. Perhaps Anubis's appearance with me was just a trick to befuddle my brain—a trick that worked *quite* well.

I was daydreaming about that, and about whether or not they had tortillas in the Land of the Dead, when I locked eyes with a girl across the plaza.

"Carter." I grabbed his arm and nodded in the direction of Zia Rashid. "Someone's here to see you."

Zia was ready for battle in her loose black linen clothes, staff and wand in hand. Her dark choppy hair was blown to one side like she'd flown here on a strong wind. Her amber eyes looked about as friendly as a jaguar's.

Behind her was a vendor's table full of tourist souvenirs, and a poster that read: NEW MEXICO: LAND OF ENCHANTMENT. I doubted the vendor knew just how much enchantment was standing right in front of his merchandise.

"You came," Zia said, which seemed a bit on the obvious side. Was it my imagination, or was she looking at Amos with apprehension—even fear?

"Yeah," Carter said nervously. "You, uh, remember Sadie. And this is—"

"Amos," Zia said uneasily.

Amos bowed. "Zia Rashid, it's been several years. I see Iskandar sent his best."

Zia looked as if he'd smacked her in the face, and I realized Amos hadn't heard the news.

"*Um*, Amos," I said. "Iskandar is dead."

He stared at us in disbelief as we told him the story.

"I see," he said at last. "Then the new Chief Lector is—"

"Desjardins," I said.

"Ah. Bad news."

Zia frowned. Instead of addressing Amos, she turned to me.

"Do not dismiss Desjardins. He's very powerful. You'll need his help—*our* help—to challenge Set."

"Has it ever occurred to you," I said, "that Desjardins might be *helping* Set?"

Zia glared at me. "Never. *Others* might. But not Desjardins."

Clearly she meant Amos. I suppose that should've made me even more suspicious of him, but instead I got angry.

"You're blind," I told Zia. "Desjardins' first order as Chief Lector was to have us killed. He's trying to stop us, even though he *knows* Set is about to destroy the continent. And Desjardins was there that night at the British Museum. If Set needed a body—"

The top of Zia's staff burst into flame.

Carter quickly moved between us. "Whoa, both of you just calm down. We're here to talk."

"I *am* talking," Zia said. "You need the House of Life on your side. You have to convince Desjardins you're not a threat."

"By surrendering?" I asked. "No, thank you. I'd rather not be turned into a bug and squashed."

Amos cleared his throat. "I'm afraid Sadie is right. Unless Desjardins has changed since I last saw him, he is not a man who will listen to reason."

Zia fumed. "Carter, could we speak in *private?*"

He shifted from foot to foot. "Look, Zia, I—I agree we need to work together. But if you're going to try to convince me to surrender to the House—"

"There's something I must tell you," she insisted. "Something you *need* to know."

The way she said that made the hairs stand up on the back of my neck. Could this be what Geb meant? Was it possible that Zia held the key to defeating Set?

Suddenly Amos tensed. He pulled his staff out of thin air and said, "It's a trap."

Zia looked stunned. "What? No!"

Then we all saw what Amos had sensed. Marching towards us from the east end of the plaza was Desjardins himself. He wore cream-colored robes with the Chief Lector's leopard-skin cape tied across his shoulders. His staff glowed purple. Tourists and pedestrians veered out of his way, confused and nervous, as if they weren't sure what was going on but they knew enough to clear off.

"Other way," I urged.

I turned and saw two more magicians in black robes marching in from the west.

I pulled my wand and pointed it at Zia. "You set us up!"

"No! I swear—" Her face fell. "Mel. Mel must've told him."

"Right," I grumbled. "Blame Mel."

"No time for explanations," Amos said, and he blasted Zia with a bolt of lightning. She crashed into the souvenir table.

"Hey!" Carter protested.

"She's the enemy," Amos said. "And we have enough enemies."

Carter rushed to Zia's side (naturally) while more pedestrians panicked and scattered for the edges of the square.

"Sadie, Carter," Amos said, "if things go bad, get to the boat and flee."

"Amos, we're not leaving you," I said.

"You're more important," he insisted. "I can hold off Desjardins for— Look out!"

Amos spun his staff towards the two magicians in black. They'd been muttering spells, but Amos's gust of wind swept them off their feet, sending them swirling out of control at the center of a dust devil. They churned along the street, picking up trash, leaves, and tamales, until the miniature tornado tossed the screaming magicians over the top of a building and out of sight.

On the other side of the plaza, Desjardins roared in anger: "Kane!"

The Chief Lector slammed his staff into the ground. A crack opened in the pavement and began snaking towards us. As the crevice grew wider, the buildings trembled. Stucco flaked off the walls. The fissure would've swallowed us, but Isis's voice spoke in my mind, telling me the word I needed.

I raised my wand. "Quiet. *Hah-ri.*"

Hieroglyphs blazed to life in front of us:

The fissure stopped just short of my feet. The earthquake died.

Amos sucked in a breath. "Sadie, how did you—"

"Divine Words, Kane!" Desjardins stepped forward, his face livid. "The child dares speak the Divine Words. She is corrupted by Isis, and you are guilty of assisting the gods."

SADIE

"Step off, Michel," Amos warned.

Part of me found it amusing that Desjardins' first name was Michel, but I was too scared to enjoy the moment.

Amos held out his wand, ready to defend us. "We must stop Set. If you're wise—"

"I would what?" Desjardins said. "Join you? Collaborate? The gods bring nothing but destruction."

"No!" Zia's voice. With Carter's help, she'd somehow managed to struggle to her feet. "Master, we can't fight each other. That's not what Iskandar wanted."

"Iskandar is dead!" Desjardins bellowed. "Now, step away from them, Zia, or be destroyed with them."

Zia looked at Carter. Then she set her jaw and faced Desjardins. "No. We must work together."

I regarded Zia with a new respect. "You really didn't lead him here?"

"I do not lie," she said.

Desjardins raised his staff, and huge cracks appeared in the buildings all around him. Chunks of cement and adobe brick flew at us, but Amos summoned the wind and deflected them.

"Children, get out of here!" Amos yelled. "The other magicians won't stay gone forever."

"For once, he's right," Zia warned. "But we can't make a portal—"

"We've got a flying boat," Carter offered.

Zia nodded appreciatively. "Where?"

We pointed towards the church, but unfortunately Desjardins was between it and us.

Desjardins hurled another volley of stones. Amos deflected them with wind and lightning.

"Storm magic!" Desjardins sneered. "Since when is Amos Kane an expert in the powers of chaos? Do you see this, children? How can he be your protector?"

"Shut up," Amos growled, and with a sweep of his staff he raised a sandstorm so huge that it blanketed the entire square.

"Now," Zia said. We made a wide arc around Desjardins, then ran blindly towards the church. The sandstorm bit my skin and stung my eyes, but we found the stairs and climbed to the roof. The wind subsided, and across the plaza I could see Desjardins and Amos still facing each other, encased in shields of force. Amos was staggering; the effort was clearly taking too much out of him.

"I have to help," Zia said reluctantly, "or Desjardins will kill Amos."

"I thought you didn't trust Amos," Carter said.

"I don't," she agreed. "But if Desjardins wins this duel, we're all dead. We'll never escape." She clenched her teeth as if she were preparing for something really painful.

She held out her staff and murmured an incantation. The air became warm. The staffed glowed. She released it and it burst into flame, growing into a column of fire a full meter thick and four meters tall.

"Hunt Desjardins," she intoned.

Immediately, the fiery column floated off the roof and began moving slowly but deliberately towards the Chief Lector.

Zia crumpled. Carter and I had to grab her arms to keep her from falling on her face.

Desjardins looked up. When he saw the fire, his eyes widened with fear. "Zia!" he cursed. "You *dare* attack me?"

The column descended, passing through the branches of a tree and burning a hole straight through them. It landed in the street, hovering just a few centimeters above the pavement. The heat was so intense that it scorched the concrete curb and melted the tarmac. The fire came to a parked car, and instead of going round, it burned its way straight through the metal chassis, sawing the car in two.

"Good!" Amos yelled from the street. "Well done, Zia!"

In desperation, Desjardins staggered to his left. The column adjusted course. He blasted it with water, but the liquid evaporated into steam. He summoned boulders, but they just passed through the fire and dropped into melted, smoking lumps on the opposite side.

"What *is* that thing?" I asked.

Zia was unconscious, and Carter shook his head in wonder. But Isis spoke in my mind. A *pillar of fire,* she said with admiration. *It is the most powerful spell a master of fire can summon. It is impossible to defeat, impossible to escape. It can be used to lead the summoner toward a goal. Or it can be used to pursue any enemy, forcing him to run. If Desjardins tries to focus on anything else, it will overtake him and consume him. It will not leave him alone until it dissipates.*

How long? I asked.

Depends on the strength of the caster. Between six and twelve hours.

I laughed aloud. Brilliant! Of course Zia had passed out creating it, but it was still brilliant.

Such a spell has depleted her energy, Isis said. *She will not be able to work any magic until the pillar is gone. In order to help you, she has left herself completely powerless.*

"She'll be all right," I told Carter. Then I shouted down to the plaza: "Amos, come on! We've got to go!"

Desjardins kept backing up. I could tell he was scared of the fire, but he wasn't quite done with us. "You will be sorry for this! You wish to play gods? Then you leave me no choice." Out of the Duat, he pulled a cluster of sticks. No, they were arrows—about seven of them.

Amos looked at the arrows in horror. "You wouldn't! No Chief Lector would ever—"

"I summon Sekhmet!" Desjardins bellowed. He threw the arrows into the air and they began to twirl, orbiting Amos.

Desjardins allowed himself a satisfied smile. He looked straight at me. "You choose to place your faith in the gods?" he called. "Then die by the hands of a god."

He turned and ran. The pillar of fire picked up speed and followed.

"Children, get out of here!" Amos yelled, encircled by the arrows. "I'll try to distract her!"

"Who?" I demanded. I knew I'd heard the name Sekhmet before, but I'd heard *a lot* of Egyptian names. "Which one is Sekhmet?"

Carter turned to me, and even with all we'd been through over the last week, I had never seen him look so scared. "We need to leave," he said. *"Now."*

33. We Go Into the Salsa Business

YOU'RE FORGETTING SOMETHING, Horus told me.

A little busy here! I thought back.

You might think it's easy steering a magic boat through the sky. You'd be wrong. I didn't have Amos's animated coat, so I stood in the back trying to shift the tiller myself, which was like stirring cement. I couldn't see where we were going. We kept tilting back and forth while Sadie tried her best to keep an unconscious Zia from flopping over the side.

It's my birthday, Horus insisted. *Wish me happy birthday!*

"Happy birthday!" I yelled. "Now, shut up!"

"Carter, what are you on about?" Sadie screamed, grabbing the railing with one hand and Zia with the other as the boat tipped sideways. "Have you lost your mind?"

"No, I was talking to— Oh, forget it."

I glanced behind us. *Something* was approaching—a blazing figure that lit up the night. Vaguely humanoid, definitely bad news. I urged the boat to go faster.

Did you get me anything? Horus urged.

Will you please do something helpful? I demanded. *That thing following us—is that what I think it is?*

Oh. Horus sounded bored. *That's Sekhmet. The Eye of Ra, destroyer of the wicked, the great huntress, lady of flame, et cetera.*

Great, I thought. *And she's following us because . . .*

The Chief Lector has the power to summon her once during his lifetime, Horus explained. *It's an old, old gift—goes back to the days when Ra first blessed man with magic.*

Once during his lifetime, I thought. *And Desjardins chooses now?*

He never was very good at being patient.

I thought that the magicians don't like gods!

They don't, Horus agreed. *Just shows you what a hypocrite he is. But I suppose killing you was more important than standing on principle. I can appreciate that.*

I looked back again. The figure was definitely getting closer—a giant golden woman in glowing red armor, with a bow in one hand and a quiver of arrows slung across her back—and she was hurtling toward us like a rocket.

How do we beat her? I asked.

You pretty much don't, Horus said. *She is the incarnation of the sun's wrath. Back in the days when Ra was active, she would've been much more impressive, but still. . . . She's unstoppable. A born killer. A slaying machine—*

"Okay, I get it!" I yelled.

"What?" Sadie demanded, so loud that Zia stirred.

"Wha—what?" Her eyes fluttered open.

"Nothing," I shouted. "We're being followed by a slaying machine. Go back to sleep."

Zia sat up woozily. "A slaying machine? You don't mean—"

"Carter, veer right!" Sadie yelled.

I did, and a flaming arrow the size of a predator drone grazed our port side. It exploded above us, setting the roof of our boathouse on fire.

I steered the boat into a dive, and Sekhmet shot past but then pirouetted in the air with irritating agility and dove after us.

"We're burning," Sadie pointed out helpfully.

"Noticed!" I yelled back.

I scanned the landscape below us, but there was nowhere safe to land—just subdivisions and office parks.

"Die, enemies of Ra!" Sekhmet yelled. "Perish in agony!"

She's almost as annoying as you, I told Horus.

Impossible, Horus said. *No one bests Horus.*

I took another evasive turn, and Zia yelled, "There!"

She pointed toward a well-lit factory complex with trucks, warehouses, and silos. A giant chili pepper was painted on the side of the biggest warehouse, and a floodlit sign read: MAGIC SALSA, INC.

"Oh, please," Sadie said. "It's not really magic! That's just a name."

"No," Zia insisted. "I've got an idea."

"Those Seven Ribbons?" I guessed. "The ones you used on Serqet?"

Zia shook her head. "They can only be summoned once a year. But my plan—"

Another arrow blazed past us, only inches from our starboard side.

"Hang on!" I yanked at the tiller and spun the boat upside down just before the arrow exploded. The hull shielded us from the brunt of the blast, but the entire bottom of the ship was now on fire, and we were going down.

With my last bit of control, I aimed the boat toward the roof of the warehouse, and we crashed through, slamming into a huge mound of ... something crunchy.

I clawed my way clear of the boat and sat up in a daze. Fortunately, the stuff we'd crashed into was soft. Unfortunately, it was a twenty-foot pile of dried chili peppers, and the boat had set them on fire. My eyes began to sting, but I knew better than to rub them, because my hands were now covered in chili oil.

"Sadie?" I called. "Zia?"

"Help!" Sadie yelled. She was on the other side of the boat, dragging Zia out from under the flaming hull. We managed to pull her free and slide down the pile onto the floor.

The warehouse seemed to be a massive facility for drying peppers, with thirty or forty mountains of chilis and rows of wooden drying racks. The wreckage of our boat filled the air with spicy smoke, and through the hole we'd made in the roof, I could see the blazing figure of Sekhmet descending.

We ran, plowing through another pile of peppers. [No, I didn't pick a peck of them, Sadie—just shut up.] We hid behind a drying rack, where shelves of peppers made the air burn like hydrochloric acid.

Sekhmet landed, and the warehouse floor shuddered. Up close, she was even more terrifying. Her skin glowed like liquid gold, and her chest armor and skirt seemed to be woven of tiles made from molten lava. Her hair was like a thick lion's mane. Her eyes were feline, but they didn't sparkle like Bast's or betray any kindness or humor. Sekhmet's eyes blazed like her arrows, designed only to seek and destroy. She was beautiful the way an atomic explosion is beautiful.

"I smell blood!" she roared. "I will feast on enemies of Ra until my belly is full!"

"Charming," Sadie whispered. "So Zia . . . this plan?"

Zia didn't look so well. She was shivering and pale, and seemed to have trouble focusing on us. "When Ra . . . when he first called Sekhmet to punish humans because they were rebelling against him . . . she got out of hand."

"Hard to imagine," I whispered, as Sekhmet ripped through the burning wreckage of our boat.

"She started killing *everyone*," Zia said, "not just the wicked. None of the other gods could stop her. She would just kill all day until she was gorged on blood. Then she'd leave until the next day. So the people begged the magicians to come up with a plan, and—"

"You dare hide?" Flames roared as Sekhmet's arrows destroyed pile after pile of dried peppers. "I will roast you alive!"

"Run now," I decided. "Talk later."

Sadie and I dragged Zia between us. We managed to get out of the warehouse just before the whole place imploded from the heat, billowing a spicy-hot mushroom cloud into the sky. We ran through a parking lot filled with semitrailers and hid behind a sixteen-wheeler.

I peeked out, expecting to see Sekhmet walk through the

flames of the warehouse. Instead, she leaped out in the form of a giant lion. Her eyes blazed, and floating over her head was a disk of fire like a miniature sun.

"The symbol of Ra," Zia whispered.

Sekhmet roared: "Where are you, my tasty morsels?" She opened her maw and breathed a blast of hot air across the parking lot. Wherever her breath touched, the asphalt melted, cars disintegrated into sand, and the parking lot turned into barren desert.

"How did she do that?" Sadie hissed.

"Her breath creates the deserts," Zia said. "That is the legend."

"Better and better." Fear was closing up my throat, but I knew we couldn't hide much longer. I summoned my sword. "I'll distract her. You two run—"

"No," Zia insisted. "There is another way." She pointed at a row of silos on the other side of the lot. Each one was three stories tall and maybe twenty feet in diameter, with a giant chili pepper painted on the side.

"Petrol tanks?" Sadie asked.

"No," I said. "Must be salsa, right?"

Sadie stared at me blankly. "Isn't that a type of music?"

"It's a hot sauce," I said. "That's what they make here."

Sekhmet breathed in our direction, and the three trailers next to us melted into sand. We scuttled sideways and jumped behind a cinder block wall.

"Listen," Zia gasped, her face beading with sweat. "When the people needed to stop Sekhmet, they got huge vats of beer and colored them bright red with pomegranate juice."

"Yeah, I remember now," I interrupted. "They told Sekhmet it was blood, and she drank until she passed out. Then Ra was able to recall her into the heavens. They transformed her into something gentler. A cow goddess or something."

"Hathor," Zia said. "That is Sekhmet's other form. The flip side of her personality."

Sadie shook her head in disbelief. "So you're saying we offer to buy Sekhmet a few pints, and she'll turn into a cow."

"Not exactly," Zia said. "But salsa is red, is it not?"

We skirted the factory grounds as Sekhmet chewed up trucks and blasted huge swathes of the parking lot to sand.

"I hate this plan," Sadie grumbled.

"Just keep her occupied for a few seconds," I said. "And don't die."

"Yeah, that's the hard bit, isn't it?"

"One . . ." I counted. "Two . . . three!"

Sadie burst into the open and used her favorite spell: "*Ha-di!*"

The glyphs blazed over Sekhmet's head:

And everything around her exploded. Trucks burst to pieces. The air shimmered with energy. The ground heaved upward, creating a crater fifty feet deep into which the lioness tumbled.

It was pretty impressive, but I didn't have time to admire Sadie's work. I turned into a falcon and launched myself toward the salsa tanks.

"*RRAAAARR!*" Sekhmet leaped out of the crater and breathed desert wind in Sadie's direction, but Sadie was long gone. She ran sideways, ducking behind trailers and releasing a few lengths of magical rope as she fled. The ropes whipped through the air and tried to tie themselves around the lioness's mouth. They failed, of course, but they did annoy the Destroyer.

"Show yourself!" Sekhmet bellowed. "I will feast on your flesh!"

Perched on a silo, I concentrated all my power and turned straight from falcon to avatar. My glowing form was so heavy, its feet sank into the top of the tank.

"Sekhmet!" I yelled.

The lioness whirled and snarled, trying to locate my voice.

"Up here, kitty!" I called.

She spotted me and her ears went back. "Horus?"

"Unless you know another guy with a falcon head."

She padded back and forth uncertainly, then roared in challenge. "Why do you speak to me when I am in my raging form? You know I must destroy everything in my path, even you!"

"If you must," I said. "But first, you might like to feast on the blood of your enemies!"

I drove my sword into the tank and salsa gushed out in a chunky red waterfall. I leaped to the next tank and sliced it open. And again, and again, until six silofuls of Magic Salsa were spewing into the parking lot.

"Ha, ha!" Sekhmet loved it. She leaped into the red sauce torrent, rolling in it, lapping it up. "Blood. Lovely blood!"

Yeah, apparently lions aren't too bright, or their taste buds aren't very developed, because Sekhmet didn't stop until her belly was bulging and her mouth literally began to smoke.

"Tangy," she said, stumbling and blinking. "But my eyes hurt. What kind of blood is this? Nubian? Persian?"

"Jalapeño," I said. "Try some more. It gets better."

Her ears were smoking too now as she tried to drink more. Her eyes watered, and she began to stagger.

"I . . ." Steam curled from her mouth. "Hot . . . hot mouth . . ."

"Milk is good for that," I suggested. "Maybe if you were a cow."

"Trick," Sekhmet groaned. "You . . . you tricked . . ."

But her eyes were too heavy. She turned in a circle and collapsed, curling into a ball. Her form twitched and shimmered as her red armor melted into spots on her golden skin, until I was looking down at an enormous sleeping cow.

I dropped off the silo and stepped carefully around the sleeping goddess. She was making cow snoring sounds, like "Moo-zzz, moo-zzz." I waved my hand in front of her face, and when I was convinced she was out cold, I dispelled my avatar. Sadie and Zia emerged from behind a trailer.

"Well," said Sadie, "that was different."

"I will never eat salsa again," I decided.

"You both did wonderfully," Zia said. "But your boat is burned. How do we get to Phoenix?"

"*We?*" Sadie said. "I don't recall inviting you."

Zia's face turned salsa red. "Surely you don't *still* think I led you into a trap?"

"I don't know," Sadie said. "Did you?"

423

I couldn't believe I was hearing this.

"Sadie." My voice sounded dangerously angry, even to myself. "*Lay off*. Zia summoned that pillar-of-fire thing. She sacrificed her magic to save us. *And* she told us how to beat the lioness. We need her."

Sadie stared at me. She glanced back and forth between Zia and me, probably trying to judge how far she could push things.

"Fine." She crossed her arms and pouted. "But we need to find Amos first."

"No!" Zia said. "That would be a very bad idea."

"Oh, so we can trust you, but not Amos?"

Zia hesitated. I got the feeling that was *exactly* what she meant, but she decided to try a different approach. "Amos would not want you to wait. He said to keep going, didn't he? If he survived Sekhmet, he will find us on the road. If not..."

Sadie huffed. "So how do we get to Phoenix? Walk?"

I gazed across the parking lot, where one sixteen-wheeler was still intact. "Maybe we don't have to." I took off the linen coat I'd borrowed from Amos's supply locker. "Zia, Amos had a way of animating his coat so it could steer his boat. Do you know the spell?"

She nodded. "It's fairly simple with the right ingredients. I could do it if I had my magic."

"Can you teach me?"

She pursed her lips. "The hardest part is the figurine. The first time you enchant the piece of clothing, you'd need to smash a *shabti* into the fabric and speak a binding charm to meld them together. It would require a clay or wax figure that has already been imbued with a spirit."

Sadie and I looked at each other, and simultaneously said, "Doughboy!"

34. Doughboy Gives Us a Ride

I SUMMONED DAD'S MAGIC TOOLKIT out of the Duat and grabbed our little legless friend. "Doughboy, we need to talk."

Doughboy opened his wax eyes. "Finally! You realize how stuffy it is in there? At last you've remembered that you need my brilliant guidance."

"Actually we need you to become a coat. Just for a while."

His tiny mouth fell open. "Do I look like an article of clothing? I am the lord of all knowledge! The mighty—"

I smashed him into my jacket, wadded it up, threw it on the pavement and stepped on it. "Zia, what's that spell?"

She told me the words, and I repeated the chant. The coat inflated and hovered in front of me. It brushed itself off and ruffled its collar. If coats can look indignant, this one did.

Sadie eyed it suspiciously. "Can it drive a lorry with no feet for the pedals?"

"Shouldn't be a problem," Zia said. "It's a nice long coat."

I sighed with relief. For a moment, I'd imagined myself having to animate my pants, too. That could get awkward.

"Drive us to Phoenix," I told the coat.

The coat made a rude gesture at me—or at least, it would've been rude if the coat had hands. Then it floated into the driver's seat.

The cab was bigger than I'd thought. Behind the seat was a curtained area with a full-size bed, which Sadie claimed immediately.

"I'll let you and Zia have some quality time," she told me. "Just the two of you and your coat."

She ducked behind the curtains before I could smack her.

The coat drove us west on I-10 as a bank of dark clouds swallowed the stars. The air smelled like rain.

After a long time, Zia cleared her throat. "Carter, I'm sorry about...I mean, I wish the circumstances were better."

"Yeah," I said. "I guess you'll get in a lot of trouble with the House."

"I will be shunned," she said. "My staff broken. My name blotted from the books. I'll be cast into exile, assuming they don't kill me."

I thought about Zia's little shrine in the First Nome—all those pictures of her village and her family that she didn't remember. As she talked about getting exiled, she had the same expression on her face that she had worn then: not regret or sadness, more like confusion, as if she herself couldn't figure out why she was rebelling, or what the First Nome had meant to her. She'd said Iskandar was like her only family. Now she had no one.

THE RED PYRAMID

"You could come with us," I said.

She glanced over. We were sitting close together, and I was very aware of her shoulder pressing against mine. Even with the reek of burned peppers on both of us, I could smell her Egyptian perfume. She had a dried chili stuck in her hair, and somehow that made her look even cuter.

Sadie says my brain was just addled. [Seriously, Sadie, I don't interrupt this much when *you're* telling the story.]

Anyway, Zia looked at me sadly. "Where would we go, Carter? Even if you defeat Set and save this continent, what will you do? The House will hunt you down. The gods will make your life miserable."

"We'll figure it out," I promised. "I'm used to traveling. I'm good at improvising, and Sadie's not *all* bad."

"I heard that!" Sadie's muffled voice came through the curtain.

"And with you," I continued, "I mean, you know, with your magic, things would be easier."

Zia squeezed my hand, which sent a tingle up my arm. "You're kind, Carter. But you don't know me. Not really. I suppose Iskandar saw this coming."

"What do you mean?"

Zia took her hand away, which kind of bummed me out. "When Desjardins and I came back from the British Museum, Iskandar spoke to me privately. He said I was in danger. He said he would take me somewhere safe and..." Her eyebrows knit together. "That's odd. I don't remember."

A cold feeling started gnawing at me. "Wait, *did* he take you somewhere safe?"

"I . . . I think so." She shook her head. "No, he couldn't have, obviously. I'm still here. Perhaps he didn't have time. He sent me to find you in New York almost immediately."

Outside, a light rain began to fall. The coat turned on our windshield wipers.

I didn't understand what Zia had told me. Perhaps Iskandar had sensed a change in Desjardins, and he was trying to protect his favorite student. But something else about the story bothered me—something I couldn't quite put my finger on.

Zia stared into the rain as if she saw bad things out there in the night.

"We're running out of time," she said. "He's coming back."

"Who's coming back?"

She looked at me urgently. "The thing I needed to tell you—the thing you need. It's Set's secret name."

The storm surged. Thunder crackled and the truck shuddered in the wind.

"H-hold on," I stammered. "How could you know Set's name? How did you even know we needed it?"

"You stole Desjardins' book. Desjardins told us about it. He said it didn't matter. He said you could not use the spell without Set's secret name, which is impossible to get."

"So how do *you* know it? Thoth said it could only come from Set himself, or from the person . . ." My voice trailed off as a horrible thought occurred to me. "Or from the person closest to him."

Zia shut her eyes as if in pain. "I—I can't explain it, Carter. I just have this voice telling me the name—"

"The fifth goddess," I said, "Nephthys. You were there too at the British Museum."

Zia looked completely stunned. "No. That's impossible."

"Iskandar said you were in danger. He wanted to take you somewhere safe. That's what he meant. You're a godling."

She shook her head stubbornly. "But he *didn't* take me away. I'm right here. If I were hosting a god, the other magicians of the House would've figured it out days ago. They know me too well. They would've noticed the changes in my magic. Desjardins would've destroyed me."

She had a point—but then another terrible thought occurred to me. "Unless Set is controlling him," I said.

"Carter, are you really so blind? Desjardins is not Set."

"Because you think it's Amos," I said. "Amos who risked his life to save us, who told us to keep going without him. Besides, Set doesn't need a human form. He's using the pyramid."

"Which you know because . . . ?"

I hesitated. "Amos told us."

"This is getting us nowhere," Zia said. "I know Set's secret name, and I can tell you. But you must promise you will not tell Amos."

"Oh, come on. Besides, if you know the name, why can't you just use it yourself?"

She shook her head, looking almost as frustrated as I felt. "I don't know why. . . . I just know it's not my role to play. It must be you or Sadie—blood of the pharaohs. If you don't—"

The truck slowed abruptly. Out the front windshield, about twenty yards ahead, a man in a blue coat was standing in our headlights. It was Amos. His clothes were tattered like he'd been sprayed with a shotgun, but otherwise he looked okay. Before the truck had even stopped completely, I jumped out of the cab and ran to meet him.

"Amos!" I cried. "What happened?"

"I distracted Sekhmet," he said, putting a finger through one of the holes in his coat. "For about eleven seconds. I'm glad to see you survived."

"There was a salsa factory," I started to explain, but Amos held up his hand.

"Time for explanations later," he said. "Right now we have to get going."

He pointed northwest, and I saw what he meant. The storm was worse up ahead. A *lot* worse. A wall of black blotted out the night sky, the mountains, the highway, as if it would swallow the whole world.

"Set's storm is gathering," Amos said with a twinkle in his eyes. "Shall we drive into it?"

35. Men Ask for Directions (and Other Signs of the Apocalypse)

I DON'T KNOW HOW I MANAGED IT with Carter and Zia yammering, but I got some sleep in the back of the truck. Even after the excitement of seeing Amos alive, as soon as we got going again I was back in the bunk and drifting off. I suppose a good *ha-di* spell can really take it out of you.

Naturally, my *ba* took this as an opportunity to travel. Heaven forbid I get some *peaceful* rest.

I found myself back in London, on the banks of the Thames. Cleopatra's Needle rose up in front of me. It was a gray day, cool and calm, and even the smell of the low-tide muck made me feel homesick.

Isis stood next to me in a cloud-white dress, her dark hair braided with diamonds. Her multicolored wings faded in and out behind her like the Northern Lights.

"Your parents had the right idea," she said. "Bast was failing."

"She was my friend," I said.

"Yes. A good and loyal servant. But chaos cannot be kept down forever. It grows. It seeps into the cracks of civilization, breaks down the edges. It cannot be kept in balance. That is simply its nature."

The obelisk rumbled, glowing faintly.

"Today it is the American continent," Isis mused. "But unless the gods are rallied, unless we achieve our full strength, chaos will soon destroy the entire human world."

"We're doing our best," I insisted. "We'll beat Set."

Isis looked at me sadly. "You know that's not what I mean. Set is only the beginning."

The image changed, and I saw London in ruins. I'd seen some horrific photos of the Blitz in World War II, but that was nothing compared to this. The city was leveled: rubble and dust for miles, the Thames choked with flotsam. The only thing standing was the obelisk, and as I watched, it began to crack open, all four sides peeling away like some ghastly flower unfolding.

"Don't show me this," I pleaded.

"It will happen soon enough," Isis said, "as your mother foresaw. But if you cannot face it…"

The scene changed again. We stood in the throne room of a palace—the same one I'd seen before, where Set had entombed Osiris. The gods were gathering, materializing as streams of light that shot through the throne room, curled round the pillars, and took on human form. One became Thoth with his stained lab coat, his wire-rimmed glasses, and his hair standing out all over his head. Another became Horus, the proud young warrior with silver-and-gold eyes. Sobek, the crocodile god, gripped his watery staff and snarled at me. A mass of scorpions scuttled behind a column and emerged on the other side as Serqet, the brown-robed arachnid goddess. Then my heart leaped, because I noticed a boy in black standing in the shadows behind the throne: Anubis, his dark eyes studying me with regret.

He pointed at the throne, and I saw it was empty. The palace was missing its heart. The room was cold and dark, and it was impossible to believe this had once been a place of celebrations.

Isis turned to me. "We need a ruler. Horus must become pharaoh. He must unite the gods and the House of Life. It is the only way."

"You can't mean Carter," I said. "My mess of a brother—pharaoh? Are you joking?"

"We have to help him. You and I."

The idea was so ridiculous I would have laughed had the gods not been staring at me so gravely.

"Help him?" I said. "Why doesn't he help *me* become pharaoh?"

"There have been strong women pharaohs," Isis admitted. "Hatshepsut ruled well for many years. Nefertiti's power was equal to her husband's. But you have a different path, Sadie. Your power will not come from sitting on a throne. I think you know this."

I looked at the throne, and I realized Isis had a point. The idea of sitting there with a crown on my head, trying to rule this lot of bad-tempered gods, did not appeal to me in the slightest. Still...Carter?

"You've grown strong, Sadie," Isis said. "I don't think you realize *how* strong. Soon, we will face the test together. We will prevail, if you maintain your courage and faith."

"Courage and faith," I said. "Not my two strong suits."

"Your moment comes," Isis said. "We depend on you."

The gods gathered round, staring at me expectantly. They began to crowd in, pressing so close I couldn't breathe, grabbing my arms, shaking me....

I woke to find Zia poking my shoulder. "Sadie, we've stopped."

I instinctively reached for my wand. "What? Where?"

Zia pushed aside the curtains of the sleeping berth and leaned over me from the front seat, unnervingly like a vulture. "Amos and Carter are in the gas station. You need to be prepared to move."

"Why?" I sat up and looked out the windshield, straight into a raging sandstorm. "Oh..."

The sky was black, so it was impossible to tell if it was day or night. Through the gale of wind and sand, I could see we were parked in front of a lighted petrol station.

"We're in Phoenix," Zia said, "but most of the city is shut down. People are evacuating."

"Time?"

"Half past four in the morning," Zia said. "Magic isn't working very well. The closer we get to the mountain, the worse it is. And the truck's GPS system is down. Amos and Carter went inside to ask directions."

That didn't sound promising. If two male magicians were desperate enough to stop for directions, we were in dire straits.

The truck's cab shook in the howling wind. After all we'd been through, I felt silly being scared of a storm, but I climbed over the seat so I could sit next to Zia and have some company.

"How long have they been in there?" I asked.

"Not long," Zia said. "I wanted to talk to you before they come back."

I raised an eyebrow. "About Carter? Well, if you're wondering whether he likes you, the way he stammers might be an indication."

Zia frowned. "No, I'm—"

"Asking if I mind? Very considerate. I must say at first I had my doubts, what with you threatening to kill us and all, but I've decided you're not a bad sort, and Carter's mad about you, so—"

"It's not about Carter."

I wrinkled my nose. "Oops. Could you just forget what I said, then?"

"It's about Set."

"God," I sighed. "Not this again. Still suspicious of Amos?"

"You're blind not to see it," Zia said. "Set loves deception and traps. It is his favorite way to kill."

Part of me knew she had a point. No doubt you'll think I was foolish not to listen. But have you ever sat by while someone talks badly about a member of your family? Even if it's not your favorite relative, the natural reaction is to defend them—at least it was for me, possibly because I didn't have that much family to begin with. "Look, Zia, I can't believe Amos would—"

"*Amos* wouldn't," Zia agreed. "But Set can bend the mind

and control the body. I'm not a specialist on possession, but it was a very common problem in ancient times. Minor demons are difficult enough to dislodge. A major god—"

"He's *not* possessed. He *can't* be." I winced. A sharp pain was burning in my palm, in the spot where I'd last held the feather of truth. But I wasn't telling a lie! I *did* believe Amos was innocent…didn't I?

Zia studied my expression. "You need Amos to be all right. He is your uncle. You've lost too many members of your family. I understand that."

I wanted to snap back that she didn't understand anything, but her tone made me suspect she had known grief—possibly even more than I.

"We've got no choice," I said. "There's what, three hours till sunrise? Amos knows the best way into the mountain. Trap or no, we have to go there and try to stop Set."

I could almost see the gears spinning in her head as she searched for some way, *any* way to convince me.

"All right," she said at last. "I wanted to tell Carter something but I never got the opportunity. I'll tell you instead. The last thing you need to stop Set—"

"You couldn't possibly know his secret name."

Zia held my gaze. Maybe it was the feather of truth, but I was certain she wasn't bluffing. She *did* have the name of Set. Or at least, she *believed* she did.

And honestly, I'd overheard bits of her conversation with Carter while I was in the back of the cab. I hadn't meant to eavesdrop, but it was hard not to. I looked at Zia, and tried to believe she was hosting Nephthys, but it didn't make any sense. I'd spoken with Nephthys. She'd told me she was far away in some sort of sleeping host. And Zia was right here in front of me.

"It will work," Zia insisted. "But I can't do it. It must be *you*."

"Why not use it yourself?" I demanded. "Because you spent all your magic?"

She waved away the question. "Just promise me you will use it *now*, on Amos, before we reach the mountain. It may be your only chance."

"And if you're wrong, we waste the only chance we have. The book disappears once it's used, right?"

Grudgingly, Zia nodded. "Once read, the book will dissolve and appear somewhere else in the world. But if you wait any longer, we're doomed. If Set lures you into his base of power, you'll never have the strength to confront him. Sadie, please—"

"Tell me the name," I said. "I promise I'll use it at the right time."

"*Now* is the right time."

I hesitated, hoping Isis would drop some words of wisdom, but the goddess was silent. I don't know if I would've relented. Perhaps things would've turned out differently if I'd agreed to Zia's plan. But before I could make that choice, the truck's doors opened, and Amos and Carter climbed in with a gust of sand.

"We're close." Amos smiled as if this were good news. "Very, very close."

36. Our Family Is Vaporized

LESS THAN A MILE FROM Camelback Mountain, we broke through into a circle of perfect calm.

"Eye of the storm," Carter guessed.

It was eerie. All around the mountain swirled a cylinder of black clouds. Traces of smoke drifted back and forth from Camelback's peak to the edges of the maelstrom like the spokes of a wheel, but directly above us, the sky was clear and starry, beginning to turn gray. Sunrise wasn't far off.

The streets were empty. Mansions and hotels clustered round the mountain's base, completely dark; but the mountain itself glowed. Ever hold your hand over a torch (sorry, a *flashlight* for you Americans) and watch the way your skin glows red? That's the way the mountain looked: something very bright and hot was trying to burn through the rock.

"Nothing's moving on the streets," Zia said. "If we try to drive up to the mountain—"

"We'll be seen," I said.

439

"What about that spell?" Carter looked at Zia. "You know ...the one you used in the First Nome."

"What spell?" I asked.

Zia shook her head. "Carter is referring to an invisibility spell. But I have no magic. And unless you have the proper components, it can't be done on a whim."

"Amos?" I asked.

He pondered the question. "No invisibility, I'm afraid. But I have another idea."

I thought turning into a bird was bad, until Amos turned us into storm clouds.

He explained what he was going to do in advance, but it didn't make me any less nervous.

"No one will notice a few wisps of black cloud in the midst of a storm," he reasoned.

"But this is impossible," Zia said. "This is storm magic, *chaos* magic. We should not—"

Amos raised his wand, and Zia disintegrated.

"No!" Carter yelled, but then he too was gone, replaced by a swirl of black dust.

Amos turned to me.

"Oh, no," I said. "Thanks, but—"

Poof. I was a storm cloud. Now, that may sound amazing to you, but imagine your hands and feet disappearing, turning into wisps of wind. Imagine your body replaced by dust and vapor, and having a tingly feeling in your stomach without even *having* a stomach. Imagine having to concentrate just to keep yourself from dispersing to nothing.

I got so angry, a flash of lightning crackled inside me.

"Don't be that way," Amos chided. "It's only for a few minutes. Follow me."

He melted into a heavier, darker bit of storm and raced towards the mountain. Following wasn't easy. At first I could only float. Every wind threatened to take some part of me away. I tried swirling and found it helped keep my particles together. Then I imagined myself filling with helium, and suddenly I was off.

I couldn't be sure if Carter and Zia were following or not. When you're a storm, your vision isn't human. I could vaguely sense what was around me, but what I "saw" was scattered and fuzzy, as if through heavy static.

I headed towards the mountain, which was an almost irresistible beacon to my storm self. It glowed with heat, pressure, and turbulence—everything a little dust devil like me could want.

I followed Amos to a ridge on the side of the mountain, but I returned to human form a little too soon. I tumbled out of the sky and knocked Carter to the ground.

"Ouch," he groaned.

"Sorry," I offered, though mostly I was concentrating on not getting sick. My stomach still felt like it was mostly storm.

Zia and Amos stood next to us, peeping into a crevice between two large sandstone boulders. Red light seeped from within and made their faces look devilish.

Zia turned to us. Judging from her expression, what she'd seen wasn't good. "Only the pyramidion left."

"The what?" I looked through the crevice, and the view

was almost as disorienting as being a storm cloud. The entire mountain was hollowed out, just as Carter had described. The cavern floor was about six hundred meters below us. Fires blazed everywhere, bathing the rock walls in blood-colored light. A giant crimson pyramid dominated the cave, and at its base, masses of demons milled about like a rock concert crowd waiting for the show to begin. High above them, eye-level to us, two magic barges manned by crews of demons floated slowly, ceremoniously towards the pyramid. Suspended in a mesh of ropes between the boats was the only piece of the pyramid not yet installed—a golden capstone to top off the structure.

"They know they've won," Carter guessed. "They're making a show of it."

"Yes," Amos said.

"Well, let's blow up the boats or something!" I said.

Amos looked at me. "Is *that* your strategy, honestly?"

His tone made me feel completely stupid. Looking down on the demon army, the enormous pyramid . . . what had I been thinking? I couldn't battle this. I was a bloody twelve-year-old.

"We have to try," Carter said. "Dad's in there."

That shook me out of my self-pity. If we were going to die, at least we would do it trying to rescue my father (oh, and North America, too, I suppose).

"Right," I said. "We fly to those boats. We stop them from placing the capstone—"

"Pyramidion," Zia corrected.

"Whatever. Then we fly into the pyramid and find Dad."

"And when Set tries to stop you?" Amos asked.

I glanced at Zia, who was silently warning me not to say more.

"First things first," I said. "How do we fly to the boats?"

"As a storm," Amos suggested.

"No!" the rest of us said.

"I will not be part of more chaos magic," Zia insisted. "It is *not* natural."

Amos waved at the spectacle below us. "Tell me *this* is natural. You have another plan?"

"Birds," I said, hating myself for even considering it. "I'll become a kite. Carter can do a falcon."

"Sadie," Carter warned, "what if—"

"I have to try." I looked away before I could lose my resolve. "Zia, it's been almost ten hours since your pillar of fire, hasn't it? Still no magic?"

Zia held out her hand and concentrated. At first, nothing happened. Then red light flickered along her fingers, and her staff appeared in her grip, still smoking.

"Good timing," Carter said.

"Also bad timing," Amos observed. "It means Desjardins is no longer pursued by the pillar of fire. He'll be here soon, and I'm sure he'll bring backup. More enemies for us."

"My magic will still be weak," Zia warned. "I won't be much help in a fight, but I can perhaps manage to summon a ride." She brought out the vulture pendant she'd used at Luxor.

"Which leaves me," Amos said. "No worries there. Let's meet on the left boat. We'll take that one out, then deal with the right. And let's hope for surprise."

I wasn't in the mood to let Amos set our plans, but I

couldn't find any fault with his logic. "Right. We'll have to finish the boats off quickly, then head into the pyramid itself. Perhaps we can seal off the entrance or something."

Carter nodded. "Ready."

At first, the plan seemed to go well. Turning into a kite was no problem, and to my surprise, once I reached the prow of the ship, I managed to turn back into a human on the first try, with my staff and wand ready. The only person more surprised was the demon right in front of me, whose switchblade head popped straight up in alarm.

Before he could slice me or even cry out, I summoned wind from my staff and blew him off the side of the boat. Two of his brethren charged forward, but Carter appeared behind them, sword drawn, and sliced them into piles of sand.

Unfortunately, Zia was a bit less stealthy. A giant vulture with a girl hanging from its feet tends to attract attention. As she flew towards the boat, demons below pointed and yelled. Some threw spears that fell short of their mark.

Zia's grand entrance did manage to distract the remaining two demons on our boat, however, which allowed Amos to appear behind them. He'd taken the form of a fruit bat, which brought back bad memories; but he quickly returned to human form and body-slammed the demons, sending them tumbling into the air.

"Hold on!" he told us. Zia landed just in time to grab the tiller. Carter and I grabbed the sides of the boat. I had no idea what Amos was planning, but after my last flying boat ride, I wasn't taking chances. Amos began to chant, pointing his staff towards the other boat, where the demons were just beginning to shout and point at us.

One of them was tall and very thin, with black eyes and a disgusting face, like muscle with the skin peeled away.

"That's Set's lieutenant," Carter warned. "Face of Horror."

"You!" the demon screamed. "Get them!"

Amos finished his spell. "Smoke," he intoned.

Instantly, the second boat evaporated into gray mist. The demons fell screaming. The golden capstone plummeted until the lines attached to it from our side yanked taut, and our boat nearly flipped over. Canted sideways, we began to sink towards the cavern floor.

"Carter, cut the lines!" I screamed.

He sliced them with his sword, and the boat leveled out, rising several meters in an instant and leaving my stomach behind.

The pyramidion crashed to the cavern floor with much crunching and squishing. I had the feeling we'd just made a nice stack of demon griddlecakes.

"So far so good," Carter noted, but as usual, he'd spoken too soon.

Zia pointed below us. "Look."

All those demons who had wings—a small percentage, but still a good forty or fifty—had launched themselves towards us, filling the air like a swarm of angry wasps.

"Fly to the pyramid," Amos said. "I'll distract the demons."

The pyramid's entrance, a simple doorway between two columns at the base of the structure, was not far from us. It was guarded by a few demons, but most of Set's forces were running towards our boat, screaming and throwing rocks (which tended to fall back down and hit them, but no one says demons are bright).

"They're too many," I argued. "Amos, they'll kill you."

"Don't worry about me," he said grimly. "Seal the entrance behind you."

He pushed me over the side, giving me no choice but to turn into a kite. Carter in falcon form was already spiraling towards the entrance, and I could hear Zia's vulture flapping its great wings behind us.

I heard Amos yell, "For Brooklyn!"

It was an odd battle cry. I glanced back, and the boat burst into flames. It began drifting away from the pyramid and down towards the army of monsters. Fireballs shot from the boat in all directions as pieces of the hull crumbled away. I didn't have time to marvel at Amos's magic, or worry what had happened to him. He distracted many of the demons with his pyrotechnics, but some noticed us.

Carter and I landed just inside the pyramid's entrance and returned to human form. Zia tumbled in next to us and turned her vulture back into an amulet. The demons were only a few steps behind—a dozen massive blokes with the heads of insects, dragons, and assorted Swiss Army knife attachments.

Carter thrust out his hand. A giant shimmering fist appeared and mimicked his move—pushing right between Zia and me and slamming the doors shut. Carter closed his eyes in concentration, and a burning golden symbol etched itself across the doors like a seal: the Eye of Horus. The lines glowed faintly as demons hammered against the barrier, trying to get in.

"It won't hold them long," Carter said.

I was duly impressed, though of course I didn't say that. Looking at the sealed doors, all I could think about was Amos, out there on a burning boat, surrounded by an evil army.

"Amos knew what he was doing," Carter said, though he didn't sound very convinced. "He's probably fine."

"Come on," Zia prodded us. "No time for second guessing."

The tunnel was narrow, red, and humid, so I felt like I was crawling through an artery of some enormous beast. We made our way down single file, as the tunnel sloped at about forty degrees—which would've made a lovely waterslide but wasn't so good for stepping carefully. The walls were decorated with intricate carvings, like most Egyptian walls we'd seen, but Carter obviously didn't like them. He kept stopping, scowling at the pictures.

"What?" I demanded, after the fifth or sixth time.

"These aren't normal tomb drawings," he said. "No afterlife pictures, no pictures of the gods."

Zia nodded. "This pyramid is not a tomb. It is a platform, a body to contain the power of Set. All these pictures are to increase chaos, and make it reign forever."

As we kept walking, I paid more attention to the carvings, and I saw what Zia meant. The pictures showed horrible monsters, scenes of war, cities such as Paris and London in flames, full-color portraits of Set and the Set animal tearing into modern armies—scenes so gruesome, no Egyptian would ever commit them to stone. The farther we went, the weirder and more vivid the pictures became, and the queasier I felt.

Finally we reached the heart of the pyramid.

Where the burial chamber should've been in a regular pyramid, Set had designed a throne room for himself. It was about the size of a tennis court, but around the edges, the floor dropped off into a deep trench like a moat. Far, far below, red liquid bubbled. Blood? Lava? Evil ketchup? None of the possibilities were good.

The trench looked easy enough to jump, but I wasn't anxious to do so because inside the room, the entire floor was carved with red hieroglyphs—all spells invoking the power of Isfet, chaos. Far above in the center of the ceiling, a single square hole let in blood-red light. Otherwise, there seemed to be no exits. Along either wall crouched four obsidian statues of the Set animal, their faces turned towards us with pearl teeth bared and emerald eyes glittering.

But the worst part was the throne itself. It was a horrid misshapen thing, like a red stalagmite that had grown haphazardly from centuries of dripping sediment. And it had formed itself around a gold coffin—*Dad*'s coffin—which was buried in the throne's base, with just enough of it sticking out to form a kind of footrest.

"How do we get him out?" I said, my voice trembling.

Next to me, Carter caught his breath. "Amos?"

I followed his gaze up to the glowing red vent in the middle of the ceiling. A pair of legs dangled from the opening. Then Amos dropped down, opening his cloak like a parachute so that he floated to the floor. His clothes were still smoking, his hair dusted with ash. He pointed his staff towards the ceiling and spoke a command. The shaft he'd come through rumbled, spilling dust and rubble, and the light was abruptly cut off.

Amos dusted off his clothes and smiled at us. "That should hold them for a while."

"How did you do that?" I asked.

He gestured for us to join him in the room.

Carter jumped the trench without hesitation. I didn't like it, but I wasn't going to let him go without me, so I hopped the trench too. Immediately I felt even queasier than before, as if the room were tilting, throwing my senses off balance.

Zia came over last, eyeing Amos carefully.

"You should not be alive," she said.

Amos chuckled. "Oh, I've heard that before. Now, let's get to business."

"Yes." I stared at the throne. "How do we get the coffin out?"

"Cut it?" Carter drew his sword, but Amos held up his hand.

"No, children. That's not the business I mean. I've made sure no one will interrupt us. Now it's time we talked."

A cold tingle started up my spine. "Talked?"

Suddenly Amos fell to his knees and began to convulse. I ran towards him, but he looked up at me, his face racked with pain. His eyes were molten red.

"*Run!*" he groaned.

He collapsed, and red steam issued from his body.

"We have to go!" Zia grabbed my arm. "*Now!*"

But I watched, frozen in horror, as the steam rose from

Amos's unconscious form and drifted towards the throne, slowly taking the shape of a seated man—a red warrior in fiery armor, with an iron staff in his hand and the head of a canine monster.

"Oh, dear," Set laughed. "I suppose Zia gets to say 'I told you so.'"

37. Leroy Gets His Revenge

Maybe I'm a slow learner, okay?

Because it wasn't until that moment, facing the god Set in the middle of his throne room, in the heart of an evil pyramid, with an army of demons outside and the world about to explode, that I thought, *Coming here was a really bad idea.*

Set rose from his throne. He was red skinned and muscular, with fiery armor and a black iron staff. His head shifted from bestial to human. One moment he had the hungry stare and slavering jaws of my old friend Leroy, the monster from the D.C. airport. The next he had sandy hair and a handsome but harsh face, with intelligent eyes that sparkled with humor and a cruel, crooked smile. He kicked our uncle out of the way and Amos groaned, which at least meant he was alive.

I was clenching my sword so tight, the blade trembled.

"Zia was right," I said. "You possessed Amos."

Set spread his hands, trying to look modest. "Well, you know… It wasn't a *full* possession. Gods can exist in many

451

places at once, Carter. Horus could tell you that if he was being honest. I'm sure Horus has been looking for a nice war monument to occupy, or a military academy somewhere—anything but that scrawny little form of yours. Most of my being has now transferred to this magnificent structure."

He swept his arm proudly around the throne room. "But a sliver of my soul was quite enough to control Amos Kane."

He held out his pinky, and a wisp of red smoke snaked toward Amos, sinking into his clothes. Amos arched his back like he'd been hit by lightning.

"Stop it!" I yelled.

I ran toward Amos, but the red mist had already dissipated. Our uncle's body went slack.

Set dropped his hand as if bored with the attack. "Not much left, I'm afraid. Amos fought well. He was very entertaining, demanding much more of my energy than I had anticipated. That chaos magic—that was *his* idea. He tried his best to warn you, to make it obvious I was controlling him. The funny thing is, I forced him to use his own magic reserves to pull off those spells. He almost burned out his soul trying to send you those warning flares. Turn you into a storm? Please. Who does that anymore?"

"You're a beast!" Sadie shouted.

Set gasped in mock surprise. "Really? Me?"

Then he roared with laughter as Sadie tried to drag Amos out of harm's way.

"Amos was in London that night," I said, hoping to keep his attention on me. "He must've followed us to the

British Museum, and you've been controlling him ever since. Desjardins was never your host."

"Oh, that commoner? Please," Set sneered. "We always prefer blood of the pharaohs, as I'm sure you've heard. But I did love fooling you. I thought the *bon soir* was an especially nice touch."

"You knew my *ba* was there, watching. You forced Amos to sabotage his own house so your monsters could get in. You made him walk into an ambush. Why didn't you just have him kidnap us?"

Set spread his hands. "As I said, Amos put up a good fight. There were certain things I could not make him do without destroying him completely, and I didn't want to ruin my new plaything quite so soon."

Anger burned inside me. Amos's odd behavior finally made sense. Yes, he had been controlled by Set, but he'd been fighting it all the way. The conflict I'd felt in him had been his attempts to warn us. He'd almost destroyed himself trying to save us, and Set had thrown him aside like a broken toy.

Give me control, Horus urged. *We will avenge him.*

I've got this, I said.

No! Horus said. *You must let me. You are not ready.*

Set laughed as if he could sense our struggle. "Oh, poor Horus. Your host needs training wheels. You seriously expect to challenge me with *that*?"

For the first time, Horus and I had the same feeling at exactly the same moment: *rage.*

Without thinking, we raised our hand, extending our

energy toward Set. A glowing fist slammed into him, and the Red God flew backward with such force, he cracked a column, which tumbled down on top of him.

For a heartbeat, the only sound was the trickle of dust and debris. Then out of the rubble came a deep howl of laughter. Set rose from the ruins, tossing aside a huge chunk of stone.

"Nice!" he roared. "Completely ineffective, but nice! It will be a pleasure chopping you to bits, Horus, as I did your father before you. I will entomb you all in this chamber to increase my storm—all four of my precious siblings, and the storm will be large enough to envelop the world!"

I blinked, momentarily losing my focus. "Four?"

"Oh, yes." Set's eyes drifted to Zia, who had quietly retreated to one side of the room. "I haven't forgotten you, my dear."

Zia glanced at me in desperation. "Carter, don't worry about me. He's trying to distract you."

"Lovely goddess," Set purred. "The form does not do you justice, but your choices were limited, weren't they?"

Set moved toward her, his staff beginning to glow.

"No!" I shouted. I advanced, but Set was just as good at magical shoving as I was. He pointed at me, and I slammed against the wall, pinned as if an entire football team were holding me down.

"Carter!" Sadie cried. "She's Nephthys. She can take care of herself!"

"No." All my instincts told me Zia couldn't be Nephthys. At first I'd thought so, but the more I considered, the more it seemed wrong. I felt no divine magic from her, and something told me I would have if she were really hosting a goddess.

Set would crush her unless I helped. But if Set was trying to distract me, it was working. As he stalked toward Zia, I struggled against his magic, but I couldn't free myself. The more I tried to combine my power with Horus's, the way I'd done before, the more my fear and panic got in the way.

You must yield to me! Horus insisted, and the two of us wrestled for control of my mind, which gave me a splitting headache.

Set took another step toward Zia.

"Ah, Nephthys," he crooned. "At the beginning of time, you were my treacherous sister. In another incarnation, in another age, you were my treacherous wife. Now, I think you'll make a nice appetizer. True, you're the weakest of us all, but you're still one of the five, and there *is* power in collecting the complete set."

He paused, then grinned. "The complete Set! That's funny! Now let's consume your energy and entomb your soul, shall we?"

Zia thrust out her wand. A red sphere of defensive energy glowed around her, but even I could tell it was weak. Set shot a blast of sand from his staff and the sphere collapsed. Zia stumbled backward, the sand ripping at her hair and clothes. I struggled to move, but Zia yelled, "Carter, I'm not important! Stay focused! Don't resist!"

She raised her staff and shouted, "The House of Life!"

She launched a bolt of fire at Set—an attack that must have cost all of her remaining energy. Set batted the flames aside, straight at Sadie, who had to raise her wand quickly to protect herself and Amos from getting fried. Set tugged at the air as if pulling an invisible rope, and Zia flew toward him like a rag doll, straight into his hand.

Don't resist. How could Zia say that? I resisted like crazy, but it didn't do me any good. All I could do was stare helplessly as Set lowered his face to Zia's and examined her.

At first Set seemed triumphant, gleeful, but his expression quickly turned to confusion. He scowled, his eyes flaring.

"What trick is this?" he growled. "Where have you hidden her?"

"You will not possess her," Zia managed, her breath choked off by his grip.

"Where *is* she?" He threw Zia aside.

She slammed against the wall and would've slid into the moat, but Sadie yelled "Wind!" and a gust of air lifted Zia's body just enough for her to tumble onto the floor.

Sadie ran over and dragged her away from the glowing trench.

Set roared, "Is this your trickery, Isis?" He sent another blast of sandstorm against them, but Sadie held up her wand. The storm met a shield of force that deflected the wind around it—the sand pitted the walls behind Sadie, making a halo-shaped scar in the rock.

I didn't understand what Set was so angry about, but I couldn't allow him to hurt Sadie.

Seeing her alone, protecting Zia from the wrath of a god, something inside me clicked, like an engine shifting into higher gear. My thinking suddenly became faster and clearer. The anger and fear didn't go away, but I realized they weren't important. They weren't going to help me save my sister.

Don't resist, Zia had told me.

She didn't mean resisting Set. She meant Horus. The falcon god and I had been wrestling with each other for days as he tried to take control of my body.

But *neither* of us could be in control. That was the answer. We had to act in unison, trust each other completely, or we were both dead.

Yes, Horus thought, and he stopped pushing. I stopped resisting, letting our thoughts flow together. I understood his power, his memories, and his fears. I saw every host he had ever been over a thousand lifetimes. And he saw my mind—everything, even the stuff I wasn't proud of.

It's hard to describe the feeling. And I knew from Horus's memory that this kind of union was *very* rare—like the one time when the coin doesn't land heads *or* tails, but stands on its edge, perfectly balanced. He did not control me. I did not use him for power. We acted as one.

Our voices spoke in harmony: "Now."

And the magic bonds that held us shattered.

My combat avatar formed around me, lifting me off the floor and encasing me with golden energy. I stepped forward and raised my sword. The falcon warrior mimicked the movement, perfectly attuned to my wishes.

Set turned and regarded me with cold eyes.

"So, Horus," he said. "You managed to find the pedals of your little bike, eh? That does not mean you can ride."

"I am Carter Kane," I said. "Blood of the Pharaohs, Eye of Horus. And now, Set—brother, uncle, traitor—I'm going to crush you like a gnat."

38. The House Is in the House

IT WAS A FIGHT TO THE DEATH, and I felt great.

Every move was perfect. Every strike was so much fun I wanted to laugh out loud. Set grew in size until he was larger than me, and his iron staff the size of a boat's mast. His face would flicker, sometimes human, sometimes the feral maw of the Set animal.

We clashed sword against staff and sparks flew. He pushed me off balance, and I smashed into one of his animal statues, which toppled to the floor and broke. I regained my balance and charged, my blade biting into a chink of Set's shoulder guard. He howled as black blood seeped from the wound.

He swung his staff, and I rolled before the strike could split my head. His staff cracked the floor instead. We fought back and forth, smashing pillars and walls, with chunks of the ceiling falling around us, until I realized Sadie was yelling to get my attention.

Out of the corner of my eye, I saw her trying to shield Zia

and Amos from the destruction. She'd drawn a hasty protective circle on the floor, and her shields were deflecting the falling debris, but I understood why she was worried: much more of this, and the entire throne room would collapse, crushing all of us. I doubted it would hurt Set much. He was probably counting on that. He *wanted* to entomb us here.

I had to get him into the open. Maybe if I gave Sadie time, she could free Dad's coffin from that throne.

Then I remembered how Bast had described her fight with Apophis: grappling with the enemy for eternity.

Yes, Horus agreed.

I raised my fist and channeled a burst of energy toward the air vent above us, blasting it open until red light once again poured through. Then I dropped my sword and launched myself at Set. I grabbed his shoulders with my bare hands, trying to get him in a wrestler's hold. He attempted to pummel me, but his staff was useless at close range. He growled and dropped the weapon, then grabbed my arms. He was much stronger than I was, but Horus knew some good moves. I twisted and got behind Set, my forearm slipping under his arm and grabbing his neck in a vise. We stumbled forward, almost stepping on Sadie's protective shields.

Now we've got him, I thought. *What do we do with him?*

Ironically, it was Amos who gave me the answer. I remembered how he'd turned me into a storm, overcoming my sense of self by sheer mental force. Our minds had had a brief battle, but he had imposed his will with absolute confidence, imagining me as a storm cloud, and that's what I'd become.

You're a fruit bat, I told Set.

No! his mind yelled, but I had surprised him. I could feel his confusion, and I used it against him. It was easy to imagine him as a bat, since I'd seen Amos become one when he was possessed by Set. I pictured my enemy shrinking, growing leathery wings and an even uglier face. I shrank too, until I was a falcon with a fruit bat in my claws. No time to waste; I shot toward the air vent, wrestling with the bat as we spun in circles up the shaft, slashing and biting. Finally we burst into the open, reverting to our warrior forms on the side of the red pyramid.

I stood uneasily on the slope. My avatar shimmered with damage along the right arm, and my own arm was cut and bleeding in the same spot. Set rose, wiping black blood from his mouth.

He grinned at me, and his face flickered with the snarl of a predator. "You can die knowing you made a good effort, Horus. But it's much too late. Look."

I gazed out over the cavern, and my heart crawled into my throat. The army of demons had engaged a new enemy in battle. Magicians—dozens of them—had appeared in a loose circle around the pyramid and were fighting their way forward. The House of Life must have gathered all its available forces, but they were pathetically few against Set's legions. Each magician stood inside a moving protective circle, like a spotlight beam, wading through the enemy with staff and wand glowing. Flames, lightning, and tornadoes ripped through the demon host. I spotted all kinds of summoned beasts—lions, serpents, sphinxes, and even some hippos charging through the enemy like tanks. Here and there, hieroglyphs glowed in the air, causing explosions and earthquakes that destroyed Set's forces. But more demons just kept coming, surrounding the magicians in deeper and deeper ranks. I watched as one magician was completely overwhelmed, his circle broken in a flash of green light, and he went down under the enemy wave.

"This is the end of the House," Set said with satisfaction. "They cannot prevail as long as my pyramid stands."

The magicians seemed to know this. As they got closer, they sent fiery comets and bolts of lightning toward the pyramid; but each blast dissipated harmlessly against its stone slopes, consumed in the red haze of Set's power.

Then I spotted the golden capstone. Four snake-headed giants had retrieved it and were carrying it slowly but steadily through the melee. Set's lieutenant Face of Horror shouted orders to them, lashing them with a whip to keep them moving. They pressed forward until they reached the pyramid's base and began to climb.

I charged toward them, but Set intervened in an instant, placing himself in my path.

"I don't think so, Horus," he laughed. "You won't ruin this party."

We both summoned our weapons to our hands and fought with renewed ferocity, slicing and dodging. I brought my sword down in a deadly arc, but Set ducked aside and my blade hit stone, sending a shock wave through my whole body. Before I could recover, Set spoke a word: *"Ha-wi!"*

Strike.

The hieroglyphs exploded in my face and sent me tumbling down the side of the pyramid.

When my vision cleared, I saw Face of Horror and the snake-headed giants far above me, lugging their golden load up the side of the monument, only a few steps from the top.

"No," I muttered. I tried to rise, but my avatar form was sluggish.

Then out of nowhere a magician catapulted into the midst of the demons and unleashed a gale of wind. Demons went flying, dropping the capstone, and the magician struck it with his staff, stopping it from sliding. The magician was Desjardins. His forked beard and robes and leopard-skin cape were singed with fire, and his eyes were full of rage. He pressed his staff against the capstone, and its golden shape began to glow; but before Desjardins could destroy it, Set rose up behind him and swung his iron rod like a baseball bat.

Desjardins tumbled, broken and unconscious, all the way down the pyramid, disappearing into the mob of demons. My heart twisted. I'd never liked Desjardins, but no one deserved a fate like that.

"Annoying," Set said. "But not effective. This is what the House of Life has reduced itself to, eh, Horus?"

I charged up the slope, and again our weapons clanged together. We fought back and forth as gray light began to seep through the cracks in the mountain above us.

Horus's keen senses told me we had about two minutes until sunrise, maybe less.

Horus's energy kept surging through me. My avatar was only mildly damaged, my attacks still swift and strong. But it wasn't enough to defeat Set, and Set knew it. He was in no hurry. With every minute, another magician went down on the battlefield, and chaos got closer to winning.

Patience, Horus urged. *We fought him for seven years the first time.*

But I knew we didn't have seven minutes, much less seven years. I wished Sadie were here, but I could only hope she'd managed to free Dad and keep Zia and Amos safe.

That thought distracted me. Set swept his staff at my feet, and instead of jumping, I tried to back up. The blow cracked against my right ankle, knocking me off balance and sending me somersaulting down the pyramid's side.

Set laughed. "Have a nice trip!" Then he picked up the capstone.

I rose, groaning, but my feet were like lead. I staggered up the slope, but before I'd closed even half the distance, Set placed the capstone and completed the structure. Red light flowed down the sides of the pyramid with a sound like the world's largest bass guitar, shaking the entire mountain and making my whole body go numb.

"Thirty seconds to sunrise!" Set yelled with glee. "And this land will be mine forever. You can't stop me alone, Horus— especially not in the desert, the source of my strength!"

"You're right," said a nearby voice.

I glanced over and saw Sadie rising from the air vent—radiant with multicolored light, her staff and wand glowing.

"Except Horus is *not* alone," she said. "And we're *not* going to fight you in the desert."

She struck her staff against the pyramid and shouted a name: the last words I'd ever expect her to utter as a battle cry.

39. Zia Tells Me a Secret

CHEERS, CARTER, FOR MAKING ME LOOK dramatic and all that.

The truth was a bit less glamorous.

Back up, shall we? When my brother, the crazy chicken warrior, turned into a falcon and went up the pyramid's chimney with his new friend, the fruit bat, he left me playing nurse to two very wounded people—which I didn't appreciate, and which I wasn't particularly good at.

Poor Amos's wounds seemed more magical than physical. He didn't have a mark on him, but his eyes were rolled up in his head, and he was barely breathing. Steam curled from his skin when I touched his forehead, so I decided I'd best leave him for the moment.

Zia was another story. Her face was deathly pale, and she was bleeding from several nasty cuts on her leg. One of her arms was twisted at a bad angle. Her breath rattled with a sound like wet sand.

"Hold still." I ripped some cloth from the hem of my pants

and tried to bind her leg. "Maybe there's some healing magic or—"

"Sadie." She gripped my wrist feebly. "No time. Listen."

"If we can stop the bleeding—"

"His name. You need his name."

"But you're not Nephthys! Set said so."

She shook her head. "A message . . . I speak with her voice. The name—Evil Day. Set was born, and it was an *Evil Day*."

True enough, I thought, but could that really be Set's secret name? What Zia was talking about, not being Nephthys but speaking with her voice—it made no sense. Then I remembered the voice at the river. Nephthys had said she would send a message. And Anubis had made me promise I would listen to Nephthys.

I shifted uncomfortably. "Look, Zia—"

Then the truth hit me in face. Some things Iskandar had said, some things Thoth had said—they all clicked together. Iskandar had wanted to protect Zia. He'd told me if he'd realized Carter and I were godlings sooner, he could've protected us as well as . . . someone. As well as *Zia*. Now I understood how he'd tried to protect her.

"Oh, god." I stared at her. "That's it, isn't it?"

She seemed to understand, and she nodded. Her face contorted with pain, but her eyes remained as fierce and insistent as ever. "Use the name. Bend Set to your will. Make him help."

"*Help?* He just tried to kill you, Zia. He's not the *helping* type."

"Go." She tried to push me away. Flames sputtered weakly from her fingers. "Carter needs you."

That was the one thing she might've said to spur me on. Carter was in trouble.

"I'll be back, then," I promised. "Don't . . . *um*, go anywhere."

I stood and stared at the hole in the ceiling, dreading the idea of turning into a kite again. Then my eyes fixed on Dad's coffin, buried in the red throne. The sarcophagus was glowing like something radioactive, heading for meltdown. If I could only break the throne . . .

Set must be dealt with first, Isis warned.

But if I can free Dad . . . I stepped towards the throne.

No, Isis warned. *What you might see is too dangerous.*

What are you talking about? I thought irritably. I put my hand on the golden coffin. Instantly I was ripped from the throne room and into a vision.

I was back in the Land of the Dead, in the Hall of Judgment. The crumbling monuments of a New Orleans graveyard shimmered around me. Spirits of the dead stirred restlessly in the mist. At the base of the broken scales, a tiny monster slept— Ammit the Devourer. He opened one glowing yellow eye to study me, then went back to sleep.

Anubis stepped out of the shadows. He was dressed in a black silk suit with his tie unknotted, like he'd just come back from a funeral or possibly a convention for really gorgeous undertakers. "Sadie, you shouldn't be here."

"Tell me about it," I said, but I was so glad to see him, I wanted to sob with relief.

He took my hand and led me towards the empty black throne. "We have lost all balance. The throne cannot be empty. The restoration of Ma'at must begin here, in this hall."

He sounded sad, as if he were asking me to accept something terrible. I didn't understand, but a profound sense of loss crept over me.

"It's not fair," I said.

"No, it's not." He squeezed my hand. "I'll be here, waiting. I'm sorry, Sadie. I truly am..."

He started to fade.

"Wait!" I tried to hold on to his hand, but he melted into mist along with the graveyard.

I found myself back in the throne room of the gods, except it looked like it had been abandoned for centuries. The roof had fallen in, along with half of the columns. The braziers were cold and rusty. The beautiful marble floor was as cracked as a dry lakebed.

Bast stood alone next to the empty throne of Osiris. She gave me a mischievous smile, but seeing her again was almost too painful to bear.

"Oh, don't be sad," she chided. "Cats don't do regret."

"But aren't you—aren't you dead?"

"That all depends." She gestured around her. "The Duat is in turmoil. The gods have gone too long without a king. If Set doesn't take over, someone else must. The enemy is coming. Don't let me die in vain."

"But will you come back?" I asked, my voice breaking. "Please, I never even got to say good-bye to you. I can't—"

"Good luck, Sadie. Keep your claws sharp." Bast vanished, and the scenery changed again.

I stood in the Hall of Ages, in the First Nome—another

empty throne—and Iskandar sat at its feet, waiting for a pharaoh who hadn't existed for two thousand years.

"A leader, my dear," he said. "Ma'at demands a leader."

"It's too much," I said. "Too many thrones. You can't expect Carter—"

"Not alone," Iskandar agreed. "But this is your family's burden. You started the process. The Kanes alone will heal us or destroy us."

"I don't know what you mean!"

Iskandar opened his hand, and in a flash of light, the scene changed one more time.

I was back at the Thames. It must've been the dead of the night, three o'clock in the morning, because the Embankment was empty. Mist obscured the lights of the city, and the air was wintry.

Two people, a man and a woman, stood bundled against the cold, holding hands in front of Cleopatra's Needle. At first I thought they were a random couple on a date. Then, with a shock, I realized I was looking at my parents.

My dad lifted his face and scowled at the obelisk. In the dim glow of the streetlamps, his features looked like chiseled marble—like the pharaoh statues he loved to study. He *did* have the face of a king, I thought—proud and handsome.

"You're sure?" he asked my mother. "Absolutely sure?"

Mum brushed her blond hair out of her face. She was even more beautiful than her pictures, but she looked worried—eyebrows furrowed, lips pressed together. Like *me* when I was upset, when I looked in the mirror and tried to convince myself things weren't so bad. I wanted to call to her, to let her know I was there, but my voice wouldn't work.

"She told me this is where it begins," my mother said. She pulled her black coat around her, and I caught a glimpse of her necklace—the amulet of Isis, my amulet. I stared at it, stunned, but then she pulled her collar closed, and the amulet disappeared. "If we want to defeat the enemy, we must start with the obelisk. We must find out the truth."

My father frowned uneasily. He'd drawn a protective circle around them—blue chalk lines on the pavement. When he touched the base of the obelisk, the circle began to glow.

"I don't like it," he said. "Won't you call on her help?"

"No," my mother insisted. "I know my limits, Julius. If I tried it again..."

My heart skipped a beat. Iskandar's words came back to me: *She saw things that made her seek advice from unconventional places.* I recognized the look in my mother' eyes, and I knew: my mother had communed with Isis.

Why didn't you tell me? I wanted to scream.

My father summoned his staff and wand. "Ruby, if we fail—"

"We can't fail," she insisted. "The world depends on it."

They kissed one last time, as if they sensed they were saying good-bye. Then they raised their staffs and wands and began to chant. Cleopatra's Needle glowed with power.

I yanked my hand away from the sarcophagus. My eyes stung with tears.

You knew my mother, I shouted at Isis. *You encouraged her to open that obelisk. You got her killed!*

I waited for her to answer. Instead, a ghostly image appeared in front of me—a projection of my father, shimmering in the light of the golden coffin.

"Sadie." He smiled. His voice sounded tinny and hollow, the way it used to on the phone when he'd call me from far away—from Egypt or Australia or god knows where. "Don't blame Isis for your mother's fate. None of us understood exactly what would happen. Even your mother could only see bits and pieces of the future. But when the time came, your mother accepted her role. It was her decision."

"To *die?*" I demanded. "Isis should've helped her. *You* should've helped her. I *hate* you!"

As soon as I said it, something broke inside me. I started to cry. I realized I'd wanted to say that to my dad for years. I blamed him for Mum's death, blamed him for leaving me. But now that I'd said it, all the anger drained out of me, leaving me nothing but guilt.

"I'm sorry," I sputtered. "I didn't—"

"Don't apologize, my brave girl. You have every right to feel that way. You had to get it out. What you're about to do—you have to believe it's for the right reasons, not because you resent me."

"I don't know what you mean."

He reached out to brush a tear from my cheek, but his hand was just a shimmer of light. "Your mother was the first in many centuries to commune with Isis. It was dangerous, against the teachings of the House, but your mother was a diviner. She had a premonition that chaos was rising. The House was failing. We *needed* the gods. Isis could not cross the Duat. She could barely manage a whisper, but she told us what she could about their imprisonment. She counseled Ruby on what must be done. The gods could rise again, she said, but it would take many *hard* sacrifices. We thought the obelisk would release all the gods, but that was only the beginning."

"Isis could've given Mum more power. Or at least Bast! Bast *offered*—"

"No, Sadie. Your mother knew her limits. If she had tried to host a god, *fully* use divine power, she would have been consumed or worse. She freed Bast, and used her own power to seal the breach. With her life, she bought you some time."

"Me? But…"

"You and your brother have the strongest blood of any Kane in three thousand years. Your mother studied the lineage of the pharaohs—she knew this to be true. You have the best chance at relearning the old ways, and healing the breach between magicians and gods. Your mother began the stirring. I unleashed the gods from the Rosetta Stone. But it will be your job to restore Ma'at."

"You can help," I insisted. "Once we free you."

"Sadie," he said forlornly, "when you become a parent, you may understand this. One of my hardest jobs as a father, one of my greatest duties, was to realize that my own dreams, my own goals and wishes, are secondary to my children's. Your mother and I have set the stage. But it is *your* stage. This pyramid is designed to feed chaos. It consumes the power of other gods and makes Set stronger."

"I know. If I break the throne, maybe open the coffin..."

"You might save me," Dad conceded. "But the power of Osiris, the power inside me, would be consumed by the pyramid. It would only hasten the destruction and make Set stronger. The pyramid must be destroyed, *all* of it. And you know how that must be done."

I was about to protest that I *didn't* know, but the feather of truth kept me honest. The way was inside me—I'd seen it in Isis's thoughts. I'd known what was coming ever since Anubis asked me that impossible question: "To save the world, would you sacrifice your father?"

"I don't want to," I said. "Please."

"Osiris must take his throne," my father said. "Through death, life. It is the only way. May Ma'at guide you, Sadie. I love you."

And with that, his image dissipated.

Someone was calling my name.

I looked back and saw Zia trying to sit up, clutching weakly at her wand. "Sadie, what are you doing?"

All around us, the room was shaking. Cracks split the walls, as if a giant were using the pyramid as a punching bag.

How long had I been in a trance? I wasn't sure, but I was out of time.

I closed my eyes and concentrated. The voice of Isis spoke almost immediately: *Do you see now? Do you understand why I could not say more?*

Anger built inside me, but I forced it down. *We'll talk about that later. Right now, we have a god to defeat.*

I pictured myself stepping forward, merging with the soul of the goddess.

I'd shared power with Isis before, but this was different. My resolve, my anger, even my grief gave me confidence. I looked Isis straight in the eye (spiritually speaking), and we understood one another.

I saw her entire history—her early days grasping for power, using tricks and schemes to find the name of Ra. I saw her wedding with Osiris, her hopes and dreams for a new empire. Then I saw those dreams shattered by Set. I felt her anger and bitterness, her fierce pride and protectiveness for her young son, Horus. And I saw the pattern of her life repeating itself over and over again through the ages, through a thousand different hosts.

Gods have great power, Iskandar had said. *But only humans have creativity, the power to change history.*

I also felt my mother's thoughts, like an imprint on the goddess's memory: Ruby's final moments and the choice she'd made. She'd given her life to start a chain of events. And the next move was mine.

"Sadie!" Zia called again, her voice weakening.

"I'm fine," I said. "I'm going now."

Zia studied my face, and obviously didn't like what she saw. "You're not fine. You've been badly shaken. Fighting Set in your condition would be suicide."

"Don't worry," I said. "We have a plan."

With that, I turned into a kite and flew up the airshaft towards the top of the pyramid.

40. I Ruin a Rather
Important Spell

I FOUND THAT THINGS WEREN'T GOING WELL UPSTAIRS.

Carter was a crumpled heap of chicken warrior on the slope of the pyramid. Set had just placed the capstone and was shouting, "Thirty seconds to sunrise!" In the cavern below, magicians from the House of Life waded through an army of demons, fighting a hopeless fight.

The scene would've been frightening enough, but now I saw it as Isis did. Like a crocodile with eyes at water level—seeing both below and above the surface—I saw the Duat entwined with the regular world. The demons had fiery souls in the Duat that made them look like an army of birthday candles. Where Carter stood in the mortal world, a falcon warrior stood in the Duat—not an avatar, but the real thing, with feathered head, sharp bloodstained beak, and gleaming black eyes. His sword rippled with golden light. As for Set— imagine a mountain of sand, doused with petrol, set on fire, spinning in the world's largest blender. That's what he looked like in the Duat—a column of destructive force so powerful that the stones at his feet bubbled and blistered.

I'm not sure what I looked like, but I felt powerful. The force of Ma'at coursed through me; the Divine Words were at my command. I was Sadie Kane, blood of the pharaohs. And I was Isis, goddess of magic, holder of the secret names.

As Carter struggled his way up the pyramid, Set gloated: "You can't stop me by yourself, Horus—especially not in the desert, the source of my strength!"

"You're right!" I called.

Set turned, and the look on his face was priceless. I raised my staff and wand, gathering my magic.

"Except that Horus is *not* alone," I said. "And we're *not* going to fight you in the desert."

I slammed my staff against the stones and shouted, "Washington, D.C.!"

The pyramid shook. For a moment, nothing else happened.

Set seemed to realize what I was doing. He let out a nervous laugh. "Magic one-oh-one, Sadie Kane. You can't open a portal during the Demon Days!"

"A mortal can't," I agreed. "But a goddess of magic can."

Above us, the air crackled with lightning. The top of the cavern dissolved into a churning vortex of sand as large as the pyramid.

Demons stopped fighting and looked up in horror. Magicians stammered midspell, their faces slack with awe.

The vortex was so powerful that it ripped blocks off the

pyramid and sucked them into the sand. And then, like a giant lid, the portal began to descend.

"No!" Set roared. He blasted the portal with flames, then turned on me and hurled stones and lightning, but it was too late. The portal swallowed us all.

The world seemed to flip upside down. For a heartbeat, I wondered if I'd made a terrible miscalculation—if Set's pyramid would explode in the portal, and I'd spend eternity floating through the Duat as a billion little particles of Sadie sand. Then, with a sonic boom, we appeared in the cold morning air with a brilliant blue sky above us. Spread out below us were the snow-covered fields of the National Mall in Washington, D.C.

The red pyramid was still intact, but cracks had appeared on its surface. The gold capstone glowed, trying to maintain its magic, but we weren't in Phoenix anymore. The pyramid had been ripped from its source of power, the desert, and in front us loomed the default gateway for North America, the tall white obelisk that was the most powerful focal point of Ma'at on the continent: the Washington Monument.

Set screamed something at me in Ancient Egyptian. I was fairly sure it wasn't a compliment.

"I will rend your limbs from their sockets!" he shouted. "I will—"

"Die?" Carter suggested. He rose behind Set and swung his sword. The blade cut into Set's armor at the ribs—not a killing blow, but enough to knock the Red God off balance and send him tumbling down the side of his pyramid. Carter bounded after him, and in the Duat I could see arcs of white energy pulsing from the Washington Monument to the Horus avatar, charging it with new power.

"The book, Sadie!" Carter shouted as he ran. "Do it now!"

I must've been dazed from summoning the portal, because Set understood what Carter was saying a lot faster than I did.

"No!" the Red God shouted. He charged towards me, but Carter intercepted him halfway up the slope.

He grappled with Set, holding him back. The stones of the pyramid cracked and crumbled under the weight of their godly forms. All around the base of the pyramid, demons and magicians who'd been pulled through the portal and knocked momentarily unconscious were starting to stir.

The book, Sadie . . . Sometimes it's helpful to have someone other than yourself inside your head, because one can slap the other. *Duh, the book!*

I held out my hand and summoned the little blue tome we'd stolen from Paris: *The Book of Overcoming Set.* I unfolded the papyrus; the hieroglyphs were as clear as a nursery school primer. I called for the feather of truth, and instantly it appeared, glowing above the pages.

I began the spell, speaking the Divine Words, and my body rose into the air, hovering a few centimeters above the pyramid. I chanted the story of creation: the first mountain rising above the waters of chaos, the birth of the gods Ra, Geb, and Nut, the rise of Ma'at, and the first great empire of men, Egypt.

The Washington Monument began to glow as hieroglyphs appeared along its sides. The capstone gleamed silver.

Set tried to lash out at me, but Carter intercepted him. And the red pyramid began to break apart.

I thought about Amos and Zia, trapped inside under tons of stone, and I almost faltered, but my mother's voice spoke in my mind: *Stay focused, dearest. Watch for your enemy.*

Yes, Isis said. *Destroy him!*

But somehow I knew that wasn't what my mother meant. She was telling me to watch. Something important was about to happen.

Through the Duat, I saw magic forming around me, weaving a white sheen over the world, reinforcing Ma'at and expelling chaos. Carter and Set wrestled back and forth as huge chunks of the pyramid collapsed.

The feather of truth glowed, shining like a spotlight on the Red God. As I neared the end of the spell, my words began tearing Set's form to shreds.

In the Duat, his fiery whirlwind was being stripped away, revealing a black-skinned, slimy thing like an emaciated Set animal—the evil essence of the god. But in the mortal world, occupying the same space, there stood a proud warrior in red armor, blazing with power and determined to fight to the death.

"I name you Set," I chanted. "I name you Evil Day."

With a thunderous roar, the pyramid imploded. Set fell crashing into the ruins. He tried to rise, but Carter swung his sword. Set barely had time to raise his staff. Their weapons crossed, and Horus slowly forced Set to one knee.

"Now, Sadie!" Carter yelled.

"You have been my enemy," I chanted, "and a curse on the land."

A line of white light shot down the length of the

Washington Monument. It widened into a rift—a doorway between this world and the brilliant white abyss that would lock Set away, trapping his life force. Maybe not forever, but for a long, long time.

To complete the spell, I only had to speak one more line: "Deserving no mercy, an enemy of Ma'at, you are exiled beyond the earth."

The line had to be spoken with absolute conviction. The feather of truth required it. And why shouldn't I believe it? It was the truth. Set deserved no mercy. He *was* an enemy of Ma'at.

But I hesitated.

"Watch for your enemy," my mother had said.

I looked towards the top of the monument, and in the Duat I saw chunks of pyramid flying skyward and the souls of demons lifting off like fireworks. As Set's chaos magic dispersed, all the force that had been charging up, ready to destroy a continent, was being sucked into the clouds. And as I watched, the chaos tried to form a shape. It was like a red reflection of the Potomac—an enormous crimson river at least a mile long and a hundred meters wide. It writhed in the air, trying to become solid, and I felt its rage and bitterness. This was not what it had wanted. There was not enough power or chaos for its purpose. To form properly, it needed the death of millions, the wasting of an entire continent.

It was not a river. It was a snake.

"Sadie!" Carter yelled. "What are you waiting for?"

He couldn't see it, I realized. No one could but me.

Set was on his knees, writhing and cursing as white energy

encircled him, pulling him towards the rift. "Lost your stomach, witch?" he bellowed. Then he glared at Carter. "You see, Horus? Isis was always a coward. She could never complete the deed!"

Carter looked at me, and for a moment I saw the doubt on his face. Horus would be urging him towards bloody vengeance. I was hesitating. This is what had turned Isis and Horus against each other before. I couldn't let it happen now.

But more than that, in Carter's wary expression I saw the way he used to look at me on our visiting days—when we were practically strangers, forced to spend time together, pretending we were a happy family because Dad expected it of us. I didn't want to go back to that. I wasn't pretending anymore. We *were* a family, and we had to work together.

"Carter, look." I threw the feather of truth into the sky, breaking the spell.

"No!" Carter screamed.

But the feather exploded into silver dust that clung to the form of the serpent, forcing it to become visible, just for an instant.

Carter's mouth fell open as the serpent writhed in the air above Washington, slowly losing power.

Next to me, a voice screamed: "Wretched gods!"

I turned to see Set's minion, Face of Horror, with his fangs bared and his grotesque face only inches from mine, a jagged knife raised above my head. I only had time to think: *I'm dead*, before a flash of metal registered in the corner of my eye. There was a sickening thud, and the demon froze.

Carter had thrown his sword with deadly accuracy. The

demon dropped his knife, fell to his knees, and stared down at the blade that was now sheathed in his side.

He crumpled to his back, exhaling with an angry hiss. His black eyes fixed on me, and he spoke in a completely different voice—a rasping, dry sound, like a reptile's belly scraping over sand. "This is not over, godling. All this I have wrought with a wisp of my voice, the merest bit of my essence wriggling from my weakened cage. Imagine what I shall do when fully formed."

He gave me a ghastly smile, and then his face went slack. A tiny line of red mist curled from his mouth—like a worm or a fresh-hatched snake—and writhed upward into the sky to join its source. The demon's body disintegrated into sand.

I looked up once more at the giant red serpent slowly dissolving in the sky. Then I summoned a good strong wind and dispersed it completely.

The Washington Monument stopped glowing. The rift closed, and the little spellbook disappeared from my hand.

I moved towards Set, who was still ensnared in ropes of white energy. I'd spoken his true name. He wasn't going anywhere just yet.

"You both saw the serpent in the clouds," I said. "Apophis."

Carter nodded, stunned. "He was trying to break into the mortal world, using the Red Pyramid as a gateway. If its power had been unleashed..." He looked down in revulsion at the pile of sand that had once been a demon. "Set's lieutenant—Face of Horror—he was possessed by Apophis all along, using Set to get what he wanted."

"Ridiculous!" Set glared at me and struggled against his

bonds. "The snake in the clouds was one of your tricks, Isis. An illusion."

"You know it wasn't," I said. "I could've sent you into the abyss, Set, but you saw the real enemy. Apophis was trying to break out of his prison in the Duat. His voice possessed Face of Horror. He was using you."

"No one uses me!"

Carter let his warrior form disperse. He floated to the ground and summoned his sword back to his hand. "Apophis wanted your explosion to feed *his* power, Set. As soon as he came through the Duat and found us dead, I'm betting *you* would've been his first meal. Chaos would've won."

"I *am* chaos!" Set insisted.

"Partially," I said. "But you're still one of the gods. True, you're evil, faithless, ruthless, vile—"

"You make me blush, sister."

"But you're also the strongest god. In the ancient times, you were Ra's faithful lieutenant, defending his boat against Apophis. Ra couldn't have defeated the Serpent without you."

"I am pretty great," Set admitted. "But Ra is gone forever, thanks to you."

"Maybe not forever," I said. "We'll have to find him. Apophis is rising, which means we'll need all the gods to battle him. Even you."

Set tested his bonds of white energy. When he found he couldn't break them, he gave me a crooked smile. "You suggest an alliance? You'd trust me?"

Carter laughed. "You've got to be kidding. But we've got your number, now. Your secret name. Right, Sadie?"

I closed my fingers, and the bonds tightened around Set. He cried out in pain. It took a great deal of energy, and I knew I couldn't hold him like this for long, but there was no point telling that to Set.

"The House of Life tried banishing the gods," I said. "It didn't work. If we lock you away, we're no better than they are. It doesn't solve anything."

"I couldn't agree more," Set groaned. "So if you'll just loosen these bonds—"

"You're still a villainous piece of scum," I said. "But you have a role to play, and you'll need controlling. I'll agree to release you—*if* you swear to behave, to return to the Duat, and not cause trouble until we call you. And then you'll make trouble only for us, fighting against Apophis."

"Or I could chop off your head," Carter suggested. "That would probably exile you for a good long while."

Set glanced back and forth between us. "Make trouble for you, eh? That *is* my specialty."

"Swear by your own name and the throne of Ra," I said. "You will leave now and not reappear until you are called."

"Oh, I swear," he said, much too quickly. "By my name and Ra's throne and our mother's starry elbows."

"If you betray us," I warned, "I have your name. I won't show you mercy a second time."

"You always were my favorite sister."

I gave him one last shock, just to remind him of my power, and then let the bindings dissolve.

Set stood up and flexed his arms. He appeared as a warrior with red armor and red skin, a black, forked beard, and twinkling, cruel eyes; but in the Duat, I saw his other side, a raging inferno just barely contained, waiting to be unleashed and burn everything in its path. He winked at Horus, then pretended to shoot me with a finger gun. "Oh, this will be *good*. We're going to have so much fun."

"Begone, Evil Day," I said.

He turned into a pillar of salt and dissolved.

The snow in the National Mall had melted in a perfect square, the exact size of Set's pyramid. Around the edges, a dozen magicians still lay passed out. The poor dears had started to stir when our portal closed, but the explosion of the pyramid had knocked them all out again. Other mortals in the area had also been affected. An early-morning jogger was slumped on the sidewalk. On nearby streets, cars idled while the drivers took naps over the steering wheels.

Not everyone was asleep, though. Police sirens wailed in the distance, and seeing as how we'd teleported practically into the president's backyard, I knew it wouldn't be long before we had a great deal of heavily armed company.

Carter and I ran to the center of the melted square, where Amos and Zia lay crumpled in the grass. There was no sign of Set's throne or the golden coffin, but I tried to push those thoughts out of my mind.

Amos groaned. "What…" His eyes clouded over with terror. "Set…he…he…"

"Rest." I put my hand on his forehead. He was burning with fever. The pain in his mind was so sharp, it cut me like a razor. I remembered a spell Isis had taught me in New Mexico.

"Quiet," I whispered. *"Hah-ri."*

Faint hieroglyphs glowed over his face:

Amos drifted back to sleep, but I knew it was only a temporary fix.

Zia was even worse off. Carter cradled her head and spoke reassuringly about how she would be fine, but she looked bad. Her skin was a strange reddish color, dry and brittle, as if she'd suffered a horrible sunburn. In the grass around her, hieroglyphs were fading—the remains of a protective circle—and I thought I understood what had happened. She'd used her last bit of energy to shield herself and Amos when the pyramid imploded.

"Set?" she asked weakly. "Is he gone?"

"Yes." Carter glanced at me, and I knew we'd be keeping the details to ourselves. "Everything's fine, thanks to you. The secret name worked."

She nodded, satisfied, and her eyes began to close.

"Hey." Carter's voice quavered. "Stay awake. You're not going to leave me alone with Sadie, are you? She's bad company."

Zia tried to smile, but the effort made her wince. "I was... never here, Carter. Just a message—a placeholder."

"Come on. No. That's no way to talk."

"Find her, will you?" Zia said. A tear traced its way down her nose. "She'd... like that... a date at the mall." Her eyes drifted away from him and stared blankly into the sky.

"Zia!" Carter clutched her hand. "Stop that. You can't…
You can't just…"

I knelt next to him and touched Zia's face. It was cold as
stone. And even though I understood what had happened, I
couldn't think of anything to say, or any way to console my
brother. He shut his eyes tight and lowered his head.

Then it happened. Along the path of Zia's tear, from the
corner of her eye to the base of her nose, Zia's face cracked.
Smaller fractures appeared, webbing her skin. Her flesh dried
out, hardening…turning to clay.

"Carter," I said.

"What?" he said miserably.

He looked up just as a small blue light drifted out of Zia's
mouth and flew into the sky. Carter backed away in shock.
"What—what did you do?"

"Nothing," I said. "She's a *shabti*. She said she wasn't really
here. She was just a placeholder."

Carter looked bewildered. But then a small light started
to burn in his eyes—a tiny bit of hope. "Then…the real Zia
is alive?"

"Iskandar was protecting her," I said. "When the spirit of
Nephthys joined with the real Zia in London, Iskandar knew
she was in danger. Iskandar hid her away and replaced her with
a *shabti*. Remember what Thoth said: 'Shabti make excellent
stunt doubles?' That's what she was. And Nephthys told me
she was sheltered somewhere, inside a sleeping host."

"But where—"

"I don't know," I said. And in Carter's present state, I was
too afraid to raise the *real* question: If Zia had been a *shabti* all

this time, had we ever known her at all? The real Zia had never gotten close to us. She'd never discovered what an incredibly amazing person I was. God forbid, she might not even like Carter.

Carter touched her face and it crumbled to dust. He picked up her wand, which remained solid ivory, but he held it gingerly as if he were afraid it too would dissolve. "That blue light," he began to ramble, "I saw Zia release one in the First Nome, too. Just like the *shabti* in Memphis—they sent their thoughts back to Thoth. So Zia must've been in contact with her *shabti*. That's what the light was. They must've been, like, sharing memories, right? She must *know* what the *shabti*'s been through. If the real Zia is alive somewhere, she might be locked up or in some kind of magic sleep or— We have to find her!"

I wasn't sure it would be so simple, but I didn't want to argue. I could see the desperation on his face.

Then a familiar voice sent a cold shiver down my back: "What have you done?"

Desjardins was literally fuming. His tattered robes still smoked from battle. (Carter says I shouldn't mention that his pink boxer shorts were showing, but they were!) His staff was aglow, and the whiskers in his beard smoldered. Behind him stood three equally battered magicians, who all looked as if they'd just regained consciousness.

"Oh, good," I muttered. "You're alive."

"You bargained with Set?" Desjardins demanded. "You let him *go*?"

"We don't answer to you," Carter growled. He stepped

forward, hand on his sword, but I put out my arm to hold him back.

"Desjardins," I said as calmly as I could, "Apophis is rising, in case you missed that part. We need the gods. The House of Life has to relearn the old ways."

"The old ways destroyed us!" he yelled.

A week ago, the look in his eyes would've made me tremble. He fairly glowed with rage, and hieroglyphs blazed in the air around him. He was the Chief Lector, and I'd just undone everything the House had worked for since the fall of Egypt. Desjardins was a heartbeat away from turning me into an insect, and the thought should've terrified me.

Instead, I looked him in the eye. Right now, I was more powerful than he was. *Much* more powerful. And I let him know it.

"Pride destroyed you," I said. "Greed and selfishness and all of that. It's hard to follow the path of the gods. But it is part of magic. You can't just shut it down."

"You are drunk with power," he snarled. "The gods have possessed you, as they always do. Soon you will forget you are even human. We will fight you and destroy you." Then he glared at Carter. "And *you*—I know what Horus would demand. You will never reclaim the throne. With my last breath—"

"Save it," I said. Then I faced my brother. "You know what we have to do?"

Understanding passed between us. I was surprised how easily I could read him. I thought it might be the influence of the gods, but then I realized it was because we were both

Kanes, brother and sister. And Carter, god help me, was also my friend.

"Are you sure?" he asked. "We're leaving ourselves open." He glared at Desjardins. "Just one more good smack with the sword?"

"I'm sure, Carter."

I closed my eyes and focused.

Consider carefully, Isis said. *What we've done so far is only the beginning of the power we could wield together.*

That's the problem, I said. *I'm not ready for that. I've got to get there on my own, the hard way.*

You are wise for a mortal, Isis said. *Very well.*

Imagine giving up a fortune in cash. Imagine throwing away the most beautiful diamond necklace in the world. Separating myself from Isis was harder than that, *much* harder.

But it wasn't impossible. *I know my limits*, my mother had said, and now I understood how wise she'd been.

I felt the spirit of the goddess leave me. Part of her flowed into my necklace, but most of her streamed into the Washington Monument, back into the Duat, where Isis would go...somewhere else. Another host? I wasn't sure.

When I opened my eyes, Carter stood next to me looking grief-stricken, holding his Eye of Horus amulet.

Desjardins was so stunned, he momentarily forgot how to speak English. *"Ce n'est pas possible. On ne pourrait pas—"*

"Yes, we could," I said. "We've given up the gods of our own free will. And you've got a lot to learn about what's possible."

Carter threw down his sword. "Desjardins, I'm not after the throne. Not unless I earn it by myself, and that's going to take time. We're going to learn the path of the gods. We're going to teach others. You can waste time trying to destroy us, or you can help."

The sirens were much closer now. I could see the lights of emergency vehicles coming from several directions, slowly cordoning off the National Mall. We had only minutes before we were surrounded.

Desjardins looked at the magicians behind him, probably gauging how much support he could rally. His brethren looked in awe. One even started to bow to me, then caught himself.

Alone, Desjardins might've been able to destroy us. We were just magicians now—very tired magicians, with hardly any formal training.

Desjardins' nostrils flared. Then he surprised me by lowering his staff. "There has been too much destruction today. But the path of the gods shall remain closed. If you cross the House of Life again..."

He let the threat hang in the air. He slammed his staff down, and with a final burst of energy, the four magicians dissolved into wind and gusted away.

Suddenly I felt exhausted. The terror of what I'd been through began to sink in. We'd survived, but that was little consolation. I missed my parents. I missed them terribly. I wasn't a goddess anymore. I was just a regular girl, alone with only my brother.

Then Amos groaned and started sitting up. Police cars and sinister-looking black vans blocked the curbs all around us. Sirens blared. A helicopter sliced through the air over the Potomac, closing fast. God only knew what the mortals thought had happened at the Washington Monument, but I didn't want my face on the nightly news.

"Carter, we have to get out of here," I said. "Can you summon enough magic to change Amos into something small—a mouse maybe? We can fly him out."

He nodded, still in a daze. "But Dad . . . we didn't . . ."

He looked around helplessly. I knew how he felt. The pyramid, the throne, the golden coffin—all of it was gone. We'd come so far to rescue our father, only to lose him. And Carter's first girlfriend lay at his feet in a pile of pottery shards. That probably didn't help either. (Carter protests that she wasn't really his girlfriend. Oh, please!)

I couldn't dwell on it, though. I had to be strong for both of us or we'd end up in prison.

"First things first," I said. "We have to get Amos to safety."

"Where?" Carter asked.

There was only one place I could think of.

41. We Stop the Recording, for Now

I CAN'T BELIEVE SADIE'S GOING TO let me have the last word. Our experience together must've really taught her something. Ow, she just hit me. Never mind.

Anyway, I'm glad she told that last part. I think she understood it better than I did. And the whole thing about Zia not being Zia and Dad not getting rescued...that was pretty hard to deal with.

If anybody felt worse than I did, it was Amos. I had just enough magic to turn myself into a falcon and him into a hamster (hey, I was rushed!), but a few miles from the National Mall, he started struggling to change back. Sadie and I were forced to land outside a train station, where Amos turned back into a human and curled into a shivering ball. We tried to talk to him, but he could barely complete a sentence.

Finally we got him into the station. We let him sleep on a bench while Sadie and I warmed up and watched the news.

According to Channel 5, the whole city of Washington

was under lockdown. There'd been reports of explosions and weird lights at the Washington Monument, but all the cameras could show us was a big square of melted snow on the mall, which kind of made for boring video. Experts came on and talked about terrorism, but eventually it became clear that there'd been no permanent damage—just a bunch of scary lights. After a while, the media started speculating about freak storm activity or a rare southern appearance of the Northern Lights. Within an hour, the authorities opened up the city.

I wished we had Bast with us, because Amos was in no shape to be our chaperone; but we managed to buy tickets for our "sick" uncle and ourselves as far as New York.

I slept on the way, the amulet of Horus clutched in my hand.

We got back to Brooklyn at sunset.

We found the mansion burned out, which we'd expected, but we had nowhere else to go. I knew we'd made the right choice when we guided Amos through the doorway and heard a familiar, *"Agh! Agh!"*

"Khufu!" Sadie cried.

The baboon tackled her in a hug and climbed onto her shoulders. He picked at her hair, seeing if she'd brought him any good bugs to eat. Then he jumped off and grabbed a half-melted basketball. He grunted at me insistently, pointing to a makeshift basket he'd made out of some burned beams and a laundry basket. It was a gesture of forgiveness, I realized. He had forgiven me for sucking at his favorite game, and he was offering lessons. Looking around, I realized that he'd tried to clean up in his own baboon way, too. He'd dusted off the one surviving sofa, stacked Cheerios boxes in the fireplace, and even put a dish of water and fresh food out for Muffin, who was curled up asleep on a little pillow. In the clearest part of the living room, under an intact section of roof, Khufu had made three separate mounds of pillows and sheets—sleeping places for us.

I got a lump in my throat. Seeing the care that he'd taken getting ready for us, I couldn't imagine a better welcome home present.

"Khufu," I said, "you are one freaking awesome baboon."

"*Agh!*" he said, pointing to the basketball.

"You want to school me?" I said. "Yeah, I deserve it. Just give us a second to…"

My smile melted when I saw Amos.

He'd drifted over to the ruined statue of Thoth. The god's cracked ibis head lay at his feet. His hands had broken off, and his tablet and stylus lay shattered on the ground. Amos stared at the headless god—the patron of magicians—and I could guess what he was thinking. *A bad omen for a homecoming.*

"It's okay," I told him. "We're going to make it right."

If Amos heard me, he gave no sign. He drifted over to the couch and plopped down, putting his head in his hands.

Sadie glanced at me uneasily. Then she looked around at the blackened walls, the crumbling ceilings, the charred remains of the furniture.

"Well," she said, trying to sound upbeat. "How about *I* play basketball with Khufu, and you can clean the house?"

Even with magic, it took us several weeks to put the house back in order. That was just to make it livable. It was hard without Isis and Horus helping, but we could still do magic. It just took a lot more concentration and a lot more time. Every day, I went to sleep feeling as if I'd done twelve hours of hard labor; but eventually we got the walls and ceilings repaired, and cleaned up the debris until the house no longer smelled of smoke. We even managed to fix the terrace and the pool. We brought Amos out to watch as we released the wax crocodile figurine into the water, and Philip of Macedonia sprang to life.

Amos almost smiled when he saw that. Then he sank into a chair on the terrace and stared desolately at the Manhattan skyline.

I began to wonder if he would ever be the same. He'd lost too much weight. His face looked haggard. Most days he wore his bathrobe and didn't even bother to comb his hair.

"He was taken over by Set," Sadie told me one morning, when I mentioned how worried I was. "Do you have any idea how *violating* that is? His will was broken. He doubts himself and . . . Well, it may be a long time. . . ."

We tried to lose ourselves in work. We repaired the statue of Thoth, and fixed the broken *shabti* in the library. I was better at grunt work—moving blocks of stone or heaving ceiling beams into place. Sadie was better at fine details, like repairing the hieroglyphic seals on the doors. Once, she really impressed me by imagining her bedroom just as it had been and speaking the joining spell, *hi-nehm*. Pieces of furniture flew together out of the debris, and *boom!*: instant repair job. Of course, Sadie passed out for twelve hours afterward, but still...pretty cool. Slowly but surely, the mansion began to feel like home.

At night I would sleep with my head on a charmed head-rest, which mostly kept my *ba* from drifting off; but sometimes I still had strange visions—the red pyramid, the serpent in the sky, or the face of my father as he was trapped in Set's coffin. Once I thought I heard Zia's voice trying to tell me something from far away, but I couldn't make out the words.

Sadie and I kept our amulets locked in a box in the library. Every morning I would sneak down to make sure they were still there. I would find them glowing, warm to the touch, and I would be tempted—*very* tempted—to put on the Eye of Horus. But I knew I couldn't. The power was too addictive, too dangerous. I'd achieved a balance with Horus once, under extreme circumstances, but I knew it would be too easy to get overwhelmed if I tried it again. I had to train first, become a more powerful magician, before I would be ready to tap that much power.

One night at dinner, we had a visitor.

Amos had gone to bed early, as he usually did. Khufu was inside watching ESPN with Muffin on his lap. Sadie and I sat exhausted on the deck overlooking the river. Philip of Macedonia floated silently in his pool. Except for the hum of the city, the night was quiet.

I'm not sure how it happened, but one minute we were alone, and the next there was a guy standing at the railing. He was lean and tall, with messed-up hair and pale skin, and his clothes were all black, as if he'd mugged a priest or something. He was probably around sixteen, and even though I'd never seen his face before, I had the weirdest feeling that I knew him.

Sadie stood up so quickly she knocked over her split-pea soup—which is gross enough in the bowl, but running all over the table? Yuck.

"Anubis!" she blurted.

Anubis? I thought she was kidding, because this guy did not look anything like the slavering jackal-headed god I'd seen in the Land of the Dead. He stepped forward, and my hand crept for my wand.

"Sadie," he said. "Carter. Would you come with me, please?"

"Sure," Sadie said, her voice a little strangled.

"Hold on," I said. "Where are we going?"

Anubis gestured behind him, and a door opened in the air—a pure black rectangle. "Someone wants to see you."

Sadie took his hand and stepped through into the darkness, which left me no choice but to follow.

The Hall of Judgment had gotten a makeover. The golden scales still dominated the room, but they had been fixed. The black pillars still marched off into the gloom on all four sides. But now I could see the overlay—the strange holographic image of the real world—and it was no longer a graveyard, as Sadie had described. It was a white living room with tall ceilings and huge picture windows. Double doors led to a terrace that looked out over the ocean.

I was struck speechless. I looked at Sadie, and judging from the shock on her face, I guessed she recognized the place too: our house in Los Angeles, in the hills overlooking the Pacific—the last place we'd lived as a family.

"The Hall of Judgment is intuitive," a familiar voice said. "It responds to strong memories."

Only then did I notice the throne wasn't empty anymore. Sitting there, with Ammit the Devourer curled at his feet, was our father.

I almost ran to him, but something held me back. He looked the same in many ways—the long brown coat, the rumpled suit and dusty boots, his head freshly shaven and his beard trimmed. His eyes gleamed the way they did whenever I made him proud.

But his form shimmered with a strange light. Like the room itself, I realized, he existed in two worlds. I concentrated hard, and my eyes opened to a deeper level of the Duat.

Dad was still there, but taller and stronger, dressed in the robes and jewels of an Egyptian pharaoh. His skin was a dark shade of blue like the deep ocean.

Anubis walked over and stood at his side, but Sadie and I were a little more cautious.

"Well, come on," Dad said. "I won't bite."

Ammit the Devourer growled as we came close, but Dad stroked his crocodile head and shushed him. "These are my children, Ammit. Behave."

"D-Dad?" I stammered.

Now I want to be clear: even though weeks had passed since the battle with Set, and even though I'd been busy rebuilding the mansion the whole time, I hadn't stopped thinking about my dad for a minute. Every time I saw a picture in the library, I thought of the stories he used to tell me. I kept my clothes in a suitcase in my bedroom closet, because I couldn't bear the idea that our life traveling together was over. I missed him so much I would sometimes turn to tell him something before I forgot that he was gone. In spite of all that, and all the emotion boiling around inside me, all I could think of to say was: "You're blue."

My dad's laugh was so normal, so *him*, that it broke the tension. The sound echoed through the hall, and even Anubis cracked a smile.

"Goes with the territory," Dad said. "I'm sorry I didn't bring you here sooner, but things have been . . ." He looked at Anubis for the right word.

"Complicated," Anubis suggested.

"Complicated. I have meant to tell you both how proud I am of you, how much the gods are in your debt—"

"Hang on," Sadie said. She stomped right up to the throne. Ammit growled at her, but Sadie growled back, which confused the monster into silence.

"What *are* you?" she demanded. "My dad? Osiris? Are you even alive?"

Dad looked at Anubis. "What did I tell you about her? Fiercer than Ammit, I said."

"You didn't need to tell me." Anubis's face was grave. "I've learned to fear that sharp tongue."

Sadie looked outraged. "Excuse me?"

"To answer your question," Dad said, "I am both Osiris and Julius Kane. I am alive *and* dead, though the term *recycled* might be closer to the truth. Osiris is the god of the dead, and the god of new life. To return him to his throne—"

"You had to die," I said. "You knew this going into it. You *intentionally* hosted Osiris, knowing you would die."

I was shaking with anger. I didn't realize how strongly I'd felt about it, but I couldn't believe what my dad had done. "This is what you meant by 'making things right'?"

My dad's expression didn't change. He was still looking at me with pride and downright *joy*, as if everything I did delighted him—even my shouting. It was infuriating.

"I missed you, Carter," he said. "I can't tell you how much. But we made the right choice. We *all* did. If you had saved me in the world above, we would have lost everything. For the first time in millennia, we have a chance at rebirth, and a chance to stop chaos because of you."

"There had to be another way," I said. "You could've fought as a mortal, without . . . without—"

"Carter, when Osiris was alive, he was a great king. But when he died—"

"He became a thousand times more powerful," I said, re-membering the story Dad used to tell me.

My father nodded. "The Duat is the foundation for the real world. If there is chaos here, it reverberates in the upper world. Helping Osiris to his throne was a first step, a thousand times more important than anything I could've done in the world above—except being your father. And I am still your father."

My eyes stung. I guess I understood what he was saying, but I didn't like it. Sadie looked even angrier than me, but she was glaring at Anubis.

"Sharp tongue?" she demanded.

Dad cleared his throat. "Children, there is another reason I made my choice, as you can probably guess." He held out his hand, and a woman in a black dress appeared next to him. She had golden hair, intelligent blue eyes, and a face that looked familiar. She looked like Sadie.

"Mom," I said.

She gazed back and forth from Sadie to me in amazement, as if *we* were the ghosts. "Julius told me how much you'd grown, but I couldn't believe it. Carter, I bet you're shaving—"

"Mom."

"—and dating girls—"

"Mom!" Have you ever noticed how parents can go from the most wonderful people in the world to totally embarrassing in three seconds?

She smiled at me, and I had to fight with about twenty different feelings at once. I'd spent years dreaming of being back with my parents, together in our house in L.A. But not like this: not with the house just an afterimage, and my mom a spirit, and my dad . . . recycled. I felt like the world was shifting under my feet, turning into sand.

"We can't go back, Carter," Mom said, as if reading my mind. "But nothing is lost, even in death. Do you remember the law of conservation?"

It had been six years since we'd sat together in the living room—*this* living room, and she'd read me the laws of physics the way most parents read bedtime stories. But I still remembered. "Energy and matter can't be created or destroyed."

"Only changed," my mother agreed. "And sometimes changed for the better."

She took Dad's hand, and I had to admit—blue and ghostly or not—they kind of looked happy.

"Mum." Sadie swallowed. For once, her attention wasn't on Anubis. "Did you really...was that—"

"Yes, my brave girl. My thoughts mixed with yours. I'm so proud of you. And thanks to Isis, I feel like I know you as well." She leaned forward and smiled conspiratorially. "I like chocolate caramels, too, though your grandmum never approved of keeping sweets in the flat."

Sadie broke into a relieved grin. "I know! She's impossible!"

I got the feeling they were going to start chatting for hours, but just then the Hall of Judgment rumbled. Dad checked his watch, which made me wonder what time zone the Land of the Dead was in.

"We should wrap things up," he said. "The others are expecting you."

"Others?" I asked.

"A gift before you go." Dad nodded to Mom.

She stepped forward and handed me a palm-size package of folded black linen. Sadie helped me unwrap it, and inside was a new amulet—one that looked like a column or a tree trunk or...

"Is that a spine?" Sadie demanded.

"It is called a *djed*," Dad said. "My symbol—the spine of Osiris."

"Yuck," Sadie muttered.

Mom laughed. "It is a bit yuck, but honestly, it's a powerful symbol. Stands for stability, strength—"

"Backbone?" I asked.

"Literally." Mom gave me an approving look, and again I had that surreal shifting feeling. I couldn't believe I was standing here, having a chat with my somewhat dead parents.

Mom closed the amulet into my hands. Her touch was warm, like a living person's. "*Djed* also stands for the power of Osiris—renewed life from the ashes of death. This is exactly what you will need if you are to stir the blood of the pharaohs in others and rebuild the House of Life."

"The House won't like that," Sadie put in.

"No," Mom said cheerfully. "They certainly won't."

The Hall of Judgment rumbled again.

"It is time," Dad said. "We'll meet again, children. But until then, take care."

"Be mindful of your enemies," Mom added.

"And tell Amos..." Dad's voice trailed off thoughtfully. "Remind my brother that Egyptians believe in the power of the sunrise. They believe each morning begins not just a new day, but a new world."

Before I could figure out what that meant, the Hall of Judgment faded, and we stood with Anubis in a field of darkness.

"I'll show you the way," Anubis said. "It is my job."

He ushered us to a space in the darkness that looked no

different from any other. But when he pushed with his hand, a door swung open. The entrance blazed with daylight.

Anubis bowed formally to me. Then he looked at Sadie with a glint of mischief in his eyes. "It's been...stimulating."

Sadie flushed and pointed at him accusingly. "We're not done, mister. I expect you to look after my parents. And next time I'm in the Land of the Dead, you and I will have words."

A smile tugged at the corner of his mouth. "I'll look forward to that."

We stepped through the doorway and into the palace of the gods.

It looked just like Sadie had described from her visions: soaring stone columns, fiery braziers, a polished marble floor, and in the middle of the room, a gold-and-red throne. All around us, gods had gathered. Many were just flashes of light and fire. Some were shadowy images that shifted from animal to human. I recognized a few: Thoth flickered into view as a wild-haired guy in a lab coat before turning into a cloud of green gas; Hathor, the cow-headed goddess, gave me a puzzled look, as if she vaguely recognized me from the Magic Salsa incident. I looked for Bast, but my heart fell. She didn't seem to be in the crowd. In fact, most of the gods I didn't recognize.

"What have we started?" Sadie murmured.

I understood what she meant. The throne room was full of hundreds of gods, major and minor, all darting through the palace, forming new shapes, glowing with power. An entire supernatural army...and they all seemed to be staring at us.

Thankfully, two old friends stood next to the throne. Horus wore full battle armor and a *khopesh* sword at his side.

His kohl-lined eyes—one gold, one silver—were as piercing as ever. At his side stood Isis in a shimmering white gown, with wings of light.

"Welcome," Horus said.

"*Um*, hi," I said.

"He has a way with words," Isis muttered, which made Sadie snort.

Horus gestured to the throne. "I know your thoughts, Carter, so I think I know what you will say. But I have to ask you one more time. Will you join me? We could rule the earth and the heavens. Ma'at demands a leader."

"Yeah, so I've heard."

"I would be stronger with you as my host. You've only touched the surface of what combat magic can do. We could accomplish great things, and it *is* your destiny to lead the House of Life. You could be the king of two thrones."

I glanced at Sadie, but she just shrugged. "Don't look at me. I find the idea horrifying."

Horus scowled at her, but the truth was, I agreed with Sadie. All those gods waiting for direction, all those magicians who hated us—the idea of trying to lead them made my knees turn to water.

"Maybe some day," I said. "Much later."

Horus sighed. "Five thousand years, and I still do not understand mortals. But—very well."

He stepped up to the throne and looked around at the assembled gods.

"I, Horus, son of Osiris, claim the throne of the heavens

as my birthright!" he shouted. "What was once mine shall be mine again. Is there any who would challenge me?"

The gods flickered and glowed. A few scowled. One muttered something that sounded like "Cheese," although that could've been my imagination. I caught a glimpse of Sobek, or possibly another crocodile god, snarling in the shadows. But no one raised a challenge.

Horus took his seat on the throne. Isis brought him a crook and flail—the twin scepters of the pharaohs. He crossed them over his chest and all the gods bowed before him.

When they'd risen again, Isis stepped toward us. "Carter and Sadie Kane, you have done much to restore Ma'at. The gods must gather their strength, and you have bought us time, though we do not know how much. Apophis will not stay locked away forever."

"I'd settle for a few hundred years," Sadie said.

Isis smiled. "However that may be, today you are heroes. The gods owe you a debt, and we take our debts seriously."

Horus rose from the throne. With a wink at me, he knelt before us. The other gods shifted uncomfortably, but then followed his example. Even the gods in fire form dimmed their flames.

I probably looked pretty stunned, because when Horus got up again he laughed. "You look like that time when Zia told you—"

"Yeah, could we skip that?" I said quickly. Letting a god into your head has serious disadvantages.

"Go in peace, Carter and Sadie," Horus said. "You will find our gift in the morning."

"Gift?" I asked nervously, because if I got one more magic amulet, I was going to break out in a cold sweat.

"You'll see," Isis promised. "We will be watching you, and waiting."

"That's what scares me," Sadie said.

Isis waved her hand, and suddenly we were back on the mansion's terrace as if nothing had happened.

Sadie turned toward me wistfully. "'Stimulating.'"

I held out my hand. The *djed* amulet was glowing and warm in its linen wrapping. "Any idea what this thing does?"

She blinked. "*Hmm?* Oh, don't care. What did Anubis look like to you?"

"What did . . . he looked like a guy. So?"

"A good-looking guy, or a slobbering dog-headed guy?"

"I guess . . . not the dog-headed guy."

"I knew it!" Sadie pointed at me as if she'd won an argument. "Good-looking. I knew it!"

And with a ridiculous grin, she spun around and skipped into the house.

My sister, as I may have mentioned, is a little strange.

The next day, we got the gods' gift.

We woke to find that the mansion had been completely repaired down to the smallest detail. Everything we hadn't finished yet—probably another month's worth of work—was done.

The first thing I found were new clothes in my closet, and after a moment's hesitation, I put them on. I went downstairs and found Khufu and Sadie dancing around the restored Great

Room. Khufu had a new Lakers jersey and a brand-new basketball. The magical brooms and mops were busy doing their cleaning routine. Sadie looked up at me and grinned—and then her expression changed to shock.

"Carter, what—what are you *wearing*?"

I came down the stairs, feeling even more self-conscious. The closet had offered me several choices this morning, not just my linen robes. My old clothes had been there, freshly cleaned—a button-down shirt, starched khaki slacks, loafers. But there had also been a third choice, and I'd taken it: some Reeboks, blue jeans, a T-shirt, and a hoodie.

"It's, *um*, all cotton," I said. "Okay for magic. Dad would probably think I look like a gangster...."

I thought for sure Sadie would tease me about that, and I was trying to beat her to the punch. She scrutinized every detail of my outfit.

Then she laughed with absolute delight. "It's brilliant, Carter. You look almost like a regular teenager! And *Dad* would think..." She pulled my hoodie over my head. "Dad would think you look like an impeccable magician, because that's what you are. Now, come on. Breakfast is waiting on the patio."

We were just digging in when Amos came outside, and his change of clothes was even more surprising than mine. He wore a crisp new chocolate-colored suit with matching coat and fedora. His shoes were shined, his round glasses polished, his hair freshly braided with amber beads. Sadie and I both stared at him.

"What?" he demanded.

"Nothing," we said in unison. Sadie looked at me and mouthed O-M-G, then went back to her bangers and eggs. I attacked my pancakes. Philip thrashed around happily in his swimming pool.

Amos joined us at the table. He flicked his fingers and coffee magically filled his cup. I raised my eyebrows. He hadn't used magic since the Demon Days.

"I thought I'd go away for a while," he announced. "To the First Nome."

Sadie and I exchanged glances.

"Are you sure that's a good idea?" I asked.

Amos sipped his coffee. He stared across the East River as if he could see all the way to Washington, D.C. "They have the best magic healers there. They will not turn away a petitioner seeking aid—even me. I think...I think I should try."

His voice was fragile, like it would crack apart any moment. But still, it was the most he'd said in weeks.

"I think that's brilliant," Sadie offered. "We'll watch after the place, won't we, Carter?"

"Yeah," I said. "Absolutely."

"I may be gone for a while," Amos said. "Treat this as your home. It *is* your home." He hesitated, as if choosing his next words carefully. "And I think, perhaps, you should start recruiting. There are many children around the world with the blood of the pharaohs. Most do not know what they are. What you two said in Washington—about rediscovering the path of the gods—it may be our only chance."

Sadie got up and kissed Amos on the forehead. "Leave it to us, Uncle. I've got a plan."

"That," I said, "sounds like very bad news."

Amos managed a smile. He squeezed Sadie's hand, then got up and ruffled my hair as he headed inside.

I took another bite of my pancakes and wondered why—on such a great morning—I still felt sad, and a little incomplete. I suppose with so many things suddenly getting better, the things that were still missing hurt even worse.

Sadie picked at her scrambled eggs. "I suppose it would be selfish to ask for more."

I stared at her, and I realized we were thinking the same thing. When the gods had said a gift . . . Well, you can hope for things, but as Sadie said, I guess you can't get greedy.

"It's going to be hard to travel if we need to go recruiting," I said cautiously. "Two unaccompanied minors."

Sadie nodded. "No Amos. No responsible adult. I don't think Khufu counts."

And that's when the gods completed their gift.

A voice from the doorway said, "Sounds like you have a job opening."

I turned and felt a thousand pounds of grief drop from my shoulders. Leaning against the door in a leopard-spotted jumpsuit was a dark-haired lady with golden eyes and two very large knives.

"Bast!" Sadie cried.

The cat goddess gave us a playful smile, as if she had all kinds of trouble in mind. "Someone call for a chaperone?"

A few days later, Sadie had a long phone conversation with Gran and Grandpa Faust in London. They didn't ask to talk to me, and I didn't listen in. When Sadie came back down to the Great Room, she had a faraway look in her eyes. I was afraid—*very* afraid—that she was missing London.

"Well?" I asked reluctantly.

"I told them we were all right," she said. "They told me the police have stopped bothering them about the explosion at the British Museum. Apparently the Rosetta Stone turned up unharmed."

"Like magic," I said.

Sadie smirked. "The police decided it might've been a gas explosion, some sort of accident. Dad's off the hook, as are we. I could go home to London, they said. Spring term starts in a few weeks. My mates Liz and Emma have been asking about me."

The only sound was the crackle of fire in the hearth. The Great Room suddenly seemed bigger to me, emptier.

At last I said, "What did you tell them?"

Sadie raised an eyebrow. "God, you're thick sometimes. What do you think?"

"Oh." My mouth felt like sandpaper. "I guess it'll be good to see your friends and get back your old room, and—"

Sadie punched my arm. "Carter! I told them I couldn't very well go home, because I already *was* home. This is where I belong. Thanks to the Duat, I can see my friends whenever I want. And besides, you'd be lost without me."

I must've grinned like a fool, because Sadie told me to wipe the silly look off my face—but she sounded pleased about it. I suppose she knew she was right, for once. I would've been lost without her. [And no, Sadie, I can't believe I just said that either.]

Just when things were settling down to a nice safe routine, Sadie and I embarked on our new mission. Our destination was a school that Sadie had seen in a dream. I won't tell you which school, but Bast drove us a long way to get there. We recorded this tape along the way. Several times the forces of chaos tried to stop us. Several times we heard rumors that our enemies were starting to hunt down other descendants of the pharaohs, trying to thwart our plans.

We got to the school the day before the spring term started. The hallways were empty, and it was easy to slip inside. Sadie and I picked a locker at random, and she told me to set the combination. I summoned some magic and mixed around the numbers: 13/32/33. Hey, why mess with a good formula?

Sadie said a spell and the locker began to glow. Then she put the package inside and closed the door.

"Are you sure about this?" I asked.

She nodded. "The locker is partially in the Duat. It'll store the amulet until the right person opens it."

"But if the *djed* falls into the wrong hands—"

"It won't," she promised. "The blood of the pharaohs is strong. The right kids will find the amulet. If they figure out how to use it, their powers should awaken. We have to trust that the gods will guide them to Brooklyn."

"We won't know how to train them," I argued. "No one has studied the path of the gods for two thousand years."

"We'll figure it out," Sadie said. "We have to."

"Unless Apophis gets us first," I said. "Or Desjardins and the House of Life. Or unless Set breaks his word. Or a thousand other things go wrong."

"Yes," Sadie said with a smile. "Be fun, eh?"

We locked the locker and walked away.

Now we're back at the Twenty-first Nome in Brooklyn.

We're going to send out this tape to a few carefully chosen people and see if it gets published. Sadie believes in fate. If the story falls into your hands, there's probably a reason. Look for the *djed*. It won't take much to awaken your power. Then the trick is learning to use that power without dying.

As I said at the beginning: the whole story hasn't happened yet. Our parents promised to see us again, so I know we'll have to go back to the Land of the Dead eventually, which I think is fine with Sadie, as long as Anubis is there.

Zia is out there somewhere—the real Zia. I intend to find her.

Most of all, chaos is rising. Apophis is gaining strength. Which means we have to gain strength too—gods and men, united like in olden times. It's the only way the world won't be destroyed.

So the Kane family has a lot of work to do. And so do you.

Maybe you'll want to follow the path of Horus or Isis, Thoth or Anubis, or even Bast. I don't know. But whatever you decide, the House of Life needs new blood if we're going to survive.

So this is Carter and Sadie Kane signing off.

Come to Brooklyn. We'll be waiting.

AUTHOR'S NOTE

Much of this story is based on fact, which makes me think
that either the two narrators, Sadie and Carter, did a great
deal of research . . . or they are telling the truth.

The House of Life did exist, and was an important part
of Egyptian society for several millennia. Whether or not it
still exists today—that is something I cannot answer. But it is
undeniable that Egyptian magicians were famed throughout
the ancient world, and many of the spells they could
supposedly cast are exactly as described in this story.

The way the narrators portray Egyptian magic is also
supported by archaeological evidence. Shabti, curved wands,
and magicians' boxes have survived, and can be viewed
in many museums. All of the artifacts and monuments
Sadie and Carter mention actually exist—with the possible
exception of the red pyramid. There is a "Red Pyramid" at
Giza, but it is only called that because the original white
casing stones were stripped away, revealing the pink granite
blocks underneath. In fact the pyramid's owner, Senefru,
would be horrified to learn his pyramid is now red, the color

of Set. As for the magical red pyramid mentioned in the story, we can only hope that it has been destroyed.

Should further recordings fall into my hands, I will relay the information. Until then, we can only hope that Carter and Sadie are wrong in their predictions about the rise of chaos. . . .

GLOSSARY

Commands used by Carter, Sadie, and others

Ha-di—"Destroy"

Ha-wi—"Strike"

Hah-ri—"Quiet"

Hi-nehm—"Join"

I-ei—"Come"

Sahad—"Open"

Tas—"Bind"

Other Egyptian Terms

Ankh a hieroglyphic symbol for life

Ba soul

Bennu phoenix

Cartouche a drawing of an oblong magical rope that contains and protects the hieroglyphs that spell out the name of a king or queen

Djed a hieroglyphic symbol that stands for stability, strength, and the power of Osiris

Duat magical realm

Hieroglyphics the writing system of ancient Egypt, which used symbols or pictures to denote objects, concepts, or sounds

Isfet chaos

Khopesh a sword with a hook-shaped blade

Ma'at order of the universe

Nome district, region

Pharaoh a ruler of ancient Egypt

Sahlab a warm Egyptian drink

Sarcophagus a stone coffin, often decorated with sculpture and inscriptions

Shabti a magical figurine made out of clay

Shesh scribe, writer, or magician

Tyet a magic knot and the symbol of Isis

Egyptian Gods and Goddesses
Mentioned in *The Red Pyramid*

Anubis the god of funerals and death

Apophis the god of chaos

Bast the cat goddess

Geb the earth god

Horus the war god, son of Isis and Osiris

Isis the goddess of magic, wife of her brother Osiris and
mother of Horus

Khons the moon god

Nephthys the river goddess

Nut the sky goddess

Osiris the god of the underworld, husband of Isis and
father of Horus

Ra the sun god, the god of order; also known as Amun-Ra

Sekhmet the lion goddess

Serqet the scorpion goddess

Set the god of evil

Shezmu demonic god of blood and wine

Shu the air god

Sobek the crocodile god

Thoth the god of knowledge

FROM *NEW YORK TIMES* BEST-SELLING AUTHOR

RICK RIORDAN

THE GREEKS AREN'T THE *ONLY* GODS IN TOWN.

HOW DO YOU PUNISH AN IMMORTAL?
BY MAKING HIM HUMAN.

FROM *NEW YORK TIMES* BEST-SELLING AUTHOR
RICK RIORDAN

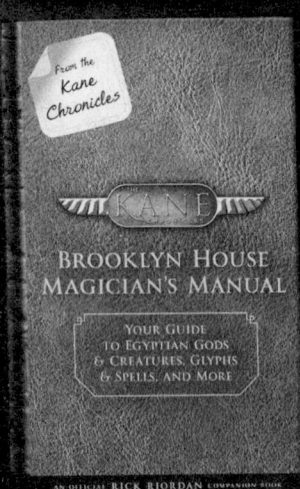

THE
SON OF
SOBEK

A Carter Kane/Percy Jackson Adventure

GETTING EATEN BY A GIANT CROCODILE was bad enough.

The kid with the glowing sword only made my day worse.

Maybe I should introduce myself.

I'm Carter Kane—part-time high school freshman, part-time magician, full-time worrier about all the Egyptian gods and monsters who are constantly trying to kill me.

Okay, that last part is an exaggeration. Not *all* the gods want me dead. Just a lot of them—but that kind of goes with the territory, since I'm a magician in the House of Life. We're like the police for Ancient Egyptian supernatural forces, making sure they don't cause too much havoc in the modern world.

Anyway, on this particular day I was tracking down a rogue monster on Long Island. Our scryers had been sensing magical disturbances in the area for several weeks. Then the local news started reporting that a large creature had been sighted in the ponds and marshes near the Montauk Highway—a creature that was eating the wildlife and scaring the locals. One reporter even called it the Long Island Swamp Monster. When mortals start raising the alarm, you know it's time to check things out.

Normally my sister, Sadie, or some of our other initiates from Brooklyn House would've come with me. But they were all at the First Nome, in Egypt, for a weeklong training session on controlling cheese demons (yes, they're a real thing; believe me, you don't want to know), so I was on my own.

I hitched our flying reed boat to Freak, my pet griffin, and we spent the morning buzzing around the South Shore looking for signs of trouble. If you're wondering why I didn't just ride on Freak's back, imagine two hummingbird-like wings beating faster and more powerfully than helicopter blades. Unless you want to get shredded, it's really better to ride in the boat.

Freak had a pretty good nose for magic. After a couple of hours on patrol, he shrieked, "FREEEAAAK!" and banked hard to the left, circling over a green marshy inlet between two subdivisions.

"Down there?" I asked.

Freak shivered and squawked, whipping his barbed tail nervously.

I couldn't see much below us—just a brown river glittering in the hot summer air, winding through swamp grass and clumps of gnarled trees until it emptied into Moriches Bay. The area looked a bit like the Nile Delta back in Egypt, except here the wetlands were surrounded on both sides by residential neighborhoods with row after row of gray-roofed houses. Just to the north, a line of cars inched along the Montauk Highway— vacationers escaping the crowds in the city to enjoy the crowds in the Hamptons.

If there really was a carnivorous swamp monster below us, I wondered how long it would be before it developed a taste for humans. If that happened . . . well, it was surrounded by an all-you-can-eat buffet.

"Okay," I told Freak. "Set me down by the riverbank."

As soon as I stepped out of the boat, Freak screeched and zoomed into the sky, the boat trailing behind him.

"Hey!" I yelled after him, but it was too late.

Freak is easily spooked. Flesh-eating monsters tend to scare him away. So do fireworks, clowns, and the smell of Sadie's weird British Ribena drink. (Can't blame him on that last one. Sadie grew up in London and developed some pretty strange tastes.)

I would have to take care of this monster problem, then whistle for Freak to pick me up once I was done.

I opened my backpack and checked my supplies: some enchanted rope, my curved ivory wand, a lump of wax for making a magical *shabti* figurine, my calligraphy set, and a healing potion my friend Jaz had brewed for me a while back. (She knew that I got hurt a lot.)

There was just one more thing I needed.

I concentrated and reached into the Duat. Over the last few months, I'd gotten better at storing emergency provisions in the shadow realm—extra weapons, clean clothes, Fruit by the Foot, and chilled six-packs of root beer—but sticking my hand into a magical dimension still felt weird, like pushing through layers of cold, heavy curtains. I closed my fingers around the hilt of my sword and pulled it out—a heavy *khopesh* with a blade curved like a question mark. Armed with my sword and wand, I was all set for a stroll through the swamp to look for a hungry monster. Oh, joy!

I waded into the water and immediately sank to my knees. The river bottom felt like congealed stew. With every step, my shoes made such rude noises—*suck-plop, suck-plop*—that I was glad my sister Sadie wasn't with me. She never would've stopped laughing.

Even worse, making this much noise, I knew I wouldn't be able to sneak up on any monsters.

Mosquitoes swarmed me. Suddenly I felt nervous and alone.

Could be worse, I told myself. *I could be studying cheese demons.*

But I couldn't quite convince myself. In the nearby subdivision, I heard kids shouting and laughing, probably playing some kind of game. I wondered what that would be like—being a normal kid, hanging out with my friends on a summer afternoon.

The idea was so nice, I got distracted. I didn't notice the ripples in the water until fifty yards ahead of me something broke the surface—a line of leathery, blackish-green bumps. Instantly it submerged again, but I knew what I was dealing with now. I'd seen crocodiles before, and this was a freakishly big one.

I remembered El Paso, the winter before last, when my sister and I had been attacked by the crocodile god Sobek. That *wasn't* a good memory.

Sweat trickled down my neck.

"Sobek," I murmured, "if that's you, messing with me again, I swear to Ra . . ."

The croc god had promised to leave us alone now that we were tight with his boss, the sun god. Still . . . crocodiles get hungry. Then they tend to forget their promises.

No answer from the water. The ripples subsided.

When it came to sensing monsters, my magic instincts weren't very sharp; but the water in front of me seemed much darker. That meant either it was deep, or something large was lurking under the surface.

I almost hoped it *was* Sobek. At least then I stood a chance of talking to him before he killed me. Sobek loved to boast.

Unfortunately, it wasn't him.

The next microsecond, as the water erupted around me, I realized too late that I should've brought the entire Twenty-first Nome to help me. I registered glowing yellow eyes as big as my head, the glint of gold jewelry around a massive neck. Then monstrous jaws opened—ridges of crooked teeth, and an expanse of pink maw wide enough to gulp down a garbage truck.

And the creature swallowed me whole.

Imagine being shrink-wrapped upside down inside a gigantic slimy garbage bag with no air. Being in the monster's belly was like that, only hotter and smellier.

For a moment I was too stunned to do anything. I couldn't believe I was still alive. If the crocodile's mouth had been smaller, he might have snapped me in half. As it was, he had gulped me down in a single Carter-size serving, so I could look forward to being slowly digested.

Lucky, right?

The monster started thrashing around, which made it hard to think. I held my breath, knowing that it might be my last. I still had my sword and wand, but I couldn't use them with my arms pinned to my side. I couldn't reach any of the stuff in my bag.

Which left only one answer: a word of power. If I could think of the right hieroglyphic symbol and speak it aloud, I could summon some industrial strength, wrath-of-the-gods-type magic to bust my way out of this reptile.

In theory: a great solution.

In practice: I'm not so good at words of power even in the best of situations. Suffocating inside a dark, smelly reptile gullet wasn't helping me focus.

You can do this, I told myself.

After all the dangerous adventures I'd had, I couldn't die like this. Sadie would be devastated. Then, once she got over her grief, she'd track down my soul in the Egyptian afterlife and tease me mercilessly for how stupid I'd been.

My lungs burned. I was blacking out. I picked a word of power, summoned all my concentration, and prepared to speak.

Suddenly the monster lurched upward. It roared, which sounded really weird from the inside, and its throat contracted around me like I was being squeezed from a toothpaste tube. I shot out of the creature's mouth and tumbled into the marsh grass.

Somehow I got to my feet. I staggered around, half blind, gasping, and covered with crocodile goo, which smelled like a scummy fish tank.

The surface of the river churned with bubbles. The crocodile was gone, but standing in the marsh about twenty feet away was a teenage guy in jeans and a faded orange T-shirt that said CAMP something. I couldn't read the rest. He looked a little older than me—maybe seventeen—with tousled black hair and sea-green eyes. What really caught my attention was his sword—a straight double-edged blade glowing with faint bronze light.

I'm not sure which of us was more surprised.

For a second, Camper Boy just stared at me. He noted my *khopesh* and wand, and I got the feeling that he actually *saw* these things as they were. Normal mortals have trouble seeing magic. Their brains can't interpret it, so they might look at my sword, for instance, and see a baseball bat or a walking stick.

But this kid . . . he was different. I figured he must be a magician. The only problem was, I'd met most of the magicians in the North American nomes, and I'd never seen this guy before. I'd also never seen a sword like that. Everything about him seemed . . . *un-Egyptian.*

"The crocodile," I said, trying to keep my voice calm and even. "Where did it go?"

Camper Boy frowned. "You're welcome."

"What?"

"I stuck that croc in the rump." He mimicked the action with his sword. "That's why it vomited you up. So, you're welcome. What were you doing in there?"

I'll admit I wasn't in the best mood. I smelled. I hurt. And, yeah, I was a little embarrassed: the mighty Carter Kane, head of Brooklyn House, had been disgorged from a croc's mouth like a giant hairball.

"I was resting," I snapped. "What do you *think* I was doing? Now, who are you, and why are you fighting my monster?"

"*Your* monster?" The guy trudged toward me through the water. He didn't seem to have any trouble with the mud. "Look, man, I don't know who you are, but that crocodile has been terrorizing Long Island for weeks. I take that kind of personal, as this is my home turf. A few days ago, it ate one of our pegasi."

A jolt went up my spine like I'd backed into an electric fence. "Did you say *pegasi?*"

He waved the question aside. "Is it your monster or not?"

"I don't own it!" I growled. "I'm trying to stop it! Now, where—"

"The croc headed that way." He pointed his sword to the south. "I would already be chasing it, but you surprised me."

He sized me up, which was disconcerting since he was half a foot taller. I still couldn't read his T-shirt except for the word CAMP. Around his neck hung a leather strap with some colorful clay beads, like a kid's arts and crafts project. He wasn't carrying a magician's pack or a wand. Maybe he kept them in the Duat? Or maybe he was just a delusional mortal who'd accidentally found a magic sword and thought he was a super-hero. Ancient relics can really mess with your mind.

Finally he shook his head. "I give up. Son of Ares? You've got to be a half-blood, but what happened to your sword? It's all bent."

"It's a *khopesh*." My shock was rapidly turning to anger. "It's supposed to be curved."

But I wasn't thinking about the sword.

Camper Boy had just called me a *half-blood*? Maybe I hadn't heard him right. Maybe he meant something else. But my dad was African American. My mom was white. *Half-blood* wasn't a word I liked.

"Just get out of here," I said, gritting my teeth. "I've got a crocodile to catch."

"Dude, *I* have a crocodile to catch," he insisted. "Last time you tried, it ate you. Remember?"

My fingers tightened around my sword hilt. "I had every-thing under control. I was about to summon a fist—"

For what happened next, I take full responsibility.

I didn't mean it. Honestly. But I was angry. And as I may have mentioned, I'm not always good at channeling words of power. While I was in the crocodile's belly, I'd been preparing to summon the Fist of Horus, a giant glowing blue hand that can pulverize doors, walls, and pretty much anything else that gets in its way. My plan had been to punch my way out of the monster. Gross, yes; but hopefully effective.

I guess that spell was still in my head, ready to be triggered like a loaded gun. Facing Camper Boy, I was furious, not to mentioned dazed and confused; so when I meant to say the English word fist, it came out in Ancient Egyptian instead: *khefa.*

Such a simple hieroglyph:

You wouldn't think it could cause so much trouble.

As soon as I spoke the word, the symbol blazed in the air between us. A giant fist the size of a dishwasher shimmered into existence and slammed Camper Boy into the next county.

I mean I *literally* punched him out of his shoes. He rocketed from the river with a loud *suck-plop*! And the last thing I saw was his bare feet achieving escape velocity as he flew backward and disappeared from sight.

No, I didn't feel good about it. Well . . . maybe a tiny bit good. But I also felt mortified. Even if the guy was a jerk, magicians weren't supposed to go around sucker-punching kids into orbit with the Fist of Horus.

"Oh, great." I hit myself on the forehead.

I started to wade across the marsh, worried that I'd actually killed the guy. "Man, I'm sorry!" I yelled, hoping he could hear me. "Are you—?"

The wave came out of nowhere.

A twenty-foot wall of water slammed into me and pushed me back into the river. I came up spluttering, a horrible taste like fish food in my mouth. I blinked the gunk out of my eyes just in the time to see Camper Boy leaping toward me ninja-style, his sword raised.

I lifted my *khopesh* to deflect the blow. I just managed to keep my head from being cleaved in half, but Camper Boy was strong and quick. As I reeled backward, he struck again and again. Each time, I was able to parry; but I could tell I was outmatched. His blade was lighter and quicker, and—yes, I'll admit it—he was a better swordsman.

I wanted to explain that I'd made a mistake. I wasn't really his enemy. But I needed all my concentration just to keep from getting sliced down the middle.

Camper Boy, however, had no trouble talking.

"Now I get it," he said, swinging at my head. "You're some kind of monster."

CLANG! I intercepted the strike and staggered back.

"I'm not a monster," I managed.

To beat this guy, I'd have to use more than just a sword. The problem was, I didn't want to hurt him. Despite the fact that he was trying to chop me into a Kane-flavored barbecue sandwich, I still felt bad for starting the fight.

He swung again, and I had no choice. I used my wand this time, catching his blade in the crook of ivory and channeling a burst of magic straight up his arm. The air between us flashed and crackled. Camper Boy stumbled back. Blue sparks of sorcery popped around him, as if my spell didn't know quite what to do with him. Who *was* this guy?

"You said the crocodile was *yours*." Camper Boy scowled, anger blazing in his green eyes. "You lost your pet, I suppose.

Maybe you're a spirit from the Underworld, come through the Doors of Death?"

Before I could even process that question, he thrust out his free hand. The river reversed course and swept me off my feet.

I managed to get up, but I was getting really tired of drinking swamp water. Meanwhile Camper Boy charged again, his sword raised for the kill. In desperation, I dropped my wand. I thrust my hand into my backpack, and my fingers closed around the piece of rope.

I threw it and yelled the command word *"TAS!"*—Bind!— just as Camper Boy's bronze blade cut into my wrist.

My whole arm erupted in agony. My vision tunneled. Yellow spots danced before my eyes. I dropped my sword and clutched my wrist, gasping for breath, everything forgotten except the excruciating pain.

In the back of my mind, I knew Camper Boy could kill me easily. For some reason he didn't. A wave of nausea made me double over.

I forced myself to look at the wound. There was a lot of blood, but I remembered something Jaz had told me once in the infirmary at Brooklyn House: cuts usually looked a lot worse than they were. I hoped that was true. I fished a piece of papyrus out of my pack and pressed it against the wound as a makeshift bandage.

The pain was still horrible, but the nausea became more manageable. My thoughts started to clear, and I wondered why I hadn't been skewered yet.

Camper Boy was sitting nearby in waist-deep water, looking

dejected. My magic rope had wrapped around his sword arm, then lashed his hand to the side of his head. Unable to let go of his sword, he looked like he had a single reindeer antler sprouting next to his ear. He tugged at the rope with his free hand, but of course he couldn't make any progress.

Finally he just sighed and glared at me. "I'm really starting to hate you."

"Hate *me*?" I protested. "I'm gushing blood here! And you started all this by calling me a half-blood!"

"Oh, please." Camper Boy rose unsteadily, his sword antenna making him top-heavy. "You can't be mortal. If you were, my sword would've passed right through you. If you're not a spirit or a monster, you've got to be a half-blood. A rogue demigod from Kronos's army, I'd guess."

Most of what this guy said, I didn't understand. But one thing sank in.

"So when you said 'half-blood'. . ."

He stared at me like I was an idiot. "I meant demigod. Yeah. What did you *think* I meant?"

I tried to process that. I'd heard the term *demigod* before, but it wasn't an Egyptian concept. Maybe this guy was sensing that I was bound to Horus, that I could channel the god's power . . . but why did he describe everything so strangely?

"What are you?" I demanded. "Part combat magician, part water elementalist? What nome are you with?"

The kid laughed bitterly. "Dude, I don't know what you're talking about. I don't hang out with gnomes. Satyrs, sometimes. Even Cyclopes. But not gnomes."

The blood loss must have been making me dizzy. His words bounced around in my head like lottery balls: *Cyclopes, satyrs, demigods, Kronos.* Earlier he'd mentioned Ares. That was a Greek god, not Egyptian.

I felt like the Duat was opening underneath me, threatening to pull me into the depths. *Greek . . . not Egyptian.*

An idea started forming in my mind. I didn't like it. In fact, it scared the holy Horus out of me.

Despite all the swamp water I'd swallowed, my throat felt dry. "Look," I said, "I'm sorry about hitting you with that fist spell. It was an accident. But the thing I don't understand . . . it should have killed you. It didn't. That doesn't make sense."

"Don't sound so disappointed," he muttered. "But while we're on the subject, you should be dead too. Not many people can fight me that well. And my sword should have vaporized your crocodile."

"For the last time, it's not *my* crocodile."

"Okay, whatever." Camper Boy looked dubious. "The point is, I stuck that crocodile pretty good, but I just made it angry. Celestial bronze should've turned it to dust."

"Celestial bronze?"

Our conversation was cut short by a scream from the nearby subdivision—the terrified voice of a kid.

My heart did a slow roll. I really was an idiot. I'd forgotten why we were here.

I locked eyes with Camper Boy. "We've got to stop the crocodile."

"Truce," he suggested.

"Yeah," I said. "We can continue killing each other after the crocodile is taken care of."

"Deal. Now, could you please untie my sword hand from my head? I feel like a freaking unicorn."

I won't say we trusted each other, but at least now we had a common cause. He summoned his shoes out of the river—I had no idea how—and put them on. Then he helped me bind my hand with a strip of linen and waited while I swigged down half of my healing potion.

After that, I felt good enough to race after him toward the sound of the screaming.

I thought I was in pretty good shape—what with combat magic practice, hauling heavy artifacts, and playing basketball with Khufu and his baboon friends (baboons don't mess around when it comes to hoops). Nevertheless, I had to struggle to keep up with Camper Boy.

Which reminded me, I was getting tired of calling him that.

"What's your name?" I asked, wheezing as I ran behind him.

He gave me a cautious glance. "I'm not sure I should tell you. Names can be dangerous."

He was right, of course. Names held power. A while back, my sister, Sadie, had learned my *ren*, my secret name, and it still caused me all sorts of anxiety. Even with someone's common name, a skilled magician could work all kinds of mischief.

"Fair enough," I said. "I'll go first. I'm Carter."

I guess he believed me. The lines around his eyes relaxed a bit.

"Percy," he offered.

That struck me as an unusual name—British, maybe, though the kid spoke and acted very much like an American.

We jumped a rotten log and finally made it out of the marsh. We'd started climbing a grassy slope toward the nearest houses when I realized more than one voice was screaming up there now. Not a good sign.

"Just to warn you," I told Percy, "you can't kill the monster."

"Watch me," Percy grumbled.

"No, I mean it's *immortal*."

"I've heard that before. I've vaporized plenty of *immortals* and sent them back to Tartarus."

Tartarus? I thought.

Talking to Percy was giving me a serious headache. It reminded me of the time my dad took me to Scotland for one of his Egyptology lectures. I'd tried to talk with some of the locals and I knew they were speaking English, but every other sentence seemed to slip into an alternate language—different words, different pronunciations—and I'd wonder what the heck they were saying. Percy was like that. He and I *almost* spoke the same language—magic, monsters, et cetera. But his vocabulary was completely wrong.

"No," I tried again, halfway up the hill. "This monster is a *petsuchos*—a son of Sobek."

"Who's Sobek?" he asked.

"Lord of crocodiles. Egyptian god."

That stopped him in his tracks. He stared at me, and I could swear the air between us turned electric. A voice, very deep in my mind, said: *Shut up. Don't tell him any more.*

Percy glanced at the *khopesh* I'd retrieved from the river, then the wand in my belt. "Where are you from? Honestly."

"Originally?" I asked. "Los Angeles. Now I live in Brooklyn."

That didn't seem to make him feel any better. "So this monster, this *pet-suck-o* or whatever—"

"*Petsuchos,*" I said. "It's a Greek word, but the monster is Egyptian. It was like the mascot of Sobek's temple, worshipped as a living god."

Percy grunted. "You sound like Annabeth."

"Who?"

"Nothing. Just skip the history lesson. How do we kill it?"

"I told you—"

From above came another scream, followed by a loud CRUNCH, like the sound made by a metal compactor.

We sprinted to the top of the hill, then hopped the fence of somebody's backyard and ran into a residential cul-de-sac.

Except for the giant crocodile in the middle of the street, the neighborhood could have been Anywhere, USA. Ringing the cul-de-sac were half a dozen single-story homes with well-kept front lawns, economy cars in the driveways, mailboxes at the curb, flags hanging above the front porches.

Unfortunately, the all-American scene was kind of ruined by the monster, who was busily eating a green Prius hatchback with a bumper sticker that read MY POODLE IS SMARTER THAN YOUR HONOR STUDENT. Maybe the *petsuchos* thought the Toyota was another crocodile, and he was asserting his dominance. Maybe he just didn't like poodles and/or honor students.

Whatever the case, on dry land the crocodile looked even scarier than he had in the water. He was about forty feet long, as tall as a delivery truck, with a tail so massive and powerful, it overturned cars every time it swished. His skin glistened blackish green and gushed water that pooled around his feet. I remembered Sobek once telling me that his divine sweat created the rivers of the world. Yuck. I guessed this monster had the same holy perspiration. Double yuck.

The creature's eyes glowed with a sickly yellow light. His jagged teeth gleamed white. But the weirdest thing about him was his bling. Around his neck hung an elaborate collar of gold chains and enough precious stones to buy a private island.

The necklace was how I had realized that the monster was a *petsuchos*, back at the marsh. I'd read that the sacred animal of Sobek wore something just like it back in Egypt, though what the monster was doing in a Long Island subdivision, I had no idea.

As Percy and I took in the scene, the crocodile clamped down and bit the green Prius in half, spraying glass and metal and pieces of air bag across the lawns.

As soon as he dropped the wreckage, half a dozen kids appeared from nowhere—apparently they'd been hiding behind some of the other cars—and charged the monster, screaming at the top of their lungs.

I couldn't believe it. They were just elementary-age kids, armed with nothing but water balloons and Super Soakers. I guessed that they were on summer break and had been cooling off with a water fight when the monster interrupted them.

There were no adults in sight. Maybe they were all at work. Maybe they were inside, passed out from fright.

The kids looked angry rather than scared. They ran around the crocodile, lobbing water balloons that splashed harmlessly against the monster's hide.

Useless and stupid? Yes. But I couldn't help admiring their bravery. They were trying their best to face down a monster that had invaded their neighborhood.

Maybe they saw the crocodile for what it was. Maybe their mortal brains made them think it was an escaped elephant from the zoo, or a crazed FedEx delivery driver with a death wish.

Whatever they saw, they were in danger.

My throat closed up. I thought about my initiates back at Brooklyn House, who were no older than these kids, and my protective "big brother" instincts kicked in. I charged into the street, yelling, "Get away from it! Run!"

Then I threw my wand straight at the crocodile's head. "*Sa-mir!*"

The wand hit the croc on the snout, and blue light rippled across his body. All over the monster's hide, the hieroglyph for *pain* flickered:

Everywhere it appeared, the croc's skin smoked and sparked, causing the monster to writhe and bellow in annoyance.

The kids scattered, hiding behind ruined cars and mailboxes. The *petsuchos* turned his glowing yellow eyes on me.

At my side, Percy whistled under his breath. "Well, you got his attention."

"Yeah."

"You sure we can't kill him?" he asked.

"Yeah."

The crocodile seemed to be following our conversation. His yellow eyes flicked back and forth between us, as if deciding which of us to eat first.

"Even if you *could* destroy his body," I said, "he would just reappear somewhere nearby. That necklace? It's enchanted with the power of Sobek. To beat the monster, we have to get that necklace off. Then the *petsuchos* should shrink back into a regular crocodile."

"I hate the word *should*," Percy muttered. "Fine. I'll get the necklace. You keep him occupied."

"Why do *I* get to keep him occupied?"

"Because you're more annoying," Percy said. "Just try not to get eaten again."

"ROARR!" the monster bellowed, his breath like a seafood restaurant's Dumpster.

I was about to argue that Percy was *plenty* annoying, but I didn't get the chance. The *petsuchos* charged, and my new comrade-in-arms sprinted to one side, leaving me right in the path of destruction.

* * *

First random thought: *Getting eaten twice in one day would be very embarrassing.*

Out of the corner of my eye, I saw Percy dashing toward the monster's right flank. I heard the mortal kids come out from their hiding places, yelling and throwing more water balloons like they were trying to protect me.

The *petsuchos* lumbered toward me, his jaws opening to snap me up.

And I got angry.

I'd faced the worst Egyptian gods. I'd plunged into the Duat and trekked across the Land of Demons. I'd stood at the very shores of Chaos. I was *not* going to back down to an overgrown gator.

The air crackled with power as my combat avatar formed around me—a glowing blue exoskeleton in the shape of Horus.

It lifted me off the ground until I was suspended in the middle of a twenty-foot-tall, hawk-headed warrior. I stepped forward, bracing myself, and the avatar mimicked my stance.

Percy yelled, "Holy Hera! What the—?!"

The crocodile slammed into me.

He nearly toppled me. His jaws closed around my avatar's free arm, but I slashed the hawk warrior's glowing blue sword at the crocodile's neck.

Maybe the *petsuchos* couldn't be killed. I was at least hoping to cut through the necklace that was the source of his power.

Unfortunately, my swing went wide. I hit the monster's shoulder, cleaving his hide. Instead of blood, he spilled sand, which is pretty typical for Egyptian monsters. I would have enjoyed seeing him disintegrate completely, but no such luck. As soon as I yanked my blade free, the wound started closing and the sand slowed to a trickle. The crocodile whipped his head from side to side, pulling me off my feet and shaking me by the arm like a dog with a chew toy.

When he let me go, I sailed straight into the nearest house and smashed through the roof, leaving a hawk-warrior-shaped crater in someone's living room. I really hoped I hadn't just flattened some defenseless mortal in the middle of watching *Dr. Phil.*

My vision cleared, and I saw two things that irritated me. First, the crocodile was charging me again. Second, my new friend Percy was just standing in the middle of the street, staring at me in shock. Apparently my combat avatar had startled him so much, he'd forgotten his part of the plan.

"What the creeping crud is *that?*" he demanded. "You're inside a giant glowing chicken-man!"

"Hawk!" I yelled.

I decided that if I survived this day, I would have to make sure this guy never met Sadie. They'd probably take turns insulting me for the rest of eternity. "A little help here?"

Percy unfroze and ran toward the croc. As the monster closed in on me, I kicked him in the snout, which made him sneeze and shake his head long enough for me to extricate myself from the ruined house.

Percy jumped on the creature's tail and ran up his spine. The monster thrashed around, his hide shedding water all over the place; but somehow Percy managed to keep his footing. The guy must have practiced gymnastics or something.

Meanwhile, the mortal kids had found some better ammunition—rocks, scrap metal from the wrecked cars, even a few tire irons—and were hurling the stuff at the monster. I didn't want the crocodile turning his attention toward them.

"HEY!" I swung my *khopesh* at the croc's face—a good solid strike that should've taken off his lower jaw. Instead, he somehow snapped at the blade and caught it in his mouth. We ended up wrestling for the blue glowing sword as it sizzled in his mouth, making his teeth crumble to sand. That couldn't have felt good, but the croc held on, tugging against me.

"Percy!" I shouted. "Any time now!"

Percy lunged for the necklace. He grabbed hold and started hacking at the gold links, but his bronze sword didn't make a dent.

Meanwhile, the croc was going crazy trying to yank away my sword. My combat avatar started to flicker.

Summoning an avatar is a short-term thing, like sprinting at top speed. You can't do it for very long, or you'll collapse. Already I was sweating and breathing hard. My heart raced. My reservoirs of magic were being severely depleted.

"Hurry," I told Percy.

"Can't cut it!" he said.

"A clasp," I said. "There's gotta be one."

As soon as I said that, I spotted it—at the monster's throat, a golden cartouche encircling the hieroglyphs that spelled SOBEK. "There—on the bottom!"

Percy scrambled down the necklace, climbing it like a net, but at that moment my avatar collapsed. I dropped to the ground, exhausted and dizzy. The only thing that saved my life was that the crocodile had been pulling at my avatar's sword. When the sword disappeared, the monster lurched backward and stumbled over a Honda.

The mortal kids scattered. One dove under a car, only to have the car disappear—smacked into the air by the croc's tail.

Percy reached the bottom of the necklace and hung on for dear life. His sword was gone. Probably he'd dropped it.

Meanwhile, the monster regained his footing. The good news: he didn't seem to notice Percy. The bad news: he *definitely* noticed me, and he looked mightily torqued off.

I didn't have the energy to run, much less summon magic to fight. At this point, the mortal kids with their water balloons and rocks had more of a chance of stopping the croc than I did.

In the distance, sirens wailed. Somebody had called the police, which didn't exactly cheer me up. It just meant more mortals were racing here as fast as they could to volunteer as crocodile snacks.

I backed up to the curb and tried—ridiculously—to stare down the monster. "Stay, boy."

The crocodile snorted. His hide shed water like the grossest fountain in the world, making my shoes slosh as I walked. His lamp-yellow eyes filmed over, maybe from happiness. He knew I was done for.

I thrust my hand into my backpack. The only thing I found was a clump of wax. I didn't have time to build a proper *shabti*, but I had no better idea. I dropped my pack and started working the wax furiously with both hands, trying to soften it.

"Percy?" I called.

"I can't unlock the clasp!" he yelled. I didn't dare take my eyes off the croc's, but in my peripheral vision I could see Percy pounding his fist against the base of the necklace. "Some kind of magic?"

That was the smartest thing he'd said all afternoon (not that he'd said a lot of smart things to choose from). The clasp was a hieroglyphic cartouche. It would take a magician to figure it out and open it. Whatever and whoever Percy was, he was no magician.

I was still shaping the clump of wax, trying to make it into a figurine, when the crocodile decided to stop savoring the moment and just eat me. As he lunged, I threw my *shabti*, only half formed, and barked a command word.

Instantly the world's most deformed hippopotamus sprang to life in midair. It sailed headfirst into the crocodile's left nostril and lodged there, kicking its stubby back legs.

Not exactly my finest tactical move; but having a hippo shoved up his nose must have been sufficiently distracting. The crocodile hissed and stumbled, shaking his head, as Percy dropped off and rolled away, barely avoiding the crocodile's stomping feet. He ran to join me at the curb.

I stared in horror as my wax creature, now a living (though very misshapen) hippo, either tried to wriggle free of the croc's nostril or work its way farther into the reptile's sinus cavity—I wasn't sure which.

The crocodile whipped around, and Percy grabbed me just in time, pulling me out of its trampling path.

We jogged to the opposite end of the cul-de-sac, where the mortal kids had gathered. Amazingly, none of them seemed to be hurt. The crocodile kept thrashing and wiping out homes as it tried to clear its nostril.

"You okay?" Percy asked me.

I gasped for air but nodded weakly.

One of the kids offered me his Super Soaker. I waved him off.

"You guys," Percy told the kids, "you hear those sirens? You've got to run down the road and stop the police. Tell them it's too dangerous up here. Stall them!"

For some reason, the kids listened. Maybe they were just happy to have something to do, but the way Percy spoke, I got the feeling he was used to rallying outnumbered troops. He sounded a bit like Horus—a natural commander.

After the kids raced off, I managed to say, "Good call."

Percy nodded grimly. The crocodile was still distracted by its nasal intruder, but I doubted the *shabti* would last much longer. Under that much stress, the hippo would soon melt back to wax.

"You've got some moves, Carter," Percy admitted. "Anything else in your bag of tricks?"

"Nothing," I said dismally. "I'm running on empty. But if I can get to that clasp, I think I can open it."

Percy sized up the *petsuchos*. The cul-de-sac was filling with water that poured from the monster's hide. The sirens were getting louder. We didn't have much time.

"Guess it's my turn to distract the croc," he said. "Get ready to run for that necklace."

"You don't even have your sword," I protested. "You'll die!"

Percy managed a crooked smile. "Just run in there as soon as it starts."

"As soon as *what* starts?"

Then the crocodile sneezed, launching the wax hippo across Long Island. The *petsuchos* turned toward us, roaring in anger, and Percy charged straight at him.

As it turned out, I didn't need to ask what kind of distraction Percy had in mind. Once it started, it was pretty obvious.

He stopped in front of the crocodile and raised his arms. I figured he was planning some kind of magic, but he spoke no command words. He had no staff or wand. He just stood there and looked up at the crocodile as if to say: *Here I am! I'm tasty!*

The crocodile seemed momentarily surprised. If nothing else, we would die knowing that we'd confused this monster many, many times.

Croc sweat kept pouring off his body. The brackish stuff was up to the curb now, up to our ankles. It sloughed into the storm drains but just kept spilling from the croc's skin.

Then I saw what was happening. As Percy raised his arms, the water began swirling counterclockwise. It started around the croc's feet and quickly built speed until the whirlpool encompassed the entire cul-de-sac, spinning strongly enough so that I could feel it pulling me sideways.

By the time I realized I'd better start running, the current was already too fast. I'd have to reach the necklace some other way.

One last trick, I thought.

I feared the effort might literally burn me up, but I summoned my final bit of magical energy and transformed into a falcon—the sacred animal of Horus.

Instantly, my vision was a hundred times sharper. I soared upward, above the rooftops, and the entire world switched to high-definition 3-D. I saw the police cars only a few blocks away, the kids standing in the middle of the street, waving them down. I could make out every slimy bump and pore on the crocodile's hide. I could see each hieroglyph on the clasp of the necklace. And I could see just how impressive Percy's magic trick was.

The entire cul-de-sac was engulfed in a hurricane. Percy stood at the edge, unmoved, but the water was churning so fast now that even the giant crocodile lost his footing. Wrecked cars scraped along the pavement. Mailboxes were pulled out of lawns and swept away. The water increased in volume as well as speed, rising up and turning the entire neighborhood into a liquid centrifuge.

It was my turn to be stunned. A few moments ago, I'd decided Percy was no magician. Yet I'd never seen a magician who could control so much water.

The crocodile stumbled and struggled, shuffling in a circle with the current.

"Any time now," Percy muttered through gritted teeth. Without my falcon hearing, I never would've heard him through the storm, but I realized he was talking to me.

I remembered I had a job to do. No one, magician or otherwise, could control that kind of power for long.

I folded my wings and dove for the crocodile. When I reached the necklace's clasp, I turned back to human and grabbed hold. All around me, the hurricane roared. I could barely see through the swirl of mist. The current was so strong now, it tugged at my legs, threatening to pull me into the flood.

I was *so* tired. I hadn't felt this pushed beyond my limits since I'd fought the Chaos lord, Apophis himself.

I ran my hand over the hieroglyphs on the clasp. There had to be a secret to unlocking it.

The crocodile bellowed and stomped, fighting to stay on its feet. Somewhere to my left, Percy yelled in rage and frustration, trying to keep up the storm; but the whirlpool was starting to slow.

I had a few seconds at best until the crocodile broke free and attacked. Then Percy and I would both be dead.

I felt the four symbols that made up the god's name:

The last symbol didn't actually represent a sound, I knew. It was the hieroglyph for *god*, indicating that the letters in front of it—*SBK*—stood for a deity's name.

When in doubt, I thought, *hit the god button.*

I pushed on the fourth symbol, but nothing happened.

The storm was failing. The crocodile started to turn against the current, facing Percy. Out of the corner of my eye, through the haze and mist, I saw Percy drop to one knee.

My fingers passed over the third hieroglyph—the wicker basket (Sadie always called it the "teacup") that stood for the *K* sound. The hieroglyph felt slightly warm to the touch—or was that my imagination?

No time to think. I pressed it. Nothing happened.

The storm died. The crocodile bellowed in triumph, ready to feed.

I made a fist and slammed the basket hieroglyph with all my strength. This time the clasp made a satisfying *click* and sprang open. I dropped to the pavement, and several hundred pounds of gold and gems spilled on top of me.

The crocodile staggered, roaring like the guns of a battleship. What was left of the hurricane scattered in an explosion of wind, and I shut my eyes, ready to be smashed flat by the body of a falling monster.

Suddenly, the cul-de-sac was silent. No sirens. No crocodile roaring. The mound of gold jewelry disappeared. I was lying on my back in mucky water, staring up at the empty blue sky.

Percy's face appeared above me. He looked like he'd just run a marathon through a typhoon, but he was grinning.

"Nice work," he said. "Get the necklace."

"The necklace?" My brain still felt sluggish. Where had all that gold gone? I sat up and put my hand on the pavement. My fingers closed around the strand of jewelry, now normal-size . . . well, at least *normal* for something that could fit around the neck of an average crocodile.

"The—the monster," I stammered. "Where—?"

Percy pointed. A few feet away, looking very disgruntled, stood a baby crocodile not more than three feet long.

"You can't be serious," I said.

"Maybe somebody's abandoned pet?" Percy shrugged. "You hear about those on the news sometimes."

I couldn't think of a better explanation, but how had a baby croc gotten hold of a necklace that turned him into a giant killing machine?

Down the street, voices started yelling: "Up here! There's these two guys!"

It was the mortal kids. Apparently they'd decided the danger was over. Now they were leading the police straight toward us.

"We have to go." Percy scooped up the baby crocodile, clenching one hand around his little snout. He looked at me. "You coming?"

Together, we ran back to the swamp.

Half an hour later, we were sitting in a diner off the Montauk Highway. I'd shared the rest of my healing potion with Percy, who for some reason insisted on calling it *nectar*. Most of our wounds had healed.

We'd tied the crocodile out in the woods on a makeshift leash, just until we could figure out what to do with it. We'd cleaned up as best we could, but we still looked like we'd taken a shower in a malfunctioning car wash. Percy's hair was swept to one side and tangled with pieces of grass. His orange shirt was ripped down the front.

I'm sure I didn't look much better. I had water in my shoes, and I was still picking falcon feathers out of my shirtsleeves (hasty transformations can be messy).

We were too exhausted to talk as we watched the news on the television above the counter. Police and firefighters had responded to a freak sewer event in a local neighborhood. Apparently pressure had built up in the drainage pipes, causing a massive explosion that unleashed a flood and eroded the soil so badly, several houses on the cul-de-sac had collapsed. It was a miracle that no residents had been injured. Local kids were telling some wild stories about the Long Island Swamp Monster, claiming it had caused all the damage during a fight with two teenage boys; but of course the officials didn't believe this. The reporter admitted, however, that the damaged houses looked like "something very large had sat on them."

"A freak sewer accident," Percy said. "That's a first."

"For you, maybe," I grumbled. "I seem to cause them everywhere I go."

"Cheer up," he said. "Lunch is on me."

He dug into the pockets of his jeans and pulled out a ballpoint pen. Nothing else.

"Oh . . ." His smile faded. "Uh, actually . . . can you conjure up money?"

So, naturally, lunch was on *me*. I *could* pull money out of thin air, since I kept some stored in the Duat along with my other emergency supplies; so in no time we had cheeseburgers and fries in front of us, and life was looking up.

"Cheeseburgers," Percy said. "Food of the gods."

"Agreed," I said, but when I glanced over at him, I wondered if he was thinking the same thing I was: that we were referring to *different* gods.

Percy inhaled his burger. Seriously, this guy could eat. "So, the necklace," he said between bites. "What's the story?"

I hesitated. I still had no clue where Percy came from or what he was, and I wasn't sure I wanted to ask. Now that we'd fought together, I couldn't help but trust him. Still, I sensed we were treading on dangerous ground. Everything we said could have serious implications—not just for the two of us, but maybe for everyone we knew.

I felt sort of like I had two winters ago, when my uncle Amos explained the truth about the Kane family heritage—the House of Life, the Egyptian gods, the Duat, everything. In a single day, my world expanded tenfold and left me reeling.

Now I was standing at the edge of another moment like that. But if my world expanded tenfold *again*, I was afraid my brain might explode.

"The necklace is enchanted," I said at last. "Any reptile that wears it turns into the next *petsuchos*, the Son of Sobek. Somehow that little crocodile got it around his neck."

"Meaning someone *put* it around his neck," Percy said.

I didn't want to think about that, but I nodded reluctantly.

"So who?" he asked.

"Hard to narrow it down," I said. "I've got a lot of enemies."

Percy snorted. "I can relate to that. Any idea *why*, then?"

I took another bite of my cheeseburger. It was good, but I had trouble concentrating on it.

"Someone wanted to cause trouble," I speculated. "I think maybe . . ." I studied Percy, trying to judge how much I should say. "Maybe they wanted to cause trouble that would get our attention. *Both* of our attention."

Percy frowned. He drew something in his ketchup with a french fry—not a hieroglyph. Some kind of non-English letter. Greek, I guessed.

"The monster had a Greek name," he said. "It was eating pegasi in my . . ." He hesitated.

"In your home turf," I finished. "Some kind of camp, judging from your shirt."

He shifted on his bar stool. I still couldn't believe he was talking about pegasi as if they were real, but I remembered one time at Brooklyn House, maybe a year back, when I was certain I saw a winged horse flying over the Manhattan skyline. At the time, Sadie had told me I was hallucinating. Now, I wasn't so sure.

Finally Percy faced me. "Look, Carter. You're not nearly as annoying as I thought. And we made a good team today, but—"

"You don't want to share your secrets," I said. "Don't worry. I'm not going to ask about your camp. Or the powers you have. Or any of that."

He raised an eyebrow. "You're not curious?"

"I'm *totally* curious. But until we figure out what's going on, I think it's best we keep some distance. If someone—*something*—unleashed that monster here, knowing it would draw both of our attention—"

"Then maybe that someone wanted us to meet," he finished. "Hoping bad things would happen."

I nodded. I thought about the uneasy feeling I'd had in my gut earlier—the voice in my head warning me not to tell Percy anything. I'd come to respect the guy, but I still sensed that we weren't meant to be friends. We weren't meant to be anywhere *close* to each other.

A long time ago, when I was just a little kid, I'd watched my mom do a science experiment with some her college students.

Potassium and water, she'd told them. *Separate, completely harmless. But together—*

She dropped the potassium in a beaker of water, and *Ka-blam!* The students jumped back as a miniature explosion rattled all the vials in the lab.

Percy was water. I was potassium.

"But we've met now," Percy said. "You know I'm out here on Long Island. I know you live in Brooklyn. If we went searching for each other—"

"I wouldn't recommend it," I said. "Not until we know more. I need to look into some things on, uh, my side—try to figure out who was behind this crocodile incident."

"All right," Percy agreed. "I'll do the same on my side."

He pointed at the *petsuchos* necklace, which was glinting just inside my backpack. "What do we do about that?"

"I can send it somewhere safe," I promised. "It won't cause trouble again. We deal with relics like this a lot."

"*We*," Percy said. "Meaning, there's a lot of . . . you guys?"

I didn't answer.

Percy put up his hands. "Fine. I didn't ask. I have some friends back at Ca— uh, back on my side who would love tinkering with a magic necklace like that; but I'm going to trust you here. Take it."

I didn't realize I'd been holding my breath until I exhaled. "Thanks. Good."

"And the baby crocodile?" he asked.

I managed a nervous laugh. "You want it?"

"Gods, no."

"I can take it, give it a good home." I thought about our big pool at Brooklyn House. I wondered how our giant magic crocodile, Philip of Macedonia, would feel about having a little friend. "Yeah, it'll fit right in."

Percy didn't seem to know what to think of that. "Okay, well . . ." He held out his hand. "Good working with you, Carter."

We shook. No sparks flew. No thunder boomed. But I still couldn't escape the feeling that we'd opened a door, meeting like this—a door that we might not be able to close.

"You too, Percy."

He stood to go. "One more thing," he said. "If this somebody, whoever threw us together . . . if he's an enemy to both of us— what if we *need* each other to fight him? How do I contact you?"

I considered that. Then I made a snap decision. "Can I write something on your hand?"

He frowned. "Like your phone number?"

"Uh . . . well, not exactly." I took out my stylus and a vial of magic ink. Percy held out his palm. I drew a hieroglyph there—the Eye of Horus. As soon as the symbol was complete it flared blue, then vanished.

"Just say my name," I told him, "and I'll hear you. I'll know where you are, and I'll come meet you. But it will only work once, so make it count."

Percy considered his empty palm. "So I'm trusting you that this isn't some type of magical tracking device."

"Yeah," I said. "And I'm trusting that when you call me, you won't be luring me into some sort of ambush."

He stared at me. Those stormy green eyes really were kind of scary. Then he smiled, and he looked like a regular teenager, without a care in the world.

"Fair enough," he said. "See you when I see you, C—"

"Don't say my name!"

"Just teasing." He pointed at me and winked. "Stay strange, my friend."

Then he was gone.

An hour later, I was back aboard my airborne boat with the baby crocodile and the magic necklace as Freak flew me home to Brooklyn House.

Now, looking back on it, the whole thing with Percy seems so unreal, I can hardly believe it actually happened.

I wonder how Percy summoned that whirlpool, and what the heck *Celestial bronze* is. Most of all, I keep rolling one word around in my mind: *demigod*.

I have a feeling that I could find some answers if I looked hard enough, but I'm afraid of what I might discover.

For the time being, I think I'll tell Sadie about this and no one else. At first she'll think I'm kidding. And, of course, she'll give me grief; but she also knows when I'm telling the truth. As annoying as she is, I trust her (though I would never say that to her face).

Maybe she'll have some ideas about what we should do.

Whoever brought Percy and me together, whoever orchestrated our crossing paths . . . it smacks of Chaos. I can't help thinking this was an experiment to see what kind of havoc would result. Potassium and water. Matter and antimatter.

Fortunately, things turned out okay. The *petsuchos* necklace is safely locked away. Our new baby crocodile is splashing around happily in our pool.

But next time . . . Well, I'm afraid we might not be so lucky.

Somewhere there's a kid named Percy with a secret hieroglyph on his hand. And I have a feeling that sooner or later I'll wake up in the middle of the night and hear one word, spoken urgently in my mind:

Carter.

THE
HEROES OF
OLYMPUS

THE LOST HERO

THE HEROES OF OLYMPUS

Book One: *The Lost Hero*

Book Two: *The Son of Neptune*

Book Three: *The Mark of Athena*

Book Four: *The House of Hades*

Book Five: *The Blood of Olympus*

The Demigod Diaries

The Lost Hero: The Graphic Novel

The Son of Neptune: The Graphic Novel

Demigods & Magicians

MAGNUS CHASE AND THE GODS OF ASGARD

Book One: *The Sword of Summer*

Book Two: *The Hammer of Thor*

Book Three: *The Ship of the Dead*

For Magnus Chase: Hotel Valhalla Guide to the Norse Worlds

9 from the Nine Worlds

THE TRIALS OF APOLLO

Book One: *The Hidden Oracle*

Book Two: *The Dark Prophecy*

Book Three: *The Burning Maze*

Book Four: *The Tyrant's Tomb*

RICK RIORDAN

THE HEROES OF OLYMPUS

I

THE LOST HERO

Disney · HYPERION

Los Angeles   New York

First Hardcover Edition, October 2010
First Paperback Edition, April 2012
New Paperback Edition, September 2019
10 9 8 7 6 5 4 3 2 1
FAC-025438-19221
Printed in the United States of America

This book is set in Adobe Caslon Pro, Trajan Pro 3/Fontspring
Designed by Joann Hill

Library of Congress Control Number for the
Hardcover Edition: 2010015469
ISBN 978-1-368-05143-9

SUSTAINABLE
FORESTRY
INITIATIVE
Certified Chain of Custody
Promoting Sustainable Forestry
www.sfiprogram.org
SFI-01054
The SFI label applies to the text stock

Visit www.DisneyBooks.com
Follow @ReadRiordan

For Haley and Patrick, always the first to hear stories.
Without them, Camp Half-Blood would not exist.

THE HEROES OF OLYMPUS

THE LOST HERO

JASON

EVEN BEFORE HE GOT ELECTROCUTED, Jason was having a rotten day.

He woke in the backseat of a school bus, not sure where he was, holding hands with a girl he didn't know. That wasn't necessarily the rotten part. The girl was cute, but he couldn't figure out who she was or what he was doing there. He sat up and rubbed his eyes, trying to think.

A few dozen kids sprawled in the seats in front of him, listening to iPods, talking, or sleeping. They all looked around his age…fifteen? Sixteen? Okay, that was scary. He didn't know his own age.

The bus rumbled along a bumpy road. Out the windows, desert rolled by under a bright blue sky. Jason was pretty sure he didn't live in the desert. He tried to think back…the last thing he remembered…

The girl squeezed his hand. "Jason, you okay?"

She wore faded jeans, hiking boots, and a fleece

snowboarding jacket. Her chocolate brown hair was cut choppy and uneven, with thin strands braided down the sides. She wore no makeup like she was trying not to draw attention to herself, but it didn't work. She was seriously pretty. Her eyes seemed to change color like a kaleidoscope—brown, blue, and green.

Jason let go of her hand. "Um, I don't—"

In the front of the bus, a teacher shouted, "All right, cupcakes, listen up!"

The guy was obviously a coach. His baseball cap was pulled low over his hair, so you could just see his beady eyes. He had a wispy goatee and a sour face, like he'd eaten something moldy. His buff arms and chest pushed against a bright orange polo shirt. His nylon workout pants and Nikes were spotless white. A whistle hung from his neck, and a megaphone was clipped to his belt. He would've looked pretty scary if he hadn't been five feet zero. When he stood up in the aisle, one of the students called, "Stand up, Coach Hedge!"

"I heard that!" The coach scanned the bus for the offender. Then his eyes fixed on Jason, and his scowl deepened.

A jolt went down Jason's spine. He was sure the coach knew he didn't belong there. He was going to call Jason out, demand to know what he was doing on the bus—and Jason wouldn't have a clue what to say.

But Coach Hedge looked away and cleared his throat. "We'll arrive in five minutes! Stay with your partner. Don't lose your worksheet. And if any of you precious little cupcakes causes any trouble on this trip, I will personally send you back to campus the hard way."

He picked up a baseball bat and made like he was hitting a homer.

Jason looked at the girl next to him. "Can he talk to us that way?"

She shrugged. "Always does. This is the Wilderness School. 'Where kids are the animals.'"

She said it like it was a joke they'd shared before.

"This is some kind of mistake," Jason said. "I'm not supposed to be here."

The boy in front of him turned and laughed. "Yeah, right, Jason. We've all been framed! I didn't run away six times. Piper didn't steal a BMW."

The girl blushed. "I didn't steal that car, Leo!"

"Oh, I forgot, Piper. What was your story? You 'talked' the dealer into lending it to you?" He raised his eyebrows at Jason like, *Can you believe her?*

Leo looked like a Latino Santa's elf, with curly black hair, pointy ears, a cheerful, babyish face, and a mischievous smile that told you right away this guy should not be trusted around matches or sharp objects. His long, nimble fingers wouldn't stop moving—drumming on the seat, sweeping his hair behind his ears, fiddling with the buttons of his army fatigue jacket. Either the kid was naturally hyper or he was hopped up on enough sugar and caffeine to give a heart attack to a water buffalo.

"Anyway," Leo said, "I hope you've got your worksheet, 'cause I used mine for spit wads days ago. Why are you looking at me like that? Somebody draw on my face again?"

"I don't know you," Jason said.

Leo gave him a crocodile grin. "Sure. I'm not your best friend. I'm his evil clone."

"Leo Valdez!" Coach Hedge yelled from the front. "Problem back there?"

Leo winked at Jason. "Watch this." He turned to the front. "Sorry, Coach! I was having trouble hearing you. Could you use your megaphone, please?"

Coach Hedge grunted like he was pleased to have an excuse. He unclipped the megaphone from his belt and continued giving directions, but his voice came out like Darth Vader's. The kids cracked up. The coach tried again, but this time the megaphone blared: "The cow says moo!"

The kids howled, and the coach slammed down the megaphone. "Valdez!"

Piper stifled a laugh. "My god, Leo. How did you do that?"

Leo slipped a tiny Phillips head screwdriver from his sleeve. "I'm a special boy."

"Guys, seriously," Jason pleaded. "What am I doing here? Where are we going?"

Piper knit her eyebrows. "Jason, are you joking?"

"No! I have no idea—"

"Aw, yeah, he's joking," Leo said. "He's trying to get me back for that shaving cream on the Jell-O thing, aren't you?"

Jason stared at him blankly.

"No, I think he's serious." Piper tried to take his hand again, but he pulled it away.

"I'm sorry," he said. "I don't—I can't—"

"That's it!" Coach Hedge yelled from the front. "The back row has just volunteered to clean up after lunch!"

The rest of the kids cheered.

"There's a shocker," Leo muttered.

But Piper kept her eyes on Jason, like she couldn't decide whether to be hurt or worried. "Did you hit your head or something? You really don't know who we are?"

Jason shrugged helplessly. "It's worse than that. I don't know who *I* am."

The bus dropped them in front of a big red stucco complex like a museum, just sitting in the middle of nowhere. Maybe that's what it was: the National Museum of Nowhere, Jason thought. A cold wind blew across the desert. Jason hadn't paid much attention to what he was wearing, but it wasn't nearly warm enough: jeans and sneakers, a purple T-shirt, and a thin black windbreaker.

"So, a crash course for the amnesiac," Leo said, in a helpful tone that made Jason think this was not going to be helpful. "We go to the 'Wilderness School'"—Leo made air quotes with his fingers. "Which means we're 'bad kids.' Your family, or the court, or whoever, decided you were too much trouble, so they shipped you off to this lovely prison—sorry, 'boarding school'—in Armpit, Nevada, where you learn valuable nature skills like running ten miles a day through the cacti and weaving daisies into hats! And for a special treat we go on 'educational' field trips with Coach Hedge, who keeps order with a baseball bat. Is it all coming back to you now?"

"No." Jason glanced apprehensively at the other kids: maybe twenty guys, half that many girls. None of them looked like hardened criminals, but he wondered what they'd all done to get sentenced to a school for delinquents, and he wondered why he belonged with them.

Leo rolled his eyes. "You're really gonna play this out, huh? Okay, so the three of us started here together this semester. We're totally tight. You do everything I say and give me your dessert and do my chores—"

"Leo!" Piper snapped.

"Fine. Ignore that last part. But we *are* friends. Well, Piper's a little more than your friend, the last few weeks—"

"Leo, stop it!" Piper's face turned red. Jason could feel his face burning too. He thought he'd remember if he'd been going out with a girl like Piper.

"He's got amnesia or something," Piper said. "We've got to tell somebody."

Leo scoffed. "Who, Coach Hedge? He'd try to fix Jason by whacking him upside the head."

The coach was at the front of the group, barking orders and blowing his whistle to keep the kids in line; but every so often he'd glance back at Jason and scowl.

"Leo, Jason needs help," Piper insisted. "He's got a concussion or—"

"Yo, Piper." One of the other guys dropped back to join them as the group was heading into the museum. The new guy wedged himself between Jason and Piper and knocked Leo down. "Don't talk to these bottom-feeders. You're my partner, remember?"

The new guy had dark hair cut Superman style, a deep tan, and teeth so white they should've come with a warning label: DO NOT STARE DIRECTLY AT TEETH. PERMANENT BLINDNESS

MAY OCCUR. He wore a Dallas Cowboys jersey, Western jeans and boots, and he smiled like he was God's gift to juvenile delinquent girls everywhere. Jason hated him instantly.

"Go away, Dylan," Piper grumbled. "I didn't ask to work with you."

"Ah, that's no way to be. This is your lucky day!" Dylan hooked his arm through hers and dragged her through the museum entrance. Piper shot one last look over her shoulder like, *911.*

Leo got up and brushed himself off. "I hate that guy." He offered Jason his arm, like they should go skipping inside together. "'I'm Dylan. I'm so cool, I want to date myself, but I can't figure out how! You want to date me instead? You're so lucky!'"

"Leo," Jason said, "you're weird."

"Yeah, you tell me that a lot." Leo grinned. "But if you don't remember me, that means I can reuse all my old jokes. Come on!"

Jason figured that if this was his best friend, his life must be pretty messed up; but he followed Leo into the museum.

They walked through the building, stopping here and there for Coach Hedge to lecture them with his megaphone, which alternately made him sound like a Sith Lord or blared out random comments like "The pig says oink."

Leo kept pulling out nuts, bolts, and pipe cleaners from the pockets of his army jacket and putting them together, like he had to keep his hands busy at all times.

Jason was too distracted to pay much attention to the

exhibits, but they were about the Grand Canyon and the Hualapai tribe, which owned the museum.

Some girls kept looking over at Piper and Dylan and snickering. Jason figured these girls were the popular clique. They wore matching jeans and pink tops and enough makeup for a Halloween party.

One of them said, "Hey, Piper, does your tribe run this place? Do you get in free if you do a rain dance?"

The other girls laughed. Even Piper's so-called partner Dylan suppressed a smile. Piper's snowboarding jacket sleeves hid her hands, but Jason got the feeling she was clenching her fists.

"My dad's Cherokee," she said. "Not Hualapai. 'Course, you'd need a few brain cells to know the difference, Isabel."

Isabel widened her eyes in mock surprise, so that she looked like an owl with a makeup addiction. "Oh, sorry! Was your *mom* in this tribe? Oh, that's right. You never knew your mom."

Piper charged her, but before a fight could start, Coach Hedge barked, "Enough back there! Set a good example or I'll break out my baseball bat!"

The group shuffled on to the next exhibit, but the girls kept calling out little comments to Piper.

"Good to be back on the rez?" one asked in a sweet voice.

"Dad's probably too drunk to work," another said with fake sympathy. "That's why she turned klepto."

Piper ignored them, but Jason was ready to punch them himself. He might not remember Piper, or even who he was, but he knew he hated mean kids.

Leo caught his arm. "Be cool. Piper doesn't like us fighting her battles. Besides, if those girls found out the truth about her dad, they'd be all bowing down to her and screaming, 'We're not worthy!'"

"Why? What about her dad?"

Leo laughed in disbelief. "You're not kidding? You really don't remember that your girlfriend's dad—"

"Look, I wish I did, but I don't even remember *her*, much less her dad."

Leo whistled. "Whatever. We *have* to talk when we get back to the dorm."

They reached the far end of the exhibit hall, where some big glass doors led out to a terrace.

"All right, cupcakes," Coach Hedge announced. "You are about to see the Grand Canyon. Try not to break it. The skywalk can hold the weight of seventy jumbo jets, so you featherweights should be safe out there. If possible, try to avoid pushing each other over the edge, as that would cause me extra paperwork."

The coach opened the doors, and they all stepped outside. The Grand Canyon spread before them, live and in person. Extending over the edge was a horseshoe-shaped walkway made of glass, so you could see right through it.

"Man," Leo said. "That's pretty wicked."

Jason had to agree. Despite his amnesia and his feeling that he didn't belong there, he couldn't help being impressed.

The canyon was bigger and wider than you could appreciate from a picture. They were up so high that birds circled below their feet. Five hundred feet down, a river snaked along the canyon floor. Banks of storm clouds had moved overhead while they'd been inside, casting shadows like angry faces across the cliffs. As far as Jason could see in any direction, red and gray ravines cut through the desert like some crazy god had taken a knife to it.

Jason got a piercing pain behind his eyes. *Crazy gods...* Where had he come up with that idea? He felt like he'd gotten close to something important—something he should know about. He also got the unmistakable feeling he was in danger.

"You all right?" Leo asked. "You're not going to throw up over the side, are you? 'Cause I should've brought my camera."

Jason grabbed the railing. He was shivering and sweaty, but it had nothing to do with heights. He blinked, and the pain behind his eyes subsided.

"I'm fine," he managed. "Just a headache."

Thunder rumbled overhead. A cold wind almost knocked him sideways.

"This can't be safe." Leo squinted at the clouds. "Storm's right over us, but it's clear all the way around. Weird, huh?"

Jason looked up and saw Leo was right. A dark circle of clouds had parked itself over the skywalk, but the rest of the sky in every direction was perfectly clear. Jason had a bad feeling about that.

"All right, cupcakes!" Coach Hedge yelled. He frowned at the storm like it bothered him too. "We may have to cut this short, so get to work! Remember, complete sentences!"

The storm rumbled, and Jason's head began to hurt again. Not knowing why he did it, he reached into his jeans pocket and brought out a coin—a circle of gold the size of a half-dollar, but thicker and more uneven. Stamped on one side was a picture of a battle-ax. On the other was some guy's face wreathed in laurels. The inscription said something like IVLIVS.

"Dang, is that gold?" Leo asked. "You been holding out on me!"

Jason put the coin away, wondering how he'd come to have it, and why he had the feeling he was going to need it soon.

"It's nothing," he said. "Just a coin."

Leo shrugged. Maybe his mind had to keep moving as much as his hands. "Come on," he said. "Dare you to spit over the edge."

They didn't try very hard on the worksheet. For one thing, Jason was too distracted by the storm and his own mixed-up feelings. For another thing, he didn't have any idea how to "name three sedimentary strata you observe" or "describe two examples of erosion."

Leo was no help. He was too busy building a helicopter out of pipe cleaners.

"Check it out." He launched the copter. Jason figured it would plummet, but the pipe-cleaner blades actually spun. The little copter made it halfway across the canyon before it lost momentum and spiraled into the void.

"How'd you do that?" Jason asked.

Leo shrugged. "Would've been cooler if I had some rubber bands."

"Seriously," Jason said, "are we friends?"

"Last I checked."

"You sure? What was the first day we met? What did we talk about?"

"It was..." Leo frowned. "I don't recall exactly. I'm ADHD, man. You can't expect me to remember details."

"But I don't remember you *at all*. I don't remember anyone here. What if—"

"You're right and everyone else is wrong?" Leo asked. "You think you just appeared here this morning, and we've all got fake memories of you?"

A little voice in Jason's head said, *That's exactly what I think.*

But it sounded crazy. Everybody here took him for granted. Everyone acted like he was a normal part of the class—except for Coach Hedge.

"Take the worksheet." Jason handed Leo the paper. "I'll be right back."

Before Leo could protest, Jason headed across the skywalk.

Their school group had the place to themselves. Maybe it was too early in the day for tourists, or maybe the weird weather had scared them off. The Wilderness School kids had spread out in pairs across the skywalk. Most were joking around or talking. Some of the guys were dropping pennies over the side. About fifty feet away, Piper was trying to fill out her worksheet, but her stupid partner Dylan was hitting on her, putting his hand on her shoulder and giving her that blinding white smile. She kept pushing him away, and when she saw Jason she gave him a look like, *Throttle this guy for me.*

Jason motioned for her to hang on. He walked up to Coach Hedge, who was leaning on his baseball bat, studying the storm clouds.

"Did you do this?" the coach asked him.

Jason took a step back. "Do what?" It sounded like the coach had just asked if he'd made the thunderstorm.

Coach Hedge glared at him, his beady little eyes glinting under the brim of his cap. "Don't play games with me, kid. What are you doing here, and why are you messing up my job?"

"You mean . . . you *don't* know me?" Jason said. "I'm not one of your students?"

Hedge snorted. "Never seen you before today."

Jason was so relieved he almost wanted to cry. At least he wasn't going insane. He *was* in the wrong place. "Look, sir, I don't know how I got here. I just woke up on the school bus. All I know is I'm not supposed to be here."

"Got that right." Hedge's gruff voice dropped to a murmur, like he was sharing a secret. "You got a powerful way with the Mist, kid, if you can make all these people think they know you; but you can't fool me. I've been smelling monster for days now. I knew we had an infiltrator, but you don't smell like a monster. You smell like a half-blood. So—who are you, and where'd you come from?"

Most of what the coach said didn't make sense, but Jason decided to answer honestly. "I don't know who I am. I don't have any memories. You've got to help me."

Coach Hedge studied his face like he was trying to read Jason's thoughts.

"Great," Hedge muttered. "You're being truthful."

"Of course I am! And what was all that about monsters and half-bloods? Are those code words or something?"

Hedge narrowed his eyes. Part of Jason wondered if the guy was just nuts. But the other part knew better.

"Look, kid," Hedge said, "I don't know who you are. I just know *what* you are, and it means trouble. Now I got to protect three of you rather than two. Are you the special package? Is that it?"

"What are you talking about?"

Hedge looked at the storm. The clouds were getting thicker and darker, hovering right over the skywalk.

"This morning," Hedge said, "I got a message from camp. They said an extraction team is on the way. They're coming to pick up a special package, but they wouldn't give me details. I thought to myself, Fine. The two I'm watching are pretty powerful, older than most. I know they're being stalked. I can smell a monster in the group. I figure that's why the camp is suddenly frantic to pick them up. But then *you* pop up out of nowhere. So, are you the special package?"

The pain behind Jason's eyes got worse than ever. *Half-bloods. Camp. Monsters.* He still didn't know what Hedge was talking about, but the words gave him a massive brain freeze—like his mind was trying to access information that should've been there but wasn't.

He stumbled, and Coach Hedge caught him. For a short guy, the coach had hands like steel. "Whoa, there, cupcake. You say you got no memories, huh? Fine. I'll just have to watch you, too, until the team gets here. We'll let the director figure things out."

"What director?" Jason said. "What camp?"

"Just sit tight. Reinforcements should be here soon. Hopefully nothing happens before—"

Lightning crackled overhead. The wind picked up with a vengeance. Worksheets flew into the Grand Canyon, and the entire bridge shuddered. Kids screamed, stumbling and grabbing the rails.

"I had to say something," Hedge grumbled. He bellowed into his megaphone: "Everyone inside! The cow says moo! Off the skywalk!"

"I thought you said this thing was stable!" Jason shouted over the wind.

"Under normal circumstances," Hedge agreed, "which these aren't. Come on!"

JASON

THE STORM CHURNED INTO A MINIATURE HURRICANE. Funnel clouds snaked toward the skywalk like the tendrils of a monster jellyfish.

Kids screamed and ran for the building. The wind snatched away their notebooks, jackets, hats, and backpacks. Jason skidded across the slick floor.

Leo lost his balance and almost toppled over the railing, but Jason grabbed his jacket and pulled him back.

"Thanks, man!" Leo yelled.

"Go, go, go!" said Coach Hedge.

Piper and Dylan were holding the doors open, herding the other kids inside. Piper's snowboarding jacket was flapping wildly, her dark hair all in her face. Jason thought she must've been freezing, but she looked calm and confident—telling the others it would be okay, encouraging them to keep moving.

Jason, Leo, and Coach Hedge ran toward them, but it was

like running through quicksand. The wind seemed to fight them, pushing them back.

Dylan and Piper pushed one more kid inside, then lost their grip on the doors. They slammed shut, closing off the skywalk.

Piper tugged at the handles. Inside, the kids pounded on the glass, but the doors seemed to be stuck.

"Dylan, help!" Piper shouted.

Dylan just stood there with an idiotic grin, his Cowboys jersey rippling in the wind, like he was suddenly enjoying the storm.

"Sorry, Piper," he said. "I'm done helping."

He flicked his wrist, and Piper flew backward, slamming into the doors and sliding to the skywalk deck.

"Piper!" Jason tried to charge forward, but the wind was against him, and Coach Hedge pushed him back.

"Coach," Jason said, "let me go!"

"Jason, Leo, stay behind me," the coach ordered. "This is my fight. I should've known that was our monster."

"What?" Leo demanded. A rogue worksheet slapped him in the face, but he swatted it away. "What monster?"

The coach's cap blew off, and sticking up above his curly hair were two bumps—like the knots cartoon characters get when they're bonked on the head. Coach Hedge lifted his baseball bat—but it wasn't a regular bat anymore. Somehow it had changed into a crudely shaped tree-branch club, with twigs and leaves still attached.

Dylan gave him that psycho happy smile. "Oh, come on,

Coach. Let the boy attack me! After all, you're getting too old for this. Isn't that why they *retired* you to this stupid school? I've been on your team the entire season, and you didn't even know. You're losing your nose, grandpa."

The coach made an angry sound like an animal bleating. "That's it, cupcake. You're going down."

"You think you can protect three half-bloods at once, old man?" Dylan laughed. "Good luck."

Dylan pointed at Leo, and a funnel cloud materialized around him. Leo flew off the skywalk like he'd been tossed. Somehow he managed to twist in midair, and slammed sideways into the canyon wall. He skidded, clawing furiously for any handhold. Finally he grabbed a thin ledge about fifty feet below the skywalk and hung there by his fingertips.

"Help!" he yelled up at them. "Rope, please? Bungee cord? Something?"

Coach Hedge cursed and tossed Jason his club. "I don't know who you are, kid, but I hope you're good. Keep that *thing* busy"—he stabbed a thumb at Dylan—"while I get Leo."

"Get him how?" Jason demanded. "You going to fly?"

"Not fly. Climb." Hedge kicked off his shoes, and Jason almost had a coronary. The coach didn't have any feet. He had hooves—goat's hooves. Which meant those things on his head, Jason realized, weren't bumps. They were horns.

"You're a faun," Jason said.

"*Satyr!*" Hedge snapped. "Fauns are Roman. But we'll talk about that later."

Hedge leaped over the railing. He sailed toward the canyon wall and hit hooves first. He bounded down the cliff with impossible agility, finding footholds no bigger than postage stamps, dodging whirlwinds that tried to attack him as he picked his way toward Leo.

"Isn't that cute!" Dylan turned toward Jason. "Now it's your turn, boy."

Jason threw the club. It seemed useless with the winds so strong, but the club flew right at Dylan, even curving when he tried to dodge, and smacked him on the head so hard he fell to his knees.

Piper wasn't as dazed as she appeared. Her fingers closed around the club when it rolled next to her, but before she could use it, Dylan rose. Blood—*golden* blood—trickled from his forehead.

"Nice try, boy." He glared at Jason. "But you'll have to do better."

The skywalk shuddered. Hairline fractures appeared in the glass. Inside the museum, kids stopped banging on the doors. They backed away, watching in terror.

Dylan's body dissolved into smoke, as if his molecules were coming unglued. He had the same face, the same brilliant white smile, but his whole form was suddenly composed of swirling black vapor, his eyes like electrical sparks in a living storm cloud. He sprouted black smoky wings and rose above the skywalk. If angels could be evil, Jason decided, they would look exactly like this.

"You're a *ventus*," Jason said, though he had no idea how he knew that word. "A storm spirit."

Dylan's laugh sounded like a tornado tearing off a roof. "I'm glad I waited, demigod. Leo and Piper I've known about for weeks. Could've killed them at any time. But my mistress said a third was coming—someone special. She'll reward me greatly for your death!"

Two more funnel clouds touched down on either side of Dylan and turned into *venti*—ghostly young men with smoky wings and eyes that flickered with lightning.

Piper stayed down, pretending to be dazed, her hand still gripping the club. Her face was pale, but she gave Jason a determined look, and he understood the message: *Keep their attention. I'll brain them from behind.*

Cute, smart, *and* violent. Jason wished he remembered having her as a girlfriend.

He clenched his fists and got ready to charge, but he never got a chance.

Dylan raised his hand, arcs of electricity running between his fingers, and blasted Jason in the chest.

Bang! Jason found himself flat on his back. His mouth tasted like burning aluminum foil. He lifted his head and saw that his clothes were smoking. The lightning bolt had gone straight though his body and blasted off his left shoe. His toes were black with soot.

The storm spirits were laughing. The winds raged. Piper was screaming defiantly, but it all sounded tinny and far away.

Out of the corner of his eye, Jason saw Coach Hedge climbing the cliff with Leo on his back. Piper was on her feet, desperately swinging the club to fend off the two extra storm spirits, but they were just toying with her. The club went right through their bodies like they weren't there. And Dylan, a dark and winged tornado with eyes, loomed over Jason.

"Stop," Jason croaked. He rose unsteadily to his feet, and he wasn't sure who was more surprised: him, or the storm spirits.

"How are you alive?" Dylan's form flickered. "That was enough lightning to kill twenty men!"

"My turn," Jason said.

He reached in his pocket and pulled out the gold coin. He let his instincts take over, flipping the coin in the air like he'd done it a thousand times. He caught it in his palm, and suddenly he was holding a sword—a wickedly sharp double-edged weapon. The ridged grip fit his fingers perfectly, and the whole thing was gold—hilt, handle, and blade.

Dylan snarled and backed up. He looked at his two comrades and yelled, "Well? Kill him!"

The other storm spirits didn't look happy with that order, but they flew at Jason, their fingers crackling with electricity.

Jason swung at the first spirit. His blade passed through it, and the creature's smoky form disintegrated. The second spirit let loose a bolt of lightning, but Jason's blade absorbed the charge. Jason stepped in—one quick thrust, and the second storm spirit dissolved into gold powder.

Dylan wailed in outrage. He looked down as if expecting his comrades to re-form, but their gold dust remains dispersed in the wind. "Impossible! Who *are* you, half-blood?"

Piper was so stunned she dropped her club. "Jason, how...?"

Then Coach Hedge leaped back onto the skywalk and dumped Leo like a sack of flour.

"Spirits, fear me!" Hedge bellowed, flexing his short arms. Then he looked around and realized there was only Dylan.

"Curse it, boy!" he snapped at Jason. "Didn't you leave some for me? I like a challenge!"

Leo got to his feet, breathing hard. He looked completely humiliated, his hands bleeding from clawing at the rocks. "Yo, Coach Supergoat, whatever you are—I just fell down the freaking Grand Canyon! Stop asking for challenges!"

Dylan hissed at them, but Jason could see fear in his eyes. "You have no idea how many enemies you've awakened, half-bloods. My mistress will destroy *all* demigods. This war you *cannot* win."

Above them, the storm exploded into a full-force gale. Cracks expanded in the skywalk. Sheets of rain poured down, and Jason had to crouch to keep his balance.

A hole opened in the clouds—a swirling vortex of black and silver.

"The mistress calls me back!" Dylan shouted with glee. "And you, demigod, will come with me!"

He lunged at Jason, but Piper tackled the monster from behind. Even though he was made of smoke, Piper somehow managed to connect. Both of them went sprawling. Leo, Jason, and the coach surged forward to help, but the spirit screamed with rage. He let loose a torrent that knocked them all backward. Jason and Coach Hedge landed on their butts. Jason's sword skidded across the glass. Leo hit the back of his head and curled on his side, dazed and groaning. Piper got the worst of it. She was thrown off Dylan's back and hit the railing, tumbling over the side until she was hanging by one hand over the abyss.

Jason started toward her, but Dylan screamed, "I'll settle for this one!"

He grabbed Leo's arm and began to rise, towing a half-conscious Leo below him. The storm spun faster, pulling them upward like a vacuum cleaner.

"Help!" Piper yelled. "Somebody!"

Then she slipped, screaming as she fell.

"Jason, go!" Hedge yelled. "Save her!"

The coach launched himself at the spirit with some serious goat fu—lashing out with his hooves, knocking Leo free from the spirit's grasp. Leo dropped safely to the floor, but Dylan grappled the coach's arms instead. Hedge tried to head-butt him, then kicked him and called him a cupcake. They rose into the air, gaining speed.

Coach Hedge shouted down once more, "Save her! I got this!" Then the satyr and the storm spirit spiraled into the clouds and disappeared.

Save her? Jason thought. *She's gone!*

But again his instincts won. He ran to the railing, thinking, *I'm a lunatic,* and jumped over the side.

Jason wasn't scared of heights. He was scared of being smashed against the canyon floor five hundred feet below. He figured he hadn't accomplished anything except for dying along with Piper, but he tucked in his arms and plummeted headfirst. The sides of the canyon raced past like a film on fast-forward. His face felt like it was peeling off.

In a heartbeat, he caught up with Piper, who was flailing wildly. He tackled her waist and closed his eyes, waiting for death. Piper screamed. The wind whistled in Jason's ears. He wondered what dying would feel like. He was thinking, probably not so good. He wished somehow they could never hit bottom.

Suddenly the wind died. Piper's scream turned into a strangled gasp. Jason thought they must be dead, but he hadn't felt any impact.

"J-J-Jason," Piper managed.

He opened his eyes. They weren't falling. They were floating in midair, a hundred feet above the river.

He hugged Piper tight, and she repositioned herself so she was hugging him too. They were nose to nose. Her heart beat so hard, Jason could feel it through her clothes.

Her breath smelled like cinnamon. She said, "How did you—"

"I didn't," he said. "I think I would know if I could fly...."

But then he thought: *I don't even know who I am.*

He imagined going up. Piper yelped as they shot a few feet higher. They weren't exactly floating, Jason decided. He could feel pressure under his feet like they were balancing at the top of a geyser.

"The air is supporting us," he said.

"Well, tell it to support us more! Get us out of here!"

Jason looked down. The easiest thing would be to sink gently to the canyon floor. Then he looked up. The rain had stopped. The storm clouds didn't seem as bad, but they were still rumbling and flashing. There was no guarantee the spirits were gone for good. He had no idea what had happened to Coach Hedge. And he'd left Leo up there, barely conscious.

"We have to help them," Piper said, as if reading his thoughts. "Can you—"

"Let's see." Jason thought *Up*, and instantly they shot skyward.

The fact he was riding the winds might've been cool under different circumstances, but he was too much in shock. As soon as they landed on the skywalk, they ran to Leo.

Piper turned Leo over, and he groaned. His army coat was soaked from the rain. His curly hair glittered gold from rolling around in monster dust. But at least he wasn't dead.

"Stupid...ugly...goat," he muttered.

"Where did he go?" Piper asked.

Leo pointed straight up. "Never came down. Please tell me he didn't actually save my life."

"Twice," Jason said.

Leo groaned even louder. "What happened? The tornado guy, the gold sword...I hit my head. That's it, right? I'm hallucinating?"

Jason had forgotten about the sword. He walked over to where it was lying and picked it up. The blade was well balanced. On a hunch he flipped it. Midspin, the sword shrank back into a coin and landed in his palm.

"Yep," Leo said. "Definitely hallucinating."

Piper shivered in her rain-soaked clothes. "Jason, those things—"

"*Venti*," he said. "Storm spirits."

"Okay. You acted like...like you'd seen them before. Who *are* you?"

He shook his head. "That's what I've been trying to tell you. I don't know."

The storm dissipated. The other kids from the Wilderness

School were staring out the glass doors in horror. Security guards were working on the locks now, but they didn't seem to be having any luck.

"Coach Hedge said he had to protect three people," Jason remembered. "I think he meant us."

"And that thing Dylan turned into..." Piper shuddered. "God, I can't believe it was *hitting* on me. He called us... what, *demigods*?"

Leo lay on his back, staring at the sky. He didn't seem anxious to get up. "Don't know what *demi* means," he said. "But I'm not feeling too godly. You guys feeling godly?"

There was a brittle sound like dry twigs snapping, and the cracks in the skywalk began to widen.

"We need to get off this thing," Jason said. "Maybe if we—"

"Ohhh-kay," Leo interrupted. "Look up there and tell me if those are flying horses."

At first Jason thought Leo *had* hit his head too hard. Then he saw a dark shape descending from the east—too slow for a plane, too large for a bird. As it got closer he could see a pair of winged animals—gray, four-legged, exactly like horses—except each one had a twenty-foot wingspan. And they were pulling a brightly painted box with two wheels: a chariot.

"Reinforcements," he said. "Hedge told me an extraction squad was coming for us."

"Extraction squad?" Leo struggled to his feet. "That sounds painful."

"And where are they extracting us *to*?" Piper asked.

Jason watched as the chariot landed on the far end of the

skywalk. The flying horses tucked in their wings and cantered nervously across the glass, as if they sensed it was near breaking. Two teenagers stood in the chariot—a tall blond girl maybe a little older than Jason, and a bulky dude with a shaved head and a face like a pile of bricks. They both wore jeans and orange T-shirts, with shields tossed over their backs. The girl leaped off before the chariot had even finished moving. She pulled a knife and ran toward Jason's group while the bulky dude was reining in the horses.

"Where is he?" the girl demanded. Her gray eyes were fierce and a little startling.

"Where's who?" Jason asked.

She frowned like his answer was unacceptable. Then she turned to Leo and Piper. "What about Gleeson? Where is your protector, Gleeson Hedge?"

The coach's first name was Gleeson? Jason might've laughed if the morning hadn't been quite so weird and scary. Gleeson Hedge: football coach, goat man, protector of demigods. Sure. Why not?

Leo cleared his throat. "He got taken by some . . . tornado things."

"*Venti*," Jason said. "Storm spirits."

The blond girl arched an eyebrow. "You mean *anemoi thuellai*? That's the Greek term. Who are you, and what happened?"

Jason did his best to explain, though it was hard to meet those intense gray eyes. About halfway through the story, the other guy from the chariot came over. He stood there glaring at them, his arms crossed. He had a tattoo of a rainbow on his biceps, which seemed a little unusual.

When Jason had finished his story, the blond girl didn't look satisfied. "No, no, no! She *told* me he would be here. She told me if I came here, I'd find the answer."

"Annabeth," the bald guy grunted. "Check it out." He pointed at Jason's feet.

Jason hadn't thought much about it, but he was still missing his left shoe, which had been blown off by the lightning. His bare foot felt okay, but it looked like a lump of charcoal.

"The guy with one shoe," said the bald dude. "He's the answer."

"No, Butch," the girl insisted. "He can't be. I was tricked." She glared at the sky as though it had done something wrong. "What do you want from me?" she screamed. "What have you done with him?"

The skywalk shuddered, and the horses whinnied urgently.

"Annabeth," said the bald dude, Butch, "we gotta leave. Let's get these three to camp and figure it out there. Those storm spirits might come back."

She fumed for a moment. "Fine." She fixed Jason with a resentful look. "We'll settle this later."

She turned on her heel and marched toward the chariot.

Piper shook her head. "What's *her* problem? What's going on?"

"Seriously," Leo agreed.

"We have to get you out of here," Butch said. "I'll explain on the way."

"I'm not going anywhere with *her*." Jason gestured toward the blonde. "She looks like she wants to kill me."

Butch hesitated. "Annabeth's okay. You gotta cut her some

slack. She had a vision telling her to come here, to find a guy with one shoe. That was supposed to be the answer to her problem."

"What problem?" Piper asked.

"She's been looking for one of our campers, who's been missing three days," Butch said. "She's going out of her mind with worry. She hoped he'd be here."

"Who?" Jason asked.

"Her boyfriend," Butch said. "A guy named Percy Jackson."

PIPER

AFTER A MORNING OF STORM SPIRITS, goat men, and flying boyfriends, Piper should've been losing her mind. Instead, all she felt was dread.

It's starting, she thought. *Just like the dream said.*

She stood in back of the chariot with Leo and Jason, while the bald guy, Butch, handled the reins, and the blond girl, Annabeth, adjusted a bronze navigation device. They rose over the Grand Canyon and headed east, icy wind ripping straight through Piper's jacket. Behind them, more storm clouds were gathering.

The chariot lurched and bumped. It had no seat belts and the back was wide open, so Piper wondered if Jason would catch her again if she fell. That had been the most disturbing part of the morning—not that Jason could fly, but that he'd held her in his arms and yet didn't know who she was.

All semester she'd worked on a relationship, trying to get

Jason to notice her as more than a friend. Finally she'd gotten the big dope to kiss her. The last few weeks had been the best of her life. And then, three nights ago, the dream had ruined everything—that horrible voice, giving her horrible news. She hadn't told anyone about it, not even Jason.

Now she didn't even have *him*. It was like someone had wiped his memory, and she was stuck in the worst "do over" of all time. She wanted to scream. Jason stood right next to her: those sky blue eyes, close-cropped blond hair, that cute little scar on his upper lip. His face was kind and gentle, but always a little sad. And he just stared at the horizon, not even noticing her.

Meanwhile, Leo was being annoying, as usual. "This is so cool!" He spit a pegasus feather out of his mouth. "Where are we going?"

"A safe place," Annabeth said. "The *only* safe place for kids like us. Camp Half-Blood."

"Half-Blood?" Piper was immediately on guard. She hated that word. She'd been called a half-blood too many times— half Cherokee, half white—and it was never a compliment. "Is that some kind of bad joke?"

"She means we're demigods," Jason said. "Half god, half mortal."

Annabeth looked back. "You seem to know a lot, Jason. But, yes, demigods. My mom is Athena, goddess of wisdom. Butch here is the son of Iris, the rainbow goddess."

Leo choked. "Your mom is a rainbow goddess?"

"Got a problem with that?" Butch said.

"No, no," Leo said. "Rainbows. Very macho."

"Butch is our best equestrian," Annabeth said. "He gets along great with the pegasi."

"Rainbows, ponies," Leo muttered.

"I'm gonna toss you off this chariot," Butch warned.

"Demigods," Piper said. "You mean you think you're . . . you think we're—"

Lightning flashed. The chariot shuddered, and Jason yelled, "Left wheel's on fire!"

Piper stepped back. Sure enough, the wheel was burning, white flames lapping up the side of the chariot.

The wind roared. Piper glanced behind them and saw dark shapes forming in the clouds, more storm spirits spiraling toward the chariot—except these looked more like horses than angels.

She started to say, "Why are they—"

"*Anemoi* come in different shapes," Annabeth said. "Sometimes human, sometimes stallions, depending on how chaotic they are. Hold on. This is going to get rough."

Butch flicked the reins. The pegasi put on a burst of speed, and the chariot blurred. Piper's stomach crawled into her throat. Her vision went black, and when it came back to normal, they were in a totally different place.

A cold gray ocean stretched out to the left. Snow-covered fields, roads, and forests spread to the right. Directly below them was a green valley, like an island of springtime, rimmed with snowy hills on three sides and water to the north. Piper saw a cluster of buildings like ancient Greek temples, a big blue mansion, ball courts, a lake, and a climbing wall that seemed to be on fire. But before she could really process all she was seeing, their wheels came off and the chariot dropped out of the sky.

Annabeth and Butch tried to maintain control. The pegasi labored to hold the chariot in a flight pattern, but they seemed exhausted from their burst of speed, and bearing the chariot and the weight of five people was just too much.

"The lake!" Annabeth yelled. "Aim for the lake!"

Piper remembered something her dad had once told her, about hitting water from up high being as bad as hitting cement.

And then—*BOOM*.

The biggest shock was the cold. She was underwater, so disoriented that she didn't know which way was up.

She just had time to think: *This would be a stupid way to die.* Then faces appeared in the green murk—girls with long black hair and glowing yellow eyes. They smiled at her, grabbed her shoulders, and hauled her up.

They tossed her, gasping and shivering, onto the shore. Nearby, Butch stood in the lake, cutting the wrecked harnesses off the pegasi. Fortunately, the horses looked okay, but they were flapping their wings and splashing water everywhere. Jason, Leo, and Annabeth were already on shore, surrounded by kids giving them blankets and asking questions. Somebody took Piper by the arms and helped her stand. Apparently kids fell into the lake a lot, because a detail of campers ran up with big bronze leaf blower–looking things and blasted Piper with hot air; and in about two seconds her clothes were dry.

There were at least twenty campers milling around—the youngest maybe nine, the oldest college age, eighteen or nineteen—and all of them had orange T-shirts like Annabeth's. Piper looked back at the water and saw those strange girls just below the surface, their hair floating in the current. They waved like, *toodle-oo*, and disappeared into the depths. A second later the wreckage of the chariot was tossed from the lake and landed nearby with a wet crunch.

"Annabeth!" A guy with a bow and quiver on his back pushed through the crowd. "I said you could *borrow* the chariot, not destroy it!"

"Will, I'm sorry," Annabeth sighed. "I'll get it fixed, I promise."

Will scowled at his broken chariot. Then he sized up Piper, Leo, and Jason. "These are the ones? Way older than thirteen. Why haven't they been claimed already?"

"Claimed?" Leo asked.

Before Annabeth could explain, Will said, "Any sign of Percy?"

"No," Annabeth admitted.

The campers muttered. Piper had no idea who this guy Percy was, but his disappearance seemed to be a big deal.

Another girl stepped forward—tall, Asian, dark hair in ringlets, plenty of jewelry, and perfect makeup. Somehow she managed to make jeans and an orange T-shirt look glamorous. She glanced at Leo, fixed her eyes on Jason like he might be worthy of her attention, then curled her lip at Piper as if she were a week-old burrito that had just been pulled out of a Dumpster. Piper knew this girl's type. She'd dealt with a lot of girls like this at Wilderness School and every other stupid school her father had sent her to. Piper knew instantly they were going to be enemies.

"Well," the girl said, "I hope they're worth the trouble."

Leo snorted. "Gee, thanks. What are we, your new pets?"

"No kidding," Jason said. "How about some answers before you start judging us—like, what is this place, why are we here, how long do we have to stay?"

Piper had the same questions, but a wave of anxiety washed over her. *Worth the trouble.* If they only knew about her dream. They had no idea....

"Jason," Annabeth said, "I promise we'll answer your questions. And Drew"—she frowned at the glamour girl—"all demigods are worth saving. But I'll admit, the trip didn't accomplish what I hoped."

"Hey," Piper said, "we didn't ask to be brought here."

Drew sniffed. "And nobody *wants* you, hon. Does your hair always look like a dead badger?"

Piper stepped forward, ready to smack her, but Annabeth said, "Piper, stop."

Piper did. She wasn't a bit scared of Drew, but Annabeth didn't seem like somebody she wanted for an enemy.

"We need to make our new arrivals feel welcome," Annabeth said, with another pointed look at Drew. "We'll assign them each a guide, give them a tour of camp. Hopefully by the campfire tonight, they'll be claimed."

"Would somebody tell me what *claimed* means?" Piper asked.

Suddenly there was a collective gasp. The campers backed

away. At first Piper thought she'd done something wrong. Then she realized their faces were bathed in a strange red light, as if someone had lit a torch behind her. She turned and almost forgot how to breathe.

Floating over Leo's head was a blazing holographic image —a fiery hammer.

"That," Annabeth said, "is claiming."

"What'd I do?" Leo backed toward the lake. Then he glanced up and yelped. "Is my hair on fire?" He ducked, but the symbol followed him, bobbing and weaving so it looked like he was trying to write something in flames with his head.

"This can't be good," Butch muttered. "The curse—"

"Butch, shut up," Annabeth said. "Leo, you've just been claimed—"

"By a god," Jason interrupted. "That's the symbol of Vulcan, isn't it?"

All eyes turned to him.

"Jason," Annabeth said carefully, "how did you know that?"

"I'm not sure."

"Vulcan?" Leo demanded. "I don't even LIKE *Star Trek*. What are you talking about?"

"Vulcan is the Roman name for Hephaestus," Annabeth said, "the god of blacksmiths and fire."

The fiery hammer faded, but Leo kept swatting the air like he was afraid it was following him. "The god of *what*? Who?"

Annabeth turned to the guy with the bow. "Will, would you take Leo, give him a tour? Introduce him to his bunkmates in Cabin Nine."

"Sure, Annabeth."

"What's Cabin Nine?" Leo asked. "And I'm not a Vulcan!"

"Come on, Mr. Spock, I'll explain everything." Will put a hand on his shoulder and steered him off toward the cabins.

Annabeth turned her attention back to Jason. Usually Piper didn't like it when other girls checked out her boyfriend, but Annabeth didn't seem to care that he was a good-looking guy. She studied him more like he was a complicated blueprint. Finally she said, "Hold out your arm."

Piper saw what she was looking at, and her eyes widened.

Jason had taken off his windbreaker after his dip in the lake, leaving his arms bare, and on the inside of his right forearm was a tattoo. How had Piper never noticed it before? She'd looked at Jason's arms a million times. The tattoo couldn't have just *appeared*, but it was darkly etched, impossible to miss: a dozen straight lines like a bar code, and over that an eagle with the letters SPQR.

"I've never seen marks like this," Annabeth said. "Where did you get them?"

Jason shook his head. "I'm getting really tired of saying this, but I don't know."

The other campers pushed forward, trying to get a look at Jason's tattoo. The marks seemed to bother them *a lot*— almost like a declaration of war.

"They look burned into your skin," Annabeth noticed.

"They were," Jason said. Then he winced as if his head was aching. "I mean . . . I think so. I don't remember."

No one said anything. It was clear the campers saw Annabeth as the leader. They were waiting for her verdict.

"He needs to go straight to Chiron," Annabeth decided. "Drew, would you—"

"Absolutely." Drew laced her arm through Jason's. "This way, sweetie. I'll introduce you to our director. He's...an *interesting* guy." She flashed Piper a smug look and led Jason toward the big blue house on the hill.

The crowd began to disperse, until only Annabeth and Piper were left.

"Who's Chiron?" Piper asked. "Is Jason in some kind of trouble?"

Annabeth hesitated. "Good question, Piper. Come on, I'll give you a tour. We need to talk."

I V

PIPER

PIPER SOON REALIZED ANNABETH'S HEART wasn't in the tour.

She talked about all this amazing stuff the camp offered—magic archery, pegasus riding, the lava wall, fighting monsters —but she showed no excitement, as if her mind were elsewhere. She pointed out the open-air dining pavilion that overlooked Long Island Sound. (Yes, Long Island, New York; they'd traveled *that* far on the chariot.) Annabeth explained how Camp Half-Blood was mostly a summer camp, but some kids stayed here year-round, and they'd added so many campers it was always crowded now, even in winter.

Piper wondered who ran the camp, and how they'd known Piper and her friends belonged here. She wondered if she'd have to stay full-time, or if she'd be any good at the activities. Could you flunk out of monster fighting? A million questions bubbled in her head, but given Annabeth's mood, she decided to keep quiet.

As they climbed a hill at the edge of camp, Piper turned and got an amazing view of the valley—a big stretch of woods to the northwest, a beautiful beach, the creek, the canoe lake, lush green fields, and the whole layout of the cabins—a bizarre assortment of buildings arranged like a Greek omega, Ω, with a loop of cabins around a central green, and two wings sticking out the bottom on either side. Piper counted twenty cabins in all. One glowed golden, another silver. One had grass on the roof. Another was bright red with barbed wire trenches. One cabin was black with fiery green torches out front.

All of it seemed like a different world from the snowy hills and fields outside.

"The valley is protected from mortal eyes," Annabeth said. "As you can see, the weather is controlled, too. Each cabin represents a Greek god—a place for that god's children to live."

She looked at Piper like she was trying to judge how Piper was handling the news.

"You're saying Mom was a goddess."

Annabeth nodded. "You're taking this awfully calmly."

Piper couldn't tell her why. She couldn't admit that this just confirmed some weird feelings she'd had for years, arguments she'd had with her father about why there were no photos of Mom in the house, and why Dad would never tell her exactly how or why her mom had left them. But mostly, the dream had warned her this was coming. *Soon they will find you, demigod,* that voice had rumbled. *When they do, follow our directions. Cooperate, and your father might live.*

Piper took a shaky breath. "I guess after this morning, it's a little easier to believe. So who's my mom?"

"We should know soon," Annabeth said. "You're what—fifteen? Gods are supposed to claim you when you're thirteen. That was the deal."

"The deal?"

"They made a promise last summer...well, long story ...but they promised not to ignore their demigod children anymore, to claim them by the time they turn thirteen. Sometimes it takes a little longer, but you saw how fast Leo was claimed once he got here. Should happen for you soon. Tonight at the campfire, I bet we'll get a sign."

Piper wondered if she'd have a big flaming hammer over her head, or with her luck, something even more embarrassing. A flaming wombat, maybe. Whoever her mother was, Piper had no reason to think she'd be proud to claim a kleptomaniac daughter with massive problems. "Why thirteen?"

"The older you get," Annabeth said, "the more monsters notice you, try to kill you. 'Round thirteen is usually when it starts. That's why we send protectors into the schools to find you guys, get you to camp before it's too late."

"Like Coach Hedge?"

Annabeth nodded. "He's—he was a satyr: half man, half goat. Satyrs work for the camp, finding demigods, protecting them, bringing them in when the time is right."

Piper had no trouble believing Coach Hedge was half goat. She'd seen the guy eat. She'd never liked the coach much, but she couldn't believe he'd sacrificed himself to save them.

"What happened to him?" she asked. "When we went up into the clouds, did he . . . is he gone for good?"

"Hard to say." Annabeth's expression was pained. "Storm spirits . . . difficult to battle. Even our best weapons, Celestial bronze, will pass right through them unless you can catch them by surprise."

"Jason's sword just turned them to dust," Piper remembered.

"He was lucky, then. If you hit a monster just right, you can dissolve them, send their essence back to Tartarus."

"Tartarus?"

"A huge abyss in the Underworld, where the worst monsters come from. Kind of like a bottomless pit of evil. Anyway, once monsters dissolve, it usually takes months, even years before they can re-form again. But since this storm spirit Dylan got away—well, I don't know why he'd keep Hedge alive. Hedge was a protector, though. He knew the risks. Satyrs don't have mortal souls. He'll be reincarnated as a tree or a flower or something."

Piper tried to imagine Coach Hedge as a clump of very angry pansies. That made her feel even worse.

She gazed at the cabins below, and an uneasy feeling settled over her. Hedge had died to get her here safely. Her mom's cabin was down there somewhere, which meant she had brothers and sisters, more people she'd have to betray. *Do what we tell you,* the voice had said. *Or the consequences will be painful.* She tucked her hands under her arms, trying to stop them from shaking.

"It'll be okay," Annabeth promised. "You have friends

here. We've all been through a lot of weird stuff. We know what you're going through."

I doubt that, Piper thought.

"I've been kicked out of five different schools the past five years," she said. "My dad's running out of places to put me."

"Only five?" Annabeth didn't sound like she was teasing. "Piper, we've all been labeled troublemakers. I ran away from home when I was seven."

"Seriously?"

"Oh, yeah. Most of us are diagnosed with attention deficit disorder or dyslexia, or both—"

"Leo's ADHD," Piper said.

"Right. It's because we're hardwired for battle. Restless, impulsive—we don't fit in with regular kids. You should hear how much trouble Percy—" Her face darkened. "Anyway, demigods get a bad rep. How'd you get in trouble?"

Usually when someone asked that question, Piper started a fight, or changed the subject, or caused some kind of distraction. But for some reason she found herself telling the truth.

"I steal stuff," she said. "Well, not really *steal*..."

"Is your family poor?"

Piper laughed bitterly. "Not even. I did it...I don't know why. For attention, I guess. My dad never had time for me unless I got in trouble."

Annabeth nodded. "I can relate. But you said you didn't really steal? What do you mean?"

"Well...nobody ever believes me. The police, teachers —even the people I took stuff from: they're so embarrassed, they'll deny what happened. But the truth is, I don't steal anything. I just ask people for things. And they give me stuff. Even a BMW convertible. I just asked. And the dealer said, 'Sure. Take it.' Later, he realized what he'd done, I guess. Then the police came after me."

Piper waited. She was used to people calling her a liar, but when she looked up, Annabeth just nodded.

"Interesting. If your *dad* were the god, I'd say you're a child of Hermes, god of thieves. He can be pretty convincing. But your dad is mortal...."

"Very," Piper agreed.

Annabeth shook her head, apparently mystified. "I don't know, then. With luck, your mom will claim you tonight."

Piper almost hoped it wouldn't happen. If her mom were a goddess, would she know about that dream? Would she know what Piper had been asked to do? Piper wondered if Olympian gods ever blasted their kids with lightning for being evil, or grounded them in the Underworld.

Annabeth was studying her. Piper decided she was going to have to be careful what she said from now on. Annabeth was obviously pretty smart. If anyone could figure out Piper's secret...

"Come on," Annabeth said at last. "There's something else I need to check."

They hiked a little farther until they reached a cave near the top of the hill. Bones and old swords littered the ground. Torches flanked the entrance, which was covered in a velvet curtain embroidered with snakes. It looked like the set for some kind of twisted puppet show.

"What's in there?" Piper asked.

Annabeth poked her head inside, then sighed and closed the curtains. "Nothing, right now. A friend's place. I've been expecting her for a few days, but so far, nothing."

"Your friend lives in a cave?"

Annabeth almost managed a smile. "Actually, her family has a luxury condo in Queens, and she goes to a finishing school in Connecticut. But when she's here at camp, yeah, she lives in the cave. She's our oracle, tells the future. I was hoping she could help me—"

"Find Percy," Piper guessed.

All the energy drained out of Annabeth, like she'd been holding it together for as long as she could. She sat down on a rock, and her expression was so full of pain, Piper felt like a voyeur.

She forced herself to look away. Her eyes drifted to the crest of the hill, where a single pine tree dominated the skyline. Something glittered in its lowest branch—like a fuzzy gold bath mat.

No . . . not a bath mat. It was a sheep's fleece.

Okay, Piper thought. Greek camp. They've got a replica of the Golden Fleece.

Then she noticed the base of the tree. At first she thought it was wrapped in a pile of massive purple cables. But the cables had reptilian scales, clawed feet, and a snakelike head with yellow eyes and smoking nostrils.

"That's—a dragon," she stammered. "That's the *actual* Golden Fleece?"

Annabeth nodded, but it was clear she wasn't really

listening. Her shoulders drooped. She rubbed her face and took a shaky breath. "Sorry. A little tired."

"You look ready to drop," Piper said. "How long have been searching for your boyfriend?"

"Three days, six hours, and about twelve minutes."

"And you've got no idea what happened to him?"

Annabeth shook her head miserably. "We were so excited because we both started winter break early. We met up at camp on Tuesday, figured we had three weeks together. It was going to be great. Then after the campfire, he—he kissed me good night, went back to his cabin, and in the morning, he was gone. We searched the whole camp. We contacted his mom. We've tried to reach him every way we know how. Nothing. He just disappeared."

Piper was thinking: *Three days ago.* The same night she'd had her dream. "How long were you guys together?"

"Since August," Annabeth said. "August eighteenth."

"Almost exactly when I met Jason," Piper said. "But we've only been together a few weeks."

Annabeth winced. "Piper... about that. Maybe you should sit down."

Piper knew where this was going. Panic started building inside her, like her lungs were filling with water. "Look, I know Jason thought—he thought he just *appeared* at our school today. But that's not true. I've known him for four months."

"Piper," Annabeth said sadly. "It's the Mist."

"Missed... what?"

"M-i-s-t. It's a kind of veil separating the mortal world from the mortal world. Mortal minds—they can't process strange stuff like gods and monsters, so the Mist bends reality. It makes mortals see things in a way they *can* understand —like their eyes might just skip over this valley completely, or they might look at that dragon and see a pile of cables."

Piper swallowed. "No. You said yourself I'm not a regular mortal. I'm a demigod."

"Even demigods can be affected. I've seen it lots of times. Monsters infiltrate some place like a school, pass themselves off as human, and everyone *thinks* they remember that person. They believe he's always been around. The Mist can change memories, even create memories of things that never happened—"

"But Jason's not a monster!" Piper insisted. "He's a human guy, or demigod, or whatever you want to call him. My memories aren't fake. They're *so* real. The time we set Coach Hedge's pants on fire. The time Jason and I watched a meteor shower on the dorm roof and I finally got the stupid guy to kiss me...."

She found herself rambling, telling Annabeth about her whole semester at Wilderness School. She'd liked Jason from the first week they'd met. He was so nice to her, and so patient, he could even put up with hyperactive Leo and his stupid jokes. He'd accepted her for herself and didn't judge her because of the stupid things she'd done. They'd spent hours talking, looking at the stars, and eventually—*finally*—holding hands. All that *couldn't* be fake.

Annabeth pursed her lips. "Piper, your memories are a lot sharper than most. I'll admit that, and I don't know why that is. But if you know him so well—"

"I do!"

"Then where is he from?"

Piper felt like she'd been hit between the eyes. "He must have told me, but—"

"Did you ever notice his tattoo before today? Did he ever tell you anything about his parents, or his friends, or his last school?"

"I—I don't know, but—"

"Piper, what's his last name?"

Her mind went blank. She didn't know Jason's last name. How could that be?

She started to cry. She felt like a total fool, but she sat down on the rock next to Annabeth and just fell to pieces. It was too much. Did *everything* that was good in her stupid, miserable life have to be taken away?

Yes, the dream had told her. *Yes, unless you do exactly what we say.*

"Hey," Annabeth said. "We'll figure it out. Jason's here now. Who knows? Maybe it'll work out with you guys for real."

Not likely, Piper thought. Not if the dream had told her the truth. But she couldn't say that.

She brushed a tear from her cheek. "You brought me up here so no one would see me blubbering, huh?"

Annabeth shrugged. "I figured it would be hard for you. I know what it's like to lose your boyfriend."

"But I still can't believe... I *know* we had something. And now it's just gone, like he doesn't even recognize me. If he really did just show up today, then why? How'd he get there? Why can't he remember anything?"

"Good questions," Annabeth said. "Hopefully Chiron can figure that out. But for now, we need to get you settled. You ready to go back down?"

Piper gazed at the crazy assortment of cabins in the valley. Her new home, a family who supposedly understood her—but soon they'd be just another bunch of people she'd disappointed, just another place she'd been kicked out of. *You'll betray them for us,* the voice had warned. *Or you'll lose everything.*

She didn't have a choice.

"Yeah," she lied. "I'm ready."

On the central green, a group of campers was playing basketball. They were incredible shots. Nothing bounced off the rim. Three-pointers went in automatically.

"Apollo's cabin," Annabeth explained. "Bunch of show-offs with missile weapons—arrows, basketballs."

They walked past a central fire pit, where two guys were hacking at each other with swords.

"Real blades?" Piper noted. "Isn't that dangerous?"

"That's sort of the point," Annabeth said. "Uh, sorry. Bad pun. That's my cabin over there. Number Six." She nodded to a gray building with a carved owl over the door. Through the open doorway, Piper could see bookshelves, weapon displays, and one of those computerized SMART Boards they have in classrooms. Two girls were drawing a map that looked like a battle diagram.

"Speaking of blades," Annabeth said, "come here."

She led Piper around the side of the cabin, to a big metal shed that looked like it was meant for gardening tools. Annabeth unlocked it, and inside were *not* gardening tools, unless you wanted to make war on your tomato plants. The shed was lined with all sorts of weapons—from swords to spears to clubs like Coach Hedge's.

"Every demigod needs a weapon," Annabeth said. "Hephaestus makes the best, but we have a pretty good selection, too. Athena's all about strategy—matching the right weapon to the right person. Let's see..."

Piper didn't feel much like shopping for deadly objects, but she knew Annabeth was trying to do something nice for her.

Annabeth handed her a massive sword, which Piper could hardly lift.

"No," they both said at once.

Annabeth rummaged a little farther in the shed and brought out something else.

"A shotgun?" Piper asked.

"Mossberg 500." Annabeth checked the pump action like it was no big deal. "Don't worry. It doesn't hurt humans. It's modified to shoot Celestial bronze, so it only kills monsters."

"Um, I don't think that's my style," Piper said.

"Mmm, yeah," Annabeth agreed. "Too flashy."

She put the shotgun back and started poking through a rack of crossbows when something in the corner of the shed caught Piper's eye.

"What is that?" she said. "A knife?"

Annabeth dug it out and blew the dust off the scabbard. It looked like it hadn't seen the light of day in centuries.

"I don't know, Piper." Annabeth sounded uneasy. "I don't think you want this one. Swords are usually better."

"You use a knife." Piper pointed to the one strapped to Annabeth's belt.

"Yeah, but..." Annabeth shrugged. "Well, take a look if you want."

The sheath was worn black leather, bound in bronze. Nothing fancy, nothing flashy. The polished wood handle fit beautifully in Piper's hand. When she unsheathed it, she found a triangular blade eighteen inches long—bronze gleaming like it had been polished yesterday. The edges were deadly sharp. Her reflection in the blade caught her by surprise. She looked older, more serious, not as scared as she felt.

"It suits you," Annabeth admitted. "That kind of blade is called a parazonium. It was mostly ceremonial, carried by high-ranking officers in the Greek armies. It showed you were a person of power and wealth, but in a fight, it could protect you just fine."

"I like it," Piper said. "Why didn't you think it was right?"

Annabeth exhaled. "That blade has a long story. Most people would be afraid to claim it. Its first owner...well, things didn't turn out too well for her. Her name was Helen."

Piper let that sink in. "Wait, you mean *the* Helen? Helen of Troy?"

Annabeth nodded.

Suddenly Piper felt like she should be handling the dagger with surgical gloves. "And it's just sitting in your toolshed?"

"We're surrounded by Ancient Greek stuff," Annabeth said. "This isn't a museum. Weapons like that—they're meant to be used. They're our heritage as demigods. That was a wedding present from Menelaus, Helen's first husband. She named the dagger Katoptris."

"Meaning?"

"Mirror," Annabeth said. "Looking glass. Probably because that's the only thing Helen used it for. I don't think it's ever seen battle."

Piper looked at the blade again. For a moment, her own image stared up at her, but then the reflection changed. She saw flames, and a grotesque face like something carved from bedrock. She heard the same laughter as in her dream. She saw her dad in chains, tied to a post in front of a roaring bonfire.

She dropped the blade.

"Piper?" Annabeth shouted to the Apollo kids on the court, "Medic! I need some help over here!"

"No, it's—it's okay," Piper managed.

"You sure?"

"Yeah. I just…" She had to control herself. With trembling fingers, she picked up the dagger. "I just got overwhelmed. So much happening today. But…I want to keep the dagger, if that's okay."

Annabeth hesitated. Then she waved off the Apollo kids. "Okay, if you're sure. You turned really pale, there. I thought you were having a seizure or something."

"I'm fine," Piper promised, though her heart was still racing. "Is there...um, a phone at camp? Can I call my dad?"

Annabeth's gray eyes were almost as unnerving as the dagger blade. She seemed to be calculating a million possibilities, trying to read Piper's thoughts.

"We aren't allowed phones," she said. "Most demigods, if they use a cell phone, it's like sending up a signal, letting monsters know where you are. But...I've got one." She slipped it out of her pocket. "Kind of against the rules, but if it can be our secret..."

Piper took it gratefully, trying not to let her hands shake. She stepped away from Annabeth and turned to face the commons area.

She called her dad's private line, even though she knew what would happen. Voice mail. She'd been trying for three days, ever since the dream. Wilderness School only allowed phone privileges once a day, but she'd called every evening, and gotten nowhere.

Reluctantly she dialed the other number. Her dad's personal assistant answered immediately. "Mr. McLean's office."

"Jane," Piper said, gritting her teeth. "Where's my dad?"

Jane was silent for a moment, probably wondering if she could get away with hanging up. "Piper, I thought you weren't supposed to call from school."

"Maybe I'm not at school," Piper said. "Maybe I ran away to live among the woodland creatures."

"Mmm." Jane didn't sound concerned. "Well, I'll tell him you called."

"Where is he?"

"Out."

"You don't know, do you?" Piper lowered her voice, hoping Annabeth was too nice to eavesdrop. "When are you going to call the police, Jane? He could be in trouble."

"Piper, we are not going to turn this into a media circus. I'm sure he's fine. He does take off occasionally. He always comes back."

"So it's true. You *don't* know—"

"I have to go, Piper," Jane snapped. "Enjoy school."

The line went dead. Piper cursed. She walked back to Annabeth and handed her the phone.

"No luck?" Annabeth asked.

Piper didn't answer. She didn't trust herself not to start crying again.

Annabeth glanced at the phone display and hesitated. "Your last name is McLean? Sorry, it's not my business. But that sounds really familiar."

"Common name."

"Yeah, I guess. What does your dad do?"

"He's got a degree in the arts," Piper said automatically. "He's a Cherokee artist."

Her standard response. Not a lie, just not the whole truth. Most people, when they heard that, figured her dad sold Indian souvenirs at a roadside stand on a reservation. Sitting Bull bobble-heads, wampum necklaces, Big Chief tablets—that kind of thing.

"Oh." Annabeth didn't look convinced, but she put the phone away. "You feeling okay? Want to keep going?"

Piper fastened her new dagger to her belt and promised

herself that later, when she was alone, she'd figure out how it worked. "Sure," she said. "I want to see everything."

All the cabins were cool, but none of them struck Piper as *hers*. No burning signs—wombats or otherwise—appeared over her head.

Cabin Eight was entirely silver and glowed like moonlight.

"Artemis?" Piper guessed.

"You know Greek mythology," Annabeth said.

"I did some reading when my dad was working on a project last year."

"I thought he did Cherokee art."

Piper bit back a curse. "Oh, right. But—you know, he does other stuff too."

Piper thought she'd blown it: McLean, Greek mythology. Thankfully, Annabeth didn't seem to make the connection.

"Anyway," Annabeth continued, "Artemis is goddess of the moon, goddess of hunting. But no campers. Artemis was an eternal maiden, so she doesn't have any kids."

"Oh." That kind of bummed Piper out. She'd always liked the stories of Artemis, and figured she would make a cool mom.

"Well, there *are* the Hunters of Artemis," Annabeth amended. "They visit sometimes. They're not the children of Artemis, but they're her handmaidens—this band of immortal teenage girls who adventure together and hunt monsters and stuff."

Piper perked up. "That sounds cool. They get to be immortal?"

"Unless they die in combat, or break their vows. Did I mention they have to swear off boys? No dating—ever. For eternity." ·

"Oh," Piper said. "Never mind."

Annabeth laughed. For a moment she looked almost happy, and Piper thought she'd be a cool friend to hang out with in better times.

Forget it, Piper reminded herself. You're not going to make any friends here. Not once they find out.

They passed the next cabin, Number Ten, which was decorated like a Barbie house with lace curtains, a pink door, and potted carnations in the windows. They walked by the doorway, and the smell of perfume almost made Piper gag.

"Gah, is that where supermodels go to die?"

Annabeth smirked. "Aphrodite's cabin. Goddess of love. Drew is the head counselor."

"Figures," Piper grumbled.

"They're not all bad," Annabeth said. "The last head counselor we had was great."

"What happened to her?"

Annabeth's expression darkened. "We should keep moving."

They looked at the other cabins, but Piper just got more depressed. She wondered if she could be the daughter of Demeter, the farming goddess. Then again, Piper killed every plant she ever touched. Athena was cool. Or maybe Hecate, the magic goddess. But it didn't really matter. Even here, where everyone was supposed to find a lost parent, she knew she would still end up the unwanted kid. She was not looking forward to the campfire tonight.

"We started with the twelve Olympian gods," Annabeth explained. "Male gods on the left, female on the right. Then last year, we added a whole bunch of new cabins for the other gods who didn't have thrones on Olympus—Hecate, Hades, Iris—"

"What are the two big ones on the end?" Piper asked.

Annabeth frowned. "Zeus and Hera. King and queen of the gods."

Piper headed that way, and Annabeth followed, though she didn't act very excited. The Zeus cabin reminded Piper of a bank. It was white marble with big columns out front and polished bronze doors emblazoned with lightning bolts.

Hera's cabin was smaller but done in the same style, except the doors were carved with peacock feather designs, shimmering in different colors.

Unlike the other cabins, which were all noisy and open and full of activity, the Zeus and Hera cabins looked closed and silent.

"Are they empty?" Piper asked.

Annabeth nodded. "Zeus went a long time without having any children. Well, mostly. Zeus, Poseidon, and Hades, the eldest brothers among the gods—they're called the Big Three. Their kids are really powerful, really dangerous. For the last seventy years or so, they tried to avoid having demigod children."

"*Tried* to avoid it?"

"Sometimes they...um, cheated. I've got a friend, Thalia

Grace, who's the daughter of Zeus. But she gave up camp life and became a Hunter of Artemis. My boyfriend, Percy, he's a son of Poseidon. And there's a kid who shows up sometimes, Nico—son of Hades. Except for them, there are no demigod children of the Big Three gods. At least, not that we know of."

"And Hera?" Piper looked at the peacock-decorated doors. The cabin bothered her, though she wasn't sure why.

"Goddess of marriage." Annabeth's tone was carefully controlled, like she was trying to avoid cursing. "She doesn't have kids with anyone but Zeus. So, yeah, no demigods. The cabin's just honorary."

"You don't like her," Piper noticed.

"We have a long history," Annabeth admitted. "I thought we'd made peace, but when Percy disappeared...I got this weird dream vision from her."

"Telling you to come get us," Piper said. "But you thought Percy would be there."

"It's probably better I don't talk about it," Annabeth said. "I've got nothing good to say about Hera right now."

Piper looked down at the base of the doors. "So who goes in here?"

"No one. The cabin is just honorary, like I said. No one goes in."

"Someone does." Piper pointed at a footprint on the dusty threshold. On instinct, she pushed the doors and they swung open easily.

Annabeth stepped back. "Um, Piper, I don't think we should—"

"We're supposed to do dangerous stuff, right?" And Piper walked inside.

Hera's cabin was not someplace Piper would want to live. It was as cold as a freezer, with a circle of white columns around a central statue of the goddess, ten feet tall, seated on a throne in flowing golden robes. Piper had always thought of Greek statues as white with blank eyes, but this one was brightly painted so it looked almost human—except huge. Hera's piercing eyes seemed to follow Piper.

At the goddess's feet, a fire burned in a bronze brazier. Piper wondered who tended it if the cabin was always empty. A stone hawk sat on Hera's shoulder, and in her hand was a staff topped with a lotus flower. The goddess's hair was done in black plaits. Her face smiled, but the eyes were cold and calculating, as if she were saying: *Mother knows best. Now don't cross me or I will have to step on you.*

There was nothing else in the cabin—no beds, no furniture, no bathroom, no windows, nothing that anyone could actually use to live. For a goddess of home and marriage, Hera's place reminded Piper of a tomb.

No, this wasn't her mom. At least Piper was sure of *that*. She hadn't come in here because she felt a *good* connection, but because her sense of dread was stronger here. Her dream—that horrible ultimatum she'd been handed—had something to do with this cabin.

She froze. They weren't alone. Behind the statue, at a little altar in the back, stood a figure covered in a black shawl. Only her hands were visible, palms up. She seemed to be chanting something like a spell or a prayer.

Annabeth gasped. "Rachel?"

The other girl turned. She dropped her shawl, revealing a mane of curly red hair and a freckled face that didn't go with the seriousness of the cabin or the black shawl at all. She looked about seventeen, a totally normal teen in a green blouse and tattered jeans covered with marker doodles. Despite the cold floor, she was barefoot.

"Hey!" She ran to give Annabeth a hug. "I'm so sorry! I came as fast as I could."

They talked for a few minutes about Annabeth's boyfriend and how there was no news, et cetera, until finally Annabeth remembered Piper, who was standing there feeling uncomfortable.

"I'm being rude," Annabeth apologized. "Rachel, this is Piper, one of the half-bloods we rescued today. Piper, this is Rachel Elizabeth Dare, our oracle."

"The friend who lives in the cave," Piper guessed.

Rachel grinned. "That's me."

"So you're an oracle?" Piper asked. "You can tell the future?"

"More like the future mugs me from time to time," Rachel said. "I speak prophecies. The oracle's spirit kind of hijacks me every once in a while and speaks important stuff that doesn't make any sense to anybody. But yeah, the prophecies tell the future."

"Oh." Piper shifted from foot to foot. "That's cool."

Rachel laughed. "Don't worry. Everybody finds it a little creepy. Even me. But usually I'm harmless."

"You're a demigod?"

"Nope," Rachel said. "Just mortal."

"Then what are you..." Piper waved her hand around the room.

Rachel's smile faded. She glanced at Annabeth, then back at Piper. "Just a hunch. Something about this cabin and Percy's disappearance. They're connected somehow. I've learned to follow my hunches, especially the last month, since the gods went silent."

"Went silent?" Piper asked.

Rachel frowned at Annabeth. "You haven't told her yet?"

"I was getting to that," Annabeth said. "Piper, for the last month...well, it's normal for the gods not to talk to their children very much, but usually we can count on some messages now and then. Some of us can even visit Olympus. I spent practically all semester at the Empire State Building."

"Excuse me?"

"The entrance to Mount Olympus these days."

"Oh," Piper said. "Sure, why not?"

"Annabeth was redesigning Olympus after it was damaged in the Titan War," Rachel explained. "She's an amazing architect. You should see the salad bar—"

"Anyway," Annabeth said, "starting about a month ago, Olympus fell silent. The entrance closed, and no one could get in. Nobody knows why. It's like the gods have sealed themselves off. Even my mom won't answer my prayers, and our camp director, Dionysus, was recalled."

"Your camp director was the god of...wine?"

"Yeah, it's a—"

"Long story," Piper guessed. "Right. Go on."

"That's it, really," Annabeth said. "Demigods still get claimed, but nothing else. No messages. No visits. No sign the gods are even listening. It's like something has happened —something *really* bad. Then Percy disappeared."

"And Jason showed up on our field trip," Piper supplied. "With no memory."

"Who's Jason?" Rachel asked.

"My—" Piper stopped herself before she could say "boyfriend," but the effort made her chest hurt. "My friend. But Annabeth, you said Hera sent you a dream vision."

"Right," Annabeth said. "The first communication from a god in a month, and it's Hera, the least helpful goddess, and she contacts me, her least favorite demigod. She tells me I'll find out what happened to Percy if I go to the Grand Canyon skywalk and look for a guy with one shoe. Instead, I find you guys, and the guy with one shoe is Jason. It doesn't make sense."

"Something bad is happening," Rachel agreed. She looked at Piper, and Piper felt an overwhelming desire to tell them about her dream, to confess that *she* knew what was happening—at least part of the story. And the bad stuff was only beginning.

"Guys," she said. "I—I need to—"

Before she could continue, Rachel's body stiffened. Her eyes began to glow with a greenish light, and she grabbed Piper by the shoulders.

Piper tried to back away, but Rachel's hands were like steel clamps.

Free me, she said. But it wasn't Rachel's voice. It sounded like an older woman, speaking from somewhere far away, down a long, echoing pipe. *Free me, Piper McLean, or the earth shall swallow us. It must be by the solstice.*

The room started spinning. Annabeth tried to separate Piper from Rachel, but it was no use. Green smoke enveloped them, and Piper was no longer sure if she was awake or dreaming. The giant statue of the goddess seemed to rise from its throne. It leaned over Piper, its eyes boring into her. The statue's mouth opened, its breath like horribly thick perfume. It spoke in the same echoing voice: *Our enemies stir. The fiery one is only the first. Bow to his will, and their king shall rise, dooming us all. FREE ME!*

Piper's knees buckled, and everything went black.

V

LEO

Leo's tour was going great until he learned about the dragon.

The archer dude, Will Solace, seemed pretty cool. Everything he showed Leo was so amazing, it should've been illegal. Real Greek warships moored at the beach that sometimes had practice fights with flaming arrows and explosives? Sweet! Arts & crafts sessions where you could make sculptures with chain saws and blowtorches? Leo was like, *Sign me up!* The woods were stocked with dangerous monsters, and no one should ever go in there alone? Nice! And the camp was overflowing with fine-looking girls. Leo didn't quite understand the whole related-to-the-gods business, but he hoped that didn't mean he was cousins with all these ladies. That would suck. At the very least, he wanted to check out those underwater girls in the lake again. They were definitely worth drowning for.

Will showed him the cabins, the dining pavilion, and the sword arena.

"Do I get a sword?" Leo asked.

Will glanced at him like he found the idea disturbing. "You'll probably make your own, seeing as how you're in Cabin Nine."

"Yeah, what's up with that? Vulcan?"

"Usually we don't call the gods by their Roman names," Will said. "The original names are Greek. Your dad is Hephaestus."

"Festus?" Leo had heard somebody say that before, but he was still dismayed. "Sounds like the god of cowboys."

"*He*-phaestus," Will corrected. "God of blacksmiths and fire."

Leo had heard that too, but he was trying not to think about it. The god of fire...seriously? Considering what had happened to his mom, that seemed like a sick joke.

"So the flaming hammer over my head," Leo said. "Good thing, or bad thing?"

Will took a while to answer. "You were claimed almost immediately. That's usually good."

"But that Rainbow Pony dude, Butch—he mentioned a curse."

"Ah...look, it's nothing. Since Cabin Nine's last head counselor died—"

"Died? Like, painfully?"

"I ought to let your bunkmates tell you about it."

"Yeah, where *are* my home dawgs? Shouldn't their counselor be giving me the VIP tour?"

"He, um, can't. You'll see why." Will forged ahead before Leo could ask anything else.

"Curses and death," Leo said to himself. "This just gets better and better."

He was halfway across the green when he spotted his old babysitter. And she was *not* the kind of person he expected to see at a demigod camp.

Leo froze in his tracks.

"What's wrong?" Will asked.

Tía Callida—*Auntie* Callida. That's what she'd called herself, but Leo hadn't seen her since he was five years old. She was just standing there, in the shadow of a big white cabin at the end of the green, watching him. She wore her black linen widow's dress, with a black shawl pulled over her hair. Her face hadn't changed—leathery skin, piercing dark eyes. Her withered hands were like claws. She looked ancient, but no different than Leo remembered.

"That old lady..." Leo said. "What's she doing here?"

Will tried to follow his gaze. "What old lady?"

"Dude, *the* old lady. The one in black. How many old ladies do you see over there?"

Will frowned. "I think you've had a long day, Leo. The Mist could still be playing tricks on your mind. How about we head straight to your cabin now?"

Leo wanted to protest, but when he looked back toward the big white cabin, Tía Callida was gone. He was *sure* she'd been there, almost as if thinking about his mom had summoned Callida back from the past.

And that wasn't good, because Tía Callida had tried to kill him.

"Just messing with you, man." Leo pulled some gears and levers from his pockets and started fiddling with them to calm his nerves. He couldn't have everybody at camp thinking he was crazy. At least, not crazier than he really was.

"Let's go see Cabin Nine," he said. "I'm in the mood for a good curse."

From the outside, the Hephaestus cabin looked like an over-size RV with shiny metal walls and metal-slatted windows. The entrance was like a bank vault door, circular and several feet thick. It opened with lots of brass gears turning and hydraulic pistons blowing smoke.

Leo whistled. "They got a steampunk theme going on, huh?"

Inside, the cabin seemed deserted. Steel bunks were folded against the walls like high-tech Murphy beds. Each had a digital control panel, blinking LED lights, glowing gems, and interlocking gears. Leo figured each camper had his own combination lock to release his bed, and there was probably an alcove behind it with storage, maybe some traps to keep out unwanted visitors. At least, that's the way Leo would've designed it. A fire pole came down from the second floor, even though the cabin didn't appear to *have* a second floor from the outside. A circular staircase led down into some kind of basement. The walls were lined with every kind of power tool Leo could imagine, plus a huge assortment of knives, swords, and other implements of destruction. A large workbench over-flowed with scrap metal—screws, bolts, washers, nails, rivets, and a million other machine parts. Leo had a strong urge to shovel them all into his coat pockets. He loved that kind of stuff. But he'd need a hundred more coats to fit it all.

Looking around, he could almost imagine he was back in his mom's machine shop. Not the weapons, maybe—but the tools, the piles of scrap, the smell of grease and metal and hot engines. She would've loved this place.

He pushed that thought away. He didn't like painful memories. *Keep moving*—that was his motto. Don't dwell on things. Don't stay in one place too long. It was the only way to stay ahead of the sadness.

He picked a long implement from the wall. "A weed whacker? What's the god of fire want with a weed whacker?"

A voice in the shadows said, "You'd be surprised."

At the back of the room, one of the bunk beds was occupied. A curtain of dark camouflage material retracted, and Leo could see the guy who'd been invisible a second before. It was hard to tell much about him because he was covered in a body cast. His head was wrapped in gauze except for his face, which was puffy and bruised. He looked like the Pillsbury Doughboy after a beat-down.

"I'm Jake Mason," the guy said. "I'd shake your hand, but..."

"Yeah," Leo said. "Don't get up."

The guy cracked a smile, then winced like it hurt to move his face. Leo wondered what had happened to him, but he was afraid to ask.

"Welcome to Cabin Nine," Jake said. "Been almost a year since we had any new kids. I'm head counselor for now."

"For now?" Leo asked.

Will Solace cleared his throat. "So where is everybody, Jake?"

"Down at the forges," Jake said wistfully. "They're working on...you know, that problem."

"Oh." Will changed the subject. "So, you got a spare bed for Leo?"

Jake studied Leo, sizing him up. "You believe in curses, Leo? Or ghosts?"

I just saw my evil babysitter Tía Callida, Leo thought. She's *got* to be dead after all these years. And I can't go a day without remembering my mom in that machine shop fire. Don't talk to me about ghosts, doughboy.

But aloud, he said, "Ghosts? Pfft. Nah. I'm cool. A storm spirit chucked me down the Grand Canyon this morning, but you know, all in a day's work, right?"

Jake nodded. "That's good. Because I'll give you the best bed in the cabin—Beckendorf's."

"Whoa, Jake," Will said. "You sure?"

Jake called out: "Bunk 1-A, please."

The whole cabin rumbled. A circular section of the floor spiraled open like a camera lens, and a full-size bed popped up. The bronze frame had a built-in game station at the footboard, a stereo system in the headboard, a glass-door refrigerator mounted into the base, and a whole bunch of control panels running down the side.

Leo jumped right in and lay back with arms behind his head. "I can handle this."

"It retracts into a private room below," Jake said.

"Oh, heck, yes," Leo said. "See y'all. I'll be down in the Leo Cave. Which button do I press?"

"Hold on," Will Solace protested. "You guys have private underground rooms?"

Jake probably would've smiled if it didn't hurt so much. "We got lots of secrets, Will. You Apollo guys can't have all the fun. Our campers have been excavating the tunnel system under Cabin Nine for almost a century. We still haven't found the end. Anyway, Leo, if you don't mind sleeping in a dead man's bed, it's yours."

Suddenly Leo didn't feel like kicking back. He sat up, careful not to touch any of the buttons. "The counselor who died—this was his bed?"

"Yeah," Jake said. "Charles Beckendorf."

Leo imagined saw blades coming through the mattress, or maybe a grenade sewn inside the pillows. "He didn't, like, die *in* this bed, did he?"

"No," Jake said. "In the Titan War, last summer."

"The Titan War," Leo repeated, "which has *nothing* to do with this very fine bed?"

"The Titans," Will said, like Leo was an idiot. "The big powerful guys that ruled the world before the gods. They tried to make a comeback last summer. Their leader, Kronos, built a new palace on top of Mount Tam in California. Their armies came to New York and almost destroyed Mount Olympus. A lot of demigods died trying to stop them."

"I'm guessing this wasn't on the news?" Leo said.

It seemed like a fair question, but Will shook his head in

disbelief. "You didn't hear about Mount St. Helens erupting, or the freak storms across the country, or that building collapsing in St. Louis?"

Leo shrugged. Last summer, he'd been on the run from another foster home. Then a truancy officer caught him in New Mexico, and the court sentenced him to the nearest correctional facility—the Wilderness School. "Guess I was busy."

"Doesn't matter," Jake said. "You were lucky to miss it. T he thing is, Beckendorf was one of the first casualties, and ever since then—"

"Your cabin's been cursed," Leo guessed.

Jake didn't answer. Then again, the dude was in a body cast. That *was* an answer. Leo started noticing little things that he hadn't seen before—an explosion mark on the wall, a stain on the floor that might've been oil...or blood. Broken swords and smashed machines kicked into the corners of the room, maybe out of frustration. The place *did* feel unlucky.

Jake sighed halfheartedly. "Well, I should get some sleep. I hope you like it here, Leo. It used to be...really nice."

He closed his eyes, and the camouflage curtain drew itself across the bed.

"Come on, Leo," Will said. "I'll take you to the forges."

As they were leaving, Leo looked back at his new bed, and he could almost imagine a dead counselor sitting there —another ghost who wasn't going to leave Leo alone.

VI

LEO

"How did he die?" Leo asked. "I mean Beckendorf."

Will Solace trudged ahead. "Explosion. Beckendorf and Percy Jackson blew up a cruise ship full of monsters. Beckendorf didn't make it out."

There was that name again—Percy Jackson, Annabeth's missing boyfriend. That guy must've been into everything around here, Leo thought.

"So Beckendorf was pretty popular?" Leo asked. "I mean —before he blew up?"

"He was awesome," Will agreed. "It was hard on the whole camp when he died. Jake—he became head counselor in the middle of the war. Same as I did, actually. Jake did his best, but he never wanted to be leader. He just likes building stuff. Then after the war, things started to go wrong. Cabin Nine's chariots blew up. Their automatons went haywire. Their inventions started to malfunction. It was like a curse, and eventually people started calling it that—the Curse of Cabin Nine. Then Jake had his accident—"

"Which had something to do with the problem he mentioned," Leo guessed.

"They're working on it," Will said without enthusiasm. "And here we are."

The forge looked like a steam-powered locomotive had smashed into the Greek Parthenon and they had fused together. White marble columns lined the soot-stained walls. Chimneys pumped smoke over an elaborate gable carved with a bunch of gods and monsters. The building sat at the edge of a stream, with several waterwheels turning a series of bronze gears. Leo heard machinery grinding inside, fires roaring, and hammers ringing on anvils.

They stepped through the doorway, and a dozen guys and girls who'd been working on various projects all froze. The noise died down to the roar of the forge and the *click-click-click* of gears and levers.

"'Sup, guys," Will said. "This is your new brother, Leo —um, what's your last name?"

"Valdez." Leo looked around at the other campers. Was he really related to all of them? His cousins came from some big families, but he'd always just had his mom—until she died.

Kids came up and started shaking hands and introducing themselves. Their names blurred together: Shane, Christopher, Nyssa, Harley (yeah, like the motorcycle). Leo knew he'd never keep everybody straight. Too many of them. Too overwhelming.

None of them looked like the others—all different face types, skin tone, hair color, height. You'd never think, *Hey, look, it's the Hephaestus Bunch!* But they all had powerful hands, rough with calluses and stained with engine grease. Even little Harley, who couldn't have been more than eight, looked like he could go six rounds with Chuck Norris without breaking a sweat.

And all the kids shared a sad kind of seriousness. Their shoulders slumped like life had beaten them down pretty hard. Several looked like they'd been physically beaten up, too. Leo counted two arm slings, one pair of crutches, an eye patch, six Ace bandages, and about seven thousand Band-Aids.

"Well, all right!" Leo said. "I hear this is the party cabin!"

Nobody laughed. They all just stared at him.

Will Solace patted Leo's shoulder. "I'll leave you guys to get acquainted. Somebody show Leo to dinner when it's time?"

"I got it," one of the girls said. Nyssa, Leo remembered. She wore camo pants, a tank top that showed off her buff arms, and a red bandanna over a mop of dark hair. Except for the smiley-face Band-Aid on her chin, she looked like one of those female action heroes, like any second she was going to grab a machine gun and start mowing down evil aliens.

"Cool," Leo said. "I always wanted a sister who could beat me up."

Nyssa didn't smile. "Come on, joker boy. I'll show you around."

• • •

Leo was no stranger to workshops. He'd grown up around grease monkeys and power tools. His mom used to joke that his first pacifier was a lug wrench. But he'd never seen any place like the camp forge.

One guy was working on a battle-ax. He kept testing the blade on a slab of concrete. Each time he swung, the ax cut into the slab like it was warm cheese, but the guy looked unsatisfied and went back to honing the edge.

"What's he planning to kill with that thing?" Leo asked Nyssa. "A battleship?"

"You never know. Even with Celestial bronze—"

"That's the metal?"

She nodded. "Mined from Mount Olympus itself. Extremely rare. Anyway, it usually disintegrates monsters on contact, but big powerful ones have notoriously tough hides. Drakons, for instances—"

"You mean dragons?"

"Similar species. You'll learn the difference in monster-fighting class."

"Monster-fighting class. Yeah, I already got my black belt in that."

She didn't crack a smile. Leo hoped she wasn't this serious all the time. His dad's side of the family had to have *some* sense of humor, right?

They passed a couple of guys making a bronze windup toy. At least that's what it looked like. It was a six-inch-tall centaur—half man, half horse—armed with a miniature bow. One of the campers cranked the centaur's tail, and it whirred to life. It galloped across the table, yelling, "Die, mosquito! Die, mosquito!" and shooting everything in sight.

Apparently this had happened before, because everybody knew to hit the floor except Leo. Six needle-sized arrows embedded themselves in his shirt before a camper grabbed a hammer and smashed the centaur to pieces.

"Stupid curse!" The camper waved his hammer at the sky. "I just want a magic bug killer! Is that too much to ask?"

"Ouch," Leo said.

Nyssa pulled the needles out of his shirt. "Ah, you're fine. Let's move on before they rebuild it."

Leo rubbed his chest as they walked. "That sort of thing happen a lot?"

"Lately," Nyssa said, "everything we build turns to junk."

"The curse?"

Nyssa frowned. "I don't believe in curses. But *something's* wrong. And if we don't figure out the dragon problem, it's gonna get even worse."

"The dragon problem?" Leo hoped she was talking about a miniature dragon, maybe one that killed cockroaches, but he got the feeling he wasn't going to be so lucky.

Nyssa took him over to a big wall map that a couple of girls were studying. The map showed the camp—a semicircle of land with Long Island Sound on the north shore, the woods to the west, the cabins to the east, and a ring of hills to the south.

"It's got to be in the hills," the first girl said.

"We *looked* in the hills," the second argued. "The woods are a better hiding place."

"But we already set traps—"

"Hold up," Leo said. "You guys lost a dragon? A *real* full-size dragon?"

"It's a bronze dragon," Nyssa said. "But yes, it's a life-size automaton. Hephaestus cabin built it years ago. Then it was lost in the woods until a few summers back, when Beckendorf found it in pieces and rebuilt it. It's been helping protect the camp, but, um, it's a little unpredictable."

"Unpredictable," Leo said.

"It goes haywire and smashes down cabins, sets people on fire, tries to eat the satyrs."

"That's pretty unpredictable."

Nyssa nodded. "Beckendorf was the only one who could control it. Then he died, and the dragon just got worse and worse. Finally it went berserk and ran off. Occasionally it shows up, demolishes something, and runs away again. Everyone expects us to find it and destroy it—"

"*Destroy* it?" Leo was appalled. "You've got a life-size bronze dragon, and you want to *destroy* it?"

"It breathes fire," Nyssa explained. "It's deadly and out of control."

"But it's a dragon! Dude, that's so awesome. Can't you try talking to it, controlling it?"

"We tried. Jake Mason tried. You saw how well that worked."

Leo thought about Jake, wrapped in a body cast, lying alone on his bunk. "Still—"

"There's no other option." Nyssa turned to the other girls. "Let's try more traps in the woods—here, here, and here. Bait them with thirty-weight motor oil."

"The dragon drinks that?" Leo asked.

"Yeah." Nyssa sighed regretfully. "He used to like it with a little Tabasco sauce, right before bed. If he springs a trap, we can come in with acid sprayers—should melt through his hide. Then we get metal cutters and ... and finish the job."

They all looked sad. Leo realized they didn't want to kill the dragon any more than he did.

"Guys," he said. "There has to be another way."

Nyssa looked doubtful, but a few other campers stopped what they were working on and drifted over to hear the conversation.

"Like what?" one asked. "The thing breathes fire. We can't even get close."

Fire, Leo thought. Oh, man, the things he could tell them about fire.... But he had to be careful, even if these were his brothers and sisters. *Especially* if he had to live with them.

"Well..." He hesitated. "Hephaestus is the god of fire, right? So don't any of you have like fire resistance or something?"

Nobody acted as if it was a crazy question, which was a relief, but Nyssa shook her head gravely.

"That's a Cyclops ability, Leo. Demigod children of Hephaestus...we're just good with our hands. We're builders, craftsmen, weaponsmiths—stuff like that."

Leo's shoulders slumped. "Oh."

A guy in back said, "Well, a long *time* ago—"

"Yeah, okay," Nyssa conceded. "A long time ago some children of Hephaestus were born with power over fire. But that ability was very, very rare. And always dangerous. No

demigod like that has been born in centuries. The last one..."
She looked at one of the other kids for help.

"Sixteen sixty-six," the girl offered. "Guy named Thomas Faynor. He started the Great Fire of London, destroyed most of the city."

"Right," Nyssa said. "When a child of Hephaestus like that appears, it usually means something catastrophic is about to happen. And we don't need any more catastrophes."

Leo tried to keep his face clear of emotion, which wasn't his strong suit. "I guess I see your point. Too bad, though. If you could resist flames, you could get close to the dragon."

"Then it would kill you with its claws and fangs," Nyssa said. "Or simply step on you. No, we've got to destroy it. Trust me, if anyone *could* figure out another answer..."

She didn't finish, but Leo got the message. This was the cabin's big test. If they could do something only Beckendorf could do, if they could subdue the dragon without killing it, then maybe their curse would be lifted. But they were stumped for ideas. Any camper who figured out how would be a hero.

A conch horn blew in the distance. Campers started putting up their tools and projects. Leo hadn't realized it was getting so late, but he looked through the windows and saw the sun going down. His ADHD did that to him sometimes. If he was bored, a fifty-minute class seemed like six hours. If he was interested in something, like touring a demigod camp, hours slipped away and *bam*—the day was over.

"Dinner," Nyssa said. "Come on, Leo."

"Up at the pavilion, right?" he asked.

She nodded.

"You guys go ahead," Leo said. "Can you... give me a second?"

Nyssa hesitated. Then her expression softened. "Sure. It's a lot to process. I remember my first day. Come up when you're ready. Just don't touch anything. Almost every project in here can kill you if you're not careful."

"No touching," Leo promised.

His cabinmates filed out of the forge. Soon Leo was alone with the sounds of the bellows, the waterwheels, and small machines clicking and whirring.

He stared at the map of camp—the locations where his newfound siblings were going to put traps to catch a dragon. It was wrong. Plain wrong.

Very rare, he thought. And always dangerous.

He held out his hand and studied his fingers. They were long and thin, not callused like the other Hephaestus campers'. Leo had never been the biggest or the strongest kid. He'd survived in tough neighborhoods, tough schools, tough foster homes by using his wits. He was the class clown, the court jester, because he'd learned early that if you cracked jokes and pretended you weren't scared, you usually didn't get beat up. Even the baddest gangster kids would tolerate you, keep you around for laughs. Plus, humor was a good way to hide the pain. And if that didn't work, there was always Plan B. Run away. Over and over.

There *was* a Plan C, but he'd promised himself never to use it again.

He felt an urge to try it now—something he hadn't done since the accident, since his mom's death.

He extended his fingers and felt them tingle, like they were waking up—pins and needles. Then flames flickered to life, curls of red-hot fire dancing across his palm.

JASON

As soon as Jason saw the house, he knew he was a dead man.

"Here we are!" Drew said cheerfully. "The Big House, camp headquarters."

It didn't look threatening, just a four-story manor painted baby blue with white trim. The wraparound porch had lounge chairs, a card table, and an empty wheelchair. Wind chimes shaped like nymphs turned into trees as they spun. Jason could imagine old people coming here for summer vacation, sitting on the porch and sipping prune juice while they watched the sunset. Still, the windows seemed to glare down at him like angry eyes. The wide-open doorway looked ready to swallow him. On the highest gable, a bronze eagle weathervane spun in the wind and pointed straight in his direction, as if telling him to turn around.

Every molecule in Jason's body told him he was on enemy ground.

"I am *not* supposed to be here," he said.

Drew circled her arm through his. "Oh, please. You're *perfect* here, sweetie. Believe me, I've seen a lot of heroes."

Drew smelled like Christmas—a strange combination of pine and nutmeg. Jason wondered if she always smelled like that, or if it was some kind of special perfume for the holidays. Her pink eyeliner was really distracting. Every time she blinked, he felt compelled to look at her. Maybe that was the point, to show off her warm brown eyes. She was pretty. No doubt about that. But she made Jason feel uncomfortable.

He slipped his arm away as gently as he could. "Look, I appreciate—"

"Is it that girl?" Drew pouted. "Oh, please, tell me you are *not* dating the Dumpster Queen."

"You mean Piper? Um..."

Jason wasn't sure how to answer. He didn't think he'd ever seen Piper before today, but he felt strangely guilty about it. He knew he shouldn't be in this place. He shouldn't befriend these people, and certainly he shouldn't date one of them. Still...Piper had been holding his hand when he woke up on that bus. She believed she was his girlfriend. She'd been brave on the skywalk, fighting those *venti*, and when Jason had caught her in midair and they'd held each other face-to-face, he couldn't pretend he wasn't a little tempted to kiss her. But that wasn't right. He didn't even know his own story. He couldn't play with her emotions like that.

Drew rolled her eyes. "Let me help you decide, sweetie. You can do better. A guy with your looks and obvious talent?"

She wasn't looking at him, though. She was staring at a spot right above his head.

"You're waiting for a sign," he guessed. "Like what popped over Leo's head."

"What? No! Well...yes. I mean, from what I heard, you're pretty powerful, right? You're going to be important at camp, so I figure your parent will claim you right away. And I'd love to see that. I wanna be with you every step of the way! So is your dad or mom the god? Please tell me it's not your mom. I would hate it if you were an *Aphrodite* kid."

"Why?"

"Then you'd be my half brother, silly. You can't date somebody from your own cabin. Yuck!"

"But aren't all the gods related?" Jason asked. "So isn't everyone here your cousin or something?"

"Aren't you cute! Sweetie, the godly side of your family doesn't count except for your parent. So anybody from another cabin—they're fair game. So who's your godly parent—mom or dad?"

As usual, Jason didn't have an answer. He looked up, but no glowing sign popped above his head. At the top of the Big House, the weathervane was still pointing his direction, that bronze eagle glaring as if to say, *Turn around, kid, while you still can.*

Then he heard footsteps on the front porch. No—not footsteps—*hooves.*

"Chiron!" Drew called. "This is Jason. He's totally awesome!"

Jason backed up so fast he almost tripped. Rounding the corner of the porch was a man on horseback. Except he wasn't on horseback—he was part of the horse. From the waist up he was human, with curly brown hair and a well-trimmed beard. He wore a T-shirt that said *World's Best Centaur*, and had a quiver and bow strapped to his back. His head was so high up he had to duck to avoid the porch lights, because from the waist down, he was a white stallion.

Chiron started to smile at Jason. Then the color drained from his face.

"You . . ." The centaur's eyes flared like a cornered animal's. "You should be dead."

Chiron ordered Jason—well, *invited*, but it sounded like an order—to come inside the house. He told Drew to go back to her cabin, which Drew didn't look happy about.

The centaur trotted over to the empty wheelchair on the porch. He slipped off his quiver and bow and backed up to the chair, which opened like a magician's box. Chiron gingerly stepped into it with his back legs and began scrunching himself into a space that should've been much too small. Jason imagined a truck's reversing noises—*beep, beep, beep*—as the centaur's lower half disappeared and the chair folded up, popping out a set of fake human legs covered in a blanket, so Chiron appeared to be a regular mortal guy in a wheelchair.

"Follow me," he ordered. "We have lemonade."

The living room looked like it had been swallowed by a rain forest. Grapevines curved up the walls and across the ceiling, which Jason found a little strange. He didn't think plants grew like that inside, especially in the winter, but these were leafy green and bursting with bunches of red grapes.

Leather couches faced a stone fireplace with a crackling fire. Wedged in one corner, an old-style Pac-Man arcade game beeped and blinked. Mounted on the walls was an assortment of masks—smiley/frowny Greek theater types, feathered Mardi Gras masks, Venetian *Carnevale* masks with big beaklike noses, carved wooden masks from Africa. Grapevines grew through their mouths so they seemed to have leafy tongues. Some had red grapes bulging through their eyeholes.

But the weirdest thing was the stuffed leopard's head above the fireplace. It looked so real, its eyes seemed to follow Jason. Then it snarled, and Jason nearly leaped out of his skin.

"Now, Seymour," Chiron chided. "Jason is a friend. Behave yourself."

"That thing is alive!" Jason said.

Chiron rummaged through the side pocket of his wheelchair and brought out a package of Snausages. He threw one to the leopard, who snapped it up and licked his lips.

"You must excuse the décor," Chiron said. "All this was a parting gift from our old director before he was recalled to Mount Olympus. He thought it would help us to remember him. Mr. D has a strange sense of humor."

"Mr. D," Jason said. "Dionysus?"

"Mmm hmm." Chiron poured lemonade, though his hands were trembling a little. "As for Seymour, well, Mr. D liberated him from a Long Island garage sale. The leopard is Mr. D's sacred animal, you see, and Mr. D was appalled that someone would stuff such a noble creature. He decided to grant it life, on the assumption that life as a mounted head was better than no life at all. I must say it's a kinder fate than Seymour's previous owner got."

Seymour bared his fangs and sniffed the air, as if hunting for more Snausages.

"If he's only a head," Jason said, "where does the food go when he eats?"

"Better not to ask," Chiron said. "Please, sit."

Jason took some lemonade, though his stomach was fluttering. Chiron sat back in his wheelchair and tried for a smile, but Jason could tell it was forced. The old man's eyes were as deep and dark as wells.

"So, Jason," he said, "would you mind telling me—ah—where you're from?"

"I wish I knew." Jason told him the whole story, from waking up on the bus to crash-landing at Camp Half-Blood. He didn't see any point in hiding the details, and Chiron was a good listener. He didn't react to the story, other than to nod encouragingly for more.

When Jason was done, the old man sipped his lemonade.

"I see," Chiron said. "And you must have questions for me."

"Only one," Jason admitted. "What did you mean when you said that I should be dead?"

Chiron studied him with concern, as if he expected Jason to burst into flames. "My boy, do you know what those marks on your arm mean? The color of your shirt? Do you remember anything?"

Jason looked at the tattoo on his forearm: SPQR, the eagle, twelve straight lines.

"No," he said. "Nothing."

"Do you know where you are?" Chiron asked. "Do you understand what this place is, and who I am?"

"You're Chiron the centaur," Jason said. "I'm guessing you're the same one from the old stories, who used to train the Greek heroes like Heracles. This is a camp for demigods, children of the Olympian gods."

"So you believe those gods still exist?"

"Yes," Jason said immediately. "I mean, I don't think we should *worship* them or sacrifice chickens to them or anything, but they're still around because they're a powerful part of civilization. They move from country to country as the center of power shifts—like they moved from Ancient Greece to Rome."

"I couldn't have said it better." Something about Chiron's voice had changed. *"So you already know the gods are real. You have already been claimed, haven't you?"*

"Maybe," Jason answered. *"I'm not really sure."*

Seymour the leopard snarled.

Chiron waited, and Jason realized what had just happened. The centaur had switched to another language and Jason had understood, automatically answering in the same tongue.

"Quis erat—" Jason faltered, then made a conscious effort to speak English. "What was that?"

"You know Latin," Chiron observed. "Most demigods recognize a few phrases, of course. It's in their blood, but not as much as Ancient Greek. None can speak Latin fluently without practice."

Jason tried to wrap his mind around what that meant, but too many pieces were missing from his memory. He still had the feeling that he shouldn't be here. It was wrong—and dangerous. But at least Chiron wasn't threatening. In fact the centaur seemed concerned for him, afraid for his safety.

The fire reflected in Chiron's eyes, making them dance fretfully. "I taught your namesake, you know, the original Jason. He had a hard path. I've seen many heroes come and go. Occasionally, they have happy endings. Mostly, they don't. It breaks my heart, like losing a child each time one of my pupils dies. But you—you are not like any pupil I've ever taught. Your presence here could be a disaster."

"Thanks," Jason said. "You must be an inspiring teacher."

"I am sorry, my boy. But it's true. I had hoped that after Percy's success—"

"Percy Jackson, you mean. Annabeth's boyfriend, the one who's missing."

Chiron nodded. "I hoped that after he succeeded in the Titan War and saved Mount Olympus, we might have some peace. I might be able to enjoy one final triumph, a happy ending, and perhaps retire quietly. I should have known better. The last chapter approaches, just as it did before. The worst is yet to come."

In the corner, the arcade game made a sad *pew-pew-pew-pew* sound, like a Pac-Man had just died.

"Ohh-kay," Jason said. "So—last chapter, happened before,

worst yet to come. Sounds fun, but can we go back to the part where I'm supposed to be dead? I don't like that part."

"I'm afraid I can't explain, my boy. I swore on the River Styx and on all things sacred that I would never..." Chiron frowned. "But you're here, in violation of the same oath. That too, should not be possible. I don't understand. Who would've done such a thing? Who—"

Seymour the leopard howled. His mouth froze, half open. The arcade game stopped beeping. The fire stopped crackling, its flames hardening like red glass. The masks stared down silently at Jason with their grotesque grape eyes and leafy tongues.

"Chiron?" Jason asked. "What's going—"

The old centaur had frozen, too. Jason jumped off the couch, but Chiron kept staring at the same spot, his mouth open mid-sentence. His eyes didn't blink. His chest didn't move.

Jason, a voice said.

For a horrible moment, he thought the leopard had spoken. Then dark mist boiled out of Seymour's mouth, and an even worse thought occurred to Jason: *storm spirits*.

He grabbed the golden coin from his pocket. With a quick flip, it changed into a sword.

The mist took the form of a woman in black robes. Her face was hooded, but her eyes glowed in the darkness. Over her shoulders she wore a goatskin cloak. Jason wasn't sure how he knew it was goatskin, but he recognized it and knew it was important.

Would you attack your patron? the woman chided. Her voice echoed in Jason's head. *Lower your sword.*

"Who are you?" he demanded. "How did you—"

Our time is limited, Jason. My prison grows stronger by the hour. It took me a full month to gather enough energy to work even the smallest magic through its bonds. I've managed to bring you here, but now I have little time left, and even less power. This may be the last time I can speak to you.

"You're in prison?" Jason decided maybe he wouldn't lower his sword. "Look, I don't know you, and you're not my patron."

You know me, she insisted. *I have known you since your birth.*

"I don't remember. I don't remember anything."

No, you don't, she agreed. *That also was necessary. Long ago, your father gave me your life as a gift to placate my anger. He named you Jason, after my favorite mortal. You belong to me.*

"Whoa," Jason said. "I don't belong to anyone."

Now is the time to pay your debt, she said. *Find my prison. Free me, or their king will rise from the earth, and I will be destroyed. You will never retrieve your memory.*

"Is that a threat? You *took* my memories?"

You have until sunset on the solstice, Jason. Four short days. Do not fail me.

The dark woman dissolved, and the mist curled into the leopard's mouth.

Time unfroze. Seymour's howl turned into a cough like he'd sucked in a hair ball. The fire crackled to life, the arcade machine beeped, and Chiron said, "—would dare to bring you here?"

"Probably the lady in the mist," Jason offered.

Chiron looked up in surprise. "Weren't you just sitting… why do you have a sword drawn?"

"I hate to tell you this," Jason said, "but I think your leopard just ate a goddess."

He told Chiron about the frozen-in-time visit, the dark misty figure that disappeared into Seymour's mouth.

"Oh, dear," Chiron murmured. "That does explain a lot."

"Then why don't you explain a lot to me?" Jason said. "Please."

Before Chiron could say anything, footsteps reverberated on the porch outside. The front door blew open, and Annabeth and another girl, a redhead, burst in, dragging Piper between them. Piper's head lolled like she was unconscious.

"What happened?" Jason rushed over. "What's wrong with her?"

"Hera's cabin," Annabeth gasped, like they'd run all the way. "Vision. Bad."

The redheaded girl looked up, and Jason saw that she'd been crying.

"I think…" The redheaded girl gulped. "I think I may have killed her."

JASON

JASON AND THE REDHEAD, WHO INTRODUCED herself as Rachel, put Piper on the couch while Annabeth rushed down the hall to get a med kit. Piper was still breathing, but she wouldn't wake up. She seemed to be in some kind of coma.

"We've got to heal her," Jason insisted. "There's a way, right?"

Seeing her so pale, barely breathing, Jason felt a surge of protectiveness. Maybe he didn't really know her. Maybe she wasn't his girlfriend. But they'd survived the Grand Canyon together. They'd come all this way. He'd left her side for a little while, and *this* had happened.

Chiron put his hand on her forehead and grimaced. "Her mind is in a fragile state. Rachel, what happened?"

"I wish I knew," she said. "As soon as I got to camp, I had a premonition about Hera's cabin. I went inside. Annabeth and Piper came in while I was there. We talked, and then—I just blanked out. Annabeth said I spoke in a different voice."

"A prophecy?" Chiron asked.

"No. The spirit of Delphi comes from within. I know how that feels. This was like long distance, a power trying to speak through me."

Annabeth ran in with a leather pouch. She knelt next to Piper. "Chiron, what happened back there—I've never seen anything like it. I've heard Rachel's prophecy voice. This was different. She sounded like an older woman. She grabbed Piper's shoulders and told her—"

"To free her from a prison?" Jason guessed.

Annabeth stared at him. "How did you know that?"

Chiron made a three-fingered gesture over his heart, like a ward against evil.

"Jason, tell them. Annabeth, the medicine bag, please."

Chiron trickled drops from a medicine vial into Piper's mouth while Jason explained what had happened when the room froze—the dark misty woman who had claimed to be Jason's patron.

When he was done, no one spoke, which made him more anxious.

"So does this happen often?" he asked. "Supernatural phone calls from convicts demanding you bust them out of jail?"

"Your patron," Annabeth said. "Not your godly parent?"

"No, she said *patron*. She also said my dad had given her my life."

Annabeth frowned. "I've never of heard anything like that before. You said the storm spirit on the skywalk—he claimed to be working for some mistress who was giving him orders, right? Could it be this woman you saw, messing with your mind?"

"I don't think so," Jason said. "If she were my enemy, why would she be asking for my help? She's imprisoned. She's worried about some enemy getting more powerful. Something about a king rising from the earth on the solstice—"

Annabeth turned to Chiron. "Not Kronos. Please tell me it's not that."

The centaur looked miserable. He held Piper's wrist, checking her pulse.

At last he said, "It is not Kronos. That threat is ended. But..."

"But what?" Annabeth asked.

Chiron closed the medicine bag. "Piper needs rest. We should discuss this later."

"Or now," Jason said. "Sir, Mr. Chiron, you told me the greatest threat was coming. The last chapter. You can't possibly mean something worse than an army of Titans, right?"

"Oh," Rachel said in a small voice. "Oh, dear. The woman was Hera. Of course. Her cabin, her voice. She showed herself to Jason at the same moment."

"Hera?" Annabeth's snarl was even fiercer than Seymour's. "*She* took you over? She did this to Piper?"

"I think Rachel's right," Jason said. "The woman did seem like a goddess. And she wore this—this goatskin cloak. That's a symbol of Juno, isn't it?"

"It is?" Annabeth scowled. "I've never heard that."

Chiron nodded reluctantly. "Of Juno, Hera's Roman

aspect, in her most warlike state. The goatskin cloak was a symbol of the Roman soldier."

"So Hera is imprisoned?" Rachel asked. "Who could do that to the queen of the gods?"

Annabeth crossed her arms. "Well, whoever they are, maybe we should thank them. If they can shut up Hera—"

"Annabeth," Chiron warned, "she is still one of the Olympians. In many ways, she is the glue that holds the gods' family together. If she truly has been imprisoned and is in danger of destruction, this could shake the foundations of the world. It could unravel the stability of Olympus, which is never great even in the best of times. And if Hera has asked Jason for help—"

"Fine," Annabeth grumbled. "Well, we know Titans can capture a god, right? Atlas captured Artemis a few years ago. And in the old stories, the gods captured each other in traps all the time. But something worse than a Titan...?"

Jason looked at the leopard's head. Seymour was smacking his lips like the goddess had tasted much better than a Snausage. "Hera said she'd been trying to break through her prison bonds for a month."

"Which is how long Olympus has been closed," Annabeth said. "So the gods must know something bad is going on."

"But why use her energy to send me here?" Jason asked. "She wiped my memory, plopped me into the Wilderness School field trip, and sent you a dream vision to come pick me up. Why am I so important? Why not just send up an emergency flare to the other gods—let them know where she is so they bust her out?"

"The gods need heroes to do their will down here on earth," Rachel said. "That's right, isn't it? Their fates are always intertwined with demigods."

"That's true," Annabeth said, "but Jason's got a point. Why him? Why take his memory?"

"And Piper's involved somehow," Rachel said. "Hera sent her the same message—*Free me*. And, Annabeth, this must have something to do with Percy's disappearing."

Annabeth fixed her eyes on Chiron. "Why are you so quiet, Chiron? What is it we're facing?"

The old centaur's face looked like it had aged ten years in a matter of minutes. The lines around his eyes were deeply etched. "My dear, in this, I cannot help you. I am so sorry."

Annabeth blinked. "You've never...you've *never* kept information from me. Even the last great prophecy—"

"I will be in my office." His voice was heavy. "I need some time to think before dinner. Rachel, will you watch the girl? Call Argus to bring her to the infirmary, if you'd like. And Annabeth, you should speak with Jason. Tell him about—about the Greek and Roman gods."

"But..."

The centaur turned his wheelchair and rolled off down the hallway. Annabeth's eyes turned stormy. She muttered something in Greek, and Jason got the feeling it wasn't complimentary toward centaurs.

"I'm sorry," Jason said. "I think my being here—I don't know. I've messed things up coming to the camp, somehow. Chiron said he'd sworn an oath and couldn't talk about it."

"What oath?" Annabeth demanded. "I've never seen him

act this way. And why would he tell me to talk to you about the gods..."

Her voice trailed off. Apparently she'd just noticed Jason's sword sitting on the coffee table. She touched the blade gingerly, like it might be hot.

"Is this gold?" she said. "Do you remember where you got it?"

"No," Jason said. "Like I said, I don't remember anything."

Annabeth nodded, like she'd just come up with a rather desperate plan. "If Chiron won't help, we'll need to figure things out ourselves. Which means...Cabin Fifteen. Rachel, you'll keep an eye on Piper?"

"Sure," Rachel promised. "Good luck, you two."

"Hold on," Jason said. "What's in Cabin Fifteen?"

Annabeth stood. "Maybe a way to get your memory back."

They headed toward a newer wing of cabins in the southwest corner of the green. Some were fancy, with glowing walls or blazing torches, but Cabin Fifteen was not so dramatic. It looked like an old-fashioned prairie house with mud walls and a rush roof. On the door hung a wreath of crimson flowers —red poppies, Jason thought, though he wasn't sure how he knew.

"You think this is my parent's cabin?" he asked.

"No," Annabeth said. "This is the cabin for Hypnos, the god of sleep."

"Then why—"

"You've forgotten everything," she said. "If there's any god who can help us figure out memory loss, it's Hypnos."

Inside, even though it was almost dinnertime, three kids

were sound asleep under piles of covers. A warm fire crackled in the hearth. Above the mantel hung a tree branch, each twig dripping white liquid into a collection of tin bowls. Jason was tempted to catch a drop on his finger just to see what it was, but he held himself back.

Soft violin music played from somewhere. The air smelled like fresh laundry. The cabin was so cozy and peaceful that Jason's eyelids started to feel heavy. A nap sounded like a great idea. He was exhausted. There were plenty of empty beds, all with feather pillows and fresh sheets and fluffy quilts and—

Annabeth nudged him. "Snap out of it."

Jason blinked. He realized his knees had been starting to buckle.

"Cabin Fifteen does that to everyone," Annabeth warned. "If you ask me, this place is even more dangerous than the Ares cabin. At least with Ares, you can learn where the land mines are."

"Land mines?"

She walked up to the nearest snoring kid and shook his shoulder. "Clovis! Wake up!"

The kid looked like a baby cow. He had a blond tuft of hair on a wedge-shaped head, with thick features and a thick neck. His body was stocky, but he had spindly little arms like he'd never lifted anything heavier than a pillow.

"Clovis!" Annabeth shook harder, then finally knocked on his forehead about six times.

"Wh-wh-what?" Clovis complained, sitting up and squinting. He yawned hugely, and both Annabeth and Jason yawned too.

"Stop that!" Annabeth said. "We need your help."

"I was sleeping."

"You're *always* sleeping."

"Good night."

Before he could pass out, Annabeth yanked his pillow off the bed.

"That's not fair," Clovis complained meekly. "Give it back."

"First help," Annabeth said. "Then sleep."

Clovis sighed. His breath smelled like warm milk. "Fine. What?"

Annabeth explained about Jason's problem. Every once in a while she'd snap her fingers under Clovis's nose to keep him awake.

Clovis must have been really excited, because when Annabeth was done, he didn't pass out. He actually stood and stretched, then blinked at Jason. "So you don't remember anything, huh?"

"Just impressions," Jason said. "Feelings, like . . ."

"Yes?" Clovis said.

"Like I know I shouldn't be here. At this camp. I'm in danger."

"Hmm. Close your eyes."

Jason glanced at Annabeth, but she nodded reassuringly.

Jason was afraid he'd end up snoring in one of the bunks forever, but he closed his eyes. His thoughts became murky, as if he were sinking into a dark lake.

The next thing he knew, his eyes snapped open. He was sitting in a chair by the fire. Clovis and Annabeth knelt next to him.

"—serious, all right," Clovis was saying.

"What happened?" Jason said. "How long—"

"Just a few minutes," Annabeth said. "But it was tense. You almost dissolved."

Jason hoped she didn't mean *literally*, but her expression was solemn.

"Usually," Clovis said, "memories are lost for a good reason. They sink under the surface like dreams, and with a good sleep, I can bring them back. But this . . ."

"Lethe?" Annabeth asked.

"No," Clovis said. "Not even Lethe."

"Lethe?" Jason asked.

Clovis pointed to the tree branch dripping milky drops above the fireplace. "The River Lethe in the Underworld. It dissolves your memories, wipes your mind clean permanently. That's the branch of a poplar tree from the Underworld, dipped into the Lethe. It's the symbol of my father, Hypnos. Lethe is not a place you want to go swimming."

Annabeth nodded. "Percy went there once. He told me it was powerful enough to wipe the mind of a Titan."

Jason was suddenly glad he hadn't touched the branch. "But . . . that's not my problem?"

"No," Clovis agreed. "Your mind wasn't wiped, and your memories weren't buried. They've been stolen."

The fire crackled. Drops of Lethe water plinked into the tin cups on the mantel. One of the other Hypnos campers muttered in his sleep—something about a duck.

"Stolen," Jason said. "How?"

"A god," Clovis said. "Only a god would have that kind of power."

"We know that," said Jason. "It was Juno. But how did she do it, and why?"

Clovis scratched his neck. "Juno?"

"He means Hera," Annabeth said. "For some reason, Jason likes the Roman names."

"Hmm," Clovis said.

"What?" Jason asked. "Does that mean something?"

"Hmm," Clovis said again, and this time Jason realized he was snoring.

"Clovis!" he yelled.

"What? What?" His eyes fluttered open. "We were talking about pillows, right? No, gods. I remember. Greek and Roman. Sure, could be important."

"But they're the same gods," Annabeth said. "Just different names."

"Not exactly," Clovis said.

Jason sat forward, now very much awake. "What do you mean, not exactly?"

"Well..." Clovis yawned. "Some gods are only Roman. Like Janus, or Pompona. But even the major Greek gods—it's not just their names that changed when they moved to Rome. Their appearances changed. Their attributes changed. They even had slightly different personalities."

"But..." Annabeth faltered. "Okay, so maybe people saw them differently through the centuries. That doesn't change who they are."

"Sure it does." Clovis began to nod off, and Jason snapped his fingers under his nose.

"Coming, Mother!" he yelped. "I mean...Yeah, I'm

awake. So, um, personalities. The gods change to reflect their host cultures. You know that, Annabeth. I mean, these days, Zeus likes tailored suits, reality television, and that Chinese food place on East Twenty-eighth Street, right? It was the same in Roman times, and the gods were Roman almost as long as they were Greek. It was a big empire, lasted for centuries. So of course their Roman aspects are still a big part of their character."

"Makes sense," Jason said.

Annabeth shook her head, mystified. "But how do you know all this, Clovis?"

"Oh, I spend a lot of time dreaming. I see the gods there all the time—always shifting forms. Dreams are fluid, you know. You can be in different places at once, always changing identities. It's a lot like being a god, actually. Like recently, I dreamed I was watching a Michael Jackson concert, and then I was onstage *with* Michael Jackson, and we were singing this duet, and I could *not* remember the words for 'The Girl Is Mine.' Oh, man, it was so embarrassing, I—"

"Clovis," Annabeth interrupted. "Back to Rome?"

"Right, Rome," Clovis said. "So we call the gods by their Greek names because that's their original form. But saying their Roman aspects are exactly the same—that's not true. In Rome, they became more warlike. They didn't mingle with mortals as much. They were harsher, more powerful—the gods of an empire."

"Like the dark side of the gods?" Annabeth asked.

"Not exactly," Clovis said. "They stood for discipline, honor, strength—"

"Good things, then," Jason said. For some reason, he felt the need to speak up for the Roman gods, though wasn't sure why it mattered to him. "I mean, discipline is important, right? That's what made Rome last so long."

Clovis gave him a curious look. "That's true. But the Roman gods weren't very friendly. For instance, my dad, Hypnos ... he didn't do much except sleep in Greek times. In Roman times, they called him Somnus. He liked killing people who didn't stay alert at their jobs. If they nodded off at the wrong time, *boom*—they never woke up. He killed the helmsman of Aeneas when they were sailing from Troy."

"Nice guy," Annabeth said. "But I still don't understand what it has to do with Jason."

"Neither do I," Clovis said. "But if Hera took your memory, only she can give it back. And if I had to meet the queen of the gods, I'd hope she was more in a Hera mood than a Juno mood. Can I go back to sleep now?"

Annabeth stared at the branch above the fire, dripping Lethe water into the cups. She looked so worried, Jason wondered if she was considering a drink to forget her troubles. Then she stood and tossed Clovis his pillow. "Thanks, Clovis. We'll see you at dinner."

"Can I get room service?" Clovis yawned and stumbled to his bunk. "I feel like ... zzzz ..." He collapsed with his butt in the air and his face buried in pillow.

"Won't he suffocate?" Jason asked.

"He'll be fine," Annabeth said. "But I'm beginning to think that you are in serious trouble."

PIPER

PIPER DREAMED ABOUT HER LAST DAY with her dad.

They were on the beach near Big Sur, taking a break from surfing. The morning had been so perfect, Piper knew something had to go wrong soon—a rabid horde of paparazzi, or maybe a great white shark attack. No way her luck could hold.

But so far, they'd had excellent waves, an overcast sky, and a mile of oceanfront completely to themselves. Dad had found this out-of-the-way spot, rented a beachfront villa *and* the properties on either side, and somehow managed to keep it secret. If he stayed there too long, Piper knew the photographers would find him. They always did.

"Nice job out there, Pipes." He gave her the smile he was famous for: perfect teeth, dimpled chin, a twinkle in his dark eyes that always made grown women scream and ask him to sign their bodies in permanent marker. (*Seriously*, Piper thought, *get a life*.) His close-cropped black hair gleamed with salt water. "You're getting better at hanging ten."

Piper flushed with pride, though she suspected Dad was just being nice. She still spent most of her time wiping out. It took special talent to run over yourself with a surfboard. Her *dad* was the natural surfer—which made no sense since he'd been raised a poor kid in Oklahoma, hundreds of miles from the ocean—but he was amazing on the curls. Piper would've given up surfing a long time ago except it let her spend time with him. There weren't many ways she could do that.

"Sandwich?" Dad dug into the picnic basket his chef, Arno, had made. "Let's see: turkey pesto, crabcake wasabi —ah, a Piper special. Peanut butter and jelly."

She took the sandwich, though her stomach was too upset to eat. She always asked for PB&J. Piper was vegetarian, for one thing. She had been ever since they'd driven past that slaughterhouse in Chino and the smell had made her insides want to come outside. But it was more than that. PB&J was simple food, like a regular kid would have for lunch. Sometimes she pretended her dad had actually made it for her, not a personal chef from France who liked to wrap the sandwich in gold leaf paper with a light-up sparkler instead of a toothpick.

Couldn't anything be simple? That's why she turned down the fancy clothes Dad always offered, the designer shoes, the trips to the salon. She cut her own hair with a pair of plastic Garfield safety scissors, deliberately making it uneven. She preferred to wear beat-up running shoes, jeans, a T-shirt, and her old Polartec jacket from the time they went snowboarding.

And she hated the snobby private schools Dad thought were good for her. She kept getting herself kicked out. He kept finding more schools.

Yesterday, she'd pulled her biggest heist yet—driving that "borrowed" BMW out of the dealership. She *had* to pull a bigger stunt each time, because it took more and more to get Dad's attention.

Now she regretted it. Dad didn't know yet.

She'd meant to tell him that morning. Then he'd surprised her with this trip, and she couldn't ruin it. It was the first time they'd had a day together in what—three months?

"What's wrong?" He passed her a soda.

"Dad, there's something—"

"Hold on, Pipes. That's a serious face. Ready for Any Three Questions?"

They'd been playing that game for years—her dad's way of staying connected in the shortest possible amount of time. They could ask each other any three questions. Nothing off-limits, and you had to answer honestly. The rest of the time, Dad promised to stay out of her business—which was easy, since he was never around.

Piper knew most kids would find a Q&A like this with their parents totally mortifying. But she looked forward to it. It was like surfing—not easy, but a way to feel like she actually had a father.

"First question," she said. "Mom."

No surprise. That was always one of her topics.

Her dad shrugged with resignation. "What do you want to know, Piper? I've already told you—she disappeared. I don't know why, or where she went. After you were born, she simply left. I never heard from her again."

"Do you think she's still alive?"

It wasn't a real question. Dad was allowed to say he didn't know. But she wanted to hear how he'd answer.

He stared at the waves.

"Your Grandpa Tom," he said at last, "he used to tell me that if you walked far enough toward the sunset, you'd come to Ghost Country, where you could talk to the dead. He said a long time ago, you could bring the dead back; but then mankind messed up. Well, it's a long story."

"Like the Land of the Dead for the Greeks," Piper remembered. "It was in the west, too. And Orpheus—he tried to bring his wife back."

Dad nodded. A year before, he'd had his biggest role as an Ancient Greek king. Piper had helped him research the myths—all those old stories about people getting turned to stone and boiled in lakes of lava. They'd had a fun time reading together, and it made Piper's life seem not so bad. For a while she'd felt closer to her dad, but like everything, it didn't last.

"Lot of similarities between Greek and Cherokee," Dad agreed. "Wonder what your grandpa would think if he saw us now, sitting at the end of the western land. He'd probably think we're ghosts."

"So you're saying you believe those stories? You think Mom is dead?"

His eyes watered, and Piper saw the sadness behind them. She figured that's why women were so attracted to him. On the surface, he seemed confident and rugged, but his eyes held so much sadness. Women wanted to find out why. They wanted to comfort him, and they never could. Dad told

Piper it was a Cherokee thing—they all had that darkness inside them from generations of pain and suffering. But Piper thought it was more than that.

"I don't believe the stories," he said. "They're fun to tell, but if I really believed in Ghost Country, or animal spirits, or Greek gods...I don't think I could sleep at night. I'd always be looking for somebody to blame."

Somebody to blame for Grandpa Tom dying of lung cancer, Piper thought, before Dad got famous and had the money to help. For Mom—the only woman he'd ever loved —abandoning him without even a good-bye note, leaving him with a newborn girl he wasn't ready to care for. For his being so successful, and yet still not happy.

"I don't know if she's alive," he said. "But I do think she might as well be in Ghost Country, Piper. There's no getting her back. If I believed otherwise...I don't think I could stand that, either."

Behind them, a car door opened. Piper turned, and her heart sank. Jane was marching toward them in her business suit, wobbling over the sand in her high heels, her PDA in hand. The look on her face was partly annoyed, partly triumphant, and Piper knew she'd been in touch with the police.

Please fall down, Piper prayed. *If there's any animal spirit or Greek god that can help, make Jane take a header. I'm not asking for permanent damage, just knock her out for the rest of the day, please?*

But Jane kept advancing.

"Dad," Piper said quickly. "Something happened yesterday...."

But he'd seen Jane, too. He was already reconstructing his business face. Jane wouldn't be here if it wasn't serious. A studio head called—a project fell through—or Piper had messed up again.

"We'll get back to that, Pipes," he promised. "I'd better see what Jane wants. You know how she is."

Yes—Piper knew. Dad trudged across the sand to meet her. Piper couldn't hear them talking, but she didn't need to. She was good at reading faces. Jane gave him the facts about the stolen car, occasionally pointing at Piper like she was a disgusting pet that had whizzed on the carpet.

Dad's energy and enthusiasm drained away. He gestured for Jane to wait. Then he walked back to Piper. She couldn't stand that look in his eyes—like she'd betrayed his trust.

"You told me you would try, Piper," he said.

"Dad, I hate that school. I can't do it. I wanted to tell you about the BMW, but—"

"They've expelled you," he said. "A car, Piper? You're sixteen next year. I would buy you any car you want. How could you—"

"You mean *Jane* would buy me a car?" Piper demanded. She couldn't help it. The anger just welled up and spilled out of her. "Dad, just listen for once. Don't make me wait for you to ask your stupid three questions. I want to go to regular school. I want *you* to take me to parents' night, not Jane. Or homeschool me! I learned so much when we read about Greece together. We could do that all the time! We could—"

"Don't make this about me," her dad said. "I do the best I can, Piper. We've had this conversation."

No, she thought. *You've cut off this conversation. For years.*

Her dad sighed. "Jane's talked to the police, brokered a deal. The dealership won't press charges, but you have to agree to go to a boarding school in Nevada. They specialize in problems . . . in kids with tough issues."

"That's what I am." Her voice trembled. "A problem."

"Piper . . . you said you'd try. You let me down. I don't know what else to do."

"Do anything," she said. "But do it yourself! Don't let Jane handle it for you. You can't just send me away."

Dad looked down at the picnic basket. His sandwich sat uneaten on a piece of gold leaf paper. They'd planned for a whole afternoon in the surf. Now that was ruined.

Piper couldn't believe he'd really give in to Jane's wishes. Not this time. Not on something as huge as boarding school.

"Go see her," Dad said. "She's got the details."

"Dad . . ."

He looked away, gazing at the ocean like he could see all the way to Ghost Country. Piper promised herself she wouldn't cry. She headed up the beach toward Jane, who smiled coldly and held up a plane ticket. As usual, she'd already arranged everything. Piper was just another problem of the day that Jane could now check off her list.

Piper's dream changed.

She stood on a mountaintop at night, city lights glimmering below. In front of her, a bonfire blazed. Purplish flames seemed to cast more shadows than light, but the heat was so intense, her clothes steamed.

"This is your second warning," a voice rumbled, so powerful it shook the earth. Piper had heard that voice before in her dreams. She'd tried to convince herself it wasn't as scary as she remembered, but it was worse.

Behind the bonfire, a huge face loomed out of the darkness. It seemed to float above the flames, but Piper knew it must be connected to an enormous body. The crude features might've been chiseled out of rock. The face hardly seemed alive except for its piercing white eyes, like raw diamonds, and its horrible frame of locs, braided with human bones. It smiled, and Piper shivered.

"You'll do what you're told," the giant said. "You'll go on the quest. Do our bidding, and you may walk away alive. Otherwise—"

He gestured to one side of the fire. Piper's father was hanging unconscious, tied to a stake.

She tried to cry out. She wanted to call to her dad, and demand the giant let him go, but her voice wouldn't work.

"I'll be watching," the giant said. "Serve me, and you both live. You have the word of Enceladus. Fail me . . . well, I've slept for millennia, young demigod. I am *very* hungry. Fail, and I'll eat well."

The giant roared with laughter. The earth trembled. A crevice opened at Piper's feet, and she tumbled into darkness.

She woke feeling like she'd been trampled by an Irish stepdancing troupe. Her chest hurt, and she could barely breathe. She reached down and closed her hand around the hilt of the dagger Annabeth had given her—Katoptris, Helen of Troy's weapon.

So Camp Half-Blood hadn't been a dream.

"How are you feeling?" someone asked.

Piper tried to focus. She was lying in a bed with a white curtain on one side, like in a nurse's office. That redheaded girl, Rachel Dare, sat next to her. On the wall was a poster of a cartoon satyr who looked disturbingly like Coach Hedge with a thermometer sticking out of his mouth. The caption read: *Don't let sickness get your goat!*

"Where—" Piper's voice died when she saw the guy at the door.

He looked like a typical California surfer dude—buff and tan, blond hair, dressed in shorts and a T-shirt. But he had hundreds of blue eyes all over his body—along his arms, down his legs, and all over his face. Even his feet had eyes, peering up at her from between the straps of his sandals.

"That's Argus," Rachel said, "our head of security. He's just keeping an eye on things . . . so to speak."

Argus nodded. The eye on his chin winked.

"Where—?" Piper tried again, but she felt like she was talking through a mouthful of cotton.

"You're in the Big House," Rachel said. "Camp offices. We brought you here when you collapsed."

"You grabbed me," Piper remembered. "Hera's voice—"

"I'm so sorry about that," Rachel said. "Believe me, it was *not* my idea to get possessed. Chiron healed you with some nectar—"

"Nectar?"

"The drink of the gods. In small amounts, it heals demi-gods, if it doesn't—ah—burn you to ashes."

"Oh. Fun."

Rachel sat forward. "Do you remember your vision?"

Piper had a moment of dread, thinking she meant the dream about the giant. Then she realized Rachel was talking about what happened in Hera's cabin.

"Something's wrong with the goddess," Piper said. "She told me to free her, like she's trapped. She mentioned the earth swallowing us, and a fiery one, and something about the solstice."

In the corner, Argus made a rumbling sound in his chest. His eyes all fluttered at once.

"Hera created Argus," Rachel explained. "He's actually very sensitive when it comes to her safety. We're trying to keep him from crying, because last time that happened... well, it caused quite a flood."

Argus sniffled. He grabbed a fistful of Kleenex from the bedside table and started dabbing eyes all over his body.

"So..." Piper tried not to stare as Argus wiped the tears from his elbows. "What's happened to Hera?"

"We're not sure," Rachel said. "Annabeth and Jason were here for you, by the way. Jason didn't want to leave you, but Annabeth had an idea—something that might restore his memories."

"That's... that's great."

Jason had been here for her? She wished she'd been conscious for that. But if he got his memories back, would that be a good thing? She was still holding out hope that they really did know each other. She didn't want their relationship to be just a trick of the Mist.

Get over yourself, she thought. If she was going to save her dad, it didn't matter whether Jason liked her or not. He would hate her eventually. Everyone here would.

She looked down at the ceremonial dagger strapped to her side. Annabeth had said it was a sign of power and status, but not normally used in battle. All show and no substance. A fake, just like Piper. And its name was Katoptris, looking glass. She didn't dare unsheathe it again, because she couldn't bear to see her own reflection.

"Don't worry." Rachel squeezed her arm. "Jason seems like a good guy. He had a vision too, a lot like yours. Whatever's happening with Hera—I think you two are meant to work together."

Rachel smiled like this was good news, but Piper's spirits plunged even further. She'd thought that this quest—whatever it was—would involve nameless people. Now Rachel was basically telling her: *Good news! Not only is your dad being held ransom by a cannibal giant, you also get to betray the guy you like! How awesome is that?*

"Hey," Rachel said. "No need to cry. You'll figure it out."

Piper wiped her eyes, trying to get control of herself. This wasn't like her. She was supposed to be tough—a hardened car thief, the scourge of L.A. private schools. Here she was, crying like a baby. "How can you know what I'm facing?"

Rachel shrugged. "I know it's a hard choice, and your options aren't great. Like I said, I get hunches sometimes.

But you're going to be claimed at the campfire. I'm almost sure. When you know who your godly parent is, things might be clearer."

Clearer, Piper thought. Not necessarily better.

She sat up in bed. Her forehead ached like someone had driven a spike between her eyes. *There's no getting your mother back,* her dad had told her. But apparently, tonight, her mom might claim her. For the first time, Piper wasn't sure she wanted that.

"I hope it's Athena." She looked up, afraid Rachel might make fun of her, but the oracle just smiled.

"Piper, I don't blame you. Truthfully? I think Annabeth is hoping that too. You guys are a lot alike."

The comparison made Piper feel even guiltier. "Another hunch? You don't know anything about me."

"You'd be surprised."

"You're just saying that because you're an oracle, aren't you? You're supposed to sound all mysterious."

Rachel laughed. "Don't be giving away my secrets, Piper. And don't worry. Things will work out—just maybe not the way you plan."

"That's not making me feel better."

Somewhere in the distance, a conch horn blew. Argus grumbled and opened the door.

"Dinner?" Piper guessed.

"You slept through it," Rachel said. "Time for the campfire. Let's go find out who you are."

PIPER

THE WHOLE CAMPFIRE IDEA FREAKED PIPER OUT. It made her think of that huge purple bonfire in the dreams, and her father tied to a stake.

What she got instead was almost as terrifying: a sing-along. The amphitheater steps were carved into the side of a hill, facing a stone-lined fire pit. Fifty or sixty kids filled the rows, clustered into groups under various banners.

Piper spotted Jason in the front next to Annabeth. Leo was nearby, sitting with a bunch of burly-looking campers under a steel gray banner emblazoned with a hammer. Standing in front of the fire, half a dozen campers with guitars and strange, old-fashioned harps—lyres?—were jumping around, leading a song about pieces of armor, something about how their grandma got dressed for war. Everybody was singing with them and making gestures for the pieces of armor and joking around. It was quite possibly the weirdest thing Piper had ever seen—one of those campfire songs that would've been completely embarrassing in daylight; but in the dark, with everybody participating, it was kind of corny and fun. As the energy level got higher, the flames did too, turning from red to orange to gold.

Finally the song ended with a lot of rowdy applause. A guy on a horse trotted up. At least in the flickering light, Piper *thought* it was a guy on a horse. Then she realized it was a centaur—his bottom half a white stallion, his top half a middle-aged guy with curly hair and a trimmed beard. He brandished a spear impaled with toasted marshmallows. "Very nice! And a special welcome to our new arrivals. I am Chiron, camp activities director, and I'm happy you have all arrived here alive and with most of your limbs attached. In a moment, I promise we'll get to the s'mores, but first—"

"What about capture the flag?" somebody yelled. Grumbling broke out among some kids in armor, sitting under a red banner with the emblem of a boar's head.

"Yes," the centaur said. "I know the Ares cabin is anxious to return to the woods for our regular games."

"And kill people!" one of them shouted.

"However," Chiron said, "until the dragon is brought under control, that won't be possible. Cabin Nine, anything to report on that?"

He turned to Leo's group. Leo winked at Piper and shot her with a finger gun. The girl next to him stood uncomfortably. She wore an army jacket a lot like Leo's, with her hair covered in a red bandanna. "We're working on it."

More grumbling.

"How, Nyssa?" an Ares kid demanded.

"Really hard," the girl said.

Nyssa sat down to a lot of yelling and complaining, which caused the fire to sputter chaotically. Chiron stamped his hoof against the fire pit stones—*bang, bang, bang*—and the campers fell silent.

"We will have to be patient," Chiron said. "In the meantime, we have more pressing matters to discuss."

"Percy?" someone asked. The fire dimmed even further, but Piper didn't need the mood flames to sense the crowd's anxiety.

Chiron gestured to Annabeth. She took a deep breath and stood.

"I didn't find Percy," she announced. Her voice caught a little when she said his name. "He wasn't at the Grand Canyon like I thought. But we're not giving up. We've got teams everywhere. Grover, Tyson, Nico, the Hunters of Artemis —everyone's out looking. We *will* find him. Chiron's talking about something different. A new quest."

"It's the Great Prophecy, isn't it?" a girl called out.

Everyone turned. The voice had come from a group in back, sitting under a rose-colored banner with a dove emblem. They'd been chatting among themselves and not paying much attention until their leader stood up: Drew.

Everyone else looked surprised. Apparently Drew didn't address the crowd very often.

"Drew?" Annabeth said. "What do you mean?"

"Well, *come on*." Drew spread her hands like the truth was obvious. "Olympus is closed. Percy's disappeared. Hera sends you a vision and you come back with three new demigods in one day. I mean, something weird is going on. The Great Prophecy has started, right?"

Piper whispered to Rachel, "What's she talking about—the Great Prophecy?"

Then she realized everyone else was looking at Rachel, too.

"Well?" Drew called down. "You're the oracle. Has it started or not?"

Rachel's eyes looked scary in the firelight. Piper was afraid she might clench up and start channeling a freaky peacock goddess again, but she stepped forward calmly and addressed the camp.

"Yes," she said. "The Great Prophecy has begun."

Pandemonium broke out.

Piper caught Jason's eye. He mouthed, *You all right?* She nodded and managed a smile, but then looked away. It was too painful seeing him and not being with him.

When the talking finally subsided, Rachel took another step toward the audience, and fifty-plus demigods leaned away from her, as if one skinny redheaded mortal was more intimidating than all of them put together.

"For those of you who have not heard it," Rachel said, "the Great Prophecy was my first prediction. It arrived in August. It goes like this:

"Seven half-bloods shall answer the call.
To storm or fire the world must fall—"

Jason shot to his feet. His eyes looked wild, like he'd just been tasered.

Even Rachel seemed caught off guard. "J-Jason?" she said. "What's—"

"Ut cum spiritu postrema sacramentum dejuremus," he chanted. *"Et hostes ornamenta addent ad ianuam necem."*

An uneasy silence settled on the group. Piper could see from their faces that several of them were trying to translate the lines. She could tell it was Latin, but she wasn't sure why her hopefully future boyfriend was suddenly chanting like a Catholic priest.

"You just...finished the prophecy," Rachel stammered. "—*An oath to keep with a final breath/And foes bear arms to the Doors of Death.* How did you—"

"I know those lines." Jason winced and put his hands to his temples. "I don't know how, but I *know* that prophecy."

"In Latin, no less," Drew called out. "Handsome *and* smart."

There was some giggling from the Aphrodite cabin. God, what a bunch of losers, Piper thought. But it didn't do much to break the tension. The campfire was burning a chaotic, nervous shade of green.

Jason sat down, looking embarrassed, but Annabeth put a hand on his shoulder and muttered something reassuring. Piper felt a pang of jealousy. It should have been *her* next to him, comforting him.

Rachel Dare still looked a little shaken. She glanced back at Chiron for guidance, but the centaur stood grim and silent, as if he were watching a play he couldn't interrupt—a tragedy that ended with a lot of people dead onstage.

"Well," Rachel said, trying to regain her composure. "So,

yeah, that's the Great Prophecy. We hoped it might not happen for years, but I fear it's starting now. I can't give you proof. It's just a feeling. And like Drew said, some weird stuff is happening. The seven demigods, whoever they are, have not been gathered yet. I get the feeling some are here tonight. Some are not here."

The campers began to stir and mutter, looking at each other nervously, until a drowsy voice in the crowd called out, "I'm here! Oh . . . were you calling roll?"

"Go back to sleep, Clovis," someone yelled, and a lot of people laughed.

"Anyway," Rachel continued, "we don't know what the Great Prophecy means. We don't know what challenge the demigods will face, but since the *first* Great Prophecy predicted the Titan War, we can guess the *second* Great Prophecy will predict something at least that bad."

"Or worse," Chiron murmured.

Maybe he didn't mean everyone to overhear, but they did. The campfire immediately turned dark purple, the same color as Piper's dream.

"What we *do* know," Rachel said, "is that the first phase has begun. A major problem has arisen, and we need a quest to solve it. Hera, the queen of the gods, has been taken."

Shocked silence. Then fifty demigods started talking at once.

Chiron pounded his hoof again, but Rachel still had to wait before she could get back their attention.

She told them about the incident on the Grand Canyon skywalk—how Gleeson Hedge had sacrificed himself when the storm spirits attacked, and the spirits had warned it was only the beginning. They apparently served some great mistress who would destroy all demigods.

Then Rachel told them about Piper passing out in Hera's cabin. Piper tried to keep a calm expression, even when she noticed Drew in the back row, pantomiming a faint, and her friends giggling. Finally Rachel told them about Jason's vision in the living room of the Big House. The message Hera had delivered there was so similar that Piper got a chill. The only difference: Hera had warned Piper not to betray her: *Bow to his will, and their king shall rise, dooming us all.* Hera *knew* about the giant's threat. But if that was true, why hadn't she warned Jason, and exposed Piper as an enemy agent?

"Jason," Rachel said. "Um . . . do you remember your last name?"

He looked self-conscious, but he shook his head.

"We'll just call you Jason, then," Rachel said. "It's clear Hera herself has issued you a quest."

Rachel paused, as if giving Jason a chance to protest his destiny. Everyone's eyes were on him; there was so much pressure, Piper thought she would've buckled in his position. Yet he looked brave and determined. He set his jaw and nodded. "I agree."

"You must save Hera to prevent a great evil," Rachel continued. "Some sort of king from rising. For reasons we don't yet understand, it must happen by the winter solstice, only four days from now."

"That's the council day of the gods," Annabeth said. "If the gods don't *already* know Hera's gone, they will definitely

notice her absence by then. They'll probably break out fighting, accusing each other of taking her. That's what they usually do."

"The winter solstice," Chiron spoke up, "is also the time of
greatest darkness. The gods gather that day, as mortals always
have, because there is strength in numbers. The solstice is a
day when evil magic is strong. *Ancient* magic, older than the
gods. It is a day when things . . . stir."

The way he said it, stirring sounded absolutely sinister—
like it should be a first-degree felony, not something you did
to cookie dough.

"Okay," Annabeth said, glaring at the centaur. "Thank you,
Captain Sunshine. Whatever's going on, I agree with Rachel.
Jason has been chosen to lead this quest, so—"

"Why hasn't he been claimed?" somebody yelled from the
Ares cabin. "If he's so important—"

"He has been claimed," Chiron announced. "Long ago.
Jason, give them a demonstration."

At first, Jason didn't seem to understand. He stepped
forward nervously, but Piper couldn't help thinking how
amazing he looked with his blond hair glowing in the firelight, his regal features like a Roman statue's. He glanced at
Piper, and she nodded encouragingly. She mimicked flipping a coin.

Jason reached into his pocket. His coin flashed in the air,
and when he caught it in his hand, he was holding a lance—a
rod of gold about seven feet long, with a spear tip at one end.

The other demigods gasped. Rachel and Annabeth stepped
back to avoid the point, which looked sharp as an ice pick.

"Wasn't that..." Annabeth hesitated. "I thought you had a sword."

"Um, it came up tails, I think," Jason said. "Same coin, long-range weapon form."

"Dude, I want one!" yelled somebody from Ares cabin.

"Better than Clarisse's electric spear, Lamer!" one of his brothers agreed.

"Electric," Jason murmured, like that was a good idea. "Back away."

Annabeth and Rachel got the message. Jason raised his javelin, and thunder broke open the sky. Every hair on Piper's arms stood straight up. Lightning arced down through the golden spear point and hit the campfire with the force of an artillery shell.

When the smoke cleared, and the ringing in Piper's ears subsided, the entire camp sat frozen in shock, half blind, covered in ashes, staring at the place where the fire had been. Cinders rained down everywhere. A burning log had impaled itself a few inches from the sleeping kid Clovis, who hadn't even stirred.

Jason lowered his lance. "Um...sorry."

Chiron brushed some burning coals out of his beard. He grimaced as if his worst fears had been confirmed. "A little overkill, perhaps, but you've made your point. And I believe we know who your father is."

"Jupiter," Jason said. "I mean Zeus. Lord of the Sky."

Piper couldn't help smiling. It made perfect sense. The most powerful god, the father of all the greatest heroes in the ancient myths—no one else could possibly be Jason's dad.

Apparently, the rest of the camp wasn't so sure. Everything broke into chaos, with dozens of people asking questions until Annabeth raised her arms.

"Hold it!" she said. "How can he be the son of Zeus? The Big Three ... their pact not to have mortal kids ... how could we not have known about him sooner?"

Chiron didn't answer, but Piper got the feeling he knew. And the truth was not good.

"The important thing," Rachel said, "is that Jason's here now. He has a quest to fulfill, which means he will need his own prophecy."

She closed her eyes and swooned. Two campers rushed forward and caught her. A third ran to the side of the amphitheater and grabbed a bronze three-legged stool, like they'd been trained for this duty. They eased Rachel onto the stool in front of the ruined hearth. Without the fire, the night was dark, but green mist started swirling around Rachel's feet. When she opened her eyes, they were glowing. Emerald smoke issued from her mouth. The voice that came out was raspy and ancient—the sound a snake would make if it could talk:

> *Child of lightning, beware the earth,*
> *The giants' revenge the seven shall birth,*
> *The forge and dove shall break the cage,*
> *And death unleash through Hera's rage.*

On the last word, Rachel collapsed, but her helpers were waiting to catch her. They carried her away from the hearth and laid her in the corner to rest.

"Is that normal?" Piper asked. Then she realized she'd spoken into the silence, and everyone was looking at her. "I mean ... does she spew green smoke a lot?"

"Gods, you're dense!" Drew sneered. "She just issued a prophecy—Jason's prophecy to save Hera! Why don't you just—"

"Drew," Annabeth snapped. "Piper asked a fair question. Something about that prophecy *definitely* isn't normal. If breaking Hera's cage unleashes her rage and causes a bunch of death ... why would we free her? It might be a trap, or—or maybe Hera will turn on her rescuers. She's never been kind to heroes."

Jason rose. "I don't have much choice. Hera took my memory. I need it back. Besides, we can't just *not* help the queen of the heavens if she's in trouble."

A girl from Hephaestus cabin stood up—Nyssa, the one with the red bandanna. "Maybe. But you should listen to Annabeth. Hera can be vengeful. She threw her own son— our dad—down a mountain just because he was ugly."

"*Real* ugly," snickered someone from Aphrodite.

"Shut up!" Nyssa growled. "Anyway, we've also got to think —why beware the earth? And what's the giants' revenge? What are we dealing with here that's powerful enough to kidnap the queen of the heavens?"

No one answered, but Piper noticed Annabeth and Chiron having a silent exchange. Piper thought it went something like:

Annabeth: *The giants' revenge ... no, it can't be.*

Chiron: *Don't speak of it here. Don't scare them.*

Annabeth: *You're kidding me! We can't be that unlucky.*

Chiron: *Later, child. If you told them everything, they would be too terrified to proceed.*

Piper knew it was crazy to think she could read their expressions so well—two people she barely knew. But she was absolutely positive she understood them, and it scared the jujubes out of her.

Annabeth took a deep breath. "It's Jason's quest," she announced, "so it's Jason's choice. Obviously, he's the child of lightning. According to tradition, he may choose any two companions."

Someone from the Hermes cabin yelled, "Well, you, obviously, Annabeth. You've got the most experience."

"No, Travis," Annabeth said. "First off, I'm *not* helping Hera. Every time I've tried, she's deceived me, or it's come back to bite me later. Forget it. No way. Secondly, I'm leaving first thing in the morning to find Percy."

"It's connected," Piper blurted out, not sure how she got the courage. "You know that's true, don't you? This whole business, your boyfriend's disappearance—it's all connected."

"How?" demanded Drew. "If you're so smart, how?"

Piper tried to form an answer, but she couldn't.

Annabeth saved her. "You may be right, Piper. If this is connected, I'll find out from the other end—by searching for Percy. As I said, I'm not about to rush off to rescue Hera, even if her disappearance sets the rest of the Olympians fighting again. But there's another reason I can't go. The prophecy says otherwise."

"It says who *I* pick," Jason agreed. "*The forge and dove shall break the cage.* The forge is the symbol of Vul—Hephaestus."

Under the Cabin Nine banner, Nyssa's shoulders slumped, like she'd just been given a heavy anvil to carry. "If you have to beware the earth," she said, "you should avoid traveling overland. You'll need air transport."

Piper was about to call out that Jason could fly. But then she thought better of it. That was for Jason to tell them, and he wasn't volunteering the information. Maybe he figured he'd freaked them out enough for one night.

"The flying chariot's broken," Nyssa continued, "and the pegasi, we're using them to search for Percy. But maybe Hephaestus cabin can help figure out something else to help. With Jake incapacitated, I'm senior camper. I can volunteer for the quest."

She didn't sound enthusiastic.

Then Leo stood up. He'd been so quiet, Piper had almost forgotten he was there, which was totally *not* like Leo.

"It's me," he said.

His cabinmates stirred. Several tried to pull him back to his seat, but Leo resisted.

"No, it's me. I know it is. I've got an idea for the transportation problem. Let me try. I can fix this!"

Jason studied him for a moment. Piper was sure he was going to tell Leo no. Then he smiled. "We started this together, Leo. Seems only right you come along. You find us a ride, you're in."

"Yes!" Leo pumped his fist.

"It'll be dangerous," Nyssa warned him. "Hardship, monsters, terrible suffering. Possibly none of you will come back alive."

"Oh." Suddenly Leo didn't look so excited. Then he remembered everyone was watching. "I mean...Oh, cool! Suffering? I love suffering! Let's do this."

Annabeth nodded. "Then, Jason, you only need to choose the third quest member. The dove—"

"Oh, absolutely!" Drew was on her feet and flashing Jason a smile. "The dove is Aphrodite. Everybody knows that. I am *totally* yours."

Piper's hands clenched. She stepped forward. "No."

Drew rolled her eyes. "Oh, please, Dumpster girl. Back off."

"*I* had the vision of Hera; not you. I have to do this."

"Anyone can have a vision," Drew said. "You were just at the right place at the right time." She turned to Jason. "Look, fighting is all fine, I suppose. And people who build things..." She looked at Leo in disdain. "Well, I suppose someone has to get their hands dirty. But you need *charm* on your side. I can be very persuasive. I could help a lot."

The campers started murmuring about how Drew *was* pretty persuasive. Piper could see Drew winning them over. Even Chiron was scratching his beard, like Drew's participation suddenly made sense to him.

"Well..." Annabeth said. "Given the wording of the prophecy—"

"No!" Piper's own voice sounded strange in her ears—more insistent, richer in tone. "I'm supposed to go."

Then the weirdest thing happened. Everyone started nodding, muttering that hmm, Piper's point of view made sense too. Drew looked around, incredulous. Even some of her own campers were nodding.

"Get over it!" Drew snapped at the crowd. "What can Piper do?"

Piper tried to respond, but her confidence started to wane. What *could* she offer? She wasn't a fighter, or a planner, or a fixer. She had no skills except getting into trouble and occasionally convincing people to do stupid things.

Plus, she was a liar. She needed to go on this quest for reasons that went way beyond Jason—and if she did go, she'd end up betraying everyone there. She heard that voice from the dream: *Do our bidding, and you may walk away alive.* How could she make a choice like that—between helping her father and helping Jason?

"Well," Drew said smugly, "I guess that settles it."

Suddenly there was collective gasp. Everyone stared at Piper like she'd just exploded. She wondered what she'd done wrong. Then she realized there was a reddish glow around her.

"What?" she demanded.

She looked above her, but there was no burning symbol like the one that had appeared over Leo. Then she looked down and yelped.

Her clothes... what in the world was she *wearing*? She despised dresses. She didn't *own* a dress. But now she was adorned in a beautiful white sleeveless gown that went down to her ankles, with a V-neck so low it was totally embarrassing. Delicate gold armbands circled her biceps. An intricate necklace of amber, coral, and gold flowers glittered on her chest, and her hair...

"Oh, god," she said. "What's happened?"

A stunned Annabeth pointed at Piper's dagger, which was now oiled and gleaming, hanging at her side on a golden cord. Piper didn't want to draw it. She was afraid of what she would see. But her curiosity won out. She unsheathed Katoptris and stared at her reflection in the polished metal blade. Her hair was perfect: lush and long and chocolate brown, braided with gold ribbons down one side so it fell across her shoulder. She even wore makeup, better than Piper would ever know how to do herself—subtle touches that made her lips cherry red and brought out all the different colors in her eyes.

She was... she was...

"Beautiful," Jason exclaimed. "Piper, you... you're a knockout."

Under different circumstances, that would've been the happiest moment of her life. But now everyone was staring at her like she was a freak. Drew's face was full of horror and revulsion. "No!" she cried. "Not possible!"

"This isn't me," Piper protested. "I—don't understand."

Chiron the centaur folded his front legs and bowed to her, and all the campers followed his example.

"Hail, Piper McLean," Chiron announced gravely, as if he were speaking at her funeral. "Daughter of Aphrodite, lady of the doves, goddess of love."

XI

LEO

Leo didn't stick around after Piper turned beautiful. Sure, it was amazing and all—*She's got makeup! It's a miracle!* —but Leo had problems to deal with. He ducked out of the amphitheater and ran into the darkness, wondering what he'd gotten himself into.

He'd stood up in front of a bunch of stronger, braver demigods and volunteered—*volunteered*—for a mission that would probably get him killed.

He hadn't mentioned seeing Tía Callida, his old babysitter, but as soon as he'd heard about Jason's vision—the lady in the black dress and shawl—Leo knew it was the same woman. Tía Callida was Hera. His evil babysitter was the queen of the gods. Stuff like that could really deep-fry your brain.

He trudged toward the woods and tried not to think about his childhood—all the messed-up things that had led to his mother's death. But he couldn't help it.

• • •

The first time Tía Callida tried to kill him, he must've been about two. Tía Callida was looking after him while his mother was at the machine shop. She wasn't really his aunt, of course —just one of the old women in the community, a generic *tía* who helped watch the kids. She smelled like a honey-baked ham, and always wore a widow's dress with a black shawl.

"Let's set you down for a nap," she said. "Let's see if you are my brave little hero, eh?"

Leo was sleepy. She nestled him into his blankets in a warm mound of red and yellow—pillows? The bed was like a cubby-hole in the wall, made of blackened bricks, with a metal slot over his head and a square hole far above, where he could see the stars. He remembered resting comfortably, grabbing at sparks like fireflies. He dozed, and dreamed of a boat made of fire, sailing through the cinders. He imagined himself on board, navigating the sky. Somewhere nearby, Tía Callida sat in her rocking chair—*creak, creak, creak*—and sang a lullaby. Even at two, Leo knew the difference between English and Spanish, and he remembered being puzzled because Tía Callida was singing in a language that was neither.

Everything was fine until his mother came home. She screamed and raced over to snatch him up, yelling at Tía Callida, "How could you?" But the old lady had disappeared.

Leo remembered looking over his mother's shoulder at the flames curling around his blankets. Only years later had he realized he'd been sleeping in a blazing fireplace.

The weirdest thing? Tía Callida hadn't been arrested or even banished from their house. She appeared again several times over the next few years. Once when Leo was three, she let him play with knives. "You must learn your blades early," she insisted, "if you are to be my hero someday." Leo managed not to kill himself, but he got the feeling Tía Callida wouldn't have cared one way or the other.

When Leo was four, Tía found a rattlesnake for him in a nearby cow pasture. She gave him a stick and encouraged him to poke the animal. "Where is your bravery, little hero? Show me the Fates were right to choose you." Leo stared down at those amber eyes, hearing the dry *shh-shh-ssh* of the snake's rattle. He couldn't bring himself to poke the snake. It didn't seem fair. Apparently the snake felt the same way about biting a little kid. Leo could've sworn it looked at Tía Callida like, *Are you nuts, lady?* Then it disappeared into the tall grass.

The last time she babysat him, Leo was five. She brought him a pack of crayons and a pad of paper. They sat together at the picnic table in back of the apartment complex, under an old pecan tree. While Tía Callida sang her strange songs, Leo drew a picture of the boat he'd seen in the flames, with colorful sails and rows of oars, a curved stern, and an awesome figurehead. When he was almost done, about to sign his name the way he'd learned in kindergarten, a wind snatched the picture away. It flew into the sky and disappeared.

Leo wanted to cry. He'd spent so much time on that picture—but Tía Callida just clucked with disappointment.

"It isn't time yet, little hero. Someday, you'll have your quest. You'll find your destiny, and your hard journey will finally make sense. But first you must face many sorrows. I regret that, but heroes cannot be shaped any other way. Now, make me a fire, eh? Warm these old bones."

A few minutes later, Leo's mom came out and shrieked with horror. Tía Callida was gone, but Leo sat in the middle of a smoking fire. The pad of paper was reduced to ashes. Crayons had melted into a bubbling puddle of multicolored goo, and Leo's hands were ablaze, slowly burning through the picnic table. For years afterward, people in the apartment complex would wonder how someone had seared the impressions of a five-year-old's hands an inch deep into solid wood.

Now Leo was sure that Tía Callida, his psychotic babysitter, had been Hera all along. That made her, what—his godly grandmother? His family was even more messed up than he realized.

He wondered if his mother had known the truth. Leo remembered after that last visit, his mom took him inside and had a long talk with him, but he only understood some of it.

"She can't come back again." His mom had a beautiful face with kind eyes, and curly dark hair, but she looked older than she was because of hard work. The lines around her eyes were deeply etched. Her hands were callused. She was the first person from their family to graduate from college. She had a degree in mechanical engineering and could design anything, fix anything, build anything.

No one would hire her. No company would take her seriously, so she ended up in the machine shop, trying to make enough money to support the two of them. She always smelled of machine oil, and when she talked with Leo, she switched from Spanish to English constantly—using them like complementary tools. It took Leo years to realize that not everyone spoke that way. She'd even taught him Morse code as a kind of game, so they could tap messages to each other when they were in different rooms: *I love you. You okay?* Simple things like that.

"I don't care what Callida says," his mom told him. "I don't care about destiny and the Fates. You're too young for that. You're still my baby."

She took his hands, looking for burn marks, but of course there weren't any. "Leo, listen to me. Fire is a tool, like anything else, but it's more dangerous than most. You don't know your limits. Please, promise me—no more fire until you meet your father. Someday, *mijo*, you *will* meet him. He'll explain everything."

Leo had heard that since he could remember. Someday he would meet his dad. His mom wouldn't answer any questions about him. Leo had never met him, never even seen pictures, but she talked like he'd just gone to the store for some milk and he'd be back any minute. Leo tried to believe her. Someday, everything would make sense.

For the next couple of years, they were happy. Leo almost forgot about Tía Callida. He still dreamed of the flying boat, but the other strange events seemed like a dream too.

It all came apart when he was eight. By then, he was spending every free hour at the shop with his mom. He knew how to use the machines. He could measure and do math better than most adults. He'd learned to think three-dimensionally, solving mechanical problems in his head the way his mom did.

One night, they stayed late because his mom was finishing

a drill bit design she hoped to patent. If she could sell the prototype, it might change their lives. She'd finally get a break.

As she worked, Leo passed her supplies and told her corny jokes, trying to keep her spirits up. He loved it when he could make her laugh. She'd smile and say, "Your father would be proud of you, *mijo*. You'll meet him soon, I'm sure."

Mom's workspace was at the very back of the shop. It was kind of creepy at night, because they were the only ones there. Every sound echoed through the dark warehouse, but Leo didn't mind as long as he was with his mom. If he did wander the shop, they could always keep in touch with Morse code taps. Whenever they were ready to leave, they had to walk through the entire shop, through the break room, and out to the parking lot, locking the doors behind them.

That night after finishing up, they'd just gotten to the break room when his mom realized she didn't have her keys.

"That's funny." She frowned. "I know I had them. Wait here, *mijo*. I'll only be a minute."

She gave him one more smile—the last one he'd ever get —and she went back into the warehouse.

She'd only been gone a few heartbeats when the interior door slammed shut. Then the exterior door locked itself.

"Mom?" Leo's heart pounded. Something heavy crashed inside the warehouse. He ran to the door, but no matter how hard he pulled or kicked, it wouldn't open. "Mom!" Frantically, he tapped a message on the wall: *You okay?*

"She can't hear you," a voice said.

Leo turned and found himself facing a strange woman. At

first he thought it was Tía Callida. She was wrapped in black robes, with a veil covering her face.

"Tía?" he said.

The woman chuckled, a slow gentle sound, as if she were half asleep. "I am not your guardian. Merely a family resemblance."

"What—what do you want? Where's my mom?"

"Ah...loyal to your mother. How nice. But you see, I have children too...and I understand you will fight them someday. When they try to wake me, you will prevent them. I cannot allow that."

"I don't know you. I don't want to fight anybody."

She muttered like a sleepwalker in a trance, "A wise choice."

With a chill, Leo realized the woman was, in fact, asleep. Behind the veil, her eyes were closed. But even stranger: her clothes were not made of cloth. They were made of *earth*—dry black dirt, churning and shifting around her. Her pale, sleeping face was barely visible behind a curtain of dust, and he had the horrible sense that she had just risen from the grave. If the woman was asleep, Leo wanted her to stay that way. He knew that fully awake, she would be even more terrible.

"I cannot destroy you yet," the woman murmured. "The Fates will not allow it. But they do not protect your mother, and they cannot stop me from breaking your spirit. Remember this night, little hero, when they ask you to oppose me."

"Leave my mother alone!" Fear rose in his throat as the woman shuffled forward. She moved more like an avalanche than a person, a dark wall of earth shifting toward him.

"How will you stop me?" she whispered.

She walked straight through a table, the particles of her body reassembling on the other side.

She loomed over Leo, and he knew she would pass right through him, too. He was the only thing between her and his mother.

His hands caught fire.

A sleepy smile spread across the woman's face, as if she'd already won. Leo screamed with desperation. His vision turned red. Flames washed over the earthen woman, the walls, the locked doors. And Leo lost consciousness.

When he woke, he was in an ambulance.

The paramedic tried to be kind. She told him the warehouse had burned down. His mother hadn't made it out. The paramedic said she was sorry, but Leo felt hollow. He'd lost control, just like his mother had warned. Her death was his fault.

Soon the police came to get him, and they weren't as nice. The fire had started in the break room, they said, right where Leo was standing. He'd survived by some miracle, but what kind of child locked the doors of his mother's workplace, knowing she was inside, and started a fire?

Later, his neighbors at the apartment complex told the police what a strange boy he was. They talked about the burned handprints on the picnic table. They'd always known something was wrong with Esperanza Valdez's son.

His relatives wouldn't take him in. His Aunt Rosa called him a *diablo* and shouted at the social workers to take him away. So Leo went to his first foster home. A few days later, he ran away. Some foster homes lasted longer than others. He would joke around, make a few friends, pretend that nothing bothered him, but he always ended up running sooner or later. It was the only thing that made the pain better—feeling like he was moving, getting farther and farther away from the ashes of that machine shop.

He'd promised himself he would never play with fire again. He hadn't thought about Tía Callida, or the sleeping woman wrapped in earthen robes, for a long time.

He was almost to the woods when he imagined Tía Callida's voice: *It wasn't your fault, little hero. Our enemy wakes. It's time to stop running.*

"Hera," Leo muttered, "you're not even here, are you? You're in a cage somewhere."

There was no answer.

But now, at least, Leo understood something. Hera had been watching him his entire life. Somehow, she'd known that one day she would need him. Maybe those Fates she mentioned could tell the future. Leo wasn't sure. But he knew he was *meant* to go on this quest. Jason's prophecy warned them to beware the earth, and Leo knew it had something to do with that sleeping woman in the shop, wrapped in robes of shifting dirt.

You'll find your destiny, Tía Callida had promised, *and your hard journey will finally make sense.*

Leo might find out what that flying boat in his dreams meant. He might meet his father, or even get to avenge his mother's death.

But first things first. He'd promised Jason a flying ride.

Not the boat from his dreams—not yet. There wasn't time to build something that complicated. He needed a quicker solution. He needed a dragon.

He hesitated at the edge of the woods, peering into absolute blackness. Owls hooted, and something far away hissed like a chorus of snakes.

Leo remembered what Will Solace had told him: No one should go in the woods alone, definitely not unarmed. Leo had nothing—no sword, no flashlight, no help.

He glanced back at the lights of the cabins. He could turn around now and tell everyone he'd been joking. *Psych!* Nyssa could go on the quest instead. He could stay at camp and learn to be part of the Hephaestus cabin, but he wondered how long it would be before he looked like his bunkmates—sad, dejected, convinced of his own bad luck.

They cannot stop me from breaking your spirit, the sleeping woman had said. *Remember this night, little hero, when they ask you to oppose me.*

"Believe me, lady," Leo muttered, "I remember. And whoever you are, I'm gonna face-plant you hard, Leo-style."

He took a deep breath and plunged into the forest.

LEO

THE WOODS WEREN'T LIKE ANYPLACE he'd been before. Leo had been raised in a north Houston apartment complex. The wildest things he'd ever seen were that rattlesnake in the cow pasture and his Aunt Rosa in her nightgown, until he was sent to Wilderness School.

Even there, the school had been in the desert. No trees with gnarled roots to trip over. No streams to fall into. No branches casting dark, creepy shadows and owls looking down at him with their big reflective eyes. This was the Twilight Zone.

He stumbled along until he was sure no one back at the cabins could possibly see him. Then he summoned fire. Flames danced along his fingertips, casting enough light to see. He hadn't tried to keep a sustained burn going since he was five, at that picnic table. Since his mom's death, he'd been too afraid to try anything. Even this tiny fire made him feel guilty.

He kept walking, looking for dragon-type clues—giant

footprints, trampled trees, swaths of burning forest. Something that big couldn't exactly sneak around, right? But he saw *nada*. Once he glimpsed a large, furry shape like a wolf or a bear, but it stayed away from his fire, which was fine by Leo.

Then, at the bottom of a clearing, he saw the first trap—a hundred-foot-wide crater ringed with boulders.

Leo had to admit it was pretty ingenious. In the center of the depression, a metal vat the size of a hot tub had been filled with bubbly dark liquid—Tabasco sauce and motor oil. On a pedestal suspended over the vat, an electric fan rotated in a circle, spreading the fumes across the forest. Could metal dragons smell?

The vat seemed to be unguarded. But Leo looked closely, and in the dim light of the stars and his handheld fire, he could see the glint of metal beneath the dirt and leaves—a bronze net lining the entire crater. Or maybe *see* wasn't the right word—he could sense it there, as if the mechanism was emitting heat, revealing itself to him. Six large strips of bronze stretched out from the vat like the spokes of a wheel. They would be pressure sensitive, Leo guessed. As soon as the dragon stepped on one, the net would spring closed, and *voilà*—one gift-wrapped monster.

Leo edged closer. He put his foot on the nearest trigger strip. As he expected, nothing happened. They had to have set the net for something really heavy. Otherwise they could catch an animal, human, smaller monster, whatever. He doubted there was anything else as heavy as a metal dragon in these woods. At least, he hoped there wasn't.

He picked his way down the crater and approached the

vat. The fumes were almost overpowering, and his eyes started watering. He remembered a time when Tía Callida (Hera, whatever) had made him chop jalapeños in the kitchen and he'd gotten the juice in his eyes. Serious pain. But of course she'd been like, "Endure it, little hero. The Aztecs of your mother's homeland used to punish bad children by holding them over a fire filled with chili peppers. They raised many heroes that way."

A total psycho, that lady. Leo was so glad he was on a quest to rescue her.

Tía Callida would've loved this vat, because it was *way* worse than jalapeño juice. Leo looked for a trigger— something that would disable the net. He didn't see anything.

He had a moment of panic. Nyssa had said there were several traps like this in the woods, and they were planning more. What if the dragon had already stepped into another one? How could Leo possibly find them all?

He continued to search, but he didn't see any release mechanism. No large button labeled OFF. It occurred to him that there might not *be* one. He started to despair—and then he heard the sound.

It was more of a tremor—the deep sort of rumbling you hear in your gut rather than your ears. It gave him the jitters, but he didn't look around for the source. He just kept examining the trap, thinking, *Must be a long way off. It's pounding its way through the woods. I gotta hurry.*

Then he heard a grinding snort, like steam forced out of a metal barrel.

His neck tingled. He turned slowly. At the edge of the pit,

fifty feet away, two glowing red eyes were staring at him. The creature gleamed in the moonlight, and Leo couldn't believe something that huge had sneaked up on him so fast. Too late, he realized its gaze was fixed on the fire in his hand, and he extinguished the flames.

He could still see the dragon just fine. It was about sixty feet long, snout to tail, its body made of interlocking bronze plates. Its claws were the size of butcher knives, and its mouth was lined with hundreds of dagger-sharp metal teeth. Steam came out of its nostrils. It snarled like a chain saw cutting through a tree. It could've bitten Leo in half, easy, or stomped him flat. It was the most beautiful thing he'd ever seen, except for one problem that completely ruined Leo's plan.

"You don't have wings," Leo said.

The dragon's snarl died. It tilted its head as if to say, *Why aren't you running away in terror?*

"Hey, no offense," Leo said. "You're amazing! Good god, who *made* you? Are you hydraulic or nuclear-powered or what? But if it was me, I would've put wings on you. What kind of dragon doesn't have wings? I guess maybe you're too heavy to fly? I should've thought of that."

The dragon snorted, more confused now. It was supposed to trample Leo. This conversation thing wasn't part of the plan. It took a step forward, and Leo shouted, "No!"

The dragon snarled again.

"It's a trap, bronze brain," Leo said. "They're trying to catch you."

The dragon opened its mouth and blew fire. A column of white-hot flames billowed over Leo, more than he'd ever tried to endure before. He felt as if he were being hosed down with a powerful, very hot fire hose. It stung a little, but he stood his ground. When the flames died, he was perfectly fine. Even his clothes were okay, which Leo didn't understand, but for which he was grateful. He liked his army jacket, and having his pants seared off would've been pretty embarrassing.

The dragon stared at Leo. Its face didn't actually change, being made of metal and all, but Leo thought he could read its expression: *Why no crispy critter?* A spark flew out of its neck like it was about to short-circuit.

"You can't burn me," Leo said, trying to sound stern and calm. He'd never had a dog before, but he talked to the dragon the way he thought you'd talk to a dog. "Stay, boy. Don't come any closer. I don't want you to get caught. See, they think you're broken and have to be scrapped. But I don't believe that. I can fix you if you'll let me—"

The dragon creaked, roared, and charged. The trap sprang. The floor of the crater erupted with a sound like a thousand trash can lids banging together. Dirt and leaves flew, metal net flashing. Leo was knocked off his feet, turned upside down, and doused in Tabasco sauce and oil. He found himself sandwiched between the vat and the dragon as it thrashed, trying to free itself from the net that had wrapped around them both.

The dragon blew flames in every direction, lighting up the sky and setting trees on fire. Oil and sauce burned all over them. It didn't hurt Leo, but it left a nasty taste in his mouth.

"Will you stop that!" he yelled.

The dragon kept squirming. Leo realized he would get

crushed if he didn't move. It wasn't easy, but he managed to wriggle out from between the dragon and the vat. He squirmed his way through the net. Fortunately the holes were plenty big enough for a skinny kid.

He ran to the dragon's head. It tried to snap at him, but its teeth were tangled in the mesh. It blew fire again, but seemed to be running out of energy. This time the flames were only orange. They sputtered before they even reached Leo's face.

"Listen, man," Leo said, "you're just going to show them where you are. Then they'll come and break out the acid and the metal cutters. Is that what you want?"

The dragon's jaw made a creaking sound, like it was trying to talk.

"Okay, then," Leo said. "You'll have to trust me."

And Leo set to work.

It took him almost an hour to find the control panel. It was right behind the dragon's head, which made sense. He'd elected to keep the dragon in the net, because it was easier to work with the dragon constrained, but the dragon didn't like it.

"Hold still!" Leo scolded.

The dragon made another creaking sound that might've been a whimper.

Leo examined the wires inside the dragon's head. He was distracted by a sound in the woods, but when he looked up it was just a tree spirit—a dryad, Leo thought they were called—putting out the flames in her branches. Fortunately, the dragon hadn't started an all-out forest fire, but still the dryad wasn't too pleased. The girl's dress was smoking. She smothered the flames with a silky blanket, and when she saw Leo looking at her, she made a gesture that was probably very rude in Dryad. Then she disappeared in a green poof of mist.

Leo returned his attention to the wiring. It was ingenious, definitely, and it made sense to him. This was the motor control relay. This processed sensory input from the eyes. This disk...

"Ha," he said. "Well, no wonder."

Creak? the dragon asked with its jaw.

"You've got a corroded control disk. Probably regulates your higher reasoning circuits, right? Rusty brain, man. No wonder you're a little...confused." He almost said *crazy*, but he caught himself. "I wish I had a replacement disk, but... this is a complicated piece of circuitry. I'm gonna have to take it out and clean it. Only be a minute." He pulled out the disk, and the dragon went absolutely still. The glow died in its eyes. Leo slid off its back and began polishing the disk. He mopped up some oil and Tabasco sauce with his sleeve, which helped cut through the grime, but the more he cleaned, the more concerned he got. Some of the circuits were beyond repair. He could make it better, but not perfect. For that, he'd need a completely new disk, and he had no idea how to build one.

He tried to work quickly. He wasn't sure how long the dragon's control disk could be off without damaging it—maybe forever—but he didn't want to take chances. Once he'd done the best he could, he climbed back up to the dragon's head and started cleaning the wiring and gearboxes, getting himself filthy in the process.

"Clean hands, dirty equipment," he muttered, something

his mother used to say. By the time he was through, his hands were black with grease and his clothes looked like he'd just lost a mud-wrestling contest, but the mechanisms looked a lot better. He slipped in the disk, connected the last wire, and sparks flew. The dragon shuddered. Its eyes began to glow.

"Better?" Leo asked.

The dragon made a sound like a high-speed drill. It opened its mouth and all its teeth rotated.

"I guess that's a *yes*. Hold on, I'll free you."

Another thirty minutes to find the release clamps for the net and untangle the dragon, but finally it stood and shook the last bit of netting off its back. It roared triumphantly and shot fire at the sky.

"Seriously," Leo said. "Could you not show off?"

Creak? the dragon asked.

"You need a name," Leo decided. "I'm calling you Festus."

The dragon whirred its teeth and grinned. At least Leo hoped it was a grin.

"Cool," Leo said. "But we still have a problem, because you don't have wings."

Festus tilted his head and snorted steam. Then he lowered his back in an unmistakable gesture. He wanted Leo to climb on.

"Where we going?" Leo asked.

But he was too excited to wait for an answer. He climbed onto the dragon's back, and Festus bounded off into the woods.

• • •

Leo lost track of time and all sense of direction. It seemed impossible the woods could be so deep and wild, but the dragon traveled until the trees were like skyscrapers and the canopy of leaves completely blotted out the stars. Even the fire in Leo's hand couldn't have lit the way, but the dragon's glowing red eyes acted like headlights.

Finally they crossed a stream and came to a dead end, a limestone cliff a hundred feet tall—a solid, sheer mass the dragon couldn't possibly climb.

Festus stopped at the base and lifted one leg like a dog pointing.

"What is it?" Leo slid to the ground. He walked up to the cliff—nothing but solid rock. The dragon kept pointing.

"It's not going to move out of your way," Leo told him.

The loose wire in the dragon's neck sparked, but otherwise he stayed still. Leo put his hand on the cliff. Suddenly his fingers smoldered. Lines of fire spread from his fingertips like ignited gunpowder, sizzling across the limestone. The burning lines raced across the cliff face until they had outlined a glowing red door five times as tall as Leo. He backed up and the door swung open, disturbingly silently for such a big slab of rock.

"Perfectly balanced," he muttered. "That's some first-rate engineering."

The dragon unfroze and marched inside, as if he were coming home.

Leo stepped through, and the door began to close. He had a moment of panic, remembering that night in the machine shop long ago, when he'd been locked in. What if he got stuck in here? But then lights flickered on—a combination of electric fluorescents and wall-mounted torches. When Leo saw the cavern, he forgot about leaving.

"Festus," he muttered. "What *is* this place?"

The dragon stomped to the center of the room, leaving tracks in the thick dust, and curled up on a large circular platform.

The cave was the size of an airplane hangar, with endless worktables and storage cages, rows of garage-sized doors along either wall, and staircases that led up to a network of catwalks high above. Equipment was everywhere—hydraulic lifts, welding torches, hazard suits, air-spades, forklifts, plus something that looked suspiciously like a nuclear reaction chamber. Bulletin boards were covered with tattered, faded blueprints. And weapons, armor, shields—war supplies all over the place, a lot of them only partially finished.

Hanging from chains far above the dragon's platform was an old tattered banner almost too faded to read. The letters were Greek, but Leo somehow knew what they said: BUNKER 9.

Did that mean nine as in the Hephaestus cabin, or nine as in there were eight others? Leo looked at Festus, still curled up on the platform, and it occurred to him that the dragon looked so content because it *was* home. It had probably been built on that pad.

"Do the other kids know...?" Leo's question died as he asked it. Clearly, this place had been abandoned for decades. Cobwebs and dust covered everything. The floor revealed no footprints except for his, and the huge paw prints of the dragon. He was the first one in this bunker since...since a long time ago. Bunker 9 had been abandoned with a lot of projects half finished on the tables. Locked up and forgotten, but why?

Leo looked at a map on the wall—a battle map of camp, but the paper was as cracked and yellow as onionskin. A date at the bottom read, 1864.

"No way," he muttered.

Then he spotted a blueprint on a nearby bulletin board, and his heart almost leaped out of his throat. He ran to the worktable and stared up at a white-line drawing almost faded beyond recognition: a Greek ship from several different angles. Faintly scrawled words underneath it read: PROPHECY? UNCLEAR. FLIGHT?

It was the ship he'd seen in his dreams—the flying ship. Someone had tried to build it here, or at least sketched out the idea. Then it was left, forgotten...a prophecy yet to come. And weirdest of all, the ship's figurehead was exactly like the one Leo had drawn when he was five—the head of a dragon.

"Looks like you, Festus," he murmured. "That's creepy."

The figurehead gave him an uneasy feeling, but Leo's mind spun with too many other questions to think about it for long. He touched the blueprint, hoping he could take it down to study, but the paper crackled at his touch, so he left it alone. He looked around for other clues. No boats. No pieces that looked like parts of this project, but there were so many doors and storerooms to explore.

Festus snorted like he was trying to get Leo's attention, reminding him they didn't have all night. It was true. Leo figured it would be morning in a few hours, and he'd gotten completely sidetracked. He'd saved the dragon, but it wasn't going to help him on the quest. He needed something that would fly.

Festus nudged something toward him—a leather tool belt that had been left next to his construction pad. Then the dragon switched on his glowing red eye beams and turned them toward the ceiling. Leo looked up to where the spotlights were pointing, and yelped when he recognized the shapes hanging above them in the darkness.

"Festus," he said in a small voice. "We've got work to do."

XIII

JASON

JASON DREAMED OF WOLVES.

He stood in a clearing in the middle of a redwood forest. In front of him rose the ruins of a stone mansion. Low gray clouds blended with the ground fog, and cold rain hung in the air. A pack of large gray beasts milled around him, brushing against his legs, snarling and baring their teeth. They gently nudged him toward the ruins.

Jason had no desire to become the world's largest dog biscuit, so he decided to do what they wanted.

The ground squelched under his boots as he walked. Stone spires of chimneys, no longer attached to anything, rose up like totem poles. The house must've been enormous once, multi-storied with massive log walls and a soaring gabled roof, but now nothing remained but its stone skeleton. Jason passed under a crumbling doorway and found himself in a kind of courtyard.

Before him was a drained reflecting pool, long and

rectangular. Jason couldn't tell how deep it was, because the bottom was filled with mist. A dirt path led all the way around, and the house's uneven walls rose on either side. Wolves paced under the archways of rough red volcanic stone.

At the far end of the pool sat a giant she-wolf, several feet taller than Jason. Her eyes glowed silver in the fog, and her coat was the same color as the rocks—warm chocolaty red.

"I know this place," Jason said.

The wolf regarded him. She didn't exactly speak, but Jason could understand her. The movements of her ears and whiskers, the flash of her eyes, the way she curled her lips—all of these were part of her language.

Of course, the she-wolf said. *You began your journey here as a pup. Now you must find your way back. A new quest, a new start.*

"That isn't fair," Jason said. But as soon as he spoke, he knew there was no point complaining to the she-wolf.

Wolves didn't feel sympathy. They never expected fairness. The wolf said: *Conquer or die. This is always our way.*

Jason wanted to protest that he couldn't conquer if he didn't know who he was, or where he was supposed to go. But he knew this wolf. Her name was simply Lupa, the Mother Wolf, the greatest of her kind. Long ago she'd found him in this place, protected him, nurtured him, *chosen* him, but if Jason showed weakness, she would tear him to shreds. Rather than being her pup, he would become her dinner. In the wolf pack, weakness was not an option.

"Can you guide me?" Jason asked.

Lupa made a rumbling noise deep in her throat, and the mist in the pool dissolved.

At first Jason wasn't sure what he was seeing. At opposite ends of the pool, two dark spires had erupted from the cement floor like the drill bits of some massive tunneling machines boring through the surface. Jason couldn't tell if the spires were made of rock or petrified vines, but they were formed of thick tendrils that came together in a point at the top. Each spire was about five feet tall, but they weren't identical. The one closest to Jason was darker and seemed like a solid mass, its tendrils fused together. As he watched, it pushed a little farther out of the earth and expanded a little wider.

On Lupa's end of the pool, the second spire's tendrils were more open, like the bars of a cage. Inside, Jason could vaguely see a misty figure struggling, shifting within its confines.

"Hera," Jason said.

The she-wolf growled in agreement. The other wolves circled the pool, their fur standing up on their backs as they snarled at the spires.

The enemy has chosen this place to awaken her most powerful son, the giant king, Lupa said. *Our sacred place, where demigods are claimed—the place of death or life. The burned house. The house of the wolf. It is an abomination. You must stop her.*

"Her?" Jason was confused. "You mean, Hera?"

The she-wolf gnashed her teeth impatiently. *Use your senses, pup. I care nothing for Juno, but if she falls, our enemy wakes. And that will be the end for all of us. You know this place. You can find it again. Cleanse our house. Stop this before it is too late.*

The dark spire grew slowly larger, like the bulb of some horrible flower. Jason sensed that if it ever opened, it would release something he did *not* want to meet.

"Who am I?" Jason asked the she-wolf. "At least tell me that."

Wolves don't have much of a sense of humor, but Jason could tell the question amused Lupa, as if Jason were a cub just trying out his claws, practicing to be the alpha male.

You are our saving grace, as always. The she-wolf curled her lip, as if she had just made a clever joke. *Do not fail, son of Jupiter.*

XIV

JASON

JASON WOKE TO THE SOUND OF THUNDER. Then he remembered where he was. It was always thundering in Cabin One.

Above his cot, the domed ceiling was decorated with a blue-and-white mosaic like a cloudy sky. The cloud tiles shifted across the ceiling, changing from white to black. Thunder rumbled through the room, and gold tiles flashed like veins of lightning.

Except for the cot that the other campers had brought him, the cabin had no regular furniture—no chairs, tables, or dressers. As far as Jason could tell, it didn't even have a bathroom. The walls were carved with alcoves, each holding a bronze brazier or a golden eagle statue on a marble pedestal. In the center of the room, a twenty-foot-tall, full-color statue of Zeus in classic Greek robes stood with a shield at his side and a lightning bolt raised, ready to smite somebody.

Jason studied the statue, looking for anything he had in common with the Lord of the Sky. Black hair? Nope. Grumbly expression? Well, maybe. Beard? No thanks. In his robes and sandals, Zeus looked like a really buff, really angry hippie.

Yeah, Cabin One. A big honor, the other campers had told him. Sure, if you liked sleeping in a cold temple by yourself with Hippie Zeus frowning down at you all night.

Jason got up and rubbed his neck. His whole body was stiff from bad sleep and summoning lightning. That little trick last night hadn't been as easy as he had let on. It had almost made him pass out.

Next to the cot, new clothes were laid out for him: jeans, sneakers, and an orange Camp Half-Blood shirt. He definitely needed a change of clothes, but looking down at his tattered purple shirt, he was reluctant to change. It felt wrong somehow, putting on the camp shirt. He still couldn't believe he belonged here, despite everything they'd told him.

He thought about his dream, hoping more memories would come back to him about Lupa, or that ruined house in the redwoods. He knew he'd been there before. The wolf was real. But his head ached when he tried to remember. The marks on his forearm seemed to burn.

If he could find those ruins, he could find his past. Whatever was growing inside that rock spire, Jason had to stop it.

He looked at Hippie Zeus. "You're welcome to help."

The statue said nothing.

"Thanks, Pops," Jason muttered.

He changed clothes and checked his reflection in Zeus's shield. His face looked watery and strange in the metal, like he was dissolving in a pool of gold. Definitely he didn't look as good as Piper had last night after she'd suddenly been transformed.

Jason still wasn't sure how he felt about that. He'd acted like an idiot, announcing in front of everyone that she was a knockout. Not like there'd been anything wrong with her *before*. Sure, she looked great after Aphrodite zapped her, but she also didn't look like herself, not comfortable with the attention.

Jason had felt bad for her. Maybe that was crazy, considering she'd just been claimed by a goddess and turned into the most gorgeous girl at camp. Everybody had started fawning over her, telling her how amazing she was and how obviously *she* should be the one who went on the quest—but that attention had nothing to do with who she was. New dress, new makeup, glowing pink aura, and *boom*: suddenly people liked her. Jason felt like he understood that.

Last night when he'd called down lightning, the other campers' reactions had seemed familiar to him. He was pretty sure he'd been dealing with that for a long time—people looking at him in awe just because he was the son of Zeus, treating him special, but it didn't have anything to do with *him*. Nobody cared about *him*, just his big scary daddy standing behind him with the doomsday bolt, as if to say, *Respect this kid or eat voltage!*

After the campfire, when people started heading back to their cabins, Jason had gone up to Piper and formally asked her to come with him on the quest.

She'd still been in a state of shock, but she nodded, rubbing her arms, which must've been cold in that sleeveless dress.

"Aphrodite took my snowboarding jacket," she muttered. "Mugged by my own mom."

In the first row of the amphitheater, Jason found a blanket and wrapped it around her shoulders. "We'll get you a new jacket," he promised.

She managed a smile. He wanted to wrap his arms around her, but he restrained himself. He didn't want her to think he was as shallow as everyone else—trying to make a move on her because she'd turned all beautiful.

He was glad Piper was going with him on the quest. Jason had tried to act brave at the campfire, but it was just that— an act. The idea of going up against an evil force powerful enough to kidnap Hera scared him witless, especially since he didn't even know his own past. He'd need help, and it felt right: Piper should be with him. But things were already complicated without figuring out how much he liked her, and why. He'd already messed with her head enough.

He slipped on his new shoes, ready to get out of that cold, empty cabin. Then he spotted something he hadn't noticed the night before. A brazier had been moved out of one of the alcoves to create a sleeping niche, with a bedroll, a backpack, even some pictures taped to the wall.

Jason walked over. Whoever had slept there, it had been a long time ago. The bedroll smelled musty. The backpack was covered with a thin film of dust. Some of the photos once taped to the wall had lost their stickiness and fallen to the floor.

One picture showed Annabeth—much younger, maybe eight, but Jason could tell it was she: same blond hair and gray eyes, same distracted look like she was thinking a million things at once. She stood next to a sandy-haired guy about fourteen or fifteen, with a mischievous smile and ragged leather armor over a T-shirt. He was pointing to an alley behind them, like he was telling the photographer, *Let's go meet things in a dark alley and kill them!* A second photo showed Annabeth and the same guy sitting at a campfire, laughing hysterically.

Finally Jason picked up one of the photos that had fallen. It was a strip of pictures like you'd take in a do-it-yourself photo booth: Annabeth and the sandy-haired guy, but with another girl between them. She was maybe fifteen, with black hair—choppy like Piper's—a black leather jacket, and silver jewelry, so she looked kind of goth; but she was caught mid-laugh, and it was clear she was with her two best friends.

"That's Thalia," someone said.

Jason turned.

Annabeth was peering over his shoulder. Her expression was sad, like the picture brought back hard memories. "She's the other child of Zeus who lived here—but not for long. Sorry, I should've knocked."

"It's fine," Jason said. "Not like I think of this place as home."

Annabeth was dressed for travel, with a winter coat over her camp clothes, her knife at her belt, and a backpack across her shoulder.

Jason said, "Don't suppose you've changed your mind about coming with us?"

She shook her head. "You got a good team already. I'm off to look for Percy."

Jason was a little disappointed. He would've appreciated having somebody on the trip who knew what they were doing, so he wouldn't feel like he was leading Piper and Leo off a cliff.

"Hey, you'll do fine," Annabeth promised. "Something tells me this isn't your first quest."

Jason had a vague suspicion she was right, but that didn't make him feel any better. Everyone seemed to think he was so brave and confident, but they didn't see how lost he really felt. How could they trust him when he didn't even know who he was?

He looked at the pictures of Annabeth smiling. He wondered how long it had been since she'd smiled. She must really like this Percy guy to search for him so hard, and that made Jason a little envious. Was anyone searching for *him* right now? What if somebody cared for *him* that much and was going out of her mind with worry, and he couldn't even remember his old life?

"You know who I am," he guessed. "Don't you?"

Annabeth gripped the hilt of her dagger. She looked for a chair to sit on, but of course there weren't any. "Honestly, Jason . . . I'm not sure. My best guess, you're a loner. It happens sometimes. For one reason or another, the camp never found you, but you survived anyway by constantly moving around. Trained yourself to fight. Handled the monsters on your own. You beat the odds."

"The first thing Chiron said to me," Jason remembered, "was *you should be dead.*"

"That could be why," Annabeth said. "Most demigods

would never make it on their own. And a child of Zeus— I mean, it doesn't get any more dangerous than that. The chances of your reaching age fifteen without finding Camp Half-Blood or dying—microscopic. But like I said, it does happen. Thalia ran away when she was young. She survived on her own for years. Even took care of me for a while. So maybe you were a loner too."

Jason held out his arm. "And these marks?"

Annabeth glanced at the tattoos. Clearly, they bothered her. "Well, the eagle is the symbol of Zeus, so that makes sense. The twelve lines—maybe they stand for years, if you'd been making them since you were three years old. SPQR— that's the motto of the old Roman Empire: *Senatus Populusque Romanus*, the Senate and the People of Rome. Though why you would burn that on your own arm, I don't know. Unless you had a *really* harsh Latin teacher..."

Jason was pretty sure that wasn't the reason. It also didn't seem possible he'd been on his own his whole life. But what else made sense? Annabeth had been pretty clear—Camp Half-Blood was the only safe place in the world for demigods.

"I, um... had a weird dream last night," he said. It seemed like a stupid thing to confide, but Annabeth didn't look surprised.

"Happens all the time to demigods," she said. "What did you see?"

He told her about the wolves and the ruined house and the two rock spires. As he talked, Annabeth started pacing, looking more and more agitated.

"You don't remember where this house is?" she asked.

Jason shook his head. "But I'm sure I've been there before."

"Redwoods," she mused. "Could be northern California. And the she-wolf...I've studied goddesses, spirits, and monsters my whole life. I've never heard of Lupa."

"She said the enemy was a 'her.' I thought maybe it was Hera, but—"

"I wouldn't trust Hera, but I don't think she's the enemy. And that thing rising out of the earth—" Annabeth's expression darkened. "You've got to stop it."

"You know what it is, don't you?" he asked. "Or at least, you've got a guess. I saw your face last night at the campfire. You looked at Chiron like it was suddenly dawning on you, but you didn't want to scare us."

Annabeth hesitated. "Jason, the thing about prophecies... the more you know, the more you try to change them, and that can be disastrous. Chiron believes it's better that you find your own path, find out things in your own time. If he'd told me everything he knew before my first quest with Percy ...I've got to admit, I'm not sure I would've been able to go through with it. For your quest, it's even more important."

"That bad, huh?"

"Not if you succeed. At least...I hope not."

"But I don't even know where to start. Where am I supposed to go?"

"Follow the monsters," Annabeth suggested.

Jason thought about that. The storm spirit who'd attacked him at the Grand Canyon had said he was being recalled to his boss. If Jason could track the storm spirits, he might be able to find the person controlling them. And maybe that would lead him to Hera's prison.

"Okay," he said. "How do I find storm winds?"

"Personally, I'd ask a wind god," Annabeth said. "Aeolus is the master of all the winds, but he's a little...unpredictable. No one finds him unless he wants to be found. I'd try one of the four seasonal wind gods that work for Aeolus. The nearest one, the one who has the most dealings with heroes, is Boreas, the North Wind."

"So if I looked him up on Google maps—"

"Oh, he's not hard to find," Annabeth promised. "He settled in North America like all the other gods. So of course he picked the oldest northern settlement, about as far north as you can go."

"Maine?" Jason guessed.

"Farther."

Jason tried to envision a map. What was farther north than Maine? The oldest northern settlement...

"Canada," he decided. "Quebec."

Annabeth smiled. "I hope you speak French."

Jason actually felt a spark of excitement. Quebec—at least now he had a goal. Find the North Wind, track down the storm spirits, find out who they worked for and where that ruined house was. Free Hera. All in four days. Cake.

"Thanks, Annabeth." He looked at the photo booth pictures still in his hand. "So, um...you said it was dangerous being a child of Zeus. What happened to Thalia?"

"Oh, she's fine," Annabeth said. "She became a Hunter of

Artemis—one of the handmaidens of the goddess. They roam around the country killing monsters. We don't see them at camp very often."

Jason glanced over at the huge statue of Zeus. He understood why Thalia had slept in this alcove. It was the only place in the cabin not in Hippie Zeus's line of sight. And even that hadn't been enough. She'd chosen to follow Artemis and be part of a group rather than stay in this cold drafty temple alone with her twenty-foot-tall dad—*Jason's dad*—glowering down at her. *Eat voltage!* Jason didn't have any trouble understanding Thalia's feelings. He wondered if there was a Hunters group for guys.

"Who's the other kid in the photo?" he asked. "The sandy-haired guy."

Annabeth's expression tightened. Touchy subject.

"That's Luke," she said. "He's dead now."

Jason decided it was best not to ask more, but the way Annabeth said Luke's name, he wondered if maybe Percy Jackson wasn't the only boy Annabeth had ever liked.

He focused again on Thalia's face. He kept thinking this photo of her was important. He was missing something.

Jason felt a strange sense of connection to this other child of Zeus—someone who might understand his confusion, maybe even answer some questions. But another voice inside him, an insistent whisper, said: *Dangerous. Stay away.*

"How old is she now?" he asked.

"Hard to say. She was a tree for a while. Now she's immortal."

"What?"

His expression must've been pretty good, because Annabeth laughed. "Don't worry. It's not something all children of Zeus go through. It's a long story, but... well, she was out of commission for a long time. If she'd aged regularly, she'd be in her twenties now, but she still looks the same as in that picture, like she's about... well, about your age. Fifteen or sixteen?"

Something the she-wolf had said in his dream nagged at Jason. He found himself asking, "What's her last name?"

Annabeth looked uneasy. "She didn't use a last name, really. If she had to, she'd use her mom's, but they didn't get along. Thalia ran away when she was pretty young."

Jason waited.

"Grace," Annabeth said. "Thalia Grace."

Jason's fingers went numb. The picture fluttered to the floor.

"You okay?" Annabeth asked.

A shred of memory had ignited—maybe a tiny piece that Hera had forgotten to steal. Or maybe she'd left it there on purpose—just enough for him to remember that name, and know that digging up his past was terribly, terribly dangerous.

You should be dead, Chiron had said. It wasn't a comment about Jason beating the odds as a loner. Chiron knew something specific—something about Jason's family.

The she-wolf's words in his dream finally made sense to him, her clever joke at his expense. He could imagine Lupa growling a wolfish laugh.

"What is it?" Annabeth pressed.

Jason couldn't keep this to himself. It would kill him, and

he had to get Annabeth's help. If she knew Thalia, maybe she could advise him.

"You have to swear not to tell anyone else," he said.

"Jason—"

"Swear it," he urged. "Until I figure out what's going on, what this all means—" He rubbed the burned tattoos on his forearm. "You have to keep a secret."

Annabeth hesitated, but her curiosity won out. "All right. Until you tell me it's okay, I won't share what you say with anyone else. I swear on the River Styx."

Thunder rumbled, even louder than usual for the cabin.

You are our saving Grace, the wolf had snarled.

Jason picked up the photo from the floor.

"My last name is Grace," he said. "This is my sister."

Annabeth turned pale. Jason could see her wrestling with dismay, disbelief, anger. She thought he was lying. His claim was impossible. And part of him felt the same way, but as soon as he spoke the words, he knew they were true.

Then the doors of the cabin burst open. Half a dozen campers spilled in, led by the bald guy from Iris, Butch.

"Hurry!" he said, and Jason couldn't tell if his expression was excitement or fear. "The dragon is back."

XV

PIPER

PIPER WOKE UP AND IMMEDIATELY GRABBED a mirror. There were plenty of those in the Aphrodite cabin. She sat on her bunk, looked at her reflection and groaned.

She was *still* gorgeous.

Last night after the campfire, she'd tried everything. She messed up her hair, washed the makeup off her face, cried to make her eyes red. Nothing worked. Her hair popped back to perfection. The magic makeup reapplied itself. Her eyes refused to get puffy or bloodshot.

She would've changed clothes, but she had nothing to change into. The other Aphrodite campers offered her some (laughing behind her back, she was sure), but each outfit was even more fashionable and ridiculous than what she had on.

Now, after a horrible night's sleep, still no change. Piper normally looked like a zombie in the morning, but her hair was styled like a supermodel's and her skin was perfect. Even that horrible zit at the base of her nose, which she'd had for so many days she'd started to call it Bob, had disappeared.

She growled in frustration and raked her fingers through her hair. No use. The do just popped back into place. She looked like Cherokee Barbie.

From across the cabin, Drew called, "Oh, honey, it won't go away." Her voice dripped with false sympathy. "Mom's blessing will last *at least* another day. Maybe a week if you're lucky."

Piper gritted her teeth. "A *week*?"

The other Aphrodite kids—about a dozen girls and five guys—smirked and snickered at her discomfort. Piper knew she should play cool, not let them get under her skin. She'd dealt with shallow, popular kids plenty of times. But this was different. These were her brothers and sisters, even if she had *nothing* in common with them, and how Aphrodite had managed to have so many kids so close in age...Never mind. She didn't want to know.

"Don't worry, hon." Drew blotted her fluorescent lipstick. "You're thinking you don't belong here? We couldn't agree more. Isn't that right, *Mitchell*?"

One of the guys flinched. "Um, yeah. Sure."

"Mmm-hmm." Drew took out her mascara and checked her lashes. Everyone else watched, not daring to speak. "So anyways, people, fifteen minutes until breakfast. The cabin's not going to clean itself! And Mitchell, I think you've learned your lesson. Right, sweetie? So you're on garbage patrol just for today, mm-kay? Show Piper how it's done, 'cause I have a feeling she'll have that job soon—*if* she survives her *quest.* Now, get to work, everybody! It's my bathroom time!"

Everybody started rushing around, making beds and folding clothes, while Drew scooped up her makeup kit, hair dryer, and brush and marched into the bathroom.

Someone inside yelped, and a girl about eleven was kicked out, hastily wrapped in towels with shampoo still in her hair.

The door slammed shut, and the girl started to cry. A couple of older campers comforted her and wiped the bubbles out of her hair.

"Seriously?" Piper said to no one in particular. "You let Drew treat you like this?"

A few kids shot Piper nervous looks, like they might actually agree, but they said nothing.

The campers kept working, though Piper couldn't see why the cabin needed much cleaning. It was a life-size dollhouse, with pink walls and white window trim. The lace curtains were pastel blue and green, which of course matched the sheets and feather comforters on all the beds.

The guys had one row of bunks separated by a curtain, but their section of the cabin was just as neat and orderly as the girls'. Something was *definitely* unnatural about that. Every camper had a wooden camp chest at the foot of their bunk with their name painted on it, and Piper guessed that the clothes in each chest were neatly folded and color coordinated. The only bit of individualism was how the campers decorated their private bunk spaces. Each had slightly different pictures tacked up of whatever celebrities they thought were hot. A few had personal photos, too, but most were actors or singers or whatever.

Piper hoped she might not see *The Poster*. It had been almost a year since the movie, and she thought by now surely everyone had torn down those old tattered advertisements and tacked up something newer. But no such luck. She spotted one on the wall by the storage closet, in the middle of a collage of famous heartthrobs.

The title was lurid red: KING OF SPARTA. Under that, the poster showed the leading man—a three-quarters shot of bare-chested bronze flesh, with ripped pectorals and six-pack abs. He was clad in only a Greek war kilt and a purple cape, sword in hand. He looked like he'd just been rubbed in oil, his short black hair gleaming and rivulets of sweat pouring off his rugged face, those dark sad eyes facing the camera as if to say, *I will kill your men and steal your women! Ha-ha!*

It was the most ridiculous poster of all time. Piper and her dad had had a good laugh over it the first time they saw it. Then the movie made a bajillion dollars. The poster graphic popped up everywhere. Piper couldn't get away from it at school, walking down the street, even online. It became *The Poster*, the most embarrassing thing in her life. And yeah, it was a picture of her dad.

She turned away so no one would think she was staring at it. Maybe when everyone went to breakfast she could tear it down and they wouldn't notice.

She tried to look busy, but she didn't have any extra clothes to fold. She straightened her bed, then realized the top blanket was the one Jason had wrapped around her shoulders last night. She picked it up and pressed it to her face. It smelled of wood smoke, but unfortunately not of Jason. He was the *only* person who'd been genuinely nice to her after the claiming, like he cared about how she felt, not just about her stupid new clothes. God, she'd wanted to kiss him, but he'd seemed so uncomfortable, almost scared of her. She couldn't really blame him. She'd been glowing pink.

"'Scuse me," said a voice by her feet. The garbage patrol guy, Mitchell, was crawling around on all fours, picking up chocolate wrappers and crumpled notes from under the bunk beds. Apparently the Aphrodite kids weren't one hundred percent neat freaks after all.

She moved out of his way. "What'd you do to make Drew mad?"

He glanced over at the bathroom door to make sure it was still closed. "Last night, after you were claimed, I said you might not be so bad."

It wasn't much of a compliment, but Piper was stunned. An Aphrodite kid had actually stood up for her?

"Thanks," she said.

Mitchell shrugged. "Yeah, well. See where it got me. But for what it's worth, welcome to Cabin Ten."

A girl with blond pigtails and braces raced up with a pile of clothes in her arms. She looked around furtively like she was delivering nuclear materials.

"I brought you these," she whispered.

"Piper, meet Lacy," Mitchell said, still crawling around on the floor.

"Hi," Lacy said breathlessly. "You *can* change clothes. The blessing won't stop you. This is just, you know, a backpack, some rations, ambrosia and nectar for emergencies, some jeans, a few extra shirts, and a warm jacket. The boots might be a little snug. But—well—we took up a collection. Good luck on your quest!"

Lacy dumped the things on the bed and started to hurry away, but Piper caught her arm. "Hold on. At least let me thank you! Why are you rushing off?"

Lacy looked like she might shake apart from nervousness. "Oh, well—"

"Drew might find out," Mitchell explained.

"I might have to wear the shoes of shame!" Lacy gulped.

"The what?" Piper asked.

Lacy and Mitchell both pointed to a black shelf mounted in the corner of the room, like an altar. Displayed on it were a hideous pair of orthopedic nurse's shoes, bright white with thick soles.

"I had to wear them for a week once," Lacy whimpered. "They don't go with *anything*!"

"And there're worse punishments," Mitchell warned. "Drew can charmspeak, see? Not many Aphrodite kids have that power; but if she tries hard enough, she can get you to do some pretty embarrassing things. Piper, you're the first person I've seen in a long time who is able to resist her."

"Charmspeak..." Piper remembered last night, the way the crowd at the campfire had swayed back and forth between Drew's opinion and hers. "You mean, like, you could talk someone into doing things. Or... giving you things. Like a car?"

"Oh, don't give Drew any ideas!" Lacy gasped.

"But yeah," Mitchell said. "She could do that."

"So that's why she's head counselor," Piper said. "She convinced you all?"

Mitchell picked a nasty wad of gum from under Piper's bed. "Nah, she inherited the post when Silena Beauregard died in the war. Drew was second oldest. Oldest camper automatically gets the post, unless somebody with more years or more completed quests wants to challenge, in which case there's a duel, but that hardly ever happens. Anyway, we've been stuck with Drew in charge since August. She decided to make some, ah, *changes* in the way the cabin is run."

"Yes, I did!" Suddenly Drew was there, leaning against the bunk. Lacy squeaked like a guinea pig and tried to run, but Drew put an arm out to stop her. She looked down at Mitchell. "I think you missed some trash, sweetie. You'd better make another pass."

Piper glanced toward the bathroom and saw that Drew had dumped everything from the bathroom waste bin—some pretty *nasty* things—all over the floor.

Mitchell sat up on his haunches. He glared at Drew like he was about to attack (which Piper would've paid money to see), but finally he snapped, "Fine."

Drew smiled. "See, Piper, hon, we're a good cabin here. A good family! Silena Beauregard, though...you could take a warning from her. She was secretly passing information to Kronos in the Titan War, helping the *enemy*."

Drew smiled all sweet and innocent, with her glittery pink makeup and her blow-dried hair lush and smelling like nutmeg. She looked like any popular teenage girl from any high school. But her eyes were as cold as steel. Piper got the feeling Drew was looking straight into her soul, pulling out her secrets.

Helping the enemy.

"Oh, none of the other cabins talk about it," Drew confided. "They act like Silena Beauregard was a hero."

"She sacrificed her life to make things right," Mitchell grumbled. "She *was* a hero."

"Mmm-hmm," Drew said. "Another day on garbage patrol, Mitchell. But *anyways*, Silena lost track of what this cabin is about. We match up cute couples at camp! Then we break them apart and start over! It's the best fun ever. We don't have any business getting involved in other stuff like wars and quests. *I* certainly haven't been on any quests. They're a waste of time!"

Lacy raised her hand nervously. "But last night you said you wanted to go on a—"

Drew glared at her, and Lacy's voice died.

"Most of all," Drew continued, "we certainly don't need our image tarnished by spies, do we, *Piper*?"

Piper tried to answer, but she couldn't. There was no way Drew could know about her dreams or her dad's kidnapping, was there?

"It's too bad you won't be around," Drew sighed. "But if you survive your little quest, don't worry, I'll find *somebody* to match up with you. Maybe one of those gross Hephaestus guys. Or Clovis? He's pretty repulsive." Drew looked her over with a mix of pity and disgust. "Honestly, I didn't think it was *possible* for Aphrodite to have an ugly child, but ... who *was* your father? Was he some sort of mutant, or—"

"Tristan McLean," Piper snapped.

As soon as she said it, she hated herself. She never, *ever* played the "famous dad" card. But Drew had driven her over the edge. "My dad's Tristan McLean."

The stunned silence was gratifying for a few seconds, but Piper felt ashamed of herself. Everybody turned and looked at *The Poster*, her dad flexing his muscles for the whole world to see.

"Oh my god!" half the girls screamed at once.

"Sweet!" a guy said. "The dude with the sword who killed that other dude in that movie?"

"He is *so* hot for an old guy," a girl said, and then she blushed. "I mean I'm sorry. I know he's your *dad*. That's *so* weird!"

"It's weird, all right," Piper agreed.

"Do you think you could get me his autograph?" another girl asked.

Piper forced a smile. She couldn't say, *If my dad survives. ...*

"Yeah, no problem," she managed.

The girl squealed in excitement, and more kids surged forward, asking a dozen questions at once.

"Have you ever been on the set?"

"Do you live in a mansion?"

"Do you have lunch with movie stars?"

"Have you had your rite of passage?"

That one caught Piper off guard. "Rite of what?" she asked.

The girls and guys giggled and shoved each other around like this was an embarrassing topic.

"The rite of passage for an Aphrodite child," one explained. "You get someone to fall in love with you. Then you break their heart. Dump them. Once you do that, you've proven yourself worthy of Aphrodite."

Piper stared at the crowd to see if they were joking. "Break someone's heart on purpose? That's terrible!"

The others looked confused.

"Why?" a guy asked.

"Oh my god!" a girl said. "I bet Aphrodite broke your *dad's* heart! I bet he never loved anyone again, did he? That's so romantic! When you have your rite of passage, you can be just like Mom!"

"Forget it!" Piper yelled, a little louder than she'd intended. The other kids backed away. "I'm *not* breaking somebody's heart just for a stupid rite of passage!"

Which of course gave Drew a chance to take back control. "Well, there you go!" she cut in. "Silena said the same thing. She broke the tradition, fell in love with that Beckendorf boy, and *stayed* in love. If you ask me, that's why things ended tragically for her."

"That's not true!" Lacy squeaked, but Drew glared at her, and she immediately melted back into the crowd.

"Hardly matters," Drew continued, "because, Piper, hon, you couldn't break anyone's heart anyway. And this nonsense about your dad being Tristan McLean—that's *so* begging for attention."

Several of the kids blinked uncertainly.

"You mean he's *not* her dad?" one asked.

Drew rolled her eyes. "Please. Now, it's time for breakfast, people, and Piper here has to start that little quest. So let's get her packed and get her out of here!"

Drew broke up the crowd and got everyone moving. She called them "hon" and "dear," but her tone made it clear she expected to be obeyed. Mitchell and Lacy helped Piper pack. They even guarded the bathroom while Piper went in and changed into a better traveling outfit. The hand-me-downs weren't fancy—thank god—just well-worn jeans, a T-shirt, a comfortable winter coat, and hiking boots that fit perfectly. She strapped her dagger, Katoptris, to her belt.

When Piper came out, she felt almost normal again. The other campers were standing at their bunks while Drew came around and inspected. Piper turned to Mitchell and Lacy and mouthed, *Thank you*. Mitchell nodded grimly. Lacy flashed a full-braces smile. Piper doubted Drew had ever thanked them for anything. She also noticed that the *King of Sparta* poster had been wadded up and thrown in the trash. Drew's orders, no doubt. Even though Piper had wanted to take the poster down herself, now she was totally steamed.

When Drew spotted her, she clapped in mock applause. "Very nice! Our little quest girl all dressed in Dumpster clothes again. Now, off you go! No need to eat breakfast with us. Good luck with…whatever. Bye!"

Piper shouldered her bag. She could feel everyone else's eyes on her as she walked to the door. She could just leave and forget about it. That would've been the easy thing. What did she care about this cabin, these shallow kids?

Except that some of them had tried to help her. Some of them had even stood up to Drew for her.

She turned at the door. "You know, you all don't have to follow Drew's orders."

The other kids shifted. Several glanced at Drew, but she looked too stunned to respond.

"Umm," one managed, "she's our head counselor."

"She's a tyrant," Piper corrected. "You can think for yourselves. There's got to be more to Aphrodite than *this*."

"More than this," one kid echoed.

"Think for ourselves," a second muttered.

"People!" Drew screeched. "Don't be stupid! She's charmspeaking you."

"No," Piper said. "I'm just telling the truth."

At least, Piper thought that was the case. She didn't understand exactly how this charmspeaking business worked, but she didn't feel like she was putting any special power into her words. She didn't want to win an argument by tricking people. That would make her no better than Drew. Piper simply meant what she said. Besides, even if she tried charmspeaking, she had a feeling it wouldn't work very well on another charmspeaker like Drew.

Drew sneered at her. "You may have a little power, Miss Movie Star. But you don't know the first thing about Aphrodite. You have such great ideas? What do you think this cabin is about, then? Tell them. Then maybe I'll tell them a few things about *you*, huh?"

Piper wanted to make a withering retort, but her anger turned to panic. She was a spy for the enemy, just like Silena

Beauregard. An Aphrodite traitor. Did Drew know about that, or was she bluffing? Under Drew's glare, her confidence began to crumble.

"Not this," Piper managed. "Aphrodite is not about this."

Then she turned and stormed out before the others could see her blushing.

Behind her, Drew started laughing. "*Not this*? Hear that, people? She doesn't have a clue!"

Piper promised herself she would never *ever* go back to that cabin. She blinked away her tears and stormed across the green, not sure where she was going—until she saw the dragon swooping down from the sky.

PIPER

"Leo?" she yelled.

Sure enough, there he was, sitting atop a giant bronze death machine and grinning like a lunatic. Even before he landed, the camp alarm went up. A conch horn blew. All the satyrs started screaming, "Don't kill me!" Half the camp ran outside in a mixture of pajamas and armor. The dragon set down right in the middle of the green, and Leo yelled, "It's cool! Don't shoot!"

Hesitantly, the archers lowered their bows. The warriors backed away, keeping their spears and swords ready. They made a loose wide ring around the metal monster. Other demigods hid behind their cabin doors or peeped out the windows. Nobody seemed anxious to get close.

Piper couldn't blame them. The dragon was huge. It glistened in the morning sun like a living penny sculpture —different shades of copper and bronze—a sixty-foot-long serpent with steel talons and drill-bit teeth and glowing ruby eyes. It had bat-shaped wings twice its length that unfurled like metallic sails, making a sound like coins cascading out of a slot machine every time they flapped.

"It's beautiful," Piper muttered. The other demigods stared at her like she was insane.

The dragon reared its head and shot a column of fire into the sky. Campers scrambled away and hefted their weapons, but Leo slid calmly off the dragon's back. He held up his hands like he was surrendering, except he still had that crazy grin on his face.

"People of Earth, I come in peace!" he shouted. He looked like he'd been rolling around in the campfire. His army coat and his face were smeared with soot. His hands were grease-stained, and he wore a new tool belt around his waist. His eyes were bloodshot. His curly hair was so oily it stuck up in porcupine quills, and he smelled strangely of Tabasco sauce. But he looked absolutely delighted. "Festus is just saying hello!"

"That thing is dangerous!" an Ares girl shouted, brandishing her spear. "Kill it now!"

"Stand down!" someone ordered.

To Piper's surprise, it was Jason. He pushed through the crowd, flanked by Annabeth and that girl from the Hephaestus cabin, Nyssa.

Jason gazed up at the dragon and shook his head in amazement. "Leo, what have you done?"

"Found a ride!" Leo beamed. "You said I could go on the quest if I got you a ride. Well, I got you a class-A metallic flying bad boy! Festus can take us anywhere!"

"It—has wings," Nyssa stammered. Her jaw looked like it might drop off her face.

"Yeah!" Leo said. "I found them and reattached them."

"But it never had wings. Where did you find them?"

Leo hesitated, and Piper could tell he was hiding something.

"In . . . the woods," he said. "Repaired his circuits, too, mostly, so no more problems with him going haywire."

"Mostly?" Nyssa asked.

The dragon's head twitched. It tilted to one side and a stream of black liquid—maybe oil, *hopefully* just oil—poured out of its ear, all over Leo.

"Just a few kinks to work out," Leo said.

"But how did you survive . . . ?" Nyssa was still staring at the creature in awe. "I mean, the fire breath . . ."

"I'm quick," Leo said. "And lucky. Now, am I on this quest, or what?"

Jason scratched his head. "You named him Festus? You know that in Latin, 'festus' means 'happy'? You want us to ride off to save the world on Happy the Dragon?"

The dragon twitched and shuddered and flapped his wings.

"That's a yes, bro!" Leo said. "Now, um, I'd really suggest we get going, guys. I already picked up some supplies in the —um, in the woods. And all these people with weapons are making Festus nervous."

Jason frowned. "But we haven't planned anything yet. We can't just—"

"Go," Annabeth said. She was the only one who didn't look nervous at all. Her expression was sad and wistful, like this reminded her of better times. "Jason, you've only got three days until the solstice now, and you should never keep a nervous dragon waiting. This is certainly a good omen. Go!"

Jason nodded. Then he smiled at Piper. "You ready, partner?"

Piper looked at the bronze dragon wings shining against the sky, and those talons that could've shredded her to pieces.

"You bet," she said.

Flying on the dragon was the most amazing experience ever, Piper thought.

Up high, the air was freezing cold; but the dragon's metal hide generated so much heat, it was like they were flying in a protective bubble. Talk about seat warmers! And the grooves in the dragon's back were designed like high-tech saddles, so they weren't uncomfortable at all. Leo showed them how to hook their feet in the chinks of the armor, like in stirrups, and use the leather safety harnesses cleverly concealed under the exterior plating. They sat single file: Leo in front, then Piper, then Jason, and Piper was very aware of Jason right behind her. She wished he would hold on to her, maybe wrap his arms around her waist; but sadly, he didn't.

Leo used the reins to steer the dragon into the sky like he'd been doing it all his life. The metal wings worked perfectly, and soon the coast of Long Island was just a hazy line behind them. They shot over Connecticut and climbed into the gray winter clouds.

Leo grinned back at them. "Cool, right?"

"What if we get spotted?" Piper asked.

"The Mist," Jason said. "It keeps mortals from seeing magic things. If they spot us, they'll probably mistake us for a small plane or something."

Piper glanced over her shoulder. "You sure about that?"

"No," he admitted. Then Piper saw he was clutching a photo in his hand—a picture of a girl with dark hair.

She gave Jason a quizzical look, but he blushed and put the photo in his pocket. "We're making good time. Probably get there by tonight."

Piper wondered who the girl in the picture was, but she didn't want to ask; and if Jason didn't volunteer the information, that wasn't a good sign. Had he remembered something about his life before? Was that a photo of his real girlfriend?

Stop it, she thought. *You'll just torture yourself.*

She asked a safer question. "Where are we heading?"

"To find the god of the North Wind," Jason said. "And chase some storm spirits."

XVII

LEO

LEO WAS TOTALLY BUZZING.

The expression on everyone's faces when he flew the dragon into camp? Priceless! He thought his cabinmates were going to bust a lug nut.

Festus had been awesome too. He hadn't blowtorched a single cabin or eaten any satyrs, even if he did dribble a little oil from his ear. Okay, a *lot* of oil. Leo could work on that later.

So maybe Leo didn't seize the chance to tell everybody about Bunker 9 or the flying boat design. He needed some time to think about all that. He could tell them when he came back.

If I come back, part of him thought.

Nah, he'd come back. He'd scored a sweet magic tool belt from the bunker, plus a lot of cool supplies now safely stowed in his backpack. Besides, he had a fire-breathing, only slightly leaky dragon on his side. What could go wrong?

Well, the control disk could bust, the bad part of him suggested. *Festus could eat you.*

Okay, so the dragon wasn't *quite* as fixed as Leo might've let on. He'd worked all night attaching those wings, but he hadn't found an extra dragon brain anywhere in the bunker. Hey, they were under a time limit! Three days until the solstice. They had to get going. Besides, Leo had cleaned the disk pretty well. Most of the circuits were still good. It would just have to hold together.

His bad side started to think, *Yeah, but what if—*

"Shut up, me," Leo said aloud.

"What?" Piper asked.

"Nothing," he said. "Long night. I think I'm hallucinating. It's cool."

Sitting in front, Leo couldn't see their faces, but he assumed from their silence that his friends were not pleased to have a sleepless, hallucinating dragon driver.

"Just joking." Leo decided it might be good to change the subject. "So what's the plan, bro? You said something about catching wind, or breaking wind, or something?"

As they flew over New England, Jason laid out the game plan: First, find some guy named Boreas and grill him for information—

"His name is *Boreas*?" Leo had to ask. "What is he, the God of Boring?"

Second, Jason continued, they had to find those *venti* that had attacked them at the Grand Canyon—

"Can we just call them storm spirits?" Leo asked. "*Venti* makes them sound like evil espresso drinks."

And third, Jason finished, they had to find out who the storm spirits worked for, so they could find Hera and free her.

"So you want to look for Dylan, the nasty storm dude, *on purpose*," Leo said. "The guy who threw me off the skywalk and sucked Coach Hedge into the clouds."

"That's about it," Jason said. "Well . . . there may be a wolf involved, too. But I think she's friendly. She probably won't eat us, unless we show weakness."

Jason told them about his dream—the big nasty mother wolf and a burned-out house with stone spires growing out of the swimming pool.

"Uh-huh," Leo said. "But you don't know where this place is."

"Nope," Jason admitted.

"There's also giants," Piper added. "The prophecy said *the giants' revenge*."

"Hold on," Leo said. "Giants—like more than one? Why can't it be just one giant who wants revenge?"

"I don't think so," Piper said. "I remember in some of the old Greek stories, there was something about an army of giants."

"Great," Leo muttered. "Of course, with our luck, it's an army. So you know anything else about these giants? Didn't you do a bunch of myth research for that movie with your dad?"

"Your dad's an actor?" Jason asked.

Leo laughed. "I keep forgetting about your amnesia. Heh. Forgetting about amnesia. That's funny. But yeah, her dad's Tristan McLean."

"Uh— Sorry, what was he in?"

"It doesn't matter," Piper said quickly. "The giants—well, there were lots of giants in Greek mythology. But if I'm thinking of the right ones, they were bad news. Huge, almost impossible to kill. They could throw mountains and stuff. I think they were related to the Titans. They rose from the earth after Kronos lost the war—I mean the *first* Titan war, thousands of years ago—and they tried to destroy Olympus. If we're talking about the same giants—"

"Chiron said it was happening again," Jason remembered. "The last chapter. That's what he meant. No wonder he didn't want us to know all the details."

Leo whistled. "So . . . giants who can throw mountains. Friendly wolves that will eat us if we show weakness. Evil espresso drinks. Gotcha. Maybe this isn't the time to bring up my psycho babysitter."

"Is that another joke?" Piper asked.

Leo told them about Tía Callida, who was really Hera, and how she'd appeared to him at camp. He didn't tell them about his fire abilities. That was still a touchy subject, especially after Nyssa had told him fire demigods tended to destroy cities and stuff. Besides, then Leo would have to get into how he'd caused his mom's death, and . . . No. He wasn't ready to go there. He did manage to tell about the night she died, not mentioning the fire, just saying the machine shop collapsed. It was easier without having to look at his friends, just keeping his eyes straight ahead as they flew.

And he told them about the strange woman in earthen

robes who seemed to be asleep, and seemed to know the future.

Leo estimated the whole state of Massachusetts passed below them before his friends spoke.

"That's . . . disturbing," Piper said.

"'Bout sums it up," Leo agreed. "Thing is, everybody says don't trust Hera. She hates demigods. And the prophecy said we'd cause death if we unleash her rage. So I'm wondering . . . why are we doing this?"

"She chose us," Jason said. "All three of us. We're the first of the seven who have to gather for the Great Prophecy. This quest is the beginning of something much bigger."

That didn't make Leo feel any better, but he couldn't argue with Jason's point. It *did* feel like this was the start of something huge. He just wished that if there were four more demigods destined to help them, they'd show up quick. Leo didn't want to hog all the terrifying life-threatening adventures.

"Besides," Jason continued, "helping Hera is the only way I can get back my memory. And that dark spire in my dream seemed to be feeding on Hera's energy. If that thing unleashes a king of the giants by destroying Hera—"

"Not a good trade-off," Piper agreed. "At least Hera is on our side—mostly. Losing her would throw the gods into chaos. She's the main one who keeps peace in the family. And a war with the giants could be even more destructive than the Titan War."

Jason nodded. "Chiron also talked about worse forces stirring on the solstice, with it being a good time for dark magic, and all—something that could awaken if Hera were sacrificed on that day. And this mistress who's controlling the storm spirits, the one who wants to kill all the demigods—"

"Might be that weird sleeping lady," Leo finished. "Dirt Woman fully awake? Not something I want to see."

"But who is she?" Jason asked. "And what does she have to do with giants?"

Good questions, but none of them had answers. They flew in silence while Leo wondered if he'd done the right thing, sharing so much. He'd never told anyone about that night at the warehouse. Even if he hadn't given them the whole story, it still felt strange, like he'd opened up his chest and taken out all the gears that made him tick. His body was shaking, and not from the cold. He hoped Piper, sitting behind him, couldn't tell.

The forge and dove shall break the cage. Wasn't that the prophecy line? That meant Piper and he would have to figure out how to break into that magic rock prison, assuming they could find it. Then they'd unleash Hera's rage, causing a lot of death. Well, that sounded fun! Leo had seen Tía Callida in action; she liked knives, snakes, and putting babies in roaring fires. Yeah, definitely let's unleash her rage. Great idea.

Festus kept flying. The wind got colder, and below them snowy forests seemed to go on forever. Leo didn't know exactly where Quebec was. He'd told Festus to take them to the palace of Boreas, and Festus kept going north. Hopefully, the dragon knew the way, and they wouldn't end up at the North Pole.

"Why don't you get some sleep?" Piper said in his ear. "You were up all night."

Leo wanted to protest, but the word *sleep* sounded really good. "You won't let me fall off?"

Piper patted his shoulder. "Trust me, Valdez. Beautiful people never lie."

"Right," he muttered. He leaned forward against the warm bronze of the dragon's neck, and closed his eyes.

XVIII

LEO

IT SEEMED HE SLEPT ONLY FOR SECONDS, but when Piper shook him awake, the daylight was fading.

"We're here," she said.

Leo rubbed the sleep out of his eyes. Below them, a city sat on a cliff overlooking a river. The plains around it were dusted with snow, but the city itself glowed warmly in the winter sunset. Buildings crowded together inside high walls like a medieval town, way older than any place Leo had seen before. In the center was an actual castle—at least Leo assumed it was a castle—with massive red brick walls and a square tower with a peaked, green gabled roof.

"Tell me that's Quebec and not Santa's workshop," Leo said.

"Yeah, Quebec City," Piper confirmed. "One of the oldest cities in North America. Founded around sixteen hundred or so?"

Leo raised an eyebrow. "Your dad do a movie about that too?"

She made a face at him, which Leo was used to, but it didn't quite work with her new glamorous makeup. "I *read* sometimes, okay? Just because Aphrodite claimed me, doesn't mean I have to be an airhead."

"Feisty!" Leo said. "So you know so much, what's that castle?"

"A hotel, I think."

Leo laughed. "No way."

But as they got closer, Leo saw she was right. The grand entrance was bustling with doormen, valets, and porters taking bags. Sleek black luxury cars idled in the drive. People in elegant suits and winter cloaks hurried to get out of the cold.

"The North Wind is staying in a hotel?" Leo said. "That can't be—"

"Heads up, guys," Jason interrupted. "We got company!"

Leo looked below and saw what Jason meant. Rising from the top of the tower were two winged figures—angry angels, with nasty-looking swords.

Festus didn't like the angel guys. He swooped to a halt in midair, wings beating and talons bared, and made a rumbling sound in his throat that Leo recognized. He was getting ready to blow fire.

"Steady, boy," Leo muttered. Something told him the angels would not take kindly to getting torched.

"I don't like this," Jason said. "They look like storm spirits."

At first Leo thought he was right, but as the angels got closer, he could see they were much more solid than *venti*. They looked like regular teenagers except for their icy white hair and feathery purple wings. Their bronze swords were jagged, like icicles. Their faces looked similar enough that they might've been brothers, but they definitely weren't twins.

One was the size of an ox, with a bright red hockey jersey, baggy sweatpants, and black leather cleats. The guy clearly had been in too many fights, because both his eyes were black, and when he bared his teeth, several of them were missing.

The other guy looked like he'd just stepped off one of Leo's mom's 1980s rock album covers—Journey, maybe, or Hall & Oates, or something even lamer. His ice-white hair was long and feathered into a mullet. He wore pointy-toed leather shoes, designer pants that were way too tight, and a god-awful silk shirt with the top three buttons open. Maybe he thought he looked like a groovy love god, but the guy couldn't have weighed more than ninety pounds, and he had a bad case of acne.

The angels pulled up in front of the dragon and hovered there, swords at the ready.

The hockey ox grunted. "No clearance."

"'Scuse me?" Leo said.

"You have no flight plan on file," explained the groovy love god. On top of his other problems, he had a French accent so bad Leo was sure it was fake. "This is restricted airspace."

"Destroy them?" The ox showed off his gap-toothed grin.

The dragon began to hiss steam, ready to defend them. Jason summoned his golden sword, but Leo cried, "Hold on!

Let's have some manners here, boys. Can I at least find out who has the honor of destroying me?"

"I am Cal!" the ox grunted. He looked very proud of himself, like he'd taken a long time to memorize that sentence.

"That's short for Calais," the love god said. "Sadly, my brother cannot say words with more than two syllables—"

"Pizza! Hockey! Destroy!" Cal offered.

"—which includes his own name," the love god finished.

"I am Cal," Cal repeated. "And this is Zethes! My brother!"

"Wow," Leo said. "That was almost three sentences, man! Way to go."

Cal grunted, obviously pleased with himself.

"Stupid buffoon," his brother grumbled. "They make fun of you. But no matter. I am Zethes, which is short for Zethes. And the lady there—" He winked at Piper, but the wink was more like a facial seizure. "She can call me anything she likes. Perhaps she would like to have dinner with a famous demigod before we must destroy you?"

Piper made a sound like gagging on a cough drop. "That's ... a truly horrifying offer."

"It is no problem." Zethes wiggled his eyebrows. "We are a very romantic people, we Boreads."

"Boreads?" Jason cut in. "Do you mean, like, the sons of Boreas?"

"Ah, so you've heard of us!" Zethes looked pleased. "We are our father's gatekeepers. So you understand, we cannot have unauthorized people flying in his airspace on creaky dragons, scaring the silly mortal peoples."

He pointed below, and Leo saw that the mortals were

starting to take notice. Several were pointing up—not with alarm, yet—more with confusion and annoyance, like the dragon was a traffic helicopter flying too low.

"Which is sadly why, unless this is an emergency landing," Zethes said, brushing his hair out of his acne-covered face, "we will have to destroy you painfully."

"Destroy!" Cal agreed, with a little more enthusiasm than Leo thought necessary.

"Wait!" Piper said. "This *is* an emergency landing."

"Awww!" Cal looked so disappointed, Leo almost felt sorry for him.

Zethes studied Piper, which of course he'd already been doing. "How does the pretty girl decide this is an emergency, then?"

"We have to see Boreas. It's totally urgent! Please?" She forced a smile, which Leo figured must've been killing her; but she still had that blessing of Aphrodite thing going on, and she looked great. Something about her voice, too—Leo found himself believing every word. Jason was nodding, looking absolutely convinced.

Zethes picked at his silk shirt, probably making sure it was still open wide enough. "Well...I hate to disappoint a lovely lady, but you see, my sister, she would have an avalanche if we allowed you—"

"And our dragon is malfunctioning!" Piper added. "It could crash any minute!"

Festus shuddered helpfully, then turned his head and spilled gunk out of his ear, splattering a black Mercedes in the parking lot below.

"No destroy?" Cal whimpered.

Zethes pondered the problem. Then he gave Piper another spasmodic wink. "Well, you are pretty. I mean, you're *right*. A malfunctioning dragon—this could be an emergency."

"Destroy them later?" Cal offered, which was probably as close to friendly as he ever got.

"It will take some explaining," Zethes decided. "Father has not been kind to visitors lately. But, yes. Come, faulty dragon people. Follow us."

The Boreads sheathed their swords and pulled smaller weapons from their belts—or at least Leo thought they were weapons. Then the Boreads switched them on, and Leo realized they were flashlights with orange cones, like the ones traffic controller guys use on a runway. Cal and Zethes turned and swooped toward the hotel's tower.

Leo turned to his friends. "I love these guys. Follow them?"

Jason and Piper didn't look eager.

"I guess," Jason decided. "We're here now. But I wonder why Boreas hasn't been kind to visitors."

"Pfft, he just hasn't met us." Leo whistled. "Festus, after those flashlights!"

As they got closer, Leo worried they'd crash into the tower. The Boreads made right for the green gabled peak and didn't slow down. Then a section of the slanted roof slid open, revealing an entrance easily wide enough for Festus. The top and bottom were lined with icicles like jagged teeth.

"This cannot be good," Jason muttered, but Leo spurred the dragon downward, and they swooped in after the Boreads.

They landed in what must have been the penthouse suite; but the place had been hit by a flash freeze. The entry hall had vaulted ceilings forty feet high, huge draped windows, and lush oriental carpets. A staircase at the back of the room led up to another equally massive hall, and more corridors branched off to the left and right. But the ice made the room's beauty a little frightening. When Leo slid off the dragon, the carpet crunched under his feet. A fine layer of frost covered the furniture. The curtains didn't budge because they were frozen solid, and the ice-coated windows let in weird watery light from the sunset. Even the ceiling was furry with icicles. As for the stairs, Leo was sure he'd slip and break his neck if he tried to climb them.

"Guys," Leo said, "fix the thermostat in here, and I would totally move in."

"Not me." Jason looked uneasily at the staircase. "Something feels wrong. Something up there..."

Festus shuddered and snorted flames. Frost started to form on his scales.

"No, no, no." Zethes marched over, though how he could walk in those pointy leather shoes, Leo had no idea. "The dragon must be deactivated. We can't have fire in here. The heat ruins my hair."

Festus growled and spun his drill-bit teeth.

"'S'okay, boy." Leo turned to Zethes. "The dragon's a little touchy about the whole *deactivation* concept. But I've got a better solution."

"Destroy?" Cal suggested.

"No, man. You gotta stop with the *destroy* talk. Just wait."

"Leo," Piper said nervously, "what are you—"

"Watch and learn, beauty queen. When I was repairing Festus last night, I found all kinds of buttons. Some, you do *not* want to know what they do. But others ... Ah, here we go."

Leo hooked his fingers behind the dragon's left foreleg. He pulled a switch, and the dragon shuddered from head to toe. Everyone backed away as Festus folded like origami. His bronze plating stacked together. His neck and tail contracted into his body. His wings collapsed and his trunk compacted until he was a rectangular metal wedge the size of a suitcase.

Leo tried to lift it, but the thing weighed about six billion pounds. "Um ... yeah. Hold on. I think—aha."

He pushed another button. A handle flipped up on the top, and wheels clicked out on the bottom.

"Ta-da!" he announced. "The world's heaviest carry-on bag!"

"That's impossible," Jason said. "Something that big couldn't—"

"Stop!" Zethes ordered. He and Cal both drew their swords and glared at Leo.

Leo raised his hands. "Okay ... what'd I do? Stay calm, guys. If it bothers you that much, I don't *have* to take the dragon as carry-on—"

"Who are you?" Zethes shoved the point of his sword against Leo's chest. "A child of the South Wind, spying on us?"

"What? No!" Leo said. "Son of Hephaestus. Friendly blacksmith, no harm to anyone!"

Cal growled. He put his face up to Leo's, and he definitely

wasn't any prettier at point-blank, with his bruised eyes and bashed-in mouth. "Smell fire," he said. "Fire is bad."

"Oh." Leo's heart raced. "Yeah, well...my clothes are kind of singed, and I've been working with oil, and—"

"No!" Zethes pushed Leo back at sword point. "We can *smell* fire, demigod. We assumed it was from the creaky dragon, but now the dragon is a suitcase. And I still smell fire...on *you*."

If it hadn't been like three degrees in the penthouse, Leo would've started sweating. "Hey...look...I don't know—" He glanced at his friends desperately. "Guys, a little help?"

Jason already had his gold coin in his hand. He stepped forward, his eyes on Zethes. "Look, there's been a mistake. Leo isn't a fire guy. Tell them, Leo. Tell them you're not a fire guy."

"Um..."

"Zethes?" Piper tried her dazzling smile again, though she looked a little too nervous and cold to pull it off. "We're all friends here. Put down your swords and let's talk."

"The girl is pretty," Zethes admitted, "and of course she cannot help being attracted to my amazingness; but sadly, I cannot romance her at this time." He poked his sword point farther into Leo's chest, and Leo could feel the frost spreading across his shirt, turning his skin numb.

He wished he could reactivate Festus. He needed some backup. But it would've taken several minutes, even if he could reach the button, with two purple-winged crazy guys in his path.

"Destroy him now?" Cal asked his brother.

Zethes nodded. "Sadly, I think—"

"No," Jason insisted. He sounded calm enough, but Leo figured he was about two seconds away from flipping that coin and going into full gladiator mode. "Leo's just a son of Hephaestus. He's no threat. Piper here is a daughter of Aphrodite. I'm the son of Zeus. We're on a peaceful..."

Jason's voice faltered, because both Boreads had suddenly turned on him.

"What did you say?" Zethes demanded. "You are the son of Zeus?"

"Um...yeah," Jason said. "That's a good thing, right? My name is Jason."

Cal looked so surprised, he almost dropped his sword. "Can't be Jason," he said. "Doesn't look the same."

Zethes stepped forward and squinted at Jason's face. "No, he is not *our* Jason. Our Jason was more stylish. Not as much as me—but stylish. Besides, our Jason died millennia ago."

"Wait," Jason said. "*Your* Jason...you mean the original Jason? The Golden Fleece guy?"

"Of course," Zethes said. "We were his crewmates aboard his ship, the *Argo*, in the old times, when we were mortal demigods. Then we accepted immortality to serve our father, so I could look this good for all time, and my silly brother could enjoy pizza and hockey."

"Hockey!" Cal agreed.

"But Jason—*our* Jason—he died a mortal death," Zethes said. "You can't be him."

"I'm not," Jason agreed.

"So, destroy?" Cal asked. Clearly the conversation was giving his two brain cells a serious workout.

"No," Zethes said regretfully. "If he is a son of Zeus, he could be the one we've been watching for."

"Watching for?" Leo asked. "You mean like in a good way: you'll shower him with fabulous prizes? Or watching for like in a *bad* way: he's in trouble?"

A girl's voice said, "That depends on my father's will."

Leo looked up the staircase. His heart nearly stopped. At the top stood a girl in a white silk dress. Her skin was unnaturally pale, the color of snow, but her hair was a lush mane of black, and her eyes were coffee brown. She focused on Leo with no expression, no smile, no friendliness. But it didn't matter. Leo was in love. She was the most dazzling girl he'd ever seen.

Then she looked at Jason and Piper, and seemed to understand the situation immediately.

"Father will want to see the one called Jason," the girl said.

"Then it *is* him?" Zethes asked excitedly.

"We'll see," the girl said. "Zethes, bring our guests."

Leo grabbed the handle of his bronze dragon suitcase. He wasn't sure how he'd lug it up the stairs, but he *had* to get next to that girl and ask her some important questions—like her e-mail address and phone number.

Before he could take a step, she froze him with a look. Not *literally* froze, but she might as well have.

"Not you, Leo Valdez," she said.

In the back of his mind, Leo wondered how she knew his

name; but mostly he was just concentrating on how crushed he felt.

"Why not?" He probably sounded like a whiny kindergartner, but he couldn't help it.

"You cannot be in the presence of my father," the girl said. "Fire and ice—it would not be wise."

"We're going together," Jason insisted, putting his hand on Leo's shoulder, "or not at all."

The girl tilted her head, like she wasn't used to people refusing her orders. "He will not be harmed, Jason Grace, unless you make trouble. Calais, keep Leo Valdez here. Guard him, but do not kill him."

Cal pouted. "Just a little?"

"No," the girl insisted. "And take care of his interesting suitcase, until Father passes judgment."

Jason and Piper looked at Leo, their expressions asking him a silent question: *How do you want to play this?*

Leo felt a surge of gratitude. They were ready to fight for him. They wouldn't leave him alone with the hockey ox. Part of him wanted to go for it, bust out his new tool belt and see what he could do, maybe even summon a fireball or two and warm this place up. But the Boread guys scared him. And that gorgeous girl scared him more, even if he still wanted her number.

"It's fine, guys," he said. "No sense causing trouble if we don't have to. You go ahead."

"Listen to your friend," the pale girl said. "Leo Valdez will be perfectly safe. I wish I could say the same for you, son of Zeus. Now come, King Boreas is waiting."

XIX

JASON

JASON DIDN'T WANT TO LEAVE LEO, but he was starting to think that hanging out with Cal the hockey jock might be the *least* dangerous option in this place.

As they climbed the icy staircase, Zethes stayed behind them, his blade drawn. The guy might've looked like a disco-era reject, but there was nothing funny about his sword. Jason figured one hit from that thing would probably turn him into a Popsicle.

Then there was the ice princess. Every once in a while she'd turn and give Jason a smile, but there was no warmth in her expression. She regarded Jason like he was an especially interesting science specimen—one she couldn't wait to dissect.

If these were Boreas's kids, Jason wasn't sure he wanted to meet Daddy. Annabeth had told him Boreas was the friendliest of the wind gods. Apparently that meant he didn't kill heroes quite as fast as the others did.

Jason worried that he'd led his friends into a trap. If things went bad, he wasn't sure he could get them out alive. Without thinking about it, he took Piper's hand for reassurance.

She raised her eyebrows, but she didn't let go.

"It'll be fine," she promised. "Just a talk, right?"

At the top of the stairs, the ice princess looked back and noticed them holding hands. Her smile faded. Suddenly Jason's hand in Piper's turned ice cold—*burning* cold. He let go, and his fingers were smoking with frost. So were Piper's.

"Warmth is not a good idea here," the princess advised, "especially when *I* am your best chance of staying alive. Please, this way."

Piper gave him a nervous frown like, *What was that about?*

Jason didn't have an answer. Zethes poked him in the back with his icicle sword, and they followed the princess down a massive hallway decked in frosty tapestries.

Freezing winds blew back and forth, and Jason's thoughts moved almost as fast. He'd had a lot of time to think while they rode the dragon north, but he felt as confused as ever.

Thalia's picture was still in his pocket, though he didn't need to look at it anymore. Her image had burned itself into his mind. It was bad enough not remembering his past, but to know he had a sister out there somewhere who might have answers and to have no way of finding her—that just drove him up the wall.

In the picture, Thalia looked nothing like him. They both had blue eyes, but that was it. Her hair was black. Her complexion was more Mediterranean. Her facial features were sharper—like a hawk's.

Still, Thalia looked *so* familiar. Hera had left him just

enough memory that he could be certain Thalia was his sister. But Annabeth had acted completely surprised when he'd told her, like she'd never heard of Thalia's having a brother. Did Thalia even know about him? How had they been separated?

Hera had taken those memories. She'd stolen everything from Jason's past, plopped him into a new life, and now she expected him to save her from some prison just so he could get back what she'd taken. It made Jason so angry, he wanted to walk away, let Hera rot in that cage: but he couldn't. He was hooked. He had to know more, and that made him even more resentful.

"Hey." Piper touched his arm. "You still with me?"

"Yeah...yeah, sorry."

He was grateful for Piper. He needed a friend, and he was glad she'd started losing the Aphrodite blessing. The makeup was fading. Her hair was slowly going back to its old choppy style with the little braids down the sides. It made her look more real, and as far as Jason was concerned, more beautiful.

He was sure now that they'd never known each other before the Grand Canyon. Their relationship was just a trick of the Mist in Piper's mind. But the longer he spent with her, the more he wished it had been real.

Stop that, he told himself. It wasn't fair to Piper, thinking that way. Jason had no idea what was waiting for him back in his old life—or *who* might be waiting. But he was pretty sure his past wouldn't mix with Camp Half-Blood. After this quest, who knew what would happen? Assuming they even survived.

At the end of the hallway they found themselves in front

of a set of oaken doors carved with a map of the world. In each corner was a man's bearded face, blowing wind. Jason was pretty sure he'd seen maps like this before. But in this version, all the wind guys were Winter, blowing ice and snow from every corner of the world.

The princess turned. Her brown eyes glittered, and Jason felt like he was a Christmas present she was hoping to open.

"This is the throne room," she said. "Be on your best behavior, Jason Grace. My father can be . . . chilly. I will translate for you, and try to encourage him to hear you out. I do hope he spares you. We could have such fun."

Jason guessed this girl's definition of fun was not the same as his.

"Um, okay," he managed. "But really, we're just here for a little talk. We'll be leaving right afterward."

The girl smiled. "I love heroes. So blissfully ignorant."

Piper rested her hand on her dagger. "Well, how about you enlighten us? You say you're going to translate for us, and we don't even know who you are. What's your name?"

The girl sniffed with distaste. "I suppose I shouldn't be surprised you don't recognize me. Even in the ancient times the Greeks did not know me well. Their island homes were too warm, too far from my domain. I am Khione, daughter of Boreas, goddess of snow."

She stirred the air with her finger, and a miniature blizzard swirled around her—big, fluffy flakes as soft as cotton.

"Now, come," Khione said. The oaken doors blew open, and cold blue light spilled out of the room. "Hopefully you will survive your little talk."

JASON

IF THE ENTRY HALL HAD BEEN COLD, the throne room was like a meat locker.

Mist hung in the air. Jason shivered, and his breath steamed. Along the walls, purple tapestries showed scenes of snowy forests, barren mountains, and glaciers. High above, ribbons of colored light—the aurora borealis—pulsed along the ceiling. A layer of snow covered the floor, so Jason had to step carefully. All around the room stood life-size ice sculpture warriors—some in Greek armor, some medieval, some in modern camouflage—all frozen in various attack positions, swords raised, guns locked and loaded.

At least Jason *thought* they were sculptures. Then he tried to step between two Greek spearmen, and they moved with surprising speed, their joints cracking and spraying ice crystals as they crossed their javelins to block Jason's path.

From the far end of the hall, a man's voice rang out in a language that sounded like French. The room was so long and misty, Jason couldn't see the other end; but whatever the man said, the ice guards uncrossed their javelins.

"It's fine," Khione said. "My father has ordered them not to kill you just yet."

"Super," Jason said.

Zethes prodded him in the back with his sword. "Keep moving, Jason Junior."

"Please don't call me that."

"My father is not a patient man," Zethes warned, "and the beautiful Piper, sadly, is losing her magic hairdo very fast. Later, perhaps, I can lend her something from my wide assortment of hair products."

"Thanks," Piper grumbled.

They kept walking, and the mist parted to reveal a man on an ice throne. He was sturdily built, dressed in a stylish white suit that seemed woven from snow, with dark purple wings that spread out to either side. His long hair and shaggy beard were encrusted with icicles, so Jason couldn't tell if his hair was gray or just white with frost. His arched eyebrows made him look angry, but his eyes twinkled more warmly than his daughter's—as if he might have a sense of humor buried somewhere under that permafrost. Jason hoped so.

"*Bienvenu*," the king said. "*Je suis Boreas le Roi. Et vous?*"

Khione the snow goddess was about to speak, but Piper stepped forward and curtsied.

"*Votre Majesté*," she said, "*je suis Piper McLean. Et c'est Jason, fils de Zeus.*"

The king smiled with pleasant surprise. "*Vous parlez français? Très bien!*"

"Piper, you speak French?" Jason asked.

Piper frowned. "No. Why?"

"You just spoke French."

Piper blinked. "I did?"

The king said something else, and Piper nodded. *"Oui, Votre Majesté."*

The king laughed and clapped his hands, obviously delighted. He said a few more sentences, then swept his hand toward his daughter as if shooing her away.

Khione looked miffed. "The king says—"

"He says I'm a daughter of Aphrodite," Piper interrupted, "so naturally I can speak French, which is the language of love. I had no idea. His Majesty says Khione won't have to translate now."

Behind them, Zethes snorted, and Khione shot him a murderous look. She bowed stiffly to her father and took a step back.

The king sized up Jason, and Jason decided it would be a good idea to bow. "Your Majesty, I'm Jason Grace. Thank you for, um, not killing us. May I ask...why does a Greek god speak French?"

Piper had another exchange with the king.

"He speaks the language of his host country," Piper translated. "He says all gods do this. Most Greek gods speak English, as they now reside in the United States, but Boreas was never welcomed in their realm. His domain was always far to the north. These days he likes Quebec, so he speaks French."

The king said something else, and Piper turned pale.

"The king says..." She faltered. "He says—"

"Oh, allow me," Khione said. "My father says he has orders to kill you. Did I not mention that earlier?"

Jason tensed. The king was still smiling amiably, like he'd just delivered great news.

"Kill us?" Jason said. "Why?"

"Because," the king said, in heavily accented English, "my lord Aeolus has commanded it."

Boreas rose. He stepped down from his throne and furled his wings against his back. As he approached, Khione and Zethes bowed. Jason and Piper followed their example.

"I shall deign to speak your language," Boreas said, "as Piper McLean has honored me in mine. *Toujours*, I have had a fondness for the children of Aphrodite. As for you, Jason Grace, my master Aeolus would not expect me to kill a son of Lord Zeus . . . without first hearing you out."

Jason's gold coin seemed to grow heavy in his pocket. If he were forced to fight, he didn't like his chances. Two seconds at least to summon his blade. Then he'd be facing a god, two of his children, and an army of freeze-dried warriors.

"Aeolus is the master of the winds, right?" Jason asked. "Why would he want us dead?"

"You are demigods," Boreas said, as if this explained everything. "Aeolus's job is to contain the winds, and demigods have always caused him many headaches. They ask him for favors. They unleash winds and cause chaos. But the final insult was the battle with Typhon last summer. . . ."

Boreas waved his hand, and a sheet of ice like a flat-screen TV appeared in the air. Images of a battle flickered across the surface—a giant wrapped in storm clouds, wading across a river toward the Manhattan skyline. Tiny, glowing figures —the gods, Jason guessed—swarmed around him like angry wasps, pounding the monster with lightning and fire. Finally the river erupted in a massive whirlpool, and the smoky form sank beneath the waves and disappeared.

"The storm giant, Typhon," Boreas explained. "The first time the gods defeated him, eons ago, he did not die quietly. His death released a host of storm spirits—wild winds that answered to no one. It was Aeolus's job to track them all down and imprison them in his fortress. The other gods—they did not help. They did not even apologize for the inconvenience. It took Aeolus centuries to track down all the storm spirits, and naturally this irritated him. Then, last summer, Typhon was defeated again—"

"And his death released another wave of *venti*," Jason guessed. "Which made Aeolus even angrier."

"*C'est vrai*," Boreas agreed.

"But, Your Majesty," Piper said, "the gods had no choice but to battle Typhon. He was going to destroy Olympus! Besides, why punish demigods for that?"

The king shrugged. "Aeolus cannot take out his anger on the gods. They are his bosses, and very powerful. So he gets even with the demigods who helped them in the war. He issued orders to us: demigods who come to us for aid are no longer to be tolerated. We are to crush your little mortal faces."

There was an uncomfortable silence.

"That sounds ... extreme," Jason ventured. "But you're not

going to crush our faces yet, right? You're going to listen to us first, 'cause once you hear about our quest—"

"Yes, yes," the king agreed. "You see, Aeolus also said that a son of Zeus might seek my aid, and if this happened, I should listen to you before destroying you, as you might— how did he put it?—make all our lives very interesting. I am only obligated to *listen,* however. After that, I am free to pass judgment as I see fit. But I *will* listen first. Khione wishes this also. It may be that we will not kill you."

Jason felt like he could almost breathe again. "Great. Thanks."

"Do not thank me." Boreas smiled. "There are many ways you could make our lives interesting. Sometimes we keep demigods for our amusement, as you can see."

He gestured around the room to the various ice statues.

Piper made a strangled noise. "You mean—they're all demigods? Frozen demigods? They're alive?"

"An interesting question," Boreas conceded, as if it had never occurred to him before. "They do not move unless they are obeying my orders. The rest of the time, they are merely frozen. Unless they were to melt, I suppose, which would be very messy."

Khione stepped behind Jason and put her cold fingers on his neck. "My father gives me such lovely presents," she murmured in his ear. "Join our court. Perhaps I'll let your friends go."

"What?" Zethes broke in. "If Khione gets this one, then I deserve the girl. Khione always gets more presents!"

"Now, children," Boreas said sternly. "Our guests will think you are spoiled! Besides, you moved too fast. We have not even heard the demigod's story yet. Then we will decide what to do with them. Please, Jason Grace, entertain us."

Jason felt his brain shutting down. He didn't look at Piper for fear he'd completely lose it. He'd gotten them into this, and now they were going to die—or worse, they'd be amusements for Boreas's children and end up frozen forever in this throne room, slowly corroding from freezer burn.

Khione purred and stroked his neck. Jason didn't plan it, but electricity sparked along his skin. There was a loud *pop*, and Khione flew backward, skidding across the floor.

Zethes laughed. "That is good! I'm glad you did that, even though I have to kill you now."

For a moment, Khione was too stunned to react. Then the air around her began to swirl with a micro-blizzard. "You dare—"

"Stop," Jason ordered, with as much force as he could muster. "You're not going to kill us. And you're not going to keep us. We're on a quest for the queen of the gods herself, so unless you want Hera busting down your doors, you're going to let us go."

He sounded a lot more confident than he felt, but it got their attention. Khione's blizzard swirled to a stop. Zethes lowered his sword. They both looked uncertainly at their father.

"Hmm," Boreas said. His eyes twinkled, but Jason couldn't tell if it was with anger or amusement. "A son of Zeus, favored by Hera? This is definitely a first. Tell us your story."

Jason would've botched it right there. He hadn't been expecting to get the chance to talk, and now that he could, his voice abandoned him.

Piper saved him. "Your Majesty." She curtsied again with incredible poise, considering her life was on the line. She told Boreas the whole story, from the Grand Canyon to the prophecy, much better and faster than Jason could have.

"All we ask for is guidance," Piper concluded. "These storm spirits attacked us, and they're working for some evil mistress. If we find them, maybe we can find Hera."

The king stroked the icicles in his beard. Out the windows, night had fallen, and the only light came from the aurora borealis overhead, washing everything in red and blue.

"I know of these storm spirits," Boreas said. "I know where they are kept, and of the prisoner they took."

"You mean Coach Hedge?" Jason asked. "He's alive?"

Boreas waved aside the question. "For now. But the one who controls these storm winds...It would be madness to oppose her. You would be better staying here as frozen statues."

"Hera's in trouble," Jason said. "In three days she's going to be—I don't know—consumed, destroyed, something. And a giant is going to rise."

"Yes," Boreas agreed. Was it Jason's imagination, or did he shoot Khione an angry look? "Many horrible things are waking. Even my children do not tell me all the news they should. The Great Stirring of monsters that began with Kronos—your father Zeus foolishly believed it would end when the Titans were defeated. But just as it was before, so it is now. The final battle is yet to come, and the one who will wake is more terrible than any Titan. Storm spirits—these are only beginning. The earth has many more horrors to yield up. When monsters no longer stay in Tartarus, and souls are no longer confined to Hades . . . Olympus has good reason to fear."

Jason wasn't sure what all this meant, but he didn't like the way Khione was smiling—like *this* was her definition of fun.

"So you'll help us?" Jason asked the king.

Boreas scowled. "I did not say that."

"Please, Your Majesty," Piper said.

Everyone's eyes turned toward her. She had to be scared out of her mind, but she looked beautiful and confident—and it had nothing to do with the blessing of Aphrodite. She looked herself again, in day-old traveling clothes with choppy hair and no makeup. But she almost glowed with warmth in that cold throne room. "If you tell us where the storm spirits are, we can capture them and bring them to Aeolus. You'd look good in front of your boss. Aeolus might pardon us and the other demigods. We could even rescue Gleeson Hedge. Everyone wins."

"She's pretty," Zethes mumbled. "I mean, she's right."

"Father, don't listen to her," Khione said. "She's a child of Aphrodite. She dares to charmspeak a god? Freeze her now!"

Boreas considered this. Jason slipped his hand in his pocket and got ready to bring out the gold coin. If things went wrong, he'd have to move fast.

The movement caught Boreas's eye. "What is that on your forearm, demigod?"

Jason hadn't realized his coat sleeve had gotten pushed

up, revealing the edge of his tattoo. Reluctantly, he showed Boreas his marks.

The god's eyes widened. Khione actually hissed and stepped away.

Then Boreas did something unexpected. He laughed so loudly, an icicle cracked from the ceiling and crashed next to his throne. The god's form began to flicker. His beard disappeared. He grew taller and thinner, and his clothes changed into a Roman toga, lined with purple. His head was crowned with a frosty laurel wreath, and a gladius—a Roman sword like Jason's—hung at his side.

"Aquilon," Jason said, though where he got the god's Roman name from, he had no idea.

The god inclined his head. "You recognize me better in this form, yes? And yet you said you came from Camp Half-Blood?"

Jason shifted his feet. "Uh...yes, Your Majesty."

"And Hera sent you there...." The winter god's eyes were full of mirth. "I understand now. Oh, she plays a dangerous game. Bold, but dangerous! No wonder Olympus is closed. They must be trembling at the gamble she has taken."

"Jason," Piper said nervously, "why did Boreas change shape? The toga, the wreath. What's going on?"

"It's his Roman form," Jason said. "But what's going on—I don't know."

The god laughed. "No, I'm sure you don't. This should be very interesting to watch."

"Does that mean you'll let us go?" Piper asked.

"My dear," Boreas said, "there is no reason for me to kill

you. If Hera's plan fails, which I think it will, you will tear each other apart. Aeolus will never have to worry about demigods again."

Jason felt as if Khione's cold fingers were on his neck again, but it wasn't her—it was just the feeling that Boreas was right. That sense of wrongness which had bothered Jason since he got to Camp Half-Blood, and Chiron's comment about his arrival being disastrous—Boreas knew what they meant.

"I don't suppose you could explain?" Jason asked.

"Oh, perish the thought! It is not for me to interfere in Hera's plan. No wonder she took your memory." Boreas chuckled, apparently still having a great time imagining demigods tearing each other apart. "You know, I have a reputation as a helpful wind god. Unlike my brethren, I've been known to fall in love with mortals. Why, my sons Zethes and Calais started as demigods—"

"Which explains why they are idiots," Khione growled.

"Stop it!" Zethes snapped back. "Just because you were born a full goddess—"

"Both of you, freeze," Boreas ordered. Apparently, that word carried a lot of weight in the household, because the two siblings went absolutely still. "Now, as I was saying, I have a good reputation, but it is rare that Boreas plays an important role in the affairs of gods. I sit here in my palace, at the edge of civilization, and so rarely have amusements. Why, even that fool Notus, the South Wind, gets spring break in Cancún. What do I get? A winter festival with naked Québécois rolling around in the snow!"

"I like the winter festival," Zethes muttered.

"My point," Boreas snapped, "is that I now have a chance to be the center. Oh, yes, I will let you go on this quest. You will find your storm spirits in the windy city, of course. Chicago—"

"Father!" Khione protested.

Boreas ignored his daughter. "If you can capture the winds, you may be able to gain safe entrance to the court of Aeolus. If by some miracle you succeed, be sure to tell him you captured the winds on my orders."

"Okay, sure," Jason said. "So Chicago is where we'll find this lady who's controlling the winds? She's the one who's trapped Hera?"

"Ah." Boreas grinned. "Those are two different questions, son of Jupiter."

Jupiter, Jason noticed. *Before, he called me son of Zeus.*

"The one who controls the winds," Boreas continued, "yes, you will find her in Chicago. But *she* is only a servant—a servant who is very likely to destroy you. If you succeed against her and take the winds, then you may go to Aeolus. Only he has knowledge of all the winds on the earth. All secrets come to his fortress eventually. If anyone can tell you where Hera is imprisoned, it is Aeolus. As for who you will meet when you finally find Hera's cage—truly, if I told you that, you would beg me to freeze you."

"Father," Khione protested, "you can't simply let them—"

"I can do what I like," he said, his voice hardening. "I am still master here, am I not?"

The way Boreas glared at his daughter, it was obvious they had some ongoing argument. Khione's eyes flashed with anger, but she clenched her teeth. "As you wish, Father."

"Now go, demigods," Boreas said, "before I change my mind. Zethes, escort them out safely."

They all bowed, and the god of the North Wind dissolved into mist.

Back in the entry hall, Cal and Leo were waiting for them. Leo looked cold but unharmed. He'd even gotten cleaned up, and his clothes looked newly washed, like he'd used the hotel's valet service. Festus the dragon was back in normal form, snorting fire over his scales to keep himself defrosted.

As Khione led them down the stairs, Jason noticed that Leo's eyes followed her. Leo started combing his hair back with his hands. Uh-oh, Jason thought. He made a mental note to warn Leo about the snow goddess later. She was not someone to get a crush on.

At the bottom step, Khione turned to Piper. "You have fooled my father, girl. But you have not fooled me. We are not done. And you, Jason Grace, I will see you as a statue in the throne room soon enough."

"Boreas is right," Jason said. "You're a spoiled kid. See you around, ice princess."

Khione's eyes flared pure white. For once, she seemed at a loss for words. She stormed back up the stairs—literally. Halfway up, she turned into a blizzard and disappeared.

"Be careful," Zethes warned. "She never forgets an insult."

Cal grunted in agreement. "Bad sister."

"She's the goddess of snow," Jason said. "What's she going to do, throw snowballs at us?" But as he said it, Jason had a feeling Khione could do a whole lot worse.

Leo looked devastated. "What happened up there? You made her mad? Is she mad at me too? Guys, that was my prom date!"

"We'll explain later," Piper promised, but when she glanced at Jason, he realized she expected *him* to explain.

What *had* happened up there? Jason wasn't sure. Boreas had turned into Aquilon, his Roman form, as if Jason's presence caused him to go schizophrenic.

The idea that Jason had been sent to Camp Half-Blood seemed to amuse the god, but Boreas/Aquilon hadn't let them go out of kindness. Cruel excitement had danced in his eyes, as if he'd just placed a bet on a dogfight.

You will tear each other apart, he'd said with delight. *Aeolus will never have to worry about demigods again.*

Jason looked away from Piper, trying not to show how unnerved he was. "Yeah," he agreed, "we'll explain later."

"Be careful, pretty girl," Zethes said. "The winds between here and Chicago are bad-tempered. Many other evil things are stirring. I am sorry you will not be staying. You would make a lovely ice statue, in which I could check my reflection."

"Thanks," Piper said. "But I'd sooner play hockey with Cal."

"Hockey?" Cal's eyes lit up.

"Joking," Piper said. "And the storm winds aren't our worst problem, are they?"

"Oh, no," Zethes agreed. "Something else. Something worse."

"Worse," Cal echoed.

"Can you tell me?" Piper gave them a smile.

This time, the charm didn't work. The purple-winged Boreads shook their heads in unison. The hangar doors opened onto a freezing starry night, and Festus the dragon stomped his feet, anxious to fly.

"Ask Aeolus what is worse," Zethes said darkly. "He knows. Good luck."

He almost sounded like he cared what happened to them, even though a few minutes ago he'd wanted to make Piper into an ice sculpture.

Cal patted Leo on the shoulder. "Don't get destroyed," he said, which was probably the longest sentence he'd ever attempted. "Next time—hockey. Pizza."

"Come on, guys." Jason stared out at the dark. He was anxious to get out of that cold penthouse, but he had a feeling it was the most hospitable place they'd see for a while. "Let's go to Chicago and try not to get destroyed."

XXI

PIPER

PIPER DIDN'T RELAX UNTIL THE GLOW OF Quebec City faded behind them.

"You were amazing," Jason told her.

The compliment should've made her day. But all she could think about was the trouble ahead. *Evil things are stirring,* Zethes had warned them. She knew that firsthand. The closer they got to the solstice, the less time Piper had to make her decision.

She told Jason in French: "If you knew the truth about me, you wouldn't think I was so amazing."

"What'd you say?" he asked.

"I said I only talked to Boreas. It wasn't so amazing."

She didn't turn to look, but she imagined him smiling.

"Hey," he said, "you saved me from joining Khione's sub-zero hero collection. I owe you one."

That was definitely the easy part, she thought. There was no way Piper would've let that ice witch keep Jason. What bothered Piper more was the way Boreas had changed form, and why he'd let them go. It had something to do with Jason's past, those tattoos on his arm. Boreas assumed Jason was some sort of Roman, and Romans didn't mix with Greeks. She kept waiting for Jason to offer an explanation, but he clearly didn't want to talk about it.

Until now, Piper had been able to dismiss Jason's feeling that he didn't belong at Camp Half-Blood. Obviously he was a demigod. Of course he belonged. But now . . . what if he was something else? What if he really was an enemy? She couldn't stand that idea any more than she could stand Khione.

Leo passed them some sandwiches from his pack. He'd been quiet ever since they'd told him what happened in the throne room. "I still can't believe Khione," he said. "She looked so nice."

"Trust me, man," Jason said. "Snow may be pretty, but up close it's cold and nasty. We'll find you a better prom date."

Piper smiled, but Leo didn't look pleased. He hadn't said much about his time in the palace, or why the Boreads had singled him out for smelling like fire. Piper got the feeling he was hiding something. Whatever it was, his mood seemed to be affecting Festus, who grumbled and steamed as he tried to keep himself warm in the cold Canadian air. Happy the Dragon was not so happy.

They ate their sandwiches as they flew. Piper had no idea how Leo had stocked up on supplies, but he'd even remembered to bring veggie rations for her. The cheese and avocado sandwich was awesome.

Nobody talked. Whatever they might find in Chicago,

they all knew Boreas had only let them go because he figured they were already on a suicide mission.

The moon rose and stars turned overhead. Piper's eyes started to feel heavy. The encounter with Boreas and his children had scared her more than she wanted to admit. Now that she had a full stomach, her adrenaline was fading.

Suck it up, cupcake! Coach Hedge would've yelled at her. *Don't be a wimp!*

Piper had been thinking about the coach ever since Boreas mentioned he was still alive. She'd never liked Hedge, but he'd leaped off a cliff to save Leo, and he'd sacrificed himself to protect them on the skywalk. She now realized that all the times at school the coach had pushed her, yelled at her to run faster or do more push-ups, or even when he'd turned his back and let her fight her own battles with the mean girls, the old goat man had been trying to help her in his own irritating way—trying to prepare her for life as a demigod.

On the skywalk, Dylan the storm spirit had said something about the coach, too: how he'd been retired to Wilderness School because he was getting too old, like it was some sort of punishment. Piper wondered what that was about, and if it explained why the coach was always so grumpy. Whatever the truth, now that Piper knew Hedge was alive, she had a strong compulsion to save him.

Don't get ahead of yourself, she chided. You've got bigger problems. This trip won't have a happy ending.

She was a traitor, just like Silena Beauregard. It was only a matter of time before her friends found out.

She looked up at the stars and thought about a night

long ago when she and her dad had camped out in front of Grandpa Tom's house. Grandpa Tom had died years before, but Dad had kept his house in Oklahoma because it was where he grew up.

They'd gone back for a few days, with the idea of getting the place fixed up to sell, although Piper wasn't sure who'd want to buy a run-down cabin with shutters instead of windows and two tiny rooms that smelled like cigars. The first night had been so stifling hot—no air conditioning in the middle of August—that Dad suggested they sleep outside.

They'd spread their sleeping bags and listened to the cicadas buzzing in the trees. Piper pointed out the constellations she'd been reading about—Hercules, Apollo's lyre, Sagittarius the centaur.

Her dad crossed his arms behind his head. In his old T-shirt and jeans he looked like just another guy from Tahlequah, Oklahoma, a Cherokee who might've never left tribal lands. "Your grandpa would say those Greek patterns are a bunch of bull. He told me the stars were creatures with glowing fur, like magic hedgehogs. Once, long ago, some hunters even captured a few in the forest. They didn't know what they'd done until nighttime, when the star creatures began to glow. Golden sparks flew from their fur, so the Cherokee released them back into the sky."

"You believe in magic hedgehogs?" Piper asked.

Her dad laughed. "I think Grandpa Tom was full of bull, too, just like the Greeks. But it's a big sky. I suppose there's room for Hercules and hedgehogs."

They sat for a while, until Piper got the nerve to ask a

question that had been bugging her. "Dad, why don't you ever play Native American parts?"

The week before, he'd turned down several million dollars to play Tonto in a remake of *The Lone Ranger*. Piper was still trying to figure out why. He'd played all kinds of roles —a Latino teacher in a tough L.A. school, a dashing Israeli spy in an action-adventure blockbuster, even a Syrian terrorist in a James Bond movie. And, of course, he would always be known as the King of Sparta. But if the part was Native American—it didn't matter what *kind* of role it was—Dad turned it down.

He winked at her. "Too close to home, Pipes. Easier to pretend I'm something I'm not."

"Doesn't that get old? Aren't you ever tempted, like, if you found the perfect part that could change people's opinions?"

"If there's a part like that, Pipes," he said sadly, "I haven't found it."

She looked at the stars, trying to imagine them as glowing hedgehogs. All she saw were the stick figures she knew— Hercules running across the sky, on his way to kill monsters. Dad was probably right. The Greeks and the Cherokee were equally crazy. The stars were just balls of fire.

"Dad," she said, "if you don't like being close to home, why are we sleeping in Grandpa Tom's yard?"

His laughter echoed in the quiet Oklahoma night. "I think you know me too well, Pipes."

"You're not really going to sell this place, are you?"

"Nope," he sighed. "I'm probably not."

Piper blinked, shaking herself out of the memory. She

realized she'd been falling asleep on the dragon's back. How could her dad pretend to be so many things he wasn't? She was trying to do that now, and it was tearing her apart.

Maybe she could pretend for a little while longer. She could dream of finding a way to save her father without betraying her friends—even if right now a happy ending seemed about as likely as magic hedgehogs.

She leaned back against Jason's warm chest. He didn't complain. As soon as she closed her eyes, she drifted off to sleep.

In her dream, she was back on the mountaintop. The ghostly purple bonfire cast shadows across the trees. Piper's eyes stung from smoke, and the ground was so warm, the soles of her boots felt sticky.

A voice from the dark rumbled, "You forget your duty."

Piper couldn't see him, but it was definitely her least favorite giant—the one who called himself Enceladus. She looked around for any sign of her father, but the pole where he'd been chained was no longer there.

"Where is he?" she demanded. "What've you done with him?"

The giant's laugh was like lava hissing down a volcano. "His body is safe enough, though I fear the poor man's mind can't take much more of my company. For some reason he finds me—disturbing. You must hurry, girl, or I fear there will be little left of him to save."

"Let him go!" she screamed. "Take me instead. He's just a mortal!"

"But, my dear," the giant rumbled, "we must prove our love

for our parents. That's what *I'm* doing. Show me you value your father's life by doing what I ask. Who's more important —your father, or a deceitful goddess who used you, toyed with your emotions, manipulated your memories, eh? What is Hera to you?"

Piper began to tremble. So much anger and fear boiled inside her, she could hardly talk. "You're asking me to betray my friends."

"Sadly, my dear, your friends are destined to die. Their quest is impossible. Even if you succeeded, you heard the prophecy: unleashing Hera's rage would mean your destruction. The only question now—will you die with your friends, or live with your father?"

The bonfire roared. Piper tried to step back, but her feet were heavy. She realized the ground was pulling her down, clinging to her boots like wet sand. When she looked up, a shower of purple sparks had spread across the sky, and the sun was rising in the east. A patchwork of cities glowed in the valley below, and far to the west, over a line of rolling hills, she saw a familiar landmark rising from a sea of fog.

"Why are you showing me this?" Piper asked. "You're revealing where you are."

"Yes, you know this place," the giant said. "Lead your friends here instead of their true destination, and I will deal with them. Or even better, arrange their deaths before you arrive. I don't care which. Just be at the summit by noon on the solstice, and you may collect your father and go in peace."

"I can't," Piper said. "You can't ask me—"

"To betray that foolish boy Valdez, who always irritated

you and is now hiding secrets from you? To give up a boy-friend you never really had? Is that more important than your own father?"

"I'll find a way to defeat you," Piper said. "I'll save my father *and* my friends."

The giant growled in the shadows. "I was once proud too. I thought the gods could never defeat me. Then they hurled a mountain on top of me, crushed me into the ground, where I struggled for eons, half-conscious in pain. That taught me patience, girl. It taught me not to act rashly. Now I've clawed my way back with the help of the waking earth. I am only the first. My brethren will follow. We will not be denied our vengeance—not this time. And you, Piper McLean, need a lesson in humility. I'll show you how easily your rebellious spirit can be brought to earth."

The dream dissolved. And Piper woke up screaming, free-falling through the air.

XXII

PIPER

PIPER TUMBLED THROUGH THE SKY. Far below she saw city lights glimmering in the early dawn, and several hundred yards away the body of the bronze dragon spinning out of control, its wings limp, fire flickering in its mouth like a badly wired lightbulb.

A body shot past her—Leo, screaming and frantically grabbing at the clouds. "Not coooooool!"

She tried to call to him, but he was already too far below.

Somewhere above her, Jason yelled, "Piper, level out! Extend your arms and legs!"

It was hard to control her fear, but she did what he said and regained some balance. She fell spread-eagle like a skydiver, the wind underneath her like a solid block of ice. Then Jason was there, wrapping his arms around her waist.

Thank god, Piper thought. But part of her also thought: Great. Second time this week he's hugged me, and both times it's because I'm plummeting to my death.

"We have to get Leo!" she shouted.

Their fall slowed as Jason controlled the winds, but they still lurched up and down like the winds didn't want to cooperate.

"Gonna get rough," Jason warned. "Hold on!"

Piper locked her arms around him, and Jason shot toward the ground. Piper probably screamed, but the sound was ripped from her mouth. Her vision blurred.

And then, *thump!* They slammed into another warm body —Leo, still wriggling and cursing.

"Stop fighting!" Jason said. "It's me!"

"My dragon!" Leo yelled. "You gotta save Festus!"

Jason was already struggling to keep the three of them aloft, and Piper knew there was no way he could help a fifty-ton metal dragon. But before she could try to reason with Leo, she heard an explosion below them. A fireball rolled into the sky from behind a warehouse complex, and Leo sobbed, "Festus!"

Jason's face reddened with strain as he tried to maintain an air cushion beneath them, but intermittent slow-downs were the best he could manage. Rather than free-falling, it felt like they were bouncing down a giant staircase, a hundred feet at a time, which wasn't doing Piper's stomach any favors.

As they wobbled and zigzagged, Piper could make out details of the factory complex below—warehouses, smoke-stacks, barbed-wire fences, and parking lots lined with snow-covered vehicles. They were still high enough so that hitting the ground would flatten them into roadkill—or skykill— when Jason groaned, "I can't—"

And they dropped like stones.

They hit the roof of the largest warehouse and crashed through into darkness.

Unfortunately, Piper tried to land on her feet. Her feet didn't like that. Pain flared in her left ankle as she crumpled against a cold metal surface.

For a few seconds she wasn't conscious of anything but pain—pain so bad that her ears rang and her vision went red.

Then she heard Jason's voice somewhere below, echoing through the building. "Piper! Where's Piper?"

"Ow, bro!" Leo groaned. "That's my back! I'm not a sofa! Piper, where'd you go?"

"Here," she managed, her voice a whimper.

She heard shuffling and grunting, then feet pounding on metal steps.

Her vision began to clear. She was on a metal catwalk that ringed the warehouse interior. Leo and Jason had landed on ground level, and were now coming up the stairs toward her. She looked at her foot, and a wave of nausea swept over her. Her toes weren't supposed to point that way, were they?

Oh, god. She forced herself to look away before she threw up. Focus on something else. Anything else.

The hole they'd made in the roof was a ragged starburst twenty feet above. How they'd even survived that drop, she had no idea. Hanging from the ceiling, a few electric bulbs flickered dimly, but they didn't do much to light the enormous space. Next to Piper, the corrugated metal wall was emblazoned with a company logo, but it was almost completely spray-painted over with graffiti. Down in the shadowy warehouse, she could make out huge machines, robotic arms, half-finished trucks on an assembly line. The place looked like it had been abandoned for years.

Jason and Leo reached her side.

Leo started to ask, "You okay...?" Then he saw her foot. "Oh no, you're not."

"Thanks for the reassurance," Piper groaned.

"You'll be fine," Jason said, though Piper could hear the worry in his voice. "Leo, you got any first aid supplies?"

"Yeah—yeah, sure." He dug around in his tool belt and pulled out a wad of gauze and a roll of duct tape—both of which seemed too big for the belt's pockets. Piper had noticed the tool belt yesterday morning, but she hadn't thought to ask Leo about it. It didn't look like anything special—just one of those wraparound leather aprons with a bunch of pockets, like a blacksmith or a carpenter might wear. And it seemed to be empty.

"How did you—" Piper tried to sit up, and winced. "How did you pull that stuff from an empty belt?"

"Magic," Leo said. "Haven't figured it out completely, but I can summon just about any regular tool out of the pockets, plus some other helpful stuff." He reached into another pocket and pulled out a little tin box. "Breath mint?"

Jason snatched away the mints. "That's great, Leo. Now, can you fix her foot?"

"I'm a mechanic, man. Maybe if she was a car..." He snapped his fingers. "Wait, what was that godly healing stuff they fed you at camp—Rambo food?"

"Ambrosia, dummy," Piper said through gritted teeth. "There should be some in my bag, if it's not crushed."

Jason carefully pulled her backpack off her shoulders. He rummaged through the supplies the Aphrodite kids had packed for her, and found a Ziploc full of smashed pastry squares like lemon bars. He broke off a piece and fed it to her.

The taste was nothing like she expected. It reminded her of Dad's black bean soup from when she was a little girl. He used to feed it to her whenever she got sick. The memory relaxed her, though it made her sad. The pain in her ankle subsided.

"More," she said.

Jason frowned. "Piper, we shouldn't risk it. They said too much could burn you up. I think I should try to set your foot."

Piper's stomach fluttered. "Have you ever done that before?"

"Yeah . . . I think so."

Leo found an old piece of wood and broke it in half for a splint. Then he got the gauze and duct tape ready.

"Hold her leg still," Jason told him. "Piper, this is going to hurt."

When Jason set the foot, Piper flinched so hard she punched Leo in the arm, and he yelled almost as much as she did. When her vision cleared and she could breathe normally again, she found that her foot was pointing the right way, her ankle splinted with plywood, gauze, and duct tape.

"Ow," she said.

"Jeez, beauty queen!" Leo rubbed his arm. "Glad my face wasn't there."

"Sorry," she said. "And don't call me 'beauty queen,' or I'll punch you again."

"You both did great." Jason found a canteen in Piper's pack and gave her some water. After a few minutes, her stomach began to calm down.

Once she wasn't screaming in pain, she could hear the wind howling outside. Snowflakes fluttered through the hole in the roof, and after their meeting with Khione, snow was the last thing Piper wanted to see.

"What happened to the dragon?" she asked. "Where are we?"

Leo's expression turned sullen. "I don't know with Festus. He just jerked sideways like he hit an invisible wall and started to fall."

Piper remembered Enceladus's warning: *I'll show you how easily your rebellious spirit can be brought to earth.* Had he managed to strike them down from so far away? It seemed impossible. If he were that powerful, why would he need her to betray her friends when he could just kill them himself? And how could the giant be keeping an eye on her in a snowstorm thousands of miles away?

Leo pointed to the logo on the wall. "As far as where we are..." It was hard to see through the graffiti, but Piper could make out a large red eye with the stenciled words: MONOCLE MOTORS, ASSEMBLY PLANT 1.

"Closed car plant," Leo said. "I'm guessing we crash-landed in Detroit."

Piper had heard about closed car plants in Detroit, so that

made sense. But it seemed like a pretty depressing place to land. "How far is that from Chicago?"

Jason handed her the canteen. "Maybe three-fourths of the way from Quebec? The thing is, without the dragon, we're stuck traveling overland."

"No way," Leo said. "It isn't safe."

Piper thought about the way the ground had pulled at her feet in the dream, and what King Boreas had said about the earth yielding up more horrors. "He's right. Besides, I don't know if I can walk. And three people—Jason, you can't fly that many across country by yourself."

"No way," Jason said. "Leo, are you sure the dragon didn't malfunction? I mean, Festus is old, and—"

"And I might not have repaired him right?"

"I didn't say that," Jason protested. "It's just—maybe you could fix it."

"I don't know." Leo sounded crestfallen. He pulled a few screws out of his pockets and started fiddling with them. "I'd have to find where he landed, if he's even in one piece."

"It was my fault," Piper said without thinking. She just couldn't stand it anymore. The secret about her father was heating up inside her like too much ambrosia. If she kept lying to her friends, she felt like she'd burn to ashes.

"Piper," Jason said gently, "you were asleep when Festus conked out. It couldn't be your fault."

"Yeah, you're just shaken up," Leo agreed. He didn't even try to make a joke at her expense. "You're in pain. Just rest."

She wanted to tell them everything, but the words stuck

in her throat. They were both being so kind to her. Yet if Enceladus was watching her somehow, saying the wrong thing could get her father killed.

Leo stood. "Look, um, Jason, why don't you stay with her, bro? I'll scout around for Festus. I think he fell outside the warehouse somewhere. If I can find him, maybe I can figure out what happened and fix him."

"It's too dangerous," Jason said. "You shouldn't go by yourself."

"Ah, I got duct tape and breath mints. I'll be fine," Leo said, a little too quickly, and Piper realized he was a lot more shaken up than he was letting on. "You guys just don't run off without me."

Leo reached into his magic tool belt, pulled out a flashlight, and headed down the stairs, leaving Piper and Jason alone.

Jason gave her a smile, though he looked kind of nervous. It was the exact expression he'd had on his face after he'd kissed her the first time, up on the Wilderness School dorm roof—that cute little scar on his lip curving into a crescent. The memory gave her a warm feeling. Then she remembered that the kiss had never really happened.

"You look better," Jason offered.

Piper wasn't sure if he meant her foot, or the fact that she wasn't magically beautified anymore. Her jeans were tattered from the fall through the roof. Her boots were splattered with melted dirty snow. She didn't know what her face looked like, but probably horrible.

Why did it matter? She'd never cared about things like that before. She wondered if it was her stupid mother, the goddess of love, messing with her thoughts. If Piper started getting urges to read fashion magazines, she was going to have to find Aphrodite and smack her.

She decided to focus on her ankle instead. As long as she didn't move it, the pain wasn't bad. "You did a good job," she told Jason. "Where'd you learn first aid?"

He shrugged. "Same answer as always. I don't know."

"But you're starting to have some memories, aren't you? Like that prophecy in Latin back at camp, or that dream about the wolf."

"It's fuzzy," he said. "Like déjà vu. Ever forgotten a word or a name, and you know it should be on the tip of your tongue, but it isn't? It's like that—only with my whole life."

Piper sort of knew what he meant. The last three months —a life she thought she'd had, a relationship with Jason—had turned out to be Mist.

A boyfriend you never really had, Enceladus had said. *Is that more important than your own father?*

She should've kept her mouth shut, but she voiced the question that had been on her mind since yesterday.

"That photo in your pocket," she said. "Is that someone from your past?"

Jason pulled back.

"I'm sorry," she said. "None of my business. Forget it."

"No—it's okay." His features relaxed. "Just, I'm trying to figure things out. Her name's Thalia. She's my sister. I don't remember any details. I'm not even sure how I know, but— um, why are you smiling?"

"Nothing." Piper tried to kill the smile. *Not* an old

girlfriend. She felt ridiculously happy. "Um, it's just—that's great you remembered. Annabeth told me she became a Hunter of Artemis, right?"

Jason nodded. "I get the feeling I'm supposed to find her. Hera left me that memory for a reason. It's got something to do with this quest. But...I also have the feeling it could be dangerous. I'm not sure I *want* to find out the truth. Is that crazy?"

"No," Piper said. "Not at all."

She stared at the logo on the wall: MONOCLE MOTORS, the single red eye. Something about that logo bothered her.

Maybe it was the idea Enceladus was watching her, holding her father for leverage. She had to save him, but how could she betray her friends?

"Jason," she said. "Speaking of the truth, I need to tell you something—something about my dad—"

She didn't get the chance. Somewhere below, metal clanged against metal, like a door slamming shut. The sound echoed through the warehouse.

Jason stood. He took out his coin and flipped it, snatching his golden sword out of the air. He peered over the railing. "Leo?" he called.

No answer.

He crouched next to Piper. "I don't like this."

"He could be in trouble," Piper said. "Go check."

"I can't leave you alone."

"I'll be fine." She felt terrified, but she wasn't about to admit it. She drew her dagger Katoptris and tried to look confident. "Anyone gets close, I'll skewer them."

Jason hesitated. "I'll leave you the pack. If I'm not back in five minutes—"

"Panic?" she suggested.

He managed a smile. "Glad you're back to normal. The makeup and the dress were a lot more intimidating than the dagger."

"Get going, Sparky, before I skewer *you*."

"Sparky?"

Even offended, Jason looked hot. It wasn't fair. Then he made his way to the stairs and disappeared into the dark.

Piper counted her breaths, trying to gauge how much time had passed. She lost track at around forty-three. Then something in the warehouse went *bang!*

The echo died. Piper's heart pounded, but she didn't call out. Her instincts told her it might not be a good idea.

She stared at her splinted ankle. *It's not like I can run.* Then she looked up again at the Monocle Motors sign. A little voice in her head pestered her, warning of danger. Something from Greek mythology...

Her hand went to her backpack. She took out the ambrosia squares. Too much would burn her up, but would a little more fix her ankle?

Boom. The sound was closer this time, directly below her. She dug out a whole square of ambrosia and stuffed it in her mouth. Her heart raced faster. Her skin felt feverish.

Hesitantly, she flexed her ankle against the splint. No pain, no stiffness at all. She cut through the duct tape with her dagger and heard heavy steps on the stairs—like metal boots.

Had it been five minutes? Longer? The steps didn't sound

like Jason, but maybe he was carrying Leo. Finally she couldn't stand it. Gripping her dagger, she called out, "Jason?"

"Yeah," he said from the darkness. "On my way up."

Definitely Jason's voice. So why did all her instincts say *Run?*

With effort, she got to her feet.

The steps came closer.

"It's okay," Jason's voice promised.

At the top of the stairs, a face appeared out of the darkness —a hideous black grin, a smashed nose, and a single blood-shot eye in the middle of his forehead.

"It's fine," the Cyclops said, in a perfect imitation of Jason's voice. "You're just in time for dinner."

LEO

LEO WISHED THE DRAGON HADN'T LANDED on the toilets.

Of all the places to crash, a line of Porta-Potties would not have been his first choice. A dozen of the blue plastic boxes had been set up in the factory yard, and Festus had flattened them all. Fortunately, they hadn't been used in a long time, and the fireball from the crash incinerated most of the contents; but still, there were some pretty gross chemicals leaking out of the wreckage. Leo had to pick his way through and try not to breathe through his nose. Heavy snow was coming down, but the dragon's hide was still steaming hot. Of course, that didn't bother Leo.

After a few minutes climbing over Festus's inanimate body, Leo started to get irritated. The dragon looked perfectly fine. Yes, it had fallen out of the sky and landed with a big *ka-boom*, but its body wasn't even dented. The fireball had apparently come from built up gasses inside the toilet units, not from the dragon itself. Festus's wings were intact. Nothing seemed broken. There was no reason it should have stopped.

"Not my fault," he muttered. "Festus, you're making me look bad."

Then he opened the control panel on the dragon's head, and Leo's heart sank. "Oh, Festus, what the heck?"

The wiring had frozen over. Leo knew it had been okay yesterday. He'd worked so hard to repair the corroded lines, but something had caused a flash freeze inside the dragon's skull, where it should've been too hot for ice to form. The ice had caused the wiring to overload and char the control disk. Leo couldn't see any reason that would've happened. Sure, the dragon was old, but still, it didn't make sense.

He could replace the wires. That wasn't the problem. But the charred control disk was not good. The Greek letters and pictures carved around the edges, which probably held all kinds of magic, were blurred and blackened.

The one piece of hardware Leo couldn't replace—and it was damaged. *Again.*

He imagined his mom's voice: *Most problems look worse than they are,* mijo. *Nothing is unfixable.*

His mom could repair just about anything, but Leo was pretty sure she'd never worked on a fifty-year-old magic metal dragon.

He clenched his teeth and decided he had to try. He wasn't walking from Detroit to Chicago in a snowstorm, and he wasn't going to be responsible for stranding his friends.

"Right," he muttered, brushing the snow off his shoulders.

"Gimme a nylon bristle detail brush, some nitrile gloves, and maybe a can of that aerosol cleaning solvent."

The tool belt obliged. Leo couldn't help smiling as he pulled out the supplies. The belt's pockets did have limits. They wouldn't give him anything magic, like Jason's sword, or anything huge, like a chain saw. He'd tried asking for both. And if he asked for too many things at once, the belt needed a cooldown time before it could work again. The more complicated the request, the longer the cooldown. But anything small and simple like you might find around a workshop—all Leo had to do was ask.

He began cleaning off the control disk. While he worked, snow collected on the cooling dragon. Leo had to stop from time to time to summon fire and melt it away, but mostly he went into autopilot mode, his hands working by themselves as his thoughts wandered.

Leo couldn't believe how stupid he'd acted back at Boreas's palace. He should've figured a family of winter gods would hate him on sight. Son of the fire god flying a fire-breathing dragon into an ice penthouse—yeah, maybe not the best move. Still, he hated feeling like a reject. Jason and Piper got to visit the throne room. Leo got to wait in the lobby with Cal, the demigod of hockey and major head injuries.

Fire is bad, Cal had told him.

That pretty much summed it up. Leo knew he couldn't keep the truth from his friends much longer. Ever since Camp Half-Blood, one line of that Great Prophecy kept coming back to him: *To storm or fire the world must fall.*

And Leo was the fire guy, the first one since 1666 when London had burned down. If he told his friends what he could really do—*Hey, guess what, guys? I might destroy the world!*—why would anyone welcome him back at camp? Leo would have to go on the run again. Even though he knew that drill, the idea depressed him.

Then there was Khione. Dang, that girl was fine. Leo knew he'd acted like a total fool, but he couldn't help himself. He'd had his clothes cleaned with the one-hour valet service—which had been totally sweet, by the way. He'd combed his hair—never an easy job—and even discovered the tool bag could make breath mints, all in hopes that he could get close to her. Naturally, no such luck.

Getting frozen out—story of his life—by his relatives, foster homes, you name it. Even at Wilderness School, Leo had spent the last few weeks feeling like a third wheel as Jason and Piper, his only friends, became a couple. He was happy for them and all, but still it made him feel like they didn't need him anymore.

When he'd found out that Jason's whole time at school had been an illusion—a kind of a memory burp—Leo had been secretly excited. It was a chance for a reset. Now Jason and Piper were heading toward being a couple again—that was obvious from the way they'd acted in the warehouse just now, like they wanted to talk in private without Leo around. What had he expected? He'd wind up the odd man out again. Khione had just given him the cold shoulder a little quicker than most.

"Enough, Valdez," he scolded himself. "Nobody's going

to play any violins for you just because you're not important. Fix the stupid dragon."

He got so involved with his work, he wasn't sure how much time had passed before he heard the voice.

You're wrong, Leo, it said.

He fumbled his brush and dropped it into the dragon's head. He stood, but he couldn't see who'd spoken. Then he looked at the ground. Snow and chemical sludge from the toilets, even the asphalt itself was shifting like it was turning to liquid. A ten-foot-wide area formed eyes, a nose, and a mouth—the giant face of a sleeping woman.

She didn't exactly speak. Her lips didn't move. But Leo could hear her voice in his head, as if the vibrations were coming through the ground, straight into his feet and resonating up his skeleton.

They need you desperately, she said. *In some ways, you are the most important of the seven—like the control disk in the dragon's brain. Without you, the power of the others means nothing. They will never reach me, never stop me. And I will fully wake.*

"You." Leo was shaking so badly he wasn't sure he'd spoken aloud. He hadn't heard that voice since he was eight, but it was her: the earthen woman from the machine shop. "You killed my mom."

The face shifted. The mouth formed a sleepy smile like it was having a pleasant dream. *Ah, but Leo. I am your mother too—the First Mother. Do not oppose me. Walk away now. Let my son Porphyrion rise and become king, and I will ease your burdens. You will tread lightly on the earth.*

Leo grabbed the nearest thing he could find—a Porta-Potty seat—and threw it at the face. "Leave me alone!"

The toilet seat sank into the liquid earth. Snow and sludge rippled, and the face dissolved.

Leo stared at the ground, waiting for the face to reappear. But it didn't. Leo wanted to think he'd imagined it.

Then from the direction of the factory, he heard a crash —like two dump trucks slamming together. Metal crumpled and groaned, and the noise echoed across the yard. Instantly Leo knew that Jason and Piper were in trouble.

Walk away now, the voice had urged.

"Not likely," Leo growled. "Gimme the biggest hammer you got."

He reached into his tool belt and pulled out a three-pound club hammer with a double-faced head the size of a baked potato. Then he jumped off the dragon's back and ran toward the warehouse.

LEO

LEO STOPPED AT THE DOORS AND TRIED to control his breathing. The voice of the earth woman still rang in his ears, reminding him of his mother's death. The last thing he wanted to do was plunge into another dark warehouse. Suddenly he felt eight years old again, alone and helpless as someone he cared about was trapped and in trouble.

Stop it, he told himself. That's how she wants you to feel.

But that didn't make him any less scared. He took a deep breath and peered inside. Nothing looked different. Gray morning light filtered through the hole in the roof. A few lightbulbs flickered, but most of the factory floor was still lost in shadows. He could make out the catwalk above, the dim shapes of heavy machinery along the assembly line, but no movement. No sign of his friends.

He almost called out, but something stopped him—a sense he couldn't identify. Then he realized it was *smell*. Something smelled wrong—like burning motor oil and sour breath.

Something not human was inside the factory. Leo was certain. His body shifted into high gear, all his nerves tingling.

Somewhere on the factory floor, Piper's voice cried out: "Leo, help!"

But Leo held his tongue. How could Piper have gotten off the catwalk with her broken ankle?

He slipped inside and ducked behind a cargo container. Slowly, gripping his hammer, he worked his way toward the center of the room, hiding behind boxes and hollow truck chassis. Finally he reached the assembly line. He crouched behind the nearest piece of machinery—a crane with a robotic arm.

Piper's voice called out again: "Leo?" Less certain this time, but very close.

Leo peeked around the machinery. Hanging directly above the assembly line, suspended by a chain from a crane on the opposite side, was a massive truck engine—just dangling thirty feet up, as if it had been left there when the factory was abandoned. Below it on the conveyor belt sat a truck chassis, and clustered around it were three dark shapes the size of forklifts. Nearby, dangling from chains on two other robotic arms, were two smaller shapes—maybe more engines, but one of them was twisting around as if it were alive.

Then one of the forklift shapes rose, and Leo realized it was a humanoid of massive size. "Told you it was nothing," the thing rumbled. Its voice was too deep and feral to be human.

One of the other forklift-sized lumps shifted, and called out in Piper's voice: "Leo, help me! Help—" Then the voice changed, becoming a masculine snarl. "Bah, there's nobody out there. No demigod could be that quiet, eh?"

The first monster chuckled. "Probably ran away, if he knows what's good for him. Or the girl was lying about a third demigod. Let's get cooking."

Snap. A bright orange light sizzled to life—an emergency flare—and Leo was temporarily blinded. He ducked behind the crane until the spots cleared from his eyes. Then he took another peep and saw a nightmare scene even Tía Callida couldn't have dreamed up.

The two smaller things dangling from crane arms weren't engines. They were Jason and Piper. Both hung upside down, tied by their ankles and cocooned with chains up to their necks. Piper was flailing around, trying to free herself. Her mouth was gagged, but at least she was alive. Jason didn't look so good. He hung limply, his eyes rolled up in his head. A red welt the size of an apple had swollen over his left eyebrow.

On the conveyor belt, the bed of the unfinished pickup truck was being used as a fire pit. The emergency flare had ignited a mixture of tires and wood, which, from the smell of it, had been doused in kerosene. A big metal pole was suspended over the flames—a spit, Leo realized, which meant this was a cooking fire.

But most terrifying of all were the cooks.

Monocle Motors: that single red eye logo. Why hadn't Leo realized?

Three massive humanoids gathered around the fire. Two

were standing, stoking the flames. The largest one crouched with his back to Leo. The two facing him were each ten feet tall, with hairy muscular bodies and skin that glowed red in the firelight. One of the monsters wore a chain mail loincloth that looked really uncomfortable. The other wore a ragged fuzzy toga made of fiberglass insulation, which also would not have made Leo's top ten wardrobe ideas. Other than that, the two monsters could've been twins. Each had a brutish face with a single eye in the center of his forehead. The cooks were Cyclopes.

Leo's legs started quaking. He'd seen some weird things so far—storm spirits and winged gods and a metal dragon that liked Tabasco sauce. But this was different. These were actual, flesh-and-blood, ten-foot-tall living monsters who wanted to eat his friends for dinner.

He was so terrified he could hardly think. If only he had Festus. He could use a fire-breathing sixty-foot-long tank about now. But all he had was a tool belt and a backpack. His three-pound club hammer looked awfully small compared to those Cyclopes.

This is what the sleeping earth lady had been talking about. She wanted Leo to walk away and leave his friends to die.

That decided it. No way was Leo going to let that earth lady make him feel powerless—never again. Leo slipped off his backpack and quietly started to unzip it.

The Cyclops in the chain mail loincloth walked over to Piper, who squirmed and tried to head-butt him in the eye. "Can I take her gag off now? I like it when they scream."

The question was directed at the third Cyclops, apparently

the leader. The crouching figure grunted, and Loincloth ripped the gag off Piper's mouth.

She didn't scream. She took a shaky breath like she was trying to keep herself calm.

Meanwhile, Leo found what he wanted in the pack: a stack of tiny remote control units he'd picked up in Bunker 9. At least he *hoped* that's what they were. The robotic crane's maintenance panel was easy to find. He slipped a screwdriver from his tool belt and went to work, but he had to go slowly. The leader Cyclops was only twenty feet in front of him. The monsters obviously had excellent senses. Pulling off his plan without making noise seemed impossible, but he didn't have much choice.

The Cyclops in the toga poked at the fire, which was now blazing away and billowing noxious black smoke toward the ceiling. His buddy Loincloth glowered at Piper, waiting for her to do something entertaining. "Scream, girl! I like funny screaming!"

When Piper finally spoke, her tone was calm and reasonable, like she was correcting a naughty puppy. "Oh, Mr. Cyclops, you don't want to kill us. It would be much better if you let us go."

Loincloth scratched his ugly head. He turned to his friend in the fiberglass toga. "She's kind of pretty, Torque. Maybe I should let her go."

Torque, the dude in the toga, growled. "I saw her first, Sump. *I'll* let her go!"

Sump and Torque started to argue, but the third Cyclops rose and shouted, "Fools!"

Leo almost dropped his screwdriver. The third Cyclops was a *female*. She was several feet taller than Torque or Sump, and even beefier. She wore a tent of chain mail cut like one of those sack dresses Leo's mean Aunt Rosa used to wear. What'd they call that—a muumuu? Yeah, the Cyclops lady had a chain mail muumuu. Her greasy black hair was matted in pigtails, woven with copper wires and metal washers. Her nose and mouth were thick and smashed together, like she spent her free time ramming her face into walls; but her single red eye glittered with evil intelligence.

The woman Cyclops stalked over to Sump and pushed him aside, knocking him over the conveyor belt. Torque backed up quickly.

"The girl is Venus spawn," the lady Cyclops snarled. "She's using charmspeak on you."

Piper started to say, "Please, ma'am—"

"Rarr!" The lady Cyclops grabbed Piper around the waist. "Don't try your pretty talk on me, girl! I'm Ma Gasket! I've eaten heroes tougher than you for lunch!"

Leo feared Piper would get crushed, but Ma Gasket just dropped her and let her dangle from her chain. Then she started yelling at Sump about how stupid he was.

Leo's hands worked furiously. He twisted wires and turned switches, hardly thinking about what he was doing. He finished attaching the remote. Then he crept over to the next robotic arm while the Cyclopes were talking.

"—eat her last, Ma?" Sump was saying.

"Idiot!" Ma Gasket yelled, and Leo realized Sump and Torque must be her sons. If so, ugly definitely ran in the family. "I should've thrown you out on the streets when you were babies, like *proper* Cyclops children. You might have learned some useful skills. Curse my soft heart that I kept you!"

"Soft heart?" Torque muttered.

"What was that, you ingrate?"

"Nothing, Ma. I said you got a soft heart. We get to work for you, feed you, file your toenails—"

"And you should be grateful!" Ma Gasket bellowed. "Now, stoke the fire, Torque! And Sump, you idiot, my case of salsa is in the other warehouse. Don't tell me you expect me to eat these demigods without salsa!"

"Yes, Ma," Sump said. "I mean no, Ma. I mean—"

"Go get it!" Ma Gasket picked up a nearby truck chassis and slammed it over Sump's head. Sump crumpled to his knees. Leo was sure a hit like that would kill him, but Sump apparently got hit by trucks a lot. He managed to push the chassis off his head. Then he staggered to his feet and ran off to fetch the salsa.

Now's the time, Leo thought. While they're separated.

He finished wiring the second machine and moved toward a third. As he dashed between robotic arms, the Cyclopes didn't see him, but Piper did. Her expression turned from terror to disbelief, and she gasped.

Ma Gasket turned to her. "What's the matter, girl? So fragile I broke you?"

Thankfully, Piper was a quick thinker. She looked away from Leo and said, "I think it's my ribs, ma'am. If I'm busted up inside, I'll taste terrible."

Ma Gasket bellowed with laughter. "Good one. The last hero we ate—remember him, Torque? Son of Mercury, wasn't he?"

"Yes, Ma," Torque said. "Tasty. Little bit stringy."

"He tried a trick like that. Said he was on medication. But he tasted fine!"

"Tasted like mutton," Torque recalled. "Purple shirt. Talked in Latin. Yes, a bit stringy, but good."

Leo's fingers froze on the maintenance panel. Apparently, Piper was having the same thought he was, because she asked, "Purple shirt? Latin?"

"Good eating," Ma Gasket said fondly. "Point is, girl, we're not as dumb as people think! We're not falling for those stupid tricks and riddles, not us northern Cyclopes."

Leo forced himself back to work, but his mind was racing. A kid who spoke Latin had been caught here—in a purple shirt like Jason's? He didn't know what that meant, but he had to leave the interrogation to Piper. If he was going to have any chance of defeating these monsters, he had to move fast before Sump came back with the salsa.

He looked up at the engine block suspended right above the Cyclopes' campsite. He wished he could use that—it would make a great weapon. But the crane holding it was on the opposite side of the conveyor belt. There was no way Leo could get over there without being seen, and besides, he was running short on time.

The last part of his plan was the trickiest. From his tool belt he summoned some wires, a radio adapter, and a smaller screwdriver and started to build a universal remote. For the first time, he said a silent thank-you to his dad—Hephaestus —for the magic tool belt. *Get me out of here,* he prayed, *and maybe you're not such a jerk.*

Piper kept talking, laying on the praise. "Oh, I've heard about the northern Cyclopes!" Which Leo figured was bull, but she sounded convincing. "I never knew you were so big and clever!"

"Flattery won't work either," Ma Gasket said, though she sounded pleased. "It's true, you'll be breakfast for the best Cyclopes around."

"But aren't Cyclopes good?" Piper asked. "I thought you made weapons for the gods."

"Bah! I'm very good. Good at eating people. Good at smashing. And good at building things, yes, but not for the gods. Our cousins, the elder Cyclopes, they do this, yes. Thinking they're so high and mighty 'cause they're a few thousand years older. Then there's our southern cousins, living on islands and tending sheep. Morons! But we Hyperborean Cyclopes, the northern clan, we're the best! Founded Monocle Motors in this old factory—the best weapons, armor, chariots, fuel-efficient SUVs! And yet—bah! Forced to shut down. Laid off most of our tribe. The war was too quick. Titans lost. No good! No more need for Cyclops weapons."

"Oh, no," Piper sympathized. "I'm sure you made some amazing weapons."

Torque grinned. "Squeaky war hammer!" He picked up a large pole with an accordion-looking metal box on the end.

He slammed it against the floor and the cement cracked, but there was also a sound like the world's largest rubber ducky getting stomped.

"Terrifying," Piper said.

Torque looked pleased. "Not as good as the exploding ax, but this one can be used more than once."

"Can I see it?" Piper asked. "If you could just free my hands—"

Torque stepped forward eagerly, but Ma Gasket said, "Stupid! She's tricking you again. Enough talk! Slay the boy first before he dies on his own. I like my meat fresh."

No! Leo's fingers flew, connecting the wires for the remote. *Just a few more minutes!*

"Hey, wait," Piper said, trying to get the Cyclopes' attention. "Hey, can I just ask—"

The wires sparked in Leo's hand. The Cyclopes froze and turned in his direction. Then Torque picked up a truck and threw it at him.

Leo rolled as the truck steamrolled over the machinery. If he'd been a half-second slower, he would've been smashed.

He got to his feet, and Ma Gasket spotted him. She yelled, "Torque, you pathetic excuse for a Cyclops, get him!"

Torque barreled toward him. Leo frantically gunned the toggle on his makeshift remote.

Torque was fifty feet away. Twenty feet.

Then the first robotic arm whirred to life. A three-ton yellow metal claw slammed the Cyclops in the back so hard, he landed flat on his face. Before Torque could recover, the robotic hand grabbed him by one leg and hurled him straight up.

"AHHHHH!" Torque rocketed into the gloom. The ceiling was too dark and too high up to see exactly what happened, but judging from the harsh metal *clang*, Leo guessed the Cyclops had hit one of the support girders.

Torque never came down. Instead, yellow dust rained to the floor. Torque had disintegrated.

Ma Gasket stared at Leo in shock. "My son...You... You..."

As if on cue, Sump lumbered into the firelight with a case of salsa. "Ma, I got the extra-spicy—"

He never finished his sentence. Leo spun the remote's toggle, and the second robotic arm whacked Sump in the chest. The salsa case exploded like a piñata and Sump flew backward, right into the base of Leo's third machine. Sump may have been immune to getting hit with truck chassis, but he wasn't immune to robotic arms that could deliver ten thousand pounds of force. The third crane arm slammed him against the floor so hard, he exploded into dust like a broken flour sack.

Two Cyclopes down. Leo was beginning to feel like Commander Tool Belt when Ma Gasket locked her eye on him. She grabbed the nearest crane arm and ripped it off its pedestal with a savage roar. "You busted my boys! Only *I* get to bust my boys!"

Leo punched a button, and the two remaining arms swung into action. Ma Gasket caught the first one and tore it in half. The second arm smacked her in the head, but that only seemed to make her mad. She grabbed it by the clamps, ripped it free, and swung it like a baseball bat. It missed Piper and Jason by an inch. Then Ma Gasket let it go—spinning it toward Leo. He yelped and rolled to one side as it demolished the machine next to him.

Leo started to realize that an angry Cyclops mother was not something you wanted to fight with a universal remote and a screwdriver. The future for Commander Tool Belt was not looking so hot.

She stood about twenty feet from him now, next to the cooking fire. Her fists were clenched, her teeth bared. She looked ridiculous in her chain mail muumuu and her greasy pigtails—but given the murderous glare in her huge red eye and the fact that she was twelve feet tall, Leo wasn't laughing.

"Any more tricks, demigod?" Ma Gasket demanded.

Leo glanced up. The engine block suspended on the chain —if only he'd had time to rig it. If only he could get Ma Gasket to take one step forward. The chain itself... that one link... Leo shouldn't have been able to see it, especially from so far down, but his senses told him there was metal fatigue.

"Heck, yeah, I got tricks!" Leo raised his remote control. "Take one more step, and I'll destroy you with fire!"

Ma Gasket laughed. "Would you? Cyclopes are immune to fire, you idiot. But if you wish to play with flames, let me help!"

She scooped red-hot coals into her bare hands and flung them at Leo. They landed all around his feet.

"You missed," he said incredulously. Then Ma Gasket

grinned and picked up a barrel next to the truck. Leo just had time to read the stenciled word on the side—KEROSENE —before Ma Gasket threw it. The barrel split on the floor in front of him, spilling lighter fluid everywhere.

Coals sparked. Leo closed his eyes, and Piper screamed, "No!"

A firestorm erupted around him. When Leo opened his eyes he was bathed in flames swirling twenty feet into the air.

Ma Gasket shrieked with delight, but Leo didn't offer the fire any good fuel. The kerosene burned off, dying down to small fiery patches on the floor.

Piper gasped. "Leo?"

Ma Gasket looked astonished. "You live?" Then she took that extra step forward, which put her right where Leo wanted. "What are you?"

"The son of Hephaestus," Leo said. "And I warned you I'd destroy you with fire."

He pointed one finger in the air and summoned all his will. He'd never tried to do anything so focused and intense —but he shot a bolt of white-hot flames at the chain suspending the engine block above the Cyclops's head—aiming for the link that looked weaker than the rest.

The flames died. Nothing happened. Ma Gasket laughed. "An impressive try, son of Hephaestus. It's been many centuries since I saw a fire user. You'll make a spicy appetizer!"

The chain snapped—that single link heated beyond its tolerance point—and the engine block fell, deadly and silent.

"I don't think so," Leo said.

Ma Gasket didn't even have time to look up.

Smash! No more Cyclops—just a pile of dust under a five-ton engine block.

"Not immune to engines, huh?" Leo said. "Boo-yah!"

Then he fell to his knees, his head buzzing. After a few minutes he realized Piper was calling his name.

"Leo! Are you all right? Can you move?"

He stumbled to his feet. He'd never tried to summon such an intense fire before, and it had left him completely drained.

It took him a long time to get Piper down from her chains. Then together they lowered Jason, who was still unconscious. Piper managed to trickle a little nectar into his mouth, and he groaned. The welt on his head started to shrink. His color came back a little.

"Yeah, he's got a nice thick skull," Leo said. "I think he's gonna be fine."

"Thank god," Piper sighed. Then she looked at Leo with something like fear. "How did you—the fire—have you always...?"

Leo looked down. "Always," he said. "I'm a freaking menace. Sorry, I should've told you guys sooner but—"

"Sorry?" Piper punched his arm. When he looked up, she was grinning. "That was amazing, Valdez! You saved our lives. What are you sorry about?"

Leo blinked. He started to smile, but his sense of relief was ruined when he noticed something next to Piper's foot.

Yellow dust—the powdered remains of one of the Cyclopes, maybe Torque—was shifting across the floor like an invisible wind was pushing it back together.

"They're forming again," Leo said. "Look."

Piper stepped away from the dust. "That's not possible. Annabeth told me monsters dissipate when they're killed. They go back to Tartarus and can't return for a long time."

"Well, nobody told the dust that." Leo watched as it collected into a pile, then very slowly spread out, forming a shape with arms and legs.

"Oh, god." Piper turned pale. "Boreas said something about this—the earth yielding up horrors. 'When monsters no longer stay in Tartarus, and souls are no longer confined to Hades.' How long do you think we have?"

Leo thought about the face that had formed in the ground outside—the sleeping woman who was *definitely* a horror from the earth.

"I don't know," he said. "But we need to get out of here."

XXV

JASON

JASON DREAMED HE WAS WRAPPED in chains, hanging upside down like a hunk of meat. Everything hurt—his arms, his legs, his chest, his head. Especially his head. It felt like an overinflated water balloon.

"If I'm dead," he murmured, "why does it hurt so much?"

"You're not dead, my hero," said a woman's voice. "It is not your time. Come, speak with me."

Jason's thoughts floated away from his body. He heard monsters yelling, his friends screaming, fiery explosions, but it all seemed to be happening on another plane of existence—getting farther and farther away.

He found himself standing in an earthen cage. Tendrils of tree roots and stone whirled together, confining him. Outside the bars, he could see the floor of a dry reflecting pool, another earthen spire growing at the far end, and above them, the ruined red stones of a burned-out house.

Next to him in the cage, a woman sat cross-legged in black

robes, her head covered by a shroud. She pushed aside her veil, revealing a face that was proud and beautiful—but also hardened with suffering.

"Hera," Jason said.

"Welcome to my prison," said the goddess. "You will not die today, Jason. Your friends will see you through—for now."

"For now?" he asked.

Hera gestured at the tendrils of her cage. "There are worse trials to come. The very earth stirs against us."

"You're a goddess," Jason said. "Why can't you just escape?"

Hera smiled sadly. Her form began to glow, until her brilliance filled the cage with painful light. The air hummed with power, molecules splitting apart like a nuclear explosion. Jason suspected if he were actually there in the flesh, he would've been vaporized.

The cage should've been blasted to rubble. The ground should've split and the ruined house should've been leveled. But when the glow died, the cage hadn't budged. Nothing outside the bars had changed. Only Hera looked different—a little more stooped and tired.

"Some powers are even greater than the gods," she said. "I am not easily contained. I can be in many places at once. But when the greater part of my essence is caught, it is like a foot in a bear trap, you might say. I can't escape, and I am concealed from the eyes of the other gods. Only you can find me, and I grow weaker by the day."

"Then why did you come here?" Jason asked. "How were you caught?"

The goddess sighed. "I could not stay idle. Your father

Jupiter believes he can withdraw from the world, and thus lull our enemies back to sleep. He believes we Olympians have become too involved in the affairs of mortals, in the fates of our demigod children, especially since we agreed to claim them all after the war. He believes this is what has caused our enemies to stir. That is why he closed Olympus."

"But you don't agree."

"No," she said. "Often I do not understand my husband's moods or his decisions, but even for Zeus, this seemed paranoid. I cannot fathom why he was so insistent and so convinced. It was . . . unlike him. As Hera, I might have been content to follow my lord's wishes. But I am also Juno." Her image flickered, and Jason saw armor under her simple black robes, a goatskin cloak—the symbol of a Roman warrior—across her bronze mantle. "Juno Moneta they once called me—Juno, the One Who Warns. I was guardian of the state, patron of Eternal Rome. I could not sit by while the descendants of my people were attacked. I sensed danger at this sacred spot. A voice—" She hesitated. "A voice told me I should come here. Gods do not have what you might call a conscience, nor do we have dreams; but the voice was like that—soft and persistent, warning me to come here. And so the same day Zeus closed Olympus, I slipped away without telling him my plans, so he could not stop me. And I came here to investigate."

"It was a trap," Jason guessed.

The goddess nodded. "Only too late did I realize how quickly the earth was stirring. I was even more foolish than Jupiter—a slave to my own impulses. This is exactly how it happened the first time. I was taken captive by the giants, and my imprisonment started a war. Now our enemies rise again. The gods can only defeat them with the help of the greatest living heroes. And the one whom the giants serve... *she* cannot be defeated at all—only kept asleep."

"I don't understand."

"You will soon," Hera said.

The cage began to constrict, the tendrils spiraling tighter. Hera's form shivered like a candle flame in the breeze. Outside the cage, Jason could see shapes gathering at the edge of the pool—lumbering humanoids with hunched backs and bald heads. Unless Jason's eyes were tricking him—they had more than one set of arms. He heard wolves too, but not the wolves he'd seen with Lupa. He could tell from their howls this was a different pack—hungrier, more aggressive, out for blood.

"Hurry, Jason," Hera said. "My keepers approach, and you begin to wake. I will not be strong enough to appear to you again, even in dreams."

"Wait," he said. "Boreas told us you'd made a dangerous gamble. What did he mean?"

Hera's eyes looked wild, and Jason wondered if she really *had* done something crazy.

"An exchange," she said. "The only way to bring peace. The enemy counts on our divisions, and if we are divided, we *will* be destroyed. You are my peace offering, Jason—a bridge to overcome millennia of hatred."

"What? I don't—"

"I cannot tell you more," Hera said. "You have only lived

this long because I have taken your memory. Find this place. Return to your starting point. Your sister will help."

"Thalia?"

The scene began to dissolve. "Good-bye, Jason. Beware Chicago. Your most dangerous mortal enemy waits there. If you are to die, it will be by her hand."

"Who?" he demanded.

But Hera's image faded, and Jason awoke.

His eyes snapped open. "Cyclops!"

"Whoa, sleepyhead." Piper sat behind him on the bronze dragon, holding his waist to keep him balanced. Leo sat in front, driving. They flew peacefully through the winter sky as if nothing had happened.

"D-Detroit," Jason stammered. "Didn't we crash-land? I thought—"

"It's okay," Leo said. "We got away, but you got a nasty concussion. How you feeling?"

Jason's head throbbed. He remembered the factory, then walking down the catwalk, then a creature looming over him —a face with one eye, a massive fist—and everything went black.

"How did you—the Cyclops—"

"Leo ripped them apart," Piper said. "He was amazing. He can summon fire—"

"It was nothing," Leo said quickly.

Piper laughed. "Shut up, Valdez. I'm going to tell him. Get over it."

And she did—how Leo single-handedly defeated the Cyclopes family; how they freed Jason, then noticed the Cyclopes starting to re-form; how Leo had replaced the dragon's wiring and gotten them back in the air just as they'd started to hear the Cyclopes roaring for vengeance inside the factory.

Jason was impressed. Taking out three Cyclopes with nothing but a tool kit? Not bad. It didn't exactly scare him to hear how close he'd come to death, but it did make him feel horrible. He'd stepped right into an ambush and spent the whole fight knocked out while his friends fended for themselves. What kind of quest leader was he?

When Piper told him about the other kid the Cyclopes claimed to have eaten, the one in the purple shirt who spoke Latin, Jason felt like his head was going to explode. A son of Mercury . . . Jason felt like he should know that kid, but the name was missing from his mind.

"I'm not alone, then," he said. "There are others like me."

"Jason," Piper said, "you were never alone. You've got us."

"I—I know . . . but something Hera said. I was having a dream. . . ."

He told them what he'd seen, and what the goddess had said inside her cage.

"An exchange?" Piper asked. "What does that mean?"

Jason shook his head. "But Hera's gamble is *me*. Just by sending me to Camp Half-Blood, I have a feeling she broke some kind of rule, something that could blow up in a big way—"

"Or save us," Piper said hopefully. "That bit about the sleeping enemy—that sounds like the lady Leo told us about."

Leo cleared his throat. "About that . . . she kind of appeared to me back in Detroit, in a pool of Porta-Potty sludge."

Jason wasn't sure he'd heard that right. "Did you say . . . Porta-Potty?"

Leo told them about the big face in the factory yard. "I don't know if she's completely unkillable," he said, "but she cannot be defeated by toilet seats. I can vouch for that. She wanted me to betray you guys, and I was like, 'Pfft, right, I'm gonna listen to a face in the potty sludge.'"

"She's trying to divide us." Piper slipped her arms from around Jason's waist. He could sense her tension without even looking at her.

"What's wrong?" he asked.

"I just . . . Why are they toying with us? Who is this lady, and how is she connected to Enceladus?"

"Enceladus?" Jason didn't think he'd heard that name before.

"I mean . . ." Piper's voice quavered. "That's one of the giants. Just one of the names I could remember."

Jason got the feeling there was a lot more bothering her, but he decided not to press her. She'd had a rough morning.

Leo scratched his head. "Well, I dunno about Enchiladas—"

"Enceladus," Piper corrected.

"Whatever. But Old Potty Face mentioned another name. Porpoise Fear, or something?"

"Porphyrion?" Piper asked. "He was the giant king, I think."

Jason envisioned that dark spire in the old reflecting pool —growing larger as Hera got weaker. "I'm going to take a wild guess," he said. "In the old stories, Porphyrion kidnapped Hera. That was the first shot in the war between the giants and the gods."

"I think so," Piper agreed. "But those myths are really garbled and conflicted. It's almost like nobody wanted that story to survive. I just remember there was a war, and the giants were almost impossible to kill."

"Heroes and gods had to work together," Jason said. "That's what Hera told me."

"Kind of hard to do," Leo grumbled, "if the gods won't even talk to us."

They flew west, and Jason became lost in his thoughts—all of them bad. He wasn't sure how much time passed before the dragon dove through a break in the clouds, and below them, glittering in the winter sun, was a city at the edge of a massive lake. A crescent of skyscrapers lined the shore. Behind them, stretching out to the western horizon, was a vast grid of snow-covered neighborhoods and roads.

"Chicago," Jason said.

He thought about what Hera had said in his dream. His worst mortal enemy would be waiting here. If he was going to die, it would be by her hand.

"One problem down," Leo said. "We got here alive. Now, how do we find the storm spirits?"

Jason saw a flash of movement below them. At first he thought it was a small plane, but it was too small, too dark and fast. The thing spiraled toward the skyscrapers, weaving and changing shape—and, just for a moment it became the smoky figure of a horse.

"How about we follow that one," Jason suggested, "and see where it goes?"

XXVI

JASON

JASON WAS AFRAID THEY'D LOSE THEIR TARGET. The *ventus* moved like...well, like the wind.

"Speed up!" he urged.

"Bro," Leo said, "if I get any closer, he'll spot us. Bronze dragon ain't exactly a stealth plane."

"Slow down!" Piper yelped.

The storm spirit dove into the grid of downtown streets. Festus tried to follow, but his wingspan was way too wide. His left wing clipped the edge of a building, slicing off a stone gargoyle before Leo pulled up.

"Get above the buildings," Jason suggested. "We'll track him from there."

"You want to drive this thing?" Leo grumbled, but he did what Jason asked.

After a few minutes, Jason spotted the storm spirit again, zipping through the streets with no apparent purpose—blowing over pedestrians, ruffling flags, making cars swerve.

"Oh great," Piper said. "There're two."

She was right. A second *ventus* blasted around the corner of the Renaissance Hotel and linked up with the first. They wove together in a chaotic dance, shooting to the top of a skyscraper, bending a radio tower, and diving back down toward the street.

"Those guys do *not* need any more caffeine," Leo said.

"I guess Chicago's a good place to hang out," Piper said. "Nobody's going to question a couple more evil winds."

"More than a couple," Jason said. "Look."

The dragon circled over a wide avenue next to a lakeside park. Storm spirits were converging—at least a dozen of them, whirling around a big public art installation.

"Which one do you think is Dylan?" Leo asked. "I wanna throw something at him."

But Jason focused on the art installation. The closer they got to it, the faster his heart beat. It was just a public fountain, but it was unpleasantly familiar. Two five-story monoliths rose from either end of a long granite reflecting pool. The monoliths seemed to be built of video screens, flashing the combined image of a giant face that spewed water into the pool.

Maybe it was just a coincidence, but it looked like a high-tech, super-size version of that ruined reflecting pool he'd seen in his dreams, with those two dark masses jutting from either end. As Jason watched, the image on the screens changed to a woman's face with her eyes closed.

"Leo . . ." he said nervously.

"I see her," Leo said. "I don't like her, but I see her."

Then the screens went dark. The *venti* swirled together into a single funnel cloud and skittered across the fountain, kicking up a waterspout almost as high as the monoliths. They got to its center, popped off a drain cover, and disappeared underground.

"Did they just go down a drain?" Piper asked. "How are we supposed to follow them?"

"Maybe we shouldn't," Leo said. "That fountain thing is giving me seriously bad vibes. And aren't we supposed to, like, beware the earth?"

Jason felt the same way, but they had to follow. It was their only way forward. They had to find Hera, and they now had only two days until the solstice.

"Put us down in that park," he suggested. "We'll check it out on foot."

Festus landed in an open area between the lake and the skyline. The signs said Grant Park, and Jason imagined it would've been a nice place in the summer; but now it was a field of ice, snow, and salted walkways. The dragon's hot metal feet hissed as they touched down. Festus flapped his wings unhappily and shot fire into the sky, but there was no one around to notice. The wind coming off the lake was bitter cold. Anyone with sense would be inside. Jason's eyes stung so badly, he could barely see.

They dismounted, and Festus the dragon stomped his feet. One of his ruby eyes flickered, so it looked like he was blinking.

"Is that normal?" Jason asked.

Leo pulled a rubber mallet from his tool bag. He whacked the dragon's bad eye, and the light went back to normal. "Yes," Leo said. "Festus can't hang around here, though, in the middle of the park. They'll arrest him for loitering. Maybe if I had a dog whistle..."

He rummaged in his tool belt, but came up with nothing.

"Too specialized?" he guessed. "Okay, give me a safety whistle. They got that in lots of machine shops."

This time, Leo pulled out a big plastic orange whistle. "Coach Hedge would be jealous! Okay, Festus, listen." Leo blew the whistle. The shrill sound probably rolled all the way across Lake Michigan. "You hear that, come find me, okay? Until then, you fly wherever you want. Just try not to barbecue any pedestrians."

The dragon snorted—hopefully in agreement. Then he spread his wings and launched into the air.

Piper took one step and winced. "Ah!"

"Your ankle?" Jason felt bad he'd forgotten about her injury back in the Cyclops factory. "That nectar we gave you might be wearing off."

"It's fine." She shivered, and Jason remembered his promise to get her a new snowboarding coat. He hoped he lived long enough to find her one. She took a few more steps with only a slight limp, but Jason could tell she was trying not to grimace.

"Let's get out of the wind," he suggested.

"Down a drain?" Piper shuddered. "Sounds cozy."

They wrapped themselves up as best they could and headed toward the fountain.

• • •

According to the plaque, it was called Crown Fountain. All the water had emptied out except for a few patches that were starting to freeze. It didn't seem right to Jason that the fountain would have water in it in the winter anyway. Then again, those big monitors had flashed the face of their mysterious enemy Dirt Woman. Nothing about this place was right.

They stepped to the center of the pool. No spirits tried to stop them. The giant monitor walls stayed dark. The drain hole was easily big enough for a person, and a maintenance ladder led down into the gloom.

Jason went first. As he climbed, he braced himself for horrible sewer smells, but it wasn't that bad. The ladder dropped into a brickwork tunnel running north to south. The air was warm and dry, with only a trickle of water on the floor.

Piper and Leo climbed down after him.

"Are all sewers this nice?" Piper wondered.

"No," Leo said. "Trust me."

Jason frowned. "How do you know—"

"Hey, man, I ran away six times. I've slept in some weird places, okay? Now, which way do we go?"

Jason tilted his head, listening, then pointed south. "That way."

"How can you be sure?" Piper asked.

"There's a draft blowing south," Jason said. "Maybe the *venti* went with the flow."

It wasn't much of a lead, but nobody offered anything better.

Unfortunately, as soon as they started walking, Piper stumbled. Jason had to catch her.

"Stupid ankle," she cursed.

"Let's rest," Jason decided. "We could all use it. We've been going nonstop for over a day. Leo, can you pull any food from that tool belt besides breath mints?"

"Thought you'd never ask. Chef Leo is on it!"

Piper and Jason sat on a brick ledge while Leo shuffled through his pack.

Jason was glad to rest. He was still tired and dizzy, and hungry, too. But mostly, he wasn't eager to face whatever lay ahead. He turned his gold coin in his fingers.

If you are to die, Hera had warned, *it will be by her hand.*

Whoever "her" was. After Khione, the Cyclops mother, and the weird sleeping lady, the last thing Jason needed was another psycho villainess in his life.

"It wasn't your fault," Piper said.

He looked at her blankly. "What?"

"Getting jumped by the Cyclopes," she said. "It wasn't your fault."

He looked down at the coin in his palm. "I was stupid. I left you alone and walked into a trap. I should've known...."

He didn't finish. There were too many things he should have known—who he was, how to fight monsters, how Cyclopes lured their victims by mimicking voices and hiding in shadows and a hundred other tricks. All that information was supposed to be in his head. He could feel the places it should be—like empty pockets. If Hera wanted him to succeed, why had she stolen the memories that could help him? She claimed his amnesia had kept him alive, but that made no sense. He was starting to understand why Annabeth had wanted to leave the goddess in her cage.

"Hey." Piper nudged his arm. "Cut yourself some slack. Just because you're the son of Zeus doesn't mean you're a one-man army."

A few feet away, Leo lit a small cooking fire. He hummed as he pulled supplies out of his pack and his tool belt.

In the firelight, Piper's eyes seemed to dance. Jason had been studying them for days now, and he still couldn't decide what color they were.

"I know this must suck for you," he said. "Not just the quest, I mean. The way I appeared on the bus, the Mist messing with your mind, and making you think I was... you know."

She dropped her gaze. "Yeah, well. None of us asked for this. It's not your fault."

She tugged at the little braids on each side of her head. Again, Jason thought how glad he was that she'd lost the Aphrodite blessing. With the makeup and the dress and the perfect hair, she'd looked about twenty-five, glamorous, and completely out of his league. He'd never thought of beauty as a form of power, but that's the way Piper had seemed—*powerful*.

He liked regular Piper better—someone he could hang out with. But the weird thing was, he couldn't quite get that other image out of his head. It hadn't been an illusion. That side of Piper was there too. She just did her best to hide it.

"Back in the factory," Jason said, "you were going to say something about your dad."

She traced her finger over the bricks, almost like she was writing out a scream she didn't want to vocalize. "Was I?"

"Piper," he said, "he's in some kind of trouble, isn't he?"

Over at the fire, Leo stirred some sizzling bell peppers and meat in a pan. "Yeah, baby! Almost there."

Piper looked on the verge of tears. "Jason...I can't talk about it."

"We're your friends. Let us help."

That seemed to make her feel worse. She took a shaky breath. "I wish I could, but—"

"And bingo!" Leo announced.

He came over with three plates stacked on his arms like a waiter. Jason had no idea where he'd gotten all the food, or how he'd put it together so fast, but it looked amazing: pepper and beef tacos with chips and salsa.

"Leo," Piper said in amazement. "How did you—?"

"Chef Leo's Taco Garage is fixing you up!" he said proudly. "And by the way, it's tofu, not beef, beauty queen, so don't freak. Just dig in!"

Jason wasn't sure about tofu, but the tacos tasted as good as they smelled. While they ate, Leo tried to lighten the mood and joke around. Jason was grateful Leo was with them. It made being with Piper a little less intense and uncomfortable. At the same time, he kind of wished he *was* alone with her; but he chided himself for feeling that way.

After Piper ate, Jason encouraged her to get some sleep. Without another word, she curled up and put her head in his lap. In two seconds she was snoring.

Jason looked up at Leo, who was obviously trying not to laugh.

They sat in silence for a few minutes, drinking lemonade Leo had made from canteen water and powdered mix.

"Good, huh?" Leo grinned.

"You should start a stand," Jason said. "Make some serious coin."

But as he stared at the embers of the fire, something began to bother him. "Leo...about this fire stuff you can do...is it true?"

Leo's smile faltered. "Yeah, well..." He opened his hand. A small ball of flame burst to life, dancing across his palm.

"That is so cool," Jason said. "Why didn't you say anything?"

Leo closed his hand and the fire went out. "Didn't want to look like a freak."

"I have lightning and wind powers," Jason reminded him. "Piper can turn beautiful and charm people into giving her BMWs. You're no more a freak than we are. And, hey, maybe you can fly, too. Like jump off a building and yell, 'Flame on!'"

Leo snorted. "If I did that, you would see a flaming kid falling to his death, and I would be yelling something a little stronger than 'Flame on!' Trust me, Hephaestus cabin doesn't see fire powers as cool. Nyssa told me they're super rare. When a demigod like me comes around, bad things happen. *Really* bad."

"Maybe it's the other way around," Jason suggested. "Maybe people with special gifts show up when bad things are happening because that's when they're needed most."

Leo cleared away the plates. "Maybe. But I'm telling you . . . it's not always a gift."

Jason fell silent. "You're talking about your mom, aren't you? The night she died."

Leo didn't answer. He didn't have to. The fact that he was quiet, not joking around—that told Jason enough.

"Leo, her death wasn't your fault. Whatever happened that night—it wasn't because you could summon fire. This Dirt Woman, whoever she is, has been trying to ruin you for years, mess up your confidence, take away everything you care about. She's trying to make you feel like a failure. You're not. You're important."

"That's what she said." Leo looked up, his eyes full of pain. "She said I was meant to do something important—something that would make or break that big prophecy about the seven demigods. That's what scares me. I don't know if I'm up to it."

Jason wanted to tell him everything would be all right, but it would've sounded fake. Jason didn't know *what* would happen. They were demigods, which meant sometimes things didn't end okay. Sometimes you got eaten by the Cyclops.

If you asked most kids, "Hey, you want to summon fire or lightning or magical makeup?" they'd think it sounded pretty cool. But those powers went along with hard stuff, like sitting in a sewer in the middle of winter, running from monsters, losing your memory, watching your friends almost get cooked, and having dreams that warned you of your own death.

Leo poked at the remnants of his fire, turning over red-hot

coals with his bare hand. "You ever wonder about the other four demigods? I mean... if we're three of the ones from the Great Prophecy, who are the others? Where are they?"

Jason had thought about it, all right, but he tried to push it out of his mind. He had a horrible suspicion that *he* would be expected to lead those other demigods, and he was afraid he would fail.

You'll tear each other apart, Boreas had promised.

Jason had been trained never to show fear. He was sure of that from his dream with the wolves. He was supposed to act confident, even if he didn't feel it. But Leo and Piper were depending on him, and he was terrified of failing them. If he had to lead a group of six—six who might not get along—that would be even worse.

"I don't know," he said at last. "I guess the other four will show up when the time is right. Who knows? Maybe they're on some other quest right now."

Leo grunted. "I bet their sewer is nicer than ours."

The draft picked up, blowing toward the south end of the tunnel.

"Get some rest, Leo," Jason said. "I'll take first watch."

It was hard to measure time, but Jason figured his friends slept about four hours. Jason didn't mind. Now that he was resting, he didn't really feel the need for more sleep. He'd been conked out long enough on the dragon. Plus, he needed time to think about the quest, his sister Thalia, and Hera's warnings. He also didn't mind Piper's using him for a pillow. She had a cute way of breathing when she slept—inhaling through the nose, exhaling with a little puff through the mouth. He was almost disappointed when she woke up.

Finally they broke camp and started down the tunnel.

It twisted and turned and seemed to go on forever. Jason wasn't sure what to expect at the end—a dungeon, a mad scientist's lab, or maybe a sewer reservoir where all Porta-Potty sludge ends up, forming an evil toilet face large enough to swallow the world.

Instead, they found polished steel elevator doors, each one engraved with a cursive letter *M*. Next to the elevator was a directory, like for a department store.

"M for Macy's?" Piper guessed. "I think they have one in downtown Chicago."

"Or Monocle Motors still?" Leo said. "Guys, read the directory. It's messed up."

Parking, Kennels, Main Entrance	Sewer Level
Furnishings and Café M	1
Women's Fashion and Magical Appliances	2
Men's Wear and Weaponry	3
Cosmetics, Potions, Poisons & Sundries	4

"Kennels for what?" Piper said. "And what kind of department store has its entrance in a sewer?"

"Or sells poisons," Leo said. "Man, what does 'sundries' even mean? Is that like underwear?"

Jason took a deep breath. "When in doubt, start at the top."

• • •

The doors slid open on the fourth floor, and the scent of perfume wafted into the elevator. Jason stepped out first, sword ready.

"Guys," he said. "You've got to see this."

Piper joined him and caught her breath. "This is *not* Macy's."

The department store looked like the inside of a kaleidoscope. The entire ceiling was a stained glass mosaic with astrological signs around a giant sun. The daylight streaming through it washed everything in a thousand different colors. The upper floors made a ring of balconies around a huge central atrium, so they could see all the way down to the ground floor. Gold railings glittered so brightly, they were hard to look at.

Aside from the stained glass ceiling and the elevator, Jason couldn't see any other windows or doors, but two sets of glass escalators ran between the levels. The carpeting was a riot of oriental patterns and colors, and the racks of merchandise were just as bizarre. There was too much to take in at once, but Jason saw normal stuff like shirt racks and shoe trees mixed in with armored manikins, beds of nails, and fur coats that seemed to be moving.

Leo stepped to the railing and looked down. "Check it out."

In the middle of the atrium a fountain sprayed water twenty feet into the air, changing color from red to yellow to blue. The pool glittered with gold coins, and on either side of the fountain stood a gilded cage—like an oversize canary cage.

Inside one, a miniature hurricane swirled, and lightning flashed. Somebody had imprisoned the storm spirits, and the cage shuddered as they tried to get out. In the other, frozen like a statue, was a short, buff satyr, holding a tree-branch club.

"Coach Hedge!" Piper said. "We've got to get down there."

A voice said, "May I help you find something?"

All three of them jumped back.

A woman had just *appeared* in front of them. She wore an elegant black dress with diamond jewelry, and she looked like a retired fashion model—maybe fifty years old, though it was hard for Jason to judge. Her long dark hair swept over one shoulder, and her face was gorgeous in that surreal super-model way—thin and haughty and cold, not quite human. With their long red-painted nails, her fingers looked more like talons.

She smiled. "I'm so happy to see new customers. How may I help you?"

Leo glanced at Jason like, *All yours*.

"Um," Jason started, "is this your store?"

The woman nodded. "I found it abandoned, you know. I understand so many stores are, these days. I decided it would make the perfect place. I love collecting tasteful objects, helping people, and offering quality goods at a reasonable price. So this seemed a good...how do you say...first acquisition in this country."

She spoke with a pleasing accent, but Jason couldn't guess where from. Clearly she wasn't hostile, though. Jason started to relax. Her voice was rich and exotic. Jason wanted to hear more.

"So you're new to America?" he asked.

"I am...new," the woman agreed. "I am the Princess of Colchis. My friends call me Your Highness. Now, what are you looking for?"

Jason had heard of rich foreigners buying American department stores. Of course most of the time they didn't sell poisons, living fur coats, storm spirits, or satyrs, but still —with a nice voice like that, the Princess of Colchis couldn't be all bad.

Piper poked him in the ribs. "Jason..."

"Um, right. Actually, Your Highness..." He pointed to the gilded cage on the first floor. "That's our friend down t here, Gleeson Hedge. The satyr. Could we...have him back, please?"

"Of course!" the princess agreed immediately. "I would love to show you my inventory. First, may I know your names?"

Jason hesitated. It seemed like a bad idea to give out their names. A memory tugged at the back of his mind—something Hera had warned him about, but it seemed fuzzy.

On the other hand, Her Highness was on the verge of cooperating. If they could get what they wanted without a fight, that would be better. Besides, this lady didn't seem like an enemy.

Piper started to say, "Jason, I wouldn't—"

"This is Piper," he said. "This is Leo. I'm Jason."

The princess fixed her eyes on him and, just for a moment,

her face literally glowed, blazing with so much anger, Jason could see her skull beneath her skin. Jason's mind was getting blurrier, but he knew something didn't seem right. Then the moment passed, and Her Highness looked like a normal elegant woman again, with a cordial smile and a soothing voice.

"Jason. What an interesting name," she said, her eyes as cold as the Chicago wind. "I think we'll have to make a special deal for you. Come, children. Let's go shopping."

XXVII

PIPER

Piper wanted to run for the elevator.

Her second choice: attack the weird princess now, because she was sure a fight was coming. The way the lady's face glowed when she'd heard Jason's name had been bad enough. Now Her Highness was smiling like nothing had happened, and Jason and Leo didn't seem to think anything was wrong.

The princess gestured toward the cosmetics counter. "Shall we start with the potions?"

"Cool," Jason said.

"Guys," Piper interrupted, "we're here to get the storm spirits and Coach Hedge. If this—*princess*—is really our friend—"

"Oh, I'm better than a friend, my dear," Her Highness said. "I'm a saleswoman." Her diamonds sparkled, and her eyes glittered like a snake's—cold and dark. "Don't worry. We'll work our way down to the first floor, eh?"

Leo nodded eagerly. "Sure, yeah! That sounds okay. Right, Piper?"

Piper did her best to stare daggers at him: *No, it is not okay!*

"Of course it's okay." Her Highness put her hands on Leo's and Jason's shoulders and steered them toward the cosmetics. "Come along, boys."

Piper didn't have much choice except to follow.

She hated department stores—mostly because she'd gotten caught stealing from several of them. Well, not exactly *caught*, and not exactly *stealing*. She'd talked salesmen into giving her computers, new boots, a gold ring, once even a lawn mower, though she had no idea why she wanted one. She never kept the stuff. She just did it to get her dad's attention. Usually she talked her neighborhood UPS guy into taking the stuff back. But of course the salesmen she duped always came to their senses and called the police, who eventually tracked her down.

Anyway, she wasn't thrilled to be back in a department store—especially one run by a crazy princess who glowed in the dark.

"And here," the princess said, "is the finest assortment of magical mixtures anywhere."

The counter was crammed with bubbling beakers and smoking vials on tripods. Lining the display shelves were crystal flasks—some shaped like swans or honey bear dispensers. The liquids inside were every color, from glowing white to polka-dotted. And the smells—ugh! Some were pleasant, like fresh-baked cookies or roses, but they were mixed with the scents of burning tires, skunk spray, and gym lockers.

The princess pointed to a bloodred vial—a simple test tube with a cork stopper. "This one will heal any disease."

"Even cancer?" Leo asked. "Leprosy? Hangnails?"

"Any disease, sweet boy. And this vial"—she pointed to a swan-shaped container with blue liquid inside—"will kill you very painfully."

"Awesome," Jason said. His voice sounded dazed and sleepy.

"Jason," Piper said. "We've got a job to do. Remember?" She tried to put power into her words, to snap him out of his trance with charmspeak, but her voice sounded shaky even to her. This princess woman scared her too much, made her confidence crumble, just the way she'd felt back in the Aphrodite cabin with Drew.

"Job to do," Jason muttered. "Sure. But shopping first, okay?"

The princess beamed at him. "Then we have potions for resisting fire—"

"Got that covered," Leo said.

"Indeed?" The princess studied Leo's face more closely. "You don't appear to be wearing my trademark sunscreen… but no matter. We also have potions that cause blindness, insanity, sleep, or—"

"Wait." Piper was still staring at the red vial. "Could that potion cure lost memory?"

The princess narrowed her eyes. "Possibly. Yes. Quite

possibly. Why, my dear? Have you forgotten something important?"

Piper tried to keep her expression neutral, but if that vial could cure Jason's memory . . .

Do I really want that? she wondered.

If Jason found out who he was, he might not even be her friend. Hera had taken away his memories for a reason. She'd told him it was the only way he'd survive at Camp Half-Blood. What if Jason found out that he was their enemy, or something? He might come out of his amnesia and decide he hated Piper. He might have a girlfriend wherever he came from.

It doesn't matter, she decided, which kind of surprised her.

Jason always looked so anguished when he tried to remember things. Piper hated seeing him that way. She wanted to help him because she cared about him, even if that meant losing him. And maybe it would make this trip through Her Craziness's department store worthwhile.

"How much?" Piper asked.

The princess got a faraway look in her eyes. "Well, now . . . The price is always tricky. I love helping people. Honestly, I do. And I always keep my bargains, but sometimes people try to cheat me." Her gaze drifted to Jason. "Once, for instance, I met a handsome young man who wanted a treasure from my father's kingdom. We made a bargain, and I promised to help him steal it."

"From your own dad?" Jason still looked half in a trance, but the idea seemed to bother him.

"Oh, don't worry," the princess said. "I demanded a high

price. The young man had to take me away with him. He was quite good-looking, dashing, strong..." She looked at Piper. "I'm sure, my dear, you understand how one might be attracted to such a hero, and want to help him."

Piper tried to control her emotions, but she probably blushed. She got the creepiest feeling the princess could read her thoughts.

She also found the princess's story disturbingly familiar. Pieces of old myths she'd read with her dad started coming together, but this woman couldn't be the one she was thinking of.

"At any rate," Her Highness continued, "my hero had to do many impossible tasks, and I'm not bragging when I say he couldn't have done them without me. I betrayed my own family to win the hero his prize. And still he cheated me of my payment."

"Cheated?" Jason frowned, as if trying to remember something important.

"That's messed up," Leo said.

Her Highness patted his cheek affectionately. "I'm sure you don't need to worry, Leo. You seem honest. You would always pay a fair price, wouldn't you?"

Leo nodded. "What were we buying again? I'll take two."

Piper broke in: "So, the vial, Your Highness—how much?"

The princess assessed Piper's clothes, her face, her posture, as if putting a price tag on one slightly used demigod.

"Would you give anything for it, my dear?" the princess asked. "I sense that you would."

The words washed over Piper as powerfully as a good

surfing wave. The force of the suggestion nearly lifted her off her feet. She wanted to pay any price. She wanted to say yes.

Then her stomach twisted. Piper realized she was being charmspoken. She'd sensed something like it before, when Drew spoke at the campfire, but this was a thousand times more potent. No wonder her friends were dazed. Was *this* what people felt when Piper used charmspeak? A feeling of guilt settled over her.

She summoned all her willpower. "No, I won't pay *any* price. But a fair price, maybe. After that, we need to leave. Right, guys?"

Just for a moment, her words seemed to have some effect. The boys looked confused.

"Leave?" Jason said.

"You mean . . . after shopping?" Leo asked.

Piper wanted to scream, but the princess tilted her head, examining Piper with newfound respect.

"Impressive," the princess said. "Not many people could resist my suggestions. Are you a child of Aphrodite, my dear? Ah, yes—I should have seen it. No matter. Perhaps we should shop a while longer before you decide what to buy, eh?"

"But the vial—"

"Now, boys." She turned to Jason and Leo. Her voice was so much more powerful than Piper's, so full of confidence, Piper didn't stand a chance. "Would you like to see more?"

"Sure," Jason said.

"Okay," Leo said.

"Excellent," the princess said. "You'll need all the help you can get if you're to make it to the Bay Area."

Piper's hand moved to her dagger. She thought about her dream of the mountaintop—the scene Enceladus had shown her, a place she knew, where she was supposed to betray her friends in two days.

"The Bay Area?" Piper said. "Why the Bay Area?"

The princess smiled. "Well, that's where they'll die, isn't it?"

Then she led them toward the escalators, Jason and Leo still looking excited to shop.

PIPER

PIPER CORNERED THE PRINCESS as Jason and Leo went off to check out the living fur coats.

"You want them shopping for their deaths?" Piper demanded.

"Mmm." The princess blew dust off a display case of swords. "I'm a seer, my dear. I know your little secret. But we don't want to dwell on that, do we? The boys are having such fun."

Leo laughed as he tried on a hat that seemed to be made from enchanted raccoon fur. Its ringed tail twitched, and its little legs wiggled frantically as Leo walked. Jason was ogling the men's sportswear. Boys interested in shopping for clothes? A definite sign they were under an evil spell.

Piper glared at the princess. "Who are you?"

"I told you, my dear. I'm the Princess of Colchis."

"Where's Colchis?"

The princess's expression turned a little sad. "Where *was*

Colchis, you mean. My father ruled the far shores of the Black Sea, as far to the east as a Greek ship could sail in those days. But Colchis is no more—lost eons ago."

"Eons?" Piper asked. The princess looked no more than fifty, but a bad feeling started settling over Piper—something King Boreas had mentioned back in Quebec. "How old are you?"

The princess laughed. "A lady should avoid asking or answering that question. Let's just say the, ah, immigration process to enter your country took quite a while. My patron finally brought me through. She made all this possible." The princess swept her hand around the department store.

Piper's mouth tasted like metal. "Your patron..."

"Oh, yes. She doesn't bring just anyone through, mind you—only those who have special talents, such as me. And really, she insists on so little—a store entrance that must be underground so she can, ah, monitor my clientele; and a favor now and then. In exchange for a new life? Really, it was the best bargain I'd made in centuries."

Run, Piper thought. *We have to get out of here.*

But before she could even turn her thoughts into words, Jason called, "Hey, check it out!"

From a rack labeled DISTRESSED CLOTHING, he held up a purple T-shirt like the one he'd worn on the school field trip —except this shirt looked as if it had been clawed by tigers.

Jason frowned. "Why does this look so familiar?"

"Jason, it's like *yours,*" Piper said. "Now we really have to leave." But she wasn't sure he could even hear her anymore through the princess's enchantment.

"Nonsense," the princess said. "The boys aren't done, are they? And yes, my dear. Those shirts are very popular—trade-ins from previous customers. It suits you."

Leo picked up an orange Camp Half-Blood tee with a hole through the middle, as if it had been hit by a javelin. Next to that was a dented bronze breastplate pitted with corrosion —acid, maybe?—and a Roman toga slashed to pieces and stained with something that looked disturbingly like dried blood.

"Your Highness," Piper said, trying to control her nerves. "Why don't you tell the boys how you betrayed your family? I'm sure they'd like to hear that story."

Her words didn't have any effect on the princess, but the boys turned, suddenly interested.

"More story?" Leo asked.

"I like more story!" Jason agreed.

The princess flashed Piper an irritated look. "Oh, one will do strange things for love, Piper. You should know that. I fell for that young hero, in fact, because your mother Aphrodite had me under a spell. If it wasn't for her—but I can't hold a grudge against a goddess, can I?"

The princess's tone made her meaning clear: *I can take it out on you.*

"But that hero took you with him when he fled Colchis," Piper remembered. "Didn't he, Your Highness? He married you just as he promised."

The look in the princess's eyes made Piper want to apologize, but she didn't back down.

"At first," Her Highness admitted, "it seemed he would

keep his word. But even after I helped him steal my father's treasure, he *still* needed my help. As we fled, my brother's fleet came after us. His warships overtook us. He would have destroyed us, but I convinced my brother to come aboard our ship first and talk under a flag of truce. He trusted me."

"And you killed your own brother," Piper said, the horrible story all coming back to her, along with a name—an infamous name that began with the letter *M*.

"What?" Jason stirred. For a moment he looked almost like himself. "Killed your own—"

"No," the princess snapped. "Those stories are lies. It was my new husband and his men who killed my brother, though they couldn't have done it without my deception. They threw his body into the sea, and the pursuing fleet had to stop and search for it so they could give my brother a proper burial. This gave us time to get away. All this, I did for my husband. And he forgot our bargain. He betrayed me in the end."

Jason still looked uncomfortable. "What did he do?"

The princess held the sliced-up toga against Jason's chest, as if measuring him for an assassination. "Don't you know the story, my boy? You of all people should. You were named for him."

"Jason," Piper said. "The *original* Jason. But then you're—you should be dead!"

The princess smiled. "As I said, a new life in a new country. Certainly I made mistakes. I turned my back on my own people. I was called a traitor, a thief, a liar, a murderess. But I acted out of love." She turned to the boys and gave them a pitiful look, batting her eyelashes. Piper could feel the sorcery washing over them, taking control more firmly than ever. "Wouldn't you do the same for someone you loved, my dears?"

"Oh, sure," Jason said.

"Okay," Leo said.

"Guys!" Piper ground her teeth in frustration. "Don't you see who she is? Don't you—"

"Let's continue, shall we?" the princess said breezily. "I believe you wanted to talk about a price for the storm spirits —and your satyr."

Leo got distracted on the second floor with the appliances.

"No way," he said. "Is that an armored forge?"

Before Piper could stop him, he hopped off the escalator and ran over to a big oval oven that looked like a barbecue on steroids.

When they caught up with him, the princess said, "You have good taste. This is the H-2000, designed by Hephaestus himself. Hot enough to melt Celestial bronze or Imperial gold."

Jason flinched as if he recognized that term. "Imperial gold?"

The princess nodded. "Yes, my dear. Like that weapon so cleverly concealed in your pocket. To be properly forged, Imperial gold had to be consecrated in the Temple of Jupiter on Capitoline Hill in Rome. Quite a powerful and rare metal, but like the Roman emperors, quite volatile. Be sure never to break that blade. . . ." She smiled pleasantly. "Rome was *after* my time, of course, but I do hear stories. And now over here—this golden throne is one of my finest luxury items.

Hephaestus made it as a punishment for his mother, Hera. Sit in it and you'll be immediately trapped."

Leo apparently took this as an order. He began walking toward it in a trance.

"Leo, don't!" Piper warned.

He blinked. "How much for both?"

"Oh, the seat I could let you have for five great deeds. The forge, seven years of servitude. And for only a bit of your strength—" She led Leo into the appliance section, giving him prices on various items.

Piper didn't want to leave him alone with her, but she had to try reasoning with Jason. She pulled him aside and slapped him across the face.

"Ow," he muttered sleepily. "What was that for?"

"Snap out of it!" Piper hissed.

"What do you mean?"

"She's charmspeaking you. Can't you feel it?"

He knit his eyebrows. "She seems okay."

"She's not okay! She shouldn't even be alive! She was married to Jason—the *other* Jason—three thousand years ago. Remember what Boreas said—something about the souls no longer being confined to Hades? It's not just monsters who can't stay dead. She's come back from the Underworld!"

Jason shook his head uneasily. "She's not a ghost."

"No, she's worse! She's—"

"Children." The princess was back with Leo in tow. "If you please, we will now see what you came for. That is what you want, yes?"

Piper had to choke back a scream. She was tempted to

pull out her dagger and take on this witch herself, but she didn't like her chances—not in the middle of Her Highness's department store while her friends were under a spell. Piper couldn't even be sure they'd take her side in a fight. She had to figure out a better plan.

They took the escalator down to the base of the fountain. For the first time, Piper noticed two large bronze sundials —each about the size of a trampoline—inlaid on the marble tile floor to the north and south of the fountain. The gilded oversize canary cages stood to the east and west, and the farthest one held the storm spirits. They were so densely packed, spinning around like a super-concentrated tornado, that Piper couldn't tell how many there were—dozens, at least.

"Hey," Leo said, "Coach Hedge looks okay!"

They ran to the nearest canary cage. The old satyr seemed to have been petrified at the moment he was sucked into the sky above the Grand Canyon. He was frozen mid-shout, his club raised over his head like he was ordering the gym class to drop and give him fifty. His curly hair stuck up at odd angles. If Piper just concentrated on certain details—the bright orange polo shirt, the wispy goatee, the whistle around his neck—she could imagine Coach Hedge as his good old annoying self. But it was hard to ignore the stubby horns on his head, and the fact that he had furry goat legs and hooves instead of workout pants and Nikes.

"Yes," the princess said. "I always keep my wares in good condition. We can certainly barter for the storm spirits and the satyr. A package deal. If we come to terms, I'll even throw in the vial of healing potion, and you can go in peace." She gave Piper a shrewd look. "That's better than starting unpleas-antness, isn't it, dear?"

Don't trust her, warned a voice in her head. If Piper was right about this lady's identity, nobody would be leaving in peace. A fair deal wasn't possible. It was all a trick. But her friends were looking at her, nodding urgently and mouthing, *Say yes!* Piper needed more to time to think.

"We can negotiate," she said.

"Totally!" Leo agreed. "Name your price."

"Leo!" Piper snapped.

The princess chuckled. "Name my price? Perhaps not the best haggling strategy, my boy, but at least you know a thing's value. Freedom is very valuable indeed. You would ask me to release this satyr, who attacked my storm winds—"

"Who attacked us," Piper interjected.

Her Highness shrugged. "As I said, my patron asks me for small favors from time to time. Sending the storm spirits to abduct you—that was one. I assure you it was nothing personal. And no harm done, as you came here, in the end, of your own free will! At any rate, you want the satyr freed, and you want my storm spirits—who are very valuable servants, by the way—so you can hand them over to that tyrant Aeolus. Doesn't seem quite fair, does it? The price will be high."

Piper could see that her friends were ready to offer anything, promise anything. Before they could speak, she played her last card.

"You're Medea," she said. "You helped the original Jason steal the Golden Fleece. You're one of the most evil villains in Greek mythology. Jason, Leo—don't trust her."

Piper put all the intensity she could gather into those words. She was utterly sincere, and it seemed to have some effect. Jason stepped away from the sorceress.

Leo scratched his head and looked around like he was coming out of a dream.

"What are we doing, again?"

"Boys!" The princess spread her hands in a welcoming gesture. Her diamond jewelry glittered, and her painted fingers curled like blood-tipped claws. "It's true, I'm Medea. But I'm so misunderstood. Oh, Piper, my dear, you don't know what it was like for women in the old days. We had no power, no leverage. Often we couldn't even choose our own husbands. But *I* was different. I chose my own destiny by becoming a sorceress. Is that so wrong? I made a pact with Jason: my help to win the fleece, in exchange for his love. A fair deal. He became a famous hero! Without me, he would've died unknown on the shores of Colchis."

Jason—Piper's Jason—scowled. "Then . . . you really did die three thousand years ago? You came back from the Underworld?"

"Death no longer holds me, young hero," Medea said. "Thanks to my patron, I am flesh and blood again."

"You . . . re-formed?" Leo blinked. "Like a monster?"

Medea spread her fingers, and steam hissed from her nails, like water splashed on hot iron. "You have no idea what's happening, do you, my dears? It is so much worse than a stirring of monsters from Tartarus. My patron knows that giants and monsters are not her greatest servants. *I* am mortal. I learn from my mistakes. And now that I have returned to the living, I will not be cheated again. Now, here is my price for what you ask."

"Guys," Piper said. "The original Jason left Medea because she was crazy and bloodthirsty."

"Lies!" Medea said.

"On the way back from Colchis, Jason's ship landed at another kingdom, and Jason agreed to dump Medea and marry the king's daughter."

"After I bore him two children!" Medea said. "Still he broke his promise! I ask you, was that right?"

Jason and Leo dutifully shook their heads, but Piper wasn't through.

"It may not have been right," she said, "but neither was Medea's revenge. She murdered her own children to get back at Jason. She poisoned his new wife and fled the kingdom."

Medea snarled. "An invention to ruin my reputation! The people of the Corinth—that unruly mob—killed my children and drove me out. Jason did nothing to protect me. He robbed me of everything. So yes, I sneaked back into the palace and poisoned his lovely new bride. It was only fair—a suitable price."

"You're insane," Piper said.

"I am the victim!" Medea wailed. "I died with my dreams shattered, but no longer. I know now not to trust heroes. When they come asking for treasures, they will pay a heavy price. Especially when the one asking has the name of Jason!"

The fountain turned bright red. Piper drew her dagger, but her hand was shaking almost too badly to hold it. "Jason, Leo—it's time to go. *Now.*"

"Before you've closed the deal?" Medea asked. "What of your quest, boys? And my price is so easy. Did you know this fountain is magic? If a dead man were to be thrown into it, even if he was chopped to pieces, he would pop back out fully formed—stronger and more powerful than ever."

"Seriously?" Leo asked.

"Leo, she's lying," Piper said. "She did that trick with somebody before—a king, I think. She convinced his daughters to cut him to pieces so he could come out of the water young and healthy again, but it just killed him!"

"Ridiculous," Medea said, and Piper could hear the power charged in every syllable. "Leo, Jason—my price is so simple. Why don't you two fight? If you get injured, or even killed, no problem. We'll just throw you into the fountain and you'll be better than ever. You *do* want to fight, don't you? You resent each other!"

"Guys, no!" Piper said. But they were already glaring at each other, as if it was just dawning on them how they really felt.

Piper had never felt more helpless. Now she understood what real sorcery looked like. She'd always thought magic meant wands and fireballs, but this was worse. Medea didn't just rely on poisons and potions. Her most potent weapon was her voice.

Leo scowled. "Jason's always the star. He always gets the attention and takes me for granted."

"You're annoying, Leo," Jason said. "You never take anything seriously. You can't even fix a dragon."

"Stop!" Piper pleaded, but both drew weapons—Jason his gold sword, and Leo a hammer from his tool belt.

"Let them go, Piper," Medea urged. "I'm doing you a favor. Let it happen now, and it will make your choice so much easier. Enceladus will be pleased. You could have your father back today!"

Medea's charmspeak didn't work on her, but the sorceress still had a persuasive voice. *Her father back today?* Despite her best intentions, Piper wanted that. She wanted her father back so much, it hurt.

"You work for Enceladus," she said.

Medea laughed. "Serve a giant? No. But we all serve the same greater cause—a patron you cannot begin to challenge. Walk away, child of Aphrodite. This does not have to be your death, too. Save yourself, and your father can go free."

Leo and Jason were still facing off, ready to fight, but they looked unsteady and confused—waiting for another order. Part of them had to be resisting, Piper hoped. This went completely against their nature.

"Listen to me, girl." Medea plucked a diamond off her bracelet and threw it into a spray of water from the fountain. As it passed through the multicolored light, Medea said, "O Iris, goddess of the rainbow, show me the office of Tristan McLean."

The mist shimmered, and Piper saw her father's study. Sitting behind his desk, talking on the phone, was her dad's assistant, Jane, in her dark business suit, her hair swirled in a tight bun.

"Hello, Jane," Medea said.

Jane hung up the phone calmly. "How can I help you, ma'am? Hello, Piper."

"You—" Piper was so angry she could hardly talk.

"Yes, child," Medea said. "Your father's assistant. Quite easy to manipulate. An organized mind for a mortal, but incredibly weak."

"Thank you, ma'am," Jane said.

"Don't mention it," Medea said. "I just wanted to congratulate you, Jane. Getting Mr. McLean to leave town so suddenly, take his jet to Oakland without alerting the press or the police—well done! No one seems to know where he's gone. And telling him his daughter's life was on the line— that was a nice touch to get his cooperation."

"Yes," Jane agreed in a bland tone, as if she were sleepwalking. "He was quite cooperative when he believed Piper was in danger."

Piper looked down at her dagger. The blade trembled in her hand. She couldn't use it for a weapon any better than Helen of Troy could, but it was still a looking glass, and what she saw in it was a scared girl with no chance of winning.

"I may have new orders for you, Jane," Medea said. "If the girl cooperates, it may be time for Mr. McLean to come home. Would you arrange a suitable cover story for his absence, just in case? And I imagine the poor man will need some time in a psychiatric hospital."

"Yes, ma'am. I will stand by."

The image faded, and Medea turned to Piper. "There, you see?"

"You lured my dad into a trap," Piper said. "You helped the giant—"

"Oh, please, dear. You'll work yourself into a fit! I've been preparing for this war for years, even before I was brought back to life. I'm a seer, as I said. I can tell the future as well as your little oracle. Years ago, still suffering in the Fields of Punishment, I had a vision of the seven in your so-called Great Prophecy. I saw your friend Leo here, and saw that he would be an important enemy someday. I stirred the consciousness of my patron, gave her this information, and she managed to wake just a little—just enough to visit him."

"Leo's mother," Piper said. "Leo, listen to this! She helped get your mother killed!"

"Uh-huh," Leo mumbled, in a daze. He frowned at his hammer. "So . . . I just attack Jason? That's okay?"

"Perfectly safe," Medea promised. "And Jason, strike him hard. Show me you are worthy of your namesake."

"No!" Piper ordered. She knew it was her last chance. "Jason, Leo—she's tricking you. Put down your weapons."

The sorceress rolled her eyes. "Please, girl. You're no match for me. I trained with my aunt, the immortal Circe. I can drive men mad or heal them with my voice. What hope do these puny young heroes have against me? Now, boys, kill each other!"

"Jason, Leo, listen to me." Piper put all of her emotion into her voice. For years she'd been trying to control herself and not show weakness, but now she poured everything into her words—her fear, her desperation, her anger. She knew she might be signing her dad's death warrant, but she cared too much about her friends to let them hurt each other. "Medea is charming you. It's part of her magic. You are best friends. Don't fight each other. Fight *her!*"

They hesitated, and Piper could feel the spell shatter.

Jason blinked. "Leo, was I just about to stab you?"

"Something about my mother . . . ?" Leo frowned, then turned toward Medea. "You . . . you're working for Dirt Woman. You sent her to the machine shop." He lifted his arm. "Lady, I got a three-pound hammer with your name on it."

"Bah!" Medea sneered. "I'll simply collect payment another way."

She pressed one of the mosaic tiles on the floor, and the building rumbled. Jason swung his sword at Medea, but she dissolved into smoke and reappeared at the base of the escalator.

"You're slow, hero!" She laughed. "Take your frustration out on my pets!"

Before Jason could go after her, the giant bronze sundials at either end of the fountain swung open. Two snarling gold beasts—flesh-and-blood winged dragons—crawled out from the pits below. Each was the size of a camper van, maybe not large compared to Festus, but large enough.

"So that's what's in the kennels," Leo said meekly.

The dragons spread their wings and hissed. Piper could feel the heat coming off their glittering skin. One turned his angry orange eyes on her.

"Don't look them in the eye!" Jason warned. "They'll paralyze you."

"Indeed!" Medea was leisurely riding the escalator up, leaning against the handrail as she watched the fun. "These two dears have been with me a long time—sun dragons, you know, gifts from my grandfather Helios. They pulled my chariot when I left Corinth, and now they will be your destruction. Ta-ta!"

The dragons lunged. Leo and Jason charged to intercept. Piper was amazed how fearlessly the boys attacked—working like a team who had trained together for years.

Medea was almost to the second floor, where she'd be able to choose from a wide assortment of deadly appliances.

"Oh, no, you don't," Piper growled, and took off after her.

When Medea spotted Piper, she started climbing in earnest. She was quick for a three-thousand-year-old lady. Piper climbed at top speed, taking the steps three at a time, and still she couldn't catch her. Medea didn't stop at floor two. She hopped the next escalator and continued to ascend.

The potions, Piper thought. *Of course that's what she would go for. She was famous for potions.*

Down below, Piper heard the battle raging. Leo was blowing his safety whistle, and Jason was yelling to keep the dragons' attention. Piper didn't dare look—not while she was running with a dagger in her hand. She could just see herself tripping and stabbing herself in the nose. That would be super heroic.

She grabbed a shield from an armored manikin on floor three and continued to climb. She imagined Coach Hedge yelling in her mind, just like back in gym class at Wilderness School: *Move it, McLean! You call that escalator-climbing?*

She reached the top floor, breathing hard, but she was too late. Medea had reached the potions counter.

The sorceress grabbed a swan-shaped vial—the blue one that caused painful death—and Piper did the only thing that came to mind. She threw her shield.

Medea turned triumphantly just in time to get hit in the chest by a fifty-pound metal Frisbee. She stumbled backward, crashing over the counter, breaking vials and knocking down shelves. When the sorceress stood from the wreckage, her dress was stained a dozen different colors. Many of the stains were smoldering and glowing.

"Fool!" Medea wailed. "Do you have any idea what so many potions will do when mixed?"

"Kill you?" Piper said hopefully.

The carpet began to steam around Medea's feet. She coughed, and her face contorted in pain—or was she faking?

Below, Leo called, "Jason, help!"

Piper risked a quick look, and almost sobbed in despair. One of the dragons had Leo pinned to the floor. It was baring its fangs, ready to snap. Jason was all the way across the room battling the other dragon, much too far away to assist.

"You've doomed us all!" Medea screamed. Smoke was rolling across the carpet as the stain spread, throwing sparks and setting fires in the clothing racks. "You have only seconds before this concoction consumes everything and destroys the building. There's no time—"

CRASH! The stained glass ceiling splintered in a rain of multicolored shards, and Festus the bronze dragon dropped into the department store.

He hurtled into the fray, snatching up a sun dragon in each claw. Only now did Piper appreciate just how big and strong their metal friend was.

"That's my boy!" Leo yelled.

Festus flew halfway up the atrium, then hurled the sun dragons into the pits they'd come from. Leo raced to the fountain and pressed the marble tile, closing the sundials. They shuddered as the dragons banged against them, trying to get out, but for the moment they were contained.

Medea cursed in some ancient language. The whole fourth floor was on fire now. The air filled with noxious gas. Even with the roof open, Piper could feel the heat intensifying. She backed up to the edge of the railing, keeping her dagger pointed toward Medea.

"I will not be abandoned again!" The sorceress knelt and snatched up the red healing potion, which had somehow survived the crash. "You want your boyfriend's memory restored? Take me with you!"

Piper glanced behind her. Leo and Jason were on board Festus's back. The bronze dragon flapped his mighty wings, snatched the two cages with the satyr and the storm spirits in his claws, and began to ascend.

The building rumbled. Fire and the smoke curled up the walls, melting the railings, turning the air to acid.

"You'll never survive your quest without me!" Medea growled. "Your boy hero will stay ignorant forever, and your father will die. Take me with you!"

For one heartbeat, Piper was tempted. Then she saw Medea's grim smile. The sorceress was confident in her powers of persuasion, confident that she could always make a deal, always escape and win in the end.

"Not today, witch." Piper jumped over the side. She plummeted for only a second before Leo and Jason caught her, hauling her aboard the dragon.

She heard Medea screaming in rage as they soared through the broken roof and over downtown Chicago. Then the department store exploded behind them.

XXIX

LEO

LEO KEPT LOOKING BACK. HE HALF EXPECTED to see those nasty sun dragons toting a flying chariot with a screaming magical saleswoman throwing potions, but nothing followed them.

He steered the dragon toward the southwest. Eventually, the smoke from the burning department store faded in the distance, but Leo didn't relax until the suburbs of Chicago gave way to snowy fields, and the sun began to set.

"Good job, Festus." He patted the dragon's metal hide. "You did awesome."

The dragon shuddered. Gears popped and clicked in his neck.

Leo frowned. He didn't like those noises. If the control disk was failing again—No, hopefully it was something minor. Something he could fix.

"I'll give you a tune-up next time we land," Leo promised. "You've earned some motor oil and Tabasco sauce."

Festus whirled his teeth, but even that sounded weak. He flew at a steady pace, his great wings angling to catch the wind, but he was carrying a heavy load. Two cages in his claws plus three people on his back—the more Leo thought about it, the more worried he got. Even metal dragons had limits.

"Leo." Piper patted his shoulder. "You feeling okay?"

"Yeah . . . not bad for a brainwashed zombie." He hoped he didn't look as embarrassed as he felt. "Thanks for saving us back there, beauty queen. If you hadn't talked me out of that spell—"

"Don't worry about it," Piper said.

But Leo worried a lot. He felt terrible about how easily Medea had set him against his best friend. And those feelings hadn't come from nowhere—his resentment of the way Jason always got the spotlight and didn't really seem to need him. Leo did feel that way sometimes, even if he wasn't proud of it.

What bothered him more was the news about his mom. Medea had seen the future down in the Underworld. That was how her patron, the woman in the black earthen robes, had come to the machine shop seven years ago to scare him, ruin his life. That's how his mother had died—because of something Leo might do someday. So in a weird way, even if his fire powers weren't to blame, Mom's death was *still* his fault.

When they had left Medea in that exploding store, Leo had felt a little too good. He hoped she wouldn't make it out, and would go right back to the Fields of Punishment, where she belonged. Those feelings didn't make him proud, either.

And if souls were coming back from the Underworld . . . was it possible Leo's mom could be brought back?

He tried to put the idea aside. That was Frankenstein thinking. It wasn't natural. It wasn't right. Medea might've been brought back to life, but she hadn't seemed quite human, with the hissing nails and the glowing head and whatnot.

No, Leo's mom had passed on. Thinking any other way would just drive Leo nuts. Still, the thought kept poking at him, like an echo of Medea's voice.

"We're going to have to put down soon," he warned his friends. "Couple more hours, maybe, to make sure Medea's not following us. I don't think Festus can fly much longer than that."

"Yeah," Piper agreed. "Coach Hedge probably wants to get out of his canary cage, too. Question is—where are we going?"

"The Bay Area," Leo guessed. His memories of the department store were fuzzy, but he seemed to remember hearing that. "Didn't Medea say something about Oakland?"

Piper didn't respond for so long, Leo wondered if he'd said something wrong.

"Piper's dad," Jason put in. "Something's happened to your dad, right? He got lured into some kind of trap."

Piper let out a shaky breath. "Look, Medea said you would both *die* in the Bay Area. And besides . . . even if we went there, the Bay Area is huge! First we need to find Aeolus and drop off the storm spirits. Boreas said Aeolus was the only one who could tell us exactly where to go."

Leo grunted. "So how do we find Aeolus?"

Jason leaned forward. "You mean you don't see it?" He pointed ahead of them, but Leo didn't see anything except clouds and the lights of a few towns glowing in the dusk.

"What?" Leo asked.

"That . . . whatever it is," Jason said. "In the air."

Leo glanced back. Piper looked just as confused as he was.

"Right," Leo said. "Could you be more specific on the 'whatever-it-is' part?"

"Like a vapor trail," Jason said. "Except it's glowing. Really faint, but it's definitely there. We've been following it since Chicago, so I figured you saw it."

Leo shook his head. "Maybe Festus can sense it. You think Aeolus made it?"

"Well, it's a magic trail in the wind," Jason said. "Aeolus is the wind god. I think he knows we've got prisoners for him. He's telling us where to fly."

"Or it's another trap," Piper said.

Her tone worried Leo. She didn't just sound nervous. She sounded broken with despair, like they'd already sealed their fate, and like it was her fault.

"Pipes, you all right?" he asked.

"Don't call me that."

"Okay, fine. You don't like any of the names I make up for you. But if your dad's in trouble and we can help—"

"You can't," she said, her voice getting shakier. "Look, I'm tired. If you don't mind . . ."

She leaned back against Jason and closed her eyes.

All right, Leo thought—pretty clear signal she didn't want to talk.

They flew in silence for a while. Festus seemed to know where he was going. He kept his course, gently curving toward the southwest and hopefully Aeolus's fortress. Another wind god to visit, a whole new flavor of crazy— Oh, boy, Leo couldn't wait.

He had way too much on his mind to sleep, but now that he was out of danger, his body had different ideas. His energy level was crashing. The monotonous beat of the dragon's wings made his eyes feel heavy. His head started to nod.

"Catch a few Z's," Jason said. "It's cool. Hand me the reins."

"Nah, I'm okay—"

"Leo," Jason said, "you're not a machine. Besides, I'm the only one who can see the vapor trail. I'll make sure we stay on course."

Leo's eyes started to close on their own. "All right. Maybe just . . ."

He didn't finish the sentence before slumping forward against the dragon's warm neck.

In his dream, he heard a voice full of static, like a bad AM radio: "Hello? Is this thing working?"

Leo's vision came into focus—sort of. Everything was hazy and gray, with bands of interference running across his sight. He'd never dreamed with a bad connection before.

He seemed to be in a workshop. Out of the corners of his eyes he saw bench saws, metal lathes, and tool cages. A forge glowed cheerfully against one wall.

It wasn't the camp forge—too big. Not Bunker 9—much warmer and more comfortable, obviously not abandoned.

Then Leo realized something was blocking the middle of his view—something large and fuzzy, and so close, Leo had to cross his eyes to see it properly. It was a large ugly face.

"Holy mother!" he yelped.

The face backed away and came into focus. Staring down at him was a bearded man in grimy blue coveralls. His face was lumpy and covered with welts, as if he'd been bitten by a million bees, or dragged across gravel. Possibly both.

"Humph," the man said. "Holy *father*, boy. I should think you'd know the difference."

Leo blinked. "Hephaestus?"

Being in the presence of his father for the first time, Leo probably should've been speechless or awestruck or something. But after what he'd been through the last couple of days, with Cyclopes and a sorceress and a face in the potty sludge, all Leo felt was a surge of complete annoyance.

"Now you show up?" he demanded. "After fifteen years? Great parenting, Fur Face. Where do you get off sticking your ugly nose into my dreams?"

The god raised an eyebrow. A little spark caught fire in his beard. Then he threw back his head and laughed so loudly, the tools rattled on the workbenches.

"You sound just like your mother," Hephaestus said. "I miss Esperanza."

"She's been dead seven years." Leo's voice trembled. "Not that you'd care."

"But I do care, boy. About both of you."

"Uh-huh. Which is why I never saw you before today."

The god made a rumbling sound in his throat, but he looked more uncomfortable than angry. He pulled a miniature motor from his pocket and began fiddling absently with the pistons—just the way Leo did when he was nervous.

"I'm not good with children," the god confessed. "Or people. Well, any organic life forms, really. I thought about speaking to you at your mom's funeral. Then again when you were in fifth grade...that science project you made, steam-powered chicken chucker. Very impressive."

"You saw that?"

Hephaestus pointed to the nearest worktable, where a shiny bronze mirror showed a hazy image of Leo asleep on the dragon's back.

"Is that me?" Leo asked. "Like—me right now, having this dream—looking at me having a dream?"

Hephaestus scratched his beard. "Now you've confused me. But yes—it's you. I'm always keeping an eye on you, Leo. But talking to you is, um...different."

"You're scared," Leo said.

"Grommets and gears!" the god yelled. "Of course not!"

"Yeah, you're scared." But Leo's anger seeped away. He'd spent years thinking about what he'd say to his dad if they ever met—how Leo would chew him out for being a dead-beat. Now, looking at that bronze mirror, Leo thought about his dad watching his progress over the years, even his stupid science experiments.

Maybe Hephaestus was still a jerk, but Leo kind of understood where he was coming from. Leo knew about running away from people, not fitting in. He knew about hiding out in a workshop rather than trying to deal with organic life forms.

"So," Leo grumbled, "you keep track of all your kids? You got like twelve back at camp. How'd you even— Never mind. I don't want to know."

Hephaestus might've blushed, but his face was so beat up and red, it was hard to tell. "Gods are different from mortals, boy. We can exist in many places at once—wherever people call on us, wherever our sphere of influence is strong. In fact, it's rare our entire essence is ever together in one place—our true form. It's dangerous, powerful enough to destroy any mortal who looks upon us. So, yes... lots of children. Add to that our different aspects, Greek and Roman—" The god's fingers froze on his engine project. "Er, that is to say, being a god is complicated. And yes, I try to keep an eye on all my children, but you especially."

Leo was pretty sure Hephaestus had almost slipped and said something important, but he wasn't sure what.

"Why contact me now?" Leo asked. "I thought the gods had gone silent."

"We have," Hephaestus grumped. "Zeus's orders—very strange, even for him. He's blocked all visions, dreams, and Iris-messages to and from Olympus. Hermes is sitting around bored out of his mind because he can't deliver the mail. Fortunately, I kept my old pirate broadcasting equipment."

Hephaestus patted a machine on the table. It looked like a combination satellite dish, V-6 engine, and espresso maker. Each time Hephaestus jostled the machine, Leo's dream flickered and changed color.

"Used this in the Cold War," the god said fondly. "Radio Free Hephaestus. Those were the days. I keep it around for pay-for-view, mostly, or making viral brain videos—"

"Viral brain videos?"

"But now it's come in handy again. If Zeus knew I was contacting you, he'd have my hide."

"Why is Zeus being such a jerk?"

"Hrumph. He excels at that, boy." Hephaestus called him *boy* as if Leo were an annoying machine part—an extra washer, maybe, that had no clear purpose, but that Hephaestus didn't want to throw away for fear he might need it someday.

Not exactly heartwarming. Then again, Leo wasn't sure he wanted to be called "son." Leo wasn't about to start calling this big awkward ugly guy "Dad."

Hephaestus got tired of his engine and tossed it over his shoulder. Before it could hit the floor, it sprouted helicopter wings and flew itself into a recycling bin.

"It was the second Titan War, I suppose," Hephaestus said. "That's what got Zeus upset. We gods were . . . well, embarrassed. Don't think there's any other way to say it."

"But you won," Leo said.

The god grunted. "We won because the demigods of"—again he hesitated, as if he'd almost made a slip—"of Camp Half-Blood took the lead. We won because our children fought our battles for us, smarter than we did. If we'd relied on Zeus's plan, we would've all gone down to Tartarus fighting the storm giant Typhon, and Kronos would've won. Bad enough mortals won our war for us, but then that young upstart, Percy Jackson—"

"The guy who's missing."

"Hmph. Yes. Him. He had the nerve to turn down our

offer of immortality and tell us to pay better attention to our children. Er, no offense."

"Oh, how could I take offense? Please, go on ignoring me."

"Mighty understanding of you..." Hephaestus frowned, then sighed wearily. "That was sarcasm, wasn't it? Machines don't have sarcasm, usually. But as I was saying, the gods felt ashamed, shown up by mortals. At first, of course, we were grateful. But after a few months, those feelings turned bitter. We're gods, after all. We need to be admired, looked up to, held in awe and admiration."

"Even if you're wrong?"

"Especially then! And to have Jackson refuse our gift, as if being mortal were somehow *better* than being a god... well, that stuck in Zeus's craw. He decided it was high time we got back to traditional values. Gods were to be respected. Our children were to be seen and not visited. Olympus was closed. At least that was *part* of his reasoning. And, of course, we started hearing of bad things stirring under the earth."

"The giants, you mean. Monsters re-forming instantly. The dead rising again. Little stuff like that?"

"Aye, boy." Hephaestus turned a knob on his pirate broad-casting machine. Leo's dream sharpened to full color, but the god's face was such a riot of red welts and yellow and black bruises, Leo wished it would go back to black and white.

"Zeus thinks he can reverse the tide," the god said, "lull the earth back to sleep as long as we stay quiet. None of us really believes that. And I don't mind saying, we're in no shape to fight another war. We barely survived the Titans. If we're repeating the old pattern, what comes next is even worse."

"The giants," Leo said. "Hera said demigods and gods had to join forces to defeat them. Is that true?"

"Mmm. I hate to agree with my mother about anything, but yes. Those giants are tough to kill, boy. They're a different breed."

"Breed? You make them sound like racehorses."

"Ha!" the god said. "More like war dogs. Back in the beginning, y'see, everything in creation came from the same parents—Gaea and Ouranos, Earth and Sky. They had their different batches of children—your Titans, your Elder Cyclopes, and so forth. Then Kronos, the head Titan—well, you've probably heard how he chopped up his father Ouranos with a scythe and took over the world. Then we gods came along, children of the Titans, and defeated *them*. But that wasn't the end of it. The earth bore a new batch of children, except they were sired by Tartarus, the spirit of the eternal abyss—the darkest, most evil place in the Underworld. Those children, the giants, were bred for one purpose—revenge on *us* for the fall of the Titans. They rose up to destroy Olympus, and they came awfully close."

Hephaestus's beard began to smolder. He absently swatted out the flames. "What my blasted mother Hera is doing now—she's a meddling fool playing a dangerous game, but she's right about one thing: you demigods have to unite. That's the only way to open Zeus's eyes, convince the Olympians they must accept your help. And that's the only way to defeat what's coming. You're a big part of that, Leo. "

The god's gaze seemed far away. Leo wondered if he really could split himself into different parts—where else was he right now? Maybe his Greek side was fixing a car or going on a date, while his Roman side was watching a ball game and ordering pizza. Leo tried to imagine what it would feel like to have multiple personalities. He hoped it wasn't hereditary.

"Why me?" he asked, and as soon as he said it, more questions flooded out. "Why claim me now? Why not when I was thirteen, like you're supposed to? Or you could've claimed me at seven, before my mom died! Why didn't you find me earlier? Why didn't you warn me about *this*?"

Leo's hand burst into flames.

Hephaestus regarded him sadly. "Hardest part, boy. Letting my children walk their own paths. Interfering doesn't work. The Fates make sure of that. As for the claiming, you were a special case, boy. The timing had to be right. I can't explain it much more, but—"

Leo's dream went fuzzy. Just for a moment, it turned into a rerun of *Wheel of Fortune*. Then Hephaestus came back into focus.

"Blast," he said. "I can't talk much longer. Zeus is sensing an illegal dream. He is lord of the air, after all, including the airwaves. Just listen, boy: you have a role to play. Your friend Jason is right—fire is a gift, not a curse. I don't give that blessing to just anyone. They'll never defeat the giants without you, much less the mistress they serve. She's worse than any god or Titan."

"Who?" Leo demanded.

Hephaestus frowned, his image becoming fuzzier. "I told you. Yes, I'm pretty sure I told you. Just be warned: along the way, you're going to lose some friends and some valuable tools.

But that isn't your fault, Leo. Nothing lasts forever, not even the best machines. And everything can be reused."

"What do you mean? I don't like the sound of that."

"No, you shouldn't." Hephaestus's image was barely visible now, just a blob in the static. "Just watch out for—"

Leo's dream switched to *Wheel of Fortune* just as the wheel hit Bankrupt and the audience said, "Awwww!"

Then Leo snapped awake to Jason and Piper screaming.

LEO

THEY SPIRALED THROUGH THE DARK in a free fall, still on the dragon's back, but Festus's hide was cold. His ruby eyes were dim.

"Not again!" Leo yelled. "You can't fall again!"

He could barely hold on. The wind stung his eyes, but he managed to pull open the panel on the dragon's neck. He toggled the switches. He tugged the wires. The dragon's wings flapped once, but Leo caught a whiff of burning bronze. The drive system was overloaded. Festus didn't have the strength to keep flying, and Leo couldn't get to the main control panel on the dragon's head—not in midair. He saw the lights of a city below them—just flashes in the dark as they plummeted in circles. They had only seconds before they crashed.

"Jason!" he screamed. "Take Piper and fly out of here!"

"What?"

"We need to lighten the load! I might be able to reboot Festus, but he's carrying too much weight!"

"What about you?" Piper cried. "If you can't reboot him—"

"I'll be fine," Leo yelled. "Just follow me to the ground. Go!"

Jason grabbed Piper around the waist. They both unbuckled their harnesses, and in a flash they were gone—shooting into the air.

"Now," Leo said. "Just you and me, Festus—and two heavy cages. You can do it, boy!"

Leo talked to the dragon while he worked, falling at terminal velocity. He could see the city lights below him, getting closer and closer. He summoned fire in his hand so he could see what he was doing, but the wind kept extinguishing it.

He pulled a wire that he thought connected the dragon's nerve center to its head, hoping for a little wake-up jolt.

Festus groaned—metal creaking inside his neck. His eyes flickered weakly to life, and he spread his wings. Their fall turned into a steep glide.

"Good!" Leo said. "Come on, big boy. Come on!"

They were still flying in way too hot, and the ground was too close. Leo needed a place to land—fast.

There was a big river—no. Not good for a fire-breathing dragon. He'd never get Festus out from the bottom if he sank, especially in freezing temperatures. Then, on the riverbanks, Leo spotted a white mansion with a huge snowy lawn inside a tall brick perimeter fence—like some rich person's private compound, all of it blazing with light. A perfect landing field. He did his best to steer the dragon toward it, and Festus seemed to come back to life. They could make this!

Then everything went wrong. As they approached the

lawn, spotlights along the fence fixed on them, blinding Leo. He heard bursts like tracer fire, the sound of metal being cut to shreds—and *BOOM*.

Leo blacked out.

When Leo came to his senses, Jason and Piper were leaning over him. He was lying in the snow, covered in mud and grease. He spit a clump of frozen grass out of his mouth.

"Where—"

"Lie still." Piper had tears in her eyes. "You rolled pretty hard when—when Festus—"

"Where is he?" Leo sat up, but his head felt like it was floating. They'd landed inside the compound. Something had happened on the way in—gunfire?

"Seriously, Leo," Jason said. "You could be hurt. You shouldn't—"

Leo pushed himself to his feet. Then he saw the wreckage. Festus must have dropped the big canary cages as he came over the fence, because they'd rolled in different directions and landed on their sides, perfectly undamaged.

Festus hadn't been so lucky.

The dragon had disintegrated. His limbs were scattered across the lawn. His tail hung on the fence. The main section of his body had plowed a trench twenty feet wide and fifty feet long across the mansion's yard before breaking apart. What remained of his hide was a charred, smoking pile of scraps. Only his neck and head were somewhat intact, resting across a row of frozen rosebushes like a pillow.

"No," Leo sobbed. He ran to the dragon's head and stroked

its snout. The dragon's eyes flickered weakly. Oil leaked out of his ear.

"You can't go," Leo pleaded. "You're the best thing I ever fixed."

The dragon's head whirred its gears, as if it were purring. Jason and Piper stood next to him, but Leo kept his eyes fixed on the dragon.

He remembered what Hephaestus had said: *That isn't your fault, Leo. Nothing lasts forever, not even the best machines.*

His dad had been trying to warn him.

"It's not fair," he said.

The dragon clicked. Long *creak*. Two short *clicks*. *Creak*. *Creak*. Almost like a pattern...triggering an old memory in Leo's mind. Leo realized Festus was trying to say something. He was using Morse code—just like Leo's mom had taught him years ago. Leo listened more intently, translating the clicks into letters: a simple message repeating over and over.

"Yeah," Leo said. "I understand. I will. I promise."

The dragon's eyes went dark. Festus was gone.

Leo cried. He wasn't even embarrassed. His friends stood on either side, patting his shoulders, saying comforting things; but the buzzing in Leo's ears drowned out their words.

Finally Jason said, "I'm so sorry, man. What did you promise Festus?"

Leo sniffled. He opened the dragon's head panel, just to be sure, but the control disk was cracked and burned beyond repair.

"Something my dad told me," Leo said. "Everything can be reused."

"Your dad talked to you?" Jason asked. "When was this?"

Leo didn't answer. He worked at the dragon's neck hinges until the head was detached. It weighed about a hundred pounds, but Leo managed to hold it in his arms. He looked up at the starry sky and said, "Take him back to the bunker, Dad. Please, until I can reuse him. I've never asked you for anything."

The wind picked up, and the dragon's head floated out of Leo's arms like it weighed nothing. It flew into the sky and disappeared.

Piper looked at him in amazement. "He *answered* you?"

"I had a dream," Leo managed. "Tell you later."

He knew he owed his friends a better explanation, but Leo could barely speak. He felt like a broken machine himself —like someone had removed one little part of him, and now he'd never be complete. He might move, he might talk, he might keep going and do his job. But he'd always be off balance, never calibrated exactly right.

Still, he couldn't afford to break down completely. Otherwise, Festus had died for nothing. He had to finish this quest —for his friends, for his mom, for his dragon.

He looked around. The large white mansion glowed in the center of the grounds. Tall brick walls with lights and security cameras surrounded the perimeter, but now Leo could see —or rather *sense*—just how well those walls were defended.

"Where are we?" he asked. "I mean, what city?"

"Omaha, Nebraska," Piper said. "I saw a billboard as we flew in. But I don't know what this mansion is. We came in right behind you, but as you were landing, Leo, I swear it looked like—I don't know—"

"Lasers," Leo said. He picked up a piece of dragon wreckage and threw it toward the top of the fence. Immediately a turret popped up from the brick wall and a beam of pure heat incinerated the bronze plating to ashes.

Jason whistled. "Some defense system. How are we even alive?"

"Festus," Leo said miserably. "He took the fire. The lasers sliced him to bits as he came in so they didn't focus on you. I led him into a death trap."

"You couldn't have known," Piper said. "He saved our lives again."

"But what now?" Jason said. "The main gates are locked, and I'm guessing I can't fly us out of here without getting shot down."

Leo looked up the walkway at the big white mansion. "Since we can't go out, we'll have to go in."

XXXI

JASON

JASON WOULD'VE DIED FIVE TIMES on the way to the front door if not for Leo.

First it was the motion-activated trapdoor on the sidewalk, then the lasers on the steps, then the nerve gas dispenser on the porch railing, the pressure-sensitive poison spikes in the welcome mat, and of course the exploding doorbell.

Leo deactivated all of them. It was like he could smell the traps, and he picked just the right tool out of his belt to disable them.

"You're amazing, man," Jason said.

Leo scowled as he examined the front door lock. "Yeah, amazing," he said. "Can't fix a dragon right, but I'm amazing."

"Hey, that wasn't your—"

"Front door's already unlocked," Leo announced.

Piper stared at the door in disbelief. "It is? All those traps, and the *door's* unlocked?"

Leo turned the knob. The door swung open easily. He stepped inside without hesitation.

Before Jason could follow, Piper caught his arm. "He's going to need some time to get over Festus. Don't take it personally."

"Yeah," Jason said. "Yeah, okay."

But still he felt terrible. Back in Medea's store, he'd said some pretty harsh stuff to Leo—stuff a friend shouldn't say, not to mention the fact he'd almost skewered Leo with a sword. If it hadn't been for Piper, they'd both be dead. And Piper hadn't gotten out of that encounter easily, either.

"Piper," he said, "I know I was in a daze back in Chicago, but that stuff about your dad—if he's in trouble, I want to help. I don't care if it's a trap or not."

Her eyes were always different colors, but now they looked shattered, as if she'd seen something she just couldn't cope with. "Jason, you don't know what you're saying. Please—don't make me feel worse. Come on. We should stick together."

She ducked inside.

"Together," Jason said to himself. "Yeah, we're doing great with that."

Jason's first impression of the house: Dark.

From the echo of his footsteps he could tell the entry hall was enormous, even bigger than Boreas's penthouse; but the only illumination came from the yard lights outside. A faint glow peeked through the breaks in the thick velvet curtains. The windows rose about ten feet tall. Spaced between them along the walls were life-size metal statues. As Jason's eyes adjusted, he saw sofas arranged in a ∪ in the middle of the room, with a central coffee table and one large chair at the far end. A massive chandelier glinted overhead. Along the back wall stood a row of closed doors.

"Where's the light switch?" His voice echoed alarmingly through the room.

"Don't see one," Leo said.

"Fire?" Piper suggested.

Leo held out his hand, but nothing happened. "It's not working."

"Your fire is out? Why?" Piper asked.

"Well, if I knew that—"

"Okay, okay," she said. "What do we do—explore?"

Leo shook his head. "After all those traps outside? Bad idea."

Jason's skin tingled. He hated being a demigod. Looking around, he didn't see a comfortable room to hang out in. He imagined vicious storm spirits lurking in the curtains, dragons under the carpet, a chandelier made of lethal ice shards, ready to impale them.

"Leo's right," he said. "We're not separating again—not like in Detroit."

"Oh, thank you for reminding me of the Cyclopes." Piper's voice quavered. "I needed that."

"It's a few hours until dawn," Jason guessed. "Too cold to wait outside. Let's bring the cages in and make camp in this room. Wait for daylight; then we can decide what to do."

Nobody offered a better idea, so they rolled in the cages

with Coach Hedge and the storm spirits, then settled in. Thankfully, Leo didn't find any poison throw pillows or electric whoopee cushions on the sofas.

Leo didn't seem in the mood to make more tacos. Besides, they had no fire, so they settled for cold rations.

As Jason ate, he studied the metal statues along the walls. They looked like Greek gods or heroes. Maybe that was a good sign. Or maybe they were used for target practice. On the coffee table sat a tea service and a stack of glossy brochures, but Jason couldn't make out the words. The big chair at the other end of the table looked like a throne. None of them tried to sit in it.

The canary cages didn't make the place any less creepy. The *venti* kept churning in their prison, hissing and spinning, and Jason got the uncomfortable feeling they were watching him. He could sense their hatred for the children of Zeus—the lord of the sky who'd ordered Aeolus to imprison their kind. The *venti* would like nothing better than to tear Jason apart.

As for Coach Hedge, he was still frozen mid-shout, his cudgel raised. Leo was working on the cage, trying to open it with various tools, but the lock seemed to be giving him a hard time. Jason decided not to sit next to him in case Hedge suddenly unfroze and went into ninja goat mode.

Despite how wired he felt, once his stomach was full, Jason started to nod off. The couches were a little too comfortable —a lot better than a dragon's back—and he'd taken the last two watches while his friends slept. He was exhausted.

Piper had already curled up on the other sofa. Jason wondered if she was really asleep or dodging a conversation about her dad. Whatever Medea had meant in Chicago, about Piper getting her dad back if she cooperated—it didn't sound good. If Piper had risked her own dad to save them, that made Jason feel even guiltier.

And they were running out of time. If Jason had his days straight, this was early morning of December 20. Which meant tomorrow was the winter solstice.

"Get some sleep," Leo said, still working on the locked cage. "It's your turn."

Jason took a deep breath. "Leo, I'm sorry about that stuff I said in Chicago. That wasn't me. You're not annoying and you *do* take stuff seriously—especially your work. I wish I could do half the things you can do."

Leo lowered his screwdriver. He looked at the ceiling and shook his head like, *What am I gonna do with this guy?*

"I try very hard to be annoying," Leo said. "Don't insult my ability to *annoy*. And how am I supposed to resent you if you go apologizing? I'm a lowly mechanic. You're like the prince of the sky, son of the Lord of the Universe. I'm *supposed* to resent you."

"Lord of the Universe?"

"Sure, you're all—*bam!* Lightning man. And 'Watch me fly. I am the eagle that soars—'"

"Shut up, Valdez."

Leo managed a little smile. "Yeah, see. I *do* annoy you."

"I apologize for apologizing."

"Thank you." He went back to work, but the tension had eased between them. Leo still looked sad and exhausted—just not quite so angry.

"Go to sleep, Jason," he ordered. "It's gonna take a few hours to get this goat man free. Then I still got to figure out how to make the winds a smaller holding cell, 'cause I am *not* lugging that canary cage to California."

"You did fix Festus, you know," Jason said. "You gave him a purpose again. I think this quest was the high point of his life."

Jason was afraid he'd blown it and made Leo mad again, but Leo just sighed.

"I hope," he said. "Now, sleep, man. I want some time without you organic life forms."

Jason wasn't quite sure what that meant, but he didn't argue. He closed his eyes and had a long, blissfully dreamless sleep.

He only woke when the yelling started.

"Ahhhgggggh!"

Jason leaped to his feet. He wasn't sure what was more jarring—the full sunlight that now bathed the room, or the screaming satyr.

"Coach is awake," Leo said, which was kind of unnecessary. Gleeson Hedge was capering around on his furry hindquarters, swinging his club and yelling, "Die!" as he smashed the tea set, whacked the sofas, and charged at the throne.

"Coach!" Jason yelled.

Hedge turned, breathing hard. His eyes were so wild, Jason was afraid he might attack. The satyr was still wearing his orange polo shirt and his coach's whistle, but his horns were clearly visible above his curly hair, and his beefy hindquarters were definitely all goat. Could you call a goat *beefy*? Jason put the thought aside.

"You're the new kid," Hedge said, lowering his club. "Jason." He looked at Leo, then Piper, who'd apparently also just woken up. Her hair looked like it had become a nest for a friendly hamster.

"Valdez, McLean," the coach said. "What's going on? We were at the Grand Canyon. The *anemoi thuellai* were attacking and—" He zeroed in on the storm spirit cage, and his eyes went back to DEFCON 1. "Die!"

"Whoa, Coach!" Leo stepped in his path, which was pretty brave, even though Hedge was six inches shorter. "It's okay. They're locked up. We just sprang you from the other cage."

"Cage? Cage? What's going on? Just because I'm a satyr doesn't mean I can't have you doing plank push-ups, Valdez!"

Jason cleared his throat. "Coach—Gleeson—um, whatever you want us to call you. You saved us at the Grand Canyon. You were totally brave."

"Of course I was!"

"The extraction team came and took us to Camp Half-Blood. We thought we'd lost you. Then we got word the storm spirits had taken you back to their—um, operator, Medea."

"That witch! Wait—that's impossible. She's mortal. She's dead."

"Yeah, well," Leo said, "somehow she got not dead anymore."

Hedge nodded, his eyes narrowing. "So! You were sent on a dangerous quest to rescue me. Excellent!"

"Um." Piper got to her feet, holding out her hands so Coach Hedge wouldn't attack her. "Actually, Glee—can I still call you Coach Hedge? Gleeson seems *wrong*. We're on a quest for something else. We kind of found you by accident."

"Oh." The coach's spirits seemed to deflate, but only for a second. Then his eyes lit up again. "But there are no accidents! Not on quests. This was *meant* to happen! So, this is the witch's lair, eh? Why is everything gold?"

"Gold?" Jason looked around. From the way Leo and Piper caught their breath, he guessed they hadn't noticed yet either.

The room was full of gold—the statues, the tea set Hedge had smashed, the chair that was definitely a throne. Even the curtains—which seemed to have opened by themselves at daybreak—appeared to be woven of gold fiber.

"Nice," Leo said. "No wonder they got so much security."

"This isn't—" Piper stammered. "This isn't Medea's place, Coach. It's some rich person's mansion in Omaha. We got away from Medea and crash-landed here."

"It's destiny, cupcakes!" Hedge insisted. "I'm meant to protect you. What's the quest?"

Before Jason could decide if he wanted to explain or just shove Coach Hedge back into his cage, a door opened at the far end of the room.

A pudgy man in a white bathrobe stepped out with a golden toothbrush in his mouth. He had a white beard and one of those long, old-fashioned sleeping caps pressed down over his white hair. He froze when he saw them, and the toothbrush fell out of his mouth.

He glanced into the room behind him and called, "Son? Lit, come out here, please. There are strange people in the throne room."

Coach Hedge did the obvious thing. He raised his club and shouted, "Die!"

XXXII

JASON

IT TOOK ALL THREE OF THEM to hold back the satyr.

"Whoa, Coach!" Jason said. "Bring it down a few notches."

A younger man charged into the room. Jason guessed he must be Lit, the old guy's son. He was dressed in pajama pants with a sleeveless T-shirt that said CORNHUSKERS, and he held a sword that looked like it could husk a lot of things besides corn. His ripped arms were covered in scars, and his face, framed by curly dark hair, would've been handsome if it wasn't also sliced up.

Lit immediately zeroed in on Jason like he was the biggest threat, and stalked toward him, swinging his sword overhead.

"Hold on!" Piper stepped forward, trying for her best calming voice. "This is just a misunderstanding! Everything's fine."

Lit stopped in his tracks, but he still looked wary.

It didn't help that Hedge was screaming, "I'll get them! Don't worry!"

"Coach," Jason pleaded, "they may be friendly. Besides, we're trespassing in their house."

"Thank you!" said the old man in the bathrobe. "Now, who are you, and why are you here?"

"Let's all put our weapons down," Piper said. "Coach, you first."

Hedge clenched his jaw. "Just one thwack?"

"No," Piper said.

"What about a compromise? I'll kill them first, and if it turns out they were friendly, I'll apologize."

"No!" Piper insisted.

"Meh." Coach Hedge lowered his club.

Piper gave Lit a friendly *sorry-about-that* smile. Even with her hair messed up and wearing two-day-old clothes, she looked extremely cute, and Jason felt a little jealous she was giving Lit that smile.

Lit huffed and sheathed his sword. "You speak well, girl— fortunately for your friends, or I would've run them through."

"Appreciate it," Leo said. "I try not to get run through before lunchtime."

The old man in the bathrobe sighed, kicking the teapot that Coach Hedge had smashed. "Well, since you're here. Please, sit down."

Lit frowned. "Your Majesty—"

"No, no, it's fine, Lit," the old man said. "New land, new customs. They may sit in my presence. After all, they've seen me in my nightclothes. No sense observing formalities." He did his best to smile, though it looked a little forced. "Welcome to my humble home. I am King Midas."

• • •

"Midas? Impossible," said Coach Hedge. "He died."

They were sitting on the sofas now, while the king reclined on his throne. Tricky to do that in a bathrobe, and Jason kept worrying the old guy would forget and uncross his legs. Hopefully he was wearing golden boxers under there.

Lit stood behind the throne, both hands on his sword, glancing at Piper and flexing his muscular arms just to be annoying. Jason wondered if *he* looked that ripped holding a sword. Sadly, he doubted it.

Piper sat forward. "What our satyr friend means, Your Majesty, is that you're the second mortal we've met who should be—sorry—dead. King Midas lived thousands of years ago."

"Interesting." The king gazed out the windows at the brilliant blue skies and the winter sunlight. In the distance, downtown Omaha looked like a cluster of children's blocks —way too clean and small for a regular city.

"You know," the king said, "I think I *was* a bit dead for a while. It's strange. Seems like a dream, doesn't it, Lit?"

"A very long dream, Your Majesty."

"And yet, now we're here. I'm enjoying myself very much. I like being alive better."

"But how?" Piper asked. "You didn't happen to have a . . . patron?"

Midas hesitated, but there was a sly twinkle in his eyes. "Does it matter, my dear?"

"We could kill them again," Hedge suggested.

"Coach, not helping," Jason said. "Why don't you go out-side and stand guard?"

Leo coughed. "Is that safe? They've got some serious security."

"Oh, yes," the king said. "Sorry about that. But it's lovely stuff, isn't it? Amazing what gold can still buy. Such excellent toys you have in this country!"

He fished a remote control out of his bathrobe pocket and pressed a few buttons—a pass code, Jason guessed.

"There," Midas said. "Safe to go out now."

Coach Hedge grunted. "Fine. But if you need me..." He winked at Jason meaningfully. Then he pointed at himself, pointed two fingers at their hosts, and sliced a finger across his throat. Very subtle sign language.

"Yeah, thanks," Jason said.

After the satyr left, Piper tried another diplomatic smile. "So... you don't know how you got here?"

"Oh, well, yes. Sort of," the king said. He frowned at Lit. "Why did we pick Omaha, again? I know it wasn't the weather."

"The oracle," Lit said.

"Yes! I was told there was an oracle in Omaha." The king shrugged. "Apparently I was mistaken. But this is a rather nice house, isn't it? Lit—it's short for Lityerses, by the way —horrible name, but his mother insisted—Lit has plenty of wide-open space to practice his swordplay. He has quite a reputation for that. They called him the Reaper of Men back in the old days."

"Oh." Piper tried to sound enthusiastic. "How nice."

Lit's smile was more of a cruel sneer. Jason was now one hundred percent sure he didn't like this guy, and he was starting to regret sending Hedge outside.

"So," Jason said. "All this gold—"

The king's eyes lit up. "Are you here for gold, my boy? Please, take a brochure!"

Jason looked at the brochures on the coffee table. The title said *GOLD: Invest for Eternity*. "Um, you sell gold?"

"No, no," the king said. "I *make* it. In uncertain times like these, gold is the wisest investment, don't you think? Governments fall. The dead rise. Giants attack Olympus. But gold retains its value!"

Leo frowned. "I've seen that commercial."

"Oh, don't be fooled by cheap imitators!" the king said. "I assure you, I can beat any price for a serious investor. I can make a wide assortment of gold items at a moment's notice."

"But..." Piper shook her head in confusion. "Your Majesty, you gave up the golden touch, didn't you?"

The king looked astonished. "Gave it up?"

"Yes," Piper said. "You got it from some god—"

"Dionysus," the king agreed. "I'd rescued one of his satyrs, and in return, the god granted me one wish. I chose the golden touch."

"But you accidentally turned your own daughter to gold," Piper remembered. "And you realized how greedy you'd been. So you repented."

"Repented!" King Midas looked at Lit incredulously. "You see, son? You're away for a few thousand years, and the story gets twisted all around. My dear girl, did those stories ever *say* I'd lost my magic touch?"

"Well, I guess not. They just said you learned how to reverse it with running water, and you brought your daughter back to life."

"That's all true. Sometimes I still have to reverse my touch. There's no running water in the house because I don't want accidents"—he gestured to his statues—"but we chose to live next to a river just in case. Occasionally, I'll forget and pat Lit on the back—"

Lit retreated a few steps. "I hate that."

"I *told* you I was sorry, son. At any rate, gold is wonderful. Why would I give it up?"

"Well..." Piper looked truly lost now. "Isn't that the point of the story? That you learned your lesson?"

Midas laughed. "My dear, may I see your backpack for a moment? Toss it here."

Piper hesitated, but she wasn't eager to offend the king. She dumped everything out of the pack and tossed it to Midas. As soon as he caught it, the pack turned to gold, like frost spreading across the fabric. It still looked flexible and soft, but definitely gold. The king tossed it back.

"As you see, I can still turn anything to gold," Midas said. "That pack is magic now, as well. Go ahead—put your little storm spirit enemies in there."

"Seriously?" Leo was suddenly interested. He took the bag from Piper and held it up to the cage. As soon as he unzipped the backpack, the winds stirred and howled in protest. The cage bars shuddered. The door of the prison flew open and the winds got vacuumed straight into the pack. Leo zipped it shut and grinned. "Gotta admit. That's cool."

"You see?" Midas said. "My golden touch a *curse*? Please. I didn't learn any lesson, and life isn't a story, girl. Honestly, my daughter Zoe was much more pleasant as a gold statue."

"She talked a lot," Lit offered.

"Exactly! And so I turned her back to gold." Midas pointed. There in the corner was a golden statue of a girl with a shocked expression, as if she were thinking, *Dad!*

"That's horrible!" Piper said.

"Nonsense. She doesn't mind. Besides, if I'd learned my lesson, would I have gotten these?"

Midas pulled off his oversize sleeping cap, and Jason didn't know whether to laugh or get sick. Midas had long fuzzy gray ears sticking up from his white hair—like Bugs Bunny's, but they weren't rabbit ears. They were donkey ears.

"Oh, wow," Leo said. "I didn't need to see that."

"Terrible, isn't it?" Midas sighed. "A few years after the golden touch incident, I judged a music contest between Apollo and Pan, and I declared Pan the winner. Apollo, sore loser, said I must have the ears of an ass, and *voilà*. This was my reward for being truthful. I tried to keep them a secret. Only my barber knew, but he couldn't help blabbing." Midas pointed out another golden statue—a bald man in a toga, holding a pair of shears. "That's him. He won't be telling anyone's secrets again."

The king smiled. Suddenly he didn't strike Jason as a harmless old man in a bathrobe. His eyes had a merry glow to them—the look of a madman who knew he was mad, accepted his madness, and enjoyed it. "Yes, gold has many uses. I think that *must* be why I was brought back, eh Lit? To bankroll our patron."

Lit nodded. "That and my good sword arm."

Jason glanced at his friends. Suddenly the air in the room seemed much colder.

"So you do have a patron," Jason said. "You work for the giants."

King Midas waved his hand dismissively. "Well, I don't care for giants myself, of course. But even supernatural armies need to get paid. I do owe my patron a great debt. I tried to explain that to the last group that came through, but they were very unfriendly. Wouldn't cooperate at all."

Jason slipped his hand into his pocket and grabbed his gold coin. "The last group?"

"Hunters," Lit snarled. "Blasted girls from Artemis."

Jason felt a spark of electricity—a *literal* spark—travel down his spine. He caught a whiff of electrical fire like he'd just melted some of the springs in the sofa.

His *sister* had been here.

"When?" he demanded. "What happened?"

Lit shrugged. "Few days ago? I didn't get to kill them, unfortunately. They were looking for some evil wolves, or something. Said they were following a trail, heading west. Missing demigod—I don't recall."

Percy Jackson, Jason thought. Annabeth had mentioned the Hunters were looking for him. And in Jason's dream of the burned-out house in the redwoods, he'd heard enemy wolves baying. Hera had called them her keepers. It had to be connected somehow.

Midas scratched his donkey ears. "Very unpleasant young ladies, those Hunters," he recalled. "They absolutely refused to be turned into gold. Much of the security system outside I installed to keep that sort of thing from happening again, you know. I don't have time for those who aren't serious investors."

Jason stood warily and glanced at his friends. They got the message.

"Well," Piper said, managing a smile. "It's been a great visit. Welcome back to life. Thanks for the gold bag."

"Oh, but you can't leave!" Midas said. "I know you're not serious investors, but that's all right! I have to rebuild my collection."

Lit was smiling cruelly. The king rose, and Leo and Piper moved away from him.

"Don't worry," the king assured them. "You don't *have* to be turned to gold. I give all my guests a choice—join my collection, or die at the hands of Lityerses. Really, it's good either way."

Piper tried to use her charmspeak. "Your Majesty, you can't—"

Quicker than any old man should've been able to move, Midas lashed out and grabbed her wrist.

"No!" Jason yelled.

But a frost of gold spread over Piper, and in a heartbeat she was a glittering statue. Leo tried to summon fire, but he'd forgotten his power wasn't working. Midas touched his hand, and Leo transformed into solid metal.

Jason was so horrified he couldn't move. His friends—just *gone*. And he hadn't been able to stop it.

Midas smiled apologetically. "Gold trumps fire, I'm afraid." He waved around him at all the gold curtains and furniture. "In this room, my power dampens all others: fire . . . even charmspeak. Which leaves me only one more trophy to collect."

"Hedge!" Jason yelled. "Need help in here!"

For once, the satyr didn't charge in. Jason wondered if the

lasers had gotten him, or if he was sitting at the bottom of a trap pit.

Midas chuckled. "No goat to the rescue? Sad. But don't worry, my boy. It's really not painful. Lit can tell you."

Jason fixed on an idea. "I choose combat. You said I could choose to fight Lit instead."

Midas looked mildly disappointed, but he shrugged. "I said you could *die* fighting Lit. But of course, if you wish."

The king backed away, and Lit raised his sword.

"I'm going to enjoy this," Lit said. "I am the Reaper of Men!"

"Come on, Cornhusker." Jason summoned his own weapon. This time it came up as a javelin, and Jason was glad for the extra length.

"Oh, gold weapon!" Midas said. "Very nice."

Lit charged.

The guy was fast. He slashed and sliced, and Jason could barely dodge the strikes, but his mind went into a different mode—analyzing patterns, learning Lit's style, which was all offense, no defense.

Jason countered, sidestepped, and blocked. Lit seemed surprised to find him still alive.

"What is that style?" Lit growled. "You don't fight like a Greek."

"Legion training," Jason said, though he wasn't sure how he knew that. "It's Roman."

"Roman?" Lit struck again, and Jason deflected his blade. "What is *Roman*?"

"News flash," Jason said. "While you were dead, Rome defeated Greece. Created the greatest empire of all time."

"Impossible," Lit said. "Never even heard of them."

Jason spun on one heel, smacked Lit in the chest with the butt of his javelin, and sent him toppling into Midas's throne.

"Oh, dear," Midas said. "Lit?"

"I'm fine," Lit growled.

"You'd better help him up," Jason said.

Lit cried, "Dad, no!"

Too late. Midas put his hand on his son's shoulder, and suddenly a very angry-looking gold statue was sitting on Midas's throne.

"Curses!" Midas wailed. "That was a naughty trick, demigod. I'll get you for that." He patted Lit's golden shoulder. "Don't worry, son. I'll get you down to the river right after I collect this prize."

Midas raced forward. Jason dodged, but the old man was fast, too. Jason kicked the coffee table into the old man's legs and knocked him over, but Midas wouldn't stay down for long.

Then Jason glanced at Piper's golden statue. Anger washed over him. He was the son of Zeus. He could *not* fail his friends.

He felt a tugging sensation in his gut, and the air pressure dropped so rapidly that his ears popped. Midas must've felt it too, because he stumbled to his feet and grabbed his donkey ears.

"Ow! What are you doing?" he demanded. "My power is supreme here!"

Thunder rumbled. Outside, the sky turned black.

"You know another good use for gold?" Jason said.

Midas raised his eyebrows, suddenly excited. "Yes?"

"It's an excellent conductor of electricity."

Jason raised his javelin, and the ceiling exploded. A lightning bolt ripped through the roof like it was an eggshell, connected with the tip of Jason's spear, and sent out arcs of energy that blasted the sofas to shreds. Chunks of ceiling plaster crashed down. The chandelier groaned and snapped off its chain, and Midas screamed as it pinned him to the floor. The glass immediately turned into gold.

When the rumbling stopped, freezing rain poured into the building. Midas cursed in Ancient Greek, thoroughly pinned under his chandelier. The rain soaked everything, turning the gold chandelier back to glass. Piper and Leo were slowly changing too, along with the other statues in the room.

Then the front door burst open, and Coach Hedge charged in, club ready. His mouth was covered with dirt, snow, and grass.

"What'd I miss?" he asked.

"Where were you?" Jason demanded. His head was spinning from summoning the lightning bolt, and it was all he could do to keep from passing out. "I was screaming for help."

Hedge belched. "Getting a snack. Sorry. Who needs killing?"

"No one, now!" Jason said. "Just grab Leo. I'll get Piper."

"Don't leave me like this!" Midas wailed.

All around him the statues of his victims were turning to flesh—his daughter, his barber, and a whole lot of angry-looking guys with swords.

Jason grabbed Piper's golden bag and his own supplies.

Then he threw a rug over the golden statue of Lit on the throne. Hopefully that would keep the Reaper of Men from turning back to flesh—at least until after Midas's victims did.

"Let's get out of here," Jason told Hedge. "I think these guys will want some quality time with Midas."

XXXIII

PIPER

PIPER WOKE UP COLD AND SHIVERING.

She'd had the worst dream about an old guy with donkey ears chasing her around and shouting, *You're it!*

"Oh, god." Her teeth chattered. "He turned me to gold!"

"You're okay now." Jason leaned over and tucked a warm blanket around her, but she still felt as cold as a Boread.

She blinked, trying to figure out where they were. Next to her, a campfire blazed, turning the air sharp with smoke. Firelight flickered against rock walls. They were in a shallow cave, but it didn't offer much protection. Outside, the wind howled. Snow blew sideways. It might've been day or night. The storm made it too dark to tell.

"L-L-Leo?" Piper managed.

"Present and un-gold-ified." Leo was also wrapped in blankets. He didn't look great, but better than Piper felt. "I got the precious metal treatment too," he said. "But I came out of it faster. Dunno why. We had to dunk you in the river to get you back completely. Tried to dry you off, but...it's really, really cold."

"You've got hypothermia," Jason said. "We risked as much nectar as we could. Coach Hedge did a little nature magic—"

"Sports medicine." The coach's ugly face loomed over her. "Kind of a hobby of mine. Your breath might smell like wild mushrooms and Gatorade for a few days, but it'll pass. You probably won't die. Probably."

"Thanks," Piper said weakly. "How did you beat Midas?"

Jason told her the story, putting most of it down to luck.

The coach snorted. "Kid's being modest. You should've seen him. Hi-yah! Slice! Boom with the lightning!"

"Coach, you didn't even see it," Jason said. "You were outside eating the lawn."

But the satyr was just warming up. "Then I came in with my club, and we dominated that room. Afterward, I told him, 'Kid, I'm proud of you! If you could just work on your upper body strength—'"

"Coach," said Jason.

"Yeah?"

"Shut up, please."

"Sure." The coach sat down at the fire and started chewing his cudgel.

Jason put his hand on Piper's forehead and checked her temperature. "Leo, can you stoke the fire?"

"On it." Leo summoned a baseball-sized clump of flames and lobbed it into the campfire.

"Do I look that bad?" Piper shivered.

"Nah," Jason said.

"You're a terrible liar," she said. "Where are we?"

"Pikes Peak," Jason said. "Colorado."

"But that's, what—five hundred miles from Omaha?"

"Something like that," Jason agreed. "I harnessed the storm spirits to bring us this far. They didn't like it—went a little faster than I wanted, almost crashed us into the mountainside before I could get them back in the bag. I'm not going to be trying that again."

"Why are we here?"

Leo sniffed. "That's what *I* asked him."

Jason gazed into the storm as if watching for something. "That glittery wind trail we saw yesterday? It was still in the sky, though it had faded a lot. I followed it until I couldn't see it anymore. Then—honestly I'm not sure. I just felt like this was the right place to stop."

"'Course it is." Coach Hedge spit out some cudgel splinters. "Aeolus's floating palace should be anchored above us, right at the peak. This is one of his favorite spots to dock."

"Maybe that was it." Jason knit his eyebrows. "I don't know. Something else, too . . ."

"The Hunters were heading west," Piper remembered. "Do you think they're around here?"

Jason rubbed his forearm as if the tattoos were bothering him. "I don't see how anyone could survive on the mountain right now. The storm's pretty bad. It's already the evening before the solstice, but we didn't have much choice except to wait out the storm here. We had to give you some time to rest before we tried moving."

He didn't need to convince her. The wind howling outside the cave scared her, and she couldn't stop shivering.

"We have to get you warm." Jason sat next to her and held out his arms a little awkwardly. "Uh, you mind if I..."

"I suppose." She tried to sound nonchalant.

He put his arms around her and held her. They scooted closer to the fire. Coach Hedge chewed on his club and spit splinters into the fire.

Leo broke out some cooking supplies and started frying burger patties on an iron skillet. "So, guys, long as you're cuddled up for story time...something I've been meaning to tell you. On the way to Omaha, I had this dream. Kinda hard to understand with the static and the *Wheel of Fortune* breaking in—"

"*Wheel of Fortune*?" Piper assumed Leo was kidding, but when he looked up from his burgers, his expression was deadly serious.

"The thing is," he said, "my dad Hephaestus talked to me."

Leo told them about his dream. In the firelight, with the wind howling, the story was even creepier. Piper could imagine the static-filled voice of the god warning about giants who were the sons of Tartarus, and about Leo losing some friends along the way.

She tried to concentrate on something good: Jason's arms around her, the warmth slowly spreading into her body, but she was terrified. "I don't understand. If demigods and gods have to work together to kill the giants, why would the gods stay silent? If they need us—"

"Ha," said Coach Hedge. "The gods *hate* needing humans. They like to be needed *by* humans, but not the other way around. Things will have to get a whole lot worse before Zeus admits he made a mistake closing Olympus."

"Coach," Piper said, "that was almost an intelligent comment."

Hedge huffed. "What? I'm intelligent! I'm not surprised you cupcakes haven't heard of the Giant War. The gods don't like to talk about it. Bad PR to admit you needed mortals to help beat an enemy. That's just embarrassing."

"There's more, though," Jason said. "When I dreamed about Hera in her cage, she said Zeus was acting unusually paranoid. And Hera—she said she went to those ruins because a voice had been speaking in her head. What if someone's influencing the gods, like Medea influenced us?"

Piper shuddered. She'd had a similar thought—that some force they couldn't see was manipulating things behind the scenes, helping the giants. Maybe the same force was keeping Enceladus informed about their movements, and had even knocked their dragon out of the sky over Detroit. Perhaps Leo's sleeping Dirt Woman, or another servant of hers...

Leo set hamburger buns on the skillet to toast. "Yeah, Hephaestus said something similar, like Zeus was acting weirder than usual. But what bothered me was the stuff my dad *didn't* say. Like a couple of times he was talking about the demigods, and how he had so many kids and all. I don't know. He acted like getting the greatest demigods together was going to be almost impossible—like Hera was trying, but it was a really stupid thing to do, and there was some secret Hephaestus wasn't supposed to tell me."

Jason shifted. Piper could feel the tension in his arms.

"Chiron was the same way back at camp," he said. "He mentioned a sacred oath not to discuss—something. Coach, you know anything about that?"

"Nah. I'm just a satyr. They don't tell us the juicy stuff. Especially an old—" He stopped himself.

"An old guy like you?" Piper asked. "But you're not that old, are you?"

"Hundred and six," the coach muttered.

Leo coughed. "Say what?"

"Don't catch your panties on fire, Valdez. That's just fifty-three in human years. Still, yeah, I made some enemies on the Council of Cloven Elders. I've been a protector a *long* time. But they started saying I was getting unpredictable. Too violent. Can you imagine?"

"Wow." Piper tried not to look at her friends. "That's hard to believe."

Coach scowled. "Yeah, then finally we get a good war going with the Titans, and do they put me on the front lines? No! They send me as far away as possible—the Canadian frontier, can you believe it? Then after the war, they put me out to pasture. The Wilderness School. Bah! Like I'm too old to be helpful just because I like playing offense. All those flower-pickers on the Council—talking about nature."

"I thought satyrs liked nature," Piper ventured.

"Shoot, I love nature," Hedge said. "Nature means big

things killing and eating little things! And when you're a —you know—vertically challenged satyr like me, you get in good shape, you carry a big stick, and you don't take nothing from no one! That's nature." Hedge snorted indignantly. "Flower-pickers. Anyway, I hope you got something vegetarian cooking, Valdez. I don't do flesh."

"Yeah, Coach. Don't eat your cudgel. I got some tofu patties here. Piper's a vegetarian too. I'll throw them on in a second."

The smell of frying burgers filled the air. Piper usually hated the smell of cooking meat, but her stomach rumbled like it wanted to mutiny.

I'm losing it, she thought. *Think broccoli. Carrots. Lentils.*

Her stomach wasn't the only thing rebelling. Lying by the fire, with Jason holding her, Piper's conscience felt like a hot bullet slowly working its way toward her heart. All the guilt she'd been holding in for the last week, since the giant Enceladus had first sent her a dream, was about to kill her.

Her friends wanted to help her. Jason even said he'd walk into a trap to save her dad. And Piper had shut them out.

For all she knew, she'd already doomed her father when she attacked Medea.

She choked back a sob. Maybe she'd done the right thing in Chicago by saving her friends, but she'd only delayed her problem. She could never betray her friends, but the tiniest part of her was desperate enough to think, *What if I did?*

She tried to imagine what her dad would say. *Hey, Dad, if you were ever chained up by a cannibal giant and I had to betray a couple of friends to save you, what should I do?*

Funny, that had never come up when they did Any Three Questions. Her dad would never take the question seriously, of course. He'd probably tell her one of Grandpa Tom's old stories—something with glowing hedgehogs and talking birds—and then laugh about it as if the advice was silly.

Piper wished she remembered her grandpa better. Sometimes she dreamed about that little two-room house in Oklahoma. She wondered what it would've been like to grow up there.

Her dad would think that was nuts. He had spent his whole life running away from that place, distancing himself from the rez, playing any role except Native American. He'd always told Piper how lucky she was to grow up rich and well cared-for, in a nice house in California.

She'd learned to be vaguely uncomfortable about her ancestry—like Dad's old pictures from the eighties, when he had feathered hair and crazy clothes. *Can you believe I ever looked like that?* he'd say. Being Cherokee was the same way for him—something funny and mildly embarrassing.

But what else were they? Dad didn't seem to know. Maybe that's why he was always so unhappy, changing roles. Maybe that's why Piper started stealing things, looking for something her dad couldn't give her.

Leo put tofu patties on the skillet. The wind kept raging. Piper thought of an old story her dad had told her . . . one that maybe *did* answer some of her questions.

One day in second grade she'd come home in tears and demanded why her father had named her Piper. The kids were making fun of her because Piper Cherokee was a kind of airplane.

Her dad laughed, as if that had never occurred to him. "No, Pipes. Fine airplane. That's not how I named you. Grandpa Tom picked out your name. First time he heard you cry, he said you had a powerful voice—better than any reed flute piper. He said you'd learn to sing the hardest Cherokee songs, even the snake song."

"The snake song?"

Dad told her the legend—how one day a Cherokee woman had seen a snake playing too near her children and killed it with a rock, not realizing it was the king of rattlesnakes. The snakes prepared for war on the humans, but the woman's husband tried to make peace. He promised he'd do anything to repay the rattlesnakes. The snakes held him to his word. They told him to send his wife to the well so the snakes could bite her and take her life in exchange. The man was heartbroken, but he did what they asked. Afterward, the snakes were impressed that the man had given up so much and kept his promise. They taught him the snake song for all the Cherokee to use. From that point on, if any Cherokee met a snake and sang that song, the snake would recognize the Cherokee as a friend, and would not bite.

"That's awful!" Piper had said. "He let his wife die?"

Her dad spread his hands. "It was a hard sacrifice. But one life brought generations of peace between snakes and Cherokee. Grandpa Tom believed that Cherokee music could solve almost any problem. He thought you'd know lots of songs, and be the greatest musician of the family. That's why we named you Piper."

A hard sacrifice. Had her grandfather foreseen something about her, even when she was a baby? Had he sensed she was a child of Aphrodite? Her dad would probably tell her that was crazy. Grandpa Tom was no oracle.

But still... she'd made a promise to help on this quest. Her friends were counting on her. They'd saved her when Midas had turned her to gold. They'd brought her back to life. She couldn't repay them with lies.

Gradually, she started to feel warmer. She stopped shivering and settled against Jason's chest. Leo handed out the food. Piper didn't want to move, talk, or do anything to disrupt the moment. But she had to.

"We need to talk." She sat up so she could face Jason. "I don't want to hide anything from you guys anymore."

They looked at her with their mouths full of burger. Too late to change her mind now.

"Three nights before the Grand Canyon trip," she said, "I had a dream vision—a giant, telling me my father had been taken hostage. He told me I had to cooperate, or my dad would be killed."

The flames crackled.

Finally Jason said, "Enceladus? You mentioned that name before."

Coach Hedge whistled. "Big giant. Breathes fire. Not somebody I'd want barbecuing my daddy goat."

Jason gave him a *shut up* look. "Piper, go on. What happened next?"

"I—I tried to reach my dad, but all I got was his personal assistant, and she told me not to worry."

"Jane?" Leo remembered. "Didn't Medea say something about controlling her?"

Piper nodded. "To get my dad back, I had to sabotage this quest. I didn't realize it would be the three of us. Then after we started the quest, Enceladus sent me another warning: He told me he wanted you two dead. He wants me to lead you to a mountain. I don't know exactly which one, but it's in the Bay Area—I could see the Golden Gate Bridge from the summit. I have to be there by noon on the solstice, tomorrow. An exchange."

She couldn't meet her friends' eyes. She waited for them to yell at her, or turn their backs, or kick her out into the snowstorm.

Instead, Jason scooted next to her and put his arm around her again. "God, Piper. I'm so sorry."

Leo nodded. "No kidding. You've been carrying this around for a week? Piper, we could *help* you."

She glared at them. "Why don't you yell at me or something? I was ordered to kill you!"

"Aw, come on," Jason said. "You've saved us both on this quest. I'd put my life in your hands any day."

"Same," Leo said. "Can I have a hug too?"

"You don't get it!" Piper said. "I've probably just killed my dad, telling you this."

"I doubt it." Coach Hedge belched. He was eating his

tofu burger folded inside the paper plate, chewing it all like a taco. "Giant hasn't gotten what he wants yet, so he still needs your dad for leverage. He'll wait until the deadline passes, see if you show up. He wants you to divert the quest to this mountain, right?"

Piper nodded uncertainly.

"So that means Hera is being kept somewhere else," Hedge reasoned. "And she has to be saved by the same day. So you have to choose—rescue your dad, or rescue Hera. If you go after Hera, *then* Enceladus takes care of your dad. Besides, Enceladus would never let you go even if you cooperated. You're obviously one of the seven in the Great Prophecy."

One of the seven. She'd talked about this before with Jason and Leo, and she supposed it must be true, but she still had trouble believing it. She didn't feel that important. She was just a stupid child of Aphrodite. How could she be worth deceiving and killing?

"So we have no choice," she said miserably. "We have to save Hera, or the giant king gets unleashed. That's our quest. The world depends on it. And Enceladus seems to have ways of watching me. He isn't stupid. He'll know if we change course and go the wrong way. He'll kill my dad."

"He's not going to kill your dad," Leo said. "We'll save him."

"We don't have time!" Piper cried. "Besides, it's a trap."

"We're your friends, beauty queen," Leo said. "We're not going to let your dad die. We just gotta figure out a plan."

Coach Hedge grumbled. "Would help if we knew where this mountain was. Maybe Aeolus can tell you that. The Bay

Area has a bad reputation for demigods. Old home of the Titans, Mount Othrys, sits over Mount Tam, where Atlas holds up the sky. I hope that's not the mountain you saw."

Piper tried to remember the vista in her dreams. "I don't think so. This was inland."

Jason frowned at the fire, like he was trying to remember something.

"Bad reputation...that doesn't seem right. The Bay Area..."

"You think you've been there?" Piper asked.

"I..." He looked like he was almost on the edge of a breakthrough. Then the anguish came back into his eyes. "I don't know. Hedge, what happened to Mount Othrys?"

Hedge took another bite of paper and burger. "Well, Kronos built a new palace there last summer. Big nasty place, was going to be the headquarters for his new kingdom and all. Weren't any battles there, though. Kronos marched on Manhattan, tried to take Olympus. If I remember right, he left some other Titans in charge of his palace, but after Kronos got defeated in Manhattan, the whole palace just crumbled on its own."

"No," Jason said.

Everyone looked at him.

"What do you mean, 'No'?" Leo asked.

"That's not what happened. I—" He tensed, looking toward the cave entrance. "Did you hear that?"

For a second, nothing. Then Piper heard it: howls piercing the night.

XXXIV

PIPER

"Wolves," Piper said. **"They sound close."**

Jason rose and summoned his sword. Leo and Coach Hedge got to their feet too. Piper tried, but black spots danced before her eyes.

"Stay there," Jason told her. "We'll protect you."

She gritted her teeth. She hated feeling helpless. She didn't *want* anyone to protect her. First the stupid ankle. Now stupid hypothermia. She wanted to be on her feet, with her dagger in her hand.

Then, just outside the firelight at the entrance of the cave, she saw a pair of red eyes glowing in the dark.

Okay, she thought. Maybe a little protection is fine.

More wolves edged into the firelight—black beasts bigger than Great Danes, with ice and snow caked on their fur. Their fangs gleamed, and their glowing red eyes looked disturbingly intelligent. The wolf in front was almost as tall as a horse, his mouth stained as if he'd just made a fresh kill.

Piper pulled her dagger out of its sheath.

Then Jason stepped forward and said something in Latin.

Piper didn't think a dead language would have much effect on wild animals, but the alpha wolf curled his lip. The fur stood up along his spine. One of his lieutenants tried to advance, but the alpha wolf snapped at his ear. Then all of the wolves backed into the dark.

"Dude, I gotta study Latin." Leo's hammer shook in his hand. "What'd you say, Jason?"

Hedge cursed. "Whatever it was, it wasn't enough. Look."

The wolves were coming back, but the alpha wolf wasn't with them. They didn't attack. They waited—at least a dozen now, in a rough semicircle just outside the firelight, blocking the cave exit.

The coach hefted his club. "Here's the plan. I'll kill them all, and you guys escape."

"Coach, they'll rip you apart," Piper said.

"Nah, I'm good."

Then Piper saw the silhouette of a man coming through the storm, wading through the wolf pack.

"Stick together," Jason said. "They respect a pack. And Hedge, no crazy stuff. We're not leaving you or anyone else behind."

Piper got a lump in her throat. She was the weak link in their "pack" right now. No doubt the wolves could smell her fear. She might as well be wearing a sign that said FREE LUNCH.

The wolves parted, and the man stepped into the firelight. His hair was greasy and ragged, the color of fireplace soot, topped with a crown of what looked like finger bones. His robes were tattered fur—wolf, rabbit, raccoon, deer, and several others Piper couldn't identify. The furs didn't look cured, and from the smell, they weren't very fresh. His frame was lithe and muscular, like a distance runner's. But the most horrible thing was his face. His thin pale skin was pulled tight over his skull. His teeth were sharpened like fangs. His eyes glowed bright red like his wolves'—and they fixed on Jason with absolute hatred.

"*Ecce,*" he said, "*filli Romani.*"

"Speak English, wolf man!" Hedge bellowed.

The wolf man snarled. "Tell your faun to mind his tongue, son of Rome. Or he'll be my first snack."

Piper remembered that *faun* was the Roman name for *satyr.* Not exactly helpful information. Now, if she could remember who this wolf guy was in Greek mythology, and how to defeat him, *that* she could use.

The wolf man studied their little group. His nostrils twitched. "So it's true," he mused. "A child of Aphrodite. A son of Hephaestus. A faun. And a child of Rome, of Lord Jupiter, no less. All together, without killing each other. How interesting."

"You were told about us?" Jason asked. "By whom?"

The man snarled—perhaps a laugh, perhaps a challenge. "Oh, we've been patrolling for you all across the west, demigod, hoping we'd be the first to find you. The giant king will reward me well when he rises. I am Lycaon, king of the wolves. And my pack is hungry."

The wolves snarled in the darkness.

Out of the corner of her eye, Piper saw Leo put up his hammer and slip something else from his tool belt—a glass bottle full of clear liquid.

Piper racked her brain trying to place the wolf guy's name. She knew she'd heard it before, but she couldn't remember details.

Lycaon glared at Jason's sword. He moved to each side as if looking for an opening, but Jason's blade moved with him.

"Leave," Jason ordered. "There's no food for you here."

"Unless you want tofu burgers," Leo offered.

Lycaon bared his fangs. Apparently he wasn't a tofu fan.

"If I had my way," Lycaon said with regret, "I'd kill you first, son of Jupiter. Your father made me what I am. I was the powerful mortal king of Arcadia, with fifty fine sons, and Zeus slew them all with his lightning bolts."

"Ha," Coach Hedge said. "For good reason!"

Jason glanced over his shoulder. "Coach, you know this clown?"

"*I* do," Piper answered. The details of the myth came back to her—a short, horrible story she and her father had laughed at over breakfast. She wasn't laughing now.

"Lycaon invited Zeus to dinner," she said. "But the king wasn't sure it was really Zeus. So to test his powers, Lycaon tried to feed him human flesh. Zeus got outraged—"

"And killed my sons!" Lycaon howled. The wolves behind him howled too.

"So Zeus turned him into a wolf," Piper said. "They call . . . they call werewolves *lycanthropes*, named after him, the first werewolf."

"The king of wolves," Coach Hedge finished. "An immortal, smelly, vicious mutt."

Lycaon growled. "I will tear you apart, faun!"

"Oh, you want some goat, buddy? 'Cause I'll give you goat."

"Stop it," Jason said. "Lycaon, you said you *wanted* to kill me first, but...?"

"Sadly, Child of Rome, you are spoken for. Since this one" —he waggled his claws at Piper—"has failed to kill you, you are to be delivered alive to the Wolf House. One of my compatriots has asked for the honor of killing you herself."

"Who?" Jason said.

The wolf king snickered. "Oh, a great admirer of yours. Apparently, you made quite an impression on her. She will take care of you soon enough, and really I cannot complain. Spilling your blood at the Wolf House should mark my new territory quite well. Lupa will think twice about challenging my pack."

Piper's heart tried to jump out of her chest. She didn't understand everything Lycaon had said, but a woman who wanted to kill Jason? Medea, she thought. Somehow, she must've survived the explosion.

Piper struggled to her feet. Spots danced before her eyes again. The cave seemed to spin.

"You're going to leave now," Piper said, "before we destroy you."

She tried to put power into the words, but she was too weak. Shivering in her blankets, pale and sweaty and barely able to hold a knife, she couldn't have looked very threatening.

Lycaon's red eyes crinkled with humor. "A brave try, girl.

I admire that. Perhaps I'll make your end quick. Only the son of Jupiter is needed alive. The rest of you, I'm afraid, are dinner."

At that moment, Piper knew she was going to die. But at least she'd die on her feet, fighting next to Jason.

Jason took a step forward. "You're not killing anyone, wolf man. Not without going through me."

Lycaon howled and extended his claws. Jason slashed at him, but his golden sword passed straight through as if the wolf king wasn't there.

Lycaon laughed. "Gold, bronze, steel—none of these are any good against my wolves, son of Jupiter."

"Silver!" Piper cried. "Aren't werewolves hurt by silver?"

"We don't have any silver!" Jason said.

Wolves leaped into the firelight. Hedge charged forward with an elated "Woot!"

But Leo struck first. He threw his glass bottle and it shattered on the ground, splattering liquid all over the wolves —the unmistakable smell of gasoline. He shot a burst of fire at the puddle, and a wall of flames erupted.

Wolves yelped and retreated. Several caught fire and had to run back into the snow. Even Lycaon looked uneasily at the barrier of flames now separating his wolves from the demigods.

"Aw, c'mon," Coach Hedge complained. "I can't hit them if they're way over there."

Every time a wolf came closer, Leo shot a new wave of fire from his hands, but each effort seemed to make him a little more tired, and the gasoline was already dying down. "I can't summon any more gas!" Leo warned. Then his face turned red. "Wow, that came out wrong. I mean the *burning* kind. Gonna take the tool belt a while to recharge. What you got, man?"

"Nothing," Jason said. "Not even a weapon that works."

"Lightning?" Piper asked.

Jason concentrated, but nothing happened. "I think the snowstorm is interfering, or something."

"Unleash the *venti*!" Piper said.

"Then we'll have nothing to give Aeolus," Jason said. "We'll have come all this way for nothing."

Lycaon laughed. "I can smell your fear. A few more minutes of life, heroes. Pray to whatever gods you wish. Zeus did not grant me mercy, and you will have none from me."

The flames began to sputter out. Jason cursed and dropped his sword. He crouched like he was ready to go hand-to-hand. Leo pulled his hammer out of his pack. Piper raised her dagger—not much, but it was all she had. Coach Hedge hefted his club, and he was the only one who looked excited about dying.

Then a ripping sound cut through the wind—like a piece of tearing cardboard. A long stick sprouted from the neck of the nearest wolf—the shaft of a silver arrow. The wolf writhed and fell, melting into a puddle of shadow.

More arrows. More wolves fell. The pack broke in confusion. An arrow flashed toward Lycaon, but the wolf king caught it in midair. Then he yelled in pain. When he dropped the arrow, it left a charred, smoking gash across his palm. Another arrow caught him in the shoulder, and the wolf king staggered.

"Curse them!" Lycaon yelled. He growled at his pack, and the wolves turned and ran. Lycaon fixed Jason with those glowing red eyes. "This isn't over, boy."

The wolf king disappeared into the night.

Seconds later, Piper heard more wolves baying, but the sound was different—less threatening, more like hunting dogs on the scent. A smaller white wolf burst into the cave, followed by two more.

Hedge said, "Kill it?"

"No!" Piper said. "Wait."

The wolves tilted their heads and studied the campers with huge golden eyes.

A heartbeat later, their masters appeared: a troop of hunters in white-and-gray winter camouflage, at least half a dozen. All of them carried bows, with quivers of glowing silver arrows on their backs.

Their faces were covered with parka hoods, but clearly they were all girls. One, a little taller than the rest, crouched in the firelight and snatched up the arrow that had wounded Lycaon's hand.

"So close." She turned to her companions. "Phoebe, stay with me. Watch the entrance. The rest of you, follow Lycaon. We can't lose him now. I'll catch up with you."

The other hunters mumbled agreement and disappeared, heading after Lycaon's pack.

The girl in white turned toward them, her face still hidden

in her parka hood. "We've been following that demon's trail for over a week. Is everyone all right? No one got bit?"

Jason stood frozen, staring at the girl. Piper realized something about her voice sounded familiar. It was hard to pin down, but the way she spoke, the way she formed her words, reminded her of Jason.

"You're her," Piper guessed. "You're Thalia."

The girl tensed. Piper was afraid she might draw her bow, but instead she pulled down her parka hood. Her hair was spiky black, with a silver tiara across her brow. Her face had a super-healthy glow to it, as if she were a little more than human, and her eyes were brilliant blue. She was the girl from Jason's photograph.

"Do I know you?" Thalia asked.

Piper took a breath. "This might be a shock, but—"

"Thalia." Jason stepped forward, his voice trembling. "I'm Jason, your brother."

LEO

LEO FIGURED HE HAD THE WORST LUCK in the group, and that was saying a lot. Why didn't *he* get to have the long-lost sister or the movie star dad who needed rescuing? All he got was a tool belt and a dragon that broke down halfway through the quest. Maybe it was the stupid curse of the Hephaestus cabin, but Leo didn't think so. His life had been unlucky way before he got to camp.

A thousand years from now, when this quest was being told around a campfire, he figured people would talk about brave Jason, beautiful Piper, and their sidekick Flaming Valdez, who accompanied them with a bag of magic screwdrivers and occasionally fixed tofu burgers.

If that wasn't bad enough, Leo fell in love with every girl he saw—as long as she was totally out of his league.

When he first saw Thalia, Leo immediately thought she was *way* too pretty to be Jason's sister. Then he thought he'd better not say that or he'd get in trouble. He liked her dark hair, her blue eyes, and her confident attitude. She looked like the kind of girl who could stomp anybody on the ball court or the battlefield, and wouldn't give Leo the time of day—just Leo's type!

For a minute, Jason and Thalia faced each other, stunned. Then Thalia rushed forward and hugged him.

"My gods! She told me you were dead!" She gripped Jason's face and seemed to be examining everything about it. "Thank Artemis, it *is* you. That little scar on your lip—you tried to eat a stapler when you were two!"

Leo laughed. "Seriously?"

Hedge nodded like he approved of Jason's taste. "Staplers —excellent source of iron."

"W-wait," Jason stammered. "Who told you I was dead? What happened?"

At the cave entrance, one of the white wolves barked. Thalia looked back at the wolf and nodded, but she kept her hands on Jason's face, like she was afraid he might vanish. "My wolf is telling me I don't have much time, and she's right. But we *have* to talk. Let's sit."

Piper did better than that. She collapsed. She would've cracked her head on the cave floor if Hedge hadn't caught her.

Thalia rushed over. "What's wrong with her? Ah—never mind. I see. Hypothermia. Ankle." She frowned at the satyr. "Don't you know nature healing?"

Hedge scoffed. "Why do you think she looks *this* good? Can't you smell the Gatorade?"

Thalia looked at Leo for the first time, and of course it was an accusatory glare, like *Why did you let the goat be a doctor?* As if that was Leo's fault.

"You and the satyr," Thalia ordered, "take this girl to my friend at the entrance. Phoebe's an excellent healer."

"It's cold out there!" Hedge said. "I'll freeze my horns off."

But Leo knew when they weren't wanted. "Come on, Hedge. These two need time to talk."

"Humph. Fine," the satyr muttered. "Didn't even get to brain anybody."

Hedge carried Piper toward the entrance. Leo was about to follow when Jason called, "Actually, man, could you, um, stick around?"

Leo saw something in Jason's eyes he didn't expect: Jason was asking for support. He wanted somebody else there. He was scared.

Leo grinned. "Sticking around is my specialty."

Thalia didn't look too happy about it, but the three of them sat at the fire. For a few minutes, nobody spoke. Jason studied his sister like she was a scary device—one that might explode if handled incorrectly. Thalia seemed more at ease, as if she was used to stumbling across stranger things than long-lost relatives. But still she regarded Jason in a kind of amazed trance, maybe remembering a little two-year-old who tried to eat a stapler. Leo took a few pieces of copper wire out of his pockets and twisted them together.

Finally he couldn't stand the silence. "So...the Hunters of Artemis. This whole 'not dating' thing—is that like *always*, or more of a seasonal thing, or what?"

Thalia stared at him as if he'd just evolved from pond scum. Yeah, he was *definitely* liking this girl.

Jason kicked him in the shin. "Don't mind Leo. He's just trying to break the ice. But, Thalia . . . what happened to our family? Who told you I was dead?"

Thalia tugged at a silver bracelet on her wrist. In the firelight, in her winter camouflage, she almost looked like Khione the snow princess—just as cold and beautiful.

"Do you remember anything?" she asked.

Jason shook his head. "I woke up three days ago on a bus with Leo and Piper."

"Which wasn't our fault," Leo added hastily. "Hera stole his memories."

Thalia tensed. "Hera? How do you know that?"

Jason explained about their quest—the prophecy at camp, Hera getting imprisoned, the giant taking Piper's dad, and the winter solstice deadline. Leo chimed in to add the important stuff: how he'd fixed the bronze dragon, could throw fireballs, and made excellent tacos.

Thalia was a good listener. Nothing seemed to surprise her—the monsters, the prophecies, the dead rising. But when Jason mentioned King Midas, she cursed in Ancient Greek.

"I knew we should've burned down his mansion," she said. "That man's a menace. But we were so intent on following Lycaon— Well, I'm glad you got away. So Hera's been . . . what, hiding you all these years?"

"I don't know." Jason brought out the photo from his pocket. "She left me just enough memory to recognize your face."

Thalia looked at the picture, and her expression softened. "I'd forgotten about that. I left it in Cabin One, didn't I?"

Jason nodded. "I think Hera wanted for us to meet. When we landed here, at this cave...I had a feeling it was important. Like I knew you were close by. Is that crazy?"

"Nah," Leo assured him. "We were absolutely destined to meet your hot sister."

Thalia ignored him. Probably she just didn't want to let on how much Leo impressed her.

"Jason," she said, "when you're dealing with the gods, *nothing* is too crazy. But you can't trust Hera, especially since we're children of Zeus. She *hates* all children of Zeus."

"But she said something about Zeus giving her my life as a peace offering. Does that make any sense?"

The color drained from Thalia's face. "Oh, gods. Mother wouldn't have...You don't remember— No, of course you don't."

"What?" Jason asked.

Thalia's features seemed to grow older in the firelight, like her immortality wasn't working so well. "Jason...I'm not sure how to say this. Our mom wasn't exactly stable. She caught Zeus's eye because she was a television actress, and she *was* beautiful, but she didn't handle the fame well. She drank, pulled stupid stunts. She was always in the tabloids. She could never get enough attention. Even before you were born, she and I argued all the time. She...she knew Dad was Zeus, and I think that was too much for her to take. It was like the ultimate achievement for her to attract the lord of the sky, and she couldn't accept it when he left. The thing about the gods ... well, they don't hang around."

Leo remembered his own mom, the way she'd assured him over and over that his dad would be back someday. But she'd never acted mad about it. She didn't seem to want Hephaestus for herself—only so Leo could know his father. She'd dealt with working a dead-end job, living in a tiny apartment, never having enough money—and she'd seemed fine with it. As long as she had Leo, she always said, life would be okay.

He watched Jason's face—looking more and more devastated as Thalia described their mom—and for once, Leo didn't feel jealous of his friend. Leo might have lost his mom. He might have had some hard times. But at least he remembered her. He found himself tapping out a Morse code message on his knee: *Love you.* He felt bad for Jason, not having memories like that—not having anything to fall back on.

"So ..." Jason didn't seem able to finish the question.

"Jason, you got friends," Leo told him. "Now you got a sister. You're not alone."

Thalia offered her hand, and Jason took it.

"When I was about seven," she said, "Zeus started visiting Mom again. I think he felt bad about wrecking her life, and he seemed—different somehow. A little older and sterner, more fatherly toward me. For a while, Mom improved. She loved having Zeus around, bringing her presents, causing the sky to rumble. She always wanted more attention. That's the year you were born. Mom ... well, I never got along with her, but you gave me a reason to hang around. You were so cute.

And I didn't trust Mom to look after you. Of course, Zeus eventually stopped coming by again. He probably couldn't stand Mom's demands anymore, always pestering him to let her visit Olympus, or to make her immortal or eternally beautiful. When he left for good, Mom got more and more unstable. That was about the time the monsters started attacking me. Mom blamed Hera. She claimed the goddess was coming after you too—that Hera had barely tolerated my birth, but *two* demigod children from the same family was too big an insult. Mom even said she hadn't wanted to name you Jason, but Zeus insisted, as a way to appease Hera because the goddess liked that name. I didn't know what to believe."

Leo fiddled with his copper wires. He felt like an intruder. He shouldn't be listening to this, but it also made him feel like he was getting to know Jason for the first time—like maybe being here now made up for those four months at Wilderness School, when Leo had just imagined they'd had a friendship.

"How did you guys get separated?" he asked.

Thalia squeezed her brother's hand. "If I'd known you were alive... gods, things would've been so different. But when you were two, Mom packed us in the car for a family vacation. We drove up north, toward the wine country, to this park she wanted to show us. I remember thinking it was strange because Mom never took us anywhere, and she was acting super nervous. I was holding your hand, walking you toward this big building in the middle of the park, and..." She took a shaky breath. "Mom told me to go back to the car and get the picnic basket. I didn't want to leave you alone with her, but it was only for a few minutes. When I came back... Mom was kneeling on the stone steps, hugging herself and crying. She said—she said you were gone. She said Hera claimed you and you were as good as dead. I didn't know what she'd done. I was afraid she'd completely lost her mind. I ran all over the place looking for you, but you'd just vanished. She had to drag me away, kicking and screaming. For the next few days I was hysterical. I don't remember everything, but I called the police on Mom and they questioned her for a long time. Afterward, we fought. She told me I'd betrayed her, that I should support her, like *she* was the only one who mattered. Finally I couldn't stand it. Your disappearance was the last straw. I ran away from home, and I never went back, not even when Mom died a few years ago. I thought you were gone forever. I never told anyone about you—not even Annabeth or Luke, my two best friends. It was just too painful."

"Chiron knew." Jason's voice sounded far away. "When I got to camp, he took one look at me and said, 'You should be dead.'"

"That doesn't make sense," Thalia insisted. "I never told him."

"Hey," Leo said. "Important thing is you've got each other now, right? You two are lucky."

Thalia nodded. "Leo's right. Look at you. You're *my* age. You've grown up."

"But where have I been?" Jason said. "How could I be missing all that time? And the Roman stuff…"

Thalia frowned. "The Roman stuff?"

"Your brother speaks Latin," Leo said. "He calls gods by their Roman names, and he's got tattoos." Leo pointed out the marks on Jason's arm. Then he gave Thalia the rundown about the other weird stuff that had happened: Boreas turning into Aquilon, Lycaon calling Jason a "child of Rome," and the wolves backing off when Jason spoke Latin to them.

Thalia plucked her bowstring. "Latin. Zeus sometimes spoke Latin, the second time he stayed with Mom. Like I said, he seemed different, more formal."

"You think he was in his Roman aspect?" Jason asked. "And that's why I think of myself as a child of Jupiter?"

"Possibly," Thalia said. "I've never heard of something like that happening, but it might explain why you think in Roman terms, why you can speak Latin rather than Ancient Greek. That would make you unique. Still, it doesn't explain how you've survived without Camp Half-Blood. A child of Zeus, or Jupiter, or whatever you want to call him—you would've been hounded by monsters. If you were on your own, you should've died years ago. I know *I* wouldn't have been able to survive without friends. You would've needed training, a safe haven—"

"He wasn't alone," Leo blurted out. "We've heard about others like him."

Thalia looked at him strangely. "What do you mean?"

Leo told her about the slashed-up purple shirt in Medea's department store, and the story the Cyclopes told about the child of Mercury who spoke Latin.

"Isn't there anywhere else for demigods?" Leo asked. "I mean besides Camp Half-Blood? Maybe some crazy Latin teacher has been abducting children of the gods or something, making them think like Romans."

As soon as he said it, Leo realized how stupid the idea sounded. Thalia's dazzling blue eyes studied him intently, making him feel like a suspect in a lineup.

"I've been all over the country," Thalia mused. "I've never seen evidence of a crazy Latin teacher, or demigods in purple shirts. Still..." Her voice trailed off, like she'd just had a troubling thought.

"What?" Jason asked.

Thalia shook her head. "I'll have to talk to the goddess. Maybe Artemis will guide us."

"She's still talking to you?" Jason asked. "Most of the gods have gone silent."

"Artemis follows her own rules," Thalia said. "She has to be careful not to let Zeus know, but she thinks Zeus is being ridiculous closing Olympus. She's the one who set us on the trail of Lycaon. She said we'd find a lead to a missing friend of ours."

"Percy Jackson," Leo guessed. "The guy Annabeth is looking for."

Thalia nodded, her face full of concern.

Leo wondered if anyone had ever looked that worried all the times *he'd* disappeared. He kind of doubted it.

"So what would Lycaon have to do with it?" Leo asked. "And how does it connect to us?"

"We need to find out soon," Thalia admitted. "If your deadline is tomorrow, we're wasting time. Aeolus could tell you—"

The white wolf appeared again at the doorway and yipped insistently.

"I have to get moving." Thalia stood. "Otherwise I'll lose the other Hunters' trail. First, though, I'll take you to Aeolus's palace."

"If you can't, it's okay," Jason said, though he sounded kind of distressed.

"Oh, please." Thalia smiled and helped him up. "I haven't had a brother in years. I think I can stand a few minutes with you before you get annoying. Now, let's go!"

LEO

WHEN LEO SAW HOW WELL PIPER AND HEDGE were being treated, he was thoroughly offended.

He'd imagined them freezing their hindquarters off in the snow, but the Hunter Phoebe had set up this silver tent pavilion thing right outside the cave. How she'd done it so fast, Leo had no idea, but inside was a kerosene heater keeping them toasty warm and a bunch of comfy throw pillows. Piper looked back to normal, decked out in a new parka, gloves, and camo pants like a Hunter. She and Hedge and Phoebe were kicking back, drinking hot chocolate.

"Oh, no way," Leo said. "We've been sitting in a *cave* and you get the luxury tent? Somebody give me hypothermia. I want hot chocolate and a parka!"

Phoebe sniffed. "Boys," she said, like it was the worst insult she could think of.

"It's all right, Phoebe," Thalia said. "They'll need extra coats. And I think we can spare some chocolate."

Phoebe grumbled, but soon Leo and Jason were also dressed in silvery winter clothes that were incredibly light-weight and warm. The hot chocolate was first-rate.

"Cheers!" said Coach Hedge. He crunched down his plastic thermos cup.

"That cannot be good for your intestines," Leo said.

Thalia patted Piper on the back. "You up for moving?"

Piper nodded. "Thanks to Phoebe, yeah. You guys are really good at this wilderness survival thing. I feel like I could run ten miles."

Thalia winked at Jason. "She's tough for a child of Aphrodite. I like this one."

"Hey, I could run ten miles too," Leo volunteered. "Tough Hephaestus kid here. Let's hit it."

Naturally, Thalia ignored him.

It took Phoebe exactly six seconds to break camp, which Leo could not believe. The tent self-collapsed into a square the size of a pack of chewing gum. Leo wanted to ask her for the blueprints, but they didn't have time.

Thalia ran uphill through the snow, hugging a tiny little path on the side of the mountain, and soon Leo was regretting trying to look macho, because the Hunters left him in the dust.

Coach Hedge leaped around like a happy mountain goat, coaxing them on like he used to do on track days at school. "Come on, Valdez! Pick up the pace! Let's chant. *I've got a girl in Kalamazoo—*"

"Let's not," Thalia snapped.

So they ran in silence.

Leo fell in next to Jason at the back of the group. "How you doing, man?"

Jason's expression was enough of an answer: *Not good.*

"Thalia takes it so calmly," Jason said. "Like it's no big deal that I appeared. I didn't know what I was expecting, but... she's not like me. She seems so much more *together.*"

"Hey, she's not fighting amnesia," Leo said. "Plus, she's had more time to get used to this whole demigod thing. You fight monsters and talk to gods for a while, you probably get used to surprises."

"Maybe," Jason said. "I just wish I understood what happened when I was two, why my mom got rid of me. Thalia ran away because of *me.*"

"Hey, whatever's happened, it wasn't your fault. And your sister is pretty cool. She's a *lot* like you."

Jason took that in silence. Leo wondered if he'd said the right things. He wanted to make Jason feel better, but this was way outside his comfort zone.

Leo wished he could reach inside his tool belt and pick just the right wrench to fix Jason's memory—maybe a little hammer —bonk the sticking spot and make everything run right. That would be a lot easier than trying to talk it through. *Not good with organic life forms.* Thanks for those inherited traits, Dad.

He was so lost in thought, he didn't realize the Hunters had stopped. He slammed into Thalia and nearly sent them both down the side of the mountain the hard way. Fortunately, the Hunter was light on her feet. She steadied them both, then pointed up.

"That," Leo choked, "is a really large rock."

They stood near the summit of Pikes Peak. Below them the world was blanketed in clouds. The air was so thin, Leo could hardly breathe. Night had set in, but a full moon shone and the stars were incredible. Stretching out to the north and south, peaks of other mountains rose from the clouds like islands—or teeth.

But the real show was above them. Hovering in the sky, about a quarter mile away, was a massive free-floating island of glowing purple stone. It was hard to judge its size, but Leo figured it was at least as wide as a football stadium and just as tall. The sides were rugged cliffs, riddled with caves, and every once in a while a gust of wind burst out with a sound like a pipe organ blast. At the top of the rock, brass walls ringed some kind of a fortress.

The only thing connecting Pikes Peak to the floating island was a narrow bridge of ice that glistened in the moonlight.

Then Leo realized the bridge wasn't exactly ice, because it wasn't solid. As the winds changed direction, the bridge snaked around—blurring and thinning, in some places even breaking into a dotted line like the vapor trail of a plane.

"We're not seriously crossing that," Leo said.

Thalia shrugged. "I'm not a big fan of heights, I'll admit. But if you want to get to Aeolus's fortress, this is the only way."

"Is the fortress always hanging there?" Piper asked. "How can people not notice it sitting on top of Pikes Peak?"

"The Mist," Thalia said. "Still, mortals do notice it indirectly. Some days, Pikes Peak looks purple. People say it's a trick of the light, but actually it's the color of Aeolus's palace, reflecting off the mountain face."

"It's enormous," Jason said.

Thalia laughed. "You should see Olympus, little brother."

"You're serious? You've been there?"

Thalia grimaced as if it wasn't a good memory. "We should go across in two different groups. The bridge is fragile."

"That's reassuring," Leo said. "Jason, can't you just fly us up there?"

Thalia laughed. Then she seemed to realize Leo's question wasn't a joke. "Wait . . . Jason, you can *fly*?"

Jason gazed up at the floating fortress. "Well, sort of. More like I can control the winds. But the winds up here are so strong, I'm not sure I'd want to try. Thalia, you mean . . . you can't fly?"

For a second, Thalia looked genuinely afraid. Then she got her expression under control. Leo realized she was a lot more scared of heights than she was letting on.

"Truthfully," she said, "I've never tried. Might be better if we stuck to the bridge."

Coach Hedge tapped the ice vapor trail with his hoof, then jumped onto the bridge. Amazingly, it held his weight. "Easy! I'll go first. Piper, come on, girl. I'll give you a hand."

"No, that's okay," Piper started to say, but the coach grabbed her hand and dragged her up the bridge.

When they were about halfway, the bridge still seemed to be holding them just fine.

Thalia turned to her Hunter friend. "Phoebe, I'll be back soon. Go find the others. Tell them I'm on my way."

"You sure?" Phoebe narrowed her eyes at Leo and Jason, like they might kidnap Thalia or something.

"It's fine," Thalia promised.

Phoebe nodded reluctantly, then raced down the mountain path, the white wolves at her heels.

"Jason, Leo, just be careful where you step," Thalia said. "It hardly ever breaks."

"It hasn't met me yet," Leo muttered, but he and Jason led the way up the bridge.

Halfway up, things went wrong, and of course it was Leo's fault. Piper and Hedge had already made it safely to the top and were waving at them, encouraging them to keep climbing, but Leo got distracted. He was thinking about bridges —how he would design something way more stable than this shifting ice vapor business if this were his palace. He was pondering braces and support columns. Then a sudden revelation stopped him in his tracks.

"Why do they have a bridge?" he asked.

Thalia frowned. "Leo, this isn't a good place to stop. What do you mean?"

"They're wind spirits," Leo said. "Can't they fly?"

"Yes, but sometimes they need a way to connect to the world below."

"So the bridge isn't always here?" Leo asked.

Thalia shook her head. "The wind spirits don't like to anchor to the earth, but sometimes it's necessary. Like now. They know you're coming."

Leo's mind was racing. He was so excited he could almost feel his body's temperature rising. He couldn't quite put his thoughts into words, but he knew he was on to something important.

"Leo?" Jason said. "What are you thinking?"

"Oh, gods," Thalia said. "Keep moving. Look at your feet."

Leo shuffled backward. With horror, he realized his body temperature really *was* rising, just as it had years ago at that picnic table under the pecan tree, when his anger had gotten away from him. Now, excitement was causing the reaction. His pants steamed in the cold air. His shoes were literally smoking, and the bridge didn't like it. The ice was thinning.

"Leo, stop it," Jason warned. "You're going to melt it."

"I'll try," Leo said. But his body was overheating on its own, running as fast as his thoughts. "Listen, Jason, what did Hera call you in that dream? She called you a *bridge*."

"Leo, seriously, cool down," Thalia said. "I don't know what you're talking about, but the bridge is—"

"Just listen," Leo insisted. "If Jason is a bridge, what's he connecting? Maybe two different places that normally don't get along—like the air palace and the ground. You had to be somewhere before this, right? And Hera said you were an exchange."

"An exchange." Thalia's eyes widened. "Oh, gods."

Jason frowned. "What are you two talking about?"

Thalia murmured something like a prayer. "I understand now why Artemis sent me here. Jason—she told me to hunt for Lycaon and I would find a clue about Percy. *You* are the clue. Artemis wanted us to meet so I could hear your story."

"I don't understand," he protested. "I don't have a story. I don't remember anything."

"But Leo's right," Thalia said. "It's all connected. If we just knew where—"

Leo snapped his fingers. "Jason, what did you call that place in your dream? That ruined house. The Wolf House?"

Thalia nearly choked. "The Wolf House? Jason, why didn't you tell me that! *That's* where they're keeping Hera?"

"You know where it is?" Jason asked.

Then the bridge dissolved. Leo would've fallen to his death, but Jason grabbed his coat and pulled him to safety. The two of them scrambled up the bridge, and when they turned, Thalia was on the other side of a thirty-foot chasm. The bridge was continuing to melt.

"Go!" Thalia shouted, backing down the bridge as it crumbled. "Find out where the giant is keeping Piper's dad. Save him! I'll take the Hunters to the Wolf House and hold it until you can get there. We can do both!"

"But where *is* the Wolf House?" Jason shouted.

"You know where it is, little brother!" She was so far away now that they could barely hear her voice over the wind. Leo was pretty sure she said: "I'll see you there. I promise."

Then she turned and raced down the dissolving bridge.

Leo and Jason had no time to stand around. They climbed for their lives, the ice vapor thinning under their feet. Several times, Jason grabbed Leo and used the winds to keep them aloft, but it was more like bungee jumping than flying.

When they reached the floating island, Piper and Coach Hedge pulled them aboard just as the last of the vapor bridge vanished. They stood gasping for breath at the base of a stone stairway chiseled into the side of the cliff, leading up to the fortress.

Leo looked back down. The top of Pikes Peak floated below them in a sea of clouds, but there was no sign of Thalia. And Leo had just burned their only exit.

"What happened?" Piper demanded. "Leo, why are your clothes smoking?"

"I got a little heated," he gasped. "Sorry, Jason. Honest. I didn't—"

"It's all right," Jason said, but his expression was grim. "We've got less than twenty-four hours to rescue a goddess and Piper's dad. Let's go see the king of the winds."

XXXVII

JASON

JASON HAD FOUND HIS SISTER AND lost her in less than an hour. As they climbed the cliffs of the floating island, he kept looking back, but Thalia was gone.

Despite what she'd said about meeting him again, Jason wondered. She'd found a new family with the Hunters, and a new mother in Artemis. She seemed so confident and comfortable with her life, Jason wasn't sure if he'd ever be part of it. And she seemed so set on finding her friend Percy. Had she ever searched for Jason that way?

Not fair, he told himself. *She thought you were dead.*

He could barely tolerate what she'd said about their mom. It was almost like Thalia had handed him a baby—a really loud, ugly baby—and said, *Here, this is yours. Carry it.* He didn't want to carry it. He didn't want to look at it or claim it. He didn't want to know that he had an unstable mother who'd gotten rid of him to appease a goddess. No wonder Thalia had run away.

Then he remembered the Zeus cabin at Camp Half-Blood —that tiny little alcove Thalia had used as a bunk, out of sight from the glowering statue of the sky god. Their dad wasn't much of a bargain, either. Jason understood why Thalia had renounced that part of her life too, but he was still resentful. He couldn't be so lucky. He was left holding the bag —literally.

The golden backpack of winds was strapped over his shoulders. The closer they got to Aeolus's palace, the heavier the bag got. The winds struggled, rumbling and bumping around.

The only one who seemed in a good mood was Coach Hedge. He kept bounding up the slippery staircase and trotting back down. "Come on, cupcakes! Only a few thousand more steps!"

As they climbed, Leo and Piper left Jason in his silence. Maybe they could sense his bad mood. Piper kept glancing back, worried, as if he were the one who'd almost died of hypothermia rather than she. Or maybe she was thinking about Thalia's idea. They'd told her what Thalia had said on the bridge—how they could save both her dad and Hera—but Jason didn't really understand how they were going to do that, and he wasn't sure if the possibility had made Piper more hopeful or just more anxious.

Leo kept swatting his own legs, checking for signs that his pants were on fire. He wasn't steaming anymore, but the incident on the ice bridge had really freaked Jason out. Leo hadn't seemed to realize that he had smoke coming out his ears and flames dancing through his hair. If Leo started spontaneously combusting every time he got excited, they were going to have a tough time taking him anywhere. Jason imagined trying to get food at a restaurant. *I'll have a cheeseburger and—Ahhh! My friend's on fire! Get me a bucket!*

Mostly, though, Jason worried about what Leo had said. Jason didn't want to be a bridge, or an exchange, or anything else. He just wanted to know where he'd come from. And Thalia had looked so unnerved when Leo mentioned the burned-out house in his dreams—the place the wolf Lupa had told him was his starting point. How did Thalia know that place, and why did she assume Jason could find it?

The answer seemed close. But the nearer Jason got to it, the less it cooperated, like the winds on his back.

Finally they arrived at the top of the island. Bronze walls marched all the way around the fortress grounds, though Jason couldn't imagine who would possibly attack this place. Twenty-foot-high gates opened for them, and a road of polished purple stone led up to the main citadel—a white-columned rotunda, Greek style, like one of the monuments in Washington, D.C.—except for the cluster of satellite dishes and radio towers on the roof.

"That's bizarre," Piper said.

"Guess you can't get cable on a floating island," Leo said. "Dang, check this guy's front yard."

The rotunda sat in the center of a quarter-mile circle. The grounds were amazing in a scary way. They were divided into four sections like big pizza slices, each one representing a season.

The section on their right was an icy waste, with bare trees and a frozen lake. Snowmen rolled across the landscape as the wind blew, so Jason wasn't sure if they were decorations or alive.

To their left was an autumn park with gold and red trees. Mounds of leaves blew into patterns—gods, people, animals that ran after each other before scattering back into leaves.

In the distance, Jason could see two more areas behind the rotunda. One looked like a green pasture with sheep made out of clouds. The last section was a desert where tumbleweeds scratched strange patterns in the sand like Greek letters, smiley faces, and a huge advertisement that read: WATCH AEOLUS NIGHTLY!

"One section for each of the four wind gods," Jason guessed. "Four cardinal directions."

"I'm loving that pasture." Coach Hedge licked his lips. "You guys mind—"

"Go ahead," Jason said. He was actually relieved to send the satyr off. It would be hard enough getting on Aeolus's good side without Coach Hedge waving his club and screaming, "Die!"

While the satyr ran off to attack springtime, Jason, Leo, and Piper walked down the road to the steps of the palace. They passed through the front doors into a white marble foyer decorated with purple banners that read OLYMPIAN WEATHER CHANNEL, and some that just read OW!

"Hello!" A woman floated up to them. *Literally* floated. She was pretty in that elfish way Jason associated with nature spirits at Camp Half-Blood—petite, slightly pointy ears, and an ageless face that could've been sixteen or thirty. Her brown eyes twinkled cheerfully. Even though there was no wind, her dark hair blew in slow motion, shampoo-commercial style. Her white gown billowed around her like parachute material. Jason couldn't tell if she had feet, but if so, they didn't touch the floor. She had a white tablet computer in her hand. "Are you from Lord Zeus?" she asked. "We've been expecting you."

Jason tried to respond, but it was a little hard to think straight, because he'd realized the woman was see-through. Her shape faded in and out like she was made of fog.

"Are you a ghost?" he asked.

Right away he knew he'd insulted her. The smile turned into a pout. "I'm an *aura*, sir. A wind nymph, as you might expect, working for the lord of the winds. My name is Mellie. We don't have *ghosts*."

Piper came to the rescue. "No, of course you don't! My friend simply mistook you for Helen of Troy, the most beautiful mortal of all time. It's an easy mistake."

Wow, she was good. The compliment seemed a little over the top, but Mellie the aura blushed. "Oh... well, then. So you *are* from Zeus?"

"Er," Jason said, "I'm the son of Zeus, yeah."

"Excellent! Please, right this way." She led them through some security doors into another lobby, consulting her tablet as she floated. She didn't look where she was going, but apparently it didn't matter as she drifted straight through a marble column with no problem. "We're out of prime time now, so that's good," she mused. "I can fit you in right before his 11:12 spot."

"Um, okay," Jason said.

The lobby was a pretty distracting place. Winds blasted

around them, so Jason felt like he was pushing through an invisible crowd. Doors blew open and slammed by themselves.

The things Jason *could* see were just as bizarre. Paper airplanes of all different sizes and shapes sped around, and other wind nymphs, *aurai*, would occasionally pluck them out of the air, unfold and read them, then toss them back into the air, where the planes would refold themselves and keep flying.

An ugly creature fluttered past. She looked like a mix between an old lady and a chicken on steroids. She had a wrinkled face with black hair tied in a hairnet, arms like a human plus wings like a chicken, and a fat, feathered body with talons for feet. It was amazing she could fly at all. She kept drifting around and bumping into things like a parade balloon.

"Not an *aura*?" Jason asked Mellie as the creature wobbled by.

Mellie laughed. "That's a harpy, of course. Our, ah, ugly stepsisters, I suppose you would say. Don't you have harpies on Olympus? They're spirits of violent gusts, unlike us *aurai*. We're all gentle breezes."

She batted her eyes at Jason.

"'Course you are," he said.

"So," Piper prompted, "you were taking us to see Aeolus?"

Mellie led them through a set of doors like an airlock. Above the interior door, a green light blinked.

"We have a few minutes before he starts," Mellie said cheerfully. "He probably won't kill you if we go in now. Come along!"

XXXVIII

JASON

JASON'S JAW DROPPED. THE CENTRAL SECTION of Aeolus's fortress was as big as a cathedral, with a soaring domed roof covered in silver. Television equipment floated randomly through the air—cameras, spotlights, set pieces, potted plants. And there was no floor. Leo almost fell into the chasm before Jason pulled him back.

"Holy—!" Leo gulped. "Hey, Mellie. A little warning next time!"

An enormous circular pit plunged into the heart of the mountain. It was probably half a mile deep, honeycombed with caves. Some of the tunnels probably led straight outside. Jason remembered seeing winds blast out of them when they'd been on Pikes Peak. Other caves were sealed with some glistening material like glass or wax. The whole cavern bustled with harpies, *aurai*, and paper airplanes, but for someone who couldn't fly, it would be a very long, very fatal fall.

"Oh, my," Mellie gasped. "I'm so sorry." She unclipped a walkie-talkie from somewhere inside her robes and spoke into it: "Hello, sets? Is that Nuggets? Hi, Nuggets. Could we get a floor in the main studio, please? Yes, a solid one. Thanks."

A few seconds later, an army of harpies rose from the pit—three dozen or so demon chicken ladies, all carrying squares of various building material. They went to work hammering and gluing—and using large quantities of duct tape, which didn't reassure Jason. In no time there was a makeshift floor snaking out over the chasm. It was made of plywood, marble blocks, carpet squares, wedges of grass sod—just about anything.

"That can't be safe," Jason said.

"Oh, it is!" Mellie assured him. "The harpies are very good."

Easy for her to say. She just drifted across without touching the floor, but Jason decided he had the best chance at surviving, since he could fly, so he stepped out first. Amazingly, the floor held.

Piper gripped his hand and followed him. "If I fall, you're catching me."

"Uh, sure." Jason hoped he wasn't blushing.

Leo stepped out next. "You're catching me, too, Superman. But I ain't holding your hand."

Mellie led them toward the middle of the chamber, where a loose sphere of flat-panel video screens floated around a kind of control center. A man hovered inside, checking monitors and reading paper airplane messages.

The man paid them no attention as Mellie brought them forward. She pushed a forty-two-inch Sony out of their way and led them into the control area.

Leo whistled. "I *got* to get a room like this."

The floating screens showed all sorts of television programs. Some Jason recognized—news broadcasts, mostly—but some programs looked a little strange: gladiators fighting, demigods battling monsters. Maybe they were movies, but they looked more like reality shows.

At the far end of the sphere was a silky blue backdrop like a cinema screen, with cameras and studio lights floating around it.

The man in the center was talking into an earpiece phone. He had a remote control in each hand and was pointing them at various screens, seemingly at random.

He wore a business suit that looked like the sky—blue mostly, but dappled with clouds that changed and darkened and moved across the fabric. He looked like he was in his sixties, with a shock of white hair, but he had a ton of stage makeup on, and that smooth plastic-surgery look to his face, so he appeared not really young, not really old, just *wrong*— like a Ken doll someone had halfway melted in a microwave. His eyes darted back and forth from screen to screen, like he was trying to absorb everything at once. He muttered things into his phone, and his mouth kept twitching. He was either amused, or crazy, or both.

Mellie floated toward him. "Ah, sir, Mr. Aeolus, these demigods—"

"Hold it!" He held up a hand to silence her, then pointed at one of the screens. "Watch!"

It was one of those storm-chaser programs, where insane thrill-seekers drive after tornados. As Jason watched, a Jeep plowed straight into a funnel cloud and got tossed into the sky.

Aeolus shrieked with delight. "The Disaster Channel. People do that *on purpose!*" He turned toward Jason with a mad grin. "Isn't that amazing? Let's watch it again."

"Um, sir," Mellie said, "this is Jason, son of—"

"Yes, yes, I remember," Aeolus said. "You're back. How did it go?"

Jason hesitated. "Sorry? I think you've mistaken me—"

"No, no, Jason Grace, aren't you? It was—what—last year? You were on your way to fight a sea monster, I believe."

"I—I don't remember."

Aeolus laughed. "Must not have been a very good sea monster! No, I remember every hero who's ever come to me for aid. Odysseus—gods, he docked at my island for a month! At least you only stayed a few days. Now, watch this video. These ducks get sucked straight into—"

"Sir," Mellie interrupted. "Two minutes to air."

"Air!" Aeolus exclaimed. "I love air. How do I look? Makeup!"

Immediately a small tornado of brushes, blotters, and cotton balls descended on Aeolus. They blurred across his face in a cloud of flesh-tone smoke until his coloration was even more gruesome than before. Wind swirled through his hair and left it sticking up like a frosted Christmas tree.

"Mr. Aeolus." Jason slipped off the golden backpack. "We brought you these rogue storm spirits."

"Did you!" Aeolus looked at the bag like it was a gift from a fan—something he really didn't want. "Well, how nice."

Leo nudged him, and Jason offered the bag. "Boreas sent us to capture them for you. We hope you'll accept them and stop—you know—ordering demigods to be killed."

Aeolus laughed, and looked incredulously at Mellie. "Demigods be killed—did I order that?"

Mellie checked her computer tablet. "Yes, sir, fifteenth of September. 'Storm spirits released by the death of Typhon, demigods to be held responsible,' etc. . . . yes, a general order for them all to be killed."

"Oh, pish," Aeolus said. "I was just grumpy. Rescind that order, Mellie, and um, who's on guard duty—Teriyaki?—Teri, take these storm spirits down to cell block Fourteen E, will you?"

A harpy swooped out of nowhere, snatched the golden bag, and spiraled into the abyss.

Aeolus grinned at Jason. "Now, sorry about that kill-on-sight business. But gods, I really was mad, wasn't I?" His face suddenly darkened, and his suit did the same, the lapels flashing with lightning. "You know . . . I remember now. Almost seemed like a voice was telling me to give that order. A little cold tingle on the back of my neck."

Jason tensed. A cold tingle on the back of his neck . . . Why did that sound so familiar? "A . . . um, voice in your head, sir?"

"Yes. How odd. Mellie, *should* we kill them?"

"No, sir," she said patiently. "They just brought us the storm spirits, which makes everything all right."

"Of course." Aeolus laughed. "Sorry. Mellie, let's send the demigods something nice. A box of chocolates, perhaps."

"A box of chocolates to *every* demigod in the world, sir?"

"No, too expensive. Never mind. Wait, it's time! I'm on!"

Aeolus flew off toward the blue screen as newscast music started to play.

Jason looked at Piper and Leo, who seemed just as confused as he was.

"Mellie," he said, "is he ... always like that?"

She smiled sheepishly. "Well, you know what they say. If you don't like his mood, wait five minutes. That expression 'whichever way the wind blows'—that was based on him."

"And that thing about the sea monster," Jason said. "*Was* I here before?"

Mellie blushed. "I'm sorry, I don't remember. I'm Mr. Aeolus's new assistant. I've been with him longer than most, but still—not that long."

"How long do his assistants usually last?" Piper asked.

"Oh..." Mellie thought for a moment. "I've been doing this for ... twelve hours?"

A voice blared from floating speakers: "And now, weather every twelve minutes! Here's your forecaster for Olympian Weather—the OW! channel—Aeolus!"

Lights blazed on Aeolus, who was now standing in front of the blue screen. His smile was unnaturally white, and he looked like he'd had so much caffeine his face was about to explode.

"Hello, Olympus! Aeolus, master of the winds here, with weather every twelve! We'll have a low-pressure system moving over Florida today, so expect milder temperatures since Demeter wishes to spare the citrus farmers!" He gestured at the blue screen, but when Jason checked the monitors, he saw that a digital image was being projected behind Aeolus, so it looked like he was standing in front of a U.S. map with animated smiley suns and frowny storm clouds. "Along the eastern seaboard—oh, hold on." He tapped his earpiece. "Sorry, folks! Poseidon is angry with Miami today, so it looks like that Florida freeze is back on! Sorry, Demeter. Over in the Midwest, I'm not sure what St. Louis did to offend Zeus, but you can expect winter storms! Boreas himself is being called down to punish the area with ice. Bad news, Missouri! No, wait. Hephaestus feels sorry for central Missouri, so you all will have much more moderate temperatures and sunny skies."

Aeolus kept going like that—forecasting each area of the country and changing his prediction two or three times as he got messages over his earpiece—the gods apparently putting in orders for various winds and weather.

"This can't be right," Jason whispered. "Weather isn't this random."

Mellie smirked. "And how often are the mortal weathermen right? They talk about fronts and air pressure and moisture, but the weather surprises them all the time. At least Aeolus tells us *why* it's so unpredictable. Very hard job, trying to appease all the gods at once. It's enough to drive anyone . . ."

She trailed off, but Jason knew what she meant. *Mad.* Aeolus was completely mad.

"And that's the weather," Aeolus concluded. "See you in twelve minutes, because I'm sure it'll change!"

The lights shut off, the video monitors went back to random coverage, and just for a moment, Aeolus's face sagged with weariness. Then he seemed to remember he had guests, and he put a smile back on.

"So, you brought me some rogue storm spirits," Aeolus said. "I suppose...thanks! And did you want something else? I assume so. Demigods always do."

Mellie said, "Um, sir, this is Zeus's son."

"Yes, yes. I know that. I said I remembered him from before."

"But, sir, they're here from *Olympus*."

Aeolus looked stunned. Then he laughed so abruptly, Jason almost jumped into the chasm. "You mean you're here on behalf of your father this time? Finally! I *knew* they would send someone to renegotiate my contract!"

"Um, what?" Jason asked.

"Oh, thank goodness!" Aeolus sighed with relief. "It's been what, three thousand years since Zeus made me master of the winds. Not that I'm ungrateful, of course! But really, my contract is so vague. Obviously I'm immortal, but 'master of the winds.' What does that mean? Am I a nature spirit? A demigod? A god? I *want* to be god of the winds, because the benefits are *so* much better. Can we start with that?"

Jason looked at his friends, mystified.

"Dude," Leo said, "you think we're here to promote you?"

"You are, then?" Aeolus grinned. His business suit turned completely blue—not a cloud in the fabric. "Marvelous! I mean, I think I've shown quite a bit of initiative with the weather channel, eh? And of course I'm in the press all the time. So many books have been written about me: *Into Thin Air, Up in the Air, Gone with the Wind*—"

"Er, I don't think those are about you," Jason said, before he noticed Mellie shaking her head.

"Nonsense," Aeolus said. "Mellie, they're biographies of me, aren't they?"

"Absolutely, sir," she squeaked.

"There, you see? I don't read. Who has time? But obviously the mortals love me. So, we'll change my official title to *god* of the winds. Then, about salary and staff—"

"Sir," Jason said, "we're not from Olympus."

Aeolus blinked. "But—"

"I'm the son of Zeus, yes," Jason said, "but we're not here to negotiate your contract. We're on a quest and we need your help."

Aeolus's expression hardened. "Like last time? Like *every* hero who comes here? Demigods! It's always about *you*, isn't it?"

"Sir, please, I don't remember last time, but if you helped me once before—"

"I'm always helping! Well, sometimes I'm destroying, but mostly I'm helping, and sometimes I'm asked to do both at the same time! Why, Aeneas, the first of your kind—"

"My kind?" Jason asked. "You mean, demigods?"

"Oh, please!" Aeolus said. "I mean your *line* of demigods. You know, Aeneas, son of Venus—the only surviving hero of Troy. When the Greeks burned down his city, he escaped to

Italy, where he founded the kingdom that would eventually become Rome, blah, blah, blah. *That's* what I meant."

"I don't get it," Jason admitted.

Aeolus rolled his eyes. "The point being, I was thrown in the middle of that conflict, too! Juno calls up: 'Oh, Aeolus, destroy Aeneas's ships for me. I don't like him.' Then Neptune says, 'No, you don't! That's my territory. Calm the winds.' Then Juno is like, 'No, wreck his ships, or I'll tell Jupiter you're uncooperative!' Do you think it's easy juggling requests like that?"

"No," Jason said. "I guess not."

"And don't get me started on Amelia Earhart! I'm *still* getting angry calls from Olympus about knocking *her* out of the sky!"

"We just want information," Piper said in her most calming voice. "We hear you know everything."

Aeolus straightened his lapels and looked slightly mollified. "Well…*that's* true, of course. For instance, I know that *this* business here"—he waggled his fingers at the three of them—"this harebrained scheme of Juno's to bring you all together is likely to end in bloodshed. As for you, Piper McLean, I know your father is in serious trouble." He held out his hand, and a scrap of paper fluttered into his grasp. It was a photo of Piper with a guy who must've been her dad. His face *did* look familiar. Jason was pretty sure he'd seen him in some movies.

Piper took the photo. Her hands were shaking. "This—this is from his wallet."

"Yes," Aeolus said. "All things lost in the wind eventually

come to me. The photo blew away when the Earthborn captured him."

"The what?" Piper asked.

Aeolus waved aside the question and narrowed his eyes at Leo. "Now, *you*, son of Hephaestus . . . yes, I see your future." Another paper fell into the wind god's hands—an old tattered drawing done in crayons.

Leo took it as if it might be coated in poison. He staggered backward.

"Leo?" Jason said. "What is it?"

"Something I—I drew when I was a kid." He folded it quickly and put it in his coat. "It's . . . yeah, it's nothing."

Aeolus laughed. "Really? Just the key to your success! Now, where were we? Ah, yes, you wanted information. Are you sure about that? Sometimes information can be dangerous."

He smiled at Jason like he was issuing a challenge. Behind him, Mellie shook her head in warning.

"Yeah," Jason said. "We need to find the lair of Enceladus."

Aeolus's smile melted. "The giant? Why would you want to go there? He's horrible! He doesn't even watch my program!"

Piper held up the photo. "Aeolus, he's got my father. We need to rescue him and find out where Hera is being held captive."

"Now, *that's* impossible," Aeolus said. "Even *I* can't see that, and believe me, I've tried. There's a veil of magic over Hera's location—very strong, impossible to locate."

"She's at a place called the Wolf House," Jason said.

"Hold on!" Aelous put a hand to his forehead and closed

his eyes. "I'm getting something! Yes, she's at a place called the Wolf House! Sadly, I don't know where that is."

"Enceladus does," Piper persisted. "If you help us find him, we could get the location of the goddess—"

"Yeah," Leo said, catching on. "And if we save her, she'd be really grateful to you—"

"And Zeus might promote you," Jason finished.

Aeolus's eyebrows crept up. "A promotion—and all you want from me is the giant's location?"

"Well, if you could get us there, too," Jason amended, "that would be great."

Mellie clapped her hands in excitement. "Oh, he could do that! He often sends helpful winds—"

"Mellie, quiet!" Aeolus snapped. "I have half a mind to fire you for letting these people in under false pretenses."

Her face paled. "Yes, sir. Sorry, sir."

"It wasn't her fault," Jason said. "But about that help..."

Aeolus tilted his head as if thinking. Then Jason realized the wind lord was listening to voices in his earpiece.

"Well... Zeus approves," Aeolus muttered. "He says... he says it would be better if you could avoid saving her until after the weekend, because he has a big party planned—Ow! That's Aphrodite yelling at him, reminding him that the solstice starts at dawn. She says I should help you. And Hephaestus ...yes. Hmm. Very rare they agree on anything. Hold on..."

Jason smiled at his friends. Finally, they were having some good luck. Their godly parents were standing up for them.

Back toward the entrance, Jason heard a loud belch. Coach

Hedge waddled in from the lobby, grass all over his face. Mellie saw him coming across the makeshift floor and caught her breath. "Who is *that*?"

Jason stifled a cough. "That? That's just Coach Hedge. Uh, Gleeson Hedge. He's our..." Jason wasn't sure what to call him: *teacher, friend, problem*?

"Our guide."

"He's *so* goatly," Mellie murmured.

Behind her, Piper poofed out her cheeks, pretending to vomit.

"What's up, guys?" Hedge trotted over. "Wow, nice place. Oh! Sod squares."

"Coach, you just ate," Jason said. "And we're using the sod as a floor. This is, ah, Mellie—"

"An *aura*." Hedge smiled winningly. "Beautiful as a summer breeze."

Mellie blushed.

"And Aeolus here was just about to help us," Jason said.

"Yes," the wind lord muttered. "It seems so. You'll find Enceladus on Mount Diablo."

"Devil Mountain?" Leo asked. "That doesn't sound good."

"I remember that place!" Piper said. "I went there once with my dad. It's just east of San Francisco Bay."

"The Bay Area again?" The coach shook his head. "Not good. Not good at all."

"Now..." Aeolus began to smile. "As to getting you there—"

Suddenly his face went slack. He bent over and tapped his earpiece as if it were malfunctioning. When he straightened again, his eyes were wild. Despite the makeup, he looked like an old man—an old, very frightened man. "She hasn't spoke to me for centuries. I can't—yes, yes I understand."

He swallowed, regarding Jason as if he had suddenly turned into a giant cockroach. "I'm sorry, son of Jupiter. New orders. You all have to die."

Mellie squeaked. "But—but, sir! Zeus said to help them. Aphrodite, Hephaestus—"

"Mellie!" Aeolus snapped. "Your job is already on the line. Besides, there are some orders that transcend even the wishes of the gods, especially when it comes to the forces of nature."

"*Whose* orders?" Jason said. "Zeus will fire you if you don't help us!"

"I doubt it." Aeolus flicked his wrist, and far below them, a cell door opened in the pit. Jason could hear storm spirits screaming out of it, spiraling up toward them, howling for blood.

"Even Zeus understands the order of things," Aeolus said. "And if *she* is waking—by all the gods—she cannot be denied. Good-bye, heroes. I'm terribly sorry, but I'll have to make this quick. I'm back on the air in four minutes."

Jason summoned his sword. Coach Hedge pulled out his club. Mellie the aura yelled, "No!"

She dived at their feet just as the storm spirits hit with hurricane force, blasting the floor to pieces, shredding the carpet samples and marble and linoleum into what should've been lethal projectiles, had Mellie's robes not spread out like a shield and absorbed the brunt of the impact. The five of them fell into the pit, and Aeolus screamed above them, "Mellie, you are *so* fired!"

"Quick," Mellie yelled. "Son of Zeus, do you have any power over the air?"

"A little!"

"Then help me, or you're all dead!" Mellie grabbed his hand, and an electric charge went through Jason's arm. He understood what she needed. They had to control their fall and head for one of the open tunnels. The storm spirits were following them down, closing rapidly, bringing with them a cloud of deadly shrapnel.

Jason grabbed Piper's hand. "Group hug!"

Hedge, Leo, and Piper tried to huddle together, hanging on to Jason and Mellie as they fell.

"This is NOT GOOD!" Leo yelled.

"Bring it on, gas bags!" Hedge yelled up at the storm spirits. "I'll pulverize you!"

"He's magnificent," Mellie sighed.

"Concentrate?" Jason prompted.

"Right!" she said.

They channeled the wind so their fall became more of a tumble into the nearest open chute. Still, they slammed into the tunnel at painful speed and went rolling over each other down a steep vent that was not designed for people. There was no way they could stop.

Mellie's robes billowed around her. Jason and the others clung to her desperately, and they began to slow down, but the storm spirits were screaming into the tunnel behind them.

"Can't—hold—long," Mellie warned. "Stay together! When the winds hit—"

"You're doing great, Mellie," Hedge said. "My own mama was an *aura*, you know. She couldn't have done better herself."

"Iris-message me?" Mellie pleaded.

Hedge winked.

"Could you guys plan your date later?" Piper screamed. "Look!"

Behind them, the tunnel was turning dark. Jason could feel his ears pop as the pressure built.

"Can't hold them," Mellie warned. "But I'll try to shield you, do you one more favor."

"Thanks, Mellie," Jason said. "I hope you get a new job."

She smiled, and then dissolved, wrapping them in a warm gentle breeze. Then the real winds hit, shooting them into the sky so fast, Jason blacked out.

XXXIX

PIPER

PIPER DREAMED SHE WAS ON THE Wilderness School dorm roof.

The desert night was cold, but she'd brought blankets, and with Jason next to her, she didn't need any more warmth.

The air smelled of sage and burning mesquite. On the horizon, the Spring Mountains loomed like jagged black teeth, the dim glow of Las Vegas behind them.

The stars were so bright, Piper had been afraid they wouldn't be able to see the meteor shower. She didn't want Jason to think she'd dragged him up here on false pretenses. (Even though her pretenses had been *totally* false.) But the meteors did not disappoint. One streaked across the sky almost every minute—a line of white, yellow, or blue fire. Piper was sure her Grandpa Tom would have some Cherokee myth to explain them, but at the moment she was busy creating her own story.

Jason took her hand—*finally*—and pointed as two meteors skipped across the atmosphere and formed a cross.

"Wow," he said. "I can't believe Leo didn't want to see this."

"Actually, I didn't invite him," Piper said casually.

Jason smiled. "Oh, yeah?"

"Mm-hmm. You ever feel like three would be a crowd?"

"Yeah," Jason admitted. "Like right now. You know how much trouble we'd get in if we got caught up here?"

"Oh, I'd make up something," Piper said. "I can be very persuasive. So you want to dance, or what?"

He laughed. His eyes were amazing, and his smile was even better in the starlight. "With no music. At night. On a rooftop. Sounds dangerous."

"I'm a dangerous girl."

"That, I can believe."

He stood and offered her his hand. They slow danced a few steps, but it quickly turned into a kiss. Piper almost couldn't kiss him again, because she was too busy smiling.

Then her dream changed—or maybe she was dead in the Underworld—because she found herself back in Medea's department store.

"Please let this be a dream," she murmured, "and not my eternal punishment."

"No, dear," said a woman's honey-sweet voice. "No punishment."

Piper turned, afraid she'd see Medea, but a different

woman stood next to her, browsing through the fifty-percent-off rack.

The woman was gorgeous—shoulder-length hair, a graceful neck, perfect features, and an amazing figure tucked into jeans and a snowy white top.

Piper had seen her share of actresses—most of her dad's dates were knockout beautiful—but this lady was different. She was elegant without trying, fashionable without effort, stunning without makeup. After seeing Aeolus with his silly face-lifts and cosmetics, Piper thought this woman looked even more astonishing. There was nothing artificial about her.

Yet as Piper watched, the woman's appearance changed. Piper couldn't decide the color of her eyes, or the exact color of her hair. The woman became more and more beautiful, as if her image were aligning itself to Piper's thoughts—getting as close as possible to Piper's ideal of beauty.

"Aphrodite," Piper said. "Mom?"

The goddess smiled. "You're only dreaming, my sweet. If anyone wonders, I wasn't here. Okay?"

"I—" Piper wanted to ask a thousand questions, but they all crowded together in her head.

Aphrodite held up a turquoise dress. Piper thought it looked awesome, but the goddess made a face. "This isn't my color, is it? Pity, it's cute. Medea really does have some lovely things here."

"This—this building exploded," Piper stammered. "I saw it."

"Yes," Aphrodite agreed. "I suppose that's why everything's on sale. Just a memory, now. And I'm sorry to pull you out of your other dream. Much more pleasant, I know."

Piper's face burned. She didn't know whether she was more angry or embarrassed, but mostly she felt hollow with disappointment. "It wasn't real. It never even happened. So why do I remember it so vividly?"

Aphrodite smiled. "Because you are my daughter, Piper. You see possibilities much more vividly than others. You see what *could* be. And it still might be—don't give up. Unfortunately—" The goddess gestured around the department store. "You have other trials to face, first. Medea will be back, along with many other enemies. The Doors of Death have opened."

"What do you mean?"

Aphrodite winked at her. "You're a smart one, Piper. You know."

A cold feeling settled over her. "The sleeping woman, the one Medea and Midas called their patron. She's managed to open a new entrance from the Underworld. She's letting the dead escape back into the world."

"Mmm. And not just *any* dead. The worst, the most powerful, the ones most likely to hate the gods."

"The monsters are coming back from Tartarus the same way," Piper guessed. "That's why they don't stay disintegrated."

"Yes. Their *patron*, as you call her, has a special relationship with Tartarus, the spirit of the pit." Aphrodite held up a gold sequined top. "No... this would make me look ridiculous."

Piper laughed uneasily. "You? You can't look anything but perfect."

"You're sweet," Aphrodite said. "But beauty is about finding the right fit, the most natural fit. To be perfect, you have to feel perfect about yourself—avoid trying to be something you're not. For a goddess, that's especially hard. We can change so easily."

"My dad thought you were perfect." Piper's voice quavered. "He never got over you."

Aphrodite's gaze became distant. "Yes... Tristan. Oh, he was amazing. So gentle and kind, funny and handsome. Yet he had so much sadness inside."

"Could we please not talk about him in the past tense?"

"I'm sorry, dear. I didn't want to leave your father, of course. It's always so hard, but it was for the best. If he had realized who I actually was—"

"Wait—he didn't *know* you were a goddess?"

"Of course not." Aphrodite sounded offended. "I wouldn't do that to him. For most mortals, that's simply too hard to accept. It can ruin their lives! Ask your friend Jason—*lovely* boy, by the way. His poor mother was destroyed when she found out she'd fallen in love with Zeus. No, it was much better Tristan believed that I was a mortal woman who left him without explanation. Better a bittersweet memory than an immortal, unattainable goddess. Which brings me to an important matter..."

She opened her hand and showed Piper a glowing glass vial of pink liquid. "This is one of Medea's kinder mixtures. It erases only recent memories. When you save your father, *if* you can save him, you should give him this."

Piper couldn't believe what she was hearing. "You want me to dope my dad? You want me to make him forget what he's been through?"

Aphrodite held up the vial. The liquid cast a pink glow over her face. "Your father acts confident, Piper, but he walks a fine line between two worlds. He's worked his whole life to deny the old stories about gods and spirits, yet he fears those stories might be real. He fears that he's shut off an important part of himself, and someday it will destroy him. Now he's been captured by a giant. He's living a nightmare. Even if he survives...if he has to spend the rest of his life with those memories, knowing that gods and spirits walk the earth, it will shatter him. That's what our enemy hopes for. She will break him, and thus break your spirit."

Piper wanted to shout that Aphrodite was wrong. Her dad was the strongest person she knew. Piper would never take his memories the way Hera had taken Jason's.

But somehow she couldn't stay angry with Aphrodite. She remembered what her dad had said months ago, at the beach at Big Sur: *If I really believed in Ghost Country, or animal spirits, or Greek gods...I don't think I could sleep at night. I'd always be looking for somebody to blame.*

Now Piper wanted someone to blame, too.

"Who is she?" Piper demanded. "The one controlling the giants?"

Aphrodite pursed her lips. She moved to the next rack, which held battered armor and ripped togas, but Aphrodite looked through them as if they were designer outfits.

"You have a strong will," she mused. "I'm never given much credit among the gods. My children are laughed at. They're dismissed as conceited and shallow."

"Some of them are."

Aphrodite laughed. "Granted. Perhaps I'm conceited and shallow, too, sometimes. A girl has to indulge. Oh, this is nice." She picked up a burned and stained bronze breastplate and held it up for Piper to see. "No?"

"No," Piper said. "Are you going to answer my question?"

"Patience, my sweet," the goddess said. "My point is that love is the most powerful motivator in the world. It spurs mortals to greatness. Their noblest, bravest acts are done for love."

Piper pulled out her dagger and studied its reflective blade. "Like Helen starting the Trojan War?"

"Ah, Katoptris." Aphrodite smiled. "I'm glad you found it. I get so much flack for that war, but honestly, Paris and Helen were a cute couple. And the heroes of that war are immortal now—at least in the memories of men. Love is powerful, Piper. It can bring even the gods to their knees. I told this to my son Aeneas when he escaped from Troy. He thought he had failed. He thought he was a loser! But he traveled to Italy—"

"And became the forebear of Rome."

"Exactly. You see, Piper, my children can be quite powerful. *You* can be quite powerful, because my lineage is unique. I am closer to the beginning of creation than any other Olympian."

Piper struggled to remember about Aphrodite's birth. "Didn't you ... rise from the sea? Standing on a seashell?"

The goddess laughed. "That painter Botticelli had quite an imagination. I never stood on a seashell, thank you very much. But yes, I rose from the sea. The first beings to rise from Chaos were the Earth and Sky—Gaea and Ouranos. When their son the Titan Kronos killed Ouranos—"

"By chopping him to pieces with a scythe," Piper remembered.

Aphrodite wrinkled her nose. "Yes. The pieces of Ouranos fell into the sea. His immortal essence created sea foam. And from that foam—"

"You were born. I remember now. So you're—"

"The last child of Ouranos, who was greater than the gods or the Titans. So, in a strange way, I'm the eldest Olympian god. As I said, love is a powerful force. And you, my daughter, are much more than a pretty face. Which is why you already know who is waking the giants, and who has the power to open doors into the deepest parts of the earth."

Aphrodite waited, as if she could sense Piper slowly putting together the pieces of a puzzle, which made a dreadful picture.

"Gaea," Piper said. "The earth itself. That's our enemy."

She hoped Aphrodite would say no, but the goddess kept her eyes on the rack of tattered armor. "She has slumbered for eons, but she is slowly waking. Even asleep, she is powerful, but once she wakes...we will be doomed. You must defeat the giants before that happens, and lull Gaea back into her slumber. Otherwise the rebellion has only begun. The dead will continue to rise. Monsters will regenerate with even greater speed. The giants will lay waste to the birthplace of the gods. And if they do that, all civilization will burn."

"But *Gaea*? Mother Earth?"

"Do not underestimate her," Aphrodite warned. "She is a cruel deity. She orchestrated Ouranos's death. *She* gave Kronos the sickle and urged him to kill his own father. While the Titans ruled the world, she slumbered in peace. But when the gods overthrew them, Gaea woke again in all her anger and gave birth to a new race—the giants—to destroy Olympus once and for all."

"And it's happening again," Piper said. "The rise of the giants."

Aphrodite nodded. "Now you know. What will you do?"

"Me?" Piper clenched her fists. "What am I supposed to do? Put on a pretty dress and sweet-talk Gaea into going back to sleep?"

"I wish that would work," Aphrodite said. "But no, you will have to find your own strengths, and fight for what you love. Like my favored ones, Helen and Paris. Like my son Aeneas."

"Helen and Paris died," Piper said.

"And Aeneas became a hero," the goddess countered. "The first great hero of Rome. The result will depend on you, Piper, but I will tell you this: The seven greatest demigods must be gathered to defeat the giants, and that effort will not succeed without you. When the two sides meet . . . you will be the mediator. You will determine whether there is friendship or bloodshed."

"What two sides?"

Piper's vision began to dim.

"You must wake soon, my child," said the goddess. "I do not always agree with Hera, but she's taken a bold risk, and

I agree it must be done. Zeus has kept the two sides apart for too long. Only together will you have the power to save Olympus. Now, wake, and I hope you like the clothes I picked out."

"What clothes?" Piper demanded, but the dream faded to black.

PIPER

PIPER WOKE AT A TABLE AT A SIDEWALK CAFÉ.

For a second, she thought she was still dreaming. It was a sunny morning. The air was brisk but not unpleasant for sitting outside. At the other tables, a mix of bicyclists, business people, and college kids sat chatting and drinking coffee.

She could smell eucalyptus trees. Lots of foot traffic passed in front of quaint little shops. The street was lined with bottle-brush trees and blooming azaleas as if winter was a foreign concept.

In other words: she was in California.

Her friends sat in chairs around her—all of them with their hands calmly folded across their chests, dozing pleasantly. And they all had new clothes on. Piper looked down at her own outfit and gasped. "Mother!"

She yelled louder than she meant. Jason flinched, bumping the table with his knees, and then all of them were awake.

"What?" Hedge demanded. "Fight who? Where?"

"Falling!" Leo grabbed the table. "No—not falling. Where are we?"

Jason blinked, trying to get his bearings. He focused on Piper and made a little choking sound. "What are you wearing?"

Piper probably blushed. She was wearing the turquoise dress she'd seen in her dream, with black leggings and black leather boots. She had on her favorite silver charm bracelet, even though she'd left that back home in L.A., and her old snowboarding jacket from her dad, which amazingly went with the outfit pretty well. She pulled out Katoptris, and judging from the reflection in the blade, she'd gotten her hair done, too.

"It's nothing," she said. "It's my—" She remembered Aphrodite's warning not to mention that they'd talked. "It's nothing."

Leo grinned. "Aphrodite strikes again, huh? You're gonna be the best-dressed warrior in town, beauty queen."

"Hey, Leo." Jason nudged his arm. "You look at yourself recently?"

"What . . . oh."

All of them had been give a makeover. Leo was wearing pinstriped pants, black leather shoes, a white collarless shirt with suspenders, and his tool belt, Ray-Ban sunglasses, and a porkpie hat.

"God, Leo." Piper tried not to laugh. "I think my dad wore that to his last premiere, minus the tool belt."

"Hey, shut up!"

"I think he looks good," said Coach Hedge. "'Course, I look better."

The satyr was a pastel nightmare. Aphrodite had given him a baggy canary yellow zoot suit with two-tone shoes that fit over his hooves. He had a matching yellow broad-brimmed hat, a rose-colored shirt, a baby blue tie, and a blue carnation in his lapel, which Hedge sniffed and then ate.

"Well," Jason said, "at least your mom overlooked me."

Piper knew that wasn't exactly true. Looking at him, her heart did a little tap dance. Jason was dressed simply in jeans and a clean purple T-shirt, like he'd worn at the Grand Canyon. He had new track shoes on, and his hair was newly trimmed. His eyes were the same color as the sky. Aphrodite's message was clear: *This one needs no improvement.*

And Piper agreed.

"Anyway," she said uncomfortably, "how did we get here?"

"Oh, that would be Mellie," Hedge said, chewing happily on his carnation. "Those winds shot us halfway across the country, I'd guess. We would've been smashed flat on impact, but Mellie's last gift—a nice soft breeze—cushioned our fall."

"And she got fired for us," Leo said. "Man, we suck."

"Ah, she'll be fine," Hedge said. "Besides, she couldn't help herself. I've got that effect on nymphs. I'll send her a message when we're through with this quest and help her figure something out. That is one *aura* I could settle down with and raise a herd of baby goats."

"I'm going to be sick," Piper said. "Anyone else want coffee?"

"Coffee!" Hedge's grin was stained blue from the flower. "I love coffee!"

"Um," Jason said, "but—money? Our packs?"

Piper looked down. Their packs were at their feet, and everything seemed to still be there. She reached into her coat pocket and felt two things she hadn't expected. One was a wad of cash. The other was a glass vial—the amnesia potion. She left the vial in her pocket and brought out the money.

Leo whistled. "Allowance? Piper, your mom rocks!"

"Waitress!" Hedge called. "Six double espressos, and whatever these guys want. Put it on the girl's tab."

It didn't take them long to figure out where they were. The menus said "Café Verve, Walnut Creek, CA." And according to the waitress, it was 9 A.M. on December 21, the winter solstice, which gave them three hours until Enceladus's deadline.

They didn't have to wonder where Mount Diablo was, either. They could see it on the horizon, right at the end of the street. After the Rockies, Mount Diablo didn't look very large, nor was it covered in snow. It seemed downright peaceful, its golden creases marbled with gray-green trees. But size was deceptive with mountains, Piper knew. It was probably much bigger up close. And appearances were deceptive too. Here they were—back in California—supposedly her home —with sunny skies, mild weather, laid-back people, and a plate of chocolate chip scones with coffee. And only a few miles away, somewhere on that peaceful mountain, a superpowerful, super-evil giant was about to have her father for lunch.

Leo pulled something out of his pocket—the old crayon drawing Aeolus had given him. Aphrodite must've thought it was important if she'd magically transferred it to his new outfit.

"What is that?" Piper asked.

Leo folded it up gingerly again and put it away. "Nothing. You don't want to see my kindergarten artwork."

"It's more than that," Jason guessed. "Aeolus said it was the key to our success."

Leo shook his head. "Not today. He was talking about ...later."

"How can you be sure?" Piper asked.

"Trust me," Leo said. "Now—what's our game plan?"

Coach Hedge belched. He'd already had three espressos and a plate of doughnuts, along with two napkins and another flower from the vase on the table. He would've eaten the silverware, except Piper had slapped his hand.

"Climb the mountain," Hedge said. "Kill everything except Piper's dad. Leave."

"Thank you, General Eisenhower," Jason grumbled.

"Hey, I'm just saying!"

"Guys," Piper said. "There's more you need to know."

It was tricky, because she couldn't mention her mom; but she told them she'd figured some things out in her dreams. She told them about their real enemy: Gaea.

"Gaea?" Leo shook his head. "Isn't that Mother Nature? She's supposed to have, like, flowers in her hair and birds singing around her and deer and rabbits doing her laundry."

"Leo, that's Snow White," Piper said.

"Okay, but—"

"Listen, cupcake." Coach Hedge dabbed the espresso out of his goatee. "Piper's telling us some serious stuff, here. Gaea's no softie. I'm not even sure *I* could take her."

Leo whistled. "Really?"

Hedge nodded. "This earth lady—she and her old man the sky were nasty customers."

"Ouranos," Piper said. She couldn't help looking up at the blue sky, wondering if it had eyes.

"Right," Hedge said. "So Ouranos, he's not the best dad. He throws their first kids, the Cyclopes, into Tartarus. That makes Gaea mad, but she bides her time. Then they have another set of kids—the twelve Titans—and Gaea is afraid they'll get thrown into prison too. So she goes up to her son Kronos—"

"The big bad dude," Leo said. "The one they defeated last summer."

"Right. And Gaea's the one who gives him the scythe, and tells him, 'Hey, why don't I call your dad down here? And while he's talking to me, distracted, you can cut him to pieces. Then you can take over the world. Wouldn't that be great?'"

Nobody said anything. Piper's chocolate chip scone didn't look so appetizing anymore. Even though she'd heard the story before, she still couldn't quite get her mind around it. She tried to imagine a kid so messed up, he would kill his own dad just for power. Then she imagined a mom so messed up, she would convince her son to do it.

"Definitely not Snow White," she decided.

"Nah, Kronos was a bad guy," Hedge said. "But Gaea is

literally the *mother* of all bad guys. She's so old and powerful, so *huge*, that it's hard for her to be fully conscious. Most of the time, she sleeps, and that's the way we like her—snoring."

"But she talked to me," Leo said. "How can she be asleep?"

Gleeson brushed crumbs off his canary yellow lapel. He was on his sixth espresso now, and his pupils were as big as quarters. "Even in her sleep, part of her consciousness is active —dreaming, keeping watch, doing little things like causing volcanoes to explode and monsters to rise. Even now, she's not fully awake. Believe me, you don't want to see her fully awake."

"But she's getting more powerful," Piper said. "She's causing the giants to rise. And if their king comes back—this guy Porphyrion—"

"He'll raise an army to destroy the gods," Jason put in. "Starting with Hera. It'll be another war. And Gaea will wake up fully."

Gleeson nodded. "Which is why it's a good idea for us to stay off the ground as much as possible."

Leo looked warily at Mount Diablo. "So . . . climbing a mountain. That would be bad."

Piper's heart sank. First, she'd been asked to betray her friends. Now they were trying to help her rescue her dad even though they knew they were walking into a trap. The idea of fighting a giant had been scary enough. But the idea that Gaea was behind it—a force more powerful than a god or Titan . . .

"Guys, I can't ask you to do this," Piper said. "This is too dangerous."

"You kidding?" Gleeson belched and showed them his blue carnation smile. "Who's ready to beat stuff up?"

XLI

LEO

LEO HOPED THE TAXI COULD TAKE THEM all the way to the top.

No such luck. The cab made lurching, grinding sounds as it climbed the mountain road, and halfway up they found the ranger's station closed, a chain blocking the way.

"Far as I can go," the cabbie said. "You sure about this? Gonna be a long walk back, and my car's acting funny. I can't wait for you."

"We're sure." Leo was the first one out. He had a bad feeling about what was wrong with the cab, and when he looked down he saw he was right. The wheels were sinking into the road like it was made of quicksand. Not fast—just enough to make the driver think he had a transmission problem or a bad axle—but Leo knew different.

The road was hard-packed dirt. No reason at all it should have been soft, but already Leo's shoes were starting to sink. Gaea was messing with them.

While his friends got out, Leo paid the cabbie. He was generous—heck, why not? It was Aphrodite's money. Plus, he had a feeling he might never be coming off this mountain.

"Keep the change," he said. "And get out of here. Quick."

The driver didn't argue. Soon all they could see was his dust trail.

The view from the mountain was pretty amazing. The whole inland valley around Mount Diablo was a patchwork of towns—grids of tree-lined streets and nice middle-class suburbs, shops, and schools. All these normal people living normal lives—the kind Leo had never known.

"That's Concord," Jason said, pointing to the north. "Walnut Creek below us. To the south, Danville, past those hills. And that way..."

He pointed west, where a ridge of golden hills held back a layer of fog, like the rim of a bowl. "That's the Berkeley Hills. The East Bay. Past that, San Francisco."

"Jason?" Piper touched his arm. "You remember something? You've been here?"

"Yes...no." He gave her an anguished look. "It just seems important."

"That's Titan land." Coach Hedge nodded toward the west. "Bad place, Jason. Trust me, this is as close to 'Frisco as we want to get."

But Jason looked toward the foggy basin with such longing that Leo felt uneasy. Why did Jason seem so connected with that place—a place Hedge said was evil, full of bad magic and old enemies? What if Jason came from here? Everybody kept hinting Jason was an enemy, that his arrival at Camp Half-Blood was a dangerous mistake.

No, Leo thought. Ridiculous. Jason was their friend.

Leo tried to move his foot, but his heels were now completely embedded in the dirt.

"Hey, guys," he said. "Let's keep moving."

The others noticed the problem.

"Gaea is stronger here," Hedge grumbled. He popped his hooves free from his shoes, then handed the shoes to Leo. "Keep those for me, Valdez. They're nice."

Leo snorted. "Yes, sir, Coach. Would you like them polished?"

"That's varsity thinking, Valdez." Hedge nodded approvingly. "But first, we'd better hike up this mountain while we still can."

"How do we know where the giant is?" Piper asked.

Jason pointed toward the peak. Drifting across the summit was a plume of smoke. From a distance, Leo had thought it was a cloud, but it wasn't. Something was burning.

"Smoke equals fire," Jason said. "We'd better hurry."

The Wilderness School had taken Leo on several forced marches. He thought he was in good shape. But climbing a mountain when the earth was trying to swallow his feet was like jogging on a flypaper treadmill.

In no time, Leo had rolled up the sleeves on his collarless shirt, even though the wind was cold and sharp. He wished Aphrodite had given him walking shorts and some more comfortable shoes, but he was grateful for the Ray-Bans that kept the sun out of his eyes. He slipped his hands into his tool belt and started summoning supplies—gears, a tiny wrench, some strips of bronze. As he walked, he built—not really thinking about it, just fiddling with pieces.

By the time they neared the crest of the mountain, Leo was the most fashionably dressed sweaty, dirty hero ever. His hands were covered in machine grease.

The little object he'd made was like a windup toy—the kind that rattles and walks across a coffee table. He wasn't sure what it could do, but he slipped it into his tool belt.

He missed his army coat with all its pockets. Even more than that, he missed Festus. He could use a fire-breathing bronze dragon right now. But Leo knew Festus would not be coming back—at least, not in his old form.

He patted the picture in his pocket—the crayon drawing he'd made at the picnic table under the pecan tree when he was five years old. He remembered Tía Callida singing as he worked, and how upset he'd been when the winds had snatched the picture away. *It isn't time yet, little hero,* Tía Callida had told him. *Someday, yes. You'll have your quest. You will find your destiny, and your hard journey will finally make sense.*

Now Aeolus had returned the picture. Leo knew that meant his destiny was getting close; but the journey was as frustrating as this stupid mountain. Every time Leo thought they'd reached the summit, it turned out to be just another ridge with an even higher one behind it.

First things first, Leo told himself. Survive today. Figure out crayon drawing of destiny later.

Finally Jason crouched behind a wall of rock. He gestured for the others to do the same. Leo crawled up next to him. Piper had to pull Coach Hedge down.

"I don't want to get my outfit dirty!" Hedge complained.

"Shhh!" Piper said.

Reluctantly, the satyr knelt.

Just over the ridge where they were hiding, in the shadow of the mountain's final crest, was a forested depression about the size of a football field, where the giant Enceladus had set up camp.

Trees had been cut down to make a towering purple bonfire. The outer rim of the clearing was littered with extra logs and construction equipment—an earthmover; a big crane thing with rotating blades at the end like an electric shaver—must be a tree harvester, Leo thought—and a long metal column with an ax blade, like a sideways guillotine—a hydraulic ax.

Why a giant needed construction equipment, Leo wasn't sure. He didn't see how the creature in front of him could even fit in the driver's seat. The giant Enceladus was so large, so horrible, Leo didn't want to look at him.

But he forced himself to focus on the monster.

To start with, he was thirty feet tall—easily as tall as the treetops. Leo was sure the giant could've seen them behind their ridge, but he seemed intent on the weird purple bonfire, circling it and chanting under his breath. From the waist up, the giant appeared humanoid, his muscular chest clad in bronze armor, decorated with flame designs. His arms were completely ripped. Each of his biceps was bigger than Leo. His skin was bronze but sooty with ash. His face was crudely shaped, like a half-finished clay figure, but his eyes glowed white, and his hair was matted in shaggy locs down to his shoulders, braided with bones.

From the waist down, he was even more terrifying. His legs were scaly green, with claws instead of feet—like the forelegs of a dragon. In his hand, Enceladus held a spear the size of a flagpole. Every so often he dipped its tip in the fire, turning the metal molten red.

"Okay," Coach Hedge whispered. "Here's the plan—"

Leo elbowed him. "You're not charging him alone!"

"Aw, c'mon."

Piper choked back a sob. "Look."

Just visible on the other side of the bonfire was a man tied to a post. His head slumped like he was unconscious, so Leo couldn't make out his face, but Piper didn't seem to have any doubts.

"Dad," she said.

Leo swallowed. He wished this were a Tristan McLean movie. Then Piper's dad would be faking unconsciousness. He'd untie his bonds and knock out the giant with some cleverly hidden anti-giant gas. Heroic music would start to play, and Tristan McLean would make his amazing escape, running away in slow motion while the mountainside exploded behind him.

But this wasn't a movie. Tristan McLean was half dead and about to be eaten. The only people who could stop it —three fashionably dressed teenaged demigods and a megalomaniac goat.

"There's four of us," Hedge whispered urgently. "And only one of him."

"Did you miss the fact that he's thirty feet tall?" Leo asked.

"Okay," Hedge said. "So you, me, and Jason distract him. Piper sneaks around and frees her dad."

They all looked at Jason.

"What?" Jason asked. "I'm not the leader."

"Yes," Piper said. "You are."

They'd never really talked about it, but no one disagreed, not even Hedge. Coming this far had been a team effort, but when it came to a life-and-death decision, Leo knew Jason was the one to ask. Even if he had no memory, Jason had a kind of balance to him. You could just tell he'd been in battles before, and he knew how to keep his cool. Leo wasn't exactly the trusting type, but he trusted Jason with his life.

"I hate to say it," Jason sighed, "but Coach Hedge is right. A distraction is Piper's best chance."

Not a good chance, Leo thought. Not even a survivable chance. Just their *best* chance.

They couldn't sit there all day and talk about it, though. It had to be close to noon—the giant's deadline—and the ground was still trying to pull them down. Leo's knees had already sunk two inches into the dirt.

Leo looked at the construction equipment and got a crazy

idea. He brought out the little toy he'd made on the climb, and he realized what it could do—*if* he was lucky, which he almost never was.

"Let's boogie," he said. "Before I come to my senses."

XLII

LEO

THE PLAN WENT WRONG ALMOST IMMEDIATELY. Piper scrambled along the ridge, trying to keep her head down, while Leo, Jason, and Coach Hedge walked straight into the clearing.

Jason summoned his golden lance. He brandished it over his head and yelled, "Giant!" Which sounded pretty good, and a lot more confident than Leo could've managed. He was thinking more along the lines of, "We are pathetic ants! Don't kill us!"

Enceladus stopped chanting at the flames. He turned toward them and grinned, revealing fangs like a saber-toothed tiger's.

"Well," the giant rumbled. "What a nice surprise."

Leo didn't like the sound of that. His hand closed on his windup gadget. He stepped sideways, edging his way toward the bulldozer.

Coach Hedge shouted, "Let the movie star go, you big ugly cupcake! Or I'm gonna plant my hoof right up your—"

"Coach," Jason said. "Shut up."

Enceladus roared with laughter. "I've forgotten how funny satyrs are. When we rule the world, I think I'll keep your kind around. You can entertain me while I eat all the other mortals."

"Is that a compliment?" Hedge frowned at Leo. "I don't think that was a compliment."

Enceladus opened his mouth wide, and his teeth began to glow.

"Scatter!" Leo yelled.

Jason and Hedge dove to the left as the giant blew fire —a furnace blast so hot even Festus would've been jealous. Leo dodged behind the bulldozer, wound up his homemade device, and dropped it into the driver's seat. Then he ran to the right, heading for the tree harvester.

Out of the corner of his eye, he saw Jason rise and charge the giant. Coach Hedge ripped off his canary yellow jacket, which was now on fire, and bleated angrily. "I *liked* that outfit!" Then he raised his club and charged, too.

Before they could get very far, Enceladus slammed his spear against the ground. The entire mountain shook.

The shockwave sent Leo sprawling. He blinked, momentarily stunned. Through a haze of grassfire and bitter smoke, he saw Jason staggering to his feet on the other side of the clearing. Coach Hedge was knocked out cold. He'd fallen forward and hit his head on a log. His furry hindquarters were sticking straight up, with his canary yellow pants around his knees—a view Leo really didn't need.

The giant bellowed, "I see you, Piper McLean!" He turned and blew fire at a line of bushes to Leo's right. Piper ran into the clearing like a flushed quail, the underbrush burning behind her.

Enceladus laughed. "I'm happy you've arrived. And you brought me my prizes!"

Leo's gut twisted. This was the moment Piper had warned them about. They'd played right into Enceladus's hands.

The giant must've read Leo's expression, because he laughed even louder. "That's right, son of Hephaestus. I didn't expect you all to stay alive this long, but it doesn't matter. By bringing you here, Piper McLean has sealed the deal. If she betrays you, I'm as good as my word. She can take her father and go. What do I care about a movie star?"

Leo could see Piper's dad more clearly now. He wore a ragged dress shirt and torn slacks. His bare feet were caked with mud. He wasn't completely unconscious, because he lifted his head and groaned—yep, Tristan McLean all right. Leo had seen that face in enough movies. But he had a nasty cut down the side of his face, and he looked thin and sickly —not heroic at all.

"Dad!" Piper yelled.

Mr. McLean blinked, trying to focus. "Pipes...? Where..."

Piper drew her dagger and faced Enceladus. "Let him go!"

"Of course, dear," the giant rumbled. "Swear your loyalty to me, and we have no problem. Only these others must die."

Piper looked back and forth between Leo and her dad.

"He'll kill you," Leo warned. "Don't trust him!"

"Oh, come now," Enceladus bellowed. "You know I was born to fight Athena herself? Mother Gaea made each of us giants with a specific purpose, designed to fight and destroy a particular god. I was Athena's nemesis, the *anti*-Athena, you might say. Compared to some of my brethren—I am small! But I am clever. And I keep my bargain with you, Piper McLean. It's part of my plan!"

Jason was on his feet now, lance ready; but before he could act, Enceladus roared—a call so loud it echoed down the valley and was probably heard all the way to San Francisco.

At the edge of the woods, half a dozen ogre-like creatures rose up. Leo realized with nauseating certainty that they hadn't simply been hiding there. They'd risen straight out of the earth.

The ogres shuffled forward. They were small compared to Enceladus, about seven feet tall. Each one of them had six arms—one pair in the regular spot, then an extra pair sprouting out the top of their shoulders, and another set shooting from the sides of their rib cages. They wore only ragged leather loincloths, and even across the clearing, Leo could smell them. Six guys who never bathed, with six armpits each. Leo decided if he survived this day, he'd have to take a three-hour shower just to forget the stench.

Leo stepped toward Piper. "What—what are those?"

Her blade reflected the purple light of the bonfire. "Gegenees."

"In English?" Leo asked.

"The Earthborn," she said. "Six-armed giants who fought Jason—the *first* Jason."

"Very good, my dear!" Enceladus sounded delighted. "They used to live on a miserable place in Greece called Bear Mountain. Mount Diablo is much nicer! They are lesser children of Mother Earth, but they serve their purpose. They're good with construction equipment—"

"Vroom, vroom!" one of the Earthborn bellowed, and the others took up the chant, each moving his six hands as though driving a car, as if it were some kind of weird religious ritual. "Vroom, vroom!"

"Yes, thank you, boys," Encedalus said. "They also have a score to settle with heroes. Especially anyone named Jason."

"Yay-son!" the Earthborn screamed. They all picked up clumps of earth, which solidified in their hands, turning to nasty pointed stones. "Where Yay-son? Kill Yay-son!"

Enceladus smiled. "You see, Piper, you have a choice. Save your father, or ah, *try* to save your friends and face certain death."

Piper stepped forward. Her eyes blazed with such rage, even the Earthborn backed away. She radiated power and beauty, but it had nothing to do with her clothes or her makeup.

"You will not take the people I love," she said. "None of them."

Her words rippled across the clearing with such force, the Earthborn muttered, "Okay. Okay, sorry," and began to retreat.

"Stand your ground, fools!" Enceladus bellowed. He

snarled at Piper. "This is why we wanted you alive, my dear. You could have been so useful to us. But as you wish. Earthborn! I will show you Jason."

Leo's heart sank. But the giant didn't point to Jason. He pointed to the other side of the bonfire, where Tristan McLean hung helpless and half conscious.

"There is Jason," Enceladus said with pleasure. "Tear him apart!"

Leo's biggest surprise: One look from Jason, and all three of them knew the game plan. When had that happened, that they could read each other so well?

Jason charged Enceladus, while Piper rushed to her father, and Leo dashed for the tree harvester, which stood between Mr. McLean and the Earthborn.

The Earthborn were fast, but Leo ran like a storm spirit. He leaped toward the harvester from five feet away and slammed into the driver's seat. His hands flew across the controls, and the machine responded with unnatural speed—coming to life as if it knew how important this was.

"Ha!" Leo screamed, and swung the crane arm through the bonfire, toppling burning logs onto the Earthborn and spraying sparks everywhere. Two giants went down under a fiery avalanche and melted back into the earth—hopefully to stay for a while.

The other four ogres stumbled across burning logs and hot coals while Leo brought the harvester around. He smashed a button, and on the end of the crane arm the wicked rotating blades began to whir.

Out of the corner of his eye, he could see Piper at the stake, cutting her father free. On the other side of the clearing, Jason fought the giant, somehow managing to dodge his massive spear and blasts of fire breath. Coach Hedge was still heroically passed out with his goat tail sticking up in the air.

The whole side of the mountain would soon be ablaze. The fire wouldn't bother Leo, but if his friends got trapped up here— No. He had to act quickly.

One of the Earthborn—apparently not the most intelligent one—charged the tree harvester, and Leo swung the crane arm in his direction. As soon as the blades touched the ogre, he dissolved like wet clay and splattered all over the clearing. Most of him flew into Leo's face.

He spit clay out of his mouth and turned the harvester toward the three remaining Earthborn, who backed up quickly.

"Bad vroom-vroom!" one yelled.

"Yeah, that's right!" Leo yelled at them. "You want some bad vroom-vroom? Come on!"

Unfortunately, they did. Three ogres with six arms, each throwing large, hard rocks at super speed—and Leo knew it was over. Somehow, he launched himself in a backward somersault off the harvester half a second before a boulder demolished the driver's seat. Rocks slammed into metal. By the time Leo stumbled to his feet, the harvester looked like a crushed soda can, sinking in the mud.

"Dozer!" Leo yelled.

The ogres were picking up more clumps of earth, but this time they were glaring in Piper's direction.

Thirty feet away, the bulldozer roared to life. Leo's make-shift gadget had done its job, burrowing into the earthmover's controls and giving it a temporary life of its own. It roared toward the enemy.

Just as Piper cut her father free and caught him in her arms, the giants launched their second volley of stones. The dozer swiveled in the mud, skidding to intercept, and most of the rocks slammed into its shovel. The force was so great it pushed the dozer back. Two rocks ricocheted and struck their throwers. Two more Earthborn melted into clay. Unfortunately, one rock hit the dozer's engine, sending up a cloud of oily smoke, and the dozer groaned to a stop. Another great toy broken.

Piper dragged her father below the ridge. The last Earthborn charged after her.

Leo was out of tricks, but he couldn't let that monster get to Piper. He ran forward, straight through the flames, and grabbed something—*anything*—from his tool belt.

"Hey, stupid!" he yelled, and threw a screwdriver at the Earthborn.

It didn't kill the ogre, but it sure got his attention. The screwdriver sank hilt-deep into the Earthborn's forehead like he was made of Play-Doh.

The Earthborn yelped in pain and skittered to a halt. He pulled out the screwdriver, turned and glared at Leo. Sadly, this last ogre looked like the biggest and nastiest of the bunch. Gaea had really gone all out creating him—with extra muscle upgrades, deluxe ugly face, the whole package.

Oh, great, Leo thought. I've made a friend.

"You die!" the Earthborn roared. "Friend of Yay-son dies!"

The ogre scooped up handfuls of dirt, which immediately hardened into rock cannonballs.

Leo's mind went blank. He reached into his tool belt, but he couldn't think of anything that would help. He was supposed to be clever—but he couldn't craft or build or tinker his way out of this one.

Fine, he thought. I'll go out blaze-of-glory style.

He burst into flames, yelled, "Hephaestus!" and charged at the ogre barehanded.

He never got there.

A blur of turquoise and black flashed behind the ogre. A gleaming bronze blade sliced up one side of the Earthborn and down the other.

Six large arms dropped to the ground, boulders rolling out of their useless hands. The Earthborn looked down, very surprised. He mumbled, "Arms go bye-bye."

Then he melted into the ground.

Piper stood there, breathing hard, her dagger covered with clay. Her dad sat at the ridge, dazed and wounded, but still alive.

Piper's expression was ferocious—almost crazy, like a cornered animal. Leo was glad she was on his side.

"Nobody hurts my friends," she said, and with a sudden warm feeling, Leo realized she was talking about him. Then she yelled, "Come on!"

Leo saw that the battle wasn't over. Jason was still fighting the giant Enceladus—and it wasn't going well.

XLIII

JASON

WHEN JASON'S LANCE BROKE, he knew he was dead.

The battle had started well enough. Jason's instincts kicked in, and his gut told him he'd dueled opponents almost this big before. Size and strength equaled slowness, so Jason just had to be quicker—pace himself, wear out his opponent, and avoid getting smashed or flame-broiled.

He rolled away from the giant's first spear thrust and jabbed Enceladus in the ankle. Jason's javelin managed to pierce the thick dragon hide, and golden *ichor*—the blood of immortals—trickled down the giant's clawed foot.

Enceladus bellowed in pain and blasted him with fire. Jason scrambled away, rolling behind the giant, and struck again behind his knee.

It went on like that for seconds, minutes—it was hard to judge. Jason heard combat across the clearing—construction equipment grinding, fire roaring, monsters shouting, and rocks smashing into metal. He heard Leo and Piper yelling defiantly, which meant they were still alive. Jason tried not to think about it. He couldn't afford to get distracted.

Enceladus's spear missed him by a millimeter. Jason kept dodging, but the ground stuck to his feet. Gaea was getting stronger, and the giant was getting faster. Enceladus might be slow, but he wasn't dumb. He began anticipating Jason's moves, and Jason's attacks were only annoying him, making him more enraged.

"I'm not some minor monster," Enceladus bellowed. "I am a giant, born to destroy gods! Your little gold toothpick can't kill me, boy."

Jason didn't waste energy replying. He was already tired. The ground clung to his feet, making him feel like he weighed an extra hundred pounds. The air was full of smoke that burned his lungs. Fires roared around him, stoked by the winds, and the temperature was approaching the heat of an oven.

Jason raised his javelin to block the giant's next strike—a big mistake. *Don't fight force with force,* a voice chided him— the wolf Lupa, who'd told him that long ago. He managed to deflect the spear, but it grazed his shoulder, and his arm went numb.

He backed up, almost tripping over a burning log.

He had to delay—to keep the giant's attention fixed on him while his friends dealt with the Earthborn and rescued Piper's dad. He couldn't fail.

He retreated, trying to lure the giant to the edge of the clearing. Enceladus could sense his weariness. The giant smiled, baring his fangs.

"The mighty Jason Grace," he taunted. "Yes, we know about you, son of Jupiter. The one who led the assault on Mount Othrys. The one who single-handedly slew the Titan Krios and toppled the black throne."

Jason's mind reeled. He didn't know these names, yet they made his skin tingle, as if his body remembered the pain his mind didn't.

"What are you talking about?" he asked. He realized his mistake when Enceladus breathed fire.

Distracted, Jason moved too slowly. The blast missed him, but heat blistered his back. He slammed into the ground, his clothes smoldering. He was blinded from ash and smoke, choking as he tried to breathe.

He scrambled back as the giant's spear cleaved the ground between his feet.

Jason managed to stand.

If he could only summon one good blast of lightning—but he was already drained, and in this condition, the effort might kill him. He didn't even know if electricity would harm the giant.

Death in battle is honorable, said Lupa's voice.

That's real comforting, Jason thought.

One last try: Jason took a deep breath and charged.

Enceladus let him approach, grinning with anticipation. At the last second, Jason faked a strike and rolled between the giant's legs. He came up quickly, thrusting with all his might, ready to stab the giant in the small of his back, but Enceladus anticipated the trick. He stepped aside with too much speed and agility for a giant, as if the earth were helping him move.

He swept his spear sideways, met Jason's javelin—and with a snap like a shotgun blast, the golden weapon shattered.

The explosion was hotter than the giant's breath, blinding Jason with golden light. The force knocked him off his feet and squeezed the breath out of him.

When he regained his focus, he was sitting at the rim of a crater. Enceladus stood at the other side, staggering and confused. The javelin's destruction had released so much energy, it had blasted a perfect cone-shaped pit thirty feet deep, fusing the dirt and rock into a slick glassy substance. Jason wasn't sure how he'd survived, but his clothes were steaming. He was out of energy. He had no weapon. And Enceladus was still very much alive.

Jason tried to get up, but his legs were like lead. Enceladus blinked at the destruction, then laughed. "Impressive! Unfortunately, that was your last trick, demigod."

Enceladus leaped the crater in a single bound, planting his feet on either side of Jason. The giant raised his spear, its tip hovering six feet over Jason's chest.

"And now," Enceladus said, "my first sacrifice to Gaea!"

XLIV

JASON

TIME SEEMED TO SLOW DOWN, WHICH WAS really frustrating, since Jason still couldn't move. He felt himself sinking into the earth like the ground was a waterbed—comfortable, urging him to relax and give up. He wondered if the stories of the Underworld were true. Would he end up in the Fields of Punishment or Elysium? If he couldn't remember any of his deeds, would they still count? He wondered if the judges would take that into consideration, or if his dad, Zeus, would write him a note: "Please excuse Jason from eternal damnation. He has had amnesia."

Jason couldn't feel his arms. He could see the tip of the spear coming toward his chest in slow motion. He knew he should move, but he couldn't seem to do it. Funny, he thought. All that effort to stay alive, and then, *boom*. You just lie there helplessly while a fire-breathing giant impales you.

Leo's voice yelled, "Heads up!"

A large black metal wedge slammed into Enceladus with a massive *thunk!* The giant toppled over and slid into the pit.

"Jason, get up!" Piper called. Her voice energized him, shook him out of his stupor. He sat up, his head groggy, while Piper grabbed him under his arms and hauled him to his feet.

"Don't die on me," she ordered. "You are *not* dying on me."

"Yes, ma'am." He felt light-headed, but she was about the most beautiful thing he'd ever seen. Her hair was smoldering. Her face was smudged with soot. She had a cut on her arm, her dress was torn, and she was missing a boot. Beautiful.

About a hundred feet behind her, Leo was standing over a piece of construction equipment—a long cannonlike thing with a single massive piston, the edge broken clean off.

Then Jason looked down in the crater and saw where the other end of the hydraulic ax had gone. Enceladus was struggling to rise, an ax blade the size of a washing machine stuck in his breastplate.

Amazingly, the giant managed to pull the ax blade free. He yelled in pain and the mountain trembled. Golden ichor soaked the front of his armor, but Enceladus stood.

Shakily, he bent down and retrieved his spear.

"Good try." The giant winced. "But I cannot be beaten."

As they watched, the giant's armor mended itself, and the ichor stopped flowing. Even the cuts on his dragon-scale legs, which Jason had worked so hard to make, were now just pale scars.

Leo ran up to them, saw the giant, and cursed. "What *is* it with this guy? Die, already!"

"My fate is preordained," Enceladus said. "Giants cannot be killed by gods or heroes."

"Only by both," Jason said. The giant's smile faltered, and Jason saw in his eyes something like fear. "It's true, isn't it? Gods and demigods have to work together to kill you."

"You will not live long enough to try!" The giant started stumbling up the crater's slope, slipping on the glassy sides.

"Anyone have a god handy?" Leo asked.

Jason's heart filled with dread. He looked at the giant below them, struggling to get out of the pit, and he knew what had to happen.

"Leo," he said, "if you've got a rope in that tool belt, get it ready."

He leaped at the giant with no weapon but his bare hands.

"Enceladus!" Piper yelled. "Look behind you!"

It was an obvious trick, but her voice was so compelling, even Jason bought it. The giant said, "What?" and turned like there was an enormous spider on his back.

Jason tackled his legs at just the right moment. The giant lost his balance. Enceladus slammed into the crater and slid to the bottom. While he tried to rise, Jason put his arms around the giant's neck. When Enceladus struggled to his feet, Jason was riding his shoulders.

"Get off!" Enceladus screamed. He tried to grab Jason's legs, but Jason scrabbled around, squirming and climbing over the giant's hair.

Father, Jason thought. *If I've ever done anything good, anything you approved of, help me now. I offer my own life—just save my friends.*

Suddenly he could smell the metallic scent of a storm. Darkness swallowed the sun. The giant froze, sensing it too.

Jason yelled to his friends, "Hit the deck!"

And every hair on his head stood straight up.

Crack!

Lightning surged through Jason's body, straight through Enceladus, and into the ground. The giant's back stiffened, and Jason was thrown clear. When he regained his bearings, he was slipping down the side of the crater, and the crater was cracking open. The lightning bolt had split the mountain itself. The earth rumbled and tore apart, and Enceladus's legs slid into the chasm. He clawed helplessly at the glassy sides of the pit, and just for a moment managed to hold on to the edge, his hands trembling.

He fixed Jason with a look of hatred. "You've won nothing, boy. My brothers are rising, and they are ten times as strong as I. We will destroy the gods at their roots! You will die, and Olympus will die with—"

The giant lost his grip and fell into the crevice.

The earth shook. Jason fell toward the rift.

"Grab hold!" Leo yelled.

Jason's feet were at the edge of the chasm when he grabbed the rope, and Leo and Piper pulled him up.

They stood together, exhausted and terrified, as the chasm closed like an angry mouth. The ground stopped pulling at their feet.

For now, Gaea was gone.

The mountainside was on fire. Smoke billowed hundreds

of feet into the air. Jason spotted a helicopter—maybe fire-fighters or reporters—coming toward them.

All around them was carnage. The Earthborn had melted into piles of clay, leaving behind only their rock missiles and some nasty bits of loincloth, but Jason figured they would re-form soon enough. Construction equipment lay in ruins. The ground was scarred and blackened.

Coach Hedge started to move. He sat up with a groan and rubbed his head. His canary yellow pants were now the color of Dijon mustard mixed with mud.

He blinked and looked around him at the battle scene. "Did I do this?"

Before Jason could reply, Hedge picked up his club and got shakily to his feet. "Yeah, you wanted some hoof? I gave you some hoof, cupcakes! Who's the goat, huh?"

He did a little dance, kicking rocks and making what were probably rude satyr gestures at the piles of clay.

Leo cracked a smile, and Jason couldn't help it—he started to laugh. It probably sounded a little hysterical, but it was such a relief to be alive, he didn't care.

Then a man stood up across the clearing. Tristan McLean staggered forward. His eyes were hollow, shell-shocked, like someone who'd just walked through a nuclear wasteland.

"Piper?" he called. His voice cracked. "Pipes, what—what is—"

He couldn't complete the thought. Piper ran over to him and hugged him tightly, but he almost didn't seem to know her.

Jason had felt a similar way—that morning at the Grand

Canyon, when he woke with no memory. But Mr. McLean had the opposite problem. He had too *many* memories, too much trauma his mind just couldn't handle. He was coming apart.

"We need to get him out of here," Jason said.

"Yeah, but how?" Leo said. "He's in no shape to walk."

Jason glanced up at the helicopter, which was now circling directly overhead. "Can you make us a bullhorn or something?" he asked Leo. "Piper has some talking to do."

PIPER

BORROWING THE HELICOPTER WAS EASY. Getting her dad on board was not.

Piper needed only a few words through Leo's improvised bullhorn to convince the pilot to land on the mountain. The Park Service copter was big enough for medical evacuations or search and rescue, and when Piper told the very nice ranger pilot lady that it would be a great idea to fly them to the Oakland Airport, she readily agreed.

"No," her dad muttered, as they picked him up off the ground. "Piper, what—there were monsters—there were monsters—"

She needed both Leo's and Jason's help to hold him, while Coach Hedge gathered their supplies. Fortunately Hedge had put his pants and shoes back on, so Piper didn't have to explain the goat legs.

It broke Piper's heart to see her dad like this—pushed beyond the breaking point, crying like a little boy. She didn't know what the giant had done to him exactly, how the monsters had shattered his spirit, but she didn't think she could stand to find out.

"It'll be okay, Dad," she said, making her voice as soothing as possible. She didn't want to charmspeak her own father, but it seemed the only way. "These people are my friends. We're going to help you. You're safe now."

He blinked, and looked up at helicopter rotors. "Blades. They had a machine with so many blades. They had six arms..."

When they got him to the bay doors, the pilot came over to help. "What's wrong with him?" she asked.

"Smoke inhalation," Jason suggested. "Or heat exhaustion."

"We should get him to a hospital," the pilot said.

"It's okay," Piper said. "The airport is good."

"Yeah, the airport is good," the pilot agreed immediately. Then she frowned, as if uncertain why she'd changed her mind. "Isn't he Tristan McLean, the movie star?"

"No," Piper said. "He only looks like him. Forget it."

"Yeah," the pilot said. "Only looks like him. I—" She blinked, confused. "I forgot what I was saying. Let's get going."

Jason raised his eyebrows at Piper, obviously impressed, but Piper felt miserable. She didn't want to twist people's minds, convince them of things they didn't believe. It felt so bossy, so *wrong*—like something Drew would do back at camp, or Medea in her evil department store. And how would it help her father? She couldn't convince him he would be okay, or that nothing had happened. His trauma was just too deep.

Finally they got him on board, and the helicopter took off. The pilot kept getting questions over her radio, asking her where she was going, but she ignored them. They veered away from the burning mountain and headed toward the Berkeley Hills.

"Piper." Her dad grasped her hand and held on like he was afraid he'd fall. "It's you? They told me—they told me you would die. They said...horrible things would happen."

"It's me, Dad." It took all her willpower not to cry. She had to be strong for him. "Everything's going to be okay."

"They were monsters," he said. "Real monsters. Earth spirits, right out of Grandpa Tom's stories—and the Earth Mother was angry with me. And the giant, Tsul'kälû, breathing fire—" He focused on Piper again, his eyes like broken glass, reflecting a crazy kind of light. "They said you were a demigod. Your mother was..."

"Aphrodite," Piper said. "Goddess of love."

"I—I—" He took a shaky breath, then seemed to forget how to exhale.

Piper's friends were careful not to watch. Leo fiddled with a lug nut from his tool belt. Jason gazed at the valley below —the roads backing up as mortals stopped their cars and gawked at the burning mountain. Gleeson chewed on the stub of his carnation, and for once the satyr didn't look in the mood to yell or boast.

Tristan McLean wasn't supposed to be seen like this. He was a star. He was confident, stylish, suave—always in control. That was the public image he projected. Piper had seen the image falter before. But this was different. Now it was broken, gone.

"I didn't know about Mom," Piper told him. "Not until you were taken. When we found out where you were, we came right away. My friends helped me. No one will hurt you again."

Her dad couldn't stop shivering. "You're heroes—you and your friends. I can't believe it. You're a *real* hero, not like me. Not playing a part. I'm so proud of you, Pipes." But the words were muttered listlessly, in a semi-trance.

He gazed down on the valley, and his grip on Piper's hand went slack. "Your mother never told me."

"She thought it was for the best." It sounded lame, even to Piper, and no amount of charmspeak could change that. But she didn't tell her dad what Aphrodite had really worried about: *If he has to spend the rest of his life with those memories, knowing that gods and spirits walk the earth, it will shatter him.*

Piper felt inside the pocket of her jacket. The vial was still there, warm to her touch.

But how could she erase his memories? Her dad finally knew who she was. He was proud of her, and for once she was his hero, not the other way around. He would never send her away now. They shared a secret.

How could she go back to the way things were?

She held his hand, speaking to him about small things—her time at the Wilderness School, her cabin at Camp Half-Blood. She told him how Coach Hedge ate carnations and got knocked on his butt on Mount Diablo, how Leo had tamed a dragon, and how Jason had made wolves back down by talking in Latin. Her friends smiled reluctantly as she recounted their adventures. Her dad seemed to relax as she talked, but he didn't smile. Piper wasn't even sure he heard her.

As they passed over the hills into the East Bay, Jason tensed. He leaned so far out the doorway Piper was afraid he'd fall.

He pointed. "What is that?"

Piper looked down, but she didn't see anything interesting —just hills, woods, houses, little roads snaking through the canyons. A highway cut through a tunnel in the hills, connecting the East Bay with the inland towns.

"Where?" Piper asked.

"That road," he said. "The one that goes through the hills."

Piper picked up the com helmet the pilot had given her and relayed the question over the radio. The answer wasn't very exciting.

"She says it's Highway 24," Piper reported. "That's the Caldecott Tunnel. Why?"

Jason stared intently at the tunnel entrance, but he said nothing. It disappeared from view as they flew over downtown Oakland, but Jason still stared into the distance, his expression almost as unsettled as Piper's dad's.

"Monsters," her dad said, a tear tracing his cheek. "I live in a world of monsters."

XLVI

PIPER

AIR TRAFFIC CONTROL DIDN'T WANT TO let an unscheduled helicopter land at the Oakland Airport—until Piper got on the radio. Then it turned out to be no problem.

They unloaded on the tarmac, and everyone looked at Piper.

"What now?" Jason asked her.

She felt uncomfortable. She didn't want to be in charge, but for her dad's sake, she had to appear confident. She had no plan. She'd just remembered that he'd flown into Oakland, which meant his private plane would still be here. But today was the solstice. They had to save Hera. They had no idea where to go or if they were even too late. And how could she leave her dad in this condition?

"First thing," she said. "I—I have to get my dad home. I'm sorry, guys."

Their faces fell.

"Oh," Leo said. "I mean, absolutely. He needs you right now. We can take it from here."

"Pipes, no." Her dad had been sitting in the helicopter doorway, a blanket around his shoulders. But he stumbled to his feet. "You have a mission. A quest. I can't—"

"I'll take care of him," said Coach Hedge.

Piper stared at him. The satyr was the last person she'd expected to offer. "You?" she asked.

"I'm a protector," Gleeson said. "That's my job, not fighting."

He sounded a little crestfallen, and Piper realized maybe she shouldn't have recounted how he got knocked unconscious in the last battle. In his own way, maybe the satyr was as sensitive as her dad.

Then Hedge straightened, and set his jaw. "Of course, I'm good at fighting, too." He glared at them all, daring them to argue.

"Yes," Jason said.

"Terrifying," Leo agreed.

The coach grunted. "But I'm a protector, and I can do this. Your dad's right, Piper. You need to carry on with the quest."

"But . . ." Piper's eyes stung, as if she were back in the forest fire. "Dad . . ."

He held out his arms, and she hugged him. He felt frail. He was trembling so much, it scared her.

"Let's give them a minute," Jason said, and they took the pilot a few yards down the tarmac.

"I can't believe it," her dad said. "I failed you."

"No, Dad!"

"The things they did, Piper, the visions they showed me..."

"Dad, listen." She took out the vial from her pocket. "Aphrodite gave me this, for you. It takes away your recent memories. It'll make it like none of this ever happened."

He gazed at her, as if translating her words from a foreign language. "But you're a hero. I would forget that?"

"Yes," Piper whispered. She forced an assuring tone into her voice. "Yes, you would. It'll be like—like before."

He closed his eyes and took a shaky breath. "I love you, Piper. I always have. I—I sent you away because I didn't want you exposed to my life. Not the way I grew up—the poverty, the hopelessness. Not the Hollywood insanity either. I thought—I thought I was protecting you." He managed a brittle laugh. "As if your life without me was better, or safer."

Piper took his hand. She'd heard him talk about protecting her before, but she'd never believed it. She'd always thought he was just rationalizing. Her dad seemed so confident and easygoing, like his life was a joyride. How could he claim she needed protecting from that?

Finally Piper understood he'd been acting for her benefit, trying not to show how scared and insecure he was. He really *had* been trying to protect her. And now his ability to cope had been destroyed.

She offered him the vial. "Take it. Maybe someday we'll be ready to talk about this again. When you're ready."

"When I'm ready," he murmured. "You make it sound like—like I'm the one growing up. I'm supposed to be the parent." He took the vial. His eyes glimmered with a small desperate hope. "I love you, Pipes."

"Love you, too, Dad."

He drank the pink liquid. His eyes rolled up into his head, and he slumped forward. Piper caught him, and her friends ran up to help.

"Got him," Hedge said. The satyr stumbled, but he was strong enough to hold Tristan McLean upright. "I already asked our ranger friend to call up his plane. It's on the way now. Home address?"

Piper was about to tell him. Then a thought occurred to her. She checked her dad's pocket, and his BlackBerry was still there. It seemed bizarre that he'd still have something so normal after all he'd been through, but she guessed Enceladus hadn't seen any reason to take it.

"Everything's on here," Piper said. "Address, his chauffeur's number. Just watch out for Jane."

Hedge's eyes lit up, like he sensed a possible fight. "Who's Jane?"

By the time Piper explained, her dad's sleek white Gulfstream had taxied next to the helicopter.

Hedge and the flight attendant got Piper's dad on board. Then Hedge came down one last time to say his good-byes. He gave Piper a hug and glared at Jason and Leo. "You cupcakes take care of this girl, you hear? Or I'm gonna make you do push-ups."

"You got it, Coach," Leo said, a smile tugging at his mouth.

"No push-ups," Jason promised.

Piper gave the old satyr one more hug. "Thank you, Gleeson. Take care of him, please."

"I got this, McLean," he assured her. "They got root beer and veggie enchiladas on this flight, and one hundred percent linen napkins—yum! I could get used to this."

Trotting up the stairs, he lost one shoe, and his hoof was visible for just a second. The flight attendant's eyes widened, but she looked away and pretended nothing was wrong. Piper figured she'd probably seen stranger things, working for Tristan McLean.

When the plane was heading down the runaway, Piper started to cry. She'd been holding it in too long and she just couldn't anymore. Before she knew it, Jason was hugging her, and Leo stood uncomfortably nearby, pulling Kleenex out of his tool belt.

"Your dad's in good hands," Jason said. "You did amazing."

She sobbed into his shirt. She allowed herself to be held for six deep breaths. Seven. Then she couldn't indulge herself anymore. They needed her. The helicopter pilot was already looking uncomfortable, like she was starting to wonder why she'd flown them here.

"Thank you, guys," Piper said. "I—"

She wanted to tell them how much they meant to her. They'd sacrificed everything, maybe even their quest, to help her. She couldn't repay them, couldn't even put her gratitude into words. But her friends' expressions told her they understood.

Then, right next to Jason, the air began to shimmer. At first Piper thought it was heat off the tarmac, or maybe gas fumes from the helicopter, but she'd seen something like this before in Medea's fountain. It was an Iris message. An image appeared in the air—a dark-haired girl in silver winter camouflage, holding a bow.

Jason stumbled back in surprise. "Thalia!"

"Thank the gods," said the Hunter. The scene behind her was hard to make out, but Piper heard yelling, metal clashing on metal, and explosions.

"We've found her," Thalia said. "Where are you?"

"Oakland," he said. "Where are you?"

"The Wolf House! Oakland is good; you're not too far. We're holding off the giant's minions, but we can't hold them forever. Get here before sunset, or it's all over."

"Then it's not too late?" Piper cried. Hope surged through her, but Thalia's expression quickly dampened it.

"Not yet," Thalia said. "But Jason—it's worse than I realized. Porphyrion is rising. Hurry."

"But where is the Wolf House?" he pleaded.

"Our last trip," Thalia said, her image starting to flicker. "The park. Jack London. Remember?"

This made no sense to Piper, but Jason looked like he'd been shot. He tottered, his face pale, and the Iris message disappeared.

"Bro, you all right?" Leo asked. "You know where she is?"

"Yes," Jason said. "Sonoma Valley. Not far. Not by air."

Piper turned to the ranger pilot, who'd been watching all this with an increasingly puzzled expression.

"Ma'am," Piper said with her best smile. "You don't mind helping us one more time, do you?"

"I don't mind," the pilot agreed.

"We can't take a mortal into battle," Jason said. "It's too dangerous." He turned to Leo. "Do you think you could fly this thing?"

"Um..." Leo's expression didn't exactly reassure Piper. But then he put his hand on the side of the helicopter, concentrating hard, as if listening to the machine.

"Bell 412HP utility helicopter," Leo said. "Composite four-blade main rotor, cruising speed twenty-two knots, service ceiling twenty-thousand feet. The tank is near full. Sure, I can fly it."

Piper smiled at the ranger again. "You don't have a problem with an under-aged unlicensed kid borrowing your copter, do you? We'll return it."

"I—" The pilot nearly choked on the words, but she got them out: "I don't have a problem with that."

Leo grinned. "Hop in, kids. Uncle Leo's gonna take you for a ride."

XLVII

LEO

FLY A HELICOPTER? SURE, WHY NOT. Leo had done plenty of crazier things that week.

The sun was going down as they flew north over the Richmond Bridge, and Leo couldn't believe the day had gone so quickly. Once again, nothing like ADHD and a good fight to the death to make time fly.

Piloting the chopper, he went back and forth between confidence and panic. If he didn't think about it, he found himself automatically flipping the right switches, checking the altimeter, easing back on the stick, and flying straight. If he allowed himself to consider what he was doing, he started freaking out. He imagined his Aunt Rosa yelling at him in Spanish, telling him he was a delinquent lunatic who was going to crash and burn. Part of him suspected she was right.

"Going okay?" Piper asked from the copilot's seat. She sounded more nervous than he was, so Leo put on a brave face.

"Aces," he said. "So what's the Wolf House?"

Jason knelt between their seats. "An abandoned mansion in the Sonoma Valley. A demigod built it—Jack London."

Leo couldn't place the name. "He an actor?"

"Writer," Piper said. "Adventure stuff, right? *Call of the Wild? White Fang?*"

"Yeah," Jason said. "He was a son of Mercury—I mean, Hermes. He was an adventurer, traveled the world. He was even a hobo for a while. Then he made a fortune writing. He bought a big ranch in the country and decided to build this huge mansion—the Wolf House."

"Named that 'cause he wrote about wolves?" Leo guessed.

"Partially," Jason said. "But the site, and the reason he wrote about wolves—he was dropping hints about his personal experience. There're a lot of holes in his life story—how he was born, who his dad was, why he wandered around so much—stuff you can only explain if you know he was a demigod."

The bay slipped behind them, and the helicopter continued north. Ahead of them, yellow hills rolled out as far as Leo could see.

"So Jack London went to Camp Half-Blood," Leo guessed.

"No," Jason said. "No, he didn't."

"Bro, you're freaking me out with the mysterious talk. Are you remembering your past or not?"

"Pieces," Jason said. "Only pieces. None of it good. The Wolf House is on sacred ground. It's where London started his journey as a child—where he found out he was a demigod. That's why he returned there. He thought he could live there, claim that land, but it wasn't meant for him. The Wolf House was cursed. It burned in a fire a week before he and his wife were supposed to move in. A few years later, London died, and his ashes were buried on the site."

"So," Piper said, "how do you know all this?"

A shadow crossed Jason's face. Probably just a cloud, but Leo could swear the shape looked like an eagle.

"I started my journey there too," Jason said. "It's a powerful place for demigods, a dangerous place. If Gaea can claim it, use its power to entomb Hera on the solstice and raise Porphyrion—that might be enough to awaken the earth goddess fully."

Leo kept his hand on the joystick, guiding the chopper at full speed—racing toward the north. He could see some weather ahead—a spot of darkness like a cloudbank or a storm, right where they were going.

Piper's dad had called him a hero earlier. And Leo couldn't believe some of the things he'd done—smacking around Cyclopes, disarming exploding doorbells, battling six-armed ogres with construction equipment. They seemed like they had happened to another person. He was just Leo Valdez, an orphaned kid from Houston. He'd spent his life running away, and part of him still wanted to run. What was he thinking, flying toward a cursed mansion to fight more evil monsters?

His mom's voice echoed in his head: *Nothing is unfixable.*

Except the fact that you're gone forever, Leo thought.

Seeing Piper and her dad back together had really driven that home. Even if Leo survived this quest and saved Hera,

Leo wouldn't have any happy reunions. He wouldn't be going back to a loving family. He wouldn't see his mom.

The helicopter shuddered. Metal creaked, and Leo could almost imagine the tapping was Morse code: *Not the end. Not the end.*

He leveled out the chopper, and the creaking stopped. He was just hearing things. He couldn't dwell on his mom, or the idea that kept bugging him—that Gaea was bringing souls back from the Underworld—so why couldn't he make some good come out of it? Thinking like that would drive him crazy. He had a job to do.

He let his instincts take over—just like flying the helicopter. If he thought about the quest too much, or what might happen afterward, he'd panic. The trick was not to think—just get through it.

"Thirty minutes out," he told his friends, though he wasn't sure how he knew. "If you want to get some rest, now's a good time."

Jason strapped himself into the back of the helicopter and passed out almost immediately. Piper and Leo stayed wide-awake.

After a few minutes of awkward silence, Leo said, "Your dad'll be fine, you know. Nobody's gonna mess with him with that crazy goat around."

Piper glanced over, and Leo was struck by how much she'd changed. Not just physically. Her presence was stronger. She seemed more... *here*. At Wilderness School she'd spent the semester trying not to be seen, hiding out in the back row of the classroom, the back of the bus, the corner of the lunchroom as far as possible from the loud kids. Now she would be impossible to miss. It didn't matter what she was wearing —you'd *have* to look at her.

"My dad," she said thoughtfully. "Yeah, I know. I was thinking about Jason. I'm worried about him."

Leo nodded. The closer they got to that bank of dark clouds, the more Leo worried, too. "He's starting to remember. That's got to make him a little edgy."

"But what if... what if he's a different person?"

Leo had had the same thought. If the Mist could affect their memories, could Jason's whole personality be an illusion, too? If their friend wasn't their friend, and they were heading into a cursed mansion—a dangerous place for demigods —what would happen if Jason's full memory came back in the middle of a battle?

"Nah," Leo decided. "After all we've been through? I can't see it. We're a team. Jason can handle it."

Piper smoothed her blue dress, which was tattered and burned from their fight on Mount Diablo. "I hope you're right. I need him..." She cleared her throat. "I mean I need to trust him...."

"I know," Leo said. After seeing her dad break down, Leo understood Piper couldn't afford to lose Jason as well. She'd just watched Tristan McLean, her cool suave movie star dad, reduced to near insanity. Leo could barely stand to watch that, but for *Piper*— Wow, Leo couldn't even imagine. He figured that would make her insecure about herself, too. If weakness was inherited, she'd be wondering, could *she* break down the same way her dad did?

"Hey, don't worry," Leo said. "Piper, you're the strongest, most powerful beauty queen I've ever met. You can trust yourself. For what it's worth, you can trust me too."

The helicopter dipped in a wind shear, and Leo almost jumped out of his skin. He cursed and righted the chopper.

Piper laughed nervously. "Trust you, huh?"

"Ah, shut up, already." But he grinned at her, and for a second, it felt like he was just relaxing comfortably with a friend.

Then they hit the storm clouds.

XLVIII

LEO

AT FIRST, LEO THOUGHT ROCKS WERE pelting the windshield. Then he realized it was sleet. Frost built up around the edges of the glass, and slushy waves of ice blotted out his view.

"An ice storm?" Piper shouted over the engine and the wind. "Is it supposed to be this cold in Sonoma?"

Leo wasn't sure, but something about this storm seemed conscious, malevolent—like it was intentionally slamming them.

Jason woke up quickly. He crawled forward, grabbing their seats for balance. "We've got to be getting close."

Leo was too busy wrestling with the stick to reply. Suddenly it wasn't so easy to drive the chopper. Its movements turned sluggish and jerky. The whole machine shuddered in the icy wind. The helicopter probably hadn't been prepped for cold-weather flying. The controls refused to respond, and they started to lose altitude.

Below them, the ground was a dark quilt of trees and fog. The ridge of a hill loomed in front of them and Leo yanked the stick, just clearing the treetops.

"There!" Jason shouted.

A small valley opened up before them, with the murky shape of a building in the middle. Leo aimed the helicopter straight for it. All around them were flashes of light that reminded Leo of the tracer fire at Midas's compound. Trees cracked and exploded at the edges of the clearing. Shapes moved through the mist. Combat seemed to be everywhere.

He set down the helicopter in an icy field about fifty yards from the house and killed the engine. He was about to relax when he heard a whistling sound and saw a dark shape hurtling toward them out of the mist.

"Out!" Leo screamed.

They leaped from the helicopter and barely cleared the rotors before a massive *BOOM* shook the ground, knocking Leo off his feet and splattering ice all over him.

He got up shakily and saw that the world's largest snowball —a chunk of snow, ice, and dirt the size of a garage—had completely flattened the Bell 412.

"You all right?" Jason ran up to him, Piper at his side. They both looked fine except for being speckled with snow and mud.

"Yeah." Leo shivered. "Guess we owe that ranger lady a new helicopter."

Piper pointed south. "Fighting's over there." Then she frowned. "No . . . it's all around us."

She was right. The sounds of combat rang across the valley. The snow and mist made it hard to tell for sure, but there seemed to be a circle of fighting all around the Wolf House.

Behind them loomed Jack London's dream home—a massive ruin of red and gray stones and rough-hewn timber beams. Leo could imagine how it had looked before it burned down—a combination log cabin and castle, like a billionaire lumberjack might build. But in the mist and sleet, the place had a lonely, haunted feel. Leo could totally believe the ruins were cursed.

"Jason!" a girl's voice called.

Thalia appeared from the fog, her parka caked with snow. Her bow was in her hand, and her quiver was almost empty. She ran toward them, but made it only a few steps before a six-armed ogre—one of the Earthborn—burst out of the storm behind her, a raised club in each hand.

"Look out!" Leo yelled. They rushed to help, but Thalia had it under control. She launched herself into a flip, notching an arrow as she pivoted like a gymnast and landed in a kneeling position. The ogre got a silver arrow right between the eyes and melted into a pile of clay.

Thalia stood and retrieved her arrow, but the point had snapped off. "That was my last one." She kicked the pile of clay resentfully. "Stupid ogre."

"Nice shot, though," Leo said.

Thalia ignored him as usual (which no doubt meant she thought he was as cool as ever). She hugged Jason and nodded to Piper. "Just in time. My Hunters are holding a perimeter around the mansion, but we'll be overrun any minute."

"By Earthborn?" Jason asked.

"*And* wolves—Lycaon's minions." Thalia blew a fleck of ice off her nose. "Also storm spirits—"

"But we gave them to Aeolus!" Piper protested.

"Who tried to kill us," Leo reminded her. "Maybe he's helping Gaea again."

"I don't know," Thalia said. "But the monsters keep re-forming almost as fast as we can kill them. We took the Wolf House with no problem: surprised the guards and sent them straight to Tartarus. But then this freak snowstorm blew in. Wave after wave of monsters started attacking. Now we're surrounded. I don't know who or what is leading the assault, but I think they planned this. It was a trap to kill anyone who tried to rescue Hera."

"Where is she?" Jason asked.

"Inside," Thalia said. "We tried to free her, but we can't figure out how to break the cage. It's only a few minutes until the sun goes down. Hera thinks that's the moment when Porphyrion will be reborn. Plus, most monsters are stronger at night. If we don't free Hera soon—"

She didn't need to finish the thought.

Leo, Jason, and Piper followed her into the ruined mansion.

Jason stepped over the threshold and immediately collapsed.

"Hey!" Leo caught him. "None of that, man. What's wrong?"

"This place..." Jason shook his head. "Sorry...It came rushing back to me."

"So you *have* been here," Piper said.

"We both have," Thalia said. Her expression was grim, like she was reliving someone's death. "This is where my mom took us when Jason was a child. She left him here, told me he was dead. He just disappeared."

"She gave me to the wolves," Jason murmured. "At Hera's insistence. She gave me to Lupa."

"That part I didn't know." Thalia frowned. "Who is Lupa?"

An explosion shook the building. Just outside, a blue mushroom cloud billowed up, raining snowflakes and ice like a nuclear blast made of cold instead of heat.

"Maybe this isn't the time for questions," Leo suggested. "Show us the goddess."

Once inside, Jason seemed to get his bearings. The house was built in a giant U, and Jason led them between the two wings to an outside courtyard with an empty reflecting pool. At the bottom of the pool, just as Jason had described from his dream, two spires of rock and root tendrils had cracked through the foundation.

One of the spires was much bigger—a solid dark mass about twenty feet high, and to Leo it looked like a stone body bag. Underneath the mass of fused tendrils he could make out the shape of a head, wide shoulders, a massive chest and arms, like the creature was stuck waist deep in the earth. No, not stuck—*rising*.

On the opposite end of the pool, the other spire was smaller and more loosely woven. Each tendril was as thick as a telephone pole, with so little space between them that Leo doubted he could've gotten his arm through. Still, he could see inside. And in the center of the cage stood Tía Callida.

She looked exactly like Leo remembered: dark hair covered with a shawl, the black dress of a widow, a wrinkled face with glinting, scary eyes.

She didn't glow or radiate any sort of power. She looked like a regular mortal woman, his good old psychotic babysitter.

Leo dropped into the pool and approached the cage. "*Hola, Tía.* Little bit of trouble?"

She crossed her arms and sighed in exasperation. "Don't inspect me like I'm one of your machines, Leo Valdez. Get me out of here!"

Thalia stepped next to him and looked at the cage with distaste—or maybe she was looking at the goddess. "We tried everything we could think of, Leo, but maybe my heart wasn't in it. If it was up to me, I'd just leave her in there."

"Ohh, Thalia Grace," the goddess said. "When I get out of here, you'll be sorry you were ever born."

"Save it!" Thalia snapped. "You've been nothing but a curse to every child of Zeus for ages. You sent a bunch of intestinally challenged cows after my friend Annabeth—"

"She was disrespectful!"

"You dropped a statue on my legs."

"It was an accident!"

"*And* you took my brother!" Thalia's voice cracked with emotion. "Here—on this spot. You ruined our lives. We should leave you to Gaea!"

"Hey," Jason intervened. "Thalia—Sis—I know. But this isn't the time. You should help your Hunters."

Thalia clenched her jaw. "Fine. For you, Jason. But if you ask me, she isn't worth it."

Thalia turned, leaped out of the pool, and stormed from the building.

Leo turned to Hera with grudging respect. "Intestinally challenged cows?"

"Focus on the cage, Leo," she grumbled. "And Jason—you are wiser than your sister. I chose my champion well."

"I'm not your champion, lady," Jason said. "I'm only helping you because you stole my memories and you're better than the alternative. Speaking of which, what's going on with that?"

He nodded to the other spire that looked like the king-size granite body bag. Was Leo imagining it, or had it grown taller since they'd gotten here?

"That, Jason," Hera said, "is the king of the giants being reborn."

"Gross," Piper said.

"Indeed," Hera said. "Porphyrion, the strongest of his kind. Gaea needed a great deal of power to raise him again —*my* power. For weeks I've grown weaker as my essence was used to grow him a new form."

"So you're like a heat lamp," Leo guessed. "Or fertilizer."

The goddess glared at him, but Leo didn't care. This old lady had been making his life miserable since he was a baby. He totally had rights to rag on her.

"Joke all you wish," Hera said in a clipped tone. "But at sundown, it will be too late. The giant will awake. He will offer me a choice: marry him, or be consumed by the earth. And I cannot marry him. We will all be destroyed. And as we die, Gaea will awaken."

Leo frowned at the giant's spire. "Can't we blow it up or something?"

"Without me, you do not have the power," Hera said. "You might as well try to destroy a mountain."

"Done that once today," Jason said.

"Just hurry up and let me out!" Hera demanded.

Jason scratched his head. "Leo, can you do it?"

"I don't know." Leo tried not to panic. "Besides, if she's a goddess, why hasn't she busted herself out?"

Hera paced furiously around her cage, cursing in Ancient Greek. "Use your brain, Leo Valdez. I *picked* you because you're intelligent. Once trapped, a god's power is useless. Your own father trapped me once in a golden chair. It was humiliating! I had to beg—*beg* him for my freedom and apologize for throwing him off Olympus."

"Sounds fair," Leo said.

Hera gave him the godly stink-eye. "I've watched you since you were a child, son of Hephaestus, because I knew you could aid me at this moment. If anyone can find a way to destroy this *abomination*, it is you."

"But it's not a machine. It's like Gaea thrust her hand out of the ground and . . ." Leo felt dizzy. The line of their prophecy came back to him: *The forge and dove shall break the cage.* "Hold on. I do have an idea. Piper, I'm going to need your help. And we're going to need time."

The air turned brittle with cold. The temperature dropped so fast, Leo's lips cracked and his breath changed to mist. Frost coated the walls of the Wolf House. *Venti* rushed in

—but instead of winged men, these were shaped like horses, with dark storm-cloud bodies and manes that crackled with lightning. Some had silver arrows sticking out of their flanks. Behind them came red-eyed wolves and the six-armed Earthborn.

Piper drew her dagger. Jason grabbed an ice-covered plank off the pool floor. Leo reached into his tool belt, but he was so shaken up, all he produced was a tin of breath mints. He shoved them back in, hoping nobody had noticed, and drew a hammer instead.

One of the wolves padded forward. It was dragging a human-size statue by the leg. At the edge of the pool, the wolf opened its maw and dropped the statue for them to see —an ice sculpture of a girl, an archer with short spiky hair and a surprised look on her face.

"Thalia!" Jason rushed forward, but Piper and Leo pulled him back. The ground around Thalia's statue was already webbed with ice. Leo feared if Jason touched her, he might freeze too.

"Who did this?" Jason yelled. His body crackled with electricity. "I'll kill you myself!"

From somewhere behind the monsters, Leo heard a girl's laughter, clear and cold. She stepped out of the mist in her snowy white dress, a silver crown atop her long black hair. She regarded them with those deep brown eyes Leo had thought were so beautiful in Quebec.

"Bon soir, mes amis," said Khione, the goddess of snow. She gave Leo a frosty smile. "Alas, son of Hephaestus, you say you need time? I'm afraid time is one tool you do not have."

XLIX

JASON

AFTER THE FIGHT ON MOUNT DIABLO, Jason didn't think he could ever feel more afraid or devastated.

Now his sister was frozen at his feet. He was surrounded by monsters. He'd broken his golden sword and replaced it with a piece of wood. He had approximately five minutes until the king of the giants busted out and destroyed them. Jason had already pulled his biggest ace, calling down Zeus's lightning when he'd fought Enceladus, and he doubted he'd have the strength or the cooperation from above to do it again. Which meant his only assets were one whiny imprisoned goddess, one sort-of girlfriend with a dagger, and Leo, who apparently thought he could defeat the armies of darkness with breath mints.

On top of all this, Jason's worst memories were flooding back. He knew for certain he'd done many dangerous things in his life, but he'd never been closer to death than he was right now.

The enemy was beautiful. Khione smiled, her dark eyes glittering, as a dagger of ice grew in her hand.

"What've you done?" Jason demanded.

"Oh, so many things," the snow goddess purred. "Your sister's not dead, if that's what you mean. She and her Hunters will make fine toys for our wolves. I thought we'd defrost them one at a time and hunt them down for amusement. Let *them* be the prey for once."

The wolves snarled appreciatively.

"Yes, my dears." Khione kept her eyes on Jason. "Your sister almost killed their king, you know. Lycaon's off in a cave somewhere, no doubt licking his wounds, but his minions have joined us to take revenge for their master. And soon Porphyrion will arise, and we shall rule the world."

"Traitor!" Hera shouted. "You meddlesome, D-list goddess! You aren't worthy to pour my wine, much less rule the world."

Khione sighed. "Tiresome as ever, Queen Hera. I've been wanting to shut you up for millennia."

Khione waved her hand, and ice encased the prison, sealing in the spaces between the earthen tendrils.

"That's better," the snow goddess said. "Now, demigods, about your death—"

"You're the one who tricked Hera into coming here," Jason said. "You gave Zeus the idea of closing Olympus."

The wolves snarled, and the storm spirits whinnied, ready to attack, but Khione held up her hand. "Patience, my loves. If he wants to talk, what matter? The sun is setting, and time is on our side. Of course, Jason Grace. Like snow, my voice is quiet and gentle, and very cold. It's easy for me to whisper to the other gods, especially when I am only confirming their own deepest fears. I also whispered in Aeolus's ear that he should issue an order to kill demigods. It is a small service for Gaea, but I'm sure I will be well rewarded when her sons the giants come to power."

"You could've killed us in Quebec," Jason said. "Why let us live?"

Khione wrinkled her nose. "Messy business, killing you in my father's house, especially when he insists on meeting all visitors. I did *try*, you remember. It would've been lovely if he'd agreed to turn you to ice. But once he'd given you guarantee of safe passage, I couldn't openly disobey him. My father is an old fool. He lives in fear of Zeus and Aeolus, but he's still powerful. Soon enough, when my new masters have awakened, I will depose Boreas and take the throne of the North Wind, but not just yet. Besides, my father did have a point. Your quest was suicidal. I fully expected you to fail."

"And to help us with that," Leo said, "you knocked our dragon out of the sky over Detroit. Those frozen wires in his head—that was *your* fault. You're gonna pay for that."

"You're also the one who kept Enceladus informed about us," Piper added. "We've been plagued by snowstorms the whole trip."

"Yes, I feel so close to all of you now!" Khione said. "Once you made it past Omaha, I decided to ask Lycaon to track you down so Jason could die here, at the Wolf House." Khione smiled at him. "You see, Jason, your blood spilled on this sacred ground will taint it for generations. Your demigod brethren will be outraged, especially when they find the bodies of these two from Camp Half-Blood. They'll believe the Greeks have conspired with giants. It will be . . . delicious."

Piper and Leo didn't seem to understand what she was saying. But Jason knew. His memories were returning enough for him to realize how dangerously effective Khione's plan could be.

"You'll set demigods against demigods," he said.

"It's so easy!" said Khione. "As I told you, I only encourage what you would do anyway."

"But why?" Piper spread her hands. "Khione, you'll tear the world apart. The giants will destroy everything. You don't want that. Call off your monsters."

Khione hesitated, then laughed. "Your persuasive powers are improving, girl. But I am a goddess. You can't charmspeak me. We wind gods are creatures of chaos! I'll overthrow Aeolus and let the storms run free. If we destroy the mortal world, all the better! They never honored me, even in Greek times. Humans and their talk of global warming. Pah! I'll cool them down quickly enough. When we retake the ancient places, I will cover the Acropolis in snow."

"The ancient places." Leo's eyes widened. "That's what Enceladus meant about destroying the roots of the gods. He meant Greece."

"You could join me, son of Hephaestus," Khione said. "I know you find me beautiful. It would be enough for my plan if these other two were to die. Reject that ridiculous destiny the Fates have given you. Live and be my champion, instead. Your skills would be quite useful."

Leo looked stunned. He glanced behind him, like Khione might be talking to somebody else. For a second Jason was worried. He figured Leo didn't have beautiful goddesses make him offers like this every day.

Then Leo laughed so hard, he doubled over. "Yeah, join you. Right. Until you get bored of me and turn me into a Leosicle? Lady, nobody messes with my dragon and gets away with it. I can't believe I thought you were hot."

Khione's face turned red. "Hot? You dare insult me? I am cold, Leo Valdez. Very, very cold."

She shot a blast of wintry sleet at the demigods, but Leo held up his hand. A wall of fire roared to life in front of them, and the snow dissolved in a steamy cloud.

Leo grinned. "See, lady, that's what happens to snow in Texas. It—freaking—melts."

Khione hissed. "Enough of this. Hera is failing. Porphyrion is rising. Kill the demigods. Let them be our king's first meal!"

Jason hefted his icy wooden plank—a stupid weapon to die fighting with—and the monsters charged.

L

JASON

A WOLF LAUNCHED ITSELF AT JASON. He stepped back and swung his scrap wood into the beast's snout with a satisfying crack. Maybe only silver could kill it, but a good old-fashioned board could still give it a Tylenol headache.

He turned toward the sound of hooves and saw a storm spirit horse bearing down on him. Jason concentrated and summoned the wind. Just before the spirit could trample him, Jason launched himself into the air, grabbed the horse's smoky neck, and pirouetted onto its back.

The storm spirit reared. It tried to shake Jason, then tried to dissolve into mist to lose him; but somehow Jason stayed on. He willed the horse to remain in solid form, and the horse seemed unable to refuse. Jason could feel it fighting against him. He could sense its raging thoughts—complete chaos straining to break free. It took all Jason's willpower to impose his own wishes and bring the horse under control. He thought about Aeolus, overseeing thousands and thousands of spirits like this, some much worse. No wonder the Master of the Winds had gone a little mad after centuries of that pressure. But Jason had only one spirit to master, and he *had* to win.

"You're mine now," Jason said.

The horse bucked, but Jason held fast. Its mane flickered as it circled around the empty pool, its hooves causing miniature thunderstorms—tempests—whenever they touched.

"Tempest?" Jason said. "Is that your name?"

The horse spirit shook its mane, evidently pleased to be recognized.

"Fine," Jason said. "Now, let's fight."

He charged into battle, swinging his icy piece of wood, knocking aside wolves and plunging straight through other *venti*. Tempest was a strong spirit, and every time he plowed through one of his brethren, he discharged so much electricity, the other spirit vaporized into a harmless cloud of mist.

Through the chaos, Jason caught glimpses of his friends. Piper was surrounded by Earthborn, but she seemed to be holding her own. She was so impressive-looking as she fought, almost glowing with beauty, that the Earthborn stared at her in awe, forgetting that they were supposed to kill her. They'd lower their clubs and watch dumbfounded as she smiled and charged them. They'd smile back—until she sliced them apart with her dagger, and they melted into mounds of mud.

Leo had taken on Khione herself. While fighting a goddess should've been suicide, Leo was the right man for the job. She kept summoning ice daggers to throw at him, blasts of winter air, tornadoes of snow. Leo burned through all of it. His whole body flickered with red tongues of flame like he'd been doused with gasoline. He advanced on the goddess, using two silver-tipped ball-peen hammers to smash any monsters that got in his way.

Jason realized that Leo was the only reason they were still alive. His fiery aura was heating up the whole courtyard, countering Khione's winter magic. Without him, they would've been frozen like the Hunters long ago. Wherever Leo went, ice melted off the stones. Even Thalia started to defrost a little when Leo stepped near her.

Khione slowly backed away. Her expression went from enraged to shocked to slightly panicked as Leo got closer.

Jason was running out of enemies. Wolves lay in dazed heaps. Some slunk away into the ruins, yelping from their wounds. Piper stabbed the last Earthborn, who toppled to the ground in a pile of sludge. Jason rode Tempest through the last *ventus*, breaking it into vapor. Then he wheeled around and saw Leo bearing down on the goddess of snow.

"You're too late," Khione snarled. "He's awake! And don't think you've won anything here, demigods. Hera's plan will never work. You'll be at each other's throats before you can ever stop us."

Leo set his hammers ablaze and threw them at the goddess, but she turned into snow—a white powdery image of herself. Leo's hammers slammed into the snow woman, breaking it into a steaming mound of mush.

Piper was breathing hard, but she smiled up at Jason. "Nice horse."

Tempest reared on his hind legs, arcing electricity across his hooves. A complete show-off.

Then Jason heard a cracking sound behind him. The melting ice on Hera's cage sloughed off in a curtain of slush, and the goddess called, "Oh, don't mind me! Just the queen of the heavens, dying over here!"

Jason dismounted and told Tempest to stay put. The three demigods jumped into the pool and ran to the spire.

Leo frowned. "Uh, Tía Callida, are you getting shorter?"

"No, you dolt! The earth is claiming me. Hurry!"

As much as Jason disliked Hera, what he saw inside the cage alarmed him. Not only was Hera sinking, the ground was rising around her like water in a tank. Liquid rock had already covered her shins. "The giant wakes!" Hera warned. "You only have seconds!"

"On it," Leo said. "Piper, I need your help. Talk to the cage."

"What?" she said.

"Talk to it. Use everything you've got. Convince Gaea to sleep. Lull her into a daze. Just slow her down, try to get the tendrils to loosen while I—"

"Right!" Piper cleared her throat and said, "Hey, Gaea. Nice night, huh? Boy, I'm tired. How about you? Ready for some sleep?"

The more she talked, the more confident she sounded. Jason felt his own eyes getting heavy, and he had to force himself not to focus on her words. It seemed to have some effect on the cage. The mud was rising more slowly. The tendrils seemed to soften just a little—becoming more like tree root than rock. Leo pulled a circular saw out of his tool belt. How it fit in there, Jason had no idea. Then Leo looked at the cord and grunted in frustration. "I don't have anywhere to plug it in!"

The spirit horse Tempest jumped into the pit and whinnied.

"Really?" Jason asked.

Tempest dipped his head and trotted over to Leo. Leo looked dubious, but he held up the plug, and a breeze whisked it into the horse's flank. Lightning sparked, connecting with the prongs of the plug, and the circular saw whirred to life.

"Sweet!" Leo grinned. "Your horse comes with AC outlets!"

Their good mood didn't last long. On the other side of the pool, the giant's spire crumbled with a sound like a tree snapping in half. Its outer sheath of tendrils exploded from the top down, raining stone and wood shards as the giant shook himself free and climbed out of the earth.

Jason hadn't thought anything could be scarier than Enceladus.

He was wrong.

Porphyrion was even taller, and even more ripped. He didn't radiate heat, or show any signs of breathing fire, but there was something more terrible about him—a kind of strength, even magnetism, as if the giant were so huge and dense he had his own gravitational field.

Like Enceladus, the giant king was humanoid from the waist up, clad in bronze armor, and from the waist down he had scaly dragon's legs; but his skin was the color of lima beans. His hair was green as summer leaves, braided in long locks and decorated with weapons—daggers, axes, and full-size swords, some of them bent and bloody—maybe trophies taken from demigods eons before. When the giant opened his eyes, they were blank white, like polished marble. He took a deep breath.

"Alive!" he bellowed. "Praise to Gaea!"

Jason made a heroic little whimpering sound he hoped his friends couldn't hear. He was very sure no demigod could solo this guy. Porphyrion could lift mountains. He could crush Jason with one finger.

"Leo," Jason said.

"Huh?" Leo's mouth was wide open. Even Piper seemed dazed.

"You guys keep working," Jason said. "Get Hera free!"

"What are you going to do?" Piper asked. "You can't seriously—"

"Entertain a giant?" Jason said. "I've got no choice."

"Excellent!" the giant roared as Jason approached. "An appetizer! Who are you—Hermes? Ares?"

Jason thought about going with that idea, but something told him not to.

"I'm Jason Grace," he said. "Son of Jupiter."

Those white eyes bored into him. Behind him, Leo's circular saw whirred, and Piper talked to the cage in soothing tones, trying to keep the fear out of her voice.

Porphyrion threw back his head and laughed. "Outstanding!" He looked up at the cloudy night sky. "So, Zeus, you sacrifice a son to me? The gesture is appreciated, but it will not save you."

The sky didn't even rumble. No help from above. Jason was on his own.

He dropped his makeshift club. His hands were covered in splinters, but that didn't matter now. He had to buy Leo and Piper some time, and he couldn't do that without a proper weapon.

It was time to act a whole lot more confident than he felt.

"If you knew who I was," Jason yelled up at the giant, "you'd be worried about me, not my father. I hope you enjoyed your two and a half minutes of rebirth, giant, because I'm going to send you right back to Tartarus."

The giant's eyes narrowed. He planted one foot outside the pool and crouched to get a better look at his opponent. "So . . . we'll start by boasting, will we? Just like old times! Very well, demigod. I am Porphyrion, king of the giants, son of Gaea. In olden times, I rose from Tartarus, the abyss of my father, to challenge the gods. To start the war, I stole Zeus's queen." He grinned at the goddess's cage. "Hello, Hera."

"My husband destroyed you once, monster!" Hera said. "He'll do it again!"

"But he didn't, my dear! Zeus wasn't powerful enough to kill me. He had to rely on a puny demigod to help, and even then, we almost won. This time, we will complete what we started. Gaea is waking. She has provisioned us with many fine servants. Our armies will shake the earth—and we will destroy you at the roots."

"You wouldn't dare," Hera said, but she was weakening. Jason could hear it in her voice. Piper kept whispering to the cage, and Leo kept sawing, but the earth was still rising inside Hera's prison, covering her up to her waist.

"Oh, yes," the giant said. "The Titans sought to attack

your new home in New York. Bold, but ineffective. Gaea is wiser and more patient. And we, her greatest children, are much, much stronger than Kronos. We know how to kill you Olympians once and for all. You must be dug up completely like rotten trees—your eldest roots torn out and burned."

The giant frowned at Piper and Leo, as if he'd just noticed them working at the cage. Jason stepped forward and yelled to get back Porphyrion's attention.

"You said a demigod killed you," he shouted. "How, if we're so puny?"

"Ha! You think I would explain it to you? I was created to be Zeus's replacement, born to destroy the lord of the sky. I shall take his throne. I shall take his wife—or, if she will not have me, I will let the earth consume her life force. What you see before you, child, is only my weakened form. I will grow stronger by the hour, until I am invincible. But I am already quite capable of smashing you to a grease spot!"

He rose to his full height and held out his hand. A twenty-foot spear shot from the earth. He grasped it, then stomped the ground with his dragon's feet. The ruins shook. All around the courtyard, monsters started to regather—storm spirits, wolves, and Earthborn, all answering the giant king's call.

"Great," Leo muttered. "We needed more enemies."

"Hurry," Hera said.

"I know!" Leo snapped.

"Go to sleep, cage," Piper said. "Nice, sleepy cage. Yes, I'm talking to a bunch of earthen tendrils. This isn't weird at all."

Porphyrion raked his spear across the top of the ruins, destroying a chimney and spraying wood and stone across the courtyard. "So, child of Zeus! I have finished my boasting. Now it's your turn. What were you saying about destroying me?"

Jason looked at the ring of monsters, waiting impatiently for their master's order to tear them to shreds. Leo's circular saw kept whirring, and Piper kept talking, but it seemed hopeless. Hera's cage was almost completely filled with earth.

"I'm the son of Jupiter!" he shouted, and just for effect, he summoned the winds, rising a few feet off the ground. "I'm a child of Rome, consul to demigods, praetor of the First Legion." Jason didn't know quite what he was saying, but he rattled off the words like he'd said them many times before. He held out his arms, showing the tattoo of the eagle and SPQR, and to his surprise the giant seemed to recognize it.

For a moment, Porphyrion actually looked uneasy.

"I slew the Trojan sea monster," Jason continued. "I toppled the black throne of Kronos, and destroyed the Titan Krios with my own hands. And now I'm going to destroy you, Porphyrion, and feed you to your own wolves."

"Wow, dude," Leo muttered. "You been eating red meat?"

Jason launched himself at the giant, determined to tear him apart.

The idea of fighting a forty-foot-tall immortal bare handed was so ridiculous, even the giant seemed surprised. Half flying, half leaping, Jason landed on the giant's scaly reptilian knee and climbed up the giant's arm before Porphyrion even realized what had happened.

"You dare?" the giant bellowed.

Jason reached his shoulders and ripped a sword out of the giant's weapon-filled braids. He yelled, "For Rome!" and drove the sword into the nearest convenient target—the giant's massive ear.

Lightning streaked out of the sky and blasted the sword, throwing Jason free. He rolled when he hit the ground. When he looked up, the giant was staggering. His hair was on fire, and the side of his face was blackened from lightning. The sword had splintered in his ear. Golden ichor ran down his jaw. The other weapons were sparking and smoldering in his braids.

Porphyrion almost fell. The circle of monsters let out a collective growl and moved forward—wolves and ogres fixing their eyes on Jason.

"No!" Porphyrion yelled. He regained his balance and glared at the demigod. "I will kill him myself."

The giant raised his spear and it began to glow. "You want to play with lightning, boy? You forget. I am the bane of Zeus. I was created to destroy your father, which means I know exactly what will kill *you*."

Something in Porphyrion's voice told Jason he wasn't bluffing.

Jason and his friends had had a good run. The three of them had done amazing things. Yeah, even *heroic* things. But as the giant raised his spear, Jason knew there was no way he could deflect this strike.

This was the end.

"Got it!" Leo yelled.

"Sleep!" Piper said, so forcefully, the nearest wolves fell to the ground and began snoring.

The stone and wood cage crumbled. Leo had sawed through the base of the thickest tendril and apparently cut off the cage's connection to Gaea. The tendrils turned to dust. The mud around Hera disintegrated. The goddess grew in size, glowing with power.

"Yes!" the goddess said. She threw off her black robes to reveal a white gown, her arms bedecked with golden jewelry. Her face was both terrible and beautiful, and a golden crown glowed in her long black hair. "Now I shall have my revenge!"

The giant Porphyrion backed away. He said nothing, but he gave Jason one last look of hatred. His message was clear: *Another time.* Then he slammed his spear against the earth, and the giant disappeared into the ground like he'd dropped down a chute.

Around the courtyard, monsters began to panic and retreat, but there was no escape for them.

Hera glowed brighter. She shouted, "Cover your eyes, my heroes!"

But Jason was too much in shock. He understood too late.

He watched as Hera turned into a supernova, exploding in a ring of force that vaporized every monster instantly. Jason fell, light searing into his mind, and his last thought was that his body was burning.

PIPER

"Jason!"

Piper kept calling his name as she held him, though she'd almost lost hope. He'd been unconscious for two minutes now. His body was steaming, his eyes rolled back in his head. She couldn't tell if he was even breathing.

"It's no use, child." Hera stood over them in her simple black robes and shawl.

Piper hadn't seen the goddess go nuclear. Thankfully she'd closed her eyes, but she could see the aftereffects. Every vestige of winter was gone from the valley. No signs of battle, either. The monsters had been vaporized. The ruins had been restored to what they were before—still ruins, but with no evidence that they'd been overrun by a horde of wolves, storm spirits, and six-armed ogres.

Even the Hunters had been revived. Most waited at a respectful distance in the meadow, but Thalia knelt by Piper's side, her hand on Jason's forehead.

Thalia glared up at the goddess. "This is your fault. Do something!"

"Do not address me that way, girl. I am the queen—"

"Fix him!"

Hera's eyes flickered with power. "I *did* warn him. I would never intentionally hurt the boy. He was to be my champion. I told them to close their eyes before I revealed my true form."

"Um..." Leo frowned. "True form is bad, right? So why did you do it?"

"I unleashed my power to help you, fool!" Hera cried. "I became pure energy so I could disintegrate the monsters, restore this place, and even save these miserable Hunters from the ice."

"But mortals can't look upon you in that form!" Thalia shouted. "You've killed him!"

Leo shook his head in dismay. "That's what our prophecy meant. *Death unleash, through Hera's rage.* Come on, lady. You're a goddess. Do some voodoo magic on him! Bring him back."

Piper half heard their conversation, but mostly she was focused on Jason's face. "He's breathing!" she announced.

"Impossible," Hera said. "I wish it were true, child, but no mortal has ever—"

"Jason," Piper called, putting every bit of her willpower into his name. She could *not* lose him. "Listen to me. You can do this. Come back. You're going to be fine."

Nothing happened. Had she imagined his breath stirring?

"Healing is not a power of Aphrodite," Hera said regretfully. "Even I cannot fix this, girl. His mortal spirit—"

"Jason," Piper said again, and she imagined her voice resonating through the earth, all the way down to the Underworld. "Wake up."

He gasped, and his eyes flew open. For a moment they were full of light—glowing pure gold. Then the light faded and his eyes were normal again. "What—what happened?"

"Impossible!" Hera said.

Piper wrapped him in a hug until he groaned, "Crushing me."

"Sorry," she said, so relieved, she laughed while wiping a tear from her eye.

Thalia gripped her brother's hand. "How do you feel?"

"Hot," he muttered. "Mouth is dry. And I saw something . . . really terrible."

"That was Hera," Thalia grumbled. "Her Majesty, the Loose Cannon."

"That's it, Thalia Grace," said the goddess. "I will turn you into an aardvark, so help me—"

"Stop it, you two," Piper said. Amazingly, they both shut up.

Piper helped Jason to his feet and gave him the last nectar from their supplies.

"Now . . ." Piper faced Thalia and Hera. "Hera—Your Majesty—we couldn't have rescued you without the Hunters. And Thalia, you never would've seen Jason again—*I* wouldn't have met him—if it weren't for Hera. You two make nice, because we've got bigger problems."

They both glared at her, and for three long seconds, Piper wasn't sure which one of them was going to kill her first.

Finally Thalia grunted. "You've got spirit, Piper." She pulled a silver card from her parka and tucked it into the pocket of Piper's snowboarding jacket. "You ever want to be a Hunter, call me. We could use you."

Hera crossed her arms. "Fortunately for *this* Hunter, you have a point, daughter of Aphrodite." She assessed Piper, as if seeing her clearly for the first time. "You wondered, Piper, why I chose you for this quest, why I didn't reveal your secret in the beginning, even when I knew Enceladus was using you. I must admit, until this moment I was not sure. Something told me you would be vital to the quest. Now I see I was right. You're even stronger than I realized. And you are correct about the dangers to come. We must work together."

Piper's face felt warm. She wasn't sure how to respond to Hera's compliment, but Leo stepped in.

"Yeah," he said, "I don't suppose that Porphyrion guy just melted and died, huh?"

"No," Hera agreed. "By saving me, and saving this place, you prevented Gaea from waking. You have bought us some time. But Porphyrion has risen. He simply knew better than to stay here, especially since he has not yet regained his full power. Giants can only be killed by a combination of god and demigod, working together. Once you freed me—"

"He ran away," Jason said. "But to where?"

Hera didn't answer, but a sense of dread washed over Piper. She remembered what Porphyrion had said about killing the Olympians by pulling up their roots. *Greece.* She looked at Thalia's grim expression, and guessed the Hunter had come to the same conclusion.

"I need to find Annabeth," Thalia said. "She has to know what's happened here."

"Thalia..." Jason gripped her hand. "We never got to talk about this place, or—"

"I know." Her expression softened. "I lost you here once. I don't want to leave you again. But we'll meet soon. I'll rendezvous with you back at Camp Half-Blood." She glanced at Hera. "You'll see them there safely? It's the least you can do."

"It's not your place to tell me—"

"Queen Hera," Piper interceded.

The goddess sighed. "Fine. Yes. Just off with you, Hunter!"

Thalia gave Jason a hug and said her good-byes. When the Hunters were gone, the courtyard seemed strangely quiet. The dry reflecting pool showed no sign of the earthen tendrils that had brought back the giant king or imprisoned Hera. The night sky was clear and starry. The wind rustled in the redwoods. Piper thought about that night in Oklahoma when she and her dad had slept in Grandpa Tom's front yard. She thought about the night on the Wilderness School dorm roof, when Jason had kissed her—in her Mist-altered memories, anyway.

"Jason, what happened to you here?" she asked. "I mean— I know your mom abandoned you here. But you said it was sacred ground for demigods. Why? What happened after you were on your own?"

Jason shook his head uneasily. "It's still murky. The wolves..."

"You were given a destiny," Hera said. "You were given into my service."

Jason scowled. "Because you forced my mom to do that. You couldn't stand knowing Zeus had two children with my mom. Knowing that he'd fallen for her *twice*. I was the price you demanded for leaving the rest of my family alone."

"It was the right choice for you as well, Jason," Hera insisted. "The second time your mother managed to snare Zeus's affections, it was because she imagined him in a different aspect—the aspect of Jupiter. Never before had this happened—two children, Greek and Roman, born into the same family. You *had* to be separated from Thalia. This is where all demigods of your kind start their journey."

"Of his kind?" Piper asked.

"She means Roman," Jason said. "Demigods are left here. We meet the she-wolf goddess, Lupa, the same immortal wolf that raised Romulus and Remus."

Hera nodded. "And if you are strong enough, you live."

"But..." Leo looked mystified. "What happened after that? I mean, Jason never made it to camp."

"Not to Camp Half-Blood, no," Hera agreed.

Piper felt as if the sky were spiraling above her, making her dizzy. "You went somewhere else. That's where you've been all these years. Somewhere else for demigods—but where?"

Jason turned to the goddess. "The memories are coming back, but not the location. You're not going to tell me, are you?"

"No," Hera said. "That is part of your destiny, Jason. You must find your own way back. But when you do... you will unite two great powers. You will give us hope against the giants, and more importantly—against Gaea herself."

"You want us to help you," Jason said, "but you're holding back information."

"Giving you answers would make those answers invalid," Hera said. "That is the way of the Fates. You must forge your own path for it to mean anything. Already, you three have surprised me. I would not have thought it possible…"

The goddess shook her head. "Suffice it to say, you have performed well, demigods. But this is only the beginning. Now you must return to Camp Half-Blood, where you will begin planning for the next phase."

"Which you won't tell us about," Jason grumped. "And I suppose you destroyed my nice storm spirit horse, so we'll have to walk home?"

Hera waved aside the question. "Storm spirits are creatures of chaos. I did not destroy that one, though I have no idea where he went, or whether you'll see him again. But there is an easier way home for you. As you have done me a great service, so I can help you—at least this once. Farewell, demigods, for now."

The world turned upside down, and Piper almost blacked out.

When she could see straight again, she was back at camp, in the dining pavilion, in the middle of dinner. They were standing on the Aphrodite cabin's table, and Piper had one foot in Drew's pizza. Sixty campers rose at once, gawking at them in astonishment.

Whatever Hera had done to shoot them across the country, it wasn't good for Piper's stomach. She could barely control her nausea. Leo wasn't so lucky. He jumped off the table, ran to the nearest bronze brazier, and threw up in it—which was probably not a great burnt offering for the gods.

"Jason?" Chiron trotted forward. No doubt the old centaur had seen thousands of years' worth of weird stuff, but even he looked totally flabbergasted. "What— How—?"

The Aphrodite campers stared up at Piper with their mouths open. Piper figured she must look awful.

"Hi," she said, as casually as she could. "We're back."

PIPER

PIPER DIDN'T REMEMBER MUCH ABOUT the rest of the night. They told their story and answered a million questions from the other campers, but finally Chiron saw how tired they were and ordered them to bed.

It felt so good to sleep on a real mattress, and Piper was so exhausted, she crashed immediately, which spared her any worry about what it would be like returning to the Aphrodite cabin.

The next morning she woke in her bunk, feeling reinvigorated. The sun came through the windows along with a pleasant breeze. It might've been spring instead of winter. Birds sang. Monsters howled in the woods. Breakfast smells wafted from the dining pavilion—bacon, pancakes, and all sorts of wonderful things.

Drew and her gang were frowning down at her, their arms crossed.

"Morning." Piper sat up and smiled. "Beautiful day."

"You're going to make us late for breakfast," Drew said, "which means *you* get to clean the cabin for inspection."

A week ago, Piper would've either punched Drew in the face, or hidden back under her covers. Now she thought about the Cyclopes in Detroit, Medea in Chicago, Midas turning her to gold in Omaha. Looking at Drew, who used to bother her, Piper laughed.

Drew's smug expression crumbled. She backed up, then remembered she was supposed to be angry. "What are you—"

"Challenging you," Piper said. "How about noon in the arena? You can choose the weapons."

She got out of bed, stretched leisurely, and beamed at her cabinmates. She spotted Mitchell and Lacy, who'd helped her pack for the quest. They were smiling tentatively, their eyes flitting from Piper to Drew like this might be a very interesting tennis game.

"I missed you guys!" Piper announced. "We're going to have a great time when I'm senior counselor."

Drew turned bug juice red. Even her closest lieutenants looked a little nervous. This wasn't in their script.

"You—" Drew spluttered. "You ugly little witch! I've been here the longest. You can't just—"

"Challenge you?" Piper said. "Sure, I can. Camp rules: I've been claimed by Aphrodite. I've completed a quest, which is one more than *you've* completed. If I feel I can do a better job, I can challenge you. Unless you just want to step down. Did I get all that right, Mitchell?"

"Just right, Piper." Mitchell was grinning. Lacy was bouncing up and down like she was trying to achieve liftoff.

A few of the other kids started to grin, as if they were enjoying the different colors Drew's face was turning.

"*Step down?*" Drew shrieked. "You're crazy!"

Piper shrugged. Then fast as a viper she pulled Katoptris from under her pillow, unsheathed the dagger, and thrust the point under Drew's chin. Everybody else backed up fast. One guy crashed into a makeup table and sent up a plume of pink powder.

"A duel, then," Piper said cheerfully. "If you don't want to wait until noon, now is fine. You've turned this cabin into a dictatorship, Drew. Silena Beauregard knew better than that. Aphrodite is about love and beauty. *Being* loving. *Spreading* beauty. Good friends. Good times. Good deeds. Not just looking good. Silena made mistakes, but in the end she stood by her friends. That's why she was a hero. I'm going to set things right, and I've got a feeling Mom will be on my side. Want to find out?"

Drew went cross-eyed looking down the blade of Piper's dagger.

A second passed. Then two. Piper didn't care. She was absolutely happy and confident. It must've shown in her smile.

"I . . . step down," Drew grumbled. "But if you think I'm ever going to forget this, McLean—"

"Oh, I hope you won't," Piper said. "Now, run along to the dining pavilion, and explain to Chiron why we're late. There's been a change of leadership."

Drew backed to the door. Even her closest lieutenants didn't follow her. She was about to leave when Piper said, "Oh, and Drew, honey?"

The former counselor looked back reluctantly.

"In case you think I'm not a true daughter of Aphrodite," Piper said, "don't even *look* at Jason Grace. He may not know it yet, but he's *mine*. If you even try to make a move, I will load you into a catapult and shoot you across Long Island Sound."

Drew turned around so fast, she ran into the doorframe. Then she was gone.

The cabin was silent. The other campers stared at Piper. This was the part she was unsure of. She didn't want to rule by fear. She wasn't like Drew, but she didn't know if they'd accept her.

Then, spontaneously, the Aphrodite campers cheered so loudly, they must've been heard all across camp. They herded Piper out of the cabin, raised her on their shoulders, and carried her all the way to the dining pavilion—still in her pajamas, her hair still a mess, but she didn't care. She'd never felt better.

By afternoon, Piper had changed into comfortable camp clothes and led the Aphrodite cabin through their morning activities. She was ready for free time.

Some of the buzz of her victory had faded because she had an appointment at the Big House.

Chiron met her on the front porch in human form, compacted into his wheelchair. "Come inside, my dear. The video conference is ready."

The only computer at camp was in Chiron's office, and the whole room was shielded in bronze plating.

"Demigods and technology don't mix," Chiron explained. "Phone calls, texting, even browsing the Internet—all these things can attract monsters. Why, just this fall at a school in Cincinnati, we had to rescue a young hero who Googled the gorgons and got a little more than he bargained for, but never mind that. Here at camp, you're protected. Still...we try to be cautious. You'll only be able to talk for a few minutes."

"Got it," Piper said. "Thank you, Chiron."

He smiled and wheeled himself out of the office. Piper hesitated before clicking the call button. Chiron's office had a cluttered, cozy feel. One wall was covered with T-shirts from different conventions—PARTY PONIES '09 VEGAS, PARTY PONIES '10 HONOLULU, et cetera. Piper didn't know who the Party Ponies were, but judging from the stains, scorch marks, and weapon holes in the T-shirts, they must've had some pretty wild meetings. On the shelf over Chiron's desk sat an old-fashioned boom box with cassette tapes labeled "Dean Martin" and "Frank Sinatra" and "Greatest Hits of the 40s." Chiron was so old, Piper wondered if that meant 1940s, 1840s, or maybe just A.D. 40.

But most of the office's wall space was plastered with photos of demigods, like a hall of fame. One of the newer shots showed a teenage guy with dark hair and green eyes. Since he stood arm in arm with Annabeth, Piper assumed the guy must be Percy Jackson. In some of the older photos, she recognized famous people: businessmen, athletes, even some actors that her dad knew.

"Unbelievable," she muttered.

Piper wondered if her photo would go on that wall some-day. For the first time, she felt like she was part of something bigger than herself. Demigods had been around for centuries. Whatever she did, she did for all of them.

She took a deep breath and made the call. The video screen popped up.

Gleeson Hedge grinned at her from her dad's office. "Seen the news?"

"Kind of hard to miss," Piper said. "I hope you know what you're doing."

Chiron had shown her a newspaper at lunch. Her dad's mysterious return from nowhere had made the front page. His personal assistant Jane had been fired for covering up his disappearance and failing to notify the police. A new staff had been hired and personally vetted by Tristan McLean's "life coach," Gleeson Hedge. According to the paper, Mr. McLean claimed to have no memory of the last week, and the media was totally eating up the story. Some thought it was a clever marketing ploy for a movie—maybe McLean was going to play an amnesiac? Some thought he'd been kidnapped by terrorists, or rabid fans, or had heroically escaped from ransom seekers using his incredible King of Sparta fighting skills. Whatever the truth, Tristan McLean was more famous than ever.

"It's going great," Hedge promised. "But don't worry. We're going to keep him out of the public eye for the next month or so until things cool down. Your dad's got more important things to do—like resting, and talking to his daughter."

"Don't get too comfortable out there in Hollywood, Gleeson," Piper said.

Hedge snorted. "You kidding? These people make Aeolus look sane. I'll be back as soon as I can, but your dad's gotta get back on his feet first. He's a good guy. Oh, and by the way, I took care of that other little matter. The Park Service in the Bay Area just got an anonymous gift of a new helicopter. And that ranger pilot who helped us? She's got a very lucrative offer to fly for Mr. McLean."

"Thanks, Gleeson," Piper said. "For everything."

"Yeah, well. I don't try to be awesome. It just comes natural. Speaking of Aeolus's place, meet your dad's new assistant."

Hedge was nudged out of the way, and a pretty young lady grinned into the camera.

"Mellie?" Piper stared, but it was definitely her: the *aura* who'd helped them escape from Aeolus's fortress. "You're working for my dad now?"

"Isn't it great?"

"Does he know you're a—you know—wind spirit?"

"Oh, no. But I love this job. It's—um—a breeze."

Piper couldn't help but laugh. "I'm glad. That's awesome. But where—"

"Just a sec." Mellie kissed Gleeson on the cheek. "Come on, you old goat. Stop hogging the screen."

"What?" Hedge demanded. But Mellie steered him away and called, "Mr. McLean? She's on!"

A second later, Piper's dad appeared.

He broke into a huge grin. "Pipes!"

He looked great—back to normal, with his sparkling brown eyes, his half-day beard, his confident smile, and his newly trimmed hair like he was ready to shoot a scene. Piper was relieved, but she also felt a little sad. Back to normal wasn't necessarily what she'd wanted.

In her mind, she started the clock. On a normal call like this, on a workday, she hardly ever got her dad's attention for longer than thirty seconds.

"Hey," she said weakly. "You feeling okay?"

"Honey, I'm so sorry to worry you with this disappearance business. I don't know..." His smile wavered, and she could tell he was trying to remember—grasping for a memory that should have been there, but wasn't. "I'm not sure what happened, honestly. But I'm fine. Coach Hedge has been a godsend."

"A godsend," she repeated. Funny choice of words.

"He told me about your new school," Dad said. "I'm sorry the Wilderness School didn't work out, but you were right. Jane was wrong. I was a fool to listen to her."

Ten seconds left, maybe. But at least her dad sounded sincere, like he really did feel remorseful.

"You don't remember anything?" she said, a bit wistfully.

"Of course I do," he said.

A chill went down her neck. "You do?"

"I remember that I love you," he said. "And I'm proud of you. Are you happy at your new school?"

Piper blinked. She wasn't going to cry now. After all she'd been through, that would be ridiculous. "Yeah, Dad. It's more like a camp, not a school, but...Yeah, I think I'll be happy here."

"Call me as often as you can," he said. "And come home for Christmas. And Pipes..."

"Yes?"

He touched the screen as if trying to reach through with his hand. "You're a wonderful young lady. I don't tell you that often enough. You remind me so much of your mother. She'd be proud. And Grandpa Tom"—he chuckled—"he always said you'd be the most powerful voice in our family. You're going to outshine me some day, you know. They're going to remember me as Piper McLean's father, and that's the best legacy I can imagine."

Piper tried to answer, but she was afraid she'd break down. She just touched his fingers on the screen and nodded.

Mellie said something in the background, and her dad sighed. "Studio calling. I'm sorry, honey." And he did sound genuinely annoyed to go.

"It's okay, Dad," she managed. "Love you."

He winked. Then the video call went black.

Forty-five seconds? Maybe a full minute.

Piper smiled. A small improvement, but it was progress.

At the commons area, she found Jason relaxing on a bench, a basketball between his feet. He was sweaty from working out, but he looked great in his orange tank top and shorts. His various scars and bruises from the quest were healing, thanks to some medical attention from the Apollo cabin. His arms and legs were well muscled and tan—distracting as always. His close-cropped blond hair caught the afternoon light so it looked like it was turning to gold, Midas style.

"Hey," he said. "How did it go?"

It took her a second to focus on his question. "Hmm? Oh, yeah. Fine."

She sat next to him and they watched the campers going

back and forth. A couple of Demeter girls were playing tricks on two of the Apollo guys—making grass grow around their ankles as they shot baskets. Over at the camp store, the Hermes kids were putting up a sign that read: FLYING SHOES, SLIGHTLY USED, 50% OFF TODAY! Ares kids were lining their cabin with fresh barbed wire. The Hypnos cabin was snoring away. A normal day at camp.

Meanwhile, the Aphrodite kids were watching Piper and Jason, and trying to pretend they weren't. Piper was pretty sure she saw money change hands, like they were placing bets on a kiss.

"Get any sleep?" she asked him.

He looked at her as if she'd been reading his thoughts. "Not much. Dreams."

"About your past?"

He nodded.

She didn't push him. If he wanted to talk, that was fine, but she knew him better than to press the subject. She didn't even worry that her knowledge of him was mostly based on three months of false memories. *You can sense possibilities,* her mother had said. And Piper was determined to make those possibilities a reality.

Jason spun his basketball. "It's not good news," he warned. "My memories aren't good for—for any of us."

Piper was pretty sure he'd been about to say *for us*—as in the two of them, and she wondered if he'd remembered a girl from his past. But she didn't let it bother her. Not on a sunny winter day like this, with Jason next to her.

"We'll figure it out," she promised.

He looked at her hesitantly, like he wanted very much to believe her. "Annabeth and Rachel are coming in for the meeting tonight. I should probably wait until then to explain..."

"Okay." She plucked a blade of grass by her foot. She knew there were dangerous things in store for both of them. She would have to compete with Jason's past, and they might not even survive their war against the giants. But right now, they were both alive, and she was determined to enjoy this moment.

Jason studied her warily. His forearm tattoo was faint blue in the sunlight. "You're in a good mood. How can you be so sure things will work out?"

"Because you're going to lead us," she said simply. "I'd follow you anywhere."

Jason blinked. Then slowly, he smiled. "Dangerous thing to say."

"I'm a dangerous girl."

"That, I believe."

He got up and brushed off his shorts. He offered her a hand. "Leo says he's got something to show us out in the woods. You coming?"

"Wouldn't miss it." She took his hand and stood up.

For a moment, they kept holding hands. Jason tilted his head. "We should get going."

"Yep," she said. "Just a sec."

She let go of his hand, and took a card from her pocket —the silver calling card that Thalia had given her for the Hunters of Artemis. She dropped it into a nearby eternal fire and watched it burn. There would be no breaking hearts in

Aphrodite cabin from now on. That was one rite of passage they didn't need.

Across the green, her cabinmates looked disappointed that they hadn't witnessed a kiss. They started cashing in their bets.

But that was all right. Piper was patient, and she could see lots of good possibilities.

"Let's go," she told Jason. "We've got adventures to plan."

LEO

LEO HADN'T FELT THIS JUMPY SINCE HE offered tofu burgers to the werewolves. When he got to the limestone cliff in the forest, he turned to the group and smiled nervously. "Here we go."

He willed his hand to catch fire, and set it against the door.

His cabinmates gasped.

"Leo!" Nyssa cried. "You're a fire user!"

"Yeah, thanks," he said. "I know."

Jake Mason, who was out of his body cast but still on crutches, said, "Holy Hephaestus. That means—it's so rare that—"

The massive stone door swung open, and everyone's mouth dropped. Leo's flaming hand seemed insignificant now. Even Piper and Jason looked stunned, and they'd seen enough amazing things lately.

Only Chiron didn't look surprised. The centaur knit his

bushy eyebrows and stroked his beard, as if the group was about to walk through a minefield.

That made Leo even more nervous, but he couldn't change his mind now. His instincts told him he was meant to share this place—at least with the Hephaestus cabin—and he couldn't hide it from Chiron or his two best friends.

"Welcome to Bunker Nine," he said, as confidently as he could. "C'mon in."

The group was silent as they toured the facility. Everything was just as Leo had left it—giant machines, worktables, old maps and schematics. Only one thing had changed. Festus's head was sitting on the central table, still battered and scorched from his final crash in Omaha.

Leo went over to it, a bitter taste in his mouth, and stroked the dragon's forehead. "I'm sorry, Festus. But I won't forget you."

Jason put a hand on Leo's shoulder. "Hephaestus brought it here for you?"

Leo nodded.

"But you can't repair him," Jason guessed.

"No way," Leo said. "But the head is going to be reused. Festus will be going with us."

Piper came over and frowned. "What do you mean?"

Before Leo could answer, Nyssa cried out, "Guys, look at this!"

She was standing at one of the worktables, flipping through a sketchbook—diagrams for hundreds of different machines and weapons.

"I've never seen anything like these," Nyssa said. "There are more amazing ideas here than in Daedalus's workshop. It would take a century just to prototype them all."

"Who built this place?" Jake Mason said. "And why?"

Chiron stayed silent, but Leo focused on the wall map he'd seen during his first visit. It showed Camp Half-Blood with a line of triremes in the Sound, catapults mounted in the hills around the valley, and spots marked for traps, trenches, and ambush sites.

"It's a wartime command center," he said. "The camp was attacked once, wasn't it?"

"In the Titan War?" Piper asked.

Nyssa shook her head. "No. Besides, that map looks *really* old. The date... does that say 1864?"

They all turned to Chiron.

The centaur's tail swished fretfully. "This camp has been attacked many times," he admitted. "That map is from the last Civil War."

Apparently, Leo wasn't the only one confused. The other Hephaestus campers looked at each other and frowned.

"Civil War..." Piper said. "You mean the American Civil War, like a hundred and fifty years ago?"

"Yes and no," Chiron said. "The two conflicts—mortal and demigod—mirrored each other, as they usually do in Western history. Look at any civil war or revolution from the fall of Rome onward, and it marks a time when demigods also fought one another. But *that* Civil War was particularly horrible. For American mortals, it is still their bloodiest conflict of all time—worse than their casualties in the two World

Wars. For demigods, it was equally devastating. Even back then, this valley was Camp Half-Blood. There was a horrible battle in these woods lasting for days, with terrible losses on both sides."

"Both sides," Leo said. "You mean the camp split apart?"

"No," Jason spoke up. "He means two different groups. Camp Half-Blood was one side in the war."

Leo wasn't sure he wanted an answer, but he asked, "Who was the other?"

Chiron glanced up at the tattered BUNKER 9 banner, as if remembering the day it was raised.

"The answer is dangerous," he warned. "It is something I swore upon the River Styx never to speak of. After the American Civil War, the gods were so horrified by the toll it took on their children, that they swore it would never happen again. The two groups were separated. The gods bent all their will, wove the Mist as tightly as they could, to make sure the enemies never remembered each other, never met on their quests, so that bloodshed could be avoided. This map is from the final dark days of 1864, the last time the two groups fought. We've had several close calls since then. The nineteen sixties were particularly dicey. But we've managed to avoid another civil war—at least so far. Just as Leo guessed, this bunker was a command center for the Hephaestus cabin. In the last century, it has been reopened a few times, usually as a hiding place in times of great unrest. But coming here is dangerous. It stirs old memories, awakens the old feuds. Even when the Titans threatened last year, I did not think it worth the risk to use this place."

Suddenly Leo's sense of triumph turned to guilt. "Hey, look, this place found *me*. It was meant to happen. It's a good thing."

"I hope you're right," Chiron said.

"I am!" Leo pulled the old drawing out of his pocket and spread it on the table for everyone to see.

"There," he said proudly. "Aeolus returned that to me. I drew it when I was five. That's my destiny."

Nyssa frowned. "Leo, it's a crayon drawing of a boat."

"Look." He pointed at the largest schematic on the bulletin board—the blueprint showing a Greek trireme. Slowly, his cabinmates' eyes widened as they compared the two designs. The number of masts and oars, even the decorations on the shields and sails were exactly the same as on Leo's drawing.

"That's impossible," Nyssa said. "That blueprint has to be a century old at least."

"'*Prophecy—Unclear—Flight,*'" Jake Mason read from the notes on the blueprint. "It's a diagram for a flying ship. Look, that's the landing gear. And weaponry—Holy Hephaestus: rotating ballista, mounted crossbows, Celestial bronze plating. That thing would be one spankin' hot war machine. Was it ever made?"

"Not yet," Leo said. "Look at the masthead."

There was no doubt—the figure at the front of the ship was the head of a dragon. A very particular dragon.

"Festus," Piper said. Everyone turned and looked at the dragon's head sitting on the table.

"He's meant to be our masthead," Leo said. "Our good

luck charm, our eyes at sea. I'm supposed to build this ship. I'm gonna call it the *Argo II*. And guys, I'll need your help."

"The *Argo II*." Piper smiled. "After Jason's ship."

Jason looked a little uncomfortable, but he nodded. "Leo's right. That ship is just what we need for our journey."

"What journey?" Nyssa said. "You just got back!"

Piper ran her fingers over the old crayon drawing. "We've got to confront Porphyrion, the giant king. He said he would destroy the gods at their roots."

"Indeed," Chiron said. "Much of Rachel's Great Prophecy is still a mystery to me, but one thing is clear. You three— Jason, Piper, and Leo—are among the seven demigods who must take on that quest. You must confront the giants in their homeland, where they are strongest. You must stop them before they can wake Gaea fully, before they destroy Mount Olympus."

"Um..." Nyssa shifted. "You don't mean Manhattan, do you?"

"No," Leo said. "The original Mount Olympus. We have to sail to Greece."

LEO

IT TOOK A FEW MINUTES FOR THAT TO settle in. Then the other Hephaestus campers started asking questions all at once. Who were the other four demigods? How long would it take to build the boat? Why didn't everyone get to go to Greece?

"Heroes!" Chiron struck his hoof on the floor. "All the details are not clear yet, but Leo is correct. He will need your help to build the *Argo II*. It is perhaps the greatest project Cabin Nine has even undertaken, even greater than the bronze dragon."

"It'll take a year at least," Nyssa guessed. "Do we have that much time?"

"You have six months at most," Chiron said. "You should sail by summer solstice, when the gods' power is strongest. Besides, we evidently cannot trust the wind gods, and the summer winds are the least powerful and easiest to navigate. You dare not sail any later, or you may be too late to stop the giants. You must avoid ground travel, using only air and sea, so this vehicle is perfect. Jason being the son of the sky god…"

His voice trailed off, but Leo figured Chiron was thinking about his missing student, Percy Jackson, the son of Poseidon. He would've been good on this voyage, too.

Jake Mason turned to Leo. "Well, one thing's for sure. *You* are now senior counselor. This is the biggest honor the cabin has ever had. Anyone object?"

Nobody did. All his cabinmates smiled at him, and Leo could almost feel their cabin's curse breaking, their sense of hopelessness melting away.

"It's official, then," Jake said. "You're the man."

For once, Leo was speechless. Ever since his mom died, he'd spent his life on the run. Now he'd found a home and a family. He'd found a job to do. And as scary as it was, Leo wasn't tempted to run—not even a little.

"Well," he said at last, "if you guys elect me leader, you must be even crazier than I am. So let's build a spankin' hot war machine!"

JASON

JASON WAITED ALONE IN CABIN ONE.

Annabeth and Rachel were due any minute for the head counselors' meeting, and Jason needed time to think.

His dreams the night before had been worse than he'd wanted to share—even with Piper. His memory was still foggy, but bits and pieces were coming back. The night Lupa had tested him at the Wolf House, to decide if he would be a pup or food. Then the long trip south to...he couldn't remember, but he had flashes of his old life. The day he'd gotten his tattoo. The day he'd been raised on a shield and proclaimed a praetor. His friends' faces: Dakota, Gwendolyn, Hazel, Bobby. And Reyna. Definitely there'd been a girl named Reyna. He wasn't sure what she'd meant to him, but the memory made him question what he felt about Piper—and wonder if he was doing something wrong. The problem was, he liked Piper a lot.

Jason moved his stuff to the corner alcove where his sister

had once slept. He put Thalia's photograph back on the wall so he didn't feel alone. He stared up at the frowning statue of Zeus, mighty and proud, but the statue didn't scare him anymore. It just made him feel sad.

"I know you can hear me," Jason said to the statue.

The statue said nothing. Its painted eyes seemed to stare at him.

"I wish I could talk with you in person," Jason continued, "but I understand you can't do that. The Roman gods don't like to interact with mortals so much, and—well, you're the king. You've got to set an example."

More silence. Jason had hoped for something—a bigger than usual rumble of thunder, a bright light, a smile. No, never mind. A smile would've been creepy.

"I remember some things," he said. The more he talked, the less self-conscious he felt. "I remember that it's hard being a son of Jupiter. Everyone is always looking at me to be a leader, but I always feel alone. I guess you feel the same way up on Olympus. The other gods challenge your decisions. Sometimes you've got to make hard choices, and the others criticize you. And you can't come to my aid like other gods might. You've got to keep me at a distance so it doesn't look like you're playing favorites. I guess I just wanted to say…"

Jason took a deep breath. "I understand all that. It's okay. I'm going to try to do my best. I'll try to make you proud. But I could really use some guidance, Dad. If there's anything you can do—help me so I can help my friends. I'm afraid I'll get them killed. I don't know how to protect them."

The back of his neck tingled. He realized someone was

standing behind him. He turned and found a woman in a black hooded robe, with a goatskin cloak over her shoulders and a sheathed Roman sword—a *gladius*—in her hands.

"Hera," he said.

She pushed back her hood. "To you, I have always been Juno. And your father has already sent you guidance, Jason. He sent you Piper and Leo. They're not just your responsibility. They are also your friends. Listen to them, and you will do well."

"Did Jupiter send you here to tell me that?"

"No one sends me anywhere, hero," she said. "I am not a messenger."

"But you got me into this. Why did you send me to this camp?"

"I think you know," Juno said. "An exchange of leaders was necessary. It was the only way to bridge the gap."

"I didn't agree to it."

"No. But Zeus gave your life to me, and I am helping you fulfill your destiny."

Jason tried to control his anger. He looked down at his orange camp shirt and the tattoos on his arm, and he knew these things should not go together. He had become a contradiction—a mixture as dangerous as anything Medea could cook up.

"You're not giving me all my memories," he said. "Even though you promised."

"Most will return in time," Juno said. "But you must find your own way back. You need these next months with your new friends, your new home. You're gaining their trust. By the time you sail in your ship, you will be a leader at this camp. And you will be ready to be a peacemaker between two great powers."

"What if you're not telling the truth?" he asked. "What if you're doing this to cause another civil war?"

Juno's expression was impossible to read—amusement? Disdain? Affection? Possibly all three. As much as she appeared human, Jason knew she was not. He could still see that blinding light—the true form of the goddess that had seared itself into his brain. She was Juno and Hera. She existed in many places at once. Her reasons for doing something were never simple.

"I am the goddess of family," she said. "My family has been divided for too long."

"They divided us so we don't kill each other," Jason said. "That seems like a pretty good reason."

"The prophecy demands that we change. The giants will rise. Each can only be killed by a god and demigod working together. Those demigods must be the seven greatest of the age. As it stands, they are divided between two places. If we remain divided, we cannot win. Gaea is counting on this. You must unite the heroes of Olympus and sail together to meet the giants on the ancient battlegrounds of Greece. Only then will the gods be convinced to join you. It will be the most dangerous quest, the most important voyage, ever attempted by the children of the gods."

Jason looked up again at the glowering statue of his father.

"It's not fair," Jason said. "I could ruin everything."

"You could," Juno agreed. "But gods need heroes. We always have."

"Even you? I thought you hated heroes."

The goddess gave him a dry smile. "I have that reputation. But if you want the truth, Jason, I often envy other gods their mortal children. You demigods can span both worlds. I think this helps your godly parents—even Jupiter, curse him—to understand the mortal world better than I."

Juno sighed so unhappily that despite his anger, Jason almost felt sorry for her.

"I am the goddess of marriage," she said. "It is not in my nature to be faithless. I have only two godly children—Ares and Hephaestus—both of whom are disappointments. I have no mortal heroes to do my bidding, which is why I am so often bitter toward demigods—Heracles, Aeneas, all of them. But it is also why I favored the first Jason, a pure mortal, who had no godly parent to guide him. And why I am glad Zeus gave you to me. You will be my champion, Jason. You will be the greatest of heroes, and bring unity to the demigods, and thus to Olympus."

Her words settled over him, as heavy as sandbags. Two days ago, he'd been terrified by the idea of leading demigods into a Great Prophecy, sailing off to battle the giants and save the world.

He was still terrified, but something had changed. He no longer felt alone. He had friends now, and a home to fight for. He even had a patron goddess looking out for him, which had to count for something, even if she seemed a little untrustworthy.

Jason had to stand up and accept his destiny, just as he had done when he faced Porphyrion with his bare hands. Sure, it seemed impossible. He might die. But his friends were counting on him.

"And if I fail?" he asked.

"Great victory requires great risk," she admitted. "Fail, and there will be bloodshed like we have never seen. Demigods will destroy one another. The giants will overrun Olympus. Gaea will wake, and the earth will shake off everything we have built over five millennia. It will be the end of us all."

"Great. Just great."

Someone pounded on the cabin doors.

Juno pulled her hood back over her face. Then she handed Jason the sheathed *gladius*. "Take this for the weapon you lost. We will speak again. Like it or not, Jason, I am your sponsor, and your link to Olympus. We need each other."

The goddess vanished as the doors creaked open, and Piper walked in.

"Annabeth and Rachel are here," she said. "Chiron has summoned the council."

JASON

THE COUNCIL WAS NOTHING LIKE Jason imagined. For one thing, it was in the Big House rec room, around a Ping-Pong table, and one of the satyrs was serving nachos and sodas. Somebody had brought Seymour the leopard head in from the living room and hung him on the wall. Every once in a while, a counselor would toss him a Snausage.

Jason looked around the room and tried to remember everyone's name. Thankfully, Leo and Piper were sitting next to him—it was their first meeting as senior counselors. Clarisse, leader of the Ares cabin, had her boots on the table, but nobody seemed to care. Clovis from Hypnos cabin was snoring in the corner while Butch from Iris cabin was seeing how many pencils he could fit in Clovis's nostrils. Travis Stoll from Hermes was holding a lighter under a Ping-Pong ball to see if it would burn, and Will Solace from Apollo was absently wrapping and unwrapping an Ace bandage around his wrist. The counselor from Hecate cabin,

Lou Ellen something-or-other, was playing "got-your-nose" with Miranda Gardiner from Demeter, except that Lou Ellen really *had* magically disconnected Miranda's nose, and Miranda was trying to get it back.

Jason had hoped Thalia would show. She'd promised, after all—but she was nowhere to be seen. Chiron had told him not to worry about it. Thalia often got sidetracked fighting monsters or running quests for Artemis, and she would probably arrive soon. But still, Jason worried.

Rachel Dare, the oracle, sat next to Chiron at the head of the table. She was wearing her Clarion Academy school uniform dress, which seemed a bit odd, but she smiled at Jason.

Annabeth didn't look so relaxed. She wore armor over her camp clothes, with her knife at her side and her blond hair pulled back in a ponytail. As soon as Jason walked in, she fixed him with an expectant look, as if she were trying to extract information out of him by sheer willpower.

"Let's come to order," Chiron said. "Lou Ellen, please give Miranda her nose back. Travis, if you'd kindly extinguish the flaming Ping-Pong ball, and Butch, I think twenty pencils is really too many for any human nostril. Thank you. Now, as you can see, Jason, Piper, and Leo have returned successfully ...more or less. Some of you have heard parts of their story, but I will let them fill you in."

Everyone looked at Jason. He cleared his throat and began the story. Piper and Leo chimed in from time to time, filling in the details he forgot.

It only took a few minutes, but it seemed like longer with everyone watching him. The silence was heavy, and for so many ADHD demigods to sit still listening for that long, Jason knew the story must have sounded pretty wild. He ended with Hera's visit right before the meeting.

"So Hera was *here*," Annabeth said. "Talking to you."

Jason nodded. "Look, I'm not saying I trust her—"

"That's smart," Annabeth said.

"—but she isn't making this up about another group of demigods. That's where I came from."

"Romans." Clarisse tossed Seymour a Snausage. "You expect us to believe there's another camp with demigods, but they follow the Roman forms of the gods. And we've never even heard of them."

Piper sat forward. "The gods have kept the two groups apart, because every time they see each other, they try to kill each other."

"I can respect that," Clarisse said. "Still, why haven't we ever run across each other on quests?"

"Oh, yes," Chiron said sadly. "You have, many times. It's always a tragedy, and always the gods do their best to wipe clean the memories of those involved. The rivalry goes all the way back to the Trojan War, Clarisse. The Greeks invaded Troy and burned it to the ground. The Trojan hero Aeneas escaped, and eventually made his way to Italy, where he founded the race that would someday become Rome. The Romans grew more and more powerful, worshipping the same gods but under different names, and with slightly different personalities."

"More warlike," Jason said. "More united. More about expansion, conquest, and discipline."

"Yuck," Travis put in.

Several of the others looked equally uncomfortable, though Clarisse shrugged like it sounded okay to her.

Annabeth twirled her knife on the table. "And the Romans hated the Greeks. They took revenge when they conquered the Greek isles, and made them part of the Roman Empire."

"Not exactly *hated* them," Jason said. "The Romans admired Greek culture, and were a little jealous. In return, the Greeks thought the Romans were barbarians, but they respected their military power. So during Roman times, demigods started to divide—either Greek or Roman."

"And it's been that way ever since," Annabeth guessed. "But this is crazy. Chiron, where were the Romans during the Titan War? Didn't they want to help?"

Chiron tugged at his beard. "They *did* help, Annabeth. While you and Percy were leading the battle to save Manhattan, who do think conquered Mount Othrys, the Titans' base in California?"

"Hold on," Travis said. "You said Mount Othrys just crumbled when we beat Kronos."

"No," Jason said. He remembered flashes of the battle—a giant in starry armor and a helm mounted with ram's horns. He remembered his army of demigods scaling Mount Tam, fighting through hordes of snake monsters. "It didn't just fall. We destroyed their palace. I defeated the Titan Krios myself."

Annabeth's eyes were as stormy as a *ventus*. Jason could almost see her thoughts moving, putting the pieces together. "The Bay Area. We demigods were always told to stay away from it because Mount Othrys was there. But that wasn't the only reason, was it? The Roman camp—it's got to be somewhere near San Francisco. I bet it was put there to keep watch on the Titans' territory. Where is it?"

Chiron shifted in his wheelchair. "I cannot say. Honestly, even *I* have never been trusted with that information. My counterpart, Lupa, is not exactly the sharing type. Jason's memory, too, has been burned away."

"The camp's heavily veiled with magic," Jason said. "And heavily guarded. We could search for years and never find it."

Rachel Dare laced her fingers. Of all the people in the room, only she didn't seem nervous about the conversation. "But you'll try, won't you? You'll build Leo's boat, the *Argo II*. And before you make for Greece, you'll sail for the Roman camp. You'll need their help to confront the giants."

"Bad plan," Clarisse warned. "If those Romans see a warship coming, they'll assume we're attacking."

"You're probably right," Jason agreed. "But we have to try. I was sent here to learn about Camp Half-Blood, to try to convince you the two camps don't have to be enemies. A peace offering."

"Hmm," Rachel said. "Because Hera is convinced we need both camps to win the war with the giants. Seven heroes of Olympus—some Greek, some Roman."

Annabeth nodded. "Your Great Prophecy—what's the last line?"

"And foes bear arms to the Doors of Death."

"Gaea has opened the Doors of Death," Annabeth said. "She's letting out the worst villains of the Underworld to fight us. Medea, Midas—there'll be more, I'm sure. Maybe the line means that the Roman and Greek demigods will unite, and find the doors, and close them."

"Or it could mean they fight each other at the doors of death," Clarisse pointed out. "It doesn't say we'll cooperate."

There was silence as the campers let that happy thought sink in.

"I'm going," Annabeth said. "Jason, when you get this ship built, let me go with you."

"I was hoping you'd offer," Jason said. "You of all people —we'll need you."

"Wait." Leo frowned. "I mean that's cool with me and all. But why Annabeth of all people?"

Annabeth and Jason studied one another, and Jason knew she had put it together. She saw the dangerous truth.

"Hera said my coming here was an exchange of leaders," Jason said. "A way for the two camps to learn of each other's existence."

"Yeah?" Leo said. "So?"

"An exchange goes two ways," Jason said. "When I got here, my memory was wiped. I didn't know who I was or where I belonged. Fortunately, you guys took me in and I found a new home. I know you're not my enemy. The Roman camp—they're not so friendly. You prove your worth quickly, or you don't survive. They may not be so nice to him, and if they learn where he comes from, he's going to be in serious trouble."

"Him?" Leo said. "Who are you talking about?"

"My boyfriend," Annabeth said grimly. "He disappeared

around the same time Jason appeared. If Jason came to Camp Half-Blood—"

"Exactly," Jason agreed. "Percy Jackson is at the other camp, and he probably doesn't even remember who he is."

Gods in *The Lost Hero*

Aeolus   The Greek god of the winds. Roman form: Aeolus

Aphrodite   The Greek goddess of love and beauty. She was married to Hephaestus, but she loved Ares, the god of war. Roman form: Venus

Apollo   The Greek god of the sun, prophecy, music, and healing; the son of Zeus, and the twin of Artemis. Roman form: Apollo

Ares   The Greek god of war; the son of Zeus and Hera, and half brother to Athena. Roman form: Mars

Artemis   The Greek goddess of the hunt and the moon; the daughter of Zeus and the twin of Apollo. Roman form: Diana

Boreas   The Greek god of the north wind, one of the four directional *anemoi* (wind gods); the god of winter; father of Khione. Roman form: Aquilon

Demeter   The Greek goddess of agriculture, a daughter of the Titans Rhea and Kronos. Roman form: Ceres

Dionysus The Greek god of wine; the son of Zeus. Roman form: Bacchus

Gaea The Greek personification of Earth. Roman form: Terra

Hades According to Greek mythology, ruler of the Underworld and god of the dead. Roman form: Pluto

Hecate The Greek goddess of magic; the only child of the Titans Perses and Asteria. Roman form: Trivia

Hephaestus The Greek god of fire and crafts and of blacksmiths; the son of Zeus and Hera, and married to Aphrodite. Roman form: Vulcan

Hera The Greek goddess of marriage; Zeus's wife and sister. Roman form: Juno

Hermes The Greek god of travelers, communication, and thieves; son of Zeus. Roman form: Mercury

Hypnos The Greek god of sleep; the (fatherless) son of Nyx (Night) and brother of Thanatos (Death). Roman form: Somnus

Iris The Greek goddess of the rainbow, and a messenger of the gods; the daughter of Thaumas and Electra. Roman form: Iris

Janus The Roman god of gates, doors, and doorways, as well as beginnings and endings.

Khione The Greek goddess of snow; daughter of Boreas

Notus The Greek god of the south wind, one of the four directional *anemoi* (wind gods). Roman form: Favonius

Ouranos The Greek personification of the sky. Roman form: Uranus

Pan   The Greek god of the wild; the son of Hermes. Roman form: Faunus

Pompona   The Roman goddess of plenty

Poseidon   The Greek god of the sea; son of the Titans Kronos and Rhea, and brother of Zeus and Hades. Roman form: Neptune

Zeus   The Greek god of the sky and king of the gods. Roman form: Jupiter

Don't miss the next book in the
mega-best-selling Heroes of Olympus series
Book Two:
THE SON OF NEPTUNE

I

PERCY

THE SNAKE-HAIRED LADIES WERE starting to annoy Percy.

They should have died three days ago when he dropped a crate of bowling balls on them at the Napa Bargain Mart. They should have died two days ago when he ran over them with a police car in Martinez. They *definitely* should have died this morning when he cut off their heads in Tilden Park.

No matter how many times Percy killed them and watched them crumble to powder, they just kept re-forming like large evil dust bunnies. He couldn't even seem to outrun them.

He reached the top of the hill and caught his breath. How long since he'd last killed them? Maybe two hours. They never seemed to stay dead longer than that.

The past few days, he'd hardly slept. He'd eaten whatever he could scrounge—vending machine gummi bears, stale bagels, even a Jack in the Crack burrito, which was a new personal low. His clothes were torn, burned, and splattered with monster slime.

He'd only survived this long because the two snake-haired ladies—*gorgons*, they called themselves—couldn't seem to kill him either. Their claws didn't cut his skin. Their teeth broke whenever they tried to bite him. But Percy couldn't keep going much longer. Soon he'd collapse from exhaustion, and then —as hard as he was to kill, he was pretty sure the gorgons would find a way.

Where to run?

He scanned his surroundings. Under different circumstances, he might've enjoyed the view. To his left, golden hills rolled inland, dotted with lakes, woods, and a few herds of cows. To his right, the flatlands of Berkeley and Oakland marched west—a vast checkerboard of neighborhoods, with several million people who probably did not want their morning interrupted by two monsters and a filthy demigod.

Farther west, San Francisco Bay glittered under a silvery haze. Past that, a wall of fog had swallowed most of San Francisco, leaving just the tops of skyscrapers and the towers of the Golden Gate Bridge.

A vague sadness weighed on Percy's chest. Something told him he'd been to San Francisco before. The city had some connection to Annabeth—the only person he could remember from his past. His memory of her was frustratingly dim. The wolf had promised he would see her again and regain his memory—*if* he succeeded in his journey.

Should he try to cross the bay?

It was tempting. He could feel the power of the ocean just over the horizon. Water always revived him. Salt water was the best. He'd discovered that two days ago when he had strangled a sea monster in the Carquinez Strait. If he could reach the bay, he might be able to make a last stand. Maybe he could even drown the gorgons. But the shore was at least two miles away. He'd have to cross an entire city.

He hesitated for another reason. The she-wolf Lupa had taught him to sharpen his senses—to trust the instincts that had been guiding him south. His homing radar was tingling like crazy now. The end of his journey was close—almost right under his feet. But how could that be? There was nothing on the hilltop.

The wind changed. Percy caught the sour scent of reptile. A hundred yards down the slope, something rustled through the woods—snapping branches, crunching leaves, hissing.

Gorgons.

For the millionth time, Percy wished their noses weren't so good. They had always said they could *smell* him because he was a demigod—the half-blood son of some old Roman god. Percy had tried rolling in mud, splashing through creeks, even keeping air-freshener sticks in his pockets so he'd have that new car smell; but apparently demigod stink was hard to mask.

He scrambled to the west side of the summit. It was too steep to descend. The slope plummeted eighty feet, straight to the roof of an apartment complex built into the hillside. Fifty feet below that, a highway emerged from the hill's base and wound its way toward Berkeley.

Great. No other way off the hill. He'd managed to get himself cornered.

He stared at the stream of cars flowing west toward San Francisco and wished he were in one of them. Then he realized the highway must cut through the hill. There must be a tunnel . . . right under his feet.

His internal radar went nuts. He *was* in the right place, just too high up. He had to check out that tunnel. He needed a way down to the highway—fast.

He slung off his backpack. He'd managed to grab a lot of supplies at the Napa Bargain Mart: a portable GPS, duct tape, lighter, superglue, water bottle, camping roll, a Comfy Panda Pillow Pet (as seen on TV), and a Swiss army knife—pretty much every tool a modern demigod could want. But he had nothing that would serve as a parachute or a sled.

That left him two options: jump eighty feet to his death, or stand and fight. Both options sounded pretty bad.

He cursed and pulled his pen from his pocket.

The pen didn't look like much, just a regular cheap ball-point, but when Percy uncapped it, it grew into a glowing bronze sword. The blade balanced perfectly. The leather grip fit his hand like it had been custom designed for him. Etched along the guard was an Ancient Greek word Percy somehow understood: *Anaklusmos*—Riptide.

He'd woken up with this sword his first night at the Wolf House—two months ago? More? He'd lost track. He'd found himself in the courtyard of a burned-out mansion in the middle of the woods, wearing shorts, an orange T-shirt, and a leather necklace with a bunch of strange clay beads. Riptide had been in his hand, but Percy had had no idea how he'd gotten there, and only the vaguest idea who he was. He'd been barefoot, freezing, and confused. And then the wolves came. . . .

Right next to him, a familiar voice jolted him back to the present: "There you are!"

Percy stumbled away from the gorgon, almost falling off the edge of the hill.

It was the smiley one—Beano.

Okay, her name wasn't really Beano. As near as Percy could figure, he was dyslexic, because words got twisted around when he tried to read. The first time he'd seen the gorgon, posing as a Bargain Mart greeter with a big green button that read: *Welcome! My name is* STHENO, he'd thought it said BEANO.

She was still wearing her green Bargain Mart employee vest over a flower-print dress. If you looked just at her body, you might think she was somebody's dumpy old grandmother —until you looked down and realized she had rooster feet. Or you looked up and saw bronze boar tusks sticking out of the corners of her mouth. Her eyes glowed red, and her hair was a writhing nest of bright green snakes.

The most horrible thing about her? She was still holding her big silver platter of free samples: Crispy Cheese 'n' Wieners. Her platter was dented from all the times Percy had killed her, but those little samples looked perfectly fine. Stheno just kept toting them across California so she could offer Percy a snack before she killed him. Percy didn't know why she kept doing that, but if he ever needed a suit of armor, he was going to make it out of Crispy Cheese 'n' Wieners. They were indestructible.

"Try one?" Stheno offered.

Percy fended her off with his sword. "Where's your sister?"

"Oh, put the sword away," Stheno chided. "You know by now that even Celestial bronze can't kill us for long. Have a Cheese 'n' Wiener! They're on sale this week, and I'd hate to kill you on an empty stomach."

"Stheno!" The second gorgon appeared on Percy's right so fast, he didn't have time to react. Fortunately she was too busy glaring at her sister to pay him much attention. "I told you to sneak up on him and kill him!"

Stheno's smile wavered. "But, Euryale..." She said the name so it rhymed with *Muriel*. "Can't I give him a sample first?"

"No, you imbecile!" Euryale turned toward Percy and bared her fangs.

Except for her hair, which was a nest of coral snakes instead of green vipers, she looked exactly like her sister. Her Bargain Mart vest, her flowery dress, even her tusks were decorated with 50% OFF stickers. Her name badge read: *Hello! My name is DIE, DEMIGOD SCUM!*

"You've led us on quite a chase, Percy Jackson," Euryale said. "But now you're trapped, and we'll have our revenge!"

"The Cheese 'n' Wieners are only $2.99," Stheno added helpfully. "Grocery department, aisle three."

Euryale snarled. "Stheno, the Bargain Mart was a *front*! You're going native! Now, put down that ridiculous tray and help me kill this demigod. Or have you forgotten that he's the one who vaporized Medusa?"

Percy stepped back. Six more inches, and he'd be tumbling through thin air. "Look, ladies, we've been over this. I don't even *remember* killing Medusa. I don't remember anything! Can't we just call a truce and talk about your weekly specials?"

Stheno gave her sister a pouty look, which was hard to do with giant bronze tusks. "Can we?"

"No!" Euryale's red eyes bored into Percy. "I don't care what you remember, son of the sea god. I can smell Medusa's blood on you. It's faint, yes, several years old, but *you* were the last one to defeat her. She *still* has not returned from Tartarus. It's your fault!"

Percy didn't really get that. The whole "dying then returning from Tartarus" concept gave him a headache. Of course, so did the idea that a ballpoint pen could turn into a sword, or that monsters could disguise themselves with something called the Mist, or that Percy was the son of a barnacle-encrusted god from five thousand years ago. But he *did* believe it. Even though his memory was erased, he knew he was a demigod the same way he knew his name was Percy Jackson. From his very first conversation with Lupa the wolf, he'd accepted that this crazy messed-up world of gods and monsters was his reality. Which pretty much sucked.

"How about we call it a draw?" he said. "I can't kill you. You can't kill me. If you're Medusa's sisters—like *the* Medusa who turned people to stone—shouldn't I be petrified by now?"

"Heroes!" Euryale said with disgust. "They always bring that up, just like our mother! 'Why can't you turn people to stone? Your *sister* can turn people to stone.' Well, I'm sorry to disappoint you, boy! That was Medusa's curse alone. *She* was the most hideous one in the family. She got all the luck!"

Stheno looked hurt. "Mother said *I* was the most hideous."

"Quiet!" Euryale snapped. "As for you, Percy Jackson, it's

true you bear the mark of Achilles. That makes you a little tougher to kill. But don't worry. We'll find a way."

"The mark of what?"

"Achilles," Stheno said cheerfully. "Oh, he was *gorgeous*! Dipped in the River Styx as a child, you know, so he was invulnerable except for a tiny spot on his ankle. That's what happened to you, dear. Someone must've dumped you in the Styx and made your skin like iron. But not to worry. Heroes like you always have a weak spot. We just have to find it, and then we can kill you. Won't that be lovely? Have a Cheese 'n' Wiener!"

Percy tried to think. He didn't remember any dip in the Styx. Then again, he didn't remember much of anything. His skin didn't feel like iron, but it would explain how he'd held out so long against the gorgons.

Maybe if he just fell down the mountain...would he survive? He didn't want to risk it—not without something to slow the fall, or a sled, or...

He looked at Stheno's large silver platter of free samples. Hmm...

"Reconsidering?" Stheno asked. "Very wise, dear. I added some gorgon's blood to these, so your death will be quick and painless."

Percy's throat constricted. "You added your blood to the Cheese 'n' Wieners?"

"Just a little." Stheno smiled. "A tiny nick on my arm, but you're sweet to be concerned. Blood from our right side can cure anything, you know, but blood from our left side is deadly—"

"You dimwit!" Euryale screeched. "You're not supposed to tell him that! He won't eat the wieners if you tell him they're poisoned!"

Stheno looked stunned. "He won't? But I said it would be quick and painless."

"Never mind!" Euryale's fingernails grew into claws. "We'll kill him the hard way—just keep slashing until we find the weak spot. Once we defeat Percy Jackson, we'll be more famous than Medusa! Our patron will reward us greatly!"

Percy gripped his sword. He'd have to time his move perfectly—a few seconds of confusion, grab the platter with his left hand . . .

Keep them talking, he thought.

"Before you slash me to bits," he said, "who's this patron you mentioned?"

Euryale sneered. "The goddess Gaea, of course! The one who brought us back from oblivion! You won't live long enough to meet her, but your friends below will soon face her wrath. Even now, her armies are marching south. At the Feast of Fortune, she'll awaken, and the demigods will be cut down like—like—"

"Like our low prices at Bargain Mart!" Stheno suggested.

"Gah!" Euryale stormed toward her sister. Percy took the opening. He grabbed Stheno's platter, scattering poisoned Cheese 'n' Wieners, and slashed Riptide across Euryale's waist, cutting her in half.

He raised the platter, and Stheno found herself facing her own greasy reflection.

"Medusa!" she screamed.

Her sister Euryale had crumbled to dust, but she was already starting to re-form, like a snowman un-melting.

"Stheno, you fool!" she gurgled as her half-made face rose from the mound of dust. "That's just your own reflection! Get him!"

Percy slammed the metal tray on top of Stheno's head, and she passed out cold.

He put the platter behind his butt, said a silent prayer to whatever Roman god oversaw stupid sledding tricks, and jumped off the side of the hill.

Turn the page to see who's who
in your favorite Riordan series.

PIPER MCLEAN
DAUGHTER OF APHRODITE

ELLA
HARPY

LEO VALDEZ
SON OF
HEPHAESTUS

GLEESON HEDGE
SATYR

CLARISSE
LA RUE
DAUGHTER
OF ARES

JASON GRACE
SON OF JUPITER

FRANK
ZHANG
SON OF
MARS

BIANCA DI ANGELO
DAUGHTER OF HADES

MIRANDA
GARDINER
DAUGHTER
OF DEMETER

CALYPSO
DAUGHTER
OF ATLAS

Ω

NICO DI ANGELO
SON OF HADES

HAZEL LEVESQUE
DAUGHTER OF PLUTO

SHERMAN YANG
SON OF ARES

THALIA GRACE
DAUGHTER OF ZEUS

LUKE
CASTELLAN
SON OF
HERMES

CARTER KANE
PHARAOH,
HOUSE OF LIFE

ZIA RASHID
SCRIBE, HOUSE OF LIFE

SADIE KANE
MAGICIAN

THE KANE
CHRONICLES

WALT STONE
HOST OF ANUBIS

⎯● SHIPS
- - - ▪ COUSINS
–·–· SIBLINGS
······● HALF-SIBLINGS
········▸ PROTECTOR
━━● PROPHECY OF SEVEN
━━▶ DARK PROPHECY

♉ PERCY JACKSON
♎ HEROES OF OLYMPUS
K KANE CHRONICLES
✦ MAGNUS CHASE
☀ TRIALS OF APOLLO

FROM *NEW YORK TIMES* BEST-SELLING AUTHOR
RICK RIORDAN

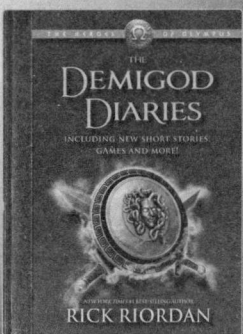

CELEBRATING 10 HEROIC YEARS
WITH A FRESH NEW LOOK!

MORE MYTHS, MAGIC, AND MAYHEM!

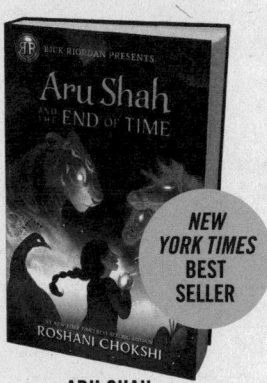

NEW YORK TIMES BEST SELLER

ARU SHAH AND THE END OF TIME
BOOK 1

ROSHANI CHOKSHI

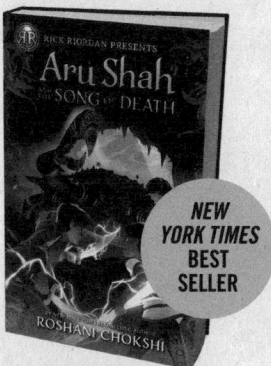

NEW YORK TIMES BEST SELLER

ARU SHAH AND THE SONG OF DEATH
BOOK 2

ROSHANI CHOKSHI

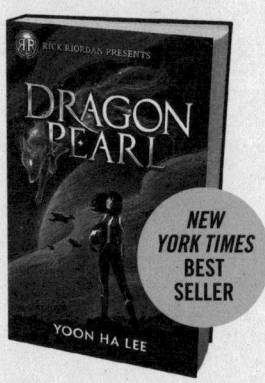

NEW YORK TIMES BEST SELLER

DRAGON PEARL

YOON HA LEE

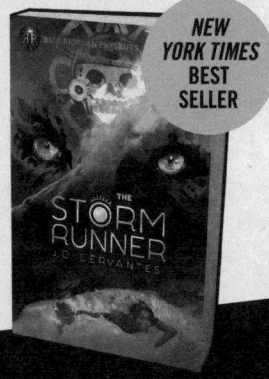

NEW YORK TIMES BEST SELLER

THE STORM RUNNER
BOOK 1

J. C. CERVANTES

THE FIRE KEEPER: A STORM RUNNER NOVEL
BOOK 2

J. C. CERVANTES

SAL AND GABI BREAK THE UNIVERSE

CARLOS HERNANDEZ

#DEMIGODGOALS • FOLLOW @READRIORDAN • Disney•HYPERION

JILL WACHTER

RICK RIORDAN, dubbed "storyteller of the gods" by *Publishers Weekly*, is the author of five *New York Times* #1 best-selling series. He is best known for his Percy Jackson and the Olympians books, which bring Greek mythology to life for contemporary readers. He expanded on that series with two more: the Heroes of Olympus and the Trials of Apollo, which cleverly combine Greek and Roman gods and heroes with his beloved modern characters. Rick also tackled the Egyptian gods in the magic-filled Kane Chronicles trilogy, and his Magnus Chase and the Gods of Asgard series is based on Norse myths. Millions of fans across the globe have enjoyed his fast-paced and funny quest adventures as well as his two #1 best-selling myth collections, *Percy Jackson's Greek Gods* and *Percy Jackson's Greek Heroes*. Rick is also the publisher of an imprint called Rick Riordan Presents, dedicated to finding other authors of highly entertaining fiction based on world cultures and mythologies. He lives in Boston, Massachusetts, with his wife and two sons. For more information, go to www.RickRiordan.com, or follow him on Twitter @camphalfblood.

THE LIGHTNING THIEF

RICK RIORDAN

PERCY JACKSON AND THE OLYMPIANS

I

THE LIGHTNING THIEF

Disney • HYPERION

Los Angeles New York

First Hardcover Edition, June 2005
First Paperback Edition, April 2006
Printed in the United States of America
60 61
FAC-025438-19221
This book is set in 13-point Centaur MT.

Library of Congress Control Number for the hardcover edition: 2005299400
ISBN 978-0-7868-3865-3 (pbk.)

Visit www.DisneyBooks.com
Follow @ReadRiordan

To Haley,
who heard the story first

CONTENTS

ONE

I ACCIDENTALLY VAPORIZE MY PRE-ALGEBRA TEACHER

Look, I didn't want to be a half-blood.

If you're reading this because you think you might be one, my advice is: close this book right now. Believe whatever lie your mom or dad told you about your birth, and try to lead a normal life.

Being a half-blood is dangerous. It's scary. Most of the time, it gets you killed in painful, nasty ways.

If you're a normal kid, reading this because you think it's fiction, great. Read on. I envy you for being able to believe that none of this ever happened.

But if you recognize yourself in these pages—if you feel something stirring inside—stop reading immediately. You might be one of us. And once you know that, it's only a matter of time before *they* sense it too, and they'll come for you.

Don't say I didn't warn you.

My name is Percy Jackson.

I'm twelve years old. Until a few months ago, I was a boarding student at Yancy Academy, a private school for troubled kids in upstate New York.

Am I a troubled kid?

Yeah. You could say that.

I could start at any point in my short miserable life to prove it, but things really started going bad last May, when our sixth-grade class took a field trip to Manhattan— twenty-eight mental-case kids and two teachers on a yellow school bus, heading to the Metropolitan Museum of Art to look at ancient Greek and Roman stuff.

I know—it sounds like torture. Most Yancy field trips were.

But Mr. Brunner, our Latin teacher, was leading this trip, so I had hopes.

Mr. Brunner was this middle-aged guy in a motorized wheelchair. He had thinning hair and a scruffy beard and a frayed tweed jacket, which always smelled like coffee. You wouldn't think he'd be cool, but he told stories and jokes and let us play games in class. He also had this awesome collection of Roman armor and weapons, so he was the only teacher whose class didn't put me to sleep.

I hoped the trip would be okay. At least, I hoped that for once I wouldn't get in trouble.

Boy, was I wrong.

See, bad things happen to me on field trips. Like at my fifth-grade school, when we went to the Saratoga battlefield, I had this accident with a Revolutionary War cannon. I wasn't aiming for the school bus, but of course I got expelled anyway. And before that, at my fourth-grade school, when we took a behind-the-scenes tour of the Marine World shark pool, I sort of hit the wrong lever on the catwalk and our class took an unplanned swim. And the time before that . . . Well, you get the idea.

This trip, I was determined to be good.

All the way into the city, I put up with Nancy Bobofit, the freckly, redheaded kleptomaniac girl, hitting my best friend Grover in the back of the head with chunks of peanut butter-and-ketchup sandwich.

Grover was an easy target. He was scrawny. He cried when he got frustrated. He must've been held back several grades, because he was the only sixth grader with acne and the start of a wispy beard on his chin. On top of all that, he was crippled. He had a note excusing him from PE for the rest of his life because he had some kind of muscular disease in his legs. He walked funny, like every step hurt him, but don't let that fool you. You should've seen him run when it was enchilada day in the cafeteria.

Anyway, Nancy Bobofit was throwing wads of sandwich that stuck in his curly brown hair, and she knew I couldn't do anything back to her because I was already on probation. The headmaster had threatened me with death by in-school suspension if anything bad, embarrassing, or even mildly entertaining happened on this trip.

"I'm going to kill her," I mumbled.

Grover tried to calm me down. "It's okay. I like peanut butter."

He dodged another piece of Nancy's lunch.

"That's it." I started to get up, but Grover pulled me back to my seat.

"You're already on probation," he reminded me. "You know who'll get blamed if anything happens."

Looking back on it, I wish I'd decked Nancy Bobofit

right then and there. In-school suspension would've been nothing compared to the mess I was about to get myself into.

Mr. Brunner led the museum tour.

He rode up front in his wheelchair, guiding us through the big echoey galleries, past marble statues and glass cases full of really old black-and-orange pottery.

It blew my mind that this stuff had survived for two thousand, three thousand years.

He gathered us around a thirteen-foot-tall stone column with a big sphinx on the top, and started telling us how it was a grave marker, a *stele*, for a girl about our age. He told us about the carvings on the sides. I was trying to listen to what he had to say, because it was kind of interesting, but everybody around me was talking, and every time I told them to shut up, the other teacher chaperone, Mrs. Dodds, would give me the evil eye.

Mrs. Dodds was this little math teacher from Georgia who always wore a black leather jacket, even though she was fifty years old. She looked mean enough to ride a Harley right into your locker. She had come to Yancy halfway through the year, when our last math teacher had a nervous breakdown.

From her first day, Mrs. Dodds loved Nancy Bobofit and figured I was devil spawn. She would point her crooked finger at me and say, "Now, honey," real sweet, and I knew I was going to get after-school detention for a month.

One time, after she'd made me erase answers out of old math workbooks until midnight, I told Grover I didn't think Mrs. Dodds was human. He looked at me, real serious, and said, "You're absolutely right."

Mr. Brunner kept talking about Greek funeral art.

Finally, Nancy Bobofit snickered something about the naked guy on the stele, and I turned around and said, "Will you *shut up?*"

It came out louder than I meant it to.

The whole group laughed. Mr. Brunner stopped his story.

"Mr. Jackson," he said, "did you have a comment?"

My face was totally red. I said, "No, sir."

Mr. Brunner pointed to one of the pictures on the stele. "Perhaps you'll tell us what this picture represents?"

I looked at the carving, and felt a flush of relief, because I actually recognized it. "That's Kronos eating his kids, right?"

"Yes," Mr. Brunner said, obviously not satisfied. "And he did this because . . ."

"Well . . ." I racked my brain to remember. "Kronos was the king god, and—"

"God?" Mr. Brunner asked.

"Titan," I corrected myself. "And . . . he didn't trust his kids, who were the gods. So, um, Kronos ate them, right? But his wife hid baby Zeus, and gave Kronos a rock to eat instead. And later, when Zeus grew up, he tricked his dad, Kronos, into barfing up his brothers and sisters—"

"Eeew!" said one of the girls behind me.

"—and so there was this big fight between the gods and the Titans," I continued, "and the gods won."

Some snickers from the group.

Behind me, Nancy Bobofit mumbled to a friend, "Like we're going to use this in real life. Like it's going to say on our job applications, 'Please explain why Kronos ate his kids.'"

"And why, Mr. Jackson," Brunner said, "to paraphrase Miss Bobofit's excellent question, does this matter in real life?"

"Busted," Grover muttered.

"Shut up," Nancy hissed, her face even brighter red than her hair.

At least Nancy got packed, too. Mr. Brunner was the only one who ever caught her saying anything wrong. He had radar ears.

I thought about his question, and shrugged. "I don't know, sir."

"I see." Mr. Brunner looked disappointed. "Well, half credit, Mr. Jackson. Zeus did indeed feed Kronos a mixture of mustard and wine, which made him disgorge his other five children, who, of course, being immortal gods, had been living and growing up completely undigested in the Titan's stomach. The gods defeated their father, sliced him to pieces with his own scythe, and scattered his remains in Tartarus, the darkest part of the Underworld. On that happy note, it's time for lunch. Mrs. Dodds, would you lead us back outside?"

The class drifted off, the girls holding their stomachs, the guys pushing each other around and acting like doofuses.

Grover and I were about to follow when Mr. Brunner said, "Mr. Jackson."

I knew that was coming.

I told Grover to keep going. Then I turned toward Mr. Brunner. "Sir?"

Mr. Brunner had this look that wouldn't let you go—intense brown eyes that could've been a thousand years old and had seen everything.

"You must learn the answer to my question," Mr. Brunner told me.

"About the Titans?"

"About real life. And how your studies apply to it."

"Oh."

"What you learn from me," he said, "is vitally important. I expect you to treat it as such. I will accept only the best from you, Percy Jackson."

I wanted to get angry, this guy pushed me so hard.

I mean, sure, it was kind of cool on tournament days, when he dressed up in a suit of Roman armor and shouted: "What ho!" and challenged us, sword-point against chalk, to run to the board and name every Greek and Roman person who had ever lived, and their mother, and what god they worshipped. But Mr. Brunner expected me to be as good as everybody else, despite the fact that I have dyslexia and attention deficit disorder and I had never made above a C– in my life. No—he didn't expect me to be *as good*; he expected me to be *better*. And I just couldn't learn all those names and facts, much less spell them correctly.

I mumbled something about trying harder, while Mr.

Brunner took one long sad look at the stele, like he'd been at this girl's funeral.

He told me to go outside and eat my lunch.

The class gathered on the front steps of the museum, where we could watch the foot traffic along Fifth Avenue.

Overhead, a huge storm was brewing, with clouds blacker than I'd ever seen over the city. I figured maybe it was global warming or something, because the weather all across New York state had been weird since Christmas. We'd had massive snow storms, flooding, wildfires from lightning strikes. I wouldn't have been surprised if this was a hurricane blowing in.

Nobody else seemed to notice. Some of the guys were pelting pigeons with Lunchables crackers. Nancy Bobofit was trying to pickpocket something from a lady's purse, and, of course, Mrs. Dodds wasn't seeing a thing.

Grover and I sat on the edge of the fountain, away from the others. We thought that maybe if we did that, everybody wouldn't know we were from *that* school—the school for loser freaks who couldn't make it elsewhere.

"Detention?" Grover asked.

"Nah," I said. "Not from Brunner. I just wish he'd lay off me sometimes. I mean—I'm not a genius."

Grover didn't say anything for a while. Then, when I thought he was going to give me some deep philosophical comment to make me feel better, he said, "Can I have your apple?"

I didn't have much of an appetite, so I let him take it.

I watched the stream of cabs going down Fifth Avenue, and thought about my mom's apartment, only a little ways uptown from where we sat. I hadn't seen her since Christmas. I wanted so bad to jump in a taxi and head home. She'd hug me and be glad to see me, but she'd be disappointed, too. She'd send me right back to Yancy, remind me that I had to try harder, even if this was my sixth school in six years and I was probably going to be kicked out again. I wouldn't be able to stand that sad look she'd give me.

Mr. Brunner parked his wheelchair at the base of the handicapped ramp. He ate celery while he read a paperback novel. A red umbrella stuck up from the back of his chair, making it look like a motorized café table.

I was about to unwrap my sandwich when Nancy Bobofit appeared in front of me with her ugly friends—I guess she'd gotten tired of stealing from the tourists—and dumped her half-eaten lunch in Grover's lap.

"Oops." She grinned at me with her crooked teeth. Her freckles were orange, as if somebody had spray-painted her face with liquid Cheetos.

I tried to stay cool. The school counselor had told me a million times, "Count to ten, get control of your temper." But I was so mad my mind went blank. A wave roared in my ears.

I don't remember touching her, but the next thing I knew, Nancy was sitting on her butt in the fountain, screaming, "Percy pushed me!"

Mrs. Dodds materialized next to us.

Some of the kids were whispering: "Did you see—"

"—the water—"

"—like it grabbed her—"

I didn't know what they were talking about. All I knew was that I was in trouble again.

As soon as Mrs. Dodds was sure poor little Nancy was okay, promising to get her a new shirt at the museum gift shop, etc., etc., Mrs. Dodds turned on me. There was a triumphant fire in her eyes, as if I'd done something she'd been waiting for all semester. "Now, honey—"

"I know," I grumbled. "A month erasing workbooks."

That wasn't the right thing to say.

"Come with me," Mrs. Dodds said.

"Wait!" Grover yelped. "It was me. *I* pushed her."

I stared at him, stunned. I couldn't believe he was trying to cover for me. Mrs. Dodds scared Grover to death.

She glared at him so hard his whiskery chin trembled.

"I don't think so, Mr. Underwood," she said.

"But—"

"You—*will*—stay—here."

Grover looked at me desperately.

"It's okay, man," I told him. "Thanks for trying."

"Honey," Mrs. Dodds barked at me. *"Now."*

Nancy Bobofit smirked.

I gave her my deluxe I'll-kill-you-later stare. Then I turned to face Mrs. Dodds, but she wasn't there. She was standing at the museum entrance, way at the top of the steps, gesturing impatiently at me to come on.

How'd she get there so fast?

I have moments like that a lot, when my brain falls asleep or something, and the next thing I know I've missed something, as if a puzzle piece fell out of the universe and left me staring at the blank place behind it. The school counselor told me this was part of the ADHD, my brain misinterpreting things.

I wasn't so sure.

I went after Mrs. Dodds.

Halfway up the steps, I glanced back at Grover. He was looking pale, cutting his eyes between me and Mr. Brunner, like he wanted Mr. Brunner to notice what was going on, but Mr. Brunner was absorbed in his novel.

I looked back up. Mrs. Dodds had disappeared again. She was now inside the building, at the end of the entrance hall.

Okay, I thought. She's going to make me buy a new shirt for Nancy at the gift shop.

But apparently that wasn't the plan.

I followed her deeper into the museum. When I finally caught up to her, we were back in the Greek and Roman section.

Except for us, the gallery was empty.

Mrs. Dodds stood with her arms crossed in front of a big marble frieze of the Greek gods. She was making this weird noise in her throat, like growling.

Even without the noise, I would've been nervous. It's weird being alone with a teacher, especially Mrs. Dodds. Something about the way she looked at the frieze, as if she wanted to pulverize it . . .

"You've been giving us problems, honey," she said.

I did the safe thing. I said, "Yes, ma'am."

She tugged on the cuffs of her leather jacket. "Did you really think you would get away with it?"

The look in her eyes was beyond mad. It was evil.

She's a teacher, I thought nervously. It's not like she's going to hurt me.

I said, "I'll—I'll try harder, ma'am."

Thunder shook the building.

"We are not fools, Percy Jackson," Mrs. Dodds said. "It was only a matter of time before we found you out. Confess, and you will suffer less pain."

I didn't know what she was talking about.

All I could think of was that the teachers must've found the illegal stash of candy I'd been selling out of my dorm room. Or maybe they'd realized I got my essay on *Tom Sawyer* from the Internet without ever reading the book and now they were going to take away my grade. Or worse, they were going to make me read the book.

"Well?" she demanded.

"Ma'am, I don't . . ."

"Your time is up," she hissed.

Then the weirdest thing happened. Her eyes began to glow like barbecue coals. Her fingers stretched, turning into talons. Her jacket melted into large, leathery wings. She wasn't human. She was a shriveled hag with bat wings and claws and a mouth full of yellow fangs, and she was about to slice me to ribbons.

Then things got even stranger.

Mr. Brunner, who'd been out in front of the museum a minute before, wheeled his chair into the doorway of the gallery, holding a pen in his hand.

"What ho, Percy!" he shouted, and tossed the pen through the air.

Mrs. Dodds lunged at me.

With a yelp, I dodged and felt talons slash the air next to my ear. I snatched the ballpoint pen out of the air, but when it hit my hand, it wasn't a pen anymore. It was a sword—Mr. Brunner's bronze sword, which he always used on tournament day.

Mrs. Dodds spun toward me with a murderous look in her eyes.

My knees were jelly. My hands were shaking so bad I almost dropped the sword.

She snarled, "Die, honey!"

And she flew straight at me.

Absolute terror ran through my body. I did the only thing that came naturally: I swung the sword.

The metal blade hit her shoulder and passed clean through her body as if she were made of water. *Hisss!*

Mrs. Dodds was a sand castle in a power fan. She exploded into yellow powder, vaporized on the spot, leaving nothing but the smell of sulfur and a dying screech and a chill of evil in the air, as if those two glowing red eyes were still watching me.

I was alone.

There was a ballpoint pen in my hand.

Mr. Brunner wasn't there. Nobody was there but me.

My hands were still trembling. My lunch must've been contaminated with magic mushrooms or something.

Had I imagined the whole thing?

I went back outside.

It had started to rain.

Grover was sitting by the fountain, a museum map tented over his head. Nancy Bobofit was still standing there, soaked from her swim in the fountain, grumbling to her ugly friends. When she saw me, she said, "I hope Mrs. Kerr whipped your butt."

I said, "Who?"

"Our *teacher*. Duh!"

I blinked. We had no teacher named Mrs. Kerr. I asked Nancy what she was talking about.

She just rolled her eyes and turned away.

I asked Grover where Mrs. Dodds was.

He said, "Who?"

But he paused first, and he wouldn't look at me, so I thought he was messing with me.

"Not funny, man," I told him. "This is serious."

Thunder boomed overhead.

I saw Mr. Brunner sitting under his red umbrella, reading his book, as if he'd never moved.

I went over to him.

He looked up, a little distracted. "Ah, that would be my pen. Please bring your own writing utensil in the future, Mr. Jackson."

I handed Mr. Brunner his pen. I hadn't even realized I

was still holding it.

"Sir," I said, "where's Mrs. Dodds?"

He stared at me blankly. "Who?"

"The other chaperone. Mrs. Dodds. The pre-algebra teacher."

He frowned and sat forward, looking mildly concerned. "Percy, there is no Mrs. Dodds on this trip. As far as I know, there has never been a Mrs. Dodds at Yancy Academy. Are you feeling all right?"

TWO

THREE OLD LADIES KNIT THE SOCKS OF DEATH

I was used to the occasional weird experience, but usually they were over quickly. This twenty-four/seven hallucination was more than I could handle. For the rest of the school year, the entire campus seemed to be playing some kind of trick on me. The students acted as if they were completely and totally convinced that Mrs. Kerr—a perky blond woman whom I'd never seen in my life until she got on our bus at the end of the field trip—had been our pre-algebra teacher since Christmas.

Every so often I would spring a Mrs. Dodds reference on somebody, just to see if I could trip them up, but they would stare at me like I was psycho.

It got so I almost believed them—Mrs. Dodds had never existed.

Almost.

But Grover couldn't fool me. When I mentioned the name Dodds to him, he would hesitate, then claim she didn't exist. But I knew he was lying.

Something was going on. Something *had* happened at the museum.

I didn't have much time to think about it during the days, but at night, visions of Mrs. Dodds with talons and leathery wings would wake me up in a cold sweat.

The freak weather continued, which didn't help my mood. One night, a thunderstorm blew out the windows in my dorm room. A few days later, the biggest tornado ever spotted in the Hudson Valley touched down only fifty miles from Yancy Academy. One of the current events we studied in social studies class was the unusual number of small planes that had gone down in sudden squalls in the Atlantic that year.

I started feeling cranky and irritable most of the time. My grades slipped from Ds to Fs. I got into more fights with Nancy Bobofit and her friends. I was sent out into the hallway in almost every class.

Finally, when our English teacher, Mr. Nicoll, asked me for the millionth time why I was too lazy to study for spelling tests, I snapped. I called him an old sot. I wasn't even sure what it meant, but it sounded good.

The headmaster sent my mom a letter the following week, making it official: I would not be invited back next year to Yancy Academy.

Fine, I told myself. Just fine.

I was homesick.

I wanted to be with my mom in our little apartment on the Upper East Side, even if I had to go to public school and put up with my obnoxious stepfather and his stupid poker parties.

And yet . . . there were things I'd miss at Yancy. The view of the woods out my dorm window, the Hudson River in the distance, the smell of pine trees. I'd miss Grover, who'd been a good friend, even if he was a little strange. I worried how he'd survive next year without me.

I'd miss Latin class, too—Mr. Brunner's crazy tournament days and his faith that I could do well.

As exam week got closer, Latin was the only test I studied for. I hadn't forgotten what Mr. Brunner had told me about this subject being life-and-death for me. I wasn't sure why, but I'd started to believe him.

The evening before my final, I got so frustrated I threw the *Cambridge Guide to Greek Mythology* across my dorm room. Words had started swimming off the page, circling my head, the letters doing one-eighties as if they were riding skateboards. There was no way I was going to remember the difference between Chiron and Charon, or Polydictes and Polydeuces. And conjugating those Latin verbs? Forget it.

I paced the room, feeling like ants were crawling around inside my shirt.

I remembered Mr. Brunner's serious expression, his thousand-year-old eyes. *I will accept only the best from you, Percy Jackson.*

I took a deep breath. I picked up the mythology book.

I'd never asked a teacher for help before. Maybe if I talked to Mr. Brunner, he could give me some pointers. At least I could apologize for the big fat F I was about to score on his exam. I didn't want to leave Yancy Academy with him thinking I hadn't tried.

I walked downstairs to the faculty offices. Most of them were dark and empty, but Mr. Brunner's door was ajar, light from his window stretching across the hallway floor.

I was three steps from the door handle when I heard voices inside the office. Mr. Brunner asked a question. A voice that was definitely Grover's said ". . . worried about Percy, sir."

I froze.

I'm not usually an eavesdropper, but I dare you to try not listening if you hear your best friend talking about you to an adult.

I inched closer.

". . . alone this summer," Grover was saying. "I mean, a Kindly One in the *school*! Now that we know for sure, and *they* know too—"

"We would only make matters worse by rushing him," Mr. Brunner said. "We need the boy to mature more."

"But he may not have time. The summer solstice deadline—"

"Will have to be resolved without him, Grover. Let him enjoy his ignorance while he still can."

"Sir, he *saw* her. . . ."

"His imagination," Mr. Brunner insisted. "The Mist over the students and staff will be enough to convince him of that."

"Sir, I . . . I can't fail in my duties again." Grover's voice was choked with emotion. "You know what that would mean."

"You haven't failed, Grover," Mr. Brunner said kindly. "I should have seen her for what she was. Now let's just worry about keeping Percy alive until next fall—"

The mythology book dropped out of my hand and hit the floor with a thud.

Mr. Brunner went silent.

My heart hammering, I picked up the book and backed down the hall.

A shadow slid across the lighted glass of Brunner's office door, the shadow of something much taller than my wheelchair-bound teacher, holding something that looked suspiciously like an archer's bow.

I opened the nearest door and slipped inside.

A few seconds later I heard a slow *clop-clop-clop*, like muffled wood blocks, then a sound like an animal snuffling right outside my door. A large, dark shape paused in front of the glass, then moved on.

A bead of sweat trickled down my neck.

Somewhere in the hallway, Mr. Brunner spoke. "Nothing," he murmured. "My nerves haven't been right since the winter solstice."

"Mine neither," Grover said. "But I could have sworn . . ."

"Go back to the dorm," Mr. Brunner told him. "You've got a long day of exams tomorrow."

"Don't remind me."

The lights went out in Mr. Brunner's office.

I waited in the dark for what seemed like forever.

Finally, I slipped out into the hallway and made my way back up to the dorm.

Grover was lying on his bed, studying his Latin exam notes like he'd been there all night.

"Hey," he said, bleary-eyed. "You going to be ready for this test?"

I didn't answer.

"You look awful." He frowned. "Is everything okay?"

"Just . . . tired."

I turned so he couldn't read my expression, and started getting ready for bed.

I didn't understand what I'd heard downstairs. I wanted to believe I'd imagined the whole thing.

But one thing was clear: Grover and Mr. Brunner were talking about me behind my back. They thought I was in some kind of danger.

The next afternoon, as I was leaving the three-hour Latin exam, my eyes swimming with all the Greek and Roman names I'd misspelled, Mr. Brunner called me back inside.

For a moment, I was worried he'd found out about my eavesdropping the night before, but that didn't seem to be the problem.

"Percy," he said. "Don't be discouraged about leaving Yancy. It's . . . it's for the best."

His tone was kind, but the words still embarrassed me. Even though he was speaking quietly, the other kids finishing the test could hear. Nancy Bobofit smirked at me and made sarcastic little kissing motions with her lips.

I mumbled, "Okay, sir."

"I mean . . ." Mr. Brunner wheeled his chair back and forth, like he wasn't sure what to say. "This isn't the right place for you. It was only a matter of time."

My eyes stung.

Here was my favorite teacher, in front of the class, telling me I couldn't handle it. After saying he believed in me all year, now he was telling me I was destined to get kicked out.

"Right," I said, trembling.

"No, no," Mr. Brunner said. "Oh, confound it all. What I'm trying to say . . . you're not normal, Percy. That's nothing to be——"

"Thanks," I blurted. "Thanks a lot, sir, for reminding me."

"Percy——"

But I was already gone.

On the last day of the term, I shoved my clothes into my suitcase.

The other guys were joking around, talking about their vacation plans. One of them was going on a hiking trip to Switzerland. Another was cruising the Caribbean for a month. They were juvenile delinquents, like me, but they were *rich* juvenile delinquents. Their daddies were executives, or ambassadors, or celebrities. I was a nobody, from a family of nobodies.

They asked me what I'd be doing this summer and I told them I was going back to the city.

What I didn't tell them was that I'd have to get a summer job walking dogs or selling magazine subscriptions, and spend my free time worrying about where I'd go to school in the fall.

"Oh," one of the guys said. "That's cool."

They went back to their conversation as if I'd never existed.

The only person I dreaded saying good-bye to was Grover, but as it turned out, I didn't have to. He'd booked a ticket to Manhattan on the same Greyhound as I had, so there we were, together again, heading into the city.

During the whole bus ride, Grover kept glancing nervously down the aisle, watching the other passengers. It occurred to me that he'd always acted nervous and fidgety when we left Yancy, as if he expected something bad to happen. Before, I'd always assumed he was worried about getting teased. But there was nobody to tease him on the Greyhound.

Finally I couldn't stand it anymore.

I said, "Looking for Kindly Ones?"

Grover nearly jumped out of his seat. "Wha—what do you mean?"

I confessed about eavesdropping on him and Mr. Brunner the night before the exam.

Grover's eye twitched. "How much did you hear?"

"Oh . . . not much. What's the summer solstice deadline?"

He winced. "Look, Percy . . . I was just worried for you, see? I mean, hallucinating about demon math teachers . . ."

"Grover—"

"And I was telling Mr. Brunner that maybe you were overstressed or something, because there was no such person as Mrs. Dodds, and . . ."

[23]

"Grover, you're a really, really bad liar."

His ears turned pink.

From his shirt pocket, he fished out a grubby business card. "Just take this, okay? In case you need me this summer."

The card was in fancy script, which was murder on my dyslexic eyes, but I finally made out something like:

Grover Underwood
Keeper

Half-Blood Hill
Long Island, New York
(800) 009-0009

"What's Half—"

"Don't say it aloud!" he yelped. "That's my, um . . . summer address."

My heart sank. Grover had a summer home. I'd never considered that his family might be as rich as the others at Yancy.

"Okay," I said glumly. "So, like, if I want to come visit your mansion."

He nodded. "Or . . . or if you need me."

"Why would I need you?"

It came out harsher than I meant it to.

Grover blushed right down to his Adam's apple. "Look, Percy, the truth is, I—I kind of have to protect you."

I stared at him.

All year long, I'd gotten in fights, keeping bullies away

from him. I'd lost sleep worrying that he'd get beaten up next year without me. And here he was acting like he was the one who defended *me*.

"Grover," I said, "what exactly are you protecting me from?"

There was a huge grinding noise under our feet. Black smoke poured from the dashboard and the whole bus filled with a smell like rotten eggs. The driver cursed and limped the Greyhound over to the side of the highway.

After a few minutes clanking around in the engine compartment, the driver announced that we'd all have to get off. Grover and I filed outside with everybody else.

We were on a stretch of country road—no place you'd notice if you didn't break down there. On our side of the highway was nothing but maple trees and litter from passing cars. On the other side, across four lanes of asphalt shimmering with afternoon heat, was an old-fashioned fruit stand.

The stuff on sale looked really good: heaping boxes of bloodred cherries and apples, walnuts and apricots, jugs of cider in a claw-foot tub full of ice. There were no customers, just three old ladies sitting in rocking chairs in the shade of a maple tree, knitting the biggest pair of socks I'd ever seen.

I mean these socks were the size of sweaters, but they were clearly socks. The lady on the right knitted one of them. The lady on the left knitted the other. The lady in the middle held an enormous basket of electric-blue yarn.

All three women looked ancient, with pale faces

wrinkled like fruit leather, silver hair tied back in white bandannas, bony arms sticking out of bleached cotton dresses.

The weirdest thing was, they seemed to be looking right at me.

I looked over at Grover to say something about this and saw that the blood had drained from his face. His nose was twitching.

"Grover?" I said. "Hey, man—"

"Tell me they're not looking at you. They are, aren't they?"

"Yeah. Weird, huh? You think those socks would fit me?"

"Not funny, Percy. Not funny at all."

The old lady in the middle took out a huge pair of scissors—gold and silver, long-bladed, like shears. I heard Grover catch his breath.

"We're getting on the bus," he told me. "Come on."

"What?" I said. "It's a thousand degrees in there."

"Come on!" He pried open the door and climbed inside, but I stayed back.

Across the road, the old ladies were still watching me. The middle one cut the yarn, and I swear I could hear that *snip* across four lanes of traffic. Her two friends balled up the electric-blue socks, leaving me wondering who they could possibly be for—Sasquatch or Godzilla.

At the rear of the bus, the driver wrenched a big chunk of smoking metal out of the engine compartment. The bus shuddered, and the engine roared back to life.

The passengers cheered.

"Darn right!" yelled the driver. He slapped the bus with his hat. "Everybody back on board!"

Once we got going, I started feeling feverish, as if I'd caught the flu.

Grover didn't look much better. He was shivering and his teeth were chattering.

"Grover?"

"Yeah?"

"What are you not telling me?"

He dabbed his forehead with his shirt sleeve. "Percy, what did you see back at the fruit stand?"

"You mean the old ladies? What is it about them, man? They're not like . . . Mrs. Dodds, are they?"

His expression was hard to read, but I got the feeling that the fruit-stand ladies were something much, much worse than Mrs. Dodds. He said, "Just tell me what you saw."

"The middle one took out her scissors, and she cut the yarn."

He closed his eyes and made a gesture with his fingers that might've been crossing himself, but it wasn't. It was something else, something almost—older.

He said, "You saw her snip the cord."

"Yeah. So?" But even as I said it, I knew it was a big deal.

"This is not happening," Grover mumbled. He started chewing at his thumb. "I don't want this to be like the last time."

"What last time?"

"Always sixth grade. They never get past sixth."

"Grover," I said, because he was really starting to scare me. "What are you talking about?"

"Let me walk you home from the bus station. Promise me."

This seemed like a strange request to me, but I promised he could.

"Is this like a superstition or something?" I asked.

No answer.

"Grover—that snipping of the yarn. Does that mean somebody is going to die?"

He looked at me mournfully, like he was already picking the kind of flowers I'd like best on my coffin.

THREE

GROVER UNEXPECTEDLY LOSES HIS PANTS

Confession time: I ditched Grover as soon as we got to the bus terminal.

I know, I know. It was rude. But Grover was freaking me out, looking at me like I was a dead man, muttering "Why does this always happen?" and "Why does it always have to be sixth grade?"

Whenever he got upset, Grover's bladder acted up, so I wasn't surprised when, as soon as we got off the bus, he made me promise to wait for him, then made a beeline for the restroom. Instead of waiting, I got my suitcase, slipped outside, and caught the first taxi uptown.

"East One-hundred-and-fourth and First," I told the driver.

A word about my mother, before you meet her.

Her name is Sally Jackson and she's the best person in the world, which just proves my theory that the best people have the rottenest luck. Her own parents died in a plane crash when she was five, and she was raised by an uncle who didn't care much about her. She wanted to be a novelist, so she spent high school working to save enough money for a college with a good creative-writing program. Then her uncle got cancer, and she had to quit school her senior year to take care of him. After he died, she was left with no money, no family, and no diploma.

The only good break she ever got was meeting my dad.

I don't have any memories of him, just this sort of warm glow, maybe the barest trace of his smile. My mom doesn't like to talk about him because it makes her sad. She has no pictures.

See, they weren't married. She told me he was rich and important, and their relationship was a secret. Then one day, he set sail across the Atlantic on some important journey, and he never came back.

Lost at sea, my mom told me. Not dead. Lost at sea.

She worked odd jobs, took night classes to get her high school diploma, and raised me on her own. She never complained or got mad. Not even once. But I knew I wasn't an easy kid.

Finally, she married Gabe Ugliano, who was nice the first thirty seconds we knew him, then showed his true colors as a world-class jerk. When I was young, I nicknamed him Smelly Gabe. I'm sorry, but it's the truth. The guy reeked like moldy garlic pizza wrapped in gym shorts.

Between the two of us, we made my mom's life pretty hard. The way Smelly Gabe treated her, the way he and I got along . . . well, when I came home is a good example.

I walked into our little apartment, hoping my mom would be home from work. Instead, Smelly Gabe was in the living room, playing poker with his buddies. The television blared ESPN. Chips and beer cans were strewn all over the carpet.

Hardly looking up, he said around his cigar, "So, you're home."

"Where's my mom?"

"Working," he said. "You got any cash?"

That was it. No *Welcome back. Good to see you. How has your life been the last six months?*

Gabe had put on weight. He looked like a tuskless walrus in thrift-store clothes. He had about three hairs on his head, all combed over his bald scalp, as if that made him handsome or something.

He managed the Electronics Mega-Mart in Queens, but he stayed home most of the time. I don't know why he hadn't been fired long before. He just kept on collecting paychecks, spending the money on cigars that made me nauseous, and on beer, of course. Always beer. Whenever I was home, he expected me to provide his gambling funds. He called that our "guy secret." Meaning, if I told my mom, he would punch my lights out.

"I don't have any cash," I told him.

He raised a greasy eyebrow.

Gabe could sniff out money like a bloodhound, which was surprising, since his own smell should've covered up everything else.

"You took a taxi from the bus station," he said. "Probably paid with a twenty. Got six, seven bucks in change. Somebody expects to live under this roof, he ought to carry his own weight. Am I right, Eddie?"

Eddie, the super of the apartment building, looked at me with a twinge of sympathy. "Come on, Gabe," he said. "The kid just got here."

"Am I *right*?" Gabe repeated.

Eddie scowled into his bowl of pretzels. The other two guys passed gas in harmony.

"Fine," I said. I dug a wad of dollars out of my pocket and threw the money on the table. "I hope you lose."

"Your report card came, brain boy!" he shouted after me. "I wouldn't act so snooty!"

I slammed the door to my room, which really wasn't my room. During school months, it was Gabe's "study." He didn't study anything in there except old car magazines, but he loved shoving my stuff in the closet, leaving his muddy boots on my windowsill, and doing his best to make the place smell like his nasty cologne and cigars and stale beer.

I dropped my suitcase on the bed. Home sweet home.

Gabe's smell was almost worse than the nightmares about Mrs. Dodds, or the sound of that old fruit lady's shears snipping the yarn.

But as soon as I thought that, my legs felt weak. I remembered Grover's look of panic—how he'd made me promise I wouldn't go home without him. A sudden chill rolled through me. I felt like someone—something—was looking for me right now, maybe pounding its way up the stairs, growing long, horrible talons.

Then I heard my mom's voice. "Percy?"

She opened the bedroom door, and my fears melted.

My mother can make me feel good just by walking into

the room. Her eyes sparkle and change color in the light. Her smile is as warm as a quilt. She's got a few gray streaks mixed in with her long brown hair, but I never think of her as old. When she looks at me, it's like she's seeing all the good things about me, none of the bad. I've never heard her raise her voice or say an unkind word to anyone, not even me or Gabe.

"Oh, Percy." She hugged me tight. "I can't believe it. You've grown since Christmas!"

Her red-white-and-blue Sweet on America uniform smelled like the best things in the world: chocolate, licorice, and all the other stuff she sold at the candy shop in Grand Central. She'd brought me a huge bag of "free samples," the way she always did when I came home.

We sat together on the edge of the bed. While I attacked the blueberry sour strings, she ran her hand through my hair and demanded to know everything I hadn't put in my letters. She didn't mention anything about my getting expelled. She didn't seem to care about that. But was I okay? Was her little boy doing all right?

I told her she was smothering me, and to lay off and all that, but secretly, I was really, really glad to see her.

From the other room, Gabe yelled, "Hey, Sally—how about some bean dip, huh?"

I gritted my teeth.

My mom is the nicest lady in the world. She should've been married to a millionaire, not to some jerk like Gabe.

For her sake, I tried to sound upbeat about my last days at Yancy Academy. I told her I wasn't too down about the expulsion. I'd lasted almost the whole year this time. I'd made some new friends. I'd done pretty well in Latin. And honestly, the fights hadn't been as bad as the headmaster said. I liked Yancy Academy. I really did. I put such a good spin on the year, I almost convinced myself. I started choking up, thinking about Grover and Mr. Brunner. Even Nancy Bobofit suddenly didn't seem so bad.

Until that trip to the museum . . .

"What?" my mom asked. Her eyes tugged at my conscience, trying to pull out the secrets. "Did something scare you?"

"No, Mom."

I felt bad lying. I wanted to tell her about Mrs. Dodds and the three old ladies with the yarn, but I thought it would sound stupid.

She pursed her lips. She knew I was holding back, but she didn't push me.

"I have a surprise for you," she said. "We're going to the beach."

My eyes widened. "Montauk?"

"Three nights—same cabin."

"When?"

She smiled. "As soon as I get changed."

I couldn't believe it. My mom and I hadn't been to Montauk the last two summers, because Gabe said there wasn't enough money.

Gabe appeared in the doorway and growled, "Bean dip, Sally? Didn't you hear me?"

I wanted to punch him, but I met my mom's eyes and I understood she was offering me a deal: be nice to Gabe for a little while. Just until she was ready to leave for Montauk. Then we would get out of here.

"I was on my way, honey," she told Gabe. "We were just talking about the trip."

Gabe's eyes got small. "The trip? You mean you were serious about that?"

"I knew it," I muttered. "He won't let us go."

"Of course he will," my mom said evenly. "Your stepfather is just worried about money. That's all. Besides," she added, "Gabriel won't have to settle for bean dip. I'll make him enough seven-layer dip for the whole weekend. Guacamole. Sour cream. The works."

Gabe softened a bit. "So this money for your trip . . . it comes out of your clothes budget, right?"

"Yes, honey," my mother said.

"And you won't take my car anywhere but there and back."

"We'll be very careful."

Gabe scratched his double chin. "Maybe if you hurry with that seven-layer dip . . . And maybe if the kid apologizes for interrupting my poker game."

Maybe if I kick you in your soft spot, I thought. And make you sing soprano for a week.

But my mom's eyes warned me not to make him mad.

Why did she put up with this guy? I wanted to scream. Why did she care what he thought?

"I'm sorry," I muttered. "I'm really sorry I interrupted your incredibly important poker game. Please go back to it right now."

Gabe's eyes narrowed. His tiny brain was probably trying to detect sarcasm in my statement.

"Yeah, whatever," he decided.

He went back to his game.

"Thank you, Percy," my mom said. "Once we get to Montauk, we'll talk more about . . . whatever you've forgotten to tell me, okay?"

For a moment, I thought I saw anxiety in her eyes—the same fear I'd seen in Grover during the bus ride—as if my mom too felt an odd chill in the air.

But then her smile returned, and I figured I must have been mistaken. She ruffled my hair and went to make Gabe his seven-layer dip.

An hour later we were ready to leave.

Gabe took a break from his poker game long enough to watch me lug my mom's bags to the car. He kept griping and groaning about losing her cooking—and more important, his '78 Camaro—for the whole weekend.

"Not a scratch on this car, brain boy," he warned me as I loaded the last bag. "Not one little scratch."

Like I'd be the one driving. I was twelve. But that didn't matter to Gabe. If a seagull so much as pooped on his paint job, he'd find a way to blame me.

Watching him lumber back toward the apartment building, I got so mad I did something I can't explain. As Gabe reached the doorway, I made the hand gesture I'd seen Grover make on the bus, a sort of warding-off-evil gesture, a clawed hand over my heart, then a shoving movement toward Gabe. The screen door slammed shut so hard it whacked him in the butt and sent him flying up the staircase as if he'd been shot from a cannon. Maybe it was just the wind, or some freak accident with the hinges, but I didn't stay long enough to find out.

I got in the Camaro and told my mom to step on it.

Our rental cabin was on the south shore, way out at the tip of Long Island. It was a little pastel box with faded curtains, half sunken into the dunes. There was always sand in the sheets and spiders in the cabinets, and most of the time the sea was too cold to swim in.

I loved the place.

We'd been going there since I was a baby. My mom had been going even longer. She never exactly said, but I knew why the beach was special to her. It was the place where she'd met my dad.

As we got closer to Montauk, she seemed to grow younger, years of worry and work disappearing from her face. Her eyes turned the color of the sea.

We got there at sunset, opened all the cabin's windows, and went through our usual cleaning routine. We walked on the beach, fed blue corn chips to the seagulls, and munched on blue jelly beans, blue saltwater taffy, and all the other free samples my mom had brought from work.

I guess I should explain the blue food.

See, Gabe had once told my mom there was no such thing. They had this fight, which seemed like a really small thing at the time. But ever since, my mom went out of her way to eat blue. She baked blue birthday cakes. She mixed blueberry smoothies. She bought blue-corn tortilla chips and brought home blue candy from the shop. This—along with keeping her maiden name, Jackson, rather than calling herself Mrs. Ugliano—was proof that she wasn't totally suckered by Gabe. She did have a rebellious streak, like me.

When it got dark, we made a fire. We roasted hot dogs and marshmallows. Mom told me stories about when she was a kid, back before her parents died in the plane crash. She told me about the books she wanted to write someday, when she had enough money to quit the candy shop.

Eventually, I got up the nerve to ask about what was always on my mind whenever we came to Montauk—my father. Mom's eyes went all misty. I figured she would tell me the same things she always did, but I never got tired of hearing them.

"He was kind, Percy," she said. "Tall, handsome, and powerful. But gentle, too. You have his black hair, you know, and his green eyes."

Mom fished a blue jelly bean out of her candy bag. "I wish he could see you, Percy. He would be so proud."

I wondered how she could say that. What was so great about me? A dyslexic, hyperactive boy with a D+ report card, kicked out of school for the sixth time in six years.

"How old was I?" I asked. "I mean . . . when he left?"

She watched the flames. "He was only with me for one summer, Percy. Right here at this beach. This cabin."

"But . . . he knew me as a baby."

"No, honey. He knew I was expecting a baby, but he never saw you. He had to leave before you were born."

I tried to square that with the fact that I seemed to remember . . . something about my father. A warm glow. A smile.

I had always assumed he knew me as a baby. My mom had never said it outright, but still, I'd felt it must be true. Now, to be told that he'd never even seen me . . .

I felt angry at my father. Maybe it was stupid, but I resented him for going on that ocean voyage, for not having the guts to marry my mom. He'd left us, and now we were stuck with Smelly Gabe.

"Are you going to send me away again?" I asked her. "To another boarding school?"

She pulled a marshmallow from the fire.

"I don't know, honey." Her voice was heavy. "I think . . . I think we'll have to do something."

"Because you don't want me around?" I regretted the words as soon as they were out.

My mom's eyes welled with tears. She took my hand, squeezed it tight. "Oh, Percy, no. I—I *have* to, honey. For your own good. I have to send you away."

Her words reminded me of what Mr. Brunner had said—that it was best for me to leave Yancy.

"Because I'm not normal," I said.

"You say that as if it's a bad thing, Percy. But you don't realize how important you are. I thought Yancy Academy would be far enough away. I thought you'd finally be safe."

"Safe from what?"

She met my eyes, and a flood of memories came back to me—all the weird, scary things that had ever happened to me, some of which I'd tried to forget.

During third grade, a man in a black trench coat had stalked me on the playground. When the teachers threatened to call the police, he went away growling, but no one believed me when I told them that under his broad-brimmed hat, the man only had one eye, right in the middle of his head.

Before that—a really early memory. I was in preschool, and a teacher accidentally put me down for a nap in a cot that a snake had slithered into. My mom screamed when she came to pick me up and found me playing with a limp, scaly rope I'd somehow managed to strangle to death with my meaty toddler hands.

In every single school, something creepy had happened, something unsafe, and I was forced to move.

I knew I should tell my mom about the old ladies at the fruit stand, and Mrs. Dodds at the art museum, about my weird hallucination that I had sliced my math teacher into dust with a sword. But I couldn't make myself tell her. I had a strange feeling the news would end our trip to Montauk, and I didn't want that.

"I've tried to keep you as close to me as I could," my mom said. "They told me that was a mistake. But there's only one other option, Percy—the place your father wanted to send you. And I just . . . I just can't stand to do it."

"My father wanted me to go to a special school?"

"Not a school," she said softly. "A summer camp."

My head was spinning. Why would my dad—who

hadn't even stayed around long enough to see me born—talk to my mom about a summer camp? And if it was so important, why hadn't she ever mentioned it before?

"I'm sorry, Percy," she said, seeing the look in my eyes. "But I can't talk about it. I—I couldn't send you to that place. It might mean saying good-bye to you for good."

"For good? But if it's only a summer camp . . ."

She turned toward the fire, and I knew from her expression that if I asked her any more questions she would start to cry.

That night I had a vivid dream.

It was storming on the beach, and two beautiful animals, a white horse and a golden eagle, were trying to kill each other at the edge of the surf. The eagle swooped down and slashed the horse's muzzle with its huge talons. The horse reared up and kicked at the eagle's wings. As they fought, the ground rumbled, and a monstrous voice chuckled somewhere beneath the earth, goading the animals to fight harder.

I ran toward them, knowing I had to stop them from killing each other, but I was running in slow motion. I knew I would be too late. I saw the eagle dive down, its beak aimed at the horse's wide eyes, and I screamed, *No!*

I woke with a start.

Outside, it really was storming, the kind of storm that cracks trees and blows down houses. There was no horse or eagle on the beach, just lightning making false daylight, and twenty-foot waves pounding the dunes like artillery.

With the next thunderclap, my mom woke. She sat up, eyes wide, and said, "Hurricane."

I knew that was crazy. Long Island never sees hurricanes this early in the summer. But the ocean seemed to have forgotten. Over the roar of the wind, I heard a distant bellow, an angry, tortured sound that made my hair stand on end.

Then a much closer noise, like mallets in the sand. A desperate voice—someone yelling, pounding on our cabin door.

My mother sprang out of bed in her nightgown and threw open the lock.

Grover stood framed in the doorway against a backdrop of pouring rain. But he wasn't . . . he wasn't exactly Grover.

"Searching all night," he gasped. "What were you thinking?"

My mother looked at me in terror—not scared of Grover, but of why he'd come.

"Percy," she said, shouting to be heard over the rain. "What happened at school? What didn't you tell me?"

I was frozen, looking at Grover. I couldn't understand what I was seeing.

"O Zeu kai alloi theoi!" he yelled. "It's right behind me! Didn't you *tell* her?"

I was too shocked to register that he'd just cursed in Ancient Greek, and I'd understood him perfectly. I was too shocked to wonder how Grover had gotten here by himself in the middle of the night. Because Grover didn't have his pants on—and where his legs should be . . . where his legs should be . . .

My mom looked at me sternly and talked in a tone she'd never used before: "*Percy.* Tell me *now!*"

I stammered something about the old ladies at the fruit stand, and Mrs. Dodds, and my mom stared at me, her face deathly pale in the flashes of lightning.

She grabbed her purse, tossed me my rain jacket, and said, "Get to the car. Both of you. *Go!*"

Grover ran for the Camaro—but he wasn't running, exactly. He was trotting, shaking his shaggy hindquarters, and suddenly his story about a muscular disorder in his legs made sense to me. I understood how he could run so fast and still limp when he walked.

Because where his feet should be, there were no feet. There were cloven hooves.

FOUR

MY MOTHER TEACHES ME BULLFIGHTING

We tore through the night along dark country roads. Wind slammed against the Camaro. Rain lashed the windshield. I didn't know how my mom could see anything, but she kept her foot on the gas.

Every time there was a flash of lightning, I looked at Grover sitting next to me in the backseat and I wondered if I'd gone insane, or if he was wearing some kind of shag-carpet pants. But, no, the smell was one I remembered from kindergarten field trips to the petting zoo— lanolin, like from wool. The smell of a wet barnyard animal.

All I could think to say was, "So, you and my mom . . . know each other?"

Grover's eyes flitted to the rearview mirror, though there were no cars behind us. "Not exactly," he said. "I mean, we've never met in person. But she knew I was watching you."

"Watching me?"

"Keeping tabs on you. Making sure you were okay. But I wasn't faking being your friend," he added hastily. "I *am* your friend."

"Um . . . what *are* you, exactly?"

"That doesn't matter right now."

"It doesn't matter? From the waist down, my best friend is a donkey—"

Grover let out a sharp, throaty *"Blaa-ha-ha!"*

I'd heard him make that sound before, but I'd always assumed it was a nervous laugh. Now I realized it was more of an irritated bleat.

"Goat!" he cried.

"What?"

"I'm a *goat* from the waist down."

"You just said it didn't matter."

"Blaa-ha-ha! There are satyrs who would trample you underhoof for such an insult!"

"Whoa. Wait. Satyrs. You mean like . . . Mr. Brunner's myths?"

"Were those old ladies at the fruit stand a *myth*, Percy? Was Mrs. Dodds a myth?"

"So you *admit* there was a Mrs. Dodds!"

"Of course."

"Then why—"

"The less you knew, the fewer monsters you'd attract," Grover said, like that should be perfectly obvious. "We put Mist over the humans' eyes. We hoped you'd think the Kindly One was a hallucination. But it was no good. You started to realize who you are."

"Who I—wait a minute, what do you mean?"

The weird bellowing noise rose up again somewhere behind us, closer than before. Whatever was chasing us was still on our trail.

"Percy," my mom said, "there's too much to explain and not enough time. We have to get you to safety."

"Safety from what? Who's after me?"

"Oh, nobody much," Grover said, obviously still miffed about the donkey comment. "Just the Lord of the Dead and a few of his blood-thirstiest minions."

"Grover!"

"Sorry, Mrs. Jackson. Could you drive faster, please?"

I tried to wrap my mind around what was happening, but I couldn't do it. I knew this wasn't a dream. I had no imagination. I could never dream up something this weird.

My mom made a hard left. We swerved onto a narrower road, racing past darkened farmhouses and wooded hills and PICK YOUR OWN STRAWBERRIES signs on white picket fences.

"Where are we going?" I asked.

"The summer camp I told you about." My mother's voice was tight; she was trying for my sake not to be scared. "The place your father wanted to send you."

"The place you didn't want me to go."

"Please, dear," my mother begged. "This is hard enough. Try to understand. You're in danger."

"Because some old ladies cut yarn."

"Those weren't old ladies," Grover said. "Those were the Fates. Do you know what it means—the fact they appeared in front of you? They only do that when you're about to . . . when someone's about to die."

"Whoa. You said 'you.'"

"No I didn't. I said 'someone.'"

"You meant 'you.' As in *me*."

"I meant *you*, like 'someone.' Not you, *you*."

"Boys!" my mom said.

She pulled the wheel hard to the right, and I got a glimpse of a figure she'd swerved to avoid—a dark fluttering shape now lost behind us in the storm.

"What was that?" I asked.

"We're almost there," my mother said, ignoring my question. "Another mile. Please. Please. Please."

I didn't know where *there* was, but I found myself leaning forward in the car, anticipating, wanting us to arrive.

Outside, nothing but rain and darkness—the kind of empty countryside you get way out on the tip of Long Island. I thought about Mrs. Dodds and the moment when she'd changed into the thing with pointed teeth and leathery wings. My limbs went numb from delayed shock. She really *hadn't* been human. She'd meant to kill me.

Then I thought about Mr. Brunner . . . and the sword he had thrown me. Before I could ask Grover about that, the hair rose on the back of my neck. There was a blinding flash, a jaw-rattling *boom!*, and our car exploded.

I remember feeling weightless, like I was being crushed, fried, and hosed down all at the same time.

I peeled my forehead off the back of the driver's seat and said, "Ow."

"Percy!" my mom shouted.

"I'm okay. . . ."

I tried to shake off the daze. I wasn't dead. The car hadn't really exploded. We'd swerved into a ditch. Our driver's-side doors were wedged in the mud. The roof had cracked open like an eggshell and rain was pouring in.

Lightning. That was the only explanation. We'd been blasted right off the road. Next to me in the backseat was a big motionless lump. "Grover!"

He was slumped over, blood trickling from the side of his mouth. I shook his furry hip, thinking, No! Even if you are half barnyard animal, you're my best friend and I don't want you to die!

Then he groaned "Food," and I knew there was hope.

"Percy," my mother said, "we have to . . ." Her voice faltered.

I looked back. In a flash of lightning, through the mud-spattered rear windshield, I saw a figure lumbering toward us on the shoulder of the road. The sight of it made my skin crawl. It was a dark silhouette of a huge guy, like a football player. He seemed to be holding a blanket over his head. His top half was bulky and fuzzy. His upraised hands made it look like he had horns.

I swallowed hard. "Who is—"

"Percy," my mother said, deadly serious. "Get out of the car."

My mother threw herself against the driver's-side door. It was jammed shut in the mud. I tried mine. Stuck too. I looked up desperately at the hole in the roof. It might've been an exit, but the edges were sizzling and smoking.

"Climb out the passenger's side!" my mother told me. "Percy—you have to run. Do you see that big tree?"

"What?"

Another flash of lightning, and through the smoking hole in the roof I saw the tree she meant: a huge, White House Christmas tree–sized pine at the crest of the nearest hill.

"That's the property line," my mom said. "Get over that hill and you'll see a big farmhouse down in the valley. Run and don't look back. Yell for help. Don't stop until you reach the door."

"Mom, you're coming too."

Her face was pale, her eyes as sad as when she looked at the ocean.

"No!" I shouted. "You *are* coming with me. Help me carry Grover."

"Food!" Grover moaned, a little louder.

The man with the blanket on his head kept coming toward us, making his grunting, snorting noises. As he got closer, I realized he *couldn't* be holding a blanket over his head, because his hands—huge meaty hands—were swinging at his sides. There was no blanket. Meaning the bulky, fuzzy mass that was too big to be his head . . . was his head. And the points that looked like horns . . .

"He doesn't want *us*," my mother told me. "He wants you. Besides, I can't cross the property line."

"But . . ."

"We don't have time, Percy. Go. Please."

I got mad, then—mad at my mother, at Grover the goat, at the thing with horns that was lumbering toward us slowly and deliberately like, like a bull.

I climbed across Grover and pushed the door open into the rain. "We're going together. Come on, Mom."

"I told you——"

"Mom! I am not leaving you. Help me with Grover."

I didn't wait for her answer. I scrambled outside, dragging Grover from the car. He was surprisingly light, but I couldn't have carried him very far if my mom hadn't come to my aid.

Together, we draped Grover's arms over our shoulders and started stumbling uphill through wet waist-high grass.

Glancing back, I got my first clear look at the monster. He was seven feet tall, easy, his arms and legs like something from the cover of *Muscle Man* magazine—bulging biceps and triceps and a bunch of other 'ceps, all stuffed like baseballs under vein-webbed skin. He wore no clothes except underwear—I mean, bright white Fruit of the Looms—which would've looked funny, except that the top half of his body was so scary. Coarse brown hair started at about his belly button and got thicker as it reached his shoulders.

His neck was a mass of muscle and fur leading up to his enormous head, which had a snout as long as my arm, snotty nostrils with a gleaming brass ring, cruel black eyes, and horns—enormous black-and-white horns with points you just couldn't get from an electric sharpener.

I recognized the monster, all right. He had been in one of the first stories Mr. Brunner told us. But he couldn't be real.

I blinked the rain out of my eyes. "That's——"

"Pasiphae's son," my mother said. "I wish I'd known how badly they want to kill you."

"But he's the Min——"

"Don't say his name," she warned. "Names have power."

The pine tree was still way too far—a hundred yards uphill at least.

I glanced behind me again.

The bull-man hunched over our car, looking in the windows—or not looking, exactly. More like snuffling, nuzzling. I wasn't sure why he bothered, since we were only about fifty feet away.

"Food?" Grover moaned.

"Shhh," I told him. "Mom, what's he doing? Doesn't he see us?"

"His sight and hearing are terrible," she said. "He goes by smell. But he'll figure out where we are soon enough."

As if on cue, the bull-man bellowed in rage. He picked up Gabe's Camaro by the torn roof, the chassis creaking and groaning. He raised the car over his head and threw it down the road. It slammed into the wet asphalt and skidded in a shower of sparks for about half a mile before coming to a stop. The gas tank exploded.

Not a scratch, I remembered Gabe saying.

Oops.

"Percy," my mom said. "When he sees us, he'll charge. Wait until the last second, then jump out of the way—directly sideways. He can't change directions very well once he's charging. Do you understand?"

"How do you know all this?"

"I've been worried about an attack for a long time. I should have expected this. I was selfish, keeping you near me."

"Keeping me near you? But—"

Another bellow of rage, and the bull-man started tromping uphill.

He'd smelled us.

The pine tree was only a few more yards, but the hill was getting steeper and slicker, and Grover wasn't getting any lighter.

The bull-man closed in. Another few seconds and he'd be on top of us.

My mother must've been exhausted, but she shouldered Grover. "Go, Percy! Separate! Remember what I said."

I didn't want to split up, but I had the feeling she was right—it was our only chance. I sprinted to the left, turned, and saw the creature bearing down on me. His black eyes glowed with hate. He reeked like rotten meat.

He lowered his head and charged, those razor-sharp horns aimed straight at my chest.

The fear in my stomach made me want to bolt, but that wouldn't work. I could never outrun this thing. So I held my ground, and at the last moment, I jumped to the side.

The bull-man stormed past like a freight train, then bellowed with frustration and turned, but not toward me this time, toward my mother, who was setting Grover down in the grass.

We'd reached the crest of the hill. Down the other side I could see a valley, just as my mother had said, and the lights of a farmhouse glowing yellow through the rain. But that was half a mile away. We'd never make it.

The bull-man grunted, pawing the ground. He kept

eyeing my mother, who was now retreating slowly downhill, back toward the road, trying to lead the monster away from Grover.

"Run, Percy!" she told me. "I can't go any farther. Run!"

But I just stood there, frozen in fear, as the monster charged her. She tried to sidestep, as she'd told me to do, but the monster had learned his lesson. His hand shot out and grabbed her by the neck as she tried to get away. He lifted her as she struggled, kicking and pummeling the air.

"Mom!"

She caught my eyes, managed to choke out one last word: "Go!"

Then, with an angry roar, the monster closed his fists around my mother's neck, and she dissolved before my eyes, melting into light, a shimmering golden form, as if she were a holographic projection. A blinding flash, and she was simply . . . gone.

"No!"

Anger replaced my fear. Newfound strength burned in my limbs—the same rush of energy I'd gotten when Mrs. Dodds grew talons.

The bull-man bore down on Grover, who lay helpless in the grass. The monster hunched over, snuffling my best friend, as if he were about to lift Grover up and make him dissolve too.

I couldn't allow that.

I stripped off my red rain jacket.

"Hey!" I screamed, waving the jacket, running to one side of the monster. "Hey, stupid! Ground beef!"

"Raaaarrrrr!" The monster turned toward me, shaking his meaty fists.

I had an idea—a stupid idea, but better than no idea at all. I put my back to the big pine tree and waved my red jacket in front of the bull-man, thinking I'd jump out of the way at the last moment.

But it didn't happen like that.

The bull-man charged too fast, his arms out to grab me whichever way I tried to dodge.

Time slowed down.

My legs tensed. I couldn't jump sideways, so I leaped straight up, kicking off from the creature's head, using it as a springboard, turning in midair, and landing on his neck.

How did I do that? I didn't have time to figure it out. A millisecond later, the monster's head slammed into the tree and the impact nearly knocked my teeth out.

The bull-man staggered around, trying to shake me. I locked my arms around his horns to keep from being thrown. Thunder and lightning were still going strong. The rain was in my eyes. The smell of rotten meat burned my nostrils.

The monster shook himself around and bucked like a rodeo bull. He should have just backed up into the tree and smashed me flat, but I was starting to realize that this thing had only one gear: forward.

Meanwhile, Grover started groaning in the grass. I wanted to yell at him to shut up, but the way I was getting tossed around, if I opened my mouth I'd bite my own tongue off.

"Food!" Grover moaned.

The bull-man wheeled toward him, pawed the ground again, and got ready to charge. I thought about how he had squeezed the life out of my mother, made her disappear in a flash of light, and rage filled me like high-octane fuel. I got both hands around one horn and I pulled backward with all my might. The monster tensed, gave a surprised grunt, then—*snap!*

The bull-man screamed and flung me through the air. I landed flat on my back in the grass. My head smacked against a rock. When I sat up, my vision was blurry, but I had a horn in my hands, a ragged bone weapon the size of a knife.

The monster charged.

Without thinking, I rolled to one side and came up kneeling. As the monster barreled past, I drove the broken horn straight into his side, right up under his furry rib cage.

The bull-man roared in agony. He flailed, clawing at his chest, then began to disintegrate—not like my mother, in a flash of golden light, but like crumbling sand, blown away in chunks by the wind, the same way Mrs. Dodds had burst apart.

The monster was gone.

The rain had stopped. The storm still rumbled, but only in the distance. I smelled like livestock and my knees were shaking. My head felt like it was splitting open. I was weak and scared and trembling with grief. I'd just seen my mother vanish. I wanted to lie down and cry, but there was Grover, needing my help, so I managed to haul him up and stagger down into the valley, toward the lights of the farm-house. I was crying, calling for my mother, but I held on to Grover—I wasn't going to let him go.

The last thing I remember is collapsing on a wooden porch, looking up at a ceiling fan circling above me, moths flying around a yellow light, and the stern faces of a familiar-looking bearded man and a pretty girl, her blond hair curled like a princess's. They both looked down at me, and the girl said, "He's the one. He must be."

"Silence, Annabeth," the man said. "He's still conscious. Bring him inside."

FIVE

I PLAY PINOCHLE
WITH A HORSE

I had weird dreams full of barnyard animals. Most of them wanted to kill me. The rest wanted food.

I must've woken up several times, but what I heard and saw made no sense, so I just passed out again. I remember lying in a soft bed, being spoon-fed something that tasted like buttered popcorn, only it was pudding. The girl with curly blond hair hovered over me, smirking as she scraped drips off my chin with the spoon.

When she saw my eyes open, she asked, "What will happen at the summer solstice?"

I managed to croak, "What?"

She looked around, as if afraid someone would overhear. "What's going on? What was stolen? We've only got a few weeks!"

"I'm sorry," I mumbled, "I don't . . ."

Somebody knocked on the door, and the girl quickly filled my mouth with pudding.

The next time I woke up, the girl was gone.

A husky blond dude, like a surfer, stood in the corner of the bedroom keeping watch over me. He had blue eyes—at least a dozen of them—on his cheeks, his forehead, the backs of his hands.

When I finally came around for good, there was nothing weird about my surroundings, except that they were nicer than I was used to. I was sitting in a deck chair on a huge porch, gazing across a meadow at green hills in the distance. The breeze smelled like strawberries. There was a blanket over my legs, a pillow behind my neck. All that was great, but my mouth felt like a scorpion had been using it for a nest. My tongue was dry and nasty and every one of my teeth hurt.

On the table next to me was a tall drink. It looked like iced apple juice, with a green straw and a paper parasol stuck through a maraschino cherry.

My hand was so weak I almost dropped the glass once I got my fingers around it.

"Careful," a familiar voice said.

Grover was leaning against the porch railing, looking like he hadn't slept in a week. Under one arm, he cradled a shoe box. He was wearing blue jeans, Converse hi-tops and a bright orange T-shirt that said CAMP HALF-BLOOD. Just plain old Grover. Not the goat boy.

So maybe I'd had a nightmare. Maybe my mom was okay. We were still on vacation, and we'd stopped here at this big house for some reason. And . . .

"You saved my life," Grover said. "I . . . well, the least I could do . . . I went back to the hill. I thought you might want this."

Reverently, he placed the shoe box in my lap.

Inside was a black-and-white bull's horn, the base jagged

from being broken off, the tip splattered with dried blood. It hadn't been a nightmare.

"The Minotaur," I said.

"Um, Percy, it isn't a good idea—"

"That's what they call him in the Greek myths, isn't it?" I demanded. "The Minotaur. Half man, half bull."

Grover shifted uncomfortably. "You've been out for two days. How much do you remember?"

"My mom. Is she really . . ."

He looked down.

I stared across the meadow. There were groves of trees, a winding stream, acres of strawberries spread out under the blue sky. The valley was surrounded by rolling hills, and the tallest one, directly in front of us, was the one with the huge pine tree on top. Even that looked beautiful in the sunlight.

My mother was gone. The whole world should be black and cold. Nothing should look beautiful.

"I'm sorry," Grover sniffled. "I'm a failure. I'm—I'm the worst satyr in the world."

He moaned, stomping his foot so hard it came off. I mean, the Converse hi-top came off. The inside was filled with Styrofoam, except for a hoof-shaped hole.

"Oh, Styx!" he mumbled.

Thunder rolled across the clear sky.

As he struggled to get his hoof back in the fake foot, I thought, Well, that settles it.

Grover was a satyr. I was ready to bet that if I shaved his curly brown hair, I'd find tiny horns on his head. But I was too miserable to care that satyrs existed, or even minotaurs.

All that meant was my mom really had been squeezed into nothingness, dissolved into yellow light.

I was alone. An orphan. I would have to live with . . . Smelly Gabe? No. That would never happen. I would live on the streets first. I would pretend I was seventeen and join the army. I'd do something.

Grover was still sniffling. The poor kid—poor goat, satyr, whatever—looked as if he expected to be hit.

I said, "It wasn't your fault."

"Yes, it was. I was supposed to *protect* you."

"Did my mother ask you to protect me?"

"No. But that's my job. I'm a keeper. At least . . . I was."

"But why . . ." I suddenly felt dizzy, my vision swimming.

"Don't strain yourself," Grover said. "Here."

He helped me hold my glass and put the straw to my lips.

I recoiled at the taste, because I was expecting apple juice. It wasn't that at all. It was chocolate-chip cookies. Liquid cookies. And not just any cookies—my mom's homemade blue chocolate-chip cookies, buttery and hot, with the chips still melting. Drinking it, my whole body felt warm and good, full of energy. My grief didn't go away, but I felt as if my mom had just brushed her hand against my cheek, given me a cookie the way she used to when I was small, and told me everything was going to be okay.

Before I knew it, I'd drained the glass. I stared into it, sure I'd just had a warm drink, but the ice cubes hadn't even melted.

"Was it good?" Grover asked.

I nodded.

"What did it taste like?" He sounded so wistful, I felt guilty.

"Sorry," I said. "I should've let you taste."

His eyes got wide. "No! That's not what I meant. I just . . . wondered."

"Chocolate-chip cookies," I said. "My mom's. Home-made."

He sighed. "And how do you feel?"

"Like I could throw Nancy Bobofit a hundred yards."

"That's good," he said. "That's good. I don't think you could risk drinking any more of that stuff."

"What do you mean?"

He took the empty glass from me gingerly, as if it were dynamite, and set it back on the table. "Come on. Chiron and Mr. D are waiting."

The porch wrapped all the way around the farmhouse.

My legs felt wobbly, trying to walk that far. Grover offered to carry the Minotaur horn, but I held on to it. I'd paid for that souvenir the hard way. I wasn't going to let it go.

As we came around the opposite end of the house, I caught my breath.

We must've been on the north shore of Long Island, because on this side of the house, the valley marched all the way up to the water, which glittered about a mile in the distance. Between here and there, I simply couldn't process everything I was seeing. The landscape was dotted with buildings that looked like ancient Greek architecture—an open-air pavilion, an amphitheater, a circular arena—except that they all looked brand new, their white marble columns sparkling in the sun. In a nearby sandpit, a dozen high school–age kids and satyrs played volleyball. Canoes glided across a small lake. Kids in bright orange T-shirts like Grover's were chasing each other around a cluster of cabins nestled in the woods. Some shot targets at an archery range. Others rode horses down a wooded trail, and, unless I was hallucinating, some of their horses had wings.

Down at the end of the porch, two men sat across from each other at a card table. The blond-haired girl who'd spoon-fed me popcorn-flavored pudding was leaning on the porch rail next to them.

The man facing me was small, but porky. He had a red nose, big watery eyes, and curly hair so black it was almost purple. He looked like those paintings of baby angels— what do you call them, hubbubs? No, cherubs. That's it. He looked like a cherub who'd turned middle-aged in a trailer park. He wore a tiger-pattern Hawaiian shirt, and he would've fit right in at one of Gabe's poker parties, except I got the feeling this guy could've out-gambled even my step-father.

"That's Mr. D," Grover murmured to me. "He's the camp director. Be polite. The girl, that's Annabeth Chase. She's just a camper, but she's been here longer than just about anybody. And you already know Chiron. . . ."

He pointed at the guy whose back was to me.

First, I realized he was sitting in the wheelchair. Then I

[62]

recognized the tweed jacket, the thinning brown hair, the scraggly beard.

"Mr. Brunner!" I cried.

The Latin teacher turned and smiled at me. His eyes had that mischievous glint they sometimes got in class when he pulled a pop quiz and made all the multiple choice answers *B*.

"Ah, good, Percy," he said. "Now we have four for pinochle."

He offered me a chair to the right of Mr. D, who looked at me with bloodshot eyes and heaved a great sigh. "Oh, I suppose I must say it. Welcome to Camp Half-Blood. There. Now, don't expect me to be glad to see you."

"Uh, thanks." I scooted a little farther away from him because, if there was one thing I had learned from living with Gabe, it was how to tell when an adult has been hitting the happy juice. If Mr. D was a stranger to alcohol, I was a satyr.

"Annabeth?" Mr. Brunner called to the blond girl.

She came forward and Mr. Brunner introduced us. "This young lady nursed you back to health, Percy. Annabeth, my dear, why don't you go check on Percy's bunk? We'll be putting him in cabin eleven for now."

Annabeth said, "Sure, Chiron."

She was probably my age, maybe a couple of inches taller, and a whole lot more athletic looking. With her deep tan and her curly blond hair, she was almost exactly what I thought a stereotypical California girl would look like, except her eyes ruined the image. They were startling gray, like storm clouds; pretty, but intimidating, too, as if she were analyzing the best way to take me down in a fight.

She glanced at the minotaur horn in my hands, then back at me. I imagined she was going to say, *You killed a minotaur!* or *Wow, you're so awesome!* or something like that.

Instead she said, "You drool when you sleep."

Then she sprinted off down the lawn, her blond hair flying behind her.

"So," I said, anxious to change the subject. "You, uh, work here, Mr. Brunner?"

"Not Mr. Brunner," the ex–Mr. Brunner said. "I'm afraid that was a pseudonym. You may call me Chiron."

"Okay." Totally confused, I looked at the director. "And Mr. D . . . does that stand for something?"

Mr. D stopped shuffling the cards. He looked at me like I'd just belched loudly. "Young man, names are powerful things. You don't just go around using them for no reason."

"Oh. Right. Sorry."

"I must say, Percy," Chiron-Brunner broke in, "I'm glad to see you alive. It's been a long time since I've made a house call to a potential camper. I'd hate to think I've wasted my time."

"House call?"

"My year at Yancy Academy, to instruct you. We have satyrs at most schools, of course, keeping a lookout. But Grover alerted me as soon as he met you. He sensed you were something special, so I decided to come upstate. I convinced the other Latin teacher to . . . ah, take a leave of absence."

I tried to remember the beginning of the school year. It seemed like so long ago, but I did have a fuzzy memory of there being another Latin teacher my first week at Yancy. Then, without explanation, he had disappeared and Mr. Brunner had taken the class.

"You came to Yancy just to teach me?" I asked.

Chiron nodded. "Honestly, I wasn't sure about you at first. We contacted your mother, let her know we were keeping an eye on you in case you were ready for Camp Half-Blood. But you still had so much to learn. Nevertheless, you made it here alive, and that's always the first test."

"Grover," Mr. D said impatiently, "are you playing or not?"

"Yes, sir!" Grover trembled as he took the fourth chair, though I didn't know why he should be so afraid of a pudgy little man in a tiger-print Hawaiian shirt.

"You *do* know how to play pinochle?" Mr. D eyed me suspiciously.

"I'm afraid not," I said.

"I'm afraid not, *sir*," he said.

"Sir," I repeated. I was liking the camp director less and less.

"Well," he told me, "it is, along with gladiator fighting and Pac-Man, one of the greatest games ever invented by humans. I would expect all *civilized* young men to know the rules."

"I'm sure the boy can learn," Chiron said.

"Please," I said, "what is this place? What am I doing here? Mr. Brun—Chiron—why would you go to Yancy Academy just to teach me?"

Mr. D snorted. "I asked the same question."

The camp director dealt the cards. Grover flinched every time one landed in his pile.

Chiron smiled at me sympathetically, the way he used to in Latin class, as if to let me know that no matter what my average was, *I* was his star student. He expected *me* to have the right answer.

"Percy," he said. "Did your mother tell you nothing?"

"She said . . ." I remembered her sad eyes, looking out over the sea. "She told me she was afraid to send me here, even though my father had wanted her to. She said that once I was here, I probably couldn't leave. She wanted to keep me close to her."

"Typical," Mr. D said. "That's how they usually get killed. Young man, are you bidding or not?"

"What?" I asked.

He explained, impatiently, how you bid in pinochle, and so I did.

"I'm afraid there's too much to tell," Chiron said. "I'm afraid our usual orientation film won't be sufficient."

"Orientation film?" I asked.

"No," Chiron decided. "Well, Percy. You know your friend Grover is a satyr. You know"—he pointed to the horn in the shoe box—"that you have killed the Minotaur. No small feat, either, lad. What you may not know is that great powers are at work in your life. Gods—the forces you call the Greek gods—are very much alive."

I stared at the others around the table.

I waited for somebody to yell, *Not!* But all I got was Mr. D yelling, "Oh, a royal marriage. Trick! Trick!" He cackled as he tallied up his points.

"Mr. D," Grover asked timidly, "if you're not going to eat it, could I have your Diet Coke can?"

"Eh? Oh, all right."

Grover bit a huge shard out of the empty aluminum can and chewed it mournfully.

"Wait," I told Chiron. "You're telling me there's such a thing as God."

"Well, now," Chiron said. "God—capital G, God. That's a different matter altogether. We shan't deal with the metaphysical."

"Metaphysical? But you were just talking about—"

"Ah, gods, plural, as in, great beings that control the forces of nature and human endeavors: the immortal gods of Olympus. That's a smaller matter."

"Smaller?"

"Yes, quite. The gods we discussed in Latin class."

"Zeus," I said. "Hera. Apollo. You mean them."

And there it was again—distant thunder on a cloudless day.

"Young man," said Mr. D, "I would really be less casual about throwing those names around, if I were you."

"But they're stories," I said. "They're—myths, to explain

lightning and the seasons and stuff. They're what people believed before there was science."

"Science!" Mr. D scoffed. "And tell me, Perseus Jackson"—I flinched when he said my real name, which I never told anybody—"what will people think of your 'science' two thousand years from now?" Mr. D continued. "Hmm? They will call it primitive mumbo jumbo. That's what. Oh, I love mortals—they have absolutely no sense of perspective. They think they've come *so-o-o* far. And have they, Chiron? Look at this boy and tell me."

I wasn't liking Mr. D much, but there was something about the way he called me mortal, as if . . . he wasn't. It was enough to put a lump in my throat, to suggest why Grover was dutifully minding his cards, chewing his soda can, and keeping his mouth shut.

"Percy," Chiron said, "you may choose to believe or not, but the fact is that *immortal* means immortal. Can you imagine that for a moment, never dying? Never fading? Existing, just as you are, for all time?"

I was about to answer, off the top of my head, that it sounded like a pretty good deal, but the tone of Chiron's voice made me hesitate.

"You mean, whether people believed in you or not," I said.

"Exactly," Chiron agreed. "If you were a god, how would you like being called a myth, an old story to explain lightning? What if I told you, Perseus Jackson, that someday people would call *you* a myth, just created to explain how little boys can get over losing their mothers?"

My heart pounded. He was trying to make me angry for some reason, but I wasn't going to let him. I said, "I wouldn't like it. But I don't believe in gods."

"Oh, you'd better," Mr. D murmured. "Before one of them incinerates you."

Grover said, "P-please, sir. He's just lost his mother. He's in shock."

"A lucky thing, too," Mr. D grumbled, playing a card. "Bad enough I'm confined to this miserable job, working with boys who don't even believe!"

He waved his hand and a goblet appeared on the table, as if the sunlight had bent, momentarily, and woven the air into glass. The goblet filled itself with red wine.

My jaw dropped, but Chiron hardly looked up.

"Mr. D," he warned, "your restrictions."

Mr. D looked at the wine and feigned surprise.

"Dear me." He looked at the sky and yelled, "Old habits! Sorry!"

More thunder.

Mr. D waved his hand again, and the wineglass changed into a fresh can of Diet Coke. He sighed unhappily, popped the top of the soda, and went back to his card game.

Chiron winked at me. "Mr. D offended his father a while back, took a fancy to a wood nymph who had been declared off-limits."

"A wood nymph," I repeated, still staring at the Diet Coke can like it was from outer space.

"Yes," Mr. D confessed. "Father loves to punish me. The first time, Prohibition. Ghastly! Absolutely horrid ten years! The second time—well, she really was pretty, and I couldn't stay away—the second time, he sent me here. Half-Blood Hill. Summer camp for brats like you. 'Be a better influence,' he told me. 'Work with youths rather than tearing them down.' Ha! Absolutely unfair."

Mr. D sounded about six years old, like a pouting little kid.

"And . . ." I stammered, "your father is . . ."

"*Di immortales*, Chiron," Mr. D said. "I thought you taught this boy the basics. My father is Zeus, of course."

I ran through D names from Greek mythology. Wine. The skin of a tiger. The satyrs that all seemed to work here. The way Grover cringed, as if Mr. D were his master.

"You're Dionysus," I said. "The god of wine."

Mr. D rolled his eyes. "What do they say, these days, Grover? Do the children say, 'Well, duh!'?"

"Y-yes, Mr. D."

"Then, well, duh! Percy Jackson. Did you think I was Aphrodite, perhaps?"

"You're a god."

"Yes, child."

"A god. You."

He turned to look at me straight on, and I saw a kind of purplish fire in his eyes, a hint that this whiny, plump little man was only showing me the tiniest bit of his true nature. I saw visions of grape vines choking unbelievers to death, drunken warriors insane with battle lust, sailors screaming as their hands turned to flippers, their faces elongating into dolphin snouts. I knew that if I pushed him,

Mr. D would show me worse things. He would plant a disease in my brain that would leave me wearing a strait-jacket in a rubber room for the rest of my life.

"Would you like to test me, child?" he said quietly.

"No. No, sir."

The fire died a little. He turned back to his card game. "I believe I win."

"Not quite, Mr. D," Chiron said. He set down a straight, tallied the points, and said, "The game goes to me."

I thought Mr. D was going to vaporize Chiron right out of his wheelchair, but he just sighed through his nose, as if he were used to being beaten by the Latin teacher. He got up, and Grover rose, too.

"I'm tired," Mr. D said. "I believe I'll take a nap before the sing-along tonight. But first, Grover, we need to talk, *again*, about your less-than-perfect performance on this assignment."

Grover's face beaded with sweat. "Y-yes, sir."

Mr. D turned to me. "Cabin eleven, Percy Jackson. And mind your manners."

He swept into the farmhouse, Grover following miserably.

"Will Grover be okay?" I asked Chiron.

Chiron nodded, though he looked a bit troubled. "Old Dionysus isn't really mad. He just hates his job. He's been . . . ah, grounded, I guess you would say, and he can't stand waiting another century before he's allowed to go back to Olympus."

"Mount Olympus," I said. "You're telling me there really is a palace there?"

"Well now, there's Mount Olympus in Greece. And then there's the home of the gods, the convergence point of their powers, which did indeed used to be on Mount Olympus. It's still called Mount Olympus, out of respect to the old ways, but the palace moves, Percy, just as the gods do."

"You mean the Greek gods are here? Like . . . in *America*?"

"Well, certainly. The gods move with the heart of the West."

"The what?"

"Come now, Percy. What you call 'Western civilization.' Do you think it's just an abstract concept? No, it's a living force. A collective consciousness that has burned bright for thousands of years. The gods are part of it. You might even say they are the source of it, or at least, they are tied so tightly to it that they couldn't possibly fade, not unless all of Western civilization were obliterated. The fire started in Greece. Then, as you well know—or as I hope you know, since you passed my course—the heart of the fire moved to Rome, and so did the gods. Oh, different names, perhaps—Jupiter for Zeus, Venus for Aphrodite, and so on—but the same forces, the same gods."

"And then they died."

"Died? No. Did the West die? The gods simply moved, to Germany, to France, to Spain, for a while. Wherever the flame was brightest, the gods were there. They spent several centuries in England. All you need to do is look at the architecture. People do not forget the gods. Every place they've ruled, for the last three thousand years, you can see them in paintings, in statues, on the most important buildings. And yes, Percy, of course they are now in your United States. Look at your symbol, the eagle of Zeus. Look at the statue of Prometheus in Rockefeller Center, the Greek facades of your government buildings in Washington. I defy you to find any American city where the Olympians are not prominently displayed in multiple places. Like it or not—and believe me, plenty of people weren't very fond of Rome, either—America is now the heart of the flame. It is the great power of the West. And so Olympus is here. And we are here."

It was all too much, especially the fact that *I* seemed to be included in Chiron's *we*, as if I were part of some club.

"Who are you, Chiron? Who . . . who am I?"

Chiron smiled. He shifted his weight as if he were going to get up out of his wheelchair, but I knew that was impossible. He was paralyzed from the waist down.

"Who are you?" he mused. "Well, that's the question we all want answered, isn't it? But for now, we should get you a bunk in cabin eleven. There will be new friends to meet. And plenty of time for lessons tomorrow. Besides, there will be s'mores at the campfire tonight, and I simply adore chocolate."

And then he did rise from his wheelchair. But there was something odd about the way he did it. His blanket fell away from his legs, but the legs didn't move. His waist kept getting longer, rising above his belt. At first, I thought he was wearing very long, white velvet underwear, but as he kept rising out of the chair, taller than any man, I realized that the velvet underwear wasn't underwear; it was the front of an animal, muscle and sinew under coarse white fur. And the wheelchair wasn't a chair. It was some kind of container, an enormous box on wheels, and it must've been magic, because there's no way it could've held all of him. A leg came out, long and knobby-kneed, with a huge polished hoof. Then another front leg, then hindquarters, and then the box was empty, nothing but a metal shell with a couple of fake human legs attached.

I stared at the horse who had just sprung from the wheelchair: a huge white stallion. But where its neck should be was the upper body of my Latin teacher, smoothly grafted to the horse's trunk.

"What a relief," the centaur said. "I'd been cooped up in there so long, my fetlocks had fallen asleep. Now, come, Percy Jackson. Let's meet the other campers."

SIX

I BECOME SUPREME LORD
OF THE BATHROOM

Once I got over the fact that my Latin teacher was a horse, we had a nice tour, though I was careful not to walk behind him. I'd done pooper-scooper patrol in the Macy's Thanksgiving Day Parade a few times, and, I'm sorry, I did not trust Chiron's back end the way I trusted his front.

We passed the volleyball pit. Several of the campers nudged each other. One pointed to the minotaur horn I was carrying. Another said, "That's *him*."

Most of the campers were older than me. Their satyr friends were bigger than Grover, all of them trotting around in orange CAMP HALF-BLOOD T-shirts, with nothing else to cover their bare shaggy hindquarters. I wasn't normally shy, but the way they stared at me made me uncomfortable. I felt like they were expecting me to do a flip or something.

I looked back at the farmhouse. It was a lot bigger than I'd realized—four stories tall, sky blue with white trim, like an upscale seaside resort. I was checking out the brass eagle weather vane on top when something caught my eye, a shadow in the uppermost window of the attic gable. Something had moved the curtain, just for a second, and I got the distinct impression I was being watched.

"What's up there?" I asked Chiron.

He looked where I was pointing, and his smile faded. "Just the attic."

"Somebody lives there?"

"No," he said with finality. "Not a single living thing."

I got the feeling he was being truthful. But I was also sure something had moved that curtain.

"Come along, Percy," Chiron said, his lighthearted tone now a little forced. "Lots to see."

We walked through the strawberry fields, where campers were picking bushels of berries while a satyr played a tune on a reed pipe.

Chiron told me the camp grew a nice crop for export to New York restaurants and Mount Olympus. "It pays our expenses," he explained. "And the strawberries take almost no effort."

He said Mr. D had this effect on fruit-bearing plants: they just went crazy when he was around. It worked best with wine grapes, but Mr. D was restricted from growing those, so they grew strawberries instead.

I watched the satyr playing his pipe. His music was causing lines of bugs to leave the strawberry patch in every direction, like refugees fleeing a fire. I wondered if Grover could work that kind of magic with music. I wondered if he was still inside the farmhouse, getting chewed out by Mr. D.

"Grover won't get in too much trouble, will he?" I asked Chiron. "I mean . . . he was a good protector. Really."

Chiron sighed. He shed his tweed jacket and draped it over his horse's back like a saddle. "Grover has big dreams,

Percy. Perhaps bigger than are reasonable. To reach his goal, he must first demonstrate great courage by succeeding as a keeper, finding a new camper and bringing him safely to Half-Blood Hill."

"But he did that!"

"I might agree with you," Chiron said. "But it is not my place to judge. Dionysus and the Council of Cloven Elders must decide. I'm afraid they might not see this assignment as a success. After all, Grover lost you in New York. Then there's the unfortunate . . . ah . . . fate of your mother. And the fact that Grover was unconscious when you dragged him over the property line. The council might question whether this shows any courage on Grover's part."

I wanted to protest. None of what happened was Grover's fault. I also felt really, really guilty. If I hadn't given Grover the slip at the bus station, he might not have gotten in trouble.

"He'll get a second chance, won't he?"

Chiron winced. "I'm afraid that *was* Grover's second chance, Percy. The council was not anxious to give him another, either, after what happened the first time, five years ago. Olympus knows, I advised him to wait longer before trying again. He's still so small for his age. . . ."

"How old is he?"

"Oh, twenty-eight."

"What! And he's in sixth grade?"

"Satyrs mature half as fast as humans, Percy. Grover has been the equivalent of a middle school student for the past six years."

"That's horrible."

"Quite," Chiron agreed. "At any rate, Grover is a late bloomer, even by satyr standards, and not yet very accomplished at woodland magic. Alas, he was anxious to pursue his dream. Perhaps now he will find some other career. . . ."

"That's not fair," I said. "What happened the first time? Was it really so bad?"

Chiron looked away quickly. "Let's move along, shall we?"

But I wasn't quite ready to let the subject drop. Something had occurred to me when Chiron talked about my mother's fate, as if he were intentionally avoiding the word *death*. The beginnings of an idea—a tiny, hopeful fire—started forming in my mind.

"Chiron," I said. "If the gods and Olympus and all that are real . . ."

"Yes, child?"

"Does that mean the Underworld is real, too?"

Chiron's expression darkened.

"Yes, child." He paused, as if choosing his words carefully. "There is a place where spirits go after death. But for now . . . until we know more . . . I would urge you to put that out of your mind."

"What do you mean, 'until we know more'?"

"Come, Percy. Let's see the woods."

As we got closer, I realized how huge the forest was. It took up at least a quarter of the valley, with trees so tall and thick, you could imagine nobody had been in there since the Native Americans.

Chiron said, "The woods are stocked, if you care to try your luck, but go armed."

"Stocked with what?" I asked. "Armed with what?"

"You'll see. Capture the flag is Friday night. Do you have your own sword and shield?"

"My own—?"

"No," Chiron said. "I don't suppose you do. I think a size five will do. I'll visit the armory later."

I wanted to ask what kind of summer camp had an armory, but there was too much else to think about, so the tour continued. We saw the archery range, the canoeing lake, the stables (which Chiron didn't seem to like very much), the javelin range, the sing-along amphitheater, and the arena where Chiron said they held sword and spear fights.

"Sword and spear fights?" I asked.

"Cabin challenges and all that," he explained. "Not lethal. Usually. Oh, yes, and there's the mess hall."

Chiron pointed to an outdoor pavilion framed in white Grecian columns on a hill overlooking the sea. There were a dozen stone picnic tables. No roof. No walls.

"What do you do when it rains?" I asked.

Chiron looked at me as if I'd gone a little weird. "We still have to eat, don't we?" I decided to drop the subject.

Finally, he showed me the cabins. There were twelve of them, nestled in the woods by the lake. They were arranged in a U, with two at the base and five in a row on either side. And they were without doubt the most bizarre collection of buildings I'd ever seen.

Except for the fact that each had a large brass number above the door (odds on the left side, evens on the right), they looked absolutely nothing alike. Number nine had smokestacks, like a tiny factory. Number four had tomato vines on the walls and a roof made out of real grass. Seven seemed to be made of solid gold, which gleamed so much in the sunlight it was almost impossible to look at. They all faced a commons area about the size of a soccer field, dotted with Greek statues, fountains, flower beds, and a couple of basketball hoops (which were more my speed).

In the center of the field was a huge stone-lined firepit. Even though it was a warm afternoon, the hearth smoldered. A girl about nine years old was tending the flames, poking the coals with a stick.

The pair of cabins at the head of the field, numbers one and two, looked like his-and-hers mausoleums, big white marble boxes with heavy columns in front. Cabin one was the biggest and bulkiest of the twelve. Its polished bronze doors shimmered like a hologram, so that from different angles lightning bolts seemed to streak across them. Cabin two was more graceful somehow, with slimmer columns garlanded with pomegranates and flowers. The walls were carved with images of peacocks.

"Zeus and Hera?" I guessed.

"Correct," Chiron said.

"Their cabins look empty."

"Several of the cabins are. That's true. No one ever stays in one or two."

Okay. So each cabin had a different god, like a mascot.

Twelve cabins for the twelve Olympians. But why would some be empty?

I stopped in front of the first cabin on the left, cabin three.

It wasn't high and mighty like cabin one, but long and low and solid. The outer walls were of rough gray stone studded with pieces of seashell and coral, as if the slabs had been hewn straight from the bottom of the ocean floor. I peeked inside the open doorway and Chiron said, "Oh, I wouldn't do that!"

Before he could pull me back, I caught the salty scent of the interior, like the wind on the shore at Montauk. The interior walls glowed like abalone. There were six empty bunk beds with silk sheets turned down. But there was no sign anyone had ever slept there. The place felt so sad and lonely, I was glad when Chiron put his hand on my shoulder and said, "Come along, Percy."

Most of the other cabins were crowded with campers.

Number five was bright red—a real nasty paint job, as if the color had been splashed on with buckets and fists. The roof was lined with barbed wire. A stuffed wild boar's head hung over the doorway, and its eyes seemed to follow me. Inside I could see a bunch of mean-looking kids, both girls and boys, arm wrestling and arguing with each other while rock music blared. The loudest was a girl maybe thirteen or fourteen. She wore a size XXXL CAMP HALF-BLOOD T-shirt under a camouflage jacket. She zeroed in on me and gave me an evil sneer. She reminded me of Nancy Bobofit, though the camper girl was much bigger and tougher looking, and her hair was long and stringy, and brown instead of red.

I kept walking, trying to stay clear of Chiron's hooves. "We haven't seen any other centaurs," I observed.

"No," said Chiron sadly. "My kinsmen are a wild and barbaric folk, I'm afraid. You might encounter them in the wilderness, or at major sporting events. But you won't see any here."

"You said your name was Chiron. Are you really . . ."

He smiled down at me. "*The* Chiron from the stories? Trainer of Hercules and all that? Yes, Percy, I am."

"But, shouldn't you be dead?"

Chiron paused, as if the question intrigued him. "I honestly don't know about *should* be. The truth is, I *can't* be dead. You see, eons ago the gods granted my wish. I could continue the work I loved. I could be a teacher of heroes as long as humanity needed me. I gained much from that wish . . . and I gave up much. But I'm still here, so I can only assume I'm still needed."

I thought about being a teacher for three thousand years. It wouldn't have made my Top Ten Things to Wish For list.

"Doesn't it ever get boring?"

"No, no," he said. "Horribly depressing, at times, but never boring."

"Why depressing?"

Chiron seemed to turn hard of hearing again.

"Oh, look," he said. "Annabeth is waiting for us."

* * *

The blond girl I'd met at the Big House was reading a book in front of the last cabin on the left, number eleven.

When we reached her, she looked me over critically, like she was still thinking about how much I drooled.

I tried to see what she was reading, but I couldn't make out the title. I thought my dyslexia was acting up. Then I realized the title wasn't even English. The letters looked Greek to me. I mean, literally Greek. There were pictures of temples and statues and different kinds of columns, like those in an architecture book.

"Annabeth," Chiron said, "I have masters' archery class at noon. Would you take Percy from here?"

"Yes, sir."

"Cabin eleven," Chiron told me, gesturing toward the doorway. "Make yourself at home."

Out of all the cabins, eleven looked the most like a regular old summer camp cabin, with the emphasis on *old*. The threshold was worn down, the brown paint peeling. Over the doorway was one of those doctor's symbols, a winged pole with two snakes wrapped around it. What did they call it . . . ? A caduceus.

Inside, it was packed with people, both boys and girls, way more than the number of bunk beds. Sleeping bags were spread all over on the floor. It looked like a gym where the Red Cross had set up an evacuation center.

Chiron didn't go in. The door was too low for him. But when the campers saw him they all stood and bowed respectfully.

"Well, then," Chiron said. "Good luck, Percy. I'll see you at dinner."

He galloped away toward the archery range.

I stood in the doorway, looking at the kids. They weren't bowing anymore. They were staring at me, sizing me up. I knew this routine. I'd gone through it at enough schools.

"Well?" Annabeth prompted. "Go on."

So naturally I tripped coming in the door and made a total fool of myself. There were some snickers from the campers, but none of them said anything.

Annabeth announced, "Percy Jackson, meet cabin eleven."

"Regular or undetermined?" somebody asked.

I didn't know what to say, but Annabeth said, "Undetermined."

Everybody groaned.

A guy who was a little older than the rest came forward. "Now, now, campers. That's what we're here for. Welcome, Percy. You can have that spot on the floor, right over there."

The guy was about nineteen, and he looked pretty cool. He was tall and muscular, with short-cropped sandy hair and a friendly smile. He wore an orange tank top, cutoffs, sandals, and a leather necklace with five different-colored clay beads. The only thing unsettling about his appearance was a thick white scar that ran from just beneath his right eye to his jaw, like an old knife slash.

"This is Luke," Annabeth said, and her voice sounded different somehow. I glanced over and could've sworn she was blushing. She saw me looking, and her expression hardened again. "He's your counselor for now."

"For now?" I asked.

"You're undetermined," Luke explained patiently. "They don't know what cabin to put you in, so you're here. Cabin eleven takes all newcomers, all visitors. Naturally, we would. Hermes, our patron, is the god of travelers."

I looked at the tiny section of floor they'd given me. I had nothing to put there to mark it as my own, no luggage, no clothes, no sleeping bag. Just the Minotaur's horn. I thought about setting that down, but then I remembered that Hermes was also the god of thieves.

I looked around at the campers' faces, some sullen and suspicious, some grinning stupidly, some eyeing me as if they were waiting for a chance to pick my pockets.

"How long will I be here?" I asked.

"Good question," Luke said. "Until you're determined."

"How long will that take?"

The campers all laughed.

"Come on," Annabeth told me. "I'll show you the volleyball court."

"I've already seen it."

"Come on."

She grabbed my wrist and dragged me outside. I could hear the kids of cabin eleven laughing behind me.

When we were a few feet away, Annabeth said, "Jackson, you have to do better than that."

"What?"

She rolled her eyes and mumbled under her breath, "I can't believe I thought you were the one."

"What's your problem?" I was getting angry now. "All I know is, I kill some bull guy—"

"Don't talk like that!" Annabeth told me. "You know how many kids at this camp wish they'd had your chance?"

"To get killed?"

"To fight the Minotaur! What do you think we train for?"

I shook my head. "Look, if the thing I fought really was *the* Minotaur, the same one in the stories . . ."

"Yes."

"Then there's only one."

"Yes."

"And he died, like, a gajillion years ago, right? Theseus killed him in the labyrinth. So . . ."

"Monsters don't die, Percy. They can be killed. But they don't die."

"Oh, thanks. That clears it up."

"They don't have souls, like you and me. You can dispel them for a while, maybe even for a whole lifetime if you're lucky. But they are primal forces. Chiron calls them archetypes. Eventually, they re-form."

I thought about Mrs. Dodds. "You mean if I killed one, accidentally, with a sword—"

"The Fur . . . I mean, your math teacher. That's right. She's still out there. You just made her very, very mad."

"How did you know about Mrs. Dodds?"

"You talk in your sleep."

"You almost called her something. A Fury? They're Hades' torturers, right?"

Annabeth glanced nervously at the ground, as if she expected it to open up and swallow her. "You shouldn't call them by name, even here. We call them the Kindly Ones, if we have to speak of them at all."

"Look, is there anything we *can* say without it thundering?" I sounded whiny, even to myself, but right then I didn't care. "Why do I have to stay in cabin eleven, anyway? Why is everybody so crowded together? There are plenty of empty bunks right over there."

I pointed to the first few cabins, and Annabeth turned pale. "You don't just choose a cabin, Percy. It depends on who your parents are. Or . . . your parent."

She stared at me, waiting for me to get it.

"My mom is Sally Jackson," I said. "She works at the candy store in Grand Central Station. At least, she used to."

"I'm sorry about your mom, Percy. But that's not what I mean. I'm talking about your other parent. Your dad."

"He's dead. I never knew him."

Annabeth sighed. Clearly, she'd had this conversation before with other kids. "Your father's not dead, Percy."

"How can you say that? You know him?"

"No, of course not."

"Then how can you say—"

"Because I know *you*. You wouldn't be here if you weren't one of us."

"You don't know anything about me."

"No?" She raised an eyebrow. "I bet you moved around

[87]

from school to school. I bet you were kicked out of a lot of them."

"How—"

"Diagnosed with dyslexia. Probably ADHD, too."

I tried to swallow my embarrassment. "What does that have to do with anything?"

"Taken together, it's almost a sure sign. The letters float off the page when you read, right? That's because your mind is hardwired for ancient Greek. And the ADHD—you're impulsive, can't sit still in the classroom. That's your battle-field reflexes. In a real fight, they'd keep you alive. As for the attention problems, that's because you see too much, Percy, not too little. Your senses are better than a regular mortal's. Of course the teachers want you medicated. Most of them are monsters. They don't want you seeing them for what they are."

"You sound like . . . you went through the same thing?"

"Most of the kids here did. If you weren't like us, you couldn't have survived the Minotaur, much less the ambrosia and nectar."

"Ambrosia and nectar."

"The food and drink we were giving you to make you better. That stuff would've killed a normal kid. It would've turned your blood to fire and your bones to sand and you'd be dead. Face it. You're a half-blood."

A half-blood.

I was reeling with so many questions I didn't know where to start.

Then a husky voice yelled, "Well! A newbie!"

I looked over. The big girl from the ugly red cabin was sauntering toward us. She had three other girls behind her, all big and ugly and mean looking like her, all wearing camo jackets.

"Clarisse," Annabeth sighed. "Why don't you go polish your spear or something?"

"Sure, Miss Princess," the big girl said. "So I can run you through with it Friday night."

"*Erre es korakas!*" Annabeth said, which I somehow understood was Greek for 'Go to the crows!' though I had a feeling it was a worse curse than it sounded. "You don't stand a chance."

"We'll pulverize you," Clarisse said, but her eye twitched. Perhaps she wasn't sure she could follow through on the threat. She turned toward me. "Who's this little runt?"

"Percy Jackson," Annabeth said, "meet Clarisse, Daughter of Ares."

I blinked. "Like . . . the war god?"

Clarisse sneered. "You got a problem with that?"

"No," I said, recovering my wits. "It explains the bad smell."

Clarisse growled. "We got an initiation ceremony for newbies, Prissy."

"Percy."

"Whatever. Come on, I'll show you."

"Clarisse—" Annabeth tried to say.

"Stay out of it, wise girl."

Annabeth looked pained, but she did stay out of it, and

I didn't really want her help. I was the new kid. I had to earn my own rep.

I handed Annabeth my minotaur horn and got ready to fight, but before I knew it, Clarisse had me by the neck and was dragging me toward a cinder-block building that I knew immediately was the bathroom.

I was kicking and punching. I'd been in plenty of fights before, but this big girl Clarisse had hands like iron. She dragged me into the girls' bathroom. There was a line of toilets on one side and a line of shower stalls down the other. It smelled just like any public bathroom, and I was thinking—as much as I *could* think with Clarisse ripping my hair out—that if this place belonged to the gods, they should've been able to afford classier johns.

Clarisse's friends were all laughing, and I was trying to find the strength I'd used to fight the Minotaur, but it just wasn't there.

"Like he's 'Big Three' material," Clarisse said as she pushed me toward one of the toilets. "Yeah, right. Minotaur probably fell over laughing, he was so stupid looking."

Her friends snickered.

Annabeth stood in the corner, watching through her fingers.

Clarisse bent me over on my knees and started pushing my head toward the toilet bowl. It reeked like rusted pipes and, well, like what goes into toilets. I strained to keep my head up. I was looking at the scummy water, thinking, I will not go into that. I won't.

Then something happened. I felt a tug in the pit of my stomach. I heard the plumbing rumble, the pipes shudder. Clarisse's grip on my hair loosened. Water shot out of the toilet, making an arc straight over my head, and the next thing I knew, I was sprawled on the bathroom tiles with Clarisse screaming behind me.

I turned just as water blasted out of the toilet again, hitting Clarisse straight in the face so hard it pushed her down onto her butt. The water stayed on her like the spray from a fire hose, pushing her backward into a shower stall.

She struggled, gasping, and her friends started coming toward her. But then the other toilets exploded, too, and six more streams of toilet water blasted them back. The showers acted up, too, and together all the fixtures sprayed the camouflage girls right out of the bathroom, spinning them around like pieces of garbage being washed away.

As soon as they were out the door, I felt the tug in my gut lessen, and the water shut off as quickly as it had started.

The entire bathroom was flooded. Annabeth hadn't been spared. She was dripping wet, but she hadn't been pushed out the door. She was standing in exactly the same place, staring at me in shock.

I looked down and realized I was sitting in the only dry spot in the whole room. There was a circle of dry floor around me. I didn't have one drop of water on my clothes. Nothing.

I stood up, my legs shaky.

Annabeth said, "How did you . . ."

"I don't know."

We walked to the door. Outside, Clarisse and her friends were sprawled in the mud, and a bunch of other campers had gathered around to gawk. Clarisse's hair was flattened across her face. Her camouflage jacket was sopping and she smelled like sewage. She gave me a look of absolute hatred. "You are dead, new boy. You are totally dead."

I probably should have let it go, but I said, "You want to gargle with toilet water again, Clarisse? Close your mouth."

Her friends had to hold her back. They dragged her toward cabin five, while the other campers made way to avoid her flailing feet.

Annabeth stared at me. I couldn't tell whether she was just grossed out or angry at me for dousing her.

"What?" I demanded. "What are you thinking?"

"I'm thinking," she said, "that I want you on my team for capture the flag."

SEVEN

MY DINNER GOES UP
IN SMOKE

Word of the bathroom incident spread immediately. Wherever I went, campers pointed at me and murmured something about toilet water. Or maybe they were just staring at Annabeth, who was still pretty much dripping wet.

She showed me a few more places: the metal shop (where kids were forging their own swords), the arts-and-crafts room (where satyrs were sandblasting a giant marble statue of a goat-man), and the climbing wall, which actually consisted of two facing walls that shook violently, dropped boulders, sprayed lava, and clashed together if you didn't get to the top fast enough.

Finally we returned to the canoeing lake, where the trail led back to the cabins.

"I've got training to do," Annabeth said flatly. "Dinner's at seven-thirty. Just follow your cabin to the mess hall."

"Annabeth, I'm sorry about the toilets."

"Whatever."

"It wasn't my fault."

She looked at me skeptically, and I realized it *was* my fault. I'd made water shoot out of the bathroom fixtures. I didn't understand how. But the toilets had responded to me. I had become one with the plumbing.

"You need to talk to the Oracle," Annabeth said.

"Who?"

"Not who. What. The Oracle. I'll ask Chiron."

I stared into the lake, wishing somebody would give me a straight answer for once.

I wasn't expecting anybody to be looking back at me from the bottom, so my heart skipped a beat when I noticed two teenage girls sitting cross-legged at the base of the pier, about twenty feet below. They wore blue jeans and shimmering green T-shirts, and their brown hair floated loose around their shoulders as minnows darted in and out. They smiled and waved as if I were a long-lost friend.

I didn't know what else to do. I waved back.

"Don't encourage them," Annabeth warned. "Naiads are terrible flirts."

"Naiads," I repeated, feeling completely overwhelmed. "That's it. I want to go home now."

Annabeth frowned. "Don't you get it, Percy? You *are* home. This is the only safe place on earth for kids like us."

"You mean, mentally disturbed kids?"

"I mean *not human*. Not totally human, anyway. Half-human."

"Half-human and half-what?"

"I think you know."

I didn't want to admit it, but I was afraid I did. I felt a tingling in my limbs, a sensation I sometimes felt when my mom talked about my dad.

"God," I said. "Half-god."

Annabeth nodded. "Your father isn't dead, Percy. He's one of the Olympians."

"That's . . . crazy."

"Is it? What's the most common thing gods did in the old stories? They ran around falling in love with humans and having kids with them. Do you think they've changed their habits in the last few millennia?"

"But those are just—" I almost said *myths* again. Then I remembered Chiron's warning that in two thousand years, *I* might be considered a myth. "But if all the kids here are half-gods—"

"Demigods," Annabeth said. "That's the official term. Or half-bloods."

"Then who's your dad?"

Her hands tightened around the pier railing. I got the feeling I'd just trespassed on a sensitive subject.

"My dad is a professor at West Point," she said. "I haven't seen him since I was very small. He teaches American history."

"He's human."

"What? You assume it has to be a male god who finds a human female attractive? How sexist is that?"

"Who's your mom, then?"

"Cabin six."

"Meaning?"

Annabeth straightened. "Athena. Goddess of wisdom and battle."

Okay, I thought. Why not?

"And my dad?"

"Undetermined," Annabeth said, "like I told you before. Nobody knows."

"Except my mother. She knew."

"Maybe not, Percy. Gods don't always reveal their identities."

"My dad would have. He loved her."

Annabeth gave me a cautious look. She didn't want to burst my bubble. "Maybe you're right. Maybe he'll send a sign. That's the only way to know for sure: your father has to send you a sign claiming you as his son. Sometimes it happens."

"You mean sometimes it doesn't?"

Annabeth ran her palm along the rail. "The gods are busy. They have a lot of kids and they don't always . . . Well, sometimes they don't care about us, Percy. They ignore us."

I thought about some of the kids I'd seen in the Hermes cabin, teenagers who looked sullen and depressed, as if they were waiting for a call that would never come. I'd known kids like that at Yancy Academy, shuffled off to boarding school by rich parents who didn't have the time to deal with them. But gods should behave better.

"So I'm stuck here," I said. "That's it? For the rest of my life?"

"It depends," Annabeth said. "Some campers only stay the summer. If you're a child of Aphrodite or Demeter, you're probably not a real powerful force. The monsters might ignore you, so you can get by with a few months of summer training and live in the mortal world the rest of the year. But for some of us, it's too dangerous to leave. We're year-rounders. In the mortal world, we attract monsters. They sense us. They come to challenge us. Most of the time, they'll ignore us until we're old enough to cause trouble—about ten or eleven years old, but after that, most demigods either make their way here, or they get killed off. A few manage to survive in the outside world and become famous. Believe me, if I told you the names, you'd know them. Some don't even realize they're demigods. But very, very few are like that."

"So monsters can't get in here?"

Annabeth shook her head. "Not unless they're intentionally stocked in the woods or specially summoned by somebody on the inside."

"Why would anybody want to summon a monster?"

"Practice fights. Practical jokes."

"Practical jokes?"

"The point is, the borders are sealed to keep mortals and monsters out. From the outside, mortals look into the valley and see nothing unusual, just a strawberry farm."

"So . . . you're a year-rounder?"

Annabeth nodded. From under the collar of her T-shirt she pulled a leather necklace with five clay beads of different colors. It was just like Luke's, except Annabeth's also had a big gold ring strung on it, like a college ring.

"I've been here since I was seven," she said. "Every August, on the last day of summer session, you get a bead for surviving another year. I've been here longer than most of the counselors, and they're all in college."

"Why did you come so young?"

She twisted the ring on her necklace. "None of your business."

"Oh." I stood there for a minute in uncomfortable silence. "So . . . I could just walk out of here right now if I wanted to?"

"It would be suicide, but you could, with Mr. D's or Chiron's permission. But they wouldn't give permission until the end of the summer session unless . . ."

"Unless?"

"You were granted a quest. But that hardly ever happens. The last time . . ."

Her voice trailed off. I could tell from her tone that the last time hadn't gone well.

"Back in the sick room," I said, "when you were feeding me that stuff—"

"Ambrosia."

"Yeah. You asked me something about the summer solstice."

Annabeth's shoulders tensed. "So you *do* know something?"

"Well . . . no. Back at my old school, I overheard Grover and Chiron talking about it. Grover mentioned the summer solstice. He said something like we didn't have much time, because of the deadline. What did that mean?"

She clenched her fists. "I wish I knew. Chiron and the satyrs, they know, but they won't tell me. Something is wrong in Olympus, something pretty major. Last time I was there, everything seemed so *normal*."

"You've been to Olympus?"

"Some of us year-rounders—Luke and Clarisse and I and a few others—we took a field trip during winter solstice. That's when the gods have their big annual council."

"But . . . how did you get there?"

"The Long Island Railroad, of course. You get off at Penn Station. Empire State Building, special elevator to the six hundredth floor." She looked at me like she was sure I must know this already. "You *are* a New Yorker, right?"

"Oh, sure." As far as I knew, there were only a hundred and two floors in the Empire State Building, but I decided not to point that out.

"Right after we visited," Annabeth continued, "the weather got weird, as if the gods had started fighting. A couple of times since, I've overheard satyrs talking. The best I can figure out is that something important was stolen. And if it isn't returned by summer solstice, there's going to be trouble. When you came, I was hoping . . . I mean— Athena can get along with just about anybody, except for Ares. And of course she's got the rivalry with Poseidon. But, I mean, aside from that, I thought we could work together. I thought you might know something."

I shook my head. I wished I could help her, but I felt too hungry and tired and mentally overloaded to ask any more questions.

"I've got to get a quest," Annabeth muttered to herself. "I'm *not* too young. If they would just tell me the problem . . ."

I could smell barbecue smoke coming from somewhere

nearby. Annabeth must've heard my stomach growl. She told me to go on, she'd catch me later. I left her on the pier, tracing her finger across the rail as if drawing a battle plan.

Back at cabin eleven, everybody was talking and horsing around, waiting for dinner. For the first time, I noticed that a lot of the campers had similar features: sharp noses, upturned eyebrows, mischievous smiles. They were the kind of kids that teachers would peg as troublemakers. Thankfully, nobody paid much attention to me as I walked over to my spot on the floor and plopped down with my minotaur horn.

The counselor, Luke, came over. He had the Hermes family resemblance, too. It was marred by that scar on his right cheek, but his smile was intact.

"Found you a sleeping bag," he said. "And here, I stole you some toiletries from the camp store."

I couldn't tell if he was kidding about the stealing part. I said, "Thanks."

"No prob." Luke sat next to me, pushed his back against the wall. "Tough first day?"

"I don't belong here," I said. "I don't even believe in gods."

"Yeah," he said. "That's how we all started. Once you start believing in them? It doesn't get any easier."

The bitterness in his voice surprised me, because Luke seemed like a pretty easygoing guy. He looked like he could handle just about anything.

"So your dad is Hermes?" I asked.

He pulled a switchblade out of his back pocket, and for a second I thought he was going to gut me, but he just scraped the mud off the sole of his sandal. "Yeah. Hermes."

"The wing-footed messenger guy."

"That's him. Messengers. Medicine. Travelers, merchants, thieves. Anybody who uses the roads. That's why you're here, enjoying cabin eleven's hospitality. Hermes isn't picky about who he sponsors."

I figured Luke didn't mean to call me a nobody. He just had a lot on his mind.

"You ever meet your dad?" I asked.

"Once."

I waited, thinking that if he wanted to tell me, he'd tell me. Apparently, he didn't. I wondered if the story had anything to do with how he got his scar.

Luke looked up and managed a smile. "Don't worry about it, Percy. The campers here, they're mostly good people. After all, we're extended family, right? We take care of each other."

He seemed to understand how lost I felt, and I was grateful for that, because an older guy like him—even if he was a counselor—should've steered clear of an uncool middle-schooler like me. But Luke had welcomed me into the cabin. He'd even stolen me some toiletries, which was the nicest thing anybody had done for me all day.

I decided to ask him my last big question, the one that had been bothering me all afternoon. "Clarisse, from Ares, was joking about me being 'Big Three' material. Then

Annabeth . . . twice, she said I might be 'the one.' She said I should talk to the Oracle. What was that all about?"

Luke folded his knife. "I hate prophecies."

"What do you mean?"

His face twitched around the scar. "Let's just say I messed things up for everybody else. The last two years, ever since my trip to the Garden of the Hesperides went sour, Chiron hasn't allowed any more quests. Annabeth's been dying to get out into the world. She pestered Chiron so much he finally told her he already knew her fate. He'd had a prophecy from the Oracle. He wouldn't tell her the whole thing, but he said Annabeth wasn't destined to go on a quest yet. She had to wait until . . . somebody special came to the camp."

"Somebody special?"

"Don't worry about it, kid," Luke said. "Annabeth wants to think every new camper who comes through here is the omen she's been waiting for. Now, come on, it's dinnertime."

The moment he said it, a horn blew in the distance. Somehow, I knew it was a conch shell, even though I'd never heard one before.

Luke yelled, "Eleven, fall in!"

The whole cabin, about twenty of us, filed into the commons yard. We lined up in order of seniority, so of course I was dead last. Campers came from the other cabins, too, except for the three empty cabins at the end, and cabin eight, which had looked normal in the daytime, but was now starting to glow silver as the sun went down.

We marched up the hill to the mess hall pavilion. Satyrs joined us from the meadow. Naiads emerged from the canoeing lake. A few other girls came out of the woods—and when I say out of the woods, I mean *straight* out of the woods. I saw one girl, about nine or ten years old, melt from the side of a maple tree and come skipping up the hill.

In all, there were maybe a hundred campers, a few dozen satyrs, and a dozen assorted wood nymphs and naiads.

At the pavilion, torches blazed around the marble columns. A central fire burned in a bronze brazier the size of a bathtub. Each cabin had its own table, covered in white cloth trimmed in purple. Four of the tables were empty, but cabin eleven's was way overcrowded. I had to squeeze on to the edge of a bench with half my butt hanging off.

I saw Grover sitting at table twelve with Mr. D, a few satyrs, and a couple of plump blond boys who looked just like Mr. D. Chiron stood to one side, the picnic table being way too small for a centaur.

Annabeth sat at table six with a bunch of serious-looking athletic kids, all with her gray eyes and honey-blond hair.

Clarisse sat behind me at Ares's table. She'd apparently gotten over being hosed down, because she was laughing and belching right alongside her friends.

Finally, Chiron pounded his hoof against the marble floor of the pavilion, and everybody fell silent. He raised a glass. "To the gods!"

Everybody else raised their glasses. "To the gods!"

Wood nymphs came forward with platters of food:

grapes, apples, strawberries, cheese, fresh bread, and yes, barbecue! My glass was empty, but Luke said, "Speak to it. Whatever you want—nonalcoholic, of course."

I said, "Cherry Coke."

The glass filled with sparkling caramel liquid.

Then I had an idea. "*Blue* Cherry Coke."

The soda turned a violent shade of cobalt.

I took a cautious sip. Perfect.

I drank a toast to my mother.

She's not gone, I told myself. Not permanently, anyway. She's in the Underworld. And if that's a real place, then someday . . .

"Here you go, Percy," Luke said, handing me a platter of smoked brisket.

I loaded my plate and was about to take a big bite when I noticed everybody getting up, carrying their plates toward the fire in the center of the pavilion. I wondered if they were going for dessert or something.

"Come on," Luke told me.

As I got closer, I saw that everyone was taking a portion of their meal and dropping it into the fire, the ripest strawberry, the juiciest slice of beef, the warmest, most buttery roll.

Luke murmured in my ear, "Burnt offerings for the gods. They like the smell."

"You're kidding."

His look warned me not to take this lightly, but I couldn't help wondering why an immortal, all-powerful being would like the smell of burning food.

Luke approached the fire, bowed his head, and tossed in a cluster of fat red grapes. "Hermes."

I was next.

I wished I knew what god's name to say.

Finally, I made a silent plea. *Whoever you are, tell me. Please.*

I scraped a big slice of brisket into the flames.

When I caught a whiff of the smoke, I didn't gag.

It smelled nothing like burning food. It smelled of hot chocolate and fresh-baked brownies, hamburgers on the grill and wildflowers, and a hundred other good things that shouldn't have gone well together, but did. I could almost believe the gods could live off that smoke.

When everybody had returned to their seats and finished eating their meals, Chiron pounded his hoof again for our attention.

Mr. D got up with a huge sigh. "Yes, I suppose I'd better say hello to all you brats. Well, hello. Our activities director, Chiron, says the next capture the flag is Friday. Cabin five presently holds the laurels."

A bunch of ugly cheering rose from the Ares table.

"Personally," Mr. D continued, "I couldn't care less, but congratulations. Also, I should tell you that we have a new camper today. Peter Johnson."

Chiron murmured something.

"Er, Percy Jackson," Mr. D corrected. "That's right. Hurrah, and all that. Now run along to your silly campfire. Go on."

Everybody cheered. We all headed down toward the amphitheater, where Apollo's cabin led a sing-along. We sang camp songs about the gods and ate s'mores and joked around, and the funny thing was, I didn't feel that anyone was staring at me anymore. I felt that I was home.

Later in the evening, when the sparks from the campfire were curling into a starry sky, the conch horn blew again, and we all filed back to our cabins. I didn't realize how exhausted I was until I collapsed on my borrowed sleeping bag.

My fingers curled around the Minotaur's horn. I thought about my mom, but I had good thoughts: her smile, the bedtime stories she would read me when I was a kid, the way she would tell me not to let the bedbugs bite.

When I closed my eyes, I fell asleep instantly.

That was my first day at Camp Half-Blood.

I wish I'd known how briefly I would get to enjoy my new home.

EIGHT

WE CAPTURE A FLAG

The next few days I settled into a routine that felt almost normal, if you don't count the fact that I was getting lessons from satyrs, nymphs, and a centaur.

Each morning I took Ancient Greek from Annabeth, and we talked about the gods and goddesses in the present tense, which was kind of weird. I discovered Annabeth was right about my dyslexia: Ancient Greek wasn't that hard for me to read. At least, no harder than English. After a couple of mornings, I could stumble through a few lines of Homer without too much headache.

The rest of the day, I'd rotate through outdoor activities, looking for something I was good at. Chiron tried to teach me archery, but we found out pretty quick I wasn't any good with a bow and arrow. He didn't complain, even when he had to desnag a stray arrow out of his tail.

Foot racing? No good either. The wood-nymph instructors left me in the dust. They told me not to worry about it. They'd had centuries of practice running away from lovesick gods. But still, it was a little humiliating to be slower than a tree.

And wrestling? Forget it. Every time I got on the mat, Clarisse would pulverize me.

"There's more where that came from, punk," she'd mumble in my ear.

The only thing I really excelled at was canoeing, and that wasn't the kind of heroic skill people expected to see from the kid who had beaten the Minotaur.

I knew the senior campers and counselors were watching me, trying to decide who my dad was, but they weren't having an easy time of it. I wasn't as strong as the Ares kids, or as good at archery as the Apollo kids. I didn't have Hephaestus's skill with metalwork or—gods forbid—Dionysus's way with vine plants. Luke told me I might be a child of Hermes, a kind of jack-of-all-trades, master of none. But I got the feeling he was just trying to make me feel better. He really didn't know what to make of me either.

Despite all that, I liked camp. I got used to the morning fog over the beach, the smell of hot strawberry fields in the afternoon, even the weird noises of monsters in the woods at night. I would eat dinner with cabin eleven, scrape part of my meal into the fire, and try to feel some connection to my real dad. Nothing came. Just that warm feeling I'd always had, like the memory of his smile. I tried not to think too much about my mom, but I kept wondering: if gods and monsters were real, if all this magical stuff was possible, surely there was some way to save her, to bring her back. . . .

I started to understand Luke's bitterness and how he seemed to resent his father, Hermes. So okay, maybe gods had important things to do. But couldn't they call once in a while, or thunder, or something? Dionysus could make Diet Coke appear out of thin air. Why couldn't my dad, whoever he was, make a phone appear?

Thursday afternoon, three days after I'd arrived at Camp Half-Blood, I had my first sword-fighting lesson. Everybody from cabin eleven gathered in the big circular arena, where Luke would be our instructor.

We started with basic stabbing and slashing, using some straw-stuffed dummies in Greek armor. I guess I did okay. At least, I understood what I was supposed to do and my reflexes were good.

The problem was, I couldn't find a blade that felt right in my hands. Either they were too heavy, or too light, or too long. Luke tried his best to fix me up, but he agreed that none of the practice blades seemed to work for me.

We moved on to dueling in pairs. Luke announced he would be my partner, since this was my first time.

"Good luck," one of the campers told me. "Luke's the best swordsman in the last three hundred years."

"Maybe he'll go easy on me," I said.

The camper snorted.

Luke showed me thrusts and parries and shield blocks the hard way. With every swipe, I got a little more battered and bruised. "Keep your guard up, Percy," he'd say, then whap me in the ribs with the flat of his blade. "No, not that far up!" *Whap!* "Lunge!" *Whap!* "Now, back!" *Whap!*

By the time he called a break, I was soaked in sweat. Everybody swarmed the drinks cooler. Luke poured ice water on his head, which looked like such a good idea, I did the same.

Instantly, I felt better. Strength surged back into my arms. The sword didn't feel so awkward.

"Okay, everybody circle up!" Luke ordered. "If Percy doesn't mind, I want to give you a little demo."

Great, I thought. Let's all watch Percy get pounded.

The Hermes guys gathered around. They were suppressing smiles. I figured they'd been in my shoes before and couldn't wait to see how Luke used me for a punching bag. He told everybody he was going to demonstrate a disarming technique: how to twist the enemy's blade with the flat of your own sword so that he had no choice but to drop his weapon.

"This is difficult," he stressed. "I've had it used against me. No laughing at Percy, now. Most swordsmen have to work years to master this technique."

He demonstrated the move on me in slow motion. Sure enough, the sword clattered out of my hand.

"Now in real time," he said, after I'd retrieved my weapon. "We keep sparring until one of us pulls it off. Ready, Percy?"

I nodded, and Luke came after me. Somehow, I kept him from getting a shot at the hilt of my sword. My senses opened up. I saw his attacks coming. I countered. I stepped forward and tried a thrust of my own. Luke deflected it easily, but I saw a change in his face. His eyes narrowed, and he started to press me with more force.

The sword grew heavy in my hand. The balance wasn't

right. I knew it was only a matter of seconds before Luke took me down, so I figured, What the heck?

I tried the disarming maneuver.

My blade hit the base of Luke's and I twisted, putting my whole weight into a downward thrust.

Clang.

Luke's sword rattled against the stones. The tip of my blade was an inch from his undefended chest.

The other campers were silent.

I lowered my sword. "Um, sorry."

For a moment, Luke was too stunned to speak.

"Sorry?" His scarred face broke into a grin. "By the gods, Percy, why are you sorry? Show me that again!"

I didn't want to. The short burst of manic energy had completely abandoned me. But Luke insisted.

This time, there was no contest. The moment our swords connected, Luke hit my hilt and sent my weapon skidding across the floor.

After a long pause, somebody in the audience said, "Beginner's luck?"

Luke wiped the sweat off his brow. He appraised at me with an entirely new interest. "Maybe," he said. "But I wonder what Percy could do with a balanced sword. . . ."

Friday afternoon, I was sitting with Grover at the lake, resting from a near-death experience on the climbing wall. Grover had scampered to the top like a mountain goat, but the lava had almost gotten me. My shirt had smoking holes in it. The hairs had been singed off my forearms.

We sat on the pier, watching the naiads do underwater basket-weaving, until I got up the nerve to ask Grover how his conversation had gone with Mr. D.

His face turned a sickly shade of yellow.

"Fine," he said. "Just great."

"So your career's still on track?"

He glanced at me nervously. "Chiron t-told you I want a searcher's license?"

"Well . . . no." I had no idea what a searcher's license was, but it didn't seem like the right time to ask. "He just said you had big plans, you know . . . and that you needed credit for completing a keeper's assignment. So did you get it?"

Grover looked down at the naiads. "Mr. D suspended judgment. He said I hadn't failed or succeeded with you yet, so our fates were still tied together. If you got a quest and I went along to protect you, and we both came back alive, then maybe he'd consider the job complete."

My spirits lifted. "Well, that's not so bad, right?"

"*Blaa-ha-ha!* He might as well have transferred me to stable-cleaning duty. The chances of you getting a quest . . . and even if you did, why would you want *me* along?"

"Of course I'd want you along!"

Grover stared glumly into the water. "Basket-weaving . . . Must be nice to have a useful skill."

I tried to reassure him that he had lots of talents, but that just made him look more miserable. We talked about canoeing and swordplay for a while, then debated the pros and cons of the different gods. Finally, I asked him about the four empty cabins.

"Number eight, the silver one, belongs to Artemis," he said. "She vowed to be a maiden forever. So of course, no kids. The cabin is, you know, honorary. If she didn't have one, she'd be mad."

"Yeah, okay. But the other three, the ones at the end. Are those the Big Three?"

Grover tensed. We were getting close to a touchy subject. "No. One of them, number two, is Hera's," he said. "That's another honorary thing. She's the goddess of marriage, so of course she wouldn't go around having affairs with mortals. That's her husband's job. When we say the Big Three, we mean the three powerful brothers, the sons of Kronos."

"Zeus, Poseidon, Hades."

"Right. You know. After the great battle with the Titans, they took over the world from their dad and drew lots to decide who got what."

"Zeus got the sky," I remembered. "Poseidon the sea, Hades the Underworld."

"Uh-huh."

"But Hades doesn't have a cabin here."

"No. He doesn't have a throne on Olympus, either. He sort of does his own thing down in the Underworld. If he did have a cabin here . . ." Grover shuddered. "Well, it wouldn't be pleasant. Let's leave it at that."

"But Zeus and Poseidon—they both had, like, a bazillion kids in the myths. Why are their cabins empty?"

Grover shifted his hooves uncomfortably. "About sixty years ago, after World War II, the Big Three agreed they wouldn't sire any more heroes. Their children were just too powerful. They were affecting the course of human events too much, causing too much carnage. World War II, you know, that was basically a fight between the sons of Zeus and Poseidon on one side, and the sons of Hades on the other. The winning side, Zeus and Poseidon, made Hades swear an oath with them: no more affairs with mortal women. They all swore on the River Styx."

Thunder boomed.

I said, "That's the most serious oath you can make."

Grover nodded.

"And the brothers kept their word—no kids?"

Grover's face darkened. "Seventeen years ago, Zeus fell off the wagon. There was this TV starlet with a big fluffy eighties hairdo—he just couldn't help himself. When their child was born, a little girl named Thalia . . . well, the River Styx is serious about promises. Zeus himself got off easy because he's immortal, but he brought a terrible fate on his daughter."

"But that isn't fair! It wasn't the little girl's fault."

Grover hesitated. "Percy, children of the Big Three have powers greater than other half-bloods. They have a strong aura, a scent that attracts monsters. When Hades found out about the girl, he wasn't too happy about Zeus breaking his oath. Hades let the worst monsters out of Tartarus to torment Thalia. A satyr was assigned to be her keeper when she was twelve, but there was nothing he could do. He tried to escort her here with a couple of other half-bloods she'd befriended. They almost made it. They got all the way to the top of that hill."

He pointed across the valley, to the pine tree where I'd fought the minotaur. "All three Kindly Ones were after them, along with a hoard of hellhounds. They were about to be overrun when Thalia told her satyr to take the other two half-bloods to safety while she held off the monsters. She was wounded and tired, and she didn't want to live like a hunted animal. The satyr didn't want to leave her, but he couldn't change her mind, and he had to protect the others. So Thalia made her final stand alone, at the top of that hill. As she died, Zeus took pity on her. He turned her into that pine tree. Her spirit still helps protect the borders of the valley. That's why the hill is called Half-Blood Hill."

I stared at the pine in the distance.

The story made me feel hollow, and guilty too. A girl my age had sacrificed herself to save her friends. She had faced a whole army of monsters. Next to that, my victory over the Minotaur didn't seem like much. I wondered, if I'd acted differently, could I have saved my mother?

"Grover," I said, "have heroes really gone on quests to the Underworld?"

"Sometimes," he said. "Orpheus. Hercules. Houdini."

"And have they ever returned somebody from the dead?"

"No. Never. Orpheus came close. . . . Percy, you're not seriously thinking—"

"No," I lied. "I was just wondering. So . . . a satyr is always assigned to guard a demigod?"

Grover studied me warily. I hadn't persuaded him that I'd really dropped the Underworld idea. "Not always. We go undercover to a lot of schools. We try to sniff out the half-bloods who have the makings of great heroes. If we find one with a very strong aura, like a child of the Big Three, we alert Chiron. He tries to keep an eye on them, since they could cause really huge problems."

"And you found me. Chiron said you thought I might be something special."

Grover looked as if I'd just led him into a trap. "I didn't . . . Oh, listen, don't think like that. If you *were*—you know—you'd never *ever* be allowed a quest, and I'd never get my license. You're probably a child of Hermes. Or, maybe even one of the minor gods, like Nemesis, the god of revenge. Don't worry, okay?"

I got the idea he was reassuring himself more than me.

That night after dinner, there was a lot more excitement than usual.

At last, it was time for capture the flag.

When the plates were cleared away, the conch horn sounded and we all stood at our tables.

Campers yelled and cheered as Annabeth and two of her siblings ran into the pavilion carrying a silk banner. It was about ten feet long, glistening gray, with a painting of a barn owl above an olive tree. From the opposite side of the pavilion, Clarisse and her buddies ran in with another banner, of identical size, but gaudy red, painted with a bloody spear and a boar's head.

I turned to Luke and yelled over the noise, "Those are the flags?"

"Yeah."

"Ares and Athena always lead the teams?"

"Not always," he said. "But often."

"So, if another cabin captures one, what do you do—repaint the flag?"

He grinned. "You'll see. First we have to get one."

"Whose side are we on?"

He gave me a sly look, as if he knew something I didn't. The scar on his face made him look almost evil in the torchlight. "We've made a temporary alliance with Athena. Tonight, we get the flag from Ares. And *you* are going to help."

The teams were announced. Athena had made an alliance with Apollo and Hermes, the two biggest cabins. Apparently, privileges had been traded—shower times, chore schedules, the best slots for activities—in order to win support.

Ares had allied themselves with everybody else: Dionysus, Demeter, Aphrodite, and Hephaestus. From what I'd seen, Dionysus's kids were actually good athletes, but there were only two of them. Demeter's kids had the edge with nature skills and outdoor stuff, but they weren't very aggressive. Aphrodite's sons and daughters I wasn't too worried about. They mostly sat out every activity and checked their reflections in the lake and did their hair and gossiped. Hephaestus's kids weren't pretty, and there were only four of them, but they were big and burly from working in the metal shop all day. They might be a problem. That, of course, left Ares's cabin: a dozen of the biggest, ugliest, meanest kids on Long Island, or anywhere else on the planet.

Chiron hammered his hoof on the marble.

"Heroes!" he announced. "You know the rules. The creek is the boundary line. The entire forest is fair game. All magic items are allowed. The banner must be prominently displayed, and have no more than two guards. Prisoners may be disarmed, but may not be bound or gagged. No killing or maiming is allowed. I will serve as referee and battlefield medic. Arm yourselves!"

He spread his hands, and the tables were suddenly covered with equipment: helmets, bronze swords, spears, oxhide shields coated in metal.

"Whoa," I said. "We're really supposed to use these?"

Luke looked at me as if I were crazy. "Unless you want to get skewered by your friends in cabin five. Here—Chiron thought these would fit. You'll be on border patrol."

My shield was the size of an NBA backboard, with a big caduceus in the middle. It weighed about a million pounds. I could have snowboarded on it fine, but I hoped nobody seriously expected me to run fast. My helmet, like all the helmets on Athena's side, had a blue horsehair plume on top. Ares and their allies had red plumes.

Annabeth yelled, "Blue team, forward!"

We cheered and shook our swords and followed her down the path to the south woods. The red team yelled taunts at us as they headed off toward the north.

I managed to catch up with Annabeth without tripping over my equipment. "Hey."

She kept marching.

"So what's the plan?" I asked. "Got any magic items you can loan me?"

Her hand drifted toward her pocket, as if she were afraid I'd stolen something.

"Just watch Clarisse's spear," she said. "You don't want that thing touching you. Otherwise, don't worry. We'll take the banner from Ares. Has Luke given you your job?"

"Border patrol, whatever that means."

"It's easy. Stand by the creek, keep the reds away. Leave the rest to me. Athena always has a plan."

She pushed ahead, leaving me in the dust.

"Okay," I mumbled. "Glad you wanted me on your team."

It was a warm, sticky night. The woods were dark, with fireflies popping in and out of view. Annabeth stationed me next to a little creek that gurgled over some rocks, then she and the rest of the team scattered into the trees.

Standing there alone, with my big blue-feathered helmet and my huge shield, I felt like an idiot. The bronze sword, like all the swords I'd tried so far, seemed balanced wrong. The leather grip pulled on my hand like a bowling ball.

There was no way anybody would actually attack me, would they? I mean, Olympus had to have liability issues, right?

Far away, the conch horn blew. I heard whoops and yells in the woods, the clanking of metal, kids fighting. A blue-plumed ally from Apollo raced past me like a deer, leaped through the creek, and disappeared into enemy territory.

Great, I thought. I'll miss all the fun, as usual.

Then I heard a sound that sent a chill up my spine, a low canine growl, somewhere close by.

I raised my shield instinctively; I had the feeling something was stalking me.

Then the growling stopped. I felt the presence retreating.

On the other side of the creek, the underbrush exploded. Five Ares warriors came yelling and screaming out of the dark.

"Cream the punk!" Clarisse screamed.

Her ugly pig eyes glared through the slits of her helmet. She brandished a five-foot-long spear, its barbed metal tip flickering with red light. Her siblings had only the standard-issue bronze swords—not that that made me feel any better.

They charged across the stream. There was no help in sight. I could run. Or I could defend myself against half the Ares cabin.

I managed to sidestep the first kid's swing, but these guys were not as stupid as the Minotaur. They surrounded me, and Clarisse thrust at me with her spear. My shield deflected the point, but I felt a painful tingling all over my body. My hair stood on end. My shield arm went numb, and the air burned.

Electricity. Her stupid spear was electric. I fell back.

Another Ares guy slammed me in the chest with the butt of his sword and I hit the dirt.

They could've kicked me into jelly, but they were too busy laughing.

"Give him a haircut," Clarisse said. "Grab his hair."

I managed to get to my feet. I raised my sword, but Clarisse slammed it aside with her spear as sparks flew. Now both my arms felt numb.

"Oh, wow," Clarisse said. "I'm scared of this guy. Really scared."

"The flag is that way," I told her. I wanted to sound angry, but I was afraid it didn't come out that way.

"Yeah," one of her siblings said. "But see, we don't care about the flag. We care about a guy who made our cabin look stupid."

"You do that without my help," I told them. It probably wasn't the smartest thing to say.

Two of them came at me. I backed up toward the creek, tried to raise my shield, but Clarisse was too fast. Her spear stuck me straight in the ribs. If I hadn't been wearing an armored breastplate, I would've been shish-ke-babbed. As it was, the electric point just about shocked my teeth out of my mouth. One of her cabinmates slashed his sword across my arm, leaving a good-size cut.

Seeing my own blood made me dizzy—warm and cold at the same time.

"No maiming," I managed to say.

"Oops," the guy said. "Guess I lost my dessert privilege."

He pushed me into the creek and I landed with a splash. They all laughed. I figured as soon as they were through being amused, I would die. But then something happened. The water seemed to wake up my senses, as if I'd just had a bag of my mom's double-espresso jelly beans.

Clarisse and her cabinmates came into the creek to get me, but I stood to meet them. I knew what to do. I swung the flat of my sword against the first guy's head and knocked his helmet clean off. I hit him so hard I could see his eyes vibrating as he crumpled into the water.

Ugly Number Two and Ugly Number Three came at me. I slammed one in the face with my shield and used my sword to shear off the other guy's horsehair plume. Both of them backed up quick. Ugly Number Four didn't look really anxious to attack, but Clarisse kept coming, the point of her spear crackling with energy. As soon as she thrust, I caught the shaft between the edge of my shield and my sword, and I snapped it like a twig.

"Ah!" she screamed. "You idiot! You corpse-breath worm!"

She probably would've said worse, but I smacked her between the eyes with my sword-butt and sent her stumbling backward out of the creek.

Then I heard yelling, elated screams, and I saw Luke racing toward the boundary line with the red team's banner lifted high. He was flanked by a couple of Hermes guys covering his retreat, and a few Apollos behind them, fighting off the Hephaestus kids. The Ares folks got up, and Clarisse muttered a dazed curse.

"A trick!" she shouted. "It was a trick."

They staggered after Luke, but it was too late. Everybody converged on the creek as Luke ran across into friendly territory. Our side exploded into cheers. The red banner shimmered and turned to silver. The boar and spear were replaced with a huge caduceus, the symbol of cabin eleven. Everybody on the blue team picked up Luke and started carrying him around on their shoulders. Chiron cantered out from the woods and blew the conch horn.

The game was over. We'd won.

I was about to join the celebration when Annabeth's voice, right next to me in the creek, said, "Not bad, hero."

I looked, but she wasn't there.

"Where the heck did you learn to fight like that?" she asked. The air shimmered, and she materialized, holding a Yankees baseball cap as if she'd just taken it off her head.

I felt myself getting angry. I wasn't even fazed by the fact that she'd just been invisible. "You set me up," I said. "You put me here because you knew Clarisse would come after me, while you sent Luke around the flank. You had it all figured out."

Annabeth shrugged. "I told you. Athena always, always has a plan."

"A plan to get me pulverized."

"I came as fast as I could. I was about to jump in, but . . ." She shrugged. "You didn't need help."

Then she noticed my wounded arm. "How did you do that?"

"Sword cut," I said. "What do you think?"

"No. It *was* a sword cut. Look at it."

The blood was gone. Where the huge cut had been, there was a long white scratch, and even that was fading. As I watched, it turned into a small scar, and disappeared.

"I—I don't get it," I said.

Annabeth was thinking hard. I could almost see the gears turning. She looked down at my feet, then at Clarisse's broken spear, and said, "Step out of the water, Percy."

"What—"

"Just do it."

I came out of the creek and immediately felt bone tired. My arms started to go numb again. My adrenaline rush left me. I almost fell over, but Annabeth steadied me.

"Oh, Styx," she cursed. "This is *not* good. I didn't want . . . I assumed it would be Zeus. . . ."

Before I could ask what she meant, I heard that canine growl again, but much closer than before. A howl ripped through the forest.

The campers' cheering died instantly. Chiron shouted something in Ancient Greek, which I would realize, only later, I had understood perfectly: *"Stand ready! My bow!"*

Annabeth drew her sword.

There on the rocks just above us was a black hound the size of a rhino, with lava-red eyes and fangs like daggers.

It was looking straight at me.

Nobody moved except Annabeth, who yelled, "Percy, run!"

She tried to step in front of me, but the hound was too fast. It leaped over her—an enormous shadow with teeth—and just as it hit me, as I stumbled backward and felt its razor-sharp claws ripping through my armor, there was a cascade of thwacking sounds, like forty pieces of paper being ripped one after the other. From the hound's neck sprouted a cluster of arrows. The monster fell dead at my feet.

By some miracle, I was still alive. I didn't want to look underneath the ruins of my shredded armor. My chest felt warm and wet, and I knew I was badly cut. Another second, and the monster would've turned me into a hundred pounds of delicatessen meat.

Chiron trotted up next to us, a bow in his hand, his face grim.

"*Di immortales!*" Annabeth said. "That's a hellhound from the Fields of Punishment. They don't . . . they're not supposed to . . ."

"Someone summoned it," Chiron said. "Someone inside the camp."

Luke came over, the banner in his hand forgotten, his moment of glory gone.

Clarisse yelled, "It's all Percy's fault! Percy summoned it!"

"Be quiet, child," Chiron told her.

We watched the body of the hellhound melt into shadow, soaking into the ground until it disappeared.

"You're wounded," Annabeth told me. "Quick, Percy, get in the water."

"I'm okay."

"No, you're not," she said. "Chiron, watch this."

I was too tired to argue. I stepped back into the creek, the whole camp gathering around me.

Instantly, I felt better. I could feel the cuts on my chest closing up. Some of the campers gasped.

[125]

"Look, I—I don't know why," I said, trying to apologize. "I'm sorry. . . ."

But they weren't watching my wounds heal. They were staring at something above my head.

"Percy," Annabeth said, pointing. "Um . . ."

By the time I looked up, the sign was already fading, but I could still make out the hologram of green light, spinning and gleaming. A three-tipped spear: a trident.

"Your father," Annabeth murmured. "This is *really* not good."

"It is determined," Chiron announced.

All around me, campers started kneeling, even the Ares cabin, though they didn't look happy about it.

"My father?" I asked, completely bewildered.

"Poseidon," said Chiron. "Earthshaker, Stormbringer, Father of Horses. Hail, Perseus Jackson, Son of the Sea God."

NINE

I AM OFFERED A QUEST

The next morning, Chiron moved me to cabin three.

I didn't have to share with anybody. I had plenty of room for all my stuff: the Minotaur's horn, one set of spare clothes, and a toiletry bag. I got to sit at my own dinner table, pick all my own activities, call "lights out" whenever I felt like it, and not listen to anybody else.

And I was absolutely miserable.

Just when I'd started to feel accepted, to feel I had a home in cabin eleven and I might be a normal kid—or as normal as you can be when you're a half-blood—I'd been separated out as if I had some rare disease.

Nobody mentioned the hellhound, but I got the feeling they were all talking about it behind my back. The attack had scared everybody. It sent two messages: one, that I was the son of the Sea God; and two, monsters would stop at nothing to kill me. They could even invade a camp that had always been considered safe.

The other campers steered clear of me as much as possible. Cabin eleven was too nervous to have sword class with me after what I'd done to the Ares folks in the woods, so my lessons with Luke became one-on-one. He pushed me harder than ever, and wasn't afraid to bruise me up in the process.

"You're going to need all the training you can get," he promised, as we were working with swords and flaming torches. "Now let's try that viper-beheading strike again. Fifty more repetitions."

Annabeth still taught me Greek in the mornings, but she seemed distracted. Every time I said something, she scowled at me, as if I'd just poked her between the eyes.

After lessons, she would walk away muttering to herself: "Quest . . . Poseidon? . . . Dirty rotten . . . Got to make a plan . . ."

Even Clarisse kept her distance, though her venomous looks made it clear she wanted to kill me for breaking her magic spear. I wished she would just yell or punch me or something. I'd rather get into fights every day than be ignored.

I knew somebody at camp resented me, because one night I came into my cabin and found a mortal newspaper dropped inside the doorway, a copy of the *New York Daily News*, opened to the Metro page. The article took me almost an hour to read, because the angrier I got, the more the words floated around on the page.

BOY AND MOTHER STILL MISSING AFTER FREAK CAR ACCIDENT

BY EILEEN SMYTHE

Sally Jackson and son Percy are still missing one week after their mysterious disappearance. The family's badly burned '78 Camaro was discovered last Saturday on a north Long Island road with the roof ripped off and the front axle broken. The car had flipped and skidded for several hundred feet before exploding.

Mother and son had gone for a weekend vacation to Montauk, but left hastily, under mysterious circumstances. Small traces of blood were found in the car and near the scene of the wreck, but there were no other signs of the missing Jacksons. Residents in the rural area reported seeing nothing unusual around the time of the accident.

Ms. Jackson's husband, Gabe Ugliano, claims that his stepson, Percy Jackson, is a troubled child who has been kicked out of numerous boarding schools and has expressed violent tendencies in the past.

Police would not say whether son Percy is a suspect in his mother's disappearance, but they have not ruled out foul play. Below are recent pictures of Sally Jackson and Percy. Police urge anyone with information to call the following toll-free crime-stoppers hotline.

The phone number was circled in black marker.

I wadded up the paper and threw it away, then flopped down in my bunk bed in the middle of my empty cabin.

"Lights out," I told myself miserably.

That night, I had my worst dream yet.

I was running along the beach in a storm. This time,

there was a city behind me. Not New York. The sprawl was different: buildings spread farther apart, palm trees and low hills in the distance.

About a hundred yards down the surf, two men were fighting. They looked like TV wrestlers, muscular, with beards and long hair. Both wore flowing Greek tunics, one trimmed in blue, the other in green. They grappled with each other, wrestled, kicked and head-butted, and every time they connected, lightning flashed, the sky grew darker, and the wind rose.

I had to stop them. I didn't know why. But the harder I ran, the more the wind blew me back, until I was running in place, my heels digging uselessly in the sand.

Over the roar of the storm, I could hear the blue-robed one yelling at the green-robed one, *Give it back! Give it back!* Like a kindergartner fighting over a toy.

The waves got bigger, crashing into the beach, spraying me with salt.

I yelled, *Stop it! Stop fighting!*

The ground shook. Laughter came from somewhere under the earth, and a voice so deep and evil it turned my blood to ice.

Come down, little hero, the voice crooned. *Come down!*

The sand split beneath me, opening up a crevice straight down to the center of the earth. My feet slipped, and darkness swallowed me.

I woke up, sure I was falling.

I was still in bed in cabin three. My body told me it was morning, but it was dark outside, and thunder rolled across the hills. A storm was brewing. I hadn't dreamed that.

I heard a clopping sound at the door, a hoof knocking on the threshold.

"Come in?"

Grover trotted inside, looking worried. "Mr. D wants to see you."

"Why?"

"He wants to kill . . . I mean, I'd better let him tell you."

Nervously, I got dressed and followed, sure that I was in huge trouble.

For days, I'd been half expecting a summons to the Big House. Now that I was declared a son of Poseidon, one of the Big Three gods who weren't supposed to have kids, I figured it was a crime for me just to be alive. The other gods had probably been debating the best way to punish me for existing, and now Mr. D was ready to deliver their verdict.

Over Long Island Sound, the sky looked like ink soup coming to a boil. A hazy curtain of rain was coming in our direction. I asked Grover if we needed an umbrella.

"No," he said. "It never rains here unless we want it to."

I pointed at the storm. "What the heck is that, then?"

He glanced uneasily at the sky. "It'll pass around us. Bad weather always does."

I realized he was right. In the week I'd been here, it had never even been overcast. The few rain clouds I'd seen had skirted right around the edges of the valley.

But this storm . . . this one was huge.

At the volleyball pit, the kids from Apollo's cabin were playing a morning game against the satyrs. Dionysus's twins were walking around in the strawberry fields, making the plants grow. Everybody was going about their normal business, but they looked tense. They kept their eyes on the storm.

Grover and I walked up to the front porch of the Big House. Dionysus sat at the pinochle table in his tiger-striped Hawaiian shirt with his Diet Coke, just as he had on my first day. Chiron sat across the table in his fake wheelchair. They were playing against invisible opponents—two sets of cards hovering in the air.

"Well, well," Mr. D said without looking up. "Our little celebrity."

I waited.

"Come closer," Mr. D said. "And don't expect me to kowtow to you, mortal, just because old Barnacle-Beard is your father."

A net of lightning flashed across the clouds. Thunder shook the windows of the house.

"Blah, blah, blah," Dionysus said.

Chiron feigned interest in his pinochle cards. Grover cowered by the railing, his hooves clopping back and forth.

"If I had my way," Dionysus said, "I would cause your molecules to erupt in flames. We'd sweep up the ashes and be done with a lot of trouble. But Chiron seems to feel this would be against my mission at this cursed camp: to keep you little brats safe from harm."

"Spontaneous combustion *is* a form of harm, Mr. D," Chiron put in.

"Nonsense," Dionysus said. "Boy wouldn't feel a thing.

Nevertheless, I've agreed to restrain myself. I'm thinking of turning you into a dolphin instead, sending you back to your father."

"Mr. D—" Chiron warned.

"Oh, all right," Dionysus relented. "There's one more option. But it's deadly foolishness." Dionysus rose, and the invisible players' cards dropped to the table. "I'm off to Olympus for the emergency meeting. If the boy is still here when I get back, I'll turn him into an Atlantic bottlenose. Do you understand? And Perseus Jackson, if you're at all smart, you'll see that's a much more sensible choice than what Chiron feels you must do."

Dionysus picked up a playing card, twisted it, and it became a plastic rectangle. A credit card? No. A security pass.

He snapped his fingers.

The air seemed to fold and bend around him. He became a hologram, then a wind, then he was gone, leaving only the smell of fresh-pressed grapes lingering behind.

Chiron smiled at me, but he looked tired and strained. "Sit, Percy, please. And Grover."

We did.

Chiron laid his cards on the table, a winning hand he hadn't gotten to use.

"Tell me, Percy," he said. "What did you make of the hellhound?"

Just hearing the name made me shudder.

Chiron probably wanted me to say, *Heck, it was nothing. I eat hellhounds for breakfast.* But I didn't feel like lying.

"It scared me," I said. "If you hadn't shot it, I'd be dead."

"You'll meet worse, Percy. Far worse, before you're done."

"Done . . . with what?"

"Your quest, of course. Will you accept it?"

I glanced at Grover, who was crossing his fingers.

"Um, sir," I said, "you haven't told me what it is yet."

Chiron grimaced. "Well, that's the hard part, the details."

Thunder rumbled across the valley. The storm clouds had now reached the edge of the beach. As far as I could see, the sky and the sea were boiling together.

"Poseidon and Zeus," I said. "They're fighting over something valuable . . . something that was stolen, aren't they?"

Chiron and Grover exchanged looks.

Chiron sat forward in his wheelchair. "How did you know that?"

My face felt hot. I wished I hadn't opened my big mouth. "The weather since Christmas has been weird, like the sea and the sky are fighting. Then I talked to Annabeth, and she'd overheard something about a theft. And . . . I've also been having these dreams."

"I knew it," Grover said.

"Hush, satyr," Chiron ordered.

"But it is his quest!" Grover's eyes were bright with excitement. "It must be!"

"Only the Oracle can determine." Chiron stroked his bristly beard. "Nevertheless, Percy, you are correct. Your father and Zeus are having their worst quarrel in centuries.

They are fighting over something valuable that was stolen. To be precise: a lightning bolt."

I laughed nervously. "A *what*?"

"Do not take this lightly," Chiron warned. "I'm not talking about some tinfoil-covered zigzag you'd see in a second-grade play. I'm talking about a two-foot-long cylinder of high-grade celestial bronze, capped on both ends with god-level explosives."

"Oh."

"Zeus's master bolt," Chiron said, getting worked up now. "The symbol of his power, from which all other lightning bolts are patterned. The first weapon made by the Cyclopes for the war against the Titans, the bolt that sheered the top off Mount Etna and hurled Kronos from his throne; the master bolt, which packs enough power to make mortal hydrogen bombs look like firecrackers."

"And it's missing?"

"Stolen," Chiron said.

"By who?"

"By *whom*," Chiron corrected. Once a teacher, always a teacher. "By you."

My mouth fell open.

"At least"—Chiron held up a hand—"that's what Zeus thinks. During the winter solstice, at the last council of the gods, Zeus and Poseidon had an argument. The usual nonsense: 'Mother Rhea always liked you best,' 'Air disasters are more spectacular than sea disasters,' et cetera. Afterward, Zeus realized his master bolt was missing, taken from the throne room under his very nose. He immediately blamed Poseidon. Now, a god cannot usurp another god's symbol of power directly—that is forbidden by the most ancient of divine laws. But Zeus believes your father convinced a human hero to take it."

"But I didn't—"

"Patience and listen, child," Chiron said. "Zeus has good reason to be suspicious. The forges of the Cyclopes are under the ocean, which gives Poseidon some influence over the makers of his brother's lightning. Zeus believes Poseidon has taken the master bolt, and is now secretly having the Cyclopes build an arsenal of illegal copies, which might be used to topple Zeus from his throne. The only thing Zeus wasn't sure about was which hero Poseidon used to steal the bolt. Now Poseidon has openly claimed you as his son. You were in New York over the winter holidays. You could easily have snuck into Olympus. Zeus believes he has found his thief."

"But I've never even been to Olympus! Zeus is crazy!"

Chiron and Grover glanced nervously at the sky. The clouds didn't seem to be parting around us, as Grover had promised. They were rolling straight over our valley, sealing us in like a coffin lid.

"Er, Percy . . . ?" Grover said. "We don't use the *c*-word to describe the Lord of the Sky."

"Perhaps *paranoid*," Chiron suggested. "Then again, Poseidon has tried to unseat Zeus before. I believe that was question thirty-eight on your final exam. . . ." He looked at me as if he actually expected me to remember question thirty-eight.

How could anyone accuse me of stealing a god's weapon? I couldn't even steal a slice of pizza from Gabe's poker party without getting busted. Chiron was waiting for an answer.

"Something about a golden net?" I guessed. "Poseidon and Hera and a few other gods . . . they, like, trapped Zeus and wouldn't let him out until he promised to be a better ruler, right?"

"Correct," Chiron said. "And Zeus has never trusted Poseidon since. Of course, Poseidon denies stealing the master bolt. He took great offense at the accusation. The two have been arguing back and forth for months, threatening war. And now, you've come along—the proverbial last straw."

"But I'm just a kid!"

"Percy," Grover cut in, "if you were Zeus, and you already thought your brother was plotting to overthrow you, then your brother suddenly admitted he had broken the sacred oath he took after World War II, that he's fathered a new mortal hero who might be used as a weapon against you. . . . Wouldn't that put a twist in your toga?"

"But I didn't do anything. Poseidon—my dad—he didn't really have this master bolt stolen, did he?"

Chiron sighed. "Most thinking observers would agree that thievery is not Poseidon's style. But the Sea God is too proud to try convincing Zeus of that. Zeus has demanded that Poseidon return the bolt by the summer solstice. That's June twenty-first, ten days from now. Poseidon wants an apology for being called a thief by the same date. I hoped that diplomacy might prevail, that Hera or Demeter or Hestia would make the two brothers see sense. But your arrival has inflamed Zeus's temper. Now neither god will back down. Unless someone intervenes, unless the master bolt is found and returned to Zeus before the solstice, there will be war. And do you know what a full-fledged war would look like, Percy?"

"Bad?" I guessed.

"Imagine the world in chaos. Nature at war with itself. Olympians forced to choose sides between Zeus and Poseidon. Destruction. Carnage. Millions dead. Western civilization turned into a battleground so big it will make the Trojan War look like a water-balloon fight."

"Bad," I repeated.

"And you, Percy Jackson, would be the first to feel Zeus's wrath."

It started to rain. Volleyball players stopped their game and stared in stunned silence at the sky.

I had brought this storm to Half-Blood Hill. Zeus was punishing the whole camp because of me. I was furious.

"So I have to find the stupid bolt," I said. "And return it to Zeus."

"What better peace offering," Chiron said, "than to have the son of Poseidon return Zeus's property?"

"If Poseidon doesn't have it, where is the thing?"

"I believe I know." Chiron's expression was grim. "Part of a prophecy I had years ago . . . well, some of the lines make sense to me, now. But before I can say more, you must officially take up the quest. You must seek the counsel of the Oracle."

"Why can't you tell me where the bolt is beforehand?"

"Because if I did, you would be too afraid to accept the challenge."

I swallowed. "Good reason."

"You agree then?"

I looked at Grover, who nodded encouragingly.

Easy for him. I was the one Zeus wanted to kill.

"All right," I said. "It's better than being turned into a dolphin."

"Then it's time you consulted the Oracle," Chiron said. "Go upstairs, Percy Jackson, to the attic. When you come back down, assuming you're still sane, we will talk more."

Four flights up, the stairs ended under a green trap-door.

I pulled the cord. The door swung down, and a wooden ladder clattered into place.

The warm air from above smelled like mildew and rotten wood and something else . . . a smell I remembered from biology class. Reptiles. The smell of snakes.

I held my breath and climbed.

The attic was filled with Greek hero junk: armor stands covered in cobwebs; once-bright shields pitted with rust; old leather steamer trunks plastered with stickers saying ITHAKA, CIRCE'S ISLE, and LAND OF THE AMAZONS. One long table was stacked with glass jars filled with pickled *things*—severed hairy claws, huge yellow eyes, various other parts of monsters. A dusty mounted trophy on the wall looked like a giant snake's head, but with horns and a full set of shark's teeth. The plaque read, HYDRA HEAD #1, WOODSTOCK, N.Y., 1969.

By the window, sitting on a wooden tripod stool, was the most gruesome memento of all: a mummy. Not the wrapped-in-cloth kind, but a human female body shriveled to a husk. She wore a tie-dyed sundress, lots of beaded necklaces, and a headband over long black hair. The skin of her face was thin and leathery over her skull, and her eyes were glassy white slits, as if the real eyes had been replaced by marbles; she'd been dead a long, long time.

Looking at her sent chills up my back. And that was before she sat up on her stool and opened her mouth. A green mist poured from the mummy's mouth, coiling over the floor in thick tendrils, hissing like twenty thousand snakes. I stumbled over myself trying to get to the trapdoor, but it slammed shut. Inside my head, I heard a voice, slithering into one ear and coiling around my brain: *I am the spirit of Delphi, speaker of the prophecies of Phoebus Apollo, slayer of the mighty Python. Approach, seeker, and ask.*

I wanted to say, *No thanks, wrong door, just looking for the bathroom.* But I forced myself to take a deep breath.

The mummy wasn't alive. She was some kind of gruesome receptacle for something else, the power that was now swirling around me in the green mist. But its presence didn't feel evil, like my demonic math teacher Mrs. Dodds or the Minotaur. It felt more like the Three Fates I'd seen knitting the yarn outside the highway fruit stand: ancient, powerful, and definitely *not* human. But not particularly interested in killing me, either.

I got up the courage to ask, "What is my destiny?"

The mist swirled more thickly, collecting right in front of me and around the table with the pickled monster-part jars. Suddenly there were four men sitting around the table, playing cards. Their faces became clearer. It was Smelly Gabe and his buddies.

My fists clenched, though I knew this poker party couldn't be real. It was an illusion, made out of mist.

Gabe turned toward me and spoke in the rasping voice of the Oracle: *You shall go west, and face the god who has turned.*

His buddy on the right looked up and said in the same voice: *You shall find what was stolen, and see it safely returned.*

The guy on the left threw in two poker chips, then said: *You shall be betrayed by one who calls you a friend.*

Finally, Eddie, our building super, delivered the worst line of all: *And you shall fail to save what matters most, in the end.*

The figures began to dissolve. At first I was too stunned to say anything, but as the mist retreated, coiling into a huge green serpent and slithering back into the mouth of the mummy, I cried, "Wait! What do you mean? What friend? What will I fail to save?"

The tail of the mist snake disappeared into the mummy's mouth. She reclined back against the wall. Her mouth closed tight, as if it hadn't been open in a hundred years. The attic was silent again, abandoned, nothing but a room full of mementos.

I got the feeling that I could stand here until I had cobwebs, too, and I wouldn't learn anything else.

My audience with the Oracle was over.

"Well?" Chiron asked me.

I slumped into a chair at the pinochle table. "She said I would retrieve what was stolen."

Grover sat forward, chewing excitedly on the remains of a Diet Coke can. "That's great!"

"What did the Oracle say *exactly*?" Chiron pressed. "This is important."

My ears were still tingling from the reptilian voice. "She . . . she said I would go west and face a god who had turned. I would retrieve what was stolen and see it safely returned."

"I knew it," Grover said.

Chiron didn't look satisfied. "Anything else?"

I didn't want to tell him.

What friend would betray me? I didn't have that many.

And the last line—I would fail to save what mattered most. What kind of Oracle would send me on a quest and tell me, *Oh, by the way, you'll fail.*

How could I confess that?

"No," I said. "That's about it."

He studied my face. "Very well, Percy. But know this: the Oracle's words often have double meanings. Don't dwell on them too much. The truth is not always clear until events come to pass."

I got the feeling he knew I was holding back something bad, and he was trying to make me feel better.

"Okay," I said, anxious to change topics. "So where do I go? Who's this god in the west?"

"Ah, think, Percy," Chiron said. "If Zeus and Poseidon weaken each other in a war, who stands to gain?"

"Somebody else who wants to take over?" I guessed.

"Yes, quite. Someone who harbors a grudge, who has been unhappy with his lot since the world was divided eons ago, whose kingdom would grow powerful with the deaths of millions. Someone who hates his brothers for forcing him into an oath to have no more children, an oath that both of them have now broken."

I thought about my dreams, the evil voice that had spoken from under the ground. "Hades."

Chiron nodded. "The Lord of the Dead is the only possibility."

A scrap of aluminum dribbled out of Grover's mouth. "Whoa, wait. Wh-what?"

"A Fury came after Percy," Chiron reminded him. "She watched the young man until she was sure of his identity, then tried to kill him. Furies obey only one lord: Hades."

"Yes, but—but Hades hates *all* heroes," Grover protested. "Especially if he has found out Percy is a son of Poseidon. . . ."

"A hellhound got into the forest," Chiron continued. "Those can only be summoned from the Fields of Punishment, and it had to be summoned by someone within the camp. Hades must have a spy here. He must suspect Poseidon will try to use Percy to clear his name. Hades would very much like to kill this young half-blood before he can take on the quest."

"Great," I muttered. "That's two major gods who want to kill me."

"But a quest to . . ." Grover swallowed. "I mean, couldn't the master bolt be in some place like Maine? Maine's very nice this time of year."

"Hades sent a minion to steal the master bolt," Chiron insisted. "He hid it in the Underworld, knowing full well that Zeus would blame Poseidon. I don't pretend to understand the Lord of the Dead's motives perfectly, or why he chose this time to start a war, but one thing is certain. Percy must go to the Underworld, find the master bolt, and reveal the truth."

A strange fire burned in my stomach. The weirdest thing was: it wasn't fear. It was anticipation. The desire for revenge. Hades had tried to kill me three times so far, with the Fury, the Minotaur, and the hellhound. It was his fault my mother had disappeared in a flash of light. Now he was trying to frame me and my dad for a theft we hadn't committed.

I was ready to take him on.

Besides, if my mother was in the Underworld . . .

Whoa, boy, said the small part of my brain that was still sane. You're a kid. Hades is a god.

Grover was trembling. He'd started eating pinochle cards like potato chips.

The poor guy needed to complete a quest with me so he could get his searcher's license, whatever that was, but how could I ask him to do this quest, especially when the Oracle said I was destined to fail? This was suicide.

"Look, if we know it's Hades," I told Chiron, "why can't we just tell the other gods? Zeus or Poseidon could go down to the Underworld and bust some heads."

"Suspecting and knowing are not the same," Chiron said. "Besides, even if the other gods suspect Hades—and I imagine Poseidon does—they couldn't retrieve the bolt themselves. Gods cannot cross each other's territories except by invitation. That is another ancient rule. Heroes, on the other hand, have certain privileges. They can go anywhere, challenge anyone, as long as they're bold enough and strong enough to do it. No god can be held responsible for a hero's actions. Why do you think the gods always operate through humans?"

"You're saying I'm being used."

"I'm saying it's no accident Poseidon has claimed you now. It's a very risky gamble, but he's in a desperate situation. He needs you."

My dad needs me.

Emotions rolled around inside me like bits of glass in a kaleidoscope. I didn't know whether to feel resentful or grateful or happy or angry. Poseidon had ignored me for twelve years. Now suddenly he needed me.

I looked at Chiron. "You've known I was Poseidon's son all along, haven't you?"

"I had my suspicions. As I said . . . I've spoken to the Oracle, too."

I got the feeling there was a lot he wasn't telling me about his prophecy, but I decided I couldn't worry about that right now. After all, I was holding back information too.

"So let me get this straight," I said. "I'm supposed go to the Underworld and confront the Lord of the Dead."

"Check," Chiron said.

"Find the most powerful weapon in the universe."

"Check."

"And get it back to Olympus before the summer solstice, in ten days."

"That's about right."

I looked at Grover, who gulped down the ace of hearts.

"Did I mention that Maine is very nice this time of year?" he asked weakly.

"You don't have to go," I told him. "I can't ask that of you."

"Oh . . ." He shifted his hooves. "No . . . it's just that satyrs and underground places . . . well . . ."

He took a deep breath, then stood, brushing the shredded cards and aluminum bits off his T-shirt. "You saved my life, Percy. If . . . if you're serious about wanting me along, I won't let you down."

I felt so relieved I wanted to cry, though I didn't think that would be very heroic. Grover was the only friend I'd ever had for longer than a few months. I wasn't sure what good a satyr could do against the forces of the dead, but I felt better knowing he'd be with me.

"All the way, G-man." I turned to Chiron. "So where do we go? The Oracle just said to go west."

"The entrance to the Underworld is always in the west. It moves from age to age, just like Olympus. Right now, of course, it's in America."

"Where?"

Chiron looked surprised. "I thought that would be obvious enough. The entrance to the Underworld is in Los Angeles."

"Oh," I said. "Naturally. So we just get on a plane—"

"No!" Grover shrieked. "Percy, what are you thinking? Have you ever been on a plane in your life?"

I shook my head, feeling embarrassed. My mom had never taken me anywhere by plane. She'd always said we didn't have the money. Besides, her parents had died in a plane crash.

"Percy, think," Chiron said. "You are the son of the Sea God. Your father's bitterest rival is Zeus, Lord of the Sky. Your mother knew better than to trust you in an airplane. You would be in Zeus's domain. You would never come down again alive."

Overhead, lightning crackled. Thunder boomed.

"Okay," I said, determined not to look at the storm. "So, I'll travel overland."

"That's right," Chiron said. "Two companions may accompany you. Grover is one. The other has already volunteered, if you will accept her help."

"Gee," I said, feigning surprise. "Who else would be stupid enough to volunteer for a quest like this?"

The air shimmered behind Chiron.

Annabeth became visible, stuffing her Yankees cap into her back pocket.

"I've been waiting a long time for a quest, seaweed brain," she said. "Athena is no fan of Poseidon, but if you're going to save the world, I'm the best person to keep you from messing up."

"If you do say so yourself," I said. "I suppose you have a plan, wise girl?"

Her cheeks colored. "Do you want my help or not?"

The truth was, I did. I needed all the help I could get.

"A trio," I said. "That'll work."

"Excellent," Chiron said. "This afternoon, we can take you as far as the bus terminal in Manhattan. After that, you are on your own."

Lightning flashed. Rain poured down on the meadows that were never supposed to have violent weather.

"No time to waste," Chiron said. "I think you should all get packing."

TEN

I RUIN A PERFECTLY
GOOD BUS

It didn't take me long to pack. I decided to leave the Mino-taur horn in my cabin, which left me only an extra change of clothes and a toothbrush to stuff in a backpack Grover had found for me.

The camp store loaned me one hundred dollars in mor-tal money and twenty golden drachmas. These coins were as big as Girl Scout cookies and had images of various Greek gods stamped on one side and the Empire State Building on the other. The ancient mortal drachmas had been silver, Chiron told us, but Olympians never used less than pure gold. Chiron said the coins might come in handy for non-mortal transactions—whatever that meant. He gave Annabeth and me each a canteen of nectar and a Ziploc bag full of ambrosia squares, to be used only in emergencies, if we were seriously hurt. It was god food, Chiron reminded us. It would cure us of almost any injury, but it was lethal to mortals. Too much of it would make a half-blood very, very feverish. An overdose would burn us up, literally.

Annabeth was bringing her magic Yankees cap, which she told me had been a twelfth-birthday present from her mom. She carried a book on famous classical architecture, written in Ancient Greek, to read when she got bored, and a long bronze knife, hidden in her shirt sleeve. I was sure the knife would get us busted the first time we went through a metal detector.

Grover wore his fake feet and his pants to pass as human. He wore a green rasta-style cap, because when it rained his curly hair flattened and you could just see the tips of his horns. His bright orange backpack was full of scrap metal and apples to snack on. In his pocket was a set of reed pipes his daddy goat had carved for him, even though he only knew two songs: Mozart's Piano Concerto no. 12 and Hilary Duff's "So Yesterday," both of which sounded pretty bad on reed pipes.

We waved good-bye to the other campers, took one last look at the strawberry fields, the ocean, and the Big House, then hiked up Half-Blood Hill to the tall pine tree that used to be Thalia, daughter of Zeus.

Chiron was waiting for us in his wheelchair. Next to him stood the surfer dude I'd seen when I was recovering in the sick room. According to Grover, the guy was the camp's head of security. He supposedly had eyes all over his body so he could never be surprised. Today, though, he was wearing a chauffeur's uniform, so I could only see extra peepers on his hands, face and neck.

"This is Argus," Chiron told me. "He will drive you into the city, and, er, well, keep an eye on things."

I heard footsteps behind us.

Luke came running up the hill, carrying a pair of basketball shoes.

"Hey!" he panted. "Glad I caught you."

Annabeth blushed, the way she always did when Luke was around.

"Just wanted to say good luck," Luke told me. "And I thought . . . um, maybe you could use these."

He handed me the sneakers, which looked pretty normal. They even smelled kind of normal.

Luke said, *"Maia!"*

White bird's wings sprouted out of the heels, startling me so much, I dropped them. The shoes flapped around on the ground until the wings folded up and disappeared.

"Awesome!" Grover said.

Luke smiled. "Those served me well when I was on my quest. Gift from Dad. Of course, I don't use them much these days. . . ." His expression turned sad.

I didn't know what to say. It was cool enough that Luke had come to say good-bye. I'd been afraid he might resent me for getting so much attention the last few days. But here he was giving me a magic gift. . . . It made me blush almost as much as Annabeth.

"Hey, man," I said. "Thanks."

"Listen, Percy . . ." Luke looked uncomfortable. "A lot of hopes are riding on you. So just . . . kill some monsters for me, okay?"

We shook hands. Luke patted Grover's head between his horns, then gave a good-bye hug to Annabeth, who looked like she might pass out.

After Luke was gone, I told her, "You're hyperventilating."

"Am not."

"You let him capture the flag instead of you, didn't you?"

"Oh . . . why do I want to go anywhere with you, Percy?"

She stomped down the other side of the hill, where a white SUV waited on the shoulder of the road. Argus followed, jingling his car keys.

I picked up the flying shoes and had a sudden bad feeling. I looked at Chiron. "I won't be able to use these, will I?"

He shook his head. "Luke meant well, Percy. But taking to the air . . . that would not be wise for you."

I nodded, disappointed, but then I got an idea. "Hey, Grover. You want a magic item?"

His eyes lit up. "Me?"

Pretty soon we'd laced the sneakers over his fake feet, and the world's first flying goat boy was ready for launch.

"Maia!" he shouted.

He got off the ground okay, but then fell over sideways so his backpack dragged through the grass. The winged shoes kept bucking up and down like tiny broncos.

"Practice," Chiron called after him. "You just need practice!"

"Aaaaa!" Grover went flying sideways down the hill like a possessed lawn mower, heading toward the van.

Before I could follow, Chiron caught my arm. "I should have trained you better, Percy," he said. "If only I had more time. Hercules, Jason—they all got more training."

"That's okay. I just wish—"

I stopped myself because I was about to sound like a

[152]

brat. I was wishing my dad had given me a cool magic item to help on the quest, something as good as Luke's flying shoes, or Annabeth's invisible cap.

"What am I thinking?" Chiron cried. "I can't let you get away without this."

He pulled a pen from his coat pocket and handed it to me. It was an ordinary disposable ballpoint, black ink, removable cap. Probably cost thirty cents.

"Gee," I said. "Thanks."

"Percy, that's a gift from your father. I've kept it for years, not knowing you were who I was waiting for. But the prophecy is clear to me now. You are the one."

I remembered the field trip to the Metropolitan Museum of Art, when I'd vaporized Mrs. Dodds. Chiron had thrown me a pen that turned into a sword. Could this be . . . ?

I took off the cap, and the pen grew longer and heavier in my hand. In half a second, I held a shimmering bronze sword with a double-edged blade, a leather-wrapped grip, and a flat hilt riveted with gold studs. It was the first weapon that actually felt balanced in my hand.

"The sword has a long and tragic history that we need not go into," Chiron told me. "Its name is Anaklusmos."

"'Riptide,'" I translated, surprised the Ancient Greek came so easily.

"Use it only for emergencies," Chiron said, "and only against monsters. No hero should harm mortals unless absolutely necessary, of course, but this sword wouldn't harm them in any case."

I looked at the wickedly sharp blade. "What do you mean it wouldn't harm mortals? How could it not?"

"The sword is celestial bronze. Forged by the Cyclopes, tempered in the heart of Mount Etna, cooled in the River Lethe. It's deadly to monsters, to any creature from the Underworld, provided they don't kill you first. But the blade will pass through mortals like an illusion. They simply are not important enough for the blade to kill. And I should warn you: as a demigod, you can be killed by either celestial or normal weapons. You are twice as vulnerable."

"Good to know."

"Now recap the pen."

I touched the pen cap to the sword tip and instantly Riptide shrank to a ballpoint pen again. I tucked it in my pocket, a little nervous, because I was famous for losing pens at school.

"You can't," Chiron said.

"Can't what?"

"Lose the pen," he said. "It is enchanted. It will always reappear in your pocket. Try it."

I was wary, but I threw the pen as far as I could down the hill and watched it disappear in the grass.

"It may take a few moments," Chiron told me. "Now check your pocket."

Sure enough, the pen was there.

"Okay, that's *extremely* cool," I admitted. "But what if a mortal sees me pulling out a sword?"

Chiron smiled. "Mist is a powerful thing, Percy."

"Mist?"

"Yes. Read *The Iliad*. It's full of references to the stuff. Whenever divine or monstrous elements mix with the mortal world, they generate Mist, which obscures the vision of humans. You will see things just as they are, being a half-blood, but humans will interpret things quite differently. Remarkable, really, the lengths to which humans will go to fit things into their version of reality."

I put Riptide back in my pocket.

For the first time, the quest felt real. I was actually leaving Half-Blood Hill. I was heading west with no adult supervision, no backup plan, not even a cell phone. (Chiron said cell phones were traceable by monsters; if we used one, it would be worse than sending up a flare.) I had no weapon stronger than a sword to fight off monsters and reach the Land of the Dead.

"Chiron . . ." I said. "When you say the gods are immortal . . . I mean, there was a time *before* them, right?"

"Four ages before them, actually. The Time of the Titans was the Fourth Age, sometimes called the Golden Age, which is definitely a misnomer. This, the time of Western civilization and the rule of Zeus, is the Fifth Age."

"So what was it like . . . before the gods?"

Chiron pursed his lips. "Even I am not old enough to remember that, child, but I know it was a time of darkness and savagery for mortals. Kronos, the lord of the Titans, called his reign the Golden Age because men lived innocent and free of all knowledge. But that was mere propaganda. The Titan king cared nothing for your kind except as appetizers or a source of cheap entertainment. It was only in the early reign of Lord Zeus, when Prometheus the good Titan brought fire to mankind, that your species began to progress, and even then Prometheus was branded a radical thinker. Zeus punished him severely, as you may recall. Of course, eventually the gods warmed to humans, and Western civilization was born."

"But the gods can't die now, right? I mean, as long as Western civilization is alive, they're alive. So . . . even if I failed, nothing could happen so bad it would mess up *everything*, right?"

Chiron gave me a melancholy smile. "No one knows how long the Age of the West will last, Percy. The gods are immortal, yes. But then, so were the Titans. *They* still exist, locked away in their various prisons, forced to endure endless pain and punishment, reduced in power, but still very much alive. May the Fates forbid that the gods should ever suffer such a doom, or that we should ever return to the darkness and chaos of the past. All we can do, child, is follow our destiny."

"Our destiny . . . assuming we know what that is."

"Relax," Chiron told me. "Keep a clear head. And remember, you may be about to prevent the biggest war in human history."

"Relax," I said. "I'm very relaxed."

When I got to the bottom of the hill, I looked back. Under the pine tree that used to be Thalia, daughter of Zeus, Chiron was now standing in full horse-man form, holding his bow high in salute. Just your typical summer-camp send-off by your typical centaur.

Argus drove us out of the countryside and into western Long Island. It felt weird to be on a highway again, Annabeth and Grover sitting next to me as if we were normal carpoolers. After two weeks at Half-Blood Hill, the real world seemed like a fantasy. I found myself staring at every McDonald's, every kid in the back of his parents' car, every billboard and shopping mall.

"So far so good," I told Annabeth. "Ten miles and not a single monster."

She gave me an irritated look. "It's bad luck to talk that way, seaweed brain."

"Remind me again—why do you hate me so much?"

"I don't hate you."

"Could've fooled me."

She folded her cap of invisibility. "Look . . . we're just not supposed to get along, okay? Our parents are rivals."

"Why?"

She sighed. "How many reasons do you want? One time my mom caught Poseidon with his girlfriend in Athena's temple, which is *hugely* disrespectful. Another time, Athena and Poseidon competed to be the patron god for the city of Athens. Your dad created some stupid saltwater spring for his gift. My mom created the olive tree. The people saw that her gift was better, so they named the city after her."

"They must really like olives."

"Oh, forget it."

"Now, if she'd invented pizza—*that* I could understand."

"I said, forget it!"

In the front seat, Argus smiled. He didn't say anything, but one blue eye on the back of his neck winked at me.

Traffic slowed us down in Queens. By the time we got into Manhattan it was sunset and starting to rain.

Argus dropped us at the Greyhound Station on the Upper East Side, not far from my mom and Gabe's apartment. Taped to a mailbox was a soggy flyer with my picture on it: HAVE YOU SEEN THIS BOY?

I ripped it down before Annabeth and Grover could notice.

Argus unloaded our bags, made sure we got our bus tickets, then drove away, the eye on the back of his hand opening to watch us as he pulled out of the parking lot.

I thought about how close I was to my old apartment. On a normal day, my mom would be home from the candy store by now. Smelly Gabe was probably up there right now, playing poker, not even missing her.

Grover shouldered his backpack. He gazed down the street in the direction I was looking. "You want to know why she married him, Percy?"

I stared at him. "Were you reading my mind or something?"

"Just your emotions." He shrugged. "Guess I forgot to tell you satyrs can do that. You were thinking about your mom and your stepdad, right?"

I nodded, wondering what else Grover might've forgotten to tell me.

"Your mom married Gabe for *you*," Grover told me. "You call him 'Smelly,' but you've got no idea. The guy has this aura. . . . Yuck. I can smell him from here. I can smell traces of him on you, and you haven't been near him for a week."

"Thanks," I said. "Where's the nearest shower?"

"You should be grateful, Percy. Your stepfather smells so repulsively human he could mask the presence of any demigod. As soon as I took a whiff inside his Camaro, I knew: Gabe has been covering your scent for years. If you hadn't lived with him every summer, you probably would've been found by monsters a long time ago. Your mom stayed with him to protect you. She was a smart lady. She must've loved you a lot to put up with that guy—if that makes you feel any better."

It didn't, but I forced myself not to show it. I'll see her again, I thought. She isn't gone.

I wondered if Grover could still read my emotions, mixed up as they were. I was glad he and Annabeth were with me, but I felt guilty that I hadn't been straight with them. I hadn't told them the real reason I'd said yes to this crazy quest.

The truth was, I didn't care about retrieving Zeus's lightning bolt, or saving the world, or even helping my father out of trouble. The more I thought about it, I resented Poseidon for never visiting me, never helping my mom, never even sending a lousy child-support check. He'd only claimed me because he needed a job done.

All I cared about was my mom. Hades had taken her unfairly, and Hades was going to give her back.

You will be betrayed by one who calls you a friend, the Oracle whispered in my mind. *You will fail to save what matters most in the end.*

Shut up, I told it.

The rain kept coming down.

We got restless waiting for the bus and decided to play some Hacky Sack with one of Grover's apples. Annabeth was unbelievable. She could bounce the apple off her knee, her elbow, her shoulder, whatever. I wasn't too bad myself.

The game ended when I tossed the apple toward Grover and it got too close to his mouth. In one mega goat bite, our Hacky Sack disappeared—core, stem, and all.

Grover blushed. He tried to apologize, but Annabeth and I were too busy cracking up.

Finally the bus came. As we stood in line to board, Grover started looking around, sniffing the air like he smelled his favorite school cafeteria delicacy—enchiladas.

"What is it?" I asked.

"I don't know," he said tensely. "Maybe it's nothing."

But I could tell it wasn't nothing. I started looking over my shoulder, too.

I was relieved when we finally got on board and found seats together in the back of the bus. We stowed our backpacks. Annabeth kept slapping her Yankees cap nervously against her thigh.

As the last passengers got on, Annabeth clamped her hand onto my knee. "Percy."

An old lady had just boarded the bus. She wore a crumpled velvet dress, lace gloves, and a shapeless orange-knit hat that shadowed her face, and she carried a big paisley purse. When she tilted her head up, her black eyes glittered, and my heart skipped a beat.

It was Mrs. Dodds. Older, more withered, but definitely the same evil face.

I scrunched down in my seat.

Behind her came two more old ladies: one in a green hat, one in a purple hat. Otherwise they looked exactly like Mrs. Dodds—same gnarled hands, paisley handbags, wrinkled velvet dresses. Triplet demon grandmothers.

They sat in the front row, right behind the driver. The two on the aisle crossed their legs over the walkway, making an X. It was casual enough, but it sent a clear message: nobody leaves.

The bus pulled out of the station, and we headed through the slick streets of Manhattan. "She didn't stay dead long," I said, trying to keep my voice from quivering. "I thought you said they could be dispelled for a lifetime."

"I said if you're *lucky*," Annabeth said. "You're obviously not."

"All three of them," Grover whimpered. *"Di immortales!"*

"It's okay," Annabeth said, obviously thinking hard. "The Furies. The three worst monsters from the Underworld. No problem. No problem. We'll just slip out the windows."

"They don't open," Grover moaned.

"A back exit?" she suggested.

There wasn't one. Even if there had been, it wouldn't

have helped. By that time, we were on Ninth Avenue, heading for the Lincoln Tunnel.

"They won't attack us with witnesses around," I said. "Will they?"

"Mortals don't have good eyes," Annabeth reminded me. "Their brains can only process what they see through the Mist."

"They'll see three old ladies killing us, won't they?"

She thought about it. "Hard to say. But we can't count on mortals for help. Maybe an emergency exit in the roof . . . ?"

We hit the Lincoln Tunnel, and the bus went dark except for the running lights down the aisle. It was eerily quiet without the sound of the rain.

Mrs. Dodds got up. In a flat voice, as if she'd rehearsed it, she announced to the whole bus: "I need to use the restroom."

"So do I," said the second sister.

"So do I," said the third sister.

They all started coming down the aisle.

"I've got it," Annabeth said. "Percy, take my hat."

"What?"

"You're the one they want. Turn invisible and go up the aisle. Let them pass you. Maybe you can get to the front and get away."

"But you guys—"

"There's an outside chance they might not notice us," Annabeth said. "You're a son of one of the Big Three. Your smell might be overpowering."

"I can't just leave you."

"Don't worry about us," Grover said. "Go!"

My hands trembled. I felt like a coward, but I took the Yankees cap and put it on.

When I looked down, my body wasn't there anymore.

I started creeping up the aisle. I managed to get up ten rows, then duck into an empty seat just as the Furies walked past.

Mrs. Dodds stopped, sniffing, and looked straight at me. My heart was pounding.

Apparently she didn't see anything. She and her sisters kept going.

I was free. I made it to the front of the bus. We were almost through the Lincoln Tunnel now. I was about to press the emergency stop button when I heard hideous wailing from the back row.

The old ladies were not old ladies anymore. Their faces were still the same—I guess those couldn't get any uglier—but their bodies had shriveled into leathery brown hag bodies with bat's wings and hands and feet like gargoyle claws. Their handbags had turned into fiery whips.

The Furies surrounded Grover and Annabeth, lashing their whips, hissing: "Where is it? Where?"

The other people on the bus were screaming, cowering in their seats. They saw *something*, all right.

"He's not here!" Annabeth yelled. "He's gone!"

The Furies raised their whips.

Annabeth drew her bronze knife. Grover grabbed a tin can from his snack bag and prepared to throw it.

What I did next was so impulsive and dangerous I should've been named ADHD poster child of the year.

The bus driver was distracted, trying to see what was going on in his rearview mirror.

Still invisible, I grabbed the wheel from him and jerked it to the left. Everybody howled as they were thrown to the right, and I heard what I hoped was the sound of three Furies smashing against the windows.

"Hey!" the driver yelled. "Hey—whoa!"

We wrestled for the wheel. The bus slammed against the side of the tunnel, grinding metal, throwing sparks a mile behind us.

We careened out of the Lincoln Tunnel and back into the rainstorm, people and monsters tossed around the bus, cars plowed aside like bowling pins.

Somehow the driver found an exit. We shot off the highway, through half a dozen traffic lights, and ended up barreling down one of those New Jersey rural roads where you can't believe there's so much nothing right across the river from New York. There were woods to our left, the Hudson River to our right, and the driver seemed to be veering toward the river.

Another great idea: I hit the emergency brake.

The bus wailed, spun a full circle on the wet asphalt, and crashed into the trees. The emergency lights came on. The door flew open. The bus driver was the first one out, the passengers yelling as they stampeded after him. I stepped into the driver's seat and let them pass.

The Furies regained their balance. They lashed their

whips at Annabeth while she waved her knife and yelled in Ancient Greek, telling them to back off. Grover threw tin cans.

I looked at the open doorway. I was free to go, but I couldn't leave my friends. I took off the invisible cap. "Hey!"

The Furies turned, baring their yellow fangs at me, and the exit suddenly seemed like an excellent idea. Mrs. Dodds stalked up the aisle, just as she used to do in class, about to deliver my F— math test. Every time she flicked her whip, red flames danced along the barbed leather.

Her two ugly sisters hopped on top of the seats on either side of her and crawled toward me like huge nasty lizards.

"Perseus Jackson," Mrs. Dodds said, in an accent that was definitely from somewhere farther south than Georgia. "You have offended the gods. You shall die."

"I liked you better as a math teacher," I told her.

She growled.

Annabeth and Grover moved up behind the Furies cautiously, looking for an opening.

I took the ballpoint pen out of my pocket and uncapped it. Riptide elongated into a shimmering double-edged sword.

The Furies hesitated.

Mrs. Dodds had felt Riptide's blade before. She obviously didn't like seeing it again.

"Submit now," she hissed. "And you will not suffer eternal torment."

"Nice try," I told her.

"Percy, look out!" Annabeth cried.

Mrs. Dodds lashed her whip around my sword hand while the Furies on the either side lunged at me.

My hand felt like it was wrapped in molten lead, but I managed not to drop Riptide. I stuck the Fury on the left with its hilt, sending her toppling backward into a seat. I turned and sliced the Fury on the right. As soon as the blade connected with her neck, she screamed and exploded into dust. Annabeth got Mrs. Dodds in a wrestler's hold and yanked her backward while Grover ripped the whip out of her hands.

"Ow!" he yelled. "Ow! Hot! Hot!"

The Fury I'd hilt-slammed came at me again, talons ready, but I swung Riptide and she broke open like a piñata.

Mrs. Dodds was trying to get Annabeth off her back. She kicked, clawed, hissed and bit, but Annabeth held on while Grover got Mrs. Dodds's legs tied up in her own whip. Finally they both shoved her backward into the aisle. Mrs. Dodds tried to get up, but she didn't have room to flap her bat wings, so she kept falling down.

"Zeus will destroy you!" she promised. "Hades will have your soul!"

"Braccas meas vescimini!" I yelled.

I wasn't sure where the Latin came from. I think it meant "Eat my pants!"

Thunder shook the bus. The hair rose on the back of my neck.

"Get out!" Annabeth yelled at me. "Now!" I didn't need any encouragement.

We rushed outside and found the other passengers wandering around in a daze, arguing with the driver, or running around in circles yelling, "We're going to die!" A Hawaiian-shirted tourist with a camera snapped my photograph before I could recap my sword.

"Our bags!" Grover realized. "We left our—"

BOOOOOM!

The windows of the bus exploded as the passengers ran for cover. Lightning shredded a huge crater in the roof, but an angry wail from inside told me Mrs. Dodds was not yet dead.

"Run!" Annabeth said. "She's calling for reinforcements! We have to get out of here!"

We plunged into the woods as the rain poured down, the bus in flames behind us, and nothing but darkness ahead.

ELEVEN

WE VISIT THE GARDEN GNOME EMPORIUM

In a way, it's nice to know there are Greek gods out there, because you have somebody to blame when things go wrong. For instance, when you're walking away from a bus that's just been attacked by monster hags and blown up by lightning, and it's raining on top of everything else, most people might think that's just really bad luck; when you're a half-blood, you understand that some divine force really is trying to mess up your day.

So there we were, Annabeth and Grover and I, walking through the woods along the New Jersey riverbank, the glow of New York City making the night sky yellow behind us, and the smell of the Hudson reeking in our noses.

Grover was shivering and braying, his big goat eyes turned slit-pupiled and full of terror. "Three Kindly Ones. All three at once."

I was pretty much in shock myself. The explosion of bus windows still rang in my ears. But Annabeth kept pulling us along, saying: "Come on! The farther away we get, the better."

"All our money was back there," I reminded her. "Our food and clothes. Everything."

"Well, maybe if you hadn't decided to jump into the fight—"

"What did you want me to do? Let you get killed?"

"You didn't need to protect me, Percy. I would've been fine."

"Sliced like sandwich bread," Grover put in, "but fine."

"Shut up, goat boy," said Annabeth.

Grover brayed mournfully. "Tin cans . . . a perfectly good bag of tin cans."

We sloshed across mushy ground, through nasty twisted trees that smelled like sour laundry.

After a few minutes, Annabeth fell into line next to me. "Look, I . . ." Her voice faltered. "I appreciate your coming back for us, okay? That was really brave."

"We're a team, right?"

She was silent for a few more steps. "It's just that if you died . . . aside from the fact that it would really suck for you, it would mean the quest was over. This may be my only chance to see the real world."

The thunderstorm had finally let up. The city glow faded behind us, leaving us in almost total darkness. I couldn't see anything of Annabeth except a glint of her blond hair.

"You haven't left Camp Half-Blood since you were seven?" I asked her.

"No . . . only short field trips. My dad—"

"The history professor."

"Yeah. It didn't work out for me living at home. I mean, Camp Half-Blood *is* my home." She was rushing her words out now, as if she were afraid somebody might try to stop her. "At camp you train and train. And that's all cool and everything, but the real world is where the monsters are. That's where you learn whether you're any good or not."

If I didn't know better, I could've sworn I heard doubt in her voice.

"You're pretty good with that knife," I said.

"You think so?"

"Anybody who can piggyback-ride a Fury is okay by me."

I couldn't really see, but I thought she might've smiled.

"You know," she said, "maybe I should tell you . . . Something funny back on the bus . . ."

Whatever she wanted to say was interrupted by a shrill *toot-toot-toot*, like the sound of an owl being tortured.

"Hey, my reed pipes still work!" Grover cried. "If I could just remember a 'find path' song, we could get out of these woods!"

He puffed out a few notes, but the tune still sounded suspiciously like Hilary Duff.

Instead of finding a path, I immediately slammed into a tree and got a nice-size knot on my head.

Add to the list of superpowers I did *not* have: infrared vision.

After tripping and cursing and generally feeling miserable for another mile or so, I started to see light up ahead: the colors of a neon sign. I could smell food. Fried, greasy, excellent food. I realized I hadn't eaten anything unhealthy since I'd arrived at Half-Blood Hill, where we lived on grapes, bread, cheese, and extra-lean-cut nymph-prepared barbecue. This boy needed a double cheeseburger.

We kept walking until I saw a deserted two-lane road through the trees. On the other side was a closed-down gas station, a tattered billboard for a 1990s movie, and one open business, which was the source of the neon light and the good smell.

It wasn't a fast-food restaurant like I'd hoped. It was one of those weird roadside curio shops that sell lawn flamingos and wooden Indians and cement grizzly bears and stuff like that. The main building was a long, low warehouse, surrounded by acres of statuary. The neon sign above the gate was impossible for me to read, because if there's anything worse for my dyslexia than regular English, it's red cursive neon English.

To me, it looked like: *ATNYU MES GDERAN GOMEN MEPROUIM.*

"What the heck does that say?" I asked.

"I don't know," Annabeth said.

She loved reading so much, I'd forgotten she was dyslexic, too.

Grover translated: "Aunty Em's Garden Gnome Emporium."

Flanking the entrance, as advertised, were two cement garden gnomes, ugly bearded little runts, smiling and waving, as if they were about to get their picture taken.

I crossed the street, following the smell of the hamburgers.

"Hey . . ." Grover warned.

"The lights are on inside," Annabeth said. "Maybe it's open."

"Snack bar," I said wistfully.

"Snack bar," she agreed.

"Are you two crazy?" Grover said. "This place is weird."

We ignored him.

The front lot was a forest of statues: cement animals, cement children, even a cement satyr playing the pipes, which gave Grover the creeps.

"*Bla-ha-ha!*" he bleated. "Looks like my Uncle Ferdinand!"

We stopped at the warehouse door.

"Don't knock," Grover pleaded. "I smell monsters."

"Your nose is clogged up from the Furies," Annabeth told him. "All I smell is burgers. Aren't you hungry?"

"Meat!" he said scornfully. "I'm a vegetarian."

"You eat cheese enchiladas and aluminum cans," I reminded him.

"Those are vegetables. Come on. Let's leave. These statues are . . . looking at me."

Then the door creaked open, and standing in front of us was a tall Middle Eastern woman—at least, I assumed she was Middle Eastern, because she wore a long black gown that covered everything but her hands, and her head was completely veiled. Her eyes glinted behind a curtain of black gauze, but that was about all I could make out. Her coffee-colored hands looked old, but well-manicured and elegant, so I imagined she was a grandmother who had once been a beautiful lady.

Her accent sounded vaguely Middle Eastern, too. She

said, "Children, it is too late to be out all alone. Where are your parents?"

"They're . . . um . . ." Annabeth started to say.

"We're orphans," I said.

"Orphans?" the woman said. The word sounded alien in her mouth. "But, my dears! Surely not!"

"We got separated from our caravan," I said. "Our circus caravan. The ringmaster told us to meet him at the gas station if we got lost, but he may have forgotten, or maybe he meant a different gas station. Anyway, we're lost. Is that food I smell?"

"Oh, my dears," the woman said. "You must come in, poor children. I am Aunty Em. Go straight through to the back of the warehouse, please. There is a dining area."

We thanked her and went inside.

Annabeth muttered to me, "Circus caravan?"

"Always have a strategy, right?"

"Your head is full of kelp."

The warehouse was filled with more statues—people in all different poses, wearing all different outfits and with different expressions on their faces. I was thinking you'd have to have a pretty huge garden to fit even one of these statues, because they were all life-size. But mostly, I was thinking about food.

Go ahead, call me an idiot for walking into a strange lady's shop like that just because I was hungry, but I do impulsive stuff sometimes. Plus, you've never smelled Aunty Em's burgers. The aroma was like laughing gas in the dentist's chair—it made everything else go away. I barely noticed Grover's nervous whimpers, or the way the statues' eyes seemed to follow me, or the fact that Aunty Em had locked the door behind us.

All I cared about was finding the dining area. And sure enough, there it was at the back of the warehouse, a fast-food counter with a grill, a soda fountain, a pretzel heater, and a nacho cheese dispenser. Everything you could want, plus a few steel picnic tables out front.

"Please, sit down," Aunty Em said.

"Awesome," I said.

"Um," Grover said reluctantly, "we don't have any money, ma'am."

Before I could jab him in the ribs, Aunty Em said, "No, no, children. No money. This is a special case, yes? It is my treat, for such nice orphans."

"Thank you, ma'am," Annabeth said.

Aunty Em stiffened, as if Annabeth had done something wrong, but then the old woman relaxed just as quickly, so I figured it must've been my imagination.

"Quite all right, Annabeth," she said. "You have such beautiful gray eyes, child." Only later did I wonder how she knew Annabeth's name, even though we had never introduced ourselves.

Our hostess disappeared behind the snack counter and started cooking. Before we knew it, she'd brought us plastic trays heaped with double cheeseburgers, vanilla shakes, and XXL servings of French fries.

I was halfway through my burger before I remembered to breathe.

Annabeth slurped her shake.

Grover picked at the fries, and eyed the tray's waxed paper liner as if he might go for that, but he still looked too nervous to eat.

"What's that hissing noise?" he asked.

I listened, but didn't hear anything. Annabeth shook her head.

"Hissing?" Aunty Em asked. "Perhaps you hear the deep-fryer oil. You have keen ears, Grover."

"I take vitamins. For my ears."

"That's admirable," she said. "But please, relax."

Aunty Em ate nothing. She hadn't taken off her head-dress, even to cook, and now she sat forward and interlaced her fingers and watched us eat. It was a little unsettling, having someone stare at me when I couldn't see her face, but I was feeling satisfied after the burger, and a little sleepy, and I figured the least I could do was try to make small talk with our hostess.

"So, you sell gnomes," I said, trying to sound interested.

"Oh, yes," Aunty Em said. "And animals. And people. Anything for the garden. Custom orders. Statuary is very popular, you know."

"A lot of business on this road?"

"Not so much, no. Since the highway was built . . . most cars, they do not go this way now. I must cherish every customer I get."

My neck tingled, as if somebody else was looking at me. I turned, but it was just a statue of a young girl holding an Easter basket. The detail was incredible, much better than you see in most garden statues. But something was wrong with her face. It looked as if she were startled, or even terrified.

"Ah," Aunty Em said sadly. "You notice some of my creations do not turn out well. They are marred. They do not sell. The face is the hardest to get right. Always the face."

"You make these statues yourself?" I asked.

"Oh, yes. Once upon a time, I had two sisters to help me in the business, but they have passed on, and Aunty Em is alone. I have only my statues. This is why I make them, you see. They are my company." The sadness in her voice sounded so deep and so real that I couldn't help feeling sorry for her.

Annabeth had stopped eating. She sat forward and said, "Two sisters?"

"It's a terrible story," Aunty Em said. "Not one for children, really. You see, Annabeth, a bad woman was jealous of me, long ago, when I was young. I had a . . . a boyfriend, you know, and this bad woman was determined to break us apart. She caused a terrible accident. My sisters stayed by me. They shared my bad fortune as long as they could, but eventually they passed on. They faded away. I alone have survived, but at a price. Such a price."

I wasn't sure what she meant, but I felt bad for her. My eyelids kept getting heavier, my full stomach making me sleepy. Poor old lady. Who would want to hurt somebody so nice?

"Percy?" Annabeth was shaking me to get my attention.

"Maybe we should go. I mean, the ringmaster will be waiting."

She sounded tense. I wasn't sure why. Grover was eating the waxed paper off the tray now, but if Aunty Em found that strange, she didn't say anything.

"Such beautiful gray eyes," Aunty Em told Annabeth again. "My, yes, it has been a long time since I've seen gray eyes like those."

She reached out as if to stroke Annabeth's cheek, but Annabeth stood up abruptly.

"We really should go."

"Yes!" Grover swallowed his waxed paper and stood up. "The ringmaster is waiting! Right!"

I didn't want to leave. I felt full and content. Aunty Em was so nice. I wanted to stay with her a while.

"Please, dears," Aunty Em pleaded. "I so rarely get to be with children. Before you go, won't you at least sit for a pose?"

"A pose?" Annabeth asked warily.

"A photograph. I will use it to model a new statue set. Children are so popular, you see. Everyone loves children."

Annabeth shifted her weight from foot to foot. "I don't think we can, ma'am. Come on, Percy—"

"Sure we can," I said. I was irritated with Annabeth for being so bossy, so rude to an old lady who'd just fed us for free. "It's just a photo, Annabeth. What's the harm?"

"Yes, Annabeth," the woman purred. "No harm."

I could tell Annabeth didn't like it, but she allowed

Aunty Em to lead us back out the front door, into the garden of statues.

Aunty Em directed us to a park bench next to the stone satyr. "Now," she said, "I'll just position you correctly. The young girl in the middle, I think, and the two young gentlemen on either side."

"Not much light for a photo," I remarked.

"Oh, enough," Aunty Em said. "Enough for us to see each other, yes?"

"Where's your camera?" Grover asked.

Aunty Em stepped back, as if to admire the shot. "Now, the face is the most difficult. Can you smile for me please, everyone? A large smile?"

Grover glanced at the cement satyr next to him, and mumbled, "That sure does look like Uncle Ferdinand."

"Grover," Aunty Em chastised, "look this way, dear."

She still had no camera in her hands.

"Percy—" Annabeth said.

Some instinct warned me to listen to Annabeth, but I was fighting the sleepy feeling, the comfortable lull that came from the food and the old lady's voice.

"I will just be a moment," Aunty Em said. "You know, I can't see you very well in this cursed veil. . . ."

"Percy, something's wrong," Annabeth insisted.

"Wrong?" Aunty Em said, reaching up to undo the wrap around her head. "Not at all, dear. I have such noble company tonight. What could be wrong?"

"That *is* Uncle Ferdinand!" Grover gasped.

"Look away from her!" Annabeth shouted. She whipped

her Yankees cap onto her head and vanished. Her invisible hands pushed Grover and me both off the bench.

I was on the ground, looking at Aunt Em's sandaled feet.

I could hear Grover scrambling off in one direction, Annabeth in another. But I was too dazed to move.

Then I heard a strange, rasping sound above me. My eyes rose to Aunty Em's hands, which had turned gnarled and warty, with sharp bronze talons for fingernails.

I almost looked higher, but somewhere off to my left Annabeth screamed, "No! Don't!"

More rasping—the sound of tiny snakes, right above me, from . . . from about where Aunty Em's head would be.

"Run!" Grover bleated. I heard him racing across the gravel, yelling, *"Maia!"* to kick-start his flying sneakers.

I couldn't move. I stared at Aunty Em's gnarled claws, and tried to fight the groggy trance the old woman had put me in.

"Such a pity to destroy a handsome young face," she told me soothingly. "Stay with me, Percy. All you have to do is look up."

I fought the urge to obey. Instead I looked to one side and saw one of those glass spheres people put in gardens— a gazing ball. I could see Aunty Em's dark reflection in the orange glass; her headdress was gone, revealing her face as a shimmering pale circle. Her hair was moving, writhing like serpents.

Aunty Em.

Aunty "M."

How could I have been so stupid?

Think, I told myself. How did Medusa die in the myth?

But I couldn't think. Something told me that in the myth Medusa had been asleep when she was attacked by my namesake, Perseus. She wasn't anywhere near asleep now. If she wanted, she could take those talons right now and rake open my face.

"The Gray-Eyed One did this to me, Percy," Medusa said, and she didn't sound anything like a monster. Her voice invited me to look up, to sympathize with a poor old grandmother. "Annabeth's mother, the cursed Athena, turned me from a beautiful woman into this."

"Don't listen to her!" Annabeth's voice shouted, somewhere in the statuary. "Run, Percy!"

"Silence!" Medusa snarled. Then her voice modulated back to a comforting purr. "You see why I must destroy the girl, Percy. She is my enemy's daughter. I shall crush her statue to dust. But you, dear Percy, you need not suffer."

"No," I muttered. I tried to make my legs move.

"Do you really want to help the gods?" Medusa asked. "Do you understand what awaits you on this foolish quest, Percy? What will happen if you reach the Underworld? Do not be a pawn of the Olympians, my dear. You would be better off as a statue. Less pain. Less pain."

"Percy!" Behind me, I heard a buzzing sound, like a two-hundred-pound hummingbird in a nosedive. Grover yelled, "Duck!"

I turned, and there he was in the night sky, flying in from twelve o'clock with his winged shoes fluttering,

Grover, holding a tree branch the size of a baseball bat. His eyes were shut tight, his head twitched from side to side. He was navigating by ears and nose alone.

"Duck!" he yelled again. "I'll get her!"

That finally jolted me into action. Knowing Grover, I was sure he'd miss Medusa and nail me. I dove to one side.

Thwack!

At first I figured it was the sound of Grover hitting a tree. Then Medusa roared with rage.

"You miserable satyr," she snarled. "I'll add you to my collection!"

"That was for Uncle Ferdinand!" Grover yelled back.

I scrambled away and hid in the statuary while Grover swooped down for another pass.

Ker-whack!

"Arrgh!" Medusa yelled, her snake-hair hissing and spitting.

Right next to me, Annabeth's voice said, "Percy!"

I jumped so high my feet nearly cleared a garden gnome. "Jeez! Don't do that!"

Annabeth took off her Yankees cap and became visible. "You have to cut her head off."

"What? Are you crazy? Let's get out of here."

"Medusa is a menace. She's evil. I'd kill her myself, but . . ." Annabeth swallowed, as if she were about to make a difficult admission. "But you've got the better weapon. Besides, I'd never get close to her. She'd slice me to bits because of my mother. You—you've got a chance."

"What? I can't—"

"Look, do you want her turning more innocent people into statues?"

She pointed to a pair of statue lovers, a man and a woman with their arms around each other, turned to stone by the monster.

Annabeth grabbed a green gazing ball from a nearby pedestal. "A polished shield would be better." She studied the sphere critically. "The convexity will cause some distortion. The reflection's size should be off by a factor of—"

"Would you speak English?"

"I *am!*" She tossed me the glass ball. "Just look at her in the glass. *Never* look at her directly."

"Hey, guys!" Grover yelled somewhere above us. "I think she's unconscious!"

"*Roooaaarrr!*"

"Maybe not," Grover corrected. He went in for another pass with the tree branch.

"Hurry," Annabeth told me. "Grover's got a great nose, but he'll eventually crash."

I took out my pen and uncapped it. The bronze blade of Riptide elongated in my hand.

I followed the hissing and spitting sounds of Medusa's hair.

I kept my eyes locked on the gazing ball so I would only glimpse Medusa's reflection, not the real thing. Then, in the green tinted glass, I saw her.

Grover was coming in for another turn at bat, but this time he flew a little too low. Medusa grabbed the stick and pulled him off course. He tumbled through the air and crashed into the arms of a stone grizzly bear with a painful "Ummphh!"

Medusa was about to lunge at him when I yelled, "Hey!"

I advanced on her, which wasn't easy, holding a sword and a glass ball. If she charged, I'd have a hard time defending myself.

But she let me approach—twenty feet, ten feet.

I could see the reflection of her face now. Surely it wasn't really *that* ugly. The green swirls of the gazing ball must be distorting it, making it look worse.

"You wouldn't harm an old woman, Percy," she crooned. "I know you wouldn't."

I hesitated, fascinated by the face I saw reflected in the glass—the eyes that seemed to burn straight through the green tint, making my arms go weak.

From the cement grizzly, Grover moaned, "Percy, don't listen to her!"

Medusa cackled. "Too late."

She lunged at me with her talons.

I slashed up with my sword, heard a sickening *shlock!*, then a hiss like wind rushing out of a cavern—the sound of a monster disintegrating.

Something fell to the ground next to my foot. It took all my willpower not to look. I could feel warm ooze soaking into my sock, little dying snake heads tugging at my shoelaces.

"Oh, yuck," Grover said. His eyes were still tightly closed, but I guess he could hear the thing gurgling and steaming. "Mega-yuck."

Annabeth came up next to me, her eyes fixed on the sky. She was holding Medusa's black veil. She said, "Don't move."

Very, very carefully, without looking down, she knelt and draped the monster's head in black cloth, then picked it up. It was still dripping green juice.

"Are you okay?" she asked me, her voice trembling.

"Yeah," I decided, though I felt like throwing up my double cheeseburger. "Why didn't . . . why didn't the head evaporate?"

"Once you sever it, it becomes a spoil of war," she said. "Same as your minotaur horn. But don't unwrap the head. It can still petrify you."

Grover moaned as he climbed down from the grizzly statue. He had a big welt on his forehead. His green rasta cap hung from one of his little goat horns, and his fake feet had been knocked off his hooves. The magic sneakers were flying aimlessly around his head.

"The Red Baron," I said. "Good job, man."

He managed a bashful grin. "That really was *not* fun, though. Well, the hitting-her-with-a-stick part, that was fun. But crashing into a concrete bear? *Not* fun."

He snatched his shoes out of the air. I recapped my sword. Together, the three of us stumbled back to the warehouse.

We found some old plastic grocery bags behind the snack counter and double-wrapped Medusa's head. We plopped it on the table where we'd eaten dinner and sat around it, too exhausted to speak.

Finally I said, "So we have Athena to thank for this monster?"

Annabeth flashed me an irritated look. "Your dad, actually. Don't you remember? Medusa was Poseidon's girlfriend. They decided to meet in my mother's temple. That's why Athena turned her into a monster. Medusa and her two sisters who had helped her get into the temple, they became the three gorgons. That's why Medusa wanted to slice me up, but she wanted to preserve you as a nice statue. She's still sweet on your dad. You probably reminded her of him."

My face was burning. "Oh, so now it's *my* fault we met Medusa."

Annabeth straightened. In a bad imitation of my voice, she said: "'It's just a photo, Annabeth. What's the harm?'"

"Forget it," I said. "You're impossible."

"You're insufferable."

"You're—"

"Hey!" Grover interrupted. "You two are giving me a migraine, and satyrs don't even *get* migraines. What are we going to do with the head?"

I stared at the thing. One little snake was hanging out of a hole in the plastic. The words printed on the side of the bag said: WE APPRECIATE YOUR BUSINESS!

I was angry, not just with Annabeth or her mom, but with all the gods for this whole quest, for getting us blown off the road and in two major fights the very first day out from camp. At this rate, we'd never make it to L.A. alive, much less before the summer solstice.

What had Medusa said?

Do not be a pawn of the Olympians, my dear. You would be better off as a statue.

I got up. "I'll be back."

"Percy," Annabeth called after me. "What are you—"

I searched the back of the warehouse until I found Medusa's office. Her account book showed her six most recent sales, all shipments to the Underworld to decorate Hades and Persephone's garden. According to one freight bill, the Underworld's billing address was DOA Recording Studios, West Hollywood, California. I folded up the bill and stuffed it in my pocket.

In the cash register I found twenty dollars, a few golden drachmas, and some packing slips for Hermes Overnight Express, each with a little leather bag attached for coins. I rummaged around the rest of the office until I found the right-size box.

I went back to the picnic table, packed up Medusa's head, and filled out a delivery slip:

The Gods
Mount Olympus
600th Floor,
Empire State Building
New York, NY

With best wishes,
PERCY JACKSON

"They're not going to like that," Grover warned. "They'll think you're impertinent."

I poured some golden drachmas in the pouch. As soon as I closed it, there was a sound like a cash register. The package floated off the table and disappeared with a *pop!*

"I *am* impertinent," I said.

I looked at Annabeth, daring her to criticize.

She didn't. She seemed resigned to the fact that I had a major talent for ticking off the gods. "Come on," she muttered. "We need a new plan."

TWELVE

WE GET ADVICE
FROM A POODLE

We were pretty miserable that night.

We camped out in the woods, a hundred yards from the main road, in a marshy clearing that local kids had obviously been using for parties. The ground was littered with flattened soda cans and fast-food wrappers.

We'd taken some food and blankets from Aunty Em's, but we didn't dare light a fire to dry our damp clothes. The Furies and Medusa had provided enough excitement for one day. We didn't want to attract anything else.

We decided to sleep in shifts. I volunteered to take first watch.

Annabeth curled up on the blankets and was snoring as soon as her head hit the ground. Grover fluttered with his flying shoes to the lowest bough of a tree, put his back to the trunk, and stared at the night sky.

"Go ahead and sleep," I told him. "I'll wake you if there's trouble."

He nodded, but still didn't close his eyes. "It makes me sad, Percy."

"What does? The fact that you signed up for this stupid quest?"

"No. *This* makes me sad." He pointed at all the garbage

on the ground. "And the sky. You can't even see the stars. They've polluted the sky. This is a terrible time to be a satyr."

"Oh, yeah. I guess you'd be an environmentalist."

He glared at me. "Only a human wouldn't be. Your species is clogging up the world so fast . . . ah, never mind. It's useless to lecture a human. At the rate things are going, I'll never find Pan."

"Pam? Like the cooking spray?"

"Pan!" he cried indignantly. "P-A-N. The great god Pan! What do you think I want a searcher's license for?"

A strange breeze rustled through the clearing, temporarily overpowering the stink of trash and muck. It brought the smell of berries and wildflowers and clean rainwater, things that might've once been in these woods. Suddenly I was nostalgic for something I'd never known.

"Tell me about the search," I said.

Grover looked at me cautiously, as if he were afraid I was just making fun.

"The God of Wild Places disappeared two thousand years ago," he told me. "A sailor off the coast of Ephesos heard a mysterious voice crying out from the shore, 'Tell them that the great god Pan has died!' When humans heard the news, they believed it. They've been pillaging Pan's kingdom ever since. But for the satyrs, Pan was our lord and master. He protected us and the wild places of the earth. We refuse to believe that he died. In every generation, the bravest satyrs pledge their lives to finding Pan. They search the earth, exploring all the wildest places, hoping to find where he is hidden, and wake him from his sleep."

"And you want to be a searcher."

"It's my life's dream," he said. "My father was a searcher. And my Uncle Ferdinand . . . the statue you saw back there—"

"Oh, right, sorry."

Grover shook his head. "Uncle Ferdinand knew the risks. So did my dad. But I'll succeed. I'll be the first searcher to return alive."

"Hang on—*the first?*"

Grover took his reed pipes out of his pocket. "No searcher has ever come back. Once they set out, they disappear. They're never seen alive again."

"Not once in two thousand years?"

"No."

"And your dad? You have no idea what happened to him?"

"None."

"But you still want to go," I said, amazed. "I mean, you really think you'll be the one to find Pan?"

"I have to believe that, Percy. Every searcher does. It's the only thing that keeps us from despair when we look at what humans have done to the world. I have to believe Pan can still be awakened."

I stared at the orange haze of the sky and tried to understand how Grover could pursue a dream that seemed so hopeless. Then again, was I any better?

"How are we going to get into the Underworld?" I asked him. "I mean, what chance do we have against a god?"

"I don't know," he admitted. "But back at Medusa's,

when you were searching her office? Annabeth was telling me—"

"Oh, I forgot. Annabeth will have a plan all figured out."

"Don't be so hard on her, Percy. She's had a tough life, but she's a good person. After all, she forgave me. . . ." His voice faltered.

"What do you mean?" I asked. "Forgave you for what?"

Suddenly, Grover seemed very interested in playing notes on his pipes.

"Wait a minute," I said. "Your first keeper job was five years ago. Annabeth has been at camp five years. She wasn't . . . I mean, your first assignment that went wrong—"

"I can't talk about it," Grover said, and his quivering lower lip suggested he'd start crying if I pressed him. "But as I was saying, back at Medusa's, Annabeth and I agreed there's something strange going on with this quest. Something isn't what it seems."

"Well, duh. I'm getting blamed for stealing a thunderbolt that Hades took."

"That's not what I mean," Grover said. "The Fur—The Kindly Ones were sort of holding back. Like Mrs. Dodds at Yancy Academy . . . why did she wait so long to try to kill you? Then on the bus, they just weren't as aggressive as they could've been."

"They seemed plenty aggressive to me."

Grover shook his head. "They were screeching at us: 'Where is it? Where?'"

"Asking about me," I said.

"Maybe . . . but Annabeth and I, we both got the feeling they weren't asking about a person. They said 'Where is *it*?' They seemed to be asking about an object."

"That doesn't make sense."

"I know. But if we've misunderstood something about this quest, and we only have nine days to find the master bolt. . . ." He looked at me like he was hoping for answers, but I didn't have any.

I thought about what Medusa had said: I was being used by the gods. What lay ahead of me was worse than petrification. "I haven't been straight with you," I told Grover. "I don't care about the master bolt. I agreed to go to the Underworld so I could bring back my mother."

Grover blew a soft note on his pipes. "I know that, Percy. But are you sure that's the only reason?"

"I'm not doing it to help my father. He doesn't care about me. I don't care about him."

Grover gazed down from his tree branch. "Look, Percy, I'm not as smart as Annabeth. I'm not as brave as you. But I'm pretty good at reading emotions. You're glad your dad is alive. You feel good that he's claimed you, and part of you wants to make him proud. That's why you mailed Medusa's head to Olympus. You wanted him to notice what you'd done."

"Yeah? Well maybe satyr emotions work differently than human emotions. Because you're wrong. I don't care what he thinks."

Grover pulled his feet up onto the branch. "Okay, Percy. Whatever."

"Besides, I haven't done anything worth bragging about. We barely got out of New York and we're stuck here with no money and no way west."

Grover looked at the night sky, like he was thinking about that problem. "How about *I* take first watch, huh? You get some sleep."

I wanted to protest, but he started to play Mozart, soft and sweet, and I turned away, my eyes stinging. After a few bars of Piano Concerto no. 12, I was asleep.

In my dreams, I stood in a dark cavern before a gaping pit. Gray mist creatures churned all around me, whispering rags of smoke that I somehow knew were the spirits of the dead.

They tugged at my clothes, trying to pull me back, but I felt compelled to walk forward to the very edge of the chasm.

Looking down made me dizzy.

The pit yawned so wide and was so completely black, I knew it must be bottomless. Yet I had a feeling that something was trying to rise from the abyss, something huge and evil.

The little hero, an amused voice echoed far down in the darkness. *Too weak, too young, but perhaps you will do.*

The voice felt ancient—cold and heavy. It wrapped around me like sheets of lead.

They have misled you, boy, it said. *Barter with me. I will give you what you want.*

A shimmering image hovered over the void: my mother, frozen at the moment she'd dissolved in a shower of gold.

Her face was distorted with pain, as if the Minotaur were still squeezing her neck. Her eyes looked directly at me, pleading: *Go!*

I tried to cry out, but my voice wouldn't work.

Cold laughter echoed from the chasm.

An invisible force pulled me forward. It would drag me into the pit unless I stood firm.

Help me rise, boy. The voice became hungrier. *Bring me the bolt. Strike a blow against the treacherous gods!*

The spirits of the dead whispered around me, *No! Wake!*

The image of my mother began to fade. The thing in the pit tightened its unseen grip around me.

I realized it wasn't interested in pulling me in. It was using me to pull itself *out*.

Good, it murmured. *Good.*

Wake! the dead whispered. *Wake!*

Someone was shaking me.

My eyes opened, and it was daylight.

"Well," Annabeth said, "the zombie lives."

I was trembling from the dream. I could still feel the grip of the chasm monster around my chest. "How long was I asleep?"

"Long enough for me to cook breakfast." Annabeth tossed me a bag of nacho-flavored corn chips from Aunty Em's snack bar. "And Grover went exploring. Look, he found a friend."

My eyes had trouble focusing.

Grover was sitting cross-legged on a blanket with

something fuzzy in his lap, a dirty, unnaturally pink stuffed animal.

No. It wasn't a stuffed animal. It was a pink poodle.

The poodle yapped at me suspiciously. Grover said, "No, he's not."

I blinked. "Are you . . . talking to that thing?"

The poodle growled.

"This *thing*," Grover warned, "is our ticket west. Be nice to him."

"You can talk to animals?"

Grover ignored the question. "Percy, meet Gladiola. Gladiola, Percy."

I stared at Annabeth, figuring she'd crack up at this practical joke they were playing on me, but she looked deadly serious.

"I'm not saying hello to a pink poodle," I said. "Forget it."

"Percy," Annabeth said. "I said hello to the poodle. You say hello to the poodle."

The poodle growled.

I said hello to the poodle.

Grover explained that he'd come across Gladiola in the woods and they'd struck up a conversation. The poodle had run away from a rich local family, who'd posted a $200 reward for his return. Gladiola didn't really want to go back to his family, but he was willing to if it meant helping Grover.

"How does Gladiola know about the reward?" I asked.

"He read the signs," Grover said. "Duh."

"Of course," I said. "Silly me."

"So we turn in Gladiola," Annabeth explained in her best strategy voice, "we get money, and we buy tickets to Los Angeles. Simple."

I thought about my dream—the whispering voices of the dead, the thing in the chasm, and my mother's face, shimmering as it dissolved into gold. All that might be waiting for me in the West.

"Not another bus," I said warily.

"No," Annabeth agreed.

She pointed downhill, toward train tracks I hadn't been able to see last night in the dark. "There's an Amtrack station half a mile that way. According to Gladiola, the westbound train leaves at noon."

THIRTEEN

I PLUNGE TO
MY DEATH

We spent two days on the Amtrak train, heading west through hills, over rivers, past amber waves of grain.

We weren't attacked once, but I didn't relax. I felt that we were traveling around in a display case, being watched from above and maybe from below, that something was waiting for the right opportunity.

I tried to keep a low profile because my name and picture were splattered over the front pages of several East Coast newspapers. The *Trenton Register-News* showed a photo taken by a tourist as I got off the Greyhound bus. I had a wild look in my eyes. My sword was a metallic blur in my hands. It might've been a baseball bat or a lacrosse stick.

The picture's caption read:

Twelve-year-old Percy Jackson, wanted for questioning in the Long Island disappearance of his mother two weeks ago, is shown here fleeing from the bus where he accosted several elderly female passengers. The bus exploded on an east New Jersey roadside shortly after Jackson fled the scene. Based on eyewitness accounts, police believe the boy may be traveling with two teenage accomplices. His stepfather, Gabe Ugliano, has offered a cash reward for information leading to his capture.

"Don't worry," Annabeth told me. "Mortal police could never find us." But she didn't sound so sure.

The rest of the day I spent alternately pacing the length of the train (because I had a really hard time sitting still) or looking out the windows.

Once, I spotted a family of centaurs galloping across a wheat field, bows at the ready, as they hunted lunch. The little boy centaur, who was the size of a second-grader on a pony, caught my eye and waved. I looked around the passenger car, but nobody else had noticed. The adult riders all had their faces buried in laptop computers or magazines.

Another time, toward evening, I saw something huge moving through the woods. I could've sworn it was a lion, except that lions don't live wild in America, and this thing was the size of a Hummer. Its fur glinted gold in the evening light. Then it leaped through the trees and was gone.

Our reward money for returning Gladiola the poodle had only been enough to purchase tickets as far as Denver. We couldn't get berths in the sleeper car, so we dozed in our seats. My neck got stiff. I tried not to drool in my sleep, since Annabeth was sitting right next to me.

Grover kept snoring and bleating and waking me up. Once, he shuffled around and his fake foot fell off. Annabeth and I had to stick it back on before any of the other passengers noticed.

"So," Annabeth asked me, once we'd gotten Grover's sneaker readjusted. "Who wants your help?"

"What do you mean?"

"When you were asleep just now, you mumbled, 'I won't help you.' Who were you dreaming about?"

I was reluctant to say anything. It was the second time I'd dreamed about the evil voice from the pit. But it bothered me so much I finally told her.

Annabeth was quiet for a long time. "That doesn't sound like Hades. He always appears on a black throne, and he never laughs."

"He offered my mother in trade. Who else could do that?"

"I guess . . . if he meant, 'Help me rise from the Underworld.' If he wants war with the Olympians. But why ask you to bring him the master bolt if he already has it?"

I shook my head, wishing I knew the answer. I thought about what Grover had told me, that the Furies on the bus seemed to have been looking for something.

Where is it? Where?

Maybe Grover sensed my emotions. He snorted in his sleep, muttered something about vegetables, and turned his head.

Annabeth readjusted his cap so it covered his horns. "Percy, you can't barter with Hades. You know that, right? He's deceitful, heartless, and greedy. I don't care if his Kindly Ones weren't as aggressive this time—"

"This time?" I asked. "You mean you've run into them before?"

Her hand crept up to her necklace. She fingered a glazed white bead painted with the image of a pine tree, one of her clay end-of-summer tokens. "Let's just say I've got no love for the Lord of the Dead. You can't be tempted to make a deal for your mom."

"What would you do if it was your dad?"

"That's easy," she said. "I'd leave him to rot."

"You're not serious?"

Annabeth's gray eyes fixed on me. She wore the same expression she'd worn in the woods at camp, the moment she drew her sword against the hellhound. "My dad's resented me since the day I was born, Percy," she said. "He never wanted a baby. When he got me, he asked Athena to take me back and raise me on Olympus because he was too busy with his work. She wasn't happy about that. She told him heroes had to be raised by their mortal parent."

"But how . . . I mean, I guess you weren't born in a hospital. . . ."

"I appeared on my father's doorstep, in a golden cradle, carried down from Olympus by Zephyr the West Wind. You'd think my dad would remember that as a miracle, right? Like, maybe he'd take some digital photos or something. But he always talked about my arrival as if it were the most inconvenient thing that had ever happened to him. When I was five he got married and totally forgot about Athena. He got a 'regular' mortal wife, and had two 'regular' mortal kids, and tried to pretend I didn't exist."

I stared out the train window. The lights of a sleeping town were drifting by. I wanted to make Annabeth feel better, but I didn't know how.

"My mom married a really awful guy," I told her. "Grover said she did it to protect me, to hide me in the scent of a human family. Maybe that's what your dad was thinking."

Annabeth kept worrying at her necklace. She was pinching the gold college ring that hung with the beads. It occurred to me that the ring must be her father's. I wondered why she wore it if she hated him so much.

"He doesn't care about me," she said. "His wife—my stepmom—treated me like a freak. She wouldn't let me play with her children. My dad went along with her. Whenever something dangerous happened—you know, something with monsters—they would both look at me resentfully, like, 'How dare you put our family at risk.' Finally, I took the hint. I wasn't wanted. I ran away."

"How old were you?"

"Same age as when I started camp. Seven."

"But . . . you couldn't have gotten all the way to Half-Blood Hill by yourself."

"Not alone, no. Athena watched over me, guided me toward help. I made a couple of unexpected friends who took care of me, for a short time, anyway."

I wanted to ask what happened, but Annabeth seemed lost in sad memories. So I listened to the sound of Grover snoring and gazed out the train windows as the dark fields of Ohio raced by.

Toward the end of our second day on the train, June 13, eight days before the summer solstice, we passed through some golden hills and over the Mississippi River into St. Louis.

Annabeth craned her neck to see the Gateway Arch, which looked to me like a huge shopping bag handle stuck on the city.

"I want to do that," she sighed.

"What?" I asked.

"Build something like that. You ever see the Parthenon, Percy?"

"Only in pictures."

"Someday, I'm going to see it in person. I'm going to build the greatest monument to the gods, ever. Something that'll last a thousand years."

I laughed. "You? An architect?"

I don't know why, but I found it funny. Just the idea of Annabeth trying to sit quietly and draw all day.

Her cheeks flushed. "Yes, an architect. Athena expects her children to create things, not just tear them down, like a certain god of earthquakes I could mention."

I watched the churning brown water of the Mississippi below.

"Sorry," Annabeth said. "That was mean."

"Can't we work together a little?" I pleaded. "I mean, didn't Athena and Poseidon ever cooperate?"

Annabeth had to think about it. "I guess . . . the chariot," she said tentatively. "My mom invented it, but Poseidon created horses out of the crests of waves. So they had to work together to make it complete."

"Then we can cooperate, too. Right?"

We rode into the city, Annabeth watching as the Arch disappeared behind a hotel.

"I suppose," she said at last.

We pulled into the Amtrak station downtown. The intercom told us we'd have a three-hour layover before departing for Denver.

Grover stretched. Before he was even fully awake, he said, "Food."

"Come on, goat boy," Annabeth said. "Sightseeing."

"Sightseeing?"

"The Gateway Arch," she said. "This may be my only chance to ride to the top. Are you coming or not?"

Grover and I exchanged looks.

I wanted to say no, but I figured that if Annabeth was going, we couldn't very well let her go alone.

Grover shrugged. "As long as there's a snack bar without monsters."

The Arch was about a mile from the train station. Late in the day the lines to get in weren't that long. We threaded our way through the underground museum, looking at covered wagons and other junk from the 1800s. It wasn't all that thrilling, but Annabeth kept telling us interesting facts about how the Arch was built, and Grover kept passing me jelly beans, so I was okay.

I kept looking around, though, at the other people in line. "You smell anything?" I murmured to Grover.

He took his nose out of the jelly-bean bag long enough to sniff. "Underground," he said distastefully. "Underground air always smells like monsters. Probably doesn't mean anything."

But something felt wrong to me. I had a feeling we shouldn't be here.

"Guys," I said. "You know the gods' symbols of power?"

Annabeth had been in the middle of reading about the construction equipment used to build the Arch, but she looked over. "Yeah?"

"Well, Hade—"

Grover cleared his throat. "We're in a public place. . . . You mean, our friend downstairs?"

"Um, right," I said. "Our friend *way* downstairs. Doesn't he have a hat like Annabeth's?"

"You mean the Helm of Darkness," Annabeth said. "Yeah, that's his symbol of power. I saw it next to his seat during the winter solstice council meeting."

"He was there?" I asked.

She nodded. "It's the only time he's allowed to visit Olympus—the darkest day of the year. But his helm is a lot more powerful than my invisibility hat, if what I've heard is true. . . ."

"It allows him to become darkness," Grover confirmed. "He can melt into shadow or pass through walls. He can't be touched, or seen, or heard. And he can radiate fear so intense it can drive you insane or stop your heart. Why do you think all rational creatures fear the dark?"

"But then . . . how do we know he's not here right now, watching us?" I asked.

Annabeth and Grover exchanged looks.

"We don't," Grover said.

"Thanks, that makes me feel a lot better," I said. "Got any blue jelly beans left?"

I'd almost mastered my jumpy nerves when I saw the tiny little elevator car we were going to ride to the top of the Arch, and I knew I was in trouble. I hate confined places. They make me nuts.

We got shoehorned into the car with this big fat lady and her dog, a Chihuahua with a rhinestone collar. I figured maybe the dog was a seeing-eye Chihuahua, because none of the guards said a word about it.

We started going up, inside the Arch. I'd never been in an elevator that went in a curve, and my stomach wasn't too happy about it.

"No parents?" the fat lady asked us.

She had beady eyes; pointy, coffee-stained teeth; a floppy denim hat, and a denim dress that bulged so much, she looked like a blue-jean blimp.

"They're below," Annabeth told her. "Scared of heights."

"Oh, the poor darlings."

The Chihuahua growled. The woman said, "Now, now, sonny. Behave." The dog had beady eyes like its owner, intelligent and vicious.

I said, "Sonny. Is that his name?"

"No," the lady told me.

She smiled, as if that cleared everything up.

At the top of the Arch, the observation deck reminded me of a tin can with carpeting. Rows of tiny windows looked out over the city on one side and the river on the other. The view was okay, but if there's anything I like less than a confined space, it's a confined space six hundred feet in the air. I was ready to go pretty quick.

Annabeth kept talking about structural supports, and how she would've made the windows bigger, and designed a see-through floor. She probably could've stayed up there for hours, but luckily for me the park ranger announced that the observation deck would be closing in a few minutes.

I steered Grover and Annabeth toward the exit, loaded them into the elevator, and I was about to get in myself when I realized there were already two other tourists inside. No room for me.

The park ranger said, "Next car, sir."

"We'll get out," Annabeth said. "We'll wait with you."

But that was going to mess everybody up and take even more time, so I said, "Naw, it's okay. I'll see you guys at the bottom."

Grover and Annabeth both looked nervous, but they let the elevator door slide shut. Their car disappeared down the ramp.

Now the only people left on the observation deck were me, a little boy with his parents, the park ranger, and the fat lady with her Chihuahua.

I smiled uneasily at the fat lady. She smiled back, her forked tongue flickering between her teeth.

Wait a minute.

Forked tongue?

Before I could decide if I'd really seen that, her Chihuahua jumped down and started yapping at me.

"Now, now, sonny," the lady said. "Does this look like a good time? We have all these nice people here."

"Doggie!" said the little boy. "Look, a doggie!"

His parents pulled him back.

The Chihuahua bared his teeth at me, foam dripping from his black lips.

"Well, son," the fat lady sighed. "If you insist."

Ice started forming in my stomach. "Um, did you just call that Chihuahua your son?"

"*Chimera*, dear," the fat lady corrected. "Not a Chihuahua. It's an easy mistake to make."

She rolled up her denim sleeves, revealing that the skin of her arms was scaly and green. When she smiled, I saw that her teeth were fangs. The pupils of her eyes were sideways slits, like a reptile's.

The Chihuahua barked louder, and with each bark, it grew. First to the size of a Doberman, then to a lion. The bark became a roar.

The little boy screamed. His parents pulled him back toward the exit, straight into the park ranger, who stood, paralyzed, gaping at the monster.

The Chimera was now so tall its back rubbed against the roof. It had the head of a lion with a blood-caked mane, the body and hooves of a giant goat, and a serpent for a tail, a ten-foot-long diamondback growing right out of its shaggy behind. The rhinestone dog collar still hung around its neck, and the plate-sized dog tag was now easy to read: CHIMERA—RABID, FIRE-BREATHING, POISONOUS—IF FOUND, PLEASE CALL TARTARUS—EXT. 954.

I realized I hadn't even uncapped my sword. My hands were numb. I was ten feet away from the Chimera's bloody maw, and I knew that as soon as I moved, the creature would lunge.

The snake lady made a hissing noise that might've been laughter. "Be honored, Percy Jackson. Lord Zeus rarely allows me to test a hero with one of my brood. For I am the Mother of Monsters, the terrible Echidna!"

I stared at her. All I could think to say was: "Isn't that a kind of anteater?"

She howled, her reptilian face turning brown and green with rage. "I hate it when people say that! I hate Australia! Naming that ridiculous animal after me. For that, Percy Jackson, my son shall destroy you!"

The Chimera charged, its lion teeth gnashing. I managed to leap aside and dodge the bite.

I ended up next to the family and the park ranger, who were all screaming now, trying to pry open the emergency exit doors.

I couldn't let them get hurt. I uncapped my sword, ran to the other side of the deck, and yelled, "Hey, Chihuahua!"

The Chimera turned faster than I would've thought possible.

Before I could swing my sword, it opened its mouth, emitting a stench like the world's largest barbecue pit, and shot a column of flame straight at me.

I dove through the explosion. The carpet burst into flames; the heat was so intense, it nearly seared off my eyebrows.

Where I had been standing a moment before was a ragged hole in the side of the Arch, with melted metal steaming around the edges.

Great, I thought. We just blowtorched a national monument.

Riptide was now a shining bronze blade in my hands, and as the Chimera turned, I slashed at its neck.

That was my fatal mistake. The blade sparked harmlessly off the dog collar. I tried to regain my balance, but I was so worried about defending myself against the fiery lion's mouth, I completely forgot about the serpent tail until it whipped around and sank its fangs into my calf.

My whole leg was on fire. I tried to jab Riptide into the Chimera's mouth, but the serpent tail wrapped around my ankles and pulled me off balance, and my blade flew out of my hand, spinning out of the hole in the Arch and down toward the Mississippi River.

I managed to get to my feet, but I knew I had lost. I was weaponless. I could feel deadly poison racing up to my chest. I remembered Chiron saying that Anaklusmos would always return to me, but there was no pen in my pocket. Maybe it had fallen too far away. Maybe it only returned when it was in pen form. I didn't know, and I wasn't going to live long enough to figure it out.

I backed into the hole in the wall. The Chimera advanced, growling, smoke curling from its lips. The snake lady, Echidna, cackled. "They don't make heroes like they used to, eh, son?"

The monster growled. It seemed in no hurry to finish

me off now that I was beaten.

I glanced at the park ranger and the family. The little boy was hiding behind his father's legs. I had to protect these people. I couldn't just . . . die. I tried to think, but my whole body was on fire. My head felt dizzy. I had no sword. I was facing a massive, fire-breathing monster and its mother. And I was scared.

There was no place else to go, so I stepped to the edge of the hole. Far, far below, the river glittered.

If I died, would the monsters go away? Would they leave the humans alone?

"If you are the son of Poseidon," Echidna hissed, "you would not fear water. Jump, Percy Jackson. Show me that water will not harm you. Jump and retrieve your sword. Prove your bloodline."

Yeah, right, I thought. I'd read somewhere that jumping into water from a couple of stories up was like jumping onto solid asphalt. From here, I'd splatter on impact.

The Chimera's mouth glowed red, heating up for another blast.

"You have no faith," Echidna told me. "You do not trust the gods. I cannot blame you, little coward. Better you die now. The gods are faithless. The poison is in your heart."

She was right: I was dying. I could feel my breath slowing down. Nobody could save me, not even the gods.

I backed up and looked down at the water. I remembered the warm glow of my father's smile when I was a baby. He must have seen me. He must have visited me when I was in my cradle.

I remembered the swirling green trident that had appeared above my head the night of capture the flag, when Poseidon had claimed me as his son.

But this wasn't the sea. This was the Mississippi, dead center of the USA. There was no Sea God here.

"Die, faithless one," Echidna rasped, and the Chimera sent a column of flame toward my face.

"Father, help me," I prayed.

I turned and jumped. My clothes on fire, poison coursing through my veins, I plummeted toward the river.

FOURTEEN

I BECOME A
KNOWN FUGITIVE

I'd love to tell you I had some deep revelation on my way down, that I came to terms with my own mortality, laughed in the face of death, et cetera.

The truth? My only thought was: Aaaaggghhhhh!

The river raced toward me at the speed of a truck. Wind ripped the breath from my lungs. Steeples and skyscrapers and bridges tumbled in and out of my vision.

And then: *Flaaa-boooom!*

A whiteout of bubbles. I sank through the murk, sure that I was about to end up embedded in a hundred feet of mud and lost forever.

But my impact with the water hadn't hurt. I was falling slowly now, bubbles trickling up through my fingers. I settled on the river bottom soundlessly. A catfish the size of my stepfather lurched away into the gloom. Clouds of silt and disgusting garbage—beer bottles, old shoes, plastic bags—swirled up all around me.

At that point, I realized a few things: first, I had not been flattened into a pancake. I had not been barbecued. I couldn't even feel the Chimera poison boiling in my veins anymore. I was alive, which was good.

Second realization: I wasn't wet. I mean, I could feel the

coolness of the water. I could see where the fire on my clothes had been quenched. But when I touched my own shirt, it felt perfectly dry.

I looked at the garbage floating by and snatched an old cigarette lighter.

No way, I thought.

I flicked the lighter. It sparked. A tiny flame appeared, right there at the bottom of the Mississippi.

I grabbed a soggy hamburger wrapper out of the current and immediately the paper turned dry. I lit it with no problem. As soon as I let it go, the flames sputtered out. The wrapper turned back into a slimy rag. Weird.

But the strangest thought occurred to me only last: I was breathing. I was underwater, and I was breathing normally.

I stood up, thigh-deep in mud. My legs felt shaky. My hands trembled. I should've been dead. The fact that I wasn't seemed like . . . well, a miracle. I imagined a woman's voice, a voice that sounded a bit like my mother: *Percy, what do you say?*

"Um . . . thanks." Underwater, I sounded like I did on recordings, like a much older kid. "Thank you . . . Father."

No response. Just the dark drift of garbage downriver, the enormous catfish gliding by, the flash of sunset on the water's surface far above, turning everything the color of butterscotch.

Why had Poseidon saved me? The more I thought about it, the more ashamed I felt. So I'd gotten lucky a few times before. Against a thing like the Chimera, I had never stood a chance. Those poor people in the Arch were probably toast. I couldn't protect them. I was no hero. Maybe I should just stay down here with the catfish, join the bottom feeders.

Fump-fump-fump. A riverboat's paddlewheel churned above me, swirling the silt around.

There, not five feet in front of me, was my sword, its gleaming bronze hilt sticking up in the mud.

I heard that woman's voice again: *Percy, take the sword. Your father believes in you.* This time, I knew the voice wasn't in my head. I wasn't imagining it. Her words seemed to come from everywhere, rippling through the water like dolphin sonar.

"Where are you?" I called aloud.

Then, through the gloom, I saw her—a woman the color of the water, a ghost in the current, floating just above the sword. She had long billowing hair, and her eyes, barely visible, were green like mine.

A lump formed in my throat. I said, "Mom?"

No, child, only a messenger, though your mother's fate is not as hopeless as you believe. Go to the beach in Santa Monica.

"What?"

It is your father's will. Before you descend into the Underworld, you must go to Santa Monica. Please, Percy, I cannot stay long. The river here is too foul for my presence.

"But . . ." I was sure this woman was my mother, or a vision of her, anyway. "Who—how did you—"

There was so much I wanted to ask, the words jammed up in my throat.

I cannot stay, brave one, the woman said. She reached out, and I felt the current brush my face like a caress. *You must go to Santa Monica! And, Percy, do not trust the gifts. . . .*

Her voice faded.

"Gifts?" I asked. "What gifts? Wait!"

She made one more attempt to speak, but the sound was gone. Her image melted away. If it was my mother, I had lost her again.

I felt like drowning myself. The only problem: I was immune to drowning.

Your father believes in you, she had said.

She'd also called me brave . . . unless she was talking to the catfish.

I waded toward Riptide and grabbed it by the hilt. The Chimera might still be up there with its snaky, fat mother, waiting to finish me off. At the very least, the mortal police would be arriving, trying to figure out who had blown a hole in the Arch. If they found me, they'd have some questions.

I capped my sword, stuck the ballpoint pen in my pocket. "Thank you, Father," I said again to the dark water.

Then I kicked up through the muck and swam for the surface.

I came ashore next to a floating McDonald's.

A block away, every emergency vehicle in St. Louis was surrounding the Arch. Police helicopters circled overhead. The crowd of onlookers reminded me of Times Square on New Year's Eve.

A little girl said, "Mama! That boy walked out of the river."

"That's nice, dear," her mother said, craning her neck to watch the ambulances.

"But he's dry!"

"That's nice, dear."

A news lady was talking for the camera: "Probably not a terrorist attack, we're told, but it's still very early in the investigation. The damage, as you can see, is very serious. We're trying to get to some of the survivors, to question them about eyewitness reports of someone falling from the Arch."

Survivors. I felt a surge of relief. Maybe the park ranger and that family made it out safely. I hoped Annabeth and Grover were okay.

I tried to push through the crowd to see what was going on inside the police line.

". . . an adolescent boy," another reporter was saying. "Channel Five has learned that surveillance cameras show an adolescent boy going wild on the observation deck, somehow setting off this freak explosion. Hard to believe, John, but that's what we're hearing. Again, no confirmed fatalities . . ."

I backed away, trying to keep my head down. I had to go a long way around the police perimeter. Uniformed officers and news reporters were everywhere.

I'd almost lost hope of ever finding Annabeth and Grover when a familiar voice bleated, "Perrr-cy!"

I turned and got tackled by Grover's bear hug—or goat hug. He said, "We thought you'd gone to Hades the hard way!"

Annabeth stood behind him, trying to look angry, but even she seemed relieved to see me. "We can't leave you alone for five minutes! What happened?"

"I sort of fell."

"Percy! Six hundred and thirty feet?"

Behind us, a cop shouted, "Gangway!" The crowd parted, and a couple of paramedics hustled out, rolling a woman on a stretcher. I recognized her immediately as the mother of the little boy who'd been on the observation deck. She was saying, "And then this huge dog, this huge fire-breathing Chihuahua—"

"Okay, ma'am," the paramedic said. "Just calm down. Your family is fine. The medication is starting to kick in."

"I'm not crazy! This boy jumped out of the hole and the monster disappeared." Then she saw me. "There he is! That's the boy!"

I turned quickly and pulled Annabeth and Grover after me. We disappeared into the crowd.

"What's going on?" Annabeth demanded. "Was she talking about the Chihuahua on the elevator?"

I told them the whole story of the Chimera, Echidna, my high-dive act, and the underwater lady's message.

"Whoa," said Grover. "We've got to get you to Santa Monica! You can't ignore a summons from your dad."

Before Annabeth could respond, we passed another reporter doing a news break, and I almost froze in my tracks when he said, "Percy Jackson. That's right, Dan. Channel Twelve has learned that the boy who may have caused this explosion fits the description of a young man wanted by authorities for a serious New Jersey bus accident three days ago. *And* the boy is believed to be traveling west. For our viewers at home, here is a photo of Percy Jackson."

We ducked around the news van and slipped into an alley.

"First things first," I told Grover. "We've got to get out of town!"

Somehow, we made it back to the Amtrak station without getting spotted. We got on board the train just before it pulled out for Denver. The train trundled west as darkness fell, police lights still pulsing against the St. Louis skyline behind us.

FIFTEEN

A GOD BUYS US CHEESEBURGERS

The next afternoon, June 14, seven days before the solstice, our train rolled into Denver. We hadn't eaten since the night before in the dining car, somewhere in Kansas. We hadn't taken a shower since Half-Blood Hill, and I was sure that was obvious.

"Let's try to contact Chiron," Annabeth said. "I want to tell him about your talk with the river spirit."

"We can't use phones, right?"

"I'm not talking about phones."

We wandered through downtown for about half an hour, though I wasn't sure what Annabeth was looking for. The air was dry and hot, which felt weird after the humidity of St. Louis. Everywhere we turned, the Rocky Mountains seemed to be staring at me, like a tidal wave about to crash into the city.

Finally we found an empty do-it-yourself car wash. We veered toward the stall farthest from the street, keeping our eyes open for patrol cars. We were three adolescents hanging out at a car wash without a car; any cop worth his doughnuts would figure we were up to no good.

"What exactly are we doing?" I asked, as Grover took out the spray gun.

"It's seventy-five cents," he grumbled. "I've only got two quarters left. Annabeth?"

"Don't look at me," she said. "The dining car wiped me out."

I fished out my last bit of change and passed Grover a quarter, which left me two nickels and one drachma from Medusa's place.

"Excellent," Grover said. "We could do it with a spray bottle, of course, but the connection isn't as good, and my arm gets tired of pumping."

"What are you talking about?"

He fed in the quarters and set the knob to FINE MIST. "I-M'ing."

"Instant messaging?"

"*Iris*-messaging," Annabeth corrected. "The rainbow goddess Iris carries messages for the gods. If you know how to ask, and she's not too busy, she'll do the same for half-bloods."

"You summon the goddess with a spray gun?"

Grover pointed the nozzle in the air and water hissed out in a thick white mist. "Unless you know an easier way to make a rainbow."

Sure enough, late afternoon light filtered through the vapor and broke into colors.

Annabeth held her palm out to me. "Drachma, please."

I handed it over.

She raised the coin over her head. "O goddess, accept our offering."

She threw the drachma into the rainbow. It disappeared in a golden shimmer.

"Half-Blood Hill," Annabeth requested.

For a moment, nothing happened.

Then I was looking through the mist at strawberry fields, and the Long Island Sound in the distance. We seemed to be on the porch of the Big House. Standing with his back to us at the railing was a sandy-haired guy in shorts and an orange tank top. He was holding a bronze sword and seemed to be staring intently at something down in the meadow.

"Luke!" I called.

He turned, eyes wide. I could swear he was standing three feet in front of me through a screen of mist, except I could only see the part of him that appeared in the rainbow.

"Percy!" His scarred face broke into a grin. "Is that Annabeth, too? Thank the gods! Are you guys okay?"

"We're . . . uh . . . fine," Annabeth stammered. She was madly straightening her dirty T-shirt, trying to comb the loose hair out of her face. "We thought—Chiron—I mean—"

"He's down at the cabins." Luke's smile faded. "We're having some issues with the campers. Listen, is everything cool with you? Is Grover all right?"

"I'm right here," Grover called. He held the nozzle out to one side and stepped into Luke's line of vision. "What kind of issues?"

Just then a big Lincoln Continental pulled into the car wash with its stereo turned to maximum hip-hop. As the car slid into the next stall, the bass from the subwoofers vibrated so much, it shook the pavement.

"Chiron had to—what's that noise?" Luke yelled.

"I'll take care of it!" Annabeth yelled back, looking very relieved to have an excuse to get out of sight. "Grover, come on!"

"What?" Grover said. "But—"

"Give Percy the nozzle and come on!" she ordered.

Grover muttered something about girls being harder to understand than the Oracle at Delphi, then he handed me the spray gun and followed Annabeth.

I readjusted the hose so I could keep the rainbow going and still see Luke.

"Chiron had to break up a fight," Luke shouted to me over the music. "Things are pretty tense here, Percy. Word leaked out about the Zeus–Poseidon standoff. We're still not sure how—probably the same scumbag who summoned the hellhound. Now the campers are starting to take sides. It's shaping up like the Trojan War all over again. Aphrodite, Ares, and Apollo are backing Poseidon, more or less. Athena is backing Zeus."

I shuddered to think that Clarisse's cabin would ever be on my dad's side for anything. In the next stall, I heard Annabeth and some guy arguing with each other, then the music's volume decreased drastically.

"So what's your status?" Luke asked me. "Chiron will be sorry he missed you."

I told him pretty much everything, including my dreams. It felt so good to see him, to feel like I was back at camp even for a few minutes, that I didn't realize how long I had talked until the beeper went off on the spray machine, and I realized I only had one more minute before the water shut off.

"I wish I could be there," Luke told me. "We can't help much from here, I'm afraid, but listen . . . it had to be Hades who took the master bolt. He was there at Olympus at the winter solstice. I was chaperoning a field trip and we saw him."

"But Chiron said the gods can't take each other's magic items directly."

"That's true," Luke said, looking troubled. "Still . . . Hades has the helm of darkness. How could anybody else sneak into the throne room and steal the master bolt? You'd have to be invisible."

We were both silent, until Luke seemed to realize what he'd said.

"Oh, hey," he protested. "I didn't mean Annabeth. She and I have known each other forever. She would never . . . I mean, she's like a little sister to me."

I wondered if Annabeth would like that description. In the stall next to us, the music stopped completely. A man screamed in terror, car doors slammed, and the Lincoln peeled out of the car wash.

"You'd better go see what that was," Luke said. "Listen, are you wearing the flying shoes? I'll feel better if I know they've done you some good."

"Oh . . . uh, yeah!" I tried not to sound like a guilty liar. "Yeah, they've come in handy."

"Really?" He grinned. "They fit and everything?"

The water shut off. The mist started to evaporate.

"Well, take care of yourself out there in Denver," Luke

called, his voice getting fainter. "And tell Grover it'll be better this time! Nobody will get turned into a pine tree if he just—"

But the mist was gone, and Luke's image faded to nothing. I was alone in a wet, empty car wash stall.

Annabeth and Grover came around the corner, laughing, but stopped when they saw my face. Annabeth's smile faded. "What happened, Percy? What did Luke say?"

"Not much," I lied, my stomach feeling as empty as a Big Three cabin. "Come on, let's find some dinner."

A few minutes later, we were sitting at a booth in a gleaming chrome diner. All around us, families were eating burgers and drinking malts and sodas.

Finally the waitress came over. She raised her eyebrow skeptically. "Well?"

I said, "We, um, want to order dinner."

"You kids have money to pay for it?"

Grover's lower lip quivered. I was afraid he would start bleating, or worse, start eating the linoleum. Annabeth looked ready to pass out from hunger.

I was trying to think up a sob story for the waitress when a rumble shook the whole building; a motorcycle the size of a baby elephant had pulled up to the curb.

All conversation in the diner stopped. The motorcycle's headlight glared red. Its gas tank had flames painted on it, and a shotgun holster riveted to either side, complete with shotguns. The seat was leather—but leather that looked like . . . well, Caucasian human skin.

The guy on the bike would've made pro wrestlers run for Mama. He was dressed in a red muscle shirt and black jeans and a black leather duster, with a hunting knife strapped to his thigh. He wore red wraparound shades, and he had the cruelest, most brutal face I'd ever seen—handsome, I guess, but wicked—with an oily black crew cut and cheeks that were scarred from many, many fights. The weird thing was, I felt like I'd seen his face somewhere before.

As he walked into the diner, a hot, dry wind blew through the place. All the people rose, as if they were hypnotized, but the biker waved his hand dismissively and they all sat down again. Everybody went back to their conversations. The waitress blinked, as if somebody had just pressed the rewind button on her brain. She asked us again, "You kids have money to pay for it?"

The biker said, "It's on me." He slid into our booth, which was way too small for him, and crowded Annabeth against the window.

He looked up at the waitress, who was gaping at him, and said, "Are you still here?"

He pointed at her, and she stiffened. She turned as if she'd been spun around, then marched back toward the kitchen.

The biker looked at me. I couldn't see his eyes behind the red shades, but bad feelings started boiling in my stomach. Anger, resentment, bitterness. I wanted to hit a wall. I wanted to pick a fight with somebody. Who did this guy think he was?

He gave me a wicked grin. "So you're old Seaweed's kid, huh?"

I should've been surprised, or scared, but instead I felt like I was looking at my stepdad, Gabe. I wanted to rip this guy's head off. "What's it to you?"

Annabeth's eyes flashed me a warning. "Percy, this is—"

The biker raised his hand.

"S'okay," he said. "I don't mind a little attitude. Long as you remember who's the boss. You know who I am, little cousin?"

Then it struck me why this guy looked familiar. He had the same vicious sneer as some of the kids at Camp Half-Blood, the ones from cabin five.

"You're Clarisse's dad," I said. "Ares, god of war."

Ares grinned and took off his shades. Where his eyes should've been, there was only fire, empty sockets glowing with miniature nuclear explosions. "That's right, punk. I heard you broke Clarisse's spear."

"She was asking for it."

"Probably. That's cool. I don't fight my kids' fights, you know? What I'm here for—I heard you were in town. I got a little proposition for you."

The waitress came back with heaping trays of food—cheeseburgers, fries, onion rings, and chocolate shakes.

Ares handed her a few gold drachmas.

She looked nervously at the coins. "But, these aren't . . ."

Ares pulled out his huge knife and started cleaning his fingernails. "Problem, sweetheart?"

The waitress swallowed, then left with the gold.

"You can't do that," I told Ares. "You can't just threaten people with a knife."

Ares laughed. "Are you kidding? I love this country. Best place since Sparta. Don't you carry a weapon, punk? You should. Dangerous world out there. Which brings me to my proposition. I need you to do me a favor."

"What favor could I do for a god?"

"Something a god doesn't have time to do himself. It's nothing much. I left my shield at an abandoned water park here in town. I was going on a little . . . date with my girl-friend. We were interrupted. I left my shield behind. I want you to fetch it for me."

"Why don't you go back and get it yourself?"

The fire in his eye sockets glowed a little hotter.

"Why don't I turn you into prairie dog and run you over with my Harley? Because I don't feel like it. A god is giving you an opportunity to prove yourself, Percy Jackson. Will you prove yourself a coward?" He leaned forward. "Or maybe you only fight when there's a river to dive into, so your daddy can protect you."

I wanted to punch this guy, but somehow, I knew he was waiting for that. Ares's power was causing my anger. He'd love it if I attacked. I didn't want to give him the satisfaction.

"We're not interested," I said. "We've already got a quest."

Ares's fiery eyes made me see things I didn't want to see—blood and smoke and corpses on the battlefield. "I know all about your quest, punk. When that *item* was first stolen, Zeus sent his best out looking for it: Apollo, Athena, Artemis, and me, naturally. If I couldn't sniff out a weapon that powerful . . ." He licked his lips, as if the very thought of the master bolt made him hungry. "Well . . . if I couldn't find it, you got no hope. Nevertheless, I'm trying to give you the benefit of the doubt. Your dad and I go way back. After all, I'm the one who told him my suspicions about old Corpse Breath."

"You told him Hades stole the bolt?"

"Sure. Framing somebody to start a war. Oldest trick in the book. I recognized it immediately. In a way, you got me to thank for your little quest."

"Thanks," I grumbled.

"Hey, I'm a generous guy. Just do my little job, and I'll help you on your way. I'll arrange a ride west for you and your friends."

"We're doing fine on our own."

"Yeah, right. No money. No wheels. No clue what you're up against. Help me out, and maybe I'll tell you something you need to know. Something about your mom."

"My mom?"

He grinned. "That got your attention. The water park is a mile west on Delancy. You can't miss it. Look for the Tunnel of Love ride."

"What interrupted your date?" I asked. "Something scare you off?"

Ares bared his teeth, but I'd seen his threatening look before on Clarisse. There was something false about it, almost like he was nervous.

"You're lucky you met me, punk, and not one of the other Olympians. They're not as forgiving of rudeness as I am. I'll meet you back here when you're done. Don't disappoint me."

After that I must have fainted, or fallen into a trance, because when I opened my eyes again, Ares was gone. I might've thought the conversation had been a dream, but Annabeth and Grover's expressions told me otherwise.

"Not good," Grover said. "Ares sought you out, Percy. This is not good."

I stared out the window. The motorcycle had disappeared.

Did Ares really know something about my mom, or was he just playing with me? Now that he was gone, all the anger had drained out of me. I realized Ares must love to mess with people's emotions. That was his power—cranking up the passions so badly, they clouded your ability to think.

"It's probably some kind of trick," I said. "Forget Ares. Let's just go."

"We can't," Annabeth said. "Look, I hate Ares as much as anybody, but you don't ignore the gods unless you want serious bad fortune. He wasn't kidding about turning you into a rodent."

I looked down at my cheeseburger, which suddenly didn't seem so appetizing. "Why does he need us?"

"Maybe it's a problem that requires brains," Annabeth said. "Ares has strength. That's all he has. Even strength has to bow to wisdom sometimes."

"But this water park . . . he acted almost scared. What would make a war god run away like that?"

Annabeth and Grover glanced nervously at each other. Annabeth said, "I'm afraid we'll have to find out."

The sun was sinking behind the mountains by the time we found the water park. Judging from the sign, it once had been called WATERLAND, but now some of the letters were smashed out, so it read WAT R A D.

The main gate was padlocked and topped with barbed wire. Inside, huge dry waterslides and tubes and pipes curled everywhere, leading to empty pools. Old tickets and advertisements fluttered around the asphalt. With night coming on, the place looked sad and creepy.

"If Ares brings his girlfriend here for a date," I said, staring up at the barbed wire, "I'd hate to see what she looks like."

"Percy," Annabeth warned. "Be more respectful."

"Why? I thought you hated Ares."

"He's still a god. And his girlfriend is very temperamental."

"You don't want to insult her looks," Grover added.

"Who is she? Echidna?"

"No, Aphrodite," Grover said, a little dreamily. "Goddess of love."

"I thought she was married to somebody," I said. "Hephaestus."

"What's your point?" he asked.

"Oh." I suddenly felt the need to change the subject. "So how do we get in?"

"Maia!" Grover's shoes sprouted wings.

He flew over the fence, did an unintended somersault in midair, then stumbled to a landing on the opposite side. He dusted off his jeans, as if he'd planned the whole thing. "You guys coming?"

Annabeth and I had to climb the old-fashioned way, holding down the barbed wire for each other as we crawled over the top.

The shadows grew long as we walked through the park, checking out the attractions. There was Ankle Biter Island, Head Over Wedgie, and Dude, Where's My Swimsuit?

No monsters came to get us. Nothing made the slightest noise.

We found a souvenir shop that had been left open. Merchandise still lined the shelves: snow globes, pencils, postcards, and racks of—

"Clothes," Annabeth said. "Fresh clothes."

"Yeah," I said. "But you can't just—"

"Watch me."

She snatched an entire row of stuff of the racks and disappeared into the changing room. A few minutes later she came out in Waterland flower-print shorts, a big red Waterland T-shirt, and commemorative Waterland surf shoes. A Waterland backpack was slung over her shoulder, obviously stuffed with more goodies.

"What the heck." Grover shrugged. Soon, all three of us were decked out like walking advertisements for the defunct theme park.

We continued searching for the Tunnel of Love. I got

the feeling that the whole park was holding its breath. "So Ares and Aphrodite," I said, to keep my mind off the growing dark, "they have a thing going?"

"That's old gossip, Percy," Annabeth told me. "Three-thousand-year-old gossip."

"What about Aphrodite's husband?"

"Well, you know," she said. "Hephaestus. The blacksmith. He was crippled when he was a baby, thrown off Mount Olympus by Zeus. So he isn't exactly handsome. Clever with his hands, and all, but Aphrodite isn't into brains and talent, you know?"

"She likes bikers."

"Whatever."

"Hephaestus knows?"

"Oh sure," Annabeth said. "He caught them together once. I mean, literally caught them, in a golden net, and invited all the gods to come and laugh at them. Hephaestus is always trying to embarrass them. That's why they meet in out-of-the-way places, like . . ."

She stopped, looking straight ahead. "Like that."

In front of us was an empty pool that would've been awesome for skateboarding. It was at least fifty yards across and shaped like a bowl.

Around the rim, a dozen bronze statues of Cupid stood guard with wings spread and bows ready to fire. On the opposite side from us, a tunnel opened up, probably where the water flowed into when the pool was full. The sign above it read, THRILL RIDE O' LOVE: THIS IS NOT YOUR PARENTS' TUNNEL OF LOVE!

Grover crept toward the edge. "Guys, look."

Marooned at the bottom of the pool was a pink-and-white two-seater boat with a canopy over the top and little hearts painted all over it. In the left seat, glinting in the fading light, was Ares's shield, a polished circle of bronze.

"This is too easy," I said. "So we just walk down there and get it?"

Annabeth ran her fingers along the base of the nearest Cupid statue.

"There's a Greek letter carved here," she said. "Eta. I wonder . . ."

"Grover," I said, "you smell any monsters?"

He sniffed the wind. "Nothing."

"Nothing—like, in-the-Arch-and-you-didn't-smell-Echidna nothing, or really nothing?"

Grover looked hurt. "I told you, that was underground."

"Okay, I'm sorry." I took a deep breath. "I'm going down there."

"I'll go with you." Grover didn't sound too enthusiastic, but I got the feeling he was trying to make up for what had happened in St. Louis.

"No," I told him. "I want you to stay up top with the flying shoes. You're the Red Baron, a flying ace, remember? I'll be counting on you for backup, in case something goes wrong."

Grover puffed up his chest a little. "Sure. But what could go wrong?"

"I don't know. Just a feeling. Annabeth, come with me—"

"Are you kidding?" She looked at me as if I'd just dropped from the moon. Her cheeks were bright red.

"What's the problem now?" I demanded.

"Me, go with you to the . . . the 'Thrill Ride of Love'? How embarrassing is that? What if somebody saw me?"

"Who's going to see you?" But my face was burning now, too. Leave it to a girl to make everything complicated. "Fine," I told her. "I'll do it myself." But when I started down the side of the pool, she followed me, muttering about how boys always messed things up.

We reached the boat. The shield was propped on one seat, and next to it was a lady's silk scarf. I tried to imagine Ares and Aphrodite here, a couple of gods meeting in a junked-out amusement-park ride. Why? Then I noticed something I hadn't seen from up top: mirrors all the way around the rim of the pool, facing this spot. We could see ourselves no matter which direction we looked. That must be it. While Ares and Aphrodite were smooching with each other they could look at their favorite people: themselves.

I picked up the scarf. It shimmered pink, and the perfume was indescribable—rose, or mountain laurel. Something good. I smiled, a little dreamy, and was about to rub the scarf against my cheek when Annabeth ripped it out of my hand and stuffed it in her pocket. "Oh, no you don't. Stay away from that love magic."

"What?"

"Just get the shield, Seaweed Brain, and let's get out of here."

The moment I touched the shield, I knew we were in trouble. My hand broke through something that had been connecting it to the dashboard. A cobweb, I thought, but then I looked at a strand of it on my palm and saw it was some kind of metal filament, so fine it was almost invisible. A trip wire.

"Wait," Annabeth said.

"Too late."

"There's another Greek letter on the side of the boat, another Eta. This is a trap."

Noise erupted all around us, of a million gears grinding, as if the whole pool were turning into one giant machine.

Grover yelled, "Guys!"

Up on the rim, the Cupid statues were drawing their bows into firing position. Before I could suggest taking cover, they shot, but not at us. They fired at each other, across the rim of the pool. Silky cables trailed from the arrows, arcing over the pool and anchoring where they landed to form a huge golden asterisk. Then smaller metallic threads started weaving together magically between the main strands, making a net.

"We have to get out," I said.

"Duh!" Annabeth said.

I grabbed the shield and we ran, but going up the slope of the pool was not as easy as going down.

"Come on!" Grover shouted.

He was trying to hold open a section of the net for us, but wherever he touched it, the golden threads started to wrap around his hands.

The Cupids' heads popped open. Out came video cameras. Spotlights rose up all around the pool, blinding us with illumination, and a loudspeaker voice boomed: "Live to Olympus in one minute . . . Fifty-nine seconds, fifty-eight . . ."

"Hephaestus!" Annabeth screamed. "I'm so stupid! Eta is 'H.' He made this trap to catch his wife with Ares. Now we're going to be broadcast live to Olympus and look like absolute fools!"

We'd almost made it to the rim when the row of mirrors opened like hatches and thousands of tiny metallic . . . things poured out.

Annabeth screamed.

It was an army of wind-up creepy-crawlies: bronze-gear bodies, spindly legs, little pincer mouths, all scuttling toward us in a wave of clacking, whirring metal.

"Spiders!" Annabeth said. "Sp—sp—aaaah!"

I'd never seen her like this before. She fell backward in terror and almost got overwhelmed by the spider robots before I pulled her up and dragged her back toward the boat.

The things were coming out from all around the rim now, millions of them, flooding toward the center of the pool, completely surrounding us. I told myself they probably weren't programmed to kill, just corral us and bite us and make us look stupid. Then again, this was a trap meant for gods. And we weren't gods.

Annabeth and I climbed into the boat. I started kicking away the spiders as they swarmed aboard. I yelled at

Annabeth to help me, but she was too paralyzed to do much more than scream.

"Thirty, twenty-nine," called the loudspeaker.

The spiders started spitting out strands of metal thread, trying to tie us down. The strands were easy enough to break at first, but there were so many of them, and the spiders just kept coming. I kicked one away from Annabeth's leg and its pincers took a chunk out of my new surf shoe.

Grover hovered above the pool in his flying sneakers, trying to pull the net loose, but it wouldn't budge.

Think, I told myself. Think.

The Tunnel of Love entrance was under the net. We could use it as an exit, except that it was blocked by a million robot spiders.

"Fifteen, fourteen," the loudspeaker called.

Water, I thought. Where does the ride's water come from?

Then I saw them: huge water pipes behind the mirrors, where the spiders had come from. And up above the net, next to one of the Cupids, a glass-windowed booth that must be the controller's station.

"Grover!" I yelled. "Get into that booth! Find the 'on' switch!"

"But—"

"Do it!" It was a crazy hope, but it was our only chance. The spiders were all over the prow of the boat now. Annabeth was screaming her head off. I had to get us out of there.

Grover was in the controller's booth now, slamming away at the buttons.

"Five, four—"

Grover looked up at me hopelessly, raising his hands. He was letting me know that he'd pushed every button, but still nothing was happening.

I closed my eyes and thought about waves, rushing water, the Mississippi River. I felt a familiar tug in my gut. I tried to imagine that I was dragging the ocean all the way to Denver.

"Two, one, *zero!*"

Water exploded out of the pipes. It roared into the pool, sweeping away the spiders. I pulled Annabeth into the seat next to me and fastened her seat belt just as the tidal wave slammed into our boat, over the top, whisking the spiders away and dousing us completely, but not capsizing us. The boat turned, lifted in the flood, and spun in circles around the whirlpool.

The water was full of short-circuiting spiders, some of them smashing against the pool's concrete wall with such force they burst.

Spotlights glared down at us. The Cupid-cams were rolling, live to Olympus.

But I could only concentrate on controlling the boat. I willed it to ride the current, to keep away from the wall. Maybe it was my imagination, but the boat seemed to respond. At least, it didn't break into a million pieces. We spun around one last time, the water level now almost high enough to shred us against the metal net. Then the boat's nose turned toward the tunnel and we rocketed through into the darkness.

Annabeth and I held tight, both of us screaming as the boat shot curls and hugged corners and took forty-five-degree plunges past pictures of Romeo and Juliet and a bunch of other Valentine's Day stuff.

Then we were out of the tunnel, the night air whistling through our hair as the boat barreled straight toward the exit.

If the ride had been in working order, we would've sailed off a ramp between the golden Gates of Love and splashed down safely in the exit pool. But there was a problem. The Gates of Love were chained. Two boats that had been washed out of the tunnel before us were now piled against the barricade—one submerged, the other cracked in half.

"Unfasten your seat belt," I yelled to Annabeth.

"Are you crazy?"

"Unless you want to get smashed to death." I strapped Ares's shield to my arm. "We're going to have to jump for it." My idea was simple and insane. As the boat struck, we would use its force like a springboard to jump the gate. I'd heard of people surviving car crashes that way, getting thrown thirty or forty feet away from an accident. With luck, we would land in the pool.

Annabeth seemed to understand. She gripped my hand as the gates got closer.

"On my mark," I said.

"No! On my mark!"

"What?"

"Simple physics!" she yelled. "Force times the trajectory angle—"

"Fine!" I shouted. "On *your* mark!"

She hesitated . . . hesitated . . . then yelled, "Now!"

Crack!

Annabeth was right. If we'd jumped when I thought we should've, we would've crashed into the gates. She got us maximum lift.

Unfortunately, that was a little more than we needed. Our boat smashed into the pileup and we were thrown into the air, straight over the gates, over the pool, and down toward solid asphalt.

Something grabbed me from behind.

Annabeth yelled, "Ouch!"

Grover!

In midair, he had grabbed me by the shirt, and Annabeth by the arm, and was trying to pull us out of a crash landing, but Annabeth and I had all the momentum.

"You're too heavy!" Grover said. "We're going down!"

We spiraled toward the ground, Grover doing his best to slow the fall.

We smashed into a photo-board, Grover's head going straight into the hole where tourists would put their faces, pretending to be Noo-Noo the Friendly Whale. Annabeth and I tumbled to the ground, banged up but alive. Ares's shield was still on my arm.

Once we caught our breath, Annabeth and I got Grover out of the photo-board and thanked him for saving our lives. I looked back at the Thrill Ride of Love. The water was subsiding. Our boat had been smashed to pieces against the gates.

A hundred yards away, at the entrance pool, the Cupids were still filming. The statues had swiveled so that their cameras were trained straight on us, the spotlights in our faces.

"Show's over!" I yelled. "Thank you! Good night!"

The Cupids turned back to their original positions. The lights shut off. The park went quiet and dark again, except for the gentle trickle of water into the Thrill Ride of Love's exit pool. I wondered if Olympus had gone to a commercial break, or if our ratings had been any good.

I hated being teased. I hated being tricked. And I had plenty of experience handling bullies who liked to do that stuff to me. I hefted the shield on my arm and turned to my friends. "We need to have a little talk with Ares."

SIXTEEN

WE TAKE A
ZEBRA TO VEGAS

The war god was waiting for us in the diner parking lot.

"Well, well," he said. "You didn't get yourself killed."

"You knew it was a trap," I said.

Ares gave me a wicked grin. "Bet that crippled black-smith was surprised when he netted a couple of stupid kids. You looked good on TV."

I shoved his shield at him. "You're a jerk."

Annabeth and Grover caught their breath.

Ares grabbed the shield and spun it in the air like pizza dough. It changed form, melting into a bulletproof vest. He slung it across his back.

"See that truck over there?" He pointed to an eighteen-wheeler parked across the street from the diner. "That's your ride. Take you straight to L.A., with one stop in Vegas."

The eighteen-wheeler had a sign on the back, which I could read only because it was reverse-printed white on black, a good combination for dyslexia: KINDNESS INTER-NATIONAL: HUMANE ZOO TRANSPORT. WARNING: LIVE WILD ANIMALS.

I said, "You're kidding."

Ares snapped his fingers. The back door of the truck

unlatched. "Free ride west, punk. Stop complaining. And here's a little something for doing the job."

He slung a blue nylon backpack off his handlebars and tossed it to me.

Inside were fresh clothes for all of us, twenty bucks in cash, a pouch full of golden drachmas, and a bag of Double Stuf Oreos.

I said, "I don't want your lousy—"

"Thank you, Lord Ares," Grover interrupted, giving me his best red-alert warning look. "Thanks a lot."

I gritted my teeth. It was probably a deadly insult to refuse something from a god, but I didn't want anything that Ares had touched. Reluctantly, I slung the backpack over my shoulder. I knew my anger was being caused by the war god's presence, but I was still itching to punch him in the nose. He reminded me of every bully I'd ever faced: Nancy Bobofit, Clarisse, Smelly Gabe, sarcastic teachers—every jerk who'd called me stupid in school or laughed at me when I'd gotten expelled.

I looked back at the diner, which had only a couple of customers now. The waitress who'd served us dinner was watching nervously out the window, like she was afraid Ares might hurt us. She dragged the fry cook out from the kitchen to see. She said something to him. He nodded, held up a little disposable camera and snapped a picture of us.

Great, I thought. We'll make the papers again tomorrow.

I imagined the headline: TWELVE-YEAR-OLD OUTLAW BEATS UP DEFENSELESS BIKER.

"You owe me one more thing," I told Ares, trying to

keep my voice level. "You promised me information about my mother."

"You sure you can handle the news?" He kick-started his motorcycle. "She's not dead."

The ground seemed to spin beneath me. "What do you mean?"

"I mean she was taken away from the Minotaur before she could die. She was turned into a shower of gold, right? That's metamorphosis. Not death. She's being kept."

"Kept. Why?"

"You need to study war, punk. Hostages. You take somebody to control somebody else."

"Nobody's controlling me."

He laughed. "Oh yeah? See you around, kid."

I balled up my fists. "You're pretty smug, Lord Ares, for a guy who runs from Cupid statues."

Behind his sunglasses, fire glowed. I felt a hot wind in my hair. "We'll meet again, Percy Jackson. Next time you're in a fight, watch your back."

He revved his Harley, then roared off down Delancy Street.

Annabeth said, "That was not smart, Percy."

"I don't care."

"You don't want a god as your enemy. Especially not that god."

"Hey, guys," Grover said. "I hate to interrupt, but . . ."

He pointed toward the diner. At the register, the last two customers were paying their check, two men in identical black coveralls, with a white logo on their backs that matched the one on the KINDNESS INTERNATIONAL truck.

"If we're taking the zoo express," Grover said, "we need to hurry."

I didn't like it, but we had no better option. Besides, I'd seen enough of Denver.

We ran across the street and climbed in the back of the big rig, closing the doors behind us.

The first thing that hit me was the smell. It was like the world's biggest pan of kitty litter.

The trailer was dark inside until I uncapped Anaklusmos. The blade cast a faint bronze light over a very sad scene. Sitting in a row of filthy metal cages were three of the most pathetic zoo animals I'd ever beheld: a zebra, a male albino lion, and some weird antelope thing I didn't know the name for.

Someone had thrown the lion a sack of turnips, which he obviously didn't want to eat. The zebra and the antelope had each gotten a Styrofoam tray of hamburger meat. The zebra's mane was matted with chewing gum, like somebody had been spitting on it in their spare time. The antelope had a stupid silver birthday balloon tied to one of his horns that read OVER THE HILL!

Apparently, nobody had wanted to get close enough to the lion to mess with him, but the poor thing was pacing around on soiled blankets, in a space way too small for him, panting from the stuffy heat of the trailer. He had flies buzzing around his pink eyes and his ribs showed through his white fur.

"This is kindness?" Grover yelled. "Humane zoo transport?"

He probably would've gone right back outside to beat
up the truckers with his reed pipes, and I would've helped
him, but just then the truck's engine roared to life, the
trailer started shaking, and we were forced to sit down or
fall down.

We huddled in the corner on some mildewed feed sacks,
trying to ignore the smell and the heat and the flies. Grover
talked to the animals in a series of goat bleats, but they just
stared at him sadly. Annabeth was in favor of breaking the
cages and freeing them on the spot, but I pointed out it
wouldn't do much good until the truck stopped moving.
Besides, I had a feeling we might look a lot better to the lion
than those turnips.

I found a water jug and refilled their bowls, then used
Anaklusmos to drag the mismatched food out of their
cages. I gave the meat to the lion and the turnips to the
zebra and the antelope.

Grover calmed the antelope down, while Annabeth used
her knife to cut the balloon off his horn. She wanted to cut
the gum out of the zebra's mane, too, but we decided that
would be too risky with the truck bumping around. We told
Grover to promise the animals we'd help them more in the
morning, then we settled in for night.

Grover curled up on a turnip sack; Annabeth opened
our bag of Double Stuf Oreos and nibbled on one halfheartedly; I tried to cheer myself up by concentrating on the
fact that we were halfway to Los Angeles. Halfway to our

destination. It was only June fourteenth. The solstice wasn't until the twenty-first. We could make it in plenty of time.

On the other hand, I had no idea what to expect next. The gods kept toying with me. At least Hephaestus had the decency to be honest about it—he'd put up cameras and advertised me as entertainment. But even when the cameras weren't rolling, I had a feeling my quest was being watched. I was a source of amusement for the gods.

"Hey," Annabeth said, "I'm sorry for freaking out back at the water park, Percy."

"That's okay."

"It's just . . ." She shuddered. "Spiders."

"Because of the Arachne story," I guessed. "She got turned into a spider for challenging your mom to a weaving contest, right?"

Annabeth nodded. "Arachne's children have been taking revenge on the children of Athena ever since. If there's a spider within a mile of me, it'll find me. I hate the creepy little things. Anyway, I owe you."

"We're a team, remember?" I said. "Besides, Grover did the fancy flying."

I thought he was asleep, but he mumbled from the corner, "I was pretty amazing, wasn't I?"

Annabeth and I laughed.

She pulled apart an Oreo, handed me half. "In the Iris message . . . did Luke really say nothing?"

I munched my cookie and thought about how to answer. The conversation via rainbow had bothered me all evening. "Luke said you and he go way back. He also said Grover wouldn't fail this time. Nobody would turn into a pine tree."

In the dim bronze light of the sword blade, it was hard to read their expressions.

Grover let out a mournful bray.

"I should've told you the truth from the beginning." His voice trembled. "I thought if you knew what a failure I was, you wouldn't want me along."

"You were the satyr who tried to rescue Thalia, the daughter of Zeus."

He nodded glumly.

"And the other two half-bloods Thalia befriended, the ones who got safely to camp . . ." I looked at Annabeth. "That was you and Luke, wasn't it?"

She put down her Oreo, uneaten. "Like you said, Percy, a seven-year-old half-blood wouldn't have made it very far alone. Athena guided me toward help. Thalia was twelve. Luke was fourteen. They'd both run away from home, like me. They were happy to take me with them. They were . . . amazing monster-fighters, even without training. We traveled north from Virginia without any real plans, fending off monsters for about two weeks before Grover found us."

"I was supposed to escort Thalia to camp," he said, sniffling. "Only Thalia. I had strict orders from Chiron: don't do anything that would slow down the rescue. We knew Hades was after her, see, but I couldn't just leave Luke and Annabeth by themselves. I thought . . . I thought I could lead all three of them to safety. It was my fault the Kindly Ones caught up with us. I froze. I got scared on the way back to camp and took some wrong turns. If I'd just been a little quicker . . ."

"Stop it," Annabeth said. "No one blames you. Thalia didn't blame you either."

"She sacrificed herself to save us," he said miserably. "Her death was my fault. The Council of Cloven Elders said so."

"Because you wouldn't leave two other half-bloods behind?" I said. "That's not fair."

"Percy's right," Annabeth said. "I wouldn't be here today if it weren't for you, Grover. Neither would Luke. We don't care what the council says."

Grover kept sniffling in the dark. "It's just my luck. I'm the lamest satyr ever, and I find the two most powerful half-bloods of the century, Thalia and Percy."

"You're not lame," Annabeth insisted. "You've got more courage than any satyr I've ever met. Name one other who would dare go to the Underworld. I bet Percy is really glad you're here right now."

She kicked me in the shin.

"Yeah," I said, which I would've done even without the kick. "It's not luck that you found Thalia and me, Grover. You've got the biggest heart of any satyr ever. You're a natural searcher. That's why you'll be the one who finds Pan."

I heard a deep, satisfied sigh. I waited for Grover to say something, but his breathing only got heavier. When the sound turned to snoring, I realized he'd fallen sleep.

"How does he do that?" I marveled.

"I don't know," Annabeth said. "But that was really a nice thing you told him."

"I meant it."

We rode in silence for a few miles, bumping around on the feed sacks. The zebra munched a turnip. The lion licked the last of the hamburger meat off his lips and looked at me hopefully.

Annabeth rubbed her necklace like she was thinking deep, strategic thoughts.

"That pine-tree bead," I said. "Is that from your first year?"

She looked. She hadn't realized what she was doing.

"Yeah," she said. "Every August, the counselors pick the most important event of the summer, and they paint it on that year's beads. I've got Thalia's pine tree, a Greek trireme on fire, a centaur in a prom dress—now *that* was a weird summer. . . ."

"And the college ring is your father's?"

"That's none of your—" She stopped herself. "Yeah. Yeah, it is."

"You don't have to tell me."

"No . . . it's okay." She took a shaky breath. "My dad sent it to me folded up in a letter, two summers ago. The ring was, like, his main keepsake from Athena. He wouldn't have gotten through his doctoral program at Harvard without her. . . . That's a long story. Anyway, he said he wanted me to have it. He apologized for being a jerk, said he loved me and missed me. He wanted me to come home and live with him."

"That doesn't sound so bad."

"Yeah, well . . . the problem was, I believed him. I tried

to go home for that school year, but my stepmom was the same as ever. She didn't want her kids put in danger by living with a freak. Monsters attacked. We argued. Monsters attacked. We argued. I didn't even make it through winter break. I called Chiron and came right back to Camp Half-Blood."

"You think you'll ever try living with your dad again?"

She wouldn't meet my eyes. "Please. I'm not into self-inflicted pain."

"You shouldn't give up," I told her. "You should write him a letter or something."

"Thanks for the advice," she said coldly, "but my father's made his choice about who he wants to live with."

We passed another few miles of silence.

"So if the gods fight," I said, "will things line up the way they did with the Trojan War? Will it be Athena versus Poseidon?"

She put her head against the backpack Ares had given us, and closed her eyes. "I don't know what my mom will do. I just know I'll fight next to you."

"Why?"

"Because you're my friend, Seaweed Brain. Any more stupid questions?"

I couldn't think of an answer for that. Fortunately I didn't have to. Annabeth was asleep.

I had trouble following her example, with Grover snoring and an albino lion staring hungrily at me, but eventually I closed my eyes.

My nightmare started out as something I'd dreamed a million times before: I was being forced to take a standardized test while wearing a straitjacket. All the other kids were going out to recess, and the teacher kept saying, *Come on, Percy. You're not stupid, are you? Pick up your pencil.*

Then the dream strayed from the usual.

I looked over at the next desk and saw a girl sitting there, also wearing a straitjacket. She was my age, with unruly black, punk-style hair, dark eyeliner around her stormy green eyes, and freckles across her nose. Somehow, I knew who she was. She was Thalia, daughter of Zeus.

She struggled against the straitjacket, glared at me in frustration, and snapped, *Well, Seaweed Brain? One of us has to get out of here.*

She's right, my dream-self thought. I'm going back to that cavern. I'm going to give Hades a piece of my mind.

The straitjacket melted off me. I fell through the classroom floor. The teacher's voice changed until it was cold and evil, echoing from the depths of a great chasm.

Percy Jackson, it said. *Yes, the exchange went well, I see.*

I was back in the dark cavern, spirits of the dead drifting around me. Unseen in the pit, the monstrous thing was speaking, but this time it wasn't addressing me. The numbing power of its voice seemed directed somewhere else.

And he suspects nothing? it asked.

Another voice, one I almost recognized, answered at my shoulder. *Nothing, my lord. He is as ignorant as the rest.*

I looked over, but no one was there. The speaker was invisible.

Deception upon deception, the thing in the pit mused aloud. *Excellent.*

Truly, my lord, said the voice next to me, *you are well-named the Crooked One. But was it really necessary? I could have brought you what I stole directly —*

You? the monster said in scorn. *You have already shown your limits. You would have failed me completely had I not intervened.*

But, my lord—

Peace, little servant. Our six months have bought us much. Zeus's anger has grown. Poseidon has played his most desperate card. Now we shall use it against him. Shortly you shall have the reward you wish, and your revenge. As soon as both items are delivered into my hands . . . but wait. He is here.

What? The invisible servant suddenly sounded tense. *You summoned him, my lord?*

No. The full force of the monster's attention was now pouring over me, freezing me in place. *Blast his father's blood—he is too changeable, too unpredictable. The boy brought himself hither.*

Impossible! the servant cried.

For a weakling such as you, perhaps, the voice snarled. Then its cold power turned back on me. *So . . . you wish to dream of your quest, young half-blood? Then I will oblige.*

The scene changed.

I was standing in a vast throne room with black marble walls and bronze floors. The empty, horrid throne was made from human bones fused together. Standing at the foot of the dais was my mother, frozen in shimmering golden light, her arms outstretched.

I tried to step toward her, but my legs wouldn't move. I reached for her, only to realize that my hands were withering to bones. Grinning skeletons in Greek armor crowded around me, draping me with silk robes, wreathing my head with laurels that smoked with Chimera poison, burning into my scalp.

The evil voice began to laugh. *Hail, the conquering hero!*

I woke with a start.

Grover was shaking my shoulder. "The truck's stopped," he said. "We think they're coming to check on the animals."

"Hide!" Annabeth hissed.

She had it easy. She just put on her magic cap and disappeared. Grover and I had to dive behind feed sacks and hope we looked like turnips.

The trailer doors creaked open. Sunlight and heat poured in.

"Man!" one of the truckers said, waving his hand in front of his ugly nose. "I wish I hauled appliances." He climbed inside and poured some water from a jug into the animals' dishes.

"You hot, big boy?" he asked the lion, then splashed the rest of the bucket right in the lion's face.

The lion roared in indignation.

"Yeah, yeah, yeah," the man said.

Next to me, under the turnip sacks, Grover tensed. For a peace-loving herbivore, he looked downright murderous.

The trucker threw the antelope a squashed-looking Happy Meal bag. He smirked at the zebra. "How ya doin', Stripes? Least we'll be getting rid of *you* this stop. You like magic shows? You're gonna love this one. They're gonna saw you in half!"

The zebra, wild-eyed with fear, looked straight at me.

There was no sound, but as clear as day, I heard it say: *Free me, lord. Please.*

I was too stunned to react.

There was a loud *knock, knock, knock* on the side of the trailer.

The trucker inside with us yelled, "What do you want, Eddie?"

A voice outside—it must've been Eddie's—shouted back, "Maurice? What'd ya say?"

"What are you banging for?"

Knock, knock, knock.

Outside, Eddie yelled, "What banging?"

Our guy Maurice rolled his eyes and went back outside, cursing at Eddie for being an idiot.

A second later, Annabeth appeared next to me. She must've done the banging to get Maurice out of the trailer. She said, "This transport business can't be legal."

"No kidding," Grover said. He paused, as if listening. "The lion says these guys are animal smugglers!"

That's right, the zebra's voice said in my mind.

"We've got to free them!" Grover said. He and Annabeth both looked at me, waiting for my lead.

I'd heard the zebra talk, but not the lion. Why? Maybe

it was another learning disability . . . I could only understand zebras? Then I thought: horses. What had Annabeth said about Poseidon creating horses? Was a zebra close enough to a horse? Was that why I could understand it?

The zebra said, *Open my cage, lord. Please. I'll be fine after that.*

Outside, Eddie and Maurice were still yelling at each other, but I knew they'd be coming inside to torment the animals again any minute. I grabbed Riptide and slashed the lock off the zebra's cage.

The zebra burst out. It turned to me and bowed. *Thank you, lord.*

Grover held up his hands and said something to the zebra in goat talk, like a blessing.

Just as Maurice was poking his head back inside to check out the noise, the zebra leaped over him and into the street. There was yelling and screaming and cars honking. We rushed to the doors of the trailer in time to see the zebra galloping down a wide boulevard lined with hotels and casinos and neon signs. We'd just released a zebra in Las Vegas.

Maurice and Eddie ran after it, with a few policemen running after them, shouting, "Hey! You need a permit for that!"

"Now would be a good time to leave," Annabeth said.

"The other animals first," Grover said.

I cut the locks with my sword. Grover raised his hands and spoke the same goat-blessing he'd used for the zebra.

"Good luck," I told the animals. The antelope and the lion burst out of their cages and went off together into the streets.

Some tourists screamed. Most just backed off and took pictures, probably thinking it was some kind of stunt by one of the casinos.

"Will the animals be okay?" I asked Grover. "I mean, the desert and all—"

"Don't worry," he said. "I placed a satyr's sanctuary on them."

"Meaning?"

"Meaning they'll reach the wild safely," he said. "They'll find water, food, shade, whatever they need until they find a safe place to live."

"Why can't you place a blessing like that on us?" I asked.

"It only works on wild animals."

"So it would only affect Percy," Annabeth reasoned.

"Hey!" I protested.

"Kidding," she said. "Come on. Let's get out of this filthy truck."

We stumbled out into the desert afternoon. It was a hundred and ten degrees, easy, and we must've looked like deep-fried vagrants, but everybody was too interested in the wild animals to pay us much attention.

We passed the Monte Carlo and the MGM. We passed pyramids, a pirate ship, and the Statue of Liberty, which was a pretty small replica, but still made me homesick.

I wasn't sure what we were looking for. Maybe just a place to get out of the heat for a few minutes, find a sandwich and a glass of lemonade, make a new plan for getting west.

We must have taken a wrong turn, because we found

ourselves at a dead end, standing in front of the Lotus Hotel and Casino. The entrance was a huge neon flower, the petals lighting up and blinking. No one was going in or out, but the glittering chrome doors were open, spilling out air-conditioning that smelled like flowers—lotus blossom, maybe. I'd never smelled one, so I wasn't sure.

The doorman smiled at us. "Hey, kids. You look tired. You want to come in and sit down?"

I'd learned to be suspicious, the last week or so. I figured anybody might be a monster or a god. You just couldn't tell. But this guy was normal. One look at him, and I could see. Besides, I was so relieved to hear somebody who sounded sympathetic that I nodded and said we'd love to come in. Inside, we took one look around, and Grover said, "Whoa."

The whole lobby was a giant game room. And I'm not talking about cheesy old Pac-Man games or slot machines. There was an indoor waterslide snaking around the glass elevator, which went straight up at least forty floors. There was a climbing wall on the side of one building, and an indoor bungee-jumping bridge. There were virtual-reality suits with working laser guns. And hundreds of video games, each one the size of a widescreen TV. Basically, you name it, this place had it. There were a few other kids play-ing, but not that many. No waiting for any of the games. There were waitresses and snack bars all around, serving every kind of food you can imagine.

"Hey!" a bellhop said. At least I guessed he was a bell-hop. He wore a white-and-yellow Hawaiian shirt with lotus designs, shorts, and flip-flops. "Welcome to the Lotus Casino. Here's your room key."

I stammered, "Um, but . . ."

"No, no," he said, laughing. "The bill's taken care of. No extra charges, no tips. Just go on up to the top floor, room 4001. If you need anything, like extra bubbles for the hot tub, or skeet targets for the shooting range, or whatever, just call the front desk. Here are your LotusCash cards. They work in the restaurants and on all the games and rides."

He handed us each a green plastic credit card.

I knew there must be some mistake. Obviously he thought we were some millionaire's kids. But I took the card and said, "How much is on here?"

His eyebrows knit together. "What do you mean?"

"I mean, when does it run out of cash?"

He laughed. "Oh, you're making a joke. Hey, that's cool. Enjoy your stay."

We took the elevator upstairs and checked out our room. It was a suite with three separate bedrooms and a bar stocked with candy, sodas, and chips. A hotline to room service. Fluffy towels and water beds with feather pillows. A big-screen television with satellite and high-speed Internet. The balcony had its own hot tub, and sure enough, there was a skeet-shooting machine and a shotgun, so you could launch clay pigeons right out over the Las Vegas skyline and plug them with your gun. I didn't see how that could be legal, but I thought it was pretty cool. The view over the Strip and the desert was amazing, though I doubted we'd ever find time to look at the view with a room like this.

"Oh, goodness," Annabeth said. "This place is . . ."

"Sweet," Grover said. "Absolutely sweet."

There were clothes in the closet, and they fit me. I frowned, thinking that this was a little strange.

I threw Ares's backpack in the trash can. Wouldn't need that anymore. When we left, I could just charge a new one at the hotel store.

I took a shower, which felt awesome after a week of grimy travel. I changed clothes, ate a bag of chips, drank three Cokes, and came out feeling better than I had in a long time. In the back of my mind, some small problem kept nagging me. I'd had a dream or something . . . I needed to talk to my friends. But I was sure it could wait.

I came out of the bedroom and found that Annabeth and Grover had also showered and changed clothes. Grover was eating potato chips to his heart's content, while Annabeth cranked up the National Geographic Channel.

"All those stations," I told her, "and you turn on National Geographic. Are you insane?"

"It's interesting."

"I feel good," Grover said. "I love this place."

Without his even realizing it, the wings sprouted out of his shoes and lifted him a foot off the ground, then back down again.

"So what now?" Annabeth asked. "Sleep?"

Grover and I looked at each other and grinned. We both held up our green plastic LotusCash cards.

"Play time," I said.

I couldn't remember the last time I had so much fun. I came from a relatively poor family. Our idea of a splurge was eating out at Burger King and renting a video. A five-star Vegas hotel? Forget it.

I bungee-jumped the lobby five or six times, did the waterslide, snowboarded the artificial ski slope, and played virtual-reality laser tag and FBI sharpshooter. I saw Grover a few times, going from game to game. He really liked the reverse hunter thing—where the deer go out and shoot the rednecks. I saw Annabeth playing trivia games and other brainiac stuff. They had this huge 3-D sim game where you build your own city, and you could actually see the holographic buildings rise on the display board. I didn't think much of it, but Annabeth loved it.

I'm not sure when I first realized something was wrong.

Probably, it was when I noticed the guy standing next to me at VR sharpshooters. He was about thirteen, I guess, but his clothes were weird. I thought he was some Elvis imper- sonator's son. He wore bell-bottom jeans and a red T-shirt with black piping, and his hair was permed and gelled like a New Jersey girl's on homecoming night.

We played a game of sharpshooters together and he said, "Groovy, man. Been here two weeks, and the games keep getting better and better."

Groovy?

Later, while we were talking, I said something was "sick," and he looked at me kind of startled, as if he'd never heard the word used that way before.

He said his name was Darrin, but as soon as I started asking him questions he got bored with me and started to go back to the computer screen.

I said, "Hey, Darrin?"

"What?"

"What year is it?"

He frowned at me. "In the game?"

"No. In real life."

He had to think about it. "1977."

"No," I said, getting a little scared. "Really."

"Hey, man. Bad vibes. I got a game happening."

After that he totally ignored me.

I started talking to people, and I found it wasn't easy. They were glued to the TV screen, or the video game, or their food, or whatever. I found a guy who told me it was 1985. Another guy told me it was 1993. They all claimed they hadn't been in here very long, a few days, a few weeks at most. They didn't really know and they didn't care.

Then it occurred to me: how long had I been here? It seemed like only a couple of hours, but was it?

I tried to remember why we were here. We were going to Los Angeles. We were supposed to find the entrance to the Underworld. My mother . . . for a scary second, I had trouble remembering her name. Sally. Sally Jackson. I had to find her. I had to stop Hades from causing World War III.

I found Annabeth still building her city.

"Come on," I told her. "We've got to get out of here."

No response.

I shook her. "Annabeth?"

She looked up, annoyed. "What?"

"We need to leave."

"Leave? What are you talking about? I've just got the towers—"

"This place is a trap."

She didn't respond until I shook her again. "What?"

"Listen. The Underworld. Our quest!"

"Oh, come on, Percy. Just a few more minutes."

"Annabeth, there are people here from 1977. Kids who have never aged. You check in, and you stay forever."

"So?" she asked. "Can you imagine a better place?"

I grabbed her wrist and yanked her away from the game.

"Hey!" She screamed and hit me, but nobody else even bothered looking at us. They were too busy.

I made her look directly in my eyes. I said, "Spiders. Large, hairy spiders."

That jarred her. Her vision cleared. "Oh my gods," she said. "How long have we—"

"I don't know, but we've got to find Grover."

We went searching, and found him still playing Virtual Deer Hunter.

"Grover!" we both shouted.

He said, "Die, human! Die, silly polluting nasty person!"

"Grover!"

He turned the plastic gun on me and started clicking, as if I were just another image from the screen.

I looked at Annabeth, and together we took Grover by the arms and dragged him away. His flying shoes sprang to life and started tugging his legs in the other direction as he shouted, "No! I just got to a new level! No!"

The Lotus bellhop hurried up to us. "Well, now, are you ready for your platinum cards?"

"We're leaving," I told him.

"Such a shame," he said, and I got the feeling that he really meant it, that we'd be breaking his heart if we went. "We just added an entire new floor full of games for platinum-card members."

He held out the cards, and I wanted one. I knew that if I took one, I'd never leave. I'd stay here, happy forever, playing games forever, and soon I'd forget my mom, and my quest, and maybe even my own name. I'd be playing virtual rifleman with groovy Disco Darrin forever.

Grover reached for the card, but Annabeth yanked back his arm and said, "No, thanks."

We walked toward the door, and as we did, the smell of the food and the sounds of the games seemed to get more and more inviting. I thought about our room upstairs. We could just stay the night, sleep in a real bed for once. . . .

Then we burst through the doors of the Lotus Casino and ran down the sidewalk. It felt like afternoon, about the same time of day we'd gone into the casino, but something was wrong. The weather had completely changed. It was stormy, with heat lightning flashing out in the desert.

Ares's backpack was slung over my shoulder, which was odd, because I was sure I had thrown it in the trash can in room 4001, but at the moment I had other problems to worry about.

I ran to the nearest newspaper stand and read the year first. Thank the gods, it was the same year it had been when we went in. Then I noticed the date: June twentieth.

We had been in the Lotus Casino for five days.

We had only one day left until the summer solstice. One day to complete our quest.

SEVENTEEN

WE SHOP FOR WATER BEDS

It was Annabeth's idea.

She loaded us into the back of a Vegas taxi as if we actually had money, and told the driver, "Los Angeles, please."

The cabbie chewed his cigar and sized us up. "That's three hundred miles. For that, you gotta pay up front."

"You accept casino debit cards?" Annabeth asked.

He shrugged. "Some of 'em. Same as credit cards. I gotta swipe 'em through first."

Annabeth handed him her green LotusCash card.

He looked at it skeptically.

"Swipe it," Annabeth invited.

He did.

His meter machine started rattling. The lights flashed. Finally an infinity symbol came up next to the dollar sign.

The cigar fell out of the driver's mouth. He looked back at us, his eyes wide. "Where to in Los Angeles. . . uh, Your Highness?"

"The Santa Monica Pier." Annabeth sat up a little straighter. I could tell she liked the "Your Highness" thing. "Get us there fast, and you can keep the change."

Maybe she shouldn't have told him that.

The cab's speedometer never dipped below ninety-five the whole way through the Mojave Desert.

On the road, we had plenty of time to talk. I told Annabeth and Grover about my latest dream, but the details got sketchier the more I tried to remember them. The Lotus Casino seemed to have short-circuited my memory. I couldn't recall what the invisible servant's voice had sounded like, though I was sure it was somebody I knew. The servant had called the monster in the pit something other than "my lord" . . . some special name or title. . . .

"The Silent One?" Annabeth suggested. "The Rich One? Both of those are nicknames for Hades."

"Maybe . . ." I said, though neither sounded quite right.

"That throne room sounds like Hades's," Grover said. "That's the way it's usually described."

I shook my head. "Something's wrong. The throne room wasn't the main part of the dream. And that voice from the pit . . . I don't know. It just didn't feel like a god's voice."

Annabeth's eyes widened.

"What?" I asked.

"Oh . . . nothing. I was just—No, it *has* to be Hades. Maybe he sent this thief, this invisible person, to get the master bolt, and something went wrong—"

"Like what?"

"I—I don't know," she said. "But if he stole Zeus's symbol of power from Olympus, and the gods were hunting him, I mean, a lot of things could go wrong. So this thief had to hide the bolt, or he lost it somehow. Anyway, he failed to bring it to Hades. That's what the voice said in your dream, right? The guy failed. That would explain what the Furies were searching for when they came after us on the bus. Maybe they thought we had retrieved the bolt."

I wasn't sure what was wrong with her. She looked pale.

"But if I'd already retrieved the bolt," I said, "why would I be traveling to the Underworld?"

"To threaten Hades," Grover suggested. "To bribe or blackmail him into getting your mom back."

I whistled. "You have evil thoughts for a goat."

"Why, thank you."

"But the thing in the pit said it was waiting for *two* items," I said. "If the master bolt is one, what's the other?"

Grover shook his head, clearly mystified.

Annabeth was looking at me as if she knew my next question, and was silently willing me not to ask it.

"You have an idea what might be in that pit, don't you?" I asked her. "I mean, if it isn't Hades?"

"Percy . . . let's not talk about it. Because if it isn't Hades . . . No. It has to be Hades."

Wasteland rolled by. We passed a sign that said CALIFORNIA STATE LINE, 12 MILES.

I got the feeling I was missing one simple, critical piece of information. It was like when I stared at a common word I should know, but I couldn't make sense of it because one or two letters were floating around. The more I thought about my quest, the more I was sure that confronting Hades wasn't the real answer. There was something else going on, something even more dangerous.

The problem was: we were hurtling toward the Underworld at ninety-five miles an hour, betting that Hades had the master bolt. If we got there and found out we were wrong, we wouldn't have time to correct ourselves. The solstice deadline would pass and war would begin.

"The answer is in the Underworld," Annabeth assured me. "You saw spirits of the dead, Percy. There's only one place that could be. We're doing the right thing."

She tried to boost our morale by suggesting clever strategies for getting into the Land of the Dead, but my heart wasn't in it. There were just too many unknown factors. It was like cramming for a test without knowing the subject. And believe me, I'd done *that* enough times.

The cab sped west. Every gust of wind through Death Valley sounded like a spirit of the dead. Every time the brakes hissed on an eighteen-wheeler, it reminded me of Echidna's reptilian voice.

At sunset, the taxi dropped us at the beach in Santa Monica. It looked exactly the way L.A. beaches do in the movies, only it smelled worse. There were carnival rides lining the Pier, palm trees lining the sidewalks, homeless guys sleeping in the sand dunes, and surfer dudes waiting for the perfect wave.

Grover, Annabeth, and I walked down to the edge of the surf.

"What now?" Annabeth asked.

The Pacific was turning gold in the setting sun. I thought about how long it had been since I'd stood on the beach at Montauk, on the opposite side of the country, looking out at a different sea.

How could there be a god who could control all that? What did my science teacher used to say—two-thirds of the earth's surface was covered in water? How could I be the son of someone that powerful?

I stepped into the surf.

"Percy?" Annabeth said. "What are you doing?"

I kept walking, up to my waist, then my chest.

She called after me, "You know how polluted that water is? There're all kinds of toxic—"

That's when my head went under.

I held my breath at first. It's difficult to intentionally inhale water. Finally I couldn't stand it anymore. I gasped. Sure enough, I could breathe normally.

I walked down into the shoals. I shouldn't have been able to see through the murk, but somehow I could tell where everything was. I could sense the rolling texture of the bottom. I could make out sand-dollar colonies dotting the sandbars. I could even see the currents, warm and cold streams swirling together.

I felt something rub against my leg. I looked down and almost shot out of the water like a ballistic missile. Sliding along beside me was a five-foot-long mako shark.

But the thing wasn't attacking. It was nuzzling me. Heeling like a dog. Tentatively, I touched its dorsal fin. It bucked a little, as if inviting me to hold tighter. I grabbed the fin with both hands. It took off, pulling me along. The shark carried me down into the darkness. It deposited me at the edge of the ocean proper, where the sand bank dropped off into a huge chasm. It was like standing on the rim of the Grand Canyon at midnight, not being able to see much, but knowing the void was right there.

The surface shimmered maybe a hundred and fifty feet above. I knew I should've been crushed by the pressure. Then again, I shouldn't have been able to breathe. I wondered if there was a limit to how deep I could go, if I could sink straight to the bottom of the Pacific.

Then I saw something glimmering in the darkness below, growing bigger and brighter as it rose toward me. A woman's voice, like my mother's, called: "Percy Jackson."

As she got closer, her shape became clearer. She had flowing black hair, a dress made of green silk. Light flickered around her, and her eyes were so distractingly beautiful I hardly noticed the stallion-sized sea horse she was riding.

She dismounted. The sea horse and the mako shark whisked off and started playing something that looked like tag. The underwater lady smiled at me. "You've come far, Percy Jackson. Well done."

I wasn't quite sure what to do, so I bowed. "You're the woman who spoke to me in the Mississippi River."

"Yes, child. I am a Nereid, a spirit of the sea. It was not easy to appear so far upriver, but the naiads, my freshwater cousins, helped sustain my life force. They honor Lord Poseidon, though they do not serve in his court."

"And . . . you serve in Poseidon's court?"

She nodded. "It has been many years since a child of the Sea God has been born. We have watched you with great interest."

Suddenly I remembered faces in the waves off Montauk Beach when I was a little boy, reflections of smiling women. Like so many of the weird things in my life, I'd never given it much thought before.

"If my father is so interested in me," I said, "why isn't he here? Why doesn't he speak to me?"

A cold current rose out of the depths.

"Do not judge the Lord of the Sea too harshly," the Nereid told me. "He stands at the brink of an unwanted war. He has much to occupy his time. Besides, he is forbidden to help you directly. The gods may not show such favoritism."

"Even to their own children?"

"Especially to them. The gods can work by indirect influence only. That is why I give you a warning, and a gift."

She held out her hand. Three white pearls flashed in her palm.

"I know you journey to Hades's realm," she said. "Few mortals have ever done this and survived: Orpheus, who had great music skill; Hercules, who had great strength; Houdini, who could escape even the depths of Tartarus. Do you have these talents?"

"Um . . . no, ma'am."

"Ah, but you have something else, Percy. You have gifts you have only begun to know. The oracles have foretold a great and terrible future for you, should you survive to man-hood. Poseidon would not have you die before your time. Therefore take these, and when you are in need, smash a pearl at your feet."

"What will happen?"

"That," she said, "depends on the need. But remember: what belongs to the sea will always return to the sea."

"What about the warning?"

Her eyes flickered with green light. "Go with what your heart tells you, or you will lose all. Hades feeds on doubt and hopelessness. He will trick you if he can, make you mistrust your own judgment. Once you are in his realm, he will never willingly let you leave. Keep faith. Good luck, Percy Jackson."

She summoned her sea horse and rode toward the void.

"Wait!" I called. "At the river, you said not to trust the gifts. What gifts?"

"Good-bye, young hero," she called back, her voice fading into the depths. "You must listen to your heart." She became a speck of glowing green, and then she was gone.

I wanted to follow her down into the darkness. I wanted to see the court of Poseidon. But I looked up at the sunset darkening on the surface. My friends were waiting. We had so little time. . . .

I kicked upward toward the shore.

When I reached the beach, my clothes dried instantly. I told Grover and Annabeth what had happened, and showed them the pearls.

Annabeth grimaced. "No gift comes without a price."

"They were free."

"No." She shook her head. "'There is no such thing as a free lunch.' That's an ancient Greek saying that translated pretty well into American. There will be a price. You wait."

On that happy thought, we turned our backs on the sea.

With some spare change from Ares's backpack, we took the bus into West Hollywood. I showed the driver the Underworld address slip I'd taken from Aunty Em's Garden Gnome Emporium, but he'd never heard of DOA Recording Studios.

"You remind me of somebody I saw on TV," he told me. "You a child actor or something?"

"Uh . . . I'm a stunt double . . . for a lot of child actors."

"Oh! That explains it."

We thanked him and got off quickly at the next stop.

We wandered for miles on foot, looking for DOA. Nobody seemed to know where it was. It didn't appear in the phone book.

Twice, we ducked into alleys to avoid cop cars.

I froze in front of an appliance-store window because a television was playing an interview with somebody who looked very familiar—my stepdad, Smelly Gabe. He was talking to Barbara Walters—I mean, as if he were some kind of huge celebrity. She was interviewing him in our apartment, in the middle of a poker game, and there was a young blond lady sitting next to him, patting his hand.

A fake tear glistened on his cheek. He was saying, "Honest, Ms. Walters, if it wasn't for Sugar here, my grief counselor, I'd be a wreck. My stepson took everything I cared about. My wife . . . my Camaro . . . I—I'm sorry. I have trouble talking about it."

"There you have it, America." Barbara Walters turned to the camera. "A man torn apart. An adolescent boy with serious issues. Let me show you, again, the last known photo of this troubled young fugitive, taken a week ago in Denver."

The screen cut to a grainy shot of me, Annabeth, and Grover standing outside the Colorado diner, talking to Ares.

"Who are the other children in this photo?" Barbara Walters asked dramatically. "Who is the man with them? Is Percy Jackson a delinquent, a terrorist, or perhaps the brainwashed victim of a frightening new cult? When we come back, we chat with a leading child psychologist. Stay tuned, America."

"C'mon," Grover told me. He hauled me away before I could punch a hole in the appliance-store window.

It got dark, and hungry-looking characters started coming out on the streets to play. Now, don't get me wrong. I'm a New Yorker. I don't scare easy. But L.A. had a totally different feel from New York. Back home, everything seemed close. It didn't matter how big the city was, you could get anywhere without getting lost. The street pattern and the subway made sense. There was a system to how things worked. A kid could be safe as long as he wasn't stupid.

L.A. wasn't like that. It was spread out, chaotic, hard to move around. It reminded me of Ares. It wasn't enough for

L.A. to be big; it had to prove it was big by being loud and strange and difficult to navigate, too. I didn't know how we were ever going to find the entrance to the Underworld by tomorrow, the summer solstice.

We walked past gangbangers, bums, and street hawkers, who looked at us like they were trying to figure if we were worth the trouble of mugging.

As we hurried passed the entrance of an alley, a voice from the darkness said, "Hey, you."

Like an idiot, I stopped.

Before I knew it, we were surrounded. A gang of kids had circled us. Six of them in all—white kids with expensive clothes and mean faces. Like the kids at Yancy Academy: rich brats playing at being bad boys.

Instinctively, I uncapped Riptide.

When the sword appeared out of nowhere, the kids backed off, but their leader was either really stupid or really brave, because he kept coming at me with a switchblade.

I made the mistake of swinging.

The kid yelped. But he must've been one hundred percent mortal, because the blade passed harmlessly right through his chest. He looked down. "What the . . ."

I figured I had about three seconds before his shock turned to anger. "Run!" I screamed at Annabeth and Grover.

We pushed two kids out of the way and raced down the street, not knowing where we were going. We turned a sharp corner.

"There!" Annabeth shouted.

Only one store on the block looked open, its windows glaring with neon. The sign above the door said something like CRSTUY'S WATRE BDE ALPACE.

"Crusty's Water Bed Palace?" Grover translated.

It didn't sound like a place I'd ever go except in an emergency, but this definitely qualified.

We burst through the doors, ran behind a water bed, and ducked. A split second later, the gang kids ran past outside.

"I think we lost them," Grover panted.

A voice behind us boomed, "Lost who?"

We all jumped.

Standing behind us was a guy who looked like a raptor in a leisure suit. He was at least seven feet tall, with absolutely no hair. He had gray, leathery skin, thick-lidded eyes, and a cold, reptilian smile. He moved toward us slowly, but I got the feeling he could move fast if he needed to.

His suit might've come from the Lotus Casino. It belonged back in the seventies, big-time. The shirt was silk paisley, unbuttoned halfway down his hairless chest. The lapels on his velvet jacket were as wide as landing strips. The silver chains around his neck—I couldn't even count them.

"I'm Crusty," he said, with a tartar-yellow smile.

I resisted the urge to say, *Yes, you are.*

"Sorry to barge in," I told him. "We were just, um, browsing."

"You mean hiding from those no-good kids," he grumbled. "They hang around every night. I get a lot of people in here, thanks to them. Say, you want to look at a water bed?"

I was about to say *No, thanks*, when he put a huge paw on my shoulder and steered me deeper into the showroom.

There was every kind of water bed you could imagine: different kinds of wood, different patterns of sheets; queen-size, king-size, emperor-of-the-universe-size.

"This is my most popular model." Crusty spread his hands proudly over a bed covered with black satin sheets, with built-in Lava Lamps on the headboard. The mattress vibrated, so it looked like oil-flavored Jell-O.

"Million-hand massage," Crusty told us. "Go on, try it out. Shoot, take a nap. I don't care. No business today, anyway."

"Um," I said, "I don't think . . ."

"Million-hand massage!" Grover cried, and dove in. "Oh, you guys! This is cool."

"Hmm," Crusty said, stroking his leathery chin. "Almost, almost."

"Almost what?" I asked.

He looked at Annabeth. "Do me a favor and try this one over here, honey. Might fit."

Annabeth said, "But what—"

He patted her reassuringly on the shoulder and led her over to the Safari Deluxe model with teakwood lions carved into the frame and a leopard-patterned comforter. When Annabeth didn't want to lie down, Crusty pushed her.

"Hey!" she protested.

Crusty snapped his fingers. *"Ergo!"*

Ropes sprang from the sides of the bed, lashing around Annabeth, holding her to the mattress.

Grover tried to get up, but ropes sprang from his black-satin bed, too, and lashed him down.

"N-not c-c-cool!" he yelled, his voice vibrating from the million-hand massage. "N-not c-cool a-at all!"

The giant looked at Annabeth, then turned toward me and grinned. "Almost, darn it."

I tried to step away, but his hand shot out and clamped around the back of my neck. "Whoa, kid. Don't worry. We'll find you one in a sec."

"Let my friends go."

"Oh, sure I will. But I got to make them fit, first."

"What do you mean?"

"All the beds are exactly six feet, see? Your friends are too short. Got to make them fit."

Annabeth and Grover kept struggling.

"Can't stand imperfect measurements," Crusty muttered. "*Ergo!*"

A new set of ropes leaped out from the top and bottom of the beds, wrapping around Grover and Annabeth's ankles, then around their armpits. The ropes started tightening, pulling my friends from both ends.

"Don't worry," Crusty told me. "These are stretching jobs. Maybe three extra inches on their spines. They might even live. Now why don't we find a bed you like, huh?"

"Percy!" Grover yelled.

My mind was racing. I knew I couldn't take on this giant water-bed salesman alone. He would snap my neck before I ever got my sword out.

"Your real name's not Crusty, is it?" I asked.

"Legally, it's Procrustes," he admitted.

"The Stretcher," I said. I remembered the story: the giant who'd tried to kill Theseus with excess hospitality on his way to Athens.

"Yeah," the salesman said. "But who can pronounce *Procrustes*? Bad for business. Now 'Crusty,' anybody can say that."

"You're right. It's got a good ring to it."

His eyes lit up. "You think so?"

"Oh, absolutely," I said. "And the workmanship on these beds? Fabulous!"

He grinned hugely, but his fingers didn't loosen on my neck. "I tell my customers that. Every time. Nobody bothers to look at the workmanship. How many built-in Lava Lamp headboards have you seen?"

"Not too many."

"That's right!"

"Percy!" Annabeth yelled. "What are you doing?"

"Don't mind her," I told Procrustes. "She's impossible."

The giant laughed. "All my customers are. Never six feet exactly. So inconsiderate. And then they complain about the fitting."

"What do you do if they're longer than six feet?"

"Oh, that happens all the time. It's a simple fix."

He let go of my neck, but before I could react, he reached behind a nearby sales desk and brought out a huge double-bladed brass axe. He said, "I just center the subject as best I can and lop off whatever hangs over on either end."

"Ah," I said, swallowing hard. "Sensible."

"I'm so glad to come across an intelligent customer!"

The ropes were really stretching my friends now. Annabeth was turning pale. Grover made gurgling sounds, like a strangled goose.

"So, Crusty . . ." I said, trying to keep my voice light. I glanced at the sales tag on the valentine-shaped Honeymoon Special. "Does this one really have dynamic stabilizers to stop wave motion?"

"Absolutely. Try it out."

"Yeah, maybe I will. But would it work even for a big guy like you? No waves at all?"

"Guaranteed."

"No way."

"Way."

"Show me."

He sat down eagerly on the bed, patted the mattress. "No waves. See?"

I snapped my fingers. *"Ergo."*

Ropes lashed around Crusty and flattened him against the mattress.

"Hey!" he yelled.

"Center him just right," I said.

The ropes readjusted themselves at my command. Crusty's whole head stuck out the top. His feet stuck out the bottom.

"No!" he said. "Wait! This is just a demo."

I uncapped Riptide. "A few simple adjustments . . ."

I had no qualms about what I was about to do. If

[281]

Crusty were human, I couldn't hurt him anyway. If he was a monster, he deserved to turn into dust for a while.

"You drive a hard bargain," he told me. "I'll give you thirty percent off on selected floor models!"

"I think I'll start with the top." I raised my sword.

"No money down! No interest for six months!"

I swung the sword. Crusty stopped making offers.

I cut the ropes on the other beds. Annabeth and Grover got to their feet, groaning and wincing and cursing me a lot.

"You look taller," I said.

"Very funny," Annabeth said. "Be faster next time."

I looked at the bulletin board behind Crusty's sales desk. There was an advertisement for Hermes Delivery Service, and another for the All-New Compendium of L.A. Area Monsters—"The only Monstrous Yellow Pages you'll ever need!" Under that, a bright orange flier for DOA Recording Studios, offering commissions for heroes' souls. "We are always looking for new talent!" DOA's address was right underneath with a map.

"Come on," I told my friends.

"Give us a minute," Grover complained. "We were almost stretched to death!"

"Then you're ready for the Underworld," I said. "It's only a block from here."

EIGHTEEN

ANNABETH DOES
OBEDIENCE SCHOOL

We stood in the shadows of Valencia Boulevard, looking up at gold letters etched in black marble: DOA RECORDING STUDIOS.

Underneath, stenciled on the glass doors: NO SOLICITORS. NO LOITERING. NO LIVING.

It was almost midnight, but the lobby was brightly lit and full of people. Behind the security desk sat a tough-looking guard with sunglasses and an earpiece.

I turned to my friends. "Okay. You remember the plan."

"The plan," Grover gulped. "Yeah. I love the plan."

Annabeth said, "What happens if the plan doesn't work?"

"Don't think negative."

"Right," she said. "We're entering the Land of the Dead, and I shouldn't think negative."

I took the pearls out of my pocket, the three milky spheres the Nereid had given me in Santa Monica. They didn't seem like much of a backup in case something went wrong.

Annabeth put her hand on my shoulder. "I'm sorry, Percy. You're right, we'll make it. It'll be fine."

She gave Grover a nudge.

"Oh, right!" he chimed in. "We got this far. We'll find the master bolt and save your mom. No problem."

I looked at them both, and felt really grateful. Only a few minutes before, I'd almost gotten them stretched to death on deluxe water beds, and now they were trying to be brave for my sake, trying to make me feel better.

I slipped the pearls back in my pocket. "Let's whup some Underworld butt."

We walked inside the DOA lobby.

Muzak played softly on hidden speakers. The carpet and walls were steel gray. Pencil cactuses grew in the corners like skeleton hands. The furniture was black leather, and every seat was taken. There were people sitting on couches, people standing up, people staring out the windows or waiting for the elevator. Nobody moved, or talked, or did much of anything. Out of the corner of my eye, I could see them all just fine, but if I focused on any one of them in particular, they started looking . . . transparent. I could see right through their bodies.

The security guard's desk was a raised podium, so we had to look up at him.

He was tall and elegant, with chocolate-colored skin and bleached-blond hair shaved military style. He wore tortoiseshell shades and a silk Italian suit that matched his hair. A black rose was pinned to his lapel under a silver name tag.

I read the name tag, then looked at him in bewilderment. "Your name is Chiron?"

He leaned across the desk. I couldn't see anything in his

glasses except my own reflection, but his smile was sweet and cold, like a python's, right before it eats you.

"What a precious young lad." He had a strange accent—British, maybe, but also as if he had learned English as a second language. "Tell me, mate, do I look like a centaur?"

"N-no."

"Sir," he added smoothly.

"Sir," I said.

He pinched the name tag and ran his finger under the letters. "Can you read this, mate? It says C-H-*A*-R-O-N. Say it with me: CARE-ON."

"Charon."

"Amazing! Now: *Mr.* Charon."

"Mr. Charon," I said.

"Well done." He sat back. "I *hate* being confused with that old horse-man. And now, how may I help you little dead ones?"

His question caught in my stomach like a fastball. I looked at Annabeth for support.

"We want to go the Underworld," she said.

Charon's mouth twitched. "Well, that's refreshing."

"It is?" she asked.

"Straightforward and honest. No screaming. No 'There must be a mistake, Mr. Charon.'" He looked us over. "How did you die, then?"

I nudged Grover.

"Oh," he said. "Um . . . drowned . . . in the bathtub."

"All three of you?" Charon asked.

We nodded.

"Big bathtub." Charon looked mildly impressed. "I don't suppose you have coins for passage. Normally, with adults, you see, I could charge your American Express, or add the ferry price to your last cable bill. But with children . . . alas, you never die prepared. Suppose you'll have to take a seat for a few centuries."

"Oh, but we have coins." I set three golden drachmas on the counter, part of the stash I'd found in Crusty's office desk.

"Well, now . . ." Charon moistened his lips. "Real drachmas. Real golden drachmas. I haven't seen these in . . ."

His fingers hovered greedily over the coins.

We were so close.

Then Charon looked at me. That cold stare behind his glasses seemed to bore a hole through my chest. "Here now," he said. "You couldn't read my name correctly. Are you dyslexic, lad?"

"No," I said. "I'm dead."

Charon leaned forward and took a sniff. "You're not dead. I should've known. You're a godling."

"We have to get to the Underworld," I insisted.

Charon made a growling sound deep in his throat.

Immediately, all the people in the waiting room got up and started pacing, agitated, lighting cigarettes, running hands through their hair, or checking their wristwatches.

"Leave while you can," Charon told us. "I'll just take these and forget I saw you."

He started to go for the coins, but I snatched them back.

"No service, no tip." I tried to sound braver than I felt.

Charon growled again—a deep, blood-chilling sound. The spirits of the dead started pounding on the elevator doors.

"It's a shame, too," I sighed. "We had more to offer."

I held up the entire bag from Crusty's stash. I took out a fistful of drachmas and let the coins spill through my fingers.

Charon's growl changed into something more like a lion's purr. "Do you think I can be bought, godling? Eh . . . just out of curiosity, how much have you got there?"

"A lot," I said. "I bet Hades doesn't pay you well enough for such hard work."

"Oh, you don't know the half of it. How would you like to babysit these spirits all day? Always 'Please don't let me be dead' or 'Please let me across for free.' I haven't had a pay raise in three thousand years. Do you imagine suits like this come cheap?"

"You deserve better," I agreed. "A little appreciation. Respect. Good pay."

With each word, I stacked another gold coin on the counter.

Charon glanced down at his silk Italian jacket, as if imagining himself in something even better. "I must say, lad, you're making some sense now. Just a little."

I stacked another few coins. "I could mention a pay raise while I'm talking to Hades."

He sighed. "The boat's almost full, anyway. I might as well add you three and be off."

He stood, scooped up our money, and said, "Come along."

We pushed through the crowd of waiting spirits, who started grabbing at our clothes like the wind, their voices whispering things I couldn't make out. Charon shoved them out of the way, grumbling, "Freeloaders."

He escorted us into the elevator, which was already crowded with souls of the dead, each one holding a green boarding pass. Charon grabbed two spirits who were trying to get on with us and pushed them back into the lobby.

"Right. Now, no one get any ideas while I'm gone," he announced to the waiting room. "And if anyone moves the dial off my easy-listening station again, I'll make sure you're here for another thousand years. Understand?"

He shut the doors. He put a key card into a slot in the elevator panel and we started to descend.

"What happens to the spirits waiting in the lobby?" Annabeth asked.

"Nothing," Charon said.

"For how long?"

"Forever, or until I'm feeling generous."

"Oh," she said. "That's . . . fair."

Charon raised an eyebrow. "Whoever said death was fair, young miss? Wait until it's your turn. You'll die soon enough, where you're going."

"We'll get out alive," I said.

"Ha."

I got a sudden dizzy feeling. We weren't going down

anymore, but forward. The air turned misty. Spirits around me started changing shape. Their modern clothes flickered, turning into gray hooded robes. The floor of the elevator began swaying.

I blinked hard. When I opened my eyes, Charon's creamy Italian suit had been replaced by a long black robe. His tortoiseshell glasses were gone. Where his eyes should've been were empty sockets—like Ares's eyes, except Charon's were totally dark, full of night and death and despair.

He saw me looking, and said, "Well?"

"Nothing," I managed.

I thought he was grinning, but that wasn't it. The flesh of his face was becoming transparent, letting me see straight through to his skull.

The floor kept swaying.

Grover said, "I think I'm getting seasick."

When I blinked again, the elevator wasn't an elevator anymore. We were standing in a wooden barge. Charon was poling us across a dark, oily river, swirling with bones, dead fish, and other, stranger things—plastic dolls, crushed carnations, soggy diplomas with gilt edges.

"The River Styx," Annabeth murmured. "It's so . . ."

"Polluted," Charon said. "For thousands of years, you humans have been throwing in everything as you come across—hopes, dreams, wishes that never came true. Irresponsible waste management, if you ask me."

Mist curled off the filthy water. Above us, almost lost in the gloom, was a ceiling of stalactites. Ahead, the far shore glimmered with greenish light, the color of poison.

Panic closed up my throat. What was I doing here? These people around me . . . they were dead.

Annabeth grabbed hold of my hand. Under normal circumstances, this would've embarrassed me, but I understood how she felt. She wanted reassurance that somebody else was alive on this boat.

I found myself muttering a prayer, though I wasn't quite sure who I was praying to. Down here, only one god mattered, and he was the one I had come to confront.

The shoreline of the Underworld came into view. Craggy rocks and black volcanic sand stretched inland about a hundred yards to the base of a high stone wall, which marched off in either direction as far as we could see. A sound came from somewhere nearby in the green gloom, echoing off the stones—the howl of a large animal.

"Old Three-Face is hungry," Charon said. His smile turned skeletal in the greenish light. "Bad luck for you, godlings."

The bottom of our boat slid onto the black sand. The dead began to disembark. A woman holding a little girl's hand. An old man and an old woman hobbling along arm in arm. A boy no older than I was, shuffling silently along in his gray robe.

Charon said, "I'd wish you luck, mate, but there isn't any down here. Mind you, don't forget to mention my pay raise."

He counted our golden coins into his pouch, then took

up his pole. He warbled something that sounded like a Barry Manilow song as he ferried the empty barge back across the river.

We followed the spirits up a well-worn path.

I'm not sure what I was expecting—Pearly Gates, or a big black portcullis, or something. But the entrance to the Underworld looked like a cross between airport security and the Jersey Turnpike.

There were three separate entrances under one huge black archway that said YOU ARE NOW ENTERING EREBUS. Each entrance had a pass-through metal detector with security cameras mounted on top. Beyond this were tollbooths manned by black-robed ghouls like Charon.

The howling of the hungry animal was really loud now, but I couldn't see where it was coming from. The three-headed dog, Cerberus, who was supposed to guard Hades's door, was nowhere to be seen.

The dead queued up in the three lines, two marked ATTENDANT ON DUTY, and one marked EZ DEATH. The EZ DEATH line was moving right along. The other two were crawling.

"What do you figure?" I asked Annabeth.

"The fast line must go straight to the Asphodel Fields," she said. "No contest. They don't want to risk judgment from the court, because it might go against them."

"There's a court for dead people?"

"Yeah. Three judges. They switch around who sits on the bench. King Minos, Thomas Jefferson, Shakespeare—

people like that. Sometimes they look at a life and decide that person needs a special reward—the Fields of Elysium. Sometimes they decide on punishment. But most people, well, they just lived. Nothing special, good or bad. So they go to the Asphodel Fields."

"And do what?"

Grover said, "Imagine standing in a wheat field in Kansas. Forever."

"Harsh," I said.

"Not as harsh as that," Grover muttered. "Look."

A couple of black-robbed ghouls had pulled aside one spirit and were frisking him at the security desk. The face of the dead man looked vaguely familiar.

"He's that preacher who made the news, remember?" Grover asked.

"Oh, yeah." I did remember now. We'd seen him on TV a couple of times at the Yancy Academy dorm. He was this annoying televangelist from upstate New York who'd raised millions of dollars for orphanages and then got caught spending the money on stuff for his mansion, like gold-plated toilet seats, and an indoor putt-putt golf course. He'd died in a police chase when his "Lamborghini for the Lord" went off a cliff.

I said, "What're they doing to him?"

"Special punishment from Hades," Grover guessed. "The really bad people get his personal attention as soon as they arrive. The Fur—the Kindly Ones will set up an eternal torture for him."

The thought of the Furies made me shudder. I realized

I was in their home territory now. Old Mrs. Dodds would be licking her lips with anticipation.

"But if he's a preacher," I said, "and he believes in a different hell. . . ."

Grover shrugged. "Who says he's seeing this place the way we're seeing it? Humans see what they want to see. You're very stubborn—er, persistent, that way."

We got closer to the gates. The howling was so loud now it shook the ground at my feet, but I still couldn't figure out where it was coming from.

Then, about fifty feet in front of us, the green mist shimmered. Standing just where the path split into three lanes was an enormous shadowy monster.

I hadn't seen it before because it was half transparent, like the dead. Until it moved, it blended with whatever was behind it. Only its eyes and teeth looked solid. And it was staring straight at me.

My jaw hung open. All I could think to say was, "He's a Rottweiler."

I'd always imagined Cerberus as a big black mastiff. But he was obviously a purebred Rottweiler, except of course that he was twice the size of a woolly mammoth, mostly invisible, and had three heads.

The dead walked right up to him—no fear at all. The ATTENDANT ON DUTY lines parted on either side of him. The EZ DEATH spirits walked right between his front paws and under his belly, which they could do without even crouching.

"I'm starting to see him better," I muttered. "Why is that?"

"I think . . ." Annabeth moistened her lips. "I'm afraid it's because we're getting closer to being dead."

The dog's middle head craned toward us. It sniffed the air and growled.

"It can smell the living," I said.

"But that's okay," Grover said, trembling next to me. "Because we have a plan."

"Right," Annabeth said. I'd never heard her voice sound quite so small. "A plan."

We moved toward the monster.

The middle head snarled at us, then barked so loud my eyeballs rattled.

"Can you understand it?" I asked Grover.

"Oh yeah," he said. "I can understand it."

"What's it saying?"

"I don't think humans have a four-letter word that translates, exactly."

I took the big stick out of my backpack—a bedpost I'd broken off Crusty's Safari Deluxe floor model. I held it up, and tried to channel happy dog thoughts toward Cerberus—Alpo commercials, cute little puppies, fire hydrants. I tried to smile, like I wasn't about to die.

"Hey, Big Fella," I called up. "I bet they don't play with you much."

"GROWWWLLLL!"

"Good boy," I said weakly.

I waved the stick. The dog's middle head followed the movement. The other two heads trained their eyes on me, completely ignoring the spirits. I had Cerberus's undivided attention. I wasn't sure that was a good thing.

"Fetch!" I threw the stick into the gloom, a good solid throw. I heard it go *ker-sploosh* in the River Styx.

Cerberus glared at me, unimpressed. His eyes were baleful and cold.

So much for the plan.

Cerberus was now making a new kind of growl, deeper down in his three throats.

"Um," Grover said. "Percy?"

"Yeah?"

"I just thought you'd want to know."

"Yeah?"

"Cerberus? He's saying we've got ten seconds to pray to the god of our choice. After that . . . well . . . he's hungry."

"Wait!" Annabeth said. She started rifling through her pack.

Uh-oh, I thought.

"Five seconds," Grover said. "Do we run now?"

Annabeth produced a red rubber ball the size of a grapefruit. It was labeled WATERLAND, DENVER, CO. Before I could stop her, she raised the ball and marched straight up to Cerberus.

She shouted, "See the ball? You want the ball, Cerberus? Sit!"

Cerberus looked as stunned as we were.

All three of his heads cocked sideways. Six nostrils dilated.

"Sit!" Annabeth called again.

I was sure that any moment she would become the world's largest Milkbone dog biscuit.

But instead, Cerberus licked his three sets of lips, shifted on his haunches, and sat, immediately crushing a dozen spirits who'd been passing underneath him in the EZ DEATH line. The spirits made muffled hisses as they dissipated, like the air let out of tires.

Annabeth said, "Good boy!"

She threw Cerberus the ball.

He caught it in his middle mouth. It was barely big enough for him to chew, and the other heads started snapping at the middle, trying to get the new toy.

"Drop it!" Annabeth ordered.

Cerberus's heads stopped fighting and looked at her. The ball was wedged between two of his teeth like a tiny piece of gum. He made a loud, scary whimper, then dropped the ball, now slimy and bitten nearly in half, at Annabeth's feet.

"Good boy." She picked up the ball, ignoring the monster spit all over it.

She turned toward us. "Go now. EZ DEATH line—it's faster."

I said, "But—"

"Now!" She ordered, in the same tone she was using on the dog.

Grover and I inched forward warily.

Cerberus started to growl.

"Stay!" Annabeth ordered the monster. "If you want the ball, stay!"

Cerberus whimpered, but he stayed where he was.

"What about you?" I asked Annabeth as we passed her.

"I know what I'm doing, Percy," she muttered. "At least, I'm pretty sure. . . ."

Grover and I walked between the monster's legs.

Please, Annabeth, I prayed. Don't tell him to sit again.

We made it through. Cerberus wasn't any less scary-looking from the back.

Annabeth said, "Good dog!"

She held up the tattered red ball, and probably came to the same conclusion I did—if she rewarded Cerberus, there'd be nothing left for another trick.

She threw the ball anyway. The monster's left mouth immediately snatched it up, only to be attacked by the middle head, while the right head moaned in protest.

While the monster was distracted, Annabeth walked briskly under its belly and joined us at the metal detector.

"How did you do that?" I asked her, amazed.

"Obedience school," she said breathlessly, and I was surprised to see there were tears in her eyes. "When I was little, at my dad's house, we had a Doberman. . . ."

"Never mind that," Grover said, tugging at my shirt. "Come on!"

We were about to bolt through the EZ DEATH line when Cerberus moaned pitifully from all three mouths. Annabeth stopped.

She turned to face the dog, which had done a one-eighty to look at us.

Cerberus panted expectantly, the tiny red ball in pieces in a puddle of drool at its feet.

"Good boy," Annabeth said, but her voice sounded melancholy and uncertain.

The monster's heads turned sideways, as if worried about her.

"I'll bring you another ball soon," Annabeth promised faintly. "Would you like that?"

The monster whimpered. I didn't need to speak dog to know Cerberus was still waiting for the ball.

"Good dog. I'll come visit you soon. I—I promise." Annabeth turned to us. "Let's go."

Grover and I pushed through the metal detector, which immediately screamed and set off flashing red lights. "Unauthorized possessions! Magic detected!"

Cerberus started to bark.

We burst through the EZ DEATH gate, which started even more alarms blaring, and raced into the Underworld.

A few minutes later, we were hiding, out of breath, in the rotten trunk of an immense black tree as security ghouls scuttled past, yelling for backup from the Furies.

Grover murmured, "Well, Percy, what have we learned today?"

"That three-headed dogs prefer red rubber balls over sticks?"

"No," Grover told me. "We've learned that your plans really, really bite!"

I wasn't sure about that. I thought maybe Annabeth and I had both had the right idea. Even here in the Underworld, everybody—even monsters—needed a little attention once in a while.

I thought about that as we waited for the ghouls to pass. I pretended not to see Annabeth wipe a tear from her cheek as she listened to the mournful keening of Cerberus in the distance, longing for his new friend.

NINETEEN

WE FIND OUT THE TRUTH, SORT OF

Imagine the largest concert crowd you've ever seen, a football field packed with a million fans.

Now imagine a field a million times that big, packed with people, and imagine the electricity has gone out, and there is no noise, no light, no beach ball bouncing around over the crowd. Something tragic has happened backstage. Whispering masses of people are just milling around in the shadows, waiting for a concert that will never start.

If you can picture that, you have a pretty good idea what the Fields of Asphodel looked like. The black grass had been trampled by eons of dead feet. A warm, moist wind blew like the breath of a swamp. Black trees—Grover told me they were poplars—grew in clumps here and there.

The cavern ceiling was so high above us it might've been a bank of storm clouds, except for the stalactites, which glowed faint gray and looked wickedly pointed. I tried not to imagine they'd fall on us at any moment, but dotted around the fields were several that had fallen and impaled themselves in the black grass. I guess the dead didn't have to worry about little hazards like being speared by stalactites the size of booster rockets.

Annabeth, Grover, and I tried to blend into the crowd,

keeping an eye out for security ghouls. I couldn't help looking for familiar faces among the spirits of Asphodel, but the dead are hard to look at. Their faces shimmer. They all look slightly angry or confused. They will come up to you and speak, but their voices sound like chatter, like bats twittering. Once they realize you can't understand them, they frown and move away.

The dead aren't scary. They're just sad.

We crept along, following the line of new arrivals that snaked from the main gates toward a black-tented pavilion with a banner that read:

JUDGMENTS FOR ELYSIUM AND ETERNAL DAMNATION
Welcome, Newly Deceased!

Out the back of the tent came two much smaller lines.

To the left, spirits flanked by security ghouls were marched down a rocky path toward the Fields of Punishment, which glowed and smoked in the distance, a vast, cracked wasteland with rivers of lava and minefields and miles of barbed wire separating the different torture areas. Even from far away, I could see people being chased by hellhounds, burned at the stake, forced to run naked through cactus patches or listen to opera music. I could just make out a tiny hill, with the ant-size figure of Sisyphus struggling to move his boulder to the top. And I saw worse tortures, too—things I don't want to describe.

The line coming from the right side of the judgment pavilion was much better. This one led down toward a small valley surrounded by walls—a gated community, which seemed to be the only happy part of the Underworld. Beyond the security gate were neighborhoods of beautiful houses from every time period in history, Roman villas and medieval castles and Victorian mansions. Silver and gold flowers bloomed on the lawns. The grass rippled in rainbow colors. I could hear laughter and smell barbecue cooking.

Elysium.

In the middle of that valley was a glittering blue lake, with three small islands like a vacation resort in the Bahamas. The Isles of the Blest, for people who had chosen to be reborn three times, and three times achieved Elysium. Immediately I knew that's where I wanted to go when I died.

"That's what it's all about," Annabeth said, like she was reading my thoughts. "That's the place for heroes."

But I thought of how few people there were in Elysium, how tiny it was compared to the Fields of Asphodel or even the Fields of Punishment. So few people did good in their lives. It was depressing.

We left the judgment pavilion and moved deeper into the Asphodel Fields. It got darker. The colors faded from our clothes. The crowds of chattering spirits began to thin.

After a few miles of walking, we began to hear a familiar screech in the distance. Looming on the horizon was a palace of glittering black obsidian. Above the parapets swirled three dark batlike creatures: the Furies. I got the feeling they were waiting for us.

"I suppose it's too late to turn back," Grover said wistfully.

"We'll be okay." I tried to sound confident.

"Maybe we should search some of the other places first," Grover suggested. "Like, Elysium, for instance . . ."

"Come on, goat boy." Annabeth grabbed his arm.

Grover yelped. His sneakers sprouted wings and his legs shot forward, pulling him away from Annabeth. He landed flat on his back in the grass.

"Grover," Annabeth chided. "Stop messing around."

"But I didn't—"

He yelped again. His shoes were flapping like crazy now. They levitated off the ground and started dragging him away from us.

"*Maia!*" he yelled, but the magic word seemed to have no effect. "*Maia*, already! Nine-one-one! Help!"

I got over being stunned and made a grab for Grover's hand, but too late. He was picking up speed, skidding downhill like a bobsled.

We ran after him.

Annabeth shouted, "Untie the shoes!"

It was a smart idea, but I guess it's not so easy when your shoes are pulling you along feetfirst at full speed. Grover tried to sit up, but he couldn't get close to the laces.

We kept after him, trying to keep him in sight as he zipped between the legs of spirits who chattered at him in annoyance.

I was sure Grover was going to barrel straight through the gates of Hades's palace, but his shoes veered sharply to the right and dragged him in the opposite direction.

The slope got steeper. Grover picked up speed. Annabeth

and I had to sprint to keep up. The cavern walls narrowed on either side, and I realized we'd entered some kind of side tunnel. No black grass or trees now, just rock underfoot, and the dim light of the stalactites above.

"Grover!" I yelled, my voice echoing. "Hold on to something!"

"What?" he yelled back.

He was grabbing at gravel, but there was nothing big enough to slow him down.

The tunnel got darker and colder. The hairs on my arms bristled. It smelled evil down here. It made me think of things I shouldn't even know about—blood spilled on an ancient stone altar, the foul breath of a murderer.

Then I saw what was ahead of us, and I stopped dead in my tracks.

The tunnel widened into a huge dark cavern, and in the middle was a chasm the size of a city block.

Grover was sliding straight toward the edge.

"Come on, Percy!" Annabeth yelled, tugging at my wrist.

"But that's—"

"I know!" she shouted. "The place you described in your dream! But Grover's going to fall if we don't catch him." She was right, of course. Grover's predicament got me moving again.

He was yelling, clawing at the ground, but the winged shoes kept dragging him toward the pit, and it didn't look like we could possibly get to him in time.

What saved him were his hooves.

The flying sneakers had always been a loose fit on him,

and finally Grover hit a big rock and the left shoe came flying off. It sped into the darkness, down into the chasm. The right shoe kept tugging him along, but not as fast. Grover was able to slow himself down by grabbing on to the big rock and using it like an anchor.

He was ten feet from the edge of the pit when we caught him and hauled him back up the slope. The other winged shoe tugged itself off, circled around us angrily and kicked our heads in protest before flying off into the chasm to join its twin.

We all collapsed, exhausted, on the obsidian gravel. My limbs felt like lead. Even my backpack seemed heavier, as if somebody had filled it with rocks.

Grover was scratched up pretty bad. His hands were bleeding. His eyes had gone slit-pupiled, goat style, the way they did whenever he was terrified.

"I don't know how . . ." he panted. "I didn't . . ."

"Wait," I said. "Listen."

I heard something—a deep whisper in the darkness.

Another few seconds, and Annabeth said, "Percy, this place—"

"Shh." I stood.

The sound was getting louder, a muttering, evil voice from far, far below us. Coming from the pit.

Grover sat up. "Wh—what's that noise?"

Annabeth heard it too, now. I could see it in her eyes. "Tartarus. The entrance to Tartarus."

I uncapped Anaklusmos.

The bronze sword expanded, gleaming in the darkness,

and the evil voice seemed to falter, just for a moment, before resuming its chant.

I could almost make out words now, ancient, ancient words, older even than Greek. As if . . .

"Magic," I said.

"We have to get out of here," Annabeth said.

Together, we dragged Grover to his hooves and started back up the tunnel. My legs wouldn't move fast enough. My backpack weighed me down. The voice got louder and angrier behind us, and we broke into a run.

Not a moment too soon.

A cold blast of wind pulled at our backs, as if the entire pit were inhaling. For a terrifying moment, I lost ground, my feet slipping in the gravel. If we'd been any closer to the edge, we would've been sucked in.

We kept struggling forward, and finally reached the top of the tunnel, where the cavern widened out into the Fields of Asphodel. The wind died. A wail of outrage echoed from deep in the tunnel. Something was not happy we'd gotten away.

"What *was* that?" Grover panted, when we'd collapsed in the relative safety of a black poplar grove. "One of Hades's pets?"

Annabeth and I looked at each other. I could tell she was nursing an idea, probably the same one she'd gotten during the taxi ride to L.A., but she was too scared to share it. That was enough to terrify me.

I capped my sword, put the pen back in my pocket. "Let's keep going." I looked at Grover. "Can you walk?"

He swallowed. "Yeah, sure. I never liked those shoes, anyway."

He tried to sound brave about it, but he was trembling as badly as Annabeth and I were. Whatever was in that pit was nobody's pet. It was unspeakably old and powerful. Even Echidna hadn't given me that feeling. I was almost relieved to turn my back on that tunnel and head toward the palace of Hades.

Almost.

The Furies circled the parapets, high in the gloom. The outer walls of the fortress glittered black, and the two-story-tall bronze gates stood wide open.

Up close, I saw that the engravings on the gates were scenes of death. Some were from modern times—an atomic bomb exploding over a city, a trench filled with gas mask-wearing soldiers, a line of African famine victims waiting with empty bowls—but all of them looked as if they'd been etched into the bronze thousands of years ago. I wondered if I was looking at prophecies that had come true.

Inside the courtyard was the strangest garden I'd ever seen. Multicolored mushrooms, poisonous shrubs, and weird luminous plants grew without sunlight. Precious jewels made up for the lack of flowers, piles of rubies as big as my fist, clumps of raw diamonds. Standing here and there like frozen party guests were Medusa's garden statues—petrified children, satyrs, and centaurs—all smiling grotesquely.

In the center of the garden was an orchard of

pomegranate trees, their orange blooms neon bright in the dark. "The garden of Persephone," Annabeth said. "Keep walking."

I understood why she wanted to move on. The tart smell of those pomegranates was almost overwhelming. I had a sudden desire to eat them, but then I remembered the story of Persephone. One bite of Underworld food, and we would never be able to leave. I pulled Grover away to keep him from picking a big juicy one.

We walked up the steps of the palace, between black columns, through a black marble portico, and into the house of Hades. The entry hall had a polished bronze floor, which seemed to boil in the reflected torchlight. There was no ceiling, just the cavern roof, far above. I guess they never had to worry about rain down here.

Every side doorway was guarded by a skeleton in military gear. Some wore Greek armor, some British redcoat uniforms, some camouflage with tattered American flags on the shoulders. They carried spears or muskets or M-16s. None of them bothered us, but their hollow eye sockets followed us as we walked down the hall, toward the big set of doors at the opposite end.

Two U.S. Marine skeletons guarded the doors. They grinned down at us, rocket-propelled grenade launchers held across their chests.

"You know," Grover mumbled, "I bet Hades doesn't have trouble with door-to-door salesmen."

My backpack weighed a ton now. I couldn't figure out why. I wanted to open it, check to see if I had somehow picked up a stray bowling ball, but this wasn't the time.

"Well, guys," I said. "I suppose we should . . . knock?"

A hot wind blew down the corridor, and the doors swung open. The guards stepped aside.

"I guess that means *entrez-vous*," Annabeth said.

The room inside looked just like in my dream, except this time the throne of Hades was occupied.

He was the third god I'd met, but the first who really struck me as godlike.

He was at least ten feet tall, for one thing, and dressed in black silk robes and a crown of braided gold. His skin was albino white, his hair shoulder-length and jet black. He wasn't bulked up like Ares, but he radiated power. He lounged on his throne of fused human bones, looking lithe, graceful, and dangerous as a panther.

I immediately felt like he should be giving the orders. He knew more than I did. He should be my master. Then I told myself to snap out of it.

Hades's aura was affecting me, just as Ares's had. The Lord of the Dead resembled pictures I'd seen of Adolph Hitler, or Napoleon, or the terrorist leaders who direct suicide bombers. Hades had the same intense eyes, the same kind of mesmerizing, evil charisma.

"You are brave to come here, Son of Poseidon," he said in an oily voice. "After what you have done to me, very brave indeed. Or perhaps you are simply very foolish."

Numbness crept into my joints, tempting me to lie

down and just take a little nap at Hades's feet. Curl up here and sleep forever.

I fought the feeling and stepped forward. I knew what I had to say. "Lord and Uncle, I come with two requests."

Hades raised an eyebrow. When he sat forward in his throne, shadowy faces appeared in the folds of his black robes, faces of torment, as if the garment were stitched of trapped souls from the Fields of Punishment, trying to get out. The ADHD part of me wondered, off-task, whether the rest of his clothes were made the same way. What horrible things would you have to do in your life to get woven into Hades's underwear?

"Only two requests?" Hades said. "Arrogant child. As if you have not already taken enough. Speak, then. It amuses me not to strike you dead yet."

I swallowed. This was going about as well as I'd feared.

I glanced at the empty, smaller throne next to Hades's. It was shaped like a black flower, gilded with gold. I wished Queen Persephone were here. I recalled something in the myths about how she could calm her husband's moods. But it was summer. Of course, Persephone would be above in the world of light with her mother, the goddess of agriculture, Demeter. Her visits, not the tilt of the planet, create the seasons.

Annabeth cleared her throat. Her finger prodded me in the back.

"Lord Hades," I said. "Look, sir, there can't be a war among the gods. It would be . . . bad."

"Really bad," Grover added helpfully.

"Return Zeus's master bolt to me," I said. "Please, sir. Let me carry it to Olympus."

Hades's eyes grew dangerously bright. "You dare keep up this pretense, after what you have done?"

I glanced back at my friends. They looked as confused as I was.

"Um . . . Uncle," I said. "You keep saying 'after what you've done.' What exactly have I done?"

The throne room shook with a tremor so strong, they probably felt it upstairs in Los Angeles. Debris fell from the cavern ceiling. Doors burst open all along the walls, and skeletal warriors marched in, hundreds of them, from every time period and nation in Western civilization. They lined the perimeter of the room, blocking the exits.

Hades bellowed, "Do you think I *want* war, godling?"

I wanted to say, *Well, these guys don't look like peace activists.* But I thought that might be a dangerous answer.

"You are the Lord of the Dead," I said carefully. "A war would expand your kingdom, right?"

"A typical thing for my brothers to say! Do you think I need more subjects? Did you not see the sprawl of the Asphodel Fields?"

"Well . . ."

"Have you any idea how much my kingdom has swollen in this past century alone, how many subdivisions I've had to open?"

I opened my mouth to respond, but Hades was on a roll now.

"More security ghouls," he moaned. "Traffic problems

at the judgment pavilion. Double overtime for the staff. I used to be a rich god, Percy Jackson. I control all the precious metals under the earth. But my expenses!"

"Charon wants a pay raise," I blurted, just remembering the fact. As soon as I said it, I wished I could sew up my mouth.

"Don't get me started on Charon!" Hades yelled. "He's been impossible ever since he discovered Italian suits! Problems everywhere, and I've got to handle all of them personally. The commute time alone from the palace to the gates is enough to drive me insane! And the dead just keep arriving. *No*, godling. I need no help getting subjects! *I* did not ask for this war."

"But you took Zeus's master bolt."

"Lies!" More rumbling. Hades rose from his throne, towering to the height of a football goalpost. "Your father may fool Zeus, boy, but I am not so stupid. I see his plan."

"His plan?"

"*You* were the thief on the winter solstice," he said. "Your father thought to keep you his little secret. He directed you into the throne room on Olympus. You took the master bolt *and* my helm. Had I not sent my Fury to discover you at Yancy Academy, Poseidon might have succeeded in hiding his scheme to start a war. But now you have been forced into the open. You will be exposed as Poseidon's thief, and I will have my helm back!"

"But . . ." Annabeth spoke. I could tell her mind was going a million miles an hour. "Lord Hades, your helm of darkness is missing, too?"

"Do not play innocent with me, girl. You and the satyr have been helping this hero—coming here to threaten me in Poseidon's name, no doubt—to bring me an ultimatum. Does Poseidon think I can be blackmailed into supporting him?"

"No!" I said. "Poseidon didn't—I didn't—"

"I have said nothing of the helm's disappearance," Hades snarled, "because I had no illusions that anyone on Olympus would offer me the slightest justice, the slightest help. I can ill afford for word to get out that my most powerful weapon of fear is missing. So I searched for you myself, and when it was clear you were coming to me to deliver your threat, I did not try to stop you."

"You didn't try to stop us? But—"

"Return my helm now, or I will stop death," Hades threatened. "That is my counterproposal. I will open the earth and have the dead pour back into the world. I will make your lands a nightmare. And you, Percy Jackson—*your* skeleton will lead my army out of Hades."

The skeletal soldiers all took one step forward, making their weapons ready.

At that point, I probably should have been terrified. The strange thing was, I felt offended. Nothing gets me angrier than being accused of something I didn't do. I've had a lot of experience with that.

"You're as bad as Zeus," I said. "You think I stole from you? That's why you sent the Furies after me?"

"Of course," Hades said.

"And the other monsters?"

Hades curled his lip. "I had nothing to do with them. I

wanted no quick death for you—I wanted you brought before me alive so you might face every torture in the Fields of Punishment. Why do you think I let you enter my kingdom so easily?"

"*Easily?*"

"Return my property!"

"But I don't have your helm. I came for the master bolt."

"Which you already possess!" Hades shouted. "You came here with it, little fool, thinking you could you threaten me!"

"But I didn't!"

"Open your pack, then."

A horrible feeling struck me. The weight in my backpack, like a bowling ball. It couldn't be. . . .

I slung it off my shoulder and unzipped it. Inside was a two-foot-long metal cylinder, spiked on both ends, humming with energy.

"Percy," Annabeth said. "How—"

"I—I don't know. I don't understand."

"You heroes are always the same," Hades said. "Your pride makes you foolish, thinking you could bring such a weapon before me. I did not ask for Zeus's master bolt, but since it is here, you will yield it to me. I am sure it will make an excellent bargaining tool. And now . . . my helm. Where is it?"

I was speechless. I had no helm. I had no idea how the master bolt had gotten into my backpack. I wanted to think Hades was pulling some kind of trick. Hades was the bad guy. But suddenly the world turned sideways. I realized I'd been played with. Zeus, Poseidon, and Hades had been set at each other's throats by someone else. The master bolt had been in the backpack, and I'd gotten the backpack from . . .

"Lord Hades, wait," I said. "This is all a mistake."

"A mistake?" Hades roared.

The skeletons aimed their weapons. From high above, there was a fluttering of leathery wings, and the three Furies swooped down to perch on the back of their master's throne. The one with Mrs. Dodds's face grinned at me eagerly and flicked her whip.

"There is no mistake," Hades said. "I know why you have come—I know the *real* reason you brought the bolt. You came to bargain for *her*."

Hades loosed a ball of gold fire from his palm. It exploded on the steps in front of me, and there was my mother, frozen in a shower of gold, just as she was at the moment when the Minotaur began to squeeze her to death.

I couldn't speak. I reached out to touch her, but the light was as hot as a bonfire.

"Yes," Hades said with satisfaction. "I took her. I knew, Percy Jackson, that you would come to bargain with me eventually. Return my helm, and perhaps I will let her go. She is not dead, you know. Not yet. But if you displease me, that will change."

I thought about the pearls in my pocket. Maybe they could get me out of this. If I could just get my mom free . . .

"Ah, the pearls," Hades said, and my blood froze. "Yes, my brother and his little tricks. Bring them forth, Percy Jackson."

My hand moved against my will and brought out the pearls.

"Only three," Hades said. "What a shame. You do realize each only protects a single person. Try to take your mother, then, little godling. And which of your friends will you leave behind to spend eternity with me? Go on. Choose. Or give me the backpack and accept my terms."

I looked at Annabeth and Grover. Their faces were grim.

"We were tricked," I told them. "Set up."

"Yes, but why?" Annabeth asked. "And the voice in the pit—"

"I don't know yet," I said. "But I intend to ask."

"Decide, boy!" Hades yelled.

"Percy." Grover put his hand on my shoulder. "You can't give him the bolt."

"I know that."

"Leave me here," he said. "Use the third pearl on your mom."

"No!"

"I'm a satyr," Grover said. "We don't have souls like humans do. He can torture me until I die, but he won't get me forever. I'll just be reincarnated as a flower or something. It's the best way."

"No." Annabeth drew her bronze knife. "You two go on. Grover, you have to protect Percy. You have to get your searcher's license and start your quest for Pan. Get his mom out of here. I'll cover you. I plan to go down fighting."

"No way," Grover said. "I'm staying behind."

"Think again, goat boy," Annabeth said.

"Stop it, both of you!" I felt like my heart was being ripped in two. They had both been with me through so much. I remembered Grover dive-bombing Medusa in the statue garden, and Annabeth saving us from Cerberus; we'd survived Hephaestus's Waterland ride, the St. Louis Arch, the Lotus Casino. I had spent thousands of miles worried that I'd be betrayed by a friend, but these friends would never do that. They had done nothing but save me, over and over, and now they wanted to sacrifice their lives for my mom.

"I know what to do," I said. "Take these."

I handed them each a pearl.

Annabeth said, "But, Percy . . ."

I turned and faced my mother. I desperately wanted to sacrifice myself and use the last pearl on her, but I knew what she would say. She would never allow it. I had to get the bolt back to Olympus and tell Zeus the truth. I had to stop the war. She would never forgive me if I saved her instead. I thought about the prophecy made at Half-Blood Hill, what seemed like a million years ago. *You will fail to save what matters most in the end.*

"I'm sorry," I told her. "I'll be back. I'll find a way."

The smug look on Hades's face faded. He said, "Godling . . . ?"

"I'll find your helm, Uncle," I told him. "I'll return it. Remember about Charon's pay raise."

"Do not defy me—"

"And it wouldn't hurt to play with Cerberus once in a while. He likes red rubber balls."

"Percy Jackson, you will not—"

I shouted, "Now, guys!"

We smashed the pearls at our feet. For a scary moment, nothing happened.

Hades yelled, "Destroy them!"

The army of skeletons rushed forward, swords out, guns clicking to full automatic. The Furies lunged, their whips bursting into flame.

Just as the skeletons opened fire, the pearl fragments at my feet exploded with a burst of green light and a gust of fresh sea wind. I was encased in a milky white sphere, which was starting to float off the ground.

Annabeth and Grover were right behind me. Spears and bullets sparked harmlessly off the pearl bubbles as we floated up. Hades yelled with such rage, the entire fortress shook and I knew it was not going to be a peaceful night in L.A.

"Look up!" Grover yelled. "We're going to crash!"

Sure enough, we were racing right toward the stalactites, which I figured would pop our bubbles and skewer us.

"How do you control these things?" Annabeth shouted.

"I don't think you do!" I shouted back.

We screamed as the bubbles slammed into the ceiling and . . . Darkness.

Were we dead?

No, I could still feel the racing sensation. We were going up, right through solid rock as easily as an air bubble in water. That was the power of the pearls, I realized—*What belongs to the sea will always return to the sea.*

For a few moments, I couldn't see anything outside the

smooth walls of my sphere, then my pearl broke through on the ocean floor. The two other milky spheres, Annabeth and Grover, kept pace with me as we soared upward through the water. And——*ker-blam!*

We exploded on the surface, in the middle of the Santa Monica Bay, knocking a surfer off his board with an indignant, "Dude!"

I grabbed Grover and hauled him over to a life buoy. I caught Annabeth and dragged her over too. A curious shark was circling us, a great white about eleven feet long.

I said, "Beat it."

The shark turned and raced away.

The surfer screamed something about bad mushrooms and paddled away from us as fast as he could.

Somehow, I knew what time it was: early morning, June 21, the day of the summer solstice.

In the distance, Los Angeles was on fire, plumes of smoke rising from neighborhoods all over the city. There had been an earthquake, all right, and it was Hades's fault. He was probably sending an army of the dead after me right now.

But at the moment, the Underworld wasn't my biggest problem.

I had to get to shore. I had to get Zeus's thunderbolt back to Olympus. Most of all, I had to have a serious conversation with the god who'd tricked me.

TWENTY

I BATTLE MY
JERK RELATIVE

A Coast Guard boat picked us up, but they were too busy to keep us for long, or to wonder how three kids in street clothes had gotten out into the middle of the bay. There was a disaster to mop up. Their radios were jammed with distress calls.

They dropped us off at the Santa Monica Pier with towels around our shoulders and water bottles that said I'M A JUNIOR COAST GUARD! and sped off to save more people.

Our clothes were sopping wet, even mine. When the Coast Guard boat had appeared, I'd silently prayed they wouldn't pick me out of the water and find me perfectly dry, which might've raised some eyebrows. So I'd willed myself to get soaked. Sure enough, my usual waterproof magic had abandoned me. I was also barefoot, because I'd given my shoes to Grover. Better the Coast Guard wonder why one of us was barefoot than wonder why one of us had hooves.

After reaching dry land, we stumbled down the beach, watching the city burn against a beautiful sunrise. I felt as if I'd just come back from the dead—which I had. My backpack was heavy with Zeus's master bolt. My heart was even heavier from seeing my mother.

"I don't believe it," Annabeth said. "We went all that way—"

"It was a trick," I said. "A strategy worthy of Athena."

"Hey," she warned.

"You get it, don't you?"

She dropped her eyes, her anger fading. "Yeah. I get it."

"Well, I don't!" Grover complained. "Would some-body—"

"Percy . . ." Annabeth said. "I'm sorry about your mother. I'm so sorry. . . ."

I pretended not to hear her. If I talked about my mother, I was going to start crying like a little kid.

"The prophecy was right," I said. "'You shall go west and face the god who has turned.' But it wasn't Hades. Hades didn't want war among the Big Three. Someone else pulled off the theft. Someone stole Zeus's master bolt, and Hades's helm, and framed me because I'm Poseidon's kid. Poseidon will get blamed by both sides. By sundown today, there will be a three-way war. And I'll have caused it."

Grover shook his head, mystified. "But who would be that sneaky? Who would want war that bad?"

I stopped in my tracks, looking down the beach. "Gee, let me think."

There he was, waiting for us, in his black leather duster and his sunglasses, an aluminum baseball bat propped on his shoulder. His motorcycle rumbled beside him, its headlight turning the sand red.

"Hey, kid," Ares said, seeming genuinely pleased to see me. "You were supposed to die."

"You tricked me," I said. "*You* stole the helm and the master bolt."

Ares grinned. "Well, now, I didn't steal them personally. Gods taking each other's symbols of power—that's a big no-no. But you're not the only hero in the world who can run errands."

"Who did you use? Clarisse? She was there at the winter solstice."

The idea seemed to amuse him. "Doesn't matter. The point is, kid, you're impeding the war effort. See, you've got to die in the Underworld. Then Old Seaweed will be mad at Hades for killing you. Corpse Breath will have Zeus's master bolt, so Zeus'll be mad at *him*. And Hades is still looking for this . . ."

From his pocket he took out a ski cap—the kind bank robbers wear—and placed it between the handlebars of his bike. Immediately, the cap transformed into an elaborate bronze war helmet.

"The helm of darkness," Grover gasped.

"Exactly," Ares said. "Now where was I? Oh yeah, Hades will be mad at both Zeus and Poseidon, because he doesn't know who took this. Pretty soon, we got a nice little three-way slugfest going."

"But they're your family!" Annabeth protested.

Ares shrugged. "Best kind of war. Always the bloodiest. Nothing like watching your relatives fight, I always say."

"You gave me the backpack in Denver," I said. "The master bolt was in there the whole time."

"Yes and no," Ares said. "It's probably too complicated for your little mortal brain to follow, but the backpack is the master bolt's sheath, just morphed a bit. The bolt is connected to it, sort of like that sword you got, kid. It always returns to your pocket, right?"

I wasn't sure how Ares knew about that, but I guess a god of war had to make it his business to know about weapons.

"Anyway," Ares continued, "I tinkered with the magic a bit, so the bolt would only return to the sheath once you reached the Underworld. You get close to Hades. . . . Bingo, you got mail. If you died along the way—no loss. I still had the weapon."

"But why not just keep the master bolt for yourself?" I said. "Why send it to Hades?"

Ares got a twitch in his jaw. For a moment, it was almost as if he were listening to another voice, deep inside his head. "Why didn't I . . . yeah . . . with that kind of fire-power . . ."

He held the trance for one second . . . two seconds. . . .

I exchanged nervous looks with Annabeth.

Ares's face cleared. "I didn't want the trouble. Better to have you caught redhanded, holding the thing."

"You're lying," I said. "Sending the bolt to the Underworld wasn't your idea, was it?"

"Of course it was!" Smoke drifted up from his sun-glasses, as if they were about to catch fire.

"You didn't order the theft," I guessed. "Someone else sent a hero to steal the two items. Then, when Zeus sent you to hunt him down, you caught the thief. But you didn't turn him over to Zeus. Something convinced you to let him go.

You kept the items until another hero could come along and complete the delivery. That thing in the pit is ordering you around."

"I am the god of war! I take orders from no one! I don't have dreams!"

I hesitated. "Who said anything about dreams?"

Ares looked agitated, but he tried to cover it with a smirk.

"Let's get back to the problem at hand, kid. You're alive. I can't have you taking that bolt to Olympus. You just might get those hardheaded idiots to listen to you. So I've got to kill you. Nothing personal."

He snapped his fingers. The sand exploded at his feet and out charged a wild boar, even larger and uglier than the one whose head hung above the door of cabin seven at Camp Half-Blood. The beast pawed the sand, glaring at me with beady eyes as it lowered its razor-sharp tusks and waited for the command to kill.

I stepped into the surf. "Fight me yourself, Ares."

He laughed, but I heard a little edge to his laughter . . . an uneasiness. "You've only got one talent, kid, running away. You ran from the Chimera. You ran from the Underworld. You don't have what it takes."

"Scared?"

"In your adolescent dreams." But his sunglasses were starting to melt from the heat of his eyes. "No direct involvement. Sorry, kid. You're not at my level."

Annabeth said, "Percy, run!"

The giant boar charged.

But I was done running from monsters. Or Hades, or Ares, or anybody.

As the boar rushed me, I uncapped my pen and side-stepped. Riptide appeared in my hands. I slashed upward. The boar's severed right tusk fell at my feet, while the disoriented animal charged into the sea.

I shouted, "Wave!"

Immediately, a wave surged up from nowhere and engulfed the boar, wrapping around it like a blanket. The beast squealed once in terror. Then it was gone, swallowed by the sea.

I turned back to Ares. "Are you going to fight me now?" I asked. "Or are you going to hide behind another pet pig?"

Ares's face was purple with rage. "Watch it, kid. I could turn you into—"

"A cockroach," I said. "Or a tapeworm. Yeah, I'm sure. That'd save you from getting your godly hide whipped, wouldn't it?"

Flames danced along the top of his glasses. "Oh, man, you are really asking to be smashed into a grease spot."

"If I lose, turn me into anything you want. Take the bolt. If I win, the helm and the bolt are mine and *you* have to go away."

Ares sneered.

He swung the baseball bat off his shoulder. "How would you like to get smashed: classic or modern?"

I showed him my sword.

"That's cool, dead boy," he said. "Classic it is." The

baseball bat changed into a huge, two-handed sword. The hilt was a large silver skull with a ruby in its mouth.

"Percy," Annabeth said. "Don't do this. He's a god."

"He's a coward," I told her.

She swallowed. "Wear this, at least. For luck."

She took off her necklace, with her five years' worth of camp beads and the ring from her father, and tied it around my neck.

"Reconciliation," she said. "Athena and Poseidon together."

My face felt a little warm, but I managed a smile. "Thanks."

"And take this," Grover said. He handed me a flattened tin can that he'd probably been saving in his pocket for a thousand miles. "The satyrs stand behind you."

"Grover . . . I don't know what to say."

He patted me on the shoulder. I stuffed the tin can in my back pocket.

"You all done saying good-bye?" Ares came toward me, his black leather duster trailing behind him, his sword glinting like fire in the sunrise. "I've been fighting for eternity, kid. My strength is unlimited and I cannot die. What have you got?"

A smaller ego, I thought, but I said nothing. I kept my feet in the surf, backing into the water up to my ankles. I thought back to what Annabeth had said at the Denver diner, so long ago: *Ares has strength. That's all he has. Even strength has to bow to wisdom sometimes.*

He cleaved downward at my head, but I wasn't there.

My body thought for me. The water seemed to push me into the air and I catapulted over him, slashing as I came down. But Ares was just as quick. He twisted, and the strike that should've caught him directly in the spine was deflected off the end of his sword hilt.

He grinned. "Not bad, not bad."

He slashed again and I was forced to jump onto dry land. I tried to sidestep, to get back to the water, but Ares seemed to know what I wanted. He outmaneuvered me, pressing so hard I had to put all my concentration on not getting sliced into pieces. I kept backing away from the surf. I couldn't find any openings to attack. His sword had a reach several feet longer than Anaklusmos.

Get in close, Luke had told me once, back in our sword class. *When you've got the shorter blade, get in close.*

I stepped inside with a thrust, but Ares was waiting for that. He knocked my blade out of my hands and kicked me in the chest. I went airborne—twenty, maybe thirty feet. I would've broken my back if I hadn't crashed into the soft sand of a dune.

"Percy!" Annabeth yelled. "Cops!"

I was seeing double. My chest felt like it had just been hit with a battering ram, but I managed to get to my feet.

I couldn't look away from Ares for fear he'd slice me in half, but out of the corner of my eye I saw red lights flashing on the shoreline boulevard. Car doors were slamming.

"There, officer!" somebody yelled. "See?"

A gruff cop voice: "Looks like that kid on TV . . . what the heck . . ."

"That guy's armed," another cop said. "Call for backup."

I rolled to one side as Ares's blade slashed the sand.

I ran for my sword, scooped it up, and launched a swipe at Ares's face, only to find my blade deflected again.

Ares seemed to know exactly what I was going to do the moment before I did it.

I stepped back toward the surf, forcing him to follow.

"Admit it, kid," Ares said. "You got no hope. I'm just toying with you."

My senses were working overtime. I now understood what Annabeth had said about ADHD keeping you alive in battle. I was wide awake, noticing every little detail.

I could see where Ares was tensing. I could tell which way he would strike. At the same time, I was aware of Annabeth and Grover, thirty feet to my left. I saw a second cop car pulling up, siren wailing. Spectators, people who had been wandering the streets because of the earthquake, were starting to gather. Among the crowd, I thought I saw a few who were walking with the strange, trotting gait of disguised satyrs. There were shimmering forms of spirits, too, as if the dead had risen from Hades to watch the battle. I heard the flap of leathery wings circling somewhere above.

More sirens.

I stepped farther into the water, but Ares was fast. The tip of his blade ripped my sleeve and grazed my forearm.

A police voice on a megaphone said, "Drop the guns! Set them on the ground. Now!"

Guns?

I looked at Ares's weapon, and it seemed to be flickering; sometimes it looked like a shotgun, sometimes a two-handed sword. I didn't know what the humans were seeing in my hands, but I was pretty sure it wouldn't make them like me.

Ares turned to glare at our spectators, which gave me a moment to breathe. There were five police cars now, and a line of officers crouching behind them, pistols trained on us.

"This is a private matter!" Ares bellowed. "Be gone!"

He swept his hand, and a wall of red flame rolled across the patrol cars. The police barely had time to dive for cover before their vehicles exploded. The crowd behind them scattered, screaming.

Ares roared with laughter. "Now, little hero. Let's add you to the barbecue."

He slashed. I deflected his blade. I got close enough to strike, tried to fake him out with a feint, but my blow was knocked aside. The waves were hitting me in the back now. Ares was up to his thighs, wading in after me.

I felt the rhythm of the sea, the waves growing larger as the tide rolled in, and suddenly I had an idea. *Little waves,* I thought. And the water behind me seemed to recede. I was holding back the tide by force of will, but tension was building, like carbonation behind a cork.

Ares came toward, grinning confidently. I lowered my blade, as if I were too exhausted to go on. *Wait for it,* I told the sea. The pressure now was almost lifting me off my feet. Ares raised his sword. I released the tide and jumped, rocketing straight over Ares on a wave.

A six-foot wall of water smashed him full in the face, leaving him cursing and sputtering with a mouth full of seaweed. I landed behind him with a splash and feinted toward his head, as I'd done before. He turned in time to raise his sword, but this time he was disoriented, he didn't anticipate the trick. I changed direction, lunged to the side, and stabbed Riptide straight down into the water, sending the point through the god's heel.

The roar that followed made Hades's earthquake look like a minor event. The very sea was blasted back from Ares, leaving a wet circle of sand fifty feet wide.

Ichor, the golden blood of the gods, flowed from a gash in the war god's boot. The expression on his face was beyond hatred. It was pain, shock, complete disbelief that he'd been wounded.

He limped toward me, muttering ancient Greek curses. Something stopped him.

It was as if a cloud covered the sun, but worse. Light faded. Sound and color drained away. A cold, heavy presence passed over the beach, slowing time, dropping the temperature to freezing, and making me feel like life was hopeless, fighting was useless.

The darkness lifted.

Ares looked stunned.

Police cars were burning behind us. The crowd of spectators had fled. Annabeth and Grover stood on the beach, in shock, watching the water flood back around Ares's feet, his glowing golden ichor dissipating in the tide.

Ares lowered his sword.

"You have made an enemy, godling," he told me. "You have sealed your fate. Every time you raise your blade in battle, every time you hope for success, you will feel my curse. Beware, Perseus Jackson. Beware."

His body began to glow.

"Percy!" Annabeth shouted. "Don't watch!"

I turned away as the god Ares revealed his true immortal form. I somehow knew that if I looked, I would disintegrate into ashes.

The light died.

I looked back. Ares was gone. The tide rolled out to reveal Hades's bronze helm of darkness. I picked it up and walked toward my friends.

But before I got there, I heard the flapping of leathery wings. Three evil-looking grandmothers with lace hats and fiery whips drifted down from the sky and landed in front of me.

The middle Fury, the one who had been Mrs. Dodds, stepped forward. Her fangs were bared, but for once she didn't look threatening. She looked more disappointed, as if she'd been planning to have me for supper, but had decided I might give her indigestion.

"We saw the whole thing," she hissed. "So . . . it truly was not you?"

I tossed her the helmet, which she caught in surprise.

"Return that to Lord Hades," I said. "Tell him the truth. Tell him to call off the war."

She hesitated, then ran a forked tongue over her green, leathery lips. "Live well, Percy Jackson. Become a true hero.

Because if you do not, if you ever come into my clutches again . . ."

She cackled, savoring the idea. Then she and her sisters rose on their bats' wings, fluttered into the smoke-filled sky, and disappeared.

I joined Grover and Annabeth, who were staring at me in amazement.

"Percy . . ." Grover said. "That was so incredibly . . ."

"Terrifying," said Annabeth.

"Cool!" Grover corrected.

I didn't feel terrified. I certainly didn't feel cool. I was tired and sore and completely drained of energy.

"Did you guys feel that . . . whatever it was?" I asked.

They both nodded uneasily.

"Must've been the Furies overhead," Grover said.

But I wasn't so sure. Something had stopped Ares from killing me, and whatever could do that was a lot stronger than the Furies.

I looked at Annabeth, and an understanding passed between us. I knew now what was in that pit, what had spoken from the entrance of Tartarus.

I reclaimed my backpack from Grover and looked inside. The master bolt was still there. Such a small thing to almost cause World War III.

"We have to get back to New York," I said. "By tonight."

"That's impossible," Annabeth said, "unless we—"

"Fly," I agreed.

She stared at me. "Fly, like, in an airplane, which you

were warned never to do lest Zeus strike you out of the sky, *and* carrying a weapon that has more destructive power than a nuclear bomb?"

"Yeah," I said. "Pretty much exactly like that. Come on."

TWENTY-ONE

I SETTLE MY TAB

It's funny how humans can wrap their mind around things and fit them into their version of reality. Chiron had told me that long ago. As usual, I didn't appreciate his wisdom until much later.

According to the L.A. news, the explosion at the Santa Monica beach had been caused when a crazy kidnapper fired a shotgun at a police car. He accidentally hit a gas main that had ruptured during the earthquake.

This crazy kidnapper (a.k.a. Ares) was the same man who had abducted me and two other adolescents in New York and brought us across country on a ten-day odyssey of terror.

Poor little Percy Jackson wasn't an international criminal after all. He'd caused a commotion on that Greyhound bus in New Jersey trying to get away from his captor (and afterward, witnesses would even swear they had seen the leather-clad man on the bus—"Why didn't I remember him before?"). The crazy man had caused the explosion in the St. Louis Arch. After all, no kid could've done that. A concerned waitress in Denver had seen the man threatening his abductees outside her diner, gotten a friend to take a photo, and notified the police. Finally, brave Percy Jackson (I was beginning to like this kid) had stolen a gun from his captor in Los Angeles and battled him shotgun-to-rifle on the beach. Police had arrived just in time. But in the spectacular explosion, five police cars had been destroyed and the captor had fled. No fatalities had occurred. Percy Jackson and his two friends were safely in police custody.

The reporters fed us this whole story. We just nodded and acted tearful and exhausted (which wasn't hard), and played victimized kids for the cameras.

"All I want," I said, choking back my tears, "is to see my loving stepfather again. Every time I saw him on TV, calling me a delinquent punk, I knew . . . somehow . . . we would be okay. And I know he'll want to reward each and every person in this beautiful city of Los Angeles with a free major appliance from his store. Here's the phone number." The police and reporters were so moved that they passed around the hat and raised money for three tickets on the next plane to New York.

I knew there was no choice but to fly. I hoped Zeus would cut me some slack, considering the circumstances. But it was still hard to force myself on board the flight.

Takeoff was a nightmare. Every spot of turbulence was scarier than a Greek monster. I didn't unclench my hands from the armrests until we touched down safely at La Guardia. The local press was waiting for us outside security, but we managed to evade them thanks to Annabeth, who lured them away in her invisible Yankees cap, shouting, "They're over by the frozen yogurt! Come on!," then rejoined us at baggage claim.

We split up at the taxi stand. I told Annabeth and Grover to get back to Half-Blood Hill and let Chiron know what had happened. They protested, and it was hard to let them go after all we'd been through, but I knew I had to do this last part of the quest by myself. If things went wrong, if the gods didn't believe me . . . I wanted Annabeth and Grover to survive to tell Chiron the truth.

I hopped in a taxi and headed into Manhattan.

Thirty minutes later, I walked into the lobby of the Empire State Building.

I must have looked like a homeless kid, with my tattered clothes and my scraped-up face. I hadn't slept in at least twenty-four hours.

I went up to the guard at the front desk and said, "Six hundredth floor."

He was reading a huge book with a picture of a wizard on the front. I wasn't much into fantasy, but the book must've been good, because the guard took a while to look up. "No such floor, kiddo."

"I need an audience with Zeus."

He gave me a vacant smile. "Sorry?"

"You heard me."

I was about to decide this guy was just a regular mortal, and I'd better run for it before he called the straitjacket patrol, when he said, "No appointment, no audience, kiddo. Lord Zeus doesn't see anyone unannounced."

"Oh, I think he'll make an exception." I slipped off my backpack and unzipped the top.

The guard looked inside at the metal cylinder, not getting what it was for a few seconds. Then his face went pale. "That isn't . . ."

"Yes, it is," I promised. "You want me take it out and—"

"No! No!" He scrambled out of his seat, fumbled around his desk for a key card, then handed it to me. "Insert this in the security slot. Make sure nobody else is in the elevator with you."

I did as he told me. As soon as the elevator doors closed, I slipped the key into the slot. The card disappeared and a new button appeared on the console, a red one that said 600.

I pressed it and waited, and waited.

Muzak played. "Raindrops keep falling on my head. . . ."

Finally, *ding*. The doors slid open. I stepped out and almost had a heart attack.

I was standing on a narrow stone walkway in the middle of the air. Below me was Manhattan, from the height of an airplane. In front of me, white marble steps wound up the spine of a cloud, into the sky. My eyes followed the stairway to its end, where my brain just could not accept what I saw.

Look again, my brain said.

We're looking, my eyes insisted. It's really there.

From the top of the clouds rose the decapitated peak of a mountain, its summit covered with snow. Clinging to the mountainside were dozens of multileveled palaces—a city of mansions—all with white-columned porticos, gilded terraces, and bronze braziers glowing with a thousand fires.

Roads wound crazily up to the peak, where the largest palace gleamed against the snow. Precariously perched gardens bloomed with olive trees and rosebushes. I could make out an open-air market filled with colorful tents, a stone amphitheater built on one side of the mountain, a hippodrome and a coliseum on the other. It was an Ancient Greek city, except it wasn't in ruins. It was new, and clean, and colorful, the way Athens must've looked twenty-five hundred years ago.

This place can't be here, I told myself. The tip of a mountain hanging over New York City like a billion-ton asteroid? How could something like that be anchored above the Empire State Building, in plain sight of millions of people, and not get noticed?

But here it was. And here I was.

My trip through Olympus was a daze. I passed some giggling wood nymphs who threw olives at me from their garden. Hawkers in the market offered to sell me ambrosia-on-a-stick, and a new shield, and a genuine glitter-weave replica of the Golden Fleece, as seen on Hephaestus-TV. The nine muses were tuning their instruments for a concert in the park while a small crowd gathered—satyrs and naiads and a bunch of good-looking teenagers who might've been minor gods and goddesses. Nobody seemed worried about an impending civil war. In fact, everybody seemed in a festive mood. Several of them turned to watch me pass, and whispered to themselves.

I climbed the main road, toward the big palace at the peak. It was a reverse copy of the palace in the Underworld.

There, everything had been black and bronze. Here, everything glittered white and silver.

I realized Hades must've built his palace to resemble this one. He wasn't welcomed in Olympus except on the winter solstice, so he'd built his own Olympus underground. Despite my bad experience with him, I felt a little sorry for the guy. To be banished from this place seemed really unfair. It would make anybody bitter.

Steps led up to a central courtyard. Past that, the throne room.

Room really isn't the right word. The place made Grand Central Station look like a broom closet. Massive columns rose to a domed ceiling, which was gilded with moving constellations.

Twelve thrones, built for beings the size of Hades, were arranged in an inverted U, just like the cabins at Camp Half-Blood. An enormous fire crackled in the central hearth pit. The thrones were empty except for two at the end: the head throne on the right, and the one to its immediate left. I didn't have to be told who the two gods were that were sitting there, waiting for me to approach. I came toward them, my legs trembling.

The gods were in giant human form, as Hades had been, but I could barely look at them without feeling a tingle, as if my body were starting to burn. Zeus, the Lord of the Gods, wore a dark blue pinstriped suit. He sat on a simple throne of solid platinum. He had a well-trimmed beard, marbled gray and black like a storm cloud. His face was proud and handsome and grim, his eyes rainy gray.

As I got nearer to him, the air crackled and smelled of ozone.

The god sitting next to him was his brother, without a doubt, but he was dressed very differently. He reminded me of a beachcomber from Key West. He wore leather sandals, khaki Bermuda shorts, and a Tommy Bahama shirt with coconuts and parrots all over it. His skin was deeply tanned, his hands scarred like an old-time fisherman's. His hair was black, like mine. His face had that same brooding look that had always gotten me branded a rebel. But his eyes, sea-green like mine, were surrounded by sun-crinkles that told me he smiled a lot, too.

His throne was a deep-sea fisherman's chair. It was the simple swiveling kind, with a black leather seat and a built-in holster for a fishing pole. Instead of a pole, the holster held a bronze trident, flickering with green light around the tips.

The gods weren't moving or speaking, but there was tension in the air, as if they'd just finished an argument.

I approached the fisherman's throne and knelt at his feet. "Father." I dared not look up. My heart was racing. I could feel the energy emanating from the two gods. If I said the wrong thing, I had no doubt they could blast me into dust.

To my left, Zeus spoke. "Should you not address the master of this house first, boy?"

I kept my head down, and waited.

"Peace, brother," Poseidon finally said. His voice stirred my oldest memories: that warm glow I remembered as a baby, the sensation of this god's hand on my forehead. "The boy defers to his father. This is only right."

"You still claim him then?" Zeus asked, menacingly. "You claim this child whom you sired against our sacred oath?"

"I have admitted my wrongdoing," Poseidon said. "Now I would hear him speak."

Wrongdoing.

A lump welled up in my throat. Was that all I was? A wrongdoing? The result of a god's mistake?

"I have spared him once already," Zeus grumbled. "Daring to fly through my domain . . . pah! I should have blasted him out of the sky for his impudence."

"And risk destroying your own master bolt?" Poseidon asked calmly. "Let us hear him out, brother."

Zeus grumbled some more. "I shall listen," he decided. "Then I shall make up my mind whether or not to cast this boy down from Olympus."

"Perseus," Poseidon said. "Look at me."

I did, and I wasn't sure what I saw in his face. There was no clear sign of love or approval. Nothing to encourage me. It was like looking at the ocean: some days, you could tell what mood it was in. Most days, though, it was unreadable, mysterious.

I got the feeling Poseidon really didn't know what to think of me. He didn't know whether he was happy to have me as a son or not. In a strange way, I was glad that Poseidon was so distant. If he'd tried to apologize, or told me he loved me, or even smiled, it would've felt fake. Like a human dad, making some lame excuse for not being around. I could live with that. After all, I wasn't sure about him yet, either.

"Address Lord Zeus, boy," Poseidon told me. "Tell him your story."

So I told Zeus everything, just as it had happened. I took out the metal cylinder, which began sparking in the Sky God's presence, and laid it at his feet.

There was a long silence, broken only by the crackle of the hearth fire.

Zeus opened his palm. The lightning bolt flew into it. As he closed his fist, the metallic points flared with electricity, until he was holding what looked more like the classic thunderbolt, a twenty-foot javelin of arcing, hissing energy that made the hairs on my scalp rise.

"I sense the boy tells the truth," Zeus muttered. "But that Ares would do such a thing . . . it is most unlike him."

"He is proud and impulsive," Poseidon said. "It runs in the family."

"Lord?" I asked.

They both said, "Yes?"

"Ares didn't act alone. Someone else—something else—came up with the idea."

I described my dreams, and the feeling I'd had on the beach, that momentary breath of evil that had seemed to stop the world, and made Ares back off from killing me.

"In the dreams," I said, "the voice told me to bring the bolt to the Underworld. Ares hinted that he'd been having dreams, too. I think he was being used, just as I was, to start a war."

"You are accusing Hades, after all?" Zeus asked.

"No," I said. "I mean, Lord Zeus, I've been in the presence of Hades. This feeling on the beach was different. It was the same thing I felt when I got close to that pit. That was the entrance to Tartarus, wasn't it? Something powerful and evil is stirring down there . . . something even older than the gods."

Poseidon and Zeus looked at each other. They had a quick, intense discussion in Ancient Greek. I only caught one word. *Father.*

Poseidon made some kind of suggestion, but Zeus cut him off. Poseidon tried to argue. Zeus held up his hand angrily. "We will speak of this no more," Zeus said. "I must go personally to purify this thunderbolt in the waters of Lemnos, to remove the human taint from its metal."

He rose and looked at me. His expression softened just a fraction of a degree. "You have done me a service, boy. Few heroes could have accomplished as much."

"I had help, sir," I said. "Grover Underwood and Annabeth Chase—"

"To show you my thanks, I shall spare your life. I do not trust you, Perseus Jackson. I do not like what your arrival means for the future of Olympus. But for the sake of peace in the family, I shall let you live."

"Um . . . thank you, sir."

"Do not presume to fly again. Do not let me find you

here when I return. Otherwise you shall taste this bolt. And it shall be your last sensation."

Thunder shook the palace. With a blinding flash of lightning, Zeus was gone.

I was alone in the throne room with my father.

"Your uncle," Poseidon sighed, "has always had a flair for dramatic exits. I think he would've done well as the god of theater."

An uncomfortable silence.

"Sir," I said, "what was in that pit?"

Poseidon regarded me. "Have you not guessed?"

"Kronos," I said. "The king of the Titans."

Even in the throne room of Olympus, far away from Tartarus, the name *Kronos* darkened the room, made the hearth fire seem not quite so warm on my back.

Poseidon gripped his trident. "In the First War, Percy, Zeus cut our father Kronos into a thousand pieces, just as Kronos had done to his own father, Ouranos. Zeus cast Kronos's remains into the darkest pit of Tartarus. The Titan army was scattered, their mountain fortress on Etna destroyed, their monstrous allies driven to the farthest corners of the earth. And yet Titans cannot die, any more than we gods can. Whatever is left of Kronos is still alive in some hideous way, still conscious in his eternal pain, still hungering for power."

"He's healing," I said. "He's coming back."

Poseidon shook his head. "From time to time, over the eons, Kronos has stirred. He enters men's nightmares and breathes evil thoughts. He wakens restless monsters from the depths. But to suggest he could rise from the pit is another thing."

"That's what he intends, Father. That's what he said."

Poseidon was silent for a long time.

"Lord Zeus has closed discussion on this matter. He will not allow talk of Kronos. You have completed your quest, child. That is all you need to do."

"But—" I stopped myself. Arguing would do no good. It would very possibly anger the only god who I had on my side. "As . . . as you wish, Father."

A faint smile played on his lips. "Obedience does not come naturally to you, does it?"

"No . . . sir."

"I must take some blame for that, I suppose. The sea does not like to be restrained." He rose to his full height and took up his trident. Then he shimmered and became the size of a regular man, standing directly in front of me. "You must go, child. But first, know that your mother has returned."

I stared at him, completely stunned. "My mother?"

"You will find her at home. Hades sent her when you recovered his helm. Even the Lord of Death pays his debts."

My heart was pounding. I couldn't believe it. "Do you . . . would you . . ."

I wanted to ask if Poseidon would come with me to see her, but then I realized that was ridiculous. I imagined loading the God of the Sea into a taxi and taking him to the Upper East Side. If he'd wanted to see my mom all these years, he would have. And there was Smelly Gabe to think about.

Poseidon's eyes took on a little sadness. "When you return home, Percy, you must make an important choice. You will find a package waiting in your room."

"A package?"

"You will understand when you see it. No one can choose your path, Percy. You must decide."

I nodded, though I didn't know what he meant.

"Your mother is a queen among women," Poseidon said wistfully. "I had not met such a mortal woman in a thousand years. Still . . . I am sorry you were born, child. I have brought you a hero's fate, and a hero's fate is never happy. It is never anything but tragic."

I tried not to feel hurt. Here was my own dad, telling me he was sorry I'd been born. "I don't mind, Father."

"Not yet, perhaps," he said. "Not yet. But it was an unforgivable mistake on my part."

"I'll leave you then." I bowed awkwardly. "I—I won't bother you again."

I was five steps away when he called, "Perseus."

I turned.

There was a different light in his eyes, a fiery kind of pride. "You did well, Perseus. Do not misunderstand me. Whatever else you do, know that you are mine. You are a true son of the Sea God."

As I walked back through the city of the gods, conversations stopped. The muses paused their concert. People and satyrs and naiads all turned toward me, their faces filled with respect and gratitude, and as I passed, they knelt, as if I were some kind of hero.

Fifteen minutes later, still in a trance, I was back on the streets of Manhattan.

I caught a taxi to my mom's apartment, rang the doorbell, and there she was—my beautiful mother, smelling of peppermint and licorice, the weariness and worry evaporating from her face as soon as she saw me.

"Percy! Oh, thank goodness. Oh, my baby."

She crushed the air right out of me. We stood in the hallway as she cried and ran her hands through my hair.

I'll admit it—my eyes were a little misty, too. I was shaking, I was so relieved to see her.

She told me she'd just appeared at the apartment that morning, scaring Gabe half out of his wits. She didn't remember anything since the Minotaur, and couldn't believe it when Gabe told her I was a wanted criminal, traveling across the country, blowing up national monuments. She'd been going out of her mind with worry all day because she hadn't heard the news. Gabe had forced her to go into work, saying she had a month's salary to make up and she'd better get started.

I swallowed back my anger and told her my own story. I tried to make it sound less scary than it had been, but that wasn't easy. I was just getting to the fight with Ares when Gabe's voice interrupted from the living room. "Hey, Sally! That meat loaf done yet or what?"

She closed her eyes. "He isn't going to be happy to see you, Percy. The store got half a million phone calls today from Los Angeles . . . something about free appliances."

"Oh, yeah. About that . . ."

She managed a weak smile. "Just don't make him angrier, all right? Come on."

In the month I'd been gone, the apartment had turned into Gabeland. Garbage was ankle deep on the carpet. The sofa had been reupholstered in beer cans. Dirty socks and underwear hung off the lampshades.

Gabe and three of his big goony friends were playing poker at the table.

When Gabe saw me, his cigar dropped out of his mouth. His face got redder than lava. "You got nerve coming here, you little punk. I thought the police—"

"He's not a fugitive after all," my mom interjected. "Isn't that wonderful, Gabe?"

Gabe looked back and forth between us. He didn't seem to think my homecoming was so wonderful.

"Bad enough I had to give back your life insurance money, Sally," he growled. "Get me the phone. I'll call the cops."

"Gabe, no!"

He raised his eyebrows. "Did you just say 'no'? You think I'm gonna put up with this punk again? I can still press charges against him for ruining my Camaro."

"But—"

He raised his hand, and my mother flinched.

For the first time, I realized something. Gabe had hit my mother. I didn't know when, or how much. But I was sure he'd done it. Maybe it had been going on for years, when I wasn't around.

A balloon of anger started expanding in my chest. I came toward Gabe, instinctively taking my pen out of my pocket.

He just laughed. "What, punk? You gonna write on me? You touch me, and you are going to jail forever, you understand?"

"Hey, Gabe," his friend Eddie interrupted. "He's just a kid."

Gabe looked at him resentfully and mimicked in a falsetto voice: *"Just a kid."*

His other friends laughed like idiots.

"I'll be nice to you, punk." Gabe showed me his tobacco-stained teeth. "I'll give you five minutes to get your stuff and clear out. After that, I call the police."

"Gabe!" my mother pleaded.

"He ran away," Gabe told her. "Let him stay gone."

I was itching to uncap Riptide, but even if I did, the blade wouldn't hurt humans. And Gabe, by the loosest definition, was human.

My mother took my arm. "Please, Percy. Come on. We'll go to your room."

I let her pull me away, my hands still trembling with rage.

My room had been completely filled with Gabe's junk. There were stacks of used car batteries, a rotting bouquet of sympathy flowers with a card from somebody who'd seen his Barbara Walters interview.

"Gabe is just upset, honey," my mother told me. "I'll talk to him later. I'm sure it will work out."

"Mom, it'll never work out. Not as long as Gabe's here."

She wrung her hands nervously. "I can . . . I'll take you to work with me for the rest of the summer. In the fall, maybe there's another boarding school—"

"Mom."

She lowered her eyes. "I'm trying, Percy. I just . . . I need some time."

A package appeared on my bed. At least, I could've sworn it hadn't been there a moment before.

It was a battered cardboard box about the right size to fit a basketball. The address on the mailing slip was in my own handwriting:

The Gods
Mount Olympus
600th Floor,
Empire State Building
New York, NY

With best wishes,
PERCY JACKSON

Over the top in black marker, in a man's clear, bold print, was the address of our apartment, and the words: RETURN TO SENDER.

Suddenly I understood what Poseidon had told me on Olympus.

A package. A decision.

Whatever else you do, know that you are mine. You are a true son of the Sea God.

I looked at my mother. "Mom, do you want Gabe gone?"

"Percy, it isn't that simple. I—"

"Mom, just tell me. That jerk has been hitting you. Do you want him gone or not?"

She hesitated, then nodded almost imperceptibly. "Yes, Percy. I do. And I'm trying to get up my courage to tell him. But you can't do this for me. You can't solve my problems."

I looked at the box.

I *could* solve her problem. I wanted to slice that package open, plop it on the poker table, and take out what was inside. I could start my very own statue garden, right there in the living room.

That's what a Greek hero would do in the stories, I thought. That's what Gabe deserves.

But a hero's story always ended in tragedy. Poseidon had told me that.

I remembered the Underworld. I thought about Gabe's spirit drifting forever in the Fields of Asphodel, or condemned to some hideous torture behind the barbed wire of the Fields of Punishment—an eternal poker game, sitting up to his waist in boiling oil listening to opera music. Did I have the right to send someone there? Even Gabe?

A month ago, I wouldn't have hesitated. Now . . .

"I can do it," I told my mom. "One look inside this box, and he'll never bother you again."

She glanced at the package, and seemed to understand immediately. "No, Percy," she said, stepping away. "You can't."

"Poseidon called you a queen," I told her. "He said he hadn't met a woman like you in a thousand years."

Her cheeks flushed. "Percy—"

"You deserve better than this, Mom. You should go to college, get your degree. You can write your novel, meet a nice guy maybe, live in a nice house. You don't need to protect me anymore by staying with Gabe. Let me get rid of him."

She wiped a tear off her cheek. "You sound so much like your father," she said. "He offered to stop the tide for me once. He offered to build me a palace at the bottom of the sea. He thought he could solve all my problems with a wave of his hand."

"What's wrong with that?"

Her multicolored eyes seemed to search inside me. "I think you know, Percy. I think you're enough like me to understand. If my life is going to mean anything, I have to live it myself. I can't let a god take care of me . . . or my son. I have to . . . find the courage on my own. Your quest has reminded me of that."

We listened to the sound of poker chips and swearing, ESPN from the living room television.

"I'll leave the box," I said. "If he threatens you . . ."

She looked pale, but she nodded. "Where will you go, Percy?"

"Half-Blood Hill."

"For the summer . . . or forever?"

"I guess that depends."

We locked eyes, and I sensed that we had an agreement.

We would see how things stood at the end of the summer.

She kissed my forehead. "You'll be a hero, Percy. You'll be the greatest of all."

I took one last look around my bedroom. I had a feeling I'd never see it again. Then I walked with my mother to the front door.

"Leaving so soon, punk?" Gabe called after me. "Good riddance."

I had one last twinge of doubt. How could I turn down the perfect chance to take revenge on him? I was leaving here without saving my mother.

"Hey, Sally," he yelled. "What about that meat loaf, huh?"

A steely look of anger flared in my mother's eyes, and I thought, just maybe, I was leaving her in good hands after all. Her own.

"The meat loaf is coming right up, dear," she told Gabe. "Meat loaf surprise."

She looked at me, and winked.

The last thing I saw as the door swung closed was my mother staring at Gabe, as if she were contemplating how he would look as a garden statue.

TWENTY-TWO

THE PROPHECY COMES TRUE

We were the first heroes to return alive to Half-Blood Hill since Luke, so of course everybody treated us as if we'd won some reality-TV contest. According to camp tradition, we wore laurel wreaths to a big feast prepared in our honor, then led a procession down to the bonfire, where we got to burn the burial shrouds our cabins had made for us in our absence.

Annabeth's shroud was so beautiful—gray silk with embroidered owls—I told her it seemed a shame not to bury her in it. She punched me and told me to shut up.

Being the son of Poseidon, I didn't have any cabin mates, so the Ares cabin had volunteered to make my shroud. They'd taken an old bedsheet and painted smiley faces with X'ed-out eyes around the border, and the word LOSER painted really big in the middle.

It was fun to burn.

As Apollo's cabin led the sing-along and passed out s'mores, I was surrounded by my old Hermes cabinmates, Annabeth's friends from Athena, and Grover's satyr buddies, who were admiring the brand-new searcher's license he'd received from the Council of Cloven Elders. The council had called Grover's performance on the quest "Brave to the point of indigestion. Horns-and-whiskers above anything we have seen in the past."

The only ones not in a party mood were Clarisse and her cabinmates, whose poisonous looks told me they'd never forgive me for disgracing their dad.

That was okay with me.

Even Dionysus's welcome-home speech wasn't enough to dampen my spirits. "Yes, yes, so the little brat didn't get himself killed and now he'll have an even bigger head. Well, huzzah for that. In other announcements, there will be *no* canoe races this Saturday. . . ."

I moved back into cabin three, but it didn't feel so lonely anymore. I had my friends to train with during the day. At night, I lay awake and listened to the sea, knowing my father was out there. Maybe he wasn't quite sure about me yet, maybe he hadn't even wanted me born, but he was watching. And so far, he was proud of what I'd done.

As for my mother, she had a chance at a new life. Her letter arrived a week after I got back to camp. She told me Gabe had left mysteriously—disappeared off the face of the planet, in fact. She'd reported him missing to the police, but she had a funny feeling they would never find him.

On a completely unrelated subject, she'd sold her first life-size concrete sculpture, entitled *The Poker Player*, to a collector, through an art gallery in Soho. She'd gotten so much money for it, she'd put a deposit down on a new apartment and made a payment on her first semester's tuition at NYU. The Soho gallery was clamoring for more of her work, which they called "a huge step forward in super-ugly neorealism."

But don't worry, my mom wrote. *I'm done with sculpture. I've disposed of that box of tools you left me. It's time for me to turn to writing.*

At the bottom, she wrote a P.S.: *Percy, I've found a good private school here in the city. I've put a deposit down to hold you a spot, in case you want to enroll for seventh grade. You could live at home. But if you want to go year-round at Half-Blood Hill, I'll understand.*

I folded the note carefully and set it on my bedside table. Every night before I went to sleep, I read it again, and I tried to decide how to answer her.

On the Fourth of July, the whole camp gathered at the beach for a fireworks display by cabin nine. Being Hephaestus's kids, they weren't going to settle for a few lame red-white-and-blue explosions. They'd anchored a barge offshore and loaded it with rockets the size of Patriot missiles. According to Annabeth, who'd seen the show before, the blasts would be sequenced so tightly they'd look like frames of animation across the sky. The finale was supposed to be a couple of hundred-foot-tall Spartan warriors who would crackle to life above the ocean, fight a battle, then explode into a million colors.

As Annabeth and I were spreading a picnic blanket, Grover showed up to tell us good-bye. He was dressed in his usual jeans and T-shirt and sneakers, but in the last few weeks he'd started to look older, almost high-school age. His goatee had gotten thicker. He'd put on weight. His horns had grown at least an inch, so he now had to wear his rasta cap all the time to pass as human.

"I'm off," he said. "I just came to say . . . well, you know."

I tried to feel happy for him. After all, it wasn't every day a satyr got permission to go look for the great god Pan. But it was hard saying good-bye. I'd only known Grover a year, yet he was my oldest friend.

Annabeth gave him a hug. She told him to keep his fake feet on.

I asked him where he was going to search first.

"Kind of a secret," he said, looking embarrassed. "I wish you could come with me, guys, but humans and Pan . . ."

"We understand," Annabeth said. "You got enough tin cans for the trip?"

"Yeah."

"And you remembered your reed pipes?"

"Jeez, Annabeth," he grumbled. "You're like an old mama goat."

But he didn't really sound annoyed.

He gripped his walking stick and slung a backpack over his shoulder. He looked like any hitchhiker you might see on an American highway—nothing like the little runty boy I used to defend from bullies at Yancy Academy.

"Well," he said, "wish me luck."

He gave Annabeth another hug. He clapped me on the shoulder, then headed back through the dunes.

Fireworks exploded to life overhead: Hercules killing

the Nemean lion, Artemis chasing the boar, George Washington (who, by the way, was a son of Athena) crossing the Delaware.

"Hey, Grover," I called.

He turned at the edge of the woods.

"Wherever you're going—I hope they make good enchiladas."

Grover grinned, and then he was gone, the trees closing around him.

"We'll see him again," Annabeth said.

I tried to believe it. The fact that no searcher had ever come back in two thousand years . . . well, I decided not to think about that. Grover would be the first. He had to be.

July passed.

I spent my days devising new strategies for capture-the-flag and making alliances with the other cabins to keep the banner out of Ares's hands. I got to the top of the climbing wall for the first time without getting scorched by lava.

From time to time, I'd walk past the Big House, glance up at the attic windows, and think about the Oracle. I tried to convince myself that its prophecy had come to completion.

You shall go west, and face the god who has turned.

Been there, done that—even though the traitor god had turned out to be Ares rather than Hades.

You shall find what was stolen, and see it safe returned.

Check. One master bolt delivered. One helm of darkness back on Hades's oily head.

You shall be betrayed by one who calls you a friend.

This line still bothered me. Ares had pretended to be my friend, then betrayed me. That must be what the Oracle meant. . . .

And you shall fail to save what matters most, in the end.

I *had* failed to save my mom, but only because I'd let her save herself, and I knew that was the right thing.

So why was I still uneasy?

The last night of the summer session came all too quickly.

The campers had one last meal together. We burned part of our dinner for the gods. At the bonfire, the senior counselors awarded the end-of-summer beads.

I got my own leather necklace, and when I saw the bead for my first summer, I was glad the firelight covered my blushing. The design was pitch black, with a sea-green trident shimmering in the center.

"The choice was unanimous," Luke announced. "This bead commemorates the first Son of the Sea God at this camp, and the quest he undertook into the darkest part of the Underworld to stop a war!"

The entire camp got to their feet and cheered. Even Ares's cabin felt obliged to stand. Athena's cabin steered Annabeth to the front so she could share in the applause.

I'm not sure I'd ever felt as happy or sad as I did at that moment. I'd finally found a family, people who cared about me and thought I'd done something right. And in the morning, most of them would be leaving for the year.

* * *

The next morning, I found a form letter on my bedside table.

I knew Dionysus must've filled it out, because he stubbornly insisted on getting my name wrong:

Dear _____ Peter Johnson _____ ,

If you intend to stay at Camp Half-Blood year-round, you must inform the Big House by noon today. If you do not announce your intentions, we will assume you have vacated your cabin or died a horrible death. Cleaning harpies will begin work at sundown. They will be authorized to eat any unregistered campers. All personal articles left behind will be incinerated in the lava pit.

Have a nice day!

Mr. D (Dionysus)

Camp Director, Olympian Council #12

That's another thing about ADHD. Deadlines just aren't real to me until I'm staring one in the face. Summer was over, and I still hadn't answered my mother, or the camp, about whether I'd be staying. Now I had only a few hours to decide.

The decision should have been easy. I mean, nine months of hero training or nine months of sitting in a classroom—duh.

But there was my mom to consider. For the first time, I had the chance to live with her for a whole year, without Gabe. I had a chance be at home and knock around the city in my free time. I remembered what Annabeth had said so long ago on our quest: *The real world is where the monsters are. That's where you learn whether you're any good or not.*

I thought about the fate of Thalia, daughter of Zeus. I wondered how many monsters would attack me if I left Half-Blood Hill. If I stayed in one place for a whole school year, without Chiron or my friends around to help me, would my mother and I even survive until the next summer? That was assuming the spelling tests and five-paragraph essays didn't kill me. I decided I'd go down to the arena and do some sword practice. Maybe that would clear my head.

The campgrounds were mostly deserted, shimmering in the August heat. All the campers were in their cabins packing up, or running around with brooms and mops, getting ready for final inspection. Argus was helping some of the Aphrodite kids haul their Gucci suitcases and makeup kits over the hill, where the camp's shuttle bus would be waiting to take them to the airport.

Don't think about leaving yet, I told myself. Just train.

I got to the sword-fighters arena and found that Luke had had the same idea. His gym bag was plopped at the edge of the stage. He was working solo, whaling on battle dummies with a sword I'd never seen before. It must've been a regular steel blade, because he was slashing the dummies' heads right off, stabbing through their straw-stuffed guts. His orange counselor's shirt was dripping with sweat. His expression was so intense, his life might've really been in danger. I watched, fascinated, as he disemboweled the whole row of dummies, hacking off limbs and basically reducing them to a pile of straw and armor.

They were only dummies, but I still couldn't help being awed by Luke's skill. The guy was an incredible fighter. It made me wonder, again, how he possibly could've failed at his quest.

Finally, he saw me, and stopped mid-swing. "Percy."

"Um, sorry," I said, embarrassed. "I just—"

"It's okay," he said, lowering his sword. "Just doing some last-minute practice."

"Those dummies won't be bothering anybody anymore."

Luke shrugged. "We build new ones every summer."

Now that his sword wasn't swirling around, I could see something odd about it. The blade was two different types of metal—one edge bronze, the other steel.

Luke noticed me looking at it. "Oh, this? New toy. This is Backbiter."

"Backbiter?"

Luke turned the blade in the light so it glinted wickedly. "One side is celestial bronze. The other is tempered steel. Works on mortals and immortals both."

I thought about what Chiron had told me when I started my quest—that a hero should never harm mortals unless absolutely necessary.

"I didn't know they could make weapons like that."

"*They* probably can't," Luke agreed. "It's one of a kind."

He gave me a tiny smile, then slid the sword into its scabbard. "Listen, I was going to come looking for you.

What do you say we go down to the woods one last time, look for something to fight?"

I don't know why I hesitated. I should've felt relieved that Luke was being so friendly. Ever since I'd gotten back from the quest, he'd been acting a little distant. I was afraid he might resent me for all the attention I'd gotten.

"You think it's a good idea?" I asked. "I mean—"

"Aw, come on." He rummaged in his gym bag and pulled out a six-pack of Cokes. "Drinks are on me."

I stared at the Cokes, wondering where the heck he'd gotten them. There were no regular mortal sodas at the camp store. No way to smuggle them in unless you talked to a satyr, maybe.

Of course, the magic dinner goblets would fill with anything you want, but it just didn't taste the same as a real Coke, straight out of the can.

Sugar and caffeine. My willpower crumbled.

"Sure," I decided. "Why not?"

We walked down to the woods and kicked around for some kind of monster to fight, but it was too hot. All the monsters with any sense must've been taking siestas in their nice cool caves.

We found a shady spot by the creek where I'd broken Clarisse's spear during my first capture the flag game. We sat on a big rock, drank our Cokes, and watched the sunlight in the woods.

After a while Luke said, "You miss being on a quest?"

"With monsters attacking me every three feet? Are you kidding?"

Luke raised an eyebrow.

"Yeah, I miss it," I admitted. "You?"

A shadow passed over his face.

I was used to hearing from the girls how good-looking Luke was, but at the moment, he looked weary, and angry, and not at all handsome. His blond hair was gray in the sunlight. The scar on his face looked deeper than usual. I could imagine him as an old man.

"I've lived at Half-Blood Hill year-round since I was fourteen," he told me. "Ever since Thalia . . . well, you know. I trained, and trained, and trained. I never got to be a normal teenager, out there in the real world. Then they threw me one quest, and when I came back, it was like, 'Okay, ride's over. Have a nice life.'"

He crumpled his Coke can and threw into the creek, which really shocked me. One of the first things you learn at Camp Half-Blood is: Don't litter. You'll hear from the nymphs and the naiads. They'll get even. You'll crawl into bed one night and find your sheets filled with centipedes and mud.

"The heck with laurel wreaths," Luke said. "I'm not going to end up like those dusty trophies in the Big House attic."

"You make it sound like you're leaving."

Luke gave me a twisted smile. "Oh, I'm leaving, all right, Percy. I brought you down here to say good-bye."

He snapped his fingers. A small fire burned a hole in the ground at my feet. Out crawled something glistening black, about the size of my hand. A scorpion.

I started to go for my pen.

"I wouldn't," Luke cautioned. "Pit scorpions can jump up to fifteen feet. Its stinger can pierce right through your clothes. You'll be dead in sixty seconds."

"Luke, what—"

Then it hit me.

You will be betrayed by one who calls you a friend.

"You," I said.

He stood calmly and brushed off his jeans.

The scorpion paid him no attention. It kept its beady black eyes on me, clamping its pincers as it crawled onto my shoe.

"I saw a lot out there in the world, Percy," Luke said. "Didn't you feel it—the darkness gathering, the monsters growing stronger? Didn't you realize how useless it all is? All the heroics—being pawns of the gods. They should've been overthrown thousands of years ago, but they've hung on, thanks to us half-bloods."

I couldn't believe this was happening.

"Luke . . . you're talking about our parents," I said.

He laughed. "That's supposed to make me love them? Their precious 'Western civilization' is a disease, Percy. It's killing the world. The only way to stop it is to burn it to the ground, start over with something more honest."

"You're as crazy as Ares."

His eyes flared. "Ares is a fool. He never realized the true master he was serving. If I had time, Percy, I could explain. But I'm afraid you won't live that long."

The scorpion crawled onto my pants leg.

There had to be a way out of this. I needed time to think.

"Kronos," I said. "That's who you serve."

The air got colder.

"You should be careful with names," Luke warned.

"Kronos got you to steal the master bolt and the helm. He spoke to you in your dreams."

Luke's eye twitched. "He spoke to you, too, Percy. You should've listened."

"He's brainwashing you, Luke."

"You're wrong. He showed me that my talents are being wasted. You know what my quest was two years ago, Percy? My father, Hermes, wanted me to steal a golden apple from the Garden of the Hesperides and return it to Olympus. After all the training I'd done, *that* was the best he could think up."

"That's not an easy quest," I said. "Hercules did it."

"Exactly," Luke said. "Where's the glory in repeating what others have done? All the gods know how to do is replay their past. My heart wasn't in it. The dragon in the garden gave me this"—he pointed angrily at his scar—"and when I came back, all I got was pity. I wanted to pull Olympus down stone by stone right then, but I bided my time. I began to dream of Kronos. He convinced me to steal something worthwhile, something no hero had ever had the courage to take. When we went on that winter-solstice field trip, while the other campers were asleep, I snuck into the throne room and took Zeus's master bolt right from his chair. Hades's helm of darkness, too. You wouldn't believe how easy it was. The Olympians are so arrogant; they never dreamed someone would dare steal from them. Their security is horrible. I was halfway across New Jersey before I heard the storms rumbling, and I knew they'd discovered my theft."

The scorpion was sitting on my knee now, staring at me with its glittering eyes. I tried to keep my voice level. "So why didn't you bring the items to Kronos?"

Luke's smile wavered. "I . . . I got overconfident. Zeus sent out his sons and daughters to find the stolen bolt—Artemis, Apollo, my father, Hermes. But it was Ares who caught me. I could have beaten him, but I wasn't careful enough. He disarmed me, took the items of power, threatened to return them to Olympus and burn me alive. Then Kronos's voice came to me and told me what to say. I put the idea in Ares's head about a great war between the gods. I said all he had to do was hide the items away for a while and watch the others fight. Ares got a wicked gleam in his eyes. I knew he was hooked. He let me go, and I returned to Olympus before anyone noticed my absence." Luke drew his new sword. He ran his thumb down the flat of the blade, as if he were hypnotized by its beauty. "Afterward, the Lord of the Titans . . . h-he punished me with nightmares. I swore not to fail again. Back at Camp Half-Blood, in my dreams, I was told that a second hero would arrive, one who could be tricked into taking the bolt and the helm the rest of the way—from Ares down to Tartarus."

"*You* summoned the hellhound, that night in the forest."

"We had to make Chiron think the camp wasn't safe for

you, so he would start you on your quest. We had to confirm his fears that Hades was after you. And it worked."

"The flying shoes were cursed," I said. "They were supposed to drag me and the backpack into Tartarus."

"And they would have, if you'd been wearing them. But you gave them to the satyr, which wasn't part of the plan. Grover messes up everything he touches. He even confused the curse."

Luke looked down at the scorpion, which was now sitting on my thigh. "You should have died in Tartarus, Percy. But don't worry, I'll leave you with my little friend to set things right."

"Thalia gave her life to save you," I said, gritting my teeth. "And this is how you repay her?"

"Don't speak of Thalia!" he shouted. "The gods *let* her die! That's one of the many things they will pay for."

"You're being used, Luke. You and Ares both. Don't listen to Kronos."

"*I've* been used?" Luke's voice turned shrill. "Look at yourself. What has your dad ever done for you? Kronos will rise. You've only delayed his plans. He will cast the Olympians into Tartarus and drive humanity back to their caves. All except the strongest—the ones who serve him."

"Call off the bug," I said. "If you're so strong, fight me yourself."

Luke smiled. "Nice try, Percy. But I'm not Ares. You can't bait me. My lord is waiting, and he's got plenty of quests for me to undertake."

"Luke—"

"Good-bye, Percy. There is a new Golden Age coming. You won't be part of it."

He slashed his sword in an arc and disappeared in a ripple of darkness.

The scorpion lunged.

I swatted it away with my hand and uncapped my sword. The thing jumped at me and I cut it in half in midair.

I was about to congratulate myself until I looked down at my hand. My palm had a huge red welt, oozing and smoking with yellow guck. The thing had gotten me after all.

My ears pounded. My vision went foggy. The water, I thought. It healed me before.

I stumbled to the creek and submerged my hand, but nothing seemed to happen. The poison was too strong. My vision was getting dark. I could barely stand up.

Sixty seconds, Luke had told me.

I had to get back to camp. If I collapsed out here, my body would be dinner for a monster. Nobody would ever know what had happened.

My legs felt like lead. My forehead was burning. I stumbled toward the camp, and the nymphs stirred from their trees.

"Help," I croaked. "Please . . ."

Two of them took my arms, pulling me along. I remember making it to the clearing, a counselor shouting for help, a centaur blowing a conch horn.

Then everything went black.

* * *

I woke with a drinking straw in my mouth. I was sipping something that tasted like liquid chocolate-chip cookies. Nectar.

I opened my eyes.

I was propped up in bed in the sickroom of the Big House, my right hand bandaged like a club. Argus stood guard in the corner. Annabeth sat next to me, holding my nectar glass and dabbing a washcloth on my forehead.

"Here we are again," I said.

"You idiot," Annabeth said, which is how I knew she was overjoyed to see me conscious. "You were green and turning gray when we found you. If it weren't for Chiron's healing . . ."

"Now, now," Chiron's voice said. "Percy's constitution deserves some of the credit."

He was sitting near the foot of my bed in human form, which was why I hadn't noticed him yet. His lower half was magically compacted into the wheelchair, his upper half dressed in a coat and tie. He smiled, but his face looked weary and pale, the way it did when he'd been up all night grading Latin papers.

"How are you feeling?" he asked.

"Like my insides have been frozen, then microwaved."

"Apt, considering that was pit scorpion venom. Now you must tell me, if you can, exactly what happened."

Between sips of nectar, I told them the story.

The room was quiet for a long time.

"I can't believe that Luke . . ." Annabeth's voice faltered. Her expression turned angry and sad. "Yes. Yes, I *can* believe it. May the gods curse him. . . . He was never the same after his quest."

"This must be reported to Olympus," Chiron murmured. "I will go at once."

"Luke is out there right now," I said. "I have to go after him."

Chiron shook his head. "No, Percy. The gods—"

"Won't even *talk* about Kronos," I snapped. "Zeus declared the matter closed!"

"Percy, I know this is hard. But you must not rush out for vengeance. You aren't ready."

I didn't like it, but part of me suspected Chiron was right. One look at my hand, and I knew I wasn't going to be sword fighting any time soon. "Chiron . . . your prophecy from the Oracle . . . it was about Kronos, wasn't it? Was I in it? And Annabeth?"

Chiron glanced nervously at the ceiling. "Percy, it isn't my place—"

"You've been ordered not to talk to me about it, haven't you?"

His eyes were sympathetic, but sad. "You will be a great hero, child. I will do my best to prepare you. But if I'm right about the path ahead of you . . ."

Thunder boomed overhead, rattling the windows.

"All right!" Chiron shouted. "Fine!"

He sighed in frustration. "The gods have their reasons, Percy. Knowing too much of your future is never a good thing."

"We can't just sit back and do nothing," I said.

"*We* will not sit back," Chiron promised. "But *you* must be careful. Kronos wants you to come unraveled. He wants your life disrupted, your thoughts clouded with fear and anger. Do not give him what he wants. Train patiently. Your time will come."

"Assuming I live that long."

Chiron put his hand on my ankle. "You'll have to trust me, Percy. You will live. But first you must decide your path for the coming year. I cannot tell you the right choice. . . ." I got the feeling that he had a very definite opinion, and it was taking all his willpower not to advise me. "But you must decide whether to stay at Camp Half-Blood year-round, or return to the mortal world for seventh grade and be a summer camper. Think on that. When I get back from Olympus, you must tell me your decision."

I wanted to protest. I wanted to ask him more questions. But his expression told me there could be no more discussion; he had said as much as he could.

"I'll be back as soon as I can," Chiron promised. "Argus will watch over you."

He glanced at Annabeth. "Oh, and, my dear . . . whenever you're ready, they're here."

"Who's here?" I asked.

Nobody answered.

Chiron rolled himself out of the room. I heard the wheels of his chair clunk carefully down the front steps, two at a time.

Annabeth studied the ice in my drink.

"What's wrong?" I asked her.

"Nothing." She set the glass on the table. "I . . . just took your advice about something. You . . . um . . . need anything?"

"Yeah. Help me up. I want to go outside."

"Percy, that isn't a good idea."

I slid my legs out of bed. Annabeth caught me before I could crumple to the floor. A wave of nausea rolled over me.

Annabeth said, "I told you . . ."

"I'm fine," I insisted. I didn't want to lie in bed like an invalid while Luke was out there planning to destroy the Western world.

I managed a step forward. Then another, still leaning heavily on Annabeth. Argus followed us outside, but he kept his distance.

By the time we reached the porch, my face was beaded with sweat. My stomach had twisted into knots. But I had managed to make it all the way to the railing.

It was dusk. The camp looked completely deserted. The cabins were dark and the volleyball pit silent. No canoes cut the surface of the lake. Beyond the woods and the strawberry fields, the Long Island Sound glittered in the last light of the sun.

"What are you going to do?" Annabeth asked me.

"I don't know."

I told her I got the feeling Chiron wanted me to stay year-round, to put in more individual training time, but I wasn't sure that's what I wanted. I admitted I'd feel bad about leaving her alone, though, with only Clarisse for company. . . .

Annabeth pursed her lips, then said quietly, "I'm going home for the year, Percy."

I stared at her. "You mean, to your dad's?"

She pointed toward the crest of Half-Blood Hill. Next to Thalia's pine tree, at the very edge of the camp's magical boundaries, a family stood silhouetted—two little children, a woman, and a tall man with blond hair. They seemed to be waiting. The man was holding a backpack that looked like the one Annabeth had gotten from Waterland in Denver.

"I wrote him a letter when we got back," Annabeth said. "Just like you suggested. I told him . . . I was sorry. I'd come home for the school year if he still wanted me. He wrote back immediately. We decided . . . we'd give it another try."

"That took guts."

She pursed her lips. "You won't try anything stupid during the school year, will you? At least . . . not without sending me an Iris-message?"

I managed a smile. "I won't go looking for trouble. I usually don't have to."

"When I get back next summer," she said, "we'll hunt down Luke. We'll ask for a quest, but if we don't get approval, we'll sneak off and do it anyway. Agreed?"

"Sounds like a plan worthy of Athena."

She held out her hand. I shook it.

"Take care, Seaweed Brain," Annabeth told me. "Keep your eyes open."

"You too, Wise Girl."

I watched her walk up the hill and join her family. She

gave her father an awkward hug and looked back at the valley one last time. She touched Thalia's pine tree, then allowed herself to be lead over the crest and into the mortal world.

For the first time at camp, I felt truly alone. I looked out at Long Island Sound and I remembered my father saying, *The sea does not like to be restrained.*

I made my decision.

I wondered, if Poseidon were watching, would he approve of my choice?

"I'll be back next summer," I promised him. "I'll survive until then. After all, I am your son." I asked Argus to take me down to cabin three, so I could pack my bags for home.

ACKNOWLEDGMENTS

Without the assistance of numerous valiant helpers, I would have been slain by monsters many times over as I endeavored to bring this story to print. Thanks to my elder son, Haley Michael, who heard the story first; my younger son, Patrick John, who at the age of six is the level-headed one in the family; and my wife, Becky, who puts up with my many long hours at Camp Half-Blood. Thanks also to my cadre of middle-school beta testers: Travis Stoll, clever and quick as Hermes; C. C. Kellogg, beloved as Athena; Allison Bauer, clear-eyed as Artemis the Huntress; and Mrs. Margaret Floyd, the wise and kindly seer of middle-school English. My appreciation also to Professor Egbert J. Bakker, classicist extraordinaire; Nancy Gallt, agent *summa cum laude*; Jonathan Burnham, Jennifer Besser, and Sarah Hughes for believing in Percy.

Can't get enough of heroes
battling monsters and mayhem?
You'll love The Kane Chronicles,
the *New York Times* #1 best-selling series
from Rick Riordan

THE
RED
PYRAMID

WARNING

The following is a transcript of a digital recording. In certain places, the audio quality was poor, so some words and phrases represent the author's best guesses. Where possible, illustrations of important symbols mentioned in the recording have been added. Background noises such as scuffling, hitting, and cursing by the two speakers have not been transcribed. The author makes no claims for the authenticity of the recording. It seems impossible that the two young narrators are telling the truth, but you, the reader, must decide for yourself.

1. A Death at the Needle

WE ONLY HAVE A FEW HOURS, so listen carefully.

If you're hearing this story, you're already in danger. Sadie and I might be your only chance.

Go to the school. Find the locker. I won't tell you which school or which locker, because if you're the right person, you'll find it. The combination is 13/32/33. By the time you finish listening, you'll know what those numbers mean. Just remember the story we're about to tell you isn't complete yet. How it ends will depend on you.

The most important thing: when you open the package and find what's inside, *don't* keep it longer than a week. Sure, it'll be tempting. I mean, it will grant you almost unlimited power. But if you possess it too long, it will consume you. Learn its secrets quickly and pass it on. Hide it for the next person, the way Sadie and I did for you. Then be prepared for your life to get very interesting.

Okay, Sadie is telling me to stop stalling and get on with

the story. Fine. I guess it started in London, the night our dad blew up the British Museum.

My name is Carter Kane. I'm fourteen and my home is a suitcase.

You think I'm kidding? Since I was eight years old, my dad and I have traveled the world. I was born in L.A. but my dad's an archaeologist, so his work takes him all over. Mostly we go to Egypt, since that's his specialty. Go into a bookstore, find a book about Egypt, there's a pretty good chance it was written by Dr. Julius Kane. You want to know how Egyptians pulled the brains out of mummies, or built the pyramids, or cursed King Tut's tomb? My dad is your man. Of course, there are other reasons my dad moved around so much, but I didn't know his secret back then.

I didn't go to school. My dad homeschooled me, if you can call it "home" schooling when you don't have a home. He sort of taught me whatever he thought was important, so I learned a lot about Egypt and basketball stats and my dad's favorite musicians. I read a lot, too—pretty much anything I could get my hands on, from dad's history books to fantasy novels—because I spent a lot of time sitting around in hotels and airports and dig sites in foreign countries where I didn't know anybody. My dad was always telling me to put the book down and play some ball. You ever try to start a game of pick-up basketball in Aswan, Egypt? It's not easy.

Anyway, my dad trained me early to keep all my possessions in a single suitcase that fits in an airplane's overhead compartment. My dad packed the same way, except he was allowed an extra workbag for his archaeology tools. Rule number one: I was not allowed to look in his workbag. That's a rule I never broke until the day of the explosion.

It happened on Christmas Eve. We were in London for visitation day with my sister, Sadie.

See, Dad's only allowed two days a year with her—one in the winter, one in the summer—because our grandparents hate him. After our mom died, her parents (our grandparents) had this big court battle with Dad. After six lawyers, two fistfights, and a near fatal attack with a spatula (don't ask), they won the right to keep Sadie with them in England. She was only six, two years younger than me, and they couldn't keep us both—at least that was their excuse for not taking me. So Sadie was raised as a British schoolkid, and I traveled around with my dad. We only saw Sadie twice a year, which was fine with me.

[Shut up, Sadie. Yes—I'm getting to that part.]

So anyway, my dad and I had just flown into Heathrow after a couple of delays. It was a drizzly, cold afternoon. The whole taxi ride into the city, my dad seemed kind of nervous.

Now, my dad is a big guy. You wouldn't think anything could make him nervous. He has dark brown skin like mine, piercing brown eyes, a bald head, and a goatee, so he looks like a buff evil scientist. That afternoon he wore his cashmere winter coat and his best brown suit, the one he used for public lectures. Usually he exudes so much confidence that he dominates any room he walks into, but sometimes—like that afternoon—I saw another side to him that I didn't really understand. He kept looking over his shoulder like we were being hunted.

"Dad?" I said as we were getting off the A-40. "What's wrong?"

"No sign of them," he muttered. Then he must've realized he'd spoken aloud, because he looked at me kind of startled. "Nothing, Carter. Everything's fine."

Which bothered me because my dad's a terrible liar. I always knew when he was hiding something, but I also knew no amount of pestering would get the truth out of him. He was probably trying to protect me, though from what I didn't know. Sometimes I wondered if he had some dark secret in his past, some old enemy following him, maybe; but the idea seemed ridiculous. Dad was just an archaeologist.

The other thing that troubled me: Dad was clutching his workbag. Usually when he does that, it means we're in danger. Like the time gunmen stormed our hotel in Cairo. I heard shots coming from the lobby and ran downstairs to check on my dad. By the time I got there, he was just calmly zipping up his workbag while three unconscious gunmen hung by their feet from the chandelier, their robes falling over their heads so you could see their boxer shorts. Dad claimed not to have witnessed anything, and in the end the police blamed a freak chandelier malfunction.

Another time, we got caught in a riot in Paris. My dad found the nearest parked car, pushed me into the backseat, and told me to stay down. I pressed myself against the floorboards and kept my eyes shut tight. I could hear Dad in the driver's seat, rummaging in his bag, mumbling something to himself while the mob yelled and destroyed things outside. A few minutes later he told me it was safe to get up. Every other car on the block had been overturned and set on fire. Our car had been freshly washed and polished, and several twenty-euro notes had been tucked under the windshield wipers.

Anyway, I'd come to respect the bag. It was our good luck charm. But when my dad kept it close, it meant we were going to need good luck.

We drove through the city center, heading east toward my grandparents' flat. We passed the golden gates of Buckingham Palace, the big stone column in Trafalgar Square. London is a pretty cool place, but after you've traveled for so long, all cities start to blend together. Other kids I meet sometimes say, "Wow, you're so lucky you get to travel so much." But it's not like we spend our time sightseeing or have a lot of money to travel in style. We've stayed in some pretty rough places, and we hardly ever stay anywhere longer than a few days. Most of the time it feels like we're fugitives rather than tourists.

I mean, you wouldn't think my dad's work was dangerous. He does lectures on topics like "Can Egyptian Magic Really Kill You?" and "Favorite Punishments in the Egyptian Underworld" and other stuff most people wouldn't care about. But like I said, there's that other side to him. He's always very cautious, checking every hotel room before he lets me walk into it. He'll dart into a museum to see some artifacts, take a few notes, and rush out again like he's afraid to be caught on the security cameras.

One time when I was younger, we raced across the Charles de Gaulle airport to catch a last-minute flight, and Dad didn't relax until the plane was off the ground. I asked him point blank what he was running from, and he looked at me like I'd just pulled the pin out of a grenade. For a second I was scared he might actually tell me the truth. Then he said, "Carter, it's nothing." As if "nothing" were the most terrible thing in the world.

After that, I decided maybe it was better not to ask questions.

My grandparents, the Fausts, live in a housing development near Canary Wharf, right on the banks of the River Thames. The taxi let us off at the curb, and my dad asked the driver to wait.

We were halfway up the walk when Dad froze. He turned and looked behind us.

"What?" I asked.

Then I saw the man in the trench coat. He was across the street, leaning against a big dead tree. He was barrel shaped, with skin the color of roasted coffee. His coat and black pinstriped suit looked expensive. He had long braided hair and wore a black fedora pulled down low over his dark round glasses. He reminded me of a jazz musician, the kind my dad would always drag me to see in concert. Even though I couldn't see his eyes, I got the impression he was watching us. He might've been an old friend or colleague of Dad's. No matter where we went, Dad was always running into people he knew. But it did seem strange that the guy was waiting here, outside my grandparents'. And he didn't look happy.

"Carter," my dad said, "go on ahead."

"But—"

"Get your sister. I'll meet you back at the taxi."

He crossed the street toward the man in the trench coat, which left me with two choices: follow my dad and see what was going on, or do what I was told.

I decided on the slightly less dangerous path. I went to retrieve my sister.

Before I could even knock, Sadie opened the door.

"Late as usual," she said.

She was holding her cat, Muffin, who'd been a "going away" gift from Dad six years before. Muffin never seemed to get older or bigger. She had fuzzy yellow-and-black fur like a miniature leopard, alert yellow eyes, and pointy ears that were too tall for her head. A silver Egyptian pendant dangled from her collar. She didn't look anything like a muffin, but Sadie had been little when she named her, so I guess you have to cut her some slack.

Sadie hadn't changed much either since last summer.

[As I'm recording this, she's standing next to me, glaring, so I'd better be careful how I describe her.]

You would never guess she's my sister. First of all, she'd been living in England so long, she has a British accent. Second, she takes after our mom, who was white, so Sadie's skin is much lighter than mine. She has straight caramel-colored hair, not exactly blond but not brown, which she usually dyes with streaks of bright colors. That day it had red streaks down the left side. Her eyes are blue. I'm serious. *Blue* eyes, just like our mom's. She's only twelve, but she's exactly as tall as me, which is really annoying. She was chewing gum as usual, dressed for her day out with Dad in battered jeans, a leather jacket, and combat boots, like she was going to a concert and was hoping to stomp on some people. She had headphones dangling around her neck in case we bored her.

[Okay, she didn't hit me, so I guess I did an okay job of describing her.]

"Our plane was late," I told her.

She popped a bubble, rubbed Muffin's head, and tossed the cat inside. "Gran, going out!"

From somewhere in the house, Grandma Faust said something I couldn't make out, probably "Don't let them in!"

Sadie closed the door and regarded me as if I were a dead mouse her cat had just dragged in. "So, here you are again."

"Yep."

"Come on, then." She sighed. "Let's get on with it."

That's the way she was. No "Hi, how you been the last six months? So glad to see you!" or anything. But that was okay with me. When you only see each other twice a year, it's like you're distant cousins rather than siblings. We had absolutely nothing in common except our parents.

We trudged down the steps. I was thinking how she smelled like a combination of old people's house and bubble gum when she stopped so abruptly, I ran into her.

"Who's that?" she asked.

I'd almost forgotten about the dude in the trench coat. He and my dad were standing across the street next to the big tree, having what looked like a serious argument. Dad's back was turned so I couldn't see his face, but he gestured with his hands like he does when he's agitated. The other guy scowled and shook his head.

"Dunno," I said. "He was there when we pulled up."

"He looks familiar." Sadie frowned like she was trying to remember. "Come on."

"Dad wants us to wait in the cab," I said, even though I knew it was no use. Sadie was already on the move.

Instead of going straight across the street, she dashed up the sidewalk for half a block, ducking behind cars, then crossed to the opposite side and crouched under a stone wall. She started sneaking toward our dad. I didn't have much choice but to follow her example, even though it made me feel kind of stupid.

"Six years in England," I muttered, "and she thinks she's James Bond."

Sadie swatted me without looking back and kept creeping forward.

A couple more steps and we were right behind the big dead tree. I could hear my dad on the other side, saying, "—have to, Amos. You know it's the right thing."

"No," said the other man, who must've been Amos. His voice was deep and even—very insistent. His accent was American. "If I don't stop you, Julius, *they* will. The Per Ankh is shadowing you."

Sadie turned to me and mouthed the words "Per *what*?"

I shook my head, just as mystified. "Let's get out of here," I whispered, because I figured we'd be spotted any minute and get in serious trouble. Sadie, of course, ignored me.

"They don't know my plan," my father was saying. "By the time they figure it out—"

"And the children?" Amos asked. The hairs stood up on the back of my neck. "What about them?"

"I've made arrangements to protect them," my dad said. "Besides, if I don't do this, we're all in danger. Now, back off."

"I can't, Julius."

"Then it's a duel you want?" Dad's tone turned deadly serious. "You never could beat me, Amos."

I hadn't seen my dad get violent since the Great Spatula Incident, and I wasn't anxious to see a repeat of *that*, but the two men seemed to be edging toward a fight.

Before I could react, Sadie popped up and shouted, "Dad!"

He looked surprised when she tackle-hugged him, but not nearly as surprised as the other guy, Amos. He backed up so quickly, he tripped over his own trench coat.

He'd taken off his glasses. I couldn't help thinking that Sadie was right. He did look familiar—like a very distant memory.

"I—I must be going," he said. He straightened his fedora and lumbered down the road.

Our dad watched him go. He kept one arm protectively around Sadie and one hand inside the workbag slung over his shoulder. Finally, when Amos disappeared around the corner, Dad relaxed. He took his hand out of the bag and smiled at Sadie. "Hello, sweetheart."

Sadie pushed away from him and crossed her arms. "Oh, now it's *sweetheart*, is it? You're late. Visitation Day's nearly over! And what was that about? Who's Amos, and what's the Per Ankh?"

Dad stiffened. He glanced at me like he was wondering how much we'd overheard.

"It's nothing," he said, trying to sound upbeat. "I have a wonderful evening planned. Who'd like a private tour of the British Museum?"

Sadie slumped in the back of the taxi between Dad and me.

"I can't believe it," she grumbled. "One evening together, and you want to do research."

Dad tried for a smile. "Sweetheart, it'll be fun. The curator of the Egyptian collection personally invited—"

"Right, big surprise." Sadie blew a strand of red-streaked hair out of her face. "Christmas Eve, and we're going to see some moldy old relics from Egypt. Do you ever think about *anything* else?"

Dad didn't get mad. He never gets mad at Sadie. He just stared out the window at the darkening sky and the rain.

"Yes," he said quietly. "I do."

Whenever Dad got quiet like that and stared off into no-where, I knew he was thinking about our mom. The last few months, it had been happening a lot. I'd walk into our hotel room and find him with his cell phone in his hands, Mom's picture smiling up at him from the screen—her hair tucked under a headscarf, her blue eyes startlingly bright against the desert backdrop.

Or we'd be at some dig site. I'd see Dad staring at the horizon, and I'd know he was remembering how he'd met her—two young scientists in the Valley of the Kings, on a dig to discover a lost tomb. Dad was an Egyptologist. Mom was an anthropologist looking for ancient DNA. He'd told me the story a thousand times.

Our taxi snaked its way along the banks of the Thames. Just past Waterloo Bridge, my dad tensed.

"Driver," he said. "Stop here a moment."

The cabbie pulled over on the Victoria Embankment.

"What is it, Dad?" I asked.

He got out of the cab like he hadn't heard me. When Sadie and I joined him on the sidewalk, he was staring up at Cleopatra's Needle.

In case you've never seen it: the Needle is an obelisk, not a needle, and it doesn't have anything to do with Cleopatra. I guess the British just thought the name sounded cool when they brought it to London. It's about seventy feet tall, which would've been really impressive back in Ancient Egypt, but on the Thames, with all the tall buildings around, it looks small and sad. You could drive right by it and not even realize you'd just passed something that was a thousand years older than the city of London.

"God." Sadie walked around in a frustrated circle. "Do we have to stop for *every* monument?"

My dad stared at the top of the obelisk. "I had to see it again," he murmured. "Where it happened..."

A freezing wind blew off the river. I wanted to get back in the cab, but my dad was really starting to worry me. I'd never seen him so distracted.

"What, Dad?" I asked. "What happened here?"

"The last place I saw her."

Sadie stopped pacing. She scowled at me uncertainly, then back at Dad. "Hang on. Do you mean Mum?"

Dad brushed Sadie's hair behind her ear, and she was so surprised, she didn't even push him away.

I felt like the rain had frozen me solid. Mom's death had always been a forbidden subject. I knew she'd died in an accident in London. I knew my grandparents blamed my dad. But no one would ever tell us the details. I'd given up asking my dad, partly because it made him so sad, partly because he absolutely refused to tell me anything. "When you're older" was all he would say, which was the most frustrating response ever.

"You're telling us she died here," I said. "At Cleopatra's Needle? What happened?"

He lowered his head.

"Dad!" Sadie protested. "I go past this *every* day, and you mean to say—all this time—and I didn't even *know*?"

"Do you still have your cat?" Dad asked her, which seemed like a really stupid question.

"Of course I've still got the cat!" she said. "What does that have to do with anything?"

"And your amulet?"

Sadie's hand went to her neck. When we were little, right before Sadie went to live with our grandparents, Dad had given us both Egyptian amulets. Mine was an Eye of Horus, which was a popular protection symbol in Ancient Egypt.

In fact my dad says the modern pharmacist's symbol, ℞, is a simplified version of the Eye of Horus, because medicine is supposed to protect you.

Anyway, I always wore my amulet under my shirt, but I figured Sadie would've lost hers or thrown it away.

To my surprise, she nodded. "'Course I have it, Dad, but don't change the subject. Gran's always going on about how you caused Mum's death. That's not true, is it?"

We waited. For once, Sadie and I wanted exactly the same thing—the truth.

"The night your mother died," my father started, "here at the Needle—"

A sudden flash illuminated the embankment. I turned, half blind, and just for a moment I glimpsed two figures: a tall pale man with a forked beard and wearing cream-colored robes, and a coppery-skinned girl in dark blue robes and a headscarf—the kind of clothes I'd seen hundreds of times in Egypt. They were just standing there side by side, not twenty feet away, watching us. Then the light faded. The figures melted into a fuzzy afterimage. When my eyes readjusted to the darkness, they were gone.

"Um..." Sadie said nervously. "Did you just see that?"

"Get in the cab," my dad said, pushing us toward the curb. "We're out of time."

From that point on, Dad clammed up.

"This isn't the place to talk," he said, glancing behind us. He'd promised the cabbie an extra ten pounds if he got us to the museum in under five minutes, and the cabbie was doing his best.

"Dad," I tried, "those people at the river—"

"And the other bloke, Amos," Sadie said. "Are they Egyptian police or something?"

"Look, both of you," Dad said, "I'm going to need your help tonight. I know it's hard, but you have to be patient. I'll explain everything, I promise, after we get to the museum. I'm going to make everything right again."

"What do you mean?" Sadie insisted. "Make *what* right?"

Dad's expression was more than sad. It was almost guilty. With a chill, I thought about what Sadie had said: about our grandparents blaming him for Mom's death. That *couldn't* be what he was talking about, could it?

The cabbie swerved onto Great Russell Street and screeched to a halt in front of the museum's main gates.

"Just follow my lead," Dad told us. "When we meet the curator, act normal."

I was thinking that Sadie never acted *normal*, but I decided not to say anything.

We climbed out of the cab. I got our luggage while Dad paid the driver with a big wad of cash. Then he did something strange. He threw a handful of small objects into the backseat—they looked like stones, but it was too dark for me to be sure. "Keep driving," he told the cabbie. "Take us to Chelsea."

That made no sense since we were already out of the cab, but the driver sped off. I glanced at Dad, then back at the cab, and before it turned the corner and disappeared in the dark, I caught a weird glimpse of three passengers in the backseat: a man and two kids.

I blinked. There was no way the cab could've picked up another fare so fast. "Dad—"

"London cabs don't stay empty very long," he said matter-of-factly. "Come along, kids."

He marched off through the wrought iron gates. For a second, Sadie and I hesitated.

"Carter, *what* is going on?"

I shook my head. "I'm not sure I want to know."

"Well, stay out here in the cold if you want, but *I'm* not leaving without an explanation." She turned and marched after our dad.

Looking back on it, I should've run. I should've dragged Sadie out of there and gotten as far away as possible. Instead I followed her through the gates.

DON'T MISS THE NEXT EXCITING
ADVENTURE IN THE

PERCY JACKSON & THE OLYMPIANS

SERIES

THE
SEA OF
MONSTERS

THE SEA OF MONSTERS

My nightmare started like this.

I was standing on a deserted street in some little beach town. It was the middle of the night. A storm was blowing. Wind and rain ripped at the palm trees along the sidewalk. Pink and yellow stucco buildings lined the street, their windows boarded up. A block away, past a line of hibiscus bushes, the ocean churned.

Florida, I thought. Though I wasn't sure how I knew that. I'd never been to Florida.

Then I heard hooves clattering against the pavement. I turned and saw my friend Grover running for his life.

Yeah, I said *hooves.*

Grover is a satyr. From the waist up, he looks like a typical gangly teenager with a peach-fuzz goatee and a bad case of acne. He walks with a strange limp, but unless you happen to catch him without his pants on (which I don't recommend), you'd never know there was anything un-human about him. Baggy jeans and fake feet hide the fact that he's got furry hindquarters and hooves.

Grover had been my best friend in sixth grade. He'd gone on this adventure with me and a girl named Annabeth to save the world, but I hadn't seen him since last July, when he set off alone on a dangerous quest—a quest no satyr had ever returned from.

Anyway, in my dream, Grover was hauling goat tail, holding his human shoes in his hands the way he does when he needs to move fast. He clopped past the little tourist shops and surfboard rental places. The wind bent the palm trees almost to the ground.

Grover was terrified of something behind him. He must've just come from the beach. Wet sand was caked in his fur. He'd escaped from somewhere. He was trying to get away from . . . something.

A bone-rattling growl cut through the storm. Behind Grover, at the far end of the block, a shadowy figure loomed. It swatted aside a street lamp, which burst in a shower of sparks.

Grover stumbled, whimpering in fear. He muttered to himself, *Have to get away. Have to warn them!*

I couldn't see what was chasing him, but I could hear it muttering and cursing. The ground shook as it got closer. Grover dashed around a street corner and faltered. He'd run into a dead-end courtyard full of shops. No time to back up. The nearest door had been blown open by the storm. The sign above the darkened display window read: ST. AUGUSTINE BRIDAL BOUTIQUE.

Grover dashed inside. He dove behind a rack of wedding dresses.

The monster's shadow passed in front of the shop. I could smell the thing—a sickening combination of wet sheep wool and rotten meat and that weird sour body odor only monsters have, like a skunk that's been living off Mexican food.

Grover trembled behind the wedding dresses. The monster's shadow passed on.

Silence except for the rain. Grover took a deep breath. Maybe the thing was gone.

Then lightning flashed. The entire front of the store exploded, and a monstrous voice bellowed: "MIIIIINE!"

I sat bolt upright, shivering in my bed.

There was no storm. No monster.

Morning sunlight filtered through my bedroom window.

I thought I saw a shadow flicker across the glass—a humanlike shape. But then there was a knock on my bedroom door—my mom called: "Percy, you're going to be late"—and the shadow at the window disappeared.

It must've been my imagination. A fifth-story window with a rickety old fire escape . . . there couldn't have been anyone out there.

"Come on, dear," my mother called again. "Last day of school. You should be excited! You've almost made it!"

"Coming," I managed.

I felt under my pillow. My fingers closed reassuringly around the ballpoint pen I always slept with. I brought it out, studied the Ancient Greek writing engraved on the side: *Anaklusmos*. Riptide.

I thought about uncapping it, but something held me back. I hadn't used Riptide for so long. . . .

Besides, my mom had made me promise not to use deadly weapons in the apartment after I'd swung a javelin the wrong way and taken out her china cabinet. I put Anaklusmos on my nightstand and dragged myself out of bed.

I got dressed as quickly as I could. I tried not to think about my nightmare or monsters or the shadow at my window.

Have to get away. Have to warn them!

What had Grover meant?

I made a three-fingered claw over my heart and pushed outward—an ancient gesture Grover had once taught me for warding off evil.

The dream couldn't have been real.

Last day of school. My mom was right, I should have been excited. For the first time in my life, I'd almost made it an entire year without getting expelled. No weird accidents. No fights in the classroom. No teachers turning into monsters and trying to kill me with poisoned cafeteria food or exploding homework. Tomorrow, I'd be on my way to my favorite place in the world—Camp Half-Blood.

Only one more day to go. Surely even I couldn't mess that up.

As usual, I didn't have a clue how wrong I was.

My mom made blue waffles and blue eggs for breakfast. She's funny that way, celebrating special occasions with blue food. I think it's her way of saying anything is possible. Percy can pass seventh grade. Waffles can be blue. Little miracles like that.

I ate at the kitchen table while my mom washed dishes. She was dressed in her work uniform—a starry blue skirt and a red-and-white striped blouse she wore to sell candy at Sweet on America. Her long brown hair was pulled back in a ponytail.

The waffles tasted great, but I guess I wasn't digging in like I usually did. My mom looked over and frowned. "Percy, are you all right?"

"Yeah . . . fine."

But she could always tell when something was bothering me. She dried her hands and sat down across from me. "School, or . . ."

She didn't need to finish. I knew what she was asking.

"I think Grover's in trouble," I said, and I told her about my dream.

She pursed her lips. We didn't talk much about the *other*

part of my life. We tried to live as normally as possible, but my mom knew all about Grover.

"I wouldn't be too worried, dear," she said. "Grover is a big satyr now. If there were a problem, I'm sure we would've heard from . . . from camp. . . ." Her shoulders tensed as she said the word *camp*.

"What is it?" I asked.

"Nothing," she said. "I'll tell you what. This afternoon we'll celebrate the end of school. I'll take you and Tyson to Rockefeller Center—to that skateboard shop you like."

Oh, man, that was tempting. We were always struggling with money. Between my mom's night classes and my private school tuition, we could never afford to do special stuff like shop for a skateboard. But something in her voice bothered me.

"Wait a minute," I said. "I thought we were packing me up for camp tonight."

She twisted her dishrag. "Ah, dear, about that . . . I got a message from Chiron last night."

My heart sank. Chiron was the activities director at Camp Half-Blood. He wouldn't contact us unless something serious was going on. "What did he say?"

"He thinks . . . it might not be safe for you to come to camp just yet. We might have to postpone."

"*Postpone?* Mom, how could it not be *safe*? I'm a half-blood! It's like the only safe place on earth for me!"

"Usually, dear. But with the problems they're having—"

"*What* problems?"

"Percy . . . I'm very, very sorry. I was hoping to talk to you about it this afternoon. I can't explain it all now. I'm not even sure Chiron can. Everything happened so suddenly."

My mind was reeling. How could I *not* go to camp? I wanted to ask a million questions, but just then the kitchen clock chimed the half-hour.

My mom looked almost relieved. "Seven-thirty, dear. You should go. Tyson will be waiting."

"But—"

"Percy, we'll talk this afternoon. Go on to school."

That was the last thing I wanted to do, but my mom had this fragile look in her eyes—a kind of warning, like if I pushed her too hard she'd start to cry. Besides, she was right about my friend Tyson. I had to meet him at the subway station on time or he'd get upset. He was scared of traveling underground alone.

I gathered up my stuff, but I stopped in the doorway. "Mom, this problem at camp. Does it . . . could it have anything to do with my dream about Grover?"

She wouldn't meet my eyes. "We'll talk this afternoon, dear. I'll explain . . . as much as I can."

Reluctantly, I told her good-bye. I jogged downstairs to catch the Number Two train.

I didn't know it at the time, but my mom and I would never get to have our afternoon talk.

In fact, I wouldn't be seeing home for a long, long time.

As I stepped outside, I glanced at the brownstone

building across the street. Just for a second I saw a dark shape in the morning sunlight—a human silhouette against the brick wall, a shadow that belonged to no one.

Then it rippled and vanished.